The Stonewycke Legacy

The Stonewycke Legacy

by

Michael Phillips
&
Judith Pella

Inspirational Press
New York

Previously published in three separate volumes:
STRANGER AT STONEWYCKE, copyright © 1987 by Michael R. Phillips and Judith Pella.
SHADOWS OVER STONEWYCKE, copyright © 1988 by Michael R. Phillips and Judith Pella.
TREASURE OF STONEWYCKE, copyright © 1988 by Michael R. Phillips and Judith Pella.

First Inspirational Press edition published in 1997.

Inspirational Press
A division of Budget Book Service, Inc.
386 Park Avenue South
New York, NY 10016

Inspirational Press is a registered trademark of Budget Book Service, Inc.

Published by arrangement with Bethany House Publishers.

Library of Congress Catalog Card Number: 96-79813
ISBN: 0-88486-169-4

Text design by Hannah Lerner.

Printed in the United States of America.

CONTENTS

STRANGER
AT
STONEWYCKE

With love and thanks to my parents
John and Norma Pella

"The kingdom of heaven is like a
treasure hidden in the ground. When
a man found it, he hid it again, and
then in his joy went and sold all he
had and bought that field."
—Matthew 13:44

CONTENTS

✵ *Introduction*

To MAN'S UNDISCERNING eye, the generations come and go, fading one into the other, ultimately passing from the face of the earth. As the march of history progresses, only the land remains, while men, women, and children grow, live, and die and then return to the earth from which they came, seemingly swallowed into nothingness by a vast uncaring universe.

In reality, however, the land is the stage upon which a drama of unparalleled eternal significance is played within the hearts of every man and woman who sets foot upon it. Unseen by those around us, often uncomprehended by ourselves, the choices and values of our earthly lives mold and determine the character we take with us into the next life.

From the time the Picts settled in northern Scotland in the seventh century, until the region was overrun by the Vikings in the ninth, and then settled throughout the following centuries by the Scots, the estate known as Stonewycke became a symbol of the enduring quality of the land. When the castle of that same name was built by Andrew Ramsay in the 1540's, his prayer was that the estate would stand as a sentinel in the north to God's goodness. His prayers for the generations who would follow him in the Ramsay line resulted in blessings and prosperity to the family throughout the next two and a half centuries, finding special fulfillment in the righteousness of his descendant Anson Ramsey in the early nineteenth century. (The spelling of the family name was changed in 1745 to Ramsey.)

But as the blessings of God follow generational lines, so also do the consequences of wrongdoing and ungodly choices. The self-will and personal greed of Ross Ramsay, brother of Adam de Ramsay, baron of Banff, also became an intrinsic factor in the family bloodline—a black stain which, unknown to Andrew, his descendant, was too strong to be rooted out entirely by the prayers that followed the stigma.

Hence, though Andrew's blood was strong in Anson, Ross's found fertile soil in Anson's sons, whose father suffered the tormenting fate of watching his own offspring turn away from the God of their fathers. The family continued to be infused by new blood; while the choices and prayers of each succeeding generation breathed new life into the heritage of godliness, at the same time self-interest strengthened the forces which opposed those prayers. The grafting into the family of James Duncan in 1845 threatened to eradicate altogether by greed and ambition what Andrew and Anson had prayed so diligently for.

Yet in the mystery of God's purpose, in James's own daughter rose the strong desire to give her life to the Almighty plan. Such yielding, however, never comes easily. Battle raged within the soul of young Maggie Duncan—the conflict found in her Ramsey bloodline was illustrative of the essential human condition. Indeed, the future of the family's heritage was at stake. Her laying down of self, and her prayers for the future of the Ramsey/Duncan lineage, rekindled for a new era the prayers begun through her ancestors, enabling the blessings of God to pass to new generations through her granddaughter Joanna.

Thus the legacy continued into the second millennium of settlement on the northern Scottish coast. And with the passage of time the tempo of life accelerated. The twentieth century brought many changes to the inheritors of the once-magnificent estate known as Stonewycke. In Great Britain the twentieth century brought the end of the Victorian Era with the Queen's death in 1901. Monarchies had come and gone countless times before, but this transfer of power was more far-reaching in its impact on the world than a mere changing of the guard from mother to son in London. A thorough-going transfiguration, the roots of which had sprouted during Victoria's lifetime, was in the process of turning society inside out.

Not only was the entire political framework of the world being revamped; cataclysmic social change, affecting every level of society, was sweeping through the once-proud center of the mighty British Empire. The growth of the Labor Party overhauled Parliament's decision-making process. Morals and literature changed dramatically. The spiritual foundation-stones of Victoria's administration eroded. Socially, economically, politically, and spiritually old norms were being thrown out. Technological breakthroughs, given momentum by the Great War against Germany, found their way into the daily lives of countless millions on both sides of the Atlantic—automobiles, electricity, airplanes, radios, urban growth, new factories, and the wild music and fashions of the 1920's.

These were profound changes. The world in the first two decades of the twentieth century was a world rushing to modernize itself. The world of Maggie's childhood was a world as distinct from that in which Joanna would raise her daughter, as the horse was distinct from the automobile. Between 1900 and 1930 stretched a gulf, not of decades, but of centuries.

Perhaps most significant for the northern shires of Scotland during this time was the final demise of the old feudal and manorial systems of land management, which had been dying a slow death for centuries. Once-proud estates gradually were sold off in parcels, were apportioned and split between heirs, or went bankrupt as their owners desperately tried to keep vast holdings together with insufficient capital. Not only economics, but social outlook had changed. While titles and nobility still mattered a great deal in Britain, they were coming to matter less. The working classes could now vote and buy land and improve their lot. The separation between the workers and the aristocracy was much narrower. No longer were the fortunes of the workers solely bound up in their dependence on the landowners and lairds who owned their houses, their lands—sometimes, it seemed, their very souls.

With such total dependency gone, the economic benefits to local lairds of the surrounding crofters and poor tenant farmers was also gone. Only the landowners who were able to cope with the changes time had brought survived in their positions of stature. They forged new, more equitable relationships with their subjects, and found other means to support their estates rather than by the blood and toil of the peasantry.

Many estates were not able to survive intact. Others, like Stonewycke, faced the new times by adapting to them rather than trying to stem the tides of change. With a wisdom supernaturally inspired, Anson Ramsey drew up a transfer document for a time which would come years after him, transferring a large portion of the Stonewycke estate to the people who lived on the land. Anson's transfer turned out to be the salvation of the proud Ramsey heritage. For in that magnanimous act was solidified a bond between the people of Stonewycke and its nobility, unique among such estates—a bond of mutual love that would see mighty Stonewycke, and all those bound to it, through years of change and regeneration.

Quietly, invisibly, the hand of God is always at work. Although we may see only a narrow individual perspective of His actions, the purpose of God goes on far beyond our limited understanding. In the Old and New Testament, God works through the generational flow of family and nation; both sin and righteousness sow seeds and harvest fruit into succeeding generations. Jesus himself came, not as a mere individual, but as a man born into the uninterrupted flow of the history of God's people. Son of God, Son of Man, Son of David, He brought God's salvation to the world through the heritage of family, through the legacy of man's ancestry and ancient birthright as the creation of our Father in heaven.

Twentieth-century mentality is often based on the present; we live in a vacuum of *now*. Yet every life is the result of a series of choices and crossroads—not only ours, but those of our ancestors for generations behind us. In the present, as in the past, each individual holds a key to the future. We stand at the crossroads of our personal histories, and the decisions we make set into motion values and attitudes that affect not only our own development as men and women made in the image of God, but the choices and decisions that will face our descendants for generations to come.

The Stonewycke saga, then, as it passes into the middle of the twentieth century, is a saga of those human choices, of the struggles of men and women to yield to the godliness to which all are called, while resisting the stain of evil that is passed down through the blood of our ancestors. It is a saga of the land, of a family, of righteousness and blessing passed down through the years as, in certain generations, the forces of good or the forces of evil gain the upper hand. And always the prayers of righteous men and women who have come before stand in the balance.

The Stonewycke saga is the story of God's work through the generations of one particular family. As the prayers of godly men and women from early in that family's history weave their way silently into the lives of future descendants, new strains of life (through such men as Ian and Alec) are grafted into the family tree just as the Gentiles were grafted into the family of God, further strengthening and solidifying God's purpose.

Stonewycke—as a home, as an estate, as a family seat—symbolizes that eternal quality of continuing life through the generations of the Ramsey and Duncan clan. Through the righteous prayers of Andrew and Anson Ramsey, and then Maggie Duncan, followed by Joanna MacNeil, the life of God moves through the generations like seeds which fall to the ground and are covered up and lie dormant—perhaps for many years—yet retain their power of growth and inherent life, waiting for the moment when the proper combination of sun, rain, and warmth sprouts them to life once more.

Though that essential life all but disappeared from the Ramsey clan during some of its darker years, the life hidden below the surface was waiting to sprout. That seed of righteousness, Anson Ramsey's transfer document, was unearthed by Anson's great-granddaughter Maggie, whose spiritual eyes were opened largely through the influence of a humble groom named Digory MacNab. Even then, the transfer document, and the very inheritance of Stonewycke itself, disappeared during the years of Maggie's lonely sojourn in America. However, the purposes of God are never lost, and through Maggie's own granddaughter Joanna, the life of Stonewycke blossomed and came to fruition once more.

The heritage continues, passing gradually from one generation to the next, with the hand of God infusing life through the answered prayers of the righteous. Man can never tell what methods God will use, nor when the fulfillment of prayers long silent will come. But God's purposes are always accomplished. The prayers of the righteous resound through the heavens, awaiting the moment when their fulfillment is at hand.

Thus, the Stonewycke legacy lives on, and moves into the future. And as it does, those of a new generation in the Ramsey/Duncan clan, and those who will be grafted into it, are imbued with a life which is given strength through the prayers and obedience of those who have come before. The only question remains: to which of the strains of their heritage will they yield their allegiance?

As the decisions surrounding that question are daily made, the future of the Stonewycke legacy is determined.

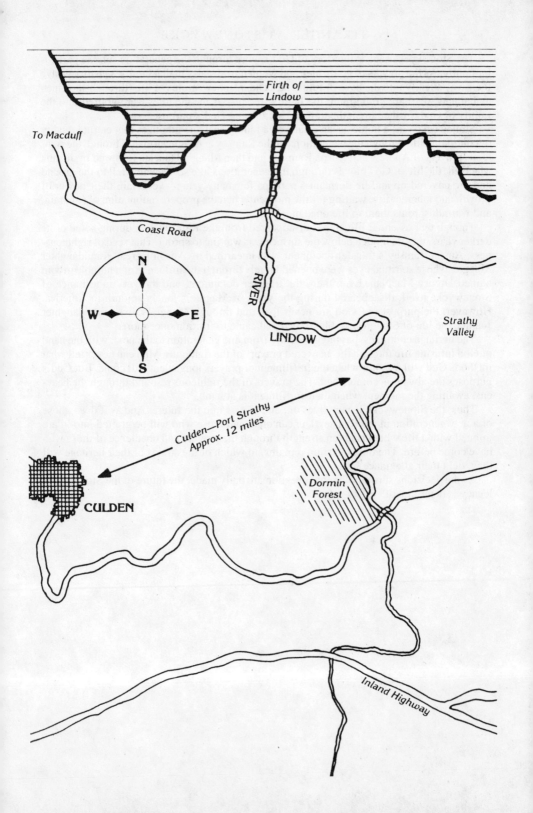

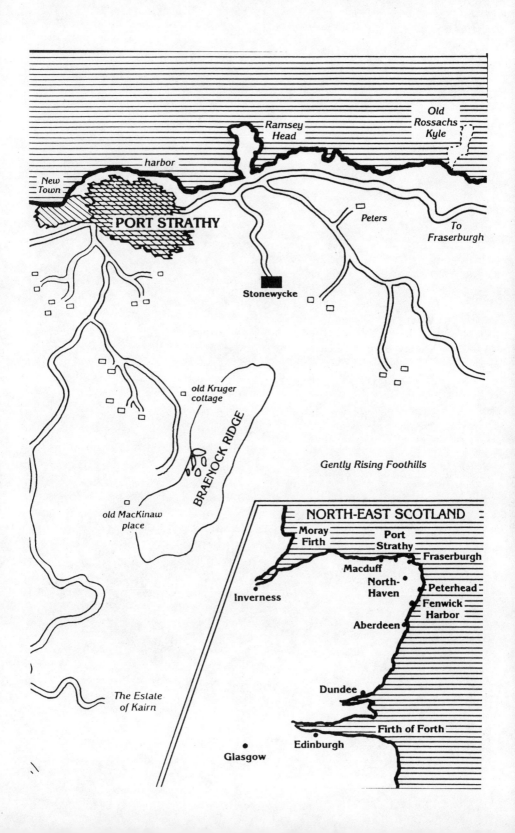

New
Town

harbor

Ramsey
Head

Old
Rossachs
Kyle

PORT STRATHY

Peters

To
Fraserburgh

Stonewycke

old Kruger
cottage

BRAENOCK RIDGE

Gently Rising Foothills

old MacKinaw
place

NORTH-EAST SCOTLAND

Moray
Firth

**Port
Strathy**

Macduff

Fraserburgh

North-
Haven

Peterhead

Inverness

**Fenwick
Harbor**

Aberdeen

*The Estate
of Kairn*

Dundee

Firth of Forth

Edinburgh

Glasgow

1 ❈ Lady Margaret

THE RECENT RAINS lent an invigorating sparkle to the clean northern landscape. White caps on the lapping dark green waves sharpened into crisp focus, and on the horizon the sapphire of the sea and the azure blue of the sky met like a narrow line on an artist's canvas.

Lady Margaret Duncan, heiress and matriarch of the centuries-old Scottish estate of Stonewycke, took a deep breath of the tangy salt air as if she fully expected it to rejuvenate her aging form. In reality, however, she cared little to push back the years. That process was reserved for those whose memories harbored discontent. She had come to savor the years as treasures, quietly at peace with the flow of her life, and with the aging it brought. The passage of time added a richness nothing else could possibly bring, the fulfillment of all that had come before. How could she ever want to go back?

She paused for a moment in her casual stroll along the beach to watch a white-winged gull swoop swiftly down toward the water. It skimmed the glistening surface for a mere second, then arched again into the sky, its quest unsuccessful. Yet it seemed not to mind. The silvery-white bird winged in a widening circle overhead until it once again spotted a potential prey.

But Lady Margaret did not witness the conclusion of the hunt. Her attention instead skipped northward, toward the horizon, where two fishing boats had appeared and were now heading in the direction of the harbor. They must have sailed immediately after yesterday's storm had abated. After a night at sea they were now on their way home. She wondered if the catch had been a good one.

Ah, yes, she was content, at home on the beach she had loved since childhood, the place she delighted in more than anywhere else. This was her Scotland, the country of her ancestors; her Stonewycke, the beloved land of generation upon generation of her own family. It was, she sometimes thought, as if God had created them just for her. Perhaps in a sense He had. For had she been the only human being in existence, He would just as fully have lavished upon her the beauty of His boundless creation, the wonder of His love.

That thought, as it had many times in the past, brought a tear to Lady Margaret's eye. The tears flowed more easily now than when she was young. A hard shell had surrounded her heart then, a shell which God had been able to break only by sending her miles from her homeland. The wilderness years across the sea had been painful, not only for her but also for her husband; the forgiveness that God had sought to implant within their hearts had not taken root easily in the soil of their independent spirits. But throughout the years of their sorrow, confusion, and aloneness, the Lord's hand upon them had never faltered.

How faithful He had been to her and Ian! If only they had been able to grasp the larger scope of God's plan for them sooner! Yet how could they, in the midst of their temporal suffering, perceive that often God's infinite answers to our finite prayers reach their victorious fulfillment only through His work in generations yet to come? As His ways are higher than our ways, so is the inexhaustible depth of His plan for reconciliation beyond the limited vision of our earthbound eyes.

Margaret and Ian now viewed their past, both the years apart and these blessed past two decades they had been allowed to share, not as one of earthly happiness, but of eternal gain. It had been a saga of God's unrelenting pursuit after the heart of man and woman, a chronicle of healing. And as the heritage of their experience continued through the lives of their grandchildren and great-grandchildren, they gave God thanks for the work He had wrought. How grateful they were for Joanna, the treasured granddaughter who had been the instrument in God's hand to bring about their reunion, and for Joanna's husband Alec, whose grafting into the family line had immeasurably strengthened the old Ramsey strain. And now, through their young children, the legacy continued into the third decade of the twentieth century.

Yes, the tears flowed more easily now, but they were tears of great joy which fell from the aged face. If Lord and Lady Duncan had known pain in their youth, it had been well-compensated for in their present contentment. *Twenty-one years ago,* she thought, *I found my husband again. But actually I found much more.* She had rediscovered the friend who had first come to Stonewycke as a mere lad of twenty. Those who knew the old couple only in passing marveled that they had not been together all their lives. Without speaking, they each knew the other's thoughts and feelings, and continually communicated with each other through the simplest gestures and glances. Though both the Lord and Lady of Stonewycke were past their mid-eighties, almost daily they could be seen upon the grassy hills about the estate, occasionally on the beach west of town, and up until recently even once or twice a year upon horseback. The companionship their heavenly Father had seen fit to deprive them of during their middle years of life had been amply restored, and a vitality and strength of body gave them back at the end of their lives the friendship and love each had stored away for so long.

Always they were deep in conversation—but not about the past, nor what might have been. They were too vitally caught up in the glories of the present to dwell long on times gone by. Every day was a new challenge. For the growth of God's life within their hearts had not stopped on that day they were reunited. If anything, it had accelerated. Often Ian now, it seemed, took the lead in spiritual matters, for with the bondage of his past finally shed, he had soared like a bird into the realms of heavenly truths. He often laughed when he thought how good a thing it was that they who wait upon the Lord could run and not be weary—especially for a man his age!

Yes, he had laughed!

These days his laughter—*their* laughter!—rang frequently within the once-somber granite walls of their beloved home, Stonewycke. But it was not their laughter alone. God had given them a wonderful family with whom to share their love, an added dimension of the old couple's joy. The marriage of Joanna and her fine man of faith had given proud old Stonewycke something it had not enjoyed in more than fifty years—the infectious sounds of childish exuberance and life reverberating through its walls. The youngest was May, and Lady Margaret often wondered if even the solid sixteenth-century castle could contain that ten-year-old girl's vibrant energy. Twelve-year-old Nathaniel was, except for his fiery red hair, most like his father. Tall and solidly built, he possessed Alec's easygoing and friendly nature, which made him an immediate favorite with whomever he met. Young Ian, at fourteen, could not have been more unlike his namesake at the same age. Slender and fine-featured, he was the scholar of the family. Margaret knew he was happy where he was—at one of Scotland's fine boarding schools for boys, showing promise for the university. His hunger for learning had never yet been satisfied, and wondrously that hunger served only to deepen his young but growing faith.

Allison, the eldest, had been reserved for last on this day in the gallery of her great-grandmother's thoughts, but not because she was the least. On the contrary, Allison at that moment weighed heaviest on Lady Margaret's mind.

With the very thought of the girl's face, a shadow passed over the old lady's countenance, encroaching upon the peacefulness of the splendid shoreline scene. *Dear Allison, what have we done wrong?* she said to herself. Perhaps too much responsibility had been placed on her as the eldest; or could it be she had not been given enough? Or was it nothing anyone had done at all, but simply the fact that she had been born into the nobility of the Stonewycke heritage?

When Lady Margaret attempted to analyze her great-granddaughter, any lasting insight into the true nature of the girl always seemed to elude her. Allison, for some reason, wore her ancestry like a shield—a shield to protect her from what, or to hide from what—that was difficult to tell.

At seventeen, Allison was not a great deal unlike her great-grandmother had been at the same age—stubborn, headstrong, willful, and independent. But there was an element present that had never been part of young Maggie's makeup. Somehow Allison seemed to take her position as heiress to a noble Scottish lineage more seriously than any of the rest of the family—too seriously. Where she had come by this strain of haughty pride, no one knew—least of all her own mother and father; no one in all the northeast of Scotland would accuse them of anything except too much humility for their high station. Allison's look of disdain revealed, without words, that she considered her family's casual mingling with the commoner elements of society to be deplorable. She kept her feelings silent for the most part, however, not wanting to be reminded that her own father, notwithstanding that he was probably the most loved and respected man in the neighborhood, had come from this so-called "common" strata of the community.

How interesting it is, thought Margaret, *that in this proud family line, the estate of Stonewycke has been passed down for four generations through the women of the family.* Each of those women, it seemed, had a unique and individual story to tell—with the possible exception of Margaret's own daughter Eleanor, who had never seen the land where her life had begun. Yet even Eleanor's contribution to the eternal plan could not be disregarded, nor could the full scope of her portion of the story be grasped this side of the life that was to come, where all stories will be made complete with the endings God purposed for them.

And now young Allison, representing the fifth generation in the continuous female line of Ramseys spanning more than a century, stood on the threshold of her own womanhood. What would the coming years bring for her?

Margaret thought of her own mother Atlanta—proud, silent, a sentinel of Scottish fortitude in the midst of what had not been a happy marriage. Had Allison inherited a high percentage of Atlanta's blood? More likely the pride—if indeed it *was* pride—so evident in her great-granddaughter, had come from Margaret's father James, if it came through the veins of the family blood at all.

Lady Margaret sighed wearily, revealing for the first time a hint of her true age. *Lord,* she prayed silently, *protect Allison and keep your loving hand upon her, and upon those who come after her. Draw them all to you, Lord, as you did me, and as you did Ian. Reveal Yourself to Allison, in your way and in your own time.*

Margaret took in another deep breath of the warm salty air and glanced about her. Unconsciously her gaze had been fixed on the hard-packed expanse of white sand as she slowly walked along. Now she looked toward the rocky cliffs in the distance. Around the swirling eddies of ocean windrafts, twenty or thirty gulls glided up and down, in and out, cavorting in the sea currents. Even from this distance she could hear their screeching calls, grating perhaps to the ear of the musician, but melody in motion to anyone in love with the sea. *What a glorious place you have given me, oh, God,* she thought, *to live out the remainder of my days! How I love this coast of Scotland with its majestic and jagged coastline, the powerful cliffs dotted with the green of heather and a dozen other wiry shrubs. There was no sight I missed so greatly in America, and no sight is more impossible for me to tire of now that I can see it nearly every day. Thank you, Lord, for bringing me back! You have been better to me than I deserve!*

She turned back toward the village. The sigh that came next was one of contentment, and the smile which accompanied it, whether she sought it or not, was a smile of rejuvenation and peace. A chuckle momentarily passed her lips. *I'd better not stray too far! The days are long past since Raven and I could gallop wherever we wanted. If I get too far from Port Strathy now, it could take me the rest of the day to get back!*

With the thought of her own youth, Allison again came to Lady Margaret's mind. But this time she felt that there was a sensitive side to her great-granddaughter, which was struggling to break free more than she allowed anyone to know. This part of her nature was no doubt at battle with the personality she opened for public view. But it would slip out unexpectedly, and the perceptive aging matriarch was quick to notice, saying to herself, "Now *there's* the real Allison. I knew she was in there!" And this hidden self had in recent months become the focus of Margaret's prayers for the girl. *Show her herself, Lord,* she prayed. *When the time is right, give her insight. Let her know you, and let her come to know herself.*

The prayer brought with it the recollection of Walter Innes's death six months earlier. When Allison took her position too seriously, the factor had never been afraid to look her in the eye and tell her exactly what he thought, even if the blood of gentility flowed through her veins. He was perhaps the only one who could hoot at her attempted arrogance, and say, "Whether ye be a leddy or no, lassie, I expect ye're none too noble t' fit o'er my knee."

The two antagonized each other whenever their paths crossed, yet loved each other no less for it. When Innes died, Allison wept the entire day, though she never allowed a soul to see, and only her puffy red eyes and solemn face gave away the depth of her feeling for the man.

Was it pride which caused her to hide this part of her nature? Sadly Lady Margaret shook her head. For if it was, it frightened the old woman to consider what humbling it would take to heal the girl.

Suddenly a shout broke the deep silence imposed by Lady Margaret's thoughts.

"Grandma!"

She turned and looked away from the sea. It was Allison, waving her hand just as her head broke over the top of the great dune bordering the shore. She ran toward her great-grandmother almost as if the latter's thoughts and prayers had drawn her. The wide and lovely smile, lighting her pretty brown eyes, hardly seemed in harmony with what must lay within, if the old lady's estimation and grave concerns were correct. To all appearances she gave every indication of being an energetic young lady who would disregard such glum notions concerning her character with a hearty laugh.

Lady Margaret returned her greeting with a wave and began walking up the dune to meet her. She returned the girl's smile and hugged her warmly. For no matter what else Allison MacNeil thought about life or herself, she must know above all things how greatly she was loved.

2 ❄ *Stonewycke*

JOANNA MacNEIL SAT at her mahogany desk in the dayroom pouring over the accounts one last time.

After a few more moments she set down her pen, propped her chin in her hand, and sighed deeply. Operating an estate like this had never seemed difficult in the fairy tales. Their family had moved up the hill to the castle after eleven years in a little cottage, just as she and Alec had dreamed. They had now been here nine years. Joanna loved Stonewycke and was no less happy than she had been in her homey cottage. She in no way regretted the move, especially knowing that her grandparents could no longer live here alone.

It was just that at times it could be such a burden.

The requirements of her position still surprised her, and she occasionally found herself lapsing back into her midwestern American timidity. Though she had been here twenty years, had picked up the local dialect noticeably, and thought of herself as a true Scot in every sense of the word, it still usually took her aback when one of the local women curtsied to her in town, or made way for her to pass in a crowd. At such times it was with a jolt that she had to remind herself who she was and of all the people who depended upon her.

Is this really me? she found herself asking. But then she reflected on how the Lord had led her to Scotland, and how she and Alec had met. What changes God had worked within her own heart for her to become the confident woman He had made! He had miraculously healed her grandmother and reunited her with her husband, and Joanna's own grandfather Dorey. When she remembered these things, her heart was filled with thanksgiving—even for the tedious paperwork which lay upon her desk.

Thank you, Lord, she said softly. *And teach me greater thankfulness of heart for these details which keep Stonewycke going.*

Suddenly the door behind her burst open.

"Mother, I've found it!" exclaimed Allison, hurrying toward her mother.

Joanna turned, smiled at her daughter's enthusiasm, and before she had the chance to say a word, found a magazine thrust onto the desktop before her. With obvious satisfaction the girl opened it to a full-page advertisement of an extremely pretty, not to mention a very expensive, evening dress. Most certainly made of satin, though the sketch made it difficult to tell, it was rather simple in design with a draped neckline trimmed in sequins, and a fitted bodice and skirt. Simple, that is, until it reached the knees, where it flared to remarkable fullness. Joanna had the good sense to keep to herself the first impression that such a dress was much too mature for her seventeen-year-old daughter.

"It's beautiful, darling," she said.

"It will be *perfect* for the Bramfords' ball!" replied Allison in high-pitched excitement. "Oh, Mother! please say I can have it!"

"Well, perhaps with a few adjustments," Joanna replied diplomatically. "We can show this to Elsie and see what she can do."

"Elsie . . . adjustments!" exclaimed the girl. "Mother, I want *this* dress—just like it is. And I don't want Elsie to make it!"

"What do you have against Elsie?"

"Mother, *please*! You wouldn't make me go to the Bramfords' in a homemade dress?" Allison's pleading tone sounded as if such would be a fate too horrible even to contemplate.

"Elsie does very professional work."

"It would be different if she were a designer," argued Allison. "But she is only a dress-maker, hardly more than a common *seamstress*."

"Allison, have you bothered to notice the price of this dress? It's fifty pounds. For many of our people, that's half a year's wages! In these times when there are so many who are suffering, I simply can't condone such frivolity—"

"I knew you'd say that!"

"It's true, dear."

"But when the nobility display their wealth, it gives the common people hope that things aren't really so bad."

Joanna had heard that worn excuse so often she didn't know whether to laugh or cry when the words came from the lips of her own daughter. How many in the aristocracy used just such an argument to justify their unnecessary opulence, and to waylay their guilt when their eyes could not disregard the widespread poverty around them? Times were hard throughout all of Britain, even all the world. But those in a position to help often did least of all.

"Allison," said Joanna after a moment's reflection, "I sincerely pray that you will give your words deep thought, and that the day will come when you will realize how empty they are. When we transferred the land to the people of Port Strathy twenty years ago, *that* was the thing which bound the nobility to the people who looked to them for guidance and sus-tenance. Giving our wealth, not displaying it, is our calling. In the meantime, we cannot pay that kind of money for a dress. These are hard times not only for the working class, but for us as well. Elsie can make the same dress for a third the cost."

"Without adjustments . . . ?" queried Allison who, seeing the war inevitably lost, hoped she might still reap a small victory.

"I'll have to give that more thought."

"I *am* seventeen."

Joanna smiled and took her daughter's hand in hers. "I know that, dear. And you are a lovely seventeen, with or without the dress. But I will keep it in mind."

"The ball is next month."

"I'll let you know in a few days."

Allison scooped up the magazine and exited, leaving Joanna once more alone. Uncon-sciously she found herself praying for her daughter. *She is so young, Lord, and has so much to learn . . .*

Her thoughts trailed off with no words to complete them.

Sometimes she wanted to shout at Allison out of her pent-up frustration: "Why can't you see! Why must you do everything your own way? Why can't you listen to what we have to teach you?"

Usually she refrained. But the unsettling realization that her daughter did not share the beliefs and priorities of the rest of the family was never far from Joanna's mind. And the older she grew, the more the distance seemed to widen between the mother and the daughter she loved so deeply.

Allison had always been the kind of girl who had to figure things out for herself. Her methods were, therefore, often fraught with obstacles and unexpected curves. When the first bicycle had come to Stonewycke, as a seven-year-old she had insisted on learning to ride it on the steepest path on the estate. Two years earlier, despite repeated warnings, only by sticking her entire hand into the hive did she learn the dangers of the bee. But as her adolescent years began to teach Allison the ways of life on more profound levels, the perils became far more hazardous and long-lasting than skinned knees and bee stings. Though Joanna firmly believed that the values of her childhood were still rooted deep inside her daughter, they became increasingly difficult to observe on the surface. One by one she seemed to be holding these values up for scrutiny, examining them, testing them, doubting them, suspicious that anything appropriate for a child could possibly be strong enough to hold her up now. Like youths in all ages, it never occurred to her that many men and women, older and wiser and with problems and anxieties more severe than hers, had discovered in those timeless principles sustenance and hope to carry them through all the dark valleys of life. Allison's young eyes seemed blinded to all but Allison herself. This fact did not so much hurt Joanna's motherly pride as it made her ache for the distance it placed between Allison and her Maker. And to make matters worse still, Allison kept such a close wall around her true self that even her mother could often no longer venture within. In fact, Allison's alienation, when displayed, seemed more directed toward her mother and Lady Margaret than anyone else, even though she had always been close to these two older women.

The girl was a paradox, that much was certain! At times she could be so warm and loving and affectionate, especially toward her great-grandmother. Then suddenly, without warning, an altogether different mood could sweep over her, during which she was cold, even embittered, toward those she loved most.

Joanna rubbed her eyes as if finally noticing the headache which had been threatening for the last two hours. Well, a new dress for Allison was simply another burden to add to the steadily growing pile. And was there a small twinge of guilt because she didn't have the money to buy her daughter the dress she wanted? Would the dress perhaps convince Allison that . . . ?

No! Joanna quickly put a stop to that seductive train of thought. Even if they had the money, she could never allow it to be spent irresponsibly. And it was a moot question regardless. There was absolutely no room in the present accounts for such a costly dress.

Indeed, the fairy tales never specified just how much money it took to run a castle. Of course, there were no Depressions in fairy tales, either. The color red was showing more and more often in the ledger these days, and last year they had begun opening the House for public tours to bring in a little additional cash. To further conserve funds, without at first realizing the consequences, they had stopped maintaining the little-used east wing of the house, with the result that it had practically gone to ruin. A carpenter had recently informed them that if something was not done—and done soon—to save the roof, it would be lost and could bring down a good portion of the adjoining wing with it.

When they had enacted Anson Ramsey's Transfer Document twenty years ago, turning over a large part of the estate to the people of the valley and drastically reducing their yearly cash income, they had never foreseen what a problem money would one day become. However, the people of Port Strathy, and the sons and daughters who had inherited the good fortunes brought upon their families by the current two generations in the Ramsey line, had never forgotten. They loved Lady Margaret and Lord Duncan and Lady Joanna and Lord Alec with a love enjoyed by few in their position. Consequently, when the net of hard times began to draw itself about the valley, the people pulled together—commoners and landowners alike—to help see one another through. Many were the small offerings of fruit and produce and fish brought up the hill "t' the Hoose," as it was still called. And with the first news carried to the village that the east wing of the castle was in need of repair, a hundred men were on hand shortly after daybreak the following morning.

Perhaps, sighed Joanna as she reflected on it, *the loss of Stonewycke would work for Allison's ultimate good.* Perhaps it was because she had always had too much that she now came to think wealth and privilege a right.

Yet at the mere thought of losing Stonewycke, a deep pang of despair swept momentarily through Joanna. She could not imagine life without Stonewycke. For good or ill, the place was woven deeply into her very being. Homeless and alone she had come to Scotland that day so long ago. Now she had been grafted into the years of her family's heritage and was an intrinsic part of the ongoing flow of Stonewycke's history. Yet times were hard, and growing harder every year. Who could tell what they might be called upon to do?

If only they could hang on to the estate until the old folks were gone! She and Alec could be happy anywhere. She knew that. She sometimes wondered if Alec would prefer living the simple life of a country vet rather than as the laird of a great property. He still refused to let anyone call him "the laird" in his hearing. He would always be just plain Alec to the people of Port Strathy. *Could it be for the best to let Stonewycke go?* Joanna wondered. *Could that be what God wanted?*

"Dear Lord," Joanna murmured aloud, "you mean more to me, to any of us, than this parcel of land and trees and stone. I would gladly give it all up to do your will, to serve you and these people you have given us more fully."

Joanna paused. Whenever she turned to the Lord in prayer, her thoughts unconsciously strayed to the daughter who tugged so constantly on her heart.

"Oh, God!" she cried out, "I would give up Stonewycke, even my own life, if somehow by it you could reach Allison!"

Joanna bowed her head, but no more words came from her lips. Only her heart silently cried out, interceding where her tongue and conscious mind could not.

"You have it in your hands, don't you, Lord?" she said after another few moments of silence. "In my mortal mind I am unable to see how you will work it out. But somehow you will provide for my daughter's needs, and also for this land. Somehow, you will bring an answer . . ."

How fortunate it was that Joanna depended on her Father in heaven! The eyes of her infinite God saw beyond the contrite woman praying at her desk, beyond the teenage girl poring over a fashion magazine, beyond the aging matriarch lying down for a rest after her afternoon's walk on the beach, beyond the inanimate granite walls of an ancient castle. His all-seeing eye did not stop there. It reached beyond the expanse of the quaint northern village of Port Strathy and the valley surrounding it. It reached beyond the rugged highlands and grassy glens, to the lowlands of Scotland, and farther down, to the very heart of that chief of all cities hundreds of miles to the south.

God's faithful answer, as so often is the case, would come from a most unlooked-for source, from a place that Joanna, even in her most wildly imaginative mood, could never have suspected. And if she could have had a glimpse of the provision of God in answer to her prayer for her daughter and for her beloved Stonewycke, she would not have recognized it as from Him.

Joanna's silent cries did not float into an empty universe to dissolve into nothingness. Even before the plea had left her aching mother's breast, it had taken root in the loving heart of God, who heard, and whose answer was already on the way.

3 ❈ *The Sinner and the Serpent*

AN OMINOUS LONDON fog drifted slowly in over the city from Southend as dusk made its appearance. Before another hour had passed, the streets and sidewalks would be slippery wet from the drizzle; residents walking home from their day's employment brandishing their trusty umbrellas, all the while flatly denied that this heavy mist was actually rain.

The young man striding purposefully down Hampstead Road behind Euston Station seemed unconcerned about the weather, for he was nearing his destination, a pub known as Pellam's, about a block away. He did, however, touch the rim of his new felt fedora a bit protectively, hoping he'd escape the drenching which was inevitable on nights such as this.

Looking across the street, he hailed a lad selling newspapers, removing a coin from his pocket as he did so. A newspaper should serve the purpose as well as an umbrella, which he did not happen to have.

"Here you go, lad," he said, flipping the coin to the boy, who caught it deftly as he ran toward him from the street.

"Thank'ee, sir," he replied with a grin as he handed him the paper. "Lemme gi' ye yer change."

"Don't trouble yourself," said the older of the two magnanimously. The boy grinned again and skipped off to peddle more of his wares. He clearly believed himself to have encountered one of London's elite, and would repeat many times over how a lord had given him a shilling for a newspaper.

The generous Logan Macintyre would be the last to refute the lad's misconception. And, dressed in a well-tailored cashmere pin stripe suit, silk necktie, and expensive wool overcoat, and, of course, the new fedora, he looked less the son of a ne'er-do-well Glasgow laborer than of a London lord. It was a ruse he was content to perpetuate as long as there were folks naive enough to accept it.

He also liked to pass himself off as thirty and, though in reality but twenty-two, he was usually as successful with this chicanery as with the other hoaxes he had pulled off in his young life. His boyish features, softly rounded about the chin with a slightly upturned nose and a thick crop of unruly brown wavy hair, might have helped dispel doubt as to his age to the more discerning. But most were fooled by his finely honed air of sophistication.

Logan paused at a corner to allow an auto to pass, then crossed the street. Glancing at his watch, he decided it was just about time. He'd soon have his shilling back—nearly the last bit of cash he had to his name. except his stake for the game—and much more along with it. For by now his partner Skittles would have everything set up to perfection.

Logan thought of his friend with an unmistakable touch of pride—like the devotion of a son for his father, though in truth he had never harbored similar feelings for his real father who had been in and out of one Glasgow jail after another. Whether Logan resented him because of what he was, or because he wasn't good enough at it to elude the police, would be difficult to determine. For his friend and mentor could hardly lay claim to an upright life of veracity and virtue. Somehow though, Logan admired him, even loved him.

Old Skittles—whose given name was the less colorful Clarence Ludlowe—was recognized in the circles of those who knew such things as the best sharp in the business. He had earned his peculiar nickname some thirty-odd years ago, before the turn of the century when the old Queen, as he called her, was still on the throne; he ran the most lucrative Skittles racket in London. He had been able to maneuver the pins with such nimble precision that even the wariest fool could not tell he was being taken. And if the game of skittles was somewhat outmoded in this modern and sophisticated era of stage plays, talkies, cafeterias, and high fashion, the old con man still maintained the status of a legend among his compatriots.

But the Depression had hit the confidence business, too. People were now more reluctant than ever to part with their money, and it took a more astute strategy to make a scheme succeed than in the old days. You had to choose not only your mark but also your partners with caution. But with the right decoy in place, it could still be like taking candy from a baby when a master such as Skittles went to work.

Perhaps it was due to their mutual respect for each other's finesse at the game that allowed Skittles and Logan to work so well together. Logan's one regret in life was that he hadn't been with his old friend in his early days. "What times we would have had!" he remarked more than once. For in his later years, Skittles had legitimized his enterprises somewhat, earning most of his income bookmaking, a practice—as long as he kept to the rules— that allowed him to operate inside the law. He was, however, known to take cash bets upon occasion, a procedure forbidden by law. For the most part the local constabulary did not scrutinize Skittles' improprieties too closely, although Logan had been stung a time or two by carelessly getting too close to a couple of cash deals.

Cooling his heels twice in the neighborhood tollbooth and once in Holloway for several days taught him more than all Skittles' remonstrations about keeping his eyes open in front of him, and guarding his flank as well. At twenty-two, he had begun to learn that important lesson and had not seen the inside of a jail in more than a year. He now left the cash bookmaking to others who might want to risk it. For himself, he would stick to what he enjoyed most. And besides, swindling another man was not strictly recognized as a criminal offense. Most magistrates based their lenient decisions on the old adage. "A fool and his money are soon parted," believing that the world will never be purged of dishonesty or swindling, and that a victim had only himself to blame for his folly. Thus, Logan committed to memory the famous quotation of eighteenth-century Chief Justice Holt—"Shall we indict one man for making a fool of another?"—to be pulled out and recited should he encounter any unenlightened bobbies who gave him a hard knock, and in the meantime he went about his activities with relish and spirit.

In another five minutes Logan reached Pellam's, and he turned into the establishment now crowded with workmen having a drink or two before boarding trains home. The setup was perfect! He glanced quickly around with pleasure. Not only was the swelling crowd suitable, but in addition, many appeared to be businessmen whose fat wallets and large egos concerning their intellectual prowess would play right into their hands. They would, no doubt, egg each other on in the emptying of their pound notes onto the bar better than Logan himself could.

Skittles, with his slick-combed hair, bulbous nose, florid cheeks, and altogether friendly countenance, sat at the bar with a frothing pint of ale in his hand, his workman's trousers and grimy leather vest completing the illusion that he was just off a hard day's work on the job. The checkered cap sitting far back on his head seemed about to topple off as a result of the animated discussion in which he was engaged with one of his neighbors. Logan passed by, and without so much as a sideglance or the least hesitation in his voice, Skittles knew he was there. The only indication he gave of his friend's presence was a momentary flash in his eyes which his companion took for the prelude to one more intoxicated tale of dubious factual content. Logan ordered a pint and seated himself in an adjacent booth.

Soon Skittles' voice rose slightly above the general din of the place. His cockney accent contained a purposefully noticeable drunken slur, but Logan knew the man was as sober as an undertaker. For far from laboring in London's streets all day, Skittles had only just now begun his night's work.

"Gawd's troth!" he said, lowering his glass to the counter with a resounding thud to emphasize his words.

"The Queen herself?" asked the man seated to Skittles' right, half incredulous, half concealing a laugh at the lunacy of the thought of this old drunk at Buckingham Palace.

"Dear old Vicky—Gawd rest 'er sowl!" exclaimed Skittles. "'Course I were but a lad then, an' much better lookin', if I do say so m'sel'."

"Incredible!" said another.

"Why, 'tis as true as Jonah slayin' Goliath!" returned Skittles in a wounded tone, but hardly had the words had time to sink in than a great laugh broke out behind him. He turned sharply around, glaring toward the source of the merriment being made at his expense.

"Hey, young fella!" he called out with feigned anger. "Are you dispargin' the word of a gent'man?"

Logan dabbed the corners of his eyes with his handkerchief and tried to look apologetic. "I'm terribly sorry," he said at length. "I couldn't help myself."

"An' you think I'm lyin', or maybe too drunk t' know me own words, is that it?" he challenged.

"In actuality I did not hear your story at all but only caught your last remark."

"An' wot of that?" Skittles had just the right edge to his voice and Logan was reminded once more of what a true pro his friend was. By now those in the immediate vicinity had begun to turn their heads in the direction of the conversation, which was steadily increasing in volume.

"Well, sir, it was, as a matter-of-fact, David who slew Goliath. Jonah was swallowed by the whale."

"He's right there, gov!" chimed in one of the men behind Logan, who was now listening intently.

"Ow, is 'e now?" said Skittles with animated gesture. "Excuse me! I must say I didn't know as we 'ad a bleedin' *parson* in our midst!"

His barbed ridicule of the dapper young know-it-all pleased the crowd, whose chuckles now began to spread out in increasing ripples throughout the room.

Unperturbed, Logan humbly shored up his defense. "I am by no means of such lofty repute, my good man. I have only a layman's knowledge in matters of a religious nature."

"Then you don't claim t' know *everythin'*?"

"Well . . ." and here Logan looked away for a moment and tried to show interest in his ale, "it would be a bit foolish of me to make such a claim, wouldn't you say?"

"So you don't know everythin'," probed Skittles further, "but you think you're a lot smarter than me, is that it?"

"I did not say that, nor would I, old man," returned Logan, taking a sip of his brew. "And as I have been something of a student in these matters, it would hardly be fitting for me to boast of my knowledge over a man who's already had—"

"*So*! We gots a prodigy in our midst!" declared Skittles mockingly.

"What's the matter, old man?" interjected Skittles' neighbor, himself a good pint past what was good for him, and still thinking about the sharp's churlish claims before Logan happened in, "Are you afraid this young man knows more'n you, an' you bein' Queen Vicky's friend 'at ye are?"

"I 'appen t' be a church-goin' man," boasted Skittles, "an' I been doin' so longer'n this wee laddie 'ere's been alive."

"Here! here!" chimed in someone from across the room.

Another laughed.

"I didn't mean to imply—" began Logan, but Skittles brashly interrupted him.

"Why, if you're such a knowin' young fella," he said, "I gots five quid in me pocket 'ere that says you can't tell me the name o' who it was wot gave Adam the apple t' eat."

"I wouldn't want to take your money so easily," replied Logan. "And besides, everyone knows it was the—"

"Say nothin' without puttin' your money on the table!" interrupted Skittles.

Logan hesitated a moment, seemingly mulling the proposition over in his mind. Then he reached a hand inside his coat, and saying, "All right, you're on, you old fool! Here's my five pounds that says it was the serpent!" he slapped a five-pound note onto the table in front of Skittles.

"I didn't ask *what* it was," said Skittles, reaching out to take Logan's money. "I bet you couldn't tell me the *name*!"

"Not so fast," returned Logan. "His name was Satan. There's the answer to your question! Satan . . . the devil . . . the serpent—whatever you want to call him. I think the ten pounds is mine!"

"Keep your 'and from off the table!" said Skittles. "My five quid still says you be wrong!"

"He's beat ye, old man!" cried someone from across the room. "He's beat ye at yer own game! Give 'im the note an' don't be a sore loser."

"Who's talkin' about losin'?" cried Skittles, spinning toward the voice. "I got another fiver I'll lay 'gainst yours wot says you're both wrong!"

The owner of the voice strode forward, placed his own note in front of Skittles and said, "The serpent's name was Satan, like the young fella said. Everyone in this room knows it. But if ye be givin' yer money away, then I'll be happy t' oblige an' take it from ye."

"Any other takers?" screamed Skittles, as if in a fit of passion. "Why can't any of you dull-witted blokes tell me the right name?"

A momentary shuffling ensued, during which several near Logan looked to him with questioning glances as if to ask, "Are ye *sure* ye got the right name, mate?" His confirming nod of self-assurance and confidence sent several hands in search of wallets. One by one, pound- and five-pound notes began accumulating on the table in front of Skittles, who continued to drink his ale and act more inebriated all the time. When the table contained some twenty or twenty-five pounds, suddenly Logan jumped up.

"Wait just a minute! Something's not right here. We've put our money on the table and have given our answer. But we still haven't seen anything but that first five-pound note of yours! I don't think you've even got this kind of money to cover these bets!"

A murmur of agreement and approval went through the crowd. By now the attention of everyone in the pub was focused in the drama with Skittles right in the middle of it.

Without saying a word, Skittles reached into his pocket and pulled forth a handful of notes, holding them aloft in a clenched fist that hid the fact that most of the bills were only flash notes. "Fifty quid, me doubting frien's!" he said. "One month's labor fit t' break the back of any son of Adam!" Then as if producing his bankroll were tantamount to winning the questionable wager, with a self-satisfied expression of well-being, he raised his glass to his lips and swallowed down the remaining third of the pint.

Looks of amazement accompanied low whistles and "ah's" as Logan slowly returned to his seat, looking around as he did so with glances to those around him which conveyed, "This old duffer's loonier than I thought!"

"Now!" concluded Skittles, "I'll put me whole wad up t' prove I'm a smarter man than the parson here!"

Within ten minutes the table was piled with the full fifty pounds in bets.

"And now," said a well-dressed man whose investment happened to be six pounds, "just where do you intend to find your proof? I don't have all night to wait for my twelve pounds!"

"Proof . . . get me a Bible," said Skittles.

A roar of laughter went up. "In this place!" yelled someone.

Logan stood and approached the bar. "My good man," he said to the pubkeeper, "would you by chance have a Bible on the premises? I need to show this well-intentioned but ignorant man where he is in error."

"The wife'll have one up t' the parlor," the man replied.

"Would you be so kind as to let us borrow it for a moment?"

The man hesitated, but immediately received such prodding from his patrons that he turned and hastened up to his flat on the second floor. In two or three minutes he returned, and handed the old, black, leather-bound volume to Logan.

"Thank you," said Logan, who immediately began flipping through the pages toward the beginning of the book.

"The Book of Genesis!" called out Skittles. "Who's name were it wot gave Adam the apple?"

"I told you before," replied Logan, all eyes upon him, "that the serpent's name was Satan. Now, if I can just find it . . ." he added, almost to himself, continuing to turn over the leaves of the Bible.

"Chapter three . . . verse 12," said Skittles.

Logan turned another page, stopped, read for a few moments in silence, then sank back to his chair looking as one stunned. By now the room had grown quiet.

"Well, what does it say?" asked the six-pound investor.

"Tell 'im, parson!" said Skittles, a grin of fiendish delight spreading over his face. Then he burst into a great peal of riotous laughter. "Read it, laddie!" he taunted. "Or shall I tell 'em wot it says?"

Slowly and deliberately, and in measured tones so that there would be no mistaking his words, Logan began to read: "And the man said, The woman whom thou gavest to be with me, *she* gave me of the tree, *and I did eat.*"

"It were *Eve*!" shouted Skittles with triumph. "*Eve* gave the bloke the apple, not the serpent!"

"You said *he*!" objected one of the many victims.

"I said, 'I say you can't tell me the name o' who it was wot gave Adam the apple.' That's wot I said, as the Lord an' Queen Vicky be my witnesses. Your young frien' there, the know-it-all parson, *he* said it were the serpent, an' then I said, 'I bet you couldn't tell me the name.'"

Again Skittles burst out in uproarious laughter, then stood, clutching at his head; though the drunkenness was all part of the deception, he had still had a bit more ale than he was accustomed to.

With the pub about equally split between the gloomy set who had taken the bait and followed Logan into the trap, and those who were now congratulating themselves that they had kept out of it, Skittles gathered up his winnings, with the humility of a peacock in full feather. He gave Logan a condescending pat on the shoulder, and a smug, "Sorry, old chap . . . you should stick t' your preachin' an' stay out of dens o' iniquity like this," and with that he half-strutted, half-staggered out of the pub.

Logan sat on for some time longer, ordering another pint and turning his dejected stares silently into the amber glass. His momentary newfound friends gave him cool glances, and the wan smile of apology on his lips whenever he did happen to look around did little to alleviate their reproachful looks. "Oh, well," he said to himself, "a fool and his money are soon parted. You gullible dolts should have known better than to believe a good-for-nothing like me!"

This was always the most difficult part of this particular dodge—knowing the right time to make an exit. Natural instinct urged him to hurry out on Skittles' heels. But that would be too obvious. However, if he waited too long, someone might eventually put two and two—or in this case five and five—together.

Therefore, he drained his drink in a leisurely fashion, glanced tiredly at his watch, and casually announced to no one in particular, "Just about time for the seven-ten." He then rose, gathered up his newspaper, set his fedora back on his head, and exited. A number of stares followed him, but no one said anything or attempted to stop him. They all appeared glad enough to let him go.

He found Skittles at their preappointed rendezvous in front of a newsstand about four blocks away. He ran forward, slapping his old friend on the back.

"You did good, lad!" laughed Skittles.

"I can never believe how they fall for it!"

"They do every time," replied the experienced sharp as he dug the wad of money from his pocket. As he did so he moved away from the stand to the darkness of an overhang at the edge of an alley. "An' this time," he went on in a subdued voice, "t' the tune of fifty quid!"

Logan could hardly restrain the whoop he felt like making as Skittles began counting off from the stack of bills. "'Ere's your 'alf, Logan. You earned it!"

Logan took the money and stood for a moment just admiring it. Most men had to work a month, sometimes two or three, at dirty, grueling labor for this kind of cash. He had gotten it all in less than an hour! *Not bad,* he thought as he pocketed the loot.

Business out of the way and the exchange settled amiably, the two men began walking, unperturbed by the darkness and the deepening foggy drizzle. Their conversation turned to what they'd do with their new-found wealth. Skittles mentioned a new dress or possibly that ornate plum hat he'd seen his wife Molly admiring in a store window the other day. Logan figured he'd better pay his long overdue rent.

Skittles stopped and laid an earnest hand on Logan's arm. "Wot you need, my young frien', is a good woman t' spen' your money on—that is, a good wife like my Molly."

Logan laughed. "That's just like a married man—wanting to wish their misery on everyone else."

"I been with Molly thirty years now, an' though there may 'ave been a bad day or two, there n'er were a bad week in the lot," replied Skittles with a tone and look in his aging eyes that was deeply sincere.

"And there's the point!" Logan slapped the newspaper he had been holding against his hand for emphasis. "How many gems like Molly do you suppose there are in this world? Not many I'll wager! No thank you," he said, shaking his head. "I don't care to take my chances."

"Well, you're a young strapper yet," said Skittles, looking dreamily into the fog. "I 'spect the day'll come when you'll fin' yoursel' someone you'll want t' settle down with."

"I doubt I'll ever become an upstanding businessman like yourself, Skits."

Now it was the older man's turn to chuckle. "There are them wot consider certain aspects o' my so-called upstandin' *business* illegal, e'en though they're pretty good about lettin' you lay out bets if you do it all properlike."

"Well, at least you run it like a gentleman."

" 'Ere's where I turn for 'ome, Logan," said Skittles as they reached a broad but deserted intersection. "Come with me an' say 'ello t' Molly. 'Ave some stew an' tatties with us."

"Another time, Skits."

"Plans?"

"Nah. It's just too early for me to be in for the night."

"Suit yoursel'."

"Good night, Skits."

"You did good at Pellam's, lad."

4 ❊ Skittles

THAT NIGHT LOGAN spent a bit more of his booty than he intended. Cards, dice, more ale, and a rather foolish sense of false invulnerability all combined to leave him penniless by the time he returned to his flat in the early hours of the morning. He had often been in this position and it caused him no great concern. A new day would bring new opportunities! He did, however, take special care as he passed his landlady's door; he would just have to avoid her for a few more days.

It was almost ten when he woke from a sound sleep. The dreary March clouds showed signs of trying to break up, allowing a few rays of sun to push through. But a steady north wind blew as if to warn that the lull in the weather would be short-lived.

As Logan swung his feet out of bed, his first thought was of food; his stomach was sending out reminders that he'd have been wiser to do more eating than gambling the night before. But even a cursory glance about his flat would have told anyone that the last thing they'd expect to find there was a decent meal. It boasted but one room, which was reasonably tidy if only because there was so little present to clutter it up. Save for sleeping, Logan did very little in these quarters. His meals he either took with Skittles and Molly or in any of a dozen public houses of which he was a frequent visitor.

His prospects for breakfast were slim if he remained where he was. In fifteen minutes he was dressed and on his way over to Skittles' place. Besides the thought of a cup of tea with something solid to go with it, he wanted to confer with his friend on a new money-making scheme, made all the more imperative by his imprudent behavior the night before after they had parted.

Skittles' flat in Shoreditch was a hearty walk for a man with benefit of neither cab fare nor breakfast. And when he reached it, the climb up the tenement's three steep flights of stairs left him panting as he gave several short raps on the door. The exercise had sharpened his appetite more than ever, but the moment Molly Ludlowe opened the door all thought of food vanished.

"Molly, what is it?" Logan exclaimed.

"'Tis Skittles," she replied. "He got 'imself beaten an' robbed last night—Ow! He's all right," she added quickly, seeing the look of panic that crossed Logan's face. "Came in about midnight—dragged 'imself all the way up these curs'd stairs!"

"Has he seen a doctor?"

"Ow, he'd 'ave none of that—stubborn bloke that he is! He'd 'ave t' be at death's door t' let a doctor go pokin' aroun' 'im—an' that's a fact!" Logan could see the pain hidden in Molly's face behind her helpless outburst of frustration.

"Did he talk to the police?"

"An' when might he 'ave done that, I ask you, Logan? He just come 'ome last night an's been in bed ever since."

She paused a moment and looked toward the floor, averting Logan's gaze, embarrassed for her shortness with her husband's friend. But she was afraid for her man, and could not help thinking that perhaps it was because of his association with Logan and others like him that Skittles got into these jams.

"Well, don't just stand there," she added at length, "come on in."

Notwithstanding the occasional rough edges around Molly's demeanor, the interior of her cheap little flat gave ample evidence that beneath her gruff cockney exterior beat the heart of a lady. Here was the kind of room anyone would count it a privilege to call home. Without the least hint of affluence, it was, even through the unmistakable signs of poverty, a place where the love that had gone into its arrangement could be felt. Crochet doilies lay on the threadbare arms of the sofa. A shelf of nic-a-bric and a few books sat against the far wall. And the pictures on the other walls—a few photos and a print or two of idyllic country scenes—had all clearly been chosen with care. It was hardly surprising that Logan felt more comfortable here than in his own flat.

"Did he lose much?" asked Logan after Molly closed the door behind him.

"Won't say. He's bein' close about the whole thing. Said the bla'arts got away clean so wouldn't do nothin' to call a bobbie."

"That's not like Skittles," replied Logan, pondering Molly's words. His friend loved a good story. And if it was true, all the better. Even if he had to embellish the actual facts, it gave him no less pleasure in the retelling. A good street mugging, especially if it was his own personal adventure, should have provided him with story material for weeks and be worth all the temporary pain. There must be some reason why he was being so tight-lipped. The moment the thought crossed his mind, Logan suspected what that reason undoubtedly was.

"Can I see him?" he asked, glancing in the direction of the closed bedroom door.

"He might be sleepin', but you're welcome t' try. He'd no doubt like t' see you."

"I won't wake him."

Logan walked to the door and opened it slowly. He could do nothing to silence the squeak of its rusty hinges, however, and even before he poked his head inside he heard a moan from the direction of the bed. He approached slowly, and even in the subdued light of the room, Logan could tell that Skittles had endured more than an ordinary mugging. His friend looked more like a prize-fighter the morning after a rough ten rounds than an aging bookmaker. His usually florid complexion had taken on a bluish-gray hue, his thick nose was cut and battered, and his eyes—nearly swollen shut—made his friendly features appear almost sinister. Without his cap he looked much older than usual, somehow shrunken from his usual stature.

At the sound of the door opening he turned his head, his eyes as wide as the swelling would permit. He glanced at the clock on the sideboard, tried to rise, then winced and fell back in pain.

"Wot does the woman think?" he bellowed—or rather snarled, for the actual sounds which emerged from his pain-thickened lips were subdued and forced. "The day's nigh gone—I'll end me days in the poor'ouse if I sleep away the bleedin' day!"

"You're feeling a mite better, I see?" said Logan hopefully.

"'Course I'm better!" And as if to substantiate the truth of his words, Skittles struggled to work his way into a sitting position, and thence to his feet. But before he could complete the undertaking, he fell back against the pillow once more. "Blimey!" he hissed in frustration.

"Won't hurt you to take a day or two off, Skits," said Logan, and as he spoke he reached down to try to rearrange one of the pillows.

"No need t' make such a fuss!" he replied, trying to shove Logan's hands away. "I'm not a baby! The only real loss is me 'at, wot fell off in the close by the shop where the bla'arts jumped me. Now," he added, trying to clutch at Logan who was still trying to fiddle with the pillows, "just give a 'and. That's all I need, an' I'll be up an' out of 'ere!"

"You just lie there!" said Logan firmly. "You should talk to a bobbie, Skits. Are you sure you didn't see the blokes?"

"I'm sure," Skittles mumbled, and turned his head away.

"Not a clue?"

Skittles only shook his head in reply.

"You're sure?"

There was still no answer, and in his friend's silence Logan perceived the answer he had suspected from the first.

"It was Chase Morgan, wasn't it? Tell the truth, Skits."

"Leave it be, Logan."

"We *can't* leave it be! Don't you see—"

Logan cut off his words sharply as Molly entered carrying a tray.

"Thought you might be able to use some food," she said to her husband. "An' there's plenty for you, too, Logan," she added.

"Breakfast in bed!" grumbled Skittles. "Now, that's takin' it a mite too far!"

"An' 'ere's a cold damp cloth for that eye," she went on, ignoring his grousing. "It'll need stitches, I shouldn't wonder."

Skittles said nothing to her last remark, but appeared to soften as he detected the concern in her voice. He reached up and gave her hand a squeeze. The look which passed between them belied their verbal sparring and was filled with tenderness. A moment or two longer Molly fussed about the meal. Then, with a gentle admonition to Logan not to overtax the patient, she departed.

The moment the door closed, Skittles turned to his young friend and said, "Don't you breathe so much as a word about Morgan t' me Molly."

"What do you take me for?" Logan replied. "But don't you see, Skits? We can't let him pull here what he did in America!"

"I've tried," said Skittles. "But wot are a couple of no-account blokes like us goin' t' do? It's cost me o'er fifty quid this week t' try t' resist 'im."

"Fifty quid!"

"I 'ad me receipts from the shop with me besides what we picked up at Pellam's," explained Skittles. "All he wants is five quid a week for 'is so-called *protection*. Look at 'ow much I'd already 'ave saved if I'd paid 'im from the start."

"It's highway robbery, Skits!"

Skittles managed a hoarse chuckle at the words.

"An' just wot do you call wot *we* do for a livin', lad?" he queried. "I s'pose I'm gettin' no more'n I deserve."

"'Tis different with us," argued Logan. "We don't hurt anybody. And we don't take from anyone who can't willingly spare it."

"An' the blokes at Pellam's? I'm sure we didn't ask t' see any of *their* bank balances."

"We didn't *force* so much as a farthing from any of them. We never even asked for their money. They took it out of their wallets and laid it on the table on their own. They were just as greedy to take your money as we were!"

Logan paused, frowned momentarily, and scratched his head. "Are you delirious or something, Skits? I've never heard you talk this way before."

"I s'pose as a fellar gets on, he starts t' give 'is life a bit more thinkin' . . ."

"Well, there's no comparing the likes of Chase Morgan with you," said Logan intractably, brushing aside the more philosophical aspects of his friend's pensive comment. "And," he added hotly, "he's not about to get away with it!"

"Just calm that Scottish blood of yours, Logan. You're not going to—" His speech suddenly broke off as he was assailed by a fit of coughing.

This only intensified Logan's rising anger.

"I'll get your money back, Skits! And I'll make sure—"

But at that moment Molly returned and Logan checked his tongue, for the present at least. Still simmering inside, he strode to the window so she wouldn't be able to observe his distress.

Parting the curtains, he pretended to occupy himself with interest in the activities in the street down below, but in truth he was listening as Molly continued to stew over her husband, while the old con man persisted in telling her he was fine.

They were the best people Logan had ever known, except perhaps for his own mother. Hearing them now—her gentle, caring tone and his tired voice growing weaker with each word he uttered—only heightened his determination. They didn't deserve any of this! As he looked out on the dingy alley below, a resolve began to grow within him.

He was not going to let them get hurt, ever again!

It was no more than they would have done for him, and *had* done for him, when, seven years ago, he had appeared practically on their doorstep. He had been fifteen and pretty cocksure of himself. But growing up in the Glasgow Gorbals, a street urchin from the time his father died when he was ten, Logan had learned to take care of himself. And even before his father's death, the older Macintyre had been in and out of Barlinnie Prison so many times that his impact upon his son's life had been minimal. His mother did her best by Logan, but her work as a cleaning lady to keep even the scant food they had in the cupboards from dwindling to nothing left Logan running free and wild, learning from a tender age to steal and pilfer food to augment his sparse diet at home.

From there it had been a short enough path to picking up the various street games— marbles, dice, cards—where he soon discovered he had some skill. He thought he fooled his mother by telling her that he had earned the money she found him bringing home by doing odd jobs in the neighborhood after school. But she had been married to one swindler too many years and knew her son was being caught in the gambling net at an early age. And she wanted no part of it.

"I'd be prood t' take an honest shillin' from ye, son," she would say. But "honest money" was much more difficult to come by, and Logan was not exactly a patient young man. Besides, he rationalized, gambling wasn't actually dishonest, just unreliable. And if he did occasionally slip in a loaded die or a marked card in the middle of a game . . . well, the other fellow would just as soon have done the same if he had been good enough to get away with it.

For all his rowdy lifestyle and bad company, however, Mrs. Macintyre's son did manage to maintain a certain good-natured air and easygoing grin, which, combined with his cocky bravado, made it difficult for people to readily dislike him. Shopkeepers in the Barrows might shake a halfhearted fist his way as he occasionally dodged away from their stands with a bulging pocket. But somehow they always found it in their hearts to forgive him. After all, they said, look what a father he had. It was a wonder the boy turned out to be as nice a chap as he was! And his gambling friends were always willing to loan him a few shillings when he was down on his luck, for he was never stingy with them.

Then he had encountered the earl's son, and from that point on everything seemed to go downhill.

Logan was a mere fifteen at the time, and the spoiled, arrogant Charles Fairgate III but a year older. The card game had been completely honest. Unfortunately for Logan, however, he was in the middle of a legitimate run of good luck. Fairgate insisted the game was rigged, and went so far as to bring his adversary up before the magistrate. With his father's support, the young heir seemed likely to win his case, especially once Logan's reputation and own paternal pedigree came to light. While Logan sat in custody awaiting the outcome, he would never have guessed the agony his mother was suffering as she saw her son on his way down the same path his father had taken. But children in the midst of their own growing pains and struggles rarely have any depth of insight into the feelings of their parents on their behalf. It takes their own parenthood, perhaps ten, fifteen, or even twenty years later to open their eyes to the true inexhaustibility of a parent's love.

For his part, Logan would have disdained any remark pointing out a similarity between himself and his no-account father; the last thing he wanted to do was follow in his footsteps. But when the magistrate finally dropped the case with a "not proven" verdict, he did pause to rethink a few things—not so deeply as his mother may have liked, perhaps, but sufficiently to realize that his life in Glasgow was going nowhere, at least toward a destination of dubious result. Nor was his announced solution to her liking, but she wisely kept her own counsel. These things took time, she tried to console herself. Perhaps he *would* find a better life in London.

The first thing to come Logan's way upon stepping off the platform in Euston Station was a crooked back-alley dice game. He should have known better, but his cocky Scots independence thought he could beat the slick London sharpies at their own game.

He soon discovered his folly; he was fleeced for all he had.

Few things are worse than finding oneself friendless and penniless in a strange city—especially a city as huge and insensitive as London. But even there, one can find occasional pockets of warmth and human kindness if one is persistent enough.

It was quite by accident that Logan stumbled upon just such a place, drifting through just the sort of neighborhood he should have been trying to avoid. From time to time he had done some running for a Glasgow bookmaker, so he was familiar with at least the rudiments of the business. Hearing his dice-playing companions mention a street in a place called Shoreditch, he decided to try his luck and see if he might find something to alleviate his desperate need of cash. There were two or three list shops on the street. Without much reason, he picked one, and walked in—trying to assume his most confident manner. It was a tiny place, hardly larger than a cigar box, and in fact had originally been used in conjunction with a tobacconist's, where one could still get a fairly decent Havana to enjoy while placing his bets.

Skittles was hardly in a position to afford another assistant, especially one as green as this kid, who looked like he would have to be reminded to wash behind his ears. But he didn't have the heart to turn the poor Scottish lad away; something inside the old man's heart took an instant liking to the runabout. Thus the seven-year friendship had begun. It had proven mutually beneficial in a number of ways. But deep inside, Logan knew he owed more to Skittles Ludlowe than he could ever possibly repay.

Molly's voice broke through the silence of his thoughts—

"Logan, we better let the ol' boy 'ave his bit of rest."

"Ol' boy is it now!" broke in Skittles. "Wot kind of thing is that t' say about your man?" The labor behind his irrascible tone only made his weakness the more pathetic.

"Come along, Logan," Molly continued, adding to her husband in the same unruffled tone, "An' you take care, or you'll fin' me callin' you worse than ol' boy!"

An hour later Logan and Molly sat together at the table, having just finished with tea and a few biscuits. Molly rose to clear away the plates and cups, and as Logan watched, his thoughts returned to his conversation with her husband the previous day. She was indeed the kind of woman men in their sometimes shady profession dreamed of having, but seldom encountered. Despite her long involvement with Skittles—and in her early years she had participated more actively in his schemes and ploys—there had yet remained a certain purity about her. She never developed the hard core that so often formed around the hearts of women in her position. Perhaps it was because her motive was a deep and abiding love for her husband rather than personal greed. Perhaps, too, it had to do with the kind of man Skittles himself was toward her.

Suddenly his eyes came back into focus on the present. He jumped up from his seat, saying, "Here, let me give you a hand, Molly!"

"Just fancy such a thing!" she replied, laying a restraining hand on his arm. "You're a well-meanin' lad, but I shudder t' think 'ow many of my dishes I'd lose afore you 'ad done with the job."

Then she paused in the midst of her efforts, with the teapot still in her hand, and turned to Logan with a grave look in her soft, brown eyes.

"He's real sick, he is, Logan," she said, setting down the teapot and sinking back into her chair.

"Oh, the old cove'll be fine," Logan assured confidently, his tone almost good enough to convince himself. "He'll be jumping out of bed and roaring like a lion by tomorrow."

"You've got t' promise me somethin', Logan," she said, her voice serious.

"Anything, dear girl."

"I don't want you gettin' yersel' 'urt too," she said.

"What in the world makes you think I'd get hurt?"

"Ow, Logan! I know all about 'at bloke Chase Morgan," she said flatly. "That Skittles may be one of London's best sharps, but he can't fool me. I 'ear the talk. I knew somethin' was goin' on. But I ought t' crown 'im for not tellin' me wot it were."

Logan knew it was no use persisting in the ruse. "You couldn't have done anything, Molly," he said.

"That may be," she replied, "but if a woman's 'usband's goin' t' come home lookin' like a piece of steak, well, she'd just like t' have some warnin', that's all."

Logan opened his mouth to reply, but she quickly cut him off.

"But the point I was tryin' to make is that I don't want anyone else gettin' 'urt. An' that means you, Logan Macintyre! I've ne'er 'ad the good fortune t' meet your mother. But so long's you're 'ere in London, I gots me own responsibility to you. An' I'd ne'er be able t' forgive myself if anythin' was t' happen to you, nor could your mother forgive me either."

"Ease your mind, Molly," he replied with a great show of earnestness. "I'm not fool enough to go getting mixed up with Morgan." He probably wouldn't have bothered lying to the wise old woman, but he had already forgotten her previous declaration that she could not be so easily misled. And the habit of trying to cover his tracks with defenses and excuses was too deeply ingrained by this time to allow any sudden changes in what were already conditioned responses.

Molly was no less fooled by Logan than she had been by her husband. Yet what more could she say? If he intended to try to get even with Morgan on behalf of his old mentor and friend, she doubted anything she might say would make him change his mind. Besides, if she pursued it he'd vehemently deny his intentions anyway, thinking all the while that he was protecting her. *Well,* she thought, *maybe it's for the best. At least he won't be worrying about me.*

Walking home that afternoon, Logan became more sure of what he had to do. Like Molly, he wanted no one else to get hurt. But his conception of how to eliminate the problem was drastically different than hers. The specifics may have still been blurry. But he was certain of one thing—Chase Morgan had to be stopped.

He took a brief detour to the neighborhood of Skittles' shop. He searched each of the back streets until suddenly he stumbled upon just what he was looking for, his friend's black and white checkered cap, hardly visible between two cans of garbage. He reached down and picked it up, dusted it off, and then before tucking it into his coat, ran his finger affectionately along the visor.

Yes, something had to be done about that low-life scum Morgan!

And Logan figured he was as good as any man to do it.

For the remainder of the day he wandered aimlessly about the streets, concentrating his thoughts on a plan which he had been toying with now and then for some time. Now, with his mark chosen, the pieces began to fit into place more quickly. His mind continued to work most of the night as he lay awake in bed. By morning he was ready to jump to his feet, hardly feeling his lack of rest.

He was ready to do what had to be done.

5 ✳ *A Scheme Takes Shape*

LOGAN HAD LITTLE difficulty finding Billy Cochran. Though it was eleven o'clock in the morning, Cochran was still sound asleep in his tiny room in the ramshackle boardinghouse on Bow Street. Pounding on the door Logan could not keep back a twinge of guilt knowing the wiry little man had likely been up all night at his favorite occupation—pub crawling. But he pounded nonetheless, for he brought important business.

After some minutes, a raspy voice snarled at him through the closed door. "Who's there? An' wot's yer blamed rush?"

"It's me, Billy, Logan Macintyre."

"Wot ye're doin' bangin' me door in at such an hour?" As Billy spoke Logan heard the click of the bolt and other fumbling noises. Then they ceased, and the door opened a bare crack. Two of the smallest eyes Logan had ever seen peered out at him, opened to no more than tiny slits, like the crack in the door out of which they were gazing, as if daylight were a mortal offense to all that was decent in the world.

"I hain't decent." The thin, unshaven face gave credence to his words.

"And I ain't the blamed king!" shot back Logan impatiently.

A bony hand reached up to scratch a sparse crop of salt-and-pepper hair. "No need t' get snappish," said Billy Cochran in a semi-wounded tone. "This better be mighty important, Logan. I was—"

"Sleeping away the day, I know, Billy! Now come on, open the door!"

There were more fumbling sounds at the chain lock, after which the door at last swung open to reveal a complete view of the odd little man behind it, now shielding his eyes from the glare of the morning's light as if it would wound him by its very brightness. In actuality the morning fog protected him from what he avoided even more—direct sunlight falling on the earth before one o'clock in the afternoon!

Only a fraction over five feet tall, Billy was thin and bony all over, with a slight hump in his back that caused his face to jut alarmingly forward. The overall effect was rather birdlike, emphasized especially by the small slits for eyes and the disproportionately large nose.

Logan stepped inside and shut the door behind him. The room had a threadbare look, not at all unlike its occupant. Somehow the small living space seemed a perfect reflection of its owner. The sparse furnishings included an iron-railed bed, chipped and rusting, a metal bedside table with a shadeless lamp on it, and a scratched and worn unpainted pine table with two unmatched chairs. Billy motioned Logan into one of the chairs, as he himself finished fastening his trousers and pulling the wide red suspenders up over his shoulders.

"Well, now as you gots me up, you better make it good, Macintyre!" The voice remained sharp and gruff, but it was as harmless as the impertinent but toothless bark of a twelve-year-old beagle.

"Skittles was attacked a couple of nights ago," Logan began gravely.

"An' is the ol' bloke okay?" Billy let go of his last suspender with a resounding snap; new wrinkles furrowed into his already creased brow. "I wondered why he 'adn't been around."

"He was battered up good. But he seems on the way up."

"Wot kinda dirty bla'art'd do somethin' like that t' ol' Skits?" exclaimed Billy, slamming his fist down on the rickety table.

"Chase Morgan, that's who!" replied Logan with conviction.

Billy sank back in the opposite chair. "I tol' Skits not t' try t' fight the man. But he 'ad some notion 'at mebbe if he stood up t' 'im, all the others'd follow 'im."

"Maybe he did have the right idea after all," said Logan. "He just went about it the wrong way."

"There hain't no way, Logan. Morgan's got ten or more of the biggest an' meanest thugs I e'er seen workin' for 'im. An' everyone knows who he's connected with in the States."

"Capone's five thousand miles away," argued Logan. "I doubt he even remembers Morgan exists. But none of that matters anyway, Billy. I've got a plan!"

"You've gots a plan . . . ?" Billy repeated, rubbing his stubbly beard skeptically. "You hain't thinkin' of pullin' some dodge on Morgan?"

"I know I can do it, Billy!" Logan's eyes flashed with enthusiasm.

"Lad," said Billy in a more cautious tone, "hain't you 'eard the ol' sayin', 'Ne'er con a con.'?"

"Sure, Billy. But I like the saying better—'It takes a thief to catch a thief.'"

"Humm . . ." was Billy's noncommittal reply.

Logan needed no further encouragement to outline his plan in detail.

"I spent the morning at the library, Billy, reading some American newspapers. Morgan has a little hobby—more like an obsession—which I'm going to make his downfall. Seems he's a dabbler in counterfeiting. He's been run out of half a dozen states, and when he finally slipped from the FBI's reach in Florida, an agent was quoted as saying that Morgan wouldn't quit till he found the perfect plate. When he was forced from the States, he went to Cuba for a while, then to South America, and after that Paris. He was almost arrested in Paris again—for counterfeiting."

"You'd think he'd learn 'is lesson," replied Billy.

"That's just it! He figures somewhere out there he's going to find the perfect plate and be set up for life. And that's where I'm going to get him!"

"An' do you 'ave the perfect snide note?" Billy's single cocked eyebrow indicated he would not be easily convinced.

With a great flourish and a smug grin to match, Logan whisked out a brand-new five-pound note from his pocket. He handed it to Billy.

"See for yourself," he stated.

Billy held the note out at arm's length, shook his head in frustration, then, pulling himself out of the chair, hobbled over the bedside where he found a pair of spectacles. He shoved them on carelessly, grumbling, "Can't see for nothin' th'out these blimey things."

He then proceeded to examine the note, first holding it close to his eyes, then at arm's length again, and finally up in the air over his head. "Well, I ne'er," he mumbled. At length he shuffled over to the only window in the room and held it up to the sunlight. He turned it over several times, and when he turned back toward Logan there was a perplexed scowl on his face.

"Where'd you get this?" he asked at last.

"The Bank of England," Logan replied, slapping his knee and laughing heartily.

"I knew it were too perfect," said Billy, unperturbed by Logan's laughter.

"Admit it, Billy! I had you fooled and you know it."

"'Course, but I'm blind as a curs'd bat!"

"I've seen those spectacles of yours! They're practically clear as glass."

"An' so wot do all your tricks prove? Nothin' is wot I say!"

"It's the perfect counterfeit note!" said Logan triumphantly. "Morgan would pay a bundle for the plates to that note."

"An' I doobt the Bank of England's sellin'!"

"You know what I'm getting at, Billy."

"Aye, an' 'tis plumb harebrained! Don't be a fool, Logan."

"You're the best, Billy, and it fooled you."

"You set me up! 'sides, I knew it couldn't be real. One look'll tell any sane man as much."

"Morgan will want to believe it so bad, it won't take that much to convince him. We'll set him up, too! When he sees this, he'll think he's found the best counterfeit notes in the world. I'll sell him the plates, slipping some real counterfeits into the package, making sure he walks right into the waiting arms of the police. I'll get all Skittles' money back, with a nice profit to boot. And the bobbies'll have a dangerous criminal off the streets."

Logan paused, the fire of anticipation still burning in his eyes.

"You're mad as a March hare, Logan."

"I need your help."

"I hain't done no snide pitchin' since I done two years in the chokey for it," Billy replied.

"You won't have to make up any bogus notes," Logan quickly assured. "I just need some help putting together a press. And . . ."—here he hesitated once more before going on—". . . I need a real plate."

"You're crazy, Logan, I tell you. He'll see you comin' all the way across the city! He puts young scamps like you in the bottom of the Thames!"

Now it was the older man's turn to pause. Logan held his peace. He was as sure of Billy's allegiance to Skittles as his own.

"Logan," Cochran went on at length, "you can get yoursel' into real trouble doin' somethin like this." For the first time the older man's voice carried a note of deep concern. "If they fin' you with the plates or the notes."

"They won't!"

Billy scratched his large nose and rubbed his hands over his scraggly face again. "I knew I should've burned all that hardware last time I were sent up," he muttered.

"Then you'll help."

"'Tis pure craziness. But then I guess wot more could you expect from a deranged Scot . . ." He paused, shaking his head. "An' 'sides, someone's got t' keep an eye on you that you don't get yoursel' locked up, or killed by Morgan."

Logan grinned and slapped the little man on the shoulder.

"'Sides," Billy added, "I s'pose I owe it t' Skittles."

It was now Logan's turn to grow serious. "There isn't a man on this side of London, leastways who knows old Skits, who doesn't owe him something."

"Okay, Logan," said Billy, "tell me wot you was thinkin'."

Logan spent the next fifteen minutes outlining his plan in more detail, after which Billy proceeded to poke a hundred holes in every careless aspect of it. Then the veteran counterfeiter set about reshaping Logan's original strategy, adding dimensions to it that Logan had scarcely considered. By the time they were through, even Billy admitted that there might be a slim possibility the harebrained scheme could work. One problem remained to be considered.

"We'll need cash for operatin' expenses," said Billy.

"There is a bit of a problem there," Logan conceded. "I sort of had t' 'borrow' that fiver there."

"I 'ave the feelin' that when word gets out about Skittles, we'll find no shortage of contributors."

"How much do you think we'll need?"

"I'll need parts for a press an' you need enough new notes t' be convincin'—a couple 'undred pounds."

"We could do it with less if we had to."

"Mebbe. But I'll start collectin' the funds regardless. I'll tell you wot t' get for the press—I'd get picked up sure if I tried it! You ought t' go out of town for wot we're needin', just in case."

Then Billy dug into his pockets and pulled out an assortment of coins, along with a fine gold pocket watch. "This ought t' get you started."

"Not your watch, Billy!" Logan knew it was the only possession of any value the man had these days, and he had many times seen him hold it up in the midst of his cronies at the pub and announce the time.

"Hain't nothin'," Billy replied carelessly, "'Sides, you can get it back for me with those so-called profits."

Logan left Billy's more convinced than ever that his plan would not fail. He was anxious to get it in motion, and yet Billy had demanded much more preliminary work than Logan had anticipated. It was going to take considerably longer to come to fruition than he had at first thought. But the first order of business was to drop by to see how Skittles was getting on.

He knocked on the door several times, but there was no answer. Everything seemed unusually quiet inside. He set his ear to the door but could not make out the slightest sound. Puzzled, he slowly descended the stairs, and as he stepped out onto the landing of the first floor, he encountered the landlady.

"Ye lookin' fer Molly an' Skittles?" she asked.

"Yes," he answered. "I wanted to see how Skittles was. He wasn't feeling too well yesterday."

"'Tis a fact!" affirmed the lady. "An worse t'day. Molly took 'im off t' the 'ospital this mornin'."

"Hospital!" exclaimed Logan, turning pale.

He waited only long enough to find out from the woman which hospital his friend had been taken to, then flew down the remaining several stairs and out the door into a freshly falling rain.

6 ❈ A Festive Evening at Stonewycke

THE LOWERING BLACK clouds seemed oblivious to the fact that it was the first day of spring. Allison sent one final glance toward the sunless sky, then yanked her drapes shut. Well, it wasn't her celebration the weather was threatening. At least she could be glad for that. Still, several of her friends would be attending, and it would have been so much nicer if the sun had shone.

The family had decided that Port Strathy was due for a holiday. Since Dorey's birthday came so near the outbreak of spring, it provided the perfect opportunity to commemorate not only his eighty-ninth birthday and the coming of spring but also the apparent easing of the hardships that had held everyone in its grip for the last two years. The winter had been a relatively mild one and everyone was optimistic, both with regard to the fishing and the crops of the Strathy valley, that the coming spring and summer seasons would be the most productive in years.

All Allison had to say about the plans was that it was about time everyone stopped acting as if life had ended because of some depression going on in London and New York. She was glad to see that her mother was dressing up the family home in a manner that showed off their position in the best possible light. They were, after all, the Duncan clan of the celebrated Ramsey stock—the closest thing to royalty, if not in the whole of northeast Scotland, then certainly for miles around. Her mother always seemed to downplay that important fact; Allison for one was delighted that on this occasion, at least, they would put on their true colors.

The whole town had been invited, as well as three prominent families from out of the area: the Arylin-Michaels from Aberdeen, the Fairgates of Dundee, and of course the Bramfords from nearby Culden. Alec had originally proposed the event strictly for local folk, but Allison had ardently argued that if they were going to have a party, she ought to be able to invite some of *her* friends, and in the end her parents consented. Thus the three families, all of whom had daughters at Allison's boarding school, were included. The fact that each of these particular friends also had dashing older brothers only slightly colored her choice. Or so she told herself, though she said nothing about this reason for her insistence to anyone.

Allison turned from the window and walked toward the mirror. She paused, smoothed out her lace dress as she took one last look, and smirked with disdain—but not without a sigh of satisfaction—that she had been able to make it turn out as well as she had. Her mother made her dress like such an absolute *infant*. At least she had extracted what was nearly an ironclad promise that she could wear the dress of her choice to the Bramfords' ball next month.

She left her room and made her way down the hall. Many of the guests had already arrived and were milling about below, for, in deference to the threatening storm, the inside of the house had also been opened to the festivities. Outside, large tables had been set up where the factor, nervously glancing toward the sky every few minutes, could not seem to make up his mind whether to continue preparations for the food and drinks that would be served, or to repair inside and there make the best of it he could, despite limitations of space.

As she approached the top of the main stairway, Allison stopped at the railing and looked down. Just then she saw Olivia Fairgate's brother entering. *There couldn't be a better moment to make my grand entrance,* she thought to herself, smiling. She glided down the stairs with all the grace that could be taught in Scotland's finest boarding schools, a noble smile on her face as if to imply, *I am the queen, come to greet my subjects.* And as intended, at least one set of eyes looked up admiringly.

"Why, Lord Dalmount, how good of you to come," she said demurely, holding out her hand with feigned timidity. And true to his breeding, the young man took the soft, dainty hand and kissed it lightly.

"The estate is hardly mine—yet," he replied in a soft voice and a chuckle, with a tinge of anxiety lest anyone should have heard Allison's flippant remark. "You must have been talking to my sister, and she sometimes says more than is good for her." Then, resuming a more relaxed countenance, he added, "But in the meantime, please just call me Charles."

"Why of course, Charles. As I said, it is nice to see you."

"I couldn't possibly resist an invitation from Stonewycke—notwithstanding the distance. They come so seldom."

"Yes, we are socially buried up here," she replied. "It has always been so. And I'm afraid large estates with old-fashioned castles on them are hardly in vogue these days."

"Going the way of the dinosaur, I suppose."

"I can't help but think it might be good to kill the old place off, and get on with the times. It is the thirties, you know."

"It has a certain provincial quaintness about it, though," he replied glancing about. And though his tone could not have been more polite, there was a certain undetectable upward tilt of his nose that indicated he shared her disdain for the ancient relics of the past. "However," he added, "I do see what you mean. Just think what could be done if the whole thing was modernized."

As they talked they had slowly made their way toward the large open parlor, where several tables of light refreshments had been laid.

"Will there be dancing later?' asked Dalmount as he lifted two glasses of punch from the tray of a passing servant.

"I think there is some kind of entertainment planned."

"*Real* dancing?" he queried, "or will we have to don our kilts and pick up our knees to the screeching sounds of the pipes?"

Allison laughed—a very musical, grown-up, and bewitching laugh. "I'm afraid you are right there! Just as with everything else about this place, my father is a traditionalist when it comes to dancing too."

"No Jan Garber or Fred Waring?"

She laughed again. "Don't I wish! But I'm afraid we will be lucky to kick up our heels to a *Gay Gordon.*"

"No ballroom dancing where I might be favored with a spin around the floor with you?"

"Surely you jest. This little fete is for the fishermen and crofters. You don't think any of them know how to jitterbug or waltz, do you? My father and mother are going to lead a round of *The Rakes of Glasgow* and *De'il Amang the Tailors* and maybe even *The Dashing White Sergeant* if they can get together enough sets of people who know it. But that's all. Do you know any of the folk dances?"

"Never bothered to learn. You?"

"Some of them. I always liked *Dee's Dandy Dance* when I was a girl, but at school we've been—oh, look!" exclaimed Allison in mid-sentence, getting more caught up in the festive mood of the day now that she saw some acquaintances from her own crowd in the midst of the local peasants, "there's Eddie Bramford outside! We must say hello." It might not exactly be the kind of party Allison would have chosen, but with Olivia's handsome, eligible brother by her side, she could overlook that fact. She linked her arm through his, and led him out through the French doors.

The garden, protected on three sides by the walls of the house and a low hedge, was rather pleasant considering the cold borne in on the winds of the gathering storm. With old-fashioned lanterns strung overhead and garlands of flowers and draped tartans of the various clans represented all about, it could almost have been a summer afternoon. But the precariously swinging lanterns and the flapping edges of the blankets served as a constant reminder that the weather would soon have its way even in this secluded spot. The children playing tag, most dressed in what seemed to Allison mere rags, had long since donned their coats.

Edward Bramford, a florid, fleshy twenty-year-old, possessed an athletic kind of attractiveness, unlike the lean, debonaire appearance of Allison's temporary companion. He lumbered up to the approaching pair and held out a thick hand to Charles.

"Grand party, Allison," he said with a good-natured grin of ridicule on his heavy face, glancing around knowingly at the other guests whom he considered beneath the dignity of his position.

"It is now that the gang's all here," Allison replied.

"I didn't realize the local gentry was going to be so well represented," he said with another sarcastic laugh. "Eh, Charles?"

"Well, Bramford," said Charles, not willing to take the bait of the joke and risk losing Allison's favor over a remark in poor taste, "will Oxford make the finals this year?"

"As long as they've got me on the offense."

"Rugby, rugby, rugby!" said Allison in mock frustration. "Is that all you men can talk about?"

"I imagine you would be more at home if we took up the subject of the lastest fashions?" rejoined Charles.

"Of course. But I hardly know when something new's out before it's two years behind the times. It is just too frustrating being stuck in such an out-of-the-way place!"

"Now really, Miss MacNeil," said Bramford, not to be diverted from a discussion of his true love, "what's wrong with rugby?"

"Nothing, I suppose . . ." replied Allison, tapping her chin thoughtfully. "That is, if I understood a whit about the game."

Thereupon Eddie Bramford launched into a description of the game detailed enough to put even an enthusiast of the game like Charles to sleep. Fortunately they were soon joined by Clifford Arylin-Michaels, the third bachelor of the little group whose presence had been secured by Allison's contrivances with Joanna and Alec. Allison was clearly the chief attraction for each of the three, and no doubt the only reason they consented to accompany their parents to an event that would otherwise bore them past endurance with all its local, boorish color.

The appearance of Arylin-Michaels fell somewhere between those of the other two men. His face was rather plain and nondescript, as was his soft-spoken voice. He also knew little about rugby, but the moment the conversation lagged, he was ready with a political expostulation about the situation on the Continent, for his father was a Conservative M.P. in the House of Commons.

Allison cared little that the conversation was dull. It was enough for the moment to be surrounded by these three young men. When her three school friends migrated toward the circle and aroused virtually no interest on the part of any of the young men, she could hardly keep her inward exhilaration from spilling onto her face. She purposefully took no notice of their hostile glances throughout the remainder of the evening.

It was difficult to tell exactly when the sun had set, for the dark afternoon had passed gradually into evening. Still the rain had not come. Though a number of guests had to leave to attend to their livestock, and a few to their fishing boats, those who remained were at last led into the ballroom, where Alec, true to Allison's prediction, marched into the center of the crowd in full Highland regalia, extemporizing an ear-deafening rendition of *Scotland the Brave* on his bagpipes, much to the delight of all present. Only Allison's small group of friends standing toward one corner was indifferent to the proceedings. The rest of Port Strathy's inhabitants whooped and clapped and sang along to the most familiar of all Scotland's tunes.

"An' noo, my friends," Alec called out when the drone from his pipes had died away, "I wad like t' invite any o' ye adventurous enough fer it, ont' the floor. Ye are the evenin's entertainment yersel's!"

Suddenly a rousing *Reel* began from the small local contingency of fiddlers and accordionists. In an instant all hands were clapping and feet stomping to the beat, and soon Alec had again filled his bag with air and was searching in wailful tones for the melody.

The *Reel* lasted about five minutes, after which Alec announced, "Let's start with *The Gay Gordons!* Men, bring your ladies onto the floor and take your positions in the center of the circle!"

But his last words could hardly be heard. No sooner had the words *Gay Gordons* left his lips than the small band had again struck up the music with their instruments and the shuffling of many feet on the hardwood floor made momentary chaos of the room. Nor did anyone present require Alec's instructions, for every native Scot—fisher, crofter, or laird—had known the favorite dance from childhood.

Soon the couples, led by Joanna and Alec, were circling the room rhythmically to the lively music. With every new stanza the men advanced to a new partner, and thus progressed around the room. Alec's laugh seemed loudest of all, and with each of the fisher or farmer wives he came to, he appeared to enjoy himself still further. The men, on their part, when they took Joanna in their arms, did so with a timid grace that was wonderful to behold. The humble pride on the faces of the hard-working men of Port Strathy told the story—for them, this was like dancing with royalty itself!

The mood was infectious. Even Allison's so-called sophisticated friends could not resist the invitation to share in the gaiety, even when it came at the hand of a crusty and red-faced old fisherman. No amount of expostulation, however, on the part of the future laird of Dalmount, could get Allison onto the floor. She stood watching the festivities in moody silence, trying occasionally to cover the mortification she felt at having her family seen mingling with such people, with snide and haughty comments intended to be witty. How could her father, *the laird,* degrade himself so!

Out-of-breath, laughing, and perspiring freely, the thirty or forty persons left on the floor burst into spontaneous applause as the music came to a loud and triumphant conclusion. No one could remember when they'd had so much fun!

"An' noo, what would ye all say t' seein' Lady Margaret an' Lord Duncan favor us wi' a sight o' their nimble feet?" said Alec above the noise, at which the clapping and shouts of encouragement grew louder still.

Knowing the futility of trying to argue, Maggie and Ian came slowly forward from where they had been standing clapping their hands and tapping their toes. Ian beamed with pleasure as his wife gently took his arm and allowed him to lead her into the center of the room. Then, as the small band softly took up the melancholy strains of *Lochnagar,* Ian tenderly slipped his hand around Maggie's waist and their aging feet began an improvisation about the floor, now a waltz, now a quick shuffle-stepping reel. Suddenly they were young again! All thought of the watching eyes were gone. The wind was on their faces, blowing down upon them from across the heather hills over which they had ridden together. Raven and Maukin stood close by, their sides heaving from the strenuous ride. For music, the birds and the breeze and the nearby rushing burn in the trees supplied more than enough. Maggie gave herself up to Ian's strong and loving arms. He swung her around, lifting her feet from the ground as she laughed as only young Maggie Duncan could laugh. *Oh, Ian, I love you!* she thought, and with the words the dying melody once again penetrated her consciousness. As her mind came back to the present, Maggie was gazing deeply into Ian's chestnut brown eyes, still thinking the same words. As if he knew her thoughts, he returned her gaze with the deep love which only two who had been through such trials as they could share. Oblivious to the music, which had by now stopped, the aging couple continued to dance a few moments longer, content in each other's arms, until the broken sounds of applause, growing steadily louder, at last awakened them. They looked around at their friends, laughed, and then Ian said, "Weel, I guess we're jist a couple o' auld lovesick fools!" That brought laughs all around, for everyone in the village knew he spoke the most perfect London-English in the entire valley.

Joanna's laugh, however, could hardly hide the tears streaming down her face at the sight of her grandmother and grandfather so happy and content together. *Thank you, Lord,* she sighed, *for bringing them together!* And indeed, as the women of Port Strathy looked on, especially those old enough to remember, Joanna was not the only one in whose eyes stood tears of joy for the lady they loved.

"An' noo, let's see if we canna get the white sergeant t' dash aboot a bit!" said Alec. "We need a set o' six—as many as we can weel fill up the floor wi'."

As the band plunged vigorously into a lively introduction to *The Dashing White Sergeant,* once again there was a great scurrying about as four or five sets of six tried to arrange themselves in lines of three, forming a great wheel about the room, with its spokes pointing toward the center. But no sooner had the dance gotten underway when suddenly Evan Hughes burst into the room, out of breath, with his hat crumpled in his hand. Mrs. Bonner, the housekeeper, trailed Hughes through the door of the ballroom.

He ran straight to Alec, who was jovially winding his way through the dance's first figure-eight, and stopped him with an urgent hand on his arm.

"There's been an accident," he began. "The schooner's run aground!"

Immediately the dancing in Alec's group came to a halt as he turned to Evan for details. One by one the other groups wound down also, and at last the music ceased, as gasps and exclamations around the room gave evidence to the severity of the news, especially for those with relatives or friends aboard.

"We'll need all the help we can git fer the rescue!" shouted Alec, and no sooner had the words fallen upon the ears of his fellow townsmen than once again the room became alive, now with no preparation for a dance but rather in preparation to battle the wind and a surly sea to save their kinsmen. The local folk never had to be told twice. Before Hughes was through with his news, a full half of them were already out of the ballroom and on their way down to the harbor.

Those remaining, however, heard as Evan continued: "Tim Peters were mindin' the helm," he said, "an' when his wife heard . . ."

He hesitated, then went on, turning toward Joanna who had joined Alec, ". . . weel, ye know her condition, my leddy."

"Yes," Joanna replied with concern in her voice, "she's had an unpleasant pregnancy—"

"Aye, she has!" broke in Hughes, "an' Doc Connally's over t' Culden."

"You don t mean . . . ?"

"Aye, my leddy!"

"She's gone into labor?"

"'Tis what I come here t' tell ye. I figured Alec here, ye know, might be a mite sight better'n nae doctor at all—that is t' say—weel . . ." And, flustered, he broke off his speech.

"I know yer meanin'," replied Alec with a smile. "But nae doobt I'll be needed at the wreck too. Hoo bad is't, Evan?"

"Can't alt'gither tell. 'Tis fearsome dark oot there! But it could be bad, my laird."

"Please, Evan, 'tis no time fer formalities! Joanna," he said, turning to his wife, "can ye see t' Mrs. Peters? Ye've had mair experience wi' human births than I."

Joanna nodded, adding, "She may not be in any real danger. Sometimes these things come and go."

"Thank ye, lass!" replied Alec with a grin. "I'll organize the men at the harbor. We'll hae t' send a fleet o' boats oot t' pick up the men, I'm thinkin'. Meantime, Evan, jist in case it *is* her time, are ye up fer a hasty ride t' Culden?"

Hughes nodded his assent and hurried away with Alec close behind him.

Now it was Joanna's turn to spring into action. She walked quickly toward Maggie where she stood anxiously watching the developments. After a few moments of hurried conversation, Lady Margaret nodded. She would take charge of the house and what guests remained. Most, however, even of the out-of-town guests, had joined the throng on its way down the road to the town, if not to help, then at least as spectators. In the meantime, Joanna turned and her eyes, flashing now in anticipation of what lay ahead, sought her daughter.

Allison felt dizzy. This was not at all how she had envisioned the conclusion of the evening. Two of her three young men had trooped off to watch the rescue efforts, while the third was even now plying his skills in an attempt to persuade her to accompany him along with the others. Her three school friends, in a group by themselves a little way away, were observing Allison's every move with jealous eyes while pretending to be completely unaware of her presence. Allison at length resigned herself to following along, that prospect being more desirable than the boredom of remaining behind listening to Clifford expound on the dangers of German rearmament, when from behind her she heard her mother's voice.

"Allison, would you come with me?"

She turned to see Joanna approaching with a determined stride.

"Uh . . . where?" she asked nervously. Now this really was too much, to have her mother speak to her like a child—and in front of her friends!

"Mrs. Peters—she may be about to have a baby."

"But—but . . ." Allison faltered, shrinking back from Joanna's penetrating eyes and the urgency in her voice.

"Allison, I may need you."

"Oh, Mother! My good dress . . . I'll spoil it!"

"Allison!" returned Joanna imperatively. "I need your help! Now, please—come with me!"

"But the guests—" attempted Allison lamely.

Lady Margaret, who had slowly come up to the two, now laid a hand gently on her great-granddaughter's shoulder. "I will see to everything here," she said. "You may go with your mother." Her words were gently spoken, but there was an immovable firmness to them at the same time which Allison could not refuse. Further resistance would be pointless. She only hoped her friends weren't watching, even though Clifford would probably recount every word to all of them!

With a sigh of martyred resignation, Allison took the coat that Mrs. Bonner held out to her and wrapped it around her shoulders. If her great-grandmother had only stayed out of it!

She might be able to argue with her mother. But Lady Margaret was like a rock. No matter how kind and gentle she appeared on the outside, down inside she could be so determined. Whenever she tried to withstand the old lady, somehow her voice always caught in her throat. Was she afraid of her? She doubted it. How could anyone be afraid of one like Lady Margaret? What was it, then? Was she intimidated by the sheer age and eminent standing of her great-grandmother, both in the family and in the community? Or was it simply an awe, a deep respect? But if that was its proper name, it was never a direction in which she allowed her thoughts to travel for long. And on this occasion she hardly had time to reflect on these things at all, for events began to sweep her along in their train.

Joanna brought the Austin around front from the garage, sounded an authoritative blast on the shrill horn, and Allison ran out into the night and climbed in beside her without a word.

As the automobile flew rattling down the hill, Allison glanced back. The last thing she saw before a bend in the road obscured her vision were several of the lanterns swinging above the courtyard garden, more agitated now in the rapidly brewing storm, a fine mist giving the lights an ethereal appearance, as if to punctuate the disastrous climax to the evening's events.

7 ❈ Allison

THE ROOM SPUN around and all the blood rushed from her head. Allison's hand trembled as she tried to grasp the edge of the coarse oak table nearby. But that was not going to help.

She was going to be sick.

I've got to get out of here, she thought.

Allison turned toward the door, threw a hasty glance back into the room, then stumbled out of the cottage into the biting rain. They were all still busy. They would never even notice that she was gone.

She tumbled forward down the incline, unconscious of the rain beating on her body, not feeling the fierce wind on her face, twice nearly twisting her ankle on the rocky ground. On she ran. The direction hardly mattered. Only that she put as much distance between herself and that hateful place as possible.

The baby had died, only moments before.

There had been nothing her mother could do. There had been nothing anyone could have done. Even if Dr. Connally had been there, the outcome would doubtless have been unchanged. The labor had suddenly come two months premature after what had been a very difficult pregnancy. Perhaps had there been a hospital nearby, there might have been a chance. But how could an infant struggling for its life hope to survive under such primitive conditions? Aberdeen was sixty miles away. Her mother might be the best midwife in the area, but some things were impossible even for Joanna MacNeil. And perhaps as Allison stumbled alone into the night, she managed to dull the sting of her own sense of failure with the realization that no one else had been able to save the child, either.

Who wouldn't get sick in that hovel? she thought, with the stupid peat smoke clogging the air so they couldn't breathe, and the disagreeably intimate proximity with all the noisome neighbor women who turned out to lend a hand to the blessed event. Some blessedness! Now they were all in there crying and praying and trying to comfort the pathetic Peters woman.

But Allison knew what had really sent her reeling from the cottage was the pitiful sight of the dead baby. She had never actually *seen* death before. The infant had scarcely been larger than the two hands of her mother that had frantically tried to pump the life back into it. And now, a quarter mile from the Peters' cottage, wind in her hair and rain streaming down her tear-stained face, Allison could not blot the sight of that tiny, limp, bluish body from her memory.

Oh, why had her mother forced her to witness such an awful thing!

Allison stopped for a moment and forced her eyes tightly shut. But it did not help. The death-child still loomed larger than life before the eyes of her mind.

She should have known better than to bring me, thought Allison, forgetting how many times in the last month she had pleaded with her mother to treat her like a grown woman rather than a child. *All those other women . . . they've seen it before. It's part of their life. But not mine. That's what people like them have to face as their lot in life. But not me! Why does my mother insist on being one of them? It's not our place! We're meant to be above—*

Her self-centered and confused thoughts were suddenly cut short as her foot snagged on a protruding scraggly heather bush. She stumbled and fell, hands and knees landing in the muddy dirt. It was not until that moment that she became aware of how cold she was. Or that she'd left her coat behind. Slowly she picked herself off the ground. Her party dress was not only soaked, now it was splattered with mud. It would serve her mother right, she thought! Now she would *have* to buy her a new dress, and it was no fault but her own. And after what she had been through this evening, Allison considered herself well-deserving of the fifty-pound dress in the magazine.

The icy cold was penetrating. But the thought of returning to the cottage for her coat never entered her mind.

Allison stood and looked about her, realizing for the first time that she had no idea in which direction she was headed. Yet above the din of the wind she could hear the faint sounds of the sea. The Peters' place was located three miles east of town, about half a mile inland on the large bluff that spread out toward Strathy Summit. Glancing about her, she realized she must have gone north from the cottage, down the slope, toward the sea. Fortunately she had gathered her wits just in time. Inching ahead, she made her way forward until before long she came to the rocky ledge atop the cliffs overlooking the sea some ninety feet below.

It was well she did not suffer the same reaction to heights as she had to blood and death. Below and to her left, Ramsey Head—now shrouded in fog and rain and nearly too black to distinguish clearly—loomed so close she could have tossed a rock onto its southern slope. She shuddered, as many would to find themselves so near the Head on such a wild night as this. Children were warned away from the place. Local folk had tale after tale of strange and mysterious sounds and disreputable doings associated with the promontory. An evil man— a murderer, they said—jumped from the top of the Head, plunging to his death in the treacherous shoal below. His body had never been recovered, undoubtedly carried far out to sea by the strong tides of the North Sea. But even after seventy years, no one cared to linger long in a place where—so the old-timers like to point out—a body might surface at any moment.

Allison did not shudder on this night, however, because of the eerie tales of past evils. Or even at this moment from the cold which had now pierced to her very bones. Rather the quiver which went involuntarily through her spine as she stood looking down on the faint white-tipped waves resounding against the rocks below was from the sight of several dozen dim lights bobbing up and down in the water offshore.

This must have been where the schooner went down, on the most hazardous stretch of coastline for miles. Growing accustomed to the darkness, she could now begin to make out lights of the rescue party on the shore as well. Now and then a muffled shout from below could be heard. But they'd have little success tonight, it seemed, with the rain and fog and high seas impairing their every effort. Turning her eyes again toward the lights from the daring fishing vessels bobbing up and down like corks in the angry waves, she thought, *They must be crazy! They'll end up in the same fix as the schooner!*

So intent was she upon the playing out of events on the water and on the shore below her that she did not hear the approach behind her until the snap of a twig revealed that she was not alone.

She started and let out a little cry.

"I didn't mean to frighten you, dear."

Composing herself quickly, almost reluctantly Allison turned. Though she was relieved, at that moment she wished the voice had belonged to almost anyone else.

"I brought your coat," Joanna continued. "You must be freezing."

"Yes . . . thank you," replied Allison, taking the coat and slipping it over her soaked dress.

"Dear," Joanna began, reaching out to her daughter not only with her hand but also with the yearning tone of her voice.

"Look!" Allison broke in with a light voice, pointing toward the sea with the arm her mother would have touched, "the schooner must have gone down off the Head."

"Allison," continued her mother, not to be deterred despite her daughter's apparent reluctance to hear her words, "forgive me for making you come tonight."

"You needed help," replied Allison coolly.

"If I had known what was going to happen . . ."

"Mother, I'm a big girl."

"You left so suddenly. I thought—"

"It looked as if you had enough help," said the daughter quickly, ". . . and I was curious about the wreck."

Joanna simply nodded, making no mention of the hurriedly forgotten coat. "Would you like to talk about what happened?"

"I don' t see what there is to talk about, Mother. A baby died. There's not much we can do about that. It happens all the time. But really, the conditions these people live in are deplorable." She turned abruptly and began a brisk walk back to their car, which was waiting at the cottage.

Joanna sighed, and followed.

Nothing more was said about the experiences of the evening, except a passing comment on Allison's part about her desperate need for a new party dress.

8 ✴ Grave Words

THE ANTISEPTIC ODOR stung at Logan's nose. This bleak hospital ward gave him the chills, and he especially didn't like seeing his friend lying between those stark white sheets. He suddenly looked so old and vulnerable.

He approached Skittles' bed with uncharacteristic timidity, his damp fedora in hand and an uncomfortable look on his face. He attempted a smile, but his eyes lacked their usual lively glint. The doleful effect could certainly not have been much of a comfort to the patient.

"How are you, Skits?" Logan's voice started to crack. It was all he could do to sound cheerful.

"I must be a goner, lad, t' 'ave landed in a pokey joint like this," replied the old bookie.

"Not a bit of it," answered Logan, still standing stiffly while nervously fingering the rim of his hat. "These days they put folks in the hospital for every little thing. Modern medicine, you know."

"I s'pose time'll tell."

"You'll be out of here before tomorrow's first race at Epsom."

Skittles gravely motioned his head to one side. "Get a chair, lad. I 'ave something t' talk o'er with you."

Logan found a chair on the other side of the ward, carried it to Skittles' bedside, and straddled it with his arms folded across the back.

"If you're worried about the shop," Logan said, "there's no need. Billy and I will take care of it. And he swore he'd do no drinking while he was in charge."

"'Tis not the shop I'm worryin'." Skittles paused to cough a deep wrenching cough. "But I s'pose the shop's got somethin' t' do with it," he began once more.

"Just tell me what it is, Skits. Anything I can do to help."

"Laying 'ere, a man's got time t' think. An' I been wondering wot I could give t' you after I'm gone . . ."

Logan opened his mouth to protest, but Skittles held up a hand to quiet him. "Just listen t' me, Logan," he said. "I thought about leavin' you the shop. But I just can't bring myself to it. I'm going t' leave it t' Billy. He'll do good by it, and give a percentage of the profits t' take care of Molly—not that you wouldn't do the same, lad. I know you would. But . . ."

He sighed, reached for a glass of water by his bedside, and took several long swallows before continuing. "I just wouldn't feel right bein' responsible for keeping you in this business—"

"What do you mean, Skits? I'm happy enough with what I do."

"Just let me finish." As he spoke, Skittles' voice was becoming more labored. Therefore Logan obeyed, albeit reluctantly. " 'Tis a rotten business we're in, Logan. Oh, maybe we ain't villainous to the core like Morgan an' 'is bunch. But when was the last time you made any *honest* money? You're a bright boy, an' you can make somethin' better of yourself. There! That's wot I wanted t' say!"

"I've made just what I want of myself," answered Logan, both in defense of himself and to try to put his friend at ease.

"You say that only because you don't know nothin' else. Get out of it!" pleaded the old man, "before it's too late. Before you wind up goin' the way of Chase Morgan."

"You can't really think that could ever happen to me?"

"I've seen many a good lad turn cold and 'ard with greed."

But even as he spoke Logan shook his head with a stubborn look which said he had stopped listening. Skittles exhaled a defeated sigh. "Guess it'll take more'n the words of an ol' reprobate like me to make you understand."

"Don't go on talking like that, Skits—" Logan's words faltered and his voice nearly broke. Steadily he bit back the rising emotion in his throat. "You're the best man I've ever known and . . . well, you just better get out of that bed in a hurry, because I need you, you crotchety old windbag!"

Logan jumped out of his chair and strode over to the window where he looked intently out as if something of great interest had suddenly caught his attention. In truth, he did not want anyone—least of all Skittles—to see the moisture filling his eyes.

"You don't need me, lad," Skittles replied with deep affection. He too brushed a hand across his misting eyes, for Logan was the son of his later years that he and Molly had never had in their youth. "Though your sentiment does me old 'eart good to 'ear it, I can't say for certain wot it tis you're needing, but it ain't the likes of me."

Logan did not reply. He knew his voice would betray him.

Silence filled the room for a few moments, each of the men struggling to maintain the long-practiced street tradition of keeping emotions well buried. When Logan again felt certain of his control, he turned and walked back to the bed.

"I almost forgot," he said, forcing a light casual tone into his words as he took the checkered cap from his pocket. "I got your hat back for you." He held it out and Skittles took it, new tears rising in his weary eyes at the sight.

"I figured you might be needing it soon," Logan added.

"Molly bought this for me ten years ago," the old man said tenderly, "to replace one just like it I lost in a—you might say in a little skirmish at Ascot. I only take it off to sleep."

He lay contemplating the cap for a minute, then held it back out to Logan.

"All I do in this place is sleep. 'Ere, Logan. Would you take care of the cap for me . . . until I need it again?"

Logan said nothing.

He reached forward, clutched the cap in his hand, and turned to leave the room.

"You'll think about it, lad . . . wot I said?" Skittles called out after him.

Logan stopped, turned, looked one last time at his friend where he lay, then nodded. "Yeah, Skits," he said. "Promise."

9 ✖ To Catch a Thief

LOGAN SPENT THE remainder of the day in consultation with Billy. The next two days were devoted to train rides, some long, some short, to various towns on the outskirts of the city. Each time he returned with several packages which he carried to a dirty one-room flat he had rented in a tenement across town from his own place.

With rising impatience to get on with the plan, Logan next submitted to Billy's habit of practicing with "dry runs" until everything was timed to perfection.

"There can't be no hitches!" Billy kept saying. "Morgan's no blimey pigeon. One whiff of a setup, Logan, an' we're dead men!"

"Why can't I just go into his place, spread a few bills around, talk it up, boast a little about how I can get as many as I need, drink a few pints, and wait for Morgan to make a move on me?"

"Oh, he'd make a move on you all right!" replied Billy mockingly. "He'd move you right int' the Thames in a lead box! Think, man! He'd see through a ruse like that five minutes after you walked in the door. We gots to make 'im come to you. The man's got to *want* that plate so bad that he's taken the bait before he e'er set 'is eyes on you. That's the key to any con, lad. Hain't Skits taught you nothin'? We gots to make 'im *want* to believe in those plates! Then he's eating out of our 'ands, not us out of 'is."

"And just how do you propose to manage such a thing?"

"That's where the rest of the boys come in. We spread a few bills round town. Discreetly. Slowly. None of your wild, fool shenanigans. We let the news of a new plate sift slowly along the grapevine. We gradually connect you with the 'earsay. Very subtle. So's no one gets the idea we're lookin' for a deal. An we keep spreadin' bills, throwing in a few bad 'uns so the thing gets talked up."

"But how long's all that going to take, Billy?"

"Doesn't matter how long. Mebbe a week or two, mebbe six months."

"Six months!"

"Settle down, Logan. Patience is the most important ingredient to this scheme. You 'ave to wait it out, dangling the hook e'er so gently, waitin' for Morgan t' get 'ungrier and 'ungrier. If we make a move before he's ready, like I said before—we're dead men! But if we can wait 'im out—no matter how long it takes—then when he pounces, we'll be ready t' reel 'im in. By then we gots 'im where we want 'im. He'll *want* to believe so bad we can slip in an amateur's plate and he'll jump at it. An' we hain't going' t' stick no amateur plate in front o' his nose. No siree! When Morgan's moment comes, he's goin' t' be feastin' his eyes on the most perfect plate I ever made. 'Course, we'll make sure the light in the place hain't too good, just in case. But e'en in broad daylight I could 'ardly tell my plate from the real one. No, Logan, if we bide our time and don't rush 'im, he'll come to you. You can be sure of that."

"And what do I do in the meantime?"

"You'll do just as I tell you," replied Billy. "I'll get the boys t' put the word out, real casual-like. And you just 'ave a good time. Don't go into Morgan's place at first. Then mebbe once or twice, then disappear for a few days. And don't say nothin'! You just keep your young mouth shut, do you understand? You don't do no talkin' till Morgan comes t' you. And then you say only what I tell you!"

The bait took three weeks to take. But then, exactly as Billy had predicted, it was Morgan who initiated a move in their direction. Logan had not been in Morgan's plush nightclub pub in four days. Billy had begun to step up the tempo and warned him to stay away. But by this time he had well coached his young protegé in what to say, for the bite on the part of Morgan could come at any time, he said.

It came about ten o'clock one evening as Logan was leaving *The Purple Pig* pub some three blocks away. Without even a word, he was suddenly sandwiched between two very large and very insistent colleagues of Morgan's who brusquely thrust him into the backseat of a waiting limousine. In less than five minutes, without a word having yet been spoken, he was escorted into the big man's office.

He had never before even seen the underworld hoodlum, and was momentarily stunned to see that he was a short man—probably no more than five foot six. Though solidly built, he had a thick appearance with little sign of a neck, and a round face that might have lent a boyish air to his overall look had it not been for his dark, glaring eyes.

Logan glanced around quickly, taking stock of his surroundings. The room in which he found himself certainly was impressive, giving every indication that Morgan's brief sojourn in the British Isles had been highly profitable thus far. Though Logan's trademark on the streets of London was his smooth tongue, his talents were stretched to their limits before the wary American gangster. And Morgan's first words immediately dispelled any further thought of his *boyish* face. He was anything but a neophyte.

"I understand you got a five-pound plate," he demanded.

"Maybe I have . . . maybe not," answered Logan, as per Billy's instructions.

"Don't play coy with me, Mr. Logan!" snapped Morgan. "For twenty pounds I can have you dropped in the river!"

Just what Billy said he'd do! thought Logan to himself. *First a vain, angry outburst, followed by a threat. "If he does that,"* Billy had said, *"he's playing right into our 'ands!"*

"Now, Mr. Logan, is the plate for sale?"

"Stall him a little longer," were Billy's instructions. *"Take it cautiously. But string him along until it begins to look dangerous."*

"Say, who are you?" Logan replied, avoiding the question.

"Who I am is none of your concern. Who I am is the man who just asked you a question. Now tell me, is—"

"And how do you know my name?"

Suddenly Morgan's fist slammed down on his desk and he jumped to his feet.

"You interrupt me again, Logan!" he shouted, "and I'll . . ." Apparently he thought better of himself. He paused, then continued. "Look. I know all about you. I've had you followed for a week. I know your name, where you drink, how badly you gamble, and where you live. And I also know about the plate. I've never heard of you. You look like a punk. But they say it's the best plate ever seen in this town, and I want it. Do you understand? Now, I'm only going to ask you nice one more time—is the plate for sale?"

"When he gives you no more choices and 'as your back to the wall, then give 'im a little more line. Not much. Just enough for us to 'ang 'im with." Okay, Billy, thought Logan, *I think this is it!*

"I . . . I hadn't really thought of selling it. I suppose I could think—"

"I don't want you to think about it. I want you to do it!" replied Morgan angrily. "Don't you understand, you little creep of a street punk? You either sell me the plate or I'll kill you. If you do it my way, I just might let you live. What do you say to two thousand pounds?"

Logan laughed outright. *"Show a cocky confidence,"* Billy had said. *"He'll 'ate you for it. But it just may save your life at the same time. No con man likes a wimp. Stand up to 'im. It's the only way to keep 'im honest at a dishonest game. Laugh at 'is first offer. He'll go at least twice as 'igh, maybe even more."*

"Two thousand!" he repeated. "The plate's worth at least ten."

"Ten thousand! What kind of a fool do you take me for?"

"Perfect five-pound notes. And you want it for a song?"

"No note's perfect!"

"And maybe mine aren't, either. But they're good enough to pass off as the real thing. And that's really all that matters, isn't it now, mate?"

"I'll give you three thousand."

"And maybe I'll just keep it. Why should I give away the golden goose for t'pence? I still ain't said the plate's for sale."

"And I said it *is* for sale!" replied Morgan, growing heated once more. "Now you look, Mr. Logan. I'll give you five thousand pounds for the blasted thing. One more word out of you and we'll put you out of your misery tonight and ransack your flat till we find it."

"You won't find it there, mate," laughed Logan.

"Then maybe we'll kill you just for the fun of it and make our own plate. Now, five thousand it is. Take it, or take your last look around at this world."

"And how do I know you'll keep your part of the bargain?"

"You don't. But you got no choice, kid. But don't worry. I don't want the word out that Chase Morgan welches on his deals. Too many people know about you already. You're safe. That is, unless you try anything stupid!"

Logan was summarily dismissed with a wave of Morgan's hand and found himself brusquely escorted through the front of the club and shoved out the door with a curt, "Mr. Morgan'll be in touch!" from one of Morgan's bouncers.

The moment he was alone Logan looked around, rippled his shoulders once or twice to figuratively dust himself off from the disquieting encounter, then exhaled a long sigh. "Whew!" he said under his breath, as he turned and walked away. "That's over!"

He walked on, turning the events of the past ten minutes over in his mind. "*Mister* Logan!" he thought, then laughed aloud. "Why, the sucker doesn't even know my real name!"

He headed immediately for Billy's, but did not reach him till after eleven, having followed the most circuitous route imaginable to shake off any potential tails.

"It was just like you said!" he exclaimed excitedly. "I didn't have to convince him of a thing."

"I tell you, Logan, if your setup's right, he's a believer long before you 'ave t' spin out your song t' 'im."

"It's going to be like taking candy from a baby!"

"Hey! Not so fast. That was the easy part," cautioned Billy. "The real game is still t' come. If he doesn't buy it all the way, and makes you demonstrate the plates, we're goners."

"He seemed ready enough to believe in it tonight."

"Threatening a kid comes easy for blow'ards like Morgan. Parting with five thousand quid in cash—that's another matter. You just don't get too smart for your own good. A little cocksure, but don't get patronizing or presumptuous. A guy like 'im 'ates that! He's got t' think you're a nitwit all the way—one with nimble fingers and a sharp eye, but still a nitwit. He's got t' think *he's* taking *you*! That's the only way a big score like this can work. And the second it's over—man, you gots t' disappear! When he finds out he's been 'ad, 'is eyes'll be flaming with vengeance! What comes next?"

"He just said he'd be in touch. What should I do?"

"Just 'ang around the neighborhood. Keep spending money."

"I'm almost out, Billy."

"Wot! Already?"

"You said to spread the bills around."

"Yeah. I guess there's no other way t' bait the hook. 'Ere's another fifty. But that's got t' last you!"

"Fifty! Sure . . . this'll last fine. But, Billy—where do you get all this money we're using?"

"Don't ask. I got it, that's all. It's part of the cost. A big setup always takes plenty of cash. Now, get outta 'ere. I gotta get some sleep. I'm not as young as you. I'll meet you at the other place tomorrow and we'll make sure everything's ready."

It was the afternoon of the third day when Logan was sent for again. The same two thugs were similarly talkative, and once more Logan found himself facing Morgan.

"I want to see the plate," he said without introductory pleasantries.

"You got the five thousand?" replied Logan.

"You're an impertinent twit, I'll say that much for you. Yeah, I got the five thousand! That is, if you can back up what you say."

"I never said anything. You gave me no choice, remember?"

"What of it! If the plate's the genuine article, you'll be on easy street for a long time. Now let's get going!"

"We can't go now."

"What do you mean, we can't go now!"

"My landlady's onto me, watches me like a hawk. I think she's put the bobbies onto me, too. The streets have been crawling with them lately."

"You never told me that!"

"You never asked!" Logan knew he was pushing Morgan to his limits of patience, but he hoped, as Billy had said, that if he demonstrated just the right amount of cheek, it might save his life.

Morgan was silent a moment, clearly in thought. "Okay, you good-for-nothing shaver, when can we go?"

"She goes into her place for the night about eight."

"Then be here at seven-thirty."

Logan turned to leave. But just as he reached the door, he heard Morgan's sinister voice behind him. It sounded more evil and threatening than it yet had.

"And, Mr. Logan," the racketeer said slowly in a menacing tone, "you better be on the level or you're a dead man. Do you understand me? I'd like nothing better than to put a hole through you if I find out you're playing games with me."

Logan turned back toward the man where he still sat behind his desk. Trying to give his voice the balance Billy had spoken of without betraying his fear, he replied: "Look, Morgan, if you want out of this deal, just say the word. I never wanted to sell in the first place. I'd be just as happy to—"

"Get him out of here!" shouted Morgan angrily. "You just be here at seven-thirty, Logan! You understand?"

Before he had a chance to say anything further, he was shoved out of the office and the door shut behind him.

At a quarter to eight that same evening, Logan was shoved into the backseat of Morgan's shiny new 1932 Rolls Royce between Morgan and one of his henchmen. The driver was the same man who had driven the limousine twice before. The other thug in the front seat Logan had not seen before. The sinister bulge in the coat pocket next to him hardly escaped Logan's attention. He knew there would be no room for mistakes tonight. The dress rehearsals were over. Billy would even now be out of the room, having perfectly set up the last details for authenticity, right down to wet ink and a couple of drying notes.

The fiat was located near the shipyards, and a drifting fog was swirling about the place. It was eight thirty-five when they arrived, and most of the side streets were reasonably quiet, all the dockside action taking place in the row of pubs along the Thames. As Logan fiddled with the lock on the door, he found himself worrying again about the unthinkable consequences should Morgan insist on an actual demonstration. Despite the fact that the plates were Billy's best, the notes themselves could not compare with the authentic workmanship of the real thing—a fact for which Billy had been compelled to spend some time in one of London's grimy prisons. But if a demonstration was required, it might still work. It would just depend on how closely Morgan felt like scrutinizing the end result.

They went inside and Logan switched on the light, his signal to Billy waiting in the alley below to make his call to the police.

"There she is," said Logan, proudly indicating the press.

Everything was perfect, looking as genuine as the detailed preparations of an experienced artist like Billy could make it. Beside the press were several crisp, new notes, mixed in with a few smudged ones, and a couple of fakes on which the ink was still wet. Under the table a box contained crumpled paper, trash, many attempted notes, some crooked, some with smeared ink, even a couple of genuine notes on which smears had been added for effect. Billy had considered the tiniest detail.

Morgan immediately approached the table and reached for one of the notes.

"Careful," Logan warned. "The ink on those top ones is still wet."

"Why didn't you warn me!" said Morgan, pulling back his hand, two of his fingertips smudged.

"I did warn you," replied Logan testily, keeping up the bravado. "Try one of these," he said, reaching toward one of the legitimate bills. "These are from yesterday. They should be dry." Of course the ink was as dry as on any of the notes issued by the Bank of England.

Gingerly, Morgan took the note and held it up by a corner to the bare light bulb hanging from the ceiling.

"Nice," he muttered. "Yes . . . very nice." He turned and again approached the table, sifting through the contents on its top with a prudent finger. "Not so good here," he said, looking at one of the fakes on which Billy had intentionally double-stamped the image.

"I'm still getting the hang of the mechanics of the press," said Logan. "Kind of a temperamental old thing."

"What about this one?" asked Morgan, pointing to a genuine note on which Billy had judiciously added two or three splotches of ink. "Looks like it should have been a good one."

"I botched it taking it out of the press," said Logan.

"Well, that'll be a problem we won't have," replied Morgan. "My men have considerably more experience at this kind of thing than you do."

A satirical response jumped to Logan's lips, but he thought better of it and held his silence.

Morgan gave the press a thorough going-over, peering in to see the plate where it sat in position. "There's ink all over the thing!" he said. "Don't you know a clean plate's the secret to a good run?"

"I was working on it today," said Logan. "Didn't see any reason to clean up. I try to run a few notes every day, so I can keep ahead."

"Idiot!" said Morgan under his breath. He was hardly aware of Logan by this time. He had swallowed the bait now, without knowing it, and was slowly being reeled in.

Next he stooped down to examine the throw-aways, fishing through the paper and trash, looking now and then at one of the rejects. As Billy hoped he would, a genuine note with some added streaks of ink caught his attention. He held it up to the light, mumbled some inaudible words to himself, then crinkled it back into a ball and threw it on the floor.

"I'd like to see the press in action," stated Morgan.

"Sure," said Logan without flinching. "But the press makes an awful racket. That's why I located here by the shipyards. You can hardly notice it in the daytime with the noises outside. More'n likely my landlady's in bed by now anyway. I doubt she'll cause us any trouble." As he spoke, Logan proceeded to make some adjustments to the press, smeared some new ink on the rubber roller and rolled out the excess on a sheet of blank paper. Then as he reached for the crank handle, he turned to one of Morgan's men who was standing by the window, and said, "Hey, mate, look down there and see if that bobby's still standing down at the corner. He's been a mite troublesome lately . . . I think the old lady put him onto me."

The man peered out into the darkness, then turned back to his boss rather than Logan, "Can't see nothin', Mr. Morgan. It's too foggy."

"Never mind," said Logan. "Just one of you keep an ear to the door. If you hear him coming up the stairs, we'll shut it down and stuff everything in the closet." With the words Logan put his hand to the crank and gave it a swift turn. An immediate grating screech filled the room, but before Logan had the chance to give the handle another full revolution, Morgan's sharp voice stopped him.

"Shut it down!" he yelled.

Logan obeyed, feigning a look of puzzlement.

"Just take out the blasted plate so I can look at it!" demanded the hoodlum. Logan did so, not once betraying his relief. Disengaging it from the press, with ink all over his hands, Logan handed the bogus plate to Morgan, who, with a look of disgust at its messy condition, took it and examined it intently. *Good thing,* thought Logan, *that the ink obscures any defects he might be able to spot. I wonder how long it will take for the police to show up.* He hoped too that they would take Billy's advice and wait for their quarry outside the building. It would never do for them to raid the room and pinch him along with Morgan.

Morgan's raspy voice broke into his thoughts. "I believe our deal was for five thousand," he said, handing the plate back to Logan.

"Deal? As I recall, you left me little choice. I would still—"

"Don't get smart with me, kid!" snapped Morgan. "I offered you five thousand. I could take that plate for nothing if I wanted. But I expect you to come up with a plate for a ten-pound note real soon."

"If you're good for your word and it's worth my while, I might be willing to deal with you again."

"You're pretty sure of yourself for a baby-faced punk!"

"I'm sure of my *merchandise,* Mr. Morgan," Logan replied evenly.

Morgan eyed Logan steadfastly, squinting slightly as his eyes seemed to probe Logan's face one last time to find any involuntary twitch that would reveal the chink in his armor. Logan returned his gaze with determination, fully aware that the next words he heard could very well be, "Kill him!"

After what seemed like an interminable period, Morgan slowly reached into his coat pocket, took out an envelope, but instead of giving it directly to Logan, he handed it to one of his men. "Give it to him, Lombardo," he said—either because he felt he was too good to make the exchange himself or from long years of keeping his own hands off the actual dirty work.

Lombardo represented the stereotype of the underworld thug. He was well over six feet tall, muscular, with a deep scar over his right eye. Morgan could not have chosen a more picturesque companion had he fabricated him according to preset specifications. He handed Logan the envelope with a scowl that seemed intended to say, "Just you wait till I get my hands on you, you little creep!" With one final gesture of cocky impudence that nettled Morgan to the very edge of his endurance with this young upstart, Logan opened the envelope and counted the notes inside. Then, as an added insult, he removed one, held it up to the light. and examined it closely.

"Can't be too careful in this business," he said.

Lombardo took a menacing step forward, but Morgan restrained him.

"Well! I guess you're as good as your word," said Logan at length, reaching into a nearby drawer as he spoke, and taking out an envelope in which he had earlier secreted several counterfeit notes. "I'll put it in here so the ink won't smear all over," he said, dropping the plate into the envelope, licking the flap and sealing it shut.

"And the other plate," said Morgan. "You weren't going to send me out ready to do only half the job, were you now, Mr. Logan?"

"Would I do a thing like that?" laughed Logan, removing the reverse plate and depositing it into a second envelope. "Here you are—two plates as agreed."

He held out the two envelopes to Morgan. Lombardo stepped forward to take them, but Logan drew in his hand, looking directly at Morgan. Morgan scowled, swore under his breath, grabbed the two plates, jammed them into his coat, and made for the door without another word. Logan exhaled an almost audible sigh of relief. It would never have done for the police to nab Morgan, with the plates and counterfeit notes in Lombardo's possession. For no doubt the hoodlum would swear complete ignorance, even backed up by his pigmy-brained flunky, who would then be trotted off to jail in his stead.

The moment the roughnecks had exited and their footsteps had died away on the steps, Logan rushed forward, caught up a screwdriver, and began to disassemble the press with all the haste he could muster. Billy had been over this phase of the operation with him many times. Time would be of the essence here. If the police were already waiting outside, he would have but a matter of minutes—probably five at most—to rid the place of every shred of evidence by the time Morgan, claiming to have been duped by a London mobster, led the constables back up the stairs to his flat.

Logan hurriedly filled the three burlap sacks he had stashed in the closet with the pieces of the press, all the notes, ink, trash, and other bits of paper. He walked to the back window and gingerly opened it. He had planned to let down the bags to the ground with a rope he had already tied outside the window. But there was already a constable positioned at the end of the alley. He should have known they would surround the building! *Why didn't Billy think of this?* he muttered, tiptoeing back from the window to take quick stock of the situation. He was trapped. But he couldn't panic. There was always a way out, if not by fast talking, then by wit or sheer daring. But there was always a way!

He could already hear the thudding of heavily booted feet on the stairs below. Morgan had wasted no time telling his story of being taken. He had probably claimed he didn't even know what was inside the envelopes. No matter what became of Morgan now. He had to get out of there!

He'd have to leave the sacks. There was no way he could be connected to anything. And who could tell, maybe they'd incriminate Morgan all the more. It was just a shame Billy would have to lose all that hard work.

He set down the bags, ducked out the window onto the fire escape, and pulled the window shut behind him. Keeping one eye on the constable below, whose back was to him, and keeping his ear atuned to the approaching police inside, he ascended the steep metal steps. Glad it was only a four-story building, he swung onto the roof just as a uniformed bobby raised the window he had just left and peered out. All his attention, however, was focused downward. Seeing nothing, and not thinking to look above him, he whistled to his companion guarding the entrance to the alley below.

But Logan could not rest yet.

With great caution he crept across the rooftop, hoping all the while that the police didn't decide to press their search. If they did, he'd have to make a run for it across the rooftops of London, and that would mean several jumps he'd rather not have to negotiate.

He sat down in the darkest corner he could find atop the building, his jump to the adjoining building well settled in his mind should it be necessary; and there he waited. Occasionally a shout broke the silence, some muffled sounds came from inside the building, and about ten minutes later he heard loud and angry protests from what he was sure was Lombardo's voice coming from the street below.

Then a police wagon roared off, followed by two automobiles, sirens piercing the night air as if to announce to all the world their capture of Al Capone's dangerous associate who had thought to find easy pickings in London.

Then all was quiet.

Still Logan sat. For two hours more he waited.

But this was indeed his lucky night. For if the police even believed Morgan's story of some phantom swindler pulling a masterful con on him, they didn't seem inclined to press it. They appeared well satisfied just to have their hands securely on Chase Morgan, with ironclad evidence to back up their arrest.

10 ❈ *Flight*

LOGAN LAY STRETCHED out on the bed in his own flat. Once more he began to count out Chase Morgan's money.

The temporary ecstasy of the feel of the notes in his fingers and the smell of more money than he had ever had in his hands at one time took his mind off the stark and dingy walls surrounding him, although it was only occasionally that he wondered what it would be like to have a real home like Skittles. But he never allowed such thoughts to progress seriously in his mind. His was not the kind of life where a man could really consider having a home or a family.

There were a few women who had been passing parts of his life. But he had never been genuinely in love. He had not been willing, or even able, to give a relationship what any kind of lasting love demanded. Besides, he was much too young to get himself "imprisoned," as he liked to phrase it. Whenever Molly heard him use the term, she acted affronted. "Wot a way t' speak of something so loverly as marriage!" she would protest, turning to Skittles with some comment like, "Is that how you think o' it too, old boy?"

Skittles would always reply wisely, and truthfully, " 'Course not! But then there ain't many men as can lay claim to such a fine ol' girl as you, Molly!"

Nothing less than a discovery so fortuitous as Skittles' could alter Logan's less than idealized attitude toward the institution of marriage. But he sincerely doubted he'd ever find someone quite like Molly. Forthright and honest, but at the same time gentle, she could be stubborn and gruff enough to keep things interesting. And how she could laugh! He knew Skittles always had a good time with Molly—which was probably why, in all their thirty years together, he had never strayed. Logan well knew that in the kind of life they led, there were sufficient opportunities.

However, at this particular moment, marriage was the furthest thing from his thoughts. He lay there, in his run-down flat, gloating over his victory. He had just completed the most successful con game of his young career. And on top of that, had fleeced the famous American gangster and sent him to jail. This could boost his reputation to the heights! For the moment Logan had entirely forgotten his original intent. Intoxicated with his success, he could not keep himself from dreaming about the prospects that might now be open to him. Who could tell—might he not even be able to take over Morgan's operation himself? Of course he'd put an end to that dirty protection racket. And he'd clean up lots of other things in the process. But that posh club, with its classy clientele—why it would be enough to set up an enterprising man for life . . .

The insistent pounding at his door suddenly woke Logan from his reverie.

"Come on in," he called.

The door opened and Billy Cochran walked in. He always seemed to have a disgruntled air about him, but his face now showed displeasure.

"Why don't you 'ave this door locked?" he reproved without preamble. "I could've been anyone!"

"Who's going to bother me?" answered Logan airily. "Morgan's on his way to prison, isn't he?"

"I saw them take 'im off with me own two eyes, bad as they may be," said Billy. "But you can't be too careful," he added, squinting and looking about, the lines in his face accentuated in the dim light.

Ignoring his cautions, Logan stuffed the money he had been holding back into its envelope and, tossing it to Billy, said, "See if this doesn't cheer you up!"

Billy caught the envelope effortlessly despite his reputed bad eyesight, and looked inside, emitting a soft whistle.

"I'd say Morgan's debt with Skittles is cleared," said Logan, grinning.

At the mention of their friend's name, Billy's hardened expression dropped and he slowly shook his head. "You 'aven't 'eard . . . I thought as much."

He walked to the bed and sat down heavily on its edge. "I just 'eard mysel'. I guess I thought you might already know."

"What is it, Billy?"

"This hain't so easy, Logan," sputtered Billy. "Skittles . . . well—he died earlier this mornin'."

For a moment Billy thought Logan had not heard him at all. For when he looked over toward him, Logan was staring blankly at the wall in front of him. The words had come too abruptly, like a fist out of nowhere, striking him senseless. As his glassy gaze gradually came back into focus, Logan slowly turned back toward Billy, his eyes filled with helpless appeal that somehow Billy's thick accent had distorted his words and that he had mistaken what he thought he heard. But the old man's small, narrow orbs—grim and filled with an agony even more pronounced because he had forgotten how to shed tears of remorse—dashed the younger man's flimsy hope.

It was true. Poor old Billy's eyes told the story. Skittles was gone.

Logan jumped off the bed. "I'll kill him," he breathed, almost softly in his wrathful distress.

It was the very quietness of his tone, the clenched understatement, that frightened Billy the most. "Logan," he began, as one entreating a child, "now don't go runnin' off an'—"

But Logan quickly cut him off, the hot blood of passion now rising in him that the dreadful news had at last sunk in. "I'll kill him!" he repeated, louder this time. "I'll kill Morgan, I tell you!"

Billy stood and caught Logan's arm, the little man holding Logan's agitated form fast in his grip.

"Hain't no way that's goin' to 'elp ol' Skits now," he said quietly, but with determination.

"Morgan murdered him!"

Billy closed his eyes, seeming to fight against his own passion for revenge, for he also loved Skittles. He, too, would have squeezed the life out of Morgan if it lay within his power. But he was old. Whether that gave him a little extra dose of wisdom, or whether it had made of him a coward, he didn't know. In any event, he understood the futility of revenge. But to assist him, Billy had something Logan had never made use of. Billy Cochran knew he had his bottle to turn to for the easing of the pain and hatred. He didn't know what Logan could do instead. Perhaps revenge was his only way to get rid of the ache inside.

"Don't stop me, Billy!" yelled Logan, and with a sudden burst of strength, he shoved Billy from him. The old ex-convict stumbled backward, lost his balance, and fell against the iron bedrail.

The shock of his temporary violent outburst, unintended though it had been, seemed to clear Logan's head. He rushed forward to assist his friend.

"Billy!" he cried. "Billy . . . I'm sorry!" Logan stooped down, stretched his arm around him, and helped him to his feet. As he did so, something deep within Logan began to crumble.

A strangled sob broke from his lips. He fought hard to bite it back, but another quickly followed. Billy reached up to pat his young friend's shoulder in sympathetic gesture. His caring action wrecked all further attempts at holding his distraught emotions in reserve. Tears started from Logan's eyes. He tried to brush them away, but the more he did so the more steadily they flowed. Hardly knowing what he was doing, Logan sagged against Billy, and his body shook as the older man laid a comforting arm on his shoulder. Neither had felt such an embrace of comfort since childhood.

Slowly Billy led Logan back to the bed, where he sat him gently down.

"Take it easy, lad," he said in a voice unaccustomed to gentleness. "'Tis a rotten shame, it is . . . but you can see, lad, can't you? Why, you're 'most a son to Molly, and it'd break 'er 'eart if somethin' was t' 'appen t' you too."

"Molly!" Logan exclaimed with renewed emotion. "I forgot about Molly. I've got to go to her!"

But Billy held him back once again. "You'd better not," he said. "Least not now. 'Tis best no one has the chance to connect you with Molly."

"But Morgan's in jail."

"E'en if he stays in jail—which hain't at all certain he will, an' you know it—but e'en if he does, he's still got boys to take care of things for 'im. I thought you understood before you got into this that you'd 'ave t' leave town for a while—"

"You said disappear. You never said get out of town," Logan interrupted, dismally shaking his head. "I hadn't thought about that."

"Well," declared Billy emphatically, "losin' five thousand quid's one thing. But landin' in jail's another. Morgan's goin' to be mad—and he's goin' to be on the lookout for you. You might 'ave t' stay away for a couple months, mebbe longer, till we see wot 'appens."

"But—"

"There hain't no other way, Logan—that is, if you value your skin."

Logan stood again and paced the room. Some sharp he was! His great scheme had accomplished nothing more than to make Morgan more dangerous than ever. Not only to himself but to Molly as well, should Morgan ever discover their connection. Skittles was dead. Molly was alone. And he could not even go to her to offer what small comfort he could—and after all she had done for him over the years.

He kicked at a chair in his frustration, sending the flimsy wooden thing flying across the room. Much as he wanted to see Morgan pay for what he had done, he felt impotent, and such a childish action was the only violence of which he was capable. He could lie, he could cheat, he could steal. But he could not murder. To do so would put him in the same class as Morgan himself. But there was something else besides, something he couldn't quite put his finger on, something inside him which told him a murderer was somehow less of a human being than any other, no matter what other crimes one might have committed. All at once he remembered what Skittles had said to him in the hospital. *"Get out,"* his friend had pleaded with him, *"before it's too late . . . before you end up going the way of Chase Morgan."*

He was different from the likes of Morgan. Wasn't he? He knew where to draw the line. He would never . . .

His thoughts drifted off to an indistinct end. Well, he *was* different! And he wasn't going to let Skittles down. Never!

Slowly he turned back toward Billy, still seated on the edge of the bed anxiously watching him pace back and forth.

"Square everything with the lads that helped us," Logan said, nodding toward the envelope which Billy still held. "Keep some for yourself and get your watch back. Then give the rest to Molly."

It seemed that abruptly Logan had resigned himself with what must be done. His voice now took on a determined tone.

"Don't worry about a thing, lad," answered Billy. "I'll take care of it. But wot about yoursel'?"

"Guess I'll need a bit for traveling."

Billy handed him two hundred pounds.

Logan recoiled. "I don't need *that* much!" he exclaimed. "I'd only lose it gambling, or doing something else just as stupid."

"Take it," insisted Billy. "You earned it. An' Molly wouldn't want to be thinkin' of you headin' off to who knows where penniless."

Logan hesitated a moment longer, then reached out and took the notes from Billy's hand. After an awkward embrace, during which even the crotchety old counterfeiter's eyes glistened with a hint of moisture, Billy left to deliver the money, and more bad news to Molly.

Through the dirty pane of his flat's only window, Logan watched him head up the mostly deserted street, sighed a long sigh when he was out of sight, then turned back into his room. He went directly to the closet, pulled a brown leather suitcase from it, and hoisted it onto the bed to begin packing. His possessions were few, so the activity occupied little of his time. When all his other worldly belongings had been stuffed inside, he laid on top the fine cashmere suit he had worn to impress Morgan, along with the silk necktie and linen shirt. Who could tell when he might need them again? Instead of such finery, he dressed himself in clothes more appropriate for travel—a brown tweed suit, with an open-collared shirt, sturdy shoes, and his well-worn dark overcoat. He picked up Skittles' checkered cap and set it rather reverently on his head. It hardly went with the rest of his attire, but at such a moment Logan could think of wearing nothing else.

"I'll never live up to it," he said to himself, "but maybe it'll bring me luck."

The new fedora—well, there just wasn't room for it. And somehow it reminded him of things he'd just as soon forget at present. He laid it on the dresser, hoping it would come by a worthier owner than Skittles' cap had. Next to the hat he placed a few notes to cover his back rent. He didn't want a disgruntled landlady setting the police on his tail, too.

As he stepped outside, the wind and rain pelted him. He pulled his overcoat tightly about his neck, looked back and forth along the street, then headed out into the nasty weather. It was no day to be traveling.

He cast a backward glance at the building where he had lived for the past year. It had never meant much to him, but now it was all he had to represent those many things that did mean so much to him in London. The falling rain, the dreary tenement, the deserted street— it all seemed such a sad ending to his seven years in the city of cities, a city he had grown to love in spite of its size and occasional filth and squalor.

I'll be back . . . and soon! he told himself, then turned away and walked down the street, not looking back again.

An hour later he found himself looking up at the entrance of Euston Station. He had arrived there almost without thinking where his steps were leading him. He still had no idea of his ultimate destination as he walked inside and strode to one of the lines.

He gradually made his way toward the front, wondering what he would say when he reached the booth. Standing before the ticket seller at last, the single word *Glasgow* seemed to come out of his mouth of its own volition.

11 ❖ Home Again

THE TRAIN RIDE was a long one.

And tedious. Despite whatever resolve he may have felt while staring out the window as the buildings and streets of London gradually gave way to the countryside of Chilterns, by the time they reached Northampton, Logan was embroiled in a heated game of cards. And as he had predicted, he had lost nearly everything before the train reached Carlisle. He had been a wealthy man in Leeds, but by the time the train had pulled into Cumberland, he had lost his shirt, just as the Duke by that same name nearly had against Bonnie Prince Charlie not far from that very spot. He built his fortune up once more by Moffat in his own home-land. But Logan had had no Culloden like the famous Duke, and by the time he reached Glasgow, he was a poor man once again.

"Just like when I left," Logan mused as he stepped off the train.

He straightened his silk necktie, buffed the toes of his black dress shoes on his pant cuffs, and made one last attempt to brush the wrinkles from the cashmere suit he had donned in honor of his homecoming. Even without the fedora, he cut a rather striking figure strutting down the street as if he owned that portion of the soot-blackened industrial city. The two days on the train, and the outbreak of sunshine eight hours north of London had served to heighten Logan's enthusiasm for life once more. Never one to stay down for long, he walked along feeling as optimistic as if he *did* own the city—and the world, if he chose. Having no money in his pockets was only a minor inconvenience to Logan Macintyre, though certainly one he would not want to advertise in his hometown. But temporary setbacks, as he always called his losses at cards and dice, in no way diminished the possibilities for the future. Though he remembered his friend fondly, and indeed, over the last two days the image of the old man's dying face had scarcely left his mind, Skittles' final words to him had yet to be driven into his heart. It would take more than a friend's death to penetrate his superficial existence with a deeper and more lasting vision of life's true values.

As he passed a public house where he had spent many an idle hour during his youth, Logan's brisk pace slowed to a stop. Through the sooty window he spied several faces he thought he recognized, sitting, as it seemed, in the very spots where he had left them seven years earlier. He turned inside, wondering if he had changed as little as they. His question was answered in short order; he sauntered toward the bar unrecognized.

He removed Skittles' cap, kept his eye on the table where three old friends sat, and waited. It took but a moment or two longer before a dawning stare of recognition began to spread over one of the faces. Logan grinned.

"Be that Logan Macintyre?" exclaimed the man.

His two cronies glanced up and peered across the room.

"Ain't no wiseacre kid no more!" said another.

Slowly Logan approached, laughing at their comments.

"Hoots! Jist look at ye!" cried the first.

"Didna anyone tell ye there was a depression on?" asked the third man, speaking now for the first time. "Where ye been, Logan, 'at ye can dress in sich fine duds?"

"London," replied Logan.

"An' hoo lang's it been since ye left Glasgow, lad?"

"Seven years."

"Ye still haen't told us hoo ye came by sich a suit," jibed another. "Hasna the Depression hit auld London yet?"

"Or maybe oor frien' here has finally found himsel' a lucrative—" with the word the speaker winked at his two friends knowingly—"line o' work!"

Logan laughed again, wanting to dispel no fancies for the moment, at least until he could once again get a feel for the lay of the land.

Drinks were bought all around, and no one so much as thought of allowing Logan to lay out a penny toward them. The fact that he *looked* wealthier than all of them put together only made them the more determined that they should finance this festive afternoon of his homecoming.

"Where's old Bernie MacPhee?" asked Logan.

"Oh, he's doin' a drag up in Barlinnie for stealin' a automobile."

"An' Danny?" tried Logan again.

"Got himsel' killed a year ago. Seems a feller didna agree that his full house were on the up-an' -up."

Logan exhaled softly at the news, somewhat deflated.

"An' what hae ye been up t' in Lonnon, Logan?"

"Me?"

But before he had the opportunity to frame a response, one of the others at the table answered for him.

"Why look at him, ye dunderhead," the man said, fingering the fine fabric of Logan's suit. "Anyone can see he's doin' jist what he set oot t' do. Ye run one o' them fancy night clubs, nae doobt, don't ye noo, Logan?"

"Well . . ." Logan began, thinking how best to answer the question. But before he had said another word, the innkeeper had shouldered his way into the group to pour refills, and the conversation was sidetracked, leaving Logan still thinking what might have been his reply. But he did not appear anxious to correct his friend's miscalculation. And when the second round was finished, he took his leave, promising to return soon to try out his London luck on them. In high spirits the three sent him on his way, sure enough in their own minds that their former acquaintance of the streets had indeed made it into the big time in London.

A light rain, never far away even on the sunniest of days in Scotland, greeted him as he left the pub. He threw on his overcoat and pulled the checkered cap down over his unruly hair. He had thought about walking around the old neighborhood for a while, but the rain forced him to turn his steps directly toward his mother's home.

Yet even as he did so, he realized for the first time that he was actually reluctant to face her. *Well, who would blame me?* he rationalized. After all, this was hardly the homecoming he had always fantasized for himself—penniless and practically running for his life. The picture his mind had usually conjured up of the event always included a Rolls Royce, a mink-clad lady on his arm, and an armload of gifts for his mother—in every way the epitome of the son who had made good. He thought fleetingly of the five thousand pounds he had handed over to Billy in London. Of course if his mother had known how he came by the money, all the outward show of success and sophistication in the world would not have impressed her. And besides, knowing the money was now in Molly's hands was worth ten Rolls Royces.

Well, tomorrow his luck would change! It was bound to—because it could hardly get much worse.

In thirty minutes he had arrived. He came to the front of the old gray granite building (he avoided calling the place a tenement, which in fact it was) where his mother lived. The front door squeaked on its hinges as he opened it, and the fifth step still had a loose board. *One's old home should always appear changed after a long absence,* he thought, but at first glance everything here was exactly as he remembered it. Everything was supposed to look different, because *he* had changed—hadn't he?

He glanced quickly down at his fine clothing as if to reassure himself. He certainly hadn't had apparel like this when he left seven years ago. Even the blokes at tile pub hadn't recognized him. For the moment he forgot, as he was prone to do, that he was nothing but a lad seven years ago.

One thing he knew for certain: the three flights up to his mother's flat had never seemed this fatiguing. He was panting heavily when he reached the final landing, and had to pause a moment to catch his breath. He raised his hand to knock on the door. That seemed the strangest sensation of all.

Suddenly his mind flooded with visions of a dirty-faced, ragamuffin boy racing up and down the steps, bounding through the door. Or more often than not, when that same youngster reached the age of thirteen or fourteen, creeping up the steps in the middle of the night and sneaking through the door so that his mother would not hear.

The temptation seized him once more to try to sneak into the flat, but he gave a mature chuckle at the idea and rapped sharply on the door instead.

His mother opened the door.

A brief moment of utter stillness ensued, like some of the moving pictures Logan had been to in London when the film had jammed and the action momentarily had ceased. Then all at once the film began running again, and Frances Macintyre smiled and took her son's hands in hers.

Logan mused that she was indeed another of the fixtures of his home that had not changed. She was nearly as tall as he, and still displayed a certain poise, though it was difficult to discern properly, covered as it was by a poorly fitting housedress of drab green.

For an instant Logan wanted to flee. Was it childlike embarrassment to once again stand in front of his mother? Or was it the manly disappointment of wanting to hang his head in shame for neglecting her all these years? How many times does a man possess five thousand pounds—right in his very hands! Yet he had not once thought to keep a little back for his mother. She had seemed so distant, almost a nonexistent memory out of his past, when he was back in London. Molly and Skittles had been everything then. But suddenly it was different. He had flown back in time and now here she was, part of his life once more. And how desperately he wished he had a few quid to buy her a new dress.

"Evening, Mum," he said, kissing her lightly on the cheek, as if he hoped the gesture could substitute for all the other things he could not do.

"Ye sure know hoo t' surprise a woman," she replied in an even contralto voice he remembered always finding so soothing. She led him inside and he noted that most of the old furnishings were still in place.

"I guess I never was one for letter writing."

"Two letters in seven years," she said without reproach. "I'm thinkin' it must be a record o' some kind fer makin' yer kin wonder whether ye be alive or dead."

As they gravitated toward the kitchen, Mrs. Macintyre set a kettle of water on the stove.

"Ye haena had supper yet?" she asked. Logan shook his head. "Weel," she said, "I got a bit left from my own. I always make more'n I need. Tomorrow I'll go t' the market an' get some real man food fer ye."

"I don't want you to make a bother for me."

"Seven years I hae been waitin' fer jist sich trouble, son! Leave me t' enjoy ye while I can."

Logan sat back and studied her as she set about her tasks, and he realized he was seeing her in a completely different light than he had before. Perhaps the years apart and his own maturity helped him to view things more objectively. At any rate, he unexpectedly noticed that his mother was still an attractive woman. But then, she was only forty-one. And even after years of hard work and poverty, Frances Macintyre could still hold her own beside the women of the world he had seen daily in London. He wondered why she had never remarried. Somehow, he had been the reason. Maybe she hadn't wanted him to turn up one day and find a new surrogate father in his home.

Before many minutes she set a dish of steaming potatoes on the table with a plate of brown bread and sliced cheese. He hadn't eaten anything all day due to his lack of funds, and fell to it with a relish that warmed the mother's heart. After he had finished everything in front of him and the second helpings that followed, she poured them both cups of hot, strong tea. It was then that he noticed her hands. They looked old. Like nothing else about her, they showed the life of toil. It seemed as if all the years of hardship and heartache had drained to those two appendages. Even old Molly's hands had never seemed so worn and wrinkled. But perhaps they were noticeable because they contrasted so sharply with her attractive, almost youthful appearance otherwise. Something about that made it all the more pitiable.

Impulsively Logan reached out and touched one of the hands which had so attracted his gaze.

Puzzled, his mother stopped with the kettle in midair. He looked up at her, and smiled—a bit embarrassed.

"It's good to be home," he said, as if he felt some words were appropriate. But he wasn't at all certain those were the exact words he wanted to say.

"'Tis good t' hae ye home, Logan."

"Don't you wonder why I've come?"

"I figured ye'd tell me when an' if ye had a mind fer it."

"I wish I'd done more for you, Mum."

"'Tweren't yer responsibility, son," she said gently, "so dinna get it int' yer mind that it were."

"I don't have any money."

Mrs. Macintyre's lips curved up into a smile—a nice smile too, considering the few occasions in her life when she had been able to practice it. "Knowin' ye as I do," she said, "I doobt that'll last fer lang."

"That's not why I've come back," he said. "But I thought you should know."

"'Tis fine wi' me, fer whate'er reasons ye came. An' noo there'll be not anither word aboot it. Ye can help oot when ye can."

She set the kettle once again on the stove. When she turned back toward him, from her wan smile Logan thought she might be on the verge of tears. She quickly sat down and took a sip of her tea. "Mr. Runyard'll be needin' some help in his restaurant," she suggested. And if her voice carried a note of hopefulness, she could perhaps be forgiven for wishing against hope that her son was at last home to stay.

"I don't know how long I'll be staying," he answered evasively.

"Oh?"

"But I'll bring some money in—"

"That weren't my meanin', son," she added hastily. "I jist knew ye'd be wantin' t' keep busy."

"I never had trouble keeping busy before."

"I know. But ye was yoonger then. An' perhaps what was keepin' ye busy wasn't the best o' things fer a grown man t' be doin'."

Then came a long silence.

They each pretended that their tea was consuming their complete interest. But a half-empty teacup can serve that purpose only so long. At length Mrs. Macintyre rose and began to clear away the supper things.

Logan jumped up to help.

"Sit doon," she said. "Ye must be tired after yer trip."

"Not a bit," he replied. "At least, not after that feast. I even thought I'd take a walk around the old neighborhood and reacquaint myself."

"'Twill be late soon—" she began, but then stopped herself. "I'll get ye a key t' let yersel' in."

"Thanks, Mum. I won't be too late. And thanks for the supper and tea."

She merely smiled as he gathered up his coat and cap. Then she walked over to a ceramic jar by the sink and took out two one-pound notes. These she pressed into Logan's hand. He began to protest, but she shook her head.

"Ye're my son," she insisted. "Let me do it fer ye."

He took the money and left, knowing all the while that his whole reason for wanting to walk about the neighborhood was simply to escape the intimacy he was so unaccustomed to—and he hated himself for it. She wanted to make up for the years of his absence by giving to him of the little she had, yet he knew it was he who should be doing for her. But because he couldn't, he found it difficult to look her in the face. At this moment he found it hard even to face himself honestly. How much easier it was to duck out into the familiar streets where every promise seemed available, especially to a man of his wit and skill.

He had little difficulty finding a back-room card game, and the cronies of his youth welcomed him with gusto, treating him with the eminence of a returning hero. Logan had no reason to doubt that tomorrow would bring changes, and there was no reason for those changes not to be for the better.

12 ❊ A New Scheme

LOGAN AWOKE THE next morning some time after ten. He had been out much later the previous night than he had anticipated.

He ambled into the kitchen where he discovered oatcakes and cheese laid out on the table for him alongside a note from his mother telling him when she expected to be home from work. Munching one of the crunchy biscuits, he wandered back into his room and set about getting dressed, this time in the tweeds, not the cashmere.

Then he began to consider his prospects for the day.

Last night's efforts had put ten pounds in his pocket, half of which he had deposited in his mother's ceramic jar. He felt much better about himself now than when he had left the evening before. Things indeed had begun to look up, despite that the light mist had turned into a distinct downpour. The weather certainly didn't beckon him to step out, though how long he could remain cooped up inside would be hard to tell. After thirty minutes he could stand it no longer. He grabbed an umbrella, not pausing to think that his mother had gone to work without hers just so that her son would have use of it, and decided to chance the storm.

The streets were nearly deserted, and his favorite pub was still empty. He bought a pint, but didn't enjoy it much without company. Feeling rather dejected he picked up a copy of yesterday's *Daily Mail* from the stand across from the pub, and returned home.

He sank down on the timeworn couch in his mother's small sitting room, propped his feet up on a low table, and tried to interest himself in London's happenings. Perhaps the paper might suggest something as to future possibilities. Dominating the front page was an account covering the opening of the trial of the Rector of Stiffkey, the clergyman whose lifestyle had lately scandalized Britain. Reading further, he learned that Britain had sent troops to Singapore to defend British interests there against the rising threat of the Japanese. On page two he read a brief account of the upcoming election in Germany and the fears of some that a former army corporal by the name of Hitler might soon take over the reins of power there. Logan recalled that Winston Churchill had once sung Hitler's praises; now it seemed that English leaders were changing their tune.

So far nothing seemed either to concern or to interest Logan very much, though it would have been a lark to have been in London for the Rector's trial. All the other news was too far removed. Singapore, Germany—even the accounts of the flagging economy failed to arouse him. His own personal financial depression seemed far more pressing, and neither the Conservatives nor the Laborites could offer him relief.

He tossed aside the paper and stood to stretch his legs. A small shelf of books caught his eye and he wandered listlessly over to it. His mother was not much of a reader, and these books had sat here untouched as long as he could remember, for he, too, had never read much. Today, however, almost without even thinking what he was doing, he found himself standing looking at the spines of the dozen or so volumes that sat here as a reminder of literacy in the midst of Glasgow's working district.

Sheer boredom led Logan to reach toward a volume and take it down—Dickens' *Bleak House.* After not much more than a moment, he replaced it with a bit of a smirk. *No wonder I never read any of these,* he thought with a droll smile. Still he removed another and then another, giving each a cursory perusal, until he came to an extremely aged black volume. The moment he took it in his hands. he could feel that this was an altogether different kind of book, bound as it was in dark, limp leather. It was a Bible, but try as he might Logan could not recall ever seeing the book on this shelf during his childhood. He was sure his mother had never mentioned it, and he certainly had never seen her read from it. If it was a recent acquisition, it was a curious one, for the book was clearly of great age. He had a friend who had dealt in old and rare books—or more precisely in *bogus* old and rare books. *I wonder what it's worth,* he thought as he unconsciously flipped through the pages. *I should probably show this to old Silky. It might be just the thing to—*

"Hello!" he exclaimed aloud as a sheet of paper fell from between the pages, "what's this?"

He stooped down, picked up the folded and yellowed paper, opened it, and saw that it was a letter, handwritten in a most illegible scrawl.

His interest piqued, he carried the Bible, along with the mysterious letter, over to the couch, where he sat down once more to attempt to decipher it. This proved to be no small task, for judging from the many misspellings and archaic expressions, the writing had obviously come from the hand of an uneducated man. The date on the letter, however, encouraged him to persevere. He was bored with nothing better to do, and one in Logan's line of work tended to look for fortune to smile upon him at every turn; through the years Logan had grown accustomed never to look the other direction no matter how unpromising the opportunity may have appeared at first glance.

March 19, 1865, he read, then continued on, making his way through the body of the letter a single word at a time.

Dear little Maggie, it began, *I dinna ken where to send this, but I pray daily that ye will write to them wha love ye at Stonewycke. I write this noo because I must explain to ye what I hae doon and why. Ye see, the treasure has weighed heavily on my heart . . .*

Logan sat up right on the couch, suddenly coming fully awake.

Yer father almost stumbled upon it one day, before his illness, that is. Weel, it set me to pondering, and I couldna keep frae thinking as hoo much trouble that treasure has already brought to this world. I thought aboot tossing it into the sea, but always I was reminded that tisna mine to destroy. I didna want to be a thief, especially from yerself, Maggie. Yet I

*feared lest another discover it and begin again the chain of terrible greed and violence. So
I hae moved it, Maggie, and hidden it where I pray none will discover that evil horde, unless
ye come back yerself, and then I'll tell ye where I had put it, 'cause 'tis yers to do with as ye
see fit.*

By now Logan was nearly perspiring, and reading as rapidly as the aged writing would
allow.

*But be assured, at this moment, Maggie, 'tis no treasure we lang fer—but 'tis only to hae
ye back in oor midst once mair. To see ye with auld Raven riding upon lonely Braenock or
the sandy beach would be worth all the gold in this world. But in yer memory I hae put it in
a spot I thocht ye loved, hoping that'll please ye. For 'tis the Lady of Stonewycke ye'll be
someday. And I'll always think of myself as yer servant.*

*Do ye remember when ye were a wee lass with Cinder, and ye tried that cliff and ye
both got stuck? Ye were always so free upon hill and sand that I didna miss ye too sore
fer some time. But then when I did, I kenned just where to find ye in the other direction.
Ye loved that path to the rock bearing yer name. And I hold sich memories of ye, dear. I
pray one day ye will read this and return to us. But 'tis all in oor dear Lord's hands, and
his will be doon.*

The letter was signed *Yers very truly, yer servant, Digory MacNab.*

Logan leaned back and let out a long, low whistle.

This was indeed a find! He might just have fallen on his feet at last! And without a hint
of any illegalities connected with the case. Maybe he would make his fortune on the up-
and-up after all!

Of course, he reasoned with himself, this letter was sixty-seven years old and who was to
say whether this Maggie might not have long since returned to claim her prize? But no, she
could clearly never have received this letter, for here it still sat after all these years. Thus, if
she had returned, with the only clue tucked away in a Bible out of sight, she would never
have found it anyway.

Hmm! This held promise! The infinite possibilities to a mind like Logan's were intriguing, to say the least.

But then, he reflected further, in that many years countless things could have intervened
in the disposition of this MacNab's treasure—excavations, building projects, erosion of the
ground. To even think that it might . . .

Well, it was preposterous!

But what if it *were* still there! Could this be the change in his fortunes he had been waiting for?

A treasure hunt! He had participated in more harebrained schemes in his time. But this
would be a first.

Yet he had hardly a clue to start with.

Or did he? Hadn't he seen a motion picture last year where the clues were hidden in just
such a note as this? And where was this Stonewycke place, anyway?

That would be a beginning. Perhaps his mother would know something about all this.
He glanced at his watch—it would be hours before she returned from work.

He stood and paced around the small room, his boredom completely dissolved by now,
thoughts tumbling rapidly out of his active brain. Now here was a project worthy of his most
diligent efforts! If it led to a dead end, what had he lost but a little time—of which he had an
abundance, anyway. But he did not want to waste a minute of that valuable time waiting
around for his mother's return. There must be something he could do in the meantime. In a
city like Glasgow, there must be scores of places to begin his research.

He turned back to the small table where he had lain the Bible, picking it up—more gingerly this time, now that it had suddenly become so valuable in his eyes. Tiny black flakes
of the crumbling leather along the edges of the spine came off into his hand. On the ornately
decorated nameplate page were inscribed the words in a florid, feminine hand:

Presented to Digory MacNab
On his tenth birthday
July 15, 1791—Port Strathy

Blimey! thought Logan. *This book is one hundred and forty-one years old!*

Running the figures quickly through his head, Logan did some further calculating. MacNab would have been eighty-four at the time of the writing of the letter. It seemed an odds-on bet that the old man went to his grave taking the secret of the treasure with him.

Logan sat pondering this turn of events another minute or two in silence. Then he jumped up, nearly forgetting his coat and cap, and hurried out.

Later that evening he scarcely gave his mother a chance to unload her basket of groceries before he began plying her with a barage of questions.

"Where did that old Bible come from?" he began.

The words sent a small spark of hope flickering in her mother's heart, until she quickly discerned that the gist of his interrogation was not spiritual in nature at all.

"It's been in an old trunk," she answered. "I finally decided t' get it oot an' put it up on the shelf with the other books."

"What trunk?" he queried.

"Jist an auld trunk o' family things."

"Who is Digory MacNab?"

"My goodness! What's sparked all this curiosity?" Mrs. Macintyre asked as she began preparations for their supper.

"Have you ever heard of a place called Stonewycke?"

"Up north, isn't it?"

"Yes," replied Logan quickly. "I did a bit of asking around today," he went on, "and I visited the library, read some old newspapers. You're right, there's a Stonewycke on the northern coast. Used to be a rather substantial estate."

"An' what's anythin' got t' do with this Stonewycke?" she asked as she cut up a few vegetables on the counter.

"Look at this," said Logan in place of an answer, thrusting the Bible in front of her, along with the letter. She scanned it hastily, gave him a noncommittal nod, and returned to her work.

"Don't you see, Mum? It must be the same Stonewycke. It was the biggest estate in those parts; then some twenty years ago most of the land was parcelled off to the tenants—given to them outright!"

"Generous lords, I'd say," commented Frances.

"Maybe. But more likely daft."

"There *are* good folk in this world, son."

"I know," conceded Logan. "But we're talking about thousands of acres of land. Why would anybody just give it away!"

"Maybe they cared more aboot their people than their ain wealth."

"Like I say—daft!"

"An' so who's the laird noo?"

"Is no laird, least none whose name I could find. The present heir is a Lady Margaret Duncan."

"There's yer Maggie, then."

"Could be . . ." he replied thoughtfully, sitting down at the table. He pulled several scraps of paper from his pockets and pored through them again. "The age would be about right," he mused, almost to himself.

"What's that ye say, son?" asked his mother, her interest in the matter growing.

"She turned up twenty years ago to claim the estate after having been in America some forty years. That would have put her in the States about the time this MacNab wrote his letter. The pieces all seem to fit."

"I dinna ken why ye're askin' me all these questions. Seems as if ye know more'n yer auld mum already."

Logan chuckled. "I couldn't help myself from finding out what I could. It caused some stir twenty years ago. The Aberdeen papers were full of it. Not only giving away all the land, but because there was some fraudulent scheme going on at the same time that the whole transfer exposed. Couple of big shots even did some time for it. And the laird before this Duncan lady had been murdered, it seems by the greedy family lawyer who was part of the fraud hoping to get his hands on the estate. The thing's positively fraught with intrigue!"

"I don't understand, son. Hoo could the lawyer hae seized the estate if there was still a living heiress?"

"That's the beauty of it, Mum!" Logan beamed triumphantly, as if he had single-handedly solved the mystery of the century. "No one knew this Margaret Duncan was alive. She had dropped completely out of sight forty years before. Don't you see? She couldn't possibly have received MacNab's letter. She probably doesn't know a thing about the treasure!"

"What's all this leading up to, son?" asked Logan's mother with just that tone in her voice which revealed that she knew all too well the answer to her own question. The gleam in her son's eye told more than any words he had spoken. "'Course ye're plannin' on informin' these Duncans o' their good fortune . . . ?"

"Of course . . . eventually." With a flourish adroitly designed to change the subject, Logan opened and spread out the letter on the table, perusing it again in detail. "I'd really like to know who this MacNab fellow was."

"He'd be some kin o' yers, nae doobt," his mother answered simply.

"Kin!"

"Why, what'd ye 'pect wi' a name like MacNab? Great Uncle maybe."

"Kin of mine?"

"'Tis my maiden name. Surely ye haena forgotten so soon?"

In fact, Logan had not forgotten. It was just that he had so little interest in his own background in his younger years that he had never taken the trouble to learn his mother's maiden name in the first place. All at once Logan's blood ran hot with exhilaration.

"My own relative," he said, continuing to ponder the implications of this latest surprising piece of information. "I should have guessed—the cagy old fox!"

"Seems ye're missin' the point o' that letter." Frances paused long enough to dump the vegetables in a kettle of bubbling water that contained six or seven potatoes, then sat down with Logan. "He says that the treasure, whate'er it be, caused nothin' but trouble an' he hid it t' spare the family more heartache. Digory MacNab didna want it t' be found again."

"Unless it was by the girl Maggie," added Logan.

"Aye. Noo the Lady Margaret o the estate. But ye said yersel' that ye weren't plannin' t' tell her—least not at first."

"Let's consider for a moment the possibility that MacNab's motives *were* pure," said Logan, once more diverting the track of the conversation away from his *own* motives. "I still don't think he would have left his letter if he truly wanted the treasure forgotten forever."

"Then he would hae wanted his Maggie t' have it."

"Or one of his own relatives," suggested Logan cautiously.

"Ye're stretchin' it a bit there, son. Ye know he intended nae sich thing."

"But once a man's dead, whatever he leaves behind comes into the hands of those of his own he leaves alive, whatever he may have intended. That's the law, Mum."

"An' ye're a fine one t' be keepin' sich a straight line!"

"The law's the law, Mum," said Logan with a tongue-in-cheek grin. "If MacNab passed on leaving no other heirs, well me being his nearest relation, that would make this Bible, and the letter, and whatever else, mine, don't you think?"

"The judge might place me ahead o' ye in that line," replied Frances with just a note of offense in her tone.

"And whatever's yours is mine, right, Mum?" rejoiced Logan cheerily, ignoring the flash of her eye. "And the letter's written quite familiarly," he went on. "I wonder if he couldn't have been related to Maggie also. An uncle perhaps, or a grandfather. That would make me—"

Here Frances laughed outright—a deep, soft laugh, not one overly filled with merriment, but pleasant to hear nonetheless.

"Believe me, Logan," she answered, dabbing her eyes on the corner of her apron, "if we had sich family connections, I'd know! Why, that'd make us kin t' lords an' ladies! 'Tis outright nonsense! This Digory was more'n likely a family servant—they got mighty attached t' those noble families back then."

"And how'd you come by the Bible?" asked Logan.

"Was in the family chest. I jist never paid it no heed till I decided t' put it oot a while back."

"I wonder if there isn't some way to confirm my relationship with the shrewd old boy."

Frances sighed, her safest reply when she knew that to say more to her son would only lead to strife. Seven years ago she had made frequent use of the habit, and it was amazing how quickly the old habit returned. For of all things, strife with her son was the last thing she desired at this moment in her life.

"Ye can look through the bureau that came t' me when yer gran'daddy passed on," she replied. The statement came somewhat grudgingly. She wanted no part in his scheme, and certainly didn't want to encourage him, but she knew he'd get to the bottom of it eventually anyway, so there was no use resisting and prolonging the inevitable. "He took great store in his family line. I never paid it much heed, but ye may find somethin'."

He was away from the table before the words had died out on her lips.

There was something in all this. Logan could feel it! It could be something big, so why shouldn't he take full advantage of such a splendid opportunity? He had no better options with which to occupy his time. And with Chase Morgan still to worry about, a trip to the north of Scotland, placing the wild Highlands between himself and his hometown, might be the perfect solution to that thorny dilemma. He doubted he could remain long in Glasgow without being traced there. If Morgan's cronies asked around Shoreditch, they were certain to discover his identity. And didn't most of his friends know of his Glasgow past? But who would think to search for him in the untamed and barren country above the Grampians?

Already the decision to go north was planted firmly in his mind. But first he had to possess all the facts possible about this estate of Stonewycke, the Duncan family, and Digory MacNab. The whole prospect was exhilarating! Who could tell what one might run across while unearthing ancient history?

Who could tell, indeed! For if Logan could have guessed what sleeping giants he was about to stir into wakefulness, a few second thoughts may have crept in with regard to the scheme hatching in his brain.

But he did not. Thus the next two days he spent—discreetly, he thought—asking more questions and stirring dust into corners that might have been better off left alone.

13 ❄ A Suspicious Caller

THE GENTLEMAN SITTING at the desk in the darkened office leaned back in his chair as he picked up the receiver of the phone. The only light in the room, coming from the street lamps outside, revealed a fashionably furnished place, though intimating that days had once been better. The man sat in shadows; his hair occasionally caught a ray of light, revealing substantial streaks of silver gray.

"I was just on my way out," he said into the phone in a low, hard tone.

He paused to listen to the voice on the other end of the line.

"Is that so . . . ?" he replied to the unseen voice, drawing out his words thoughtfully. "Inquiring about Stonewycke, you say?"

More listening.

"A treasure . . . then the rumors we heard are true . . . ?"

He leaned forward, grabbed a pencil, and drew a pad toward him.

"What was the name . . . ? Macintyre . . . from London, you say . . . ? No, no, don't do anything just yet. We don't want to scare him off. I'll make some inquiries here. For now we'll let him do the footwork for us. But don't let him out of your sight."

Another pause followed.

"He did?"

The man rubbed his chin reflectively. "Well, you do the same. Just remember, it's a sleepy little burg. Make sure he gets off at Strathy; then you go on to the next town and double back. I want no one to know of our interest in the matter. Report back to me regularly."

Another question interrupted him. After a brief pause he resumed: "Use that code we used in the last project we worked on together. Is that all, Sprague? All right. Just be sure he doesn't get on to you."

Without another word he replaced the receiver.

Notwithstanding the periodic raising of his eyebrows during the course of the conversation, if he was in any way excited over the prospects raised by the phone call, he did not show it. Instead, he continued to sit at his desk, absently tapping his pencil against the solid walnut top.

In fact, though his surface appearance seemed perfectly nonchalant, inside he was more than enthusiastic over this turn of events. He had been looking for just such a break. At this point he had no idea where it might lead, but he felt certain that he would somehow be able to use these tidings to his advantage. He had carried out some research of his own through the years and had heard a local legend about some ancient horde from the Pict era over a thousand years ago supposedly connected with the Stonewycke property. Intriguing though it was, he had always considered it nothing but a straw in the dark. Perhaps he had been wrong. A fellow from London asking about a treasure, then heading north by train—certainly bore looking into!

He picked up the phone receiver once more, hastily looked for a number in the card file on his desk, gave the operator the city and number, then sat back to wait. After about a minute he sat forward attentively.

"Hello," he said, in a different voice this time. "Yes, yes—it's me . . . I know, it's been a long time . . ."

He tapped the pencil impatiently while he listened for another minute to the man he had called.

"I—I certainly will," he said. finally getting a word in. "But perhaps until then, you might help me out . . . No, no!" he laughed, "I only want a bit of information. Yes . . . Do you know of a young fellow by the name of Macintyre, early twenties, I'd say, likes to hang around where there's some action in the back room, if you know what I mean?"

The voice on the line rambled on again for some time, with an occasional question or comment interspersed on the part of the listener.

"A sharp . . . can't say as I'm surprised . . ."

More listening.

". . . a bookie? . . . oh, an old counterfeiter. Hmmm . . ."

All at once the gentleman's impatience with his talkative informant changed to rapt interest. "He did what?" he exclaimed. "To Chase Morgan . . . !"

After another pause the man chuckled, the first crack in his otherwise steely demeanor. "It's a good thing Morgan can afford clever lawyers. Three months in jail isn't much, but for a man like Chase it's enough. I should think he'd want Macintyre! . . . How much? . . . I'm sure some low-life goon will take him up on his offer and try to collect, if Morgan doesn't find him first . . . My interest? A different matter altogether. A friend of mine was making inquiries—didn't think he was on the up-and-up, but the deal he offered sounded too good to pass up . . . Yes, you're right there," he laughed. "Morgan should have been as smart. Certainly, I'll come by next week . . . Thanks for your assistance."

The thing was becoming more fascinating by the moment, thought the man as he hung up the phone. A confidence man like this Macintyre was bound to be up to something . . . something shady, no doubt! It was lucky for him his man in Glasgow had stumbled into the middle of it. Well, *stumbled* was not exactly the right word, he reflected further. After all, Sprague had been hired for the express purpose of gathering information. And he had definitely hit the jackpot in Glasgow!

14 ❈ Errand Day in Port Strathy

ALLISON TAPPED HER foot impatiently as she leaned with folded arms against the parked Austin.

She and her younger brother had driven their great-grandmother into town for several errands; she did not mind so much waiting for her, but Nat had run off just as Lady Margaret was due to be finished. He had probably gone down to the harbor to pass the time with those fishermen whom he seemed to adore, would lose all track of time, and she would be forced to go all the way down there to fetch him.

As a child she had not really noticed. But now that she had grown into a refined young lady of seventeen, it became clearer to her worldly-wise eyes with each passing day that there was absolutely nothing in this provincial town to interest her. The main street of Port Strathy had not changed in fifty years, possibly even longer. The chandlery, Miss Sinclair's Mercantile, the office next door—now occupied by Strathy's first resident doctor—all were as staid and static in their appearance as ever.

The fish processing plant was the town's newest addition, having been built not long before Allison's birth. But it wasn't much to boast about for one like Allison MacNeil. Nor was the "New Town" which had sprung up around it. The entire vicinity was permeated with the distasteful odor of fish, and if it had swelled the population of the town by some two hundred, they were of an even more undesirable breed than the fishers and farmers. The rows of company houses they occupied were in many cases as poor as the abandoned crofters' cottages in the Highlands, and a rowdy district had grown up alongside them, with two new pubs where loud music and heavy-fisted brawls were not uncommon.

Allison looked about and sighed heavily. Still no sign either of her great-grandmother or Nat. But what was there at home for her to hurry back to? She doubted she'd ever be able to forgive her parents for taking her away from school; it had been her only touch with civilization. As much as everyone else in the family might enjoy the company of those dull fishers and ignorant crofters, she certainly had more respect for her own position than that. If her father was from that class, he was different. He had struggled to get an education, to better himself, to rise above the station of his birth.

And Allison intended to do the same. That is, she did not intend to be dragged back to those depths by remaining buried here in Port Strathy all her life. Let her mother prattle about the merits of the simple life; Allison wanted no part of it. What she wanted was the life her family's position and standing entitled her to. She should be wearing silk and fine linen, not this outlandish checkered shirt with dungarees. But she had no reason to dress up;—she would never run into Charles—or even Eddie Bramford here.

She glanced up again, this time noticing a plain girl about her own age crossing the street. *If I remain in Port Strathy much longer,* she thought to herself, *I will be certain to end up like Patty Doohan.* Of course, Patty had no choice. She was a commoner, an orphan raised by an older sister who worked in the plant. Watching the girl approach, Allison could hardly believe they had been childhood friends. But there had been so few girls her age in the area, and Patty had seemed, at the time, the best of the lot. She could have been pretty, with her rich chestnut hair and large dark brown eyes. But she let her hair hang in a most unfashionable manner, and her eyes seemed to droop like the eyes of a sad, tired bassett hound. What they could have had in common back then, Allison couldn't even imagine. Fortunately, she had now grown beyond such juvenile relationships. If Patty had no choice about her direction in life, Allison did, and she intended to make use of it.

Or did she? Allison sighed once more. Well, maybe not for the time being. But one day she *would* be able to make her own choices, and then she'd show everyone!

"Hi, Allison," said Patty rather shyly as she came close. Perhaps she, too, was remembering the days not so long ago when they had played and laughed together.

"Hello, Patty," replied Allison. "How are you?" she asked, as a matter of course, in a tone that implied that it did not matter.

"Jist fine." She held out the basket she was holding. "Been shoppin'. Miss Sinclair's got some real fine apples this week."

"Oh, has she? I'll have to tell the cook so she can purchase some for us." Allison emphasized the word *cook* heavily. She wouldn't want Patty to think she did the shopping herself.

"I thought ye was away at that boardin' school."

"Oh, I was, but I'm rather old for school now." As she spoke Allison was not the least aware of the upward tilt of her nose. "I'm just biding my time here before I go to London for the season."

"Oh," said Patty flatly. Then as if an afterthought, she added, "How nice."

What an awkward conversation, thought Allison. *If only I had some excuse not to just stay here, or if Patty would be on her way.*

An uncomfortable moment or two of silence followed. At length Patty said goodbye, and turned to go.

"It was good t' see ye, Allison," she called back with a smile.

Allison forced a smile in return, but no words of farewell would come. She had not particularly enjoyed seeing her old friend, for more reasons than she could even name or understand.

Not many minutes after Patty's retreating figure had disappeared in one direction, Nat appeared ambling casually toward her down the street in the other. He was munching an apple and seemed to be thoroughly enjoying the first fine spring day since the storm the night of the celebration when the schooner had gone down.

"Well, it's about time!" Allison snapped when he was within earshot. "You're lucky I didn't have to come fetch you."

"What's your rush? Grandma's not back yet."

"She'll be along," replied Allison defensively. "I just didn't want her to have to wait on you."

Nat grinned good-naturedly, but before his sister could retort with another caustic remark, she saw her great-grandmother emerging from the mercantile carrying a small parcel. Nat hurried to her side, relieving her of the package, took her arm, and led her across the street to the car.

For all her frail appearance, the old woman walked with a sure, steady gait, hardly requiring the assistance of her young great-grandson. But she patted the boy's hand and smiled her thanks to him.

"Well, children," said Lady Margaret rather breathlessly, "I think I've finished with everything. I do appreciate your carting me about."

"Glad to do it, Grandma," replied Nat, while inside Allison wondered what he meant by the words. It was *she,* not Nat, who was doing the carting.

"Your great-grandfather thinks I should take up driving one of these," she said, tilting her head to indicate the auto. "But," she chuckled gaily, "I'd sooner take to horseback riding again."

The younger folk laughed with her. Whether she could have mounted one of the spritely coursers in their stables was a question their father, Alec, would not allow to be answered. But both of them had heard many times of the three wonderful mares, Cinder, Raven, and Maukin, which Lady Margaret and Grandpa Dorey had ridden all over this very countryside in their youths.

Nat proceeded to help his great-grandmother into the front seat of the car. He then walked around in order to climb in behind the wheel, leaving the rear seat for Allison. But she put out her hand to prevent him from opening the door.

"What do you think you're doing?" Allison inquired pointedly.

"Aw, come on, Ali," pleaded Nat. "I can do it."

"That may be. But you can practice with Daddy, not with me."

"Aw, Ali!"

"The car is my responsibility, and I won't leave it in the hands of a child. And don't call me Ali!"

Brushing past him, Allison climbed into the driver's seat, and Nat into the back. She turned the key in the ignition, but the engine only turned over limply, then made not another sound. The Austin seemed to have no intention of moving from the spot where it sat. Again Allison tried to coax it to life, this time pumping furiously on the accelerator. Still there was no response. Slapping at the steering wheel, she opened the door and climbed out, with Nat on her heels. Wrenching up the bonnet of the car, she stared at the jumble inside. Nat elbowed her aside, and she had no choice but to defer to him. He had, after all, learned something about the workings of engines from Mr. Innes before his death.

Nat reached in and began tapping and wriggling various parts that he considered the most likely offenders.

"Here, hold this back," he said, indicating a greasy hose.

Allison wrinkled her nose distastefully, then plunged her hand into the grimy mess. In a moment Nat seemed satisfied with his work.

"Go around and try it again," he said.

She laid the hose down according to her brother's instruction, then brushed her hair from her eyes, smudging her nose as she did so, and climbed in once more behind the wheel.

But despite Nat's efforts, nothing happened. She rejoined Nat, who had procured several tools from the boot and was about to take a wrench to what he thought might be a loose connection.

"Mr. Innes would know what to do," he said, almost to himself and with a hint of sadness in his voice.

For the first time of the afternoon, Allison's expression softened. Each of the MacNeil children, in their own way, had been attached to the kind old factor, and Allison knew what her brother must be feeling to miss him at such a moment. They exchanged a rare, momentary, tender look.

But just as quickly Allison's expression resumed its look of superiority, and she barked out rather gruffly, "Maybe you've hit *something* this time . . . I'll try again."

But the Austin continued to make the same obstinate protestations. And since automobiles were few in Port Strathy, and the nearest automobile mechanic more than twenty miles away in Fraserburg, the options before the three stranded travelers looked to be rather limited.

Allison jumped out of the car a third time, angry by now, looked around helplessly, and gave the tire a futile, surly kick.

15 ※ *Stranger in a Strange Land*

LOGAN HAD STEPPED off the schooner that morning a bit shaky in the knees and even more so in the stomach, wondering why he had abandoned the train in Aberdeen in favor of the sea route. He had never been attracted to the sea-faring life—and now he knew why. Even worse, he had not been able to interest a soul onboard in a friendly little game of poker. He had reached the conclusion that if these fisher types were all so intent upon hanging on to their money, it would be dull sojourn indeed in this place called Port Strathy.

For his stomach's sake, and in an attempt to disprove his first impression of these northern folk, the first thing Logan did upon touching firm, dry land was to spy out the local pub.

Had he been seeking only a drink and a round or two of cards, he would no doubt have ended up at one of the establishments of the New Town, where his enterprising nature might have been more fully satisfied. However, as he was in need of a place to stay as well, he was directed to the only respectable inn in the place—the Bluster 'N Blow.

The fact that the history of the establishment dated back nearly two hundred years impressed Logan very little. Always looking ahead, to him anything that old was a step backward rather than into the future where real life was to be lived. He had had quite enough of old buildings—mostly the rat-infested tenements of Glasgow and London. The ultimate dream, to Logan Macintryre, would be to take up residence in one of the fashionable new West End apartment complexes, complete with every modern convenience.

He thus viewed the Bluster 'N Blow as neither quaint nor respectable. But since it was the only available hostelry, he'd have to make do. If he, however, was unimpressed with the inn, the innkeeper was quite taken with his new customer. For though Logan was dressed only in his tweeds, he appeared every inch a dapper gentleman, and Sandy Cobden knew a man of means when he saw one.

"Afternoon, sir," said the innkeeper. "An' what might I be doin' fer ye?"

Logan strode jauntily to the counter and perched himself on one of the tall stools. "I'd like a room, my good man," he said, "and something to soothe my sea-tossed insides."

"Ah, ye must hae jist come in on the schooner."

"That I did," replied Logan. "I should have waited for the train, but then I'd have had to finish the last of the trip overland, and I was anxious to get here."

Cobden laughed. "Ye see why we dinna get many visitors," he said, and as he spoke the innkeeper brought a bottle of his best Glenfidich Scotch up from under the counter. "Ye're lucky e'en t' hae a schooner t' ride after the accident several weeks ago. But take a drap o' this. It'll be jist the thing fer yer stomach," he added, pouring out a dram for his guest. "So, ye've come from Aberdeen, have ye . . . ?" queried Cobden, drawing out his tone in order to elicit some response. He took what he considered his "position" in the community with the utmost seriousness, and was therefore ever vigilant for whatever bits of gossip he might stumble across.

"Farther than that, I'd say—London, actually."

"I thought so!" declared Cobden, "the moment I heard yer accent."

In reality he had thought no such thing, for even after seven years in London, Logan had not entirely lost his Scottish tongue. He spoke with just enough mixture of the various dialects to which he had been exposed that his speech readily would have confounded the most experienced British linguist. Without revealing a thing, Cobden's curiosity was more than aroused by this well-dressed Londoner with the Scottish brogue. But he restrained himself from further questioning for the moment. He preferred to gather his information by more subtle means.

Instead, he busied himself with buffing the counter and wiping several glasses, while Logan sipped his Scotch and wondered that such energy could be summoned from so huge a bulk of a man. At length Logan finished his drink and took a coin from his pocket.

"Are you a sporting man, Mr.—?" Logan paused, as no introductions had as yet been forthcoming.

"Cobden's the name—Sandy Cobden." The innkeeper laid down his cloth and thrust a hand toward his visitor, shaking the smaller man's hand vigorously.

Logan, smiling a bit wanly, recovered his hand and introduced himself. "Well, as I was saying, Mr. Cobden, might you be a sporting man?"

"I'm na too sure if I take yer meanin'."

"I thought we'd lend a little interest to our tête-à-tête and toss a coin for my drink. Tails, I pay double, and heads, it's on the house."

"Why not?" agreed Cobden.

Logan flipped his gold sovereign high into the air, catching it crisply on the back of his left hand with his right over it. When he uncovered it, the face of George the Third leered up at them. "Sorry, old chap," he apologized, pocketing his coin.

"Not a bit o' it!" grinned Cobden in his most congenial manner. "Yer drink would hae been on the house anyway, ye bein' all the way from London, an' all."

"That's mighty friendly of you."

"We're a friendly little toon, Port Strathy is." Cobden resumed his labors, then after a moment's pause, in an off-handed way, asked, "So . . . hoo lang will ye be stayin' wi' us?"

"It's hard to say just how long my business will detain me," replied Logan noncommitally.

"Business, ye say . . ." Cobden mused, half to himself, half hoping his puzzled expression would draw something further from the stranger. He was remembering the last time such a dapper-looking fellow had come to Strathy on business some twenty years ago. That time it had meant nothing but trouble for the town. He hoped it would be different this time. But this young man certainly looked friendly enough, Cobden decided. And if there was one thing Sandy Cobden prided himself on, it was his keen ability to judge character.

"I thought I'd have a look about the place before dinner," Logan went on, ignoring Cobden's query. He was not quite certain how he was going to proceed on his quest, and he wanted to make sure he had a good feel for the town before he said anything. "Would you be so kind as to take my suitcase up to my room? I should be back in an hour or so."

Logan strode confidently from the inn.

He might not know how to begin this latest project that had brought him so far off the beaten path. But one thing appeared certain—it was going to be a breeze. These cuddys wouldn't know a good dodge if it jumped out and kissed them. Why, that Cobden fellow still had no idea he had been fooled by the most elemental of cons—a double-headed coin!

Yes . . . he felt instinctively that his luck was taking a turn for the better. It only remained to find old Uncle Digory's treasure and hop aboard the next schooner or train back to civilization.

The first order of business, therefore, was to locate these Stonewycke people. They might prove his most difficult obstacle, however, for if they were of the cultured aristocracy, they were likely to be far more worldly-wise than that Cobden or the sea-folk he had encountered on the schooner. But notwithstanding whatever potential snags lay in his path, Logan's confidence was running high as he walked along the cobbled street, noting the rustic buildings of gray granite and the coarsely clad residents he met along the way.

Ambling past Sinclair's Mercantile and looking in the window, he heard a shout from farther down the street. He glanced up just at the moment when an animated young lady had aimed a fierce blow to her Austin's tire.

He took in the scene with amused interest. The girl in blue jeans and sandy blonde hair with a smudge across her nose was certainly in keeping with the general motif of the town, though the auto was somewhat out of place, despite its antiquity and obvious state of disrepair.

All at once, without really thinking, Logan turned and started toward the Austin. His best ploy in a place like this would be to ingratiate himself with these country folk. And what better place to begin than with these stranded wayfarers?

16 ❧ Introductions

ALLISON HAD DUCKED her head into the car to explain the situation to her great-grandmother; she did not, therefore, immediately notice the approach of the stranger. When she did look up, he had gone past her and was greeting Nat in a cheerful tone.

"Good afternoon," he said.

Nat wiped a grimy hand across his sweaty forehead and grinned.

"Having problems?" inquired the stranger.

Nat nodded, and the man continued, "I've some small skill in mechanics. If you like, I'll have a look."

"Sure," replied Nat eagerly. "I'm not doing much good."

He stepped up to the bonnet, affording Allison a closer view of his features. No doubt he was a stranger, she thought, not only in the unfamiliarity of his face, but also because of his general carriage and the polished finesse of his actions. No fisherman would have removed his jacket with such care, even if it had been a well-tailored tweed such as this man's. Folding it neatly, he laid it on the car, then proceeded to roll up the sleeves of his fine linen shirt. He definitely did not possess the brawny physique Allison was accustomed to seeing on the fishers and farmers around Strathy. She might have taken him for a scholar, but the tone of his voice and a peculiar look in his eye did not quite concur with that conclusion. There was a boldness about him, as if he feared nothing and, in fact, invited challenge with relish.

The fact that the newcomer was young and good-looking was not lost on her, but for the moment she could not help feeling perturbed that she had thus far gone completely unnoticed as he concentrated on the more practical aspects of the situation. *And however bold and confident his appearance,* she asked herself, *how much does he really know about automobiles?* Her doubts along that line were preempted when he called out to Nat from under the bonnet.

"Give her a try."

Nat brushed past Allison and slipped in behind the wheel. Then miraculously came the sudden roar of the engine.

Nat whooped and hopped out. "Thanks, mister," he said.

"Glad to be of assistance."

"What was wrong with it?"

The man replied with a technical explanation involving wires and sparks, connections and cylinders, which greatly impressed Nat, whose budding love affair with things mechanical had been cut short by Mr. Innes's death. Allison, however, could make little of it.

"Where'd you learn all that?" asked the youth with admiration.

"Oh . . . here and there," replied the stranger, a bit evasively, thought Allison. Though she could not possibly have known, her misgivings were sound, for he had in fact gained most of his knowledge of cars from his involvement in a rather lucrative, albeit illegitimate, auto racing enterprise some two years earlier. This, of course, he wisely kept to himself.

"Our factor knew all about cars," said Nat, "and he was teaching me all he knew, but . . . he died a while ago, and no one in Strathy knows more than I do."

"That's too bad." The man brushed his hands together, then held one out to Nat. "I'm Logan Macintyre. I may be here a while, if you'd ever like a few pointers."

"Thanks." Nat took Logan's hand and shook it awkwardly. He was hardly used to being treated on equal terms as this man was now doing. "I'm real pleased t' meet ye. Nat MacNeil's my name."

Finally Allison could no longer stand to remain in anonymity. She stepped boldly forward, clearing her throat daintily.

"Oh, that's my sister, Ali," Nat added, almost as an unnecessary afterthought.

"Allison," she corrected with a disapproving cocked eyebrow directed at her brother. "We are very much in your debt, Mr. Macintyre," she added in her most mature tone, smiling prettily.

It was a pleasant smile, and ought to have had a very positive effect on the stranger, even though it was tinged with an indiscernible trace of haughtiness, which Allison could not have helped even had she wanted to. The smile did, in fact, largely make up for her appearance in his mind, though as he looked fully upon her, Allison was acutely aware of her old clothes and messy hair. Had she known of the smudge of grease across her cheek, she would have turned a bright shade of pink.

But after a moment or two Allison began to gain the distinct impression that this man was looking at her as if she were a little girl, and might at any moment reach out and pat her condescendingly on the head. At last she thought she knew what the peculiar look was that she had noted earlier—it was the unmistakable air of superiority. It was a wonder she had not drawn the conclusion sooner, as familiar as she was with that very bearing. And she found it especially distasteful in someone who treated Nat as more his equal than herself. However, her hastily formed judgment was confused by his congenial reply.

"Don't think of a debt to me," he said. "Actually, I haven't been able to tinker with a car for some time, and I rather enjoyed myself." Had Allison been able to read deeper into the truth of his statement, she would have known that after his close brush with the law two years ago he had sworn never to touch another automobile in his life.

Maybe I misjudged him, Allison thought. *He might deserve Port Strathy's best welcome after all.*

"Now that you've managed to get our car running," she offered, "can we give you a lift anywhere?"

"Oh, no thanks. I'm staying at the inn down the street, and don't have anyplace else to go."

"Then you *are* new here?" Allison observed.

"Just arrived today."

"What brings you here?" put in Nat.

"I'm sure it's none of our business, Nat," reproved Allison.

"You must be visitin' friends, though," ventured Nat, ignoring Allison's remonstration.

"I don't know a soul in town," answered Logan, apparently not as disturbed by the inquisitive nature of the youth as his older sister assumed he might be. "Except you folks," he added.

"Then we can repay you by having you to our place for dinner," declared Nat.

"That's not necessary," answered Logan, taken aback momentarily by the unexpected display of hospitality.

"Sandy Cobden's cooking leaves a great deal to be desired since Mrs. Cobden died," came a new voice from inside the automobile. Logan had not at first realized there were other passengers. He stooped down and tilted his head to have a look at the new speaker.

A brief silence ensued as the two surveyed one another. Before he spoke, Logan cleared his throat, somewhat nervously Allison thought, and as he did, she noted a slight sagging of the cool composure he had thus far assumed.

"In that case," he said, recovering himself as best as he was able, "perhaps I had better take you up on your kind offer."

"Jolly good!" exclaimed Nat.

"We shall be pleased to have you, young man," said the woman in the Austin.

"Mr. Macintyre," said Allison in a rather lofty tone, "may I present my great-grandmother, Lady Margaret Duncan."

17 ❋ *The Lady and the Sharp*

LOGAN SAT BACK in the rear seat of the Austin as it left the small town and headed up the steep coast road.

If he hadn't been one who had trained himself to take in stride whatever life chanced to throw him, he might have been knocked off balance a bit with the sudden turn of events. As it was, he sat back and reveled in his good fortune.

His fortuitous stumbling upon the very people he sought had momentarily been lost upon him as he and the old lady had first exchanged glances. For when his eyes met those of Lady Margaret, a very odd and unfamiliar sensation passed through him. Even if he had tried, he couldn't have explained what it was he felt. He might have made a faltering attempt to describe it as like being suddenly stripped naked before one who knew you better than you knew yourself, as if the lady had been able to perceive to the very depths of his being. It seemed in that passing moment of time as if she had possessed the ability to read him more accurately than if his whole life had been boldly printed upon his shirt front—better than

Skittles, better than his mother, better even than himself. He had an unnerving premonition that possibly he had opened the door to more than he bargained for.

But just as quickly the sensation passed. Logan was not of the temperament to ponder such things deeply. He was content to allow it to pass without further reflection. And if there was any truth to the unsettling foreboding, if she did know of his motives or his duplicity, the pleasant smile which followed immediately made clear that she would never have held any of these things against him. The only acquiescence he gave to the uncomfortable feelings her penetrating eyes had elicited was an unconscious and barely perceptible faltering of his self-command.

It was only the beginning of an afternoon filled with unexpected sensations. But at the moment Logan climbed into the automobile, the remainder of this landmark day still lay ahead of him. As he settled into his seat, he took a few moments to regather his equanimity. And now as Allison maneuvered the Austin up that oft-trod road southeast of town, Logan's eyes took in the wonders of the rugged seascape terrain on his left.

In a few more minutes they turned off the road to the right, away from the sea, through a slight wooded area, still climbing, until suddenly looming before them was the great, gray-brown ancient castle known as Stonewycke. They sped through an ornate open iron gate, and for a moment all his worldly savoir-faire fled. Even a modern sophisticate such as Logan could not help being awed by the four-hundred-year-old edifice.

And with the awe came a fleeting sense of defeat. Suddenly things were happening he hadn't planned on. Who was he, a mere mortal, to think of pitting his puny wiles against this place? Here for the first time an impression of history came over him. The walls of this fortress had withstood storms and armies and revolutions, and the lives and deaths of hundreds of mortals no better nor stronger than he. Yet here it stood, outlasting them all. Logan had faced up to many obstacles in his life—poverty and failure among them. But here was something he could never hope to conquer—inanimate, yet commanding.

He struggled to clear his head. These kinds of thoughts would never do.

But then a voice, soft and dreamy, seeming to float down from the heavens, caught his attention as if his very thoughts had been read:

"Child of loud-throated war! the mountain stream
Roars in thy hearing; but thy hour of rest
Is come, and thou art silent in thy age:
Save when the wind sweeps by and sounds are caught
Ambiguous, neither wholly thine nor theirs. . . ."

Logan glanced around and saw that the words had come from Lady Margaret. The peculiar feeling he had had when he first met her in town tried to intrude upon him once more. But this time he shook the spell away, and looked back toward the castle.

He was himself again. He had to be wary. Something about this place, and especially something about that lady, was unnerving him. He couldn't let that happen. This was business. This was his big chance. He'd just have to call to his aid all those years on the tough streets of London. Why, this place couldn't throw anything at him in a year like what one day in the big city did. He had to keep his head about him.

"Nice poem, m'lady," he commented, in a tone perceptibly more distant than he had thus far used.

"William Wordsworth wrote it about another castle," Lady Margaret replied. "But to me it has always captured the soul of our Stonewycke."

"That's what you call the place?"

"The name goes back to the time of the Picts. But the castle's only been here less than half that time."

Suddenly Allison braked to a jerky stop at the doorstep of the great mansion.

"How does it stand after four hundred years?" asked Logan.

"You are familiar with the history of our home I see, Mr. Macintyre," said Lady Margaret, evidently pleased.

Only then did Logan realize his blunder. "Oh, no more than most," he quickly replied, hoping to repair his error. "You said it had been here less than half of the last thousand years, so I naturally figured—"

"I see," she replied.

I had better be more careful, thought Logan. *I don't want to arouse any suspicions this early in the game.* It had been a lucky break to stumble upon the Duncans as he had, even if it was a small town. But he couldn't trust to luck, not with something this important at stake. He had to use his wits and his brains. And he needed to think of something fast, some reason for being here, for no doubt at dinner there would be questions flowing his way.

His hosts ushered him into the mansion through huge oaken doors, which were easily twice his height and seemed as thick as his head. *I'd better not have to make any quick escapes,* he thought wryly.

The larcenous side of Logan's nature could hardly help noting the finery that greeted him as he stepped across the threshold. Some of the pieces in the entryway had to be nearly as old as the house itself. That hall tree, for example, if it was authentic, might be worth a thousand pounds. And nestled on a shelf in the middle of the ornate antique piece stood a gilt-edged vase—he couldn't even venture a guess as to its probable value. Then there was the artwork. While they passed down a long corridor, he glanced into several rooms to his right and left. In one his eyes focused on a magnificent portrait of a highland chieftain that reflected a distinct Raeburn touch. Logan had a passing knowledge of art, for in his line of work one usually managed to acquire at least a cursory knowledge in a wide variety of potentially useful fields. If that painting was an original . . .

He did note, however, from the very moment he entered the place, that it was not opulent in its display of finery. Now that he looked around further, in fact, everything was quite simple. And that very simplicity convinced him that what he did see could be nothing but the real thing. The place had no hint of anything fake about it. And these people must be the real thing, too. People didn't have to flaunt their wealth or position when the blue of their blood ran as deeply as the Duncans'.

From the corridor they stepped into a large parlor, and all at once it seemed to Logan that they had stepped again back into the twentieth century. The room was furnished with several low comfortable sofas, three rocking chairs, a couple of slender-legged tables, and three electric lamps in two of the corners and against a third wall. Magazines and newspapers were strewn about, and a large console radio stood along the adjacent wall. This was clearly where the family spent a great deal of time. A roaring fire blazed in a huge hearth that occupied nearly the entire far wall.

"Some digs," said Logan with a low whistle.

"Please make yourself comfortable, Mr. Macintyre," said Allison. "I'll go and find my parents." Then turning to Nat, she added in what the young boy thought was a snooty tone, "Nat, you go tell Claire we'll have a guest for dinner."

None too pleased at having to leave Logan, whom he considered his own personal discovery, and even less pleased at being ordered about by his big sister, Nat nevertheless complied. Then Allison followed him from the room.

After the departure of the young people, Logan found it extremely difficult to make himself comfortable as Allison had encouraged him to do. He was not quite ready to spend an extended amount of time alone with this intimidating lady, despite the fact that it was she he had come to Port Strathy to find. He would no doubt be able to like her; she seemed pleasant enough. But her effect on him thus far had been disconcerting and he could not help being— he hated to admit this—just a little afraid of her.

Had he been alone and at liberty to do so, he would probably have laughed outright at the very suggestion of such a thing. Why . . . she was just a frail old lady, after all! There could not be a sinister fiber in her entire being. On the contrary, she struck him as thoroughly kind, gentle, and compassionate. He had no doubt imagined the whole thing—probably a hangover from his seasickness! Had he given the matter deeper consideration, he might have discovered that it was these very qualities of virtue which caused his inner self to squirm. But Logan did not consider such things deeply, least of all introspective matters to do with his own emotions. Instead, he strolled toward the hearth and pretended to be engrossed in the procedure of warming his hands.

"For all her grandeur," the voice he had been hoping not to hear said, "we do have a time keeping this old place warm."

"I can imagine," replied Logan, hoping the conversation would drift to topics no more threatening than the weather. "Installing central heating would be rather a difficult task."

"We have done so in the sleeping quarters," she said. "It would have been too hard on the children without it. I don't know how I survived it as a child."

"Then you've been here all your life?" He knew he might regret this line of questioning, but he couldn't help himself.

"Not exactly. I had a sojourn in America. A rather long sojourn, actually. But I shan't easily forget my childhood here."

"You sound as if you love the old place."

Lady Margaret laughed a bright, merry laugh. The tones were almost musical, and obliterated all sense of her great age in a single instant.

"The love of Stonewycke is rather a family inheritance," she said, in the same melodic voice, which sounded cheery and youthful. "You've heard of some families which inherit a family curse? Well, we Stonewycke women pass along a deep regard for this home, this estate, these people, and this land. At least—" she paused momentarily, and the hint of a cloud passed rapidly across her brow as Allison's face suddenly came into her mind. She left the sentence unfinished, glanced up at Logan, smiled, and just as quickly the momentary shadow disappeared and she resumed. "It runs in the blood, like genes and chromosomes and personality traits. But do forgive me; I laughed only because your comment struck me as so understated."

"I suppose having a place where you belong is pretty important," offered Logan, suddenly feeling a hint of the discomfort returning.

"Yes it is. But in all the places I've been, sometimes almost beyond memory of this, where my sense of belonging began, I've learned over the years that there is something even more important . . ."

She paused thoughtfully, then walked toward one of the rocking chairs and sat down, rocking gently back and forth as she continued to speak. "And where might be such a place for you, Mr. Macintyre—if it's not too forward of me to ask?"

He didn't mind her asking. What he minded was the feeling that she must certainly already know the answer.

"I should have said," he replied, "that belonging must be important to *some* people. In my case, I prefer to keep my options open, so I'm free to move about. I suppose I haven't found a place where I *want* to belong yet."

"I detect a Glasgow ring to your accent, and even, strange as it may seem, a bit of cockney."

This lady doesn't miss much, thought Logan. She'd make an *honest* fellow nervous. He was going to have to be *very* careful.

"Born in Glasgow," he answered. "Been in London the last seven years."

"But still no roots?"

"I've plenty of time."

"Yes . . . I suppose you do," she answered thoughtfully. Had she felt a little freer with their new acquaintance, she might have added, "But time, Mr. Macintyre, is a fickle commodity. It can deepen the hurts, or it can heal them, depending on what you do with it." As it was she said nothing.

The tone of her words disturbed Logan, but he was saved from having to ponder it further by the arrival of Allison. At her side was a lovely woman whom Logan immediately took for her mother. She was three inches taller than Allison, slim of figure, and carried herself in a manner worthy of her station. Her auburn hair, streaked lightly with gray and pulled back in a simple bun, framed a face of delicately chiseled features. Though there was a youthfulness about her, delicate crow's-feet at the corners of her eyes hinted at her forty-two years. She was dressed simply in a navy woolen skirt and pale blue sweater. Logan was again struck by the understated simplicity of this family. But Mrs. MacNeil required no ornaments to announce her breeding. It flowed unmistakably with her every move and proclaimed to anyone perceptive enough to notice it that she had been born to the grandeur of Stonewycke. Had Logan read his Glasgow newspapers more closely, of course, he would have realized that things are not always as obvious as they appear.

She stepped toward him and held out a hand, smiling, "Mr. Macintyre, I'm so pleased to meet you. Allison has told me how you helped them on the road today. It was very kind of you."

Logan stepped awkwardly forward to take her proffered hand. The American accent which spilled fluidly from her mouth came so unexpectedly that, when coupled with the easy grace of her manner, the sophistication which had seemed so refined in London among the Ludlowes and Cochrans fled him.

"I . . . well, it was no real trouble," he stammered. "I had nothing better to occupy my time."

"We'd still be stuck in Port Strathy," put in Nat, who had come back into the parlor behind his mother, "if you hadn't come along."

"Well, we couldn't have that," laughed Mrs. MacNeil. "And we are certainly happy you have accepted our hospitality."

"I'm sure the honor's entirely mine, ma'am," answered Logan, recovering his possession.

"Dinner won't be for some time," she added. "Perhaps you would enjoy having the children show you about the grounds in the meantime."

Logan replied enthusiastically to the suggestion. Allison, however, begged to be excused from the excursion.

So Nat, who could not have been more fully pleased with the turn of events, led their guest back outside. Breathing in a great draught of the country air, Logan disguised his sigh of relief as a delight for the out-of-doors. More relieved than he would have imagined for the respite from the conversation, he decided this would be the perfect opportunity to question the youth away from the scrutiny of the adults. Thus he could better prepare himself for the more formidable assault of the masters of Stonewycke.

18 ✴ Disclosures

ALLISON SCRUBBED HER face until it shone.

Of course all the while she told herself that it actually *needed* scrubbing and that her great-grandmother would not have approved of her coming to dinner, especially in the presence of a guest, with a dirty face and dressed in worn denim. In no way, she tried to convince herself, did her present actions have anything to do with the guest in particular.

But it wasn't every day a handsome young man ventured to set foot in Port Strathy, even if he was arrogant and treated her like a child. Although she had to admit that was partly her own fault, for she hadn't exactly presented her best side today, what with grime on her face and dressed in old clothes.

She'd make up for it at dinner. She'd make certain he wouldn't be able to neglect her. *I wonder how long he's staying?* she thought. *And what could have brought him to Strathy?* He had been rather vague about it. She laid down her washcloth and tapped her lips thoughtfully as she tried to place his name. There were the banking Macintyres down in Edinburgh. They were quite wealthy and had weathered the banking problems in '29 better than most. They'd had a daughter in one of the schools she had attended. A year behind her, as she recalled. She wished now she'd been friendlier with her.

Yes, that must be it. He had something of the look of a financier, although she could hardly picture his youthful face in a pin stripe suit and vest sitting behind a desk. The thought brought a laugh to her lips. But he did carry himself with the refinement of someone with breeding. There was a certain worldliness about him too, and she liked that. Of course it made his condescension toward her all the more grating.

Well, she would command his interest tonight, and it would be no child that he saw.

She looked fully into the mirror on her wall, turning her head back and forth to gain her best advantage. She did not have to lie to herself when she concluded that the face which met her gaze was a pretty one. Picking up her brush, she began to arrange the silky golden waves that fell to her mid-back. She twisted and turned her hair in many styles and shapes, some absolutely ghoulish, some rather alluring. In the end she left it to hang in its most natural manner, which was becoming in its own way. But she did wish she could do something about the paleness of her skin. Next year—she didn't care what her mother said!—she was going to wear lipstick.

She pulled open the vanity drawer where she had secretly laid a tube of pale pink, called "passion flower." They might not even notice if she wore some tonight. And even if they did, they would never embarrass her in front of a guest. And later . . . they could do what they chose.

Slowly she lifted off the cap, and with the painstaking effort of inexperienced and nervous fingers, attempted to dab the color onto her lips.

Leaning back, she surveyed the effect. *Hmmm . . . not bad at all,* she thought. She pinched her cheeks till they matched the color on her lips. Too bad she was cursed with that infernal Duncan pale skin! A hundred years earlier it might have been in vogue. But modern women preferred to glow with health and vitality. They were not frail and helpless as were their predecessors. *Today's women,* thought Allison, *are capable and independent, able to stand on their own two feet.*

Allison thought she carried the effect off rather well, and if she lied about anything as she completed her toilette, it was the worldly maturity of the girl seated at the vanity. No amount of lipstick or verbal prattle about self-sufficiency could hide the lingering child within seventeen-year-old Allison MacNeil. As the eldest of the family, a great deal of maturity had been expected of her, and she had grown to expect it even more so from herself. She refused to be less than the adult woman she hoped to become, and if childish insecurity tried occasionally to surface, she repressed it beneath a veneer of grown-up hauteur. The facade, however, was only skin-deep, though she protected it well—protected it especially against the comparisons with the two women who had raised her in the Duncan heritage. At such distinctions she steadfastly refused to look. The time of her unmasking had not yet come.

The selection of a dress proved to be more difficult than the choice of hairdo. She pulled open her wardrobe door and began sorting through the clothes hanging before her. The white eyelet was too frilly, the navy organdy too grim, the tartan too . . . well, too gauche.

Allison walked over to her bed and flopped down upon it. Even if he *was* one of the banking Macintyres, he could hardly be worth all this trouble!

Then sighing, she rose, and once again lifted her eyes to survey the wardrobe. At length she settled on the pink and white floral cotton with its A-line skirt and flared elbow-length sleeves. Her father had once commented on how grown-up she looked in it. His opinion on most things mattered next to nothing to her, but on this particular occasion she hoped maybe he was right. It was a calculated risk she was willing to take.

After slipping the dress on her trim figure, she decided the choice had been a good one. She walked to the door, refraining purposely from taking one final satisfied look in the mirror. She opened the door, then hesitated and turned back into the room for that one last look.

She looked pretty, indeed. This Logan Macintyre would take notice tonight!

She descended the main stairway as gracefully as each of the Duncan women had before her. But when she passed the portrait of Lady Atlanta Duncan that hung on the wall where the staircase curved around, Allison's step faltered momentarily. The austere face, looking as if it had been chiseled in white marble, seemed to stare down upon her in mockery. "How do *you*," she seemed to be saying, in that proud, restrained voice she knew her great-great-grandmother must have had, "presume to carry the mantle of your Duncan heritage?"

Allison puckered her mouth stubbornly at her fancy, hitched her shoulders as straight and tall as her regal ancestor's, and proceeded on her way, giving a defiant backward glance at the portrait.

A pleasant fragrance, emanating from several bowls of flowers, filled the dining room. Logan wondered if they always ate this way, or if today marked some special occasion. Surely the finery had not all been laid out for the benefit of a guest they had just picked up on the road and invited home for dinner. Sterling, crystal, expensive china, and fine linen all graced the long flower-bedecked table. It was quite a spread, indeed.

Seeming to anticipate his silent question from his puzzled gaze, Mrs. MacNeil spoke. "Perhaps you would have preferred eating in the kitchen," she said. "We usually do, to be quite truthful. But we so seldom have guests to entertain that before we knew it . . . well— we had the dining room all opened and dressed."

Logan commented that he'd enjoy himself regardless, but asked them to forgive him if he chanced to pick up the wrong fork. While his hostess chuckled over his pleasant-natured humor, the rest of the family began to enter. Lady Margaret appeared on the arm of an elderly gentleman whom Logan took for her husband, Lord Theodore Duncan. Logan recalled having read that he had recently inherited the family title, Earl of Landsbury, from an older brother who had died. He noted that though the white-haired old man carried himself with dignity, there was a marked self-effacing humility about him. When Logan referred to him as "Your Lordship," he had demurred, almost bashfully, saying something about how meaningless such titles could be at times. And indeed, everyone but his wife referred to him simply as *Grandpa Dorey,* and thus Logan settled on "Sir" as the safest appellation.

Lord Duncan sat at the head of the table, and Lady Margaret at the opposite end. Logan sat to Lady Margaret's right, and Mrs. MacNeil and her eldest daughter flanked him. He did not fail to observe the change in Allison. *She'd be quite attractive,* he thought, *if it wasn't for that smug self-centered manner of hers.* Across the table sat Nat and a younger sister, Margaret, whom all simply called May. A vivacious ten-year-old, she looked more like her mother and great-grandmother, despite her age and dark curls, than either of the other offspring Logan had yet met. She had apparently been very aptly named. Next to May sat an empty chair.

For some time Logan was spared the grilling he had feared by the constant jabbering of little May. There was no end of information which poured forth concerning neighbors, house pets, events at school, and a hundred other trivialities. The two older people, especially Lord Duncan, encouraged her along, and laughed merrily over her endless anecdotes.

About fifteen minutes into the meal, they were interrupted as a man poked his head into the room.

"The Johnsons' mare had a lovely filly," he announced as he entered and walked toward the table. From his coarse dress, tousled pale hair, and sweat-streaked face, Logan assumed that he must be one of the workmen.

"Oh, can we see her, Daddy?" chimed May.

"Of course ye can, lassie," he replied. "We'll go oot t'morrow mornin'."

So, Logan mused to himself, *the elegant, highbred Mrs. NacNeil is married to a common country fellow.* The prospects for amusement here became more and more interesting by the moment. However, as he surveyed the man further, Logan concluded that he'd be best to reserve any hasty judgments regarding this powerfully built man until he was better acquainted. He could see at a glance that it would not do to cross the fellow.

"Alec," said Mrs. MacNeil, "this is our guest, Mr. Logan Macintyre. From London."

"Pleased t' make yer acquaintance, Mr. Macintyre," said Alec, approaching the table with outstretched hand. Logan stood and shook it. The big man's hand seemed to swallow his own as it wrapped around it in a firm grip, which was followed by a vigorous and friendly shake. "Ye're most welcome in oor hoose!"

Oh, Daddy, for heaven's sake! thought Allison as her father brushed past her. *Coming into the dining room smelling of the barnyard! And with a guest, too!* She tried to ignore the proceedings by directing her interest toward her plate, but Allison could hardly hide her embarrassed displeasure. Her father's country ways, untamed by position, title, modest wealth, or the fact that he lived as laird in a prestigious mansion,was a constant source of chagrin to her elevated sensibilities. *Why can't he act befitting his station,* she thought, *instead of always having to play the country bumpkin!*

"Dinner is still warm, Alec," said his wife.

"I'll be along directly," he replied.

He disappeared, only to return ten minutes later, washed, with hair combed, and dressed in corduroy trousers, an open-collared cotton shirt, and a slightly worn Eaton jacket. Even with the improvements of his attire, he hardly seemed to befit the station of a country squire.

MacNeil took the empty place which had been reserved for him. His presence at once added a distinctive energy to the atmosphere in the room, not unlike that provided by young May, but on a higher level, more substantial, the incidents related with more meaning. By his speech and mannerisms he revealed himself even more as a country-bred man than before. Yet that appeared to in no way affect the attitudes of the others toward him. They all deferred to him; even the earl spoke in a deferential manner when addressing the younger man. He was the obvious master of Stonewycke, but it was not an authority he demanded or required. It was simply there, without anyone's having thought about it, given unconsciously simply by virtue of the person he was. Logan noted, however, a considerable cooling on the part of Allison the moment her father sat down across the table from her.

This crowd is most unusual! thought Logan. *I wonder what other surprises are waiting behind these ancient stone walls.*

He had not been looking forward to the inevitable moment when he should become the central topic of conversation. But when it came it took him almost by surprise, for it came more like the whisper of a breeze than the hurricane he had expected.

The main course had been served—a steaming, juicy salmon—when Nat, no doubt feeling himself the resident expert on the stranger, opened the discussion in Logan's direction.

"Mr. Macintyre knows all about cars," he said to his father, the only one at the table not yet informed of the incident in town.

"Do ye, Mr. Macintyre," said MacNeil. "Weel, if ye intend t' stay here in Port Strathy, ye'll find nae dearth o' work in that area."

"I haven't seen many autos about," said Logan.

"There be only a handful o' autos, t' be sure," replied Alec, "but we hae oor share o' tractors, threshers, an' the like. All needin' repairin' e'en more than the auld oxen an' draught horses."

"Maybe *you're* in the wrong field," suggested Lady Margaret playfully.

MacNeil gave a great laugh.

"Hoots! I'd sooner wrestle wi' a stubborn Gallowa' or a huge Clydesdale any day than wi' one o' them mystical engines."

"You work with animals then, Mr. MacNeil?" asked Logan.

"Aye, do I! I'm a veterinarian."

"And what do you do for a living, Mr. Macintyre—that is, when you're not tinkering with autos?" It was Allison who spoke.

Fortunately for Logan he had spent the afternoon giving that very question considerable thought. For he had known it would come sooner or later, and he wanted to be ready with a well-formulated response. He may not have been eager for an inquisition with himself at the center. But at least if it came, he would be amply prepared for it.

"I'm in finance—investments, mostly," he replied. "However, at the moment I'm on an extended leave from my firm."

"Ye willna find much in that line aroun' here," said MacNeil.

"Looking for new investment opportunities?" suggested Allison, ignoring her father's comment.

"I'm really not at liberty to divulge anything," replied Logan, content to maintain the charade, but Allison thought she detected the hint of a knowing look in his eyes.

"Can't imagine what could interest anyone aroun' here whose business was bankin'," insisted Allison's father.

"But it is a lovely spot for vacationing," said Lady Margaret, entering the discussion for the first time. As she did so, her eyes drifted to Logan's. Somehow he picked up the impression that he was being rescued, spared the ordeal of answering any more uncomfortable questions.

Well, I don't need rescuing, lady, he thought stubbornly. *And I won't be intimidated either!*

Out loud he said, "I'm here neither strictly for business nor pleasure." His tone held a hint of defiance, as if he would not be daunted by their questions and would maintain a sense of his own strength of presence in spite of these very unexpected surroundings. "Mine is, you might say, an errand of . . . well, I suppose you might call it an errand of sentiment," he went on, now opening the door shrewdly in the direction of his choice, and hoping that someone would take the bait and lead him where he wanted to go. "My mother has a keen interest in our family heritage, and I am now in the process of tracing a branch of our family that seems to have led me to this area. You see, my mother is quite aged now."—he silently hoped his mother would forgive him for coloring the facts a bit, and was glad none of those present would ever have occasion to meet his mother, who could not have been a day older than Mrs. MacNeil—"and she resorts to using me as her feet, so to speak."

A butler began clearing away the dishes while a maid, who also doubled as the cook, set bowls of berries and cream at each place.

"How very fascinating!" said Mrs. MacNeil, smiling in a most mysterious way. "My own introduction to Port Strathy came as a result of a very similar purpose . . ." She glanced toward her husband with a twinkle in her eye. "However," she went on, "I got much more than I would ever have anticipated."

The whole family seemed greatly amused, and enjoyed a merry laugh over her statement. Logan stirred a lump of sugar into the coffee the maid had just poured for him. He was considering an appropriate response to Mrs. MacNeil's humorous remark, when Lady Margaret spoke.

"Please excuse us, Mr. Macintyre," she said. "We don't mean to leave you out of our family jocularity. It is a long story, though interesting I'm sure one day any of us would be happy to relate it to you."

"I shall look forward to it," exaggerated Logan diplomatically.

"Perhaps," offered MacNeil, "we can be o' some assistance t' ye in yer quest."

"Thank you, sir, but I'm sure folks like yourselves could not have known *my* relatives," answered Logan, skillfully allowing himself to be led down the very path he had hoped to steer the conversation from the beginning .

"This is a small town," said Mrs. MacNeil, "and being in our position I daresay we know just about everyone, especially the families that have been here a long time."

"I haven't a great deal to go on," he replied unpretentiously. "There is, of course, the family name, and we have record of an uncle—a great-great-great uncle, to be exact—who may have lived in this area."

"If I may ask, Mr. Macintyre, what was the name?"

"Why certainly," replied Logan. "My mother's maiden name, the one we are in the process of tracing, is MacNab."

"MacNab . . ." repeated Lady Margaret, her interest clearly piqued. When Logan nodded, she continued in a faltering voice, obviously attempting to call up remembrances from a past that was growing all too hazy from the march of years gone by. "And this uncle of yours . . . do you know his name?"

"Why, yes," replied Logan. "It was Digory MacNab."

The words had but left his lips when he saw that Lady Margaret had turned suddenly pale.
"Grandmother, what is it?" asked Joanna, alarmed. "Alec, hand me that pitcher of water."
But before her husband could comply, Lady Margaret appeared to regain her composure.
"No, no, Joanna . . . please. I'm fine." Then turning to Logan, she smiled weakly and went on in a soft voice. "I have not heard that name in years. It rather took me by surprise."
"Who is he, Grandma?" asked May, unabashed.
But seeming to ignore the question, Lady Margaret reached across the table and grasped Logan's hand in hers.
"You are related to him . . ." she said. It was not a question, but rather a statement spoken deliberately and with a touch of wonder. "*You* are Digory's nephew!" Again the words were in the same tone, her face gazing at him as if she wanted to weep, or laugh, or gather him into her arms. After a moment, she recovered herself, released his hand, straightened herself in her chair, and smiled. "Forgive me for taking on so. But this is like meeting a ghost—a most welcome and pleasant ghost!—from the past."
"I didn't intend to shock you."
"Only a shock in a most gratifying and wonderful way," she assured.
"Then you knew him?"
"He was groom, right here at Stonewycke, when I was a girl. He made quite an impact on me."
"No!" exclaimed Logan. "Why, that's positively uncanny! I mean that I should chance upon you in town as I did, then be led to this very spot!" Logan judged it best that he verbalize the coincidence before anyone else thought of it and had their suspicions aroused.
"We dinna believe in coincidences aroun' here," said MacNeil.
His statement, unprepared as he was for it, startled Logan to such an extent that he had difficulty maintaining his own composure. It sounded almost threatening.
"What my husband means," interposed Mrs. MacNeil, "is that we believe in a Lord and God who is the great Master Planner of life. With Him there are no accidents, no events without deeper meaning, no coincidences."
So that was all he meant! Logan exhaled a sigh of relief and almost broke out laughing. For a moment he had feared they were on to him. But now, he hardly knew whether to laugh or stiffen up his defenses all the more. On top of everything else, he found he had landed in the middle of a bunch of religious zealots!

19 ❇ *Conversations in the Bluster 'N Blow*

IN THE MIDDLE of the night the weather turned stormy and violent. The winds off the North Sea pelted the coast with such force that three trees on the bluff east of town were uprooted and crashed into the sea below. By morning the sky was still so black that sunrise offered only a whimper of protest against the dark, a pathetic streak of light swallowed up in minutes by the fierce, gray, rolling clouds.

By noon Logan had had all he could take of the vacant, deathly quiet inn, and of Sandy Cobden's company. What he wouldn't have given for an evening with Skittles at some pub like Pellam's! It looked as if the weather might be trying to break up a bit, so he donned his overcoat and cap and made his escape.

He wandered over to the New Town, but the place was all but deserted. He engaged one of the innkeepers in a game of cribbage, but when Logan won two games and several shillings, the innkeeper lost interest in any further contests of luck and wit. He was heading back toward town when the storm, with redoubled force, opened up once more upon Port Strathy. In minutes Logan was drenched through to the skin. Any notions of further exploration were firmly quelled.

He opened the Bluster 'N Blow's stout door, but it was the wind which forced him inside. Cobden was busy as always, this time sweeping the floors.

"Looks as if the storm ootraced ye. Mr. Macintyre," said the innkeeper.

"There wasn't even a warning," replied Logan, then looking down at the puddle he was making on the clean floor, added, "Sorry about the floor. Looks like I've made a new mess for you." He stripped off his overcoat and jacket and cap and hung them on a rack to dry.

"Canna be helped . . . 'tis the wettest spring we've had in years." Without missing a stroke of his perpetual labor, the innkeeper continued. "There's a good blaze in the hearth where ye can dry off."

Logan thanked Cobden and was turning gratefully toward the warmth of the fire when he heard some commotion. Someone had entered from the kitchen, and the swinging door had clattered shut behind him.

"Tabby ought t' be jist fine in a day or twa," said the newcomer.

Hearing a familiar voice, Logan turned and saw the broad hulk of Alec MacNeil, at the moment rifling through a black valise.

"Good afternoon, Mr. MacNeil," said Logan.

Alec looked up from his search with a friendly grin on his face. "Logan! Good t' see ye again!"

All over again Logan was stirred by the vibrant energy that seemed to flow from this unlikely landed gentleman. Who would possibly have guessed his position and esteem in the community from seeing him in his manure-caked rubber boots and working clothes? "Been makin' some house calls," he added before returning his attention to his valise. "Ah, here we be!" He held up a small pill box. "She should be better afore ye finish these, Sandy. But use them all onyway." He gave the box to the innkeeper.

"Thank ye kindly, Alec," said Cobden. "I hate t' admit it, but auld Tabby's been a right fair companion since the missus passed on." He set his broom against a wall and wiped his hands on his dingy apron. "Let me fix ye gents a pot o' tea . . . or a hot toddy, if ye'd rather?"

"Tea would be wonderful, thank ye, Sandy," said Alec. "I dinna like the idea o' goin' back oot in that storm. Ye'll join me, willna ye, Logan?"

They found seats as near the fire as possible. "That is," said Alec with a touch of jovial gruffness, "I'll let ye join me if ye'll leave off the *Mr. MacNeil* wi' me. Everyone in the toon calls me Alec, an' I'd be pleased t' have ye do the same!"

Logan smiled his assent and sat down opposite his unlikely companion. They exchanged conversation as Cobden served them their tea and then retreated to his labors. Logan meanwhile tried to fathom this Alec MacNeil, Doctor of Veterinary Medicine. It had come out in the conversation the previous evening that his father had been a fisherman; yet here was Alec, as he insisted on being called, married into one of Scotland's ancient titled families. Logan had known men in similar positions, common men who had married money and position. Though they lived well and were able to draw upon certain advantages as a result of their appropriated position, there yet remained a sense in which they maintained a subordinate place in the scheme of things, especially in the eyes of their peers. Logan had never met such a man he did not disdain; it seemed as if they had forfeited the pride of their manhood for wealth.

But Alec MacNeil fit no such pattern. What had seemed obvious around the dinner table— the deference of his family toward the authority of his character—was no less apparent here with Cobden, who, though their exchange was as of equals, nevertheless treated Alec with a visible respect. MacNeil had relinquished nothing of his manhood in his marriage, and instead seemed to command the totality of the Stonewycke prestige and whatever else may have gone along with it.

"That auld Austin's been runnin' like a top since ye tinkered wi' her, Logan," said Alec, taking a gulp of his steaming tea.

"Glad to hear it. But you've got to watch that magneto and especially keep the spark plugs clean. Otherwise it won't crank."

Alec held up his hand and laughed good-naturedly. "I'm afraid I dinna ken one end o' an engine from the other. But I'll pass yer instructions on t' Nathaniel—he's likely goin' t' be the mechanic o' the family."

"He did seem to have a knack for it." Logan cupped his cold hands around his steaming cup and drank deeply. "I offered to give him some pointers," he added, "and the offer still stands whenever he's free."

"That's kind o' ye," replied Alec. "So ye think ye may bide a wee wi' us here?"

"I'd like to learn more about my uncle Digory and the place where he spent his life. Possibly I might be able to meet one or two old-timers who knew him."

"'Tisna many yoong folks these days who hae such an interest in their family histories."

"I'm doing this for my mother," stated Logan. "But I have to confess that since I've discovered who Uncle Digory was, I am growing more and more intrigued with him."

"He seemed rather a simple man, from what little I've heard," commented Alec.

"Perhaps that's the very thing that interests me. There must be more under the surface. and I wouldn't want to miss it."

"Could be. It'd be Lady Margaret who'd help ye best. We'd all be pleased fer ye t' take up her invitation to speak with her further on the subject. I suppose she was too tired last night t' help ye much."

"I don't want to put a strain on her."

Silently Logan wondered if it indeed had been fatigue which had restrained her conversation last night at dinner. At times she could be most ebullient, then suddenly would draw back as if the conversation had approached shaky ground. Once he had asked an innocuous question about her parents. All at once the tables were reversed and it was as if she were being discomforted by him. Her eyes darkened for a flickering instant, a look had passed over her face which he couldn't identify, and then just as quickly she had laughed lightly and said there must be more interesting topics to discuss. The conversation had then moved into a different track, but before he left she had promised him another interview regarding Digory. He knew it would have been unwise to press further just then. Whether he was anticipating seeing her again with fear or with eagerness, Logan couldn't really tell. It all would depend on which aspects of her mysterious nature presented themselves to him.

"Oh, she's hale an' hearty enough," Alec was saying. "But at that age, I suppose some days are jist better than others."

At that moment the door opened and a new face entered the room. Logan, seated facing the door, saw her first. She was a tall woman, and though not exactly fat, bore a muscular frame uncommon in women. Her storm-tousled thick brown hair, streaked with gray, framed a hard-working but not entirely unattractive face. She had a healthy glow about her and a certain liveliness in her sea-blue eyes that made it difficult to fix her exact age, though it was nearer forty than fifty. She was dressed in worn dungarees with wide navy suspenders hitched up over a chambray work shirt. She had already hung a heavy red-and-black checkered coat and battered wide-brimmed hat on Sandy's coat rack. In her arms she carried a sleek, silky-coated Irish setter.

"There ye are, Alec MacNeil!" she said in a voice as husky as her physique.

"Why, Jesse . . . hello!" exclaimed Alec, turning. "What have we here?" He had risen and was now giving the dog a friendly pat. The animal gave a pathetic wag of her tail. Then first Logan noticed a thick rag wrapped around her forepaw.

"Luckie got tore up pretty bad," replied Jesse. "I saw yer car parked oot front an' thought I might save a trip up t' yer surgery."

Alec took the setter called Luckie into his arms and carried her over to the rug in front of the hearth. Logan watched closely as the doctor cleaned the wound, all the while speaking in soothing tones to the animal. Luckie did not protest, hardly whimpering at what must have been a painful process. It seemed that Alec MacNeil's uncanny charisma extended even to the animals of Port Strathy.

The woman apparently noticed Logan's rapt interest in the process and sidled toward his table. In hushed tones, as if she did not want to disturb a master at work, she said, "Wouldn't trust my Luckie t' no one else."

"He appears to know what he's doing," commented Logan, following her example and speaking in a subdued voice.

"Mind if I take a load off?" she said, and without waiting for a reply, plopped rather ungracefully onto the bench opposite Logan. "Ye're new here, aren't ye?"

"Yes. Came yesterday. The name's Logan Macintyre." He held a hand out to the woman.

"Jesse Cameron here," she replied, grasping his hand firmly and shaking it vigorously. She then proceeded to fill Alec's abandoned cup with hot tea, taking a long, satisfied swig. "Ah! That warms the body good! 'Tis a muckle storm oot there! Nae doobt the mercury's dropped twenty degrees since yesterday." She took another drink of Alec's tea. "We may as weel scrap the season completely. I doobt it'll let up fer days."

"Bad for the crops, is it?" offered Logan, feeling bound to hold up the other end of the conversation, though he had the distinct impression that she would do just fine without him.

"Crops!" she rejoined, as if the word were an insult. "Rain in spring doesna bother the farmers! 'Tis the draughts in August that sen's them t' an early grave. Oh, a flood might slow things up a mite. But as far's the weather goes, the farmers haena a thing t' worry aboot. But a fisher! The slightest ruffle on the deep blue surface o' life, is enough t' louse things up fer him fer weeks!"

"You're a fisher . . . ah, fisherwoman?"

"That surprises ye? Ye canna hide't from me, young man! But 'tisna so odd as ye may think. Womenfolk aroun' here are as hearty as their men, ye ken." Her tone contained no defensiveness, but she spoke firmly, as if she had made the statement so many times it had become a fact from mere repetition at the mouth of Port Strathy's resident thick-skinned and opinionated expert on women's rights. "Women hae always worked alongside their men aroun' here. The fact that my man's dead an' gone doesna mean I should let the best trawler in Strathy go."

"By no means! I agree completely," said Logan. This was quite some woman, he had to admit. "I meant no offense."

"O' course ye didna, lad," she answered without guile or sarcasm. "There's many strangers, city folk mostly, who might. Lord knows, I've had my troubles, companies in Aberdeen no wantin' t' contract oot t' a woman. Had t' prove mysel' o'er an' o'er."

"I understand. It must be difficult," said Logan. "My mother supported my family since I was a child, so I know what you mean." Actually, it was only at that very moment that Logan had ever given so much as a thought to what his mother had been through all those years. But he'd make up for it when he found old Digory's treasure, he told himself.

"I'm no complainin', mind ye," Jesse went on. "An' I've done right weel. 'Course e'erybody's havin' a struggle these days. An' these storms dinna help neither."

By now Alec had rejoined the two. "'Tis a muckle storm, Jesse!" he said. "I hope no one was oot when't struck?"

"The only casualty I know o' is poor Luckie there," replied Jesse. "E'erybody's been more fearsome careful since the schooner cracked up. We were o'er haulin' some equipment— 'bout the only thing ye can do in the rain—when a hook flew back an' grabbed hold o' auld Luckie."

"You take your dog onboard your boat?" asked Logan.

"Ye heard o' sea-farin' cats, haena ye? Well, we hae oorsel's a sea dog. Couldna keep her off, if the truth be known!"

"Weel," put in Alec, "this storm may be a blessin' fer Luckie. 'Tis best she stays in fer a day or twa. She lost some blood, so keep her warm. I'll send doon some powders tomorrow fer ye t' put on the wound. I sewed it up with some stitches I had in my bag. I think it'll do fer her. Bring her aroun' t' the hoose in aboot a week so I can remove them."

"Thank ye kindly, Alec. I dinna ken what I'd do wi'oot Luckie."

She slid her frame off the bench, gathered Luckie into her arms and made ready to leave. She paused at the door. "Will we be seein' more o' ye, Logan?" she asked across the room. But then, as was her custom, she waited for no reply, and continued, "If ye're o' a mind t' bide a wee in Strathy, come doon t' the harbor an' I'll show ye hoo a real fishin' boat is run."

Logan laughed and said he'd be sure to look her up.

When Jesse Cameron and Luckie had gone, Alec turned to Logan and said, "That is a remarkable woman. Lost her husban' t' the sea ten years ago. She refused t' give up everythin' they had worked an' died fer, so she took it o'er. Operates two trawlers noo an' pulls a man's weight in a man's business, so they say of her doon in the New Town. Each an' every person in Strathy hae nothin' but respect fer her. But when she first started, none o' the men fer miles wanted t' work fer a woman. There was no blamin' them, I suppose— 'tis a dangerous business, fightin' the sea. But she's made't work an' is noo one o' the most successful fishers—man or woman—in all o' this part o' the coastline."

"How'd she get on her feet if no one would work for her?"

"She's tenacious," answered Alec. "At first she went oot by hersel', an' all the others thought she had gone crazy o'er the death o' her man. But she was determined not t' lose the business. When they saw what she was doin', one or two that needed the work took a chance wi' her. An' noo, when they're oot on the sea, they hardly know she's a woman. One thing she is, she's the boss! An' she runs her boats like any tough man'd have t'. She takes nothin' from no one. Ye ought t' take her up on her offer—ye'd find it a grand learnin' experience. I went oot on the sea one night wi' her. I'll never forget it as long's I live."

Alec drained the tea which Jesse had left behind, and then rose. "Weel, rain or no, I best be gettin' back t' my work. Was nice t' visit wi' ye, Logan."

Logan rose and shook his hand.

"An' dinna ye forget," said Alec, tossing the words over his shoulder as he exited, "ye're welcome at the hoose any time!"

Logan leaned back against the hard support of the wooden bench. No, he would hardly forget that invitation. But he'd have to be judicious in his steps so as not to appear over-anxious. He had to contrive some way to make frequent comings and goings to and from Stonewycke seem quite natural. As intimidating as she might be, he had to get close to Lady Margaret. And he was certain he'd be able to handle her once he had his bearings a little more solid. He'd been in tighter jams. Her penetrating eyes were no match for Chase Morgan's thugs, and he'd outwitted them.

Yes, he thought, the old lady was the key. She had known Digory. If there were clues to where the old boy had hidden whatever treasure he'd been talking about, she would be the one to put him on the right track. Somehow those clues were locked in Lady Margaret's head, though she might not even realize it—especially if she'd never received any communication from old Uncle Digory. He first had to find out if any other letter had been sent. If not, then the clues he sought might lie in some altogether obscure thing the old boy had said to her, or in a place they may have gone together. Though the treasure may be hidden, he was certain it was still here. He could feel it!

Too bad she wasn't younger; he could charm the answers from her. As it was he'd have to use some finesse to entice her to open up to him. He had already noticed that there were some areas of her youth at Stonewycke she was reticent to speak of—but those might be the very things he needed to know about.

Well, he did have time. But he would like to find the loot while he was young enough to enjoy it.

20 ✦ On the Sea with Jesse Cameron

BY FRIDAY IT had rained almost solidly for two days. It wasn't the rain so much as the fact that he had lost all his cash in a card game on the first evening that caused the time to drag slowly for Logan. There was nothing to do, and the rain forbade any casual exploration. The weather notwithstanding, he had toyed with the notion of a walk up the hill to

Stonewycke. But he ruled out the idea on the grounds that a man doesn't brave a severe storm merely to enjoy casual conversation about a virtually unknown relative who has been dead some sixty-odd years.

Around midmorning, however, the clouds began to break up. Logan hurriedly finished his breakfast, grabbed his coat, and headed outdoors. That afternoon, if the weather held, he would walk up to Stonewycke. He'd simply excuse himself on the basis of needing to stretch his legs after the storm had forced him indoors for so long—a perfectly acceptable excuse. And he would time his visit so that he might be able to wheedle a dinner invitation in the process.

Until then, and with his encounter with Jesse Cameron in the back of his mind, he wandered down toward the harbor. Some thirty or forty boats, ranging from six-foot dories to hundred-foot vessels, were tied up to the docks, gently rocking up and down in the decreasing swell. Apparently he had not been the only one to notice the changes overhead, for the whole place was a bustle of activity, the fishing community apparently determined not to let this lull pass them by and go to waste. Shouts from dozens of fishermen, the clatter of gear being hauled aboard the boats, and the purring from some and the sputtering from other engines warming up filled the salty air. A few of the sailors who had been involved in the card game shouted friendly greetings to him. They had every reason to be friendly, thought Logan; they had each profited greatly from his foolishness. He would not underestimate their acumen at cards the next time.

Just then a more feminine call, though by no means softer, rose above the others.

"Weel, Logan!" called out Jesse Cameron. "So ye decided t' give us a look. Welcome t' ye!"

"Thank you," replied Logan. "Trying to squeeze in some fishing between storms?"

"We got t' make a run when we can," she replied. "But they say it may hold fer a day or twa."

Jesse was perched aft near the wheelhouse of a 50–foot double-ended craft called the *Little Stevie*. She momentarily turned from Logan and shouted to a crewman who was bent forward, with a frustrated scowl on his lined and weathered face, over the winch.

"Hoo's it goin', Buckie?" she called. "We dinna want t' be the last ones oot."

"I got it," he drawled uncertainly. "But I dinna ken if it'll hold wi' the weight o' the fish."

"You're about to be taking off?" interjected Logan.

"Aye, that we are!" answered Jesse. "We got t' take advantage o' e'ery minute possible." Then swinging back toward Buckie, she said, "I'll do it. Let's get underway."

Suddenly there was a flurry of activity as the crew of three sprang into action. "Hurry up, yoong fella!" Jesse called to Logan.

"What?" replied Logan, puzzled.

"Ye're comin' wi' us, arena ye?"

"I . . . I don't—"

"'Tis what ye're here fer, ain't it?"

"I hadn't really intended—" began Logan, feeling very uncharacteristically like a tenderfoot whelp.

"Come along!" Jesse interrupted, and reaching out a sturdy arm, hauled Logan aboard the *Little Stevie* before he had a chance to object. Logan looked about him, feeling altogether useless and out of his element—and not enjoying the sensation. Even Luckie, favoring her injured foot but otherwise appearing none the worse for the wear, was scurrying about as if she were an invaluable member of the crew.

Jesse quickly took up her position in the wheelhouse, Buckie cast off the remaining lines, and Jesse began maneuvering the boat out of the narrow mouth of Port Strathy's harbor. Logan braced his body against the starboard rail; he hoped he had not let himself in for more than a day at sea; he had heard of these boats spending days, even weeks, on the water before returning. But never one to brood over the lot life might cast him, if he was going to sea, he would enjoy himself.

The sharp, pungent sea air proved invigorating, as if it could scrape clean the cloudy residue of a spotted city life. The sight of the great wave of fishing boats was moving indeed. Within twenty minutes they had broken free of the neck of the harbor and found themselves surrounded only by the white-capped azure sea below, and above, a blue sky, marked heavily with white and gray clouds which still seemed uncertain about their future. With the wind tossing his hair and beating against his face, Logan found that he could appreciate just such an outdoor life, however alien it was to him. There was the same freedom and challenge here that he relished on the streets of London.

He turned and watched Jesse through the window of the wheelhouse. Yes, he could see it in her eyes, that same flash of enthusiasm which he'd seen pass through old Skittles' eyes as they embarked on their con in Pellam's. It was a thirst for adventure, the love of the chase, the pursuit of the quarry with nothing to rely on but daring, wit, and skill.

Yes, he and Jesse Cameron could hardly appear more dissimilar on the surface. Yet down inside, they were the same. Her life was spent chasing the fish, and fighting against those who would take her self-respect and personhood from her because she was a woman. He, on the other hand, sought more elusive prey. But they were each driven in the same way, though perhaps toward different ends.

His thoughts were shattered as the mistress of the vessel shouted out several more orders. He could feel the excitement even in her voice. He could almost imagine that she was old Skits, setting up a con to lure the fish into their nets. In another couple of minutes Buckie replaced her at the wheel and she joined Logan where he stood.

"Ye're a city fella, ain't ye?" she asked.

Logan nodded.

"Weel, ye look as though ye can take the water. There canna be another life like it!"

"I half believe you," replied Logan, laughing.

"Ye'll be a believer by the time we dock this evenin'."

"We'll be out only a day?"

"Aye. We're only rigged fer a short haul. What do ye ken aboot boats?"

"Very little," said Logan. "I have gathered that this is a *fishing* vessel, however," he added with a grin.

Jesse let forth a great, booming laugh, as hearty and invigorating as the crisp air. "Ye're a good sport, mate!" she said.

"What kind of fish are we after?"

"We'll take what we can get," replied Jesse. "After a storm like this, wha knows what'll blow oor way. The *Little Stevie* is a drifter, an' we used t' gill net the herrin' wi' her. But I converted her into a sidetrawler so we can fish fer cod or haddock in the spring."

"What's the difference?"

"Doon in Aberdeen they're findin' trawlin' t' be more productive. I'm thinkin' that after twa centuries or so, the herrin's gettin' wise. Some folks'll keep gill nettin' till they drop. But I've always kept my eyes open t' new advances." She paused and rubbed her hands together. "Come on in oot o' the wind fer a spell, an' I'll pour ye a cup o' hot coffee."

They went into the wheelhouse where a wooden bench large enough to seat two or three was strung against the aft wall. Jesse found a large thermal flask and poured out three tin cups of steaming brew.

"I drink coffee at sea," she said, handing one of the cups to Buckie at the wheel and the other to Logan. "These flasks are handy inventions, but they jist dinna do justice t' tea. I'll brew ye a proper pot o' tea after we cast the net, if there be time." She took a large gulp from her cup, apparently impervious to the burning of the liquid. Logan felt rather dainty by comparison as he cautiously sipped at his.

"I'm curious," he said at length. "Most boats seem to have feminine names. How did yours come by such an unusual epithet?"

A soft smile enveloped Jesse's lined mouth as a tender look filled her eyes. Logan would have thought from her expression that they were sailing on a glassy sea under a warm summer's sun. And perhaps it was just such a day that now filled her memory. "My husband closed the deal on this boat the day after oor son was born. So we, o' course, named it 'Little Stevie' after the boy."

"And your husband was *big* Stevie?"

"'Twas the boy's grandfather . . . my own father, Stevie Mackinaw." She said the name almost dreamily, and with a touch of sorrow.

"Have you been in fishing all your life?"

"Oh no," laughed Jesse. "I'm new at it compared t' most o' the folks ye find hereaboot. My daddy came from a long line o' crofters. They were tenants right on the Stonewycke lands fer generations. They herded sheep an' scratched oot a few bushels o' oats a year on the poorest piece o' moorlan' ye could imagine. Hoo they did I'll ne'er ken. Finally when my daddy was but a lad an' orphaned at that, the laird turned him oot."

"Just like that? After generations?"

"Wasna a crueler, more arrogant man than James Duncan, the laird then. Figured he couldna turn a profit w' jist a lad workin' the land—an' wha kens but maybe he was right. It might hae killed my daddy had he kept workin' that rocky groun'. As it was he wandered aboot, homeless an' penniless, an' near t' starvin' 'cause he was too prood t' take handoots. Finally, na that lang after James Duncan died, the Lady Atlanta found oot what had happened, an' gave my daddy a small piece o' land o'erlooking the coast, atween Strathy Summit an' the toon."

"These are the same Duncans that inhabit the estate now?" asked Logan innocently.

"Aye. But they're a different breed, these are." Jesse refilled the tin cups, then handed the flask to one of the other hands out on deck. Coming back inside she took up the end of the conversation where she had left off. "They love the land as much as the rest o' us. An' Lady Margaret always did care. Somethin' different aboot that lady. Why, my daddy used t' say that when he was a lad—"

"He knew Lady Margaret back then?" Logan nearly spilled his coffee, but struggled to keep up the nonchalance of his exterior.

"Only as weel's a crofter could know the daughter o' the laird. There werena all the mixin' then like ye see nowadays. But Lady Margaret took a special likin' t' my daddy's mother, an' the family in general. He always said 'twas 'cause o' her that he taught me the ways o' the Lord as he did. T' tell ye the truth, I always fancied that my daddy was a mite in love wi' Lady Margaret. I think that's why he married so late in life. But I guess fate was against him, though I'm sure the Lord's hand was in't as weel, 'cause a year after he married, his wife died havin' me. I brought him sorrow from the day I was born."

"You must be exaggerating," said Logan, intrigued.

"I ne'er took t' the land. I always sat on the cliffs an' looked oot t' sea. He shouldna hae been surprised when I married a fisherman. 'Course I was only a bairn, hardly sixteen at the time, an' it meant me leavin' home, 'cause Charlie was one o' them itinerant fishers, hirin' himsel' oot fer seasonal work. My daddy was none too happy an' I left wi'oot very frien'ly feelings atween us."

"I'm sure he's very proud of you now."

"He's been dead some four years noo," said Jesse. "Luckily we patched it up when I came back after my Charlie died—that was in 1919, after the war, ye ken. We had some good years t'gether, Daddy an' me. The Lord used the loss o' my husban' an' son t' mellow me oot some—made me learn t' appreciate all the things a yoong girl used t' scoff at."

"You don't mean you went back to a farming life like your father?"

"Na, na," replied Jesse. "I meant the things my father used t' tell me when I was yoong that I had nae use fer then. Things aboot God an' nature, aboot God's love fer His children, things we've all heard from oor mothers an' fathers, but which we pay no attention t'. Till we get older an' wiser, perhaps—an' then we start rememberin' an' seein' the truth o' it. Or until some catastrophe smacks us in the face an' makes us listen. I don't know why we willna listen till we get oorsel's int' trouble. But it took the loss o' my Charlie an' my boy t' wake me up."

"And even after what happened to them, you stayed in fishing?" asked Logan, trying to change the direction of the conversation off this uncomfortable subject.

Jesse rose and crossed the small open space of floor to the wheel where she stood next to Buckie, looking out on the vast expanse of blue all about them.

"It grows on ye, Logan," she said wistfully. Her gaze out toward the open sea, and her contented sigh said the rest.

Some time before noon the *Little Stevie* crept to a stop. Jesse told Logan they were ready to shoot the net over the side.

He found a place well out of the way, then watched as the crew expertly lowered the trawl, by means of rope suspended on gallows hitched to the starboard side of the boat. Jesse and Buckie were giving particular attention to the troublesome winch located amidship. To Logan's untrained eye everything appeared to be going smoothly, but Buckie looked none too pleased. Once again he attempted some adjustments on the winch, this time with screwdriver in hand.

When the net was finally in place, Jesse disappeared and Logan guessed by the steam emitted from the smokestack that she was firing up the engines. When she rejoined him, the *Little Stevie* was again underway, this time with one of the other crew members at the wheel.

"Noo we can relax a wee," she said. "We'll trawl fer three or so hours afore we haul in the catch. Time t' give oor attention t' the galley—I hope ye're hungry."

Logan had hardly thought about food until that moment. But with the suggestion of a meal he realized he was starving. At the same time it dawned on him that the undulating sea had in no way affected his insides as it had on the schooner. Mentally he patted himself on the back and began to wonder what fortunes a man of his unique talents might make aboard luxury ocean liners.

Jesse set a fine table, even in the cramped galley, which was located directly under the wheelhouse. Smoked fish, oatcakes, and fresh tea heated over the engine boiler, at that moment tasted as fine to Logan as any meal he had taken in London.

He liked the company too. If Jesse had an occasionally overbearing nature, her warmth and forthrightness softened any other rough edges. Perhaps she was just a coarse version of Molly Ludlowe. No doubt that was why he had in this short time felt such an attachment to her. He found himself talking to her as he would have to Molly or Skittles, and a time or two caught himself just as he was about to reveal too much of who he was and what he was about in Port Strathy.

And when he slipped back into his familiar ruse of hypocrisy, he could not keep back a surge of unfamiliar guilt, as if he were—of all things!—actually *lying*. The experience was novel to him, and most disconcerting. But he managed to salve these pricks of conscience by telling himself that when he found Digory's treasure, he'd buy Jesse Cameron a new boat— one with a modern diesel engine and motorized winches and even radio equipment. She had talked about them, and had gone so far as to show him a picture of one she had clipped from a magazine and pinned up in the wheelhouse.

"Dinna ken what I'd do wi' a radio, though," she had laughed. "Don't know who else in the fleet'd be able t' talk t' me. Not a single one o' them has radios neither, except the *MacD*, an' he's never oot when the fish are runnin', anyway."

But Logan thought to himself, *I'll get the whole fleet radios!*

That morning he hadn't given the welfare of Port Strathy's fishing fleet a moment's thought. But now he felt oddly bound up in their well-being. Shortly, that bond was to grow yet stronger, as the invisible forces working upon the soul of young Logan Macintyre zeroed in on him ever more closely.

It came about two hours after they had eaten.

Buckie had earlier noted that the wind seemed to be picking up, though at the time all had agreed they still had time for another hour or two's trawl. And the few other boats they could see in the distance seemed to be holding. But by half past two the sky had blackened and the *Little Stevie* was riding ten-foot swells. There was nothing else to do but haul in the net and head for home. Every hand was needed by this time, as the wind now suddenly whipped up to double its force. The battle of net, fish, and human strength pitted against wind, wave, and rocking boat was a torturous and dangerous one. As Logan lent his inexperienced hands to the task, he noticed for the first time in his life how soft they were.

Halfway through the job the rain began to fall. Now the ropes became twice as difficult to handle, and the decks too slippery to get a strong foothold. To seasoned fishers, such hazards were commonplace enough, and with one's wits firmly intact, presented no obstacle which could not be dealt with. Logan, however, was hard pressed merely to remain upright, and all the more to shoulder his share of the increasingly heavy and cumbersome load.

The foul weather had one positive point, though. The fishing grounds that day had been especially fertile, and the net was bulging. Logan had taken a position near the starboard rail, holding a rope fast while two of the other men swung the net past the starboard stanchion in order to lift it in—all the while the wind swinging it murderously overhead. At the very moment when the heavy load was at its apex over the deck, the winch gave way from the weight and added tension of movement.

Suddenly the rope gripped in Logan's hand lurched forward without warning.

"Let go!"

Scarcely hearing the shout, Logan found himself yanked off his feet; even the rubber boots Jesse had fitted him with could offer no traction on the wet deck to prevent him from altogether losing his footing.

In another instant he was flying overboard, then plunged into the icy sea.

As an angry wave engulfed him and pulled him under, his first thought was that now he wouldn't be able to get Jesse a new boat. His second was the realization that he couldn't swim. And the third, following almost instantly in succession after the others as his head broke through the surface only to be overwhelmed by another wave, was that he was going to die and never see his mother again.

Again his head bobbed to the surface. Logan gulped for air, but took in little more than a mouthful of the freezing salt water. Frantically he looked around for the *Little Stevie,* but could see nothing except water and sky. He tried to yell, but only a sputtering gurgle emerged; his panic-stricken lungs were already filling with the salty water. Another huge wave crashed over him, and all went black. Floundering and flailing to reach the surface, the only sensation he could afterward recall was the sense of being pulled upon by an evil force intent upon drawing him down . . down . . . down.

Gradually the will to fight slackened. He could feel the downward force tightening its grip. He began to relax. It would be so much easier to give in . . . to let it have its way with him. If only he could just go to sleep . . . then he could be warm again . . . then he could wake up and everything would be—

Suddenly a strong pair of arms wrapped themselves around him. These were not the arms of the downward force. These arms, though he barely felt them, were strong and were pulling him up . . . up . . . out of the sea!

Within seconds after he had gone over, Jesse had a life rope around her waist and had plunged over the side after him. And though Logan's benumbed senses told him he was not being rescued because he was still surrounded by thousands of fish, in fact he now lay on the deck in the midst of the catch of the day.

He must have lost consciousness for only two or three minutes, for Jesse was still pounding his back and pumping sea water from him when he awoke. He rolled over, then coughed and gagged for a few moments, but it was some time before he could speak. When words finally came out, they were little more than a weak wheeze.

"I'm sorry," he gasped

"Hoots!" exclaimed Jesse. " 'Tis my own fault. I should hae known better than t' place ye there!"

The incident had given the toughened sea woman a scare as nothing else could. It had been many years since her husband and son were lost to the sea, but she still had occasional nightmares in which she pictured them floundering helplessly in the icy North Sea waters. Her son had been but ten at the time, and he'd now be nearly Logan's age if he had lived. The thought made her shudder, and also angry with herself for not taking better care of her young guest. Thus her gruff tone contained more hidden meaning than Logan could have guessed. As Jesse looked at Logan lying before her, in her mind's eye he was her own son. And it would be a sensation she would long remember.

She and Buckie helped Logan below, where Buckie found him some blankets and dry clothes, then poured him a cup of hot tea. After changing out of her own drenched things in the wheelhouse, Jesse poked her head in to see how he was doing. He looked up over his second cup of hot tea with a solemn expression he seldom wore.

"I owe you, Jesse," he said in a tone to match his look. "I'll repay you somehow. I won't forget."

"There'll be nae talk o' repayin'," she replied crustily. "At sea everyone gives their all— that's what's expected o' us. Couldn't survive no other way." But beneath her words, the voice of Jesse Cameron betrayed that she, too, had been touched by the emotion of the incident. To save a fragile human being's life, for the fragile human animal, may be just as awesome a thing as to see your own snatched from the very door of death. In any case, neither would Jesse soon forget this day. Perhaps the heartaches of her own life had prepared her for this moment when she would become a vessel in God's hands, instigating the purifying work of redemption in the heart of this boy who could almost be her own son.

Logan watched as she poured a cup of tea, recalling what Alec had said about her. He had to agree. A remarkable woman she was, indeed.

21 ❖ Allison in New Town

ALLISON PARKED THE Austin on High Street, the main thoroughfare connecting Port Strathy proper with New Town, right across from one of its two public houses. The second stood at the other end of the street. She remained in the car, hoping that somehow Mr. Macintyre would make an appearance so she would be spared having to get out and go hunting around for him.

She had been shopping in the Mercantile when her mother had called. The tractor had broken down and neither the men, Nat, nor Alec could get it operational again as they usually managed to do. And since they could afford to lose no more time with the spring planting, she asked Allison to inquire about town and try to find Mr. Macintyre. Would he be interested, she was told to ask him, in being of further service to them, at a fair wage this time?

When the call ended, Allison slammed down the receiver and stormed out of the store without a single word of explanation to Miss Sinclair. Now she was a common errand girl! She had her own plans. It was early, her mother said, and there was sufficient time for her to deliver Mr. Macintyre and still meet Sarah Bramford. But the whole thing nevertheless upset her—even if her mother did promise to call the Bramfords to inform them she would be a little late.

The only hope was that this errand might afford her an opportunity to better acquaint herself with the mysterious Logan Macintyre. Though after the revelation of his common heritage the other night, she wondered why she even wanted to bother. The great-nephew of a groom! Really, she had better prospects than that!

But there was something incongruous about him . . . an intriguing side. He was no dolt, however common his heritage. He carried himself with aplomb. If she hadn't known his background, she would have been rather proud to display him to her friends. And that unique accent, with just a hint of Scots tempered with the genteel London sound—it all came off rather pleasantly.

It was irksome how he all but ignored her. The rest of the family had, of course, monopolized him shamefully. Perhaps it wasn't his fault. Who could tell but that he had been attracted to her, had even wanted to speak to her, but had been unable to in the awkward surroundings of a family dinner?

Maybe she could turn this inconvenient request of her mother's to her own advantage after all!

At the Bluster 'N Blow, however, Allison's inquiries were met with a shake of the head. "Came in last night," said Cobden, "wi'oot e'en informin' me he wasna plannin' t' be here fer dinner. Came in late, passed the time wi' the few customers I had at the time, then went t' his room, an' a few minutes later was back in new duds, an' then was gone t' the New Toon—jist like that. I dinna think he e'en came back fer the night."

"That was last night, Mr. Cobden," said Allison impatiently. "What about today?"

"I' ain't seen him since."

"He hasn't left town?"

"Na, na," the innkeeper shook his head. "His gear's all still here."

Allison waited to hear no more. Without a word of thanks, she bounded from the inn and set out for New Town, where she now sat, growing more irritable with each passing moment. After observing the deserted streets for about as long as she could stand, she was about to get out and head for one of the pubs, when the door she had been watching opened and several figures ambled out.

There could be no doubt that one was the man she sought. That checkered cap of his was pushed well back on his head and his face sported a day or two's growth of beard. His suit, which might at one time have been a fine one, was wrinkled with a long night of wear. In his mouth he sported a cigar, which he appeared to be enjoying immensely. With him were three or four locals. They were all laughing, but with their eyes squinting against the glare of the sun, looking brashly out of place on a sunny Saturday morning.

Allison stepped out of the Austin and approached waving to him. "Mr. Macintyre," she called in a tight voice, taking no pains to conceal her contempt.

Logan looked up, removed the cigar, and smiled. Well, at least there was nothing wrong with his smile, thought Allison. Why did everything else about him have to be so entirely wrong?

"Why, Miss MacNeil," he said, "this is a pleasure. What brings you out on a fine morning like this?"

She could not tell whether his joviality was from being drunk or from simple high spirits. "I was looking for you," she replied coolly.

"Ah," he intoned, with a knowing glance and a wink to one of the other men, "can I be of further assistance to your family, or to yourself perhaps?"

Before she could answer, the men with Logan began to wave and call out. At first she thought the commotion was directed at her. But to her even greater chagrin, she then realized they had hardly noticed her at all, and were instead calling to a woman crossing from the other side of the street.

"Mornin', Liz," said one of Logan's cronies.

"Hello, Jimmy . . . boys," the woman replied. As she approached and greeted them, her eyes strayed to the newcomer as she appraised him with a thoughtful smile.

It took all the self-restraint Allison could muster to keep her snort of disgust to herself. Wasn't that just like Liz Doohan, Patty's elder sister? Dressed in a simple cotton frock and maroon cloth coat that clashed dreadfully with her red hair, she looked frumpy but may have been pretty a few years earlier. But working women aged faster than most, and it hardly became her now to flirt with men right out on the street. For all her caustic notions of superiority, Allison would no doubt have been surprised to know that Liz Doohan was but twenty-six.

A lively banter had sprung up between Logan's small group and Liz, who was now being told by Logan's shipmates of the previous day and how well their young friend from London had taken to the sea, mercifully omitting his adventure in the water. Allison's presence had been altogether forgotten.

"Am I the only one who has t' work t'day?" asked Liz with a mock pout.

"Grounded fer repairs," answered Jimmy.

"An' the weather's so cockeyed." added Buckie, "that another storm could blow in on us afore noon."

"Mr. Macintyre," interrupted Allison, approaching with a huffy gait. "If you don't mind . . ."

"Oh, Miss MacNeil. What was it you were wanting?"

He may not have intended for his tone to sound condescending, but in her present mood Allison could hardly interpret it as otherwise.

"There is trouble with our tractor," she answered, rankled even further by the turn of events, "and we would like to *employ* your services." She emphasized the word so there could be no possible mistaking her own patronizing attitude.

"Glad to be of assistance," he replied good-naturedly.

"It *is* rather pressing. Do you suppose you can tear yourself away?"

He turned to his friends. "Duty calls," he said. "I'll give you a chance to get even tonight."

"Ye deserve the win," said Buckie with a laugh. "Especially after yer day yesterday."

"But we willna begrudge ye yer offer," laughed Jimmy.

"It was nice t' meet ye, Logan," purred Liz; "maybe I'll see ye aroun' again . . . ?"

"No doubt," he answered with a noncommittal grin.

Finally, with the fishers all slapping Logan fraternally on the back as if they had known him for years, they parted company.

Allison drove Logan back to the inn for a change of clothes, saying hardly a word. She dropped him off, then returned to the Mercantile for something she had forgotten as a result of her agitated departure from the store after her mother's call. Why she was so angry she could not exactly say. Was it because he had tramped about all night in the most disreputable section of town? Or because he persisted in humoring her as if she were nothing but a child? Or was the real reason that she wanted to be noticed like he had noticed Liz Doohan? That she could never admit! Liz was . . . a *nobody*. How could he pay more attention to her than to an heiress like herself! He must be blind to the way things really were!

And I had entertained ideas of presenting him to my friends. Never! He'll have to beg first!

At the thought, a sly smile crept across Allison's lips. Perhaps that was not such a bad idea. In fact, it would be rather splendid to have that arrogant southerner groveling at her feet. Of course, she'd turn him down flat. But what a pleasure it would be!

Returning to the inn, she found Logan outside leaning casually against a post, arms folded across his chest. The manner in which he surveyed the town gave every impression that he thought he owned the place. His face was shaven and one could hardly tell he had been awake all night.

All at once Allison realized that while his self-assured, I-don't-need-anyone manner irritated her, in an odd sort of way it drew her, too. One could not help being attracted to someone so independent. Wasn't that the very thing she herself wanted to be?

Considering the matter further, she decided that after she had him begging, she might grant him the privilege of her attentions—for a while, at least. There could be nothing permanent, of course. He didn't have the blood to match her breeding.

22 ❈ *The Door Is Opened*

AN OLD CLUNK of a tractor was a far cry from race cars or street automobiles, but Logan determined to put on a convincing show that he knew what he was about. If Skittles had taught him one thing it was that man had been given a tongue to make up for what he lacked in actual skill. Logan had bluffed his way through stickier situations than this. Only this time he had to come up with a working tractor in the end. If he could do it, he knew this would be his ticket into Stonewycke.

Allison dropped him in front of a large stone structure behind the house that she referred to as the stable. The tractor was sitting outside. Allison spun the Austin around and sped off, leaving him coughing in a cloud of dust. If the family did not fit his expectations of the occupants of Stonewycke, Allison did, for she was out of harmony with the rest of the family. In fact, she was the only one who came close to matching his expectations. She paraded her position around like she was the daughter of the king. What a contrast there was between her looks of superiority toward Jesse Cameron's crew, and the manner in which her father had received Jesse herself! Maybe Alec was still one of the townspeople at heart. But Logan could not imagine even Lady Margaret treating the common folk with such derision.

Where, then, had Allison acquired such attitudes, he wondered, if not from her own family? One thing was sure—Allison MacNeil had something to prove. But he wasn't at all sure what it was. She had everything she could possibly want. Her mother and great-grandmother were the most respected women in the community, and thus she herself would surely have been accepted with a certain sense of stature by the townsfolk. Yet she seemed to disdain it all.

Well, he concluded, *Allison may be an enigma in a family full of enigmas, but it doesn't rest on me to try to figure them all out.* He had a hidden treasure to find, and then he'd be out of this place.

Even as he was still watching the Austin speed away, Logan found himself being hailed by Fergusson Dougall, Stonewycke's factor since the passing of Walter Innes.

"Ye must be Macintyre!" said the factor, moving as hastily as he was able toward Logan where he stood puzzling over his thoughts. To have described the man's movement would have been difficult; it resembled a waddle more than a walk, for Dougall was an extremely bulky man, whose weight over the years had settled mostly into his lower regions, the end result being a most unwieldly pear-shape configuration. His round, sunburned face with sagging jowls was friendly, and his voice carried an unpretentious, almost self-effacing tone.

"That I am," replied Logan, turning and extending his hand, which was quickly engulfed in Dougall's beefy paw.

"Weel, I'm the factor," he said, his voice almost reminiscent of an apology. "Fergusson Dougall at yer service, but everyone jist calls me Fergie, an' ye're welcome t' do the same, Mr. Macintyre."

"Thank you. And it's Logan."

"I'm obliged t' ye fer comin'," said Dougall, relieved that the tedious formalities were dispensed with and anxious to get to the business at hand. "This here's the tractor—the troublesome beast!" he began, then chuckled, producing a great jiggling effect in the regions of his stomach. "'Course I needna be tellin' *you* that!"

Logan laughed at the factor's wit, but the humor which struck him was the irony of the man's words. For in reality, Logan had never before that very moment laid eyes on a tractor in his life.

"Well, let's have a look," said Logan, then hung back a moment hoping Dougall would take the initiative and open the engine's bonnet, for he was even uncertain how to go about that most basic of operations.

Fergie did so. Logan peered inside, discovering to his great relief that he recognized most of the basic parts, though their arrangement was somewhat bewildering at first. He turned back and picked up a couple of the tools that had been laid out on the ground in preparation for the arrival of the tractor "expert."

"Does she start at all?" he asked.

"Nothin' but a cough an' a sputter."

"Hmmm," pondered Logan. "Let's hear it."

The factor moved toward the tractor but apparently had not driven it personally on many occasions. His difficulty in climbing up into the high seat would have been humorous had the sight not been sadly pathetic, and he would not have accomplished the task without a helpful boost from Logan. It took him a moment to get the cantankerous shift lever into neutral. But when he did and the attempted start was made, his description of the result could not have been more accurate. Another look at the engine made Logan wonder that the thing had ever run at all.

"I shouldna wonder if nothin' can be done wi' it," said the factor. "We always left the engine work t' Walter—in fact, he wouldna hardly let anyone else touch his engines, 'ceptin' Nat. He treated them jist like they was livin' things, like he did the horses. I know farmin', but I neither ken nor do I like these contraptions."

"The time will come, Fergie," said Logan philosophically, "when you won't be able to survive without them."

Logan proceeded to tinker with the engine until it began to make sense to him. Gradually the puzzle of its operation came clear to him, not without several more attempts at starting it. Within an hour he had located the problem, and as he had feared, a new part was going to be needed. He was determined, however, to get the engine functional. Who could tell how long it might take to get the new part, if it could be obtained at all? He didn't have that kind of time.

He therefore unbolted the carburetor, then turned to Fergie and said, "I'm pretty sure she needs a new coil. If this one's not bad already, it will be soon. So you'll need to order one wherever you get parts around here. In the meantime I'm going to try to clean up the carburetor. If the coil's got any life still left in it, that might help to get it going."

Nodding as if he understood every word, Fergie followed each move of the young man who more and more appeared to him a mechanical expert with every moment that passed.

"Where s young Nat?" asked Logan as he rummaged through the tool box sitting beside the tractor in search of a certain tool.

"He an' Alec went oot t' the field after the tractor broke doon, t' check the state o' the soil after all the rain. Be back any minute noo, I shouldna think."

Logan proceeded to do what he could to clean up the carburetor, removing accumulated grime from the tiny valves and carefully scrutinizing every inch of it. "Probably hasn't been adjusted recently," he said, more to himself than anyone else, but Fergie responded quickly.

"Adjusted?"

"These carburetors have to be adjusted almost constantly. I take it Mr. Innes didn't pass on that bit of information? Well, I'll do what I can. I think we've got the tools here to do at least a workable job. In the meantime, do you have any extra diesel?"

Dougall scurried off into the stone building and in a few moments returned carrying a small red can.

"Ah, perfect!" said Logan, opening the can and splashing a bit of the oily reddish-gold liquid onto the offending mechanism. "I think with an adjustment here and there, and with all the cracks and crevices and holes and jets cleaned out, we just *may* get this thing running again—that is if the coil isn't altogether gone already."

In five minutes, after several final adjustments and another thorough cleaning, Logan bent over the tractor's engine and reinstalled the carburetor into position.

"That's it, my friend!" he called out at length, giving his back a stretch but remaining in front of the engine. "Time to give the old bucket of bolts a try . . . and keep your fingers crossed!"

Summoning both his pride and all the discipline possible for his overtaxed frame, Dougall managed to scramble up onto the seat without assistance and immediately tried the starter. Logan held his breath as the engine coughed once, then again, and at last kicked into activity.

"Give it a little more throttle!" shouted Logan above the racket, reaching in to adjust the carburetor.

The factor did so.

Within thirty seconds the engine settled down and began, if not exactly to purr, at least to chug rather steadily along.

Sensing victory over the uncanny beast, the free-spirited factor gave a whoop and stood to jump out of the driver's seat. In his excitement his portly leg knocked against the gear-shift lever, sending the tractor into gear and suddenly lurching forward. His corpulent bottom side came crashing back into the seat and he barely managed to keep from falling off the tractor completely. Logan, still standing directly in front *of* it, wrenched his body to the side only missing by inches having the runaway vehicle crush his leg under its massive wheel. As he did so he tripped over the tool box, twisting his ankle in the process. He crumpled to the ground as the tractor rumbled dangerously past.

Fergie managed to grind the lever back out of gear and slam on the worn brakes, then laboriously catapulted his bulk off the tractor—a procedure which nearly cost him more damage to his entire frame than Logan, who was still lying on the ground, had suffered.

"Oh, dear Lord!" cried the factor. In the melee, he had been slammed to his seat at the moment Logan had jumped free, and he thought he had run directly over the young man. "I've killed him!"

"I'm nowhere near dead, man," replied Logan, turning onto his side. Fergie, however, refused to be comforted and continued to loudly bemoan his stupidity.

"I'm fine, Fergie," insisted Logan, in a voice intended to sound weak but brave. "Just help me to my feet."

Fergie put his thick arm around Logan and pulled him up, but as soon as Logan reached an upright position and tried to test out his own weight, his left foot slipped under him.

"Ye've broken yer ankle!" wailed the factor. "Dinna ye move a step," he said, taking firm hold of Logan again and easing him back to the ground. "I'll get ye help." The moment he had Logan comfortable, he ran off like a charging elephant, making more noise than speed, puffing laboriously.

His ankle did hurt, but it was certainly not broken. Logan knew that much. It was probably not sprained, either. He could walk on it right now if he wanted, and it would be fine in a couple of days. But if he had received this much sympathy from the factor, how much might he garner from the members of the family? Might they even feel duty-bound to nurse him back to health? This could be his key into the good graces of the family. He would be stupid to turn his back on such a fortuitous gift.

Within moments Joanna MacNeil, little May, and two farmhands came running from the direction of the house. Dougall was hobbling along at the rear, panting awfully, and mopping his brow with a huge red handkerchief.

Joanna was the first to reach Logan's prostrate form, and he smiled weakly at her.

"I'm terribly sorry for causing you this trouble," he said.

"It's certainly no fault of yours," she answered, kneeling at his side. "I should never have asked Allison to bring you here. May I have a look? I'll be able to tell if it's broken or not." She began to roll up his right pantleg.

"It's the left ankle," he corrected her, making a mental note that he was going to have to remember that fact as well.

Gently Joanna manipulated the injured foot, with Logan wincing at all the appropriate moments.

"It doesn't appear to be broken," she announced, clearly relieved, "but you must have sprained it badly. If you don't mind I'll have Harry and Russell here carry you to the house. Then I'll call for the doctor."

"I don't want to put you to the trouble. If someone could just—"

"Nonsense! You're not going anywhere. Don't even think it. This is the least we can do." And without further argument, she instructed the two sturdy men to take him in hand.

He was carried into the house and upstairs to a guest room on the second floor. They laid him on top of a made-up four-poster, while Joanna remained downstairs to use the phone. When the men left him alone, he looked about, nodding his head approvingly. This would do quite nicely! The Duke of Windsor himself would find little to complain about in a setup like this. The room was Victorian and very expensive. But like everything else at Stonewycke, it was tastefully simple. He wondered how long a sprained ankle should keep one immobile, and what other symptoms he should display. The doctor could be trouble. But if he was like the rest of the rustics in this out-of-the-way place, he shouldn't be too difficult to convince. He couldn't remain on his back for long. But then if he played his cards right, by the time his *injury* was healed, he'd have another reason to stay at Stonewycke.

Soon a light knock came to the door and Joanna entered carrying a tray with tea.

"Forgive me for leaving you so long," she said, pouring the tea. "I've been trying to soothe poor Fergie."

For the first time Logan felt a pang of guilt at his subterfuge. The factor was a nice fellow, and well-meaning. He was sorry to put him through this. *But he'll get over his worry,* Logan told himself. When this was behind them, the man would be more beholden to him than anyone on the estate, which could prove a tangible asset later on. And he would make it up to the factor somehow, just like to Jesse. After all, it was Dougall who had inadvertently landed him right into the middle of the biggest opportunity of his life. Yes, he owed him too!

In the meantime, it felt rather nice to have the Lady MacNeil wait on him. He let her stir two lumps of sugar and some cream into his cup, then arrange his pillows while he painfully pulled himself up on the bed. He'd have to be careful not to overdo it, however, for these people would sympathize more with brave fortitude than with sniveling.

"Fergie tells me this all happened because of your good fortune with the tractor," she said.

He laughed softly. "Good for the tractor, that is," he said.

"You do seem to be quite a mechanical wonder, Mr. Macintyre."

"I guess I've always been handy in that way," he replied modestly.

She tapped her chin thoughtfully but said nothing more. To make conversation, Logan launched into an account of his experiences aboard the *Little Stevie.* When he laughed at his trip overboard, she laughed with him and commented that she had had a similar "baptism" into Port Strathy life, only hers was more figurative: midwifing in a barn with manure up to her knees. She related in full the story of the calf-birthing and how she had been reluctantly pressed into service by a very cross vet by the name of Alec MacNeil. The doctor arrived in the midst of their laughter over the story.

He complimented Joanna on keeping the patient in good spirits. When he examined the ankle he noted the lack of swelling, the only symptom Logan was unable to feign. But everything else met with his apparent medical satisfaction, and his final diagnosis was even somewhat more severe: there could possibly be a pulled muscle or torn ligament, injuries which might not produce overt swelling but could be even more serious than a sprain. He parted with the final instructions to apply ice and to stay off the foot for two days, calling him after that time if it was still able to bear no weight. He left a small bottle of pain pills, and upon taking two Logan immediately fell asleep, aided no doubt by the fact that he had not slept in well over thirty-six hours.

Dark shadows had begun to crisscross the bed when Logan awoke some hours later. His sleep had been a heavy one, yet somehow not entirely refreshing. Unaccustomed to the pull of conscience, he attributed the uneasiness he felt to the effects of the drug. He remained groggy and disoriented for several minutes, but by the time he heard the knock at the door, he had regained his full faculties.

Joanna entered, followed by Alec. She was carrying another tray, this one burdened with several steaming bowls and another pot of tea.

"I hope you've slept well," she said.

"Yes, thank you. I did. Those pills must've been strong."

Joanna reached over to arrange his pillows.

"Lady MacNeil, you don't have to wait on me like this."

Then Alec spoke for the first time. "Logan," he said, "my wife's a born nurse. She wouldna be happy wi'oot servin' others. So dinna try t' stop her—ye'll only end up wi' a fight on yer hands." He chuckled as he watched her, but there was an unmistakable look of pride in his eyes.

"Well . . ." Logan conceded reluctantly, letting her set his dinner in place.

"Ye worked more o' yer wonders wi' oor tractor, I understan'?"

"Nothing much," replied Logan. "I got her started, but she's going to need a new coil. I'm almost certain of that."

There was a slight pause; then Alec spoke again. "Logan," he began in a more business-like tone, "I came up here, o' course, t' see hoo ye're farin', but also, my wife an' I hae been talkin'—"

"Please," interrupted Logan, "you have been more than hospitable, but I have no intention of taking advantage of your kindness. There's no reason why someone can't drive me down to the inn."

"We wouldna think o' na such thing, Logan," said Alec sternly, "an' dinna insult us by inferrin' that we'd sen' ye away in yer present state."

Logan was taken aback by the rebuke, and hardly knew how to react to it. But when Alec spoke again, his voice had softened perceptibly. "Noo, ye'll be stayin' here as long as it takes t' git ye on yer feet, an' we'll hear nae more aboot it. But that's not what Joanna an' I were talkin' aboot. Ye see, we hae a good bit o' machinery here, an' some o't it's gettin' rather auld, an' it's all been sorely neglected since oor auld factor died a few months ago. What's more, Walter made himsel' almost indispensable t' the crofters an' farmers and fishers, too. Everyone's been managin', I s'pose, like they'd manage wi'oot a vet if they were forced t'. But 'tis a lot easier t' have someone aboot wi' a special touch who can eliminate the headaches that come when ye hae t' do somethin' y'ere not trained fer. Well, that's a roundaboot way o' sayin' that we'd like t' hire ye here at Stonewycke, t' work fer us an' t' lend ye oot t' the others in Port Strathy that might be able to make use o' yer services. We know ye hae important work in London, but ye said ye was on leave, an' we'd be pleased fer ye t' consider it. We'd give ye room an' board an' ten pounds a month in salary."

Logan doubted that even his smoothest talking could have conjured up a better offer. Still, he did not want to appear too anxious.

"You don't owe me this, you know," was his reply.

"We know that, Mr. Macintyre," said Joanna. "We need your service, pure and simple. It has been a struggle since Walter left us. As much as Fergie has a heart of gold, there are just too many things he doesn't know yet. We understand that you did not come here intending to settle. But perhaps you could try it for a month or two, or at least long enough to teach Fergie some of what you know—"

"Oh, my lady," broke in Logan, "my reasons for coming here wouldn't be a factor in my decision. This is a wonderful place and you are all very kind. It might be nice to be away from the rush of London for a time." He took a long, thoughtful swallow of tea, and when he spoke again he sounded as if his decision were being made even as he spoke. "As I told you, I am more or less between assignments, and have no pressing date when I must be back, and . . ." Here he chuckled lightly as if an amusing thought had just occurred to him. "My mother would certainly be thrilled to hear that I was *plannin' t' bide a wee in the muckle toon o' my ain oncle Digory.*"

They both laughed at his attempt at the local dialect. "It sounds right fine on ye, lad!" said Alec.

"Yes . . . this might be just what I'm looking for."

"Then ye'll do it?" asked Alec, grinning.

Logan paused just long enough for effect, then nodded. Both men shook hands while Joanna poured her new mechanic another cup of tea.

Logan fell asleep that night feeling extremely satisfied with himself. Everything couldn't have gone more smoothly if he had planned each minute detail. Here he was, an employee of Stonewycke. He could now freely roam about the estate, and even more importantly, he'd have opportunity to work his way closer to Lady Margaret.

Suddenly a dark thought entered his mind. What if, as an employee, the family stood more aloof to him? It was only natural that they would keep their distance from the hired help. But, then, nothing thus far had indicated that these people did anything according to the book. Perhaps they treated their employees like family as well.

No matter. He had come this far. He would manage any further obstacles that presented themselves. Things were going perfectly. Almost too perfectly. If he had been back on the streets of London, Skittles would probably tell him to watch his backside; when things went this well, it was time to suspect a setup.

But Logan didn't follow that train of thought even for another moment. There was no one here who could possibly be setting him up. No one even knew he had come. Who could possibly be interested in him? No, he was in the driver's seat, and everything was moving just as he wanted it to. He lay back on the luxurious feather bed and smiled contentedly.

23 ❧ Another Stranger in Town

ROY HAMILTON WAS not accustomed to taking in boarders.

His pub on New Town's High Street was a drinking establishment, nothing else. He did have the spare room next to his living quarters upstairs. But he used it for storage and, to tell the truth, he'd just as soon have kept it that way. The minute you started letting in boarders, you had nothing but headaches. The profit was in drink, and that's the way he intended to keep it.

He rinsed off another dish and dropped it in the drainer. It wasn't washing the extra dishes that was so bad. After all, he had to do that anyway, although it was mostly only glasses. But now he'd have to sweep out that room occasionally and maybe even change the sheets, not to mention cooking the man's meals. Hamilton was a bachelor, a thin man who ate only slightly more often than he washed himself, which was not three times a day by the remotest stretch of anyone's imagination. But then his customers did not expect cleanliness, only liquor, and a pretty poor grade of spirits it was that he served.

He would have refused the man outright. Started to, in fact, with a wave of the hand before he had even completed his question. But then the stranger had unfolded a thick wad of bank-notes, and Roy Hamilton would have been a fool to refuse *them*. Maybe he *could* reconsider, he had said. The man had begun to peel several notes off the stack and hand them across the counter, and the end of it all was that now he had a guest. A most peculiar guest, to be sure, a man who guarded his privacy and offered few words. About the only thing he had said was what almost sounded like a threat, that the innkeeper was to say nothing about either his presence or his bankroll. But for this man's price, he could give him the room and keep his mouth shut.

Why he hadn't gone to the Bluster 'N Blow where visitors usually stayed in Port Strathy, Hamilton did not know. He had asked at the first, but the man had been most uncommunicative on the subject. And he remained untalkative. Last night he had done his drinking off in a corner, alone. He hadn't even been interested in giving the local folk a chance to relieve him of some of that cash he had stuffed in his pockets. At least that other stranger, the young fellow, had been free with his money—he lost a good deal the last time he was in Hamilton's place, though the innkeeper heard he won a bundle at MacFarlane's pub just down the street the other night.

Hamilton washed up the remainder of the dishes, flicked a cockroach off the drainboard, then dried his hands on his grimy apron. Well, with times being so bad, maybe he ought to give some more thought to this taking in of boarders. The man hadn't really been that much trouble. The room was just sitting there, and if it meant a little more work, it might be worth it if his guests paid him half as much as this Sprague bloke had.

Ross Sprague puffed at his Cuban cigar, then downed the last drink of his rum-braced tea.

It was not his habit to imbibe alcoholic beverages so early in the morning, but it was the only way to kill the taste of that garbage the innkeeper had called breakfast. He should have expected a hick town like this to have only one decent hotel. He had grown up in a town no bigger than Port Strathy. And his childhood in the dusty prairie town had taught him the limitations of little one-horse watering holes like this. That town had had only one hotel, run by Mae Wadell, whose reputation was none too sterling in Aldo, Oklahoma. He had learned a few things at Wadell's, but the most valuable lesson learned was the quickest way out of Aldo. When he left at seventeen, he swore he'd never go back—and he never did. He had come a long way since the Aldo days and Mae Wadell's wild place. Now he was forty-five, and liked fine cigars, expensive Scotch, and hotels that weren't crawling with vermin, like this fleabag.

Unfortunately, Macintyre had arrived first and procured the better establishment. Though when Sprague had looked in at the place called the Bluster 'N Blow upon arriving yesterday, it didn't appear to be much of an improvement over this sleazy joint. He supposed he ought to consider himself lucky that Macintyre was still here. If he lost him, it would be his head! He hadn't intended on giving Macintyre a four-day lead, but storms and a few other entanglements he'd just as soon forget had held him up. He hadn't been too worried, however, for if this Macintyre was on some sort of a treasure hunt, it was bound to take him some time. He doubted the fellow had much to go on, and from what he had been able to learn of Macintyre's activities since his arrival, he did not appear to have gotten much closer.

What puzzled Sprague more than anything was why his boss had been so adamant about his sticking to Macintyre. Sprague rubbed a hand over his thinning gray-blonde hair. Why would a successful man like his boss want to waste time on some rumors about a ridiculous ancient treasure—no doubt entirely mythical? Pure greed, he supposed. The man had nearly lost everything in the Wall Street crash, and that had made him more conscious than ever of retaining his old wealth and power. But he was already making his way back to the top, with a classy flat in London's West End and a business that boasted branches not only in London but also Paris and Berlin. He was never satisfied, and no doubt that's what would make him a success again. But the whole thing still seemed peculiarly out of his line, and Sprague could not help but think there was something personal involved, something more than business—revenge, perhaps. Or did his boss know something more than he was telling?

Sprague was being paid well for his services, well enough not to ask questions. But things were beginning to get puzzling, and he could hardly keep from being curious. First, he was sent to Glasgow to make discreet—very discreet!—inquiries into various property owners, specifically of Scottish coastal property, and even more specifically into the holdings of what had formerly been the vast Duncan estate. He had been told to get the names of every property owner in the valley and along the coast. He figured his boss was looking to buy some country place with a view and wanted to make a killing by closing in on someone who had been particularly hard hit by the crash. It was logical. Everyone with a few bucks these days was scouting around for the chance to benefit by picking up the pieces.

Then he was suddenly told to drop everything and follow this Macintyre fellow. Sure that this so-called treasure was supposed to be located on the Duncan property, Macintyre had come here. There was a connection. But why would an intelligent man like his boss fall for what could be no more than a con game by a petty, small-time crook?

The best move, he thought, would be to stop Macintyre before he clued anyone in about the treasure—pay him off, do whatever it took. If there was any validity to the treasure fairy tale, and the Duncans were tipped off, it would put the lid on any possible sale. As it was, it seemed that the Duncan clan was in bad enough shape financially that they might be more than willing to sell if the price was right. Why didn't his boss just put Macintyre on ice for a while, move in smoothly and make the Duncans an offer they couldn't refuse? Then he could find the treasure later, without any need to hide a thing. If there was no treasure, then at least he had his beach house—or castle, rather.

But his boss was just that—the boss. If he wanted him to tail Macintyre till doomsday, Sprague would do it. But he personally felt they were wasting their time.

Sprague inhaled the smoke from his cigar two or three more times. No, they sure didn't have smokes like this in Aldo. Maybe in Muskogee, but even if they'd had them there, he hadn't had the money in those days to buy them. Thanks to a generous boss, he now possessed an unlimited supply—so who was he to question the man's judgment?

Stick to Macintyre. Keep a low profile.

Those were his orders. And Ross Sprague followed orders. That's how he got to where he was today. And he'd keep following orders until eventually *he* was the one *giving* the orders.

24 ❊ *Visitors*

LOGAN WAS RESTLESS.

Now that he didn't *need* this injured ankle, he was stuck with it. He couldn't very well hop out of bed and proclaim a miracle. The doctor had said two days off his feet, and that meant he couldn't get up until tomorrow. Even then, he'd have to remember to limp somewhat for a week or so.

Out of sheer boredom he picked up one of the three books Lady MacNeil had brought up to him. *After all,* he thought, *the last time started flipping through books, I stumbled onto Digory's letter.* Maybe he'd find a further clue to the location of the treasure here, perhaps even a hint of what the treasure actually was. Who could tell? The events of his life seemed somehow ordered since he had arrived here. He would hardly be surprised at this point if a clue jumped right off the page.

Mrs. MacNeil had offered to have him carried down to the library or a sunlit dayroom where he might see better. But pretending an injury for business was one thing; letting people carry him around was quite another. He would just brave it out right here. He had taken the books, not having the heart to tell her he had no interest in reading.

But interested or not, he was going crazy just lying there. Not knowing his preferences, she said, she had brought a variety. Dickens' *Great Expectations,* however apropos the title, he quickly tossed aside. He remembered teachers trying to force it down him. A hasty flipping through the book revealed no notes or letters, and that was that. Next was Scott's *Guy Mannering.* Who could possibly plow through the small print, and all those anachronisms? He turned it upside down and let the pages hang as he gave it a shake or two. No clues there either. Of course the whole thing was absurd! What was he thinking, that right under her nose the proprietress of the estate was going to tell him where the treasure was so he could steal it from them?

He laughed aloud. The isolation had already made him come unhinged!

Finally he reached for the third book, a volume of poems by George MacDonald. Although the name sounded vaguely familiar, Logan couldn't quite place him—a Scot, he thought, perhaps nineteenth century. He wasn't sure. He had never been much on poetry, but these were short and uncluttered and at least looked more palatable than the other two books. He opened the book to the middle. One of the nice things about books like this was that you didn't have to start at the beginning and read to the end. And when someone asked you how you liked the book, you could spout off a few things about a poem—maybe the only one you read—and they'd never be the wiser.

Skimming the page, he noticed a reference to boats, and thinking this as good a place as any to start, he sought the beginning of the verse:

Master, thou workest with such common things—
Low souls, weak hearts, I mean—and hast to use,
Therefore, such common means and rescuings,
That hard we find it, as we sit and muse,
To think thou workest in us verily:
Bad sea-boats, we and manned with wretched crews—
That doubt the captain, watch the storm-spray flee.

Thou art hampered in thy natural working then
When beings designed on freedom's holy plan
Will not be free: with thy poor, foolish men,
Thou therefore hast to work just like a man.

But when, tangling thyself in their sore need,
Thou hast to freedom fashioned them indeed,
Then wilt thou grandly move, and godlike speed.

Logan stopped reading.

These were nothing but religious poems. There was no treasure here—just old-fashioned notions of piety! He should have known!

Actually, Logan had nothing personal against religion. His mother had been religious on and off, and went through bouts of dragging him to church when he hadn't made his escape fast enough on Sunday mornings. But never in his life had he felt any particular need for religion.

Bad sea-boats, we and manned with wretched crews. . . . Yes, he supposed that described him. At least he had been told as much on those few Sundays when he had ventured into church. "Ye're a bad apple, Logan Macintyre. Settle doon afore ye wind up in hell!"

No thanks, he thought. He had no use for such fanatical pessimism. If they wanted to be prisoners of that kind of fear, that was their choice. But he didn't need it. He was free. With the thought, the words came back into his mind, and he looked back onto the page to see exactly what the poet had said. *Thou art hampered in thy natural working then when beings designed on freedom's holy plan will not be free.* . . .

What did the man mean? What a strange thing to say?

He was free, wasn't he? He prided himself on that fact. Footloose and fancy free; he had always taken pleasure in being just that sort of man. Whatever freedom this old-fashioned writer was talking about, he certainly wasn't referring to someone like himself. Logan Macintyre was free, was on the track of a treasure which was going to put him on easy street, and nothing was going to stop him.

He closed the book just as a sharp knock came at the door, jerking him out of his momentary reverie.

It would be a relief to have some company. He had never been a deep thinker and had no intention of starting now. No old dead poet was going to start filling his mind with foolish fancies. Somehow he was sure it was the kind of thing Lady Margaret would know all about. The poem almost reminded him of that peculiar look in her eyes. It wouldn't surprise him if she knew the old bloke who wrote it.

"Come in," he called.

The door opened and Allison ushered in an entourage that appeared as out of place within the grand walls of Stonewycke as she had on the streets of New Town. With her were Jesse Cameron, Buckie Buchannan, and Jimmy MacMillan.

"It looks like ye're na havin' a run o' much luck here in Strathy," said Jesse, taking his hand and shaking it heartily.

"Ha!" laughed Jimmy who had been involved in the poker game at MacFarlane's. "Dinna be talkin' t' this bloke aboot luck. He's got plenty o' it!"

"Aye," added Buckie with a friendly grin. "He's got enough Port Strathy siller in his pockets t' stay in bed a month."

"What a surprise!" said Logan, laughing with the banter.

"Ye dinna think oor best crew member would get laid up an' rate no visit from his mates?" said Jesse with mock astonishment.

"If you don't mind," came Allison's cool voice, noticeably out of concert with the other congenial tones, "I'll be leaving you to your . . . visitors, Mr. Macintyre." Then turning toward Jesse, "I trust you can find your own way out when you are through?"

"Yes, mem," replied Jesse, with the quiet respect of one who knew her place when she was put in it. "Thank ye, m'leddy."

Favoring those in the room with one final aloof glance, which left Logan with the impression that she was appraising how they would handle their temptation to carry out the family silver, Allison turned crisply and exited.

"Pull up some chairs," he said to his guests. When he saw Buckie glancing all about and then giving a soft whistle, he added, "Some digs, huh?"

"Who says the bloke ain't lucky!" said Jimmy as he straddled a delicate Queen Anne chair.

Jesse and Buckie took two other chairs, launching immediately into a conversation about the weather, fishing prospects, and the latest repairs being undertaken aboard the *Little Stevie*. A week earlier such topics would have held no meaning whatsoever for Logan, but now he found himself interested in even the most trivial details. From firsthand experience he now knew how vitally important the weather was to the fishermen, and since his "voyage," he had now and then found his eyes straying toward the sky with a concern he would never have felt before. Would those clouds bring rain? From which direction was the wind coming? Could the *Little Stevie* take another gale? Thus Logan found himself listening with more attentiveness than he could have thought possible.

Before anyone realized it, an hour had passed. Jesse was the first to rise.

"We didn't mean t' take all yer time, an' we still got plenty t' do today," she said.

"My time!" said Logan. "Time's all I've got!"

She laughed. "The soft life's gettin' t' ye already?"

"I'd sooner be out on your deck in a rainstorm than caged up in here," Logan replied.

A serious look passed over Jesse's face, one Logan had not seen her wear previously. "The Lord spared ye once, my frien'," she said, "an' it's no wise t' be temptin' the likes o' Him afore ye figure oot what He saved ye fer."

Logan's unresponsive stare apparently urged her to explain further.

"When we're oot on the water an' a squall breaks oot, sometimes a clap o' thunder'll break an' I'll swear we're all goners. Or sometimes a flash o' lightnin'll break almost from a clear sky. Weel, sometimes somethin' happens like that in life, too. Somethin' terrible will fall wi' oot warnin'. An' from that time on, everythin' is changed. Life can no more be what it was afore. Like when my Charlie an' my boy was lost. An' the result depen's on hoo ye respon' t' the invadin' storm o' trouble. What do ye do after the echo o' the thunder has died away? Is yer life better than it was . . . or worse? Do ye let Him use the bolt o' lightnin' t' open yer eyes, or do ye keep them shut?"

"I'm afraid I don't really understand what you're talking about, Jesse," said Logan in an apologetic tone.

"Weel, I'll see if I canna be a mite more plain-spoken, lad," she replied. After a short pause, she resumed. "I dinna believe in accidents. Everythin' is t' a purpose. Jist like yer comin' here, an' like yer accident on the boat, an' maybe like yer accident here, too, fer all I ken. Dinna ye see, lad? The Lord's tryin' t' get yer attention. 'Tis the bolt o' lightnin' in yer own life. He's tryin' t' wake ye up. An' that's what I said in the beginnin', that ye'd be wise t' figure oot what He's tryin' t' save ye fer afore He runs oot o' patience an' leaves ye t' yer own devices."

Logan was silent, trying to ponder her words, but in truth they barely reached past the surface of his mind.

"We almost forgot," put in Buckie in a lighter tone; "we got presents."

"Presents! It's not my birthday, Buckie!" laughed Logan.

"'Twas Jesse's idea, but we all agreed 'twas a good one," replied the first mate, stuffing his hand into his pocket and withdrawing three cigars. "We thought ye might like a fine smoke," he added, laying them on the bed.

Logan picked one up and sniffed it lingeringly. "Ah," he said, "*that* is a good cigar!"

"I brought ye somethin'," said Jimmy, "but I left it wi' the cook. We smoked some o' the catch ye helped wi'."

"I hardly *helped!*"

"Ye was there, an' that's enough," said Jesse, and Logan could tell she meant it sincerely. Then she proceeded to take a small package from her pocket. "The lads thought ye might be able t' fin' some use fer these."

It was a deck of cards. Logan slipped them out of the box and fanned them out expertly; his fingers obviously had more than a passing acquaintance with the game. Suddenly he broke into an uproarious laugh. Each card bore a picture of a fish on its back.

He looked up at Jesse and noted a definite twinkle in each eye.

All at once he felt very odd. He bit his lip and looked hastily down, pretending to examine the cards more closely. He didn't know what this feeling inside him was, nor what he should say. When at last he did speak, his voice felt hollow. He couldn't say what he felt without saying too much.

"Thanks. You are all . . . you're good friends," was all he said, but when he ventured a glance at Jesse, he knew she understood.

Telling him to visit them at the boat again sometime, even though he was now an important man and working for the estate, they left, and again Logan found himself alone.

He lay quietly on the bed, feeling very strange—not a little deceptive, certainly ill at ease, and at the same time, very heavy. He fingered the deck of cards and sniffed at another cigar. Suddenly he knew what felt heavy—it was his blasted left foot, sound and whole as it was.

"So what was I *supposed* to do?" he half yelled to himself, throwing back the blankets and jumping out of bed.

Pacing back and forth over the Persian carpet, he continued to argue with himself. "They'd understand! They'd do the same in my shoes if they had the chance. These are big stakes! Friends or no friends, I've come too far to start getting wishy-washy now!"

Then, as if resolving his temporary ambivalence, he grabbed up one of the cigars, bit off the end, which he spat out on the floor, lit it, and puffed dramatically. It wasn't *that* great a cigar, anyway. It certainly wasn't as if they had spent their last penny on it. He puffed again and tried to blow the smoke into a ring. But despite all his efforts, that was one trick Skittles had not been able to teach him.

Poor old Skittles . . .

Why did things have to change? Why couldn't he be back in London where he belonged, among people he belonged with? Everything had been simple enough there. He had known what he wanted and how to get it. There were no deeper questions of life back there—at least, not many. Now here was Jesse trying to talk to him about thunderbolts from heaven, and some ancient poet yapping about foolish men who didn't want to be free! It was all such nonsense!

Suddenly he heard a noise outside the door.

Like a naughty child, he leaped back under the covers, his heart racing. The cigar had lost all its flavor. Never before had he felt so much like a common sneak.

25 ⁂ *The Greenhouse*

LEAVING LOGAN WITH his friends, Allison returned downstairs in a none-too-pleasant frame of mind. It was disgraceful how they were all treating the man—giving him the best guestroom, waiting on him hand and foot, allowing his coarse and smelly friends the run of the house.

Yet all those things had not irritated her half as much as her mother asking her to show the visitors up to Macintyre's room. They had servants for such tasks!

Her mother and father both knew what sort of person he was; Allison had made a point of telling exactly how she had found him in town the other day when they had mentioned they were going to hire him. If *she* had tried to befriend such a person, they would have objected strenuously.

When she reached the bottom of the stairs, she was carrying a taut, sour expression on her face, which Joanna could hardly have missed. The perceptive mother had a vague idea of the cause, for she had seen the protest in her daughter's eyes the moment she had been asked to escort Logan's guests upstairs. Joanna often doubted whether or not she was approaching her daughter's problems wisely, thrusting her into situations that would challenge and expose her arrogant attitude for what it was. She'd hoped that when Allison saw herself in her true light, it would have a much greater impact than a mother's preaching. Joanna told herself over and over to exercise patience and to stand faithful in prayer for her daughter—those would be her greatest weapons against this thing that was eating away at Allison. But sometimes it was so hard to keep from saying what sprang to her mind.

"Mother!" said Allison in a remonstrative tone, as a master rebuking a servant. "How could you? It's hardly suitable for a member of the family to be showing a mere employee his guests! How do you expect to maintain order around here? And *such* guests!"

The arrogant tone of her daughter's words taxed Joanna's resolve to the limit. *Perhaps what she needs is a good hard spanking!* Joanna thought to herself. But instead she took a breath, then answered calmly, "I hadn't thought of that."

"You wouldn't, Mother," replied Allison. "Sometimes you just let them walk all over you!"

"Do I . . . ?"

Allison nodded, looking as though she were expecting a verbal attack from her mother on another flank. But then Joanna went on in the same controlled voice. "I'm on my way out to the greenhouse." With the words, Allison noticed for the first time the basket her mother was carrying. "Dorey said there were some lovely rhododendrons ready to pick. Would you care to join me?"

Allison hesitated.

There seemed no threat in the invitation. Still it was a little odd. Why hadn't her mother given her the usual sermon on treating everyone as equals? She and her mother used to take walks over the grounds all the time. Why had they stopped, she wondered? She was about to make some excuse for refusing when suddenly she found herself saying, "Yes."

It was not a day particularly conducive to a morning stroll. A steady wind had arisen and was now blowing in from the north, filled with portents of another rainstorm. It whipped Allison's hair in her face, and she pulled her sweater snugly about her. It would have been impossible to talk as they walked without yelling in one another's ears.

The moment they stepped into the greenhouse, they seemed to enter another realm altogether. The glass walls immediately cut off the roar of the wind and they were surrounded by a still, quiet, humid warmth.

Joanna smiled as she looked about.

"I remember the first time I came into this place," she said reflectively. "Your father and I had sneaked onto the grounds through a breach in the hedge. I was trembling when we came through this door, and with good reason, for I was a common trespasser—an unwelcome interloper."

"I've heard the story many times, Mother."

"Yes . . . I suppose you have." Joanna took down a pair of shears from a hook on the wall. "I guess I'm telling you now because I hoped it would help you understand why I feel as I do toward the folk around here."

"Because you were one of them once?"

"Yes. I was an outsider too. A commoner. I have never *stopped* being 'one of them,' as you put it." She walked to several rhododendron bushes laden with large deep red blossoms. "I suppose it's my own background that made me realize there wasn't anything magical about being a *Duncan*. And when I began to learn about some family history, I learned there wasn't even anything very *desirable* about it."

"Mother! How can you say such a thing?"

"There's nothing special about us, dear, except in God's eyes—where every one of His children is infinitely special." Joanna clipped one of the blooms and laid it in her basket. "Several hundred years ago a man by the name of Ramsay happened to save a king's life, and the king gave him some land and a title for his reward. It could have happened to anyone."

"But it didn't."

"Andrew Ramsay, then, was special. He was a courageous man who placed another's life above his own. *That* was special and he deserved what he got. But the rest . . . in a sense, they belonged no more to that reward than I belonged in the greenhouse that day."

"We've *earned* our place by faithfully administering the estate," argued Allison.

"You know," said Joanna, attempting a new train of thought, "your brother wants to go to America; he may decide to live there permanently. Nat has no interest in being a country squire—I think he'd much rather be a fisherman. Thus, the mantle of Stonewycke will no doubt fall to you, Allison."

Allison had never heard her mother talk like this. It was a little sobering, even frightening. Allison did not like fear, and she responded by trying to protect herself with a hard, cool shell. For the moment she said nothing.

"I agree with you in one sense," Joanna continued. "We do have a unique responsibility to the community. They look to us for a kind of stability and leadership, which is a good thing when wisely used. But it is not because of who *we* are, or even what we are, but rather because of what *Stonewycke* is, what it represents in the minds of the people and in the history of this community, what it has always stood for. Allison, *we* have been placed here as servants to the folk around us. To serve—that is the highest calling of all."

"*I knew* you would find a way to twist it around to that," retorted Allison angrily. "No one expects servanthood from us, least of all the people in Port Strathy. They like to flaunt their resident nobility, just like all common people do. I think it embarrasses them the way this family sometimes behaves, acting as if we were not better than they."

"And you do think we're better?"

"Maybe *better* was an unwise word. But yes, we're supposed to be set apart, higher in society. It's for their good too, don't you see? They *need* us to be above them."

"And you think we should lord it over them because of our position?"

"Do you know what the real problem is, Mother?" asked Allison, ignoring her mother's question.

Joanna simply raised her eyebrows inquisitively, knowing her daughter's answer was going to come no matter what she said.

"I think you're afraid of what your position really means, afraid you won't be able to measure up to *real* nobility." Joanna stared, too stunned by her daughter's reasoning to respond. "I think you're hiding behind all this servant rhetoric!" Allison added in one final outburst.

Joanna closed her eyes and let the shears slip from her hand. "Oh, Allison . . ." she breathed, the pain evident in her voice. "I . . . I can see we can't talk about this," she tried to go on, then stopped. Her lip trembled as she tried to hold back the tears, for she knew they would not draw Allison's sympathy, and might even induce her contempt.

Joanna could not utter another word. She was hurt, disappointed, even a little angry in a quiet sort of way, and afraid of what, at that point, she might say—what terrible things might lash out at her own daughter.

She turned, and still clutching the basket of Dorey's lovely flowers, hurried out of the greenhouse.

Allison watched, but her own fancied indignation on the side of truth shielded her from feeling her mother's poignant and heart-wrenching emotion. She hadn't noticed the soft shuffling sound behind her, and had no idea someone had entered the greenhouse by the back door while she had made her cruel speech to her mother.

"I didn't mean to intrude," came a soft, aged voice.

Startled at the sound, she jerked herself around, glaring at whoever had the gall to frighten her so. It was Dorey.

"Oh, Grandpa," she said, quickly rearranging her features into a look of deference, for he was one of her elders whose opinion she still respected. "You frightened me."

"You frightened me, dear," he replied in a calm tone, sounding not at all like one who had been frightened in anything like a normal manner.

"Me?"

Appearing to ignore her questioning tone, Dorey hobbled slowly over to the place where Joanna had dropped the shears. He inched his frame gingerly down and picked them up. "They'll rust if they lay there and chance to get wet," he said quietly. He laid them carefully on a worktable.

"Were . . ." Allison began hesitatingly, "were you here the whole time?"

"I haven't yet fallen into the habit of common eavesdropping."

"I'm sorry, Grandpa. That's not what I meant."

"When I came in, you and your mother were too intent on one another to notice me. I was rather at a disadvantage, and at the moment I tried to make my presence known, your mother walked out."

"She's impossible to talk to," said Allison with a defensive edge to her voice.

"A common malady between mothers and daughters, I expect," said the old man.

"I'm afraid she didn't understand me."

"I think she understands you only too well," replied Dorey, his brow furrowed with a rebuke his soft-spoken voice did not carry. "As I also understood you."

"What do you mean?" she asked. She really didn't want to ask the question, but somehow it almost seemed expected, and she could not help herself.

He came toward her and took her hands into his—gnarled old hands, coarse with their work in the soil and trembling slightly with age. But his grasp was firm and warm, filled with a love he knew his great-granddaughter was unwilling to acknowledge openly.

"I heard something in your voice," he said, his voice forever soft, as a man who gave little credit to his own wisdom. "I see it now in your eyes, and it does frighten me, my dear, dear Ali." He was the only one she permitted to call her by that name. "As much as we would like to, we cannot forget that *his* blood flows through your veins. But I saw it so clearly in your eyes just now. They were *his* eyes . . . I could never forget them."

"Whose, Grandpa?" Allison's voice trembled a bit now too. Her great-grandfather was as lucid a man as there ever was, but she knew he had suffered greatly and had had some mental disorder many years ago; and every now and then, not often, he said something that reminded her of that fact.

"James Duncan's," he replied tightly. The name would always be difficult for him to say.

"He was rather a scoundrel, wasn't he?"

"He was your great-great-grandfather," was Dorey's only reply. He brought her hands to his wrinkled lips and kissed them softly.

"Mother didn't get any pink rhodies," Allison said with a forced tightness in her voice. She blithely released herself from Dorey's grasp, picked up the shears, and flitted about the flowers like a butterfly.

Dorey shook his head sadly. "Will you apologize to your mother?" he asked.

"I don't see why," said Allison, frantically clipping blossoms.

"You hurt her terribly."

"I didn't mean to."

"We never mean to hurt those we love," he said as he let out a weary sigh. "But it happens only too often. You mustn't let such things fester between you."

"Well . . . I suppose I should have used a different tone," she conceded, though reluctantly, appearing to do so only to please her grandfather. "That should be enough pink ones, don't you think?" She dropped the shears on the table and skitted to the door. "Luncheon should be ready soon, Grandpa, so don't be too long."

She was out the door and gone before he could even reply.

Dorey sighed heavily. "Dear Lord," he prayed softly, "don't let her go that way—his way. Draw her to you early in her life, my Father, so that she may have that many more years to enjoy your love. She needs you so. Help her to realize her need . . ."

As he passed, he thought of a young man so many, many years ago, and what it had taken for him to acknowledge his need for God. The thought made him wince in pain for Allison.

But the dread was even greater when he recalled James Duncan's terrible glint in his dear Ali's eyes.

"Do whatever you must, Father." They were hard words to say. And perhaps would have been impossible if he did not know he was saying them to a loving and merciful God.

26 ❈ The Stable

LOGAN GRIPPED THE cane and took a few tentative steps. He looked up and smiled at Joanna who was watching encouragingly.

"I should think it'll be taking my full weight in no time," he said, holding out his left foot.

"Don't rush it, Logan."

"I'm anxious to start work," he replied. And in his own context, the words were truthfully spoken.

"Believe me, we are anxious to have you, but the doctor did say that if the muscles have been damaged, another injury could recur more easily."

"I'll be careful."

It was now the third day since the "accident," and he at last had official permission to be up and about. The doctor had dropped by with the cane yesterday, just after his visitors had left, and fortunately discovered Logan lying in bed. After resisting the idea at first, Logan then decided that the cane would be a nice touch. It lent him rather a distinguished air, and even a bit of sympathy that might work to his advantage later. The old recurring injury ploy might play into his hands at some future time, who could tell? He recalled a crony in London who had his shoulder shattered during the Great War. He was as fit as anyone until he wanted to impress a lady or dodge a bill collector. Then, how he could favor that shoulder—it was masterful!

All Logan wanted right now, though, was to get some fresh air and exercise. Being waited on in this kingly room had been splendid for a while. But he couldn't take another day of it.

"Would it be in order for me to have a look around my new work area?" he asked.

"By all means," replied Joanna. "I'll accompany you if you like."

"You're too kind. But I can manage, and I'm certain you have other responsibilities."

"At least let me help you down the stairs. It might be a little tricky with that cane."

Logan simply smiled, and set off with her slowly down the corridor.

In five minutes they had reached the rear exit nearest the stable. There Joanna left him, pointing the way, and Logan limped—careful to continue favoring his left foot, though he could see no one watching him—the rest of the way alone.

The front section of the huge stone structure had been walled off to serve as a garage and workshop of sorts. He swung open the wooden doors, large enough to admit a vehicle— motor cars and farm machinery now, but in days past coaches and wagons must have passed through them. In the foreground was a large, open room, very old, with a floor of compressed dirt and cobwebby open-beamed walls and ceiling. Scattered randomly about were the machines of farm labor—some old and rusted, others still in use. A broken-down wooden wagon against one wall must have been fifty or more years old. He recognized a primitive threshing machine from a picture he had seen; it looked as if it might still be in working order. Several plows were on the floor, and a couple of other attachments for the tractor whose purpose he did not know. Neither the Austin nor the tractor was present, but the room was large enough to hold them both. In the near corner to his right, the modern era clearly predominated with the presence of tools and equipment obviously intended for working on motorized engines. An old tire leaned against the wall; a rusted-out fender and containers of oil and diesel stood nearby. *This must have been Innes's niche,* thought Logan. He had a friend who ran a small automobile garage, and it looked just like that corner.

As Logan made his way into the depths of the room, the years seemed to slowly turn back the farther he went. A stone fire pit with an ancient bellows overhead spoke of times past when a blacksmith worked with the groom to shoe horses or mend a wagon wheel. Logan wandered toward it and reached out for the wooden lever which opened and closed the bellows. It was tight with age, but he managed to force some air through it, raising a small cloud of ash dust in the fire pit.

Suddenly it dawned on him that his uncle Digory must have worked in this place, walked in day after day just as he had done, even stood on this very spot, possibly maneuvering the bellows for a muscular blacksmith who stood over a roaring fire hammering useful shapes out of crude iron.

He looked around the enclosure. Now it was no more iron shoes and iron-rimmed wooden wheels, but rubber tires and inanimate machines. No more horses and oxen and hand-driven plows, but automobiles and tractors and the mechanisms of a modern age. An involuntary twinge of sadness pricked Logan's heart with the thought. He had never considered it before, but there was something appealing about the ancient methods, something melancholy about witnessing their passing.

He took a deep breath, as if searching for the faint, lingering smells of a time now past. Then with one final glance about him and an involuntary sigh, he continued deeper into the building, arriving at length to a wall which ran from floor to ceiling. It appeared to be of relatively recent date, erected some two-thirds of the way from one end of the structure to the other, no doubt to section off the modern garage from the originally purposed stables, for which there was an ever-dwindling need.

He pushed open the door in the middle of the wall and stepped inside.

The snort of a horse startled him, but then all was quiet again except for the shuffling feet of several animals. He seemed to have taken still another step backward in time, for here were the more traditional surroundings of agrarian life. No doubt this was the place where his uncle had spent most of his time. Flies buzzed about, the fragrance of sweet-smelling hay mingled with the odor of horseflesh filled the air, and an occasional snort from the equine residents broke the stillness. How many worlds apart this was from the life Logan knew on the streets of London! Yet the spell that had come over him while standing at the bellows deepened. There was something vital and elemental in the air about him. Again he sucked in a deep draught of air, but this time it filled him with an intense pleasure rather than sadness. There was a quality of earthiness here, something wholesome, something basic, something invigorating—as if here, and nowhere else, one might discover the very foundation-stone of life. Here there was quiet. Here there was peace. Here one might actually shut out the world and settle into a calmness of spirit unknown on the busy streets and fast-paced thoroughfares of life.

He thought of the stately grandeur of the castle he had just left, which stood not a hundred yards away. Though the people occupying it might seem rather docile, the castle itself emanated a severe, even harsh sense of authority. There it stood, cold, immovable, unfeeling—a sentinel to times past, a reminder of turbulent and violent times in Scottish history. What had Lady Margaret quoted? "Child of loud-throated war . . . !" All the crystal and satins and velvets could not hide the grim undercurrent of stormy and self-motivated violence that had characterized so many eras of Scotland's past, giving birth to the many castles such as this one.

Yet in the midst of that formidable tower of unbending might, surviving alongside it, stood this stable—a soothing, protective element against the grimness of the castle itself. With the thought, Logan was reminded of the words Lady Margaret had spoken at dinner that first evening.

"I spent many hours in Digory's stable," she had said. "I loved horses, but perhaps even more I loved the peace and respite it offered me." Digory had been her only real friend, she had said, and she had longed for his world to be hers. But always she had been compelled to return to the sobering realities of life within the castle.

"But surely your family must have cheered the place somewhat?" Logan had asked.

At that moment a subtle change had momentarily come over her—that darkening of her eyes and faltering of the conversation. She had quickly shaken off whatever the spell had been, and curious though he had been, Logan had felt restrained from pursuing any further.

Now here he was in Digory's world, that place which the young girl had shared with him and longed to be more a part of. Did the man himself somehow embody the very qualities of the place? The peacefulness and serenity and calm? Why had Lady Margaret as a child sought out his uncle?

Musing over these thoughts, Logan strolled past the stalls where the horses were kept. Many were empty now, a further reminder that the estate was not what it once had been; but there were five or six fine specimens: two grand bays, a black mare with three white socks, and a trim chestnut he knew must be a thoroughbred. He began to move on, then stopped at the chestnut's stall and reached in to rub her silky nose. She whinnied and stamped her hoof.

"I'd bet you'd turn a pretty penny at Epsom," Logan said aloud.

"We've only raced her locally," came a voice behind him.

Startled, Logan turned sharply. "Lady Margaret . . . good afternoon."

"I'm sorry to have startled you."

"I must have been too absorbed to hear you coming."

"You have an eye for good horseflesh."

"I've spent some time at the racetrack." He patted the mare again. "What's her showing been?"

Before replying, she held out an open hand to the animal, revealing two lumps of sugar. The chestnut lapped them greedily and stamped her foot again. "She came off quite well," Lady Margaret continued, "a national champion. But I'm afraid the racing circuit is rather strenuous on both beasts and owners. Last year we decided to breed her instead. Come here."

Glowing with eagerness, she took Logan's free arm and led him to the next stall. "There's her foal. A beauty, isn't he?"

Still only a mangy colt, the animal nevertheless showed in every powerful sinew the evidence of noble breeding. The young stallion was a deep amber color with a pale tan star on his nose.

"He's magnificent!" said Logan, and the awe in his voice was genuine. "You really ought to race him!"

Margaret laughed with his enthusiasm.

"Why, you should hire someone to take him around. I'd beg for the job myself if I knew anything about horses."

"He's already been sold." She spoke the words sadly, even regretfully. Logan sensed that the animals meant far more to her than a mere business enterprise.

"Did Digory teach you to love horses so?" asked Logan. Had he been able to analyze the change, he would have been surprised to find that the question sprang from a real desire to know the answer rather than as part of his scheme. Subtly, he was being lured into an affinity for this life he had unwittingly become part of.

"Digory emanated such a love for everything that I suppose it was bound to rub off," replied Lady Margaret. "I had almost forgotten how much he meant to me. Somehow, your coming here brought it all suddenly back. He was the first one to call me *Maggie* when I was still a child, barely able to walk."

She paused, the memory clearly an emotional one. Her eyes filled with tears, then she laughed. Logan joined in with her.

"Oh, Logan, I can't think of him without wanting to weep! It makes me happy and sad at the same time. He was such a good man. He taught me about so much besides horses."

"How was that?"

"Mostly by his life. He was not a man of many words or great intellect. But he lived what he believed, and I think it shaped me as a child more than anything else in my life. My mother used to scold me, saying it was unseemly for me to spend so much time with a common groom, much less receive instruction from him. Though deep down, she liked Digory too.

Everyone did, possibly with the exception of my father, though I think even he bore Digory a kind of respect. Digory couldn't help what he did. He was not trying to foist anything off on me. Just being around him was a learning experience. Sometimes he didn't have to say a word. You could see in the way he treated the animals, or in that glowing peace which was always in his eyes, that there was a difference in him not found in the average man. So many in our station of life look down on what they call the common man. But often real common-ness lies in those the world counts greater. True nobility is a matter of the heart, Logan. And I can tell you, your uncle Digory was no common man. He was a true aristocrat. When he spoke, every word possessed substance and came from a heart of love."

"Then he was an educated man?"

"Oh no, by no means," replied Margaret. "I doubt he ever read a book in his life, except for his Bible, of course. But then, that was the only book he ever needed. From it he gleaned the words of life, and those he imparted to others, especially to me, with more profound and simple wisdom than I've heard from many a clergyman."

"I wouldn't doubt that," Logan replied with more than a touch of cynicism.

"Are you a religious man, Logan? . . . I may call you Logan, may I not?"

"Of course. Please do!" Logan said, nodding. "I haven't been inside a church," he went on, "since the last time a pompous vicar told me I'd better mend my ways or go to hell. I was fourteen at the time and figured my ways didn't need mending."

"And are you still of that mind?" she asked simply. Her tone was benign, almost inno-cent, but he knew what she was driving at.

"I'm not saying I'm perfect," he countered defensively, "but I'm no less perfect than anyone else, especially that vicar. What would Digory have said to that?"

"Probably nothing," replied Lady Margaret.

Logan was noticeably astonished by the answer.

"In all the time I knew him," she went on, "I never heard him argue morals or theology with anyone. I suppose he understood that you couldn't get someone to believe or to see the holes in their own values by badgering them to death. Only God, not man, can change a person's heart."

"Then what's the use of sermons and preachers and churches and all that rigmarole?"

"Sometimes very little. But we never know the vehicle God may use in making His changes—it might occasionally even be something as outlandish as a sermon in church."

As she finished speaking, a small smile crept onto her face and it gradually broadened into a mischievous grin. Logan grinned, too. He hated to admit it, but he liked the old lady's style. Then she continued, "Tell me, Logan, do you believe in God?"

"Sure," he answered quickly. Too quickly, for it was in the manner of one who had never really given the question about what belief in God might entail, and still didn't care to think about it.

"I'm sure that would have pleased Digory," replied Margaret, not allowing her voice to reveal that she knew perfectly well what was behind Logan's answer.

They had begun to walk toward the farther end of the stable, and presently came to a steep stairway in the most distant corner. It was in a state of considerable disrepair, and from the dust and cobwebs covering it, Logan surmised that it had not been used in many years. He glanced toward the top, but saw only a closed door.

"That's where Digory lived," said Margaret, noting his interest.

"Really?" said Logan, his original scheme suddenly reemerging into prominence in his mind. He studied the stairway again, this time with heightened interest. The steps were nar-row and steep, and there was no evidence they had ever had a railing. *For an old man,* he thought, *it looks rather unsafe.*

"Does that surprise you?"

"I suppose I would have thought that a servant held in such high regard would have warranted something . . . better."

"It was only I who had any special regard for Digory. Nonetheless, this was where he *chose* to live. He loved his horses, and no doubt he also loved the sounds and smells of the stable itself, as I did myself. Only I wasn't fortunate enough to live right here."

"How long did he work at Stonewycke?"

"All his life," replied Margaret. "His father was groom here before him. Digory sort of inherited the position."

"That was all he inherited," he said wryly, almost to himself, and when he realized what he had said, he immediately regretted it. "Forgive me," he added quickly. "I didn't mean—"

She smiled. "You're right, though. It doesn't seem like much for a man who gave his entire life in service to a family—a tiny, drafty room above a stable. No possessions to pass on except an old black Bible. Not much of a fortune, wouldn't you say?"

Logan's heart perked up immediately at the word. He glanced up and returned the look in Lady Margaret's eyes for a moment. *Is she baiting me? What could she possibly know?* he thought. "A Bible, you say . . . ?" he said at length.

"Yes. I won't easily forget that," she replied, glancing again up the stairs. Her voice contained no hint of hidden motive. Gradually Logan relaxed. *It must have been nothing,* he said to himself. "It was quite worn with use," she went on, "I remembered once when he became ill, he asked me to read to him from it. I wonder what ever became of it?"

"I believe I may have it," said Logan. He almost wondered at himself for being so free with the information. Yet what reason could he have to conceal it? And it would only go the worse for him if it was later discovered that he'd said nothing after the Bible had been mentioned.

"You . . . ?" said Margaret.

"Yes. There was an old Bible among my mother's possessions. In a chest of family heirlooms, that sort of thing."

"Of course," mused Margaret. "I suppose when he died, someone must have packed up his few belongings and sent them to his relatives."

"Yes, I imagine so. It was the Bible, in fact, that put me on course to Port Strathy."

"Would it be possible for me to see it? It would mean a great deal to me."

"By all means. Alec was kind enough to retrieve my belongings from the inn, so I'll get it for you when I return to my room."

They continued walking about the stable, admiring the horses once again, and Logan was wondering how best to bring up the subject of the room again. Perhaps he was being overly cautious. It would be no more incongruous for him to want to take a peek at Digory's room than for Lady Margaret to request a look at his Bible. But before he had a chance to verbalize his request, she brought up the subject herself.

"You must want to see Digory's room as much as I want to see his Bible," she said. "To be perfectly truthful, I would very much like to see it again myself. I haven't been in there since that time he was ill."

"Never?"

"I left Scotland rather suddenly shortly afterward, and then I was gone some forty years. When I returned . . . well, I hate to admit it, but I hadn't given it much thought until now. While Digory's presence remained with me, some other things grew rather dim. And of course, the general disrepair of the place, not to mention my age, has discouraged exploration."

"So no one has been up there in all that time . . . ?" Logan tried to sound casual, but he feared a slight tremor in his voice might betray his eagerness.

"I'd see no reason for anyone to. We certainly didn't need the space for anything. Of course someone had to gather his things when he died."

"Yes, that's true . . ."

"My mother, probably."

"Lady Atlanta?"

"My, but you are well versed in our family history already!"

"I just try to pay attention," laughed Logan.

Since the revelation of the room, Logan had harbored the hope that perhaps Digory had simply hidden the treasure in his own private little flat above the stable. Perhaps it was not too bright a move, but then Digory was a simple man whose whole world seemed to be his horses and that black Bible. He might not have been cunning enough to think of a more creative spot. Could it be possible that he had hidden it in a manner that anyone superficially gathering his belongings would have overlooked it? And overlooked any clues he might have left, hoping for young Maggie's return? If no one had disturbed anything since then . . .

He had to get into that room!

Suddenly his mind reeled from the idea which would make him a rich man. As calmly as he was able, he turned his gaze from the broken stair and back again toward Lady Margaret.

"I was wondering," he began, "and it may be an entirely presumptuous thing for me to even ask, but Mrs. MacNeil mentioned that I was to receive room and board as part of my wages. Would you think it might be possible for me to stay in Digory's old room?"

Margaret smiled. Why the idea struck her as so perfect, she could not tell. Was it because this young man was of the same blood as her dear old friend? She could not deny that she felt a peculiar bond with him. She had almost from the very first. Thus, it was right for him to live where Digory had spent most of his simple existence. And who could tell, she reflected further, but that some of the old man's life, the life of the spirit. might yet haunt the place and turn the young man, still a boy in so many ways, toward Digory's God, who had become her own God as well?

"I think it would be very possible," she answered at length. "The steps will have to be repaired of course, and the room cleaned up no doubt."

"I can do the work myself," he offered, perhaps too eagerly.

"I'll send someone over to help you. You'll not want to do a great deal until your leg heals."

"Thank you, Lady Margaret," Logan replied sincerely. "This means a great deal to me."

She left him in high spirits over the prospects of seeing her old groom's room made habitable again.

Logan continued to stare up at the closed door at the top of the stairs, then leaning his cane against a wall, tried to pry loose a couple of the boards that seemed to be rotten. Most of the framing was still sound. It wouldn't take much to make the stairway fully navigable.

Again, he had to compliment himself on the perfect setup. Even if the treasure was not up there, the place might reveal any number of clues. According to Lady Margaret, the old fellow was nothing less than a saint. What would a man like that do with a treasure? But actually Logan did not believe in saints—everybody had an angle. What had been Digory MacNab's? It could not have been pure goodness of heart—Logan found such a notion difficult to swallow. But then, why hadn't he touched the treasure for his own use? More than likely the old duffer had died waiting for the loot to cool off enough for him to use it. But that wouldn't explain the cryptic letter to Maggie.

The whole puzzle was perplexing.

But was it really necessary to figure it all out? It hardly mattered what the man's motives were, except insofar as it might lead Logan to the location of the treasure. Yet in spite of himself, he could not help being profoundly struck by the ambiguous complexity of the man who was his ancestor. He had to keep telling himself that the man's personality had nothing to do with it. It didn't matter if he was a saint or sinner. No matter what he was, it would surely please him greatly to see his great-great-great nephew prosper for a change.

Engrossed in thought, Logan heard, barely in time, the squeak of the door between garage and stable. He grabbed his cane and spun around.

27 *Heated Words*

IT WOULD RAIN before the day was out, but Allison thought she would have a couple of hours for a ride.

Every heir to the Stonewycke legacy could ride, and Allison was no different. She didn't care that much for horses, but riding did prove some distraction from the nearly intolerable prison that home had become.

As she walked through the old wooden stable doors, still standing open, she thought of the days long past when her great-grandmother had been a girl, when Stonewycke's stable boasted the finest stock in several shires and a full staff to care for them—groom, stable boys, and blacksmith.

Today there were only six horses. All good ones, certainly. But there was no staff to speak of. Her father—she shuddered at the thought—cared for the horses, and Nat and a couple of the field hands cleaned out the stable when they could be spared. Mr. Dougall looked in from time to time, but when Allison thought of her father feeding and rubbing down horses, and her brother, who might one day bear the family title, mucking out the stalls, she wanted to scream.

None of the other families she knew lived like that. The Bramfords had a far smaller estate, but it was fully *and* properly equipped. Imagine Edward Bramford IV sweeping up horse droppings! The thing was inconceivable. Her mother preached about hard times and economy, but Allison knew her parents really, deep inside, *enjoyed* living this way. They would have carried on as commoners even if Stonewycke were as prosperous and mighty as it had been in its days of glory.

Someday, she thought, *I may, as Mother said, be the mistress of Stonewycke. And then things will be different!*

As she yanked the door open into the interior of the stable itself, she noticed a light on. Perhaps there'd be someone around, after all, to saddle up her mount.

"Hello," she called, "is anyone in here?"

"It's me, Miss MacNeil," said Logan, hobbling out from the corner. "Good afternoon."

She nodded curtly and walked to the saddle rack where she began to examine several before selecting one. She started to lift it off, then cast a quick glance at Logan.

"Do you mind, Mr. Macintyre?"

"Of course not," he replied, "that is, if you're in no hurry." He smiled slightly and held up his cane to remind her of his infirmity.

"Oh, I had forgotten. I'm sorry." Rather than remorse, her voice seemed to contain a note of annoyance.

Logan, however, was determined to be friendly. Although this girl was the most tedious person he had met in a long while, he was not going to let her sour disposition intimidate him.

"Please, Miss MacNeil," he said, "everyone around here seems to be calling me Logan. Why don't you do the same?"

"Mr. Macintyre," she replied haughtily, "I hope the congeniality of my family does not cause you to forget who you are, and who *we* are. And I especially hope you do not plan to take advantage of their kindness. You are an employee here, nothing more. And it would be wise for you not to forget your *place*."

For a brief moment he could only gape in astonishment at the rebuke.

The next moment he burst into a great laugh. She could not mean it! It was altogether too ridiculous!

"How dare you laugh at me!" she cried in a passion of anger.

"My . . . my place! Ha, ha, ha—don't you know that sort of thing went out with Victoria? Ha, ha!"

"Maybe it went out on the back streets you call home," Allison said, still enraged, "but persons of proper breeding still know to whom their respect is due."

If there was one thing Logan despised it was snobbery. He believed that he was as good as any man, pauper or king. He refused to take arrogance without countering it, especially when it was directed at him. This attitude had gotten him into trouble before, and no doubt would again.

His laugh subsided quickly and he glared back at Allison. His next words were controlled and cool. "And I suppose you think you are just the one to remind me of my *place*?"

"If I must."

"It's you, *my lady,* who needs to be put in her place. And I think *I'm* the one who's going to have to do that!" Though he, too, was angry by now, his tone was measured, and not without a touch of tongue-in-cheek. But Allison did not enjoy his humor, especially that it came at her expense.

"You dare!" she seethed. "I will have your job."

"It would be well worth it, *my lady,"* he replied. "To lose my job in order to see you put in *your* place, I would consider it a more than equitable trade."

Allison rankled at his sarcastic use of her title, and Logan, thoroughly enjoying her reaction, continued. "I must be honest with you, *my lady*; it's high time someone was. You are the worst snob I have ever known, Miss Allison MacNeil."

"How dare you!" she shrieked.

"Whatever you may think," he went on, "being a Duncan does not give you the right to walk around treating people like dirt. If you hadn't noticed, this is the twentieth century. We are not your feudal serfs."

"I don't have to listen to this!" she fumed. "Leave this stable at once!"

"And if I don't?" said Logan, leaning back against the saddle rail and cocking his head slightly to one side.

"Leave this place at once!" repeated Allison. "You have no rights here. I command you to leave!"

"You command me!" laughed Logan. "You are so insufferable I can hardly keep from laughing. You're living in the Dark Ages, Miss MacNeil."

In a white heat of passion, Allison grabbed a saddle off the rack and marched down the row of stalls, stopping at the black mare's. She heaved the saddle onto the horse, who stamped its foot, none too pleased at the brusque treatment. She began to untie her, thinking to lead her outside and saddle her there.

But Logan, not yet finished, hobbled after her. "Do you mean to tell me I'm the first person to inform you of this flaw in your character?"

Dropping her hand from the latch of the stall door, her only response was a furious but speechless expulsion of breath.

This conversation had not gone as Allison had intended. After impressing him with her superiority, she had planned to relent just a bit, grant him the privilege of calling her by her first name, and perhaps even invite him along on her ride. Now she was too enraged even to speak.

With fingers none the nimbler, trembling uncontrollably, Allison attempted to secure the saddle. She gave the girth such a taut yank that the mare jerked away. But with Logan's final words she spun around, looking as full of energy as the lively filly she was saddling.

"Flaw in my character!" she repeated indignantly. "Who do you think you are that you can talk to me like this!" Her voice had grown icy cold and full of the imagined pride of her superiority, as if she dared him to venture an answer.

With the change, Logan had suddenly seemed to have enough. He could never out-argue or out-yell someone so passionate and volatile as this. Maybe she would listen to reason.

His tone moderated and his voice softened. "Who do I think I am? I'm just someone who was trying to be friendly," he said. "I only suggested that you call me by my first name, not that we marry and spoil the precious Duncan bloodline."

She bristled, and he quickly added, "I suppose I was only hoping that your cool and formal behavior toward me did not spring out of something personal you might have against me. And I thought perhaps if you called me by name—"

"Personal?" she asked, cocking her eyebrow, confused but wary. "I have no reason to have anything personal against you—I hardly know you. It's you who has been making personal remarks, when *you* hardly know *me.*"

He nodded thoughtfully at her point, then said, "However, I gathered from what you said that I might not be good enough for you to become acquainted with."

She restrained a satisfied smile. He was attempting to concede, to back down. He *did* acknowledge her superiority after all.

"Well . . ." she answered, drawing the word out in a coquettish manner, "I might make an exception—with you."

"You would!" He clasped his free hand to his heart and beamed stupidly. "You really would do that—for me?" He was mocking her, but she did not catch it at first.

"Why, of course," she began, "I don't see why I shouldn't—"

Suddenly she stopped, seeing his face, which could contain itself no longer, at last break out into a smile.

Realizing she'd been the butt of his joke, she tried to stammer out something further. But taken so off her guard, nothing would come, and the next words were Logan's.

"Why? you ask." His laughing had given way to a brutal seriousness. "Because, my lady, it's you who's not good enough for *me!*"

His cruel words were meant to sting, and they hit Allison all the more severely when he spun hotly around and limped away. She wanted to scream something after him, the final insult which would put the lowlife in his place. But she wouldn't give him the satisfaction. She let him think his words didn't bother her at all. Which they didn't, of course!

She stared silently after him, and when he reached out to open the rear door of the stable which led outside, she suddenly noticed his limp, favoring his right foot. Hadn't it been the left that was injured? She continued watching in silence until the door had closed behind him, then ran quickly toward it and peered out through a crack. There could be no mistake: he was favoring his right foot, putting his weight on the left. How curious! She'd have to observe him again, later in the day, to see if the limp of their new mechanic had changed.

Slowly she walked back to the stall and turned her attention to the mare, finished saddling her, then walked her outside and mounted.

What could the man's game be, anyway? Why fake an injury? To get the job? It hardly seemed reasonable. He hadn't appeared that desperate for work. Her parents almost had to beg him to take it. Why then? Was he trying to ingratiate himself to the family? He had certainly not tried to get into her good graces with his behavior today!

She'd have to watch him and say nothing to her family. Nor would she confront Macintyre. At least not yet. She would bide her time for now. With someone as arrogant and self-assured and plain-spoken as this man, she would want some distinct advantage over him. In the meantime, she would keep her eyes open and try to find out what he was up to. Perhaps she ought to get on friendly terms with him. That might not be so easy after the things they had said today. But if he confided in her, there could be no telling what she might discover. And if she went to her parents with something definite against him, it might teach them to respect her opinion a little more.

She dug her heels into the mare's flanks and galloped off, eagerly anticipating the days ahead. The challenge of a bit of mystery was always invigorating—especially when the prey was such a cocky beast. Yes, the next few days and weeks might prove most interesting. And if nothing else, her schemes would relieve her boredom.

28 ❈ The Hunt Begins

IT TOOK TWO days, with the demands of Logan's other new duties as Stonewycke's mechanic, to repair the stairs to Digory's room. He had done most of the work himself, since spring planting had required the attention of the other hands. Thus when he had hammered the final board into place, he was all alone.

He gingerly navigated the steps, not out of fear either for their weakness or that of his ankle, but out of anticipation of what lay beyond the closed door at the top. What might his uncle's room reveal to him? Would this prove the end of his quest? He had but to turn the latch to find the answer.

He reached out, placed his hand on the ancient iron bar, twisted it downward, and pushed open the rough-hewn door, creaking on its hinges, nearly decayed from disuse. The light inside was dim and shadowy. High on the adjacent wall was a single window, large enough only to admit a whisper of the morning's light that shone outside. Logan had come prepared for near-blackness, and now he held aloft the kerosene lantern he had been carrying in his other hand. Suddenly a rapid fluttering sound filled the room. Logan stepped aside and ducked as a bat flew directly toward him, missing his head by inches, escaping through the door into the stable.

The large room was covered with a thin dirt-film from neglect, with cobwebs hanging everywhere. Stepping fully inside, Logan saw that there were in actuality two rooms. The one in which he stood contained a small cast-iron stove and a bed with a rat-eaten straw mattress. The other, little more than an alcove where the roof of the stable sloped down to the floor, but in which a small gable added enough height to stand at the near end of the room, contained a rough pine table and a single chair. An empty shelf had probably contained books or eating utensils. Between the two rooms stood a wide-open doorway. Two people would have felt extremely cramped in these quarters, but for a single man, with simple tastes, it might be satisfactory.

At least, thought Logan dryly, he had holed up in worse places in London. He set the lamp on the table and walked about, coughing as his feet stirred up years of settled dust. Everything he touched was covered with a thin layer of gray. But of one thing he was certain—there were no personal items lying about that might have belonged to old Digory. Whoever had cleaned out this room had done a thorough job years ago. They appeared to have left nothing but dirt and dust. Still, he remained undaunted. He would clean away the dirt and see what might lie beneath.

Logan turned and bounded down the steps to fetch a broom. By now he had abandoned his cane and any pretense of a limp. When he saw Lord and Lady Duncan approach the stairway, he did not panic, only slowed to a gait which might be considered respectable for one so recently recovered from an injury such as his. He was pleased to see them, for he had feared his employment might slow up his interaction with Lady Margaret as he became more of a fixture around the place.

"We heard you were nearly done with the repairs to the stairs," Lady Margaret said.

"Just nailed on the last board a moment ago," replied Logan, grinning with enthusiasm.

"Lady Margaret has not rested since you began your work," said Lord Duncan. As he spoke he glanced merrily at his wife and gave her hand an affectionate squeeze.

"Well, sir," replied Logan, "the work on the stairs may be finished, and I believe the steps are sound enough for you to venture a trip on them. However, my lady, it is terribly dusty up there. I was, in fact, on my way to get a broom just now."

"You seem to be getting along on your ankle quite well. A remarkably quick recovery," said Dorey.

"Yes . . . I suppose it was," said Logan. "It's feeling almost back to normal now."

"A little dust won't hurt me," said Margaret, not to be deterred from her mission. "And once you have cleaned up the place and moved in yourself, I wouldn't dream of intruding upon your privacy."

"That would hardly be a problem," said Logan. "You may feel free to intrude upon me any time. But I can understand how you would want to see it as it is."

Standing aside, Logan allowed them to proceed up the stairs; then he followed. Lady Margaret walked first through the open door, and soon all three were standing in the midst of the small main room. Turning around, Lady Margaret surveyed her surroundings, and a vague look of disappointment gradually came over her face.

"What is it, my dear?" asked Lord Duncan, closely in tune with his wife's moods.

"I don't know exactly what I expected," she replied. "I should have realized that a room is nothing more than that—walls and a few sticks of furniture. Without even an article of his lying about, it's almost lost all connection to him. I suppose I had hoped for some sweet memories to be rekindled. But there is nothing of Digory left here—it's only a room."

Then she turned expectantly toward Logan. "More than in these four walls, his memory resides in you, Logan. And that's how it should be. The legacy a man or woman leaves is propagated through his descendants, not through his possessions; through the emotions and spiritual values he passes on, not through the things he owned. Digory had no children of his own. But somehow I think you are meant to be his progeny—the one to carry on his memory."

Logan swallowed hard.

She made it sound like a great honor had been bestowed upon him—to sustain the memory and legacy of a great man, who was, in fact, nothing more than a common groom, a poor man who lived a life of comparative insignificance. Yet she indeed did see him as nothing less than great, a man worthy of all admiration and respect and honor.

Despite his efforts to harden his heart against intrusion, Logan could not keep from squirming under the responsibility her statement placed upon him. He found he could not easily brush aside her words. Then he thought of something.

"Wait here a moment," he said, as he turned and hurried down again to the stable, where he had already deposited his carton of belongings.

When he returned a minute later he was carrying an ancient and worn black book—Digory's Bible. Except for his removal of the letter, it was exactly as he had found it in Glasgow.

"Oh dear," said Lady Margaret as she took it into her hands. Her lips trembled as she tried unsuccessfully to speak. At last, with effort, she said, "He would sit over there," she pointed a hand toward the alcove, "at the table, the lamp sitting almost exactly where it sits now, with this book open before him. Dear Lord . . ." she closed her eyes and smiled. "I can almost hear his soft voice with its thick brogue as he would read to me when I was a child. I could hardly understand him.—But Digory . . . the words remained within my heart, and they grew and flowered, as you knew they would. I hope you can see the fruits of your undaunted faith . . ."

"He does, my dear Maggie . . . he does," murmured Dorey.

There ensued a long silence among the three, each who had come for his own reasons to that bare room where had dwelt a simple man of faith. Even Logan was caught up in that moment of poignant reflection. He glimpsed old Digory for the man he was, the man he himself had tried so hard not to see. He could visualize him just as Lady Margaret had described, bent over his Bible, his wrinkled lips saying the words that were so precious to him, hoping that somehow he could touch others. But he probably would not have given himself credit to think that anything about his own life would have had a lasting impact on others so many years later. All at once it occurred to Logan that the old groom would hardly have relished the idea of one such as Logan being his only progeny. If Digory had been such a saint, the notion of a con man like him being his descendant hardly seemed right.

But Logan shook himself free from the spell. He could not let himself be influenced by the lady's tender memories. He forced his mind back onto his ignoble course, realizing even as he did so that such an action was becoming harder and harder. The more caught up he became in the personalities of Digory and Lady Margaret, and the more the whole aura of this stable and these people and the whole of Stonewycke itself settled around him, the less easily he could shake off faint hints of something speaking to him that he had ignored all his life—the voice of his conscience. Was this place getting to him? No! He would not admit that. He had his job to do, and this was just one more obstacle to be overcome. If the problem were his conscience, he could deal with it as he had with Chase Morgan.

Yet . . . these people were not easy to dismiss—the ghostly image of Digory MacNab, no less real and compelling at this eerie moment than the Lady Duncan who stood right before him. But he had to dispel these thoughts, these feelings of fidelity and honor and respect for the dead. There was too much at stake. And as he tried to convince himself to remain on course with his original purpose, he did not wonder that he could be so greedy, nor did he even attach to his attitude that heinous label. But despite his resistance, the low, soft, persistent voice of his conscience and the One who created the conscience were moving closer and closer to the heart of Logan Macintyre.

The next words he spoke came from his lips with great difficulty, as if he knew the deceit that was in them, spoken as from a man who was trying desperately to pull his mind out of a deep trance.

"I wish I had your memories to draw from," he said, his voice feeling thick and heavy in his mouth. But an opportunity like this might not come again, and he had to find out all he could before this window to the past closed up and was gone.

"And I wish there were a better way for me to share them with you," said the lady. "He so loved his horses, as well as his Bible," she went on in a dreamy tone. "I remember how he pampered our two horses, Raven and Maukin. Do you remember them, Ian?"

The old man nodded, tears standing in his eyes. "Remember? How could I forget what those two horses meant to the two of us?"

"I think that's why they were so special to Digory. I think he took pride in those two above all the others because of you and me, dear."

"No doubt you're right," said her husband.

"But in a way, the horses were his whole life in those later years," continued Margaret. "I hardly remember him leaving the stable."

"Never?" said Logan in surprise.

"At least not often. He was so old, even when I was a girl. He cared for the horses, but there were younger men to do the driving and riding. He was so arthritic. There was one time, however . . ."

Suddenly she retreated, as if an exposed nerve had been touched, a memory too painful to speak of casually.

But Logan felt instinctively that these were the very words he must hear. He might hate himself for it later, but he had to press on. "What happened?"

She glanced at her husband. Logan could not read the look that passed between them, but Lord Duncan's brow knit tightly together.

"We rode out to the granite pillars of Braenock Ridge," she answered, as if she were making herself answer because she did not want to be ruled by dark memories. "I should never have made him go, but . . . I needed his help . . . I couldn't do it alone. I . . . think that's why he became ill later. It was an awful night."

The old man reached out and touched her arm tenderly. The sense that she had caused his sickness had obviously been a pain she had borne a long time.

"Braenock Ridge?" queried Logan. "Is that around here?"

"A few miles to the south," answered Lady Margaret, composing herself.

"Not a nice place," put in Lord Duncan grimly. "It grows only gorse and wiry heather and that only on the bit of soil between the rocks. The rest is dreary peat moor intermingled with treacherous bogs."

Margaret smiled at her husband, seeming to have overcome her temporary melancholy. "Spoken like a true lover of flowers and forest," she said. "But the moor has its merits. It was Digory, in fact, who instilled an appreciation for Braenock in me. He thought it might hold a particularly tender place in God's heart because it was so tenacious. You could find an occasional primrose there, but there weren't many. If you did find one, it was hardier than the ones in the valley. It did not give up because of the ugliness of its surroundings, but became even more precious because of them."

"Oh, lass," laughed Lord Duncan playfully, "I shall have to take a walk and have another look at this veritable Garden of Eden of yours!"

"Yes, I should like to see it again also," replied Margaret. Then turning to Logan, she apologized. "Mr. Macintyre, I'm afraid we've taken up too much of your time with our old folks' meanderings."

"I've enjoyed every minute," replied Logan. "I should like to talk again sometime."

"By all means. And thank you for allowing us to visit your new quarters."

Logan saw them safely down the steps, then he hurried off in his own direction. He knew he had pressed the woman enough on the subject of Braenock Ridge for one day. But he had to discover more. There had been something in her tone, in the way her voice had faltered, that made him feel it imperative to explore this place which Digory had apparently thought so much of.

29 ❊ Braenock Ridge

FOR ONE INEXPERIENCED on horseback, the best way to reach Braenock was on foot. At least that was Fergie's opinion.

"What do ye want t' be goin' oot there fer, lad?" asked the factor. "Nothin' there but rocks an shrubs an' bogs fer yer horse t' break his leg on."

"Just curious," replied Logan vaguely. "Sounds like an interesting place."

"The ruin's all growed o'er."

"Ruin?"

"Aye. 'Tis what all the foreigner's be wantin' t' see oot there. A thousand years ago, maybe more, there was some Pict village there, oot by the boulders."

"Really?" said Logan, trying to appear interested in what looked to be the prelude of a boring history lecture. All he wanted to know was how to get there.

"Aye. But the village was wiped oot by maraudin' Vikings. In a single bloody massacre, so 'tis said, every man, woman, an' bairn was killed. Jist because the Vikings thought the Picts had gold . . ."

At the word Logan's interest suddenly came alive.

"Gold, you say?"

"Personally, I think the gold was jist added t' the story t' liven it up a bit. If ye ask me, 'twas all done fer a crust o' bread. That's what they did in them days."

"How would I get there?" asked Logan. "Is there a road?"

"Weel, there's a road o' sorts fer a ways. After that ye got no more'n an auld shepherd's trail, an' that's mostly growed o'er too. There be little traffic oot there these days. No one lives oot there anymore."

"You mean someone used to?"

"Jesse Cameron's daddy lived oot there when he were a lad, an' the Grants, an' the MacColls, but they moved clean oot o' the valley noo. That were years ago. No one's lived there in my time. Jist canna support life on a bog that's either too arid or too wet."

After further effort, Logan at length was able to extract sufficiently specific directions from the factor, continually interspersed with odd bits of local memorabilia. But it was late afternoon before Logan could get away from his duties to make his solitary trek to the moor.

A gray sky loomed overhead and a chilly south wind blew down from the mountains. A gust threatened his checkered cap and he reached quickly for it, planting it more firmly down upon his head. With the motion came a thought of Skittles. The pain of his death had seemed to grow distant, as had thoughts of Molly and old Billy. He wondered what they were doing. And for the first time in a long while a fleeting picture of Chase Morgan's face came into his mind. He shivered and gave a violent kick to a pebble at his feet. His revenge over the ganster had availed him absolutely nothing, after all. Even his anger had not been appeased. He knew that if he ever saw Morgan, he'd give him no better treatment than that pebble. So what good had it all done? Molly had some money to get her through a tough time. But as Billy had warned, it had not brought Skittles back. Instead, it had only separated Logan from those he cared for.

Funny, thought Logan as he walked along, how such an insignificant act as touching a hat could produce so many memories. He had been here less than two weeks. But his memories of London seemed as far removed as Lady Margaret's memories of Digory. Would he never see his friends again, as Lady Margaret had never seen Digory again after she left

Scotland nearly sixty years ago? It seemed inconceivable that he would never return to London. But then, perhaps she had felt the same way.

Lady Margaret . . .

His thoughts always seemed to come back to her. Why had she left Scotland so suddenly, as she told him? What did it have to do with the treasure? Or was it completely unrelated? He remembered that Digory had stated in his letter that the treasure had wrought so much evil. Yes, Digory would have thought it evil indeed that his dear little Maggie would have been forced to leave Stonewycke. But people such as Digory—poor, and filled with religious fancies—always saw things in black and white, always considered money evil, and blamed the ills of the world on "filthy lucre" and "mammon," as they called it. But it did not have to be that way. If Logan found the treasure, he was certain it would be different. He would make it different.

Logan was relieved of his thoughts for a time as the road steepened and he had to focus his complete attention on his steps. He left the road as Fergie had described and struck off on the shepherd's trail. The rock-strewn path crept like a beaten cur through a gray blanket of dormant heather, most of it overtaken completely by the spindly shrubbery. It was hard to imagine that in summer this whole hillside would break out into a vivid purple, like a royal robe spread out over the neglected patch of isolated ground. Now it lay grim and dank, more like a shroud than a king's mantle, and the wind whistled a lonely tune over the silent earth. Logan had to agree with Lord Duncan—it was, indeed, a dreary and inhospitable place. Beyond the abundance of heather, he could see large patches of bracken, the inevitable result of hundreds of years of overgrazing. No wonder this place was now deserted of human life, for even the poor sustenance sheepherding had provided was removed—perhaps forever.

As Logan's gaze swept the horizon, it finally rested on a misshapen heap of granite boulders jutting up from the moor about a half mile off. He veered off the path and struck a line through the heather directly toward the rocks. The spot where a band of cut-throat Vikings had murdered an entire village was an ominous place to begin his own modern-day treasure hunt, but it was the most logical one, and Logan would not be cowed by some ancient legend.

In ten minutes he had come to the foot of the granite mounds that loomed a good twenty feet above him. He looked them up and down like a mountain climber studying a new challenge. But Logan was no mountain man, and he dearly hoped he'd not be called upon to climb these, for their sides had been worn smooth by the weather. Smooth, that is, on their exposed surfaces. But they were still jagged and treacherous at the points where the huge rocks leaned upon one another in apparently random fashion. Five or six major stones stood out from the rest, none looking more inviting than any of the others.

It took him twenty minutes to circle the entire area, exploring, poking, and prodding around the overgrown heather and bracken at the bases of the silent towers. He had no idea what he might be looking for, guided only by Lady Margaret's painful memory of a day she and her groom had come out to this very place. She had said she "made" him go. What could have been the mission that had drawn her out to this desolate corner of the estate?

At length Logan sat down on a small stone. Once more he glanced all about him. On both sides of him stood the granite pillars. In front of him was a sunken little hollow, seemingly which once might have been large enough to walk into but was now all overgrown with brush. He'd looked everywhere obvious, and now had no idea what to do next. Perhaps this seeming lead out to Braenock meant nothing, was no more than a red herring in his search. Yet somehow inside he sensed that this place had something to do with the treasure, or at least had at one time. Had the Picts truly buried their gold somewhere here, only to have it discovered centuries later? And where was it now? *What were you trying to tell Maggie, Uncle Digory?* thought Logan. *She said you loved horses. And in your letter you even mentioned riding. And a cliff . . . and some path. If you moved it, then it must not be here. It must have something to do with the horses,* thought Logan; *somewhere Maggie rode, or you and she rode together. But if not here, then where?*

Finally Logan rose with a sigh.

There was nothing more he could do here. He just didn't know enough yet.

Striking out in a different direction than the way he had come, Logan walked south from the pillars several hundred yards farther, then began to descend the ridge westward, hoping to pick up the road by which he had come at a more southerly point than where he had left it. As he tramped along with no path now to guide him, he spied in the distance what looked like a broken-down house. He continued on toward it, and coming closer saw that at one time indeed it must have been one of the crofters' cottages Fergie had told him about. Fences had at one time enclosed a small garden and no doubt a modest stockade of household animals. A couple of dry stone dikes ran away from the house, standing, despite their antiquity, nearly to their original height. The house itself, like all those abandoned hovels throughout the highlands and lowlands of Scotland, was roofless but still displayed four stout, stone walls, impervious to wind, weather, and time. It was a sad and melancholy reminder of a time gone by when the land, however poor, had been able to sustain the life of those poor tenant crofters who worked it with the sweat of their brow and the love of their hands.

Could this place be where Jesse Cameron's father was born and raised? wondered Logan. *She said it was out here. And if it was, Lady Margaret had been here, too.* "She must have been well acquainted with the whole valley and the hills that surrounded it," murmured Logan. "No wonder she is so fond of horses; she must have ridden here, and all about, by the hours." *Raven and Maukin,* he remembered, *the horses she mentioned. And Digory spoke of a horse named Cinder.* If the treasure has something to do with where she rode, it could be *anywhere!*

Arriving no closer to a conclusion than when he had begun his afternoon's outing, Logan left the abandoned cottage, made for the valley road, and thence back toward Port Strathy.

30 ❈ *Telegram from the Fox*

So, MACINTYRE HAD entrenched himself in the old castle!

Ross Sprague made a hasty departure from the Bluster 'N Blow where he had gleaned this nugget of information from the talkative innkeeper. *Well, the kid is a smooth operator, indeed,* thought Sprague as he ambled down the cobbled sidewalk of Strathy's main street. He would never have thought that Macintyre could have managed to get that close to the town's resident nobility. He wondered how he had done it, and if it meant he was any closer to the treasure.

It had been only a few days since Sprague's arrival in Port Strathy, and nothing of great import had occurred. He had managed to keep tabs on his young quarry mostly by listening in on the village gossip and occasionally asking a few innocuous-sounding questions. It seemed Macintyre had been making quite a name for himself around the card tables, and despite the fact that he had recently fleeced several of the locals, he appeared to be held in rather high regard. He had become a regular mascot on one of the fishing boats and now was setting up housekeeping with the town highbrows.

Well, Logan Macintyre, thought Sprague as he turned into the mercantile, *enjoy it while you can—it won't last.*

Sprague got no particular thrill out of hurting people. When it came time for him to walk in and ruin all of Logan's hard-wrought labors and plans, he would feel no sense of elation or particular pleasure. In fact, he would probably not feel a thing. He never became emotionally caught up in his work, and was thus considered by some as downright cold-blooded. But a man didn't get ahead by allowing his emotions to rule him, he reasoned. And that's exactly what Sprague's goal was—to get ahead. He would do whatever was necessary to achieve that end. Tailing a kid from London was nothing compared to what one of his particular calling was usually asked to do. He expected his boss would have him let Macintyre find the treasure, and then Sprague would jump in at that moment and take possession. It was a pretty standard plan that should work, especially with a man like Sprague in command. He was neither greedy, nor angry, nor vengeful—emotions that usually fouled up even the best-planned scheme.

Sprague suspected his boss's interest in this whole affair had roots in the nonreasonable—revenge was the most likely candidate. Probably something had happened years ago and he felt he had some score to settle. But that was hardly Sprague's concern. He was a man who could do his job. He'd walk in, cool as you please, and take what he came for. He'd do whatever he had to. If it meant not only retrieving the treasure but also getting rid of Macintyre, well, so be it. It wouldn't be the first time. Sprague was not squeamish. This Macintyre kid was not a bad sort. Sprague had known a lot worse in his business. But that would not prevent Sprague from successfully completing his assignment.

And he was ready to find out exactly what that assignment was going to be. He didn't like working in the dark, as his boss was forcing him to do on this case. With this sudden change in Macintyre's living situation, things could start happening pretty fast, and Sprague wanted to be prepared.

He walked up to the cluttered counter. The woman behind it was about his own age, although her rough appearance made her appear older. She was seated in an old captain's chair thumbing through a catalog of boats and fishing equipment.

"Mornin' t' ye," said Jesse Cameron, filling in while Olive Sinclair stepped out for a moment.

"Hello," said Sprague in a tone not unpleasant, but nonetheless laced with a certain arrogance. "I was told you have a telegraph here."

"Aye we do." She laid aside her catalog and rose, motioning him to follow. "Olive put it back here," she added as they entered a small back room crowded with a roll-top desk, stacks of cartons, and a narrow table which held the telegraph equipment. "It doesna get too much use in these parts, but the auld laird had t' hae one." Jesse blew away a layer of dust to punctuate her point. "Jist fix yer message doon on this," she went on, handing him a small piece of paper.

Sprague cleared a space on the corner of the desk in order to find room to write, then he chewed at the end of his pencil for a moment while he clarified in his mind the code he and his boss had settled upon. Finally he scribbled several lines on the paper and handed it back to Jesse.

"Noo, let me read it back t' ye, so's I know I hae e'ery word aright." She cleared her throat and began in an oratorical tone: "*To Hawk: The pigeon is in nest. The robins are blind. The worm remains hidden. When and how will fox strike? Signed T.H.E. Fox.*"

Jesse paused and cast a puzzled glance at her customer. "That's what ye're wantin' sent, Mr. Fox?" she asked, trying with little success to subdue the incredulity of her voice.

"Birdwatchers," Sprague offered by way of explanation. "My employer is one of those—what's the fancy name?—ornithologist, that's it! And a bit eccentric, too."

"Oh . . . I see." But the way Jesse drew out the words seemed to indicate that she did not see at all, but was willing to let the matter drop. "Noo," she went on more briskly, "Olive'll send it soon's she gets back."

"But this is urgent."

"Weel, I canna run the machine, but Olive'll be back directly."

"I expect it to go out today."

"Dinna ye worry aboot that." Jesse impaled the telegram decorously on the outgoing spindle. "I'll make sure Olive checks this first thing."

"And I'll be expecting an answer. Deliver it to Roy Hamilton's place."

Sprague turned smartly and strode from the store, leaving Jesse shaking her baffled head and wondering just what the world was coming to.

Sprague glanced at his watch. Well, if the telegraph was par with the rest of the service in this little village, he'd better not expect an answer until tomorrow. That would mean another whole day of sitting around this hick town. He'd end up going crazy before he had any real work to do. That wire might spur his boss to some action. But what could he do before Macintyre located the treasure?

Actually, Sprague hoped the telegram from London would tell him to abort the whole crazy mission. There couldn't be any treasure. And even if there was, there were certainly easier ways of earning that kind of money.

Whatever the reply to his wire, he'd have to figure out a more foolproof way to keep track of Macintyre now that he was situated at Stonewycke. He couldn't very well hang about the place without attracting attention.

Sprague decided to spend the rest of the day assessing the castle's staff. There must be at least one person out there whom he could buy, someone who could deliver regular communiques about Macintyre's activities, and especially someone who wasn't apt to run off at the mouth.

Glad for the prospect of some activity, Sprague turned into Hamilton's pub in much better spirits than when he had left an hour ago.

31 ⁂ An Unexpected Invitation

ALLISON SAW HIM in the kitchen.

But standing as he was in the dim glow of the banked fire in the hearth, with eerie shadows reflecting off his face, he looked so much like a thief in the night that she was at first timid to approach.

In the two days since their fiery conversation, she had given Logan Macintyre a great deal of thought. She had not been able to help herself. How could a man make her so angry, and yet so fascinate her all at the same time? Perhaps that accounted for some of her present timidity.

But she couldn't let this opportunity pass. She couldn't tolerate a situation in which she had no leverage, no control. Thus, something had to be done to reestablish her supremacy over him. She had been looking for him for the last twenty-four hours, always just missing him. Or at times, as now, she would come upon him unobserved, but, losing her resolve, would quickly depart.

Shyness could never be accounted to Allison MacNeil as one of her faults. Had there been a morsel of it in her personality, it would have been considered, in her case, a virtue. But shyness was not what had held Allison back, it was more a case of stubbornness and pride. It galled her to make up to him—he was such an incorrigible cad. He should be crawling to her, not the other way around. And yet the very fact that she knew he would never do such a thing almost compelled her to make the first move. She had never met anyone quite so . . . so impossibly aloof from what she considered the strength of her own personality. He could not have cared less what she thought of him. She hated him for it, of course! And yet, at the same time, she couldn't help feeling . . .

Well, she didn't know what she felt!

She just had to remind herself that there was a purpose behind her decision. She would turn the tables on him, put her feminine wiles to work, and in the end—well, whether she made sure the arrogant Mr. Logan Macintyre received his just desserts, or whether she granted him mercy . . . that would remain to be seen.

Amid such a jumble of emotions, Allison cleared her throat to announce her presence, and stepped boldly into the room as if, indeed, he were a thief and she were about to apprehend him. But when he turned to face her, she instantly softened her expression, remembering that she planned to try out a new tack on him this time.

"Good evening, Mr. Macintyre," she said sweetly. "May I be of assistance?"

"Hello, Miss MacNeil," he replied, not showing that he had been disturbed by the sudden intrusion, nor displaying his surprise at her congenial tone. "I hope my fumbling about hasn't dragged you all the way down here?"

"Not at all," she answered in her most pleasant manner. "The sounds of the kitchen hardly penetrate to the next room, much less into the rest of the house. I was simply in the mood for a cup of tea."

"I can't seem to locate the light switch," he went on, asking himself even as he said the words what she could possibly be up to by being so friendly. "The cook said I might avail myself of the kitchen if I should ever miss a meal. I'm afraid I worked up a healthy appetite today."

"It's quite a walk out to Braenock Ridge." As Allison spoke she laid her hand on the elusive light switch. The bulb flashed on as the last word escaped her lips, and the illumination revealed her dismay at having said something she would have just as well kept quiet.

"I didn't know you kept such careful track of the activities of your hired *help*."

"Well, I . . ."—the last thing she wanted him to know was that she had been asking after him—"I had need of the car and wasn't sure it was in working order." The lie was too obvious but she couldn't help that now. She probably should have come right out and told the truth at that point, but she was so unused to such honesty that it simply did not occur to her. "We had kidney pie tonight," she changed the subject adroitly. "The cook's is every bit as good cold as it is hot."

"Thank you for the advice."

Logan crossed the room to the stove, where he found a covered crock. He decided to let the slip about Braenock pass, for she was obviously flustered enough without his adding to it. What was on her mind, anyway? And why was she so nervous . . . and so friendly all at once? It was rather interesting to think that the grand Lady Allison had been asking about him. The whole thing intrigued him, and since he could find no threat in her actions, he decided to play along.

"Kidney pie!" he announced, lifting the lid of the bowl. "Shall I also put on a kettle for tea?"

"That's woman's work," she replied, bustling up to the stove as if she were actually accustomed to standing there. She checked the waterline of the kettle, then turned on the burner.

Resisting a strange urge to comment sarcastically on her uncharacteristic words, he, instead, suddenly reached out and took her hands in his.

"Funny," he said, "I would never have associated these hands with work—of *any* kind." She tensed, but did not pull away. "I'm sorry," he said, almost embarrassed now himself. "I didn't mean to startle you. But they are lovely hands. I doubt they were meant for menial tasks." Slowly, almost reluctantly. he loosened his grasp and she let her hands drop to her sides.

She then flitted, with almost too much affectation, to a cupboard where she took out cups and saucers and plates.

"And what of *your* hands, Mr. Macintyre?" she asked airily. "They do not feel like rough, workingman's hands, either."

"No. As I mentioned earlier, I have lately been busying myself in investments and finance, an occupation which develops callouses only where they cannot be observed."

"I had forgotten."

Allison set the crockery on the table, and by the time she had cut off two slabs of the kidney pie, the kettle was whistling.

"I'm glad to see that you are joining me," Logan said casually.

Allison poured the tea and they seated themselves at the old round table nestled in a warm corner of the vast kitchen. Had there been an intelligent mouse perched in the rafters above, a creature who knew the inner motives and designs of the two seated at that table, he might have thought the scene a very incongruous one indeed. Neither fit very well into the environs of a homey country kitchen, despite the fact that it was the kitchen of an ancient castle. Something about that setting, for the moment at least, seemed to soften all the rough and selfish edges both had accumulated in their short lives.

They chatted easily for a time about various inoffensive topics—the quality of the food, the castle, the weather, the horses, the countryside. Forgetting herself, Allison even laughed a time or two—a free, easy laugh. In those moments, the contours of her eyes and face seemed to change. A freshness and innocence flashed upon her. She looked as though she could be kind and warm, if only she would let herself be. And the way she tightened up immediately afterward, as if even the sound of laughter coming from her own mouth was too revealing, too threatening, caused Logan to wonder what she was hiding with the veneer of haughty distance she seemed bent on wearing.

"From the way you talk," Logan observed, "I detect that you have a deep attachment for this country."

"Does that surprise you?"

"Well . . ." he hesitated, not wanting to renew the previous tension between them.

"Speak freely, Mr. Macintyre."

"Until now I've sensed you're not particularly happy with your life here at Stonewycke."

"You're very observant." She sipped her tea as if she expected to be prodded to reveal her inner feelings.

"I see a girl who has everything, and I ask myself, what could possibly be missing that makes you so unhappy?"

"You're not going to start preaching to me, are you, Mr. Macintyre?"

"Heavens no!" He threw his hands up in mock surprise at such an idea.

"Good," she said crisply, suddenly reverting to her old self. "I get enough of that already. As if I were some kind of heathen or something."

"I think I see now," he said, drawing out the words thoughtfully. "It is the family that is the source of contention."

Allison said nothing, and there followed a moment of silence during which Logan wondered if he'd overstepped his bounds. Then suddenly she jumped up. "It's getting late," she said in a voice higher pitched than usual, apparently ignoring what he had said.

"Forgive me," he said quickly, laying his hand on her arm so she would not leave. "I spoke out of line."

"Not at all." She seemed to be struggling with whether to admit the truth in what he had said and thus allow him to see further into her real self than she had planned, or to lash out against his words in angry denial and self-defense. The mask of her outer self was momentarily stretched so thin that Logan might have seen something akin to desperation in her eyes as she wrestled with how to reply. Then just as suddenly the look vanished, and she said in a cool, controlled tone that kept her from either of the two emotion-charged extremes: "You simply made an observation, however far from the mark. Do not worry about offending me, Mr. Macintyre. My family is *wonderful.*" The final word was spoken with such an emphasis as to drain it of the sincerity inherent in the statement.

Allison wanted to flee. She didn't care for observations like his and wasn't used to such honesty. None of her friends were this open with her. She intimidated them into a sort of subservience which kept everything on a superficial level. But this man refused to be intimidated by her. And yet even as he probed in his most discomforting way, he was not without a certain sympathetic, even tender side which seemed concerned lest his—

But what was she thinking! Hadn't he been downright cruel in his outbursts in the stable earlier? *Tender? Logan Macintyre! Pshaw! The man . . . why, he is insufferable!*

She was about to frame some caustic word which would again put him in his place when the thought of her friends came again to her and made her recall her original purpose in seeking Logan out. She became calm inside, reminding herself that she could be more successful by keeping up the front. Concentrating her attention on her previous intent, she let herself forget her awkwardness under his questioning and whatever else she might feel toward him.

She sat down once more, but Logan could sense that the previous pleasant mood had retreated, and the pretense was back again in full force. The words, however, when they came from the mouth, were agreeable enough.

"I've enjoyed our conversation, Mr. Macintyre," she said, pouring out some fresh tea.

"So have I."

"I'm afraid you might have misunderstood me on our last meeting."

"I feel certain I must have," he replied.

He thought, even as he spoke, that he had understood her quite well *then*. It was *now* that confused him—this changeableness, the flip-flops of her moods, the brief glimpses of a character she seemed desperate to hide, the congeniality followed by unspoken flashes of anger. What was going on inside the hidden inner self of this attractive young girl who seemed so in need of friendship, even love, but who so violently resisted any attempt by another to draw near on a human level? She was intriguing, despite his confusion; Logan would no doubt have been highly amused to learn that her own feelings for him were very similar.

"I'd like to make that up to you in some small way," said the congenial Allison.

"If there was any need for restitution," he replied in cavalier manner, "you have already done that tonight."

"I was thinking of some other way," went on the designing and contrived Allison.

"It isn't necessary," replied the wary Logan.

"I know," she said, touching her chin as if she were uncertain how to proceed; in reality the scheming side of her nature was now fully into place. "You may even think me forward in suggesting this, but . . . I feel justified in that I'm certain you must long for the company of people your own age—everyone around here is so ancient. Well—there is to be a gathering of some of my school friends this Saturday at Lord Bramford's estate. And I thought you might like to accompany me."

Logan could not help wondering what he could possibly want with the company of a roomful of teenagers like Allison. And the way in which the invitation was phrased sounded as if she thought she were doing him a great favor in asking him. It hinted at the condescension so evident in their earlier encounters. Yet, could it be possible that she was sincere? He doubted it! Something in her tone . . .

But on the other hand, he could hardly resist such an opportunity to find out more of what made the complex Allison MacNeil tick. He could ignore the irritation stirred by her tone; after all, old habits die hard. And he was inclined to accept the invitation regardless. The enigma of this young lady was positively too fascinating, even though at the same time he was fully aware he could get burned by getting too close. Hers was not an emotional nature to be toyed with.

"That's a very kind invitation," he replied slowly, after a pause. "But I really doubt that I'd fit in."

"You deport yourself quite well—that is, you'd hardly know—"

"Hardly know I wasn't *really* of the same stock?" He shouldn't have said it, but he couldn't resist. He waited for her fiery response.

Instead, "No . . . that's not what I meant to say—I mean . . ." she said, then broke off, flustered.

He responded with a good-natured grin. Realizing that he was not disposed to making an argument out of it, she returned his smile.

"That is to say," she went on, the mask dropping again for a moment, "you would have no problem fitting in. I'm sure of it."

Logan was sure of it, too. He had mixed with such crowds before, and knew all the proper moves. How else could he be invited into the richest gambling salons or into the action around the wealthiest card tables? Still, he was hesitant. He reminded himself that he had to remain cognizant of his purpose in coming to Stonewycke, that he could not jeopardize his plan in any way, especially by becoming too involved with any of these people.

"I don't know," he said, looking her full in the eyes, seeing if he could find the real Allison somewhere.

"I'd . . I'd really like you to go with me," she said, returning the gaze.

He stared back, still wondering. *She was something!* he thought.

"I doubt your parents would approve of your being escorted by one of their employees," he said.

At this Allison laughed, and the bitterness of her tone only added to the paradox.

"Believe me," she said, "my parents like nothing better than the mixing of the classes. You needn't worry about them!"

"Well, then, if they approve, I'd be happy to escort you."

She rose.

"Now it really is getting late. Thank you."

He stood and bowed grandly. "My pleasure."

She seemed to float to the door, then stopped, turned, and added casually, as if she had just thought of the trifling matter. "The affair is black tie. I hope that won't present a problem for you."

"Not at all," replied Logan.

The young lady fairly waltzed through the corridors back to her room. She was quite pleased with herself. She had managed Mr. Macintyre quite well. But more than that—though the haughty Allison would never admit such a thing—she was extremely pleased at the prospect of being with this man. The sensitive Allison had enjoyed him immensely this evening and could almost forget that he was of low birth.

The haughty Allison hoped he'd see fit to keep that fact quiet on Saturday. She also found herself wondering what her friends would think of her dating such a person. It might even be considered rather chic, she told herself. It had always amused her friends to go "slumming," as they called it, while on holiday.

Whatever happened on Saturday, it was sure to be a memorable evening. The three days until then were positively going to drag by. At least she had gotten her new gown—not the exact one she had wanted, but close enough.

It would dazzle everyone. Including Logan Macintyre.

32 ✵ Glasgow Red Dog

THERE IS A pride often associated with those who have known poverty, a pride that can be the result of stubborn pigheadedness rather than stemming from anything noble.

Logan Macintyre possessed just such a pride, however mixed it was with a colored sense of morality. He would make his own way in the world whatever it took. No handouts for him. He would rather "earn" his money in a poker game, employing questionable methods of skill, than to take a few shillings from a sympathetic friend. Even with Molly and Skittles, he had adroitly turned their acts of charity toward him into situations of mutual benefit. If they fed him when he was penniless, he reasoned that they needed his youth and energy in order to make their various schemes successful.

Thus, when Logan assessed his meager finances immediately following Allison's invitation, he found them sorely wanting for the necessities he supposed such an occasion would require. To ask Alec, the only likely candidate, for the loan of a tuxedo was out of the question. Not only was Alec several sizes larger than Logan, but it would have been too degrading to attend such an affair in a borrowed suit. Logan was extremely conscious of appearances. What money he had possessed had always gone toward the very best in attire. His tailor in London was reputed to have outfitted the Duke of Marlborough at one time. These things were important to Logan.

Unfortunately, he did not just now have the funds to meet these standards. But he did know where he might quickly acquire them. So the next evening found him at Hamilton's place, around a coarse table with several of his recent acquaintances, among them Buckie, a few other fishers, and a farmer or two. The stakes were not high, but he needed to raise only ten or fifteen pounds, and that should be possible. So confident was Logan of his success that he had already made arrangements with a tailor in Aberdeen for a fitting, and had requested the following day off from his employment at Stonewycke.

Buckie dealt the first hand, and bets were laid on the table.

Ale and pleasant conversation, however trivial, conversation mingled with the business of poker. It was a congenial, easygoing group; none were apt to flare up angrily at their companions. Logan played a straight game, not caring whether he won or lost, just making sure he kept his stake in readiness for the real game, which would come later. He was simply lubricating the pursestrings for the time being.

Tonight Logan had a difficult time making himself forget how much he liked these simple country folks. It was especially hard to forget that Buckie had helped save his life. He would make it up to them all, he reminded himself. Now, he had to have the money, and this was the only way he knew to get it. He'd give them all a more than fair chance to win every shilling back later. But his once-benumbed conscience had been raising it's head more often of late, and it took more than a concerted effort to squelch its insistent reminders that what he was about to do was wrong.

"I'm rather tired of poker," he said at length, leaning back in his chair with a yawn. "What about something else?"

"What did ye have in mind, mate?" asked one of the men.

"You ever hear of Glasgow Red Dog?"

"Canna say I have."

"Any of the rest of you?" asked Logan, looking around the table.

They all shook their heads.

"It's simple enough really. And everyone makes just as much money as he wants. You're not even playing against each other, in a manner of speaking."

"Sounds too easy," said Buckie, with a skeptical expression.

"It is! But it's a good way to make a lot of money. That is, if you're sharp. But everyone's playing with the same chances. Shall I explain it?"

Shrugs and nods followed. Logan pulled out the cards Jesse had given him.

"Here, Buckie," said Logan, "try it. I'll deal you five cards, just like in poker." He did so. "Now, you look at your hand, and if you think you can beat the card I'm about to turn up, in the same suit, then you place a big bet, anywhere from a shilling up to the size of the pot. If you win, you collect the amount of your bet from the pot on the table. If you lose, your bet stays on the table."

Buckie surveyed his cards. He had a queen, a jack, two nines, and a six.

"What do you have?" asked Logan. Buckie laid his cards down on the table. "Well, that's a fair hand, Buckie, but not great. What do you think your chances are of beating this top card in the same suit?"

"I dinna ken," said Buckie slowly. "I'd say, maybe fifty-fifty."

"And how much would you bet?" asked Logan.

"I'd say a shillin'."

"Well, then, let's see how you'd have fared." Logan turned over the top card of the deck. "An eight of clubs. Your nine of clubs wins. You would then take a shilling out of the pot . . . or however much you had bet."

Nods of approval and general laughter spread around the table.

"What do you all say?"

"Let's gi' yer game a try," said Buckie.

"Okay," said Logan. "Everyone put in a shilling to start. Then from now on you can bet from a shilling to whatever's on the table."

Each tossed a shilling into the middle of the table and Logan dealt each man five cards. Each then took their turn betting, all starting with shilling bets, followed by Logan's displaying the top card off the deck against each hand. Two of the men won, four lost, including Logan; as the second round began, the pot stood at eight shillings, and Logan passed the deck to Buckie.

"Your deal," he said, and the game continued.

With every, successive hand the pot grew larger, occasionally dwindling temporarily when a five or ten shilling bet was won, but steadily rising. With every hand, Logan's bet remained the same—one shilling—never varying.

At the end of an hour, the table contained some four pounds.

It was now the turn of a farmer by the name of Andy McClennon. He surveyed his hand for some time, obviously in doubt, then looked at his own money in front of him, an amount of about four and a half pounds. The cards in his hands were good ones, and at length he said, "I bet the size o' the pot!"

Exclamations followed and raised eyebrows. It was the first such bet that had been made.

"The size o' the pot, man. Ye're loony!" said Buckie.

"I got nothin' smaller than a ten, Buckie, an' three faces!" said Andy excitedly. "Hoo can I lose?"

The dealer turned over the jack of hearts. Andy's face fell.

"Blimey!" he shouted in a disgusted voice, throwing down his ten of hearts onto the table. "The one low suit I had!"

"Sorry, Andy," said Logan, and general condolences were mumbled around the table.

By this time, with the judicious use of his stake money and his slight winnings from the preliminary poker game, Logan had slowly boosted his cash to approximately five pounds. For the next several rounds the mood at the table was subdued, each man greedily eyeing the money on the table, but at the same time somewhat sobered by Andy's plight. Three hands later, the first of the moments Logan had been waiting for had come. Having carefully scrutinized every card on the table before him, and holding an ace, two kings, a jack and a nine, he knew there was only one card still out—the queen of diamonds—which could beat his hand—his own nine of diamonds. Deciding the risk to be worth it, he took the chance.

"I bet four pounds," Logan announced.

"That's nearly all ye got in front o' ye, Logan," reminded Buckie.

"Ye done nothin' but one shillin' bets all the game," said Jimmy, hardly hiding his perplexity.

"Just a difference in styles, I guess," said Logan.

"An' yet noo ye're layin' doon four pounds!"

"This is just my time to live dangerously," said Logan with a laugh. "Come on, Andy, turn up the card."

Andy flipped over the top card—a king of spades. Logan's black ace was higher.

"If that don't beat all!" exclaimed Jimmy. "It's like he knew what was comin' all along."

"You all saw that Andy was dealing me straight," said Logan. gathering in his winnings, leaving eight pounds in front of him, and only four in the center of the table.

Disbelieving shakes of the head followed. However, concurrent with Andy's dejection were several eyes twinkling with renewed enthusiasm. If Logan could do it—and they all saw that the game was fair—so could any one of them. And there was still plenty of money to win. Logan had been right. You could win just as much as you wanted.

Once again bets of five or ten shillings began to flow, with now and then a one-pounder thrown in. The size of the pot ebbed and flowed, steadily rising over the course of time. And once again, hand after hand Logan's bet remained the same—a single shilling.

Still he bided his time, waiting for another opportunity, watching the cards being played like a hawk, memorizing each as it was displayed, then carefully eyeing his own hand. He now had enough in front of him to go for broke—*when* the right moment came. He could not be overanxious. He couldn't even risk it if a single card was out. He'd have to wait for what Skittles always called a lead-pipe cinch.

After another hour, the moment came. His own stash stood at about eight and a half pounds. The pot was now something slightly over seven.

The hand he'd been dealt was not all that strong on the surface of it—a king, two jacks, a ten, and a seven. It happened, however, that as Jimmy, immediately to his right, was dealing, he was the last man to play. Therefore, when time for his bet came, twenty-four cards were displayed on the table. With his own five, more than half the deck was known to him. Every heart above his seven of hearts was out, as were all the spades over his ten, and so on.

When his turn came, therefore, Logan was confident.

"I bet the size of the pot!"

"Ow!" whistled Jimmy. "Not again! Logan, ye'll put us oot o' the game!"

"Or maybe myself!" suggested Logan with a wry grin.

"Somehow I doobt that," said Andy sarcastically. He didn't exactly think this clever fellow from London was cheating. But he didn't like the idea of his betting nothing but one shilling until . . . wham!—the pot was suddenly empty.

"Weel . . . what'll it be, Jimmy?" said Buckie, anxious to get on with it.

Slowly and dramatically Jimmy lifted the card and threw it down in front of Logan.

"Ten o' diamonds!" exclaimed Buckie. "Tough t' beat, Logan!"

"Not for a king of diamonds," returned Logan, laying down his entire hand on the table beside the ten.

"Somehow I knowed it!" said Andy. "I jist knowed it!"

"Weel, lad," said Buckie, with a sigh, "I guess that's the end o' this game, seein' as hoo Logan has all oor hard-earned cash." They all began to rise, and Buckie gave Logan a friendly slap on the back. "Ye're the luckiest bloke I e'er seen!"

"I'd be happy to give you fellows a chance to get even," offered Logan, stuffing the sixteen or so pounds—mostly in coin—into the pockets of his coat.

Buckie laughed. "Na doobt . . . na doobt! But ye always seem t' come oot on top!"

"Like you said," replied Logan, "I guess I'm just lucky."

"An' I already dipped sorely int' this week's grocery cash," Buckie went on. "I'll hae the de'vil t' pay wi' me wife as't is."

Logan could not keep a pang of guilt from rising, but he quickly dismissed it with the thought, *I'll make it up to you fellows. Just you wait and see. I'll find that treasure, and I'll do right by you all.*

Andy McClennon, dour of disposition and in much less friendly tones than the others, added, "Seems t' me ye made fairly certain we'd no hae the means t' get e'en wi' ye."

"I can assure you—" Logan began, but Buckie did not give him the opportunity to finish.

"Come on, Andy," he said, laying a hand on the poor crofter's shoulder. "Dinna be a sore loser. 'Twas a fair game. We all knew what we was gettin' int'. Logan's as guid a man as one o' oor own, an' I'll be hearin' nae different. Noo, what aboot those drinks ye mentioned, Logan?"

"What! I mentioned no drinks."

"Dinna they do that in London?" said Buckie, winking knowingly at Jimmy. "Why, here in Strathy, man, the winner buys fer e'eryone!"

Logan laughed heartily. "Well, you've got me there, my friend," he said, glad to be able to buy his way graciously out of the potentially awkward situation with only a few pints.

The laughter and Buckie's good sportsmanship seemed to appease any further unrest, except perhaps in Logan's inexperienced conscience. Rising and shoving their chairs back, the rest of the group ambled over to refill their glasses, for Roy was not in the habit of serving his guests at their tables unless absolutely necessary. Bringing up the rear, Logan passed the small table where a lone customer sat, quietly sipping a brandy. Catching Logan's eye, he gave him a sly half grin.

"Those yokels don't even know what hit them," said Ross Sprague in a soft, almost conspiratorial tone.

"What do you mean by that?" asked Logan in a tone made more defensive by the guilt he was trying to repress. "There was nothing crooked about that game. We all had the same chance."

"Except that you knew the game. I can spot a sharp a mile off." But as Logan opened his mouth to speak, Sprague held up his hand. "Oh, don't worry. Your secret's safe with me."

"To what do I owe that honor?"

"You and me live by the same motto, young fellow," Sprague replied. "It was stated very succintly by an American actor, W. C. Fields: 'Never give a sucker an even break.' Why, you had that game in the palm of your hand. That last hand—you couldn't lose! Well done, I must say."

Logan shrugged noncommitally. "Leave it to an American to sum it up so well." He started forward once more.

"Have a drink on me, kid," Sprague called after him.

Logan nodded his thanks, but after the encounter, his ale did not taste very good. He didn't like to think of friends like Buckie as "suckers." He didn't like to think that he might live by such a motto, even if he had never quite put it in those words. And since he didn't like to think of such things, he didn't.

Instead, he poured more than his usual measure of Hamilton s foul-tasting brew down his throat, and for the time at least, it dimmed the pangs of his conscience.

He didn't return home that night.

Somehow the thought of that unaffected loft where his simple, honest ancestor had dwelt was not appealing to Logan just then. Instead, he staggered up the street, where Sandy Cobden, against his better judgment, rented him a bed for the night. Logan made his way up the stairs weak-kneed, fell upon the bed, and drifted into a restless sleep, filled with the kind of dreams dragons might have while perched upon their ill-gotten treasures. In fact, at one point a dragon came into his dream, dressed in a grand tuxedo, with a plain fisher wife on his arm, carrying in her other hand an empty basket, which he knew had been intended for groceries.

But even in his sleep, when the dragon turned his direction, Logan shut the eyes of his mind even tighter, refusing to look at its face.

33 ❈ *The Party*

LOGAN CALLED FOR Allison at five o'clock sharp.

He was invited by Joanna into the formal parlor where they engaged in a very awkward conversation for several minutes before Allison finally made her entrance.

He hadn't realized until that moment what a lovely *woman* she was. He had always known she was pretty, but tonight she seemed to have matured far beyond her seventeen years. Before, she had been an attractive *girl,* but now her budding womanhood was given full reign. Some of it, to be sure, was affected by Allison. But what struck Logan was the natural beauty and grace which could not be feigned, a hint of the loveliness and poise of her handsome mother. Logan could only think that what she tried to put on with grown-up airs only detracted from what naturally dwelt within.

Her golden, silky hair was piled in curls atop her head, some of them falling daintily about her face. Tufts of baby's breath were tucked about the curls like a crown. Her gown of periwinkle blue strongly resembled the one she had discovered in the catalog, only its stark severity had been softened by demurely flowing butterfly sleeves that fell to her mid-arm, and a satin belt around the waist, clasped with satin rosebuds. The overall effect had been to Allison's satisfaction, the price to Joanna's, and thus a very stunning compromise had been negotiated. An ancient strand of pearls that had been her great-grandmother's graced her lovely, porcelain-smooth neck.

At that moment, Logan did not feel so bad about his winnings of the other night. He had been to Aberdeen and had purchased a tuxedo, if not the finest evening attire to be had in that provincial city, certainly more than adequate for whatever he would encounter north of London.

There was little call for a florist in Port Strathy, but Logan had engaged Dorey's willing assistance to fashion a corsage of creamy white orchids, nurtured with love in the laird's own greenhouse. He fastened the blossoms about Allison's tiny wrist.

When he helped Allison into her rabbit-fur stole, he noted a tear glistening in Joanna's eye. He wondered if it was simply the sentimentality of a mother seeing her daughter looking so grown-up, or if it had other more remote origins. Was she having last-minute misgivings about letting her precious daughter go off with a man they barely knew? She had given her approval, but perhaps was now having second thoughts.

Well, it was too late for that now, and perhaps Joanna sensed that fact as well. For she bid them goodbye and did not even remain in the doorway while Logan maneuvered the Austin down the long drive and out through the iron gates.

The Bramford estate, located a few miles southwest of Culden, was one of those early Victorian country homes which, from the passage of years, could have either taken on a quaint historical charm, or have become a run-down white elephant. In the Bramfords' case, due to yearly maintenance and an ongoing familial interest in the estate, the former was happily true, and the home was one of the more elegant in the entire region.

The continued foul weather had prevented much in the way of outdoor festivities, and even as Logan and Allison stepped out of the Austin, leaving it to be parked by an attendant, dark clouds could be seen massing overhead. But that hardly dampened the party spirits of the young people gathered inside. Music, heavy with brass and drums, blared from the ballroom, creating a scene quite alien to the affairs the same room had seen in the days of Queen Victoria. The youths danced in a fashion that left Lady Edwina Bramford, who was positioned by the door greeting guests as they arrived, with a bewildered look on her highly refined face. She smiled thin smiles at the constant stream of arrivals, most of whom she did not even know, wondering how long her motherly duties would force her to remain in such close proximity to this unseemly display of modern merrymaking. She was from the old school, where young ladies *did not* wriggle around thus on the dance floor, and where *gentlemen* politely asked the favor of a young lady before a dance, not with a slick, "Come on, baby, let's dance." There had hardly been a polite word spoken, in her estimation, all evening. And these were the flower of the nation's populus, the offspring of the very best—lords and ladies, financial magnates, military leaders. What was the world coming to if the children of the land's elite had completely forgotten how to behave?

Thus, when Logan and Allison walked toward the ballroom door, it was little wonder that she was pleasantly surprised. Allison would have strode into the room without giving the woman a passing glance, but Logan took Lady Bramford's hand, kissed it respectfully, and bowed with what she could only consider very gallant taste.

"I am honored, my lady," he said when introductions had been made.

"We are pleased you could come, Mr. Macintyre," replied Lady Bramford. "I haven't heard your name mentioned, but you must know my son from Oxford."

"I'm afraid I haven't had the pleasure of his acquaintance, nor that of the remainder of your esteemed family."

"Mr. Macintyre is a friend . . . of my family," broke in Allison, feeling an explanation was due before Logan was accused of party-crashing. "I hope it was all right for me to invite him."

"Of course, Allison, my dear," replied Lady Bramford. "I'm certain any friend of your family must be of the most sterling character."

At length Allison steered Logan onto the dance floor. A five-piece band was beating out Fred Waring's version of the 1927 hit *My Blue Heaven,* and the glossy parquet floor was alive with other dancers shimmering in brilliant color and displaying the wealth they represented. There were many friendly calls of greeting to Allison who, in return, waved and generally behaved as if the Bramfords' ball had been given exclusively for her benefit. And, whereas the greetings had been largely lodged at Allison, the curious glances and muttered comments of *Who is that she's with? . . . quite a handsome chap, don't you think?* were reserved for Logan. The looks sent his way by a number of the young men, while not exactly hostile, were nevertheless guarded, as if to imply, *He's too suave . . . he must be up to no good.* The girls, on the other hand, all wondered where Allison had found such a gorgeous man outside their circle, some asking themselves whether he might be fair game or whether Allison had him already sewed up.

Saundra Bramford, as hostess, took the opening initiative with the new arrivals.

"Allison, dear," she said, approaching them graciously, as if she were a model for one of the new fashion magazines. All the years of training and dental work had paid off, for her natural homeliness was hardly evident beneath the exterior gloss. When she turned her head toward Logan and smiled, showing perfect caps, he might not have noticed her striking resemblance to her lumbering football-playing brother. But unfortunately, Eddie Bramford turned up almost at the same instant, accentuating the similarities in comic paradox—where he was thick and imposing like a mountain, she was thin and imposing like a tree. Yet despite their handicaps, they remained a good-natured pair.

"I'm so glad you could make it," Saundra went on. "It's such a long ride, and in this abominable weather. And you even managed to bring a guest." Here she smiled at Logan.

"I hope you don't mind," Allison replied as if it really didn't matter anyway. "This is Logan Macintyre. Logan, these are our hosts, Saundra and Eddie—I should say *Edward*—Bramford."

"Macintyre . . ." mused Eddie. "Didn't you play for King's College."

"I'm afraid not," Logan answered politely, not elaborating on the fact that he had played nothing for any college, had never so much as set foot on the campus of an institution of higher learning.

"Now don't you go talking rugby, Eddie," Saundra scolded. "You said you were cousins . . . ?" she prompted, wanting to know immediately where Allison and this good-looking Logan Macintyre stood.

"No relation whatsoever," said Allison.

"I'm in the employ of the MacNeils," Logan offered, part of him warming up to the challenge of keeping up the charade, another part curious to see how Allison might handle herself if he revealed just what a low fellow he was. He had agreed to come with her, but he didn't want to give her *too* much control over him.

"What line are you in, Macintyre?" asked Eddie.

Logan opened his mouth to answer, but it was Allison's voice that rushed in ahead of his. "He's in investments," she said.

Logan snapped his mouth shut, wondering just what he would have said given the chance. As it was, he could not call Allison a liar, so he was forced to play the game.

"Investments," parroted Bramford. "A sticky business these days."

"We've weathered the crisis quite well."

"And what firm would that be?"

"Oh, look!" broke in Allison conveniently, "Punch—I'm simply dying of thirst!" She grabbed Logan's arm and dragged him toward the refreshment table.

Logan handed her a glass of the sweet red liquid but Allison stared into it as if it were the furthest thing from her mind. As Logan set the glass back on the table, his lips bent into a smile. *Why not?* he said to himself. He took her hand and tugged her toward the dance floor.

"Shall we dance?" he said. It was more of a command than a question.

She started at the initial gesture and glanced toward him, not a little bemused. In picturing this evening beforehand in her mind, somehow she had never envisioned what it would actually be like to have Logan Macintyre take her in his arms and dance with her. She had thought about what she would wear, about which perfume to choose, about what her friends would say, and about how she might flirt with Logan just enough to raise the attention of, say, Charles Fairgate. But of the moment when they would inevitably move around the dance floor, holding one another close, keeping time to the strains of the music, her face but inches from his shoulder—that was a moment she had not fully considered. Perhaps she was afraid of the effect such a moment might have on her.

The band had just begun playing *Girl of My Dreams,* and Logan gripped her waist for the waltz with rather more strength than she was accustomed to. She wondered if he was angry, but when he spoke his voice was smooth and pleasant.

"I think, Ali, my dear," he said, "that you should have gone for broke. Why stop at a mere investment broker? You could at least have given me an earldom."

"I thought you'd *thank* me," she replied.

"Thank you?"

"I only thought to save you undue embarrassment."

He chuckled softly in her ear, which was resting very near his lips. *Embarrassment for whom,* he wondered—*herself or me?* But he said nothing further. He had invested too much in this suit to see the evening degenerate into an argument. Besides, he wanted to enjoy himself. This young vixen was not altogether without her charm. Whatever her motives had been, he decided, she had apparently resolved to make the best of the situation, for she snuggled closer to him as the tune progressed. For all their discord of a few days earlier, they seemed to move like a single dancer, in almost perfect unison. Wary as they had been of one another, neither had to be forced to enjoy floating over the dance floor. Nor did they say a word for some time. On they danced, and Allison had just rested her head softly against Logan's chest and shoulder when Logan felt a firm tap on his shoulder, intruding into his contented thoughts.

He loosened his hold on Allison and spun around to behold an uncomfortably familiar face out of his past. Suddenly the years fell away in his mind, and he was fifteen, sitting in a card game, trying out his skill against the wealthy son of a lord. And after seven years, his adversary—though older and wiser, and now a man—had not changed. If anything, his dark and arrogant good looks had become even more pronounced.

Charles Reynolds Fairgate III! thought Logan, managing to keep his expression as cool as ever. *If he recognizes me, the jig's up! He would love nothing better than to expose me now after he couldn't make the charges stick the last time!*

"I hope you don't mind, old chap," said the man who had caused Logan several anxious days in jail. He nodded toward Allison, and Logan was momentarily relieved. *Perhaps, this far away, in this setting, after seven years, he won't recognize me,* thought Logan. But then almost as if reading his mind, Fairgate's brow wrinkled in puzzlement. "Have we met before?" he asked.

"I don't think so," Logan replied, thrusting out his hand. "Macintyre's the name." He cringed inwardly even as the name left his lips but he could see no way to avoid it. He only hoped Fairgate's memory for names was as fuzzy as it apparently was for faces. Besides, back in those days, Logan went by so many aliases that perhaps he could sneak his real name by with minimal risk.

"Hmm . . ." muttered the young lord thoughtfully. Then in a different vein, "Allison," he said, "I've been waiting for a dance with you."

"By all means, Charles." She stepped away from Logan, betraying a twinge of disappointment, which surprised her more than anyone, and into Fairgate's arms.

Logan stepped back, folding his arms, and watched the couple swing away from him. He tried to keep a nonchalant smile in place, but it was not as easy as it once might have been. He had rather enjoyed that last dance, or more accurately, had enjoyed holding Allison in his arms.

No doubt most observers would have felt the two made a fine couple, he thought. She probably had brought him here as part of a scheme to work her wiles on Fairgate. It would be just like her, he thought. But as he watched them, Logan could not help but think there was something sharp and dissonant about Fairgate's harsh, angular features next to Allison's soft loveliness. It grated against Logan's sensitivities, even as he tried to convince himself that he should not care whom Allison danced with. He would not be here that much longer. He would be gone and that would be that.

With the thought of his business in Port Strathy came the jarring reminder that Fairgate's sudden appearance could prove a major dilemma. If he should chance to remember their previous association, and revealed what he knew, it might be difficult for Logan to talk his way out of. But Logan was not left to his thoughts, or his aloneness, for long. The moment Allison melted away with Fairgate, several girls swarmed toward him. The first to lay claim was Saundra Bramford.

"We are very progressive around here, Mr. Macintyre," she said. "The girls are not expected to have to wait to be asked. And I especially, as hostess, must see that my guests are properly cared for."

All for progress, Logan took Saundra's slim arm just as the slow beat reverted to a swing. For that Logan should have been thankful, for the Bramford girl, in many years of trying to teach her cloddish brother to dance, had nearly forgotten how to do anything but lead. But Logan soon found himself being handed off from girl to girl to girl, and it was not until the call for dinner sounded that he saw Allison again.

Following dinner, Logan and Allison found themselves together for several more dances. Whenever the music turned to a slow tune, each unconsciously sought the other out, trying, however, to make their encounters seem accidental. But whenever Allison was in the company of another man, Logan found himself with no scarcity of society girls, for they seemed ever available. He was frequently the object of scowls from the young men whose dates seemed far too intrigued with Allison's mysterious friend.

He managed to avoid any further contact with Fairgate, though Angela Cunningham, who had accompanied the young lord of Dalmount, always seemed to migrate toward Logan whenever Charles was with Allison. The last thing Logan wanted to do was attract Fairgate's attention. But Miss Cunningham, in addition to being rather pretty herself, was precocious and difficult to refuse.

When the huge grandfather clock in the entryway chimed ten o'clock, Logan began to give thought to the trip home. It had taken a good hour to drive to the Bramford estate, but since their arrival a fresh rainstorm had descended and the roads, already poor, might add still another hour to the return. The MacNeils had said nothing to him about when they expected their daughter home, but he did not want to take any chances with their good graces.

He determined to seek out Allison at the first opportunity. However, when next the music stopped, it was to the sharp ringing of a spoon against a crystal glass. A gradual hush fell over the crowd, the band stopped playing, and all eyes turned toward where Lady Bramford stood on the platform beside the band.

"Children," she said, "I have an announcement." She paused, as if for effect, then continued. "I've just had word that our road is washed out. I'm afraid you are all quite stranded—"

Before she could finish, a great cheer rose from the young people, for in their youthful estimation, the most perfect end to an evening such as this would be not to have it end at all.

Lady Bramford, none too pleased at the prospects, but attempting to make the best of it, cleared her throat daintily. When that had no effect on the reveling group, the cornet player blasted a shrill note, bringing silence. "As I was saying," she continued, "you will be our guests until morning, at which time we will be able to send a crew out to repair the road. Accommodations will be prepared for you all—I hope you won't mind being a bit crowded."

Far from minding, the guests doubted that anything could be more exciting! Logan, however, was hardly looking forward to another twelve hours of such highbrow company. He would have given anything to be able to spend the night with the fishermen at Hamilton's.

The next hour was spent telephoning families with the news, made all the more frantic by the fear that the phone line would go out any minute.

"I know, Mum, it's a rotten go, but what can I do?" . . .

"Yes, Father, you'll have to mention the conditions of the roads in the next House session. Until then . . . we'll just *have* to make do." . . .

"It's terrible—but somehow, Mother, I'll survive it."

And so went the calls until scores of parents were feeling sorry for their hapless children. And the children themselves did little to dissuade such feelings, knowing that no parent would feel very comfortable with the thought that their children were having a *good* time.

By midnight the sleeping accommodations had been arranged—the young ladies in the east wing, the men in the west.

It would be hours before slumber would descend in either wing, however. To the east, sleep was forestalled by the endless gossip concerning the evening. Who had danced with whom, and how often. Wasn't Saundra Bramford's engagement to be announced tonight? What had happened? And why was her beau so conspicuously absent?

Logan's name came up frequently in the various rooms of the east wing. Who was the dashing stranger? Why hadn't anyone heard of his family before this? Could he be from the Continent? No, he had an unmistakable Scottish accent. But hadn't someone said he was from London? Too bad of Allison to keep him all to herself.

On her part, Allison wasn't quite sure how to react to all the attention Logan had generated among her friends. She had brought him for this very purpose, but now that it had worked so well, she had mixed feelings about the whole thing. He *was* her discovery, and the raves of the other young ladies naturally reflected on her. But they detracted from her in a sense, as well. She wouldn't have minded so much if during her sallies among the other young men, he had been idle and disconsolate at her absence. But he hadn't appeared to miss her company in the least.

She joined halfheartedly into the girlish banter around her, and was downright sullen as she finally snuggled down under the blankets to try to find some solace in sleep. What she had expected from the evening, she couldn't quite specify. Had she brought Logan Macintyre here hoping to make him fall in love with her? Was she irritated because she was unexpectedly beginning to fall in love with him? No—of course not! That was ridiculous! He was nothing! A commoner! And a brash egotist as well! She refused to think about it anymore.

And with such a turmoil of confusions and questions rattling around in her brain, Allison drifted into an uneasy but dreamless sleep.

Logan had other matters occupying his mind at that moment. The young men, not given to gossip, had found more practical means of passing their time. By some ill stroke of the draw, Logan had been housed with the boorish Clifford Arylin-Michaels and Charles Fairgate. His first thought was that the young lord had purposefully machinated the seemingly coincidental accommodations in order to get him alone to question him, or perhaps for some other purpose yet to be named.

Somehow he did not perceive Fairgate as a man who ever fell victim to mere chance. But as the young lord said nothing, there was no way for Logan to find out what he knew without dangerously jogging his memory. His only choice for the present was to continue playing the innocent, and hope that what Fairgate knew about his Glasgow background would not come to light.

A few minutes after they were settled, Eddie Bramford and two others whom Logan did not know came into the room.

"It's too early for sleep," said Bramford, brandishing a deck of cards. "Anyone game?"

Fairgate nodded his assent, but Arylin-Michaels abstained on the grounds that he was too intelligent to participate in low games of "chance." Then several eyes turned to Logan. What he most feared was to get involved in a game which would simulate that situation so many years ago and which might therefore refresh Fairgate's memory all too keenly. He had changed a lot from the coarse and grubby fifteen-year-old he was then. But not enough to stand up to a test this severe.

"I think I'll pass," he said, punctuating his words with a convincing yawn and stretch. "I'm awfully tired."

"Aw, come on," prodded Bramford. "You stole all our girls tonight. The least you can do is give us a chance to get even." His voice revealed his cheerful nature.

"I hope you don't think I was trying to—"

"No," interrupted Bramford. "We'd never hold a little thing like that against you. It's hardly your fault if those crazy girls—you know they're all younger than us *men!*"—he looked around at his two friends knowingly and with a sly grin—"all go a bit featherheaded the minute they lay eyes on someone new."

Logan laughed, looking quickly from face to face. They all seemed in accord except for Fairgate. His look, fairly well concealed but evident to one like Logan whose business required a knowledge of faces and their masks, revealed that he had indeed not forgotten Logan's advances in the directions of his Angela Cunningham. His silence was all the more foreboding, knowing what Logan knew he knew, and he wondered what revenge the young lord might even now be planning.

"I'm not really much of a card player," said Logan.

"We'll be more than happy to teach you," replied Fairgate, speaking now for the first time and looking him evenly in the eyes.

"I . . . I really—"

"We won't take no for an answer," insisted Bramford, "except from Clifford, because he's a wet blanket, anyway."

Seeing that to continue with his resistance would only raise more questions than to give in, Logan resigned himself to his fate.

The five, including Bramford's Oxford cronies Raymond Crawford and Mitchell Robertson, sat in a circle on the floor since there was no table in the room large enough for the gamesters. Ray produced a box of chips and began placing stacks in front of each player.

"I'm afraid," said Logan, making one final attempt to retreat, "that I haven't come prepared with much ready cash—"

"Not to worry," said Bramford. "We know you're good for it."

Logan didn't even want to think about what the progression of chips were worth, and he certainly wasn't about to ask. Perhaps, being but the *sons* of wealth, these fellows might have little *real* wealth at their fingertips. The stakes might not be that high. But who could tell? He'd just have to put it out of his mind, and concentrate on playing like an amateur, making sure he neither won nor lost too much, and making sure the attention stayed on someone else when the pot grew large.

Bramford dealt out the first hand, identifying the game as five-card draw. Each player threw a white chip into the pot. Logan had no idea if it represented a shilling, a quid, or a hundred pounds, but he tossed it in as if it were worth only the wood from which it had been made.

The game progressed without incident. The pots remained small, the hands nothing much more than an occasional full house or straight, and Logan managed to lose an occasional big one for the sake of appearances, always gradually winning back his losses over the following several hands in small enough chunks that his profile in the game remained obscure.

Whether Fairgate was watching him he could not tell, but the longer the game went the more he remembered why Fairgate had been such a perfect setup seven years earlier. Not only was his manner irritating and conceited—a fact which had only grown worse with the passage of time—his poker playing was of the worst sort. It was all Logan could do not to forget that he was supposed to be an inexperienced gambler. He simply could not pass up such an opportunity to outplay these "golden boys." Especially Fairgate.

At length the hand Logan had been waiting for came. With deuces wild—a typical university trick, Logan told himself, which had no part in men's poker, but which he would take full advantage of since it was the house rule—he had drawn two cards to a jack-high full house. Bramford and Crawford were out. Robertson had raised twice, and he and Fairgate had both remained in. After Robertson's second raise, Fairgate had raised again. Robertson folded. His eyes gleaming with the old magic, Logan threw in the calling chip, hesitated a moment, then threw in another blue.

"Let's see how good your hand really is, Fairgate. I'll raise you again."

"You're a cocky one, aren't you, Macintyre," replied Fairgate. "On the poker table as well as the dance floor. But this time I don't think you can beat me. In fact, Macintyre," he added with a slight curl to his already scornful lip, "I think you're bluffing. I don't think you're quite man enough for our game. I don't know where you come from, though I could swear I've seen you before. But one thing you'll soon learn is not to mix where you don't fit. So I'm going to call your bluff, Macintyre."

With the words he brazenly tossed a final blue chip into the middle of the floor, and with a flourish abandoned protocol and displayed his cards for all to see—a queen-high straight.

"Beat that, Macintyre!" he said with a sneer, looking Logan deeply in the eyes, as if still trying in vain to recall the connection his mind seemed intent on making.

Logan returned his gaze, debating within himself. After a pause of several moments, he laughed, almost nervously, and said, "You're right, Fairgate; you're a better man than I!" With that he threw his winning cards face-down onto the rest of the discarded deck. "You win!"

34 ✖ *The Drive Home*

ALLISON WAS GLAD when the final goodbyes had been said and they could finally get away. She wasn't quite sure what to make of the events of the previous evening, or where exactly she now stood with Logan. By inviting him, she had hoped to gain ground both in the estimation of her friends and in Logan's eyes. But it seemed he had in fact been the one to become the talk of the ball, not her. She had hoped to play the new appreciation Logan would surely have for her to an advantage; now she realized she was in no position to do any such thing. If anything, he now held the upper hand.

The rain had let up for a short while that morning, allowing workmen to repair the damaged section of road. But by the time Allison and Logan reached the Lindow Bridge, the clouds had amassed again. Below, as the Austin plodded across the ancient wooden structure, they could see the waters of the river lapping nearly at a level with the road. Allison had never seen the river this high before, but she had heard of other floods in the valley that had ripped away bridge, road, and anything else within several hundred feet of the river's shores. Already the mighty rush of water was making the pilings of the bridge creak and sway dangerously. Allison held her breath as they crossed, wondering what the road ahead would be like.

Logan slowed the car through a muddy bog shortly beyond the bridge, then suggested they turn back. But Allison made light of the weather.

"Oh, this is nothing. It gets this way every spring." She could hardly disguise the fact that she was more than a little frightened to be slipping and sliding around the road as they were. But she wanted to get home, and she could not betray her inner anxieties to a man of the world like Logan.

Logan proceeded forward. The road was muddy, in some places covered completely with water, but still navigable. The Austin crept along like some strange amphibious creature. All at once a deafening crack of thunder shook the landscape, and the sky belched forth an almost instantaneous deluge of fresh rain. It fell so hard and thick that the automobile's small windshield wipers were hopeless to fulfill their intended task. Logan could see nothing ahead of him.

"Ali," he said, "put your head out the window and let me know when I have to turn."

"What?"

"I said stick your head out—"

"I *heard* what you said. You must be joking. I'll be drowned!"

"Would you rather end up in a ditch alongside the road?"

"It's miles till the road turns."

"I saw a bend in the road just ahead."

"Impossible!"

Logan blew out a sharp breath. "Ali, *you* are impossible!"

"Don't call me Ali!"

"I'll call you anything I please," he retorted, the tension of trying to drive in the storm undermining his usual patience. "And unless you want me to think of something even more unpleasant, you had better—"

He broke off as the steering wheel suddenly jerked out of control and the wheels of the car lurched over the edge of the muddy road. Logan pumped furiously on the water-soaked brakes. But he hardly needed to. The car bumped to a jerky stop, its two front tires off the road in a ditch full of water, its engine dead. Logan turned the key, but it only coughed and sputtered in response.

"Now look what you've done," said Allison smugly.

Logan turned his head and stared at her, his burning eyes saying more than could any words.

She turned away, perhaps humbled by the sound of her own outburst. "Now what?" she asked in a more contrite tone.

"I suggest we sit here until the storm passes."

"That could take forever!"

"Well, what do you expect me to do? Stop the rain? Would you prefer to walk for help in this downpour?"

Pouting, Allison folded her arms and stared out the window as if she could see something. Finally, keeping her eyes focused ahead, she said, "I suppose I should have helped when you asked. I'm . . . I'm sorry I blamed you."

"Don't worry about it," he replied. "It'll be alright."

Trying the key in the ignition again, Logan jammed his foot on the accelerator and pushed to the floor. Much to his surprise, the engine revved right up. He threw the gearshift into reverse and let out the clutch, but nothing followed except the sickening sound of helplessly spinning wheels in the mud of the road.

"Don't say a thing!" he growled in frustration.

"I wasn't going to," she replied, sounding truly hurt. When he turned to look, he saw her lip quivering. "What are we going to do, Logan?" she said after a moment.

"We'll get out," he said confidently. "I'll flag someone down. At best we can walk."

"Logan, it's Sunday morning. No one will be out, especially in this weather. We should have driven down to the Inland Highway, even if it was longer."

"Don't worry. Remember, I'm a lucky fellow."

She glanced at him and managed a laugh.

"You see," he said, sounding as cheerful as if the sun had been shining, "it won't be so bad if we keep our spirits up. Trust me. I've been in tighter spots than this!"

"Yes, I imagine you have!" she said, with a tease in her voice.

Now it was his turn to laugh. "Ah, you are finding out my secrets."

"Logan, do you think the river will flood?" she asked, serious again. "If it does, the water will head right down this road and turn it into a new river."

He didn't want to think of that. Instead, he reached out and gently touched her hand. Something in her vulnerability had touched him. It was a side of Allison MacNeil he had not seen before this moment. Suddenly he saw her without all the pretense and affectation. Again he wondered what made her surround herself with such a hard wall. He wondered, too, what more there might be to the *real* Allison MacNeil that he was still unable to see.

She did not pull her hand away. But neither did she look over at him. The moment passed in silence. Awkwardly Logan lifted his hand from hers and, hugging his overcoat about him, opened the door of the car and stepped out into the fury of the storm.

Wind lashed rain into his face like sharp needles. The sky was so dark that it could have been evening instead of morning. Where he stood, water lapped at his ankles. His shoes and new tuxedo trousers were ruined. He plodded back onto the surface of the road, though it was hardly visible through the water running over the top of it. It seemed to have risen in just the few minutes since they had come along. He looked around, trying to survey their options. Then he spied an object floating down the ditch stream on the other side of the road, that appeared to be a piece of wood. Hastening toward it, he stooped down and pulled it out. It was no tree branch, but an old piece of milled lumber, ragged at one end. Of course it could have broken free from anything, but Logan immediately thought of the bridge. If the bridge was about to give way, there would certainly be no more travelers along the road. And if the Lindow was rising as quickly as he feared, he and Allison could never outrun, or more likely, *outwalk* the flood. They *had* to get that car moving before the river broke its boundaries and spread out over the entire Strathy Valley. It was their only hope, even if it was a slim one. And they had to do so before the water level on the road became too deep to drive.

Clutching the board, Logan turned back toward the car. It seemed to be settling even deeper into the muddy ditch already, water up to its fender. It would take a miracle to get it out, but Logan knew he had to try.

Allison was anxiously looking out the window for him when he approached. Anxiety was etched all over her face. Logan ducked his head through the window and smiled as if to allay her fears, suddenly realizing the responsibility that faced him. He knew she was depending on him, and that awareness both humbled and intimidated him. He tried to infuse his voice with its usual confidence.

"Get behind the steering wheel," he instructed Allison. "I'm going to use this board as leverage. I'll shove when you try to back it out. But hit it easy . . . not too much throttle."

He walked around to the front of the Austin and knelt down in the water, jammed the end of the board into the ground and tested it by lifting until it hit the bumper. "Start the engine," he yelled to Allison, "and push down on the accelerator as easy as you can."

She did so. As the wheels began to spin, Logan bent his full weight on the board against the Austin bumper, trying to rock it backward enough for the rear tires to grab. But it was no use. Other than rocking the car back and forth, he accomplished nothing. The slick rubber tires simply spun through the tracks they had made for themselves in the mud.

"Once more!" he called out in desperation, giving the board every ounce of strength he possessed. The car did not budge. However the board, lodged none too securely in the loose soil, slipped, and the thrust of the motion threw Logan off his balance. The next instant he was on his back in the little stream.

Within seconds Allison had shut off the ignition and, without thinking, jumped out of the car to his aid.

"Oh, Logan . . . Logan!" she cried. "Are you hurt?" Struggling through the water and rough surface of the ground to reach him, she never noticed that the rain quickly soaked her pretty curls, or that the muddy water was splattering her expensive new dress.

Logan looked up at her from his position with a grin. It was difficult to distinguish his body from the mud and debris covering him.

"So much for this lucky fellow," he said with a laugh.

"You're not hurt?" she said, holding out her hand.

"Nothing but my pride," he replied.

At last a smile broke from Allison's lips, which soon became a giggle, and finally erupted into a great laugh. "This is hardly the time for a swim, Mr. Macintyre," she said as he took her hand.

He laughed with her. Their predicament was made all the more ridiculous in that she was unable to pull him out on the first attempt. Her thin shoes and inexperience were no match for the mud, and on the second effort, with a great flying slip of her foot where she had tried to anchor it, she lost hold and flew into the water next to him.

He burst into a great roar of laughter.

"You did that intentionally!" she cried in her old petulant tone.

"Even if I had thought of it," he replied, still laughing, "I would never have dared!"

"And why is that?"

"You should know! You've been watching me like a hawk, ready to pounce on me if I step out of line," Logan replied playfully.

"I guess I have been rather cross with you," she said, smiling. "I'm sorry."

"Fine time to apologize, now that you have me at such a disadvantage!"

She laughed again. "You should see yourself! Lying in the mud in a brand new tuxedo, with—"

"How do you know it's new?"

"What do you take me for, a complete fool? I know new clothes when I see them. You're not so very clever, you know."

"So—I've been found out!"

"Logan Macintyre unmasked!"

"And what else do you know about me?" he asked.

"Just that I'm glad you stopped by to help us fix our car in town."

"I'm glad too," he returned. "And I'm glad you wanted me to go to the Bramfords' with you."

"Even though it ended like this?"

Logan laughed again. "I wouldn't miss this for anything! How many people around here have had the chance to see the uppity Miss Allison MacNeil—"

"Watch yourself, Logan," Allison warned.

"Sorry. How many people have the chance to see the charming and beautiful Miss Allison MacNeil—"

"That's better!"

"—have a chance to see her in an expensive new evening dress, lying in a mud puddle in the pouring rain? Now I ask you . . . would *you* miss this?"

"Careful!" she said, with a teasing gleam in her eye, then splashed a handful of water in his direction.

He turned away, but not before she had splashed him again.

Then a pause came. Logan was the first to speak. "You know, Ali—I mean, Allison—"

"It's all right. You can call me Ali," she replied. "It sounds good in your mouth too, just like in Grandpa Dorey's."

"Thank you. What I was going to say was that I like you best like this."

"What! All covered with mud and soaked to the skin?" She tried to sound affronted, but it was a difficult facade to maintain with fresh laughter attempting to escape from her lips.

"You know what I mean," he went on, trying to be serious. "I like how you laugh—really laughing, like you mean it."

"I suppose it's pointless to remain angry at this point."

"Were you truly angry with me all this time?"

"Not *all* the time. But you can be infuriating."

"I thought perhaps you were just angry at the world in general." His words were sincere, completely without any mocking tone which might have characterized them a couple of weeks earlier.

She sensed the sincerity of his remark, but found she was unable to easily frame a reply. It was not easy to open up that part of her life which had been shut tight for so long.

"We're going to catch pneumonia if we stay here much longer," she said, repressing everything her heart wanted to cry out.

Logan struggled to his feet, then leaned over, took her offered hand, and pulled her up. However, he did not quickly release her hand, but instead kept it cupped in his.

"Ali," he said, "let's not let things go back to the way they were."

"I'm . . . I'm afraid that when we get back, that somehow, all this will seem like a dream . . . and we'll—"

"But it can be different now. We don't have to fight anymore."

"Has it really changed? I mean, is it really different?"

"It could be. Sometimes mud and grime have an odd way of cleansing. When we do get cleaned up and back into our old clothes, who knows what might happen?"

Suddenly an urge came over Logan to tell her everything. He hesitated, not for fear of the failure of his scheme, but because he desperately didn't want her angry at him all over again. Instead, saying nothing, he leaned forward and kissed her lightly on her rain-streaked lips.

It was over so quickly, Allison was not even sure that it had happened. But she knew that it had, and that it had been nice. She had enjoyed it so much, in fact, that she let herself forget the deception of his injured foot. There had to be an explanation, she told herself. Better that she wait for him to tell her when he was ready. She was feeling so wonderful, none of that seemed to matter anymore. Oh, she didn't want to go back and then find it impossible to recapture this special moment. Why couldn't it last? Could things be different, like he had said?

Logan released her hand and they made their way back toward the car, still not knowing what they'd do.

"Can I ask you something?" Logan said after a moment.

"Yes, of course," she answered softly.

"Why do you hate to be called Ali?"

"I don't hate it. But only my great-grandfather calls me that. Why have you wanted to call me that?"

"At first, partly because it made you angry, I suppose. But mostly now because it seems to fit you better."

"That's funny," she answered thoughtfully. "Grandpa Dorey always says that too. Why?"

"Allison sounds like some frail little girl. You know the kind, with pale skin and a dainty voice to match." He saw her bristle slightly, then added quickly, "I'm not saying that about you. Why does everyone think that kind of young lady is more to be desired than one with spirit—as a friend of mine used to say, 'with a little spunk.' That's an *Ali*—a girl with spunk. Like you."

"I suppose people like the dainty, quiet sort," sighed Allison, "because they are the ones who are good and saintly and kind."

"You can't really believe that. Why, look at your mother and great-grandmother."

"Exactly! That's just what they are like!" she retorted as if she were lodging an accusation.

"Lady Margaret seems pretty spirited, even shrewd, for a woman over eighty! I bet she was something when she was your age!"

"I suppose," said Allison in a dejected voice. "But don't you see? That's just it. I can't measure up to what she was, and that's what they're all expecting of me. I can't even measure up to my own name, just like you said. I've tried so hard, but it's impossible. Spunky, spirited girls, as you call them, just can't be very good Christians."

"Well, I wouldn't know anything about that. My mother was pretty religious, though I've never had any use for it. But I think what you said is wrong. Look at Jesse Cameron. The way she talks, I'd imagine *she's* a Christian. At least she sounds religious enough. But you should hear her bellow and whoop aboard her boat—and she's the furthest thing from frail I can think of. Yet I've seldom been treated with more kindness. No, Ali, I think you're wrong about what you said."

"Well, one thing I'm not wrong about," she said, changing the uncomfortable subject, "is that we're going to drown if we stand here and philosophize much longer."

"How far is it back to Stonewycke?" asked Logan.

"Probably seven or eight miles."

"Well, we've got to get moving. That water's rising fast, and Noah had a better chance of finding a fellow traveler than we have."

"I wish I could pray," said Allison.

"I only wish I believed there was someone up there who could hear."

She stared at him with mild surprise. "You don't believe in God?" She had never actually known anyone honest or impertinent enough to admit such a thing.

"I don't know. I suppose neither of us has had much use for the other in the past," replied Logan.

As Allison passed the car door, she turned aside and reached for the handle.

"What are you doing?" asked Logan.

"Getting an umbrella. If we are going to walk all the way home, we could use it," she replied innocently.

Logan laughed. "In this downpour! I doubt it'll do us much good," he said, then reached for her again and pulled her toward him.

He studied her face intently for a moment, then said, "Let's stay . . . friends." He wanted to kiss her again. But, of all things for Logan Macintyre, he felt strangely bashful. The kiss before had been on impulse, done before he even realized what he was doing. Now there seemed to be more between them. And a kiss now meant more also. More than he was certain he could give.

But she was already replying to his words; perhaps she had not even noticed the awkward moment that had just passed.

"I'd like that, Logan," she had said. "I truly would."

In fact, she *had* noticed. But like Logan, Allison was confused and timid. Too many new emotions were assailing her all at once.

Actually the emotions weren't new at all. But for so long she had tried to repress things like honesty and sincerity and tenderness that she felt more comfortable pretending they didn't even exist.

Yet she couldn't deny that these past fifteen minutes with Logan had been wonderful; she had felt a freedom to be herself, unlike any other time she could remember. Still, to give up her protective shield, even for the sake of Logan, would mean facing some difficult things.

Logan had come close to hitting the core of her inner conflict, without his even knowing it. How miserably she had always failed to measure up to what her family expected of her! Didn't they know she could not be like them? She couldn't be perfect—a saint. How could Logan know how much deeper it all went? To him it looked merely like a twist in her personality.

They walked along, each deep in thought. The falling away of their fear and reserve toward each other had opened them unexpectedly toward their inner selves as well. And now Logan found his thoughts turning to the man who had sent him here in the first place—his uncle Digory. According to Lady Margaret, he was surely a man who could pray when things got tight. He found himself almost wishing he were here now to send up a few words heavenward on behalf of the stranded party-goers. *Why, if we get out of this mess,* Logan thought, *I might even read some of that old Bible of yours.*

All at once Allison grasped his arm. "Logan . . . listen!"

"What is it?" Logan listened hard, and faintly in the distance could make out a sound he could not place. It wasn't the noise he had been hoping for—an engine. Rather, there was a creaking sound, as of wood, mingled with an intermittent *clop-splash . . clop-splash.* He could not recognize it.

He did not have to ponder long, however, for in a few moments, from the mist of the thick downpour emerged the last thing he would have expected to see—a rickety old haywagon, pulled by two great, gray, tired-looking, wet draught horses.

Both he and Allison broke into simultaneous yells, accentuated with a jump of joy on Allison's part and a fist-pounding of relief on Logan's. But even in his ecstasy, the first thing that returned to Logan's mind was the thought of what he had vowed to himself in connection with Digory's Bible.

Was it possible that someone could actually have *heard* those thoughts? Could there really be a God ready to intercede, even for unbelievers and doubters?

He'd have to think about this a little more. He wasn't ready to call this a miracle. But it certainly did cast a cloud—even heavier than the one in the sky—over his previously comfortable unreligious notions.

35 ❈ Back to Stonewycke

INTO VIEW CAME Fergusson Dougall, perched atop the hardwood seat, looking like anything but a guardian angel. Allison clambered aboard, threw her arms around him, and kissed him unabashedly on the cheek.

"God be praised!" said the factor, when they had briefly related the story of their car trouble. "Weel, the folks sent me oot t' look fer ye, seein' as ye were overdue an' the river was risin' fast. Actually, I was the only one available. Yer father left early this mornin' t' help some o' the farmers clear oot. Most o' the lowlan' crofts are already under water. Ye're lucky the road's mostly on high land or ye wouldna hae made it this far."

"And how's everything at home?" asked Allison.

"All's fine, but wet, at the hoose, but we've already lost two or three hunnert acres o' the new plantin'. 'Twas poor timin' fer a flood." As he spoke, Fergie had been driving at a healthy clip, but as he finished, he slowed to nearly a stop. He stood, gazed off ahead of him and to his left, and then continued. "I didna think I'd get back on the Culden road. Look oot there." He pointed down the valley toward the sea; where yesterday had been green farmland, now stood a huge, brown lake. Any traces of the road were completely obscured.

"We'll go as far as we can, then skirt aroun' t' Braenock. I ken a few sheep trails an' sich like. It'll take hours, but we'll eventually strike the Fenwick Harbor road. We can be thankful I brought a wagon, not an automobile."

"Sheep trails, Fergie!" said Allison dismally. "Can even a wagon travel on them?"

"If worse comes t' worst, I tossed a couple saddles in back an' we can unhitch the horses an' ride. Leastways we willna drown."

"Did you happen also to toss in some dry clothes and rain gear back there?" asked Logan, almost facetiously, hardly relishing the misery of spending several more hours in their soaking party clothes.

"Aye," answered Fergie, quite pleased with himself, "Lady Joanna fixed us up right weel. There'll be a deserted cottage or twa where ye can change."

They traveled along a somewhat decent surface of road for about half an hour, the rain still pouring relentlessly. But even in that short time they gained considerable elevation and seemed to have left the flood far behind. But then the road veered left again, beginning a gradual descent toward the valley, now a lake, then disappeared. Fergie led the horses eastward, off the road. Now their way became so rough with potholes, mud, rocks, and shrubbery that it took nearly an hour to traverse a mile; the three passengers bounced mercilessly against the hard board seat of the wagon, but Fergie doggedly encouraged the two horses forward.

At last they ascended a small rise and there in a shallow hollow before them, on the edge of Braenock Ridge, stood a small stone cottage, meshing perfectly with the barrenness of the moor and the bleakness of the weather. Even inhabited, it could not have been much to look on, but now it was like recalling a sad memory. In places the mortar between the stones had long since crumbled away, leaving gaps in the walls which made the boarded-up windows appear even more pathetic and hopeless. Adjacent to the cottage stood the remains of what had no doubt once been a cattle byre. Only three stone walls still stood, and any thought of a roof was long since gone. Over the cottage, however, a roof still remained. But even it was sagging, and would collapse before many more years, leaving this poor home but an abandoned shell like so many thousands of others scattered throughout the poorer regions of that northern country.

The moment they walked inside, it was clear that, even though the structure of a roof was still present, the thatch upon it was in such poor repair that it could not hope to keep out such a rain. Numerous muddy puddles on the floor marked the presence of each hole above. The dirt floor was in hardly better condition than the ground outside, except that there was no wind, and one small corner did remain which had somehow escaped time's destruction. Allison entered first, made her way through the maze of puddles to the only dry spot to be found, and changed into the corduroys, plaid flannel shirt, fresh socks, and heavy boots her mother had packed for her. Then, throwing a mackintosh over her shoulders, she stepped outside while Logan went in and changed into similar attire, provided from Alec's oversized wardrobe. Greatly to their relief, Fergie suggested that they take a few extra moments to enjoy the cold meals Lady Joanna had included.

The dry corner of the hut, while not cozy by most standards, seemed to welcome the three travelers, who unwrapped sliced cheese, fresh baked bread, oatcakes, and crisp red apples, accompanied by a flask of hot tea to wash it all down. When the humble but delicious fare had been consumed, no one seemed particularly anxious to brave the elements quite so soon again. Fergie leaned against a wall and lit his pipe, but had barely taken three puffs before he was sound asleep. Logan reached over, removed the still smoking pipe from his hand, and set it on the dirt floor beside him.

Allison hugged her knees to her body to ward off the chill.

"Perhaps I should try to build a fire," Logan suggested.

"You'd never find any wood dry enough," said Allison, taking up the flask of tea and refilling their cups. "Perhaps this will help."

"Thank you." Logan stared at the dirt floor a moment, then said, "Is this Stevie Mackinaw's cottage?"

"How do you know about him?"

"Jesse Cameron told me a few things."

"Oh. I had forgotten you were friends." Her tone contained a hint of its old hauteur, but she must have been aware of it too, for her next words were more mellow. "Lady Margaret was quite close to the Mackinaws when she was a girl. They lived a little ways from here, farther up onto Braenock. This was the old Krueger place, I think. She used to come out to both places a lot, from what she's said."

"Yes. Jesse mentioned that. She also said she thought Stevie Mackinaw was in love with your great-grandmother. But the feelings must have been only one-sided."

"That doesn't surprise me," sighed Allison. "Everyone—especially the crofters—loves her. It was probably even more so when she was young and beautiful. Did you know it was love that forced her from Scotland?"

"No. I haven't heard much about your family's history."

"Lady Margaret married Grandpa Dorey against her father's wishes; he was furious, vowed to get back at them, even once tried to kill Grandpa."

"And that's what forced them away?"

"My great-grandmother sailed for America, but Grandpa Dorey stayed behind to clear his name of a murder in which James Duncan had implicated him. He was to follow later, but his father-in-law schemed against their plans until in the end, each thought the other was dead. This is how my mother explained it all to me. Neither my great-grandmother nor Grandpa Dorey talk much about it, but my mother has spent hours getting the facts from them, writing it down so the story of their love for each other and the legacy of their sacrifice for the land and for Stonewycke won't ever be lost. In fact, all my life I have memories of my mother quizzing my great-grandmother and great-grandfather for details. Pictures of them sitting side by side in front of a fire, talking, as it seemed to a little girl, for hours on end. It's been something that has been really important to my mother. I think she almost looks upon it as her mission in life to preserve the legacy. As if it were Lady Margaret and Grandpa Dorey—or Maggie and Ian, as they were known when they were young—who were the central characters of the story, and her role was more to make certain their story was preserved and passed on to future generations."

She stopped and was silent for a few moments.

"So what happened?" asked Logan. "Lady Margaret was in America, and . . . ?"

"It drove Grandpa Dorey mad. Lady Margaret remained in exile for forty years, thinking there was nothing left for her here."

"What made her finally come back?"

"Actually my mother came first, while my great-grandmother was in a coma in America. My mother knew nothing about the family in Scotland. She came here blindly, merely hoping to fulfill her grandmother's last wish before she lapsed into unconsciousness."

"She knew nothing about the family or the inheritance which would have been hers?"

"That's why she says she got more than she bargained for."

"I guess so—quite a bit more!" Logan took a swallow of his tea as he considered Lady Joanna's stroke of fortune.

"But none of that means anything to *them*." Allison's words were mixed with reproach, with the old tone returning once more. But to the more sensitive observer, there was also an unmistakable touch of envy, of which even Allison was unaware. "Why, the prestige of Stonewycke means nothing to them. They gave away half the estate to the tenants. There was even a treasure—"

"A treasure?" Logan's voice was so calm that Allison could not have guessed that he had nearly dropped his cup at her words.

"When she returned home, Lady Margaret looked where she had hidden it before she left Scotland, but it was gone. And no one ever made any other attempts to locate it—not to say that it even exists! But it just proves all the more how little they all care for our family position. They'd all be just as content in some fisher's hut! My own parents lived in nothing more than a little cottage for years. I was born there, can you imagine? I've lived at Stonewycke only half my life."

"Are you saying your great-grandmother may have *imagined* the treasure?" Logan could not help it if the question was ill-timed. He *had* to ask!

"You know how old people's memories are," Allison replied. "What does it matter?"

"Nothing . . . certainly—nothing at all!" replied Logan hastily, perhaps a bit too hastily. "Simply a curiosity." He tried to interest himself in his tea for the next few moments, his racing thoughts circling once again about the person of Lady Margaret.

No, the old lady's memory is just fine, he told himself. There *must* have been a treasure—must *still* be a treasure. She had seen it. She had placed it somewhere. And now it was gone.

That was no surprise to Digory MacNab's great-great-great nephew, who had read the old groom's letter and confession. But this was a new bit of news, to learn that Lady Margaret had hidden the treasure before she had been forced out of the country. Could it be possible that only she and Digory had known of its existence originally? Why wouldn't she tell her husband on their parting, for surely such a valuable find could have helped save him from the clutches of James Duncan?

Logan wondered if he'd ever have the chance to find out the entire story. He couldn't go about asking too many questions. He would have to content himself to pick up bits and pieces however he could. He hoped that one of those pieces would lead him to the treasure. Nothing else mattered.

Or did it?

Suddenly the thought of Allison came back into his mind. Had the events of this day changed anything? With the mere mention of the treasure, all at once his thoughts had flown off wildly, completely forgetting the brief moments of intimacy they had shared. It was as if he had become two separate persons—the old Logan, still intent on nothing but the treasure, and the part of him which could hardly ignore a growing attachment to this place and its people, Allison in particular. And even Allison, he recalled, had suddenly reverted to tones reminiscent of her old self the moment she began talking about her family. *Was this part of the curse of the treasure to which Uncle Digory had alluded,* Logan wondered? While everyone sought the treasure for the wealth it would bring, was it, in fact, a messenger of evil? What was the treasure, anyway? Was it something which could bring fulfillment and peace and lasting meaning to life? Or was it instead something which, as Digory had said, would best serve the family legacy by being thrown into the sea or destroyed? *What could be the real treasure?*

Again Logan dragged his thoughts back to the present. Once again thoughts of the treasure had pulled him away from Allison, in just a few seconds of time. What a strange lure it had on him!

What did matter now? Only the treasure? Or were there new factors to consider? He tried to dismiss the matter from his mind. He didn't want to have to think about how these new relationships might figure into his scheme. He hadn't planned on them—nor had he planned on Allison. A few weeks ago in Glasgow when he had concocted all this, he saw himself simply walking into Port Strathy, finding the long, lost treasure, and waltzing out again with no one being the wiser and himself being a good deal richer. But now for the first time he began to wonder just how easy it was going to be to walk away from here.

Logan's thoughts were interrupted as Fergie suddenly started awake. "Hae I been sleepin'?" he exclaimed. "Ye shouldna hae let me drop off like a fool bairn," he continued in a fluster. "We must be goin'."

They all rose, packed up everything, clutched their raingear as close to their bodies as possible, and shouldered their way back out into the storm.

The rain had abated somewhat, but their way—now a sheep path, now simply open moor with treacherous peat bogs to beware of—became increasingly difficult to navigate the farther across Braenock Ridge they went, making for the higher ground of the road across Strathy Summit to their northeast. They had been on their way from the cottage no more than an hour when Fergie finally stopped the animals.

"Can't go no farther wi' this wagon," he announced. "We'll hae t' come back fer it when the weather clears."

Fergie stepped down and proceeded to unhitch the wagon and saddle the two horses, while Allison and Logan gathered supplies and strapped them on behind one of the mounts. The young couple rode together, while Fergusson, weighing nearly as much as the two others combined, rode the other horse. The portly factor took the lead, a sight to see astride his animal, his ponderous bulk bouncing and swaying with every step, while Allison, with Logan behind her, followed.

Once they left the wagon behind, the going became easier, for the narrow paths and steep inclines of the high moor were far more suitable for horseback than for the awkward vehicle. The flooded valley was by now far behind them, but even the high country had not been left untouched by the storm. Great portions were covered with water, little streams were going every which way, and Logan occasionally found himself being splashed by water and mud from the horse's heavy hooves.

Once they abandoned the wagon, they no longer had to go all the way to the Summit road, and they struck due north instead, directly through toward Stonewycke from the back side. At one time there had been a rather worn trail, though steep in parts, which they were now following. As they went, gradually Allison and Logan began talking again, and it seemed they were about to fall back into the free and easy manner of the earlier part of the day. However, Allison was cold and tired and growing extremely weary of this journey, which it seemed would never end. She had begun to wish she had never been invited to Saundra and Eddie's ball in the first place.

A pause had come in their conversation and Allison had drifted into a somewhat irritable mood from the cumulative effects of the weather and her exhaustion. Oblivious to the flying mud and inexperienced rider behind her, she began unconsciously to pick up the pace whenever their way allowed.

"Ali, must you splash through *every* puddle!" said Logan at length, his tone cheerful, while he reached up to brush a fresh splat of mud from his cheek.

"What right have *you* to complain?" she snapped in reply.

"I was only joking," he laughed, not aware of his peril at the mercy of her changing mood. "I haven't a single complaint about this day." As he said the words he loosened his grip from the edge of the saddle and placed his arm around her waist, hugging her close.

"What do you think you're doing?" she barked in an outraged tone.

"I don't know . . . I just—" he faltered, bewildered by her outburst.

"Just because you stole an unguarded kiss from me, Logan, at a time when my defenses were down," she said snappily, "does not mean that you now have total license with me."

"I had no intention—" he began, but broke off, stubbornly refusing to swing pliantly with her moods. He didn't need to defend himself, he decided. "What's gotten into you?" he asked instead.

"Things may have gotten out of hand today, but—"

"Is that what you call it?"

"Well, it's easy to forget yourself in that kind of situation," she answered matter-of-factly, as if *now* she had come to her senses. "But I'm not some empty-headed trollop like that Angela Cunningham, who would positively swoon at the merest nod from a man."

"You can't be stewing over the party? I thought those games were behind us. We had decided to be friends."

"Friends," she smugly informed him, "don't go pawing at one another."

"I suppose you're right," he said with an air of defeat. He wasn't sure if she was right or not, but he saw no sense in arguing further. He had learned from past experience that the haughty Allison was not open to reason. And he didn't want to get into any more shouting matches with her. Even if she reverted back to her old self, it didn't mean he had to.

For the next ten minutes the only sounds either could hear was the *clop-splash . . . clop-splash* of the horses' hooves, and the steady raindrops falling on the ground and puddles all about them. Neither said a word.

At length Allison sighed. "Logan," she said, realizing she had perhaps been a little unfair, "I . . . I—" she wanted to apologize, but it was new territory for her. "Well . . . we'll be getting home soon, and . . . I have to maintain . . . you know, there's a certain dignity expected with my . . . the position I'm in. And I'm just not certain . . . that is—"

"Say no more, my lady," Logan broke in, with no rancor in his voice. "We are entering the real world, as we feared. And in that world, you are an heiress and I the offspring of a mere groom. You know, of course, that I don't give a fig for such distinctions of class. But I understand that they have been with you all your life."

"Life . . ." she murmured, repeating him, but with a pensive tone. Then after a moment, she added more emphatically, "I hate it!"

"What, Ali?" he asked as the wind had carried off her words.

"Nothing," she answered glumly. "How can you be so understanding?"

"I've seen something special in you today, Allison MacNeil," he answered earnestly, "but I have also seen a very confused and mixed-up young lady. I'm willing to be patient until you sort out the two."

"How kind of you!" she snapped sarcastically. Then she dropped her head, confused and possibly a little ashamed, and added, "Oh, forget it!"

They fell silent again, and remained so until the gray walls of Stonewycke broke through the gray mist of the storm.

The castle was not exactly a welcoming sight. It had been built four hundred years before, not to welcome but to strike fear into the spirits of any who dared approach it. But Allison was glad, nonetheless, to see it.

She needed the protection of its thick granite walls just now, for her own personal walls were growing far too weak for her liking.

36 ※ *Grandpa Dorey*

B UT EVEN STONEWYCKE'S thick walls did not prove fortress enough for Allison. However much she tried to shut out every outside element that attempted to intrude upon her inner being, she could never fully shut out herself. And her own thoughts, and nothing else, caused her unrest.

For years she had allowed the flow of her existence to be determined by her confused and often conflicting emotions. Even after she had reached an age where serious thought began to be possible, she continued to steadfastly avoid analyzing why she acted as she did, why she felt as she did, and what her responses to life should possibly entail. In short, she avoided looking honestly in the quiet of her own soul at the most basic of life's questions: *Who am I, and what should I be about?*

Since her earliest childhood years, she had known two things: that her family believed in God's active participation in their lives, and that her family held a position of importance and esteem. As a child she adopted the external appearance of pursuing her parents' spiritual values. Yet as she grew into her teen years, without revealing it to any observers, more and more she began to sense a divergence between what she came to term her "religious" parents and her own inner spiritual void. How could she know of the turmoil and struggles and periods of doubt that her parents and great-grandparents had experienced on the way to their present lives of faith? All she knew was that they spoke and acted as if God were an intimate friend, while to her "religion," as she called it, was dry and impersonal. The end result of this divergence was the feeling that somehow there was something wrong with her intrinsic being. She was out of step. Something about her was incomplete and inadequate. She was supposed to be like them, but wasn't. Yet she couldn't help it. And, of course, the more this feeling grew upon her, the more she tried to hide it from view, both from her parents and great-grandparents, and even from herself.

Added to this was the knowledge that everyone looked up to her mother and father, the matriarch and patriarch of the community, Lady Margaret and Grandpa Dorey, with a love and veneration akin to that given to royalty. The fact could hardly escape her that the family line had come down from the Lady Atlanta through the women of the family—all solid, virtuous, strong, capable, and—in Allison's mind—far more religious and compassionate toward Strathy's common folk than she. And now here she stood, next in line to wear that mantle, and yet totally lacking the attitudes and qualities which set her mother and great-grandmother apart in people's minds. They would all expect her to be like them, to be just as good and selfless and wise and strong and godly. Yet down inside, Allison knew all too well that she was none of those things. And maybe never could be.

The result was a growing feeling of pressure, from about her tenth year on, to be something she was not. In the bewildered, hurting inner self of a girl struggling to enter into her own womanhood, young Allison through the next several years came to resent the very things she wanted most to be. What she considered to be her inability to measure up to standards set before her in both matters of spirituality and her place in society, caused her to begin tearing away at those very foundations of virtue and holiness.

Thus her own spiritual and personal insecurity, by the time she was fifteen, had taken the form of an independence that seemed bent on carving out a life for herself which was at odds with everything previous generations stood for. In her innermost being—a part of herself by now so hidden that even she did not know of its existence—she still hungered desperately for the reality of a friendship with God such as she witnessed daily in her mother and father, and even more so in the older people. But on the surface level of her daily life, she resisted their attempts to say that God was a "personal" God. *He's not personal to me,* she thought, *and I don't need Him! I can make it just fine on my own; I don't need them OR Him.*

And in the same way she seemed determined to rebel against the very attributes within her mother and great-grandmother that others so admired, even resenting their goodness and qualities of strong character. To defend her own insecurity, she tore at the very roots of her being, seeking to find refuge in being someone of importance. She scoffed at her father's common origins and her mother's identification with the poor of the community. Because she was not secure in who she was, she attempted to elevate her stature in the eyes of the world, clinging to an elusive sense of superiority. But even her seemingly egotistical pride could not conceal to perceptive eyes that deep inside remained a pain which nothing but a personal encounter with the God of her fathers and mothers could heal.

And now, at seventeen, she still had not allowed herself to reflect on these matters. When thoughts of conscience came, she quickly dismissed them as childish carryovers from the outmoded values of her elders. She did not need them, she tried to convince herself. This was a new age, and she would be her own person. She did not recognize the steady tapping on the door of her heart. Her hour had not yet come, but it was nigh at hand. The prayers of the generations before her were on the verge of being fulfilled in her. For no word from the mouth of the Lord returns void, but always accomplishes that which He pleases. The prayers of the righteous avail much in the lives of their descendants, for the Lord pours out His love and mercy to the third and fourth generation of those who love Him and keep His commandments. The prayers young Maggie prayed in her exile—fulfilled in part in the life of her granddaughter, whose more recent prayers for her own daughter combined with them in the mysterious stream of God's mighty purpose—now came to bear on the heart of young Allison MacNeil, resistant to God, yet chosen by Him to share in the inheritance of the saints.

And the instrument in God's hand to begin this process of healing was one in whom the treasured generational flow of righteousness was also silently at work. How could the nearly crippled old Digory MacNab have foreseen that his quiet prayers in his lonely loft would stretch across the years, down through time, to unlock the hearts of both his own posterity and that of his beloved Maggie, for whom the humble witness of his life had accomplished so much? But no man can ever know how far his prayers and the impact of his life will reach. In the infinite provision of God's wisdom, the prayers of the righteous always come full circle, though none but the God who inspires them will ever know the full stories of their impact.

For now, in the somber solitude of a cheerless upstairs room in the austere castle known as Stonewycke, and in the darkened stable loft where the spirit of a godly man's prayers still dwelt, the loving heavenward cries of former generations were at last coming to bear upon the hearts of two young people. The Hound of Heaven, who had been stalking them all their lives long, was closing in.

Allison stood quietly staring out her window into the dreary wet below. What she was thinking she hardly knew herself. Her mind was more confused now than it had been two days ago. She had been so looking forward to that party. Now the mere memory of it left a bitter taste in her mouth. Everything was all wrong now! Life had been smooth enough—a little boring, perhaps, but at least predictable—before. But now that he had come, it was all mixed up! Why couldn't he have left well enough alone, left them to get home by themselves without having to meddle with their car? He had no right to interfere! And who was he, anyway? Supposedly the nephew of some stupid old groom. She doubted it! He was a fake. Limping with the wrong foot! But of course everyone thought he was wonderful, thanking him for getting her home safely. Why, you'd have thought he was the son of the Prime Minister, the way her father treated him. But that was just like him, just like them all! Always making over the peasants and ignoring her. Didn't anybody care that she had almost been swept away by the flood? What if that bridge had given way? Then what would they think of their precious Logan Macintyre? What a fool she had been to let him kiss her! Now he would think she felt something for him. He'd begin to take liberties. And, of course, she hadn't felt anything for him. She couldn't have! He was a nobody. He had no family. No position. What she had felt was nothing more than—well, it was nothing at all! She had been cold and afraid. Everything was just an accident! It meant nothing! She couldn't trust her feelings for him. She'd been emotionally caught up in the party and the storm, it just all—

Allison turned away from the window, hesitated a moment, then fled her room. She could take no more of this inner mental wrestling with herself. Everything was all a jumble!

She couldn't go outside. It was wet and cold. Even worse, she might run into *him*. And that would never do. She wanted no more chance meetings. Who could tell what he might do?

Perhaps a good book would liberate her overactive mind and help her to concentrate on other things. She turned and walked toward the library.

As she opened the great oaken door of the austere, book-lined room, Allison stopped short. There stood her great-grandfather in front of a shelf of first editions of Scott. He had been reaching up for one of the volumes when he heard the door open, and turned. Escape was impossible for Allison, who did not think she wanted to see anyone. But when he smiled, she realized that a small part of her at least was glad to see him.

"Ali, how nice to see you," he said in that soft and sincere tone he used most often these days.

"Hello, Grandpa Dorey," she answered, trying to be friendly but her voice betraying a touch of formality. "I didn't mean to interrupt you," she added, as she made to retreat.

"You haven't at all," he said hastily. "Do come in and sit down." He let his hand fall from the shelf and moved to one of the comfortable brocaded chairs positioned for the use of readers. He sat down, indicating an adjacent one to her. "I've been hoping I'd see you," he went on, his whole demeanor indicating that this encounter was much more to his liking than a leather-bound Sir Walter Scott.

"Oh?"

"I wanted to see how you were after your ordeal."

"What ordeal, Grandpa?"

"Your mother told me about the unfortunate events of two days ago. I'm sorry the party and all that followed turned out such a disappointment for you."

"Disappointment?" She may have placed many labels on that day, but somehow "disappointing" would not have been one of them. "I suppose it was rather disastrous," she went on after a brief pause, "but—well, it wasn't so bad."

Dorey chuckled softly. "I had nearly forgotten the capacity you young people have for making the most out of everything. A rather godly attribute, too, when you think about it. For after all, He originated the truth that it is possible for all things to work for good—though of course on a much higher plane." In truth, he had forgotten no such thing. He knew perhaps better than anyone that the older one becomes the more clear that truth becomes, and that often the young are utterly blind to it—as he had once been. But he had been feeling a gentle prodding to speak to her for some time, and thus made the most of the opportunity when it at length presented itself.

In her present rather befuddled state, it rankled Allison that her great-grandfather had chosen to turn what might have been a pleasant conversation into another religious dissertation. He was usually less irritating in that regard than any of them. Thus she took a more biting tone than she ordinarily would have with him.

"I don't see how you, of all people, can say that, Grandpa."

"I'm not sure I understand you."

"After all you've been through," said Allison, "how can you claim that God works everything for good?"

"I didn't exactly say He *does* work everything for good," Dorey replied. "I said *it is possible* for all things to work for good."

"Don't split hairs, Grandpa. What's the difference?"

"A great deal, my dear. God works things for good only when we allow Him to. The Bible says He works all things for the good of those who love Him if they are living according to His purpose. That's a rather big if."

Allison smiled oddly. She could tell what he was driving at. But she was not going to be sidetracked.

"That may very well be," she said. "It's all too pious sounding for me. But I still want to know how you can say that all things have worked for your good after the rotten deal you had?"

He smiled and nodded, not at all affronted by the turn of the conversation.

"The fact is, my dear, that of all people, I may know it best. When I was young I was determined to make my life go the way *I* thought was best. I ignored the Lord, and—you're right—things did not turn out very well. But as I gradually and painfully realized the futility of what I was trying to do, more and more I saw the necessity of giving the Lord my life— all of it, not just bits and pieces here and there. Then *He* was able to take the reins, so to speak, and begin working everything that happened for my good. And now here I am, content and happy, surrounded by my dear family, at peace and rest, more ready than I ever could have been in the past to be with my Lord. My life is a perfect example of that truth. So perhaps I was amiss before when I said that young people have the capacity to do the same thing. It may be that it is the passage of years that allows one's eyes to be opened."

"But, Grandpa," insisted Allison, "your life has been anything but happy!"

"Oh, my dear," sighed Dorey, "happiness is not what we were put on this earth to strive for, or to achieve. It may come our way; it may not. But we are called to something so much greater."

"Like what?"

"To know Him! If it takes heartache and loss for us to know Him, the price is a small one to pay for the timeless and eternal treasure of that relationship. Ali, do you know that I would not trade one hour, not one minute of my past for years and years and years of earthly happiness! I was such a stubborn young man. It took those years of grief to break the shell of my stubborn pride. And I am so thankful He loved me enough to see the job through."

He stopped momentarily, and Allison could almost detect a glow on his face. Though she could hardly grasp the depth of his words, she could sense how truly he meant what he said. He really was, as he said, *thankful* for the ups and downs of his life. The look on his face sobered her, and took from her the desire to pick his words apart. She could feel the reality in what he was telling her, although her conscious mind was unable to apprehend it fully.

"So you see, Ali," he went on, "it is God who turns evil or unhappiness or confusion or heartache into good, even when the recipient is unaware of His hand."

Allison knew his statement was directed at her, but she had to ask regardless. "Do you really think God's hand is on me?"

"In everything you do, my dear."

"But I don't always try to live by His purpose, like you said. So how can His hand be on me? How can He be working good in my life?"

"Because He has a purpose for you, Ali. The day will come when you will see His hand guiding you."

"If only I could believe that, Grandpa," sighed Allison, in a rare relaxing of the stoic pretense which she showed the world. "But—"

"He loves you, Ali!" said Dorey tenderly, taking his great-granddaughter's hand in his. "And so do I, and the rest of the family."

"I just don't know, Grandpa . . ." she said, her voice unsteady. "It's so hard to believe that when I've been so . . . you know."

He gently patted her hand with his, old and gnarled as it was. "There are many who are praying on your behalf, Ali. I am praying that you will know His love . . . and mine, toward you. You are not alone. You can take strength from that."

Allison's eyes were moist now, but she fought the compelling urge to break down. She had to maintain her composure! "I . . . I know I must be a terrible disappointment to you," she blurted out.

"Oh, Ali," replied Dorey in a voice full of both anguish and compassion, tears standing in his ancient eyes, "you have never been that! God forgive us if we have somehow led you to think so!"

"Maybe not to you, Grandpa," she said, "but I know Mother and Father don't think I measure up to the grand family traditions." There was not a trace of accusation in her voice, only broken, self-inflicted hurt.

"I think you misunderstand them, Ali. I know your father thinks the world of you. He—"

Suddenly the door burst open, and Allison was rescued from having to show the tears which seemed determined not to stay where they belonged. The door she had opened toward the heart of her great-grandfather quickly shut, and she returned to normal.

Nat's red head popped into the library and, breathless, he said: "Oh, there you are, Allison! You've got a visitor."

37 ⁂ Unexpected Guest

AS SHE DESCENDED the stairs, Allison quickly scanned her appearance. She probably should have taken a few minutes to change her clothes, but maybe it would be no one important.

She had donned her kilt of the green Duncan plaid and a navy cashmere sweater that morning, mostly for warmth. The navy blue knee stockings and oxfords only added to the schoolgirl look. As she thought about her clothing, it momentarily dawned on Allison how quickly her mind had shifted from the deep, emotional concerns of the morning to the trivial. Actually, she was relieved to be able to think of something of no more lasting significance than her clothes. The conversation with her great-grandfather had further stirred up thoughts she preferred to keep in place. She didn't like all this meditation! The yearnings which had always been buried deep inside her were now stirring into activity. But like all awakenings, the birth of spiritual consciousness would not occur without the pain of the breaking of the shell which enclosed it. And before the process was complete, the being in whose heart that embryo lay would more than once seek refuge in the comfortable womb of the past, resisting the painful process of being born again.

Allison walked into the family sitting room. There by the great hearth, thumbing through a recent copy of *The Strand,* stood Charles Fairgate. Inwardly Allison cringed with mortification. This schoolgirl look was the last image she wanted to portray to him!

"I hope you don't mind my coming without an invitation," he said, laying aside the magazine and approaching her.

"Of course not," replied Allison, trying to sound cheerful. "But if I'd known you were coming, I would have dressed more suitably. As you can see, I just threw something on to keep warm—this dreadful old castle, you know. So drafty!"

"You look exquisite," said Fairgate.

"Don't fib, Charles," replied Allison, trying to hide her embarrassment, not over his comment but from how she looked. "But I am surprised to see you out in this awful weather."

"It's settled down quite a bit since yesterday," he replied. "Even the sea is calming rather nicely. And besides, what's a bit of weather where friendships are concerned?"

He moved to a sofa where he reclined easily. She sat in an adjacent chair, strangely uncomfortable with his visit thus far, though she couldn't say why.

"I went directly to Aberdeen after the Bramfords' ball," he went on after they were settled. "My family has some interests in the shipyards. Waiting for me there was a telegram requesting my presence in London next week. A friend of mine was about to take his new yacht out on a shakedown cruise the moment the storm let up. I convinced him to take it north. I said to myself that I couldn't go to London, which would surely detain me for weeks, without seeing Allison once more. So when the winds died down yesterday morning, we sailed stopping off at Peterhead, and here we are. He's moored down at the harbor right now."

"That's very flattering of you, Charles," said Allison, still uncomfortable, but warming to Fairgate's charm. He had never been this attentive to her before.

"I didn't mean it entirely to flatter you."

"Oh?"

"I must admit I do have an ulterior motive."

"Sounds suspicious," she replied, her old coyness gaining the upper hand.

"I hoped I might be able to pry you out of this grim nest. What would you say to an exhilarating sail to Inverness, then a train to London?"

"My, that *is* a daring proposal! I hardly know what to think."

"You'll have a grand time."

"I'm sure I would." Allison laughed just at the thought of it. Just to imagine what it might be like sent a tingle through her—the exciting thrill of high society life which Charles was sure to be a part of. "But alas," she added, inexplicably feeling less regret than her tone indicated, "you know my parents. They are extremely old-fashioned—they hardly let me out of the house without a proper chaperone."

"The party at the Bramfords' must have been quite an exception, then," he said tightly. "I don't believe I saw a chaperone with you and Mr. Macintyre."

"Oh, that . . ." she said with a nervousness she couldn't hide and which Fairgate duly noted, to his further annoyance. "Mr. Macintyre is . . . a trusted family employee."

"Rather remarkable, isn't it, for one so young to acquire such trust?" His eyebrow cocked slightly, revealing that he saw only too well through this amplification of the truth. What he tried not to reveal was that the mere mention of Logan Macintyre was an irritation to him. "And it's funny," he went on, "I cannot seem to recall ever hearing his name mentioned before in connection with Stonewycke."

"He hasn't personally been here long, of course," said Allison, "but his family has been in the . . . uh, service of our family for . . . er, years. Several generations, in fact."

"Well, it is remarkable nevertheless," repeated Fairgate.

"You might say he is a bit remarkable, that is . . . in the area of maturity. He's rather like . . . a big brother to me. That's all."

Fairgate didn't much care for the look in her eye or the tone of her voice. He had labored under the same reaction with Angela Cunningham two days ago when Macintyre's name had been mentioned. Angela, however, had been less subtle. She had rambled on incessantly about the dashing newcomer on the drive home, hardly trying to hide the fact that she was attempting to make her beau jealous—and succeeding rather admirably in one so cocky as Charles Reynolds Fairgate III.

Until now Charles had had things pretty much his own way. Though he had been working his way toward the heartstrings of Stonewycke slowly, the future earl of Dalmount was anything but subtle when it came to his ultimate design. He already dared to envision himself as the future laird of Stonewycke, and looked forward to the time when he might once again extend its boundaries and reestablish its preeminence in northern Scotland. If neither Alec nor Joanna dreamed what was in the mind of the young man who came calling upon occasion, neither did Allison, despite all her seemingly worldly wisdom. She enjoyed his company, and flattered herself that he seemed moderately interested in her. But she had no true sense of his eventual aspirations.

Fairgate on his part, had enjoyed himself juggling the attentions of the two very lovely and high-bred young women. Angela was pretty enough, but her family was no match for Allison's in prestige and status. She was a pleasant distraction while Fairgate was biding his time. He could afford to wait a year or two until Allison matured. He would gradually work himself into a more intimate friendship with her simpleton vet of a father, until the appropriate moment came. He knew he was the most eligible and sought-after bachelor in his social circle—though he wondered why the people at Stonewycke did not seem aware of that fact—and had the pick of the available debutantes. He could thus afford the impropriety of being seen with two women at once.

Such had been his plan, at least. But he hadn't planned on this Macintyre fellow suddenly coming in and brazenly rocking his comfortable little boat. Most provoking of all was that in a single evening, Logan had threatened him on both feminine fronts and came dangerously close to cleaning him out at cards. It was just lucky for him he'd drawn that straight on the last hand.

He didn't like being put in this position by anybody, even a nobody who would never get far in his pursuits. The fact was, no matter how far Logan might reasonably get, he had already cast a shadow on Fairgate's parade. And Charles Reynolds Fairgate was not the sort to share anything, especially the limelight. Thus he arrived at this madcap idea of attempting to spirit Allison away for a visit to London. He knew it could not hope to succeed. But perhaps the mere thought of a romantic flight south with him would implant sufficient thoughts of him in Allison's mind to waylay the wiles of Macintyre. If only he could recall why he was so certain he knew him!

"We shall miss you," Fairgate said coolly. "Perhaps when you are a little *older* . . ."

The jab struck its mark, and Allison pulled herself up with all the self-importance a seventeen-year-old could muster. "I can jolly well go to London whenever I please," she asserted with emphasis, "chaperone or not. It's high time my parents got out of the Dark Ages, anyhow. But as it happens, I don't fancy a sail anywhere in this weather, or a long train ride either. And I was already considering traveling to London later in the year."

"Then perhaps I shall meet you there," said Charles, a bit more warmly.

"Perhaps . . ." Now it was Allison's turn for a calculated cooling of her tone.

The conversation drifted to more benign topics while they had tea. Then Allison invited Fairgate to accompany her on a walk about the place. As they walked through the gallery, he could not help but be impressed at the originals by Raeburn, Reynolds, and Gainsborough. On the wall hung the sword reputed to have been a gift from Bonnie Prince Charlie to Colin Ramsey, who gave his life in the would-be king's futile cause.

But Fairgate's mind was only half on the valuable antiquities, though he had to admit he wouldn't mind possessing them. He could not keep himself from sulking vengefully over the impertinent so-called trusted servant Logan Macintyre. Not only was Logan's position right on the estate and so close to Allison dangerous, but as Angela Cunningham had left him she had slipped in a final crafty thrust with her incisive tongue. "I really must renew my acquaintance with Allison MacNeil," she had said with a more than knowing glint in her cunning eye. "I think I'll run up there next week while you are gone, Charles dear, and pay a little visit." She well knew that Charles had not missed the underlying message that it wasn't Allison she was particularly interested in seeing.

So, Macintyre would have both young things within his clutches, would he? And Charles himself did indeed have to go to London—it could not be avoided. *Lucky in cards, lucky in love.* Charles mused as he pretended to keep up a passing interest in what Allison was showing him.

That card game the other night at Bramfords' still stuck in his craw. Even if he had won, something in Macintyre's supercilious manner had annoyed him, and it only added to Fairgate's account against him. He did not like losing, at cards any more than with women, and he was the type who did not easily forget his losses at either. But to win, and yet to walk away with the distinct impression that the other had nevertheless maintained some unspoken and invisible advantage over him—that was worse than an outright defeat.

Lucky at cards . . .

Subconsciously Fairgate began to tick off his past losses at the gaming tables. Something about Macintyre had unsettled him since the moment he had laid eyes on him. Why could he not shake that nagging feeling that they had met?

Of course—they *had* met! All at once the scene flashed through his mind's eye as if it were yesterday.

How could he have possibly forgotten?

The recollection struck him with such impact that he gasped audibly.

"What is it, Charles?" asked Allison in the midst of an explanation of the history of the fine Raeburn clan chieftan hanging in the formal parlor.

"What?" replied Charles in a detached tone, then suddenly recalling himself, "Oh . . . nothing . . . I—I just banged my shin on this chair." He laughed lightly, trying to cover himself.

"My great-grandmother always makes over this portrait," Allison went on. "It's of her great— let's see, it would be her great-great-grandfather Robert Ramsey. Tradition has it that he and his mother helped hide Prince Charlie for a few days after the '45, on his way from Skye to France."

"Very interesting," commented Fairgate politely. Then, as if his mind had not been intent on the very subject for the last hour but it had just occurred to him, he added casually, "I say, it just crossed my mind that it would be terribly impolite of me to come all this way and not give my regards to your Mr. Macintyre."

An hour earlier Allison would have gone to whatever lengths she could manage to avoid such a meeting, and to avoid having to lay eyes on Logan herself. But her brief foray into the regions of healthy self-reflection had already faltered as a result of Fairgate's presence. The threat to her emotions was not nearly so great now. It might even be enjoyable to watch the two men spar because of her.

After a brief pause as Allison considered the implications of Fairgate's statement, she smiled, and led him toward the corridor which would take them to the ground floor and outside to the stable.

"How well do you know Macintyre?" asked Fairgate, diligently trying to keep his voice sounding indifferent.

"Well . . . he is, as I said, of a family which has been—"

"But *he* hasn't been here long?"

"No . . . not long really."

"So you personally haven't been acquainted with him for many years?"

"Not really . . . No, not exactly. Why all the sudden interest in a mere hired hand?"

"Oh, just curious. His face struck me the other night somehow, that's all. Just curious."

Without another mention of him they made their way outside, Fairgate anticipating the encounter with relish.

38 ❈ Confrontation

LOGAN HAD NOTED Fairgate's arrival. Whether it irritated him because of Allison, or whether it worried him because of himself, he didn't exactly know. But he did know that the heir's appearance at Stonewycke was not a welcome sight.

Allison was growing to mean something to him.

He could scarcely admit it to himself, but he had hardly stopped thinking of her since yesterday. Her abandoned laughter in the rain and mud beside the broken-down Austin still lingered in his ears. To find himself stymied with his work because his mind was filled with the pretty face of a young lady was an altogether new sensation to Logan Macintyre. Even her petulance reminded him of a jewel that, with the rough edges smoothed out, would be precious beyond price. He had enough of his own rough edges to worry about, so he could hardly be too critical. What was it old Skittles used to say? "Molly and me are like two rocks in a tumbler sometimes. But if we stick together we'll soon end up smooth and shiny."

Like rocks in a tumbler . . . yes, that could describe his relationship with Allison—if he wanted to presume so far as to call it a relationship at all. Up and down, now arguing, now laughing, now self-protective, now opening up. The process was as new to Logan as it was to Allison.

Logan was still valiantly trying to maintain his single-mindedness toward his goal. But it was becoming more difficult with each passing moment.

Fairgate had added a whole new dimension to the scenario—jealousy, although Logan would have disdained giving it that name. He tried to look at it more pragmatically, like a card game. Did he want to fold or raise? The stakes were clear. It was a simple decision, not some emotional ordeal, he desperately tried to convince himself. Could his three jacks beat whatever Fairgate held? It would cost him to find out. It could well cost him Allison. But even so, he could retreat and nothing would be changed. Logan could still get his treasure, and leave Fairgate with Allison.

Thus he tried to reason with himself. But the fact of the matter was that it *was* an emotional response. He could not be entirely pragmatic about it. The price of losing Allison to a contemptible fellow like Fairgate was enough to raise the hair on the back of his neck. Therefore, when he saw the two approach, looking every inch the ideal aristocratic couple, foolhardy though it would be and little chance as he had, he knew he would call Fairgate's bluff. He pretended not to see them coming and went on with what he was doing.

Logan glanced up from his work on Jesse Cameron's power winch as they pushed open the stable doors. He didn't like the fact that they had apparently sought him out. Fairgate did not strike him as the type to make friendly calls, and the look on Allison's face displayed not a hint of any previous familiarity with him; the glassed-over look of her former shell was firmly back in place. Regardless, Logan attempted the gesture of a friendly welcome, not unlike he supposed his uncle might have welcomed visitors to *his* stables.

"Hello," he said, wiping his hands on a cloth. "What brings you all the way out here?" He extended his hand to Charles, who took it in a gentlemanly fashion. The handshake was firm and sincere, if one judged merely by the feel of its grasp. But over the years Logan had developed the habit of assessing a man more by the look in his eye, and Fairgate's glance was cold and hard, with a hint of cunning, which Logan did not like.

"Charles dropped by on his way to Inverness," said Allison lightly, "and he wouldn't have forgiven himself if he had not at least given you his greetings." Her voice was too pleasant, too easygoing. She and Fairgate did indeed seem most suitably matched.

"Very considerate of you, Fairgate," Logan replied, on his guard.

"Well, I've always thought a night of gambling instills a certain bond between men," said Charles. "Don't you agree?"

"I suppose so," replied Logan warily.

"Charles sailed here from Aberdeen," put in Allison. "Isn't that daring?" She was playing her own little game, pitting the sensitivities of the two against one another, unaware of the more perilous war of nerves going on between the men.

"It must have been—for you, Fairgate," said Logan, "especially in this weather."

"It heightens the challenge, but then you'd know all about that sort of thing, wouldn't you, Macintyre?"

"I'm afraid I know nothing about sailing."

"I was talking about challenges."

The real intent of Fairgate's words was becoming clear, assisted by the sly glow of anticipated victory in his eye. So, he had at last remembered their former acquaintance and was now going to make his adversary pay! That had to be the purpose of this contrived little meeting. Well, there was no way out of it. There was nothing for Logan to do except remain cool. "Whatever 'appens," Skittles always said, "don't bolt. Always play the dodge to the end—unless the Bobbies are breathin' down your neck."

"Ah yes . . . the challenge of the sea," said Logan. "I was on a fishing vessel recently and almost lost my neck from the challenge." He laughed, trying to divert the attention from Fairgate's probing remarks.

"A fascinating life—the sea," replied Fairgate. "But then it runs in my family. It has since the days we built frigates for Queen Elizabeth. Drake sailed one of our vessels."

"How positively intriguing."

"In fact, I'm off now for Glasgow to oversee the launching of our new liner."

"You didn't say anything about Glasgow," intruded Allison, a bit confused at the direction and stilted quality of the conversation. Around her eyes could be seen a slight cracking of the shell. She wasn't sure she liked what Fairgate was doing to Logan.

"I don't look forward to it, though," continued Charles, heedless of Allison's remark. "It's a rum city, that. Have you ever been there, Macintyre?"

"Once or twice."

"Then you know. A worse city there never was—for civilized folks, that is."

"I'm sure you're right."

"Gentlemen have to watch what they're about in that city."

Logan said nothing, only returned Fairgate's gaze. The cards had been laid face down on the table, and now only the eyes betrayed the steely determination of the bluff.

"No telling when you're going to be fleeced," went on Fairgate, probing Logan's eyes. Still Logan did not reply, but his blood was starting to run hot.

"Why, I remember one time—"

"I don't mean to sound rude," Logan broke in, glancing over at Allison with an easy laugh intended to convey warmth and hopefully enlist her support in halting Fairgate's runaway reminiscing about the past. "But I promised Jesse I'd get this winch to her this afternoon."

"Don't let us keep you from your work, by all means," said Fairgate. But he had no intention of releasing this grip he had by now so forcibly seized. "You know, Macintyre," he went on, as if the thought had just occurred to him, "since the other evening at Bramfords', I've had the strangest sensation that I've met you before."

"I've never been in this area before in my life."

"Could it have been in Glasgow?"

"I suppose anything's possible," returned Logan bravely, deciding to face it squarely.

"Something about your face reminds me of that city."

"I have a terrible memory for such things myself."

"There was one fellow," Charles pressed relentlessly, clearly enjoying every moment. "You resemble him somewhat." Here he paused and laughed. "But of course, it couldn't have been you." He laughed again. "He was a grubby little street waif . . . and it was some years ago. Fancied himself a card sharp." As the words flowed from Fairgate's mouth, his good humor gradually turned into an icy stare of hatred, even while his mouth kept up its smile for Allison's benefit. "And he proved it by cheating me out of a tidy sum. Spent a few days in jail for it as I remember."

He turned to Allison, who was now more bewildered as she found herself torn between the two men. The old Allison stood beside her companion while he grilled a low employee; the new, squirmed with compassion and genuine sympathy for Logan. "Quite something, wouldn't you say, my dear?" laughed Fairgate merrily. "Can you imagine, a runny-nosed little kid trying to slick me and get away with it?"

He threw his head back and roared with laughter.

"Of course getting thrown in the clink wasn't anything new to *him,* for it came out in court that his father was a dirty jailbird too—"

"That's enough, Fairgate!" Logan exploded. Had Fairgate chosen any subject other than his father, Logan might have been able to let it pass. But he had spent too much time trying to dissociate himself from that man, too much time trying to forget his past, to hear Fairgate's accusation calmly.

Even then, Logan might have been able to restrain further outbursts had it not been for the silky, smug grin of satisfaction that spread across Fairgate's patrician face. That look caused Logan to lose his cherished control.

"Enough?" sneered Fairgate. "Enough! After what you did to me, infinitely your superior in every way, and you say *enough!"*

"Yes!" snapped Logan, "and I say it again—enough, or you'll be sorry you ever opened your mouth."

Fairgate roared with laughter again. *"I'll* be sorry! This really is too much, Macintyre! And what are you going to do if I persist?"

"To find that out," replied Logan, "you'll have to call my hand. But in the meantime, you leave my father out of it."

"Oh, so that's it! Your father! Sensitive whelp you are, I must say. But I hardly see what's to defend. The man was nothing but a lowdown—"

Logan lunged forward, his hand knotted into a fist and his eyes full of rage. The blow nearly felled the fine lord, but as it reached its mark and he staggered back, he caught himself against the work table and remained on his feet. Fairgate made no counterattack, only stood his ground and grinned back toward his assailant. Then he turned, almost casually toward Allison, who was looking on with horror. "So, Allison," he said, bringing his hand to his chin to stop a small trickle of blood, "at last we see the true colors of your houseguest. Or should I say your *trusted* family employee?"

White with mingled rage and chagrin for what he had done, Logan shot a glance at Allison. He had nearly forgotten her presence. And suddenly he knew why Fairgate still wore his proud grin. Logan had played right into his hand. He had proved with his angry outburst that every word Fairgate had said about him was true. Fairgate had raised the bet to the limit, had called Logan's hand, and had won it all. In that single act of violence, Logan had undone everything. And Fairgate's unmistakable victory was only punctuated by his refusal to reciprocate in kind. He was the gentleman, Logan the cad.

Allison had been so shocked by the turn of the confrontation that she merely stood gaping, hardly noticing Fairgate's words. When she did speak, all pretense and command was gone. The sensitive side of her nature was struggling desperately to absorb what had happened. She tried to answer, but her voice had not yet caught up with events.

"People of our station must take care for such riffraff," Charles advised, pressing his advantage to the full.

"He's . . . he's not a houseguest . . ." said Allison at length, still lagging behind Fairgate's half of the exchange. But her sentence ended unfinished as Logan swung around and strode from the stable.

Seeing her gaze following him, yet more sure of himself than ever, Fairgate chuckled cockily. "Let him go, Allison," he said. *"He* can mean nothing to *us* now."

But the words were unwisely spoken. He had pressed Allison too soon to make a choice between the victor and the vanquished, and like most sensitive women, Allison allowed her heart to follow Logan in the pain of his defeat.

Coming awake suddenly, without realizing what she did or why, Allison turned and ran after him. "Logan!" she called. "Logan!"

Whether her voice was not loud enough or whether he chose to ignore it, Logan kept walking, and was soon out of sight behind the stable.

She stopped and watched him silently, while Fairgate walked slowly up behind her from the open stable door.

"Let him go," he repeated in the same self-important tone. "He has deceived you, Allison. If I were you, I'd go and check the family silver."

She spun around, her face flushed with anger.

"What could you possibly know about him? He has behaved nothing but honorably since he came to us!" she lashed out.

"So, you're going to take up the cause for a common street swindler! Come now, Allison, it doesn't become you."

"You think I am somehow obligated to take your side against him?" she snapped. "Because you are more of a man . . . of better blood. Is that it?"

"Allison, Allison," he tried to soothe. "Men from his, shall we say, 'origins,' never do amount to anything. He's a deceiver . . . a swindler. I shouldn't be surprised to learn he's a thief. I ask you again, just what do you really know about him? And why is he here? That's another question one might reasonably ask." He gently placed a calming hand on Allison's shoulder.

She stood a moment longer, staring at the last place she had seen Logan, then, her anger at Fairgate subsiding, she shrugged off his touch, turned, and sat down on the bench next to the stable wall. What he said did make sense after all.

"He didn't exactly *lie* to us, Charles," she said finally. "That is, no one really *asked* about his background. And some uncle of his, or great uncle, used to work here."

"How convenient," said Fairgate sarcastically.

Allison shot him a questioning glance as another defense of Logan rose to her lips. She apparently thought better of it, however, sighed, and finally threw up her hands and said, "Oh, I don't know what to think."

"Any man who withholds information about a prison record—" Charles knew very well that Logan's few days in the custody of the court could not even broadly be termed a *prison record,* but he saw no reason to take particular pains to clarify this point—"well . . . such a man is practicing deception. There's just nothing else you can call it. You ought to inform your parents immediately."

"You don't know my parents," said Allison. And even as she spoke a picture leaped into her mind of how her family would receive such information. She especially saw her grandmother in her mind. Lady Margaret had always taken such pains with the poor and downtrodden, the "grubby street waifs" of the world. When they heard that he was an ex-convict, what would that matter to her elders? Hadn't Lord Duncan, the most revered man in all of Strathy, spent months in prison? No one here would turn Logan out, no matter what he had done.

For the last seven or eight years of her life, Allison had taken great pains to do just the opposite of what the rest of her family might. She had resented their compassion and had tried to rise above what she considered their family weakness. Yet doing so had never brought Allison peace. It had, in fact, produced just the opposite reaction. With a dual personality, she looked with disdain on her mother and great-grandmother and their charitable attitudes, but at the same time, the deepest part of her nature felt guilty for not being more like them.

Suddenly she had a chance to reach out to someone just like they would. And if she didn't, she had no doubt that Logan would walk right out of Port Strathy. But she was not ready to lose him. She could admit that now. She didn't want to lose the happiness she had felt with him for those brief moments on the road back from Culden. She had tried to hide from it, pretend it hadn't happened. She had been horrible to him afterward. But with Charles standing here now, suddenly everything was coming clear. She had never felt that way around him—all the titles and numbers after his name meant nothing. Maybe Logan was just the nephew of a groom. But she had *felt* something! And she couldn't just let it go. She had to find out what the feelings he had stirred in her meant.

She jumped up and started back toward the stable door.

"Where are you going?" asked Charles.

"I'm going after him."

"To make him face the music?"

"No. To apologize. You . . . you were very unkind to him, Charles." The words had been difficult to say to someone so imposing as Charles Fairgate. She knew her change of heart would "get around." But oddly, it felt rather liberating to stand up for something important.

"You'll never find him now," said Charles, coming up next to her.

"Just you watch me!"

"Don't be a fool, Allison."

They were inside the stable now and Allison was hurrying toward the stalls in back. The heavy clouds had returned overhead, and all at once a crack of thunder echoed outside.

"You'll not catch him," said Fairgate, hastening after her. "He's made a run for it. He probably has other warrants out for him."

"That's cruel, Charles."

"Where are you going, Allison?" he asked as she rushed through the rear door of the workshop. Something had gone wrong with his plan and he was not liking it.

"I'm going to saddle a horse and ride after him. He can't have gone far."

"It's starting to rain!"

Allison had already grabbed a saddle and thrown it atop her favorite—the bay mare. Rain was certainly the least deterrent for her at this moment; she had, in fact, very pleasant memories of rain. She only hoped it was not too late to recapture some of them.

She quickly tightened the saddle, opened the stall door, and led the horse out. She paused to throw a macintosh over her shoulders and jam a hat on her head. When she finally mounted, small droplets had begun to fall in earnest. But she welcomed the rain. The look in her face showed it clearly as she turned in the saddle toward Charles, who still stood inside, utterly baffled at the inexplicable change that had come over her.

"Have a nice sail, Charles," she called out, "and give my regrets to everyone in London!"

Without awaiting an answer, she dug her heels into the horse's flanks, galloped off, and was soon out of sight.

39 ❧ The Healing Rain

ALLISON FOUND LOGAN tramping across a wet stretch of moorland about a quarter of a mile behind Stonewycke.

He turned when he heard the horse making its way through the shrubbery. She pulled up beside him and slid gracefully off the bay. He continued to walk. Allison grabbed the reins and jogged to catch up. "Logan . . . please!" she called after him.

"You still don't know enough to get in out of the rain," he said, still walking, staring straight ahead.

"I don't care about the rain!" she answered passionately. "I wanted to apologize. It was just awful what Charles said to you."

Logan stopped. That was the last thing he had expected her to say. Of course, how could he have any idea what to expect from her? He had all but concluded that everything which had happened two days ago was a mirage, when suddenly it seemed possible their blossoming friendship had meant something to her after all.

But until this very moment it had not occurred to him how Allison would conflict with his designs. Logan had always maintained a hard and fast rule—one he had learned from Skittles: *Never hustle a friend.* He might lie, cheat, and steal from anyone else. But with his friends—of which, to be sure, there were few—he had always been open and honest.

Were these people his friends? Was Allison his friend?

The latter question hardly needed an answer. The sincere expression on her face was more convincing in his soul than any reasonings he could have made with himself. She had never been honest with anyone, not even herself. And yet her face said that she wanted to change that—with him. She was trying to be forthright. How could he lie to her anymore?

His thoughts had taken the merest seconds. Now he turned abruptly and faced her.

"Allison, everything he said about me was true."

"I'm sure you would have told us if we had asked."

"How do you know that?"

"It doesn't matter. I don't want to know what you would have done. And no one in my family will care, either. That's all in the past, anyway. I know just what my great-grandmother would say—that none of us are perfect, least of all me. And besides, none of them need know what Fairgate accused you of. I'll not tell."

"Why?"

"There's no reason. And besides, who's Charles Fairgate that I should believe him over you?"

"He's someone who knew me many years ago."

"I don't care. That was then, now is now."

"I'm not sure I understand," said Logan, still reeling from this sudden turnaround.

Allison paused a moment, and when she spoke again there was a quiet seriousness in her tone. "I haven't behaved in a way I'm proud of these last couple of days."

"Don't worry about it."

"I do worry about it. Sometimes the person I am isn't very nice. And . . . I'm sorry. Logan, *I do* want to be your friend."

"Thank you. You don't know how much that means to me. But there's still so much you don't understand."

"What does it matter? Don't spoil it, Logan Macintyre, or I might run out of sweetness for you yet. A girl can be only so nice in one day." She laughed, and he joined her.

Then Allison swung back up upon the bay. "Now!" she called down to him. "Get up here with me, and let's go for a ride!"

"But it's raining," he protested with another laugh.

"That never stopped us before."

He laughed, reached up and took her offered hand, and swung up behind her. He hadn't forgotten his earlier decision to be honest with her. But why spoil the moment with confessions and revelations? They could wait for a more opportune time.

Allison led the mare eastward, away from the flooded low country. The rocky ground rose steadily until they reached the Fenwick Harbor road which, had they followed it, would have led them to Aberdeen. They rode north instead, toward the sea. As they trotted along, the wind increased in force and the droplets of rain became larger and larger. A ragged flash of lightning lit the afternoon sky, followed almost the same instant by a crack of thunder.

"That was close by!" shouted Allison. "Right over on the coast, I'd say."

It was not much longer until they reached the Port Strathy road, with Ramsey Head directly to their right off the shoreline, shrouded in mist and clouds. Allison could not hold back a shudder at the granite promontory that would always be associated with evil doings.

"It might not be a bad idea to think of turning toward Stonewycke," said Logan. "If we wait much longer we'll get soaked again."

"I don't mind if you don't," said Allison cheerily. "But you're probably right."

They rode on past the Head. There had been a time, even during Lady Margaret's childhood, when the place had been used for pleasant afternoon walks and picnics, despite its ancient history as a hideout for smugglers and shipwreckers. But since then, it had reverted to its former ways in the minds of the local inhabitants. The caves surrounding it were well known to house occasional drunks and derelicts who were unconcerned about the dark legends of the place. And every Halloween, a report would begin to circulate of a body popping up among the jagged and treacherous sea rocks.

"Cold?" asked Logan, concerned over Allison's sudden silence.

"No, it's just this place, I suppose."

"What about it?"

Allison tried to relieve her nervousness by relating a portion of the history of the place. For the first time he discovered that the murderer who had killed himself had been involved in the events of Lord and Lady Duncan's early history, news that on first hearing struck him as incredulous.

All at once, as if to emphasize the heavy, ominous feeling that had descended upon them, a figure darted out onto the road from the very point in which they had been staring, coming it seemed directly from the trail down to the shore at Ramsey Head.

Allison reined in the mare, and there beside them stood Jesse Cameron. She had been running and now stopped with her hand to her chest, trying to catch her breath again before she could speak.

40 ❈ *Tragedy*

"Jesse!" exclaimed Logan. "What's all the hurry?"

"There's been an accident," she replied between gasps. "Some children were a playin' in one o' them sea caves on the Head. I don't know what the parents was thinkin' t' let them oot on a day such as this. But one o' them—young Harry Stewart—got himsel' hurt an' couldna climb oot. Alec happened t' be at my place seein' t' one o' my goats when the other young'un came fer help. Weel, he went doon t' lend a hand. He was gone sae lang I went doon. An' the cave they were in was all blocked up wi' rocks!"

"How—" asked Allison anxiously, "what do you mean?"

"Looks like one o' them tall pinnacles up above't may hae been struck by that blast o' lightin', an' when it fell, it must hae dislodged the boulders that formed the walls o' the cave. 'Tis all I can think o'. But Logan, man, they're trapped inside. I'm goin' t' toon t' get the others."

"How can you be certain it was the right cave?" Allison's voice was shaky. Many new emotions were assailing her all at once.

"The boy—oh, here he is noo—" a boy of about eleven came trotting out onto the road. He was smudged and wet and trembling with fear, exhaustion, and cold. Jesse put her thick arm around the child. "Tommy's certain. An' we'd hae seen them by noo. I'm sorry, Lady Allison. I canna believe otherwise."

"You think they might be . . ." Allison managed to say in a weak whisper, then stopped, swaying unsteadily in the saddle.

Logan caught her and held her tightly with one arm. Then with his free hand he took charge of the reins.

"Could you hear them?" he asked.

"No," Jesse answered, "but wi' the wind an' the noise o' the sea, not t' mention the solid rock blockin' up the mouth o' the cave, 'tis not surprisin'. There's still reason t' hope fer the best."

"You look spent already, Jesse," said the practical Logan. "You best take the boy back to your place and we'll ride for help."

"I'm going to my father," said Allison firmly, and, springing back to life, she wrenched the reins from Logan and dug her heels into the bay.

"Lass, ye canna do that," Jesse called. "Yer mother'll hae worry enough!"

But it was too late. The riders were already well out of earshot, even if Allison had been listening. Jesse wasted no more time trying to yell after them. Perhaps the two young folks could do something while she went for help. In the meantime she hurried back down the hill to her house, deposited the boy, hastily saddled her own horse, and rode for town.

Allison's bay found the going slow down the trail to the neck connecting the Head to the mainland. From there the animal had to thread her way cautiously up the muddy incline of Ramsey Head. In summer, the terrain on this, the leeward side of the promontory, was green with heather and bracken, dotted here and there with a handful of trees, bent and contorted by the constant sea winds. But at this time of year the foliage was brown and wet, beaten down by the steady barrage of rain. From the bleak face of nature, it would have been difficult to surmise that spring had already come to this region—come, and then seemingly given way again to winter without a hint of anything in between.

The horse was surefooted enough on this turf, but when they had climbed the path toward the seaward side, the hard and rocky surface, stripped of nearly all vegetation and slick with rain, became impossible to traverse. Several caves crowded this part of the promontory, some merely large crevices formed by the haphazard placement of boulders and cliffs, others extending well into the depths of the Head, bored through the rock over thousands of years by the constant contact with the sea. The floors of most were under water either part or all of the time, but there were a few high enough to remain snug and dry even at high tide. Those most challenging to Strathy's children were the ones accessible during low tide, but whose floors sunk below the ocean's surface as the tide came in.

"We'll have to leave the horse here," she called back to Logan over her shoulder. Though he was only inches from her, the wind velocity forced her to yell in order to be heard.

They dismounted and made their way along a narrow footpath skirting the circumference of the bluff some fifty feet above the water's edge. In a few minutes they rounded a curve, reaching the outermost point of the promontory, and were suddenly met with the full force of the wind and the open expanse of the sea. The gray waters frothed white around the edges like the mouth of a mad dog. The rain-filled blasts lashed at Allison's face, whipping her hair into a tangled mass about her head.

"There it is!" shouted Allison, pointing to a spot some distance down the path below a steep grade. They could make out the scattered rubble on the ledge, broken shards from the larger rocks that had been dislodged. A spike of stone, larger than a tree, lay against the wall of the mountain as if some giant had leaned his walking stick against a garden wall. On closer inspection, Allison saw that the cave was indeed one of the rock crevices. When the spike had fallen, its movement had displaced the boulders forming the walls of the cave, as Jesse had described.

Before they reached their destination, they had to traverse a steep descent which dropped about ten feet, where the trail had once been. Allison scrambled down with little difficulty, too intent on her father's peril to pay the least attention to her own. But Logan, afraid for her safety, was paying closer attention to the dropoff to the sea fifty feet below, just beyond the ledge. Into his imagination came a vision of the legendary murderer flying off a spot just like this to his death on the sharp rocks below. Even as he shook his head to rid his mind of the ominous picture, his foot slipped, and he had to struggle and claw at the precarious surface to keep himself from falling. He let out an involuntary cry which, muffled by the gale, went unheard by Allison several feet ahead. With trembling knees he followed slowly, none too confident they could accomplish anything even if they could reach the cave alive, resisting the great urge to turn around and run.

Slipping and sliding, and walking where possible, they made their way farther, till at last they neared the place where the cave-in had occurred. Still racing ahead, Allison began to yell for her father. But the wind carried her voice off as a vanishing puff of smoke.

She came to the heap of rock and immediately began to tear at the jagged slab of stone with her bare hands. Seeing her pathetic gesture, Logan set his hands also to the task, but nothing budged, save a few inconsequential stones. Her bravado tempered somewhat, she looked helplessly at Logan. She didn't have to speak for him to know what she was thinking. Even if the whole town turned out, they'd have difficulty moving these stones. And what good would the entire town do anyway? Only a handful of people could move about safely on the ledge that faced the cave.

In an agony of despair Allison stood back and began pacing around the area. Where was everyone? Why was it taking them so long to get here? All at once her eyes filled with tears.

"Daddy . . ." she murmured.

It had been so long since she thought about him as she once had when a child, how much he meant to her, how she needed him. She had been so cold to him in recent times, so independent, so unfeeling. What would happen now if she never had the chance to make it up to him?

"Oh, please . . . please," she whispered, hardly realizing her distraught mind was forming a prayer for the first time in years, "please don't let anything happen to him."

Logan went to her side.

"You have to believe he's safe," he said gently. "We'll get him out."

"Oh, Logan," she wailed, "I'm so afraid I won't ever get a chance to tell him—"

She could not go on. A sob choked out her words. She turned away, embarrassed at the show of emotion.

Logan laid a hand on her shoulder to comfort her, but said nothing.

"I've never been much of a daughter to him," she blurted out, crying now. "I don't think I've ever told him how proud I am to have him for my father."

"He must know."

"Oh, how could he know?" she wailed despondently. "I've let him think I'm ashamed of him because of his common birth. I've just been all mixed up, Logan," she confessed. "Why, he's better than a hundred highbred men together. It's just that—" she sniffed and brushed a sleeve across her nose, all pretense at playing the sophisticated role now gone. "Oh, I was so blind . . . I've been so confused. Why did I treat him like that?"

"Don't think of it now," said Logan lamely. He did not know any words of real comfort to give, so he settled for hollow phrases he had heard others give. Yet even as he spoke, he knew his words were empty, and wished he could offer more to soothe her aching heart. "It won't be long until he'll be right here next to you, and then you can make everything right."

"Oh, Logan," she cried, "if only I could do something *now*!" She turned her face back toward the rock wall and shouted with all her might, "Daddy, can you hear me!"

41 ❊ Rescue

ALEC LAY SPRAWLED on the bare rock in pitch darkness. A trickle of blood ran out of a deep gash on his head.

At last he tried to move, slowly and painfully. His head may have been the most seriously injured, but his shoulder and foot had also been grazed by the falling rock. Feeling a sharp throb in his head, he brought his hand to the wound and felt the sticky moistness of blood. He could see nothing around him and might reasonably have feared blindness until his eyes adjusted and he began to distinguish dim shadows.

"Harry!" he called, thinking of the boy the moment his head began to clear.

"I'm here, Mr. MacNeil."

"Are ye safe, boy?"

"Aye, sir. 'Tis jist my leg hurts sorely."

"Stay where ye are, Harry, an' I'll get t' ye."

Alec rolled over and attempted to pull himself up. He barely reached his knees when everything solid seemed to melt from under him and he crumbled back to the ground. "'Tis goin' t' take me a minute or twa, lad. Can ye wait?"

"Aye, sir," said the boy, but his voice trembled with each word. "Mr. MacNeil, do ye think we're stuck in here fore'er?"

"Not a bit o' it, lad," Alec replied as buoyantly as he could make his voice sound. "We'll be oot o' here afore supper. Jesse'll get help an' they'll clear away the rock before we know it." He paused, then added, trying to conceal his concern, especially with the rising tide in the back of his mind, "Hoo lang hae I been lyin' here, lad?"

"A powerful lang time, sir. I thought ye was—" Harry's voice broke, and the remainder of his thought hardly needed to be spoken. Then he added in a tearful rush, "Oh, I'm glad I'm na here alane!"

"Noo, lad," said Alec, "ye wouldna hae been alane whate'er had happened. Our Lord's here wi' ye—wi' us both, lad. He'll ne'er leave us alane—ye ken that, dinna ye, lad?"

"Aye, sir, but I'm guessin' I forgot for a bit."

Alec's smile was unseen in the darkness, but it could be heard in his gentle words. "I'm thinkin' the Lord understan's that. But let's remember t' remin' one another o' it."

"Aye, sir," said Harry.

"I'm comin' t' ye noo," said Alec, praying silently for strength.

He crawled along the floor of the cave for a foot or two until he came to an upright wall. He could not tell if it was the wall of the cave or merely a section of the rubble that had shut them in. At least it was solid enough to hold his weight. Groping at one protruding rock after another, he pulled himself to a standing position. Everything spun before him, and he felt fresh blood flow into his eyes, obscuring what little vision he had. He wiped a hand across his eyes, then steadied himself for a moment before beginning to inch his way along the wall toward the boy's voice. His foot throbbed, seemingly in rhythm with the ache in his head. He must have twisted it during the fall.

It took him five long, torturous minutes to reach Harry. When he finally did so, he nearly collapsed on the ground beside him. He rested a moment, then tried to examine the boy's leg.

It was a definite break, but there was little he could do. It was a wonder the poor boy had not yet fainted from shock. His medical instinct forced him to make some attempt to help, no matter how feeble it turned out to be. But he had not even come across a piece of driftwood he could use as a splint. He lurched to his feet, and, after instructing Harry to keep perfectly still, began groping about the cave. Vagrants and wanderers often camped out around here. Perhaps some sticks from an old campfire might be lying around.

After some searching, his hands lit upon several pieces of charred wood. They were irregular, and it took some skill to suit them to his purpose. But with the aid of his shirt, torn into strips, he made them work. He had made better splints for injured kittens, but at least the boy's every movement would not incapacitate him.

When he had done all he could do medically, he turned his attention to their plight. After loosening a few of the smaller stones and forcing his shoulder several times against the large ones, he realized there was no way a single man, especially an injured one, was going to be able to begin to budge the debris. Not a man given to fits of hopelessness, he limped back and forth across their narrow prison for several minutes, thinking and praying, wishing there were something he could *do*. Strong as his faith was, it was agony to Alec MacNeil simply to sit and wait for the hand of the Lord to act, without being able to participate in the process himself.

At length, so that his agitation would not further upset the boy, he sat down once more next to Harry, reaching his arm around him to give the child both warmth and comfort. There was nothing else to do but to wait and pray, and give what strength he could to the frightened child.

When he started awake after some time, he wasn't certain if the sounds he heard were from his dreams or from somewhere beyond the blackness. He cocked his head and listened intently.

There it was again! A high-pitched sound, almost like the wail of the wind, yet there was a desperate human quality about it. He jumped up, forgetting his injured foot, and nearly fell again to the ground. Supporting himself as best he could, he hobbled as quickly as his head and foot would allow to the mouth of the cave.

The sound came again, more distinct now, yet seemingly still as part of his dream. Yet he was almost certain he could make out the single unlikely word:

Daddy!

He shouted out a reply, and Harry's small voice joined his own. "We're here! We're all right!"

The sound of her father's voice filled Allison with an unabashed and childlike joy such as she had not recently allowed herself to feel.

"He's safe!" she exclaimed, throwing her arms around Logan and squeezing him as if he had been the object of her anxieties. The tears were flowing freely now, but she seemed unconcerned and did not try to hide them. She stood back, looked into his eyes, laughed with relief, then embraced him again.

All at once a loud clamor reached them from above the wail of the wind. It was the approach of the rescue party. Logan and Allison fell apart awkwardly, trying quickly to regain their composure. But Allison hardly cared what the others might think. In a single bound, she had, for the moment at least, moved beyond that. Her embarrassed reaction was merely a response of habit, and now as the men came, she ran toward them with an uncharacteristic exuberance. For the first time in her life she realized how glad she was to see men of this sort, men like her father, men of brawn, men of loyalty to their kind, the kind of men her arrogant eyes had always been blind to. Suddenly, the inner door of her spirit was flung open to the truth that her parents and great-grandparents had always stressed, that the simple and common people of the valley of Strathy embodied the true and lasting Stonewycke heritage. How glad she was that these men came to rescue her father, not the smooth-of-speech, silky-of-dress, dainty-of-hand Charles Fairgates she had known.

Seven men appeared around the bend in the path, each a shining specimen of Port Strathy's manhood. Burly and muscular, they represented the fishing and farming communities. They carried rope, picks, crowbars, long lengths of metal pipes, and anything else they thought might aid in the excavation.

"Oh, thank you! thank you!" cried Allison. "Do hurry. They're all right . . . I heard them!"

Dislodging the great stone spar that had caused the mishap in the first place proved rather a simple matter when eight strong backs, including Logan's, were thrust against it. With a booming crash which rose even above the din of wind and waves, the spar tumbled to the sea.

But the boulders blocking the entrance were another matter. Six of the men climbed to a point above the cave, and, using pipes and crowbars as levers, attempted to separate the largest of the rocks. They inched it slowly apart, but before an opening even six inches had been made, the strength of the laborers gave out and the rocks snapped back together.

"We'll ne'er be able t' keep the rocks open lang enough fer them t' crawl through!" yelled Jimmy MacMillan from his perch overhead.

Logan, waiting below, shook his head in despair. The thing looked so hopeless! Glancing around, his eyes focused on a foot-long length of pipe lying on the ground where one of the men had abandoned it. He ran to it, caught it up, and hurried back to the site.

"I have an idea," he shouted. "Spread the rocks apart again. I'll try to wedge this pipe between them!"

Again the men set their shoulders to the bars, this time with yet greater determination, and again the rocks were pried apart—five, six, seven inches. Logan could hear Alec and Harry shouting encouragement from deep within the cavity. He scrambled toward the small opening, placing himself in the middle of the temporary breach they had made, and gripped the pipe firmly in his fingers, waiting for the exact moment when the pipe could be wedged in perpendicularly so that it would hold the rocks apart. No one needed to tell him that if the men above lost their traction, or if the pipe proved inadequate, his arm, and perhaps half his body, would be crushed in an instant.

. . . Nine inches . . . eleven . . .

Logan set the pipe into place. It was still a little crooked.

"Another inch or two!" he shouted, hiding his fear.

Carefully the men continued to increase the pressure. At last the opening was wide enough and Logan jammed the pipe securely in place.

"Back off slightly!" called Logan. He removed himself from the hole as the men eased the tension on their bars, everyone holding his breath during the tense moments, waiting to see if the bar would hold. At that moment Logan found himself worried more about saving himself than about saving Alec and the boy.

"It's holding!" cried Jimmy.

Alec needed to hear no more. Now it was his turn to spring into action.

"Help me wi' the boy!" he called out.

Still closest to the opening, Logan peered into the blackness below. Gently, but with great haste, Alec lifted Harry into the breach where Logan took his outstretched arms and pulled him up to safety.

"A rope!" called Logan out behind him, and in moments felt Alec tugging on the bottom of the line he had fed through. Several men joined him, holding the upper end of the line secure, while Alec pulled his bulky frame, not without some difficulty, through the narrow opening. Within three minutes more, he was standing safely on the ledge with the others. A great cheer went up. Alec greeted them with a smile and a wave of the hand, then turned back, picked up a length of wood, and with a great blow knocked the pipe loose. The rocks crashed firmly and permanently together.

"We canna be havin' anyone else gettin' trapped in there!" he said.

He turned back to face the small and happy crowd, but then swayed unsteadily. Abandoning the reluctance that had come upon her at the sight of him, Allison ran forward and threw her arms around him. "Daddy," she said, "you're hurt!"

"Allison, lass," Alec answered stroking his daughter's hair. "I thought I was jist dreamin' when I heard yer voice."

"No, Daddy. I was here, and I'm so happy you're safe. Here, let me help you."

Logan stepped forward to lend some support to the brawny veterinarian, but he almost wished he had remained in the background when Alec turned his attention toward him.

"Thank ye, Logan, fer what ye did there. It took a good bit o' courage, an' jist may ha' saved my life!"

The temporary glow and sense of satisfaction with having done a brave deed suddenly vanished. The words *a good bit o' courage* resounded in his brain like a painful gong intended to humiliate him before the whole world. He had almost forgotten who he really was, and why he had come. So caught up in his happy ride with Allison and the struggle to free Alec and young Harry, he had temporarily blanked his true self out of his mind. But now, reminded so graphically of his deception by Alec's thanks, he felt like throwing his hands over his ears. Those were the last words he wanted to hear, for he knew he deserved none of them.

"There were others who did as much," he answered.

"Aye, an' I'll be thankin' them, too. But ye're a stranger an' so it means even more comin' from yersel', riskin' yer life fer a man ye hardly know. I'll na be forgettin'."

The clamorous approach of the men who had been scrambling down from their perch on the rocks above relieved Logan of the necessity to make any further response.

But his conscience was not relieved of the fact that Alec's praise was both unmerited and unfounded. He was a liar and a con man, and, if his plan to make off with the family's lost treasure succeeded, he would also be a thief. He deserved no praise.

He was far from brave. And he knew it. Because he lacked the most fundamental courage of all—the courage simply to tell the truth.

42 ❀ New Dawn

SUNSHINE SPILLED IN through Allison's window. At first she noticed nothing unusual about it. She rolled over in her bed, yawned and gave a great stretch, and then realized it was the first ray of sun she had seen in days.

She sprang out of bed, ran to the window, and flung open the drapes. Yes! Spots of blue were piercing the gray covering overhead. Allison did not mind the rain. Indeed, in the last few days it had been friendly to her. But it had also wrought havoc in the valley and along the coast. And it was because of the storm that her father had been trapped in the cave.

But it was just like Grandpa Dorey had said—God had turned a seeming tragedy to good. Her father would be in bed a day or two with his injuries, but he would be fine. And out of his accident a profound wonder had occurred. When Allison had looked upon her father after he had been delivered from his tomb, much of the superficiality of her former shell had fallen away. She suddenly saw clearly what was truly important. All those things in her father she had tried so hard to reject were in reality the very qualities in life which mattered. For so long she had shunned her family. Yet now she knew she would be lost without them. Her father, in all the commonness of his upbringing, his occupation, his clothes, and his unrefined speech, represented all that she had disdained. Yet none of them—especially her gentle and soft-spoken father—had ever done anything other than pour their love out to her.

How could she have been so selfish . . . so blind?

At this moment, however, she didn't want to burden herself down with all the questions and the guilt which they produced. Instead, now was a time to shed the superficiality of the past, start over, and try to make it up to them as best she could.

Hurriedly Allison dressed in her prettiest spring dress of pale pink. What did she care if she had to throw a white sweater over her shoulders to ward off the chill that continued to linger in the air? She felt like the earth must when the first tiny crocus pushes past the snow covering the stubborn spring sod, or like a butterfly breaking out of its cocoon. She didn't know what was coming or even what she wanted to happen next. All she sensed was that a new day in her life had come. The sun was shining, the old shell had fallen away, and anticipation fairly throbbed within her breast.

She hastened from her room, down the hall, and around a corner toward her father's recovery chamber. Whatever it was she had to do in order to make a new beginning, she knew it had to begin here. The door was closed, and as Allison stood there hesitating, wondering whether to knock or walk in, the door opened of its own accord and she stepped back. Dorey, moving with exaggerated quietness, appeared. He quickly put his finger to his lips when Allison began to speak. Then he stepped across the threshold and closed the door softly behind him.

He placed his arm around Allison and led her down the corridor before speaking. "I stepped in to see when he wanted breakfast," he said at length, "but he was sound asleep. Your mother said he had quite a restless night, so I thought it best to leave him be."

"I was hoping to see him," said Allison, "but I know he needs his rest."

"If I know your father, he will be up soon. Then the battle will begin to convince him to remain in bed for another day or two."

Allison smiled. Her father had never been sick a day in his life. He was up at dawn every day and continually on the move from that moment, riding, or driving all over the district tending his four-legged patients. He did sleep, it was true, but on many nights he was interrupted at all hours by emergencies large and small. He might grumble a bit then, but to be *forced* to stay in bed was quite another matter. No, she was sure he would not take kindly to a day in bed. Such thoughts reminded Allison of the boundless love in his nature that more than equalled his energy, and his hearty laughter, and his capacity to make friends with everyone. She had not allowed herself to notice such qualities of his character before, qualities which made of him no *common* man indeed, but rather a great one. How much she had missed!

"Oh, Grandpa Dorey, will he ever be able to forgive me?" she asked, as if her great-grandfather had been privy to all her thoughts.

"What are you speaking of, lass?"

"My father," she answered. "I've been so cruel and selfish to him, acting as if I were too good for him, when all along it was just the other way around. I wouldn't blame him if he hated me."

"Ali, dear, your father doesn't know how to hate. And I know that he has long since forgiven you for anything which may have required it. He is not a man to carry a sense of wrong. But it wouldn't hurt for you to ask him to forgive you if you feel it is necessary. He could not respond any way but with the loving arms of true fatherhood. And perhaps you need to do it for the cleansing it will bring to you. Then all the hurts you have been carrying can be put behind you."

"It couldn't be *that* easy."

"You can only ask to know for certain. I know your father, I think as well as I have known any man. But my telling you of his love for you can never take the place of your knowing that love for yourself—just as it is with our Father in heaven. That's why you are right to go to him."

"And you think he'd not be angry with me?"

"Oh, my dear, that's the last thing he'd be! A man who has known great forgiveness usually has a greater capacity to forgive. Your father has felt the touch of God's love in his own life. He'll withhold nothing from you."

"Oh, Grandpa, I hope that's true, because there are several others I must ask forgiveness from after him. I've been so foolish!" She stopped and looked up into his aged eyes of wisdom with the youthful eyes of entreaty.

He hugged her to him, then said, "Come, dear. Let's walk farther and talk."

They continued along the hall to the main staircase and then down, with Dorey leaning on Allison's arm, exiting the house, and emerging into the crisp spring morning. The sky was a brilliant blue, with scarcely a cloud except for two or three billowy white clusters— clean and sharply defined. Dorey breathed deeply of the fresh, cold air.

"Ah," he sighed, "there'll be new blossoms now. It is truly spring at last. How I love springtime! Lord, how I thank you for your seasons!"

They made their way past the leafless, flowerless rose garden, then down the slope of the lawn toward the rear of the castle.

"Tell me, my dear," Dorey said as they continued to walk at a leisurely pace, "what has been happening with you?" His voice was casual, conversational, but a tingle of something akin to excitement coursed through his aged body. "Am I right in sensing that there is a springtime of new birth seeking to blossom within your heart as well as in the earth all about us?"

"I don't know, Grandpa," she answered. "I don't feel very much like my old self lately. But seeing Daddy in such danger yesterday magnified it. Suddenly I didn't want to be that way anymore—how I have been for so long. Maybe I began to see myself as I truly was. And I found myself wanting to change."

She sighed, then went on. "But I don't know if I can. I just don't have the kind of nature that can be good and kind, like my mother or great-grandmother. I don't think I ever will no matter how hard I try."

"Have you talked to the Lord about this, Ali?"

"I don't think He'd listen to me," she answered. "I haven't prayed to Him much lately, and haven't been much of a Christian."

"Then, if you care to take the advice of an old man, it seems to me that you ought to deal with that before you go trying to do something as big as changing your nature. You see, Ali, it is God who changes natures. You'd not get very far on your own. Your mother, and my Maggie—they would never say *they* had good and kind natures either. They both had to come to this point in their lives when they laid down who they were on their own and began to let God remake them according to *His* design. That's why it's God you need to talk to first."

"But why would He listen to *me*—?"

She stopped short, for she knew the question hardly needed an answer. "Yes, I know," she said, more to herself than to Dorey, "He always listens. Maybe that's what I'm afraid of—facing God after so long. Grandpa, I'm not even sure I really am a Christian!"

By now they had come to a small courtyard. Dorey paused and pushed in the gate.

"Let's sit in here a moment," he said, leading her into the enclosure. "Look," he said, pointing. "There are new shoots on the oak tree. I shall be able to come out here next week to plant the annuals." The carved marble bench under the tree was dry, and he motioned for her to sit next to him there.

"May I ask you a question, Ali?" he said after a moment.

She nodded.

"You have a kind and loving father, do you not?" She nodded again, this time with more emphasis.

"And if you went up to his room this moment to ask, you believe he would forgive you and love you completely, don't you."

"It's hard . . . But yes, I do believe it."

"Do you think your heavenly Father, who sacrificed His Son for us, would have less capacity to love and forgive?"

"I wouldn't blame Him," she answered, tears welling up in her eyes. "I've been so awful! All my life I've wanted to be like mother, and like your Lady Margaret. All I ever see is how giving and kind they are. And everyone knows how much they have given their lives and the wealth of their heritage for the common people. Yet I'm nothing like that! I can't possibly ever measure up to what they must expect me to be like. I've been cold and distant and arrogant. Oh, how I've prayed to be like them, Grandpa! But down deep inside there's such a fear . . . that I . . . that I never will be. I feel like . . . like I've let the family down!"

She hardly spilled out the words before a torrent of weeping assailed her. She hadn't realized what pain her confession would bring until it was at last spoken.

The sudden gush of tears and uncontrollable sobs did not surprise Dorey. He had seen the turmoil building for some time, and now, even as she wept, silently closed his eyes in thanksgiving to his Lord for bringing it at last to a head so the deep healing of her heart could begin.

He drew her to him, and quietly stroked her head as it lay on his shoulder. She cried for several minutes, until the surface of Dorey's jacket was quite damp. Then she lifted her head, sniffed, and dried her eyes on his offered handkerchief.

"Oh, Grandpa, what am I going to do?"

"Simply ask your heavenly Father to help you," he answered. "He wants nothing more than to help His children."

"But . . . I don't even know if I am His child . . ."

"Then let's take care of that first," said the old man, taking her hand in his. "Come, dear, let's pray. . . ."

43 ✳ *The Prayers of the Righteous*

IAN AND MAGGIE walked hand in hand up their favorite little knoll near the house. Their shoes were wet by the time they reached the top, and they were nearly out of breath. But it was always to this place they came when they had a special joy to share.

Indeed, though the stillness surrounding them would hardly have indicated it, they each knew there were multitudes of angels rejoicing with them on this great day for the Duncan clan, when their dear child Allison had been welcomed into the fold of God.

Lady Margaret both rejoiced and wept at the news. Part of her, however, was saddened as well at what had oppressed the girl for so long.

"I knew she was troubled," she told her husband, "by some of the things she saw in the rest of us. It was clear her resentments and shows of pride were coming from her own insecurity. If only I had been more sensitive, how much pain might have been avoided. The dear child!"

"I won't have you blame yourself," Ian gently rebuked. "You did everything God gave you to do. You could hardly sacrifice what He wanted of you in order to shield another from a very necessary pain."

"How do you mean?"

"The Lord gave to you and Joanna the vision of what serving these people of Strathy means. To you fell the blessing of giving a portion of Stonewycke's heritage back to them. Allison felt she was supposed to live up to that tradition. But she couldn't. And therefore she turned that very thing into a false sense of pride that God had to break. You could not have avoided it for her. Your legacy, in a sense, proved the tool in His hands to break through into Allison's heart."

"All things do indeed work for good, don't they, my dear husband?"

"There are many things only He can do. And certainly one of those is knowing a person's mind and heart, and then doing whatever is necessary to open that heart to His love. Only the Lord could identify that something in Allison—whether it was rebellion or fear or insecurity—made her feel so oppressed by the rest of us. Only God could identify that, and then reach in and heal it."

"Oh, Ian, I'm so glad she's whole again! I remember how fresh and clean I felt when at last I released the terrible burden of unforgiveness toward my father. When at last I was able to give it up, even though I was not yet with you, I felt my spirit could soar!"

"I'm glad for her, too. But it will not be easy for her. She is with her father right now on one of the difficult errands God has compelled her to do. You had to forgive your father; she has to ask her father's forgiveness. And that can sometimes be even harder. I suspect she will want to see you and Joanna next. And that will not be easy for her either."

"But now she won't be alone," added Maggie, as if she were encouraging Allison herself. "With the Lord's Spirit now inside her, she will have a strength to face such challenges she hasn't had before."

"That is exactly what I told her."

"And a strength to grow into the new nature He has fashioned for her. When I look back on our lives, Ian, I marvel at that very thing—how the Lord gave us such new natures! Do you remember what we were like?"

He laughed. "How could I ever forget? I was so caught up in myself."

"We both were! And yet here we are, at least in some small measure, beginning to reflect Him. Oh, He has been *so* good to us!"

They walked along for a while, gradually making their way back down the hill toward the house, when Ian stopped and slowly bent his aging body down to the ground. With deft, experienced fingers, he pushed back a tuft of grass.

"Look, Maggie!"

When she had stooped down next to him, he indicated with almost a sense of joyful reference a tiny yellow primrose, so small that few casual strollers would have seen it.

"Winter is coming to an end," said Maggie, her words sounding oddly prophetic.

They rose and continued on.

"You know," said Ian at length, "there's another element in this change in Allison that I continue to puzzle over."

Maggie glanced up inquisitively. "You're not thinking of our new mechanic friend?"

"Aye," replied Dorey with a twinkle in his eye. "Somehow I think he has more to do with the unlocking of Allison's heart than even she knows. She mentioned him a number of times when I was talking with her. You do know whom he reminds me of, don't you?" he asked.

"Why, of course, Ian—you!"

He laughed. "I only hope he can be a better influence on Allison than I was on you."

"Nonsense! Don't you even think such a thing," she chided.

"But it just goes to show again how the Lord uses the most unlikely instruments."

"I know! Just imagine—old Digory's descendant."

"I was actually thinking of his background. It's as if he just turned up here out of nowhere. We really know nothing about him. I sometimes almost imagine him to be an angel, planted here at this time for the very purpose of triggering these changes in Allison's heart."

Maggie became silent for a moment. "He is a puzzling fellow," she then said. "From the moment I laid eyes on him, I could see Digory in him. His eyes drew me. Yet I've sensed something else, too—something I can't quite put my finger on. I don't know whether it alarms me or excites me. But it seems that there is more to him than we know."

"Of one thing we can be sure. He is intrinsically bound up in the Lord's present work in Allison—and, for that matter, of the whole estate!"

"We must remember to pray diligently for Mr. Macintyre," said Maggie solemnly. "Angel or not, there can be no doubt that God sent him to us, not only for Allison's benefit, but also because of the work the Lord is carrying out in him. Whatever his future at Stonewycke, I sense that he is troubled. We must pray earnestly, for there is no doubt but that he is among us by God's design."

44 ✠ *Ramsey Head Again*

LOGAN SPENT THAT same morning brooding over the events of the previous day.

The quest which had brought him here was becoming increasingly difficult to fulfill— not because he couldn't find the treasure, but because it was becoming harder and harder to keep his mind on its business. Suddenly all sorts of new emotions were bearing in upon him from many unexpected directions. Every time he thought of resuming his search, and then packing up and leaving town in the dead of night as a rich man, he could not help but cringe inwardly.

He threw down the tool he'd been cleaning, jumped up, and began to pace about the stable. He couldn't keep his mind on anything! True to the half-hearted vow he'd made with himself, he had dug out old Digory's Bible that morning and tried to read it. But he couldn't make sense out of it. Vaguely familiar passages from childhood occasionally stood out. But the rest of it might as well have been Greek. He was too troubled to concentrate on it, anyway. Whenever he tried to read something, the phrase Jesse had said to him kept coming back into his mind: *Things aboot God, things we've all heard from oor mothers but which we pay no attention t', till we get older an' wiser an' then we start rememberin'* . . . His brain was too full to read, to think . . . to do anything. He had then thrown down the Bible and gone downstairs where he hoped some work would take his mind off his dilemma. But work proved as impossible as reading, and even cleaning up rusted tools turned out to be more taxing than his restive mind could cope with.

All his life he had looked out for only one person—himself. The instinct to survive was deeply ingrained, and with it a certain mistrust of others. Because his own motives were often self-seeking and larcenous, he naturally suspected the same of everyone else—and experience more often than not proved him right.

Yes, he admitted, this Duncan clan seemed congenial and hospitable enough—now. But they, like anyone, he tried to convince himself, had the capacity to turn on someone who proved a threat. What was to make him think they'd treat him any differently? The risk of revealing his motives was too great. Even if he hadn't done anything strictly illegal, people with the power and prestige of the Duncans could find some charge against him and make it stick.

Logan knew he was risking their friendship, which was, for some reason he could not quite identify, difficult to give up—not only theirs, but also that of Jesse and others. And to continue on his chosen course of action would mean to give up Allison, too. Whether she would ever accept someone from his station might be doubtful, but that made it no easier to forget the moments they had had together.

Did none of the last two weeks matter? Was it all a mere distraction, one of the obstacles he anticipated in seeking out this lost treasure? How could everything change so quickly? What Jesse had said kept coming back to haunt him: *I don't know why we willna listen t' truth till we get oorsel's int' trouble, or until some catastrophe smacks us in the face an' wakes us up.* But he didn't want to hear it! He had no time for all that now. And that old poet talking about bad boats and wretched crews and freedom. Was he one of the poor, foolish men who refused to be free?

No! He *would* be free. The treasure would give him freedom. With it he could help all these people who had been kind to him and have plenty left over for himself. It was his rightful inheritance anyway! It had last been in Digory's possession. It did not belong to anyone. It had belonged to an ancient people and whoever found it—well, possession is nine-tenths of the law. Everyone knew it. He would not listen to these doubts any longer, all these ridiculous religious fancies that somehow got stirred up in his brain.

Survival. That's what it amounted to. No more!

He had to survive, and he knew only one way to do it.

Logan sat down, picked up an oily rag, and began to wipe down the scythe he had been sharpening for Alec.

He could take uncounted chances with a deck of cards. He had done so for years. He was good at it. But he had never gambled with his emotions, never let his personal feelings emerge far enough to lay them on the table. The mere thought of giving up his quest for Digory's treasure in exchange for friendship, even love, was so unimaginably foreign to his nature that he could hardly believe such a thing was occurring to him. No, he was not ready for a risk like that!

The incident yesterday on Ramsey Head proved it. When he had been dangerously wedged between those crushing rocks, the only thing that had mattered was saving his own skin. Alec MacNeil could have rotted in that cave, with his daughter too, for all he had cared. Now was no time to start getting soft. He came here to do a job, and he had to stick with it. For the moment he conveniently forgot how in those tense moments of fear he had silently prayed for Alec's rescue, and how good he had felt when it was over, until Alec's praise had sent his conflicting emotions spinning.

"'Each man for himself,'" Logan murmured to himself, quoting Chaucer, "'there is none other.'"

He had picked up the words once in a pub, and though he knew very little about Chaucer, he did recall the bloke who had recited the verse. He'd been a dandy of a man by the name of Charles E. Franklin, rather good-looking for his age, which had at the time been about sixty. Extremely slick with dice, well-dressed, he claimed to have worked the Riviera and America for some years. He boasted that he had married and divorced a duchess and earned several thousand pounds selling real estate that didn't exist, and had once even sold a so-called gold-manufacturing machine to some gullible American.

Logan had admired the man from afar for some time, for he was not without a reputation, and it had been quite an honor to meet him that night. But later that evening, Logan had encountered Franklin again, passed out drunk in an alley where several street urchins were picking his pockets.

The sight of his fallen hero had been sickening, for he was fallen in every sense of the word. The self-reliant man had no one but a near-stranger to pick him up and haul him off to his dingy one-room flat, filled with dusty momentos of a life that was quickly passing.

When he had recalled the quotation, sitting there in Stonewycke's stable, he hadn't expected to conjure up the whole scene. He had hardly remembered how that evening had ended until just now as it flooded his mind. *Bad boats and wretched crews . . .* That certainly described Franklin!

"Well," Logan thought, trying to shrug off this newest wave of reflection, "you have to pay a price for everything, especially independence."

But was it independence or cowardice that was driving him? The question pierced his mind before he had time to hide from it. For the first time in his life, Logan Macintyre was truly confused. He didn't know the answer.

Out on Ramsey Head, when Alec had praised his courage, Logan knew how close he had been to running. Yet he had never before considered himself a coward. He had stood up to Chase Morgan, hadn't he? Was it the danger he had wanted to run from, or something else? Was it because he didn't care about these people . . . or because he *did?*

Logan threw down the scythe, and its point stuck in the dirt floor. He rose again and unconsciously began pacing. This questioning and confusion were too much! He should never have gotten involved. He should have stayed at the inn, found out what he could, retrieved the treasure, and then left. It had been a mistake to come live at the castle. He had to get out of here! He turned and headed toward his loft to pack his things.

Halfway up the stairs he stopped and closed his eyes tightly, as if to halt the careening assault of thoughts.

He had to get away from here . . . to think.

No! He had to *stop* thinking!

Frustrated, Logan spun around and raced down and to the bay's stall. He managed, despite his inexperience, to saddle her, opened the stall door, mounted, and rode off, having no idea where he was going or what he would do. He just knew he had to get away. *Perhaps I will never return,* he thought with a trace of a smile. Then horse stealing could be added to his many other indiscretions, and the Duncans could prosecute him on those grounds.

It was not really coincidence that his path led him to Ramsey Head. Its mournful awe drew him. In many ways it was similar to the moor he had visited days ago—lonely, barren, and dangerous. But where the moor had been dead and impotent, Ramsey Head seemed to stir with an energy and even a certain power. Perhaps it was from its constant contact with the life of the sea. And now Logan knew why he had come here.

He tied the horse where the path began to narrow. He could have ridden farther—in fact, it appeared that at one time wagons or carts might have traversed the Head. But today he wanted to be alone, to walk unassisted. He turned up the path along the grassy side of the promontory; he wasn't quite up to the challenge of the rocky seaward side today. It was the top he sought, where he could be alone—completely alone. The beauty all about him slowly muted his previous thoughts. He hoped that perhaps, in the midst of the grandeur of this place, surrounded on all sides by grass and wind and sky and sea, his confusion would be clarified. It was the first time in his life he had sought out nature for nature's sake.

The grass was still slick from the rain, and he did not negotiate the summit without slipping many times. But after a ten- or fifteen-minute hike, after which he found himself puffing lightly, with splotches of mud and bits of bracken clinging to his tweed work clothes, he stepped at last onto the crown of Ramsey Head's highest point.

As he crested the top and the sapphire of the sea spread out before him in all directions, he breathed deeply, and let out a silent exclamation of incredulity. It was a sight like he had never seen, and its impact on him was profound. He simply stood and gazed, his heart and mind at last quiet enough to receive the voice of peace that had been silently shouting to him through the created world all along.

Yesterday the sea had been gray and angry, but now it wore a completely new face. Rough whitecaps still beat against a shimmering blue. No boats were out yet, no doubt because of the strong wind which still lashed at the coast. Directly below lay the spot where they had been yesterday. Without the mist and rain to obscure his vision, he could see just how treacherous had been their position. Had he or Allison fallen when they were scrambling around on that ledge, they would not have survived for a moment. The mere thought sent a chill into the pit of his stomach, and he recalled again the tale of the murderer who had fallen, probably from that very spot. This was not a friendly place, nor a comforting one. Why had he come here? What sort of solace had he hoped to find?

At length Logan looked about for a rock to sit on. He'd have a short rest, then head back. There was nothing for him here, and he didn't want to waste any more time thinking. It was beautiful, and he could enjoy that. And it had helped to clear his head. He should have known all along what to do. It was simple enough. When he got back, he'd pack up his things, and when the house was asleep tonight, he'd slip away. If he walked all night he might make Fenwick Harbor by morning, and from there he'd get a train or schooner to Aberdeen and thence to London. The treasure had been a bad idea; it was probably just imaginary, anyway. At any rate, it would be easier to leave it behind, and with it any necessity for wearisome sensitivities and awkward confessions. He'd been a fool. He'd put too much into the pot on a bad hand, and it was now time to cut his losses, quit while he still had seed money for the next opportunity, and get out of the game.

But he would have to keep his mind off what he might be leaving behind. It wasn't only the treasure; there was Allison.

He couldn't dwell on that! It was for the best. He couldn't stop to consider what they would think of him sneaking away like a criminal. What did he care what they thought? He would never see any of them again, anyway. What did it matter what Allison thought? He'd never been good enough for her; she had made that clear from the start. She would probably breathe a sigh of relief to learn that he was gone.

Walking about fifty feet farther along the crest, he came to a large rock and sat down. As far as he could see in both directions the rugged coastline stretched into the distance. He had never thought much of the sea, but this truly had to be one of the rare high points of creation. Unconsciously his thoughts turned to the rock he was sitting on. For some reason it struck him as oddly out of place. It had a strangely sculptured look, as if it had at one time been chiseled toward some shape, then abandoned. He could not quite make out what the shape reminded him of. It was probably nothing, only an accident of nature.

As he rose to leave, his foot stepped on the matted bracken and weeds surrounding the rock and struck something hard underneath. Absently he kicked at the foliage and saw that buried beneath the surface of the tangled weeds was a smooth, flat board—hardly the sort of thing one would expect to find on this wild, uninhabited piece of earth. Maybe some children had dragged it up here with the intention of building a little hideaway.

Idle curiosity, coupled with a desire to divert his mind from its uncomfortable and confusing thoughts, made Logan bend down and scrape away the plants in order to excavate the board. When at length he was able to pull it free from the tangled roots and undergrowth, he found it to be only about two feet long by some six or eight inches wide. The edges had at one time been sanded smooth and the corners carefully rounded, but many years under the wet ground had caused some rotting, and Logan could pinch off small chunks of wood with his fingers. There were holes in the center where it had apparently been nailed to another board. Turning it over in his hand, Logan discovered the most curious feature of all— carved letters spread out across the length of the wood. This was no random piece of scrap. Someone had made this very carefully and had designed it as some sort of plaque or inscription. Logan brushed away the dirt and grass and saw that the letters were still almost legible, though time and the weather had taken their toll. With a curious finger Logan dug away at the encrusted buildup until the two names *Raven* and *Maukin* began to appear before him.

At first glance they struck no chord of familiarity to him, but he was certain this sign had to be a marker of some sort—for a grave, perhaps. But the names were hardly human. Had this been the burying place for some child's favorite pets? Two dogs, perhaps? A dog and a cat?

Raven and Maukin . . . where had he heard those names?

Suddenly Logan knew it was no child who had dug a grave at the top of Ramsey Head. ". . . I remember how he had pampered our horses, Raven and Maukin," Lady Margaret had once said.

It couldn't be! Yet what else could the plaque and this strangely crude rock signify? A grave for two beloved animals! If he had been anywhere else, Logan would not have believed such a thing possible. But at Stonewycke, where loyalties ran deep, where sympathies were out of step, where a hard-working vet was laird of the land, where the landowners gave away the largest portion of their once-vast estate to the poor crofters and villagers, where the heiress of the family lived forty years in a foreign land only to return to live out her golden years as matriarch of the family—this was certainly a place where anything could happen! Nothing at Stonewycke fit the expected patterns. So why not a grave on a high and windy promontory overlooking the sea?

Had Lady Margaret herself buried her favorite animals up here? No, that was unlikely. Surely she would have mentioned it. Her mother, the Lady Atlanta? Possibly. Could she have perhaps sought to enshrine the memory of her daughter after her flight to America with a loving tribute in the form of an honored grave at some place the young Maggie loved? *It could be,* thought Logan. *It would be just the sort of thing some mothers would do. Was Lady Atlanta the emotional sort,* he wondered? Would she have suffered the loneliness of her latter years in silence, or would she have tried to find outlets through which she could remember her Maggie?

Instead, a picture filled Logan's mind of an old man, the trusted family groom who had cared for these two beloved horses all their lives, perhaps with tears filling his aged eyes, bending over a roughly hewn hunk of wood, carving out the names of the horses he had loved as his way to remember the young girl he would never see again.

Was it possible, thought Logan, that the two horses were actually buried right here beneath his feet? It hardly seemed possible that the old groom would have hauled the carcasses of two huge beasts all the way up here. Yet it would be possible for a wagon to navigate the Head. And if Lady Atlanta had backed his scheme, with several of the hands assisting, it would not have been out of the question. He had heard of stranger happenings in London.

Logan tucked the board under his arm, turned, and began his downward trek off the small mountain to the point where he had tethered the horse. Maybe he should follow this one last lead, if not to the treasure, at least a little deeper into the past of Lady Margaret and his remarkable ancestor.

He'd give it one more day. He could not resist the challenge of a new set of puzzling questions.

45 ❈ *Crossroads*

MARGARET, JOANNA, AND Allison sat around the large oblong table in Stonewycke's kitchen.

This was Joanna's favorite spot in the entire castle, for its homey warmth reminded her of the little kitchen in the cottage she and Alec had shared in the early years of their marriage. It also stirred the memories of her first days in Port Strathy with dear Nathaniel and Letty. They were gone now, but their memory was all the more special because in their home Joanna had given her life to the Lord. She recalled the quiet joy of that day as clearly as if it had only just occurred. She did not think there could possibly be another day so profoundly meaningful, though her wedding day and the birth of her children came close. Yet the moment of her own rebirth went beyond even these milestone events, perhaps because it enriched them and added still more to their meaning.

Yet Joanna now realized there could come another moment as significant to her as that memory of so long ago at the Cuttahay's—the day, after so many years of inner conflict and struggle, when her own daughter came to the point of repentance and new birth. Only parents can know the depth to which their own children can bring heartache or joy by their responses to life, by their growth, by their sorrows, by their victories. Suddenly mother and daughter became what they had never before been able to be—sisters, born of the same Father.

Joanna reached across the table and took her daughter's hand. She smiled.

"Allison," she said, "I just don't know what to say. I'm sorry for whatever grief I ever caused you."

"Mother, I know I don't need to ask your forgiveness," said Allison, tears welling up in her eyes. "I know now how much you have loved me. But Daddy said that though I wouldn't *have* to, I should anyway."

"Forgiveness is a healing balm," said her great-grandmother, "a duty that proves to be as much for our own good as it is for another's."

"That's just what Daddy said," replied Allison. "Mother, will you forgive me? I know I've caused you nothing but sadness these last several years."

"Oh, Allison . . ." said Joanna tenderly, weeping in the fullness of her motherhood. She rose and went to her daughter. Allison rose also, and Joanna embraced her gently. "Of course I forgive you, dear," she said softly, still crying tears of joy and healing. "And believe me, any grief you may have caused me is far outweighed by my love for you. I'm so sorry for anything I may ever have done to hurt you."

They clung to one another for some time, as if to make up for the past breach and in anticipation of their future together.

When the tender moment had played itself out, Joanna resumed her seat and Allison struggled to bring up the subject that had been nagging at her but which she knew she had to bring into the open.

"I want so much to change," she said. "I always wanted to be like both of you. But I felt that I failed. And Grandpa Dorey helped me understand that God could use that failure to help me depend on Him. What I guess I'm trying to say, again, to both of you is that I'm sorry. I'm sorry for blaming you for my own inadequacies. And I don't know how much better I can do, but with God's help I'm going to try."

"Dear," said Margaret, "God does want us to change—to become molded into the image and character of Christ. But what makes you think you must someday become like your mother or me?"

"You are the kind of women God wants. You are the kind of women Stonewycke has always had—generous, kind, loving."

"Oh, dear, your mother and I are nothing of the sort! Whatever good you may see in us is not *us* at all. It is His work in us!"

Allison shook her head. "I suppose I've used all the rest of you as an excuse not to take responsibility for myself and my own attitudes. I could get away with being a beast while blaming it on you. That's why I have to both ask your forgiveness and forgive you, too."

"And forgive yourself," added Margaret. "When I was in America I was able to forgive my father. But the time came in my life when I had to accept the Lord's forgiveness for myself, too. The healing that God is always trying to carry out in families, even through the generations, is a forgiveness that extends in many directions—out toward others, inward from others, and outwardly to God as well as inwardly from Him. Only by forgiving and receiving forgiveness in all these ways will true wholeness come to us. We cannot leave any stone unturned, any relationship unhealed, any person unforgiven, if we want God to have His full way with us. And it is through forgiveness and healing that God is able to extend His plan and purpose for a family down through future generations of time. I do not doubt for a moment that my forgiving of my own father is one of the reasons the three of us are sitting here today. God himself only knows what the impact will be, Allison, of the forgiveness now blossoming in your heart.

"But healing is never without profound consequences. I do not doubt that as the history of Stonewycke continues down through the years, Allison, you will play a vital role in it, and that this moment when three generations of Duncan women can join in oneness with the Lord will prove a pivotal crossroads time. Perhaps that is why the Lord has spared me so long, so that I could share this moment with you. Allison, in the name of our Father, I tell you that I love you, and I give you my blessing as you carry on the Duncan line. I do not know how much longer I shall be among you—"

Joanna reached across the table and took her grandmother's hand. There were tears of admiration and love in her eyes.

"—but however long it is, I will be praying fervently for the continued godly faith of this family, and for you, Allison, as you carry that legacy into the future. I bless you, my child. May the Lord truly be with you!"

All three were silent. As Lady Margaret had been speaking, an aura had seemed to come over her, her entire lifetime focused into that single moment when she passed to her grand-daughter and great-granddaughter that life which had sustained her so long. She had been the Lady of Stonewycke, but seemed to sense that now the moment had come to transfer that heritage into their hands.

Joanna first broke the silence, though her eyes remained wet for some time to come. "So you see, dear, you don't have to be like anyone to please God. You are a unique creation. Whatever gifts and whatever personality you have, *He* gave you for *His* purposes. He will not expect you to be like either of us. Stonewycke will face challenges in your lifetime that we have not known. Times change; we live in a modern world. He wants you to be *you*. Of course He wants us to change where we have been self-centered. He wants to bring healing. But He will not change the special nature He gave you. He only wants it channeled for His purpose."

"You make it sound easy, Mother."

"Be assured," laughed Margaret, "it is *not* easy—far from it! Especially when you resist, as I did for many years. But in the laying down of self is true healing born. And in that laying down is the only path along which you will find true joy and peace."

The conversation was abruptly interrupted with a sound from the scullery door. Allison looked up at the instant when Logan Macintyre had just stepped across the threshold.

Joanna, on the opposite side of the table and facing her daughter, did not immediately see who had just walked in. But she noted a strange interplay of emotions cross Allison's face—initial surprise, as if his arrival was very unexpected though welcome, then a flicker of concern followed by a smile. The smile was unlike any Joanna had ever seen from Allison—shy, a bit awkward, even uncertain.

All these images flashed by in no more than an instant. But in that time, the discerning mother saw, before even the daughter realized it, that Allison was in love.

46 ❈ The Lady and the Seeker

LOGAN HAD NOT expected to find three women seated thus. And to the usurper, the man who had come in guile and deceit, they appeared not as three women merely having tea and pleasant conversation, but rather as the mighty first line of defense to their ancestral home. Indeed, his reaction was not far off the mark. For something of a delicate glow yet hovered in the air, which he could feel rather than see, a sense that he had stumbled unknowingly onto holy ground. As indeed he had. For where healing, forgiveness, and new birth are at work, there the Lord surely is. It put him immediately in an exposed position, and he hesitated momentarily.

His eyes strayed toward Allison. He quickly jerked them away, but not before he had caught a glimpse of her smile. There was something different in her face; that much he could see. In so many of her previous smiles he had detected traces of motive or cunning; today her face shone with a purity he had not seen there before.

Why had she chosen this moment to smile at him like that? It nearly undid his resolve to play out this last hand and get away from here. But he had to keep his wits and not melt, smile or no smile. These people were not going to get to him any more!

He yanked on his composure. He had business here. Nothing but business.

He had come directly to the house after leaving Ramsey Head. Entering through the kitchen, as was his custom now that he was accepted about the grounds as an employee, he had hoped to find a servant whom he might send after Lady Margaret, inquiring if he might beg a moment of her time. Though disconcerting, this unexpected turn would at least save time.

"Excuse me," he said. "I didn't mean to barge in."

"The kitchen belongs to everyone!" said Joanna cheerily. "There are plenty of places to go in this old house if we expected privacy. What can we do for you?"

"I had hoped to speak with Lady Margaret."

Allison's disappointment, though she tried to hide it, was apparent.

"Certainly, Logan, what is it?" the lady asked.

Logan hesitated. Somehow he would have felt safer if he could have gotten the old lady alone. She was cagy enough. But he wasn't sure he was up to braving a series of questions from all three. The women of this family, after all, were a pretty stalwart breed. He didn't like to cross them with unfavorable odds.

Joanna, perhaps sensing his misgivings, quickly rose.

"If I'm not needed," she said, "I have a few things to attend to. Please excuse me." Then turning to Allison, she added, "I could use your help, Allison . . ."

Allison moved back her chair and retreated with her mother. In the shyness of her change and the uncertainty of her true feelings, she had not uttered a word to Logan.

"Would you like some tea, Mr. Macintyre?" asked Lady Margaret when they were alone. "It's still quite hot."

But before he could say anything, she was on her feet and taking a cup and saucer from the cupboard. *Why did she have to be so hospitable?*

"Now . . ." said the lady, seated again, and pouring the steaming tea from the pot into Logan's cup.

Logan had carried the board from Ramsey Head into the kitchen with him, setting it against his chair as he sat down. He now picked it up and held it out to his hostess.

"I found this today on the top of Ramsey Head."

She took the wood and examined it with gradually dawning wonder spreading over her face.

"Raven and Maukin . . ." she murmured.

She laid it on the table, still gazing at the carved names. "Where on the Head did you find it?"

"At the very top, right on the crest."

"How very like him."

"You think it was Digory who put this up there?"

"Who else? It would have been so like him to do such a thing. And I think I even recognize a trace of his hand in the letters. He knew how Raven and I loved to romp along the beach and up and down the shore for miles. It was only natural for him to place a memorial to the animal where the view of the sea was the most spectacular."

"Of course! I see it now," said Logan, in a detached tone as if a great discovery had suddenly come upon him. He was just then thinking of Digory's letter and the reference to the girl Maggie riding along the sea.

"Pardon me?"

"Oh . . . nothing . . . it just makes sense when you put it that way. Tell me, Lady Margaret, do you think it possible that the horses are actually buried there? Could that be what this plaque signified?"

"Hmmm . . . that would be something indeed. Quite an undertaking. But he was reasonably strong for his age. He and I dug big holes before."

"What?"

"Nothing of significance. I was just thinking out loud. I was just reflecting on how it would be the sort of thing he would do, the sentimental old dear! Did it for me, no doubt." She dabbed her eyes. Thoughts of Digory always brought tears.

"And in his mind it would be only fitting that Maukin should be laid to rest there also," she concluded.

"I don't mean to sound disrespectful of the dead, Lady Margaret," ventured Logan, "but the whole thing does seem rather bizzare. I mean, they were only animals."

"Very special animals. He knew what they symbolized to Ian and me. They were almost a symbol of our love. We rode those two horses everywhere. And too, it was our mutual love for horses that strengthened the bond between Digory and me."

She stopped and smiled that peculiar smile of hers, which Logan had yet to fathom. Filled with mystery, wisdom, and sympathy, it was always disconcerting to him, especially today.

"Digory was a man of hope," she went on. "Perhaps he felt that in keeping alive the memory of the animals which had been so dear to me, he was also keeping alive the hope that I might one day return."

"It seems rather an absurd and sentimental gesture for a man who was supposed to have faith in God. If he wanted you to return, why didn't he just pray for it instead of carrying dead horses around the countryside and erecting memorials to a life that was gone and past?"

Logan could see that his statement pierced the lady's heart. He hadn't intentionally tried to hurt her. Yet in his present mood, impertinence was but one more tool to insure his isolation, and thus his survival.

When she replied with gracious calm, he had to admire her, though it almost made him angry at the same time. Could *nothing* rankle this lady?

"I did not know you were an authority on the subject of how men of faith live out their hope, Mr. Macintyre," she said, with just the merest hint of a challenge in her tone.

"You know very well I make no claim to be!" rejoined Logan, prepared to accept the challenge. "But even to an infidel like me, it sounds like the good Digory MacNab had more faith in a couple of dead horses than in that God he was so fond of."

Suddenly Logan was sick of the whole lot of them, and their prattle about God. The new air of belligerence in his attitude felt good. It made what he was going to do that much easier. The religious sops! He'd had enough.

Lady Margaret smiled, only this time it was an open smile and filled with amusement.

"I have the impression, Logan," she said, the smile gone from her lips but lingering in her lively eyes, "that you are trying to strike up an argument with me."

"Why should I want to do that?" he replied rather too hastily. He was noticeably on the defensive, the cool aplomb of the confidence man wearing thin as his battle to hang on to his past identity increased.

"That's exactly what puzzles me. I sense that a change has come over you, but I don't know why." She fingered her cup thoughtfully. "You are struggling with something, aren't you?"

Logan barked out a sharp, hollow laugh. "I can't imagine what would give you that idea. I only want to understand my distant relative better."

"I only wish that were so. But there's more to it. Something else is on your mind." Margaret sipped her tea, then set the cup softly on its saucer. "If you were simply seeking to know your uncle Digory," she went on, "then I think you would try to *understand* his faith and not ridicule it—for to understand Digory you must understand his faith. They are too much bound up in one another even to be considered separately."

"Then to ridicule his faith is to ridicule him?" queried Logan, "and that angers you?"

"You take me wrong, Logan. It doesn't anger me—rather, it hurts me. But not for Digory's sake, nor even for mine. It hurts me for *your* sake."

"Mine!"

"You are afraid, Logan. You are afraid to understand Digory's God."

She *was* challenging him! However sweet and charming, this was still a boldfaced challenge.

"I think you are running from God," she went on. "I once knew a man who tried to run from God. But he knew no peace until the moment he stopped."

"You've got it all wrong, Lady Margaret. But perhaps it is hard for you to understand someone who has no need for religious crutches. Your faith may be fine for people like you and Digory. I won't belittle you for it. But so far I've left God alone, and He's been kind enough to return the favor." Even as Logan spoke the words, the memory of his hastily spoken vow on the flooded road shot through his mind. He hadn't wanted to be left alone then.

Well, that was then—he had been caught up in the moment. It had been a foolish and sentimental reaction. *He could take care of himself.*

Yet the words reverberated through his brain with a hollow and foreign sound. He was lying even to himself. What about all the times in his life when he *hadn't* been able to make it alone? The time his mother had helped him out of the jam over the Fairgate fiasco, and later when Skittles had taken him in as a fifteen-year-old who knew no more about the streets of London than an innocent babe. And how many times when his luck had run sour would a friend lend him a quid?

But that had nothing to do with God! That was people—he had done the same thing for his friends! It had nothing to do with God or Digory or Lady Margaret or any of it!

But she was speaking again. "Many people consider religion a crutch, Logan. But that's because they don't grasp that what it *really* boils down to is a relationship, an intimate friendship. I have not chosen to live my life as a Christian primarily because I am weak and He is strong and I am unable to get through life on my own. Though of course that is true—we all *are* weak, and *can't* make it on our own, and we *do* need His help. And someday you will see those truths in your own life. But primarily, Logan, something even greater draws me: simply the fact that He is the God who made me, who knows me, who loves me . . . and I can *know* Him intimately! Oh, Logan, I hate to think where I would be if He left me alone!"

"I haven't done too badly," he said steeling himself against her passionate words of truth.

"You are entirely satisfied with your life?"

"Completely!" His voice sounded firm and confident. Who besides Logan could have been aware of the stark hypocrisy behind it?

"You are a very fortunate young man," she answered, and Logan knew that she saw through him as if his very soul had been naked.

But rather than feeling a sense of conviction, he withdrew yet further into the fortress he was trying to build around himself. It angered him to sit there exposed and foolish before the self-righteous old woman! She had no right to do this to him!

"Yes . . . *very* fortunate!" he repeated, glaring at her. Then stood quickly and strode from the kitchen without another word.

He didn't have to take insults like that from anyone, even the grand Lady of Stonewycke. For the moment the irony was lost on Logan that she had not insulted or belittled him in any way. She had, in fact, been nothing but kindly in her tone. It would have made it easier on him in that moment had she responded in kind and tried to crush him beneath her noble heel. He could have taken that . . . understood it. But not this, not kindness in exchange for his rudeness.

The crisp air of the early evening jolted him like a slap to a man in panic. That was one thing he couldn't do—panic. He had to pull himself together. He had to think clearly. He had given himself one more day, and he needed to make the best use of it.

He crossed the lawn in the direction of the stable when a figure came striding toward him, arm raised in a wave.

"Logan, there ye are!" It was Jesse Cameron.

"Jesse," he said without enthusiasm. Here was a friend who had saved his life, to whom he had pledged his loyalty. But now he wanted no friends in Strathy, no ties.

"I've got a telegram fer ye." Her voice was grave and in her eyes was a look of deep concern.

"I suppose you've read it," snapped Logan as he whipped the envelope from her hand.

"That 'tisna my habit," she replied, and Logan could see he had hurt her. "Telegrams 'most always bring bad news, ye ken."

He wished he had the guts to say he was sorry. Her friendship had meant something to him. But he could not flinch now. This was no time for repentant deeds like apologies. No time even for smiles. He let her turn and walk away just as he had left Lady Margaret—saying nothing, giving nothing. As she went he watched her—sadly, but with resolve.

When she had walked dejectedly out of sight, he turned his attention to the telegram. He looked at it for a long and agonizing moment. No one knew he was here except his mother. And only one or two of his London friends knew how to get in touch with her.

With a shaking hand he ripped open the flap. He would not be able to cope with it just now if something had happened to his mother. But the telegram was not from Frances Macintyre.

LOGAN

CHASE MORGAN HAS LEARNED WHERE YOU ARE STOP HE IS STILL IN THE CHOKEY BUT THAT WILL NOT STOP HIM STOP KEEP A LOOKOUT AND BE CAREFUL STOP

BILLY COCHRAN

47 ❊ A Deal at the Bluster 'N Blow

AT LAST SOMETHING was starting to happen. Sprague had begun to fear he might just end up rotting in this hick town.

Sprague's contact at Stonewycke had just passed on an interesting report. Early that afternoon Macintyre had gone off alone. Although that was not altogether unusual in the context of his job, this time he had ridden by horse to a lonely, uninhabited spot called Ramsey Head—hardly a likely place for the services of a mechanic. The field hand from the estate said Macintyre had returned empty-handed except for a piece of wood he was carrying. Curious, Sprague had concluded that this excursion must have ended with the same result as the one Macintyre had taken several days ago to Braenock Ridge. Perhaps they were both wild goose chases. But the piece of wood was interesting; obviously Macintyre bore continued watching. It certainly indicated that he had not abandoned the hunt. If he was sticking to it after all this time, possibly he was on to something.

But sitting idly about was getting to him. For a diversion, after hearing what the man had to say, Sprague decided to have a walk out to the promontory himself. By the time he arrived dusk was approaching; he had no time for a thorough appraisal, but it looked as likely as any place to hide a treasure. But with no map or specific instructions, it might as well have been a needle in a haystack. Therefore, there remained no alternative but to watch Macintyre. He was still the one with the clues—whatever they might be.

Following his afternoon trek, Sprague returned to the Bluster 'N Blow. When Logan had moved up the hill to Stonewycke, Sprague saw no further reason to remain at Roy Hamilton's dingy place. The Bluster 'N Blow was only a step or two above it, but at least it was clean and the food was edible. He now sat at one of the rough tables in the common room stirring his coffee and waiting for his dinner to be served. He was also anxiously awaiting the arrival of the inn's two new guests. They had checked in while he was out. But sneaking a look at Cobden's register, he had learned their names: Frank Lombardo and Willie Cabot.

Sprague's boss had mentioned Morgan's interest in Macintyre. He definitely recognized Lombardo's name as one of Morgan's transplants from the Chicago crowd. It was only too bad they had found Macintyre before Sprague had finished his business with the London con man. If they got to him first, it would be the end of Macintyre, and the end of Sprague's mission. And his boss didn't like excuses. His motto had always been, "Get it done. Whatever you have to do—just get it done." Even if Morgan's men put an end to Logan, his boss would blame Sprague. "If you want to work for me, Sprague," he would say, "getting it done is the only thing I care about."

So he would have to try to handle these two somehow.

Sprague lifted his cup to his lips and drank deeply of the strong black brew. They never could make good coffee on this island.

But he quickly forgot the bitter taste in his mouth when, peering over the rim of his earthenware cup, he saw the two newcomers enter the room. Both were veritable hulks, typical of the thugs Morgan liked to surround himself with.

"Evening, gentlemen," said Sprague in an easygoing, friendly tone.

The two stopped cold, and a flicker of recognition crossed Lombardo's swarthy face. Sprague had met him some years ago, but he had not thought the younger man would remember. Not that it mattered.

"You talkin' to us?" answered Lombardo with an accent that combined Bronx, Sicilian, and a touch of cockney with a most curious result.

"None other," replied Sprague, though an answer was academic since there were no others in the place.

"Do we know you?"

"It's possible. Have you ever been to Chicago?"

"What'd you want?" Lombardo's voice grew menacing and his eyes grew wary. Sprague had never been mistaken for a cop before, but Lombardo appeared more blessed with muscles than with brains.

"Come on, Lombardo, do I look like a Fed?"

At that moment Sandy Cobden burst into the common room bearing a tray laden with Sprague's dinner.

"Here ye go, Mr. Sprague," said the innkeeper, setting the heavy tray down with a deep sigh. "Hope I didna keep ye waitin' too long. Ne'er hae acquired the knack fer kitchen work. My missus used t' do all that in years past. Noo that she's gone I jist dinna get much chance t' practice. We can go fer months wi'oot a single guest. It picks up a wee in summer, but here tis April an' sich a foul one at that, an' I've more guests at one time than . . . than I dinna ken when."

He turned to his other guests as he emptied the tray of its burden, setting plates and bowls before Sprague. "I'll be bringin' yer supper in directly," he said. "Jist hae yersel's a seat."

He paused in his steady chatter, perhaps expecting a *thank you*, but since none was immediately forthcoming, he swept up his tray and bustled away.

"Sprague?" ruminated Lombardo thoughtfully.

"Five years ago," prompted Sprague, "Leighton Club, Chicago."

"That place was only open to a very special clientele."

"That's right."

"Well, if you really was there, then you'll know the maitre d'."

Sprague shook his head as if he were placating a child. "Benny Margolis. Do you want a description, too?"

"No, I guess you're on the level."

"Have a seat," Sprague went on, confident that his estimation of Lombardo's intelligence was not too far wrong. "Your silent friend, too ."

The two hoods took seats opposite Sprague, barely squeezing their brawny frames into the narrow, high-backed bench. Cobden returned with their meal and the three spent the next few minutes engrossed in their food.

At length Lombardo spoke, his words muffled as he continued to chew a large hunk of meat pasty.

"Prohibition . . . them were the days," he said. "I took it on the lam right after the crash—figured they wouldn't be able to afford it no more, and I was right—they repealed it lickity-split."

"You should have stuck around. As I hear it the mob doesn't need boot-legging to keep it going."

"Yeah . . . well, I had other reasons too," replied Lombardo cryptically.

"So," Sprague went on, pushing back his empty plate and pouring himself another cup of coffee, "then you migrated to England and hooked up with Morgan—?"

"What about Morgan?" broke in Cabot sharply, breaking his long silence.

"Relax," said Sprague, then turning to Lombardo, "tell your friend to take it easy. I've got a business proposition for you, but we won't get anywhere if you keep jumping down my throat."

"Okay," replied Lombardo. "Put a lid on it, Willie."

"Don't tell me what to do," growled Cabot. He was apparently beginning to feel the imbalance of being the odd man out as the only Britisher among these two Americans. "Don't forget who we're working for, Frank."

"You got me wrong," said Sprague, feeling the need to placate the Londoner. "I figured I might be able to help you out."

"What'd you know about us?"

"Why don't I begin at the beginning?" said Sprague, adopting his most congenial tone. "Here, have a cup of coffee."

"Ain't there nothin' stronger?" put in Lombardo.

"Later; I'll buy. In the meantime . . ." Without completing his sentence, Sprague poured out coffee for his companions. "Now," he began again, "as it happens we all have the same interest here in Port Strathy. And that happens to be a third-rate con artist by the name of Macintyre—"

"Macintyre!" repeated Morgan's men in unison.

"That's right, boys. I'm afraid this is a small country and word gets around fast. Morgan wants Macintyre's skin, and I know that's what you're doing here."

"What's your interest in him?"

"I want him, too. Only I need him alive and well."

"So what's this business proposition of yours?"

"Like I said, I need Macintyre in one piece. So it seems that at the moment, we are somewhat at cross purposes. When I'm through with him, you fellows can do what you please. Now, I'm willing to make it worth your while to hold off for a spell—say one thousand pounds apiece?"

"What do you want with him?" asked Cabot, determined not to let his guard down so easily.

"The specifics aren't important. Let's just say he has some information I need—that is, he will have soon," answered Sprague.

"Two thousand pounds . . . that must be some information he has!" said Lombardo, stuffing a thickly buttered bannock into his mouth.

"Not the sort of thing that would be of interest to you or me," answered Sprague evasively, "but there are some highly placed individuals who are anxious to have it."

"I don't know," said Cabot.

"Aw, com'on," prodded Lombardo, "it ain't like we're not going to do Morgan's job—we'll just tell him we got delayed a few days."

"Exactly how long?" asked Cabot.

"That's the rub," replied Sprague, "I can't pin it down exactly."

"Two days," said Cabot, answering his own question, "then we move in."

"I'm afraid if we pressure him, he'll bolt. Then neither of us will get what we want—and you'll be out a cool thousand." Sprague directed this last remark to Lombardo, whom he judged as most sympathetic.

"We got Morgan to think of," said Lombardo, almost apologetically. "He's not a man you try to con. And if we don't bring him Macintyre's head, he'll have ours."

Sprague leaned back on the bench to ponder his dilemma.

Even if he withheld Macintyre's whereabouts, this town was so small that they'd locate him in an hour if they put their minds to it, however vacant that part of their anatomy was. His only chance had been to deal with them, and that would have worked if it hadn't been for that hardnose Cabot. There was no way of knowing how close Macintyre was to finding the loot, if it existed. He might even have already found it and was only sticking around to avert suspicion.

Sprague knew he now had no choice but to force Macintyre's hand! If he had nothing, well, they were both out of luck. Sprague knew his boss would be none too pleased. But in part it was his fault, too. Hadn't he said he would take care of Morgan? Obviously his slick manuevering had not worked too well in that arena, so he couldn't blame Sprague.

"Give me three days," bargained Sprague, "and you get *two* thousand each." It wasn't *his* money, Sprague reasoned to himself.

The two hoodlums looked at each other, then nodded toward Sprague. Lombardo appeared much more satisfied with the deal than his cohort, who looked as if three days was an interminably long wait for his sport.

48 ❈ Digory's Clues Unfold

LOGAN STARED ONCE more at Billy's telegram.

Somehow he had let himself forget about the threat of Morgan, which had been hanging over him for weeks. As he reread the words he felt as if a heavy boulder were resting on his shoulders.

After receiving the telegram, Logan had climbed the steep, narrow steps to Digory's room. Now he slumped into the coarse, straight-backed chair that had probably been there when the groom had occupied these same quarters.

He had just told Lady Margaret what a lucky man he was, spitting the words out defiantly. Some luck!

This turn of events left him no alternative but to get out of Port Strathy as fast as possible. If Morgan knew he was here, no doubt a couple of his thugs would be hot on his tail, if they weren't here already. His own sense of panic was dulled by the events of recent days, but suddenly Logan thought of Morgan's hoodlums tainting the quiet peacefulness of Port Strathy. These were dangerous and merciless men—look what they had done to Skittles! And now they were coming to Port Strathy . . . and Logan had brought them here!

Even if he left immediately, the men looking for him would cause trouble. And these locals would be foolish enough and loyal enough to stand up to the thugs. They could be hurt trying to protect him, never realizing that he had double-crossed them himself.

As much as Logan wanted to convince himself that they cared no more for him than he cared for them, he could not do so. Jesse Cameron had saved his life at the risk of her own. Lady Margaret would no more turn on him than his own mother would. He had little doubt Alec would stand up to anyone who threatened one he loved. And Allison . . . that look he had seen in her eyes an hour ago could not quickly be erased from memory. She *had* changed after Fairgate's visit! She cared about him. And she too would protect him.

How could he put all these people in danger? Yet the only other alternative was to confront Morgan's men, possibly even give himself up to them, or perhaps draw them away from Strathy. That's what he'd have to do: set up some kind of decoy to lure them out of town. Then if they got him, at least it wouldn't have to involve his new friends.

Friends! He could hardly believe he'd called them that. He desperately wanted to believe that he didn't care about what happened to the people in this town. He had lied to them, cheated them, was about to steal from them and put them in grave danger. Yet he still cared about them. Were they indeed his friends? If so, how could he be so dishonest with them?

Evening shadows now darkened the room, but Logan had no heart to light a lamp. He leaned forward on the old pine table, resting his head in his hands.

He *did* care! It made him cringe to think of any one of them being touched by Morgan's evil. He hated himself for what he was doing. He was in debt to these folks, just as he was to many others in his life.

He remembered Lady Margaret's words: *I hate to think where I would be if He left me alone!*

Was he not only in debt to these people but to God also?

Then as Logan raised his head, his eyes fell upon Digory's old Bible on the table. Instinctively he touched the worn cover. It reminded him of the promise he made on that flooded road: *If we get out of this mess, I might even read that old Bible . . .*

He had opened it a time or two. But he had done just what Lady Margaret had said—he was not trying to understand, he was trying to pick it all apart. He was as false in his half-hearted attempt to carry out that vow as he was with everything else. He was doing just what he despised others for doing—trying to use God to get him out of a jam when things were going sour, like some benevolent magistrate in the sky, without getting personally involved, without any relationship with Him as Lady Margaret had said. He had always considered such an attitude hypocrisy, and yet he was guilty of the same thing. Well, neither Lady Margaret's words nor the earnestness of her voice mattered. He wasn't going to do what he did when they were out in the flood and go blubbering to God now.

Yet what if she was right? What if he was running from the only person who could help resolve this dilemma and rescue him and his friends from terrible danger? What if all this was happening, as Jesse would no doubt say, just as a way of God's getting his attention? What if the only way out of his confusion was through the one door he was refusing to open—the door of his own heart?

"Oh, God . . . !" he cried, but nothing else would come. He laid his head softly down on the table, and in the quiet stillness of the evening, Logan Macintyre began weeping tears of bitter remorse.

When he lifted his head a few minutes later, his eyes were red, but he felt no healing balm. His tears had been acid on an open wound, for he knew nothing about him had changed. He was alone and in a despair of suffering, seeing for the first time in his life the sinner he truly was. But he would not give in.

Logan sighed a comfortless sigh. His eyes strayed back to the Bible and he again thought of his uncle. Logan had never before truly envied another man. When he had said that he had been satisfied with his life, on the surface he had been speaking the truth so far as he knew it. Yet now he found himself envying old Digory. Here was a man who had been the picture of simplicity. It was evident in this very room where he had dwelt. Logan could almost feel the impact of his unpretentious life in the soul of the place he had inhabited.

"He loved his horses and his Bible," Lady Margaret had said.

A man without struggles, without the complications of modern life, without people chasing him, without the sham of a false personality tearing at him—it must have been easy for him to follow his God.

Yet . . . was that true? Is it ever *easy* to lay one's life down? Though every man's sacrifice is different, does not every man truly sacrifice when he lays his *self* on the altar and chooses to follow the path God has laid out for him? Is it ever *easy,* even for a man like Digory? Was he not wrapped up in the struggles and heartaches of those he loved? Did his heart not ache for his little Maggie? Did not the decision he had to make about the treasure tear at him, too?

All at once Logan caught an image of the old groom bent over his Bible, agonizing over what to do, forced in the end by his love for the girl and his loyalty to the family he had served to hide a priceless treasure in order to keep them from further heartache, evil, and self-generated suffering.

He loved his horses and his Bible. . . .

Digory had sacrificed at least some of his natural simplicity for those he loved. But Logan knew even in his present confusion that if his life had become too complicated to cope with right now, he had only himself to blame. With a frustrated gesture he shoved Digory's Bible aside. If peace was to be found there, he deserved none of it. He would never be like Digory. He could never be devoted to others. And he deserved none of Digory's peace. Fatigue began to wash over him. He rose to his feet and shuffled to the bed where he stretched out, fully clothed, on the straw mattress. His eyes drooped and sleep seemed but a moment away, yet his mind continued to race in confused, anguished disarray.

I deserve no peace, he thought. If he had promised to read the words in that old Book, he had lied.

He was a liar! That was how he lived. He had no horses, no peaceful stable, no Bible. He had nothing—but himself! And a rotten self it was. The old poet, Mac—something, whatever his name was—had been right. *Low souls, weak hearts . . .* That was certainly him! A bad sea—boat with a wretched crew—none other but himself. He was low, weak, and wretched! A poor, foolish man, made to be free but running from the very freedom Lady Margaret said was the source of Digory's peace—and her own. He was a fool, but he couldn't help himself. All he had to keep him going was the hope of a treasure—a dirty, stinking treasure.

Maybe that was what he deserved. He had given his heart to this mammon, so his reward would be the anguish of seeing his lust for riches fulfilled while his soul remained tormented in the hell of his own selfishness. There would be no peace for him, only the suffering of the rich man whose tongue could not be cooled amid the flame. Digory had given up the treasure for love. Now his wretched and selfish descendant would turn his back on love, for the treasure . . . would unearth that which had brought evil . . . and would loose more evil into the world and upon himself.

No horses, no Raven, no Maukin, no peace, no quietness of spirit for the descendant. He, Logan Macintyre, whom no doubt old Digory had prayed for without knowing his name, was about to undo what this man of faith had done—he was about to dig up the pain, the heartache, the self of mammon which Digory had tried so hard to banish from the reach of any hands but Maggie's.

No horses . . . no Bible . . .

Suddenly Logan jerked out of his groggy, half sleep.

His body trembled from the abrupt awakening from a much needed rest. But words tumbled wildly through his brain . . . *it was not the first time he'd dug a large hole.* Where had he heard that?

He leaped out of bed. Groping in the darkness, his hands fumbled over the table and fell onto the Bible. He flung it open to the spot where he had replaced the letter after loaning it to Lady Margaret, the very page where it had been hidden by the old groom. Still trembling, now for other reasons, he took the letter out. What had Digory said? It had been a long time since Logan had read it. Groping farther, Logan found the lamp and matches. He lit it. The bright glow pained his eyes momentarily, but he forced them to study Digory's scrawl.

I hae moved it, Maggie, and hidden it where I pray none will discover . . .

No, thought Logan . . . further . . . where did he move it?

To see ye with auld Raven . . . lonely Braenock . . . the sandy beach . . . I hae put it in a spot I thocht ye loved . . .

There was the mention of Raven again!

. . . that cliff and ye both got stuck . . . sand . . . the other direction . . .

The other direction from the sand! Of course! It had to be Ramsey Head! It was in the other direction from town than the sandy beach. What else could the cliffs mean?

Ye loved that path to the rock bearing yer name.

That's it! That's it! cried Logan—the rock bearing your name . . . *Ramsey* Head! He buried the treasure on Ramsey Head somewhere near, or in, the very graves of the beloved horses. No one but Maggie could know those secrets the two of them shared—the horses, the love for the path, the time she got stuck riding there. He had done it! He had located the treasure! Unconsciously his eyes continued reading, *I pray one day ye will read this and return to us . . .*

He folded the letter hastily, wanting to hear no more. Not now. Not when he was on the verge of unearthing what might be millions! He would not condemn himself for being the one to keep Digory's prayer from being answered, for being the one to keep the letter hidden from the one whose eyes it was intended for.

He began pacing the room, a cold sweat breaking out over his body. How could he have known, at that moment, that the last line of the letter was the most important of all, the line he had not allowed himself to read: *But 'tis all in oor dear Lord's hands, and his will be doon.* The direction the bad boats of men's hearts sail is not always dependent upon the temporal plans of their wretched souls, but instead on the direction of the winds of God's Spirit that blows upon the waters, guiding them toward the harbor their blind eyes cannot see.

Even as his mind was racing with how to carry out the final stage in his long-awaited scheme, Logan found it incongruous that he should discover the location of the treasure just at the moment he had almost grown to detest any further mention of it.

Yet he could not stop himself. He could not leave it buried as Digory had. He was compelled to go on. But another compulsion, one whose promptings he was altogether unfamiliar with, told him to go back to the table and look again, this time at the Bible rather than the letter. Reluctantly, he obeyed. The book was still opened to the page where the letter had rested all those years. Then his eyes fell on something he had not noticed before. The Bible was opened to the sixth chapter of Matthew. He had never paid any attention to that fact before. And there on the yellowed page, seemingly for the first time, yet he knew that could not be the case, he noticed that one certain verse had been underlined. How odd that Digory would mar this book he so loved, that one—and only one—small passage would be so marked. Carefully Logan bent down and read the fine print:

"For where your treasure is, there will your heart be also."

Logan snapped the Bible shut. He knew he had not been intended to find peace or comfort from these pages. Digory, a man of peace, had left his final admonition to anyone who would seek that which his letter revealed—one doomed to tear Logan apart.

He turned away from the table and clasped his head between his hands in a fresh turmoil of confusion and indecision. He *couldn't* stop now! To do so would mean to relinquish so many other things! Maybe they were things he was not even sure he wanted anymore. And if he had thought deeply about it, he probably would have admitted he loathed them now. His past life was fading into a mist behind him, and with many backward glances of longing he watched all he had once loved retreat from him. And as he looked to the future, he was afraid of the unknown, afraid as Lady Margaret had said, to understand Digory's God. He was afraid to depend on Another, even though his own attempts to help himself had failed so miserably. He was afraid to go forward, but realized it was almost too late to go back, stuck at a crossroads of life's journey. He realized, without framing it consciously in his mind, that to repent of his past now would mean a complete changeabout, would mean to turn on the path and begin moving in a whole new direction. But making that turn was something he could not do . . . not alone . . . not yet.

Logan grabbed his heavy coat from the hook behind the door and ran down the steps into the stable.

49 ✺ *The Turn*

THE AIR WAS oppressively warm and the evening was so still that Logan could hear his heart thudding within his chest. He hardly needed his coat. The wind and chill of the morning had been almost welcome compared to this. It foreboded more ill weather to come, though that fact hardly mattered to Logan at this moment. He would be gone from here before the storm broke. All this mental turmoil would be behind him. He'd be rich. And he'd be gone.

He had descended from his room with a resolute determination. His mind cried out for him to stop, but he refused to listen. From the tool rack he grabbed a shovel, then walked past the stalls of horses. He would not risk the commotion it might cause to take out a mount at this time of night. When he stepped outside, intuitively he clung to the shadows as he crept stealthily along the sides of the buildings. *'Tis only fitting,* he mused, *that I act the part of the thief for this, my final job at Stonewycke.* Looking over his shoulder, he crossed an open space to the point where, he recalled, a breach in the great hedge surrounding the courtyard existed.

In the morning, early, he'd go into town and leave specific instructions with the innkeeper that he had to leave for Aberdeen immediately, and then Edinburgh. He'd say he was expecting friends and they could be directed to follow him. He would give him the names of two hotels in each of the cities. Thus when Morgan's hoodlums came looking for him, they would follow his trail south and would not have *to force* any information from anyone. His one final favor to these people would be to avoid a confrontation or bloodshed in Port Strathy. These arrangements done, he would return to Ramsey Head, retrieve the treasure, or as much of it as he could reasonably take with him, and make his way on foot along the coast toward Fraserburg and then possibly Peterhead. He would lay low there for a long while; he'd have left no trail to lead anyone to him, and eventually he'd catch a schooner bound straight through for London.

The face of Allison kept intruding into his mind, but he forced it from him. His plan may have been foolproof. But inside he was miserable. He walked steadily faster, as if tiring his body would keep the voices of conscience and old ladies and old grooms and old poets at bay.

But he could not keep the words and images from that day out. Something had begun to open within him, and now that the door was ajar, a torrent of unwelcome thoughts pressed to find entrance.

"I think you are running from God," the lady had said.

If she could only see him now! Half walking, half running along the road, shovel in hand, his motives hidden by darkness, on his way to steal that which was rightfully hers. What a picture he made!

Was she right? Was this flight symbolic of his running away from truth . . . running away from God? Was he using the treasure and the supposed threat of Morgan's thugs as just another excuse not to face up to himself—who he was, what he was doing? Was he trying to bolster his cowardice with noble-sounding gestures, thinking what a brave man he was to save the town from Morgan's men and put them on his own trail, when in reality he was afraid to stand up to the most basic truth of all—the truth of his own sinfulness, the truth of his need for God? Afraid . . . that was all he was. A coward.

"I knew a man who tried to run from God . . ." Lady Margaret's words echoed in his mind. *"But he knew no peace until the moment he stopped . . ."*

What was his life—what had his life *always* been but a sham? A giant con game played upon no one but himself. What he had taken for contentment had been nothing more than a thick protective wall to enclose his fears and insecurities. He had seen that very thing in Allison and had been quick to identify it. But in himself he had been blind to it—until now. He had been hiding . . . running . . . covering up the truth of his ugly nature.

Did he want to stop running? Did he want to stop the sham, the con? Did he want to break down the walls with which he had been trying to protect his heart?

Logan was physically running now, gripping the shovel so tightly that his hand and arm muscles ached. His whole body was drenched with perspiration, but even he—self-reliant, calm, cocky Logan Macintyre—could not mistake the tears streaming down his face for sweat from his forehead. He was crying, and he knew it. Yet somehow in the anguish which precedes new birth, he could not be ashamed. They were tears, if not of comfort, yet of healing, and it felt good to unleash them.

What would it be like, he wondered, just once, to make the kind of selfless sacrifice that his uncle had? After all, Digory MacNab's blood ran in his veins also. Could it . . . be possible that . . . perhaps he *might* be able to know the peace and freedom that the old groom must have had? Again the words of the old poem came into his mind, *Thou hast to freedom fashioned them indeed.* Had he been made for freedom, and refused it all along?

Could he make the necessary sacrifice? Could he lay down his self? Could he give up the treasure?

He would gladly do so to have the joy in his heart that Lady Margaret had. But would he have the courage to face them, to expose himself for what he was, to face their rejection, and possibly prosecution? Would he have the courage to make amends for the life he had lived, to repay those he had swindled? Could he make such a gigantic change?

Gradually Logan's pace slowed, and he came to a halt. All was still and silent around him. The only sound he could hear was the breathing of his own lungs, and the distant call of the sea where he was headed. Silent tears of decision continued to flow.

He could go on like this all the rest of his life—blindly running and hiding, seeking one elusive treasure after another, playing con after con on himself, always trying to convince himself of what Lady Margaret had known was a bold-faced lie from the beginning—that he needed no one else. But now that his eyes were open to his true self, could he continue on in that way? Could he go back to his former life and ignore what his heart was prompting him to do?

Logan sank to his knees. "Oh, God . . . !" he cried, throwing the shovel from him and burying his face in his hands. "God, help me! Forgive me for what I've been . . . help me become . . . a true man!" And with the words Logan broke down into an impassioned fit of penitent sobbing.

It was ten minutes before he rose. The tears had dried and the prayers of his heart had soothed his agitated spirit. He picked up the shovel, took one last look down the road on which he had been headed, took a deep breath, turned, and began walking in the opposite direction. He had a more important treasure awaiting him at Stonewycke.

As he retraced his steps back toward the estate, the awful burden which had been bearing down upon him all day lightened by degrees. Yet he knew in one sense he had only begun. For the first step in beginning to live differently would be to make reparations for the wrong he had done. For a life such as Logan's, that would be no easy matter. And the first step might be the hardest of all—to come clean before the people he had been trying to hoodwink.

But he did not have long to think about these things, for before he was halfway back he saw a figure dart behind a thick clump of broom.

"Who's there?" he called, stealing cautiously forward.

Then two men, large and imposing, stepped out from the cover of the bush. It was dark, and on first glance Logan registered no recognition. Then gradually it began to dawn on him. He had sat between them, long ago it seemed, in a fancy Rolls Royce. Here were Chase Morgan's henchmen, sooner than he had expected. He did not have long to ponder, however, when another voice yelled behind him.

"It's time we talked, Macintyre!"

Logan spun around.

Though he had seen Ross Sprague in Hamilton's pub, Logan did not now recognize him. What he did recognize was the pistol Sprague held in his right hand.

Logan hardly thought about his next act. It was generated instinctively, from panic rather than logic. Remembering the shovel he still held, he swung mightily at Sprague's arm. The impact knocked the gun loose and into the heather and Sprague into the ditch on the side of the road. But the other two were on him in a moment. Logan barely had time to hope that if they had guns they might be reluctant to use them this near the house. Clumsily he wielded the shovel at once as a battle-ax and lance. He thrust forward, clipping Cabot in the head and knocking him temporarily unconscious. Lombardo, left alone in the attack, charged Logan. Had he gotten a firm hold on him, Logan would surely have been finished. But the big man, thinking through his attack none too clearly, simply rushed at Logan angrily, with all the deftness of a wild bull. Logan let him come, then at the last moment, stepped aside, shoved the shovel into Lombardo's oversized torso, and pushed with all his might. The uncoordinated goon was taken completely off his guard, stumbled over a rock, and crashed off the road somewhere near his cohort Sprague.

Logan did not even wait for Lombardo to land. The last thing Logan wanted was to bring danger to Stonewycke. But for the first time in his life he realized—with a humility that was new to him—that he was in over his head. He could handle this alone no longer. He needed the help of his friends.

He threw down the shovel and ran for the house.

50 ✹ The Confession

THOUGH THE EVENING was well advanced toward night, Lady Margaret and Joanna were sitting alone together in the kitchen. Ever since their talk with Allison, Joanna had felt a growing urgency to find out as much as possible from her grandmother about the family's history and her own life. She had long been gathering what information she could and writing it down, knowing that in her grandmother's memory lay the wealth of the Ramsey and Duncan heritage that might someday be lost. In giving her blessing to Allison, and passing along of her legacy to the two younger women, Margaret had, Joanna sensed, released something of the energy of her life, sending it into the future through the lives of her descendants. Now her time was coming to move on into that next phase of her life with God, which only death could bring. Heartbreaking though this realization was to Joanna, she knew of its necessity. Yet she could not look into her grandmother's face, seeing there a gradual fading of the embers of life, without tears rising in her own eyes. It was a crossroads which must come, but God would help her to live through it with victory, for it would bring a sadness to her greater than any she had ever known.

Their quiet conversation was interrupted by a knock on the door. Logan had gone to the only place in the castle where a light was still burning.

Despite the late hour, the family gathered immediately in the drawing room upon his urgent request. They were all there except the younger children.

Dorey reclined on the divan, Joanna took a seat in one of the great winged-backed chairs, her face displaying clear anxiety over whatever Logan's plight might be. Lady Margaret, clad in a quilted, satin dressing gown, took her place next to her husband. Alec stood easily by the hearth, his arm resting on the high mantle. Logan admired the calm and utter peace in his expression and wondered if he'd ever possess such a quality. Allison sat stiffly on the stone skirt of the hearth, a trace of fear showing out of her blue eyes but also a brave attempt to appropriate a calm like her father's, whom she resembled in so many other ways.

Part of Logan had wanted to flee after his attack. Yet another side of him knew he needed help.

But more than that, at last he knew he had to make right the terrible wrongs he had done, and even planned to do against these people. He had struggled too hard on the road out there to come to this decision, and now he must not turn away from it.

Now, however, as he stood before them, he had no idea what to do or say. It was rather an imposing array of lairds and ladies, representing a span of four generations in the Ramsey and Duncan line. He felt more than simply foolish. He felt low, insignificant, petty. And worse, he had probably brought danger right to their doorstep, though it was unlikely his pursuers would breach the security of the estate.

Logan's glance moved from face to face, resting momentarily on Allison's, where he could not keep from lingering a moment longer than he wanted. Their eyes locked for an instant, during which a hundred unspoken words—apologies, pleas, explanations—passed between them.

Logan jerked his gaze away. She figured strongly in why he had come back, but he could not think of that now. It would only confuse the more urgent issues.

"You must be thinking I have gone crazy," he said, in a voice that was taut and thin. "Perhaps what I want to say could have waited until morning. I only know that *I* could not have waited. I may have brought danger here, but it is too late for me to bemoan that now— I only hope I can make you understand how very sorry I am."

His words were met with puzzled looks all around. Then Alec spoke.

"I'm afraid we're a bit in the dark, lad," he said. "That is, ye might do best if ye started at the beginnin'."

Logan nodded, then took a deep breath. "I have presented myself falsely to you," he began, each word spoken deliberately as if to insure they were not misunderstood. And though Logan felt none of the release he expected from the confession, he went on. "I have spent my entire life in lies and cheating. Honesty and dishonesty have all been one to me. When I'm not gambling, I swindle innocent folk in any other way I can. That's how I make my living, not in investments, as I tried to make you believe."

"We appreciate that you have seen fit to tell us this, Logan," said Lady Margaret, to whom it came as no surprise. "But it changes nothing in how we feel toward you." She looked at him intently, with the same penetrating gaze he had encountered on his first day in Port Strathy. But now for the first time he felt from the look what had been at its root all along, a great heart of compassion and understanding.

"How can that be?" said Logan, both astonished and frustrated. "I know you people detest dishonesty. I'm a thief; don't you understand that?"

"I understand," she replied with that mystery in her voice which he had yet to fully grasp. "And we do detest dishonesty. But I see honesty in you now, and that means everything. What can we do for you?"

Logan shifted his weight on his feet, flustered and uncertain what to say. He had expected rejection, and possibly could have handled that. But he didn't know what to do with *this!* "You don't understand," he began again more firmly. "That's why I came *here*—to Stonewycke. It was no accident that I met you. I planned it. I intended to swindle you! All of you—but you in particular, Lady Margaret."

He looked around, the old part of his nature almost defying them to accept him now. But just before his eyes turned toward Allison, they faltered and looked away. He couldn't bear to see the changed expression he knew must be on her face. Instead, he forced his gaze back to Lady Margaret. He knew he had wronged her more than any by presuming on her love for Digory.

"And Digory . . . the Bible?" she asked.

"Oh, they're real enough."

"Then if you have committed some crime against us," she replied, "I am quite unaware of it."

"I lied to you! That ought to be enough. I didn't come here to research my family roots. I never gave a thought to anything like that until I found a letter written by my great-great-great uncle Digory—a letter written to you, Lady Margaret. The letter mentioned a treasure, and I came here in hopes of finding it—a treasure rightfully belonging to you—and to steal it from under your nose."

At the mention of the treasure, Margaret's face turned pale. It was as if a ghost out of her childhood had suddenly reappeared. Ian perceived the change and reached out to take her hand.

A long, silent pause followed. Logan stared down at the Persian carpet, for he could stand their eyes upon him no longer.

"And though it's too late to undo my falsehood to you," he said at length, "I want to apologize . . . to say how sorry I am." It was not easy to get the words out. The attempt was a new one for him. "I want to try somehow to make it up to you. You have all been . . . so . . . kind—you have treated me like I was one of the family when I did not deserve it." He stopped. If he said more he would likely break down again.

Finding her breath again, it was Lady Margaret who spoke next. "And did you complete your plan, Logan?"

He shook his head in reply. "But can you forgive me?" he blurted out, almost like a child.

Joanna stood and walked toward him. She led him to a chair, then sat down beside him. She rested her hand gently on Logan's shoulder while she silently prayed that the Lord would give them the words with which to comfort and show the way toward healing.

"Oh, Logan," said Lady Margaret, "do you know us so little yet that you do not know that our hearts are overflowing with love toward you? Of course we forgive you!"

"A confession such as yours, Logan," added Dorey, "is from the heart and is a clear sign of repentance. Believe me, I know about the need to repent. I ran from God for years before I accepted His forgiveness. So not only do we forgive you, so does God."

"How can you both say that!" This new outburst came from Allison, who looked ravaged with hurt and indignation. "How can you forgive him so easily? We believed him and he *lied* to us. We thought he was our friend and he deceived us. How can we trust him now? How do we know he hasn't just come to us because he's in some kind of trouble?"

"Oh, Allison . . . dear," Joanna began, but before she could utter another word Logan broke in.

"I am in trouble, but that's not why I've come to you—"

"How can we ever believe you again!" said Allison.

"I know I don't deserve it."

"I trusted you!" Allison exclaimed tearfully, the hurt clearly evident in her voice. "How can I be expected to forgive you now, Christian or no Christian? I just don't see how I can." She turned and fled the room.

"Logan," said Joanna, sensing the pain in his heart as he watched her go, but knowing he was unable to reach out to her, "you must try to understand Allison . . . she's young, and—"

"But what she said is right."

"I should go to her now," Joanna added, "but I know she didn't mean those things. Her heart will be able to forgive you, too. Just give her time." She gave his shoulder a motherly pat, then turned and left the room after her daughter.

"Come o'er here an' sit ye doon, lad," said Alec, drawing Logan to an overstuffed chair opposite the divan where Lord and Lady Duncan sat. Alec pulled a straight-backed medieval chair next to him. "Lad," he said when they had settled themselves, "do ye think forgiveness has anythin' t' do wi' merit? Wi' whether we *deserve't?* Weel, it doesna. It has t' do wi' only one thing—a contrite an' repentant heart. Where do ye think any o' us would be if God took the attitude wi' us that He'd forgive us if we deserved it?"

"I can imagine you forgiving me much easier than I ever could God," said Logan.

"It is from Him that we learn forgiveness, Logan," said Lady Margaret. "The first step of all is to accept *His* forgiveness."

"The first step of what?"

"Of committin' yer whole life t' Him," replied Alec. "That's what He wants from us. An' only by givin' Him yer life can forgiveness an' peace an' healin' come."

"I know now that I do want to be different, to be honest, to be upright. I want to be forgiven for all I've done. But it's hard for me to think of God as wanting anything to do with someone like me. I already told you. I'm not good, like you people. I've done dishonest things, *illegal* things." ·

"We ha' all been there t' one degree or another. Before God no one's free from sin. The Bible says that 'God commends his love toward us in that while we were *yet* sinners, Christ died fer us.' Dinna ye see, Logan. *Sinners* are His chief interest!"

"Calling all people sinners is just a religious way of talking. But nobody really believes everybody's just as bad as everybody else. What could you have done *really* sinful?"

"I strongly doubt, young man," put in Dorey before Alec had a chance to reply, "that you've spent any more time in the jails than I have—London and Glasgow both. I'm not proud of it. But God reached out to me, and I was in as despicable shape as anyone could have been at the time."

"And Logan," added Alec with an intensity in his voice, "I once killed a man."

Any argument that may have been posed on Logan's lips melted away to nothing, and he gaped in silence. The thing couldn't be true—surely he had misunderstood! Yet he could see in Alec's earnest blue eyes that it *was* so—beyond all reason. And yet despite such a crime, Alec still spoke about God as if He were his friend. It hardly seemed possible.

"The court exonerated me, but it made it no easier t' live wi' such a thing, knowin'—"

Alec closed his eyes and swallowed hard. It was still heart-wrenching to discuss it, and he wouldn't have except for Logan's benefit. "—Knowing that wi' my own hands I had destroyed a human life. I'm only tellin' ye this so ye can see jist hoo great God's love is fer us. When I came t' Him, He didna look at my deed an' say, 'Sorry, 'tis a bit too much fer me t' forgive!' No, Jesus had *already* died for that deed. He was merely waitin' fer me t' realize it, repent o' what I had done, an' let His love come int' my heart in place o' my old selfish nature. His love had nothing t' do wi' what I had done. His love's great enough t' cover the worst an' the best o' us. But we *all* need that love abidin' in oor hearts equally."

"I've never really heard it said like that before," confessed Logan. "But how did you know it was true—I mean, really *know*?"

"A dear friend first told me," Alec replied. "Then one night I knew in my heart that He *did* love me an' had answered my prayer an' had forgiven me. I guess ye could say He spoke t' me in a quiet sort o' way. Once ye take the step o' askin' His forgiveness an' invitin' Him t' dwell wi' ye in yer heart fer the rest o' yer life, He'll not leave ye alone."

"I've never thought of God like that before—so close."

Almost as if by common consent, the three older persons laid their hands on Logan and bowed their heads. Feeling both a slight embarrassment, yet at the same time the warmth of their love, Logan closed his eyes. Dorey was the first to speak.

"Father," he began, "we all thank you for bringing Logan here to live among us. Thank you that his heart is open to you."

He stopped. After a moment Alec prayed, "Oh, Lord, keep yer lovin' hand on oor friend Logan. Reveal yer love t' him in a special way. An' show him the way through this present trouble in his life, usin' us, yer servants, in any way ye see fit. Help him t' accept yer forgiveness in his heart. Thank ye fer yer great love, Lord. Amen."

"Help me, Lord," said Logan simply. "Help me to live as you want me to. Please dwell in my heart like you do in these people's. And thank you for forgiving me for what I have been . . . Amen."

He looked up just as Joanna came back into the room. She smiled at him as she approached. Alec held out his hand for her, and she took it gratefully.

"Hoo's oor daughter?" he asked.

"I couldn't find her," replied Joanna. "I looked all over the house. She must want to be alone. She's probably gone for a walk outside."

She sighed. "Maybe the cool evening air will settle her emotions."

"She has every right to hate me," said Logan. "I talked about being friends—but I've proved myself nothing more than a liar to her."

He looked solemnly at Allison's parents. "I want you to know that whatever happens, I never meant to hurt her. I . . ."

His voice faltered. He wanted to tell them that he cared for her, cared for her more than even he was sure he wanted to admit. But he left unspoken the words of his heart, rose, and began to leave the room.

"I'm going to pack my things," he said. "I'll leave in the morning. I appreciate all you've done for me. I appreciate what you've said and done this evening, and your praying with me. But it's best that I leave. There are . . . some men . . . looking for me. Men from out of my past. It would not be fair of me to stay. Lady Margaret, I will leave you the Bible, with Digory's letter. I know it will mean a great deal to you. His memory—and yours—will always be special to me. But it is best this way . . ."

He paused and tried to look up at the four of them where they stood watching him through eyes of love. He felt the filling of his tear ducts and would have to make his exit soon.

"If only . . . if I could do all this over again, I . . ." but he left his words unfinished, turned quickly, and fled from the house.

51 ❈ Abduction

THE SLIVER OF a moon had broken through the clouds, but it shed no light on the deepening night. As Logan crossed the yard, the quickly moving clouds rolled past, obliterating it once more. The air was heavy. In the distance he heard a faint rumble of thunder.

Was he running once again—this time perhaps not from God, but from people? Why had he been so afraid to open up and tell them everything? He knew they would have accepted him with open arms, would have prayed with him, would have done whatever they could to help. What made it so difficult to receive the help and love of one's fellows?

Suddenly a sound arrested Logan's attention. He stopped and listened again. Was it Allison? He wasn't sure he wanted to meet her right now.

He glanced all about, but saw nothing. It was just as well. What could he say, anyway? As he walked on he reviewed all their times together. They had made no promises or commitments to one another. But then they were both too self-centered for that. He immediately rebuked himself for thinking ill of her; he knew there was more to Allison than that. He had seen glimpses at first, but then after that day when Fairgate came to call she had seemed genuinely different. Was she fighting a battle within herself—just as he was?

He walked on. He didn't want to leave. But what else could he do? He and Allison had merely had a brief glimpse of what might have been. What was he thinking, anyway? He could never settle down—even for love. The very thought of the word sent an electric charge through his body. It was not something he had encountered much of in his hard life on the streets. He had not even sought it, nor wanted it—until now, when it seemingly lay so close within his grasp. And yet his chance for love was all but gone.

Logan reached the stable door and opened it wide enough to let himself through. All was pitch black and still, except for an occasional snort from one of the horses in back. He had never known until now what a comforting sound that was. No wonder his uncle had so loved his animals and his little world here!

Before he had a chance to secure the door behind him, he again heard a sound, like the shuffling of feet. Again he thought of Allison. But before he had the chance to wonder what she might be doing in the stable, another voice broke through the silence. Logan froze.

"Don't do anything funny, Macintyre," it said. "I have a .38 aimed right at your head." It was the same voice he had heard with Lombardo's earlier.

So, the walls of mighty Stonewycke were not impenetrable after all!

"Who are you? What do you want?" Logan struggled to keep the tremor from rising in his voice.

"Sprague's the name," said the intruder coolly. "But it won't mean anything to you. You have something I want—at least I hope you have it. If not . . . then I'll be *very* disappointed. You see, Macintyre, I have a fondness for buried treasure."

How could Morgan have found out about that? Logan wondered. But it hardly mattered now.

"Where is Allison?"

"You mean that sweet young thing that was roaming around out here an hour ago?"

"Where is she?" was Logan's only reply as he started to spin around.

"Hold it!" barked Sprague. "You turn around real slow and keep your hands where I can see them."

Logan complied. "What have you done with her?" he shouted, feeling a mixture of rage and self-derision for getting her mixed up with men who were likely murderers.

"Don't worry. She's safe and sound—*for now.* You cooperate and give me what I want, and you'll have your little mistress back." Sprague's threat needed no further embellishment.

"And what is it you want?"

"I told you. I want that treasure."

"That's all?"

Something didn't fit. If this man were from Morgan, settling the score against him would count for far more than some elusive treasure. He might want the loot anyway, if it chanced to come his way. But Morgan was the type who would want Logan's blood. Morgan would want revenge.

"I'm not a greedy man," Sprague was saying, "nor a violent one. I can, in fact, be most conciliatory."

"I won't tell you a thing until I know the girl is safe."

Sprague clicked his tongue in mocking rebuke. "It hurts my feelings, sonny, that you won't trust old Uncle Ross."

"You'll get nothing until I see with my own eyes that she is alive and well and will go free unharmed."

52 ❊ *The Abandoned Cottage*

ALLISON SQUIRMED AGAINST the rough stone wall of the deserted cottage.

Except for the blaze in the fire pit, there was no light in the single room of the hut. But it showed enough to reveal the cruel, menacing faces of her abductors. They were strangers, and, though she had heard them refer to one another as Cabot and Lombardo, the names meant nothing to her. Logan's name, however, had come up once or twice.

They had grabbed her in the courtyard behind the house, hustled her out through the gap in the hedge, shoved her into the backseat of a car, and driven her here. They were about half a mile from the moor, as close as any automobile could get to it. The old cottage had not been occupied for years, and though so many of them were alike and it was difficult to see, she was sure this was the same hut where she and Logan and Fergie had taken refuge. Now, it seemed it had become Allison's prison.

She shivered, as much from fear as from the descending cold of night. An icy wind had started to blow down from the moor, stirring up the stagnant air of the last several hours, portending a new storm.

"Cold, little lady?" asked the man named Lombardo gruffly, but not without a flicker of genuine concern.

Allison nodded, but she would never tell them she was also scared. *Oh, Lord,* she prayed, *please give me courage. I need you now more than ever!*

Lombardo slipped off his jacket and laid it roughly over her. She knew she should acknowledge the gesture, but with her hands numb from the cords that tightly bound them, and her arms still aching from their rough handling when they captured her, she could muster up little thanks.

"You're a bowl of mush," jeered Cabot to his comrade.

"Well, we don't want her to croak on us."

"No one ever croaked from a little cold."

"Aw, shut up!" growled Lombardo as he lumbered back to his place on the other side of the fire.

The jacket didn't help much, but it was something.

"What do you want with me?" Allison asked. "My family doesn't have any money."

"Hmm, that's a thought," said Cabot ominously. "Too bad we don't have time for a side venture."

"Please just let me loose, then go away—no one will come after you."

"You're awful generous," laughed Cabot.

Allison slumped back and fell silent. This seemed a harsh way to test her new faith, especially after she had failed so dreadfully when Logan had been confessing to her parents. If she hadn't run out acting so stupidly, none of this would have happened. She prayed once more, and continued to pray for help until she fell into a restless sleep.

A sudden rush of cold air awakened her. The door had been pushed open, but in the distorted light of the flames and the haze of sleep, she could not make out the newcomers. At last her eyes came into focus.

"Logan!" she cried, relieved and exultant, forgetting all past anger.

"Allison!" He rushed forward, stumbling over a piece of wood in the darkened room, and falling to his knees. She could see that his hands were tied. He made his way toward her, and, raising his hands to her, brushed her cheek as if to make certain she was real. Then, closely examining her from head to foot, he asked, "Are you all right?"

"Oh, yes. I'm so glad to see you!"

"I'm sorry to have gotten you into this. I hardly deserve your forgiveness, but I *am* sorry."

"Oh, Logan," she said, "all that's behind us. I treated you so rudely!"

Sprague interrupted before either could speak further. "Sorry to break up this warm little reunion," he said sarcastically, "but I don't think we're quite finished with our deal, Macintyre."

Logan turned. He had little faith that Sprague would spare them once he had his precious information, but Logan had few options.

"Let Allison go. Then I'll tell you."

"What kind of fool do you think I am?" laughed Sprague. "Once she's gone, you might tell me anything! She's my only insurance that you'll tell me the truth."

Logan looked at Allison and sighed. Well, it had been worth a try. But Sprague was no dummy.

"There's a place called Ramsey Head," he said.

"Yeah?"

"It's buried at the top."

"How will I find it?"

"You'll see when you get there. It's under a large rock, part way chiselled to look like the head of a horse."

Sprague grabbed Logan by the shirt and dragged him to his feet.

"I'll see, because you're going to show me!"

"Then Allison comes too."

But Cabot stepped forward. "No go, Sprague," he said. "You start moving them around and you're asking for trouble. There might be people out looking for the girl by now. I'm not letting Macintyre out of my sight. You go check it out. But believe me, my friend, if you find it and try to double-cross us and skip town—we'll find you!"

"What if it's not there?" asked Sprague.

"We won't have at them till you get back."

"That's going to waste time," argued Sprague.

"You're not running this show anymore. We've done our part and I'm taking no more chances on losing Macintyre. You've got two hours. If you're not back by then, I'll just assume you don't need Macintyre anymore."

"Two hours! You must be crazy! I'll need help. Who knows how deep the stuff's buried."

Cabot gestured with his gun toward Lombardo. "You go with him. I'll watch these two."

"Don't tell me what to do!" grumbled Lombardo. "This is your idea. So you go!"

Cabot eyed his accomplice intently, then rose, apparently thinking it fruitless to push the point. Where could the two kids go, anyway? Even Lombardo should be able to handle that. But Sprague just might try to skip. Maybe it was good for him to go, to keep an eye on Sprague—and the loot.

There was at least some comfort in the fact that they had some time to spare, and Allison tried to be thankful for that. Logan had come. Perhaps the Lord had sent him. She was no longer alone. And when Lombardo pushed him down next to her, she felt a warm peace from his nearness.

"Logan," she said softly, "you're not the only one who has things to be sorry about. I haven't treated you fairly either. From the very beginning I judged you. When you hurt your foot, I knew it was fake."

"You did?"

"Yes. But believe me, I didn't keep quiet about it for any noble reasons. I planned to wait till the right time, then use it against you. Don't ask me why. I'm not even certain myself. Let's just say I was a different person back then. Not a very nice person. Everything was so twisted in my mind."

"I asked for it," Logan replied. "I badgered you—"

"It's enough that we forgive each other," Allison interrupted. "And I *do* forgive you. Something's happening inside me, Logan—"

"Hey!" broke in Lombardo's sharp voice, "what're you two whispering about."

"Just passing the time," Logan replied.

"Well, no funny business, that's all!" He waved his gun in the air to add emphasis to his words.

"We can't do any harm talking, can we?"

Lombardo grunted and fell silent.

Logan said nothing for a few moments. Allison wondered what he was thinking. She wanted to tell him that what she had felt that day in the rain was *not* mere accident, as she had said earlier. But she didn't know how to begin. Then she noticed that he was working his hands, within his bonds, back and forth. Quickly she jerked her gaze away, not wanting to alert Lombardo's attention.

"Logan," she said at length, "you know all those things I said earlier about our time together, you know, coming home from the Bramfords'?"

He nodded.

"I was wrong to try to make so little of that. It *was* a special moment for me. I didn't mean what I said later."

"You mean if I tried to steal another kiss from you, you wouldn't slap me?" he teased.

"Logan . . . please. You'll embarrass me," she replied with good-natured chiding in her tone.

"Now," said Logan more softly, "how are you at acting sick?"

"Maybe as good as you," she answered with a coy smile.

"Well, give it a try—and make it look good."

Allison doubled over and let out a terrible groan. She repeated it over and over several times, but still Lombardo paid no attention. Finally Logan intervened.

"Help her!" he cried in a most convincing tone. "She's in pain . . . please."

"That's an old dodge," said Lombardo callously. "I wasn't born yesterday."

Allison rolled over onto her side, still moaning.

"Come on, lady," said Lombardo, "it's the oldest trick in the book."

"You can't just let her lie there!" yelled Logan. "What if your friends come back and she's dead? They'll feed you to the cops, while they make off with the loot."

"This better not be some game." Lombardo hitched his frame to its feet, then motioning with the gun at Logan, added, "You get way over there."

Logan complied, and still Lombardo had taken no notice that the cords binding his hands had loosened considerably. The big man bent down beside Allison and tapped her shoulder.

"All right, lady, what's wrong?" he asked.

"My stomach," gagged Allison.

Lombardo had been careful to keep Logan, who had moved to the far end of the wall, in his sight. But for the single moment while he took Allison's arm to pull her up from the ground, he let his gun hand drop.

Logan's next move was so quick and unexpected that even the split second it would have taken to raise the gun was not enough. Logan sprang across the space between them, his weight momentarily stunning the hoodlum.

"Ali . . . run!" he shouted. He knew he was no fighter, and this man was nearly twice his size. There might be only a few seconds for her to escape.

Allison scrambled to her feet, but instead of taking flight looked about for a way to help Logan. In the meantime, Lombardo had regained what wits he had, and tried to aim his gun. Logan caught his arm and flattened it to the ground. They struggled for another minute, until, with a horrifying crack, the pistol fired.

For a frightening instant everything stopped. Then Logan raised his hand, the weapon gripped tightly between his fingers. Lombardo stared, shocked both that he had fired and that this amateur had been able to wrestle the gun from him. Then he backed slowly away. Pale and trembling, with his right arm pressed against his side, Logan steadied the gun in his left hand toward Lombardo.

"Ali, go!" he repeated.

"Are you all right?"

"Yes, yes! I'm fine," he answered with a weak smile. "You have to run for help."

"I'm not leaving you."

"*You have* to. Don't you understand? There's no one else. I'll keep him here. You're the only one who can do this."

"But you're hurt!"

"It's nothing much," he lied, thankful that his jacket hid the spreading red beneath his shirt. "I would only slow you down. Just go. I'll be fine."

Then he turned to his prisoner and said, "Untie her, Lombardo."

With hesitancy Allison at last approached the door. With her hand on the latch, she turned and looked back, her eyes pleading with Logan. Reading her unspoken, "Are you sure?" Logan nodded and said, "Now, make a run for it."

The moment she cleared the rickety wooden step of the cottage, she broke into a run, a prayer on her lips, and an ache in her heart that she might not get back with help in time.

53 ❈ *Looking Death in the Eye*

PAIN SEARED THROUGH Logan's side as if a red-hot iron had been thrust through his chest.

Sitting on the ground, he had to raise one knee in order to rest the arm that held Lombardo's pistol. When the slug had first hit him there had been no pain, only a jolt and an instant feeling of weakness. That's how he knew he'd been hit bad. He'd seen flesh wounds; they were the worst of all. The deeper the bullet, or so he'd been told, the greater the shock, the less the pain. But the stabbing throb had followed soon enough, and if the slug didn't kill him, he'd no doubt faint eventually from sheer agony and loss of blood, and then Lombardo would finish him off. In either case, he was a dead man.

He had never been hurt like this, never knew this kind of physical torture. Already his vision was blurring and his hand was so weak it shook. Then Lombardo stirred and Logan tensed.

"Don't, Lombardo," warned Logan in a voice thin and dry.

"You're not going to make it, Macintyre. You're half gone already."

"I can still pull this trigger."

"You don't have the stomach for it," taunted the hoodlum.

"Maybe not. But I'm beyond caring, so I might be able to do what I don't have the stomach for."

Lombardo sat back quietly. Logan's point made sense, and was well taken. What was the hurry? He would faint soon enough anyhow. Lombardo's chief worry now was what to say when his cohorts came back. If they found no treasure, and discovered the girl escaped and Logan dead, they would be none too pleased. True, Morgan's mission would have been accomplished. But then the girl was loose to point the finger at them, and Sprague would be furious. He did not relish a tangle with that man. If the kid died, maybe he should split and try to get back to Morgan first, with his side of the story.

Meanwhile, Logan sat with his own thoughts. He knew Lombardo was not far wrong. He could never pull this trigger. Here he was again trying to be something he was not. He had always hated guns and had never used one in his life. But something else was also operating within Logan at that moment, which Lombardo could not possibly realize—a stubborn determination not to let Allison or her family down again. He didn't know if he could take another man's life. But he did know that he had to keep Lombardo here long enough to give Allison enough time for a clean escape. The thought of this hulk getting away too soon and catching her was enough to make Logan think that he just might be able to kill. He hoped it wouldn't come to that.

Perspiration dripped into his eyes and he dashed it away with his free hand, a hand as cold and clammy as death itself. His eyes began to droop and he forced them open. He had to hang on!

As the minutes ticked away, Logan had to work harder and harder to keep his brain from freezing in a jumble of fog. His head already felt too light, as if it were three or four feet above his shoulders. Every once in a while Lombardo would appear distorted and distant, like the view through the wrong end of a telescope.

How long had it been, he wondered? Where would Allison be? But all perception of time was gone. It felt like hours, but it might have been only minutes. His wounded body screamed out for release, but he steeled himself against surrender. He could not lie down and go to sleep, though every fiber of his being cried out for rest.

Oh, God, help me!

Suddenly his head jerked up. His brain had begun to swirl about as consciousness started to leave him. Seeing his advantage, Lombardo inched forward. Logan thrust out the pistol.

"I'm warning you, Lombardo. I *will* use this." But Logan's voice sounded hollow and far away. He wasn't even certain his finger any longer was touching the trigger.

"You're a goner, Macintyre."

No! Logan tried to shout. But it was a wicked dream. He heard no sound come out of his mouth. His tongue and lips were so dry they felt glued shut, and the room spun sickeningly around him.

How long . . . how long had it been . . . ?

Allison, I'm sorry . . . I tried . . . I love you . . . but I can't . . .

When Logan was next aware of anything, he was sprawled out on the hard, earthen floor of the deserted cottage. He lifted his head long enough to see that Lombardo was gone; then he let it fall in despair. The fire had burned low. He had no sense of time. He did not even bother to wonder why the hoodlum had left him alive. Could it be that even a criminal like him had no stomach for cold-blooded murder? His friends would hardly be so kind.

He was alive. But barely. He knew it would not be long now.

Logan had not often thought about death. He was young and it had always seemed so distant. He had always scorned deathbed confessions. He thought of his last conversation with Skittles. His dying friend had said, "You're a bright boy, and you can make somethin' better of yourself."

Well, Skits, he thought feebly, *guess I let you down again.*

They had never talked about religion. And now Logan regretted that, for it seemed a shame that it should have been missing from their close relationship. But of course, he had not been interested in God, not seen so many things clearly back then.

Deathbed confessions . . . Now Logan understood what they were all about. They had to be real because a man could not be insincere when he was dying—it was no time for lies or games or false promises. Skittles had tried so urgently to get him to listen, but he had brushed it off.

Now it was his turn, and there was no one for him to talk to. Was his life passing before his eyes? Was this what it was like? He knew what he wanted now, and only wished he had time to prove he was worthy of the same faith as Digory's and Lady Margaret's and all the rest of them. He only wished he had time to make amends to all those he had hurt, to those he had swindled, to Buckie and Jimmy and how many others. If it took a lifetime, he wanted to undo the results of his former lifestyle. But now it was too late . . . there was no time left . . .

Logan drew a ragged breath.

"God, forgive me for what I have been, for what I have done," he prayed in a hoarse whisper. "Forgive me for ignoring you for so long. Let me die with the peace I know only you can give—"

He stopped suddenly with a fit of coughing that sent renewed pain shooting through his body.

Then he was silent. He could hardly think. But in those moments that he knew would be his last, he recalled Alec's words: *"One night I jist knew in my heart that He did love me an' that He had forgiven me."* With the thought Logan felt the peace he had yearned for.

Logan knew the same voice that had spoken to Alec. In some mysterious and miraculous and unfathomable way, God had accepted to His heart a liar, a thief, a swindler, a no-good, self-centered young man who had lived his entire life for no one but himself.

It was all Logan needed to know.

He closed his eyes. He had seen into God's heart of love—and was ready to die.

54 ❈ *The Stretching of Allison's Faith*

ALLISON RAN HARD the entire three miles between the deserted Krueger place and Stonewycke's gates.

Had she taken the road, the way would have been easier, but longer, and she feared she might run into the other two men. She had therefore struck out over the moor and, despite the darkness of the night, had miraculously made it without breaking her leg in a peat bog. Even as the imposing walls of Stonewycke's outer perimeter came into view, she was not sure she could make it. Her chest heaved frightfully and a painful stitch tore at her side. But the rain did not begin until she was in sight of the castle.

The ever-present thought of Logan forced her to keep going. *Please, God,* she prayed over and over as she ran, *please don't let him be hurt seriously. Protect him, Lord . . . keep your hand upon him.*

She pushed open the ancient gate and paused a brief moment to catch at least one more breath with which to go on. Glancing up at the house, she found two or three lights still on. It must be nearly midnight.

The kitchen door was still unlocked. She entered, frantically calling for her mother. Footsteps hurried along the corridor above, then down the stairs. More lights flashed on. As her mother reached her, Allison collapsed into her arms, crying and trembling. Alec was but two paces behind his wife, the anxiety of the night etched clearly on his face.

"Lass," he said, "oh, lass, what's happened? I've been oot lookin' fer ye this last hour."

"It's awful, Daddy!" she cried, now finding his strong arms enfolding her as well. "It's Logan—"

"What's he done?" exclaimed Alec, his proud Scottish blood on the rise.

"He's hurt, Daddy . . ." replied Allison. "There are some men, bad men. They kidnapped me. Then they brought Logan. We were both tied up. Logan got loose and overpowered the man so I could escape. But he was shot—he wouldn't tell me how bad. Oh, I'm so scared!"

"Shh," soothed Alec, concerned by Allison's disjointed explanation.

"What men?" asked Joanna.

"I don't know, but they wanted Logan. They made him tell where the treasure is. Two of them left. I think they had orders to kill us once they found the treasure. If they get back before help comes, I'm afraid—" She burst into tears.

"Where is he?" asked her father, his mind clearing.

"At the old Krueger cottage."

"All right, we'll go fer him," said Alec, springing into action. "I'll get the truck from Fergie an' gather up a few men on the way. We'll be there in no time."

He started down the hall, but Allison ran after him.

"I'm going with you," she stated.

"Lass, there's no tellin' what we'll find."

"I don't care. I have to go. I can't let him think I didn't care enough to come back."

"Let her go, Alec," Joanna said with an understanding smile. "This is something she has to do. The Lord will protect you both."

"Ye must do whate'er I tell ye."

"Of course I will," replied Allison earnestly. "But let's go!"

Within twenty minutes, the truck was brought out and the farmhands who lived on the estate were awakened, and they set out for the deserted cottage. On the way Alec tried to get what additional information from Allison he could. He sent Fergie into town to gather assistance in order to apprehend the men who had gone to Ramsey Head, if they were still there.

The truck bounced and clattered over the old, rutted dirt road they had to use for the final leg of the short journey. Allison sat on the edge of the front seat, clinging tensely to the dashboard, trying to peer through the rain.

Suddenly she saw something, a dark and shadowy figure, moving toward them.

"Look!" she exclaimed. "Daddy, stop . . . it's Logan!"

Alec ground the truck to a halt and jumped out, Allison at his side. They ran forward.

But it was not Logan, only Frank Lombardo trudging heavily through the rain, soaked to the skin, utterly lost. In spite of the certain disaster awaiting him, he was actually relieved to see a sign of human life through the dismal night.

"It's him!" cried Allison. "That's the man!"

Alec needed no further explanation. He stepped forward, grabbed Lombardo's arms, and pushed him against the truck. With two other burly crofters now backing Alec and ready at the first sign of a struggle, Lombardo surrendered without a fight.

"Where is he?" screamed Allison. "What have you done to him?"

"If you mean Macintyre," replied the subdued Lombardo, "I didn't do nothin' to him. He just died, that's all—at least he's dead by now. You saw for yourself. He's the one who attacked me, and the gun just went off."

"No! Daddy . . . no!"

"Dinna ye give up hope yet, lassie," said Alec. "Ye jist keep prayin' hard."

But Lombardo scoffed at the words. "It's too late fer prayin'. I tell you, he's a goner. But it weren't my fault."

Without further conversation, Alec took the prisoner toward the back of the truck and made him climb up. "Can you handle him?" he asked his men. One of them, sitting in the back with his hunting rifle on his lap, wielded it knowingly and nodded.

As they approached the cottage, it looked more deserted than ever. Nonetheless, Allison was out of the truck even before it had come to a full stop and racing toward the door. *Lord,* she prayed, afraid for what she might find, *help me to face this with strength.*

The fire had died to all but a few pitiful embers and it was almost dark inside. But the next moment Alec came up behind her holding a lantern. Allison saw Logan lying on the hard earth, deathly still, his skin ashen as if the fire of his life, too, had died. She rushed forward and fell to her knees beside him.

"Logan!" she wept, gently lifting his head. "Oh, Logan . . . please don't be dead."

For several agonizing moments there was no response. She grasped his hand. It was still warm with life. With tears of anguish and love in her eyes, she leaned down, kissed him, and laid her head on his chest. "Logan . . . Logan . . ." she said, softly this time. "Logan . . . I love you!"

A flutter, though faint, stirred in his chest. She looked up at her father helplessly, then back to the prostrate form.

Slowly Logan's eyelids opened, but the merest crack. A pathetic, crooked smile bent his lips.

"Ali . . ." he breathed. "Ali . . . is that you?"

"Oh yes! Logan . . . yes, it's me! Oh, thank you, Lord!"

". . . told you I was a lucky fellow . . ."

"Oh, Logan! . . . hush now . . . please . . ." rebuked Allison with joy in her voice.

Alec knelt down and gently lifted Logan into his arms, and, with Allison beside him, murmuring words of love and encouragement into his ear, carried him to the truck.

55 ✼ The Fate of the Bonnie Flora MacD

FRANK LOMBARDO WAS securely in the custody of the local authorities. But the search party that climbed Ramsey Head found another kind of justice had been meted out to Willie Cabot. He was found lying next to a hastily dug hole with a bullet through his heart.

Ross Sprague it seemed had escaped justice altogether. A search for Ross Sprague was mounted, but to no avail. No one had thought to look north toward the sea until it was too late—although the rising storm would have discouraged even the most tenacious pursuer.

Sprague, meanwhile, had hired a thirty-foot fishing vessel, one sentimentally styled *Bonnie Flora MacD* after the prince's daring lady, under the name Albert Smith. Even that did not arouse suspicions until a day or two after the escape. Port Strathy's law-abiding community was simply not equipped to deal with crime at this level—a fact that worked to Sprague's benefit.

Sprague was no seaman, but he thought his cursory knowledge would suffice him for the short distance which would be required of him. When the rain began to fall and the wind rise, his confidence began to wane somewhat. But he knew he couldn't turn back. The once sleepy little burg of Port Strathy was wise to him by now, no doubt. So he steered the crusty old boat due north against the gale, cursing the cagy yokel who had rented him the craft. The five-pound rental fee had been highway robbery, for the vessel was barely seaworthy. But the fellow owned several boats, and this one had been equipped with a radio—its chief selling feature, as far as Sprague was concerned. Anyway, Sprague could not complain too heartily about the fee since he had no intention of returning the crazy old tub.

The minute Cabot had decided to tag along, Sprague knew there would be trouble. Not only was the Englishman surly and disagreeable, he was also greedy. The moment he had laid eyes on the cache of wealth buried underneath the rock on Ramsey Head, he had gone wild. No court would ever acquit Sprague on the grounds of self-defense, but he knew instinctively that had he not taken care of Cabot, he would never have made it to the mainland alive.

But he had made it, and nothing would stop him now. His boss had better be there to meet him! He didn't relish the idea of a submarine, but it was the safest means of undetected escape. His boss's connections in Berlin had paid off; this was, after all, the surest getaway. They'd be looking for him all up and down the coast, probably watching all the roads, and he'd be safe and sound where none of those yokels would ever think to even consider—under the sea. He didn't like Germans, and never had. But he could put up with them for a few days if that was the price for becoming a rich man.

A fifteen-foot wave crashed against the side of the boat, sending a column of spray over the deck and lifting it dangerously starboard. Sprague grabbed the wheel and forced the vessel around a few degrees in order to break away from the rough water. The compass told him he was off course. It was almost midnight. He better get her going right if he planned to make his rendezvous.

He would never have considered himself greedy, but then he had never had much to be greedy about. So why was he risking his neck on this stupid little boat in the middle of the night? Couldn't he just as well have paid off some farmer for a wagon and a couple of horses and hightailed it away on some back road to Aberdeen or Inverness, and then by way of some freighter to a nice safe South American country where he could spend the rest of his days a wealthy man?

Why, then, was he out in this storm?

Sprague answered his own question, although this time it was not the safety of the sub which convinced him, but rather the memory of his boss's face. He was not the kind of man who would let a man like Sprague get away with a double-cross. His boss had the kind of resources that could ferret out a traitor in the most remote lands. He was not the kind of man you betrayed, if you wanted to stay alive. It probably would have been next to impossible to fence the loot he had unearthed, anyway. He was being well paid for his services, and now he had also arranged some insurance for a bit of a raise from his boss. So in the end he reached the same conclusion as before—he may not like it, but this was no doubt the best way.

Sprague glanced at his watch. It was the time to make contact. He flipped the switch on the radio, turned the necessary dials, and began tapping out the appropriate Morse Code. After a few minutes he received a response, though faint. At least someone was out there. Sprague knew his boss wouldn't back out if he smelled money. He tapped out another message: "difficult to read . . . repeat message." If only he knew German, he thought, and could talk to them.

A minute later came the reply, still choppy, but he got the vitals. The rendezvous sub was three miles offshore, north by northeast.

Sprague looked again at the compass. He was still way off course. Cursing, he struck his fist angrily against the panel. Then he gaped with disbelief. The instrument needles were spinning wildly.

It was broken!

The no good piece of junk was broken! How long had he been steering blindly? Where was the sub?

Perspiration beaded on Sprague's forehead as the cold dread of panic seized him. His hands shook as he grabbed the wheel. But he had no idea where to steer. He didn't even know in which direction the land lay! He could have been heading anywhere—

Suddenly he heard a sickening crack.

The craft lurched and shivered. Sprague was tossed off his feet, struck his head against the bulkhead, and knew no more. Perhaps he was better off that way, for the old fishing trawler was taking water fast.

56 ※ *The Guest of the* Admiral Mannheim

"HERR COMMANDER," CALLED the young lieutenant as he removed his heavy headset.

"Ja, Lieutenant," replied the commander of the *Admiral Mannheim* wearily. It was already midnight, and he had been up since before dawn maneuvering his submarine to its present locale some three miles off the coast of Scotland in the North Sea. He hadn't liked the assignment from the first. It was dangerous in such shallow water. But his superiors had made it clear: *This man is worth keeping happy. Do whatever he says.* And the commander was one who could follow orders, whether he happened to like them or not. That was how one got ahead in the German navy. So he would carry out his duty and ask no questions.

"It's been half an hour, mein Herr, and I have not been able to raise our contact again. Shall I continue to signal?"

Commander Von Graff sighed and, as if he planned to ignore his officer's query, ordered the periscope up. Leaning heavily on the horizontal bars, he scanned the storm-tossed seas above. On nights like these he was thankful for submarine duty. The other-worldliness of traveling fifty fathoms below the turmoils on the surface never failed to thrill him. And to do so in this craft, one of the Fatherland's finest, equipped with all the newest technology as part of the newly revitalized German military, only added to the dreamlike dimension. Of course, even if Hitler were elected and, as some predicted, poured three or four times as much into more sophisticated equipment, that would still not enable him to see more than a few yards on a night like this.

Von Graff stood back from the periscope and turned toward his subordinate. "The wind is blowing twenty to thirty knots up there," he said, "and he probably has nothing but a fishing radio. But . . . you had better keep up the signaling, if for no other reason than we shall have trouble from our *guest* if we don't."

"Ja wohl, mein Herr," replied the lieutenant obediently, but there was a smirk on his lips that the commander could hardly miss.

"You do not approve?" asked Von Graff with a knowing smile.

"Are you asking my opinion, mein Herr?"

The commander nodded.

"Then I would candidly say," the young officer went on, "that the German Reich could do well enough without *American* financiers getting involved in it."

Von Graff laughed, though without making a sound.

"Someday that *will* be so," he said, turning suddenly serious. "But in the meantime we will have to suck in our pride and kiss the boots of men like our *guest*. We are still paying for the foolishness of 1918, but it shall not be so much longer."

"What were you saying?" came a caustic voice from behind the two men.

The commander swung around. "Ah, mein Herr," he said with an air of cool politeness, "we were discussing the status of your associate."

"Which is?"

"We have had no radio contact for the last thirty minutes. In this storm . . . anything might have happened."

"Well, you just better find him," retorted the newcomer. "I'm paying you good money for this excursion."

"The *Reich* is paying me," rejoined the commander with just enough emphasis on the word *Reich* to give it added, sinister meaning.

"I'm pumping enough money into the Reich to make it all one to me," said the American.

"Be assured that we will do everything possible to reach your friend, Herr Channing."

Jason Channing turned sharply and strode from the bridge. Those arrogant Germans! You'd think losing a war would have taught them some humility. But fourteen years later they were still strutting around as if they owned the world. Well, maybe this time they'd make it—at least that's what Channing was banking on.

When he had lost nearly everything in the crash three years ago, he had been despondent. It was not easy for a man of sixty to think about starting over. But he'd never been the type to jump off a ledge because of a little setback. Thus he hung on to a hope that something would come along. And it had, during a trip to Munich at the invitation of some friends. While in Berlin he had heard Adolf Hitler speak to a crowd of union workers. Channing had found himself almost caught up in the frenzy of the gathering—the man was mesmerizing! Admittedly some of the things he said, if you listened closely enough, bordered on insanity. But Hitler himself had such a depth of charisma that he could get away with it. After the speech, Channing met the upcoming Nazi leader at a cocktail party. He was again struck with his absolute command—here was a man, he had little doubt, who *could* carry out his wild schemes. And since Channing was tired of his recent defeats, and the system that had brought them about, he decided to hitch his wagon to the brilliant rising star of Adolf Hitler.

It took Channing a year or so to recoup his losses, which, when he began liquidating his properties, proved to be less disastrous than at first report. Soon he was again able to wield the kind of power he craved. It didn't quite compare to the old days yet. But it was a start.

This business with Sprague had taken him off course for a time, but it was a long past-due debt. And after all, revenge was as sweet as power. The moment the name of Stonewycke had surfaced in his life again, he knew he would not be able to let it go. He did not like to lose.

He had lost only twice in his life. The crash had been the most recent loss, and he had switched national allegiance because of it. The other had been some twenty years before, when a pretty little bit of nothing by the name of Joanna Matheson had denounced him to his face. He had lost to a frail, stupid woman, and that fact had goaded him all these years far more than the loss of any fortune.

Now it was beginning to seem as if he may have been defeated again—this time in his attempt to settle the debt with Stonewycke. But he'd bury them for this—he'd not rest until every one of them was a dispossessed pauper.

Channing came to his cabin door, kicked it open and went inside. Lying on the small desk was the flimsy paper, Sprague's last communication. It wouldn't acquit the Duncan clan in his mind, but Channing reread it nonetheless. "Am aboard boat. Our package is secure. Rendezvous at midnight."

It did not seem possible to have come so close to such wealth and lose it so quickly. Had Sprague's boat indeed gone down in the storm? Sprague was too cold and calculating not to have covered all his angles. Was there a hidden meaning in the message? First of all, the specific use of the word *our* was not in keeping with their boss-employee relationship. Being a calculating man himself, Channing was well able to guess his intent. He was no doubt planning to cut himself in on the action. His lackey had seen the wealth and had decided that his boss should share it. What did he mean by "secure"? If he was planning on striking a deal, had he only brought aboard part of the loot, to insure his own continued safety? If so, what had he done with the rest of it?

Of course, he didn't want to give Sprague too much credit. He was not exactly a brilliant man, Channing noted. Before, he had always done what he was told. Perhaps the message meant nothing more than it said.

Channing refused to admit complete defeat.

If Sprague had gone down with his boat, so be it. But it didn't mean all was lost. Channing might still get his hands on the treasure. The only obstacle was to figure out just what Ross Sprague might have done with it.

A knock came to the door.

Channing rose and answered it.

"We're unable to reach your colleague," said the commander. "What would you like us to do?"

Channing thought for a moment, then replied. "Hold your position for another hour, and keep trying the radio. If there's no contact by then, head back out to sea."

57 ❊ *The Legacy Continues*

THREE WEEKS PASSED.

The first had been agony for Allison as Logan semiconsciously struggled against death. Fever, delirium, and pain marked the slow passage of days, while Allison attended him faithfully, leaving his side only when she herself could ward off sleep no longer. She had been stretched and tested in her new faith beyond the capability of her tender years. The strength of the bloodline of her ancestors rose up from within her, and both Ian and Alec marveled silently at the resemblance she had suddenly taken to their own two wives—in both the look in her eyes and the depth of her character. She had indeed, in a short period of time, stepped fully into her heritage as the next in the proud line of Ramsey women.

Even more significantly, through her late-night vigils of prayer next to Logan's bed, she stepped fully into her heritage as God's child, as his woman of valor. More clearly and personally than ever did she at last grasp the truth of the words she had heard since infancy: "Though I walk through the valley of the shadow of death, I will fear no evil, for thou art with me. . . ." Never had a darker valley loomed before young Allison MacNeil and when it was over, a lasting glow of maturity flashed in her eyes from within.

At last came the morning when Logan awoke from his travels in the netherlands. Allison had nodded off to sleep where she sat. He looked up, saw her, and closed his eyes again, content to know that she was near him. When she awoke she saw that a change had passed. He seemed to be breathing easier, and the trace of a smile remained on his lips. With her heart beating anxiously within her breast, she rose and approached him. Her presence awakened him again. He smiled up at her. Though welcome beyond words, the sight accentuated all too clearly his pale, drawn complexion and his thin, wasted frame. She saw more clearly than ever what a terrible ordeal had passed.

"Oh, Logan . . . !" she said, weeping tears of joy.

"It seems I am a patient here once more," he said softly.

"Yes, but this time I think you'll remember which foot to limp on," she replied, laughing through her tears. She felt such an exuberant joy she could not contain herself.

"I wish it were only my foot that hurt." He winced as he tried to move. "I thought for a while I was going to receive *new* life and *eternal* life all in the same package."

"Logan, I'm so happy for you. Mother and Daddy told me about their talk with you, and the prayer you prayed. I'm so sorry I ran away."

"I think we'll both be learning about this new life for a long time to come," he said. "I tell you, Ali, on that night I didn't think I had much of a life to give to God. But I learned something since—God knows a man's heart, and you can't fool Him. And when you think you're dying, you don't *want* to fool Him any longer."

"I'm so thankful for all that's happened."

"Yes," he agreed. "But I'm afraid I've just caused more trouble for your family."

"Oh no! You are already like a son to them. You know how they are—it gives them pleasure to serve you. It does me too, more than you know!"

As the first week had been agony, the following weeks were bliss for Allison. Logan was strictly charged by the doctor to remain in bed, and had not the strength to argue the admonition. Allison was with him most of the time. She read to him, often from the Bible, frequently, too, from the old Scottish poet whose poem about the man-boats so tugged at his heart during his days of indecision. Usually they wound up discussing what they'd read. Sometimes Lady Margaret or other family members would join in, gently opening new insights to both of them concerning their new faith. Dorey quipped that he had a captive audience and likened the atmosphere, more philosophically, to that of his greenhouse. God was providing them a time of respite through which to grow and become strong and extend their roots down. But soon, like Dorey's precious plants, they would be transplanted into the harsher elements of life outside the greenhouse, where wind and rain and snow and sun would beat upon them, helping them to grow stronger yet.

As wonderful as such discussions were, even more memorable were the long talks between Allison and Logan when they were alone, sometimes lasting until late at night. They poured out their beings to one another, as each had never done to another before. Both, in their own way, had hidden their deepest selves for so long. Suddenly there was so much to say, so much to share, so much to try to understand. Their spirits linked together inextricably and the love that had begun between them solidified upon the strongest foundation of love a man and woman can have—the love of God.

Thus, when Logan was at last given leave for an outdoor excursion, the turn of the conversation was not altogether unexpected by either of them.

They walked to the wild and tangled walled garden at the back of the house which Ian and Maggie had loved so much. Summer, as early as the spring had been late, had come full force to Stonewycke. The great old birch was heavy with fresh green foliage, and the untrimmed rhododendrons and azaleas lent splashes of vivid orange, red, and lavender to the woodsy surroundings. Tangled ivy wound around the feet of the bench where Logan and Allison sat. No more perfect setting could have been dreamed for what followed.

"Ali," began Logan when they had finished talking about the lovely garden and the warmth of the weather the past several days, "now that the direction of my life has changed, I've tried to think what I will do with myself. I have no education, no money, and very few talents that could be marketed in an *honest* world."

"You have more to offer than you think," said Allison. "And I know your position here will always be open to you."

"Yes . . ." Logan said, drawing out the word thoughtfully, "and I am grateful to your father for it. But there's not a great deal of future in repairing another's tools and equipment. I had hoped to have more to offer—that is . . . were I ever to settle down, it would be nice to have better prospects."

"Settle down?" Allison cared nothing for prospects. Those days were past for her. All she wanted was the man she loved.

"You know I've never been one to worry about position," Logan went on. "I never thought any nobleman was better than me in any way. But now I'm seeing—"

"Logan, *I'm* not making you feel awkward about your background, am I? That part of me's dead and buried. I don't care about class or distinctions anymore."

"I know. But still, opportunities for someone like me are . . . well, limited. What can I do other than work with my hands for a few quid a month? That's no way to . . . I mean, I could hardly expect . . . well, that would hardly be a suitable life for a man with a wife . . . like you."

"Oh, Logan!" exclaimed Allison in tearful and joyous frustration, "you dear, dear fool! I love you! Do you think that matters? It's different with us. We don't need position. Besides, there is a family precedent we have to keep up, you know. Such things did not stop my mother and father."

"Your father is a different man than I," replied Logan. "I have things hanging over my head. Things which make me far less worthy."

"I love and respect my father," Allison replied passionately. "More than ever in my life, now that I truly see him for the man of truth and integrity and courage he is. But you are every bit the man he is, Logan Macintyre."

"Oh, Ali, I don't know how you can say that . . . how you could believe such a thing. But I thank you, and I love you from the bottom of my heart for it. I do so want to marry you . . . if you'll have me. I will wait . . . or you can have me as I am."

She threw her arms around him. "I would not take you any other way, Logan, than just how you are. Because that is how God made you. And it is the person you are that I fell in love with!"

He winced with pain at the exuberance of her embrace, but quickly recovered and drew her to him, kissing her tenderly. "Thank you, Ali," he whispered in her ear. "Thank you! Thank you for accepting me. Thank you for loving me."

"God has been good to us, Logan—seeing us through all that has happened and bringing us to this."

They were silent a moment. Then Logan spoke again; this time his voice registering concern. "But your parents—" he began. "What will they say?"

"Oh, Logan, they love you! Social barriers mean nothing to them. I should know that better than anyone. Remember, they've been through it themselves."

"Then I should talk to your father," said Logan.

"My parents will be happy for us," said Allison gleefully; "I know it!"

"I wish I had your confidence just now."

"They love you already—as I do," she replied.

"Logan," she went on, "we will always be together—imagine it!"

"That brings up another matter," Logan began, then hesitated. He had not been looking forward to this part. "As soon as I've recovered, I must go to Glasgow to see my mother and give her a personal invitation."

"Of course."

"And after that, to London."

Allison frowned. "I've told you about Molly," Logan went on. "She's been like a mother to me, and I must see her—I want to share with her . . . well, all the changes in my life. And especially tell her about you."

"Are you certain you have to go to London?" asked Allison, her voice quivering. "I don't think I could keep from worrying about you."

"This is not the sort of thing you tell a dear friend in a telegram or a letter. But I will be very careful."

"I want to go with you, then."

"Your parents are gracious and perhaps progressive," he replied, "but that would be asking too much. Besides, I won't be gone long."

"I'll hate every minute of it."

Logan took her hand in his. "I still have a few more days to recuperate," he laughed. "And I'll need you beside me every minute!"

Later that evening, when Logan was alone, he heard a gentle knock on the door. His welcome was followed by the entrance of Dorey, looking more solemn than Logan had ever seen him. He walked in, clearly with some purpose on his mind, and sat down next to Logan's bedside.

"I want to talk to you, Logan," he began.

"Certainly," replied Logan.

"Alec has told me of your conversation with him. I want first to offer you my congratulations, and to say—on behalf of Lady Margaret and myself—welcome to the family. We could not be more happy for you and Allison."

Somehow, thought Logan, *his face and tone do not indicate great joy.*

"But I would be gravely remiss if I did not warn you that I think you are making a serious mistake by wanting to return to London alone."

"Because of the danger?" asked Logan.

"More than that, because of the separation it would mean between you and your future wife. You know, I believe, something of the story of my past?"

Logan nodded.

"We all know the Lord has used it for good," Dorey went on, "but I was so young and foolish. It was impetuous of me to send Maggie to America while I remained behind myself. Good . . . yes," he sighed; "the Lord used it to strengthen us. But I just don't want to see you make a mistake you might regret."

Logan nodded again, receiving the words of wisdom from this man he had grown to respect.

"Take her with you, Logan," he concluded. "Now that the Lord has brought you together, do not let anything happen to interfere with your love."

"I will think about what you have said," said Logan. "You may be right. Thank you."

Dorey rose and extended his arm. The two men clasped hands and shook them firmly. "The Lord bless you, son," said Dorey at last. "I meant what I said. Welcome into this family. I have no doubt that great good will come to Stonewycke and its descendants through the virtues you bring to the line. I pray the Lord's fullest blessings on you and your marriage."

It was now Logan's turn to fight back the tears rising in his eyes. God had indeed prospered him beyond anything he deserved by bringing him into the wealth of this heritage.

The following afternoon Logan and Allison once again walked in the walled garden. Circumstances had kept them apart the entire morning.

"I spoke to your father last night," said Logan quietly.

"And?" replied Allison expectantly.

"It was just like you said."

"He smiled and shook your hand . . . am I right?"

"Well, yes . . . in a way," said Logan with a smile. "He smiled. Then he gave a great roar of laughter. Then he embraced me in a huge bear hug that nearly burst my wound open again. When I winced, he jumped back, a pained look of apology on his face. Then he laughed again. And then . . . finally, he *did* shake my hand!"

Allison laughed. "That's just like Daddy! So warm . . . so boisterous!"

"And I had a visit from Dorey too, late last night."

"Yes?"

"We talked about several things. He welcomed me into the family, and gave me his blessing. He truly is a remarkable man."

They walked on, hand in hand, saying nothing for several minutes. Finally Logan broke the silence.

"Do you still want to go with me to London?"

"Oh, Logan, do you mean it?" exclaimed Allison.

"If you want to. I've already spoken to your mother. She said she would be free to accompany you."

"How wonderful. I can't wait!"

"We'll have a great time. I'll show you all the sights of the big city! Molly will love you both!"

Turning, they walked back toward the garden gate. "Oh, Logan," Allison said, "I've never been happier."

"Neither have I, Ali," he replied, bending to kiss her forehead. "God has given me everything. What more could be left?"

"Only more of the same!"

They left the garden and, laughing like two children, walked toward the great castle where they had found treasure beyond compare—not only each other but also the fullness of God's love.

Lady Margaret, having seen them approach, walked to meet them. She reached out, took each of their hands in one of hers, gazed deeply into Allison's eyes, then turned to Logan and did the same. She needed to speak no words. The love which she felt and the prayer of her heart for their well-being was written all through her face. They saw, received, and understood.

After a moment, she turned with them, and the three, still hand in hand, walked into the house to join the rest of the family.

SHADOWS
OVER
STONEWYCKE

To my father, Denver Phillips,
and his good friend, Warren Dowling,
both of whose wartime experiences
fell upon my eager boyhood ears.

CONTENTS

❊ Introduction

OUT OF CONFLICT and crisis frequently emerge life's most significant periods of inner growth. Indeed, according to the Scriptures, from diversity are fortitude and spiritual stamina born.

Allison and Logan's story in Book 1 of The Stonewycke Legacy was a happy one. Yet their coming together cannot be viewed as an end, but rather as the beginning of an ongoing journey that, if it is to build a permanent relationship of love, will encompass more than simply living "happily ever after."

Certainly a deep joy has its part in this journey, but a truly God-divined path will be richly filled with trials as well. The long-haul character of life's most meaningful relationships and experiences is often overlooked by our short-sighted vision which views only the now. We make decisions lightly, little considering the day-by-day lifetime of dedication necessary to carry them out. Nor do we adequately foresee the unavoidable adversities which will build inner resiliency and strength of character that enables us to persevere in those aspects of life to which we have pledged ourselves.

In no two areas of life do our decisions and surface expectations run aground from lack of awareness of the long-haul than in marriage and spiritual dedication. The commitment required to transform a loving marriage into a lifetime partnership of sustained growth and mutual fulfillment parallels the commitment required to sustain one's Christian life following the one-time decision to follow Christ.

Neither commitment to marriage nor to God comes easy. The decision can be made in a moment. Living out the commitment to that decision, after the gloss fades, over the course of decades—that requires something altogether different than a burst of enthusiasm. That sort of lifetime commitment requires *daily* dedication to endure, to stick with the decision over the long-haul.

It is no surprise, then, that so often in the Bible God uses marriage as the perfect illustration or "type" of what being a Christian is really like. Entering into a marriage covenant, and giving one's life to Christ (as His "bride") are similar in a host of ways.

Little wonder, therefore, that when Logan Macintyre and his new bride Allison MacNeil begin to falter in their new lives as Christians, their marriage relationship also starts to waver. They must both learn that most fundamental of lessons: that commitment requires sacrifice, that love requires the laying down of one's *own* preconceptions, and that only in denying one's *self* and surrendering all to the Lord will true fulfillment come.

Their story, and their struggle, is not a unique one. All husbands and wives—and all Christians—must eventually pass through the same refining process if they are to discover what true commitment is—to one another and to the Lord.

That process of growth is the soil out of which maturity is able to blossom.

1 ⁂ *Man in the Shadows*

THE SHRILL BLAST of an auto horn blared through the hushed foggy night.

A young man making his stealthy way down the empty street started involuntarily, then paused for a moment. He hugged the concrete wall to his right, keeping well within the shadows. As the car passed, he exhaled a sharp breath and continued on, his heart thudding a hard rhythm within his chest. He had told himself a thousand times there was nothing to be afraid of. No one could have any idea what he was up to. It wasn't as if he were sneaking around in enemy-occupied territory. Yet such analysis was unable to quiet the pounding of his heart.

There was no way he could have been followed! He had taken every precaution, every side street, used all the old ruses. But if someone had by chance slipped up at headquarters—enemy territory or not—it might mean his neck. There were, after all, dangers he knew nothing about. He hated to admit it, but he really knew very little about this game.

He glanced at his wristwatch, but could not make out the tiny hands in the surrounding darkness. The blackout, meant to deter the German Luftwaffe, provided excellent cover for sneaking unnoticed through the streets, even though it did make his watch impossible to read. He had to find out the time. He couldn't be late. And he had another several blocks to go before reaching the bridge.

The hour was late; the deserted streets bore clear witness to that. But you couldn't judge the hour by the activity—Londoners turned in early these days. Since war with Germany had become a reality over a year ago, the people toiled to the limits of human endurance to prepare their small island against the encroaching threat of Adolph Hitler. Seventy-hour work weeks left little physical reserve for walking at night—except for those whose work began at these nefarious hours.

This particular night crawler knew all about factory work. He had put in his own share of long, tedious hours. He'd pushed pencils and brooms. He'd sat behind cluttered, wearisome desks as well as cleaned them. So despite his frayed nerves on this night, the change from his past seven years of drudgery was welcome. Now he wondered how he'd tolerated the monotony for that long.

He had tried to stick to a routine. He'd tried to hold a "normal" job. But it had been no use. His fingers and feet and senses had never gotten over their itch. All that time he had thought he was finished with occupations requiring eyes in the back of his head. But now it looked as if such employment had not finished with *him*. How great that sense of exhilaration felt—just like the old days!

True, there was an added dimension to what he was doing these days: fear. A wrongly spoken word, a mistaken contact, even an overly curious neighbor, could land him squarely in a prison camp or in front of a firing squad. This was no game, as it had been before.

Yet the terror only served to heighten the challenge, the thrill. At least now he was *doing* something—something useful, he hoped.

Suddenly the roar of an automobile broke into his thoughts as it rounded a corner and sped his way. He crouched out of sight and waited. The headlamps were dimmed according to blackout regulations, but in the dull flicker of illumination it afforded, the time on his watch was clearly evident. It was three minutes to eleven.

The man jumped out of his temporary shelter the instant the car was past, and immediately quickened his pace. His rendezvous was to take place at eleven sharp. If he missed it, he could not only endanger his contact, but would almost certainly quell his superior's willingness to confer another such assignment on him.

All at once he heard footsteps. A regular beat of leather soles against the hard pavement, seemingly in perfect rhythm with his own, echoed behind him. His heart raced again, even as his feet slowed to a stop. He paused before a closed shop window, pretending to look at the wares behind the glass. It was hardly a believable ploy since he could barely make out whether he was observing shoes, teapots, or women's hose. But at least it would tell him if the time had come to start worrying again.

The footsteps continued, getting louder. A short pudgy man came indistinctly into view, strolled by, tipping a gray derby hat and breaking the intense quiet of the night with a jaunty, "Evenin', mate!"

As the innocuous little man passed into the invisible silence, the edgy night-walker shook his head and reminded himself that he had to keep his cool. That had always been his major asset. He needed it now more than ever.

Even as the man's retreating steps were swallowed up by the night, in the distance the faint sounds of a ship's horn could be heard from upriver, its deep-rumbling tone carried through the sound-dulling fog. The familiar echo reminded him of Big Ben, now strangely silent because of the war, and brought home to him more graphically than ever the fact that he was late. The man hastened on.

In four minutes he stood at the foot of London Bridge. A more fitting place could not have been chosen for such a meeting—especially at this hour! Wreaths of gray fog clung to the towering steel. The night was calm, and the fog swirled about in slow motion, weaving in and out of the pilings below and the steel columns above the bridge, obscuring the topmost spires—an eerie reminder that strange, almost cosmic forces were hurling world events toward an unknown end.

The scene was straight out of a cheap spy novel. But this was no story; there was a war on, and this kind of thing happened from the necessity born of the times. Though he had a penchant for adventure, he would have liked the place better in the sunlight, buzzing with traffic and life. It was crazy to send him alone to such a deserted place. It was too obvious, too great an invitation for foul play.

He peered into the fog, then began walking straight ahead. He had gone perhaps a hundred and fifty feet when he realized the bridge wasn't deserted at all. At first he thought it might be his contact, but as he drew closer he saw that he was approaching a young couple. A soldier and a young lady were standing arm in arm, gazing out upon the Thames.

What brought them out so late? he wondered absently, momentarily allowing his thoughts to drift away from his own concerns. No doubt the fellow had been called up and this was their last night together before he was shipped off to some distant part of the war. The scene was a melancholy one; there were probably tears in the girl's eyes.

Or perhaps the soldier was home on leave and the words being softly spoken were of blissful happiness at the reunion. The war made all of life a drama, and every man and woman occupied a private little corner of the stage on which to play out his or her personal destiny.

This man's destiny at the moment, however, was farther along the bridge. He had no time to philosophize over two young lovers, nor stew about his own unfitness to be a soldier.

Instinctively he glanced once more at his watch, forgetting it would do him little good. It had to be time for his meeting. Past time. He knew he was late. Where was his contact? This was the place—center of the span. Eleven p.m.

The man slowed his pace, walked a little farther. Behind him the romancing couple ambled away, and he was left alone. Finally he stopped altogether. He turned his eyes toward the river, of which he could catch but an occasional glimmer as the black slow-moving current glided silently through the fog and darkness. An occasional dull foghorn in the distance broke the heavy silence.

"Good evening, mein Herr," said a voice suddenly out of the empty night behind him. The accent was decidedly German. Though the tone was quiet and the words evenly spoken, he could not help nearly jumping out of his skin. He had heard no approaching steps, and thought he was completely alone. "The river is grand under the night sky, is it not?" the foreign voice went on.

What would old Skits think to see me so jumpy? he thought to himself, but to the stranger he replied, "It is grand any time of the day," making every effort to infuse his voice with a calm his heart did not feel. He could not betray that he had been startled.

The code phrases of introduction were particularly ridiculous just now, but at least they gave the two men assurance that they had each found the right person.

"I am Gunther," said the contact, a tall, lean, middle-aged man dressed in a heavy wool overcoat and slanted felt hat that shadowed an austere, pock-marked face. Had the young man been able to make out the features under the felt brim more clearly, his fear would only have been the greater. It was not a friendly face. "Who are you?"

"Macintyre—" The instant the word passed his lips, Logan Macintyre realized his foolish blunder.

"—Trinity, that is," he added hastily. They had been given code names—his was *Trinity* and his contact was *Gunther.* How could he have done something so stupid? He must be slipping, losing his touch, forgetting that whatever the cloak of solemnity over this business, it was, deep down, nothing more than a complicated con game. His error had not gone unnoticed.

"I see they send me a novice," said Gunther, shaking his head.

"Don't worry. I know what I'm doing."

"Hopefully that will not matter," replied Gunther.

Logan wrinkled his brow. He didn't like to think that he had come all the way across town, risking who could tell what hazards, only to be told that his part in this assignment was relatively unimportant.

Yet who was he trying to kid? That fact had been clear enough from the beginning. They had said, "We need a stand-in . . . a body. You won't have to know anything, do anything. We just need somebody they don't know."

Logan had desperately wanted to believe it would be more than that. He had probably even imagined all the need for secrecy and stealth in getting here. He glanced at Gunther. It was dark, but he could see it in his eyes nonetheless: it had not even mattered that he had used his real name instead of the code.

"Where are we going?" asked Logan, glad to change the subject.

"We will walk as we talk," replied his companion, ". . . to avoid eavesdroppers."

There wasn't a soul in sight, and Logan could not imagine a possible hiding place a hundred and fifty feet above the icy Thames. But he did not argue the point.

"Now, about your assignment . . ." continued Gunther, who was already a pace ahead.

Logan took a deep breath and turned to follow Gunther as he strode away. No matter what he did tonight, or how trivial his task, he was determined to prove his worth.

2 ❄ *The Hills of Stonewycke*

THE MORNING WAS especially crisp and vivid. Fresh snow had fallen during the night, covering the hills and valleys of Stonewycke and the Strathy Valley with a clean, sparkling layer of white.

Though the sky was blue and the sun shone brightly, the air was frigid as only January in northern Scotland could be. Even the faintest hint of wind would have given the air cruel fingers with which to reach in and lay hold of the very marrow of one's bones. But on this particular morning the wind was quiet, and Allison did not mind the frosty chill as she traipsed along the icy path. She had been out walking at this same early hour every morning for the last week, hoping that the barren frozen landscape of her surroundings would in some miraculous way instill a new peace into her consciousness.

She sighed, then stooped down to scoop up a handful of the snow, and her thoughts were diverted to the more pleasant paths of her childhood. How she and her brothers and sister had always delighted when the first snows had fallen! Little May, the youngest of the four, had been too small to join in to much of the winter mayhem, but occasionally their mother would bundle up the little one and Allison would take her for a wild ride down the hill on the sled.

And the snowball fights!

Her brothers were merciless as they stood behind their stockpiled cache of icy ammunition, pelting whomever chanced by, regardless of age, sex, or religion. Occasionally they grudgingly admitted that even she had a pretty good arm for a girl.

Allison smiled. Those had been happy times. Her mother and father had made Stonewycke a joyful place to grow up. But just as quickly as the involuntary movement tugged at her lips, it began to fade.

They were all grown up now. Sled rides and snowball fights and stories read by Mother and Daddy while the four of them snuggled cozily under a blanket seemed far in the past these days. And if the years themselves had fallen short in the maturing process, the war was rapidly finishing the job. Ian, the eldest, a pilot in the RAF, was stationed in Africa, and Nat was with the 51st Highland Division of Scotland. After distinguishing themselves in France at the time of the Dunkirk evacuation, Nat's division was being reassigned and Nat hoped for a place in a newly formed commando unit. Both were men now, seasoned soldiers, yet Nat was not yet even twenty-one years old.

Time was passing so quickly. Allison was now twenty-five. The war had come suddenly to dominate their lives, changing them all, forcing maturity upon them perhaps before its rightful time, pushing them onto paths they might otherwise never have chosen. Yet Allison wondered if she could truly lay the blame for her own mixed-up life on this war. If she questioned herself honestly, she had to admit that her confusion had begun long before Adolf Hitler had stormed through Poland. She couldn't pinpoint the exact moment. There was not a particular day she remembered when she could say, "Then it was when the joy began to fade . . . when things began to unravel." It had come upon her gradually, and the moments of discontent remained so mixed with alternating seasons of joy that she was still not entirely certain what was happening.

Before her thoughts progressed further, she glanced down at her palm still holding its handful of snow, now unconsciously molded by her gloved fingers into a round ball. With a swift motion she flung it into the air, watching it arch back to earth, falling with a silent puff of white spray into a snowbank. If only she could cast her tensions away so easily!

What had gone wrong? It had all started out so wonderfully!

During those weeks and months following his near-fatal wound, she and Logan had been blissfully in love. Everything had fallen perfectly into place for them—their meeting, their new spiritual priorities, their hopes for the future. The first injection of *realism,* if such it could be called, into the idyllic season of the budding of their young love came when her mother and father counseled them to wait rather than rush immediately into marriage. They were young—especially Allison, only seventeen at the time. And Logan needed time to establish a living, a legitimate one, capable of supporting a family.

They had waited, Logan perhaps more patiently than Allison. The trip to London was made as planned. Allison, Joanna, and Logan had seen much, met some of Logan's old friends, and had a pleasurable time cementing their new relationships one with another. Even Joanna and Allison seemed to have discovered each other in many respects for the first time. After their return to Stonewycke, Logan once again took up his duties as mechanic to the estate and surrounding crofts.

At length the wedding was planned for February 1933, almost a year from the day Logan had entered into their lives. Ironically, in hindsight, it also coincided closely with Hitler's rise to power in Germany. If that had any significance at the time, Allison was certainly unaware of it. The forebodings from the Continent did not become ominous for several years to come.

However, the death that previous December of her great-grandfather suddenly made a February wedding seem unthinkable. Who could possibly plan a wedding with the loss of such a beloved family patriarch so fresh? With old Dorey's passing at ninety, the whole community mourned. Yet in spite of the loss of her beloved, Lady Margaret would have them wait no longer than the summer. And so the much anticipated event finally took place in June of 1933.

It was a day long remembered in the environs of Port Strathy, rivaled only by the wedding of Joanna and Alec in the scope of its hospitality. But unlike Joanna's, which was held in the local church, Allison's took place on the estate itself, in the lovely gardens tended by Lord Duncan, in special tribute to the beloved man.

There could not have been a more perfect day. Allison cherished no more misguided notions about class distinctions, and the whole valley was present, from poorest to wealthiest, from refined to most humble. Patty Doohan was bridesmaid, along with Sarah Bramford and Olivia Fairgate. Allison wore her mother's exquisite wedding dress of sculptured lace and pearls; Logan looked even more debonair than usual in his pinstriped dark blue tuxedo and tails. Several times throughout the day he was heard to say, *If only Skittles could see me now!* But notwithstanding the absence of his old friend, he had managed to bring Molly Ludlowe north by train, as well as his mother from Glasgow. Joanna welcomed them warmly as they had her when she visited them before the wedding. She made them feel completely a part of the family and after the ceremony, both stayed on with her in the castle for a week.

Everyone commented on what a striking couple the two newlyweds made. The wait had done them good, for now Allison was sure that it was not only in appearance that they were so perfectly suited. There were many ways in which they complemented each other. Logan enjoyed Allison's independent spirit, but was not intimidated by it. Allison both admired and needed the strong masculine protection and leadership Logan gave, and at the same time could not help loving his easygoing, lighthearted nature. They had seemed so right for each other. Could it be that the very qualities that had originally drawn them together had now turned against them?

Something her great-grandfather had said to her before his death came back with increasing frequency these days: "I believe God has brought you and Logan together, my dear. I see a bond growing between the two of you that reminds me of your great-grandmother and me when we were your age. Your love will surely count for much in the Kingdom. But—" Here Dorey's ancient brown eyes deepened with intensity; Allison knew he spoke not mere words but feelings born out of his depth of experience. "But the path He has laid out for you may not be free from pain and sorrow."

Allison had been touched by the words at the time, for she loved and highly respected her great-grandfather. But, in the idealism of youth, it was easy to shrug them off as springing more from the pessimism of old age than any reality she needed concern herself with.

Yet as the words came back to her on many occasions these days, she had grown to see them as the result of his wisdom, not any misplaced elderly melancholia. The deep sensitivity that had worked its way into his nature through the years of his solitude had given him vision to perceive what lay down the road for the young couple. Dorey and Logan had also spoken privately together for an hour while Dorey lay in the bed from which he would not arise.

Allison had always wondered if that last conversation between the two men had somehow concerned the same matter. Logan had been solemn and subdued afterward, but never revealed to a soul what had transpired between them.

If Dorey had sensed trouble in the union, the logical question Allison found herself asking was: Why had he done nothing to prevent it? Allison had come to respect him more than she might at one time have cared to admit; they would have listened to his counsel.

Yet even as she debated with herself, she knew what he would have said. *Child,* she could hear his voice saying, *this love is ordained of God. It is to be. It may be a love that will know sorrow, that is true. Of that kind of love I am intimately familiar. But while we are upon this earth, it is our response to the sorrows the Lord sends that carve out the cavity within our natures to hold the joy He pours into them. The greater the sorrows, the greater the possible joys, and the greater our potential service to Him. Love your young man, and marry him, and serve the Lord with him. And when sorrows come, as they surely will, let them deepen your love and enlarge your capacity to receive God's life.*

Yes, that is what Dorey would have said.

And she could not imagine, even now, life without Logan. She had loved him then, and she loved him still.

Yet, could she be sure that love would be enough?

3 ❈ South to London

NOT LONG AFTER the wedding, Logan began to grow restive.

Working as the estate mechanic had been all right for Logan Macintyre, bachelor, ne'er-do-well, and sometimes con man. But as son-in-law to nobility, he began to see the grease on his hands from a different perspective. He cared nothing at all for class distinctions; neither did the family into which he had been grafted in the tradition of Ian Duncan and Alec MacNeil apply any pressure for him to "better himself." Yet pride is a strange phenomenon, often showing neither logic nor sense, and assuming a variety of intricate disguises. Slowly Logan's self-respect began to dwindle. He felt like a leech, taking but never giving, living off the family spoils and offering nothing substantive in return. He had fended for himself all his life, and now he was reduced to taking what the lower side of his nature called "handouts" from his wife's family.

He did not doubt their love and their acceptance of him. Yet he could not keep from feeling less a man for being under the protective covering of Stonewycke. To keep his eroding respect for himself intact, he needed to make something of himself and his marriage on his own.

"But, Logan," Allison tried to tell him, "you work hard, and more than earn your way."

"Do you think we'd ever afford a place like this on fifteen pounds a month?" he rejoined caustically. He hadn't wanted to argue, but he was frustrated—mostly with himself.

"Well, maybe not . . . but, then, none of us could actually afford Stonewycke, if you think about it." Allison had tried to lighten the heavy atmosphere, but Logan was in no mood, especially since he had just arrived at a decision that would not make Allison happy.

"I want to move to London," he said flatly.

Allison stared into his face blankly. The greatest irony about his statement was that only a couple of years before, Allison had longed to escape the boredom—as she considered it then—of Stonewycke. She had dreamed of an exciting life in the city. Edinburgh would have suited her fine. But London! That would have been the fulfillment of all she could have desired!

But now, with new priorities, new commitments—not only to Logan, but also to family, to land, and not least of all to her faith—she had come at last to feel an intrinsic part of everything that Stonewycke represented. How could she even think about leaving at this particular moment? Lady Margaret was ailing, and her mother feared she might not be with them much longer.

A time of tension followed. Logan was unhappy where he was, that was clear. Allison was miserable for him, but she could not bear the thought of leaving. Without anything settled, life managed to go on, but a strained silence came to characterize what had once been a relationship full of laughter and shared joys.

One day about a month later, Logan received a mysterious letter. He opened it privately and not until that evening did he show it to Allison. She bit her lip as she read it, then looked up at him, unable to speak.

"I'm going to take the job," he said with finality, leaving Allison little room for refutation.

The letter was from a friend in London who was opening a restaurant. He had offered Logan a position.

"But you have work *here,*" she replied.

"Work, maybe. But no future."

"How can you say that? Someday you'll—"

"Someday I'll what? Be an even better mechanic! Don't you see, Allison? Sometime I'll have to get out on my own."

"But why, Logan? Why now? We're in the middle of a depression. We're secure here for the present. Why risk that?"

"It's just something I have to do."

"But what do you know about the restaurant business? It doesn't make sense for you to jump at the first thing to come along."

"You said it—we're in a depression. I'm lucky to have such an offer."

"But things couldn't possibly be as good for us in London as they are here."

"There's just no way I can make you understand," he said, throwing down the letter and stalking away.

Allison might have continued to rebel at the idea, but the following day her mother and great-grandmother took her aside for a long, soul-searching conversation. When she left them she knew what she must do.

"Stonewycke will still be here once he knows what he wants to do with his life," they reminded her. "Stonewycke will always be here. And we will be here for you, too."

Perhaps she had known all along what her answer to Logan must be, but the two older women had guided her in the right direction, helping her to see where her true love must lie.

Leaving Strathy had not been easy—for either Allison or Logan. Tears had flowed that day without restraint. For despite Logan's determination to stand on his own two feet, he had developed—perhaps more than he realized on the conscious level—a deep love for old Stonewycke. Not only was it the place where his dear ancestor Digory had lived, but it was also filled with recent memories. Here Logan had met his God. Here, on these lovely heather hills, his and Allison's life together had begun. And here they had pledged their lives to each other.

Logan did not carelessly walk away from all this, but he was doing what he felt he had to do. What made it the hardest on him was his certainty that he did not have the family's approval in his decision. Logan still had much to learn about the family into which he had come. Had he been able to summon the courage to reveal his hidden fears and motives openly to Alec and Joanna and Lady Margaret, he would have quickly discovered their understanding and compassion to be far-reaching and filled with tenderness. They would no doubt have supported him, perhaps even applauded his high principles, though they might well, at the same time, have cautioned him to be heedful of pride. Above all, they would have held him up in prayer while wrapping him in the understanding arms of love.

But Logan had lived too long encased in a protective shield designed to mask his innermost feelings. It went against his very nature to open his soul and reveal all. And the door seemed to shut all the more tightly when his feelings of inferiority began to harass him. God was at work, slowly peeling back one layer of his inner being at a time. But Logan was not yet ready to yield himself entirely up to the process and say, "Thy *complete* will be done with me."

Once Allison had resigned herself to the change, she and Logan settled down to their new lives and found renewed happiness in each other. They located a flat in Shoreditch, not far from Molly Ludlowe. It was no Stonewycke, and was noticeably threadbare for a girl who had grown up, if not with wealth, at least in a comfortable home, free from want. Allison made a commendable attempt to turn the tiny place into a home. She painted the dingy rooms, hung curtains, and arranged a few prints she had brought from Scotland. Here and there were scattered reminders of Strathy.

Almost to Allison's surprise, after some time had passed she began to find the city life appealing. She had always sensed that the agrarian nature had not run quite so deeply in her blood as in her mother and her ancestors. And when that truth bore in upon her even more forcibly after a couple of years in the city, she was not certain whether to be happy or sad. She hoped she was not an anomaly in the strong line of Stonewycke matriarchs that had maintained their vigilant watch over the northern valley for more than a century. Certainly the same Ramsey and Duncan blood coursed through her veins. Yet she found herself thrilled to dress up to attend a play or a concert—not a frequent occurrence, since Logan would accept very little financial help from her family—almost as happy as she knew Lady Margaret had been to walk the Scottish hills.

Even in the midst of the worldwide depression, the young couple managed to live adequately. Logan's personality insured his success in his friend's enterprise. Despite their gradual drifting apart, Allison found plenty to occupy her time. Many of her former acquaintances, having finished school or married, had come south to the social and financial hub of the world, and she began to mix with them as before.

But Allison's friends did not appeal to Logan, and he shied away, keeping more and more to himself. Not that he minded their blue blood, or so he told himself. Such things had never bothered him before. But he wanted to make something of himself. He wanted more in life than had previously been his, and he didn't want to slide into it like the Bramfords and the Fairgates and the Robertsons. He could hardly help resenting their genteel ways. His motives were not ones of greed; he simply wanted to better his lot, to stand on his own two feet. And at the same time, by virtue of his marriage, he felt compelled to provide Allison with a standard of life he thought she deserved. Mixing with her friends only seemed to emphasize his deficiencies. He would become something first; then he would be able to walk in such circles with head high.

In the meantime, just a few months after their move to the city, Lady Margaret went to join her beloved Dorey. Her death was painless and peaceful; with the confidence of one going home at last, she joyfully relinquished this life and embraced the real life of eternity. And although the family mourned, they found joy amidst their tears in the certainty that they would all, at last, be reunited.

Allison grieved for her great-grandmother's passing, then threw herself with renewed vigor into her schedule of social activities. Keeping busy seemed to alleviate the pain of her loss, but gradually her life and Logan's began to follow divergent paths. Too proud to admit his own insecurities, Logan put up a front toward the outside world, and without realizing it at first, toward Allison as well. Wrapped up in her own activities, she was unable to see the forces gnawing away at him until their communication had already broken down. When at length Allison began to sense that perhaps her husband was not as content as he seemed, she was unable to get him to open up in order to find what was bothering him.

The situation was aggravated by Logan's unstable employment status. The restaurant position, after a hopeful beginning, soon fell short of Logan's expectations for advancement. He had conceived of himself as a public relations man and head maitre d'. But when the restaurant did not grow as anticipated, he found himself nothing more than a low-paid waiter, with little hope that more would be offered. His personality and connections had little trouble landing him jobs, even in the midst of hard times, but they led nowhere. Money was scarce and talented people were out of work everywhere. He took a position in a brokerage firm, but sitting behind a desk all day hardly suited his adventurous disposition. Besides, the investment trade was in terrible straits. Then came a string of dead-end jobs—shoe salesman, cab driver, hotel desk clerk, night watchman/janitor—each one appearing better than the last, but none in the end measuring up to Logan's high hopes.

Though the first five years of their marriage followed this pattern, they were not years without occasional moments of happiness. The foundation of love begun in their first days together helped transcend the tensions of their present lives. But time ate away at their faltering relationship, and the closeness they had once shared was not sufficient in itself to bolster a sagging foundation. Involved in personal frustrations, both Allison and Logan were too preoccupied to see that the focus of their lives had dramatically shifted. No longer were they putting the other first in their considerations, and no longer were they jointly looking for guidance from the God to whom they had committed their lives. Thus they were unable to see that He alone could deliver their marriage from the pitfalls toward which it was certainly bound.

Letters back to Stonewycke veiled the problems. But during the two or three visits Joanna and Alec made during the time, the hidden frustrations could not help surfacing. Allison's parents tried to intercede, but both Logan and Allison had so slipped back into their former tendencies that they were unable to listen humbly enough and let go of pride and selfishness enough to see the true nature of their need.

4 ❈ The Coming of War

CURIOUSLY, IN SPITE of the difficulties she and Logan had had, Allison found herself longing for a child. A baby, she hoped, would pull the two of them together, give them a common focus in life and perhaps renew their love. But for over four years this gift was denied them.

Then in 1938, coinciding frighteningly with what Churchill called Hitler's rape of Austria and later invasion of Czechoslovakia, Allison found that her prayers were answered. She could have wished for happier times to bring her new daughter, Joanna, into the world. But despite the tensions throughout Europe from Germany's aggressive movements, Allison could not have been happier to welcome her mother into their simple London flat. Joanna would be staying to share the Christmas season with Allison and Logan and her new granddaughter.

The child for a time drew her parents together again, but the change was temporary at best. Only a year later, in the fall of 1939, war finally came to France and Britain. By now the mask of their love had worn so thin that they had to admit all was not well. For Logan, the war only deepened his feelings of having failed—himself, his wife, and now his growing family. The moment hostilities were declared, he tried to enlist. His prison record, however, came back to haunt him. Though by most standards his offenses were minor ones, the mere hint of his having been involved in counterfeiting, coupled with his unexplained four months in Germany in 1929, placed Logan in what British Recruitment considered a "high risk" category. Logan could not divulge the details of the con he had been working on in Germany for fear of repercussions to friends; so, while his peers marched proudly off to fight the Germans, he had to bear the shame of remaining behind. No matter what he turned his hand to, it seemed he failed. He began to look back with longing to his pre-marriage days with Skittles and Billy. True, what he was doing then was not a virtuous pursuit. But he had been good at it—and enjoyed it.

At least the financial worries of the depression years were now past since jobs were plenteous in wartime Britain. The war immediately spawned whole new industries, and now Logan took a low-level position in a munitions factory, hoping in time to move up. If he couldn't join the war effort as a soldier, then he might as well do what he could behind the lines, and profit from it as well. However, the hoped-for advancement never came, and after nearly a year the assembly-line job had become pure drudgery. Allison had begun to think that perhaps he had settled down, though deep inside she knew him too well to believe he could be happy at such employment for long.

In the spring of 1940, he came home early one day, casually planted a kiss on Allison's cheek, and began to play with little Joanna, now a toddler, as if there were nothing unusual in his appearance in midafternoon.

"Logan," the inquisitive Allison asked, "you're never home before six or six-thirty." She tried to sound casual, but feared her voice betrayed her concern. "Is . . . anything wrong?"

"I've got a new job."

"They've moved you to a new department?"

Logan understood the thrust of her questioning well enough. They had been through the process enough times for him to sense her dissatisfaction with his unstable job situation without her having to say a word. But not inclined to argue just now, he too attempted to strike a casual attitude, as if they had never spoken of such things before.

"No," he answered, "that factory job wasn't for me. I have a friend who's found me something . . . more interesting. It's perfect. No more job changes for a long time."

"Logan—" Allison began, her voice thinning in frustration. Then she stopped herself. "What is it?" she asked.

"It's in an office . . ." He hesitated a moment; Allison sensed immediately that he was holding something back.

"You've never liked office work."

"This is different. I'll be working for the government." There was a slight defensiveness in his tone.

"The government? But I thought—"

"What's the matter, don't you believe me?" he snapped. "Why the third degree? I'll be doing something to help the country!"

"Of course I believe you. It's just—"

"Don't worry. I'm making more money than at the factory."

"How could you say such a thing? You know your happiness means more than money to me."

"Your trips to Harrods would not seem to indicate that. Even with rationing, you've managed to run up a sizable bill."

"Logan—!" she protested, then turned away, biting her lip.

Logan immediately regretted his harsh, defensive words. Haltingly he reached out to lay his hand on her shoulder, but she tensed beneath his touch.

"I'm sorry," he said.

"I'm only interested in you, Logan," she replied in a trembling voice. "I just want so badly for you to be happy, and for us—to be . . ."

"My dear Ali," he replied gently, gathering her into his arms, "that's all I want, too—for you—for us both."

Thus the brief argument over Logan's job ended, heated words giving way to the love for one another still struggling to surface. Yet notwithstanding, no lasting understanding between them was to be found. Allison's specific questions with regard to Logan's new position were forgotten in the immediacy of one brief moment of blissful togetherness. But he never did open to her further. And desiring no renewal of the tension, Allison swallowed her hurt and did not ask again, though with the passage of every new day she longed more than ever to know, to share his life. As still more time passed, a deep-set fear began to gnaw away at the edges of Allison's consciousness—the dread that perhaps he had returned to his old ways. He occasionally spoke of his new "job," but always in the most vague and general terms. And what governmental position, she thought, would require such odd and irregular hours, and seemingly so much secrecy? Yet she steadfastly refused to believe he had reverted back to his life on the streets, and made a concerted effort to push such possibilities from her mind.

In the summer of 1940, England began to gear up for the expected German invasion of the tiny island, essentially all that stood in Hitler's way of a total conquest of Europe. With many in like circumstances, Allison made plans to leave London with their daughter, intending to return to the safety of Stonewycke until the danger of enemy attack had passed. In vain she tried to convince Logan to join her. But he insisted that his job responsibilities were too important to leave now. Again she questioned him without success as to the nature of what he did. His sudden loyalty, she said, hardly seemed characteristic of the man who had had no fewer than a dozen jobs in five years and had had little qualms about leaving any of them. Still he would reveal nothing, leaving Allison to make the journey north alone, and fearing the worst.

"Well, I should at least have your office number in case I need to reach you," she said at length with resignation in her voice. Such was not, however, her only reason for making that request.

"I'll be sure to call you two or three times a week," he answered evasively.

"But what if there's an emergency? How will I get hold of you?"

"Nothing's likely to happen," he replied, then paused. "Well . . . here's a number, then. But only for an emergency, nothing else." He quickly jotted a phone number down on a slip of paper and handed it to her.

"Maybe I shouldn't go, Logan," Allison sighed as she took the paper. "I don't want to leave you here alone. All this talk of invasion is probably just an overreaction. Last year everyone left the cities so worried, and nothing ever came of it."

"It's different now that France has fallen," said Logan. "The Nazis are only forty miles away, and they have no reason to hold back. Everyone knows Hitler's only waiting for the right time to attack."

Allison sighed again. "I suppose you're right. And you'd no doubt be happier if I went away," she said, voicing the fear that was more real to her than any Nazi invasion.

Logan turned away, shaking his head in frustration. "It has nothing to do with that!" he said angrily. Yet even as he spoke the words, he could not honestly say there was no truth in the accusation. Instead, he lamely added, "This is wartime, Allison. We both have things we have to do. Everyone is making sacrifices. Your father and brothers are in the army. You and your mother volunteer your time. Why can't you let me have the chance to do my part, too?"

"I didn't know your job had anything to do with the war," said Allison, trying to be sympathetic.

"I didn't say it did—exactly. But at least here in London I might have the opportunity to do something."

"You *were* doing something at the munitions factory—"

"Are you going to start on that again?"

Allison sighed. "I guess it is best I go. We can't seem to talk about much of anything these days."

"We might be able to if you could only trust me a little."

Allison said nothing.

"Besides, the fact is, it's just not safe in London right now."

At that moment a waking cry came from the next room. Allison turned to go, and thus the conversation was kept from escalating further.

Allison tarried in London another week, hoping somehow to convince Logan to leave with her. But in this effort she met with no success, and as the days passed she knew it would be foolhardy to expose their daughter any longer to the terrible German air raids. They had begun in early July and mounted in severity as the summer progressed.

So in the end Allison returned north to Stonewycke. She arrived at her beloved home and fell into her mother's arms hurt, confused, and even a bit lonely. But she dried the tears of her first day, by the second was able to breathe deeply again of the fragrant sea air, and on the third took baby Jo out for a walk. Inside, however, she remained silently afraid, wondering what her husband was doing during her absence, and what she would find upon her return.

5 ❊ *Mother and Daughter*

JOANNA SAW HER daughter in the distance as she crested the top of the snow-covered hill. Even from here Joanna could see the pensive, troubled expression—not at all like her usual confident self. Times had changed. Her daughter was a woman now, with all the cares of adulthood pressing upon her.

It had been almost six months since her daughter and granddaughter had come to Stonewycke to escape the bombing in London. The year 1940 had been difficult, not only for their family, but for all of Britain. London had nearly been lost under the assault of the German air attack, and the threat of invasion remained ever present.

It had been an especially hard time for Allison. Not only had the distance separated her from her husband, but their parting had not been on the best of terms. Of course it was wartime, and many women were having to deal with such anxieties. There were thousands who had lost their husbands. Unfortunately, such knowledge made it no easier for Allison. At least when I had kissed Alec farewell, thought Joanna, the embrace was tender, and each of us was sure of our abiding love. If only Allison possessed such a memory to carry her through!

Logan had spent two weeks at Strathy during Christmastime. But Joanna sensed the awkwardness he felt, acutely feeling the absence of the other men, away at war while he comfortably celebrated a holiday with the women. Had that been his only discomfort, of course, the atmosphere might have been better. But the sensitive mother could tell there was still tension between Allison and Logan and if anything, it had worsened.

If only they could shed their insecurities and self-centered motives, thought Joanna. Yet how much better would she have done at their age? Their faith may have cooled, but Joanna was certain it was not completely cold. They only needed something to remind them of life's real priorities, and then to nudge them back along the right path. Hopefully something would come out of this difficult time to accomplish that. Joanna regretted that she could not be that instrument. But as respectful as the young people were, they did not always heed her words of wisdom.

Dear Lord, Joanna silently prayed, *I know they both have hearts for you. Do what you must to mature them out of themselves. Refocus their eyes, Lord, onto the needs of each other, and onto you.*

How often Joanna wished she possessed the compelling wisdom of her grandmother! But Lady Margaret was gone, and even after many years, sometimes when stumbling upon a familiar object or a dearly loved place, Joanna would often find herself in tears. There was nothing about the estate that had not in some way been touched by dear Maggie. Joanna doubted she would ever cease to feel her loss.

Then Joanna smiled softly to herself. *Grandma left her wisdom, too,* she thought. *As her presence and the memory of her smile linger in places and things so does her spirit linger through all the grounds of Stonewycke. Perhaps her wisdom, too, passed down from God through her, lingers in those of us whom she loved.*

"Oh, Lord," whispered Joanna, "I know she left me with a spiritual heritage that is not dependent on my own strength or insight. Through her I learned that my strength is in you. When I call on you, you are there. Continue her legacy, Lord. If it be your will, transfer the cloak of her wisdom to me, as she prayed on the very day of her death. And, like your servant Elisha, let me be faithful to serve you with it. Give me your wisdom, Lord God. And make me your faithful and obedient daughter."

Even as she voiced the prayer, as she had done on numerous occasions previously, Joanna's thoughts went back to that day eight years earlier. No doubt sensing that her time was short and desiring her final moments to be spent with her dear granddaughter, Lady Margaret had called Joanna to her bedside. She smiled, for there was no fear in her, and took Joanna's hand in hers.

"I remember," the peaceful old woman had said in a faint voice, "another time I thought I was dying. Even in my delirium back then I knew I could not die without passing on to you the heritage of Stonewycke, though I was nearly too late. But God spared me, and it was as though He had given me a second life. How many times since then have I given Him thanks for allowing me to live these later years of my life with you, and with my Ian!"

"He must have known that I still had much to learn from you," said Joanna lovingly.

"You have learned well, my dear child. You have been an inspiration to me as well. I can go in peace to my rest."

"Oh, Grandma!" Joanna closed her eyes as they filled with tears.

"You will no doubt cry much in the next days, Joanna. How I wish I could be there to comfort you! But you will have our Lord to rely on. Remember His words, 'I must go away, that the Comforter can come.' Let Him comfort you, my dear, for it is now my time to go away. You will not begrudge me going to my Ian?"

"No, Grandma," said Joanna, with a smile through her tears. "Tell dear Dorey I love him more than ever."

"I will, child. I think he knows'"

"I will miss the two of you," said Joanna, weeping afresh.

"I have asked myself what final words I would leave you with. But I think I have given you all I have to give. If not, I suppose it is too late now."

She chuckled softly. "Twenty-two years ago I gave you the heritage of my family, though you hardly knew what it meant at the time. You had to come to Scotland to discover it for yourself."

Margaret paused. The lengthy speech was clearly taking its toll, but she struggled to continue. "But now, Joanna," she went on, "I leave you with the most important gift of all—the very sustenance and lifeblood of Stonewycke—the one inheritance that can never leave you: the love and hope of our Lord. I pray our heavenly Father will pass on to you a hundredfold whatever I might have. I think what you will face in this modern twentieth-century world will far surpass anything we of previous generations could imagine. But I know His strength will be equal to it, and He will remain faithful to you."

By now Margaret's eyes were flashing with the fire of her younger years, and tears streamed down Joanna's face. The fire, however, was not of youth but rather the final swelling glow of a dying ember, as the light from this life faded into the light of the life to come. When Joanna looked up through her glistening eyes a moment later, the dear lady's eyes were closed and she slept peacefully. Joanna bent down and kissed the wrinkled cheek, then rose to leave the room.

When she returned in two hours to bring her tea, Maggie had breathed her last breath and her peacefulness was not of this world.

Joanna fell upon her knees and quietly wept. For so many generations the continuation of the Stonewycke bloodline had lain with the woman. Alec was a strong, godly, man, worthy to head a great house. Yet in that moment Joanna knew that, as the next woman in the Ramsey/Duncan lineage, a heavy responsibility now rested on her shoulders. Thus at forty-three, she became matriarch of the proud and ancient family. From that moment she was always conscious of the memory of both Atlanta and Margaret, seeking not only to follow the guidance of their God and hers, but aware of their spirit, their love for Stonewycke, and their legacy living on through her.

Now, at fifty-one, the gray had taken over more of her hair. She was a grandmother herself. Her husband and two of her sons were out of the country fighting in a fearful war. And her eldest daughter's marriage, begun with such high hopes, was charting a dangerous course through rocky water, and she seemed powerless to help.

She looked up, saw Allison drawing near, raised her hand in a wave, and smiled warmly.

"Good morning, dear," said Joanna. "Do you mind some company?"

"Of course not. I was just out . . . you know, thinking."

"It is a beautiful day for that," replied Joanna.

"But the more I think, and even try to pray, the more confusing it all becomes," said Allison in frustration.

Joanna reached around her daughter's shoulder and gave her a hug as they continued to walk slowly.

Allison sighed deeply, glancing away into the distance. In her heart she knew her words to be, though true, only a shadow of the whole truth. She realized that she had offered no more than perfunctory prayers, having somehow convinced herself that God expected her to work everything out for herself. She had drifted from her Father, she knew that. How to recapture the intimacy she had once known was another matter. That was a path she had never walked. And admitting to her mother the void that had crept into her heart would have been more difficult still.

But Joanna was not Maggie's granddaughter for nothing.

"He will speak," she said at length, "but you must be open to hear Him. God's guidance always involves both His speaking and our listening."

Allison did not reply for a moment. "Mother," she said abruptly, as if she had not heard Joanna's words, "what do you think will happen if Logan and I can't . . . well, work things out?"

"There is always a solution, Allison."

"I . . . I'm just not sure that's true—marriages do break up, you know."

Joanna winced inwardly. She tried hard to mask the stab of pain at the thought.

"I really hoped the months apart would improve things. But Christmas showed me nothing has changed. I really don't think he loves me anymore."

"Oh, Allison, dear! That can't be true!"

"He barely talks to me," said Allison, her eyes filling with tears.

"He's been through many changes in the last few years," said Joanna. "A whole new lifestyle, both spiritually and socially. Perhaps we've expected too much of him too quickly."

"Are you defending him, Mother?" Allison shot back, a hint of anger surfacing through her tears of hurt.

"I'm only saying there are always two sides to every problem. It always helps to try to look at things from the other person's perspective. I know he's been under a great deal of pressure, both from the war and trying to find a job he's happy with. But I'm sure his motives still spring from his love for you."

"I tried to believe that for a while. But you don't know what it's been like, Mother. And his job! That's part of his problem!"

"You mean his not finding anything lucrative? Times have been—"

"I don't care how much money we have. I just want him—like it used to be. But I'm afraid he's gone back to his old life."

"You don't really think so!"

"Why else has he been so mysterious about it?"

"Have you asked him?"

"Every time I so much as hint at trying to find out what he does, he explodes with his usual evasiveness. I just can't trust anything he says."

"I know it may be especially difficult just now," said Joanna slowly. "But once you begin to doubt someone you love, a close relationship can fall apart quickly. Perhaps if you *could* trust him and—"

"How can I? He lied to me, Mother!" Allison burst out. "When I left London, months ago, he gave me a phone number. He said never to use it except for an emergency. So I never did. It was supposed to be his office number."

"And?"

"All during the time he was here at Christmas I tried to drag out of him some of the details about his job, but he was more evasive than ever. So last week I called the number. I just had to know! Mother, the number he gave me was for Billy Cochran's shop!"

"Is that so terrible?" asked Joanna.

"Don't you see? He lied! He told me he was working for the government, but he's just back into the old life—I know it."

"There may be some other explanation. Maybe he wasn't allowed to give out the office number and knew Billy would be able to reach him."

"Oh, Mother, if only that were true! But there's more! After the call to Billy's, I decided to try the apartment. Ever since he told me he had a position with the government, I couldn't help wondering. There was something in his tone that didn't ring true. I found myself—well, I didn't know what to think. I didn't want to think the worst. But when I called, someone I didn't know answered—in our apartment! Someone with a distinct German accent!"

"Allison, what are you saying?"

"I don't know, Mother. But if he is working for the government, I can't help wondering just what government. He's been acting more and more strange . . . distant—upset about not being able to get into the army. He's said some things—"

Allison paused and took a deep breath, then exhaled slowly and thoughtfully. "Well," she said at length, "I suppose what he's doing doesn't matter all that much anyway. Our problems began long before now."

Joanna kept further thoughts to herself. For all she knew, her daughter's assessment could be right. Yet from the very beginning she had seen a core of rectitude in Logan. Lady Margaret had seen it too, even when he had first come to Stonewycke with fraudulent intentions. She had sensed something amiss in his motives back then, but she had not failed to sense the heart of honor that beat within him—the heritage of Digory's blood, her grandmother had always maintained.

Whatever secret Logan now possessed, Joanna knew he would never use it to intentionally hurt his family or those he loved, especially Allison.

Yet it was possible, she had to admit to herself, that his perception of honor could have become confused and distorted amid the pressures and struggles of his present situation. Some men even convince themselves their wives will be better off without them, and use such wrong rationalizations for their own self-centered ends. She prayed such would not happen with Logan.

Could he possibly return to his old life? His turnabout had been so complete. He even made financial restitution wherever possible, and was still faithfully repaying a loan he had obtained from her and Alec in order to clear off one sizable old debt. His initial faith may have cooled, but had it gone so far? Was he trying to right his past wrongs by allowing himself to become involved in new present ones?

No! She would not believe it! She had talked to Allison about trust, and now here she herself was starting to doubt her son-in-law. She would not believe it! He was a good man, an honorable man, a faithful man to his wife and young daughter! She *would* believe that! She had to!

Allison's last words had been spoken with such finality that Joanna could not find an easy response.

Perhaps the time for words was past. She gave her daughter another hug, then released her. The women parted in silence. Allison continued along the crusty path toward their home. Joanna watched her go for a moment, then turned in the opposite direction.

Ten minutes later she stood before a simple marker, her warm breath sending white clouds into the frosty morning air. The words on the stone were simple—Maggie had wanted it that way, to match her husband's. No frills, no quotations, not even *Lady*. The stone read: Margaret Ramsey Duncan 1846–1933.

How could future generations, from that humble inscription, know all that she had meant— first as Maggie, later as Lady Margaret—to this valley? *I must be faithful to my journal,* Joanna thought to herself. *Maggie and what she had stood for must not be forgotten.*

Joanna glanced at the small family plot. To the right of Maggie and Ian lay James and Atlanta Duncan. Toward the rear of the fenced, well-kept grounds, with a larger stone than the rest, lay the grave of Anson Ramsey, flanked by his wife and two sons. But this was not the time to dwell on the past; the present contained cares enough. *Oh, Grandmother!* thought Joanna, glancing down at Maggie's grave again, *what would you do for Allison and Logan if you were alive?*

Joanna sighed. She knew the answer. Maggie would tell her to trust God, just as she herself gave that same advice to Allison. Who else but God was capable to heal and restore her daughter's marriage, and most important of all, to revive both Allison's and Logan's waning faith? He had worked mightily in Maggie's life. He had reunited her and Ian. He had saved Ian from the turmoil of his middle years. He had brought her to Scotland against all odds. How could she doubt that the same God who had been so repeatedly faithful in the past would not work in this new generation as He had in those of the past?

Silently Joanna prayed the prayer that could only be born out of one's deep relationship with the Lord through the years:

Oh, God, do whatever you must to bring them back to each other . . . and back to you. Take them where you must, take them through what you must, bring to them whatever joys and sufferings you must, so that in the end, Lord, their eyes are fully opened to your love for them.

And even as Joanna turned and slowly followed Allison back to the ancient family castle known for centuries simply as Stonewycke, she had done what Maggie herself would have done. Even in what she considered her own weakness, she had performed the one vital act, the most important single thing she could have done for her daughter and son-in-law: she had given them in prayer into the hands of God.

The granite walls of Stonewycke gave her comfort when she entered them a few moments later; she sensed once again that the Spirit of the living God dwelt here still. He who had profoundly touched and changed so many lives in the past would not fail to touch the lives of future generations through the prayers of those who had come before, through her own prayers, and through prayers yet to be prayed. God's ways were beyond finding out. But of one thing she could be certain: the prayers of His people would never go unheeded.

6 ❈ Recruitment

THE TELEPHONE'S INSISTENT ringing echoed through the cold London flat.

Logan paused at the open front door, hesitating. He was running late and couldn't afford a delay. He started to close the door, then thought, What if it's headquarters? Could there have been a change in plans?

Still the phone rang, and again.

"Blast!" he said with a frustrated sigh, slamming the door behind him and reentering the apartment.

He reached the phone and picked up the receiver on the sixth ring. His heart sank when he heard the voice on the other end.

"Logan, dear? Hello! It's me—Allison!"

"Ali," replied Logan, doing his best to instill enthusiasm into his tone. But this was the worst possible time for a call. He was too keyed up about his meeting with Gunther coming up to give her the kind of attention she would expect.

"Are you okay, Logan?"

"Sure, of course . . . fine."

"You sound . . . funny, just now."

"It's just a surprise, that's all. I didn't expect to hear from you."

"I miss you so much, Logan."

"I miss you too . . . of course," Logan replied. The words were true, in spite of their troubles.

"Do you?"

"You know I do! How could you—?" He stopped himself. He couldn't get into an argument about it now.

"Logan, why don't you come to Scotland?"

"I can't just leave. You know that. Especially now. There are important things going on." His words made him remember his pressing appointment. He glanced at his watch.

"What could be more important than your own family? Your daughter is growing so fast, and you have hardly seen her in—"

"Don't start on me, Ali—" interrupted Logan. How could he make her understand what he hardly understood himself? He loved her. He loved them both. Yet at the same time maybe it was easier to be away, not reminded every time they tried to talk of the tensions which so easily sprang up between them. As he hesitated, searching for the right words, the clock on the mantel chimed the quarter hour.

"Allison, let's not talk about it right now," he continued lamely.

"When is there ever going to come a time when you will talk about it?" she retorted. The bitterness in her voice was not even disguised.

The line was silent a moment. He attempted to pacify her.

"Sometime when we're together," he said, his tone hinting at past tenderness. "Talking by phone when we're four hundred miles apart is hardly the best way."

"But there'll never come a good time. Even when we're together you won't talk. You were here just three weeks ago. But you might as well have been a thousand miles away!"

The accusation sent Logan back behind his wall of self-preservation. "I have to go," he said flatly. "I've got an appointment. We'll talk about it sometime later."

"By then it may be too late!" she said stiffly, and before he could utter another word, a loud click was heard on the other end of the line.

The knot in Logan's stomach grew tighter as he approached Euston station and his rendezvous with Gunther.

He should have let the phone ring; now was no time to be beset with personal problems! He had to concentrate on the business at hand! But try as he might, he could not erase from his mind the mental picture of Allison slamming down the phone, and probably bursting into tears of mingled anguish and anger.

Why did she have to call right then? She certainly managed to make things difficult for him! At last he had found a job he was suited for, and one he liked. If he had to keep it secret from his wife, thousands of other men did no less, and their wives didn't fly into an uproar over it. Why couldn't she be proud of him for once, instead of always badgering him to "talk things over"? There was nothing to talk over if she wouldn't trust him!

Who was he trying to kid? Skits would have seen right through his facade in a second. For the first time he found himself glad his old mentor wasn't there. He would have had no kind words for Logan, trying to pass off tight security as an excuse to avoid communication with his wife. He wouldn't have believed it any more than Allison did.

But why couldn't she just trust him! His past life made his need for her confidence more imperative than for other men. He had to sense that she believed in him, that she wanted him to succeed.

But sometimes he had the feeling she was just waiting for him to slip up, to backslide, to drift into his old "techniques" for raising cash—especially between jobs when money was tight. Not that he wasn't tempted. How many times had he strolled past an old hangout, only to feel his heart race at the thought of how easy it would be to strike up a card game and bring home a nice thick bankroll to tide them over?

If the years of frustration had dulled his relationship with God, they had not negated the moral commitments that had sprung from that commitment. Moreover, his morality seemed about the only thing he had left to offer Allison.

If he was going to work so hard to keep straight, he thought, the least she can do is keep her suspicions in check every time some tiny questionable uncertainty arises in her mind.

Well, he stubbornly said to himself, *I'm not going to quit the only job, I seem cut out for just to please her.*

He'd been waiting too long for this chance. It had taken two months since that first meeting with Gunther on London Bridge in November. There'd been two failed attempts. He had almost begun to fear that the whole thing would fizzle out. And if this assignment went, so would his new job. This deal with Gunther was his one chance to make good, to convince them to keep him on. He hoped he wasn't placing too much hope in one assignment. But he couldn't help thinking that some of the higherups were watching him, and that if he showed well and displayed some pluck, well—it would lead to bigger things.

It had been pure luck he'd landed in the midst of all this in the first place. After being rejected twice by the army, he had resigned himself to sitting out the war in some wretched factory with women and men too old to make a difference anywhere else.

Then came the phone call from Arnie Kramer.

He had known Arnie in the old days, and, though a public-school boy he was a decent enough fellow and a fair hand around a card table. Now Kramer was no longer Arnie, but *Arnold,* and a major at that. He worked for the Intelligence Corps. The years had been good to him, he said. He'd settled down, moved up quickly, and now was having more fun *in* the system than he'd ever dreamed of when trying to fleece it with all his penny-ante games. The stakes were higher, and the game sometimes got dangerous. But the thrill was there, and sometimes there could be money in it. He was doing a bit of recruiting, he said, and could they possibly meet? Logan agreed.

"But the army won't have me," said Logan after he had listened to the opening gambit of his friend's proposal, certain that he must have been misinformed about his availability for active service.

"The *regular* army—bah!" said Kramer with the usual disdain of one corps for another. "If *they* rejected you, that's as good a recommendation as you could get!"

"What exactly is it you want me to do?" asked Logan, his interest piqued.

Kramer leaned his hefty frame forward, and lowered his voice to a conspiratorial whisper, a sparkle of merriment in his small dark eyes. It was just like the old days, only now Logan was the prey. And now Logan had no idea he was being reeled in by one who had grown just as shrewd in the ancient game as he. "Just a bit of cloak and dagger, Logan, m' lad!"

"Spying?"

Arnie nodded.

"You've got to be kidding! What do I know about that?"

Kramer threw his head back and laughed heartily. "Why, man, you've been doing it all your life!"

"Cons, maybe. But hardly spying!"

"Same thing. Only now you won't have to worry about ending up in an English prison for it."

Logan touched his moustache thoughtfully. "I don't know . . ." he said hesitantly, though his heart was racing with excitement. "I've got a family now, Arnie."

"Believe me," answered Kramer in his buoyant style, "you'll be in far less danger than all the blokes out on the battlefield. And you'll work in London—no separation from your family. Of course, you won't be able to tell your wife what it's about. But you'll be doing your country a great service, and she'll forgive you in the end."

"What'll I tell her?"

"We'll arrange a cover story, naturally. No problem. We do it all the time. Security and all that, you know."

"I hate to lie to her."

Kramer laughed again. "That hardly sounds like the Logan Macintyre I used to know. Reformed, eh?"

"I suppose I have changed a bit . . ." Logan replied, stumbling over the words. He wished he had the guts to say more. But in a moment the opportunity was past. After all, this was hardly the time or place to start talking about God.

"Very commendable," said Kramer. "I've changed too, Logan, my man. But look at it this way—the secrecy is for your family's protection as well as for yours and ours." Kramer tried to keep his tone lighthearted, but from under his thick brown eyebrows he was eyeing his quarry. The only reason they wanted Logan was because he was sure never to be recognized by any of the opposing agents. They didn't need *him* in the strict sense of the word. Anyone would do. But Arnie had always liked Logan, had seen him cool under fire, even if only during card game hustles, and had made up his mind that Logan was his man. Therefore, he eyed him carefully, not wanting to bring him in too quickly. Logan had to *want* it—the essence of a good con. So Arnie waited. "Don't turn me down, Logan. You'll be perfect for this work."

Logan didn't turn Major Arnold Kramer down. He wasn't about to miss out on a chance like this! He knew he'd be perfect for the work. He hardly needed Arnie to tell him that! At least, the work would be perfect for *him*.

How could he refuse when he'd been hoping for an opportunity like this for the last six years?

Allison would, or *should,* understand. If she loved him, she would be able to accept him and what he did—no questions asked.

The impasse was a classic one, each expecting the other to make the move that would right the relationship and settle the rocking boat of their marriage. Allison expected confidence and open sharing; Logan expected blind trust.

The love which had drawn them together was still there, but was buried beneath so many layers of selfishness and stubbornness that it surfaced upon rarer and rarer occasions. Yet as Logan sat silently next to the tall, sinister-looking Gunther on the speeding train, his thoughts focused on Allison rather than on what lay ahead. This did happen to be one of those infrequent moments when he fell into self-reflection, and he found himself wondering if he had done all he should have to make the marriage work.

She was probably right—he was a louse. He didn't deserve someone like her. But he'd make it up. He'd tell her everything. As soon as this assignment was over, he'd dash up to Scotland. Maybe even stay awhile. They had always been happy there. He was certain they'd be able to patch everything up.

Just as quickly as the contemplative mood had come, it passed. With his marriage satisfactorily resolved in his mind for the moment, he could now turn his concentration upon the task at hand.

7 ❈ The Assignment

GUNTHER WAS A German agent now controlled by British intelligence, MI5. His double agency was, of course, unknown to the Germans—one of a number of similar closely guarded secrets.

Once Gunther had been enlisted to the British side, MI5 began to develop an intricate plan to use him to infiltrate Germany's spy network. If Gunther's defection could be kept secret from Berlin long enough to plant up to a half-dozen experienced Britons throughout mainland Europe, the benefits to the Allied cause could conceivably shorten the war considerably.

The German had represented to his superiors in the Abwehr, the intelligence branch of the German military, that he had recruited several subagents. When, two months ago, they had radioed that they wanted to meet one of these recruits, British intelligence had to produce someone to fit the bill without risking any of their knowledgeable experienced men. Until the legitimacy of Gunther's position was absolutely assured, MI5 had to play cat-and-mouse, insuring that the setup was sound. They could not risk putting a man who had vital information into the hands of the Abwehr. What if, after all, Gunther's defection was nothing more than an elaborate trick to lure a couple of ranking British spies into German hands?

Then Arnie Kramer had thought of Logan. His criminal record would make him an ideal recruit for the Germans. Kramer had his *own* little private network of eyes and ears throughout London, and had done his homework well on Logan. He knew Logan was down on his luck—marriage going sour, rejected by the army, unable to hold a job. He was the perfectly believable candidate for jumping ship. All MI5 would have to do would be to alter the name on Logan's record, and everything else about his past should suit the Germans fine.

Of course, Kramer didn't think it would do to reveal the entire scope of the plan to Logan. No need for him to know that he was nothing more than a decoy, so that if Gunther's loyalties were still to the east of the Channel, they could torture Logan all they wanted to and never get anything vital out of him. If Gunther was for real, and the plan held up, Logan would be in no danger, and they could easily substitute experienced men for the infiltration of the Abwehr later on. If there was danger . . . well, better one like Logan be sacrificed for the good of the cause than any vital information be lost.

So Kramer made his devious offer to his old friend, played out his role of offering Logan a favor most believably, and suddenly Logan was a British spy—or at least so he chose to think. He didn't much like the name Kramer handed him. But *Lawrence MacVey* suited his Scottish accent, and he went along with it.

"You won't need to know a word of German, mate!" said Kramer. "Old Gunther'll have them krauts so anxious to have you they won't care about details like that. Everything's so topsy-turvy anyway, you can't tell who's who anymore by what language they're using.

France is where most of the action is, and the French and English and German all mix up there so much—blimey! The tongue in a man's mouth means nothing!"

It'll be a lark, thought Logan, and he wasn't getting paid badly either. The first meeting on London Bridge with the German had instilled in him the seriousness of the situation. But he was still game to play out his hand. Gunther had briefed him thoroughly on what he was to do at the meeting with the Germans—which essentially amounted to nothing—and now they just had to carry it out. The Germans would be watching Logan, Kramer would be watching Gunther, and Gunther would no doubt be watching for the safety of his own backside. Little did Logan realize that he had been "brought in" for nothing more than this simple "one-act play" being staged for the Germans. But just as little did Kramer realize that when the time came to drop the curtain to end Logan's brief performance, plans would change, and the single act would become a complex drama involving many actors, dozens of curtain calls—all carried out with inexperienced Logan Macintyre occupying center stage.

Two meetings subsequent to London Bridge had aborted. The first had been blown, of all things, by Scotland Yard, who had not been informed that the trawler was in the hire of MI5. Contrary to Arnie's steadfast assurances, Logan nearly wound up back in jail. The second time a heavy fog had prevented their making contact with the German sub.

Now he and Gunther were about to make a third attempt. Their train was within minutes of Cleethorpes, a fishing village on the northeast coast of England, where MI5 had another trawler ready to carry them to a rendezvous with a German U-boat in the North Sea.

As the train jerked to a stop at the tiny coastal station, Logan stole a glance at his associate. *He is a cool number,* thought Logan with mingled admiration and intimidation. He knew very well that Logan was a complete novice. Yet the fact seemed not to bother him. It was almost as if—

No, that is too crazy even to consider! Logan argued with himself. Arnie would never have sold me out! He guaranteed that Gunther was completely dependable.

Logan's mind went back to his second meeting with his old friend, as if trying to reassure himself now that it was too late to back out. Kramer had laid out the plan to him. "Dependable," he'd said; ". . . all ours. Nothing to worry about, Logan!" Gunther had proved himself on several missions, Arnie had added. "There's no question he's with us . . . no question!" According to the major, Gunther had gone to work for the Germans in the first place under some duress and had been very cooperative right from the beginning when British intelligence had captured him within two hours of his parachute landing.

Might his cooperative spirit been just a bit too convenient? Logan found himself wondering. But he dismissed the thought from his mind. He didn't even want to think what might happen if, once they were aboard the sub, Gunther decided to betray him to the Nazis.

That was the trouble with this business—you could never really trust anyone.

Gunther rose from his seat, gathering his belongings from the upper compartment. Logan followed him down the aisle, and soon they stepped out into the chill evening air. He looked around and was at least relieved that it was a clear night. No fog would abort this meeting.

"It's the *Anna Marie,* isn't it?" said Gunther, glancing furtively about.

"What?"

"The trawler," said Gunther tersely, as if the failure to read his mind was a serious flaw. "The trawler is the *Anna Marie?*"

"Yes, that's it," replied Logan. *What is this?* he thought. Surely Gunther wasn't quizzing him at this late hour! But just as surely he didn't need to be reminded of the name of the trawler.

The two walked silently on. Logan drew his overcoat tightly around him. The streets were deserted, but Logan knew it was more than the January cold that kept them in. The east coast of England had been hit hard by the Luftwaffe. Not as dramatically this far north as farther south, but the fear of attack was always present. What would these simple townsfolk think if they knew that but a few miles away, in their placid fishing waters, a Nazi submarine lay awaiting reports from two supposed spies?

What would they do if they thought *he* was one of them? No doubt, shoot first, and ask questions later.

A brisk ten-minute walk brought them to the dock. It reminded Logan of Port Strathy. Fifteen or twenty boats of varying sizes bobbed up and down at their moorings. No human being was in sight; the only sounds were the creakings and groanings and bumpings and scrapings from the docks, boats, and ropes—all accompanying the gentle slap-slap-slap of the water against the sides of the rocking vessels. A single boat pulling out to sea at this hour was certain to arouse suspicion, and no doubt MI5, with their intense mistrust of all other agencies, had informed none of the locals of what was about to transpire.

The *Anna Marie* sat silently waiting in the seventh slip down, an innocent-enough looking forty-foot trawler. Though MI5 had procured the ship, Gunther had hired the crew, which consisted of two sailors. They had been kept in the dark about the purpose of the mission, but were Nazi sympathizers quite willing, for the right price, to carry out a mission of dubious intent with sealed lips. Logan would have preferred an Admiralty man at the helm, but Gunther had convinced Kramer that the Germans would too easily spot a Navy man. "Perhaps," Logan told Kramer at the time, "but would they have any more difficulty spotting an MI5 man?"

"You, my boy," Kramer had replied, "that's the difference! I've seen you hob-nob with society one minute, and the next pass yourself off as a coal miner. The Germans will be plum pudding for you, putty in your hand, as it were. Why else do you think I recommended you for the job?"

Logan tried to catch hold of Arnie's confidence in him. He wished Gunther would do the same.

Gunther approached the boat, making no apparent effort to muffle the echoing of his boots as they walked out to the slip. He stopped, leaned forward, and called out in a low but clear voice, "Is there anyone aboard?"

Logan cringed. That German accent—it was going to get them all strung up if he blurted out something in the wrong crowd.

Before he had a chance to worry further, a figure appeared from below. In the darkness Logan could make out a man shorter than himself, small and wiry. An electric torch suddenly flashed on its beam, seemingly aimed directly for Logan's eyes. It blinded him momentarily.

"What's yer business?" came a harsh voice in a gravelly whisper.

"If the fishing is good—especially the herring—we'd like to engage your boat." It was the prearranged code phrase. Any Cleethorpes fisherman worth his salt knew there to be no herring off the coast at this time of year.

"Oh yeah—that is, ah . . . the fishing is good, especially at night," came the nearly muffed reply.

Gunther grimaced with disgust at another incompetent. Even though he had already spoken twice with the man, he liked to play the little game with code phrases carried off to perfection.

He said nothing further, but swung aboard the trawler. Logan followed. In a moment his feet were planted firmly on the deck. He glanced about to take in his surroundings. He had had no formal training in the spy business, but Arnie had done his best to instill in him some practical tricks of the trade. The foremost principle was to examine your surroundings so that you had at least two possible plans of retreat and escape in mind at all times. You could never tell when a setup would turn on you. When that happened, a second or two delay could be the difference between getting away and landing in prison camp.

What Logan saw was a typical fishing vessel, not unlike Jesse Cameron's, though a little smaller, complete with all the nets, ropes, and other gear essential to earning one's livelihood at sea. The reek of fish was everywhere; there could certainly be no doubt as to the authenticity of this craft! Vessels such as these had made a success of the evacuation of Dunkirk the year before, and since then the British had commandeered several for use in patrolling the coast. There was no way to tell, from a quick look about, whether this was a permanent MI5 craft, or was being used just for the night.

The three men headed for the cabin, located aft. Logan could not help being reminded of his first experience aboard Jesse Cameron's boat, on that crisp northern morning when she had shanghaied him aboard her trawler. It had turned out one of the most memorable days of his life. He had learned a great deal that day, about more than fishing. The fact that he had almost drowned did not in the least diminish the value of the experience.

But though the *Anna Marie* evoked such pleasant memories, it had little else in common with the *Little Stevie* on this chill and sinister night. On that day years ago he had been disappointed to have the cruise off Strathy's harbor come to an end. Tonight, however, he was praying for the hours to pass quickly and to get the whole thing safely over with.

At the same time, he was looking for an escape route should the whole operation blow apart.

8 ※ *Interview at Sea*

"SO, HERR MACVEY," began Colonel von Graff. "You do not mind if I use your real name? I find code names so tedious."

They had located the German submarine without difficulty, had been taken below, and Logan at last found himself face-to-face with the stern German officer who could well determine his fate. The man spoke perfect English, but with a thick accent.

"You're the boss," replied Logan, striking a cocky, halfway belligerent attitude. Arnie had told him not to grovel; they would buy his story more readily if he didn't make it too easy for them, and maybe respect him more in the process. "No one respects a weakling!" he had added.

"As I was saying," continued the colonel, "I have noted in your file—"

"File! You blokes have a file on me?" exclaimed Logan in angry offense. He knew perfectly well they would check his record, but he was warming up to the game.

"Do not be offended, Herr MacVey. It is standard procedure—merely routine. The Abwehr trusts no one, even its own."

"So I've heard," said Logan caustically.

"You do not approve?" said the colonel, raising one eyebrow.

"One does what one has to do," replied Logan. "I suppose you Germans are no different."

"Indeed. And it would seem doing what might be considered somewhat—how do you say, irregular?—is something you are familiar with."

"Just what's that supposed to mean?" snapped Logan.

"Only that I took note of your prison record with interest," replied the colonel.

Logan leaned against the bulkhead, folded his arms across his chest, and sent his gaze directly toward the colonel's, as if challenging him to make an issue of his record. Logan and von Graff were in a tiny cabin, alone. Gunther had departed to some other part of the sub while the colonel carried out his interrogation. Logan had refused the chair that had been offered when the interview began five minutes earlier and merely stood with his back to the wall. The colonel sat at a small wooden table bolted to the floor.

Colonel Martin von Graff, an average-sized but imposing man in his late forties, carried a physique primed to military fitness, more than an equal match to most men regardless of size. His brown, close-cut hair was graying slightly at the temples, adding an element of venerability to his square, taut, clean-shaven face. His clear, precisely clipped speech accentuated his confident nature. He was accustomed to issuing orders and being obeyed. He was clearly a man not easily crossed or lied to.

"The dirty Crown," said Logan, pointedly slurring his last word with disgust; "tossed me into the chokey—half the charges were trumped up, and I didn't have a fancy title to get me off."

"The son of a Glasgow laborer," added von Graff, "himself in jail several times for petty theft."

How much information did Arnie let them have? wondered Logan. They just better have left out all mention of Allison and Stonewycke.

"It's the only way a poor blighter can get ahead in this rotten country," said Logan.

"You hope to find something better in Germany?"

"There's something to be said for a place where a house painter can rise to power."

Von Graff winced. The Germans did not like to be reminded that their Führer had once been a common laborer. Even as the words were past his lips, Logan realized this was not to be the best approach. The Nazis weren't like the Communists, proud of a working man's heritage.

"Hitler also has a prison record," Logan added smugly.

"And so you feel your crimes were of a *political* nature?"

"In Britain only Jews and noblemen get anywhere." The words nearly choked Logan, but he had to move the interview toward ground to which this Nazi could relate. He had to try to appeal to the man's Teutonic prejudice so as to take the attention off himself. "The only crime is that a man with white skin and pure breeding has to rob and steal to keep starvation from killing him, while the *Jews* control all the money."

"I see," said the colonel, without affect.

This man gives the word cool *new meaning,* thought Logan. Either he indulged in no political or racial fancies, or he had them as precisely under control as he did everything else about him.

"Look," said Logan impatiently, "did you call me here to discuss anything besides my prison record?"

"Indeed I did," answered von Graff. "But what I have in mind will involve some sensitive areas that a man without scruples—"

"I get your drift," interrupted Logan.

"You have reformed of your life of crime, I take it, Herr MacVey?"

"I have no intention of stealing from the Reich, if that's what you mean."

"What exactly brought about this reform—your marriage, perhaps?"

"My marriage?"

"My report indicates you were married in 1933 to an Allison Bently of Yorkshire, after which you desisted from your criminal activities."

What is this? thought Logan. He and Arnie had never discussed this aspect of his life and past in relation to what would be placed in his record. Somehow he had assumed that all mention of his marriage had been eliminated. Well, if Arnie had falsified the records, at least he had had the foresight to alter the names and places. That is, *if* he had indeed changed them. What if von Graff was baiting him, throwing out misinformation to catch him up? To see how far Logan was willing to carry the truth?

"Listen," answered Logan at length, "I want my family left out of this. They have nothing whatever to do with my political viewpoints. Besides, my wife and I haven't been together in months."

"A divorce . . . ?"

"Not yet—but my wife had nothing to do with any of this, see? And I want it kept that way—or I don't deal."

"There is no reason for her to be involved," replied von Graff.

A rap came on the door, and an aide entered with a tray containing a coffeepot and cups. "Will that be all, mein Colonel?" he asked. The colonel dismissed him briskly, and he turned and exited.

"I wish I could offer you something stronger, but it is best we keep our heads about us," said the colonel as he poured out the coffee from an antique silver urn that could not have looked more out of place aboard a German war sub. "Do you take anything?" he asked Logan.

"Cream and sugar," answered Logan.

"Two lumps?"

Logan nodded.

Suddenly the whole tenor of the meeting had changed. This was no longer a confab of spies, but a tea party. Von Graff had ceased for the moment being a military man, and instead was carrying out the role of host at an elegant dinner party. Logan recalled that the title "von" indicated nobility, and he wondered if in the colonel's case it was more than merely an inherited appellation. Yes, the man's nature was honed sharp, like a deadly weapon. But he had risen to his position without forgetting to bring along his silver coffee service and fine china. His wit and savoir-faire were perhaps restrained in these austere surroundings, but as he was served, Logan could easily picture von Graff moving gracefully about at an elite cocktail reception.

Still, through it all there remained something unchanged in his eyes, a raw chill that belonged to the battlefield, and it was visible even as he spoke in an apparently social vein.

"You British will never learn how to drink coffee properly," he said, handing Logan the Wedgewood cup and saucer.

"We've always been resistant to change," replied Logan noncommittally.

"You hope that by adding cream and sugar you will make the coffee taste like tea?"

"Maybe."

"But alas, the two drinks are as different as . . ."

The colonel's sentence was completed by the knowing glance in his eyes.

"You're right. Nothing can turn coffee into tea."

"So it is with life," von Graff went on in a philosophical tone. Logan smiled at how deftly the colonel had maneuvered the conversation back to cases. "I was going to say a moment ago, as different as the Germans and the British. Throw in a pinch of this ideology or a dash of that doctrine and you still have what you began with—in your case an Englishman, born and bred. You can't alter a man's heritage any more than cream and sugar will alter the basic flavor of coffee."

"Hardly an Englishman!" corrected Logan. "A Scot, to be specific. And no true Scotsman would ever consider himself an *Englishman.* All true Scots would agree—the union of 1707 be hanged!"

"So the Scots, the Irish, and the Welsh would align themselves with fascism as a means to an end?"

"Why not?"

"They are hardly fascist."

"I can't believe that ideology would matter a fig to Hitler if he could get any of the Commonwealth countries to turn on England."

"And is nationalism *your* motivation, Herr MacVey?" asked von Graff.

"Does it matter?"

"You spoke earlier of poverty and Jews," said the colonel. "I wonder if you are a zealot."

Logan leaned forward, peering intently into his interviewer's eyes to give added emphasis to his words.

"To tell you the truth, von Graff," he said, "I have only one ideology, and that's Lawrence MacVey!"

Logan had slipped very comfortably into his role, and hardly balked at such an outright lie, and did not even stumble over the use of the strange name. "I figure that deep down you Germans are just like me, and that's why I'm here."

Von Graff laughed—not a merry laugh, but a dry response to a droll witticism.

"Hitler wrote in *Mein Kampf,*" he said, " 'The conviction of the justification of using even the most brutal weapons is always dependent on the presence of *fanatical* belief in the necessity of the victory of a revolutionary new order on this globe.' The Third Reich is such a new order, and the extent of the Führer's fanatical belief has only begun to be seen."

"Are you saying, then, that my observation regarding the Reich's motivations is incorrect?"

"It is correct," answered the colonel. "But I would hasten to suggest that if you should ever meet the Führer, you not put it quite so succinctly."

He rose, refilled the coffee cups, then began again.

"I must say, I am relieved, Herr MacVey. An opportunist is so much easier to work with than a zealot. However, opportunists do possess one serious drawback."

"Which is?" asked Logan.

"Since they have no loyalties, it is forever difficult to predict when—and if—a sweeter opportunity will lure them away."

"Not in my case," Logan assured the colonel coolly. "I'm no zealot, but I'll die before I sleep in the same bed with Britain. It has nothing to do with ideology. It has everything to do with me, and what they did to me. There are only two sides in this war—Britain and her cronies against your Fatherland. That leaves me with only one choice. It helps, though, that I expect to be well-compensated for my services."

"The Reich expects such compensation to be well-earned."

"And that brings us back to the beginning," said Logan, "which is why I've been asked here. Certainly not for the stimulating conversation I've provided. You could have had that in Berlin."

"You'd be surprised, mein Herr," replied von Graff pensively. "You'd be surprised . . ."

He raised his cup of black coffee to his lips and drained off the remainder of its contents. "I believe this is a superb time to come to the point of our little meeting," he added, changing back into his brisk military voice.

"Then I pass muster?"

"Time will tell, Herr MacVey. But for now, as you might say, Why not?"

Logan could think of a hundred reasons why he should not have passed his interviewer's scrutiny, but none of them mattered as long as von Graff bought his act. He restrained a relieved sigh. Everything was going well enough; Arnie would be proud of him.

Taking advantage of the brief pause in the conversation, von Graff bent over and shuffled through some papers in a briefcase that sat on the floor next to him. In a moment he withdrew a large-sized folded sheet, pushed aside the coffee things, and opened it out on the table. It was a map of England.

"This is where I want you to begin," said the colonel, his slim, neatly manicured finger pressed against the southeast coast of England. "Sussex, Kent, and Essex," he continued. "I want everything you can get on coastal defenses. Specifically the location of anti-aircraft guns and the status of the electrically controlled land mines. Also, detailed damage reports after bombings. Finally, I want you to take a copy of this map and update it for us. As you can see, it is a few years old."

"Sounds as if you haven't given up hopes of invasion," Logan prompted coyly.

"Keep in mind, MacVey," replied von Graff, "that yours is the task of reporter, not interpreter. Many a good spy has failed because he has tried to second-guess his superiors."

"I'll keep that in mind," Logan answered. But if von Graff expected humility to accompany such a reply, he got none from Logan.

"Entrench yourself in that region," continued the colonel. "I'm certain you'll have no problem establishing a cover. When you leave here tonight, you will take with you a wireless transmitter—you do know how to operate a wireless, I take it?"

"Of course," Logan lied. Actually he had never seen one at close quarters before. But Arnie would handle all that.

"Here is your code and its key," von Graff said, handing him a thick folder along with the map. "Continue to use the same code name—Trinity, wasn't it?"

Logan nodded.

"An interesting choice. A covert reference to the *Third* Reich, perhaps?"

"Pretty clever, wouldn't you agree?" replied Logan. But even as he spoke he was thinking of how the name really had come about. Von Graff would have been surprised, and probably appalled.

One Sunday morning Logan and Allison had attended a little church not far from their Shoreditch flat. He had already encountered Arnie Kramer, and his thoughts were full of the major's offer. He could hardly remember a thing about the service itself. But as he sat there silently with Allison at his side, he found himself thinking that if he wanted to do this spy thing right, he ought to come up with a code name for himself. "You'll be taking on many names and characters from here on out," Arnie had told him. Then he chuckled reassuringly. "But don't worry, the same old Logan Macintyre will always be there somewhere!"

While Logan sat in church, unable to focus his mind on the sermon, his eye fell upon the word *Trinity* engraved in ornate script upon a window. Since his thoughts of late had never been far from his potential new occupation, he immediately perceived the parallel between Arnie's statement and the spiritual manifestation represented by the window. He chided himself at his cheek in comparing what he was doing with anything spiritual. Yet when he had to give a code name, *Trinity* was the name that came to his lips.

So now, here he was telling lies to a Nazi colonel, using a name he had stolen from a stained-glass window. None of it made much sense. But maybe somehow the name, which had nothing whatever to do with the Third Reich, would force some sanity or meaning into the topsy-turvy world in which Logan Macintyre now found himself entangled.

9 ❋ *Unexpected Twist*

"HE HAD WHAT!" exploded Kramer.

"A box . . . a transmitter, I told you."

"You were supposed to stick close. I told you not to let MacVey be alone with the krauts!"

"They took me away," replied Gunther defensively. "I had no choice."

Kramer looked away, thinking for a moment. Then he went on.

"So you heard nothing of what went on?"

"No. Only what Trinity told me on the way back."

"Trinity . . . MacVey . . . Mac—!" burst out Kramer again, but caught himself. "This was only supposed to be a one-time operation. What am I supposed to do with a novice in the middle of a cauldron of Nazis?"

"It might not be a completely lost cause," said Gunther.

Kramer rose from his chair, eyeing his companion momentarily, then ambled slowly to the window, his back to Gunther, and looked out on the street below. There was something else about this new twist he didn't like. He was further than ever from being able to assess Gunther's true loyalties. For all he could tell, *he* was the one who had been set up, and now Gunther had him just where he wanted him. That's what he hated about this bloody business—you never really *knew,* at bottom, where people's loyalties lay! Double agents, triple agents, quadruple agents! And there was Logan, the unsuspecting amateur, right in the middle of it as the wild card!

Blast! If he only had one of his own men in it! He should probably pull the plug on Logan, get him out of it, cover his tracks, and hang Gunther out to dry. It was just too risky. If this German wasn't on the level, there was too much at stake, especially if they were now able to manipulate Logan.

He didn't like it! He wasn't tightly in control, and that made him nervous. But on the other hand, what if Gunther *was* solidly in their camp? He could ill afford to blow such a perfect defection. Maybe they could still pull out Logan as planned with Arnie's boys operating the radio. But Gunther had said he had the impression the Abwehr was going to want to deal directly with Trinity, which would get sticky if they insisted on more face-to-face meetings. They had to get Logan out; he didn't know anything of these affairs, con man that he was. He just hadn't counted on it going so far. Logan had been supposed to keep quiet, let Gunther handle it. Now, here he was all signed up as a German agent, coming back to England with a wireless and a full set of orders, for heaven's sake! The thing was ridiculous!

"So, what makes you so optimistic?" asked Arnie, turning. His face revealed little of his doubt to the German.

"I see no problem with keeping Trinity in," replied Gunther.

"Keep him in! Why, that would mean—"

Kramer stopped. He had to keep his wits about him. He still wasn't completely sure whom he was talking to. If Gunther still belonged to the Germans, it could be to his advantage to have a novice as his protege.

"He doesn't have the experience for this kind of thing," he said finally.

"But he has conquered the biggest obstacle already. They trust him."

"Ha! You believe that? Then you are more of an idiot than I thought, mein lieber Freund."

"They gave him a wireless and instructions."

"It's a setup, I tell you. How long have you been in this business, Gunther?"

"Long enough!" snapped the German.

"Long enough to recognize a checkup, an audition, when you see one?"

Kramer stopped. Perhaps he had already said too much. After all, Gunther was riding high in his own trial balloon at this very moment. Kramer didn't want to push him too hard and blow him back across the Channel if he truly was theirs.

Gunther did not reply, and was left to his own reflections. He too was thinking what a complex and subtle business this was.

Kramer turned his back again, thought for a couple minutes, then opened his mouth to speak. When he spun back around, however, Gunther was gone. He had left the room silently; Kramer had not even heard the door.

He sighed deeply. Who could tell, though? Maybe Gunther was right. Logan *had* handled himself pretty well. If the Abwehr contact had at least thought him worth testing, that might be a good sign. Perhaps his old friend Logan might prove more useful than he had first anticipated.

Keep him in—a novel idea! Maybe a good one. They could manage Gunther.

No one could say Major Arnold Kramer had advanced to his present position by being afraid to go out on a limb occasionally.

10 ⁂ Short Furlough

IT WAS ONE of those crisp days of April when the chill in the air is a sufficient reminder that the last snow has only recently thawed. But accompanying the brisk temperature was a bright persistent sun, and had he been on land, better yet in the countryside, there would have been a fragrance of flowers in the air, speaking with conviction that spring had arrived.

As he leaned against the rail, sucking in the tangy salt breezes, Logan recalled another spring nine years ago when he had sailed northward on this very schooner. Then he had come bearing lies and deception, and a plan to swindle the most prominent family in town. As the schooner slid into its slip in Port Strathy's harbor, on this spring day of 1941, Logan somehow felt that very little had changed.

He found himself almost wishing Arnie hadn't so willingly granted permission for this brief leave. But things had been going so well, he was probably glad to reward Logan in this way. Logan had contacted von Graff upon several occasions by wireless, had fed him what information Arnie had supplied, and on the whole Kramer seemed pleased with the way things were developing. He had had Gunther reassigned farther north temporarily so as to remove at least one element of chance from Logan's activities. He'd let some of the other boys keep an eye on him for a while; Kramer himself would have his hands full keeping tabs on Logan and von Graff, at least until Logan knew how to handle himself in the spy game.

As he was handing Logan his official papers for the trip north, Kramer had rather off-handedly mentioned that he had had an ulterior motive, aside from all else, for giving Logan a brief respite.

"What's up?" asked Logan, curious.

"You never told me you could speak French," said the major.

"You never asked."

"It's a good thing I was looking over your personnel file." Kramer absently tapped a manila folder lying on his desk. "How good are you?"

"Not bad, I suppose," said Logan modestly.

"Level with me, Logan."

"They always said I had a knack for it."

"By which they meant what?"

"That I didn't have an English accent, I suppose. It came natural to me."

"And where did you pick it up?"

"I was there for a couple years in '29 and '30."

"On what business?"

"You know how it was back then, Arnie. Things had begun to get a little touchy for me. So in order to promote my continued freedom, I decided to see what the Continent had to offer. A friend and I had a pretty decent setup in Le Mans in the racing game until the gendarmes got onto us. Then I drifted down to the Riviera. I didn't make my fortune, but I did pick up the language."

"Well, I mentioned you to the boys in *SOE*."

"Sorry—I haven't got all your initials down yet."

"Special Operations Executive," replied Kramer. "They specialize in overseas espionage, sabotage, that sort of thing. They need operatives who speak French, especially now with the Continent totally in the hands of the Germans and the role of the underground so crucial."

He paused and glanced at Logan.

"What are you suggesting, Arnie?" Logan asked.

"I don't know, but it made sense to me. You've done well so far. But the training's rather stiff, and only a fraction of those who can speak the language manage to pass. It's an elitist outfit."

"You can't seriously be considering *me*!"

"Why not? You've shown some guts recently. You might be good at it. So I had them put your name on the roster for the next training session. It's coming up in a month."

Logan knew only a little about the SOE, but since that conversation with Arnie Kramer, he had tried to remember everything he'd heard. They operated behind enemy lines, constantly walking the tightrope between a hazardous freedom and capture. In case of the latter, torture was certain, death probable. The missions were of the highest importance, yet at the same time were as close to suicide assignments as the British could offer. Few operatives returned without having at least flirted with death. It was a long way from petty con games, or even posing as a German spy in a quiet English port town.

As Logan looked up at the harbor of Port Strathy, he recalled that his first thought after hearing Arnie's proposal about the SOE was of his family. He would be seeing them soon. And as difficult as his marriage had been over the last few years, down inside he still wanted it to work. He couldn't keep lying to Allison. In a few minutes he would again be holding her in his arms. He'd been thinking about what Kramer had said during the whole of his voyage north, and finally he knew what his answer had to be.

No, Arnie Kramer, he thought to himself, *this is one assignment I cannot accept.*

The schooner's crew was already busy casting the ropes out to catch the dock's moorings. Out on the wharf Logan saw several familiar faces. He returned their friendly greetings, gradually warming to the idea of his return, realizing that perhaps it was not like the first time at all. He was no stranger coming to Stonewycke this time. These people were his friends; he was part of this little community, and he held nothing but goodwill in his heart for these people.

Where was Allison? Civilian communications were so haywire since the war. He wondered if she'd even received his telegram. He probably should have telephoned. But as much as he hated to admit it, he'd been just a bit afraid to talk to her. Their last conversation still haunted his memory.

He quickly scanned the faces lining the shore again, but then suddenly his eyes were diverted to the street running adjacent to the Bluster N' Blow. Allison's dark golden hair seemed to reflect the crimson of the sun itself, and her cheeks held a rosy glow from her hurried pace. The moment her blue eyes spotted him on the deck of the waiting boat, her lips broke into a warm, lively smile and her step quickened still further.

"Ali!" he shouted, running down the barely situated gangway. All his earlier ambivalence dissolved at the sight of his wife, nor was he embarrassed at the good-natured cheer that rose from the crowd of onlookers as he rushed forward and took her into his arms.

"Oh, Logan!" she exclaimed.

He could find no immediate words. He wrapped his arms tightly around her and held her close, then bent down to kiss her. But as his lips met hers, there were tears in her eyes. He felt tears rising in his own as well.

"We must look like a couple of ninnies," he said at last.

"It'll give all the people something to talk about for the next week," replied Allison. "We're improving the morale of the neighborhood!"

Logan laughed.

As they stood together for a lingering moment, forgotten were the tensions, the doubts, the harsh words, and the pain of recent meetings. Seemingly for a few brief careless minutes they were once again newlyweds, jubilant in their love and in the sheer joy of being together. They turned, and hand-in-hand walked back along the street to the car.

Logan jumped behind the wheel of the old Austin. It started right up, another reminder that this day was different than that on which he and Allison had first met, when the old car had stubbornly coughed and sputtered until Logan appeared with his timely mixture of expertise and good luck.

As he wheeled the car around, he reflected back to that earlier time. Like that finicky Austin, their first encounters had been but sputtering attempts toward relationship, each antagonizing the stubborn pride of the other. When the day of the flood came, it was as if the water itself had begun a cleansing process within them. They were soon to learn, however, that such inner cleansing had nothing to do with the flood. Rather, it was God himself who was washing them clean, and drawing them together in the process, as He drew their spirits toward His heart of love. He who would become their Lord was tearing down the walls that each had erected, though in the years since that time, without knowing it, they had both built them back up again.

But for the moment, as they flew out of Port Strathy and up the hill toward the ancient estate, their thoughts were filled with the good times of their youth.

"Tell me—" began Allison, but at the same moment Logan had also tried to speak. They laughed.

"You go ahead," said Allison. "What were you going to say, Logan?"

"It's not that important."

"I want to hear," she insisted. "I've waited so long just to hear your voice since . . ."

She hesitated, and Logan said nothing.

"Oh, Logan, I'm so sorry about what I did on the phone!" she added.

"Forget it. Everything's forgiven," replied Logan. "Let's both just forget the past and start out new."

"Logan, how I wish . . ." But even as she spoke, Allison paused, as if some sudden assurance had stolen upon her. "Yes, we can, can't we? Oh, it's so good to see you . . . I'm so glad you're home!"

The word *home* stung Logan with an odd sensation. Yes, there was a part of him that had felt like he was coming home as the schooner rounded the head and pointed its bow into the bay. Yet another part of him . . .

Even as the thought darted into his mind he silently cursed himself for spoiling the sweet mood of their reunion.

"I'm glad too, Ali," he said, and left it at that.

Then followed a silence. Logan could not shake the cloud that had suddenly showed itself on his horizon. The quiet would have become awkward had they allowed it to linger on, but Allison interceded in time.

"You should see little Joanna," she said. "You won't recognize her. She's so big, and talks all the time. She'll soon be two—just imagine!"

"I've thought of nothing else," he answered, "except you."

She slipped her arm through his and snuggled closer.

"We had a letter from Dad yesterday," she said, trying to fill him in on family news.

"How is he?"

"He says he's healthy and all. But he hasn't seen Ian, which is a disappointment to him—they're both in North Africa, you know, and he was hoping they'd see more of each other. He can't say much about the war, but Mother sensed some discouragement. About all he had to say on the bright side was that he'd been studying camels and was fascinated."

Logan laughed. "Always the vet! Your dad is really quite a guy."

"Yes," sighed Allison, thinking of how long it took her to discover that fact. She now knew what a wonderful man her father was—even more so now that he was absent from her.

"Things haven't gone so well in Africa," continued Logan, "since the Germans sent in Rommel a couple of months ago. He's pushed the British troops back nearly all the way to the Egyptian border."

"Do you think . . . is Dad in any danger?"

"Of course not!" Logan replied with all the confidence he could muster. "That was stupid of me to say."

"No! I want to know what's going on. I hate it when the government and newspapers try to whitewash everything. How do you have such current information? We have to struggle for every tidbit we get up here."

"Oh . . . well." Logan quickly sought in his head for a plausible explanation other than that he'd heard it at MI5. "I met a talkative soldier on the train," he lied, hating himself for it.

"Well I wish I'd meet a talkative soldier some time." She hadn't seemed to notice his momentary hesitation. "But he probably wouldn't have told *me* anything—no one will say anything to a woman about the war."

"It can't be as bad as all that. This is a new age. Women are in all kinds of vital positions." *Even intelligence,* he was about to say, but thought better of it.

"Probably not. I'm sure I just imagined it. But it's so frustrating! Sometimes I wish I were a man, Logan, so I could *do* something. I'd rather be part of the fight than sitting around rolling bandages and collecting tin."

"That's important too, you know. Keeps the morale high, for the boys to know the women are waiting for them at home—so I've been told."

"That's so old-fashioned, Logan! We'd rather be part of it all."

As Allison spoke, they drove through the open iron gates of Stonewycke. Logan chuckled as he braked the car in front of the courtyard fountain. The image of Allison dressed in army fatigues, hefting a rifle over her shoulder, was an amusing one indeed.

But the passionate words of his young wife also touched Logan's heart. She had so much spirit, such vitality and energy! Yes, she no doubt *would* make a good soldier—strong and courageous, even daring.

As they climbed out of the car, the large front door opened and Joanna walked out and hurried toward Logan.

He turned and faced her.

"Logan!" she said, "it's so good to see you! Welcome back!"

He paused a moment, then bowed deeply, and rose. "Charming, as always, Lady Mac-Neil!" he said, with exaggerated tone and a twinkle in his eye.

The women both eyed each other with a grin. Each then took an arm, and Logan, as if exulting in his triumphant return, led the way toward the house, all three laughing in the joy of his irrepressibly buoyant spirit.

11 ❊ *Like Old Times*

IN HER DESPERATION to have everything right again between them, Allison forgot a principle she knew only too well—that wounds do not often heal so readily. Seeing Logan again, with the old lilt in his step and sparkle in his eye and wisecrack on his tongue convinced her that she could lay aside all the fears and doubts about their marriage that had been plaguing her. They were together now, and that was all that mattered. He had come to her. He had known she needed him, and had left London and all that had been so important to him—for her.

Alas, the next few days only aided Allison in her blissful misconception. Patience had never been one of her greatest assets, and she could not wait for the depth of discernment which might have allowed her to see that the ground under her feet was not as smooth as she wanted it to be. But for the blessed present, spring had come to the land, and to the soul of young Allison Macintyre.

As the coming of growth and green, planting and blossoms, warmth and rain gradually took over the Strathy countryside, so did joy and apparent happiness surround the young couple. As if reacquainting themselves with one another, as well as old haunts and old memories together, they walked for miles, both visiting old friends and simply enjoying the glorious coastline and inland beauty. On horseback they rode upon the surrounding hills and along the sandy beach, just as Maggie and Ian had done some seventy-five years before. Though all upon it had changed, the land had not, still possessing a power to move, a power to invoke reflection, a power to open the spirit to the heart of its Creator.

Once again talk flowed easily between them. Neither seemed to notice, or care, that amid all the profusion of conversation, they subconsciously avoided anything that hinted at the deep or the personal. Neither wanted to threaten the precarious balance of relationship that seemed to be growing once more between them. Instinctively they realized it too tender a thing yet to be examined directly without endangering its frail life. Therefore they kept in constant motion. Joanna commented one evening that she had hardly seen Logan again since the day of his arrival, and had not had the chance to sit down and talk with him about anything.

He laughed it off.

"Ah, my dear mother-in-law," he said flippantly, "these are not the days for serious conversation. The world is at war, and darkness surrounds us on all sides. These are the times, rather, when we must laugh and make merry. For tomorrow we may, as the saying goes— well, perhaps the remainder of said proverb had best remain unspoken. Nevertheless, I do not choose to add to the world's gloom with serious reflection, introspection, and pontification. My calling has always been to bring a little levity to the world!"

He lifted his glass, to Allison's delight, and Joanna joined in the laughter at his speech. However, as it subsided, neither of the two young people noted the deep anxious furrow of concern that remained in her brow.

One day the sun rose especially warm. A cool breeze would no doubt later come blowing in off the ocean as a reminder of recently departed winter. A few clouds dotted the sky, but Logan, undaunted, walked into the kitchen about ten to see if he could cajole the cook into preparing a basket for an outdoor feast.

Twenty minutes later, he emerged with the basket over his arm and a carefree smile on his face. He found Allison in the family parlor sewing while listening to the radio. She looked up as he entered, and her look of concentration immediately brightened.

"What have we here?" she asked cheerfully.

"This, *mon chèri,*" replied Logan with a humble bow and tip of his cap, "is a *celebration de vivre*—a celebration of life! Come join me, fair maiden!"

"Logan . . . what?" exclaimed Allison, delighted, yet still puzzled.

"An old-fashioned Scottish picnic, what else!"

He reached out, took her hand, and pulled her from her seat up to his side.

"Did you prepare that all by yourself?" asked Allison, peeking into the basket.

"I had some help. Now come, before the weather changes."

"We'll still need coats."

"What else were coats invented for?" he answered playfully. "I remember reading all about it. *Voila!* The coat has been invented; now the world can picnic!"

"Logan, you *are* crazy!" exclaimed Allison, dropping her sewing and jumping up. "I'll get the baby ready."

In ten minutes they were all three in the Austin bumping along a back road that ran south behind the estate. Though rutted and unpaved, the road traversed mostly flat terrain with acres of crop land spreading out to the right and left. Already the farmers were out in the fields plowing and preparing the earth for spring planting. Allison and Logan waved at old Fergie, the estate's factor, as he huffed and puffed, carrying his jelly-like frame across the newly made furrows back to his truck.

After some distance the road veered toward the west, and the cultivated land gave way to low-lying hills covered with now dormant heather. The Austin groaned and labored its way up and down one incline after another, and at the top of one Logan stopped for a few minutes to let it cool down a bit.

"Where are we going?" asked Allison, finally able to contain her curiosity no longer.

"A secret place," answered Logan, grinning as he started up the engine and pulled back onto the road.

"I grew up here, Logan. How can you have a secret spot that I know nothing about?"

"Just you wait, my dear."

Allison sat back expectantly as the familiar countryside of her home rolled past. The day was going to be a magical one; she sensed it in the very air around them. In the four days since Logan had returned to Stonewycke, her confidence in their relationship had grown tremendously. She was more sure of Logan than she had been for some time, and knew that this afternoon would be the perfect time to bring up a subject she now felt certain he would be enthusiastic about. It had been on her mind constantly ever since she had received his telegram, and now the time was right. Perhaps God had at last arranged everything perfectly for the plan that had been in the back of her mind for months.

All at once the car came to a stop. Deep in thought, Allison had scarcely noticed that they had slowed and pulled off the road. Glancing around, she realized that the place was indeed unfamiliar to her. The ground had turned rocky, and the road, which had been gradually disintegrating, now disappeared altogether.

"All ashore!" declared Logan. "We've a wee hike before we reach our destination."

He hopped out of the car and in a moment was lifting the sleeping baby off Allison's lap with one hand, while he helped Allison out with the other.

"I'll get the basket," said Allison.

Logan hoisted his daughter, waking now to the activity around her, onto his shoulders, the child giggling with glee. "Daddy!" she squealed happily.

The sight brought tears to Allison's eyes. It was so right, so perfect. She had waited so long for this reunion, this rekindling of their love, for the old Logan to surface once again. This was where they belonged. Why had they fought so much . . . why had they even gone to London? This was their life. God had given them a wonderful family and a beautiful home in Scotland. There was no reason for them not to be content. And as she observed her husband and daughter together, Allison sighed, never doubting that they would be together like this from now on.

She followed Logan through a small wood, and after about ten minutes the densely packed pine trees opened out into a secluded little meadow. Three sides remained walled by the wood, and on the fourth, below a steep bank, the icy cold Lindow River splashed and danced on its way to the sea.

"How on earth did you find this place?" asked Allison when they paused in the middle of the lush green grass of the meadow. "It's beautiful!"

Logan smiled, feeling quite pleased with himself. "Your mother told me about it last night when I asked her where a good spot for a picnic might be. I wish I could say it was my own discovery. But honesty forces me to fess up!"

Allison laughed. "You always were a shrewd one, Logan. But I wonder why she never told us about it, or brought us here."

"I asked her that myself," replied Logan. "She told me she always thought it would bring more pleasure to the one who made the discovery on his own. She said she and Alec used to bring you children near here all the time, hoping that one day you would make the discovery. But so far Ian is the only one to have found it."

"But she told you?"

Logan laughed. "I suppose she figured with my ignorance of the country life and my city ways, I would never find it on my own. Besides, I told her I wanted someplace special."

"So that's it," said Allison. She put her arms around Logan and lightly kissed his cheek. "Thank you."

But the youngster, still perched atop her daddy, had no patience for tender love scenes, and called out, "Daddy, down!"

Logan swung her gently into his arms, and then with a great fatherly hug and kiss set her on the ground where she immediately took off gleefully through the grass. Logan turned to assist Allison with the picnic things.

"Your mother said some old folks she knew by the name of Cuttahay first showed her this spot," said Logan as he shook out the blanket and spread it on the grass.

"Oh yes. The Cuttahays were the first friends Mother had here in Port Strathy," said Allison.

"Well, apparently they used to come here when they were courting. Old Mr. Cuttahay used to strip off his shirt, dive into the water, then swim to the other side and back, just to impress his sweetheart," said Logan. As he spoke he stood up and sauntered toward the riverbank.

Allison giggled. "I can hardly imagine old Nathaniel diving into the Lindow." Then she gasped, "Logan, what are you doing?"

As Allison spoke, Logan had dramatically begun to tear off his coat and shirt.

"I can impress my lassie, too!"

Allison burst into disbelieving laughter.

"But the water's freezing. You'll catch your death of cold!"

"I'm a rugged fellow," said Logan, making ready to dive.

"But you don't need to impress me, Logan," she said, with as much earnestness as her mirth would allow.

"I don't?" he replied. Though his face continued to smile as he glanced back at her, his voice momentarily sounded as if a small part of him truly was surprised with her statement.

Had Allison been more secure within herself concerning their relationship, his simple question might have slipped by almost unnoticed. She might even have continued the light-hearted banter in kind. However, his tone stung her, and before she even realized what was happening, she had blurted out words she quickly regretted.

"Logan, I don't think you've ever really known me!" Her lip trembled as she spoke, as she fought back tears.

Logan stepped back from the edge of the bank, his merry mood suddenly gone. He gathered up his things, hurried to Allison's side and knelt down on the blanket, facing her.

"I was only joking," he said. The fib came so easily to his lips. His inner self excused it on the grounds that lying was better at the moment than strife.

"Oh, never mind about it," replied Allison, forcing a bright smile to her face, and hastily wiping her eyes dry. "I'd better get the baby."

She jumped up and went off after their daughter, spending some time helping the child pick flowers and chase a butterfly. Allison prolonged the diversion long enough to regain her self-control.

When she returned Logan had laid out lunch, and the three ate while Logan and Allison chatted about things inconsequential, using the antics of their daughter as a protective shield to keep the conversation light. But a stilted air settled over the remainder of the afternoon, as if each saw that despite the surface merriment, the hurts and stresses continued to simmer as though in a covered pot. Yet both Allison and Logan clung determinedly to the surface appearance of cordiality, not wanting the cover to blow off again, desperate to avoid a confrontation.

Had Allison considered it carefully, she would have altogether forgotten about what she had hoped to discuss with Logan. However, the peaceful meadow, filled with pleasant ghosts from the past, and the reassuring roar of the river, along with the semblance of congeniality between them, all combined to lull her into a forgetful state of security. I won't let my own emotions out, she thought; only mention the thing and then let it drop.

The three finished lunch, walked about the meadow, hiked through a portion of the wood, and then returned to the blanket to partake of the sweet shortbread the cook had baked the day before. Logan stretched himself out, leaning lazily against an old stump, while little Joanna climbed sleepily into his lap.

"You are a dear thing, my sweet little lass," he said, lovingly stroking her mass of amber-colored curls. "I often wonder how I could have deserved such a blessing."

"Lady Margaret would have said that we don't deserve God's blessings," replied Allison, "but we receive them only because He loves us so."

"Or would she perhaps quote my old progenitor Digory to say it?" laughed Logan. "She did like to tell me about him. I suppose she thought it would make me more receptive to know that spiritual blood flowed in my veins. The dear old lady—I still miss her."

"Don't we all!"

"I can just hear her say it, like you said. And the words were never truer than in my case." Logan reached out and took Allison's hand. "Why am I not more thankful, more receptive to His blessings to me?"

"I know," said Allison. "Since I've come back home, though I've grumbled and complained more than I should, I now see I have everything anyone could want."

"And you're happy, Ali?" Logan, too, had forgotten to take care of dangerous ground.

"Now that you're here with me, Logan, I'm more than happy—I'm ecstatic!"

Logan sighed, then reached out his arm and drew her close. Allison laid her head peacefully against him, and the next several minutes were spent just quietly listening to the lovely sounds of spring.

"For the first time in a long time, Logan," said Allison at length, "I feel we can begin to think of the future."

"Not many want to do that during wartime," replied Logan. "It's dangerous to make plans when everything is so uncertain."

"But it's different for us," answered Allison confidently. "I know you've felt bad about not getting into the army, about not having a job you liked, about not doing anything you felt was important, but now I see that maybe God planned it that way for us."

"Oh?"

"I can't say why! but I really believe we've been given something special, something better than jobs or wealth or anything, and we'd be foolish not to accept it and take advantage of it."

"How do you mean 'take advantage of it'?" asked Logan, unable to restrain the caution creeping into his tone. "Accept what?"

"Accept who we are, where we are, and then try to have the very best family we can have."

"I see . . ."

"Like it's been these last few days, Logan."

"They have been wonderful."

"And now that you're going to stay—"

"Allison—"

But she hurried on. unable, or unwilling, to hear her hopes contradicted.

"Logan," she said excitedly, "I've found the perfect job for you—right here in Port Strathy. I've been dying to tell you, but it wasn't confirmed until yesterday."

"You went out and *found* me a job?"

"It wasn't exactly like that," she hurriedly replied. "But I heard that Mr. Thomas, who manages the fish plant, was retiring. I just knew you'd be right for the job, so I spoke to—"

"I already *have* a job, Allison."

"Yes, but this is here, and now that you're staying—"

"That's another thing. Whoever said I was staying?"

"But it only makes sense to—"

"I'll tell you what makes sense," interrupted Logan, the measured calm of his voice finally breaking and giving way to the simmering anger rising within him. "It makes sense that a man finds his own jobs, and that he has some say in where he lives!"

"But I thought—"

"Allison," he said slowly and calmly. He closed his eyes and tried to force the anger from his tone. When he continued, a certain forced gentleness had returned to his voice. He deeply wanted to make her able to understand. "I'm sorry if I let you think that. But I never said we were going to live here. I'm not sure myself what the future holds. But right now I'm doing something I enjoy and I'm not ready to make a change."

"You're never sure! And while you're trying to decide what to do with your life, your daughter and I bounce about never knowing what tomorrow will bring. What kind of life do you think it's been for us?"

"Is that really how it's been for you?"

"Yes."

"But we've been in the same flat in London for years."

"With no sense of permanency. We never could feel settled, for at the drop of a hat you might take a job in South America. We are always on the edge, Logan. I'm always wondering what you're going to be doing next. All I want is a real home."

"No, Allison. All you want is to live here at Stonewycke!"

"Is that so terrible?"

"But don't you see—this is *your* home. It's not mine—or *ours.*"

"Why can't it be yours?"

"Because it's *not* mine! You're the heir, the daughter. I'm nothing but the distant off shoot of a hired hand. I've got to make something of myself—on my own! Don't you see? How else can I stand on my own two feet? I thought you understood that when you married me!"

"I thought I understood a lot of things when we got married."

"What's that supposed to mean?"

"Just that I thought I knew you, that's all."

"Oh, fine! So you wouldn't have married me in the first place if you'd known that some-day I wanted to be a man in my own right, on my own terms! You wanted me to be satisfied tinkering with farm equipment all my life?"

"I didn't say I wouldn't have married you, Logan."

"You just as well as said it! I may not know where everything fits, or exactly what I want to spend the rest of my life doing. But I would certainly expect more loyalty than that from a wife!"

"So it's my fault you can't hold a job?"

"I've held my jobs! And been good at them, too! No thanks to you, always out gallivant-ing around with your society friends."

"You leave my friends out of it! If it weren't for them, I'd have gone crazy in London, thanks to you!"

"You see what I mean? That's some loyalty from a wife!"

"What do you expect when you never talk, don't even tell me what you do?"

"You never showed any interest! Then whenever I did try to say anything about my work, all you did was criticize it and tell me I ought to go back to Stonewycke. Is it any wonder I couldn't find anything that seemed right?"

"If you'd stick to something, maybe it would become right."

"How can I do that when I don't know what it is I want to stick to?"

"Logan, you're thirty-two years old. Don't you think it's time you decided?"

The words tore painfully into Logan, for they exposed a part of him he desperately sought to avoid. Were he to face the full implication of Allison's words honestly, he feared he might have to admit that their problems truly were his fault, stemming from his inability to accept the responsibilities that life had given him. Therefore, he lashed angrily out at her instead.

"And if I don't, if it takes me some time to find the right thing, then you are going to do it for me, is that it? You can't wait for me to make my own way?"

"Oh, Logan, sometimes you can be so immature!"

Had he not been holding baby Joanna in his arms, Logan would at that moment have jumped up and stalked away. But though his entire body was taut, he remained where he was. The child stirred and whimpered restlessly, even though he had fought to keep his voice low. Logan stroked her hair and tried to quiet her; the muscles in his jaw twitched as he clenched his teeth, but he remained silent.

"It's an excellent job, Logan," Allison continued, trying to sound calm, as if to make up for her cruel outburst. "Very well-paying, and not without prestige in this town."

"But I don't *want* it!"

"You just said you don't know what you want," pleaded Allison.

"When are you going to realize that I can't live by the patterns you devise? A man has got to live his own life!"

"I don't understand you!" replied Allison, growing tearful. "Aren't we supposed to want the same things?"

"But you seem to think you're in a better position to determine my future than I am."

"I was just trying to help."

"Don't kid yourself, Allison! You were trying to get me to do what you thought would be best—what would be best for *you*. How many times have you stopped to ask yourself what might be best for *me*?"

"I thought it would be best for you."

"I think you're deceiving yourself. Just because I'm unsure of my future doesn't mean I have to jump to your side of the fence and take anything that's offered."

"I didn't know we were on different sides!"

"Well, the way you treat me like a little child who can't even make his own decision, I don't know what else you'd call it!"

He deposited the baby in her arms, jumped up, and started to walk away. If they hadn't had to drive home together, he would have kept going.

"We can't talk anymore, can we, Logan?" said Allison. Silent tears dropped from her eyes.

"We were doing fine until you started trying to maneuver and manipulate my life." As he spoke he did not turn to face her. He knew his words were only half the truth. Even in the midst of his anger, he knew she was right about two things. She *had* only been trying to help, and he *was* immature. But why couldn't she just accept him like he was and let him find his own help? He was as good a husband as a lot of men. Why couldn't she just lay off?

In the meantime, the child had awakened fully, whining and crying, as if sensing the element of strife that surrounded her.

The once-peaceful afternoon was over. The picnic was packed away in silence, and they departed Letty and Nathaniel Cuttahay's lovely little meadow.

A sense of defeat and loss pervaded the ride home. Not a word was spoken, though neither Allison nor Logan yet fully realized just what they had lost.

12 ✽ A Time for Reflection

LOGAN AND ALLISON entered the great old house together, but as soon as Allison had gone upstairs and disappeared round a corner, probably to have a good cry in some private place, Logan swung around and exited the house.

He left the Austin parked in front—after all, it wasn't *his* car to take at will—and set off on foot. The notion of walking and thinking did not exactly appeal to him, but it beat hanging idly about the old castle. And unfortunately he couldn't stop the flow of whatever might come into his mind. Hopefully if he kept on the go, the thoughts wouldn't get too deep. He'd had enough of that for one day!

He headed off in the general direction of town, though he didn't really care to run into anyone he knew. But maybe after the two-and-a-half-mile trek, he'd be ready for some distractions. He might even check out the action at the Bluster 'N Blow, or down at Hamilton's.

The fine spring day had grown blustery, and an edge of chill accompanied the northeasterly breezes. Only patches of blue could be found in the sky now. Logan hitched his collar up around his neck, remembering as he did so his playful attempt to "impress" Allison earlier at the Lindow. That water would have been cold!

The gesture may have been a foolish one. But Logan had to face it—he did want to impress Allison; he had been trying to do so for the last nine years. She may *say* he didn't have to, but it looked otherwise to him. Why else had she used her influence to get him a job? What other reason was there for her always hounding him about moving back to Stonewycke? His own choices weren't good enough for her.

But were they even good enough for him?

Was his own insecurity about who he was coming back to haunt him? He'd always walked with a cocky step and a confident word on his tongue. But down inside, didn't he really know that he would never measure up alongside this family? He'd been stupid to think he could change, adapt, become one of them. He was a man of the streets, an ex-crook, a card sharp, nothing more than a common confidence man.

Could it ever be different? He had tried. Maybe he could be more respectable, more able to fit into Allison's world, if he could just settle on some definite course for his life. But in all this time he hadn't found anything that "clicked."

Many reasons why flooded his mind. He didn't want to think that they were nothing more than cheap excuses. He had no education, for one thing, and no capital with which to start anything. He could borrow from his in-laws, but that had its drawbacks, especially for one trying to stand on his own. His prison record was terribly limiting, for eight out of ten potential employers wouldn't think of hiring an ex-convict.

Was it his fault he had only one talent, and that that talent happened to function best in areas of somewhat disputable legality? What could a man do? Wasn't God supposed to take care of all that, make him fit in somewhere else?

There must be something out there that could satisfy him as much as his old life had. He had been happy in the old days, happier than he had been at any recent time, that was for sure.

A smile crept onto his face as he thought of some of the antics he and Skittles had carried out. As if it were yesterday, he could still clearly see his dear old friend perched upon a pub stool playing the part of the drunken braggart, challenging any who dared contradict his profound scriptural knowledge. The old Adam and Eve gag had truly been one of the best! Like taking candy from a baby! And with him playing his part of the innocent bystander with cool aplomb, together they had made quite a financial killing.

And there was the ever-faithful accident victim routine, in which Skittles would collapse in front of a car in slow-moving traffic, convincing the unsuspecting driver that he had nearly killed a helpless old man. At the most opportune moment Logan would appear as an eyewitness. After fifteen minutes of Skittles' moaning, the driver was more than willing to make an on-the-spot cash settlement rather than risking a possible lawsuit.

It was not the most original ploy, and used at one time or another by every street hustler worth his salt. But he and Skittles had been one of the best duos around; they had raised the con to the level of an art form.

And there were many others. There was hardly a gambler in London who could match Logan's flair and nimble fingers with a deck of cards. He'd been good, and it had been fun. He couldn't help that.

Intellectually, he knew his old ways were inconsistent with the new life God had given him, and with the life of integrity he had tried to establish since. Yet he couldn't keep from smiling as he recalled those days, nor hold back a sense of disappointment from stealing over his heart as he realized what a failure his supposed "new" life was by comparison. Had it all been an illusion? Had God for some reason not come through for him as He seemed to for others? Was he himself somehow to blame for this failure?

Of course, right now he *did* like what he was doing. It was legitimate, and it even had something of the same thrill as his old lifestyle. Arnie was right; he *was* good at it, tailormade for the job. But what would happen after the war was over? What then? He'd be right back where he began.

Logan came to a small wooden bridge and paused in the middle to watch the tiny stream rush toward the west where it would deposit its winter runoff into the Lindow. The bridge was still fairly new; the flood ten years ago had washed the old one away. He had been so sure of himself back then when he and Allison fell in love, so certain everything would work out perfectly for them.

Was it now time at last to admit that it hadn't, maybe that it couldn't, and cut his losses?

He let out a dry, bitter laugh. *Still the gambler, eh, Logan?* he silently rebuked himself. *Know when to raise, when to hold steady, when to fold.* His strategies worked around the gaming tables; could they be applied to life as well? Was it time to fold, to throw in his cards, admit that it had all been a gigantic mistake?

It seemed that he and Allison had done all they could. Maybe it would be different if they could communicate. But today only proved once again that any attempt to talk about things that mattered only led them back along the same bitter paths of discord. Perhaps it was true, after all, that they both wanted different things in life. How could a man and woman possibly stick together and make a go of it if they had opposite goals? They had struggled for over seven years trying to hang on to the thrill of their initial love, but it had long since worn too thin to sustain them anymore. And if they were going different directions in life, how could they ever hope to regain it?

By now Logan had reached the environs of Port Strathy. He tried to focus his attention on his surroundings. He *had* to get his thoughts going in another direction, for they only seemed to be leading him into a dark abyss, and he dreaded to think what might lie at the end. But the town was quiet at this hour and offered little hope of distraction. The farmers had not yet returned home from the fields, and the fishers were inside resting before their night runs. Many of the men were gone, off to fight in the war, or to lend their services to the more lucrative factories in the south. The war had even changed Port Strathy. When it was over, no doubt many of those very men would not want to return to this slow-paced, poverty-bound northern valley. Others would have no choice but be forever separated from their earthly home. He had heard that the Peters clan had already lost two sons. Jimmy MacMillan, his old fishing and poker cronie, had been killed at Dunkirk. They said he had dragged ten wounded men to safety during the mass evacuation and was going back for more when a mortar struck him down. How many more would die before it ended?

But at least they died honorably, thought Logan morosely. Maybe Jimmy was even a little to be envied. He went off to war and died a hero. His life meant something. And though his loved ones left behind would mourn his passing, they could also swell with pride at the mention of his name. The only use he himself could be was to skulk around in dark alleys. Even if a stray bullet chanced his way and killed him, the military and MI5 and all official agencies would disavow any connection with him in order to protect other agents in the field. He would be a nothing, a nonentity, not a hero. All Allison would get was a letter from some magistrate stating that her husband's body had been discovered, the apparent victim of a street mugging. Everything would fit in her mind too: once a street hoodlum, always a street hoodlum.

"So much for diversion," mumbled Logan glumly.

Unconsciously he struck out on the path leading to the harbor. Maybe a visit with Jesse Cameron would help. But even as the thought came to him and her animated face rose in his mind s eye, he wondered to himself if he really wanted to see the feisty fisherwoman. She certainly would not let him get away with mere superficial chitchat.

No, he couldn't deal with that just now. Instead, he took the street westward. He'd go out on the beach and sit on a lonely sand dune for a while till he got his thoughts straightened out. Right now he didn't want to see anybody!

Passing the harbor and then crossing the wide stretch of flat sandy beach that rose gradually fifty yards inland to rolling dunes, Logan caught the heavy odor of fish from the processing plant. Suddenly the sounds of the machinery inside and the squawking of the perpetual gathering of gulls around the refuse bins invaded his consciousness as well.

Just what he needed! A not-so-subtle reminder of today's blow-up with Allison. A reminder that he didn't *have* to die some inglorious death on a dirty back street in Northampton or Brighton. A reminder that if he would just give in and be what they all expected of him, he could make everyone happy. A reminder that a whole new life awaited him as manager of Port Strathy's major industry. A reminder that if he would only—

But it wasn't what *he* wanted. He shook his head in frustration.

And from his self-centeredness, anger arose to join his feelings of being abused and misunderstood. Did Allison really know him so little that she could think he'd be happy there? *She is the selfish one,* he thought. Her husband couldn't be a war hero, so at least she could make him into a prestigious pillar of the community. *Her* community! To make *her* look good! To give *her* security and contentment.

But what about *him*? What about what *he* wanted? What about his own happiness and sense of worth?

Yet, who could blame her? Everyone would agree that she deserved so much better than what she got, and Logan would be the first to concur. She would have made any of her public school friends proud as their wife. She had been courted by the cream of the crop before he came along. Today, she could have been the wife of a lord or a financier. But instead she was stuck with a nobody, a hoodlum, and worse. She wanted more for him because *she* deserved more. Yet the truth would always be that she would never have more than a second-rate loser for a husband. And there was nothing he could do about it. He was what he was. He couldn't change his past, his common blood, his street-wise ways. He was not one of *them,* never would be, never could be. He was a hustler. He would never be able to fit into Allison's mold, even if he wanted to. Right now he wasn't sure he *did* want to. But even if he did, even if he took the job, even if he became utterly respectable on the outside, it would never change the person he was inside.

Again came the conviction—Allison deserved better. She would be better off without him. Then she could be free. And he could follow his own life without having to carry around the guilt of knowing he didn't measure up to what she needed.

Logan came to an impasse in his thoughts. What to do? They both wanted the other to be happy. There still flowed love between them. Yet each was unable to sacrifice personal goals and personal contentment toward that end. Happiness for the other, yes—but while preserving their own individual goals for life. Was such a thing possible? Probably not.

Why couldn't marriage be that way? Why couldn't *both* people be happy? Why did *one* have to give everything up, lose his identity, in order for the other to be content? It *must* be possible for a marriage to work so that both husband and wife were satisfied. Molly and

Skits had certainly enjoyed that kind of marriage. And he had known others too. What was the secret?

Maybe it all boiled down to whether the marriage was meant to be in the first place. And if not . . . then probably all the scheming in the world wouldn't make it work.

Was that where he and Allison stood at this moment—in a marriage that had never been meant to be in the first place, and was therefore doomed to fail no matter what either of them did? Not a pleasant thought!

Logan sighed, stood slowly, and headed back down the hill of sand the way he had come. Again he avoided the harbor. He couldn't see Jesse right now, or anyone for that matter. He almost wished he had the guts to go down to Roy's in Old Town and get plastered. But he hadn't yet sunk so low as to go out on a drunken binge.

He supposed he should pray. But he couldn't make his mind focus enough for that. All he could see was his pitiful self, his failure as a husband, and the terrible thing he knew he was going to have to do before many more hours had passed.

13 ❋ A Mother's Advice

WHEN SHE AND Logan had parted, Allison rushed upstairs. She gave the child to the nurse, then sought the silence of the library where she could unburden her pain behind stacks of silent, unseeing books.

By the time she emerged some time later, it had grown dark and stormy outside. She heard the steady pelting of rain against the windows, but all throughout the house was quiet. She hadn't been aware of the passage of time and was now unsure how late it was. Had everyone gone to bed? She found herself wondering where Logan was, or if he was still there at all.

Her heart ached at that final thought. She knew she had been wrong to make him angry. But it was such a little thing! Why did he have to be so stubborn, so proud? Allison knew they could be happy here at Stonewycke. Why couldn't he see that! What difference did a job make? Why did he always fly off the handle at any mention of it? Especially when all she was ever trying to do was help! *Being together*—that's what was important. Loving each other. Why couldn't he see that? Why couldn't he—?

She couldn't finish the thought. She had felt certain of his love when he had stepped off the schooner four days ago. But now . . .

Suddenly Allison heard the floor creak behind her. She started and spun around, her heart pounding. But the disappointment was clearly evident on her face when she saw it was not Logan at all.

"There you are, Allison."

"Mother."

"I saw the car in front, but I didn't see you and Logan return," said Joanna. "Dinner will be ready soon."

"I—we . . ." Allison began, but the tears, which had only been checked on the surface, rushed forth again. She bit her lip and screwed her eyes shut, but nothing could stop them from flowing afresh as if the well-springs of her sadness had not abated a drop from the last hour's crying.

"Dear, what is it?" said Joanna, approaching. But she hardly needed to ask the question. She had sensed that her daughter and son-in-law had all along been running from their problems and that sooner or later a painful confrontation must occur. For the moment, however, she said nothing more. She placed an arm around Allison, led her to one of the library chairs. and sat down quietly next to her, comforting her with the nearness of motherly love.

Gradually Allison managed a tearful account of the afternoon. She told her mother everything, from the joyful discovery of the secluded meadow to the final angry outburst of emotion. She ended with the question she had already posed to herself many times.

"Mother, why can't we work things out?"

Joanna knew the reason. But was her daughter ready to hear it?

"Allison," she began, "there has to be some self-sacrifice in a marriage. If you both stubbornly try to hang on to your own personal desires, you might never work things out. People so often mistake what marriage really is all about. It's not *getting*. It's *laying down* your life for the other."

"Well, I've sacrificed plenty!" exclaimed Allison. "I willingly left home and went to London. I've lived in that crummy flat, where my friends are embarrassed to visit me. I've put up with his starting a new job practically every week, and when he's between jobs, living on a budget that makes rationing look like wealth. What has Logan ever sacrificed?"

"Is it truly sacrifice, dear, when you expect something in return?"

"There you go sticking up for him again!" retorted Allison.

"I'm not sticking up for either of you," returned Joanna, her calm, soft-spoken voice rising slightly. "You both just have a lot to learn about marriage, that's all. And about what sacrifice *really* means. You say you love him and he loves you, yet I haven't seen either of you demonstrate the kind of love for each other that Paul says is to characterize a marriage, the kind of love Jesus had for the Church, the kind of love that lays down its life for the other. That's what marriage is—laying down your life, not having things comfortable and how you want them."

"But I've tried so hard, Mother!" replied Allison, breaking into fresh tears.

"Oh, my dear child," said Joanna, taking her weeping daughter into her arms, gently stroking her head. After a few moments she said, "You can't make a marriage work without facing that simple fact of what sacrifice really means. And then you have to ask God to help you do it. It's not easy, Allison—for anyone. It hasn't been easy for me. But God can and will help, once you reach that point of being willing to lay everything down. Only He can give you the strength to do what it might take to heal your relationship. True loving sacrifice goes so against our human grain that it is impossible for us to do alone."

"I've prayed and prayed, Mother." Allison sniffed and wiped her reddened eyes with a handkerchief provided by her mother. "But what's the use, when Logan doesn't care and won't talk about it? I'm sure he doesn't pray about any of it. I'm afraid he's gotten away from his faith. I thought it would only make things worse if I hounded him about it, so I just let it go—maybe I let mine slip too, I don't know. But we are still Christians, Mother. Shouldn't that mean something?"

"Being a Christian is no magic cure-all," answered Joanna. "Especially in a marriage. Belief counts for far less than a willingness to put the other person first. When things happen within us, and the lines of communication break down, God is still there, but we get out of tune to the sound of His voice. Then we give ourselves preeminence over others, and before you know it, some deep problems have set into our lives."

"So then what are you supposed to do?"

"Two things. You have to try to start listening for the quiet sound of God's voice, and be sure to do what He says. And then you have to look for opportunities to put others first, in your case, Logan."

"Oh, but what does it matter, unless Logan is listening to God also? I can't force him to make our marriage work if he doesn't care!"

"It has to start with someone, Allison."

"But why does it always have to be me?"

"I'm sure Logan would think *he's* the one holding it together."

"That's crazy!"

"Maybe to you. But we all think we're being more unselfish than perhaps in reality we are—including Logan, *and* including you. Besides, I believe he still does care, dear. But regardless, it doesn't mean *you* should stop caring."

"Why does it have to be so hard?" said Allison, shaking her head hopelessly. She rose slowly. "I better check on the baby. I don't even know how long it's been since I left her with the nurse."

"Allison," Joanna called hurriedly after her daughter, before she had completely disappeared out the door. "Would it help for the three of us to talk together?"

"I doubt Logan would ever agree to such a thing," Allison replied, and then was gone.

Joanna sat alone in the library for several more moments. It is all so clear! she pondered. How can they be so blind to such an elemental scriptural principle? They were both afraid to admit their own personal responsibility for contributing to their problems and lack of communication. Why was taking responsibility such a fearsome thing? Why was the first instinct always self-defense, followed by laying blame on another?

Yet, what could be worse than watching their marriage destroyed?

Joanna felt the frustration of one who knows that the time for words might well be over. Nevertheless, with deep faith she bowed her head, knowing that time for prayer was never past.

14 ❈ A Season for Parting

SLOWLY LOGAN RETRACED his steps along the sandy shore back toward town.

It was seven-thirty in the morning, and already he had been up for well over two hours. Hardly knowing where else to go, he walked to town in the darkness of pre-dawn, and was on the beach, slowly sauntering along alone with his thoughts as the sun gradually crept up in the east.

In the obscure distance, indistinct through the settled fog, the vague outlines of fishing boats in the harbor could be seen as he approached. High in the sky the fog was thin, showing every promise of burning off as the day advanced. But it clung to the water thickly, lending an eerie quietude to the early morning. The partially visible masts of Port Strathy's fleet resembled some ancient ghostlike wraiths whose bodily mass had mostly vaporized from the face of the earth. All around, the water was still. Not a breath of wind remained from the short-lived storm of the previous night, and through the mist the surface of the sea was almost glasslike until it reached the very shore, where it suddenly curled into activity as the sand came up from underneath to meet it.

Logan observed these things as one unable to focus on their ethereal and yet common beauty. With his eyes he beheld, while his mind was elsewhere.

His future was before him; his past had faded from his memory almost as the boats had faded through the fog. Everything was now, and his decision was a heavy weight, which, sadly, he took it upon himself to bear alone.

Allison had not seen Logan since they parted after returning from their picnic. He had been absent at both dinner and breakfast, and from the look of him one might easily have supposed he had neither eaten nor slept in all that time. His hair was rumpled, his face sported a two-day growth of beard, and the white shirt he wore under a navy sweater vest was creased and wrinkled, as were his slacks. If he had slept, he must have been fully clothed at the time. Dark circles ringed his eyes.

She sat in the family room, making a poor pretense of sewing again. It was an eternal job these days, for no one dared throw out old clothes when new things were so hard to come by. But Allison's thoughts were far too occupied to make much good of her fingers, wartime necessities notwithstanding. She had been alternately mad and worried over Logan, and still, when she looked up and saw him standing there, couldn't quite resolve which of the two emotions to give the upper hand.

It might have eased her anger a little had she known he had passed the night in the stable in his uncle Digory's old room. The thought had never occurred to her, hardly surprising since Logan did not talk much about how deeply special that place had remained to him. From the very beginning, even when he had come as a confidence man out to swindle this family, it had always represented an element of simplicity and purity toward which he might turn—qualities in which he knew he was seriously lacking. Always when he entered that room, he seemed to feel some of the gentle spirit of the old groom, hoping that it might somehow touch him and jar him back to those things that were important and meaningful in life.

It would no doubt have fanned the flames of her anger to have known some of the paths of his thoughts as he sat there alone, however.

The spirit of Digory's old home had done little for him last night. All he had for his efforts was a pounding head, a sore back, and an empty ache in his heart, which his early-morning walk to town and back had done nothing to resolve. Despite his awareness of his own personal shortcomings, he could not keep from blaming Allison for her independent attitude and her lack of support. His was not a healthy mind-set for reconciliation.

Allison could see from his face that he had come seeking her.

For a moment neither said a word. Unconsciously both seemed to know what was coming next, but neither could open their mouths to speak. It was, after all, Logan who had arrived at the decision and made the effort to come find her, and it was he, therefore, who first broke the silence.

"Allison," he said, "there is no way I can take that job." His mouth had gone dry as cold ashes. That wasn't what he had planned to say, but the other words stuck in his throat.

"It was wrong of me to try to force it on you. I'm sorry."

"I understand. There are things you want, and that you ought to have, and it's not possible for me—"

"I only want us to be happy again."

"Do you really think that's possible anymore?"

"Yes, it is!" she insisted in an imploring tone. "It doesn't matter where—here or in London. You'll find the right job. You don't need my help."

"But you're forgetting, I already have a job."

"What kind of job must it be that you can't even tell me what it is?" said Allison, her irritation gaining the upper hand at the prick of an old wound.

"I thought it didn't matter to you as long as we were happy," he rejoined, sharply poking at a sore spot within him.

"How can I be happy when I know you don't trust me enough to tell me what you're doing—when I live in fear that it's so bad you are ashamed to tell me?"

"I've told you over and over that it's nothing like that," he answered. "You're the one without any trust!"

"No trust!" exclaimed Allison, incredulous. "I left my home and went to London with you, didn't I?"

"Ha! Left your home, but you remind me of the fact every week. And even so, you keep doubting me. Because I was once a con, you will always doubt me."

"And you blame me, when you hide from me what you're doing? What else am I supposed to think?"

"I don't know what you're supposed to think. All I know is that trust has got to start with you."

"Me! Why does it always have to start with me?"

"Because a wife has got to trust her husband."

"And a husband doesn't have to trust his wife? What kind of a partnership is that?"

"I never said marriage was a partnership."

"Oh, I see! So it's a dictatorship, where the husband rules the roost, is that it?"

"I didn't say that, either! You know me better than that."

"Do I? Sometimes I wonder!"

"What's that supposed to mean?"

"It means I just don't think I know you anymore, Logan. You don't trust me, but don't think there's anything wrong with it. Yet you expect blind trust out of me. Hardly a fair arrangement, if you ask me!"

"All I know is that if a wife doesn't trust her husband, there's nothing left between them. Trust has got to start with the wife. Maybe my past makes that impossible for you. But I just know I can't live with it anymore."

Allison was silent, fuming, angry, hurt, wanting to yell at him and hold him all at once. In her confusion she sat speechless. Logan stood before her stiff and awkward, wanting also to hold her, but knowing the time for that had passed.

"It's more than just a lack of trust," he finally went on, painfully forcing each word from his lips. "I realized it for the first time yesterday, though it's been there all along. We want different things. We're going different directions in life. We have different goals, different needs, different expectations. I suppose I was just never meant to be the kind of family man you want and need. I'm sorry for all that. I wanted to be. I tried to be. But it's just not working—"

"Logan, no."

"Please, Allison, let me finish."

"No, I won't! I know what you're going to say, and it's not right!" She jumped up and looked directly into his eyes. "I still love you, and I know you still love me, Logan. And that's all that is important."

"I'm not even sure of that anymore."

"I don't believe it!"

"Sure, maybe part of us still has that love, but if neither of us can trust each other, if we can't talk about anything without arguing, then what does it matter? Love or not, it's falling apart. You must see that."

"We can make it work," said Allison. "If you could only see that I want so badly to trust you."

"There we are again," replied Logan. "If only *I* could see. You *want* to trust me. But admit it—you don't." He turned and walked to the stone hearth where a fire sent rays of warmth into the room. He could face her no longer. "I think we need some time apart," he finally added.

"We've already been separated for months," Allison protested lamely, "and what good has it done?"

"That was different. For this past year we've been deceiving ourselves into thinking it was nothing but the inconvenience of wartime. It's time we faced reality. We're no good for each other. Not now. We're cut out of different cloth. Reality—do you understand me? No fairy tale romances, but reality. This time there may be no passionate dockside reunion."

"How can I understand what you are saying? This is all so ridiculous. I love you and you still love me. There *has* to be some other way."

"Allison, you have to start looking at things as they really are, not how you *want* them to be. You want to think that a kiss and hug and a few apologies will cure everything. But then what happens the next time I come home with a new job, or the next time you get irritated at me because you can't stand our flat? What then? To make this work, a lot of changes would have to happen. And I haven't heard you say a word about changing. I'm not sure you're willing to change that much. I know I've got lots of problems in this relationship. Probably most of them, for all I know. I realize I'm not as communicative about my work as you'd like. I'm aware of a lot I've done wrong. But right now I don't know if I can change who I am. And I'm at the point that I know when to quit kidding myself. Allison, it's just not going to work, don't you see?"

"Logan, I know we have problems—"

"Until last night, I never thought I'd be saying this," he interrupted. He closed his eyes. Each word was an agony of effort. "Allison," he continued, "I'm leaving . . ."

He forced his eyes open. It was too cowardly to say such a thing without looking directly at her. "I pray it won't be forever, but we both have to face that possibility."

"I won't let you do this!" she cried.

"Allison, don't. You have to believe me when I say that I truly consider this the best thing I could do for you."

"How could it be?"

"You'll be free of me, free of the heartache, free of the problems. You'll finally be able to be the person you should be."

He dropped his gaze, turned, and walked from the room.

With each step he took, Allison wanted to run after him, grab him, somehow force him to stay. But she stood still as stone, huge tears of grief silently welling up from within her and overflowing her eyes.

Was it pride that kept her rooted to the floor? Or was it the awful certainty that he meant what he said, and that nothing she could do would be able to stop him in the end?

15 ✠ *Final Interview*

JOANNA REREAD HER letter from Alec.

This was not the first time they had been parted. There had been an earlier war. But they had a granddaughter now, and Alec was too old for this sort of thing. She wished he'd never volunteered.

Somehow it seemed she should be immune, but the pains of war were to be borne not only by the young. The old, perhaps, carried even more than their share. Especially mothers and fathers. She wished Alec were here, yet she was proud that he had not fallen back on his age as an excuse to exempt him from serving his country. When his old regiment had been called up, desperate for veteran officers, he had jumped to the call immediately. A few months ago he had been promoted to full colonel for his heroism while in Libya during the taking of Bardia and Tobruk, notable British victories in North Africa. Maybe she didn't wish he hadn't volunteered; he was a man to be proud of. Unfortunately, Bardia and Tobruk were to be among the last British victories in Africa for some time. She couldn't help being anxious.

Alec said nothing in his letter about his heroism or exploits. Joanna could sense immediately that his normal robust optimism was missing. He was a natural leader of men. But it was not in his nature to lead them to their deaths. The weight of the burden was bearing down upon him.

He asked Joanna, as he always did, for her prayers. But now even the scrawl of his handwriting seemed to bear the signs of desperate entreaty. He had made an obvious attempt to lighten the letter with a humorous account of his attempt to purchase a gift for Joanna in an Arab bazaar in Cairo. It had been a wild farce in two languages, each at top pitch. Alec had been more than willing to pay the original asking price until his guide reminded him not to offend the seller by doing thus. Even at the end, once all the dust had settled and he found himself walking away from the booth with the desired item in hand, he was not sure whether he had come away with a bargain, or had himself been taken. But it hardly mattered; he had offended the man anyway, for as he walked away he heard the Egyptian spit at his back. He was sure, however, that it had nothing to do with the sale.

"Joanna," he wrote, "these people hate the British as much, probably more, than they do the Germans. I guess they *know* what we are like—they have had a hundred years of our tyranny—and they can't believe the Nazis could be worse. It's all so ironic, yet we fight on here. But I doubt the British Empire will survive this war, even if we somehow are able to win. And that seems so doubtful as I write."

He went on to say, for the tenth or twentieth time, that he missed her, that he longed for a time to sit and talk over with her all the experiences and sensations he was encountering daily. "This land is so foreign," he added at the end. "The people are indeed mysterious, but no less so than I must appear to them. Yet I also feel a strange kinship with these Arabs. Is it because it was here, in this ancient part of the world, that God chose to live out His human existence? I think I am coming to understand so much better many things I read in His Word. Oh, I have so much to share with you. but how can I possibly write it all on paper? I need you, and yet I can't say how much longer it will be until we are together. This war is far from over, my dearest. Sometimes I fear it has only begun. But God sustains me. In the words of Paul, *I am troubled on every side, yet not distressed; perplexed, but not in despair; persecuted, but not forsaken; cast down, but not destroyed!"*

A tear fell from Joanna's eye onto the paper. She quickly brushed it away so as not spoil the ink. Who knew when the next precious letter might come? These little pieces of paper with the familiar writing on them were now the most treasured of her possessions.

She wiped at the stubborn flow from her eyes, picked up her own pen, and took a clean sheet from the desk at which she sat in her great-grandmother Atlanta's own dayroom. A bright, crackling fire blazed warmth upon her, almost making her forget the chill that had come over the land outside.

She wrote in the fine hand her husband had always admired, and for which he would scan each day's bag of envelopes as if ten thousand pounds were waiting in the one addressed in the proper hand.

My dearest Alec,

I have read your letter a dozen times and more in the week since I received it. Each word is almost as precious to me as the memory of your own dear face. Your final words have given me so much encouragement. Isn't that typical? Here you are at war, facing who knows what dangers, while I am safe in our dear old Stonewycke. Yet it is you who are encouraging me. It is cold outside, but a cheery fire helps me to keep my spirits up. We have had rain, then warm sun, then a chilling, all in twenty-four hours. Our beloved Scotland's weather, you know! What you wouldn't probably give for some of our cold! Oh, Alec, I love this old place, this dear Stonewycke! Sitting here brings me such peace sometimes. There is a heritage . . . a legacy to this place that makes me feel part of ancient truths, ancient people, roots and strengths that extend far beyond my own vision.

I feel something of the same thing being married to you. For you, dear Alec, are like Stonewycke in so many ways—strong, solid, immovable.

You bring me strength, you have loved me so, you have helped make me who I am by believing in me, loving me, trusting me, and giving yourself for me. *You* are my Stonewycke— my peace, my heritage. Though I forget all else, I will never cease to thank God for you, my dear! I cannot imagine life without you.

Events of late have made me more aware than ever of the special gift He has given us, and especially of the sacrifices of love you have made for me. You know of the struggles of Allison and Logan. I fear their floundering relationship is not improving. I pray there is some truth to the adage that things are always darkest just before the dawn. I know that God must have brought them together for a purpose—

Joanna glanced up from her desk at the soft tap on the dayroom door. She laid down her pen and turned.

"Come in," she said.

Logan's appearance was considerably improved since his encounter with Allison several hours earlier. He had bathed, combed his hair, and shaved. He wore a tweed suit, fresh white shirt and necktie. In his hand he held the checkered cap that had once belonged to his old friend Skittles, and over his arm was slung a woolen overcoat. Joanna realized immediately that he was dressed for travel, though even without the clothes she would have been able to read in his eyes and by his demeanor that he had come to say goodbye.

"I hope I'm not disturbing you, Lady Joanna," he began formally.

"Not at all," answered Joanna. "Would you care to sit down?"

"I think I'll stand, if you don't mind." He paused, shifting his hat to his other hand and took a deep breath before continuing. "I did not want to leave without seeing you first."

"You are leaving, then?"

"Yes, I'm afraid so."

"I'm sorry your visit must be so short. I sense this wasn't in your plan."

"No, it wasn't, Lady Joanna. You see, Allison and I—"

He stopped, raising his eyes momentarily to the high-vaulted ceiling. Joanna could tell he was on the very edge of self-control, desperately fighting to retain his grasp on his emotions.

"It's not working out between us," he went on, blurting out the words and forgetting his formality. "I came to you today because I want you to understand that the last thing I would ever want to do is hurt Allison. I don't take lightly—"

He stopped, unable to continue. Sensing his emotion, Joanna rose and went to him. She took his arm and gently led him to the sofa where she urged him to sit. She took the place beside him and laid her hands on his, which were cold and trembling.

"You don't plan to come back, do you, Logan?" she said at length.

"I don't know." He closed his eyes, squeezing back tears. "I would still like to believe in miracles, Joanna. But I doubt one is possible in this case. Our wants and needs are so different, and we can't even talk civilly about it. I'm sure the fault is mine, but what can I do? I've tried to change, to be the kind of husband she wants. But she deserves something more, and it would have been better for me never to have married her in the first place."

"But you *did* marry, Logan," said Joanna. "You have a child. You opened yourself to those responsibilities. This isn't a game of cards where you can throw in your hand if things fail to go your way." She saw him visibly wince at her apt analogy. "The last thing I want to do is speak harshly to you when you are hurting. Believe me, I feel for the pain you are going through. And it's hardly in my nature to criticize. But since it seems that for now I'm the only one left, then I must speak clearly to you."

"I deserve everything you have to say," Logan replied contritely. "I can't help it if I'm not made for the kind of life Allison wants. And because of my mistake, it's making us both miserable."

"There are no mistakes with God. Marriage is a unity, Logan, a symbol of the unity that is to exist between believers and their Lord. Do you know what unity is? It's not like and like. It's a joining of opposites. It's not unity unless there is diversity coming together. That's what marriage is meant to be—diversity, differences that come together and join as one."

"But we're *too* different!"

"There's no such thing as *too* different. The greater the differences, the greater the unity, therefore the greater the love."

"It's no use, Joanna. What you say may be right. But we're *not* unified."

"That's true, but not because the marriage was a mistake but because the two of you aren't committed to making it work, to achieving the unity God intended in the face of your very diverse personalities."

"But how long are we supposed to go on being miserable?"

"You think being unhappy is a valid excuse for breaking a sacred vow?"

"That's not fair, Joanna," replied Logan. "You make it sound like I'm slapping God in the face because I'm admitting that Allison and I can't get along."

"That's exactly what you're doing. *He's* the one who brought you together, and now you're turning your back on something that was clearly His doing."

"But I can't believe God expects us to go through the rest of our lives in misery just because we made the mistake of getting married in the first place."

"I told you, there are no mistakes with God. You both gave your future to Him, and your marriage was the result. But even if it was a mistake, once married, your marriage then became part of God's perfect plan for each of you. You can't go back and undo it. He has already taken up your marriage, drawn it into His plan. It is now the same as if He had intended it all along. So even if I admit to its being a mistake back then—which I don't—it is still a more serious mistake to turn your back on it now. Logan, maybe there are times when dissolving a marriage seems to be a tragic necessity. Only God knows. But I do know that, contrary to how freely men and women—even Christians—allow their marriages to break up, God's plan is for reconciliation, not separation. He ordained marriage, and He intends for husbands and wives to stay together. Don't make the mistake of disobeying God's command for the sake of a little temporal happiness."

"So you think God expects people to be miserable just to stick together even if they no longer love each other?"

"I don't know what God expects," replied Joanna. "But I do know that His people are not free to choose the kind of life they think best suits them. Your life is no longer your own. As a Christian you are no more at the center of the decision-making process. God's instructions must take preeminence. Then we must put others ahead of ourselves. That is always God's way. I would say the very same thing to Allison. The life of the Christian is a life of denying yourself—there can be no true happiness without that.

"To answer your question, no, I don't think God wants us miserable. But love has far less to do with marriage than most people think. People say they no longer love each other and use that as an excuse for walking away from a marriage. But love has nothing to do with it. It's a matter of obedience. Are they going to obey the Lord, or not? Are they going to commit themselves to the marriage, in obedience to God, or not? People were making a go of ordinary— even dull—marriages for centuries before this modern notion of *being in love* became such a part of it. People back then understood commitment. They understood that every marriage relationship has its problems and you make the best of it. People nowadays understand so little about what marriage really means at its core. And I'm afraid so do you, Logan. Every marriage is hard. Every two people are incompatible in many ways. A happy marriage is not one that doesn't have those things, but one where you learn to put the other first and thus use those incompatibilities as opportunities for serving your mate. That's what makes a marriage work."

"Well maybe I'm just not cut out for that," said Logan. "You might be right. But maybe I don't have what it takes either for marriage *or* for being a Christian. I only know I can't be happy until I figure out just where Logan Macintyre belongs!"

"But don't you see? You'll *never* be happy while putting yourself first. That's not the way happiness works. The world is upside-down from God's way. The only path to happiness, Logan, is by giving yourself, sacrificing yourself, for others—even for Allison. There just is no happiness apart from that. There's only more misery with yourself as ruler of your own life."

"But what about Allison? She's unhappy, too. She can't be content while I'm trying to figure out what I'm supposed to do. I'm doing this for her as much as myself."

"Oh, Logan, don't fool yourself. The best thing for Allison is for you to be by her side. If you're going to do this, then at least be man enough to take responsibility for it on your own shoulders. That's nonsense about it being for Allison's best. There is only one best for a couple, and that's for each to lay down his life for the other."

"Okay! It's selfish of me. It's my decision. I hate myself for it, but right now I can't see any other way!" As he spoke, he pulled himself to his feet.

Joanna knew the conversation was over. She rose also after a brief awkward pause, then put her arms around him in a loving, motherly hug.

"Logan, I will always love you as a son. But in that love I must honestly tell you that God will not let you off so easily. His love is too great to do that. You can turn your back on it now, but because of His loving grace, He *will* one day bring you back to face this again."

Tears had gathered in the corners of Logan's eyes, but he walked to the door in silence and did not allow them to overwhelm him. Once there, he paused, and turned back to his mother-in-law.

"Goodbye, Joanna."

She could see the struggle within him. He turned again, and hurried out the door, as though he might lose his resolve if he hesitated any longer. But when the door clicked shut, it seemed to announce that, for now at least, the time for reflection, for self-evaluation, and for repentance was past.

Tearfully Joanna returned to her desk. But she could not bring herself to write the kind of letter due a struggling soldier at war. Then she recalled the words of hope that Alec had quoted: *Perplexed, but not in despair . . . cast down, but not destroyed.*

Was I too hard on Logan? she wondered. She had certainly not said what he wanted to hear. Yet he had to be told the truth, hard or not. No good could come of glossing over it. Perhaps the day would come when her words would come back to his mind, and perhaps then they would penetrate deep enough to have impact. For now, there was but one thing she could do.

Joanna fell to her knees beside the sofa. To the Source of hopeful promises she would turn in prayer. Her Lord would sustain her, and more, He would not allow Logan to be destroyed by his own self-will. Her prophetic final statement to her son-in-law was more than mere words. She had spoken the truth. God would not let go of His dear child.

16 ❈ Training

THE DARK ROOM suddenly blazed with light.

Logan had been sleeping heavily, and in the first moments, seemed only able to respond in slow motion. He lifted his head from his pillow. Men were pushing their way into his room. To his groggy senses they sounded like an army. Well-armed as the intruders were, however, there were but three of them.

"Get up!" one of them shouted.

Clumsily Logan swung his feet out of bed.

"Qu'est-ce que c'est? What is this?" he asked in French, his voice still thick with sleep.

"Who are you?" demanded the man who had spoken before, belligerently ignoring Logan's question.

Logan propped his elbows on his knees and rubbed his face with shaky hands. "Maurice Baudot . . ." he said sluggishly. "Je m'appelle Maurice Baudot," he repeated, as if with more certainty.

"D'où venez-vous?"

"Avignon . . . I'm from Avignon." Logan rubbed his eyes and tried to shake the sleep from his head.

"What is your business here?"

"I am a wine merchant . . ."

All at once his interrogator's cruel look faded into a smile. He handed his rifle to one of his companions and drew up a chair, which he proceeded to straddle comfortably.

"You forgot that we changed your occupation last night," said the man, now in a friendly voice. "Otherwise, not a bad show. You even remembered to reply in French, which is not easy for a Britisher waking from a dead sleep."

"Thanks," said Logan indifferently. "Now can I go back to sleep?" He was already halfway to his pillow.

"And I loved your groggy act," chuckled the man. "Sometimes the quickest tip-off is a steady flow of answers that are *too* well rehearsed."

"You call that an *act*!" said Logan, "after you had me traipsing over twenty-five miles of mountains yesterday followed by four hours of deciphering instructions?"

The early morning intruder was one of Logan's Special Operations instructors, and their exchange one of many such mock-up exercises. In the intelligence training course that Logan had begun three months earlier, he could never tell from which direction his readiness was to be assaulted next. The course was nearly at its conclusion, and he had been made proficient in a variety of activities, from blowing up bridges to walking down a street looking as inconspicuous as possible. He was nearly ready to set out on the path he had chosen.

It was odd. He had never actually made a conscious decision to take Arnie up on his offer. When he had left Allison at Stonewycke, he had headed aimlessly south. He spent a few days in

Glasgow, and, though his mother was undemanding, requiring of him no tedious explanations, he soon could not bear the quiet, pensive atmosphere the visit seemed to thrust upon him. He didn't want to think of anything. At least not so soon. He had to keep moving, and so before many days had elapsed he had said farewell to his childhood home, and was on the road again.

It took him two drifting weeks to reach London, and the first stop he made was at Arnie's office. He had never said to himself, "I'm going to London and take that job." But perhaps he knew all along that that's what he was eventually going to do. For one thing, the danger of the assignment no longer troubled him. Perhaps he felt, without knowing it, that he had less to live for now. When he walked into Arnie's office, all he wanted to do was get away, to forget. What better way to do so than in the shadowy, unreal world of the espionage game?

As soon as his visitors departed, Logan fell quickly back to sleep. If nothing else, during the last months he had been kept too exhausted to think of anything beyond the rigors of the training. Some time soon he would turn his attentions back toward his problems with Allison. But for now, he was just too tired.

When Logan completed his training a week later, he was entitled to a leave before entering the field. He wanted none of that, however, and requested an immediate assignment. Thus, before the week was out, he found himself standing before one Major Rayburn Atkinson on a secret RAF air base in the south of England.

Atkinson, a career man in the regular army, was the consummate military personality. He had received three field promotions during the Great War, and the Victoria Cross for heroism during the second Battle of the Marne in 1918. It seemed as though the second "war to end all wars" would prove his swan song, however, for at its very beginning at Dunkirk, Atkinson received wounds resulting in a left arm amputation and a blinded left eye. But he was not the kind of man to be easily placed out of the action on some dusty shelf. He fought the military bureaucracy as valiantly as he did the Germans, and it was not long after his recovery that a place was found in this vital department of Intelligence. He was now the key liaison between agents and their government. It was his responsibility to apprise agents of their assignments, and see to it that they were properly equipped for their tasks. In short, a good many of the agents sent on dangerous missions into enemy territory depended on Major Atkinson for their very lives.

It would not have been difficult for Logan to find himself intimidated by this iron-willed man, and Atkinson seemed determined to do just that. He sat, stiff-backed, behind his desk, his pinned-up sleeve seeming more a badge of honor than of shame. The black patch over his left eye said as much as the steel-gray right eye, which spoke of boldness, courage, and not a little defiance.

"I see you finished training only less than a week ago," he said in a voice that was no less commanding despite its low volume.

"Yes, sir," Logan replied, standing at attention in front of the desk, with all the respect this old soldier deserved.

"You refused the leave to which you were entitled?"

"Yes, sir. I had just had a lengthy leave three months earlier."

"Your record indicates you have a wife."

"Yes, sir."

"Yet you turned down a leave prior to embarking on a dangerous assignment from which no one can be certain you will return."

"I've waited a long time to get actively involved in the war," said Logan somewhat defensively. "I doubt that it will wait for me forever."

"I've seen many an eager soldier in my day, lad, and none who were healthy and red-blooded as you appear to be were ever known to miss a chance to be with their wives or lovers before shipping out unless something was amiss at home."

Logan did not reply. He had no desire to elaborate on his marital problems with this officer whom he barely knew.

"It is one thing for a regular soldier to hit the battlefield with problems on the home front occupying his mind," said the major. "But for one in your position, it could prove nothing less than suicide."

"I assure you, Major, I know where my duty lies, and I am fully able to keep my concentration on my job."

"Well it is *my* duty to insure that any escaping is done from the other end," Atkinson said firmly, though his voice never rose above its original soft tone. "That's not what this unit is about. Do you understand?"

"I understand, sir."

Atkinson leaned back in his swivel chair, and for a long moment allowed his eye to move up and down in a thorough examination of this would-be agent standing before him.

"I seriously wonder if you do, Macintyre."

"Sir?"

"I'm going to be frank with you, young man," he said, then paused.

He leaned forward, his eye still focused on Logan, though now it rested only on his face, intently probing Logan's eyes. Logan did not flinch, though he desperately wanted to look away. He didn't want to betray the anger rising within him.

"I have my doubts about you, Macintyre," continued the major. "To put it succinctly, I don't think you have what it takes for this job."

"Meaning no disrespect, sir," answered Logan, "but it would have been nice if someone would have mentioned that before I *successfully* completed three months of training."

"For one thing, Macintyre, screening volunteers is not my job. If it were, you can be certain I would have voiced my doubts. For another thing, as far as your success during training is concerned, I believe it would be a small enough matter for a man of your diverse talents and background to succeed in such a situation. I think you would understand my meaning if I used the old expression 'bluff your way through.' But I don't believe you are tough enough to succeed in a *real* situation."

"I had to survive on the streets before I was ten years old."

"You lack discipline," countered Atkinson. "And you lack staying power. According to your record, the only thing you've ever done that's lasted longer than a year is your marriage—and now it appears as if that is failing also. How can we be certain that you won't get out there where it can be rough, and decide it's too much for you? Or worse, what if you get captured? How long could you hold up under torture?"

"Can any man truly answer those questions, Major?"

"It helps to have a sound track record."

"Does this mean you're going to blackball me?"

"If Major Kramer hadn't so highly recommended you, yes. I'd tell you to go back to I-Corps and continue with the work you were doing for them. But I've known Arnold a long time, and I respect his opinion."

Atkinson opened a folder that had been lying in front of him and leafed quickly through several pages. "It says here you were classified as a sharpshooter during training."

"I guess I did something right," replied Logan, forgetting himself in the relief of apparently being accepted—though reluctantly—by this hard-nosed army major.

Atkinson opened his desk drawer and took out a small automatic pistol. Before Logan even had a chance to wonder what was coming next, the major tossed the weapon in Logan's direction. Logan reacted swiftly and caught it in one smooth motion.

"Tell me something, Macintyre—have you ever *killed* anyone?"

Logan's mind froze in place for a moment as he stared down at the major's gun. He was thinking of the last time—besides his training—when he had held a similar weapon. He had been sitting in a deserted cottage holding a pistol on one of Chase Morgan's men. He had to keep the man prisoner long enough to allow Allison to get safely away. The only problem was that he was himself slowly succumbing to a serious wound. But he had threatened Lombardo that he would kill him if he tried anything. Logan's threat, however, was never to be proven, for he passed out and the hoodlum escaped, fortunately not in time to overtake Allison. Logan had never touched a gun either before or after that moment. He had never physically harmed anyone in his life. He'd never even been involved in a common fistfight. He'd always used his mouth, and had managed to talk his way out of many jams. He'd recently been exposed to hand-to-hand combat techniques during his training, but that was different, and the major knew it. Steadily he returned the man's gaze, then said, "No, I haven't."

"You probably think I'm a real hard case, don't you, Macintyre?"

Logan pointedly did not respond.

"There's a reason for that," the major went on. "I'm responsible for the men I send out. I don't like to lose any—even cocky con men. Unfortunately, I lose too many just from the natural hazard of the job. But as much care as I try to take, I still have trouble sleeping at night. There's no way I could send out an incompetent."

"Will you allow me to be frank with you, Major?" asked Logan steadily.

Atkinson nodded solemnly.

"I have spent more than half my life defying the law," Logan began resolutely, "and more time in jail for it than I care to admit. There used to be a noble character or two in my family— at least on one side of it. I have one ancestor who was held in rather high esteem by some pretty grand people. But in less than half a lifetime I've managed to disgrace the whole lot. And when I tried to establish some kind of honest life, I royally botched the job. Now I've got a chance to change all that. Well, Major, you were right when you said that it would have been easy for me to bluff my way through SOE training. But I'm not bluffing about this—"

Logan's gaze momentarily turned hard and serious. "I don't plan to disgrace my family again. I intend to bring some honor to the name of Logan Macintyre or—"

"Die trying?" interjected Atkinson.

"If that's what it takes."

There followed a long, heavy silence.

Logan could say no more. It was up to the major now. If only he could read that steely gray eye.

At length the major lifted a thick brown paper packet from his desk. He hefted it in his hand, apparently in thought, for a few seconds, then handed it out to Logan.

"This is your assignment," he said.

Logan reached across the table and took the packet in his hand and began to open it.

"You will commit the contents to memory," said Atkinson. "We will be sending one million francs with you to be distributed to various contacts as indicated in the papers you are now holding. You will be dropped by parachute some forty miles north of Paris. Your contact is Henri Renouvin in the city. His address and code identification phrases are all in there." He cocked his head to indicate the packet. "Renouvin's network just lost its radio operator, so, since you fared well enough in that area during training, one of your duties will be to train a new one for them. Their radioman was captured, so we are also sending new codes—it's far too much to memorize; you'll have to carry them. But you don't want to be caught with them on you. The organization there has taken quite a bit of battering lately, so we'll be looking for you to pull them back together."

Atkinson paused to hand Logan another smaller envelope. "In here you'll find your French identity card, travel permit, ration book, and one hundred thousand francs for your personal use. Your cover name is Michel Tanant. From here on out you are to erase Logan Macintyre from memory. He no longer exists. You are now a bookseller from Lyon. Your cover is convenient in that Renouvin owns a bookstore in Paris, and thus your contact with him will not arouse undue suspicion. You will have a day or two to completely familiarize yourself with Tanant's background. I've instructed your training officer to devise some drills and tests for you so that by the time your life is on the line, his identity will be ground into you deeper than your own. From now on, your final training is to be taken with the utmost seriousness. No more bluffs, Macintyre. It's deadly serious. Do I make myself clear?"

Logan nodded.

"There is one other item in that envelope you ought to be aware of—a cyanide tablet. I believe you know what to do with that, though I pray you'll never have to use it. Oh, this is for you also."

He took something from his desk drawer, and when he held his hand out, Logan saw a lieutenant's star. "You can't wear this, or even take it with you, but the title is official nonetheless. You're hardly regular army, but you'll no doubt be dealing from time to time with escaped British POW's and other personnel, and we felt some rank would serve you well— not to mention its usefulness should you ever be captured."

Logan stared quietly at the gold star before taking it. Until this moment he had not wanted to believe he was officially in His Majesty's Armed Services. Suddenly he was an officer.

"Have you any questions?" asked the major.

"Dozens," replied Logan, "but probably none that you need answer, or would care to."

"Well, read through and memorize your material first. It ought to fill in the gaps. Then report back here day after tomorrow. I'm afraid I can't give you more time than that. We'll have our final briefing then. There will be a Whitley bomber ready for you that evening."

"I'll be ready by then."

Atkinson leveled his gaze once more on Logan. "Yes . . . I think you just might be." He paused a moment, still riveting his single eye straight ahead.

"I don't know whether to like you or not, Macintyre," he finally added. "But in either case, I wish you the best. You just might make it, after all."

He stood and extended his hand.

The gesture, preceded as it had been by the softly spoken words, were the only acquiescence he gave that perhaps he was slowly gaining faith in this untried, unproven would-be spy.

17 ❄ The Drop

BRIGHT STARS DOTTED the clear night sky.

It was a perfect night for flying, but Logan secretly wished for a few more clouds to cover the lone parachute that would soon be floating down from the heavens to the earth below. Not a few agents more experienced than he were captured the instant their feet touched the ground. Logan did not want to be one of them.

Crouched over the opening of the Whitley's fuselage, at about six hundred feet in the air, Logan could just barely make out some of the distinct features of the landscape below. He caught a glimpse of one or two farmhouses, but because of the blackout and the fact that it was three a.m., he couldn't tell whether they were occupied or deserted. He hoped he would not have need of them, for a small reception committee was to meet him at the drop site to see that he got safely on his way to Paris. Beyond the farmhouses, Logan saw a stretch of open countryside, fringed with a belt of trees.

"We're goin' t' try an' land ye close t' that clump o' trees, so ye willna be far frae cover," came the voice of the plane's navigator from behind where Logan sat.

"Not *too* close, I hope," said Logan. He could not keep his knees from trembling a bit at the thought of the jump that lay ahead, but the warmly familiar burr of the navigator's Scottish accent helped soothe his natural fear. The fact that the navigator happened to be a fellow countryman was perhaps a small blessing, but a blessing nonetheless. "By the way," added Logan, "I'm from Scotland too."

"I thought I heard a wee bit o' the Glaswegian in yer tone, but no enocht, t' be sure. Ye been awa too lang, laddie!"

"Yes, perhaps I have," mused Logan.

"Noo," continued the navigator good-naturedly, "ye needna worry aboot oor pilot's aim. He's one o' the best, an' he'll see that ye land as gently as if ye were one o' his ain bairns—an' Joe's got three o' them, so he kens what he's aboot!"

Logan smiled. "I've a child of my own back home," he said. It felt good to get his mind momentarily off what he was about to do.

"Do ye noo?" The navigator's ruddy face spread into a warm grin. "Weel, he'll have good reason t' be prood o' ye when he sees ye next."

"It's a she . . . my daughter."

With each word, Logan's tone grew with pride. Perhaps he did not think of himself as a father often enough.

"Weel, in that case, ye better make good an' certain ye jump clear o' them trees!"

Then came the pilot's shout: "Get ready!"

Logan had made four practice jumps in training. But they had not become easier with repetition. The supreme moment of terror when he had to leap out into thin air, certain each time that he would meet his death, was a fear far beyond any he had ever known on the ground. It was a totally unnatural thing for a man to do. Those practice jumps had been the most paralyzing experiences of his life, no matter that each lasted only about fifteen seconds from the moment he left the plane to the instant his body hit the ground. And they had been done on lighted, well-secured fields in England. His reception committee of French resistance fighters couldn't guarantee that they'd be able to use any lights, and from the dark look of the ground below, Logan had to assume he was going to have to jump blind. Not knowing where the ground was in a fall of twenty feet per second could result in two broken legs—or worse.

Logan sat on the edge of the bomb port, his legs dangling outside the plane. He double-checked his rubber helmet and body pads, and made sure his small suitcase was firmly attached to his pack. Then the navigator attached his parachute strap to the static line. If all went well, the weight of his body would automatically open the chute. If it didn't, he'd have to grab the cord himself and hope for the best.

"She's in tiptop shape," assured the navigator, as if he had read Logan's thoughts.

"Go!" cried the pilot from the cockpit.

Logan could not hesitate a moment now, for even a delay of two or three seconds could carry him miles off course and most likely into the trees.

"I hate this . . ." he breathed, as he let his body slip through the port.

"God bless ye, laddie!" shouted the navigator, but Logan only heard the words fading quickly away from him as if in a dream.

The draft of the plane threw him violently back, and that jolting was followed almost immediately by a hard jerk on his armpits. The chute had opened safely—as they usually did.

If jumping from the plane had been terrifying, then those next few seconds made up for it slightly. With the deafening racket of the plane's engines quickly fading into the distance, suddenly Logan was surrounded by a deep ethereal silence. The overwhelming sense of peace and well-being was almost so great as to make the terror of jumping worth it. Unfortunately, it was all too brief.

As much as he would have liked the silent sensation of floating weightless to go on and on, time was ticking rapidly away in unforgiving seconds, not eons, and he had to force his attention to the earth, slanted away below him. He thought he caught a brief glimpse of figures on the edge of the wood, but he couldn't be certain. All was black below him, but he thought he saw a deeper blackness, which must be the ground. Closer and closer it loomed, rushing at him like a giant speeding train. He bent his knees in readiness, trying with all the intensity he could muster to judge the moment of impact.

Suddenly his feet slammed against the solid ground at fifteen mph.

He let his knees buckle to absorb the blow, and in the same motion rolled to his side.

His body rolled over itself, distorting his perceptions, and in another instant he felt the silky parachute floating down upon him. Instead of the soft earth, his shoulder hit a rock and he cried out in pain. At least it wasn't my head, he thought with indistinct gratitude.

In a couple of seconds he lay still, trying to right his senses. But before he had a chance to settle back into a normal state of awareness and determine "up" from "down," he heard shouts.

"Dear Lord," he murmured, "please be with me." It was the first prayer he had uttered in a long time, and though it had popped out without forethought, never had he meant a prayer more sincerely.

The approaching voices were near now—and they were speaking French.

He felt hands untangling him from his chute and the lines.

"Bonsoir! Bonsoir, mon ami! Michel Tanant, n'est-ce pas? You made it!"

In his relief and exhilaration at seeing friendly, smiling faces, Logan forgot his recognition code. He jumped to his feet and grasped the fellow's hand, shaking it fervently.

"Oui, monsieur!" answered Logan. "Yes, I'm Michel Tanant!"

Logan could hardly contain his ebullience at having successfully completed this hazardous and enervating stage of his mission. He was safely in France! But the better part of his adventures still lay ahead.

18 ❊ Allison's Resolution

SPRING HAD COME and gone at Stonewycke, and now autumn was nipping impatiently at the heels of summer. And while Logan was taking his first steps on French soil, Allison strolled pensively along paths lined with brilliant purple heather.

In the months since she and Logan had parted, Allison had experienced a wide gamut of emotional changes, ranging from self-pity to sympathy for Logan, to anger, to despair, to renewed love for her husband. They came and went in no particular order, returning at will, one following another in unpredictable fashion.

At this particular moment, walking with a gentle warm breeze at her back, Allison's present state was one of something akin to a gloomy hopelessness. For four months she had not heard a single word from Logan. Perhaps that was partly her own fault, she reasoned while in a more tender mood. For at first she had stubbornly refused to make any attempt to correspond. *He* had left her. She wasn't about to demean herself by begging him to return, and she felt that even a neutral newsy letter might be construed as such.

But three weeks ago, in one of her sympathetic frames of mind, she had decided to write him, ostensibly to inform him that their daughter had caught cold and had been ill for two weeks. An angry mood followed when she received absolutely no reply from Logan. A while later that was replaced by worry: what if something had happened to him?

She tried another letter, this one studiously devoid of anything approaching the personal. Still no answer.

It had now been a week since her third letter, and she knew there would be no answer to that one, either.

Pausing in her walk at the crest of a small knoll, she surveyed the view. She had come west of the castle about a mile, taking no road but rather traipsing across open fields of heather and gorse. She had descended a bit from where the walls of Stonewycke stood, yet she still stood high enough to see some sparkle from the sea off to the north. Allison thought of how much she had grown to love this place. Why couldn't Logan feel the same way about it?

But he had to have his busy city and flashy jobs! He didn't care about anyone's happiness but his own. The day he left he'd said he realized he wasn't cut out to be a family man. And so, that was it—it was too much effort for him to try, and so much easier just to forget the whole thing. What did it matter to him if *she* was miserable, and that their child was abandoned to a broken home? Oh no, it was perfectly all right as long as Logan Macintyre was happy!

Suddenly, in the midst of her thoughts, it dawned on Allison how quickly her despair had turned into anger. It was the first time she had seen the transformation so clearly. How could she feel sorry for him one moment and despise him the next?

It was not right of her. Even in the midst of her irritation with Logan, she suddenly realized her own attitude was not all it should be either.

But then, how could it be? Nothing about this whole mess was right. Everything was so cockeyed, so mixed up. How could she possibly figure anything out if she couldn't even decide whose fault it was?

At that moment, her eye caught an especially vibrant clump of heather. Taking a few steps to reach it, she bent down and plucked off a twig.

"I should pick a bunch to take home," she murmured under her breath, as she immediately began to break off more branches and fashion them into a little rustic bouquet.

She had several in her hand when all at once she stopped. She had been thinking of something before she spotted the heather. It had seemed important. What was it? . . .

Oh yes—blame . . . fault.

No wonder she had allowed her attention to be diverted!

Why was the laying of blame so important to her? What was it her mother had said? *You both have a lot to learn about marriage.* If Allison was going to lay blame, it was on both of them. Could she trust her mother's perceptions? All this time she had blamed Logan for everything. Was it possible she was just as much at fault? Did she truly have as much to do with their problems as he? Did she really understand marriage that little? Was Logan right— she did not let herself *see* things as they really were?

She wanted so desperately for things to be ideal, perfect, problem-free. Maybe she had let herself be blinded to realities. If that was true, then she would have to face that fact squarely.

Oh, God, she prayed silently, *help me to see . . . help me to understand. Show me what to do!*

Allison paused in her anguished prayer. She had prayed many times before. She had poured out her heart to God over the course of the last eight years upon many occasions. And she believed that He heard. But something happened to Allison in that moment following her heart's cry which had never happened before.

For the first time, she paused to listen . . . to *hear* the voice of God in response. Rather than continuing her *own* petitions, she waited, silencing her mind, her heart, her voice—and listened. Her heart was at last ready to receive the truths He had been waiting to give. The first answer came through the words of Allison's mother.

Allison, there has to be some self-sacrifice in a marriage, she had said. At the time Allison had argued, defending herself on the grounds of what she thought she had given up. All at once now she saw that she had completely misunderstood her mother's words. Joanna had not been speaking of externals at all, but of heart attitude, of having her mind and heart fixed in an orientation of submissive and loving sacrifice. What a far different thing that was than giving up this or that while maintaining a resistant and self-centered posture!

If you both stubbornly try to hang on to your own personal desires, you might never work things out.

How right her mother had been! *People so often mistake what marriage really is all about.* That was certainly true of her! She had wanted to get out of it what was best for *her*. Laying down her life for Logan, in loving and sacrificial service to him, whether she ever received anything in return, had *not* been her idea of marriage! She had expected Logan to go at least halfway—maybe even just a little more. After all, the husband was to be the leader, the provider. Wasn't it *his* responsibility to care for the wife, and make the marriage pleasant for her?

Oh, she had had it all backward! She *had* been placing false expectations on him—expecting him to serve her! Both her mother and Logan had been right! Her eyes had been blinded. But now in response to the cry of her heart, God was beginning to open them at last.

There was something else her mother had said, only the other day. She had scarcely been paying attention at the time, had not even wanted to hear. But now the words came ringing back:

"You are responsible only for yourself, your own reactions, your own responses. You cannot expect Logan to do his part. Your eyes must be focused only on your self-sacrifice to him, not his to you. Nor can you gauge what you give by what you expect to receive in return, nor by what you think you deserve.

"Marriage is not a fifty-fifty proposition as so many modern thinkers would have us believe, Allison. Each partner must give everything, expecting nothing in return, to make a marriage work. The standard has got to be one hundred percent-zero percent—from each person's vantage point. The moment you say, 'I'll only go ninety-nine percent of the way and I'll expect the other to do his fair one percent share,' the false and selfish expectations begin to creep in, and the whole marriage begins to be undermined. That one percent you place on the other is the open door to every problem in every marriage. You've got to sacrifice, lay down, give, and love the full one hundred percent. God established marriage, and in His economy, that's the only way it can work. Whenever man tries to make it work using a different formula, it can only end in self-centeredness, disappointment, and misery."

As bits and pieces of her mother's passionate plea came back to her, Allison's eyes gradually filled with tears. She had, indeed, been guilty of expecting Logan to go not one percent, not ten or twenty percent, but fifty percent of the way—probably even more! She had expected him to meet *her* needs, to love *her,* to sacrifice for *her.* And what small so-called sacrifices she had thought she had made had all come grudgingly from within her, and she had held them against him. Everything she had done had been self-motivated!

Well, now it was time to turn it around. God had spoken to her. And now He was indeed showing her what to do. He had given no easy answer. But then she had not asked for one.

Oh, but how hard it would be to go back, to humbly have to admit defeat, to admit wrong attitudes! How easy it would be to expect Logan to share in the blame! How easy it would be to become angry with him all over again if he listened to her words of contrition and then turned upon her a haughty reply! How could she possibly keep from expecting from him at least a fifty percent response, or ten, or even one?

She didn't know if she could face him with apology in her mouth and renewed commitment to laying down of self in her heart. Especially if his response was hostile or skeptical, as perhaps he had every right to be.

Then, as if she were struck by some heavenly bolt, a kind of revelation dawned upon her. God had not told her to succeed. He had only said to take the first step!

That's all she had to do! What became of it, Logan's response, what she would do next—that was all God's concern.

She had to go back to London. That much was clear. She had to find Logan; she had to talk to him; she had to make herself vulnerable even to his possible rejection, and she had to tell him of her commitment to be to him at last a wife after God's fashion.

What he would say, what she would do then, she did not know. For one of the first times in her life, she truly felt in God's hands. He would guide her steps. She was sure that somehow He would restore their marriage.

But the first step had to be her obedience.

19 ❄ Back to London

WORLD EVENTS APPEARED in perfect accord with the direction Allison believed God wanted her to take. In June of 1941, Hitler shifted the force of his interest away from Britain. His mighty Wehrmacht and stunning Luftwaffe suddenly did an about-face and turned upon Russia. It would be for historians to debate why he made such a move, and perhaps for the Third Reich to lament. But with the fifteen-thousand-mile Russian front to occupy his troops, Hitler could not now hope to win the tiny island forty miles across the sea west of France, one of the few bastions of freedom now left in Europe. Thus, Britain was granted a respite after nearly a year of relentless blitzkrieg. And for Allison, it meant that she could return to London that autumn to make an attempt to heal the wounds of her marriage.

As Allison waited for her cab in front of Victoria Station, she was horrified at what met her gaze.

Yes, the Battle of Britain had been won, but it had been a victory for which the brave British people had paid dearly. In many places heaps of brick and stone lay where familiar buildings had once stood. She had heard that the civilian death toll ranged in the multiple thousands. Huge portions of old Londontown lay in rubble. Ancient cathedrals had been gutted, parts of St. Paul's and the House of Commons were destroyed, and bombs had even fallen dangerously close to Buckingham Palace.

Yet amid all the destruction it was evident that the British people themselves were largely untouched, at least in their undaunted spirits, which, under the leadership of Winston Churchill, remained typically stoic and courageous. Perhaps it was because they knew there was no time for despair—the hedonist enemy may have been turned from their door, but he was by no means defeated.

"Where to, mum?" asked the cabby as Allison ducked inside the black automobile.

"To 314 Clemments Street," said Allison.

"Right-o!" replied the cabby. "Been away long, mum?"

"Throughout most of the bombing, I'm afraid."

"Oh, I wouldn't be ashamed of that, wot with the little one and all." He cocked his head toward little Joanna, who inched a little closer to her mother while under the scrutiny of this stranger. "Many's the wife wot got out of the city last year."

"I never imagined it would be so bad," said Allison while the cab maneuvered into the traffic.

"It were a livin' inferno at times," replied the cabby, "but we'll kick the tar out o' them krauts yet! I 'spect yer 'usband's out doin' jist that, eh, mum?"

Allison did not answer, pretending not to hear. Yet she had to ask herself: was the reason for her silence that she was ashamed of Logan? She didn't know, but at least she finally had the courage to face the question. Or was her reluctance a further reminder that she didn't even *know* what Logan was doing?

No, she was not ashamed. She knew Logan had anguished over being perceived as a coward for not being able to get into the army. But *she* knew he was a brave man.

She had to remember to tell him that. There was so much more he must know. Since leaving Scotland, it seemed she was growing and changing minute by minute. With every humbling she was able to bring to bear upon herself, God seemed to give her more insight concerning Logan and their relationship. She was coming to understand how self-sacrifice and humility went hand-in-hand, and thus she could see how her pride had been a terrible barrier in their marriage. And when some of her old thinking tried to creep in, telling her that Logan was a proud and stubborn man too, she could remind herself that she was only responsible for *her* responses.

And with these changes within herself, Allison's love for Logan was restoring itself as well.

She could hardly wait to see him! She cautioned herself, saying she couldn't expect overnight changes. But it would be good just to be with him again, and she held an assurance in her heart that she would be able to accept things as they were. As silent and uncommunicative as he wanted to be was fine with her. She just longed to be his wife again!

All at once the cab jerked to a stop. Her heart raced within her and her stomach fluttered. She couldn't help it—she was nervous.

"'Ere you go, mum," said the cabby, opening the door. Allison climbed out, while he rushed around to the boot of the car for her suitcases . "Please, 'low me to carry these up fer ye, mum."

At the door of her apartment she paid him and thanked him for his kindness.

She waited until he had gone before raising her hand to knock. When no answer came, she pulled out her key and glanced at her watch.

"Daddy here, Mummy?" asked her daughter.

"I don't know, honey," replied Allison. She hadn't wanted to barge in unannounced. But it was only four-thirty in the afternoon. He was no doubt still at work.

She inserted the key, but the door did not open. A panic seized her. But there was their name, still on the door! She tried it again, gave the key half a twist to the right, then jammed it forward, twisting it to the left. The lock clicked and the door opened. It had been so long she had forgotten about the trick to the lock. Still, it seemed a little tighter than usual.

A dank chill greeted her the moment she stepped across the threshold, and a mildewy odor permeated the air. A more objective visitor would immediately have realized she was stepping into a place that had not been occupied for some time—months perhaps, or more. There had been no heat turned on to dry out the dampness, nor had the windows been opened to air out the stale odors. Yet Allison clicked on the lights and wandered half through the place before the truth dawned on her that Logan was gone.

From all appearances he might have never been here after leaving Stonewycke in April. Or if he had been back, his stay had been brief, for it had been weeks and weeks since anyone had been here. He must have paid the rent up in advance, and then left. Slowly, painfully, the reality began to settle in upon Allison—he had gone away, and not even bothered to tell her.

For once she didn't care for her own sake—it didn't matter how he wanted to treat her. She could cope with it, even love him in spite of it now. But he had a child. Didn't he feel any responsibility for their daughter? That was the painful question.

She had been receiving regular checks from him all along—at least she always assumed they were from Logan, though they had always been cashier's checks, with no name upon them but her own, accompanied by nothing, not even a note. Yet was there no duty laid to his charge beyond money? What if something happened—an emergency? The recent illness had proved minor. But what if it had been something worse? Had he stopped caring for *everything*?

Already, without even noticing what she was doing, Allison had slipped back into the old pattern of casting blame onto Logan. Suddenly she realized what she'd been doing. This was not going to be easy—changing all her old ways and habits of thinking!

"Where Daddy?" Jo's pleading voice interrupted Allison's thoughts. She sank down onto the sofa, then looked full into the sweet blue eyes that were reminding her more and more of her great-grandmother Maggie's.

"Oh, dear little pumpkin," she said, "your daddy loves you . . . and me. But he's not here right now. It's only that he's a little confused—"

She had to stop, for tears had begun to rise to the surface of her eyes, accompanied by a thick knot in her throat. "Oh, my little darling, what are we going to do?"

She sat, taking the child onto her lap, and held her tight while she wept softly. It was not many minutes before she awoke to the selfish element in her tears. No one would have blamed her for crying at that moment, but she had not given a single thought to Logan.

Where was *Logan*? What was *he* going through? He was no cold, unfeeling man without human emotions and compassion as her old self tried to tell her. He needed her love, her prayers, not her accusations. Yet even as she tried to lift him up before his Father and hers, some deep inner resistance prevented her from saying the words The struggles would be many before she would be able to completely forget the hurts of the past, the seeming unfairnesses. She wanted to pray for him, but the thoughts and words would not focus.

In the midst of her mental tussle, a noise outside the apartment door distracted her.

Her ears perked up at the sound. She jumped to her feet, hoping against everything her rational mind told her that it might be Logan. The doorknob was rattling, as if someone were fitting a key into the lock. Her heart leapt into her throat. She stood staring at the door.

The next moment it swung open, and there stood the bent and wizened figure of Billy Cochran. He stopped short in his tracks, looking every bit as surprised as Allison did disappointed.

"Well, I'm blowed!" he exclaimed when he found his voice. "I sure didn't mean t' barge right in on you, Miz Macintyre." His normally irascible tone was noticeably softened, almost deferential. Lady Allison Macintyre was the only member of the nobility he had ever known personally, and notwithstanding that most people in the twentieth century gave not a fig for such distinctions, Billy could still remember a time when it was not thought comical for a man to bow in such a presence. Though his hunched back seemed to give the appearance of that action, in fact he merely afforded to Allison what respect the tone of his voice could command.

"That's all right, Mr. Cochran," answered Allison kindly. She had always considered him a sweet old man, no matter that her perception had often amused Logan. In point of fact, Cochran's heart was made of gold, though, except in the presence of the wife of his friend Logan, he seemed bent on giving exactly the opposite impression with his surly manner. "Do come in," she added with a smile, hoping her reddened, puffy eyes were not too noticeable.

Billy shuffled rather awkwardly into the room, removed his hat, and stood fingering its rim for some moments before speaking.

"'Tis right nice t' see you agin, Miz Macintyre," he said, managing a smile that to anyone else would have looked even more alarming than his usual scowl. "If I'd—"

"I don't mind," replied Allison. "Are you . . . looking in on the place for Logan?"

"That's right, mum. 'Course, now as yer back, I'll be leavin' you t' yer privacy."

"I appreciate what you've been doing. Tell me, Mr. Cochran, how long has it been since—"

Allison paused. It was hard to admit to a relative stranger that she had no knowledge of her husband's recent activities. But she had to know.

"—since you started coming by?"

"Now, lemme see . . ." He screwed up his face in deep thought and silently counted his fingers. "April, it would of been when I came the first time. That'd be—"

"Four months," sighed Allison, at last accepting the reality of the situation. Their apartment had not seen Logan for almost as long as she. "Please sit down, Mr. Cochran," she went on; "that is, if you have a moment."

"Don't mind if I do, mum. Them stairs is mighty steep." He lowered his small frame into a chair adjacent to Allison's. Then, as if the act of sitting down next to this gentlewoman brought them into, if not equal status, then at least closer proximity, he appeared to relax, and said in a more personal tone, "Miz Macintyre, there hain't nothin' wrong, is there?"

For a brief moment Allison attempted to put on her secure and self-assured mask. But there was something in the old man's eyes—a deep, almost fatherly concern—that made her suddenly blurt out the fears from the depths of her heart.

"Oh, Mr. Cochran, I haven't seen or heard from Logan in four months! I don't know what to think. Can you tell me anything? What is he doing? Where is he?"

Billy frowned, and thoughtfully scratched his large nose. "I didn't think it were so bad," he mused, mostly to himself. "If ye're beggin' me pardon, mum, I don't mean t' be so forward, but you see, Logan did talk a mite t' me afore 'e left. Didn't give me no details, but 'e said there was some problems, that is, atween you an' him, mum."

"What did he say?" she asked anxiously. "Do you know where he went?"

"Didn't say much, I'm feared t' say. Just that 'e was goin' away fer a bit, an' would I check in on things every now an' then." Billy took a long slow breath. "But 'e was real mysterious 'bout it. Wouldn't give me so much as a clue."

"Don't you have any idea, Mr. Cochran?" pleaded Allison. "Was he—has he been involved, you know . . . with his old life?"

"No!" answered the ex-counterfeiter emphatically. "I'd swear on it with me life!"

"Have you noticed anything unusual when you've been here?"

"Only stumblin' in on you today, Miz Macintyre," he replied. "'Cept that 'e ast me t' pick up 'is mail, but there hain't been a stitch of it."

"None?"

Cochran shook his head.

"But I've written," Allison went on. "Surely my letters have arrived."

"Not so's I seen them."

Allison leaned forward excitedly as a new idea came to her. "Mr. Cochran, is it possible Logan could be in the city—coming here only to pick up the mail?"

"'Tis a wild notion, if I may say so, mum. Not that Logan hain't experienced at layin' low. But I doubt 'e could do it 'thout *me* findin' out. 'Sides, 'e gave me the distinct impression as 'e was leavin' town fer a spell."

"But it *is* possible he's still in London?"

Slowly, somewhat regretfully, Billy cocked his head to indicate doubt.

"Now, mum, would you be permittin' me to speak openly?"

"Yes, of course." Despite her affirmation, Allison's voice contained a trace of hesitancy, as her old self sought to hide from the truth.

"'Tis like this, mum," Billy began. "This 'ere world is pretty crazy these days, an' anythin's liable t' happen. An' I hain't sayin' you ought not t' hope fer the best. I know Logan'll be back. I'd wage me last bob on it. But I'm thinkin' you'll be only 'urtin' yerself if you don't accept things as they are right now, an' that's that he's long gone, who knows where. I mean, you'd not be doin' you or that dear wee girl there no good if you go beside yerself at every sound you hear, or every distant face that might resemble Logan."

"You're saying to give up on him?"

"No, mum. The bloke'll be back. You can count on that. I'm only sayin' there's no tellin' how much longer he's bound t' be gone. In the meantime, you gots t' go on with your life. You gots t' let things 'appen as they may."

"You're probably right, Mr. Cochran."

"But Logan's comin' back, you don't 'ave to worry none about that!"

"How can you be so certain?"

"'Cause I *know* the blighter. Oh, he's got 'is problems t' be sure, jist like the rest of us. But there hain't a finer, more honorable man aroun'—what'd give 'is life fer a friend if he had t'—than Logan Macintyre. An' he loves you too, an' that's a fact!"

When the conversation waned, Allison rose, asked Billy to stay for some tea, which the small, unstocked kitchen was still able to supply, to which he heartily agreed. When he left an hour later, Allison embraced him warmly. Never before, at least within the old man's memory, had anyone expressed such a feeling toward him, and the act of affection flustered and pleased the dear man more than he cared to show. He forced out his stammered goodbyes, insisting that Allison call on him if she needed anything at all.

He would have been further embarrassed, and perhaps pleased, had he known that he had come as an answer to Allison's prayers. Hours after he had departed, while she lay upon her bed in the dark, she played over again his words of encouragement in her mind.

Perhaps tomorrow, or next week, she would despair again. But for now, God had sent, through her husband's old friend, a sustaining message of hope.

20 ⁂ *Rue de Varennes*

THE GUSTY BREEZE rising off the Seine was unable to dispel the summer warmth of the city. Logan had long since removed his jacket and tucked it into his knapsack, which he had slung French-style over one shoulder. As he walked down the Champs-Elysees, he could not shake a deep oppression that came not from the heat but from the sights his eyes beheld.

Along the historic avenue the German occupation forces were playing out their daily noontime ritual. The garrison of the Kommandant von Gross-Paris, with colors flying in the air and a band beating out victorious notes, marched in arrogant affirmation of their rule. It was one of those sights that would not soon fade from Logan's memory. To him it looked as if the Nazi jackboots would literally tramp out the spirit of the mighty French capital. He remembered the grand City of Lights in the late twenties when he had been there. They had called it "Gay Paree" then, and it had certainly been just that. Of course back then the French were still cocky with *their* victory over the Germans. How could they know that within a score of years *they* would be the vanquished, or that their hated oppressors would march unopposed in the very shadow of the Arc de Triomphe?

It hardly mattered that few passers-by stopped to watch the spectacle. The grim looks he saw upon so many of the faces said all there was to say. Marshall Pétain, leader of the so-called government, now exiled to Vichy, had said shortly after the Germans marched into Paris: "Is it not enough that France is defeated? Must she be dishonored as well?" Yet it had largely been the apathy of the French people that had made for such an easy victory for Hitler. A peculiar and unpredictable nation politically, perched precariously through the centuries between England and Spain or between England and Germany, she was ill-suited temperamentally to step into the role of ally to her longtime adversary. The French were much later than the English to see the evil of the Third Reich, and on the day France fell, Frenchmen cheered and toasted Pétain's armistice.

Yet by this time Logan could see a pervading shadow of shame on many of the faces around him. The truth was now clear; but now it was too late. They were a nation vanquished, and their pride was trampled underfoot. They could not believe with their exiled leader that it was wisdom rather than cowardice "to come to terms with yesterday's enemy." Yet what could they do against this foe when even their most honored military hero had capitulated?

There were Frenchmen, however, who did believe there was something they could do. Feeling that old Pétain had betrayed them, though their numbers were yet few, these would never cease to fight for the freedom of their Paris, their France. "Liberty, equality, fraternity" were no shallow words to them, but a slogan that ignited the inner fires of their nationalistic fervor. Charles de Gaulle, an obscure but patriotic general, had fled to Britain, now the home of Free France, where he slowly was being joined by those of his countrymen determined to keep up the fight. Other patriots had chosen to remain in France. Whether by choice or necessity, theirs was the task to which de Gaulle had called them in the wake of the fall of France in 1940: "Whatever happens, the flame of French resistance must not die, and will not die."

It was a small group of such Frenchmen Logan now sought. He turned his back on the parading soldiers, and pointed his steps toward the bank of the Seine.

One twenty-four, rue de Varennes. The address had been pressed permanently into his memory during the hours of memorization in England. Behind that unassuming door lay the headquarters of a resistance operation that had sprung up nearly a year ago. Their numbers were unknown, but they had been effective enough to warrant a good portion of the money Logan now carried securely in a money belt beneath his shirt.

They had recently come on hard times. Two weeks ago their radio operator, along with a handful of others, had been captured. As far as London could tell no one had talked, but a lot of damage could be done in a short time, especially where German interrogators were concerned. If the bookstore on the rue de Varennes had been compromised, Logan could be walking into a dangerous situation. Of course, I am only a bookseller from Lyon, he reminded himself. How could I know this place has ties to the Resistance?

When he came within two blocks of the bookstore, he grew vigilant. The narrow street appeared innocent enough, with four or five casual strollers stopping now and then at the various shops—a grocer, a chemist, a cafe—all typically Parisian. A woman leaned out from her second-floor apartment window, exchanging a few words with the grocer's wife about the new ration regulations. Some children were skipping rope in an alleyway singing a pleasant, childish ditty. For a moment Logan began to question his original impression of the occupation. But life did go on, after all. What else could people do? Children had to play, and women had to discuss the price of bread, even if the Nazis roamed the streets.

Logan could see nothing suspicious about. Slowly he approached the bookstore, nestled between the cafe and the chemist. There was no name, merely the words *La Librairie* printed in plain roman lettering across the door.

Logan opened the door and walked in. Immediately a bell clanged overhead. Stepping inside, he saw that no one, not even the proprietor, was present. He took a moment to appraise his surroundings—a tiny room where barely five persons could browse comfortably among the stacks and shelves of hundreds of volumes. There appeared little order to the categories of books, or at least it gave such an impression because there was so much crammed into the small available space. The musty smell of old books and dust heightened the assurance that it was, indeed, a bookstore.

Logan had no time to reflect further, for in but a second or two the proprietor himself appeared. Logan had well learned the name Henri Renouvin, though he had been given no description or history of the man. In all his attempts to visualize him in his mind, he had never come even close to this small, compact bookseller in his mid-forties who stood before him. Logan had been looking for a tough embattled soldier of the night, not a simple shop-keeper, which was exactly what this man appeared to be. His thinning blond hair, dimpled chin, and wire-rimmed glasses, which framed sensitive blue eyes, all gave the impression of an intellectual.

"Puis-je vous aider? May I help you?" he asked in a friendly, unassuming tone, as if the encounter were nothing more out of the way than a businessman greeting a potential customer.

"Oui," answered Logan, "that is, if you are Henri Renouvin."

"I am."

"Then you will be pleased to hear the messages I bear," continued Logan in perfect idiomatic French, using the recognition phrase he had learned from the file back at headquarters: "My Aunt Emily from Lyon wanted you to know she has recovered from her illness."

"Ah, oui!" answered Renouvin, his quiet features suddenly animating into life. "It is good news. She is a fine woman like her daughter Marie!"

"Marie, too, sends her greetings and is sorry she was unable to write."

Renouvin stepped up to Logan and gave him a firm welcoming pat on the shoulder as they exchanged handshakes.

"We were not even certain our message got through," Renouvin went on. "The radio has been nearly useless since we lost Jacques, though we must try to communicate. You cannot imagine how welcome you are! But come into the back—it is not good to talk out here."

"Is it safe for me to remain?"

"Oui, oui, most certainly," replied Renouvin, leading Logan as he spoke through a curtained doorway into a dimly lit room that was as dominated with rows and piles of books as was the store itself. In addition to the books were stacks of crates and cardboard boxes, a roll-top desk nestled between more books against one wall, and a small table that had three of the wooden crates situated around it, apparently to be used in lieu of chairs.

Renouvin motioned Logan to one of these crates, and while he seated himself, the bookseller took two heavy pottery cups from a shelf nailed haphazardly on the wall over the table. "Would you like a bowl of coffee?" he asked. "It is actually only ersatz, that horrible brew they expect us to drink these days, while no doubt the real coffee goes to Berlin. But it is freshly brewed at least."

"Merci," replied Logan. "You seem pretty certain there is no danger here."

Renouvin sat on a crate opposite Logan's. "There is always danger in Paris these days, my friend. But we are very careful, and it helps that the Boche* are not too smart. That must sound ridiculous from a man who has just lost four valuable workers."

Renouvin sighed heavily. "But it was not carelessness or stupidity that brought about their demise."

"They were betrayed?"

"It is a strong possibility. But fortunately, only Jacques knew about *La Librairie* and other incriminating locations where we conduct our business. He died before the Boche got anything out of him." Renouvin paused reflectively. "But," he began again in a lighter tone, "tell me about yourself."

"I am Michel Tanant," said Logan, "bookseller from Lyon."

"Clever touch! Do you know anything of the book trade?"

---

*Boche—French slang for Germans.

"Very little."

"No matter, as long as your skills in, shall we say, *other areas* are adequate."

"I hope they are," said Logan. But his inner confidence was still struggling to match the apparent importance this man was placing in him.

"You are British?"

"My accent is that bad?"

"Non, non!" said Renouvin apologetically. "It is quite good, in fact. It will fool the Germans easily, and many Frenchmen will not give you a second look. Whoever placed you from Lyon knew his business. Your accent resembles that usually found in the Alpine region of the south."

Logan drained off the last of his ersatz coffee, grimacing in spite of himself.

"Please forgive me, Michel, mon ami, for serving you such a dreadful brew," said Renouvin. "When the war is over and we are free again, you will come to my house and I will offer you the best French coffee you have ever had."

Logan smiled. It was going to be easy to like this man who spoke with the good-natured congeniality of one without a care in the world. How could anyone guess that he was daily but a breath away from death, and that he held in his brain enough information to bring down hundreds of others also? Yet perhaps it was the very aura of angelic innocence surrounding him that had kept him alive these many months. Logan knew he would long for the time he could visit this man without guile and enjoy pleasant, even trivial conversation. But now, such notions were out of the question. This cup of coffee was not a luxury at all. There was much to be done, and much danger hanging over them despite the innocent look of things.

The urgency of their business must also have been pressing itself upon Renouvin, for he leaned intently forward and began to give Logan a brief synopsis of the operation at *La Librairie*.

"Now that poor Jacques is gone," he began, "there are only five of us who know of the bookstore. Each of us has a circuit of agents that operate blind, for the most part. If any is captured, he knows only one or two names at most, and the identities of the five of us are known only among ourselves. My network, for example, knows me as *L'Oiselet,* little bird, and can contact me only through a post office box. None of them know anything about the bookstore or that I am involved with others like myself. The five of us who operate our little networks out of *La Librairie* are something like the hub of a wheel, from which many, many spokes go out. If the Nazis have any knowledge of L'Oiselet, which they do not, there is no way they can connect him to Henri Renouvin, bookseller. All the pieces are separate. That is why Jacques's capture and death did not compromise *La Librairie*. As for myself, I act mostly as a collector and disseminator of information. My four associates do more of the footwork of the organization, and are thus more exposed than I. You will meet each of them in due time. But for now, mon ami, we must get you settled. You are tired and hungry, non?"

Logan was certainly that, and more, though it was only then, with the concerned words of this kindly gentleman, that he realized just how taxing his two-day journey to Paris had been. He had eaten but scantily since his drop. Though he had a pocketful of perfectly good, however forged, ration coupons, he had not mastered the local idiosyncrasies well enough to use them with confidence, despite his training in current regulations. He had nearly blown his cover in his fumbling novice attempt last night at dinner, and had ended up with nothing more than bread and coffee. Since then he had managed only a few turnips plucked from the fields this morning on his way into the city. Sleep had posed an additional problem; even for a city lad like himself, Paris was an intimidating place, and it was hardly worth the effort to try to locate a hole to curl up in for a while.

Renouvin set Logan up in a hotel a few blocks from the bookstore, with effusive regrets that he could not open up his own small flat to him. Such a plan would have been to court danger needlessly, however, and they both realized it. He then saw to it that Logan had a nourishing meal, while filling him in on more details of his organization. And while Renouvin had been genuinely concerned about Logan's rest, he talked with him far into the evening.

When Logan at last finally did lie down on his cheap hotel bed, he hardly noticed how hard and coarse it was. He fell soundly asleep within minutes, and it is doubtful even a Gestapo raid could have wakened him.

21 ❈ *The Resistors*

THOUGH THE BRIGHT morning sun shone with a particular brilliance outside, Henri Renouvin's back room remained dim. But the figures gathered around his little table more than preferred their present business to remain ensconced in shadows.

"It's not like Jean Pierre to be late." The voice seemed to echo through the small room. It was an animated voice, full of vigor and haste, medium-pitched, though its owner's massive build gave him the appearance of a *basso profundo.*

"Keep your voice down, Antoine!" said Henri, looking over toward the table from where he stood at the sink filling a coffeepot with water.

Though a bear of a man, towering over six feet and weighing in excess of two hundred pounds, the speaker Antoine jumped up agilely from where he sat on a rickety crate barely able to sustain his weight, and began pacing nervously on the tiny floor space the cluttered room allowed. Every ounce of the man seemed a powerhouse of energy in constant motion, whether sitting or standing. His lively manner belied his fifty years, as did his thick, unruly black hair and beard, which held not a trace of gray. Even his eyes were alive and vibrant, emanating a love of life that seemed impervious to his present agitation. He appeared to be a man who both laughed and wept easily and without shame.

"I tell you, I don't like this," said Antoine, making a supreme effort to quell the natural booming timbre of his voice. "And where is Lise? Something must be wrong! Claude, you were the last to see her. She said nothing about being late for today's gathering?"

"Non," answered the third man in the room.

"Is that all you have to say?" exclaimed Antoine, as if he had been somehow cheated by the brevity of Claude's reply.

"Oui, Antoine," answered Claude quietly, apparently unaffected by his companion's anxiety. He was of about Henri's diminutive stature. However, at that point any resemblance ended. At thirty, the man was sinewy and muscular, and, but for several deep scars about his face, might have been handsome. One scar, in particular, situated over his left eye and causing it to droop slightly, gave him an especially sinister air. This impression of lurking evil was compounded by a crooked nose and dark eyes that flashed hatred just as Antoine's sparkled with life. Claude had received his scars, if not his hatred also, at the hands of the Gestapo when he had been captured with Antoine's wife and daughter. He had been severely tortured before finally getting away in the escape plot which had killed Antoine's daughter.

"You talk too much, Claude," snapped Antoine sarcastically. "Are you not even worried for our comrades?"

"I am more concerned about this Anglais we will soon be forced to entertain," replied Claude. His every word was uttered with effort, as if speaking wasted energy that could better be used for more lethal tasks.

"Forced," rejoined Antoine. "He brings us a million francs! For that I will kiss his feet."

"You don't think his money comes without strings?" returned Claude darkly. "In return he will expect to control our operation."

"He did not strike me as that sort," put in Henri.

"Who cares?" said Antoine extravagantly. "With that kind of money we will be able to do much damage to the Boche. Tell me that bothers you, Claude."

In response, Claude just shook his head grimly, with the barest hint of a smile on his face.

"Ha, ha!" laughed Antoine. "There is nothing you like better than killing our enemy, eh, mon ami?"

"I think perhaps he likes it *too* much," muttered Henri under his breath.

Claude bristled. "What do you know, Monsieur Mouse?" he sneered. "You sit here all day safe in your little bookstore—"

"Claude!" remonstrated Antoine, ominously halting his pacing.

"Never mind!" said Henri, with a self-deprecating wave of his hand. "Maybe he is right. Who knows?"

"None of us risks more or less than the others," Antoine replied firmly with a pointed look toward Claude.

"So be it," said Claude in a tone that made it uncertain if his words represented apology or condescension. "But I won't do the bidding of this Anglais," he continued resolutely, "no matter how much money he brings."

As if Claude had planned the timing of his last word, the discussion ended abruptly when the bell over the outer door clanged loudly. The three men started, then went rigid, none moving for some time, as if fearing this intruder might validate their earlier fears.

At last Henri stirred into motion. As the proprietor, he must greet everyone who came through his door. He set the coffeepot on the hot plate, then strode through the curtain to the front of the store.

In less than a moment he reappeared, beaming with relief. He was followed by a priest, who entered the dingy room with an air of practiced grace and aplomb, like a man well accustomed to socializing.

Antoine fairly leaped from his chair and took the newcomer in a huge embrace. "Jean Pierre!" he exclaimed.

"What a reception!" the man replied, breathless from the zeal of Antoine's greeting. "And I am only half an hour late."

"What kept you, mon père?" said Henri. "You know ordinarily we set our clocks by you."

"The Boche can sometimes be just as punctual," said the priest. "They were at my door at seven a.m. sharp." He wore a cool composure even as he delivered what could be none other than shocking news.

"Mon Dieu!" exclaimed Antoine. "What happened?"

The priest gathered his black cassock around him and lowered his trim, stately frame onto one of the crates. Everything about the man spoke of a noble breeding, a *savoir-faire* that seemed to stand in sharp contrast with his priestly calling. Even his handsome, Patrician features were smooth and unlined, refuting on the surface the venerability that one might automatically associate with his holy robes. Only his gray hair, though thick, hinted at his forty-nine years.

"Ah, merci," said Jean Pierre as Henri set a steaming cup of ersatz coffee before him. "You really must not be so concerned for me," he added, noting Henri's pained expression of concern. "Once or twice a month the Gestapo try to make life difficult for me, rousting me out for questioning, occasionally arresting me. It has become almost a ritual I depend on. They put me through their ridiculous little barrage of interrogation, then release me because they never have enough evidence to hold me. I think they are naturally skeptical of anyone whose business it is to do good in the world."

"Someday they may get lucky," warned Antoine.

"But I have more than mere luck on my behalf, eh, mon ami?"

"Those collaborators in your congregation will not stick their necks out for you indefinitely, mon père," cautioned Henri.

"It was not collaborators of whom I spoke, Henri," said Jean Pierre. "There is a heavenly Protector who will never fail me."

"And what about the rest of us?" challenged Claude, disgruntled as always by Jean Pierre's composure, as well as his irritating habit of making absurd references to a higher power.

"He will protect even you, Claude," smiled the priest, with more fondness than disdain.

"Nevertheless, Jean Pierre," said Antoine, "and I mean no disrespect, but do you think it wise for you to have come directly here? How can you be certain you were not followed?"

"You know I am always followed," answered the priest. "But the last thing the Gestapo suspect is a priest visiting his favorite bookstore."

"Mon Dieu!" exploded Claude rising. "Do you mean you led them here, and they are watching us? They may have seen the rest of—"

"Relax, my friend," assured the priest, scarcely raising the volume of his voice despite the other man's angry outburst. "You may rest assured that in honor of today's special significance, I gave my shadow the slip long before I came anywhere near the rue de Varennes."

He paused and glanced around the room, as if noticing for the first time that something was out of place. "Where is Lise?" he asked.

Henri merely shook his head and sighed. Antoine continued with his pacing, and Claude, who had reluctantly resumed his seat, only grunted, as if the priest's question was in itself proof of some point he had just made.

Before anyone had the opportunity to answer, the bell clanged again. All movement in the back room stopped once more as Henri made his way to the front, with only slightly less trepidation than before.

22 ❧ First Meeting

LOGAN HAD OVERSLEPT on his first night in Paris.

It was little wonder, for he had not slept soundly in days. Even prior to leaving England, he had been so steeped in his preparatory efforts and so keyed up in anticipation of this mission that he had slept little. But though he might be justified in sleeping so long, to sleep so soundly in the midst of this Gestapo-infested city was nothing short of pure folly, or so he told himself as he hastened out of bed. He would have to be more careful of that in the future.

He had hoped to have time to unpack and study the layout of the hotel, but that would have to wait. He was already late for his scheduled appointment with Renouvin. He dressed quickly, found he was too late for the stale roll and coffee provided to guests on the premises, ate a hurried breakfast in a cafe across from the hotel, then headed toward the rue de Varennes. Knowing he was a good thirty minutes late, his most difficult task was to walk casually and take a sufficiently roundabout route; to run or even rush his walk could mean death to an agent. Any appearance of haste could do nothing but draw attention to him, and that was the last thing any agent wanted behind foreign lines, where all eyes were suspicious.

When he pushed open the door of the bookstore, setting off the overhead bell, he had only a moment to wait before Renouvin emerged to greet him. Henri's face was tense, missing its usual affable smile.

"I'm sorry to be late, Henri," said Logan, assuming his tardiness the cause of the man's anxiety.

"Think nothing of it," replied Renouvin, attempting a smile for his guest's benefit. "It appears everyone is late this morning. Come back and meet my compatriots."

That morning in Renouvin's storeroom Logan met the oddest-matched aggregate of men he could possibly imagine. He studied each in turn as he was introduced to them, wondering how the suave, urbane priest, the dark, dangerous Claude, and the vibrant, boisterous Antoine could have come to be associated with the mild-mannered bookseller, Henri Renouvin. If it was true that politics bred strange bedfellows, then perhaps the politics of resistance carried the old adage to the extreme. Common cause, common hatreds, common fears were enough to bring both villains and saints together against a universal enemy.

He immediately noted the air of tension in the room. Henri told him that the fifth member of their group was also late, and they were growing concerned. Henri poured out coffee for everyone, and they took up again the debate they had begun before Logan's arrival: whether they should do anything about their comrade's absence.

"If she isn't here in ten minutes," declared Antoine, "I'm going to look for her."

"You must use discretion," cautioned Henri. "Haste in our business can always lead to danger."

Jean Pierre smiled. The idea of the big emotional man using discretion seemed altogether incongruous. But he said nothing.

"Lise knows how to take care of herself," said Claude bluntly.

"Which means we should ignore the fact that she might be in danger?" shot back Antoine.

"Which means that if she can't cover her tracks, there's nothing we can do to help her anyway," replied Claude. "Like I said, she can take care of herself."

"You're not going to have much of an organization if you all don't try to take care of one another," said Logan, but he regretted his words almost before they were out of his mouth.

"Who are you to judge us, Anglais?" sneered Claude.

"For once I agree with Claude," boomed Antoine, forgetting Henri's previous injunction to be quiet. "We *do* take care of each other, and we are a good organization!"

"I didn't mean—" began Logan, but Claude quickly cut him off.

"We know what you mean, Anglais!" he seethed. "You think your English money gives you the right to tell us what to do."

"You're all wrong," returned Logan. For a brief moment his eyes locked with Claude's in what was nothing less than a power struggle between two proud men who had never seen each other five minutes before.

"For heaven's sake!" exclaimed Henri. "This gets us nowhere!"

"And certainly does not help Lise," added Jean Pierre, "whom I believe is our main concern at the moment."

"You're right, mon père," said Logan, calming. "But I think at the outset I should make one thing clear. What Claude said is not true. The last thing I want to do is tell any of you what to do. That's not what I was sent here to do. I want to help—that's all."

"C'est bien, Monsieur Tanant," said the priest diplomatically. "And help is exactly what we need at the moment. We would be fools not to accept it."

The heated atmosphere relaxed, and Henri opened his mouth to make another suggestion regarding their absent member, when the bell in front again arrested their attention.

Henri jumped to his feet, but before he could enter the store, the curtain swept aside. From the relieved exclamations on the part of the men in the storeroom, Logan surmised it to be Lise, who now hurriedly entered the room.

A petite woman of no more than thirty years of age, on first glance she appeared rather plain. She had, in fact, arranged herself to achieve exactly that effect. She wore a simple gray wool skirt and cardigan sweater over a white cotton blouse, with thick, serviceable shoes on her feet. Her brown hair was pulled haphazardly back into a pony tail that reached midway down her back, and she wore no makeup, not even a trace of lipstick. But before the war, when she had dressed for an evening at the theater or the opera, the beauty she so carefully downplayed, now that her city was crawling with Germans, had been clearly evident. Even then, however, it was not immediately discernible in her high cheekbones or perfectly chiseled nose or her intriguing widow's peak. Nor was it her eyes, black and shimmering as onyx, which first drew attention. Rather, her first attraction was her quiet, unaffected charm, her sensitivity, and chiefly the intense fervor in her contralto voice when she spoke of things that mattered.

Everyone except Logan spoke at once with their relieved greetings. Antoine embraced her in a hug that nearly swallowed her small frame, while Jean Pierre took her hands in his and squeezed them tenderly.

"Mon cher," said the priest when the others had quieted. "You are in trouble, non?"

"Not I so much, mon père," she answered, "but there is trouble."

"Sit down," said Henri, ever the thoughtful host. "Have some coffee and tell us about it."

She let Henri guide her to a chair, but all the while her eyes rested on Logan. She had known there would be a stranger in their midst this morning; that was the purpose of the meeting. But still she studied Logan, as if, despite what anyone else said, she must draw her own conclusions regarding his merit. Logan found himself squirming under her scrutinizing gaze. Instinctively he knew it was important to be accepted by her, not so much because she held any particular power in the group, but rather because he immediately sensed that she was the kind of person whose opinion was worthwhile.

"You can speak in front of Monsieur Tanant, Lise," prompted Henri.

She gave Logan a final glance, as if to say, *I still haven't decided, but I must speak anyway.*

"Madame Guillaume is being watched," she began, then paused to take a sip of Henri's coffee. "She took in two escaped British airmen yesterday, and now she is beside herself with anxiety. She called me this morning when she thought she saw the Gestapo again prowling about the neighborhood."

"Why didn't you get the airmen out immediately?" asked Henri.

"They refused to go."

"What! " cried Antoine, jumping up from the seat he had only a moment before taken. "The idiots! Don't they know they endanger her life? It has always been understood that the protection of the safe-house proprietors comes first. The airmen could only be arrested again—*she* could be shot!"

"They must understand," said Lise, "though they do not speak a word of French, and Mme. Guillaume knows no English. My own is so limited I could do nothing to remedy the situation. They are very agitated and ill. I think they have spent many very difficult weeks getting this far from Germany. Their uniforms were filthy and torn when they arrived, and Madame took them and burned them. Now they seem to think that if they go out wearing the civilian clothes she gave them, especially while the place is under surveillance, they will be arrested as spies. It's obvious they have been through a terrible ordeal. I believe they would be more reasonable otherwise. But they are so desperate for the rest and so reluctant to go out on the run again."

"It is still no excuse," Antoine said staunchly.

"I have nearly convinced them to leave," continued Lise, "but now I have no more available safe houses. I spent the last hour trying to contact everyone I knew, and no one can squeeze in even two more. Henri, I was hoping you or one of the others might have something."

Henri did not waste even the moment necessary to answer her. He was on the phone by the roll-top desk almost before her request was completed. He asked the operator for several numbers while everyone watched expectantly.

"Allô!" he said at last into the receiver. "M. Leprous? I thought you might want to know that my friend M. L'Oiselet brought by two books for you. Shall I drop them by your house?" There was a pause while Henri listened. He nodded his head slowly, his mouth spreading into a grin. "Merci . . . and au revoir," he said. He hung up the phone and turned back to the group with a satisfied smile on his face. "Voilà!" he said. "It is arranged."

He jotted down the address on a slip of paper and handed it to Lise.

"Oh, Henri! You are a savior," exclaimed Lise, and the intensity of her dark eyes lightened a moment. Her gravity it appeared might also contain room for some laughter under the right conditions. "Now I only have to get the men out of there," she added, as if it were a small matter.

"Why don't you take M. Tanant with you," suggested Jean Pierre off-handedly. "As an Englishman, perhaps he could be of some help with them."

"Merci, but I can take care of it, mon père."

Logan couldn't tell if it was defensiveness or mistrust in her tone. Then she added, "There is no need to involve anyone unnecessarily." If there was apology in her voice, it was more than likely directed at the priest.

"He has come to help us, Lise," replied Jean Pierre firmly, but at the same time gently. "I think we should let him do that, don't you?"

She hesitated for a second, though it seemed much longer, as the entire room waited in silence.

In the meantime, Logan found himself growing steadily more perturbed with this bunch. He had risked his neck to come here for their sakes, and now three out of five of them were treating him as if he were but one step removed from the Germans. He was not yet sure of the priest, whom he thought might simply be testing him, however civilly he chose to do it. Logan was just about to tell this woman, who was so arrogantly assessing him with her critical eyes, that she need not do him any favors, when she spoke.

"If he is willing . . ." she said.

It might have been nice to hear, "Merci, it would be helpful to have him come," instead of the grudging consent she finally gave. But he had not come here for thanks or appreciation. If he could help, that would be the best way to prove his loyalty and good intentions. So he swallowed his annoyance and merely nodded his assent.

A few minutes later, he found himself walking down the rue de Varennes with a very silent resistance agent at his side.

23 ❈ First Assignment

THEY WALKED FOR ten minutes before Lise finally turned toward Logan and spoke.

"I bear you no grudges, M. Tanant."

"You're not afraid I have come to impose my will on your organization?"

A corner of her mouth curved upward, amused. It was not a smile, but was as close as she had yet come.

"I see Claude has accosted you already," she said. "He is forever thinking someone is trying to take over our operation. He imagines bogeymen everywhere. But I have no such fear. Even if it were your intention, you won't get far with Claude and Antoine."

"Then, what are you afraid of?" asked Logan. "From me, that is?"

"It has more to do with trust than fear."

"You don't trust me?"

"Trust is a commodity I have learned to dole out skeptically and scantily this last year."

She paused as a bicycle-powered velo-taxi came into sight. She waved a hand and it stopped. After she gave their destination to the driver and she and Logan had settled themselves into the rickshaw-like seat, she took up her speech again. "I don't like it, M. Tenant. I despise this world in which I must exist. I despise what it forces us to become. But it is the only world I have left. I must live in it and still keep my honor. Someday I hope things will be different . . ." She said no more, leaving whatever else there may have been of the thought unfinished. She was not accustomed to revealing her heart to many.

"I think I understand," replied Logan, saying no more. He allowed the sincerity in his voice and eyes to say the rest.

In another twenty minutes they had reached the building in which Madame Guillaume occupied a small flat. They had departed the cab a block away and walked the rest of the way to the building so they could reconnoiter the area. Lise feared that if the Gestapo did indeed have the place under watch, it might look suspicious for her to return so soon after her last visit. But a thorough examination of the street revealed that either Mme. Guillaume was mistaken or else the Gestapo had given up. Logan unwillingly reminded himself that there was one other possibility—that the Nazis had already raided the place. But he said nothing.

Inside the building, all appeared peaceful and normal. They climbed the stairs to the second floor, and Lise led the way to the door, where she knocked using a prearranged signal—two knocks, a pause of two seconds, and two more quick knocks. Only a minute passed before there was a response from inside, but to Logan it seemed inordinately long.

At last the door opened a crack. The woman on the other side smiled broadly when her eyes lighted on Lise. She opened the door the rest of the way and hurriedly ushered them in.

She was a gentle old soul, plump and wrinkled, with eyes that drooped slightly at the corners, giving her a sorrowful look like a woebegone basset hound. Yet whenever she smiled, the expression of her face was warm enough to make up for the eyes, and if there was indeed sorrow in her life, it seemed to make up for that too.

"Ah, Lise! I did not think you were ever coming back," said the woman as she placed a chubby arm around Lise and propelled her into the living room.

"Have you seen any more of the Gestapo?"

"Non, thank goodness!" she replied. "I think it was a neighbor. I heard rumors that he was a collaborator, but I could not believe it. He has lived next to me for twenty years. We made too much noise last night getting the Anglais gentlemen in here. He must have reported me."

"But they are not watching you now," said Lise. "If that is so, why have they not yet made a move against you?"

"It is most peculiar."

"Where are your men?" asked Logan. Whatever the Germans were up to, he doubted there was time to sit around analyzing it.

"This is M. Tanant," said Lise, in response to the other woman's questioning look. "He is here to help us."

"Welcome to my house, Monsieur," said the lady. "Please come this way."

They followed her down a short hall and into a dimly lit bedroom. There were two beds in the room, and on each a man was lying. A youth of about eighteen years was bent over one of the beds holding a cup for its occupant.

"That is my nephew, Paul," explained Mme. Guillaume, motioning toward the boy. "I was afraid to be here alone if the Boche should come, so I asked him if he would stay with me."

Logan marveled at the woman. She appeared so fainthearted; what could have prompted her to take on such a harrowing task? No doubt she was like so many of her courageous countrymen and women who saw a need and did not stop to wonder whether she had the heart for it before offering her aid.

Logan did not have the chance to ponder this long, for the men on the beds required his attention. One had already started up to a sitting position at the unexpected intrusion. His eyes darted nervously toward these newcomers, and did not rest until he realized he recognized one of them. The other man simply lifted his head off the pillow and let it fall back in fatigue.

"Tisna the Germans, is it noo, Bob?" he said in a voice that sounded as if he hardly cared anymore.

"I'm definitely no German!" answered Logan in English, striding up to the man's bedside. "An' what else cud I be but a muckle Scotsman just like yersel', lad!" he added, in the thickest brogue he could muster.

"Hoots!" exclaimed the man. "I must hae deed an' gone to haeven! Whaur be ye frae? I'm a MacGregor mysel' o' Balquhidder." As he spoke the sallow Scottish face spread into a huge grin, perhaps the first in many weeks.

"Logan Macintyre o' Glasgow," said Logan, not even realizing his error in revealing his real name. The Highland airman stretched out to take Logan's extended hand, then, thinking better of it, instead threw his arms all the way around Logan in an emotional embrace.

There were tears in MacGregor's eyes as he fell back on his pillow. "I'm thinkin' ye're as close as I'll be coming t' me bonny Highland fer some spell, laddie!"

"'Tis muckle nonsense, man!" exclaimed Logan. "We're here t' get ye back on yer way. Are ye up fer it?"

MacGregor glanced over at his companion. "What do ye say, Bob?"

The one whom MacGregor addressed as Bob rose and extended his hand toward Logan. He was as worn and emaciated as his companion, and his clothing was the same coarse garb that Mme. Guillaume had provided. There was, however, a certain cool refinement about him that the Scotsman had lacked.

"I'm Robert Wainborough," he said in a genteel Eaton voice.

Logan knew the name. The elder Wainborough was an M.P. and a baronet. But Robert had carried the name to new heights as an ace R.A.F. pilot and hero of the Battle of Britain.

"Well, Wainborough," said Logan, too hurried and anxious to be impressed by this celebrity before him, "shall we be on our way?" His words were half statement, half question.

"Look, old man," he replied, then paused as he sat back tiredly on the bed and reached for a pack of cigarettes, "we don't want to endanger these people. We're ready to go. But this is the first real roof we've had over our heads since we flew that German coop two months ago. We thought here was a place where we could rest a bit, and start to feel like human beings again. We've been dodging patrols, living in ditches, stealing food—Lord, it's been miserable!"

He paused and lit his cigarette with a shaky hand. "When they told us we had to leave here before we'd even had a full night's sleep—it was more than we could bear!"

"I understand," said Logan solemnly, but he wasn't sure he actually did any more than he had really understood Lise earlier. He had been through his own trials and doubts, it is true, but he wondered if it was possible that he would ever understand either Wainborough or Lise in the way their words were truly meant. But before he had the chance to reflect further on what his future might hold, he was jolted back to reality; Wainborough was speaking again.

"Would you please explain it to them?" he said. "I flunked French at Eaton—never had much of an aptitude for languages."

"I'm sure they know, Wainborough," replied Logan. But he turned back to Lise and briefly related all that had passed between them. Then to his countryman he said, "I wish you could stay and recuperate longer, but we better start thinking about being on our way."

"Mac is in rotten shape," said Wainborough, "though he'd never admit it."

"Can you walk, Mac?"

"Point me in the direction o' me bonny Balquhidder, an' then try t' stop me, lad!" he replied with more spirit than energy. With the words he gathered his remaining strength and, with the help of Paul and Wainborough, got himself into a sitting position.

Logan turned to Lise. They spent a few moments discussing details of a plan that was beginning to form in Logan's mind. It was several miles to the new safe house, but a tram ran about four blocks from the Guillaume place that would take them almost to the doorstep of their destination. They had merely to get the soldiers safely those four blocks. Logan wished they could move under the cover of darkness, but there was no time to wait for nightfall. Besides, roaming the city at night presented its own hazards. At length Logan turned back to the R.A.F. boys.

"Have you lads seen *Gone with the Wind* yet?"

"What?" exclaimed Wainborough. "Have you gone daft, man? What do we care about movies for now?"

Logan smiled. "Have you seen it?"

Both men nodded, but cast each other puzzled looks as they did.

"Well, you two are about to play Ashley Wilkes, and I'll assume the role of Rhett Butler after a questionable evening at Belle Watling's place."

Yet another moment longer the airmen remained confused, until the light dawned on MacGregor as he remembered the scene where Rhett saved Ashley from the Union soldiers by claiming he and Ashley had just spent a drunken evening at a house of ill repute.

"I got ye!" said Mac.

"Then why don't you explain it to our bemused war hero?" said Logan with good-natured sarcasm, "while I attend to a few other details."

24 ❊ *Déjà Vu*

THE MORNING WAS well-advanced when three drunken rousters, well doused with Mme. Guillaume's last bottle of sherry, made their wobbly way down the stairs to the first floor and out onto the sunlit street. They could not have made a better job of it had several bottles of the sherry been inside them rather than merely splashed about their head and clothes. Even Wainborough got into character and could have passed an audition for the part with ease.

They had no sooner exited the building, squinting painfully from the blast of light, when a French policeman loomed up before them. Logan did not falter a moment, but he dared not look at his companions' faces to see their reactions.

"Bonjour, Monsieur Le Gendarme!" said Logan, affecting an extravagant bow, nearly stumbling into the man's arms.

The policeman looked disdainfully down his long nose at the three. "It is early for such behavior, non?" he said sternly.

"Oui . . ." answered Logan, "unless you have been at it all night, eh?" he chuckled, hoping to appeal to this man's natural French love of a good time.

"You are fortunate I am in a generous mood," said the policeman. "But get yourselves home quickly—the Germans are not so benevolent."

"Merci beaucoup! Vous êtes très bien . . . You are a good man, most kind," Logan rattled on. Then he thrust out the bottle of sherry he was holding. "Please share a drink with us."

"Get on your way before I lose my patience!"

Logan bowed again with a sickening grin; then he and his companions staggered on their way.

"You've got nerve, old chap," said Wainborough, beginning to reevaluate his opinion of this Scotsman who had come to rescue him. "I just aged ten years, but you didn't even flinch."

"What'd ye expect?" exclaimed MacGregor. "He's a Scot, isn't he?" He didn't bother to admit that his own heart had nearly stopped at first sight of the gendarme.

Glancing in a shop window, Logan saw that Lise and Paul were behind them at some distance in case they happened to need someone to run interference for them. But he did not kid himself about the danger. He knew too much was at stake for them to risk their organization for the three of them. If serious trouble came, they would be on their own. The loss of three Britons was a small price to pay to keep their network functional. He knew they would help if they could, but they could not compromise their larger work.

By now they had turned down another street, a wider avenue with more midday traffic— mostly bicycles and pedestrians, though there were also a few automobiles. Logan scrutinized their surroundings, thinking that the tram line should not be too much farther, when part way down the street he spied some commotion. A German van had pulled to a stop in the middle of the thoroughfare. His stomach lurched as he saw the S.S. soldiers barricading the street.

"We're finished!" moaned Wainborough.

Just as they passed a narrow alley, Logan nudged his companions into it, even though he saw immediately it was a dead-end.

"Wait here," he said, then stepped back onto the sidewalk and ambled to an adjacent shop window, where he paused as if shopping. In a moment Lise and Paul were at his side, feigning the same activity.

"What's going on?" asked Logan.

"Looks like a snap check," answered Lise. "I doubt it has anything to do with us. It's just a rotten coincidence. The tram stops around the corner *beyond* the barricade."

"Then we have to get past it," said Logan. Not only did they want the tram, but he now saw that a similar barricade was being installed at the other end of the street from where they had just come. They were trapped between the two groups of soldiers. "Those Germans are thorough!" he said.

"And our friends have no papers!"

"I know," said Logan grimly. He rubbed his chin thoughtfully, as if the action might magically prompt some solution to their fix. "We need a diversion," he said at length.

"What do you suggest?" said Lise.

Logan had expected some opposition, or at least some hesitation on her part in going along with him. But she seemed perfectly willing to follow his lead, perhaps because she was wise enough to know this was no place for a debate, or because she had no idea of her own to suggest.

Logan thought a moment more, then said, "How are you at being hit by a car?"

She cocked a questioning eyebrow toward him, perhaps already regretting her decision to allow Logan to play out his hand.

"I have never had the experience, so I do not know," she replied.

"You'll do fine. I'd do it myself, but since I know the dodge, I'll have to play the eyewitness."

He glanced once more up and down the street. There were few cars, so the timing would be even more crucial, and the chances of having their deception seen all the more dangerous.

"Okay," he said finally, "we'll all amble slowly toward the barricade as if we don't know one another. When a likely vehicle pulls up to the barricade, just step out and drop in front of it. But *please* make certain it's already almost at a stop. You'll also have to try to gauge a moment when the soldiers are absorbed with someone else and not noticing the car as it approaches."

"Oui," replied Lise. "I see what you are getting at. It's crazy, but it just might work."

Then Logan turned to Paul. "You must get into the line, Paul, and get the people stirred up. A discreet word here and there ought to do it, and keep moving so no one can pinpoint the trouble to you. Can you handle that?"

The boy nodded, warming to the excitement of being thus used to outwit the Boche.

Logan then returned to the alley, briefed his countrymen on their part in the ploy, and verbally gave them the address of the safe house should they become separated.

Paul moved into place in the line where already thirty or forty pedestrians were shuffling about, along with two cars. Logan judged it would not take much to incite them, for they were already cross and surly at this bothersome inconvenience. Soon Lise crossed the street, hoping that by doing thus she would divert attention from the side where the airmen would be making their escape.

A shiny black sedan pulled up to the roadblock. It would be the perfect pigeon. Out of the corner of his eye, Logan watched Lise. She was making no move. Why was she waiting?

The glare on the windshield shifted and Logan saw that the car was occupied by a German officer—nothing less than a general!

Good girl! thought Logan. She had her head about her!

The general's car pulled around the crowd, up to the barricade, and was allowed to pass. As the soldiers, four of them in all, were replacing the barricade, an older gray Renault pulled up. Logan held his breath. Lise stepped off the sidewalk.

In a moment she was down in such a commotion of squealing breaks, agonized screams, and crowd noise that Logan feared she might have actually been hit. He berated himself for coming up with the fool plan, but no matter what happened he couldn't fold now. Back in England, he and Skittles only faced a few days in jail if their scam failed. But now five lives depended on success, and there was no place to bolt to even if he wanted to.

"Someone's been killed!" came a cry from the crowd; Logan thought he recognized Paul's tenor voice.

"Mon Dieu! she's been hit!"

"There's blood! Someone help her—the girl's dead!"

"No, she's still breathing, she needs a doctor."

The voices were from many different quarters now, as the throng pressed in around the scene.

"Hey, don't push . . . someone took my wallet!"

"It's the Germans' fault!"

Curses and accusations and commotion grew, leveled both toward the Boche and between the volatile Frenchmen themselves. Pushing and shoving gave way to an occasional outbreak that looked as though it could turn the scene into an ugly mob, enough to draw two of the S.S. men from their posts into the disorderly fray. A third stepped well away from the barricade to better view the melee. A quick glance to his right showed that Wainborough and MacGregor were inching their way closer to the roadblock. Just as he was about to make his move, Logan remembered his jacket, still reeking of sherry. Tearing it off and dropping it on the ground, he rushed up to the fourth soldier, who was still firmly planted at his post.

"Please," he said, his face and tone filled with frantic entreaty, "I'm a doctor. I must get to the girl, but I can't get through the crowd. Help me!"

"Folge ihm!" the soldier grunted, pointing to the third S.S. man.

Logan shook his head, pretending not to understand, and grabbing the man's arm. "Please help me!" he said, and managed to get the man a few steps away from his position.

"Hans!" called the German to his comrade. But the third soldier was too engrossed in the noisy spectacle to hear.

"Stupid Französisch!" he said, swearing an oath vehemently at Logan, then striding hotly up to the man he had called Hans. "Take this doctor and see what he can do."

A surreptitious glance showed Logan that he had given his airmen enough time to get past the barricade. But they still had to get the few yards to the next street and around the corner out of sight.

"Oh, merci . . . merci!" exclaimed Logan effusively. He put an arm around the man, plying him with what hollow praise he could dream up.

Mac and Wainborough had broken into a trot, and Logan caught a glimpse of pain etched onto Mac's homely countenance. But the Scot hadn't made it this close to home to give up so easily. If they were spotted now, running, they would be dead ducks. Logan had to keep the German's attention another twenty or thirty seconds, yet his experience told him he had already carried the con beyond its natural limits. The soldiers would get suspicious before long.

"If you want to help," shouted the German in broken French, "then go *help!*"

Logan could stall no longer. The third soldier had taken him in tow and was shoving him through the crowd. He couldn't even chance a look over his shoulder. He breathed a quick prayer that he had bought his charges sufficient time. When he heard no outbursts at the barricade, he realized he had—the flyboys had make it! He also saw that Paul had made his exit too, sneaking to the head of the line, and passing through the quick inspection; perhaps he would be able to help the Anglais.

Now Logan could turn his energy to getting himself and Lise out of there.

Scarcely a minute or two had elapsed since the gray sedan had slammed on its brakes. As Logan elbowed his way through the crowd with the aid of his S.S. escort, he saw that Lise was only just then pulling herself to a sitting position. She shook her head groggily, while rubbing her face with her hands. Her nose was smudged, and a scrape across her cheek looked real enough, with genuine blood oozing from it. *She is definitely no amateur*, thought Logan to himself.

"Mademoiselle," he said, kneeling down beside her, "I am a doctor. Where are you hurt?"

"I will call an ambulance," said the German, seeming to be genuinely concerned.

"Non . . . non!" replied Lise. "I will be fine. I only had the wind knocked from me."

"Can you walk?" asked Logan.

"Oui. Just give me a hand." She began to pull herself unsteadily to her feet as a cheer rose from the crowd. Then she winced sharply in pain as her left knee buckled. "I think it is my hip," she said.

"I should examine you in my office," said Logan, the conscientious medical man. "It is not far—only around the corner."

"I'll call a car," offered the helpful German.

"Do not trouble yourself," said Lise, rising again on her feet. "I can manage to walk that far." She bravely smiled her thanks, then limped off with Logan's steadying arm around her. The barricade was parted for them and no one even bothered to look at their papers.

The half-block past the barricade and around the corner seemed to take hours. The urge to make a run for it was almost overpowering. But Lise and Logan kept up the ruse of doctor and patient until they were well on their way down the next street. They hoped they would be in time to catch Paul and the two refugees, but speed was always a sure way of arousing attention. They did not break into a jog until they were well out of sight, when they saw the tram coming to a stop a hundred yards ahead.

Two minutes later Logan sank gratefully onto a back seat of one of the vehicles. MacGregor, Wainborough, Paul, and Lise were all safely aboard as well, scattered throughout the car.

Barring any further interference from the Germans, they were home free, at least for this particular episode.

25 ❈ New Compatriots

LOGAN STIRRED THE saccharin into his coffee.

The adventure of the day was successfully over. MacGregor and Wainborough were settled into their new safe house. They could now look forward to several days of recuperation before they were moved along to the next stage of the escape line—probably Marseille in unoccupied France—and then, with the help of a guide, over the Pyrenees into Spain. Their trek was far from over, but if they were lucky they'd be home for Christmas. The snow would be piled high in the glens of MacGregor's Balquhidder, and icy wind wafting down from the mountains. His little cottage would be filled with the warm, sweet, comforting smell of peat, while his mother tended a bubbling pot of tatties and neeps. . . .

"You are deep in thought, M. Tanant," said Lise, setting a plate of bread and cheese on the table.

They had come to her flat after leaving the airmen. It was closer than the bookstore, and she thought Logan might want to see the wireless that was secreted there. He glanced up absently, hardly realizing his mind had wandered so far from the present.

"Oh, I was just thinking of home," he said. "Scotland, you know," he added with a light ironical laugh. "I suppose I was thinking more of MacGregor's home than of any home I have ever known. You know, country kitchens, peat fires, heather blooming on the hills, a cow mooing softly in the byre—the poverty-stricken but romantic Scottish highlands which everyone since Robbie Burns has loved to write and sing about?"

"What was *your* home like?" asked Lise.

"More along the line of soot-covered brick buildings for miles on end, air filled with the sharp metallic sounds of industry, smokestacks spewing out black smoke, and that singular odor only a seaport slum can produce," replied Logan. "I'm a city fellow, born and bred. Glasgow. But I'm not complaining. The city was good to me, and I rather liked it. Maybe I would have been better off in the open air and barren hills and fields; who knows?"

He paused and lifted his eyes to Lise, who had been listening with great intensity. "What about you? Are you from Paris?"

"I too am a city girl," she replied, then paused. She looked as if she was about to say more, but instead rose to refill their coffee cups.

"And . . . ?" said Logan.

She took the coffeepot from the stove and began pouring into the cups, appearing not to have heard him.

"What is there to say?" she sighed at length. "What there is of my life is all too apparent—intrigue and death, killing, deception . . . a hell of uncertainty. As for my past life, what good does it do to remember when I was alive and my days were filled with laughter? Those times are gone, and it seems they will never return."

She had spoken with such sorrow and pain; Logan had not expected the emotion it roused within him. Yet her voice contained courage too, consistent with the tough shell he had begun to associate with her.

"You are so sure the past will never come again?"

"The old France is dead, M. Tanant," she replied with sadness. "And I died a year ago when the Germans marched beneath the Arc de Triomphe," she replied, "and the fragrance of the chestnuts along the Champs-Elysees was replaced with the stench of Nazis. I died when they took my family to a concentration camp."

"I'm sorry. I didn't know."

"Do you want to know about my life now, M. Tanant?"

"You are Jewish?"

"Perhaps you object to helping us?"

"Why should I?"

"Many people do, even fellow Frenchmen."

"I am not one of them."

"Jewish educators were among the first to be 'purged,'" she went on, apparently satisfied. "Naturally the Nazis fear the intelligentsia, for it is the thinking man who can see their vile propaganda for what it is. My father was a professor of Talmud—a very subversive threat, that! He cared only for his Torah and keeping the Sabbath."

She paused and shook her head. "My poor parents—I haven't kept the Sabbath since their death, and somehow I think that fact grieves them as much as all these atrocities in the world." She set down the coffeepot and sat down in a chair across the table from Logan. "Even after they removed him from the university, he said we must forbear in peace. Then two or three of his colleagues disappeared, men who had spoken out against the Reich. He made the mistake of trying to intervene. He believed, right to the end, that all men were basically good, and he tried to deal with the Nazis as if they were reasonable men. A neighbor who watched the Gestapo carry them off said my father wore an incredible look of surprise on his face."

"How did you manage to keep out of their clutches?"

"Pure chance, I suppose. I was away when they raided our home. When I returned, it was over and my parents were gone. I would have waited for them to return, except that a neighbor told me what happened. She said the Gestapo would surely come back for me. I called Henri— he and my father grew up together. He made inquiries for me and learned that my parents and sister had been taken to Drancy, a camp just outside Paris. After that we heard no more until the letter came to Henri informing him that my parents had died in what they called an influenza epidemic. Nothing was said about my sister. I still don't know if she is alive or dead—"

She broke off suddenly, her voice faltering, but she tightened her jaw and did not let her emotions take control.

"I would like to change the subject," she said after a brief pause.

"I'm sorry," said Logan again.

Lise attempted to smile, but the action was by no means a bright one; it did not even reach up into her eyes, but was filled with gentleness and sincerity.

"Do you mind if I call you Michel?" she finally asked. "After what we have been through today, formalities seem ridiculous."

"I don't mind," he replied, "especially since I only know your first name."

"Some life, oui?" said Lise. "And *that* is not even my real one. I cannot tell you my name, and I must forget yours."

"Forget mine?" said Logan, puzzled.

"You surely are not unaware of your error today at Mme. Guillaume's. You were so intent on giving courage to your countrymen—"

"I'd already forgotten!" exclaimed Logan, chuckling as he recalled his slip up.

"I did not want to say anything and draw further attention to it. But do not worry, I have already forgotten it also."

"I won't worry," he replied playfully. "I think I can trust you."

"You British!" she scolded. "You are so naive! But you will learn your lessons soon enough if you remain long in Paris. You should have left your *trust* back in England. It is too heavy a burden to carry here in France. Even the best intentioned comrade could spill his guts under the tortuous thumb of the Gestapo. Trust your companions only as far as you must—for your sake and theirs."

"That's what they mean when they call this a lonely life?" said Logan. "Though it has not seemed such to me yet."

"It will, Michel, it will. Then it will begin to eat away at you."

She stopped, trying to shake off the gloom that had begun to settle about her.

"So tell me about *La Librairie*," said Logan in a lighter tone. "How did such a menagerie manage to come together under one roof?"

Again Lise's lips twitched into a smile, this time accompanied by a soft chuckle.

"If you did that more often, maybe things would not appear so grim," Logan commented.

"Perhaps . . ." She seemed to meditate a moment on Logan's reference to her hidden emotions, then shook away the reflective mood to answer his question. "You think us an odd assortment? It's all quite logical, actually. Of course, you already know of my connection to Henri. Antoine is Henri's brother-in-law, married to Henri's sister before she was killed by the Gestapo. They are not as different as it appears on the surface. Henri is the mild and gentle one; Antoine is boisterous and gentle. But both have soft hearts and nerves of steel. I would trust my life to either of them."

"Quite a statement coming from one who trusts nobody."

She cocked an eyebrow at his friendly jibe. "There are no consistencies in this business," she said smugly. "That is another thing you will have to learn."

"Speaking of inconsistencies, tell me about Claude."

"He is a shadow that stands out, even in a world of shadows," replied Lise. "The only thing I know of him is that he turned up one day with Antoine's daughter. He was with Antoine's wife and daughter when they were all three captured, and Claude was the only one to escape. I think he is a survivor, and manages to do so by keeping to himself."

"Was he in love with the girl?"

"She was most certainly in love with him. But I find it difficult to imagine such an emotion as love with the heart of one such as Claude. Though, who can say what may lie under that stone wall of his? And who am I to talk, you would perhaps say?"

"There is something immensely different between his wall and yours," said Logan. "At least that is how I perceive it. I can't quite describe it yet, but ask me when I know each of you better."

"Don't count on knowing Claude better—you, of all people. He despises the British."

"For letting France fall?"

"Nothing so pragmatic."

"What did we ever do to him?"

"Perhaps a simple difference in ideology," answered Lise. "Claude is a Communist."

"They are a wild and dangerous lot, especially now that Hitler has invaded Russia. Why do you people keep him around?"

"Antoine feels a loyalty toward him, for his daughter's sake, no doubt. But perhaps in the case of a man like Claude, it is sometimes wise to have him where you can keep an eye on him, non?"

"I hope you're right," said Logan with some skepticism. "Now, what about the most fascinating member of your secret little enclave?"

"Jean Pierre?" As she said the priest's name, Lise's taut features momentarily softened. "An incredible man. His father was Baron Olivier de Beauvoir of Belgium. Jean Pierre, for better or worse, is the only one of us whose life is an open book. Before entering the priesthood, his face appeared on the pages of every society paper in Europe. He was present at all the social events, and even considered to be something of a philanderer. I must say," she added with a smile of affection, "he still manages to be in attendance at as many parties as possible. 'For the cause,' he always says with a coy grin. His family has been in Paris for two generations, accumulating their vast wealth in the textile industry. His brother Arthur, now head of the family, is in quite tight with von Stülpnagel, the military governor of France. Jean Pierre is truly cut out of a different *cloth* than the rest of his family, in more ways than one."

"Is his brother a collaborator, or is it some kind of front?"

"How Jean Pierre wishes it were a front! But Arthur de Beauvoir is making a fortune off the German occupation—a true profiteer. Poor Jean Pierre! I suppose he will die one day trying to atone for his brother's sins."

"The Germans have arrested him several times, have they not?"

"Merely a show," replied Lise. "They hope eventually to break him down, and bring him over to their side with his brother. But they do not know Jean Pierre! He could never be one of them but he is too well-connected for them to hold him. It drives the Germans crazy! They know he is involved in the escape route, but they can do nothing about it—unless they apprehend him in the very act."

"I appear to have fallen into quite an assemblage!" said Logan.

"And despite what anyone says, it will be for you to take the reins and lead us."

"What!" protested Logan immediately. "That's not my game."

"Quelle bêtise! Nonsense!" replied Lise. "I saw you in action, Michel. You are the man for the job."

"The man for what job?"

"Leading our small group."

"I came here merely to deliver some money and teach someone how to operate a wireless, not to join your band permanently."

"Perhaps your commander did not tell you all."

"I was sent on assignment to help you however I could, but—"

"The help we need, Michel, is leadership."

"I didn't know the job was vacant."

"Henri is the closest we have to a *leader*. But he would be the first to admit that he is not capable of making *La Librairie* a truly far-reaching and effective weapon against the Nazis. He lacks the audacity, the *élan* necessary—qualities, I might add, you seem to possess in abundance."

"What about Jean Pierre?"

"He is too visible."

"Claude and Antoine would have something to say against your views."

"Claude would submit to no one, that is true. But he himself could not garner the loyalty of an ant," Lise replied with conviction. "And Antoine, though he has the heart of a hundred patriots, knows he is no leader."

"That is exactly how I feel about myself. I've always worked with one or two others only. I'm not your man." Logan knew that the sort of leadership Lise spoke of demanded more than he was willing to give. The thrill and excitement of this work were appealing enough, but not the responsibility for others. Had he looked more deeply into himself, he might have quickly seen a connection between his refusal to entertain thoughts of responsibility in this situation, and his failure in his marriage. Instead, he offered Lise another suggestion.

"What about you?" he asked.

"Face it, Michel. Whether it's here or in some other circumstance, you were meant to lead. Even if you try to hide from the inevitable, the day will come when it will find you."

The words had a strange ring of familiarity to them. Into his mind darted a fragment of something Joanna had said as he was leaving Stonewycke.

Now it was Logan's turn to change the subject.

"I'd better start instructing you on this wireless, as long as you're the one who's going to be taking it over."

She nodded her consent, and for the next hour he gave her some initial instruction, ending with the words, "I'm scheduled to transmit to London tomorrow. I'll give you your first actual experience in being *La Librairie's* new radio operator."

By the time he returned to his hotel that evening, Logan was exhausted. He stopped on the way for a quick dinner, then took a moment to call Henri from the hotel phone. It was nine o'clock by the time he dragged himself up the stairs to his room.

He kicked off his shoes and literally fell into bed. Almost immediately the moment his head hit the pillow, however, it seemed as if his mind suddenly came awake, though his body screamed out for sleep. For half an hour he fought with himself, turning back and forth, then finally swung out of bed, hoping a few paces around the room would help. All he managed to do was stub his toe against his suitcase in the darkness.

To kill time, he switched on a light, flung open the suitcase lid, and began to unpack his few things. His hand fell upon two shirts and he lifted them out.

They were French made, as were the trousers and handkerchiefs that followed. These were not really *his* things. They belonged to Michel Tanant. Razor, soap, socks—all of French origin. In addition there were several book catalogues Henri had provided him with last evening to further validate his Lyon identity. And if all this was not sufficient, his wallet was stuffed full of additional reminders—the name and number of Tanant's unit in the French army were stamped on his demobilization papers. His work permit stated that his occupation was book-seller and that he was employed at *La Ecrit Nouvelle* in Lyon. With this was the ticket he had supposedly used to travel from Lyon to Paris, officially stamped. London missed no details. He even carried a much-worn photo of Tanant's parents, now dead, whose graves the Gestapo could find in a churchyard outside Lyon—if they chose to check so closely.

Logan smiled mordantly. Taking everything together, Michel Tanant's life appeared to be on more solid ground than Logan Macintyre's. How nice it would be to be able to wrap himself up so completely in the person of this exemplary Frenchman that, as Atkinson had said, he could erase his own name from his mind.

But that was easier fantasized than carried out in reality.

To forget who he really was would mean forgetting Allison too. Could he ever do that? Did he *want* to? He had been successful over the last several months of pushing her toward the most obscure corners of his mind. He could have spoken of her to Lise, but he hadn't, though he had thought of her once or twice during the conversation. But he hadn't even mentioned that he was married.

He had told Allison that he needed time to think about their relationship. Yet he had run off to an environment where he did not even have to be himself, much less meditate on the problems of one Logan Macintyre, distant Scotsman from out of his past. It would be so easy just to let Logan die a slow and silent death. Everything he needed for his new life was right in this bag.

Oh, Allison, Allison! he thought. *This war has made everything so easy for me, easy to forget the past, easy to run away. I wonder if you'll ever understand why I must continue with what I am doing, even though it might tear us apart. You may hate me when I return— I wouldn't blame you if you already despised me. But that's a chance I guess I'll have to take.*

Suddenly he shoved aside the suitcase, only half empty. He *had* to sleep. He wouldn't be thinking such stupid, morbid, defeating thoughts if he wasn't so bloody tired!

He lay back again on the bed more determinedly than before. But he was able to find only fitful rest throughout the rest of the night, until the light of dawn pierced through the blackout shades. What sleep he did get was filled with ghoulish images and nightmares, featuring alternately Claude's sneering countenance, S.S. soldiers gunning Logan down while he was trying to run a roadblock, and Allison's lovely face—but only her face, floating as in a fog above him, crying out to him, but he could not answer.

And in her eyes were the tears of endless weeping.

26 ❊ *Face in the Crowd*

Allison LOOKED ACROSS the table at her old friend Sarah Bramford, now Sarah Fielding, wife of a well-to-do shipping magnate. The years had been kind to Sarah, though she had never been a particularly pretty girl. Today she was strikingly attractive in her ex-quisite Dior silk suit and rich fox stole, obviously selected from the season's new collection and priced well beyond the limits of clothing rations.

Allison tried not to think of the fact that her own dress was two years old, and had hardly been in style even then, notwithstanding that the lovely silk print did possess stylish lines and was the nicest dress she owned. If everything else in her life had been right, she would probably not even have noticed, because clothes, after all, had very little to do with her present frame of mind.

"You should have seen my Wally's face when the sheik asked him if *I* could be part of his harem!" Sarah paused to giggle in the midst of her story about her adventures on one of her husband's recent trips to the Middle East. "Oh, but those Arabs are charming," she added with a coy wink.

"My father is in Egypt," said Allison, attempting to keep her focus on the luncheon conversation as the two women sat in the plush dining room of London's Green Velvet Restaurant. "He is fascinated with the Arabs, but doesn't think they like the British much."

"They like our money, though," replied Sarah knowingly.

"They'd just as soon have German marks as British pounds."

"But as long as we still control the canal at Suez," said Sarah, "they'll be our friends. My Wally says that's why the fighting in North Africa is so crucial—keeping the sea lanes open."

"At the rate that Rommel is going, all the fighting might not matter much longer."

"What defeatest talk!" exclaimed Sarah, with more emphasis than she felt. "Don't let old Winnie Churchill hear you. Now, no more politics or war talk. It's positively depressing." She took a dainty sip of tea as if to emphasize the more vital things in life. "You haven't said a word about my dress, Allison—isn't it scrumptious?"

"It certainly is," answered Allison with proper enthusiasm. "How on earth do you manage it these days?"

"Oh, Allison, don't be so naive. If you know the right people, you can manage anything."

At that moment a waiter came to replenish their pot of tea. "Will there be anything else, ladies?" he asked.

Sarah shook her head and the man departed.

"I wore this to the Fairgate's for tea last week," she continued, as if the announcement were tantamount to the capture of the German high command. "Olivia and her mother practically drooled all over it. Have you been to their new city place over by Hyde Park? It's on Portland Place."

"No, I haven't," replied Allison.

"Oh, well, you must. By the way, did you hear that Charles was wounded recently?"

"No. How serious is it?"

"He's being sent home, but it's not terribly dreadful. Of course he *will* be decorated, so I hear." Sarah sipped again at her tea. "I can't tell you how thankful I am that Wally's back has kept him out of the military. You must feel the same way about Logan."

Allison did not reply immediately.

This was only the second time she had seen Sarah since her return to London, and she had not yet found the opportunity to bring up the subject of Logan. Actually, there had probably been any number of opportunities; she had just not found the courage.

By all appearances, it seemed that Sarah Bramford Fielding had everything—clothes, status, a happy marriage, and was even a reasonably nice person to boot, if you could overlook the superficiality of her interests, and a slightly oversized ego. But she was pleasant enough to be around.

Allison had never spoken of her marital problems to her friends, always choked by her own version of ego, better labeled pride. Yet over the last months Allison had been taking strides toward new levels of maturity. Bit by bit that very pride was being beaten down by the hammer of difficulties, and the reality of true personhood was slowly being built within her. She was learning the folly of living in a manufactured world of shallow whimsy. That world of empty priorities had blinded her to Logan's need until it was too late, and now she was about to let it supersede her own need. She couldn't let that happen. She couldn't let one more acquaintance drift off into trivialities because she lacked the courage to speak out the concerns of her heart. She needed a friend just now—a real friend. If they could but pierce the surface of their relationship, it was possible Sarah could be such a friend. They had known each other for years, but they had never attained any depth with one another. Dresses and parties and school and men and fashions had dominated their conversations, but nothing beyond. Was it possible there could be more between them? *Should* be more?

With the question Allison found herself wondering if she had purposely avoided substance in her friendships in order to keep from having to look too deeply within herself. Did she even know how to share her heart with Sarah? What about her faith in God? Was that something she could talk about to another?

These were suddenly new questions for Allison. But they were questions whose answers she did not want to postpone any longer. Reality could only emerge between them one way. And all at once it seemed imperative to Allison that she be a *real* person, with *real* emotions, rather than trying to cover up the hurts she was struggling with inside.

"You know, Sarah," she said, "Logan and I have been having some problems."

"What is it?" asked Sarah, her high forehead creased with concern.

"It's been going on for some time, I guess," Allison went on, hesitantly, but gaining in confidence as she saw genuine feeling etched on her friend's face. "We've been separated for the last few months."

Uttering the statement was perhaps the hardest thing she had ever done in her life. Yet once it was out, she felt oddly relieved. Perhaps sitting opposite her was a friend to help her shoulder some of the burden.

"Allison, I'm so sorry," said Sarah. "Why have you waited so long to say anything?"

"It's not an easy thing to admit. I didn't know what—you know, what you might think of me."

"Nonsense. It changes nothing between us."

"Everyone wouldn't agree. A broken marriage is the kiss of death to some people. You're different in their eyes from that moment on."

"Well, I won't tell a soul if that's how you want it."

"Thank you. It's hard to admit one's failings. I guess I want people to think well of me."

"I suppose I know what you mean," sympathized Sarah. "Everyone gets together and *talks,* but nobody says what they're really thinking, what's really hurting them inside."

"For so long I've tried to keep anyone from seeing deep inside me, but lately I've been so alone. I think what I really just need is a friend—someone to confide in. We've known each other for so long that—"

"That it's about time we started to act like it," Sarah finished Allison's sentence for her. "If I let myself admit it, I need that kind of friend too."

"You?"

"I suppose my marriage itself is fine—most of the time," said Sarah. "But believe me, the London social set is the most shallow mob you ever want to see, and sometimes I'm no better."

"Remember, this is me, Sarah. I used to be a part of all that—or at least wanted to be."

"You never did quite fit in though, as much as you tried. Especially in recent years. And I mean that as a compliment!" Sarah smiled again, then added, "I always thought it had something to do with Logan."

"Not at first," replied Allison. "The focus of my life changed when I really tried to give my life to the Lord. It happened with Logan and me together about the same time, just before we were married. God began to teach me new priorities and attitudes, and before I knew it I began to feel out of place with all the gossip and backbiting and petty jealousies and flaunting of wealth that went on among us. I was the worst of the lot!"

"I did see a change in you, Allison, but I guess I was too stupid to say anything."

"We all try to put on a front of self-sufficiency. Just because I was taking being a Christian seriously doesn't mean I changed overnight, either."

"You'll never know how many times when I was with your family that I wanted to ask what made them all so . . . I don't know—different . . . complete, I suppose is the best way to describe it."

"You really felt that way?"

"Your great-grandmother always made me feel so special and loved. I knew she was a religious lady and I couldn't help wondering if that had anything to do with it. But I was always too embarrassed to ask. You know how it's embarrassing to talk about spiritual things. It shouldn't be, I suppose, but it is. You think people will laugh at you for being interested in religion. So many people think it's only for old people."

"I know. That's what I always thought, before I really knew what living closely with the Lord could mean in my life."

"But even though Lady Margaret *was* old," Sarah continued, "I always wished I could have that sparkle in my life that she had."

"So did I," said Allison with a tender smile as she recalled her many struggles over that very thing, and her eventual reunion on a deeper level with her great-grandmother. "But she would say there was no reason why we couldn't have what she did. It was simply a matter of making a choice about one's priorities and attitudes."

"It hardly seems *that* simple."

"It was her choice to let the Spirit of Christ fill her with a new outlook on life that made her who she was," replied Allison. "And that same thing happened to me nine years ago. I gave my life to God too, and for a time, things were different. I had new values and perspectives, and it really did change my attitude toward everything. Unfortunately, I allowed too many external pressures to rob that original dedication from me. I guess it happened so slowly I didn't notice. Then as things started going sour between Logan and me, I began looking in other directions for help. It took Logan's leaving to shake me up enough to begin looking in the right direction again. I'm trying to bring the Lord back into my life, but I don't know what He is planning to do with my marriage—I haven't seen or heard from Logan in five months."

"Dear, you must be miserable!"

"I'd be lying if I tried to say I wasn't. But God is giving me strength to face it, a little bit at a time. I wish I could describe it better so you could understand."

"I would like to hear more," replied Sarah.

"You would?"

"Who wouldn't want the kind of contentment Lady Margaret had? But let's talk more on the way."

"On the way where?"

"I want to surprise you."

"But the nurse is expecting me back."

"Give her a call and tell her you'll be a little late," said Sarah firmly. "You don't want to miss this."

"I feel as if I'm being kidnapped," laughed Allison.

"I didn't think I'd have to kidnap you to get you to my designer."

"What's this all about, Sarah?"

"I know a new dress won't solve your problems, Allison. And maybe it's silly to worry about what you look like. But sometimes a woman needs something new, just to feel good about herself. What do you say—it couldn't hurt, could it?" She winked and smiled.

"I could never afford—"

"Ta, ta, dear girl! This one is on my Arabian sheik!"

The next couple of hours proved a heaven-sent boon for Allison. The new dress proved the least of her delight. Rather, it was the transformation of her friendship with Sarah brought on by the newfound honesty that had flowed between them.

Late in the afternoon they left the elegant offices where Allison had been fitted for her new outfit, diligently searching the street for a taxi—not a frequent sight in those days of petrol rationing. They had walked halfway down the block when Allison stopped suddenly, her gaze focused intently on a newspaper stand across the street.

"Allison, what is it?" asked Sarah.

"That man over there—I've seen him before."

"Oh . . . ?" The revelation hardly seemed startling to Sarah.

"I saw him once with Logan."

Allison hadn't given the incident a single thought since before the blitz. It had taken place long before she had returned to Stonewycke, but now it all came back to her clearly. She and Logan were to meet for lunch at a west-end restaurant. She'd arrived a few minutes early and was speaking to the maitre d' about a table, when she spotted Logan already seated at the far end of the room. With him was a man whose austere, pock-marked face was not easy to forget. Even had the face been of more ordinary features, she could hardly have erased from her mind the reaction on the countenances of both men when they saw her approach. The stranger cut off his speech immediately and made his departure with only a curt tip of his hat for Allison's benefit. When she questioned Logan about him, his response was evasive and vague. She knew that the meeting must have something to do with his mysterious job, but Logan would say nothing, and there the matter dropped. She had hardly thought of it again until the same man should suddenly appear out of the past, bringing it all vividly back to her.

Without thinking, she stepped suddenly out into the street toward the newsstand, causing several passing autos to slam on their brakes. Hardly taking a notice, she hurried on across.

"Sir!" she called out as she approached.

The man made no response.

"I say, there at the newsstand!" she called again, reaching the other side of the street and hurrying up to where he stood.

He glanced up, a cloud of uncertainty passing over his face for an instant. As it did, Allison could see the split-second hesitation as he debated within himself what he should do. At last it appeared as if it was more compulsion than decision that forced his eyes to acknowledge her.

"Sir," she said when their eyes met, "may I please speak with you?"

But in the next instant, another cloud passed over his countenance, this time one of sudden recognition. The magazine he had been browsing fell from his hands, he turned on his heel, and quickly rushed away.

"Please—I must talk to you!" cried Allison after him.

She had taken little notice of the gathering afternoon crowd till that moment. But now suddenly it seemed as though the sidewalk was swarming with people—all bent on preventing her from catching up with the elusive stranger. Weaving her way in and out, she managed to keep him in sight for about half a block. Then suddenly he was gone.

27 ❄ Billy's Assistance

"Y E'RE TALKIN' CRAZINESS, Miz Macintyre—if I might be so blunt," said Billy Cochran.

"But you might be able to find out who he was."

"An' just how do y' propose I'd be doin' that?"

"Logan used to tell me some of the things you and he'd done together," said Allison, "when he was in a good mood and wanted to make me laugh. The way he tells it, *you* could do anything!"

"Pshaw!" said Billy, but not without a flicker of pride in his eye at the compliment from an old friend.

"But I just *can't* let it go, Billy—even if it's just one chance in a hundred. Aren't long shots in the nature of your business?" she added demurely.

Billy smiled. Here was Logan's wife trying to con *him*!

The incident at the newsstand had been plaguing Allison for a whole day; now she could stand it no longer. Until that afternoon with Sarah she had resigned herself to simply biding her time until Logan saw fit to contact her. But now suddenly she realized she might be able to take steps to contact him! Billy had once cautioned her against the futility of trying to get a lead on Logan's well-cooled trail. But now everything was changed. This would be no aimless poking about—there was now something concrete to go on. She had seen a man who knew Logan, and probably knew what work he was involved in. If she could only talk to him!

Billy, however, had been none too optimistic, and had done his best to convince her against it when the next day she ventured into his list shop.

"Even allowin' fer the possibility—" said the grizzled old man.

"Then you admit, it *is* possible!"

"I admit to nothin', young lady. I'm just saying that a quick glimpse of a face in a crowd, disappearin' as fast as it showed itself, is 'ardly much evidence to lay a bet on, even for a 'undred-to-one nag."

"He knows where Logan is," pleaded Allison. "I'm sure of it. I could see it in his eyes."

"Even if it were possible to locate Logan through an old acquaintance, this 'ere bloke hain't likely the man to help you. You don't know 'is name, where he lives—nothin'! And you said yerself, he didn't appear none too friendly."

"But you could do it, Billy! I know you could, even without all that information. The police do it all the time, and Logan always says you were two or three steps ahead of the law."

"I'm not so sure ye're graspin' his meanin'," said Billy with a chuckle.

"However he meant it," insisted Allison, "you're the man for the job. You care about Logan. That's more than the police would do."

"Maybe 'tis them wot ought t' help you."

"You know I can't go to them."

Before Billy could answer her, the phone rang and took his attention for a few moments.

"First call I've 'ad all day," he said, hanging up. "With the race tracks closed on account of the war, I don't get much action—'cept a cricket or rugby match now and then." He paused, jotted down something in a notebook, then turned back to the problem at hand. "I suppose ye're right; the police hain't the ones t' help you, for more reasons than one."

"But *you* can help me, Billy."

He raised his eyebrows as if the idea were too outlandish to consider.

"Miz Macintyre . . . I'm thinkin' that maybe the strain of the last few weeks has been too 'ard on you. You hain't thinkin' straight."

"You know more about this city's underworld than anyone—at least anyone *I* know."

"You hain't still thinkin' Logan's gone back t' the old life?"

"No. I believe you when you say he's not. But he still might be in some kind of trouble, and that's the logical place to start. Besides, the man I saw Logan with, and saw again at the newsstand today, did not look like he came from Chelsea."

Billy rubbed the stubbly beard on his chin for a moment. In his mind Lady Allison MacNeil Macintyre was as sweet and gentle—and innocent—as any lady he had ever known. Yet more than once Logan had hinted at the presence of a wide stubborn streak that could surface in her. And now Billy could see it more than clearly in her determined blue eyes. She was not about to be moved, now that her mind was set. But perhaps with his experience he might be able to interject some practicality into her wild scheme.

All at once he recalled a similar time when it was Logan who had approached him with a crazy idea of a sting to swindle Chase Morgan. Now it was his wife taking up where he left off. Maybe she wasn't as innocent as he made her out to be. *Both them young folks gots a stiff-necked streak in them,* he said to himself. *'Tis hardly no wonder they're havin' problems.* Logan had not listened to Billy's voice of reason ten years ago, though he had submitted enough to Billy's instruction to keep him clear of disaster.

Billy glanced up at Allison. Yes, he could tell she was going to go ahead with her hunt for her husband with or without his help. Perhaps he owed it to Logan to try to keep her out of trouble, too.

Billy removed his spectacles, which he wore constantly now, and wiped the lenses off on his sleeve. Methodically he rubbed the grime on them around in a circle, then placed them again on his nose and peered once more at his friend's wife, as if somehow his little delay might have changed things. It had not. Her eyes were just as determined as ever.

"Ye're askin' for trouble, missy," he finally replied, but there was an air of defeat clearly in his tone. "If this feller is as crooked as you think, he hain't goin' t' take kindly t' bein' dogged about London. An' even if you do find 'im, you'll probably end up regrettin' it in the end. But wot'll be more likely is you'll find 'im an' then he won't know any more about Logan's whereabouts as I do."

"You'll help me, though, won't you, Billy?"

"I'm an old fool is wot I am," he replied. But how could he refuse her pleading eyes? And he would never be able to face Logan again if he left her to her own resources, and something was to happen to her.

They began back at the newsstand. The vendor, however, was no more communicative with Billy than he had been with Allison when she had questioned him the day before. But at least they could surmise that if the stranger frequented the newsstand, then he must have reason to be often in this part of the city. If they were lucky, either his work or residence might be close by. They spent the better part of the next two days methodically visiting shops, hotels, and taverns in the nearby precincts hoping something would turn up.

By the end of the second day, Allison's voice was hoarse with repeating the man's description, and poor Billy's old arthritic limbs ached as they seldom did these days. At four o'clock they came to the door of a tobacconist shop. Billy declared that this would be his last stop for the day, and Allison gave him no argument. She was footsore, tired, and discouraged, and wanted nothing more just then but to go home, soak her feet, and play with her little girl, whom she feared she had been neglecting of late.

The pungent odor of rich blends of tobacco filled the air inside the shop, and for the hundredth time Allison forced out a description of the man she had almost begun to think was only a figment of her imagination.

"Tall, ye say?" said the stocky, balding proprietor.

"Yes," replied Allison hopefully, "and rather thin, too—bony, actually."

"Spoke with a German accent, did he?"

Allison paused. Had she ever heard them speak? No—but she recalled several phone calls Logan had received from a man whose accent was unmistakable.

"It's possible," she replied.

"Well, I reported him."

"Reported him?"

"I didn't like the looks of him, so I turned him in to the War Office," said the tobacconist. "They said as how they couldn't pick up every bloke who didn't *look* right on account of the tens of thousands of innocent refugees who came here before the war fleeing from that madman Hitler. They needed more to go on to arrest a bloke than a man's looks, they said. Well, *I* say round 'em all up, and then there'll be no doubts!"

"So, you have the man's name?" said Allison, too impatient to listen to the man's biased political ramblings.

"I do that; he had his own particular blend he ordered. He'd call me up and say, 'Prepare me so-and-so's a blend, I'll pick it up this afternoon.' No one's willin' to wait around these days and have a nice bit of conversation. Everything's done on the phone—no waiting."

"What was the man's name?" asked Allison, whose throat had suddenly gone very dry.

"I can remember without even looking in my ledger, on account of having reported him, you know. Smith was the name, a Mr. Hedley Smith."

Allison cast a woeful look at Billy. The new-found information hardly increased the chances of locating a man with a phony name.

Now it was Billy's turn to step forward.

"And 'ave you gots an address in your records, by any chance?" he asked.

"'Course I do! What kind of businessman do you think I am?" the tobacconist replied, flipping through the pages of his ledger, while Billy craned his head to try to see for himself. "Like I said, no one wants to wait. Some blokes even call and tell me to deliver the stuff. 'Send a pound of Mr. Smith's Carolina blend over to such-and-such a place.'"

"An' where did you send our Mr. Smith's when he called?"

The man hesitated, suddenly growing wary. "Say, I don't know as I should be giving out that information."

"Look 'ere," said Billy, pulling himself up to every inch of his diminutive stature, "this young woman and I are from Immigration an' we 'ave reason t' believe yer first suspicions about this man could be correct."

"You don't *look* much like Immigration officials."

"'Course we don't!" exclaimed Billy at the silly notion. "You don't expect us t' be walkin' around tippin' off the blokes we's after with fine duds an' a nice gov'mental accent, now do ye?"

"Let me see your identification."

Without a second's hesitation, the old confidence man pulled out his worn leather wallet and flashed it quickly before the stubborn shopkeeper's eyes. Skittles' old list-shop license, which Billy carried around with him for luck, looked official enough for most similar purposes if not scrutinized too closely.

The man behind the counter appeared satisfied, and wrote the address on a slip of paper.

All Allison's fatigue was gone when they exited the shop. "How far is it?" she asked excitedly. "Shall I call a taxi?"

"I thought we was done for the day!"

"Oh, Billy, we can't quit now! I wouldn't be able to rest knowing we are this close."

"Just funnin' you, Miz Macintyre," said Billy with a crooked but warm smile. "But the address may prove just as phony as the *Smith*. But let's take the tube t' Charing Cross. Cheaper and just as quick, an' puts us close t' where we wants t' go."

Bunker Street, it turned out, looked none too respectable, presenting a string of seedy hotels and seedier-looking pubs, broken here and there with grimy shops and dirty tenement buildings. They followed the street numbers until they came to the one the tobacconist had written down. They stopped, then glanced puzzled at one another. The chipped, worn number was painted on the bricks above the door of The Blue Crow Pub. Had the shopkeeper made a mistake, or was the address as false as the man's name?

"You best wait out 'ere, mum, whilst I goes in an' 'ave a look about," said Billy protectively.

Allison scanned the area; across the street a couple of men as rundown and seedy as the neighborhood were leering at her.

"I'll go in with you," she replied.

The Blue Crow was practically vacant. The few men present could not have been of the sturdiest caliber, and the room reeked of stale odors. Allison willingly hung back while Billy approached a man whose stained and dingy apron gave indication that he was the one in charge. They exchanged a few quiet words; then Billy thanked him and led Allison back out into the fresh air.

"No luck?" asked Allison.

"I gots me a feelin' the bloke knows the man, but he sure hain't goin' t' talk t' us about it. I've a bad feeling about that place."

They had started on their way once more, but Allison grabbed Billy's arm. "We can't leave it at that," she implored.

"There's no suckin' blood from a turnip."

"Offer him money—anything!"

"I tried that, mum."

"There must be a way."

"Let's be gettin' home," suggested Billy wearily. "Mebbe after a good rest, we'll come up with somethin'."

They started off, but after another few steps, Allison stopped suddenly again.

"Oh drat!" she exclaimed.

"Mum?"

"I lost my earring. I'm sure I had it when I went into that place. I'd best go back and check. I must have dropped it."

"Ye sure, mum?" said Billy, who had not seen her hand quickly snatching away the earring only a moment before.

"I'll only be a moment," said Allison, running off, not giving Billy the opportunity either to argue or to accompany her.

"Let me go," he protested.

But it was too late. She was already at the door of the place she had entered so reluctantly only five minutes earlier.

"Here it is!" she said triumphantly, exiting a few moments later, just as Billy was about to go in after her.

Billy never realized he had been taken in by the sweet Mrs. Macintyre. Had he known, he might have stayed in the next few evenings, anxiously awaiting whatever might develop from Allison's return dash into the pub. As it was, he was out and not to be reached when Allison needed him most.

She knew leaving her phone number with the pubkeeper was foolhardy at best, as was telling him she had vital information for the man they were seeking, Mr. *Smith*—which she spoke with sufficient emphasis to let him know that they both knew more than they were letting on. If the man was German, which she by now had every reason to suspect, she hoped her bait might be enough to bring him out of hiding.

Her little scheme worked. The next evening her phone rang. A man with a decidedly German accent wanted to meet her at nine p.m. In no position to argue, she scribbled down the location. Her heart was pounding when she hung up the phone. Thankfully, the rendezvous would not take place on Bunker Street. The man had instead given her the name of a different pub, The Silver Stallion, down by the river—not far from the docks. The man must like odd colored animals, thought Allison to herself. Her attempt at humor, however, was but a thin mask over her rising fear that she had gotten herself into more than she bargained for.

She tried to call Billy several times, but to no avail. Finally, as eight o'clock drew near, she had no choice but to leave the baby with her neighbor and strike out alone.

28 ❈ The Foggy Riverfront

THE NIGHT WAS dark and misty with a light fog. An evening wind had begun to blow in from the mouth of the Thames, swirling the gathering mist about the deserted streets.

Allison would be able to take the tube only part of the way. The dimly lit underground station proved just slightly less portentous than the somber open air. During the blitz these stations had been a thriving beehive of activity as thousands of Londoners sought shelter from the incessant German bombs. Many had slept regularly in whatever corner of a tube station they could find. Even now Allison observed several men dozing off on benches or in out-of-the-way corners, but now they were more likely homeless drunks than citizens fearful for their lives.

Allison got off at Tower Hill. Slowly she walked up a long flight of stairs and into the dark night. Billingsgate Market to her right was by now long deserted, but she suspected The Silver Stallion to be in that direction. There was no one about as she began walking south toward the river. It was not far; already she could hear sounds of an occasional ship or barge passing by, sounding their muted horns in warning.

She reached the river at eight-thirty. To her right, just past the Billingsgate, was London Bridge. On her left, in the vague distance through the fog, she could make out the imposing spires and turrets of Tower Bridge. Everything looked so silent and sinister in the fog and dark. Why had the man asked her to come here? *Why had she agreed?* What a fool she must be! The whole idea was stupid. She should never be here by herself. The man could be dangerous, whether or not he was a friend of Logan's. But she had come too far to turn around now. If only Billy were here!

"Dear Lord," she prayed, hardly realizing that she had not taken the time to pray about finding Logan since first spotting the stranger while with Sarah, "forgive me if I am being foolish. But please help me to learn something of Logan. Protect me, Lord."

Some ten minutes' walk more brought her alongside the Billingsgate. At least now there were a few people about here—mostly seamen, none of whom, to her relief, bothered her. None of the pubs displayed the sign she sought. At last she walked inside one to ask if she was anywhere near The Silver Stallion.

The pubkeeper gave her a peculiar smile, then laughed.

"Sure, lady," he said. "You's near it all right. Though what you'd want there I can't think!" He laughed again.

"Where is it, please?" asked Allison.

"Straight on down, miss," replied the man, still chuckling to himself.

Allison hurried out. At the next cross-street, all activity seemed to cease. Slowly she walked across. In the distance she could see nothing but dark, silent, run-down buildings. *Surely there's no pub down there,* she thought. Yet this was in the direction the man had pointed.

Slowly she continued on, her eyes scanning the buildings through the mist. They looked more like warehouses than anything, although there were signs of bomb damage all about, so it was difficult to tell. Everything had grown ominously silent around her.

Allison stopped. This was absurd. There couldn't possibly be any pub around here. She looked around one last time, walking slowly back and forth. What was that just ahead? It looked like it could be a sign. She approached. Yes—there was an old sign above the door. But the place was dark, its windows and doors boarded up. She reached the door. In the darkness she could barely make out a few letters on the old and dilapidated marker that must have at one time invited patrons to enter: *Si—Stal——*was all she could read. But that was enough! She had been led here under false pretenses. She'd been an idiot—she had to get out of here!

Allison turned to retrace her steps.

She had not even seen the black figure step out from between two buildings just beyond where she stood.

The moment she began to run an arm shot out from behind and caught her in a vise-like grip. Allison screamed.

"There's no one to hear you, Frauline," said a sinister gravelly voice. Notwithstanding his words, he clamped his hand tightly across her mouth. "I will do the talking for the moment," the accented voice went on, "but when you are required to speak, remember that I have a weapon pressed into your back."

He jabbed his pistol fiercely into her ribs to emphasize the veracity of his words. "Now, who are you, and why are you following me?"

"I'm Allison Macintyre," said Allison when the man released his fingers. She said no more, not only because her lips were trembling, but also because she hoped the mention of her name would signify her interest to the man.

"Is that supposed to mean something to me?" he snapped. It obviously did not.

"I'm only trying to find my husband," she managed to say.

"What's that to me?"

"You know him."

"Says who?"

"I've seen the two of you together. I had hoped you might be able to tell me where he is."

"His name?"

"Logan Macintyre."

"The name means nothing to me."

"But I saw you together in a restaurant, several months ago," she said in desperation. "You were talking at a table, but when I came, you stopped, and then left quickly."

An agonizing moment of silence passed. Allison could not tell if he was trying to recall the meeting or contemplating the best method for her demise.

"Ah, so that is why I recognized you at the newsstand," he said finally. "Trinity is your husband."

There was a faint hint of would-be laughter in Gunther's voice, as if the incident might be comical if the stakes weren't so deadly serious.

"Trinity? I don't understand," said Allison.

"You don't need to understand. You need only forget you ever saw me."

"Where is my husband?"

"I don't know, and I don't care."

"How do you know him?"

"We had business together once."

"What is he doing?"

"You ask too many questions."

"I have to know."

"You have to know nothing! These are dangerous times, made all the more dangerous by interfering fools."

"I am his wife!"

"If you persist in your questioning and idiotic sleuthing," said Gunther, "you will endanger the lives of many people, your husband included."

"Why? Why can't you tell me?"

"Listen to me, Frau Macintyre, you are treading upon dangerous ground. Stop, or you will find yourself with more trouble than you know what to do with. I would not like to see you dead, but I myself would kill you in order to save my own neck. Don't make me do that!"

"I will go, then!" answered Allison. "I have only one more question. Is my husband safe?"

"No one is *safe* in this dark world," Gunther replied shortly. "What is *safe*? Everything is, how do you say it here, topsyturvy? To my knowledge, no ill has come to your Trinity. But I have not seen him for months, and he is in a dangerous game." He paused. "Now, I want you to start walking," he said, slowly releasing his arm from around her neck. "You will go back the way you came—I will be watching you. Do not turn around. For you to see my face again could someday mean your death."

His tone left no doubt that his surveillance would not end with her departure from this riverfront street that night. "You will forget my face . . . you will forget this meeting. You will forget all about me, for that matter, and about your husband also. We will all live much longer if you do so."

Allison's heart had climbed up into her throat and her legs felt like rubber. Yet they somehow managed to propel her slowly away from the awful deserted place, and from the man who might be either friend or enemy—she could not guess which. Of only one thing she was fairly certain, that he honestly knew no more of Logan's whereabouts than he had told her. The entire ordeal of this search had been a dangerous dead-end. She was no closer to finding Logan now than when she had begun. Only now she knew he was involved in something secretive, and that danger might now come to her as well.

Despite Gunther's stern injunction, she could never forget what had happened. To forget Logan altogether was unthinkable! What kind of man would suggest such a thing to a wife?

But if she could not find him or help him, there was one thing she *could* do on Logan's behalf. Something she should have thought of much sooner.

Later that night, back in the safety of her own home, Allison knelt down at her bedside and began a ritual that would continue daily for many, many months.

"Father," she prayed, "I don't know where Logan is or what he is involved in. Neither do I know where his heart is. But as you have always cared for us while we were straying through dark and shadowy valleys, care for him, Lord. As you watched over Lady Margaret and Dorey during the long years of their separation, watch over Logan. Don't let him wander far from you. Bring him continually into contact with your presence, even if at times he is unable to recognize your hand in his life. Protect him, God. Strengthen his faith again. And strengthen my own! Help me to be faithful in this commitment to prayer, and to selflessly give myself to the rebuilding of our marriage."

29 ❧ Eyes Across the Sea

"AND YOU SAY there's no way either of them could have seen you?"

"How many times 'ave I got to say it, mate? What kind of fool blighter does you take me for! The lady was scared clean out her skin. And as for that kraut—"

"Watch your mouth, you old fool! Don't forget you're not in England now. Over here even the walls have ears. I don't pay you what I pay you and then bring you all the way over here to have you shoot your mouth off and get us both thrown in some stalag. I pay you to keep me informed of the movements of that family and otherwise to keep silent."

"My apologies," replied the old lackey, just a hint of sarcasm underlying the respectful tone of his voice.

The man to whom he was reporting was in reality just past seventy and several years the senior of his cockney underling. But he bore himself with such peremptory authority, and the mere sound of his voice was so commanding, that few dared to cross him. To all appearances he was a man confident of always getting what he wanted.

"As I was sayin'," the man went on, "I'd been keepin' my eye on the girl like you said. Still nary a word on her man, but she's takin' up livin' in his old flat. Then she met that German fellow."

"Hmmm . . . most interesting," said the other with a wave of the hand, speaking almost to himself. He leaned back from his desk and thought for a minute or two. This was an interesting business! What could *she* possibly have to do with a German? They were the most intriguing lot! Ever since reading about the marriage in the papers, he'd been curious as to what new possibilities might open up to him. Might there be something in this he could use? Even as he thought to himself, his intense black eyes glowed with a fire deeper than any human flame. *I will bide my time,* he concluded. *As I always do.* He had spent thousands of pounds over the years, in the hopes of ultimately satisfying the demon that still tormented him and fed the fires which looked out of his eyes. Yet ultimate victory had always eluded him.

At length he exhaled sharply and looked up at the man still standing in front of his desk. From a drawer he pulled out a thick envelope.

"Here is your fare back, and a little extra for your trouble," he said. "Now you keep her under watch. I want to be able to get to her any time I want her. Is that clear?"

"All clear, mate."

"And one more thing. You ever call me *mate* again, and I'll have your throat slit. Is *that* clear?"

"Clear enough . . . sir."

30 ❧ Rescue

A RAW WIND beat mercilessly upon the streets of Paris that chill November afternoon.

The porter pushing his cart of beef down the avenue Foch hitched his frayed woolen coat more tightly about him. That was his only acquiescence to the icy cold, however, and he continued to shuffle along in the same sluggish, unhurried manner that he apparently used every day, no matter what the weather. He gave every indication of being both bored and worn out, whether from life's hardships or the German occupation, it was impossible to tell.

But why should he have hurried? His meat consignment was designated for S.S. headquarters—who else ate meat in Paris these days but the Germans? And it wouldn't kill them to wait.

An especially forceful rush of wind struck him at that moment, nearly tearing his beret from the thick gray hair underneath. He grabbed at the beret with more speed than any of his other movements would have indicated was possible, and firmly clamped it back in place. Then, hunching his shoulders up and lowering his head, like a ram, into the wind, he continued on.

In another several minutes he came to the first checkpoint for the main building, which housed both a small facility for holding certain of their more important prisoners and the administration offices for the German S. S.—Schutz Staffeln, the elite police force organized by Heinrich Himmler.

"Bonjour, Monsieur Sergeant," he said in a gravelly mumble as he tipped his beret slightly.

"What have you there, old man?" barked one of the three guards standing closest by, who was in truth only a corporal.

The porter raised his bushy eyebrows as if he didn't know what to make of a question with such an obvious answer, for large shanks of meat were in plain view under the haphazardly placed canvas tarp. He stared at the guard with a deadpan expression; then finally a slow grin appeared between the tufts of his tangled gray beard, as a deep guffaw began to rumble from somewhere deep in his throat.

The guard stepped brusquely forward. "You imbecile!" he spat. "Lift some of that up— let me see under it!"

"Ah," said the porter, brightening with understanding. He pulled the flap back and proceeded to shove several of the shanks this way and that. "Eh, bien?" he said when the procedure was over, wiping his hands on the grimy blood-stained apron that hung beneath his coat. "Fine cuts, non? Very lean!"

"Get on your way!" ordered the guard. "Dummkopf Französischer!"

"Merci," replied the porter, summoning the energy to continue on, shoving his cumbersome burden ahead of him.

He crossed the large cobbled courtyard, pausing once to let a squad of marching soldiers pass. He then shoved on, going around to the service entrance with his load. There the supply clerk checked his clipboard for the delivery authorization, apparently unconcerned that he was an hour and a half late according to the regular schedule, put a mark on the page, and let the porter pass inside the building.

"No wonder the old fool's so much later than the usual man," thought the guard as he watched the door close behind him. "Never seen a delivery man move so slow!"

Still ambling along at his snail's pace as if the only thing that mattered in life was placing one foot in front of the other, the porter moved down the length of one corridor, then another, pausing now and then to let soldiers pass, but meeting very few. Apparently his information had been correct, that the place would be nearly deserted during this precise time when the serving of dinner overlapped with the rotation of personnel on and off duty. Since they had to check in and out in the front of the building, the service and prison areas toward the rear were, for about a twenty-minute period, devoid of activity except for a skeleton maintenance crew. A silent observer might have questioned why he seemed to be moving away from the kitchen area where food deliveries were normally taken.

His twists and turns soon brought him to an altogether silent wing of the building, and at length he arrived at an intersection of two corridors, where he stopped, glanced furtively over his shoulder, then to his right and left.

Apparently satisfied that he was alone, he suddenly seemed to spring to life, as if his veins had just been pumped with blood from a man thirty years younger. Quickly he pushed his cart into a dark alcove, unloaded about half its contents, which he stashed in a corner on the floor, then lifted a large bundle that had been stowed beneath the meat in a hidden compartment. In the seclusion of the alcove he began to remove the outer layers of his porter's attire, including the gray wig and beard.

Logan was especially glad to get rid of the uncomfortable beard, though he laid it neatly with the other items, for he would have need of it again. From the bundle, he took the uniform of an S.S. sergeant, which he hurriedly put on. Within moments the old porter was transformed into a member of Hitler's elitist corps of protectors of the Third Reich. He placed the porter's things into the bundle, tying all together securely. At the very last he strapped on his sidearm.

Finally, taking up the bundle under his arm and inhaling a deep breath, he stepped back out into the dimly lit corridor. With stiff military bearing and purposeful stride, though no one was nearby to witness them, he walked about ten yards to a flight of stairs, which he descended into the detention area of the building. At the bottom of the steps stood a locked door with a small barred window placed at eye level, and a single buzzer on the doorpost.

Logan set the bundle down out of sight, then withdrew a handkerchief and small vial from his pocket. He saturated the cloth with a few drops from the vial, then, keeping the handkerchief out of view, stepped up and pressed the buzzer. He only hoped the German he had learned in training and had been practicing so diligently in his spare time would pass the ultimate test.

In a moment a face appeared at the window.

"Ja?" said the guard from inside. "Was wollen Sie?"

"Ich bin hier für die Gefangene Übertragung gekommen," replied Logan.

"No one told me of a transfer of prisoners."

"I've got the order right here." Logan took a folded paper from his breast pocket and held it up to the window.

The guard opened the door and Logan stepped inside.

"Immer Sicherheit! Jeden Tag Sicherheit!" complained the guard. "Every day they preach to me about security. Then they don't tell me what's going on. So what am I supposed to do?"

"Why don't you call upstairs?" said Logan, manifesting considerable impatience at this guard who displayed fewer stripes on his shoulder than he. "But be quick about it. I haven't got all day!"

The guard turned to the wall behind him where the phone hung. But he progressed no farther, for the instant his back was turned Logan stepped forward and, grasping his body with one arm, with his free hand jammed the handkerchief over his nose. In three seconds the guard went limp and slumped to the floor.

Quickly Logan dragged his unconscious body out of sight, then returned to the guard desk, grabbed up the keys, and scanned the pages of the roster. Finding the information he sought, he retrieved his bundle from outside, firmly closed the outer door, and went into the prison cell block.

Here he encountered the long hallway he had been told to expect, with locked doors running down each side, similar to the one through which he had just passed. He resisted the temptation to look into each tiny window; from the groans and whimpers he heard, he knew what kind of sight would greet his eyes. Unfortunately, he could not now help all these poor men to escape. He had come for three in particular, and so must harden himself to the pitiful sounds, trying to assure himself that one day he would see them all free.

Three-quarters of the way down the corridor he paused. He stepped up to the window of the door and saw a man sitting on his bunk, huddled against the wall with his legs pulled up to his chest, a single blanket wrapped around his shivering body. For the first time it suddenly dawned on Logan how icy cold these dark dungeons were; his own adrenaline had been pumping so hard he was almost in a sweat. Hearing a sound at his door, the man looked up.

He was Reuven Poletski, a Jew, one of the driving forces of the Warsaw resistance movement. He was a man of average size and undistinguishing features. However, his dark hair and thick brown eyebrows appeared especially vivid against the prison pallor of his skin. But he did not appear the fierce leader of men his reputation had made of him—that is, until he glanced up and his eyes met those of the man he supposed to be an S.S guard. They were filled with such contempt and defiance that Logan almost forgot who he really was and hesitated for a moment opening the door.

But the silent exchange lasted less than a second before Logan swung into action, unlocking the door and thrusting it open.

"Reuven Poletski?" he said.

"I am," replied the prisoner in what Logan took for Polish. He proudly squared his shoulders and stood courageously to meet whatever fate was in store for him.

"I'm with the Resistance," said Logan in French. "I've come to get you out of here."

"This is some trick," said Poletski, also in French, eyeing Logan warily.

"We haven't time for a cross-examination."

"I will not go without my wife and son," answered the Pole resolutely.

"Don't worry. We will get them out, too. That's my business."

"I can't believe this."

"You're a very important man, Monsieur Poletski. We certainly cannot let the Nazis have you without a fight. Now hurry."

Reuven Poletski and his family had been in the process of escaping Poland after an enormous price tag had been placed on Poletski's head. They had made it as far as Paris, and had been staying with friends until false papers and a guide out of the city could be arranged for them. But a suspicious neighbor, a collaborator, had turned them in. They had been in Gestapo hands only three days before *La Librairie,* which since Logan's arrival had been steadily gaining a reputation for successful escape operations, had been called in. Poletski had to be freed, for he knew enough to bring down the entire Warsaw resistance structure. And now with his family also in custody, there was no telling how long he could hold out. Even three days was pushing it.

"I want you to know," said Poletski, as he gathered what meager items of clothing he had, and speaking with a proud edge to his voice, "that were it only myself, I would never have left Poland—and as soon as they are safe in London, I will return."

"That's fine, Poletski," replied Logan. "But first we have to get you out of here. Come on, we haven't much time. This thing was planned for the only twenty-minute gap we could discover in this place. In another ten, these corridors will be crawling with Germans again."

Quickly they located Poletski's wife and sixteen-year-old son. Logan unlocked their door, Poletski explained excitedly, and in three or four minutes the small party was assembled once more at the guard's station. Hastily Logan changed back into his porter's clothes, while the three Polish refugees put on the Nazi uniforms Logan had smuggled into the building in his bundle.

"We hardly look like S.S. men," said Poletski, surveying the ill-fitting uniforms on the diminutive frames of his wife and son.

Logan took a second look. The son was nearly as tall as he was himself, and Madame Poletski filled out the uniform admirably, better than he had expected.

"Don't worry. You look fine. By the time you get to the outside gate, they won't give you a second thought. It'll be me they'll be after."

Notwithstanding Logan's assurances, Poletski was clearly nervous, though for his wife and son, not himself. How could he not be? It was insanity to attempt an escape right from under the noses of the S.S.; certain torture and death awaited them if they failed.

When they were ready to leave the detention area on the final leg of their journey to freedom, Logan paused by the unconscious guard, stooped down, and gave him another dose of chloroform from the handkerchief.

"That should hold him until we're away from here," he said.

"We would be safer if he were dead," said Poletski.

"I don't operate that way," replied Logan, rising from the floor. He opened the door and led the three escapees out of the detention block, up the stairs, and to the alcove where Logan retrieved his meat cart.

Moving quickly, they kept to the same service corridors by which Logan had come. As Logan led the way, he filled Poletski in on what to do the moment they exited the building and made for the guardhouse.

As they rounded a tight corner, Logan took the lead, and suddenly found himself face-to-face with a German officer. Immediately slapping on a toothy ingratiating grin, he tipped his beret and said in his gravelly porter's voice, "Bonjour, mon Captain." He only hoped Poletski, who had not yet come around the corner, had heard him and taken his cue.

Almost the same instant from behind him Logan heard a sharp German command: "Move aside, Porter!"

It was Poletski, getting admirably into his character.

"Pardonnez-moi, Monsieur!" Logan replied, with profound humility, making an overdone attempt to move the cart aside. But he seemed to catch one of the wheels on one of the floor stones, causing the cart nearly to overturn. He righted it before catastrophe struck; but during the entire several seconds the captain, now pinned against the wall, was forced to attend to the errant cart, while the three other soldiers passed by on the other. Logan's smile at his discomfort was fortunately hidden beneath the tufts of his beard. Poletski and his family had marched past Logan and cart and the captain with all the precision and hauteur of the German conquerors they were dressed up to be. In the meantime, the S.S. captain hurried on down the hall in the opposite direction, just thankful to have made it by the maniac of a meatporter without breaking his neck.

At last they reached the final door. Poletski shook his head doubtfully.

"We can't possibly get out of the compound," he said. "It was pure luck we made it this far."

"Have faith, Monsieur Poletski."

"Do you plan to hide us in that thing?" he asked, cocking his head dubiously toward the meat cart.

"I have something a bit more creative in mind," said Logan. "Now, as I was starting to tell you when we were interrupted by that captain in the hallway, you let me get about fifty meters beyond the gate—three minutes should do it . . . "

Two minutes later the guards at the main gate looked up to see the old porter once more shuffling across the courtyard, pushing his now empty cart at his unhurried, sluggish pace. He paused, and nodded his head toward the corporal.

"You want to check again, non?" he said, fumbling at the ties on the tarp.

The guard looked under one edge of the canvas, then gave the cart a harsh shove.

"Get on with you, crazy old man!"

Logan said nothing, just lumbered past the gate.

For the first time he was painfully conscious of each slow, methodical step, as he listened intently behind him. But he knew that if he even picked up his pace imperceptibly, he might raise the suspicions of whatever guards were still eyeing him.

He was almost to the corner of the adjacent building when his cue came.

From inside the courtyard he heard the sound of urgent commanding shouts and the sound of running feet on the pavement.

Logan started to walk faster, but he dared not turn around. If he had, he would have seen a tall S.S. officer, followed by two shorter ones, run breathlessly up to the guardhouse and ask in frantic German, "Did a porter just come by here . . . pushing a meatcart?"

"Ja, mein Herr," answered the corporal.

Logan was now out of sight and breaking into a run.

"And you let him pass? Imbecile!" shouted Poletski. "He is a Resistance agent. We will have to go after him."

"What do you want us to do, mein Herr?"

"You have done enough already! Call inside and have them check the prison compound. We will soon be back with the agent. Come, men!"

The two others with him silently obeyed, and all three ran out of the compound and down the street in the direction Logan had gone.

When the corporal emerged from the guardhouse after making his call a minute later, the evening was once again silent. There was no sign either of the porter or the three officers in pursuit of him.

31 ❊ Arnaud Soustelle

THE CLOSING MONTHS of 1941 were turbulent ones in Paris. If the German occupation had turned France upside-down, these months turned it inside-out.

Hitler's invasion of Russia had stirred new fervor among French Communists. A demonstration protesting the German breach of faith with Russia, a former ally, turned into a riot in August. Two Communists were executed for their part in the protest. Then followed what, in a world fraught with perfidy, seemed to be the height of betrayal to French patriots, whether they were Communist or Gaullist—hundreds of Frenchmen enlisted, forming a military division to *join* the German army in the fighting on the Russian front.

When a German soldier was gunned down in a back alley, apparently by a Communist, the Nazi's reacted by taking a number of hostages. But when still another soldier was murdered, the S.S. retaliated with savage recriminations, including the execution of a dozen of these innocent French hostages. Paris became a powder keg, ready to explode on many fronts at once. The hit-and-run tactics of the French Resistance fighters only angered the Germans all the more. For every French prisoner they took or hostage they executed, however, it seemed two were miraculously set free. Each time the scenario was different, but the Resistance agents seemed able to penetrate the most secure of their installations. Always there was a disguise, always a diversion. Yet the diversity made it impossible to detect ahead of time what was about to happen. Eventually talk began to circulate among S.S. and Gestapo headquarters that the escapes were all the work of a single man. A dedication began to grow to discover his identity and put a stop to his sabotage of the Third Reich's attempt to consolidate its stranglehold on Paris.

Attacks on both sides continued sporadically through the fall and winter. Controversy and discord were everywhere. The indifference of the general public was one of the most disheartening factors for those involved in the Resistance. While a handful of patriots were sacrificing their lives toward the hope of liberation, a much greater majority of Frenchmen were going on with their lives under the German occupation as if nothing had happened. And an alarming number actually fell in with the Nazis. The patriots did not know whom to hate more—the Nazis or their collaborators. How, they asked themselves, can watching the deaths of their innocent countrymen not turn the hearts of such vile traitors—if such opportunists even have hearts?

Arnaud Soustelle was among the worst of this ignoble breed.

Prior to the war he had already begun to acquire a reputation as an inspector of police with a total lack of moral scruples. For even a small bribe he would turn in a trusting friend, he could beat information out of the most stubborn of suspects, and he took special delight in devising ever more inhumane ways to torment Jews.

When the Germans came in 1940, Soustelle lost no time in hitching his loyalties to the Nazi wagon. Hitler's racism suited him well, and armed with his particular talents and a loyal retinue of informants and connections who would do anything for a price, Soustelle found himself openly welcomed by the German occupiers. He was soon serving in the Sicherheitsdienst, or simply the S.D. This security agency for the Nazi party operated in the same ignominious capacity as the Gestapo, though the S.D. more willingly welcomed civilian nationals within its ranks. Arnaud had thus far proved an extremely valuable agent for his native knowledge of the city, and his policeman's savvy served him well.

Today, however, walking down the avenue Foch with a light snowfall dusting the shoulders of his new overcoat, Soustelle felt a slight twinge of a very uncharacteristic emotion: trepidation. It was not a feeling the tough forty-five-year-old Frenchman was used to, or liked. At six feet tall, broad of chest with icy gray eyes and hawk-like nose, it was ordinarily *he* who instilled fear in others.

But it was no small matter to be summoned to S.S. headquarters, especially when he was well aware of recent failures having to do with leads he had given them. These Nazis were an unforgiving lot. Forgetting all his successes, they would probably boot him out (no doubt to some labor camp in Germany) if he wasn't careful. But, he reminded himself, as he would his superiors, he had not yet exactly failed. He had merely not yet completely succeeded. But he would. Of that they could be certain.

Thoughtful, he slipped his hand into his pocket, took out a chunk of black licorice, and popped it into his mouth. It was a habit he had acquired many years earlier, and now almost continually he had a thick wad of the stuff churning about inside his mouth. Where most men smelled of tobacco, Soustelle perennially reeked of the bitter-sweet odor of licorice.

Chewing on the candy, he continued to wonder what was in store for him as he walked. He passed the main gate unimpeded, crossed the courtyard, and entered the building. This particular part of the compound had once been a fine townhouse occupied by a wealthy Parisian. He proceeded directly up a wide stairway, paying no attention to the intricate balustrade or the expensive flocked wallpaper. In another few moments he paused before a large oak door, and, before knocking, tossed another licorice drop into his mouth. He would have argued vehemently that it was not a nervous habit, but however coincidental it was, he seemed to devour many more during times of stress.

"Herein!" came a feminine voice from inside.

"I have an appointment with the general," said Soustelle upon entering.

"Yes, Herr Soustelle," said the secretary. "General von Graff is expecting you. Go right in."

Soustelle neither paused nor hesitated. He opened the door to the inner office and stepped smartly inside the spacious room, clicking his heels sharply together while stiffly raising his right hand in the air.

"Heil Hitler!"

"Heil Hitler," replied von Graff in the more casual tone of one who does not have to try so hard to prove his loyalty.

The fortunes of Martin von Graff had altered dramatically in the last several months. He had never been completely content in the Abwehr. For one thing, he could never tolerate Admiral Canaris, that perpetual intriguer who ruled military intelligence, regardless of the fact that they were both Navy men. One never knew where one stood with the old man and, moreover, one never quite knew where the old man stood. However, lately the vacillating Canaris was leaning too dangerously toward anti-Nazism to suit von Graff. Not that he was a fanatic himself, but he was not about to risk being in the wrong camp when the Führer's designs reached their victorious climax—as they certainly must. Thus, taking masterful advantage of the constant in-fighting between the Abwehr and the Gestapo, von Graff had secured his present position in the S.S. hierarchy, upon recommendation of Heinrich Himmler himself.

Landing the Paris assignment had been a coup far beyond his hopes as a relatively new S.S. recruit. Here in the cultural hub of the world, he felt as if there might be life beyond the war, after all. Hitler was adamant that the reputation of Paris should not decline during his wartime regime—hoping, no doubt, to make it a showcase of Third Reich "culture" later. Thus the arts continued to flourish. Von Graff attended the theater or opera nearly every night, and considered himself treated to fine performances each time.

Yes, things were going well for him. He was not about to let recent setbacks destroy everything.

He leaned back in his chair and focused his cold, unrelenting gaze upon the unscrupulous French collaborator before him.

"Well, Herr Soustelle," said von Graff, "I hope it is *good* news you have for me today."

"These things take time, mon General," hedged Soustelle.

"Time, Soustelle . . . ?" Von Graff let his words trail off with an ominous impression. "In the *time* since we borrowed you from the S.D., we have lost three more major prisoners, which does *not* include last night's loss of that Jew Poletski and his family. That makes six in two months, Herr Soustelle. I need not tell you how bad that looks."

He was thinking as much about his own reputation as Soustelle's. To have these escapes coincide so inconveniently with his own arrival in Paris was most unfortunate.

"So you see," he went on, "your talk of time does not put me at ease. Time is going by and you seem to be getting nowhere."

"I assure you, mon General, I have my best people on it," replied Soustelle. "I have one reliable informer in the Resistance who is almost certain these particular escapes are originating with one network, masterminded by one certain crafty man."

"Exactly as we have suspected!" von Graff burst out—whether in pleasure or frustration, it was hard to tell.

"Yes, mon General."

"And who is this one crafty individual?"

"If I knew that, you and I would not be standing here sweating today, now would we?"

"You have a great deal of nerve *for a Frenchman*," said von Graff caustically—he did not like how close to the mark Soustelle's jibe had been.

"My nerve is what makes me good at what I do," said Soustelle, his boldness rising once more. He had been foolish to fear this man. "And why I seldom fail."

"So *you* say! Thus far I have witnessed none of your reputed ingenuity."

Von Graff rose from his chair and walked to the window behind his desk. Snow had begun to pile up in the gutters; the busy late afternoon traffic, mostly bicycles and pedestrians, hurried along to homes or cafes where they might find some warmth.

"You know nothing about this man?" asked the general at length. It galled him that anyone, even one of the crowd below, could be the culprit, perhaps spying on him at this very moment, and yet he was no closer to finding him than if he were on another planet.

"Very little," answered Soustelle. "But there are already whisperings of him circulating in the streets. It seems your six are only the most famous of his escapees. Many others have benefited from his aid—especially Jews, escaped prisoners of war, foreigners who could not get out when the city was first occupied."

"He is mocking us!" shouted von Graff, slamming his hand down upon the desk.

"He will be ours in time, I assure you."

"Time! Time! Meanwhile, he sets people free, and we look like fools!"

"We are already laying a trap for this traitor the people consider a folk hero. His own cleverness will be his downfall."

"Folk hero! Bah!"

"I have heard the code name *L'Escroc* used."

"L'Escroc . . . ?" repeated von Graff thoughtfully. "The swindler."

"Oui. They say it is the Germans he is swindling—out of their prize prisoners."

Von Graff glanced out the window at the people below once more, then spun around and flashed his piercing glint upon the Frenchman. "I want him, Soustelle; do you understand?"

"I understand perfectly. And you shall have him. I want him, too."

"I am glad we agree on that," he said with a touch of sarcasm in his tone. "I understand there is great need for S.D. units on the Eastern Front—they may soon have to draw them from Paris itself, or so I understand."

"So I have heard," replied Soustelle, returning the general's piercing gaze. He would play the man's subtle little war of nerves. He was not afraid.

"It is very cold in Russia this time of year."

"So my Russian acquaintances have said," replied Soustelle, still calmly. As he spoke a tremendous urge came upon him to dig into his pocket. But another piece of licorice would have to wait. He comforted himself with the knowledge that this new S.S. general might just have the Russian front looming in *his* future as well.

Once he was again outside, Soustelle strode down the avenue doggedly, with large determined strides, arms swinging widely. His cheeks bulged with licorice.

He would find this *L'Escroc*! He would ferret him out of whatever resistance hole he was hiding in. He would find him, or . . .

There was no *or*! He *would* find him! This fool had gone too far when he threatened the comfort and advancement of Arnaud Soustelle.

32 ✢ L'Escroc

LOGAN GLANCED ACROSS the table at Henri, who was thoughtfully buttering a slice of bread.

They were enjoying a light lunch at Chez Lorainne, the cafe across from Logan's hotel, where he had become something of a regular customer of late. The conversation between the two men, however, was not as light as the meal. This had been their first major dispute since joining forces nearly four months ago.

Henri took a bite of bread with frustrating deliberation, chewing carefully, thoroughly, as he just as methodically considered his response to the current problem that faced them.

"No matter what has been done, Michel," he said at length, "he is one of us and we must help him."

"I disagree, Henri," Logan replied flatly. "This resistance business brings many strange birds together. But we must draw the line somewhere. And I draw it when it comes to aiding a cold-blooded and merciless killer."

"There are many among us who would take issue with you. A war necessitates the letting of blood."

"Are you one of them, mon ami?"

Henri sighed and stared at the bread on his plate as if he might escape to the solace of food once more. But instead he turned his gaze back to Logan.

"Boche are Boche," he said. "What difference does it make how they die?"

"You don't honestly believe that."

"Last week we blew up a train carrying German soldiers," returned Henri. "What is the difference between that and killing one in the Metro?"

Logan leaned heavily against the hard wooden back of the booth where he sat. He scrutinized Henri for a moment. *Here is a sensitive man, a feeling and compassionate man,* he thought, *caught in the ugly net of war, forced to say and do things he would never say and do under any other circumstances.* In peacetime, Logan doubted he would so much as speak harshly to a dog. He was probably the sort of man who would alter his footfall at the last moment to avoid stepping on a beetle on the sidewalk. He was a gentle man . . . a good man. Yet here he was talking about killing a trainload of men as if it were scarcely more out of the ordinary than an afternoon's walk down to the market.

"What a business!" sighed Logan at length.

"Acts of sabotage . . . acts of murder—it gets very mixed up, Michel. And to be truthful," Henri went on in a faraway voice that almost made it sound as though he wished he could say the same about himself, "I do not say you are wrong to question it."

"There is something intrinsically inhuman and atrocious about stabbing a lone man in the back, a man who is unsuspecting and probably doing nothing more sinister than enjoying a few days leave in Paris. That is murder, and I'll have no part in it. That is worlds away from helping condemned men and women to their freedom."

Logan did not like to be faced with the more glaring inconsistencies of his present vocation. He had steadfastly refused to use or carry a weapon, though perhaps he had not examined his moral code thoroughly. Probably it amounted to nothing more than a carry-over from the old days when avoiding the seamier side of his "profession" had somehow assuaged his conscience. He had never been a street fighter, though he knew he could fight. But to go beyond that . . . he didn't know, and was perhaps afraid of placing himself in the position where he'd find out.

He had avoided looking at the wider implications of what he was doing—that he was fighting in a cruel war, and that death was an intrinsic part of the process. If the axiom of guilt by association was true, then was he not equally culpable as this friend of Claude's whom they were now discussing?

He should have known that eventually he would face such an impasse, especially when dealing with such a vicious character as Claude. They had not found so much as an inch of common ground in four months, and had only avoided a blow-out because they studiously stayed out of each other's way. But the uneasy peace could not last forever, especially once Logan began to suspect Claude's part in the street killings of German soldiers. He had hinted to one or two of the others about getting rid of him, but he had never actively pursued such a notion because deep down Logan knew Claude served a vital function in the *La Librairie* network. Claude was the sabotage expert, and if he were not around to lay the bombs that blew up trains, they might try to enlist Logan for the job.

For now, however, Logan could not let himself wade through the overall moral questions of what he was involved in. Somehow he had to keep as much as possible black and white, and, failing that, he would just have to focus on the vile enemy they were all, Claude included, fighting.

"Bien entendu," Logan finally conceded with a ragged sigh. "Tell me about Claude's companion."

"He calls himself Louis," said Henri. "He was an officer in the French army and served courageously with the defenders of the Maginot Line in '40. He eluded capture when the defense finally broke, and made his way to the mountains, where he fought with the Marquis until about six months ago, when he came to Paris in an attempt to enlist support for the guerrilla fighters."

"Why don't his Communist friends help him?"

"One of his Communist friends *is* helping him," replied Henri pointedly. "He came to Claude, and Claude has come to us. Do you think this resistance will get anywhere if we maintain all these petty differences?"

"I suppose you're right."

"Besides, Louis' regular contacts are being too closely watched right now," added Henri.

"What does he want?"

"A new identity and all the falsified documents to go along with it. He wants to get to the unoccupied zone where he won't be such a hot property. I think Jean Pierre's man can accommodate us with the printing."

"No," interjected Logan quickly. "I don't want to risk Jean Pierre in this—in fact, I'm still not sure we ought to risk *anyone.*"

"Look at it this way, mon ami," said Henri, his quiet voice taking on a shrewd yet fatherly quality. "Louis is a marked man and, if he remains in Paris, is sure to be caught eventually. He knows a great deal, even more about *La Librairie* than is safe. So unless you are willing to put a bullet through his head, our only recourse is to do what we can to get him out of here."

"Adroitly phrased! Beneath all that genteel facade, you are a cagey old fox, Henri." Logan shook his head in defeat, but let his lips turn up in an affectionate smile.

"You are L'Escroc. Perhaps I should be Le Renard, eh?" He winked and sent Logan a knowing grin in reply. "The fox; what do you think?"

Judging from his response, Logan did not join in the amusement. "You do not like your new-found fame, do you, Michel?" said Henri more seriously.

"Fame is not very healthy in this work," replied Logan. "Even a back table in a deserted cafe is too risky a place to be discussing such things."

"I am sorry, Michel. I would have said nothing if I thought there was the slightest chance—"

"I know, Henri," said Logan apologetically. "I suppose the whole thing isn't setting altogether well with me. It is not only the notoriety and the danger that accompanies it, but also being thought too highly of. We all work together and take the same risks. I deserve no special honor."

"If glory were all you had to worry about, then your problems would indeed be small ones."

"What do you mean?"

"L'Escroc is bound to be something of a scapegoat too," said Henri gravely. "Don't be fooled. Those who whisper the name about the streets after there has been a particularly notable escape—whether it was your doing or not—care less for your glory than to have the attention of the Germans focused on someone besides themselves."

"Wonderful comrades we have out there," said Logan dryly.

"To most of them L'Escroc is an idea, a symbol. I think a good many of them would watch their tongues a little more closely if they really thought of him as a real person."

"I suppose this being a symbol wouldn't be so bad if some good could come of it, like bringing together some of the factions."

Henri contemplated his food once more in thought, then looked up. "Yes," he said slowly, almost regretfully. "But believe me, a symbol is a benefit in work such as this. I can't say it would heal all the wounds and unite the French people. But it does provide a rallying point, a symbol of hope. And that is the last thing the Germans want here in Paris. They will do everything in their power to crush it."

Saying nothing, Logan merely raised his eyes at Henri's words as their full implication settled in upon him.

"The very thing that could sustain us," said Henri, "could also destroy us. 'Entertaining hope means recognizing fear,' " he added, then paused and smiled, as if recalling a pleasant memory. "My wife is a bit 'touched in the head' over Browning, but I never thought I'd be quoting him in the midst of my present circumstances."

"You've never mentioned being married," said Logan in some astonishment.

"That is perhaps the greatest shame of this life—that we are not able to be together. Every day I pray that I will be spared long enough to see her again."

"Where is she?"

"Just before the Boche came, I was able to get Marcelle and our children south, where a friend ran a fishing boat out of Cannes. He got them to England."

"Why didn't you go with them?"

"What! And leave my precious books to the Nazis?" His eye twinkled mischievously.

"I think you and our friend Poletski are cut from the same cloth," said Logan.

"Once my family was safe," Henri went on, "how could I turn my back on my country? I was too old for the army but knew there would be many other tasks to be done, and a battle-field of sorts upon which to serve right here in Paris."

"Your wife must love you very much."

"Of course! She is my wife."

"It does not necessarily follow that she must love you. Many wives stop loving their husbands."

"Ah, Michel, that shows how little you truly understand marriage. No wife ever stopped loving her husband, when he was truly loving *her* as a man was intended to love a woman."

"Are you saying people do not fall in love, and then out of it again?"

"Michel! Michel! What has falling in love to do with marriage? Nothing! You are not married, n'est-ce pas?"

"Actually, I am married," replied Logan.

"Then for your sake—and your wife's—I hope that someday soon you leave behind this foolishness about being 'in love.' No marriage can survive unless it gets past that and to the love of sacrifice. Ah, but you are young!"

"But you said your wife loved you. I assume you love her?"

"Of course! of course! We are in love now because we first learned how to sacrifice ourselves one to the other. We have learned to serve, to lay down our lives, to wash each other's feet, so to speak. You don't do those kinds of things year after year unless you are determined to love. Not *in* love, but *determined* to love."

"Hmm," mused Logan. "I guess I always thought love had to come first in a marriage."

"Non, mon ami. Love—that comes second! First comes commitment, sacrifice. Then, and *only* then, comes *true* and lasting love. That is why my wife and I *are* now in love."

Logan said no more. He had certainly been given plenty to think about.

33 ❖ A Quiet Supper

WHEN HENRI AND Logan parted, Logan set out on his bicycle to make necessary contacts to begin arranging things for Louis. A printer was his first stop. The man on the left bank was not as good as Jean Pierre's man, but his work would be adequate, and Logan was firm about not involving the priest. He had never discussed the moral complexities of such matters with him, but Logan didn't think it would be fair to place a priest in such a compromising position. He wasn't altogether comfortable with the decision he had just made regarding the fugitive Louis, but now that he had made it, he would handle everything on his own.

Since the printing of the identity papers would take three days, Logan next set about locating a safe house for Claude's friend while he waited. It was five o clock in the afternoon when he finally trudged up the stairs of Lise's building on his last task of the day. He had a pocketful of messages to be radioed to London that evening.

She looked down with some dismay at the sheaf of papers Logan held out to her once he had stepped inside her apartment.

"I'm sorry," he apologized. He knew the longer the radio was transmitting at one time, the greater the risk of detection.

"It's not that," said Lise. "But there were detector vans out last night and I had to shut off. I still have a good deal from yesterday to send."

"Do you think they're onto you?" asked Logan.

"No. I think it was just a general sweep of the area."

"Well, I'll stick around as lookout while you send."

"It's still some time before I can transmit."

"Then why don't we go have some dinner while we wait—I'm starved."

She smiled. "It's a long time since I ate in a restaurant for pleasure, without it being for some kind of rendezvous."

"Let's make a point of forgetting all about the underground."

"We can try," she replied.

They walked down the stairs and to a cafe about two blocks away. Since it was Friday, the place was quite busy, and Logan found himself enjoying the festive activity around him. By all appearances he and Lise were just two friends relaxing after a hard week, not a British agent and a Resistance radio operator. The concierge welcomed them warmly and did not even notice their sudden consternation when several German officers entered shortly afterward and sat down only two tables away.

But they were innocents tonight and had no reason to fear the Germans. At least not for another hour. Besides, the presence of the officers only reinforced their determination to avoid mention of their underground existence.

In the months since Logan had come to Paris, he and Lise had worked frequently together, spending countless hours over the wireless, not to mention a wide variety of other missions. Though Lise had softened her original attitude toward Logan considerably, not since that first evening in her apartment had she revealed any more of her heart to him. It was as though she was embarrassed at having exposed a chink in her armor, and now wanted to make up for that lapse by proving such incidents were rare.

She was a complex woman, indeed, and Logan was intrigued by her.

But if Lise had not opened up to Logan, it was not for his lack of trying. The very mystery surrounding this young Frenchwoman compelled him to probe deeper. He was curious to know what thoughts hovered behind those keenly sensitive dark eyes. What did she think about L'Escroc? What were her deeper motives for what she did? Had she ever been in love? What were her political leanings? What did she think about *him*?

Intuitively Logan sensed that her perceptions would be wise and valuable, as well as interesting. If only she could be induced to express them more freely!

When the meal was finished and the coffee served, Logan leaned contentedly back, sipping at the ersatz brew, not even noticing any longer its loathsome taste.

"Tell me, Lise," he began casually, "what did you do before the war?"

"I was a teacher."

"A teacher. Hmm . . . What did you teach?"

"A dozen eight- and nine-year-old girls."

"Really?"

"Does that surprise you?"

Logan set down his cup and gave the question a moment's consideration before replying. "No," he said finally, "not now that I think of it. In fact, I can just picture them sitting around you in the Place du Trocadéro, faces scrubbed and smiling, looking up at you from the grass in frank admiration."

"What makes you think they would admire me?"

"Oh, I just know they would," Logan replied. "You possess an air of security, and they must surely have hung on every word you said. I have a daughter of my own, and I know she would like you."

His statement raised an obvious flicker of surprise in her normally controlled features. Logan had not intended to mention his daughter and had done so almost unconsciously.

"I guess it's my turn to surprise you," he said lightly.

"Yes, I suppose you did," she replied. "But come, it is time we got back."

They paid their bill, then walked out into the icy winter night. Only after walking a half block in silence did Lise attempt to return to the previous conversation.

"I have never thought of you as a family man," she said as they walked.

"I suppose I'm not really much of one."

"Your daughter must be very proud of you—or at least she will be when she learns of your great courage here and all the people you have helped."

"She's much too young to know what is going on. But I do hope that one day she'll find out what I did in the war, and have some reason to be proud. The Lord only knows how little else there is for her to be proud of."

"She will, Michel," said Lise with sincerity. "Someday she will look up at you with the same admiring eyes you have pictured on my students."

"I don't know . . . What does a child care about Nazis and tyranny and war?" Logan paused, questioning for the first time the validity of his motives for coming to France.

"And your wife?" Lise asked. "She is aware of what you do . . . she is proud?"

Logan did not answer. Instead he sighed deeply.

"I'm sorry . . . I only thought the wife of L'Escroc must be a proud woman."

"She knows nothing about L'Escroc," Logan blurted out finally. "She doesn't even know I'm in Paris."

"I see," replied Lise. Now it was her turn to be silent. They did not know each other well enough yet for her to probe further. At length, she sought to return the conversation to the subject of Logan's daughter, which she hoped would remove the heaviness that had descended upon them.

"But your little girl . . . you seem to think that when she is older she will not be able to understand your absence from her now. But surely when you explain—"

"Why should she? I'm not even sure I do."

Logan paused again. He had not given his family much thought in weeks. If he had hoped that by ignoring it, the problem would somehow resolve itself, he now found he was mistaken. He was just as confused about where everything stood as he was when he left Stonewycke—perhaps more so.

"I'm probably kidding myself with all this about making her proud of me," he finally added in frustration. "I think it's just a lot easier to be here doing this than back there, that's all. What's there to be proud of in that?"

"Does it take more courage to be a father than it does to be a soldier?" asked Lise pensively.

She did not actually expect an answer. But Logan stopped, then reached out and touched her arm to stop her, too. She turned back and looked at him. She could not tell if he was angry, hurt, or reprimanded by her words. She had not meant them to elicit any of those responses. The question had been merely a philosophical one, but now she wondered if she'd been wise to voice it.

A variety of reactions were surging through Logan, though anger was not one of them. His first instinct was to rebuff the whole notion. But he couldn't do that, for he had just admitted to its truth. Instead, he attempted to steer the conversation afield.

"Where did you obtain all that wisdom?" he asked.

Not one to probe where she was uninvited, Lise let him have his diversion. "No doubt from the Talmud," she answered. "My father had no sons to whom he could pass on his great learning. But that hardly mattered to him. He was just as content to pour himself into his daughters. I did not attend the yeshiva, but I know as much Talmud as any man."

They fell silent for the remainder of the walk to Lise's apartment. A light snow began to fall and they quickened their pace, arriving just at the time they were supposed to contact London. If it had been in either of their minds to ponder or further discuss any of the questions raised by their conversation, they were impeded by the sudden rush of successive events.

34 ❊ Caught

THE TRANSMITTING THAT evening began on a smooth note, despite the fact that a new girl was being broken in on the London end and their messages were received with agonizing delay.

Logan paced back and forth in front of the window, pausing every now and then to peek out the blackout shade. In the frosty, darkened streets below little activity could be detected. The midnight curfew would begin in little more than an hour, and most of the cautious Parisians had retired indoors long before this, leaving only a handful of cyclists and pedestrians hurrying along to catch the last trains at eleven.

Logan glanced at his watch. He had wanted to cut off communications much sooner than this, but Lise had been confident yesterday's incident had not been aimed toward them. Besides, messages were piling up. Most of them were too urgent to wait. And with all the dangers that constantly beset them in their daily work, it seemed hardly necessary to allow something so minor to cause them to change their plans.

"How much longer?" Logan called out to Lise, who was intent on her work.

"I'm sorry it's taking so long."

"I know it's not your fault, but curfew is coming up."

Lise didn't reply immediately, for a message was just then coming through. Logan turned his attention back to the window.

Suddenly he snapped the shade closed. "Shut down! There's a van!"

Instantly Lise clicked off the machine, in the middle of the poor London trainee's painstaking reply to one of their messages. She jumped up and joined Logan at the window. Turning out the light in the room, then peering out the merest crack in the shade, they could see the detector van at the far end of the street. Rounding the corner behind it came another.

They watched, holding their breath. Had they only pinpointed the general whereabouts of the wireless sounds, or would the vans screech to a halt right in front of Lise's building?

Both vehicles stopped at the end of the street. Unless there was another wireless transmitting on this same block—an unlikely prospect—the Germans had only been able to zero in on the street. They would begin a house-to-house search.

"Let's get out of here!" said Logan, already grabbing their coats and quickly stuffing the London messages, which he hadn't had a chance to read, into his pocket, while tossing the rest into the coal stove.

"Michel, we can't leave the radio."

Logan paused and looked at the precious instrument.

Yes, it was indispensable to their work, and who could tell when London could send them a new one? But was it valuable enough to risk their lives over? He glanced out the window once more. As he had guessed, the German detection squad was now moving from building to building, and if they carried out their search with customary Nazi thoroughness, there might still be a few moments to attempt a rescue of the wireless.

"Is there a back way out of here?" he asked after a momentary pause.

"An old fire escape, up to the roof and down also."

Logan thought for a moment. "The roof might work," he said, "but we might be trapped." He paused, then went on. "No, we'd better chance it on the street. Get a box for the radio."

In less than two minutes the radio was packed into a cardboard box and the two were rushing out the door and down the hall to a large window. As he wrestled it open, the resulting squeak seemed ear-splitting in the quiet night, and Logan prayed the Nazis didn't have enough manpower to patrol every back exit while their vans crept along the front of the street.

The window opened onto the metal fire escape as Lise had indicated. Carefully they stepped out onto the metal grating, tiptoeing so as not to reveal their presence.

Slowly—very slowly—they made their way down the two flights and into the littered, darkened alley, one end of which led to the street fronting Lise's building on which the Germans were at this moment conducting their raid. Hugging the dirty brick wall, they crept in the opposite direction toward the next block.

Just as they reached the end Logan stopped abruptly and jumped back against the dark recess of the wall, shoving Lise back also.

"Gestapo," he whispered.

"We better give it up," said Lise. "If we stow the wireless in one of these garbage bins, and pretend to be a couple in love and out late, we still might get past."

"Maybe we'll have to," replied Logan, "but I'm not quite ready to give up on the radio yet."

The next instant, however, gave Logan pause to reconsider his daring. The night-call of a prowling tom cat nearly sent him into Lise's arms with panic. He grinned nervously at his reaction, and the twinkle in Lise's eyes told him he had given her a rare moment of amusement. But the serious urgency of the moment did not allow them to revel long in humor. They were trapped in an alley, with the Gestapo watching the street on the one end, and the street swarming with Germans from the two vans on the other. Even if they did stash the radio, there appeared little hope they would get by without at least being detained for questioning, during which time the alley was bound to be turned inside out and the radio discovered.

Suddenly Logan's eyes lit up.

He set the box on the ground, took out the wireless, and hid it behind a trash bin. Then he handed the empty carton to Lise. She gave him a puzzled look, but in the months of their association she had learned to accept his occasional odd behavior without question.

"Hold that box open," he said, "and stay right beside me."

Then he turned his attention to the old tom that had taken up a position on a ledge just above the trash bin, calmly observing all the strange goings-on below.

"Come here, kitty," said Logan in the loudest whisper he dared. "Come, kitty—I've got something nice for you." He attempted to give his voice a sappy inviting sound, but the cat, scrawny and mangy and as hungry as being homeless during wartime could make him, made no move except to wash his face.

"Come, Monsieur le matou," joined in Lise. Her voice too was sweet, and this time the animal looked up with some interest.

Slowly the cat stood, taking notice of the box for the first time, seemingly tempted by the unknown contents inside. Noiselessly he jumped onto a pile of trash nearby. Lise made an untimely jerk with the box and the animal froze. But before it could leap back to safety, Logan's hand shot out and grabbed it by the tail. The tom hissed and spat, while its back leg clawed Logan's wrist and its front paw whipped a vicious scratch across his cheek. But Logan did not let loose his grasp, and pulled the clawing, furious animal toward him, deposited him into the box, and snapped the lid quickly shut.

"Now what?" asked Lise, handing Logan the box, which the caged animal was beating against from inside, letting out deep pained cries.

"Now we can be on our way," said Logan. "But please, look more distraught for your poor sick *matou*, your beloved pet who has taken ill."

With bravado Logan led her out of the alley and into the street, where they were promptly stopped by the vigilant Gestapo.

"Arrêtez!" shouted one of the three standing nearby, who followed his command by running toward them, gun drawn.

Logan and Lise stopped in their tracks.

"What is in that box?" asked the man in very poor French.

"In here?" replied Logan innocently. "Why, only a sick cat we are taking to the veterinarian. We would have waited till morning, but my wife could not sleep for all the poor beast's awful cries."

"Open it up."

"Please, Monsieur Officer, it is nearly crazy since I put him into the box. I had the devil to pay just trapping it inside. You can see the scratches it gave me." Logan pointed to the blood on his cheek and held out his wrist toward the man.

"I said open it up—now!" repeated the man.

Logan cracked the lid, and with a disgusted grunt the agent bent over to peer into the box. Seeing hope of freedom, the tom lurched toward the opening. Logan's hand slipped from the lid with the animal's movement, and the cat came screaming out of its prison into the German's face. He leaped back with an angry curse, and the cat fled once more for the alley.

"Quel dommage!" exclaimed Logan, partly in apology to the startled German, and partly as if bemoaning his own ill luck. "Now I must trap the animal all over again."

"Just see that you do it before curfew," growled the angry agent, in an attempt to regain some of his lost dignity. "Fool animal-loving Frenchmen!" he muttered.

"Merci," said Logan with great sincerity. "You have a kind heart!"

He and Lise turned back into the alley after the lost cat. Once back under the cloak of darkness, Logan retrieved the wireless, set it back into the box, then waited several minutes more to allow for a plausible cat search.

"I hope these Germans are as gullible as customs officials on whom I used to see seamen pull this ruse," said Logan.

"You think they will let us stroll right by?"

"Let's hope so," answered Logan. "But why don't you go back the other way. They'll question you but eventually let you go. No sense both of us running the risk of getting caught with this thing."

"No, Michel. We are in it together."

"But we still have to get the radio across town—and before midnight."

"Perhaps not," said Lise. "Do you remember the cafe where we had dinner? The concierge there is a sympathizer."

"Do you think he will keep our *package* temporarily?"

"I think we ought to try him."

"Then let's go."

The Germans glanced up with little more than a curious interest at the couple as they came back out of the alley carrying their box. No one seemed to express much astonishment that they had found the wild cat so soon. They waved the Frenchman and woman on. They had been posted here to stop Resistance agents, not sentimental cat-lovers.

In less than ten minutes they were inside the cafe. The concierge was sweeping, preparing to close the moment the two or three of his remaining customers departed. From the look on his face he was not altogether pleased at the two new arrivals.

He listened to their highly sensitive request with even more skepticism. Sympathizer though he was, the concierge was also by necessity a very cautious man. He had a family and a decent little business. He was in sympathy, but not anxious to get involved in any underground activities. He was certainly not sympathetic enough to die for this cause. And there could be no other penalty for being caught with a wireless. In the end, however, Logan managed to convince him that his help would only be required for twelve hours. He would himself be back first thing in the morning to retrieve it.

"What could happen, after all, in such a short time? You will be asleep, and so will the Germans," said Logan.

Once the last of the customers had exited, the concierge took the box to his basement where he stowed it in a spot that he felt was safe, even should the Gestapo mount a full-scale raid of the place. Logan made a mental note of the place, for it was sure to come in handy again.

He and Lise then bade the man good night with profuse thanks, and departed. Once outside, Logan looked at his watch. He had but twenty minutes to get home. They made it back to Lise's apartment, sneaking behind the two detection vans that had progressed beyond her building and farther down the street. He retrieved his bicycle, then set off.

The frigid wind whipped across his face like fingers of ice. It had stopped snowing long ago, but the temperature must have dropped ten degrees since dinner. Logan's gloved fingers nearly froze around the handle grips, and even the exertion of pedaling twenty miles an hour did not help neutralize the cold. He tried to focus his mind on the events of the day in order to forget his discomfort.

First there had been the disquieting news about Claude's friend Louis. By now the wheels were in motion to help him, whether it was the right thing to do or not.

Suddenly the face of Alec jumped into Logan's mind. What would his father-in-law think of him helping a man who had knifed a German in the Metro? In the years of his association with Alec, Logan had often measured his own responses by how his father-in-law—a man he greatly admired—might react. But there were too many gray areas to make any clear sense of his present moral dilemma. Perhaps things would become clearer once he met Louis face-to-face. Perhaps not. It was, after all, wartime. And moral dilemmas were all the more thorny during war.

And Logan also faced the wireless problem. He had to retrieve it in the morning, but what would he do with it if he had found no new safe location from which he and Lise could operate? Her apartment could no longer be relied upon. Perhaps by the light of day the concierge would be less faint-hearted and would agree to keep it a bit longer. But the radio couldn't remain out of use for long. There were important communiques that had to be relayed to London. Logan had a pocketful of them right now. They would need responses. Without a wireless in operation, their underground activities would be seriously crippled.

The pressing needs of his present situation managed to divert Logan's mind from the wind biting into his skin. He was so absorbed in trying to sort out all the possible locations for his radio that he paid little attention to the condition of the streets. About halfway home, accelerating downhill, he rounded a corner and suddenly hit a patch of black ice. The front wheel of his bicycle twisted out of control, jerking the handlebars loose in his hands. The bicycle slid sideways out from under him, and Logan was sent sprawling up against the cement post of a street lamp.

Logan lay dazed for several moments before he could take stock of his situation. The side of his face and his shoulder were badly bruised. He forced himself to try to stand, but the left side of his body refused to cooperate. He glanced at his watch. The hands were moving steadily toward midnight.

He forced himself to his feet, ignoring the pain of his scrapes and bruises, then hobbled to where his bike lay. He stooped down to pick up the precious bicycle. A few spokes were bent, but otherwise it seemed usable. By the time he once again straddled the seat and set off again, more slowly, it was already midnight.

As soon as the opportunity presented itself, Logan turned off the main avenue he had been following and began to make his way by means of side streets, keeping to the shadows.

Three blocks from his place he had no choice but to cross a wide boulevard. It was only ten minutes past twelve. If he was lucky, he might—

"Halt'" came a sharp German voice at Logan's back.

For a split instant many thoughts flew through Logan's mind. Could he outwit the bullet that was sure to follow if he kept going and tried to make a dash for it? What was the current discipline for breakers of the curfew? If I'm lucky, perhaps only deportation to a forced labor camp in Germany, he thought glumly.

His cover was solid, his papers flawless, forgeries though they were. Might he be so lucky as to get by with a mere warning?

Suddenly his heart stopped. He still had the slips of incriminating papers in his pocket! Those wireless messages were worth a firing squad at the very least.

He was just about to make a run for it when the German shouted for him to stop a second time.

Without thinking it over, suddenly reason took over and he slammed on his brakes. There was no sense getting killed. If Skittles had taught him one thing, it was never to give up until he'd fully played out his hand.

35 ✣ *Interrogation*

LOGAN LOOKED ABOUT the small room for the twentieth time.

Despite the hour, he had been unable to relax enough to sleep though he was extremely tired. He had been here for hours, imprisoned in what he took to be a holding cell. It was certainly far better than the dungeonlike accommodations where they had kept Poletski downstairs.

It was not the first time he had scanned the room for some possible escape route. But since being deposited there five hours earlier, all his attempts to come up with some way out had proved equally futile.

He had been taken straight to the S.S. headquarters on the avenue Foch, and he could not miss the irony that less than a week ago he had rescued three inmates from this very place. Now *he* was the prisoner, and if he were to remain locked in this room with only a bed and chair, his stay would no doubt be a long one. There were not even sheets on the bed—only a small blanket. Someone obviously planned the accommodations to deter escape through the window, though it was covered with steel bars, or, failing that, the possibility of hanging oneself from the bare light fixture in the ceiling.

Logan was not yet ready for such extremes.

As far as he knew he was still believed to be nothing more than a common curfew breaker. Except for a cursory frisk for weapons, he had not been searched.

His messages had not been discovered, and the moment he had been left alone he set about destroying them. He tore each one into tiny bits, then, prying the window open a crack through the bars, shoved them out where the scraps floated to the ground, mingling inconspicuously with the falling snow.

Yet he could not feel completely relieved. He was worried about this long wait. Any good confidence man knows that a delay in a scam plays against the con man. The primary rule was swiftness—never give the victim the chance to think.

In this case the victim—though he laughed inwardly at the inaptness of the analogy—was the Nazis, and the longer they mulled over what to do with this curfew breaker, the more chance they might have to discover his true intentions. He would have been immensely relieved to know that the long delay was due to nothing more sinister than bureaucratic foul-up. The efficient Nazis had locked him up, then simply forgotten about him. He could thank the opening of Verdi's opera *La Traviata* for that; the cocktail party that had followed had occupied many officers, leaving headquarters short-staffed until late into the night.

By six o'clock a.m. he had gone over every inch of the room several times, fixed his cover story firmly in his mind, and was beginning to wonder about breakfast when he heard a key in the lock.

He began pacing nervously across the room like the harried, supposedly innocent citizen he was pretending to be. But when the S.S. captain walked in, in his trim black uniform, Logan was in complete possession of himself. The German was a young man for an officer, several years Logan's junior, though his fair skin and blonde hair made him appear even younger. But for all his youthful appearance, his well-defined jaw was as firm as if it were set in granite, and his Aryan blue eyes were more reminiscent of ice than they were of the sky or the sea.

"Vous êtes, Michel Tanant?" he said in the polished French of either an educated man or a skilled con artist. Logan guessed from the captain's bearing that it was the former.

"Oui," replied Logan, then added in a frazzled voice, "Please, I've been kept here all night. I don't understand."

"You have violated the curfew."

"Oui, but—"

"Sit down!" ordered the captain.

Logan hesitated, then, complying like a whipped puppy, slumped down on the edge of the bed. The captain sat on the single chair and shuffled through a sheaf of documents that Logan recognized as his identity papers which had been confiscated upon his arrest. *Have they discovered some flaw in them?* he wondered. Even good forgeries were never perfect.

"I am Captain Neumann," said the man. "Your papers appear to be in order. I see no reason to detain you. However, there are a few questions I would like to ask you. Afterward it may be possible for you to go."

"Thank you, Captain," said Logan with immense gratitude. "I assure you that if it had not been for my accident I would have—"

"You are from Lyon?" broke in Neumann impatiently.

"Oui."

"What is your mother's name?"

"Marie."

"How many sisters has she?"

"Two."

"What are their names?"

"Why, Aunt Suzanne and Aunt Yvonne . . . "

The captain was employing a method of interrogation popular with the Germans during snap controls or at roadblocks or borders. A suspect found himself bombarded with a barrage of questions any innocent man ought to be able to answer without thought. If a suspect stumbled or faltered over any reply, he stood immediately accused.

Logan's cover had included none of the previous information, but it didn't matter. The captain would never check up on any of it. He was not even listening to the answers, only scrutinizing Logan's demeanor while responding. As Logan rattled off his answers, he did not hesitate, but answered as if such names had always been part of his life, not merely thought up that instant.

"Where do they live?"

"My aunts?"

"Yes."

"Aunt Suzanne lives in Lyon, but Aunt Yvonne married an artist and now lives in Arles—you know, following in the footsteps of Van Gogh and all that—"

"Where is your father?" interrupted Neumann, not the least bit interested in turning this interrogation into a conversation.

"He's dead."

"And your mother, Michelle . . . ?"

"It's Marie—and she's dead also."

"Buried in Lyon where your Aunt Yvonne lives?"

"No, she's the one in Arles—with the artist." Then Logan added, as in a wounded tone, "I simply don't understand the meaning of all this."

"Your mother is buried in Lyon?"

"Yes. Next to my father. But please—"

"That is all, Monsieur Tanant," said the captain crisply, rising. "You will come with me."

"But where—?"

"Quickly!" snapped the captain. Logan jumped up obediently.

They exited the tiny room. That, at least, was a small relief. Logan still had no idea what was to become of him. Neumann had left the impression that he was about to be released, but then that could be only another clever trick—raise a man's confidence so that he lets down and gets sloppy.

Logan knew he had been scrupulously careful with his responses. Perhaps too much so. There was such a fine line, and one could not always tell when or if he might have inadvertently crossed it.

He and Neumann walked side by side. Logan was quick to note that the captain did not think him a dangerous enough prisoner to draw his gun. Still, he would never be so foolish as to attempt a break in the heart of S.S. headquarters with dozens of armed soldiers close at hand. Using a surreptitious disguise was one thing. But a pitched race through these halls was quite another. He'd never make it to the end of the corridor.

Nevertheless, he would remain watchful and ever vigilant of his surroundings. One could never tell when an acceptable opportunity might arise.

They turned a corner and Logan saw the main stairway just ahead. His hopes began to rise.

Three officers were ascending and had just reached the landing. Suddenly Logan's short-lived hopes plummeted. There, at the top of the stair, was the last person Logan had ever expected to see again—Colonel Martin von Graff!

Only now Logan could plainly see it was *General,* and he wore the uniform and insignia of the S.S. rather than the Abwehr. If he recognized him, Logan was finished.

But General von Graff and his companions walked briskly past, only exchanging salutes with Neumann.

It seemed too good to be true, thought Logan, as he walked steadily on toward the door. They had met in person only that one time. Much had happened since. It was possible he had—

"Captain Neumann," came von Graff's commanding but cultured voice from behind them.

Logan felt the blood drain from his face. All the disciplined training in the world could not have prevented it. Desperately he tried to gather back his composure. There was always a way out—a bluff! He had to think fast!

Neumann turned smartly to face his superior. "Ja, mein General?" he said.

"Why do you have this man?" he asked, eyeing Logan.

"He was caught violating curfew," answered Neumann. "He was brought in last night for questioning."

"I see . . ."

Von Graff paused, apparently in thought, most likely trying to remember where he had seen the face before, and then analyzing this unexpected turn in the same way that Logan was also doing at that very instant.

"Take him to my office," von Graff finally said decisively. "I must take care of a small matter and then I will be there. I will be ten minutes at most—remain with him the entire time!"

"Ja, mein Herr!"

Logan understood enough German to know what had transpired. But he still did not know whether this was a boon or a disaster.

Von Graff continued on his way, and Neumann took his prisoner more firmly in tow back down the corridor the way they had come. Apparently there was more to this Michel Tanant than met the eye. And young Captain Neumann kept well hidden his own queasy stomach—for he had been about to release him!

36 ❈ Unsought Reunion

"THIS IS AN unexpected surprise," said von Graff with understated irony, turning to Logan for the first time.

When he had entered the room a few moments earlier, he had gone straight up to Neumann and exchanged a few words. The captain gave his superior the particulars of Logan's arrest. Then von Graff dismissed the captain and Neumann turned briskly and left the room. Logan found it difficult to read his controlled expression.

"It is for me also," Logan replied.

The conversation was carried on in English, and Logan decided to leave it that way. Undoubtedly von Graff knew that Logan was proficient in French and there was little he could do about that. But he thought it might somehow work to his advantage if he underplayed his limited knowledge of German for the time being. In the ten minutes he had been sitting alone in silence with Neumann awaiting the general's arrival, Logan had been hastily trying to collect his wits and figure some way out of this jam he found himself in. Was his cover blown completely? Or might he possibly resurrect his old *Trinity* identity by which von Graff had known him and play out that game a little longer? Could there be some plausible reason for Trinity to be in Paris and still in league with the Nazis? If so, could he make von Graff buy it? Or had the S.S. already linked him to the underground?

"Naturally, explanations will have to be made," said von Graff.

"Naturally."

Maybe he could tell him that he had been found out by MI5 and forced to flee London. Yes . . . that could work—*if* the Trinity they had brought in to replace him had made no transmissions to Germany in the last two days. The schedule with the Abwehr when *he* had been Trinity several months ago had been one transmission a week, on Tuesdays. It was now Saturday morning. He might be in the clear. Of course all that could have changed. For all he knew MI5 might already have disposed of Trinity. When Logan had gone into the SOE they had decided to keep Trinity as a notional agent because he had been bringing in some valuable intelligence. Gunther had even begun to be slightly jealous at the Abwehr's favoring of this new recruit. Yet, in the time since he had left, Trinity could have easily played out his usefulness. In hindsight, it was foolish to have kept such a loose end active. But who could have guessed that an agent working undercover in Paris would stumble into such a coincidence?

Still, if he could just make this all work for him, he might land on his feet. He would have to feel von Graff out. If the jig *was* up, well . . . he supposed he couldn't have expected this to go on forever. Many agents were glad to last as long as he had. He tried not to think of the consequences awaiting failure. Naturally, his cyanide was in his other suit—but perhaps that was lucky too, for it would have been a dead giveaway.

If only he wasn't so tired! He hadn't slept in over twenty-four hours, and now he wished he had dozed off a bit during the last five. But he had been too keyed up. Logan knew he had to remain alert now more than ever, for he would not easily fool von Graff.

The general took in a sharp breath, the muscles tightening around his neck. Then he walked around behind his desk and sat down. At length he looked up, eyes glinting.

"Come now, Herr MacVey," he said tightly. "Are you trying to play cat and mouse with me? Do you wish to feel me out before you make any commitments?"

The man was shrewd, there was no mistaking that. He had guessed Logan's motives exactly and now there was nothing else for Logan to do but forge ahead, hoping that the story he contrived would somehow coincide with facts.

"Can you blame me, General?" said Logan. "Intelligence types aren't exactly the most trusting of individuals, and I see you are with the S.S. now—that makes it even worse."

"You have nothing to fear from us . . . if you have nothing to hide."

"Do you think that tin soldier you have out there would have believed me if I had told him I was a British subject working for the Abwehr?" asked Logan cynically. "They would have laughed me right into Fresnes Prison, and then directly before a firing squad. I figured that by sticking to my French cover, I just might get released. And then I could have continued with my original plan."

"Which is?"

"I was on my way to Berlin—to see you, actually."

"And what brought on this sudden urge for camaraderie?"

"I had to dog it out of England, that's what. MI5 raided my place and just about had a noose around my neck. But luckily I gave them the slip. That was two days ago."

"And so you decided to go to Berlin without contacting us first?"

"What else could I do? They had my wireless, and I gathered from the MI5 blokes who arrested me that Gunther was not long for this world either."

"They've captured Gunther?" Von Graff was truly surprised at this revelation.

"They didn't use names, but he's the only agent connected to me," answered Logan.

"Don't you know an interrogator's trick when you see one?" said von Graff derisively. "They tell you they have one of your comrades, and that he has been talking freely, in hopes that it will loosen your own tongue."

Logan knew the trick well, but he didn't admit that to von Graff. Instead, "Why those blighters!" said Logan, shaking his head in self-recrimination.

"I hope their ploy was unsuccessful."

"I didn't tell them a thing."

"Then continue on with your remarkable story. How did you escape?"

"You don't believe a word I'm saying, do you?"

"Time will tell, Herr MacVey. Go on."

"They let me go, thinking, I suppose, that I would lead them to some higher-ups. They had a couple of clowns on me, but I ditched them within the hour."

"And . . . ?"

"There isn't much more to say. I hired a couple of sympathizers I knew who owned a trawler, and they got me across the Channel to France."

"Where did you get these papers? Excellent forgeries, I might add."

"I still have friends in London from the old days," said Logan. "You know I did a drag in prison a few years back on a counterfeiting charge. I know a chap who has made that racket an art form."

Logan could hardly believe that the answers to von Graff's probing questions kept coming. His mind was growing so numb from fatigue that it felt as if he were running on the last fume of a very empty tank of petrol. Every now and then his eyes would lose their focus and he would have to jerk them back to attention. He tried to appear alert, but it was no use hiding his fatigue from von Graff—the general could see it plainly and was using it to his fullest advantage.

"Why the break in communications before that?" von Graff said quickly, as if·hoping the sudden change in tact would catch his victim off guard.

It very nearly did. Logan was about to answer with another madeup alibi when all at once a warning went off in his head. Was it something in the general's tone, or that imperceptible squint which suddenly appeared in his eyes, as if he were watching for the answer Logan might make to this question with even more scrutiny than usual? Something from outside himself nudged him into wakefulness. His head had become so dull that he had nearly fallen into one of the oldest traps in the book—if, indeed, it was a trap. But he had no time to deliberate. He must reply immediately, or von Graff would know he was lying.

"General, really . . ." sighed Logan with a soft chuckle. "That's a rather simpleton's trick for a man of your expertise and intelligence. You know very well that I sent my usual message—that is, unless you're out of touch with the Abwehr these days."

"You seem to have an answer for everything, Herr MacVey."

"That's because there is an answer for everything."

"*If* your story is true."

Logan jumped up, took two quick strides to von Graff's desk and slammed his fist angrily on the polished surface.

"If you don't want to believe me, fine!" he shouted. "At this point I don't give a farthing! All I want is a bed and a few minutes sleep—then you can shoot me for all I care. I just wonder if this is how you treat all the agents who give so much for your bloody Reich!"

"It would be much simpler just to radio London," said the general calmly.

"Go ahead—by all means!" replied Logan, irate now. "I don't know why you didn't do that in the first place rather than play all these little games of yours. I just about got myself hung for you—but do I get any thanks? No, instead I'm treated like a bloody snake!"

"I have been sorely amiss, Herr MacVey," said von Graff humbly. "I apologize."

"Oh, cut the bull!" snapped Logan. "I said I was sick of your games."

"Then let me be frank with you." Von Graff's eyes caught Logan's and held them for a tense moment. The true test had come, and Logan knew it. He returned the stare, but it did not last long. Von Graff relaxed and continued. "I believe you," he said. "It would take too much nerve to make up such a tale knowing that every point can and will be verified. Nevertheless, I had to be fully convinced before I could convince my superiors."

"Okay," said Logan contritely. "My outburst may have been uncalled for—I've had a harrowing week, and I'm nearly burnt out."

"I understand," replied von Graff, "and you may consider this interview at an end. I will have Captain Neumann take you to some very comfortable quarters down the hall where you can rest while I make arrangements for a hotel for you."

"What about Berlin?"

"You have found me here. There is hardly any need to continue to Berlin, is there?"

"I suppose not," said Logan, "as long as you've got something for me to do. I don't want to sit out the war in some hotel room."

"That can be arranged. But surely you want some rest and recuperation first. And what better place for that than the City of Lights?"

"I could live with that," said Logan, smiling. "Yes, that sounds just fine."

Neumann was summoned and Logan followed him to another room, which was indeed quite finely appointed, probably serving as temporary quarters for visiting officers and the like. He was given fresh linens, a breakfast tray containing foods most Parisians had not seen in two years, and even a change of clothes. He was suddenly being given the VIP treatment. But he refused to let it go to his head, for when Neumann finally departed, Logan heard the firm turn of the outer lock on the door.

Oh well, he thought. He very nearly *had* come to the point where he no longer cared. All he wanted was some sleep. In a few hours he could face once more all the lies and deceptions. Then he would worry about Gunther's response to von Graff's unbelievable query.

Then he would wonder what had become of his planned rendezvous with Louis. And then he could ponder over how he would explain all this to Henri . . . if he got the chance.

But for now, he just stretched out on the delightfully soft bed and fell instantly to sleep.

37 ❈ Speculations

SOMETIMES ARNIE KRAMER longed for the clear-cut life of the front lines. When two opposing battalions meet and shoot it out, he thought, you know who are the winners and who are the losers. No matter what, you can always tell the enemy. He's the bloke on the other end of your rifle.

But in I-Corps it was never that easy.

Kramer brought his Scotch and soda to his lips for another gulp, then glanced over the rim of the glass at his companion. What would Atkinson make of it all? But there was no reading that flinty eye. Arnie would just have to spell it all out and then wait for his measured, soft-spoken response. He hoped he wouldn't be too slow about it. Time was precious, and Kramer had already wasted an hour driving to the airbase and Atkinson's office.

"It was rather a giant mess to trust to the telephone," replied Kramer, taking another swallow of his drink.

"Just begin at the beginning, and give it to me," said Atkinson. "Don't leave anything out."

Kramer studied his drink a few moments more, deep in thought. Then he began.

"I've got an agent, a double, named Gunther. Some months ago his Abwehr contacts required him to expand his network and introduce them to one of his sub-agents. We set up an imaginary agent, code name Trinity, and dug up a bloke to present to the Jerrys. I opted to bring in new blood for the operation because at the time we weren't sure of Gunther's loyalty and I didn't want to risk one of our own boys. The meet came off a bit too successfully. The Abwehr was so impressed with our Trinity that they sent him off with his own wireless and a questionnaire. We've been operating the Trinity cover ever since."

"And?"

"Well," continued Kramer hesitantly. He liked Atkinson and knew he was a good man, but his reputation for ruthless perfectionism was daunting. Kramer did not like admitting a blunder to him.

He drained off the last of his drink and resumed with a deep sigh. "The fellow we brought in was good. He played the Trinity game for a while, fed the Germans some good bogus info. But I figured there was no reason for him not to go on to bigger and better things. Then, too, it became known that he could speak fluent French. Immediately the French section wanted him, and I saw no reason to keep him. Besides, I knew he wanted more action. So I had HQ bring in someone else to cover Trinity's wireless."

"What became of Trinity?"

"Well, Ray, that's the problem."

Kramer chuckled dryly, but he knew his attempt at humor wouldn't help. Major Atkinson leaned back in his chair, staring down at Arnie with fire in his eye.

"Are you trying to tell me I've got a man in occupied territory with an MI5 skeleton in his closet?" seethed Atkinson. His own code name was Mother Hen, and not without good reason. Protecting his agents was everything to the major, and seeing any of them in trouble tore him apart. And when something came up that he thought he should have known about, he made no attempt to disguise his anger.

Kramer nodded reluctantly. "And the closet door has just been thrown open."

"Talk plainly, Arnie," said Atkinson in a controlled tone despite his distress. "Who is Trinity? And how in the blazes could you have kept me blind about this?"

"Trinity was a gold mine for us," answered Kramer. "It just did not seem possible that there could ever be a conflict between the two operations."

"What if the Abwehr wanted to meet with your Trinity?"

"We'd stall them. If that wasn't possible, then we'd have Trinity imaginarily arrested by MI5, thus taking him out of commission as far as the Abwehr was concerned."

"What about my first question? Who is Trinity?"

"Logan Macintyre."

"Good Lord!" breathed Atkinson. "What kind of danger is he in?"

"That's one of the many things I'm not sure of."

Kramer took a folded paper from his coat pocket. "Gunther got this about three hours ago." He handed it over to Atkinson.

The major read the decoded words incredulously:

TRINITY ARRIVED SAFELY FRANCE STOP VERIFY CIRCUMSTANCES RE DEPARTURE ENGLAND STOP IS YOUR PRESENT STATUS SECURE END

"What did your agent Gunther do?" asked Atkinson.

"He feigned bad reception, which luckily with this blustery weather we've been having was perfectly believable. He told them to contact him later. They arranged to radio back in twenty-four hours. That's tomorrow evening."

"So they bought it?"

"I hope so."

"What do you propose to do now?" asked Atkinson.

"Before I make that decision, I'd like to know just what Trinity, that is, Macintyre, is up to. I don't want Gunther to give them any information that would compromise him." Kramer glanced down at his empty glass, wondering if Atkinson would break out the bottle again. "Have you been in regular contact with him? Have there been any irregularities?"

"Our most recent communication was last night as per schedule. But it was cut off prematurely."

"Then it's possible the Nazi's may have picked him up?"

"Anything is possible in the underground," said Atkinson. "We haven't heard a thing since then. To tell you the truth, I've been concerned."

"If they did pick him up," mused Kramer, "isn't it possible he invoked the Trinity cover for protection?"

"He'd never get away with it if he were caught red-handed operating a wireless." Atkinson paused, sipping his own drink, though with more disinterest than his companion. "Perhaps someone else has assumed the Trinity identity," he said at length.

"Impossible," stated Kramer firmly. "Gunther and Macintyre and I are the only ones who know about it. And Cartwright, of course, my new Trinity. No, it's got to be Macintyre himself. And I'd like to know why."

"What are you implying, Arnie?"

"Don't get me wrong, I like him. He and I were old friends. That's why I pulled him into this business in the first place. But the Germans can turn our boys just as easily as we can theirs." Though he said nothing, Kramer was thinking of his conversation with Gunther in which the German told him of his brief meeting with Logan's wife. He didn't like it. Wives only muddied an agent's existence. And he couldn't help wondering if there wasn't more to the Macintyre woman's tracking of Gunther than met the eye.

"Macintyre turned! I don't believe that for a minute." The major was incensed at the very thought. "I may have had doubts about Macintyre at first. And I wasn't even particularly nice to him. But I never doubted his loyalty. Besides, he's proved himself. The charge doesn't fit with facts. He's been in Paris four months, yet the Germans think he's only just arrived. And regardless of all that, what advantage would it be to the Germans to use the Trinity cover in this way? It just doesn't fit."

"All right," conceded Kramer. "But say he was arrested last night, and assume further that he broke under torture. What if he made promises to the Germans, compromising Gunther in the process? Their radio message could just be part of some cunning ploy."

Atkinson opened his desk drawer, took out the bottle of Scotch, and walked around to Kramer's chair and refilled his glass.

"Steady, old boy," he said, setting the bottle down and leaning on the edge of his desk. "I think you're getting a bit gun-shy about this whole business. Intrigue's the name of the game—we just have to outwit the Nazis on this one—for Macintyre's sake."

Kramer gulped his drink. "Something's going on over there, and I don't know anything about it and you don't know anything about it. Doesn't that make you a bit nervous, Ray?"

Atkinson did not answer immediately. Instead, he shuffled through a stack of papers on his desk, finally removing one and handing it over to Kramer.

"Look at this, Arnie," he said. "It's a recommendation for the George Cross for Macintyre."

Kramer's thick eyebrows arched in surprise and his mouth fell open.

"It's all 'most secret' right now—the details of his activities," Atkinson went on, "but you read these reports and *then* tell me you suspect him of disloyalty or even breaking. The guy has become one of the underground's key operatives, the hub of dozens of activities. Something's going on in Paris, of that you are right. And we better give Macintyre all the support we can."

"Well," said Kramer, surprised at such high praise coming from a man like Atkinson, and yet not a little proud of his protege, as he considered Logan, "at the very least it was foolhardy of him to fall back on the Trinity cover after four months' separation."

Atkinson gave a short dry chuckle. "Now *that* does sound like Macintyre!"

"So what do you suggest we do now," asked Kramer, "in order to give him that support you are talking about?" He was quite willing to dump the decision into Atkinson's lap.

"When the Abwehr contacts Gunther," said the major without hesitation, "have him verify Macintyre's story."

"But we have no idea what his story is!"

"Yeah, you're right." Atkinson paused and thought for a moment before continuing. "Then you and I are just going to have to get inside his skin and figure out what alibi he would have given the Germans," he went on. "They must have been convinced, whatever he told them, or they wouldn't have wired Gunther. I would say if he was picked up, it was probably for something completely unrelated to his espionage activities. He's too careful to get caught in the middle of a wireless operation."

"Like picking a pocket or cheating at cards," quipped Kramer.

"Whatever . . . But afterward something must have gone sour and he saw the resurrection of his old Trinity identity as a way to cover his tracks."

"Actually," said Kramer, a sly gleam creeping into his eyes, "if we could pull this off, it could prove quite to our advantage. What a boon to have an inside man in Paris!"

"You're a crass opportunist," grunted Atkinson with disgust. "You'd be asking him to walk a dangerous tightrope. *If* we can clear him with the Germans, I want him pulled out of France at the first opportunity."

"Sure, Ray, sure."

But as he said the words, Kramer's tone was not at all convincing. The gleam was still in his eye. *I knew Logan was made for this business when I brought him in,* he thought to himself.

38 ❊ *An Elite Soirée*

LOGAN WAS READING his third back issue of *The Signal,* France's collaborationist magazine. It was revolting fare, but since he was forced to play the part of a Nazi, it could do no harm to keep abreast of the latest propaganda.

Neumann had provided the reading material to keep Logan amused during his enforced stay at S.S. headquarters. Technically, so he was told, Logan was not a prisoner. But the room remained faithfully locked nevertheless. He had not laid eyes on von Graff since they had parted late yesterday morning. He did not know if Gunther had been contacted, but he assumed that since his status had not changed, he must still be in limbo. There was a good chance they had not been able to reach him yet, but if they had, he hoped Gunther was quick on his feet.

It was only a matter of time before the jig was up, however, if he didn't succeed in getting word to somebody on the outside. But how could he get a message to Henri? By now they probably assumed him captured and would have already begun to break up the network. The rule for a captured agent was to make every effort to give his comrades forty-eight hours to disband before breaking down. It had now been well over thirty. But even if *La Librairie* still were intact, how could he get word to them from this prison?

The real question, however, echoed in Logan's mind: Will Gunther have enough wits about him to give me the kind of support I need? Gunther had never respected Logan or been friendly toward him. But just good sense ought to tell him that more was at stake than Logan's life. In the Abwehr's eyes, Gunther was Logan's mentor. If Logan became discredited, Gunther could be blown as well.

The uncertain waiting was hardest of all to bear. If only he could be sure of his status so he would know how to play himself. Then he might formulate some plans. If he was blown, then he ought to be thinking about an escape. If by some miracle they *had* bought his story, he should be thinking more definitely how to use it to his advantage.

What wouldn't he be able to do for the Resistance effort from inside the S.S.! He grinned to himself. What a coup that would be!

Absently his eyes turned to the magazine lying in his lap. Suddenly the grin on his face faded. There on the page was a grotesque drawing of a hideous ghoul digging his fingernails into the world globe. Underneath read the caption, "Le Juif et la France." The accompanying article raved about evil Jewish global intentions, accusing the Jews of having started the war, and rallying the French people to take strong and determined action against this dangerous threat.

Logan's mind turned to the honorable Poletski. He had brought with him reports of dire atrocities committed against Polish Jews by the Germans. Thousands had disappeared without a trace. He had used a term unfamiliar to Logan, and to all civilized men—death camps. The idea was inconceivable to Logan. Surely Poletski is an alarmist, he thought at first. Yet how could a man exaggerate unless he had seen something with his own eyes to start the tale growing?

Logan shook his head. The article and the thought of Poletski reminded him what a deadly business this was. Too often he tended to think of it as a mere lark. He was glad for the sobering look at the article.

"Lord," he prayed, not caring that he hadn't offered a prayer in months, "let me make it through this. Let me have this victory. I'll do anything just to be allowed one more crack at helping to defeat these evil Nazis!"

At that moment a knock on the door interrupted him.

When Captain Neumann entered, he made no mention of communication with London. Logan could hardly ask, thus risking the appearance of being too anxious. Yet by Neumann's polite demeanor, it seemed that his cover was probably still holding up. And he also might have read a positive message in Neumann's greeting.

"Heil Hitler!" said the captain with the customary salute.

Caught off guard, Logan gaped silently for a moment until it dawned on him that he was meant to return the blasphemous greeting. Cringing inside, he forced out the words.

"Heil Hitler," he said with nominal enthusiasm, raising his arm partially in salute. He pretended to have just been awakened from a brief nap, and Neumann appeared satisfied.

Neumann addressed Logan in French, either because he knew no English or von Graff had not informed him of the "guest's" true nationality.

"The general," began Neumann, "wishes you to accompany him to a function this evening."

"A function?"

"Yes. A birthday party for a local personage." Neumann held out his arm, over which were draped several items of clothing. "The general sent this evening attire for you to wear." He laid the items over the back of a chair. "He hopes the fit is correct."

"I'm sure it will be," said Logan, strolling to the chair and fingering the fine fabric.

"I will return for you in an hour, then."

Logan nodded.

Neumann departed, locking the door obediently behind him. Logan went to the adjoining bathroom to wash, then changed into the black tuxedo.

As he stood before the mirror combing his hair, Logan was suddenly reminded of another tuxedo he had worn many years ago. At first it seemed completely incongruous that such a memory should assail him at this particular moment. But he had been playing a part then too—until the drive home, that is.

Coming home from the party in the rain that morning had been magical. He and Allison had muddied themselves in the rain and rising floodwaters, and in the process had become friends and put their incessant feuding behind them. At that moment he had seen beyond her hard veneer and had glimpsed instead into the heart of a vibrant, loving young woman. He had come to discover both vulnerability and tenderness there, and had determined to know more of that side of Allison MacNeil. Now, so far removed from everything but such sweet memories, it seemed inconceivable that they could be separated by such vast distances, distances not measured only in miles. Where had they gone wrong? What, or who, was to blame? Was it really over between them?

That morning in the pouring rain everything had seemed so right. If only they could go back.

But here he was stuck in Nazi headquarters, so up to his neck in deceit that he wondered if there would ever be a way out. With every twist he only got in deeper. What would Allison think of him going to a Nazi birthday party! Her doubts and misgivings about him certainly appeared well-founded now. No matter how much he told himself that his actions were justifiably necessary in order to counter the evil of the enemy, there were times when he could begin to understand her confusion. He got confused at times himself. What worried him most was that he did this kind of thing so well. He was, he had to admit, a born con man. He enjoyed it! Yes, he had winced at the "Heil Hitler." But he had done it, and convincingly. And tonight he would attend the party and be the best Nazi there!

Why? Because his life depended on it. But there was more to it than that, and he knew it. And there was more to it than his revulsion toward the Nazis. He would play out the charade with his best flair and style because it was a challenge. Even if this double life was confusing with all its gray areas, he still had to admit that he loved the *challenge*.

That's what he had been searching for all those years in London. That's what Allison had never been able to understand. And the real irony was that probably on that rainy day in Scotland ten years ago, Allison had been a kind of challenge too.

How about that, Allison? he thought. *Maybe you're right about me. What a chump I really am. I suppose I deserve all this Nazi company!*

By the time Neumann arrived for him, Logan was ready to throw himself into this latest ruse. He did not let his thoughts probe any deeper into his motives for now. Whether self-serving or noble, what did it matter now, anyway? He had no choice but to go through with it.

Logan was driven to a stately townhouse a few miles outside Paris in the fashionable suburb of Neuilly. The moment he entered the villa, he was immediately struck with the display of wealth all about him, a stark contrast to his four months among the deprivation and poverty of wartime Paris. What he saw could best be described as a spectacle, a grand effort to prove that "gay Paree" had survived the coming of the new regime. All the men were in full black-tie dress—no frayed and mended old models, but perfectly new and stylish suits and tuxedos. The German soldiers present were in their finest dress uniforms, the officers loaded down with decorations from this and the last war. The women were outfitted in the latest Paris fashions, bedecked with mink and jewels. The effect was dazzling, combined as it was with the light from three huge crystal chandeliers.

What drew Logan's eyes most, however, was the long refreshment table laid out with platters of roast pheasant, duck, and beef and finished off with bowls of caviar and dozens of other rich dishes—all complemented with the finest French champagne. And to think his friends in some of the poorest sections of Paris were living on bread and cheese and turnips!

"I trust you are well rested," said General von Graff, walking up suddenly behind him and greeting him.

"Very," replied Logan, "enforced though it was."

"Please, I hope you are not one to hold grudges." Von Graff paused to respond to the friendly greeting of a passerby. "Let this evening be as a way of a peace offering."

"I must say, you Germans know how to throw a soirée."

Von Graff laughed dryly as if Logan's statement had been intended as a joke. "Your host actually is a Frenchman, and the guest of honor also—Baron de Beauvoir."

Logan restrained a reaction to the name de Beauvoir. He knew it must be Jean Pierre's brother. But before he had time to think through the implications further, von Graff spoke up again.

"I shall introduce you if you wish. However, for the present I would like to keep your British origins under wraps."

"I should think it would be quite a feat for you to introduce a British convert to your friends."

"Perhaps; but if you'll indulge me this evening," said the general, adding cryptically, "It may be more advantageous to keep it quiet for now."

"Whatever you say."

"Apparently your French is quite good. So I thought I would say you are a merchant from Casablanca, Monsieur Dansette."

Logan nodded his consent, though inwardly balking at yet another identity to keep straight.

They approached a small knot of people and von Graff introduced Logan. Common pleasantries were exchanged and soon the conversation turned into the inevitable current of war news. But Logan's attention had wandered, finally arrested by a familiar face across the room. The man at whom he found himself staring stood holding a glass of champagne and engaged in animated conversation with a uniformed German and two ladies. Except for his clerical garb, he seemed quite in keeping with the events of the evening and perfectly comfortable with this upper-class crowd. With his tall, graceful form and handsome, distinguished features, Logan could easily see him as he once must have been—the society playboy. Logan wondered what had happened to lead him into the priesthood. But his musings were suddenly interrupted.

"I see you have noticed our resident cleric," said von Graff with a cynical edge to his voice.

Logan hadn't realized he had been staring so intently nor that it had been noticeable, something he would have wished to avoid. He jerked his eyes away, berating himself for his carelessness, but making the most of his indiscretion.

"Yes," he replied. "He's rather out of place here, isn't he?"

"He is, but not because of his collar or cassock."

"How cryptic of you, General," chuckled Logan. "Why, my imagination soars with the possibilities inherent in such a statement."

"The good priest is a member of the Resistance," elaborated von Graff. However, he did not join in Logan's amusement.

"You must be jesting!" exclaimed Logan, appearing genuinely surprised with such a far-fetched statement.

"But it is true."

"Why isn't he in chains?" asked Logan. "Or do you make it a policy to invite the Resistance to your soirées?"

"It is only a matter of time before Monsignor de Beauvoir will have his prison quarters."

"De Beauvoir?"

"He is our host's brother."

"Ah . . . I see," said Logan, nodding his head. "How intriguing. Blue blood blinds the Nazis to a man's affiliations."

"Nothing of the sort!" snapped von Graff. "I'd put him in irons this instant if I could get some concrete evidence against him. He's a thorn in our flesh. And look at him! He shows up at these gatherings as if to flaunt his impervious position, and no doubt to gather what intelligence he can for his Resistance friends."

"A crafty devil . . . for a holy man," said Logan admiringly.

"Even Satan fell from grace," replied von Graff caustically, "as will this priest—sooner or later."

Logan couldn't help thinking of the old Genesis dodge he and Skittles used to run in London, and wondering how the scheme might go off in a setting like this. But to von Graff he said, "What about his brother, the baron? Is he also a patriot?"

"Baron de Beauvoir is much too pragmatic for such folly—he's making far too much money off the Germans to be able to afford patriotism. But regardless, he'd not wish to see his brother shot, if he could help it—which, believe me, he can."

"Well, General, I'm thoroughly absorbed. Could you manage an introduction?"

"Of course."

As they approached, Logan was the only one who noticed the brief flicker of consternation that passed across the priest's face when he saw him at von Graff's side. But he betrayed no other indication of his surprise at seeing his former colleague in these surroundings.

"Enchanté, Monsieur Dansette," he said graciously, extending his slim cultured hand to Logan. "How is Casablanca these days? It has been years since I was there."

"Dirty and crowded as always," replied Logan. "Paris is a refreshing breath of air by comparison."

"Yes, even despite our Teutonic guests."

Von Graff rankled at the slur, but Logan only smiled.

"You are bold, Monsignor," said Logan.

"Priests and old men can get away with anything," laughed Jean Pierre.

"But not for long, de Beauvoir," seethed von Graff. "Not for long . . ."

"Oh, General," countered the priest good-naturedly, "I hope your contact with the French will, if nothing else, serve to improve the dour German sense of humor. Or should I say *lack* of it?" He paused, took a breath, and began again in a new vein. "And your manners, too. Look, poor Monsieur Dansette, a guest to our country and to my brother's home, and he does not even have a glass of champagne in his hand. Nor, I suppose," he added, turning toward Logan, "have you partaken of the fine table my brother sets?"

"As a matter of fact I have not," replied Logan, more interested, however, in what might be in store for him at this gathering other than food. "I did only just arrive, though," he added.

"Then come along, let me be your guide."

"You need not trouble yourself, Monsignor," put in von Graff. "I will see to Monsieur Dansette's comfort."

"I insist," said Jean Pierre, taking Logan's arm. "I'm sure it has been a long enough time since Monsieur Dansette has been treated to true Parisian hospitality."

He whisked Logan away, keeping up a stream of trivial chatter until they reached the table. There was no one close by, but as he spoke he retained the light, social timber to his voice, though lowering its volume, smiling and chuckling at appropriate intervals. Logan responded in kind, as if they were still talking about the weather or the food.

"You don't know how glad I am to find you here," said Logan.

"Nor you, how *surprised* I am to find you," replied Jean Pierre. "We thought you had been arrested, and here I find you on the arm of an S.S. officer, a general no less—and looking well and fit, I might add."

"I *was* arrested," said Logan, defensiveness creeping into his disguised tone. Despite Jean Pierre's social tone, he could sense the accusation in his words.

"The Nazis have changed their style, then."

"How do you mean?"

"Wining and dining their prisoners."

"It's a long story and there is not time for it now—"

At that moment a couple strolled up to the priest's elbow.

"You must try the paté," said the priest to Logan, slicing off a slab and laying it on the plate Logan had picked up. "It's delightful. My brother employs the finest culinary staff in Europe."

"You are most kind," exaggerated Logan.

"But stay away from the caviar," rejoined Jean Pierre. "All the skill in the world cannot disguise the fact that it's not Russian. Alas, for the ravages of war!"

As the couple moved away, Logan took up the previous conversation where it had been interrupted.

"You must get a message to London for me," he said.

"How can you ask such a thing?"

"What do you mean?"

"What am I to think?" said the priest, a sadness suddenly entering his voice. "You are quite friendly with the Nazis—even a magician could not have performed such a feat in such a short time. You have had previous association with them, that is obvious. Perhaps even in the last four months."

"Jean Pierre!" Logan's voice rose dangerously. He had to clench his teeth to keep it under control. He paused until he could respond without drawing attention to himself. "You must believe me! You've *got* to send that message. I'm a dead man if you don't."

But the conversation progressed no further, for at that moment von Graff rejoined them.

"Ah," he said, "I had no idea a trip to the refreshment table could be so lengthy."

There was something odd in his tone. Did he suspect, or was it simply his natural distrust of anything out of the ordinary?

"I'm afraid," Jean Pierre answered casually, "that I have monopolized Monsieur Dansette's time with a discussion on the merits of Russian caviar over other continental varieties."

"I had no idea you were a gourmet, Monsignor," said von Graff.

"Oh, I have many talents," answered Jean Pierre airily. "But I try to keep most of them hidden."

"So I've heard."

"In fact, I was just trying to persuade our guest from Casablanca to join me at the rectory tomorrow for a truly excellent meal. Even the Pope has marveled at my delectable crepes."

"Of course I told him that would be impossible," said Logan, "under the *constraints* of my present circumstances."

"You must not be such a slave driver, General," prompted Jean Pierre.

But von Graff's attention strayed momentarily as his aide approached, appearing rather flustered.

"General, these just arrived," he said, holding out two slips of paper. "I did not think you'd want them to wait."

Logan surmised his charade was about to come to an abrupt end. He glanced about for an escape exit, even though as he did so, he realized the futility of such an effort.

In the meantime von Graff had perused the messages, and as he finished the last his color paled noticeably, though he was quick to resume his military facade.

"Bad news?" queried Jean Pierre.

"No," he replied coolly, "only rather shocking. Japan has just bombed Pearl Harbor in the Hawaiian Islands. It seems that America will now enter the war."

"Is that inevitable?" asked Logan.

"It is inevitable that America will declare war on Japan. Probably she has already done so," answered von Graff. "I have little doubt that the Führer will honor the Reich's treaty with Japan and declare war in turn on the United States."

"Mon Dieu!" breathed the priest.

"Germany has gained a formidable ally."

"Formidable enough to stand against the might of America?" countered Jean Pierre.

"Japan has not been defeated for three thousand years," replied the general, "so why not?"

However, his tone lacked essential conviction, and his initial response to the telegram indicated deeper doubts. If he did not sense then, he soon would know that America's entry into the war must mean Germany's ultimate defeat.

Logan had been so absorbed in this recent development that he had nearly forgotten his own plight. But von Graff's next words brought it immediately back to mind. The ending to Logan's speculations came on a much more positive note than he had anticipated.

"By the way, Monsieur," he said to Logan, "I am going to instruct my aide to have Neumann secure a hotel room for you. He can drive you there tonight if you wish."

"Thank you, General," Logan replied calmly, as if he had expected nothing else.

Yet, all the while he was shouting with exuberance inside, he knew this news was a mixed victory. He would still be under their thumb, and no doubt under surveillance, too. Had he really been set free, or had his trap only been enlarged?

39 ❈ Luncheon at the Rectory

LOGAN JERKED UP in his bed, drenched with perspiration. He swung his feet out of bed, then sat there on the edge with his head resting in his trembling hands, trying to catch his breath.

It had only been a nightmare . . . nothing but a dream. But he couldn't help feeling foolish for the fright it gave him.

It had been so real! He was still breathing hard, like the man running through the city streets. He hadn't had a dream like that since he was a child.

Glancing at the bedside clock he saw it was seven a.m. He stood, walked slowly to the window, and pulled open the blackout shade. No wonder it seemed so much earlier than seven. Outside the sky was dark and brooding. The clouds were heavy laden with winter storms, and the icy blasts they held were almost palpable, even as Logan stood there in his warm hotel room.

Wakefulness gradually coming to him, he threw on the bathrobe von Graff had provided him, then called down to the front desk and asked for a pot of coffee to be brought up. The activity helped to steady him, and before long he nearly succeeded in forgetting about the unsettling interruption to his sleep.

In a few minutes the waiter came with the coffee. For the first time since arriving late last night, Logan began to consider his surroundings. The waiter, dressed in a trim hotel uniform, pushed a cart covered in white linen bearing a silver coffee service, fine china, and a silver vase containing a red rose bud. This was no cheap hotel, Logan thought to himself. He had pulled scams in places like this, but never stayed in one! The waiter bowed politely, and when Logan attempted to give him a tip, he shook his head.

"Ne vous dérangez pas," he said. "It is already taken care of."

Logan raised his eyebrows in astonishment. "Merci," he replied as the fellow left.

Logan had figured von Graff knew how to live. But this was too much. He poured out a cup of the steaming brew and unconsciously raised it to his lips for a sip.

The first taste nearly choked him. It was the real thing! He had not tasted coffee like this in months!

He sat down and gazed about him. The windows were covered with velvet drapes, the floor with a thick Persian carpet. He sat on a satin-covered Chippendale chair. It had been so late when he came in last night that he had been too tired to notice. But now he could see that von Graff had spared nothing for his British double agent. What was that insidious Nazi up to, anyway?

Logan finished his coffee. No sense letting it go to waste. He poured himself another cup.

For the moment von Graff was the least of his problems. He still had to get in touch with London, and it seemed that his only avenue, Jean Pierre, had suddenly grown hostile toward him, or at least suspicious. Though he had good reason. After von Graff had intervened last night at the refreshment table, they never had another moment alone. Had Logan's final plea softened the priest's reticence?

There was no way of knowing. But if Jean Pierre did not believe him, and succeeded in turning the rest of *La Librairie* against him, and Logan tried to make contact with them, he could be in as much danger there as in S.S. headquarters.

What wouldn't Claude give for a chance to slit his throat as a traitor!

If he could just see Lise . . .

But immediately he shook that idea from his head. If von Graff had him under surveillance, it would be tricky trying to explain everything to her.

There had to be another way.

What an irony, he thought. He had only been superficially trained in this business, got into it almost by accident through Arnie. Now here he was in the classic jam of a spy—caught in no man's land. Mistrusted by both sides, either of which would kill him in a second if they broke his cover. Caught in a foreign land with no friend to trust him. These past four months he'd been arranging escapes for refugees. But now that he was caught in the middle, he himself had no safe house to go to.

He sipped at the coffee, and in his mind went over every detail he could recall of the last few days, trying to find an angle. What would von Graff be looking for? How would he have to change his habit patterns to keep from looking the least bit suspicious? If he chanced to see anyone he knew, he'd have to be especially on his guard. And what had Gunther told von Graff anyway?

The scenes from de Beauvoir's birthday party marched through his mind. His talk with Jean Pierre—all at once he saw it!

Jean Pierre had given him his escape route! He tried to recall his words verbatim:

". . . I was just trying to persuade our guest from Casablanca to join me in the rectory tomorrow for a truly excellent meal . . ."

That was it! Just what he was looking for. The only thing he could be accused of was accepting the kind invitation of this fascinating priest.

He instantly jumped up, forgetting all about the coffee, and prepared to dress and set out immediately.

But what was he thinking? It was still early morning. No time had been specified. How early did he dare call? He paced the room several times, trying to work it out in his mind, considering all the consequences of various actions. Finally he paused by the phone. He'd have to risk it. Calling would be easier to explain than showing up at an empty rectory.

The velo-taxi dropped Logan at the rectory door. As he walked up to the ancient oak door, he saw a black Renault sedan pull up across the street. It had followed him, none too discreetly, from the hotel. But he had covered his bases. There was nothing to worry about.

Jean Pierre welcomed him warmly. Logan found himself wondering if the priest had had a change of heart, or if the greeting was only for the benefit of the housekeeper who had led Logan to the drawing room. When she departed, the priest remained congenial, though his mood was tempered with more solemnity than was customary in the usually debonair cleric.

"I hoped you would catch my subtle cue," he said as he directed Logan to a chair, while he himself took an adjacent one.

"To be honest," replied Logan, "I didn't at first. I wondered if I'd ever see you again after our conversation last night."

"It would not have been fair of me to pass judgment under those circumstances—at least not without a full hearing of your story. I make no guarantees, however, other than listening to what you have to tell me."

"Thank you for that much," said Logan, "though I still don't know what I can say to convince you of my loyalty."

"Perhaps you ought to tell me everything from the beginning," suggested the priest.

Logan began with his MI5 work in London and proceeded to do exactly that, from his first meeting with Gunther to his ill-timed encounter with von Graff after his arrest two days ago. When he was through, Jean Pierre rubbed his chin for several minutes before saying anything in reply. At length he rose and walked slowly to the window.

"I see you did not come alone," he said.

"That couldn't be helped," answered Logan. "Von Graff wouldn't trust his own mother. At least I'm out of that place. But there should be nothing incriminating about me coming here today."

"Incriminating, no . . . but you can believe von Graff will be suspicious."

"I'll just tell him I couldn't resist the thought of getting something on an underground priest."

"Just don't play it too cocky, my friend. Von Graff is nobody's fool."

"I have discovered that."

Jean Pierre continued to stare absently outside. "Look over there," he said after a moment. Logan joined him at the window. The priest cocked his head toward the corner opposite that at which the black sedan was parked. A man who would have been husky even without his thick layers of winter clothing leaned against a lamppost, puffing on a cheroot. "There's my shadow," he said with a coy grin.

"They have someone on you all the time?"

"In a manner of speaking," replied Jean Pierre. "They are easily gotten rid of, however, and I give them the slip whenever their presence would be . . . cumbersome."

He chuckled softly. "The Gestapo is not unlike a charging rhinoceros. Very dangerous to be sure, but not altogether smart. However, they might be smart enough to find out whether we in fact did have our meal here today, so perhaps we ought to retire to the kitchen for the sake of our cover."

"Of course," agreed Logan. But as they walked together down a corridor toward the back of the rectory, he added in a graver tone, "You may be right about the rhinoceros analogy. But don't underestimate them, Jean Pierre. They're not altogether stupid. That is exactly what they would like us to think."

The priest ushered Logan into the kitchen, where they found the housekeeper busily engaged in the process of brewing coffee for the priest and his guest.

"Ah, Madarne Borrel," said Jean Pierre, "that is so kind of you. But I have promised my guest that I would prepare him one of my specialties."

"Oui, mon Père," replied the housekeeper. "But if you are planning to make crepes, we have but one egg. You're likely to end up with pancakes instead."

"We'll have to make do," said Jean Pierre. "Now, if you would like to take the morning off, I see no reason why you shouldn't."

"Merci, mon Père," Mme. Borrel answered enthusiastically, scurrying off and leaving the two men alone.

"She is a fine lady," said Jean Pierre, "and completely loyal. But it is best we take no chances." As he spoke, he took out bowls, utensils, and all the necessary ingredients, and immediately began pouring and mixing.

"You amaze me, Jean Pierre," said Logan at length.

"Anyone can make crepes."

"That's not what I meant. The way you've handled yourself—last night, and today . . . I find it remarkable."

"Because I am a priest?"

"Yes, I suppose so. All the deception and cover and evasion tactics. You couldn't have learned to be so proficient at this double life in the seminary."

"Here, take this and oil it thoroughly," said the priest, handing Logan a heavy griddle. As Logan fell to his task, Jean Pierre continued.

"No, none of what I do was learned there, believe me," he said. "Nor did I acquire it in my days before conversion in a life of crime." He paused while he cracked the single precious egg into one of the bowls. "It's a matter, I suppose, of doing what must be done."

"Why do you do it at all?" asked Logan. "It does not follow that it must be done by you. In your position, no one would blame you for staying out of the whole thing."

"Yes, I could have." His attention was momentarily diverted to the task of properly beating his egg, but Logan wondered by the intense look in Jean Pierre's eyes if he wasn't using the diversion to consider the many ramifications to his position. He hoped he wasn't trying to think of some elusive response because he still didn't trust Logan. When he finally spoke again, it was in a thoughtful tone. "Thomas Jefferson once said, 'Resistance to tyrants is obedience to God.' I have often thought about that since the war began. It is a weighty idea."

"I have never thought of it in quite those terms," said Logan. "I suppose if I was really put to it, I would have to admit that right now, with what I am doing, the last thing I feel is obedient to God."

"You doubt the morality of our methods?"

"I try not to, but sometimes I find myself doubting them. Yet it's more a personal reaction I'm speaking of than a response to our methods. Inside me, things are a little insecure."

"War brings insecurity to us all."

"Helping people escape is one thing. Being involved with killers is another. I just don't know what's right."

"The morals of the Resistance, then, are important considerations for you."

"Several years ago I tried to dedicate my life to God. Not in the way you have, I suppose—but I was sincere. I truly wanted to change. Yes, it was very important to me." He paused and shook his head. "I don't know what happened."

"The war, Michel—it changes us . . . it changes everything."

"That may be true. But whatever it was with me happened long before the war ever came along."

Logan turned and looked intently at Jean Pierre. "Yet now I'm afraid that what has happened to me since the war began will make those changes irreversible, that somehow I will never be able to go back." He stopped and tried to assume a lighter attitude. "I'm sorry for burdening you with all this. I don't know what possessed me."

Jean Pierre tapped a floury finger against his stiff white collar. "This sometimes has a way of loosening a man's tongue. Perhaps the Gestapo ought to get rid of their whips and employ a few more priests in their interrogation rooms."

Jean Pierre began to spoon his batter onto the hot griddle while Logan watched in silence. At length he began to speak again. He did not know Jean Pierre in depth, but all at once he knew he had to talk to someone. It was perhaps more than underground business that had drawn him to seek the priest out that morning.

"Last night I had a dream," he began slowly. "Actually it was more like a nightmare. I awoke in a dreadful fright."

"Do you want to tell me about it?" Jean Pierre asked as he took two crocks of jam from a cupboard and handed them to Logan. Then he walked with the plate of crepes over to the kitchen table.

"I think I had better tell someone," sighed Logan, taking a chair and facing the priest. He had been so successful in ignoring his internal struggles that he had only at this moment realized how terribly oppressive they had become. The dream had brought it all out into the light and he could no longer push it from his mind. So as Jean Pierre dished up the crepes, Logan launched into an account of his disturbing night.

"It was rather simple, actually," Logan began, then took a thoughtful sip of the coffee his host had just poured, followed by a bite into the delicious crepe. He nodded his approval across the table. "Simple, but a little spooky too. It was too real and too bizarre all at once. I was running—at least a man was running who was meant to be me, though he bore no resemblance to me. I watched as if I were part of the audience at the cinema. But the appearance of the man changed, depending on who was chasing him. But there was always someone at his heels—von Graff was there, Gunther, Arnie, Henri, you for a moment, and even my father! That was probably the strangest part of the dream. My father died when I was ten. Before that he was in jail most of the time. I hardly knew him. I haven't thought of him more than a half-dozen times since then, and certainly not lately. And here he pops up in my dreams. I suppose Freud would have a heyday with that!

"Anyway, these people kept chasing me. Or at least they kept chasing the apparition that was supposed to be me. I was running. It wasn't like those childhood nightmares where you are terrified because you can't go any faster than a crawl. The skies were dark. I assume it was night. And we ran through city streets, narrow and close. The buildings were grimy stone and brick, like the sooty ones back in Glasgow. I was so tired. I wanted desperately to stop, but I knew I couldn't. So I just kept going. The darkness and bleakness was oppressive. I thought I would die if it kept going like that without a change.

"Suddenly my running legs broke out into the clean air. Now it *was* me that was running, but I felt light and free. The oppression of the dark city was gone. The air was clean and refreshing, the sun warm and bright. I was running on soft, pure, white sand, with a sparkling ocean immediately to my right. It was just like the grand beach of home—"

Without even realizing he had done so, Logan had used the unlikely word to describe Port Strathy, a place he hadn't felt at home in for some time. But he went right on.

"I knew I was saved at last. But for some reason I couldn't stop running. The sand stretched out forever in front of me. Soon a woman came running onto the beach from the side and she too began to chase me. All the men from the city had left the dream with the coming of the sunlight and the beach. She began to call my name. She called and called.

"Suddenly the voice broke through into my consciousness—it was Allison, my wife. I was so glad to hear her voice! But still I didn't stop. I couldn't stop. When she at last caught up to me, she took my arm and finally I stopped. But when I spun around to face her, I disappeared.

"Again I was watching the dream from the outside, rather than playing the part in it. I could see my body fade away, and my clothes fell like limp empty rags at her feet. I started to leave the dream world and drift back into consciousness. But before I did I saw Allison's face, this time close up. Huge tears were falling from her eyes as she sank down on her knees and wept over the clothes lying in the sand.

"Then I woke up."

Logan chuckled nervously. "Pretty loony, isn't it?" he said, suddenly feeling foolish again over the whole thing.

"Dreams are the only way a sane man can express his insanity," observed Jean Pierre. "Considering the kind of life you have been living these past months, I'm surprised it was as subdued as it was. I can, however, understand your consternation over it. But I don't think I would want to venture an interpretation."

Logan said nothing. He was afraid the interpretation was all too obvious. He finished his crepes. They did indeed live up to his expectations, and he was glad to concentrate on them for a while. But at length he spoke again.

"I came to France to forget myself."

"And now you are perhaps afraid you have been too successful?" The priest's intelligent, noble eyes held Logan's for a long moment. Deep within them Logan could discern a kind understanding, an empathy that Logan would not have expected from the society priest.

Finally Logan turned away and sighed deeply.

"Maybe so," he said without much conviction. "I like what I'm doing. For the first time in my life I feel I'm involved in something truly meaningful . . . worthwhile. But I was more content and sure of myself when I was cheating people at cards or swindling them out of their money. If what I am doing is a good thing, why is it so filled with confusion?"

"Perhaps because there is a greater good to be considered, Michel," said Jean Pierre after some thought.

"I don't understand."

"You said before that I have the ideal excuse for staying out of the Resistance," Jean Pierre went on. "But the priesthood, in my opinion, should never be an excuse to be *unin-*

volved, but rather an open door into greater involvements in the hurts of people and the world. Believe me, my clerical superiors have often urged me to take a more neutral stand. They argue that God is no respecter of persons, that His love and judgment are meted out equally to the just and the unjust. I should not take sides, therefore, but let justice come from the hand of God. They are right, of course; God *is* no respecter of persons. The Bible does say, 'Resist not evil, but turn the other cheek.' Yet justification for my position can be found in the Scriptures also; James says, 'Resist the devil and he will flee from you.' I realize each of these passages can be interpreted in many ways. But perhaps that is occasionally the reason for our confusion, as you have expressed, because God leaves it to us to hear His voice in each of our hearts. I know without a doubt that God has called me to this work we are doing. Though I am criticized for forsaking my holy calling, I know that any other path *for* me would be less than God intended. I do not judge my brothers who choose to serve the Lord or their brothers on more neutral grounds. And I do not judge you either, Michel. I only say all this because you alluded to your—what shall I call it?—your attempt to live a more godly life."

Logan nodded. "I suppose that's as good a description of it as anything."

"It is something you still desire?"

"Yes," replied Logan without deep emotion. "I always wanted to be closer to Him. But I never seemed able to fit in. I once had a pair of alligator shoes; I loved those shoes and they cost me a bundle. They hurt my feet from the first day I got them, but I wore them every day for a month until I couldn't stand it any longer and finally had to throw them out. I guess living as a Christian was a little like that for me."

"Faith is tossed aside at a much greater price than a pair of shoes."

Logan stared moodily down at his plate. He had never before considered that he had abandoned his faith until just this moment. Had he discarded it like the shoes? The whole thing had come upon him so gradually that he had not really considered it gone at all. But now he could see that perhaps he had walked away from it.

"But what does that have to do with the greater good you spoke of?" he asked, almost unintentionally trying to shift the conversation away from the personal.

"It is just this," replied Jean Pierre, "as a man with a *heart* toward God—never mind where your mind and emotions might be right now—have you considered that you may have wandered onto a different path without realizing it? Yes, what you are doing is good, and for me it is my calling, *my* greater good. Perhaps for you, there is another greater good. Something you have yet overlooked, which no doubt begins with your retrieving what you tossed aside—that is, if you truly do still desire it in your life."

"But then the question is, what do I *do*? What is *my* greater good to which *I* am called?"

"I cannot answer that for you, Michel. But I am certain it is waiting for you."

"Perhaps the priesthood?" said Logan dryly.

Jean Pierre chuckled. "That would be an irony! You the priest, me the secret agent!"

"But this all comes so naturally to me, playing the games, the cons, the masquerade. How can it be wrong?"

"There are many questions I have no answers to. I cannot say it *is* wrong. You must sort through your own confusion. It must be a signal of something, though I cannot say of what. Remember one thing, however. Certain things are natural because they come from God. Others are natural because they originate in our natural man. And these must be overcome. Do you mind if I quote you another scripture?"

"By all means," answered Logan.

" 'Do not be conformed to this world,' Paul said, 'but be transformed by the renewing of your mind, so that you may prove what is that good, and acceptable, and perfect will of God.' "

Logan whistled softly as the words struck a responsive chord in his mind, if not in his heart.

"We are meant to change," went on Jean Pierre. "We are meant to grow into an understanding of what God's will for us is by this transformation process. Perhaps you tried to wear the shoes, so to speak, without allowing the transformation to renew your heart and mind. Thus, the spiritual life you wanted never quite *fit*."

"I've never thought of it like that before," said Logan. "I'm not sure I understand it completely."

"Food for thought," said Jean Pierre. "God will give understanding in its proper season."

"And in the meantime?" sighed Logan.

"It was our Lord who wisely said that each day has troubles enough of its own to worry about."

Logan nodded. He had plenty to think of for now, and would be glad to switch mental gears for a while.

"Perhaps the first thing you could do," said Jean Pierre, "is to get von Graff to have *you* replace my shadow!" He laughed at the suggestion and Logan joined him.

"I'm glad you mentioned von Graff's name! I'd almost forgotten the most important thing of all. That's why I had to see you. You've got to get a message to London for me."

"About your latest *change* in circumstances?"

"Yes. Von Graff implied they'd been contacted and my story verified. But they have no idea what tale I spun out when I was captured."

"It would seem from your release everything has satisfactorily fallen into place."

"Maybe. They might have guessed about my having been caught and said just enough to satisfy the Germans but leaving the details vague. But there is another option."

"Which is?" said the priest.

"That they haven't found out a thing about me yet, and von Graff decided to let me go, like a piece of bait on a hook, to see what would come of it."

"Hmm," said Jean Pierre, "it wouldn't be the first time he's used a ploy like that. They are fond of these little mental cat-and-mouse games, those Germans."

"In any case, I've got to make sure they know back home what happened and what I said. Whatever my present status, von Graff won't let it go indefinitely without absolute confirmation."

"What do you want me to do?"

"Does Lise have the wireless operational again?"

"Yes, I believe so."

"In her apartment?"

"No, it's been moved."

"Have her get word to Mother Hen. Tell him I was taken, that to save my hide I resurrected *Trinity*."

"Trinity? Oh yes, your cover in England. Please, go on."

"Tell Mother Hen that I was forced to become Trinity again, and to let the word out that Trinity's cover was broken by the English last Wednesday and that they assume he escaped to France by boat on his way to Germany. Be sure they cut off all further broadcasts from the Trinity angle. If whoever they had replace me as Trinity in England tries to contact the Germans again, I'm finished. Do you have all that?"

Jean Pierre repeated everything to Logan exactly as he had heard it.

Both men were silent for several moments, deep in their own thoughts. The times were indeed perilous.

"You know," Logan said at length, with a mischievous glint in his eye, "that idea you had a while ago isn't a bad one—my being your shadow."

"Don't jest with the Gestapo, mon ami!" said Jean Pierre.

"It could be done," said Logan, rubbing his hands together in anticipation. "Just think of the possibilities!"

"Think of the dangers," rejoined Jean Pierre seriously.

"I will," said Logan, returning to a solemn tone. "In that you can trust me . . . I will undertake nothing with von Graff lightly."

40 ✵ New Role

"HOW HAVE YOU found Paris, Herr MacVey?" General von Graff asked when Logan saw him later that same afternoon.

His voice contained no more guile than that of a concerned host as he sat back in his own desk chair and looked across the room at Logan.

"Perhaps you ought to ask your watchdogs that question," replied Logan, a pointed edge in his tone.

"You must forgive my little foibles."

"I thought you had confirmed my loyalty."

"But, Herr MacVey, the moment I set you free, what is the first thing you do but stretch my confidence to its limits?"

Logan wrinkled his brow, perplexed. Then slowly, as if awareness were just then dawning, he nodded in understanding.

"You mean my visit to the priest?" he said.

"What am I to think?"

"That I was bored and thought such a fascinating cleric would offer an intriguing diversion, so I decided to take him up on his invitation at his brother's party."

"A plausible explanation."

"Believe me, General, if I had anything to hide, I wouldn't have allowed my tail to have so easy a time of it."

"Why did you not confer with me first?"

"I *thought* I was a free man."

"Oh you Britishers—you have no concept of what it means to live in a police state." Von Graff sighed. "No one is free these days," he continued after a moment. His cultured tone contained the merest hint of regret, but he resumed in a different vein. "So . . . I trust you had a pleasant diversion?"

"He's as remarkable as everyone thinks," answered Logan honestly enough.

"Did your conversation touch on political issues?"

"He didn't confide in me about his Resistance activities, if that's what you mean," answered Logan. "But it wouldn't surprise me if he did in time."

"Oh . . . ?"

"I thought you would want me to make the most of the contact, so I subtley let it be known that my true sympathies were not with the Nazis."

Von Graff leaned forward, his eyes obviously demanding an explanation.

"As a new face in town," Logan explained, "I felt I might be successful where others have failed. I let slip that I thought Pétain was possibly not acting in the best interests of the French people."

"And?"

"You know yourself, General, that these things take time. But de Beauvoir did extend me another invitation."

"And you think you can hand us the priest?"

"General, you set your sights too low." Logan shook his head as if patronizing a child. "If the priest is anything, he is only a small cog. Don't let your personal vendetta against him blind you to the overall picture. De Beauvoir is but a link. Yet lubricated properly, he could be instrumental in aiding us to pull in the entire chain."

"And you would like to do the lubricating."

"I could pull it off, and you know it."

"The idea does contain some merit."

"But no more of this watchdog business," said Logan firmly.

"Why should it bother you so, Herr MacVey?"

"Like you said, I've been spoiled. I've grown accustomed to my freedom and it makes me nervous to have a hound on my tail. But more than that, de Beauvoir is no moron. He'd sense a setup in a minute. He is already well aware of his own Gestapo shadow. Moreover, I might be able to penetrate the Resistance, but they can smell Gestapo a mile off. The minute they did, my life would be history."

"So you want, as the French say, *carte blanche*?"

"That's the only way I'll agree to it," said Logan, gambling that deep inside, the general would find it within himself to respect someone who played the game hard, like the Germans themselves did. He carried his bluff out with all the poise and just the proper dose of cockiness, just as Skittles had taught him. "You don't want a few couriers or radio operators, General," he went on, getting into the stride, "you want to pull down the structure at the top. The leadership is the heartthrob of these kinds of movements—you take away the leaders, and the rest will wither away on the vine."

Von Graff nodded his assent. The fellow knew what he was talking about, that much was certain.

"I could use my British citizenship to win their trust—and from there I know I could get to the leaders."

Von Graff rubbed his clean-shaven chin thoughtfully, considering all the aspects to Logan's daring proposal. The recent escapes had lately lowered his esteem in the eyes of his mentor and superior, Himmler, and he knew he needed to bring in some results—and soon. Here was an opportunity to cement his value to his Nazi masters. He hardly knew this MacVey, and he wasn't quite sure what to make of him. The communication from Gunther had been too vague to set him completely at ease. And MacVey himself seemed a bit too independent. But von Graff's instincts told him to take a chance with him.

Logan waited just long enough to allow von Graff to mull the whole thing over in his mind, then voiced the words that would solidify him in the general's mind as no patriot, and just the sort of man the Nazis were fond of.

"But, General," he said, "I don't intend to go a step further unless certain guarantees are made which will, shall we say, make this whole venture worth my while."

"You think you are in a position to dictate to a general of the Reich what he is about?" shouted von Graff, slamming his hand down on his desk. "If we find your proposal useful, you *shall* carry it out. Do I make myself clear?"

"Perfectly, General," replied Logan, concealing a smile. He had probed closer to the general's frustration point than he realized.

"Certainly you shall be paid," von Graff went on, calming. "But let there be no mistake— *I* shall be the one issuing the orders."

The general paused, but before he could say anything further, a knock came at his door.

He glanced up, distracted and perturbed by the untimely interruption.

"Come in!" he called out.

Arnaud Soustelle stepped into the office with an apologetic yet confident look on his face. "Pardonnez-moi, Monsieur General, but your secretary is gone and I thought you would not mind if I came in unannounced."

"What is it, Soustelle?" said von Graff. "As you can see, I am with someone at the moment."

Soustelle now turned and noticed Logan for the first time. He glanced in his direction and eyed him quickly, but taking in every detail with his policeman's scrutiny.

"Oh, then again, many pardons," said the Frenchman effusively. "I will return at a more convenient time."

"This time is as convenient as any," said von Graff. "Herr MacVey is working for me."

"MacVey . . . ? An Anglais?" Soustelle's tone was heavy with speculation.

Logan stood and extended his hand in an almost extravagant effort at cordiality. "Enchanté, Monsieur Soustelle."

Soustelle took Logan's offered hand with obvious reserve, eyeing him now with deeper and more sinister perusal. The English were far from his favorite nationality at any time, but especially now. He might have been surprised to know that French collaborators were similarly at the bottom of Logan's list.

"Now, what do you want?" asked von Graff, who was either unaware or unconcerned with the unspoken tension between his two henchmen.

"This regards the assignment you have had me working on," replied Soustelle.

"The business with L'Escroc?"

Soustelle's eyebrows shot up, astonished at von Graff's candor before this Englishman. Fortunately, the general's attention was focused on Soustelle's reaction, and so Logan's own imperceptible intake of air went unnoticed. To him, at least. Soustelle, a man with certain reptilian attributes of vision, had noted Logan's reaction even as he eyed the general.

"Yes, General," replied the Frenchman, now glancing directly at Logan. His voice, as well as his look, contained something Logan could not readily identify. But the Frenchman clearly did not like to see his primary assignment treated so casually by his superior.

"Continue, Herr Soustelle," pressed von Graff abruptly.

"I have just discovered," Soustelle went on, now focusing on the general once more, "that a strong possibility exists that L'Escroc is a British agent."

"You have confirmation?"

"No confirmation. *Everything* about that man comes only from rumors and hearsay. I have a dozen people circulating about the streets of Paris in search of any more direct clue. But until today they have turned up nothing. There must be only a small handful who know his identity, and they're keeping very tight-lipped. But my source on the British angle is very reliable."

"Who might that be?"

Almost unnoticeably Logan leaned forward.

"The chauffeur of a well-known French family," Soustelle went on, "gave me the information. It appears this family has a son in the French army who was a prisoner of war in Germany until he escaped. He made it to Paris, where he was recaptured and sent to Fresnes. But while he was being transferred back to Ravensbruck, he escaped again. We believed that L'Escroc had aided in this escape, and now the chauffeur has confirmed it. He overheard his employers talking of that matter. One of them made mention of his nationality."

"You would think the fool would keep it a secret."

"Most assuredly," agreed Soustelle. "Apparently it was a fluke."

Logan remembered the incident vividly. Yes, he had blundered . . . forgotten himself in a moment of weakness—now he realized just *how* serious it had been!—when the lad he was helping mentioned a cellmate who happened to be a Glasgow acquaintance of Logan's. Luckily Logan had been wearing the disguise of an old train conductor at the time, and even if he had lapsed into English momentarily, at least he could not have been identified.

"Well, Soustelle," von Graff was saying, "this is an interesting piece of information. But does it bring you any closer to apprehending the scoundrel?"

"I think if I brought in this French family for interrogation . . . ?"

"Why do you need my permission?"

"They are not without influence."

"Haul them in!" ordered the general, "and bleed them for everything they know. See how far their influence gets them in an S.S. interrogation chamber."

The boy's family knew nothing. That much Logan knew. The whole thing had been arranged through go-betweens. He would have to try to get word out before Soustelle got to them. He shifted uncomfortably in his chair as he turned the dilemma over in his mind.

Logan's movement drew von Graff's notice.

"Do you have something on your mind, Herr MacVey?" he asked.

"L'Escroc . . ." mused Logan. "The Swindler—an interesting code name. Who is it?"

"That," replied von Graff, "is what I hoped Herr Soustelle would tell me." He cast the Frenchman a sharp look.

"I am this close!" Soustelle said, gesturing with his thumb and index finger to punctuate his words.

"That is not close enough!"

"This fellow seems to have caused quite a furor," put in Logan casually. "What has he done?"

"Our prisoners slip through our fingers like sand," answered von Graff. "And when they are gone, that name lingers in the air as if to mock us."

"Are you certain there *is* such a man?" probed Logan. "You know how underground movements love to create legends out of thin air, as a way of banding their people together."

"An interesting theory, Herr MacVey."

"Bah!" exclaimed Soustelle. "He is real. I can smell his presence in Paris. And soon I will crush him!"

"And how many more months will you need, Herr Soustelle?" said von Graff with enough emphasis to indicate his low regard for Soustelle's promises, and to point toward the Frenchman's peril in the general's eyes.

"You say he's British?" asked Logan.

"What is that to you?" snapped Soustelle.

"Nothing, of course," replied Logan. "It is none of my business. You seem to have the situation well in hand."

"What is in that conniving mind of yours, Herr MacVey?" asked von Graff.

"Really, I would not presume upon Monsieur Soustelle's territory," said Logan.

"Let me attempt to read your thoughts, Herr MacVey," said von Graff.

"There is a saying, 'It takes a thief to catch a thief.' Perhaps it could also go, 'It takes an Englishman to catch an Englishman.'"

"Perhaps," said Logan with a smile. "Notwithstanding the fact that I am a Scot and no Englishman, you have the general idea. Boche and Français and Anglais do not think alike. It might be I could assist you, Monsieur Soustelle, with whatever nationalistic insights I might possess."

"I do not require the assistance of anyone," replied Soustelle implacably.

"I will decide that," returned von Graff. "My perception is that a little assistance might be precisely what you need. But actually, Soustelle, I think you can continue as you have been doing. Interrogate the family if you wish. Herr MacVey can assist you from his sphere of influence."

"His sphere?" queried Soustelle suspiciously.

"I plan to use MacVey *inside* the Resistance itself," answered the general. "He could well make contact with L'Escroc himself."

Logan chuckled, but only he knew the true source of his amusement.

"Let's not get ahead of ourselves, General," he said. "First I have to get in. Then we can think how best to set our sights on such a prize catch."

41 ❊ Doubts

THAT SAME AFTERNOON, even as Logan sat in von Graff's office, Jean Pierre made his way purposefully down the rue de Varennes toward *La Librairie*. He had carried off one of his many methods of working himself free from his ever-vigilant attendant. Had his business with his four comrades been less serious, he would have been chuckling to himself at the thought of the befuddled Gestapo agent still loitering about the W.C. at the Eiffel Tower waiting for him to exit, not realizing that he was long gone.

But his business today *was* serious, and thus he found no amusement in what he had done. It had been a matter of necessity and he had already forgotten it.

As much as he was inclined to believe Tanant's story, his loyalty must lie with *La Librairie* first. He liked Michel, but how well did he really know him? The others had risked their lives one for the other; he knew where they stood. He owed them a full disclosure of what had taken place, so they could all have a say in any decision that must be made. Thus he had contacted Henri, and the impromptu meeting had been hastily arranged.

The others were all waiting when he walked into Henri's back room.

"Well, what is this news you have of our missing Monsieur Tanant?" asked Claude somewhat cynically. "Have you seen him?"

"Yes, is he safe?" said Lise, who, like the others, had heard nothing concerning Logan since he had left her three nights before and could not help but wonder if she was in any way responsible.

"Please," enjoined Henri, "at least allow the good priest to be seated. I'm sure he will tell us everything in good time."

"Thank you all for coming on such short notice," said Jean Pierre, seating himself and taking the offered cup of coffee from Henri. "Perhaps my worries are unfounded and all is exactly how it appears on the surface. But I owed you all an explanation of what I learned. If we should be in any danger, we must all know at once. If not, that should be a decision we make together."

"Worries . . . danger? What evils do such words portend, Jean Pierre?" asked Henri with grave concern in his voice.

"Our speculations concerning Michel were correct. He was picked up by the S.S. for breaking curfew on his way home last Friday night after leaving you, Lise."

"Did they imprison him?" asked Antoine.

"Yes," replied Jean Pierre, "but only for a short time."

"He is free, then?" asked Lise.

"Apparently so. But that is where the whole thing grows fuzzy. I chanced to see him at my brother's birthday celebration."

"What was he doing there?" asked Claude, his suspicious tone saying more than his words.

"That is the part which worries me," admitted Jean Pierre. "It was an extremely gala event, collaborators and Germans almost exclusively. And there who should I see, well-dressed and jovial, and in the company of a German general no less, was our own Michel Tanant."

"Mon Dieu!" exclaimed Henri. "That does not sound like him."

"I have told you all along," said Claude angrily, "that we knew nothing about this so-called *Monsieur* Tanant"—and as he said it, he spat out the word venomously— "but none of you would listen! Now he is in league with the Boche, and *La Librairie* is in danger!"

"We do not know that, Claude," put in Antoine, willing to hear arguments in Logan's favor as well as the accusations against him before passing judgment. "For myself, I want to hear the rest of Jean Pierre's story."

"I was naturally on my guard," went on the priest. "Like you, Claude, I did not like the look of it. We barely had a chance to speak last evening at the party. But the moment we were alone he began insisting that I get a message to London for him. He said he was in danger, and that the whole thing with the Germans was a facade."

"A facade, no doubt, invented on the spot the moment he saw you!" said Claude.

"Perhaps, mon ami. Perhaps. But if he *is* telling the truth, then if we do not back him up and get his message to London, it may not only mean Michel's death, it may bring yet more danger to the rest of us."

"What did you do?" asked Henri.

"In the presence of the general, I threw out an invitation for today, to see what might come of it."

"And?"

"Michel was at my door before ten."

"Alone?"

"We each had a Gestapo agent watching from a distance."

"Well, that is a good sign, that they are having him followed," said Henri. "At least if there is collusion with the Boche going on, it must not have progressed too far. They apparently do not yet trust him fully."

"Unless the tail was all part of the scheme," said Claude. "And let me guess, Jean Pierre! He told you he was 'playing along' with them, *pretending* to be sympathetic to their cause. He probably told you he was going to pretend to turn so he could infiltrate the Resistance for them and feed back information. Am I on the mark, mon père?"

Jean Pierre was silent a moment. The others all awaited his response, but his lack of a quick reply told them Claude's perception had been correct.

"What else would you have expected him to say under the circumstances?" went on Claude. "All this time he has been setting up this moment, gaining our confidence, even helping a few people to escape. But now! Now comes the moment for which he was sent into our midst—sent by the Germans! He fakes an arrest, tells us that he was captured and was 'forced' to fake a turn and that he now has to play along with them. All the while this has been his plan from the first day when he walked through this door of yours, Henri. And now that it has reached this stage, he can come and go with the Germans as he pleases, and in the meantime he has equal access through the Paris underground. A most convenient arrangement, I must say, and very cunning for the Boche to have devised!"

Claude's point seemed well taken. The others pondered his words for several moments.

"I want to know what he wanted you to tell London," said Henri at length.

"I'm afraid that only adds to the perplexity," replied Jean Pierre. "It is indeed a rather incredible tale." The priest then proceeded to tell his comrades everything Logan had said about his Trinity cover and what he had been forced to tell von Graff.

"It is too incredible *not* to believe," said Antoine.

"Bah!" shot back Claude. "You are a gullible fool! He will have us all before the Boche firing squad if we allow him back among us!"

"Claude!" said Lise, speaking now for the first time since hearing Jean Pierre's story. "Whatever your views, you have no right to say such a thing to your comrade! Your bitter protestations make me inclined to believe Michel as well—if only to spite you for your unfounded accusations!"

"You may seal your fate if you like," said Claude. "But I will trust him no more than I ever have. I will watch my flank even in my sleep. If *La Librairie* goes down, I will not go with it! Our safest course is to eliminate him, and you all know it! What can have so captivated you about this Britisher to blind your eyes, I do not know!"

"No one will be eliminated without proof," said Jean Pierre. "We will all be wary. But we cannot pass judgment too hastily."

"Jean Pierre is right," said Henri. "We have all missed one of the key ingredients to this unexpected turn of events. That is, if Michel is indeed telling the whole truth, think what benefits could be gained *for us* in having L'Escroc able to come and go inside S.S. headquarters unhindered! This may be the best thing ever to happen for the Resistance in Paris."

"Well, I'm going to transmit his message to Mother Hen just as he gave it to Jean Pierre," said Lise. "He has done much for the cause, and perhaps we owe it to him to do that much. Was that all he asked of us, Jean Pierre?"

"There was just one other thing," replied the priest. "He wanted you to meet him as soon as it could be arranged."

42 ❊ Seeds of Vengeance

WHEN LOGAN LEFT von Graff's office that Monday afternoon, December 8, 1941, he was feeling more than usually pleased with himself. War had been raging in at least two corners of the world, and now all at once—with the outbreak of hostilities between Japan and the United States—it looked as if all four would now be involved. His own tiny home-land across the Channel to the west was taking a terrible beating. Yet Logan could not help feeling that he, at least, had just won a small victory. The misfortune of being caught the previous Friday night was turned suddenly around and now looked like it might prove for-tuitous indeed for the fortunes of L'Escroc.

Somehow he had just managed to pull off the biggest swindle of his life since Chase Morgan. Immediately as the thought formed in his mind, he recalled his prayer while at S.S. headquarters. Could what happened have been God's way of answering that prayer for deliverance? Logan had no doubts about God's capacity to answer prayer. But over the course of the past year or two, he had never really imagined God's blessing to be on his life or what he was involved in. After all, he had not even seen Allison in . . . he didn't even know how long. He had made some halfhearted attempts to get Arnie to contact her to let her know he was okay. And since coming to France, things had been moving so fast. How could God possibly have anything to do with him anymore. The prayers he had offered arose more from desperation than from faith. And if he were following the wrong path, as Jean Pierre had suggested, then why would God help him now?

The whole thing was puzzling, and called into his mind many random images out of his past—conversations with Lady Margaret and Dorey and his in-laws, and even with Allison during their first blissful days together as young believers in a God who could be an inti-mate friend. It had all faded since then. God seemed once again remote. Yet he had prayed . . . and now this turn of events with von Graff.

Did God still care about him? He continued to search his mind for something that might answer the question, but he could not get that realm of his thoughts to come altogether into focus. He would have to talk to Jean Pierre again.

He turned down rue Leroux deep in thought. He should have taken a tram, but the clean, crisp winter air felt good. The sun had come out earlier, warming the icy atmosphere, and in spots melting the snow. He could take his time. He still had over two hours until his next rendezvous. That would give him plenty of time to circle around, double back, and make sure no eyes were upon him that shouldn't be.

He hoped Jean Pierre had been able to set it up with Lise as they had arranged before he left the rectory that morning. He wanted to see her, knowing it would be a far less trouble-some contact to explain—if they happened to be spotted—than a meeting with Henri.

Even then, if Lise agreed to see him, the meeting in the Left Bank Cafe was to appear as nothing more than a chance encounter by two strangers. Logan had purposefully chosen a cafe in a part of Paris where he had never been before. From now on he would have to avoid those places he had frequented before. One chance word which revealed that he had been in Paris months before running into von Graff would land him into hot water with the S.S. It would be tricky; he had met a lot of people. But Paris was a huge city, and it would not be impossible. It helped that Lise had relocated since the raid near her apartment.

Logan paused at a newsstand to buy a paper. He would need it for his meeting with Lise. While glancing around, waiting for his change, he sensed he was being watched. He paused before continuing on, peering casually at the headlines, while out of the corner of his eye trying to focus on the faces off in the distance to see if his instinct had been correct.

He could see no one he recognized. Yet as he walked on, the feeling became stronger and stronger. Whoever it was behind him was good. And he was certain there was *someone* back there!

Could this be von Graff's doing again? He thought the near promise he'd managed to extract was as close to a guarantee as he was likely to get that there would be no surveil-lance. The possibility that the general had gone back on his word was not altogether remote. But that same instinct which told him someone was following him also told him his tail had nothing to do with von Graff.

Logan walked on another block, turning over in his mind several options for losing the unwelcome shadow. Whatever precautions he and Lise took, he still couldn't be followed to the cafe. Somehow he had to find out who was back there, and why. He at least had to know if it was friend or foe.

Lost in thought, Logan was suddenly nearly smashed into by a young girl who had lost control of her bicycle. She was already on her way down when she brushed by him. He reached out a hand, but he was too late to prevent a nasty spill. The incident came about so unexpectedly that it caught Logan's tail by surprise, and he drew a bit too close. As Logan stooped down to help the girl up, he managed to catch a brief glimpse of a furtive figure scuttling back into the shadows between two buildings. Everything happened too quickly for him to see the face or make out any details. But the size and bearing of the man bore an uncanny resemblance to someone Logan hardly knew but knew he didn't like.

Logan helped the girl to her feet, saw her safely off once again on her bicycle, then continued on himself, crossing the busy street just in front of a passing tram. Hidden momentarily by the large vehicle, Logan broke into a run and ducked into an alley way on the other side. Peering around the corner, he saw the bewildered Frenchman looking up and down the street for his quarry once the tram had passed. Then he turned in Logan's direction. Logan pulled back inside, picked his best spot, and waited.

The moment the ex-detective entered the opening of the alley Logan leaped out, grabbed him by his jacket, and yanked him into the dark recesses of the passage. It was risky business in broad daylight, but no one in Paris these days had much taste for getting involved in petty street crimes that might bring them face-to-face with their Nazi occupiers.

"Okay, Soustelle! What are you doing following me?" said Logan, as with one swift motion he slammed the Frenchman up against the wall, his nose pressed into the rough brick.

Soustelle merely growled in reply, struggling to free himself. He was larger than Logan, and probably would have made quick work of an all-out fistfight or street brawl and left Logan unconscious in a matter of seconds. But Logan was younger and lighter, and had learned a number of swift-moving tricks as part of his training.

"I will kill you for this, Anglais!" snarled Soustelle.

Logan wrenched one of the man's arms back, then swung his own arm around Soustelle's neck in a grip that would have made it impossible for the burly Frenchman to move without the risk of getting his neck broken. Thus the battle, what there was of one, was brief, leaving the former gendarme helpless and at the mercy of one he considered a puny runt half his own size.

He made a few further vain attempts to struggle free.

"C'est assez! commanded Logan. "That's enough! I don't want to break your neck, but I think you know I can from this position."

"Allez au diable!" spat Soustelle, panting.

"Not before I find out what your game is, Monsieur Soustelle," rejoined Logan. "Why are you following me?"

"You are an Anglais. That is reason enough!"

Logan jerked Soustelle's neck painfully. "Think again, Soustelle! What are you up to? And consider the consequences before you answer. I know von Graff didn't put you up to this."

Soustelle moaned, beads of sweat dripping down his brow. "What do you know?" he said, "and what does von Graff know!"

"You think I'm going to usurp your territory, is that it?" said Logan.

Soustelle remained doggedly silent.

"Well, perhaps I may do just that," Logan went on. "Or, we can work together. That is your choice. But if I catch you or anyone else on my tail again, you will be very sorry, Monsieur. Not only will you have to answer to me, you will also have to explain to von Graff and the S.S. just why you chose to countermand their orders. And you well know that once you have fallen into disfavor with the Germans, you will wish that I had broken your neck here and now. So what is it going to be, Soustelle?"

"I would sell my soul to the devil before I would work with an Anglais!" spat Soustelle.

"That will be a fine arrangement with me," said Logan. "I half thought you had already made such an agreement with him. In the meantime, I will do what I have to do. And I won't see you behind me again, will I?"

Logan punctuated his final words with a stiff jab upward of Soustelle's arm. The Frenchman winced in pain, but remained proudly silent, even in temporary defeat. Logan yanked once more.

"All right! All right! Have it your way!" he growled, his voice seethed with hatred.

Logan immediately slackened his hold.

"I'm going to let you go," said Logan. "I want you to turn to your right and walk down the street, and keep walking. This incident can be our little secret, but if I so much as see you look back, I will go directly to the general. Is that clear?"

Defiantly Soustelle nodded.

"You will pay for your arrogance, Monsieur MacVey!" he said. "You will live, and perhaps die, regretting this day!"

Even as he spoke, however, he began walking away from Logan and did not turn back, shuffling off down the sidewalk in mingled shame and fury. Logan watched him until he was out of sight.

His last glimpse was of the Frenchman digging his hand into his pocket, then tossing something into his mouth.

Soustelle continued down the street. His pride would not let himself show so visible a reaction to his defeat; but inside, his entire being pulsed with an indignation that quickly became a seething cauldron of hate.

He stuffed another licorice into his mouth and ground it mercilessly between his teeth, stained indelibly from the juices of his habit.

The arrogant Anglais would soon pay for his impudence!

It was not long, however, before the Frenchman began to examine his hatred with an eye toward its practical implications. This MacVey possessed the confidence of General von Graff, that much was apparent. Thus the threats in the alley were not idle. Von Graff may not have *said* it in so many words, but the implication was still there—MacVey was the darling of the S.S., and he must be placated at all costs.

"Le quel salaud!" spat Soustelle. "The dirty dog!"

But that's how it was. The French were nothing to the Germans—serfs and slaves, hated for their victory in the first war, despised for their defeat in the second!

But the British—they were different. Even Hitler admired them. And how much better an Anglais turned Nazi! Oh yes, they would do anything to keep him content, thinking nothing of stepping on a lowly French policeman in the process!

Yes, Soustelle told himself, I had better leave the Anglais alone—for the time being, at least. He would get around to Monsieur MacVey when the time was right. His chief objective for the present must be catching that other dog, L'Escroc. In doing that he would inflict more damage to MacVey's esteem in the eyes of the S.S. than anything else, not to mention raising his own. After that could come the real vengeance—the kind a man like Soustelle hungered after.

His footsteps soon quickened. He had another task ahead of him that afternoon which would help satiate that gnawing appetite after evil. He hailed a velo-taxi to take him across town. There lived the employers of a certain chauffeur; judicious dealing with them would bring him one step closer to his diabolical goal.

43 ❈ Friendship Renewed

LOGAN ORDERED A café au lait from the garcon in the little cafe where he and Lise were to meet. Despite his run-in with Soustelle, he had arrived five minutes early and Lise was not yet there.

He sipped his warm drink, spent a few moments reading his newspaper, but before long set it aside to concentrate on his drink in what seemed a bored, detached manner. All the while, however, he remained acutely aware of each person who came and went from the small sidewalk cafe.

In about five minutes Lise entered. She took a table ten feet away from Logan, though she paid him little heed. When the garcon came, she gave him her order, while glancing causally about. Her roving eyes were arrested by the newspaper lying on Logan's table. She stood and walked over to him.

"Pardon, Monsieur," she said, "but I have not read a newspaper in two days. Would it be an imposition if I borrowed yours while I waited for my order?"

"Not in the least," replied Logan, handing her the paper. "But perhaps you would prefer more human companionship?" He smiled up at her as any Frenchman might at a pretty girl. "You are welcome to join me."

"I would not want to impose," she answered. However, the coquettish tone of her voice would tell anyone who by chance was listening that she had indeed hoped from the start for such an invitation from this handsome stranger.

"To tell the truth," said Logan, "the prospect of having coffee alone is rather a dreary one."

"In that case . . ." she said, pulling out the chair opposite Logan.

For the following fifteen minutes the conversation progressed as it might had they indeed only just met. For both it was a frustrating span of time, for each was eager to get on with what really mattered. But they played out the charade until they had completed their hot drinks and Logan could make the request anyone observing them might expect.

"Well, I must be on my way," he said, rising.

"It was very nice to meet you," Lise replied. "I'm sorry you must go so soon."

Logan paused, seeming to consider his words, then added, "Would you care to join me? I have no particular commitments at the moment."

Lise nodded with a smile, and they left the cafe together. Even von Graff would only suspect that Logan had simply sought out some female companionship to brighten his stay in Paris. The ensuing relationship between the two should then appear quite natural.

As they began walking down the sidewalk, Logan could tell that beneath Lise's well-controlled cover, she was tense and even more reserved than usual. He waited until they had walked a good distance from the cafe and he was certain they weren't being followed, then said, "Lise, what's wrong?"

"There is much to discuss and so little time," she replied evasively.

"You too are worried about my Nazi ties?"

"We all are, Michel. How can you expect us—"

"*All?*" interrupted Logan.

"Jean Pierre told us everything."

"But I only just saw him this morning."

"He set up a meeting immediately afterward. We were all there. We discussed the situation, and what we should do about . . . you."

"And what did you decide?" asked Logan caustically.

"Come on, Michel, what did you expect us to do?" said Lise. "We had all confided in you; we thought we knew you. Now this. Jean Pierre owed it to all of us to let us share in the decision. You must know how it looks to the rest of us."

"You didn't answer my question."

"We didn't really decide anything, if that's what you mean."

"And so," asked Logan coldly, "are you not going to send the message I gave to Jean Pierre? Are you going to keep England in the dark about me and let me dangle and see what happens? Is that how you treat your comrades?"

"We risk our lives for our comrades," returned Lise sharply. "You know that! The question is whether you *are* a comrade. The underground is a dangerous business. You get killed for small mistakes. We have to take every precaution. You would do no different in our shoes."

Logan was silent. She was right, and he knew it. Still, it hurt.

"And you?" he said at length. "Do you trust me? Or do you think I'm Boche too?"

Now it was Lise's turn to walk along in silence. Logan held his breath, afraid to say anything further. He did not want to press, though something inside him had to know. How he hated this feeling of alienation that the war brought to everything—separation from friends, from family, even from oneself. This kind of work was lonely enough, and he had come to appreciate the feeling of camaraderie that had been developing between them. Now suddenly it was gone. Would he face the same cold reception from Henri? Jean Pierre had seemed so open, yet apparently he still doubted Logan, too. She was right—there *was* a great deal to discuss, and time was too short.

His thoughts were finally broken by her answer to his question.

"I don't know," she said. "I have to be truthful. I'm a little shaken by what Jean Pierre told us."

"But as I told him, it was all a dodge."

"A plausible enough explanation."

"A *true* explanation!" insisted Logan.

"I pray everything *is* just as you say," said Lise. "Time will clarify it all, as it has a way of doing."

"And in the meantime, I'm on my own?"

"No. I said I didn't know what to believe. That does not mean I will automatically disbelieve you. I *want* to believe you, and will do what I can for you until you give me reason to do otherwise."

"That's magnanimous of you, I must say," said Logan sarcastically.

Lise sighed. "I'm sorry. I know you want something more out of me—"

"A little trust would be nice!"

"Trust is an expensive commodity during wartime. Unfortunately—perhaps, as you say, through no fault of your own—your credibility has been damaged for a time. You will have to earn back our trust. But please, Michel, do not be offended. Try to see that you would feel just the same toward me."

"You will send my message?" asked Logan, hardly satisfied, but resigned to the way things stood.

"Yes. But you had already asked Jean Pierre to do that. Why did you want to see *me*?"

"I suppose because out of all the others, I thought you—and Henri—would be the ones most likely to believe me. I guess I had to know what you thought. And I knew it would be far less likely to raise suspicions by being seen with you—a man and a woman in Paris, you know—than with Henri. I didn't want to endanger him . . . or the group."

"Is that all?" asked Lise.

"At the time—this morning when I was with Jean Pierre—yes. But since then something's come up. I was with the general again this afternoon and I learned of some people who are in terrible danger. You've got to get word to them . . . and soon."

"Who are they?"

"Have you heard of the Gregoire family?"

"Yes, of course."

"You must get a warning to them that the Gestapo is likely to visit them soon."

"How do you know this?" asked Lise, still cautious.

"That's not important for now. If you find you can trust me, then I'll fill you in on everything too. Just answer me this: do you know a Frenchman, a collaborator, by the name of Soustelle?"

"I have heard the name. An evil man. But I have not met him."

"He is in league with von Graff. If he gets to this family before your people do, I fear for the result."

Logan and Lise had been walking toward a little park. It was too cold and icy to sit and relax, though patches of grass peeked through the snow in places, and children were tossing crusts of bread to the pigeons. Logan marveled that they had bread to spare. Maybe, he thought, they are trying to fatten up the birds for this evening's stew pot.

All at once a young man stepped into their path, hailing Lise with a friendly greeting.

"Bonjour, Paul," Lise replied. Then turning to Logan she made introductions, presenting Logan as Michel Tanant.

Logan immediately recognized the young man as Mme. Guillaume's nephew who had assisted them in transporting the two British airmen when Logan had first arrived in Paris.

"I thought it would look better," explained Lise, "if it appeared you two were just meeting for the first time."

"Yes, I suppose you're right," agreed Logan. "These last four months can't exist for me any longer. It must from now on be as if I only arrived in Paris this week. But is there some reason you set up this meeting today?"

"Henri thought that since your contact with *La Librairie* must be more limited now," said Lise, "a courier would be useful for you. Paul is willing to help, and has far fewer ties to the underground. He will raise no suspicions."

"It is nice to see you have such a high regard for my safety," said Logan, "dubious member of your clandestine entourage though I am." A trace of his former humor came through in the words.

"We have our own interests to protect," replied Lise. "And that includes our investment in you. If you are not on the up-and-up, you will be dead before you know what we know. Claude will see to that. And if you are still with us, then we owe you a great deal and we must do our best for you."

"I do wish I could talk to Henri," said Logan.

"You realize that is impossible for now. He has too much at stake. Too many lives depend on him. Now, tell me about this Soustelle."

Logan briefly recounted what he had heard in von Graff's office regarding the parents of the French soldier he had helped escape. Ever since leaving the general's office earlier, he had been pondering how he might get to them before Soustelle. Now the perfect opportunity seemed to present itself.

"Do you know where the Gregoires live?" he said to Paul.

The young man nodded

"Can you go there and warn them? Their lives may depend on your speed."

"It would be quickest to telephone them," he said.

"Never trust the telephone, Paul. The government controls the system, and I'm certain that in the case of the Gregoires, their phone is under Gestapo scrutiny by now. But you'd best dig up some kind of disguise; a delivery boy ought to do."

"Oui, Monsieur!" he said eagerly. "Just like L'Escroc, eh?"

Logan tensed. Was it possible Paul knew of L'Escroc's identity? He glanced toward Lise and noted a hint of consternation in her face as well. No, he couldn't know. It must have been but another example of how L'Escroc's reputation had seized the fancy of many patriots throughout Paris. Quickly Logan dismissed it and returned to the problem at hand.

"Be careful not to compromise yourself," he cautioned. "The situation is very dangerous. Can you handle it?"

"Oui, Monsieur!"

"All right then . . . be off!" said Logan. "You can find out how to reach me through Lise. When we meet again we will set up some kind of regular contact point. Good luck, Paul!"

The boy turned and sped off on his bicycle.

When he was out of sight, Logan glanced at Lise, as if seeking some reassurance that this obviously untried youth could perform the task given him.

"Yes, he is young," she replied, correctly reading his look. "But we have little more than the young to rely on, with so many of our men in German prisons or dead. But Paul is not as naive as he may appear. He has helped us before. I am sure we can count on him."

"I hope you're right," said Logan. "It seems he is my only lifeline at present."

But neither Logan nor Lise could know that as he sped away from them, all the experience or savvy in the world could not get Paul to the Gregoire family ahead of the villainous Frenchman.

44 ❈ *The Old Gentleman*

EVEN WHILE LOGAN and Lise were talking in the cafe, Soustelle had made all the necessary arrangements.

He and his soldiers were storming the Gregoire townhouse while Paul was still pedaling frantically across town. And by the time Paul knocked in vain on the ornate door, Soustelle was preparing to confront Monsieur Gregoire in an interrogation chamber of a small building adjacent to the S.S. headquarters where the S.D. often performed their dirty work.

Except for the actual arrest, Soustelle had decided to handle the entire matter himself. He would notify von Graff upon its successful conclusion. Thus he had ordered the S.D. agents to drag the prisoner into the chamber, then dismissed them. He was now alone with the wealthy Frenchman, who had made a fortune manufacturing perfume.

Gregoire was about seventy, with white hair and a clean-shaven face of nearly transparent skin, though it was deeply creased with wrinkles. Because of a touch of arthritis in his vertebrae, his neck jutted forward slightly, and a mild case of Parkinson's caused his head to tremble constantly on its seemingly precarious perch. The effect would have been pitiful had it not been for his proud, lively eyes and firm, determined chin. He was a man who had known little trouble in his life, having inherited an already successful business from his father. He had enjoyed a genteel existence with his wife and family, reputed to be a gentleman however tenacious he might be in the marketplace. But with the occupation of the city and the imprisonment of his only son, Gregoire had quickly learned the harsh realities of life. They were soon to become much harsher.

Soustelle strutted back and forth in front of the aged Frenchman as he sat with all the decorum he could muster under the circumstances.

"We know you are connected with the underground," said Soustelle, pausing to focus his cold gaze at his prisoner.

"That is not true!" exclaimed the proud Gregoire.

Soustelle's fleshy hand suddenly shot out, striking the older man's pale face with a savage blow. Gregoire was knocked momentarily off his seat, but caught his balance before falling to the floor, and doggedly resumed his place.

"Tell me about your son," demanded Soustelle.

"I only did what any father would do. You are a Frenchman; you should understand." Soustelle spat on Gregoire's expensive Italian shoes.

"I understand my duty! Now tell me—who helped him escape?"

"I do not know—it was all arranged through the post."

Soustelle delivered another punishing blow, which stung the old man's ear, drawing blood. "Lies!" snapped the Nazi henchman. "Give me names!"

"I know none to give."

"What about L'Escroc?"

Gregoire said nothing.

"You *will* talk!" said Soustelle with icy menace.

He strolled in a casual, off-hand manner to a table where his hand laid hold of a policeman's nightstick. Tapping it meaningfully in his hand, he strutted before the old man several times, a gleam of profound relish in his eyes, and, oddly enough, no licorice churning in his mouth.

"You *will* give me names," he said.

Still Gregoire remained silent.

Incensed by the man's effrontery not to be intimidated, Soustelle set to work with his club. The gentle, aged face—bloodied and purple from the Frenchman's blows—was unrecognizable within the span of but a few moments. When the old man fell to the floor, Soustelle aimed several more blows at his kidneys. But by now, even if Gregoire had known anything, he was more determined than ever not to utter a word to this evil man some would dare call his countryman.

"So be it!" spat Soustelle. "There are other methods to loosen stubborn tongues!"

Gregoire rolled over and looked up with terror at his captor.

"Yes, Gregoire," laughed Soustelle. "Your wife is in the next room. Perhaps the sound of her cries will make you talk, eh?"

"Please, no!" begged Gregoire with a pathetic whimper, all his determination to resist suddenly swallowed by panic. "Not my wife . . . she is not well."

"Then give me names! Tell me who is this L'Escroc!"

"I tell you I know nothing. Do you not think I would talk—especially now—if only I could?"

"Have it your way then."

Soustelle stalked from the room, that sinister gleam still in his eyes.

Gregoire crawled from the cold hard floor toward the door through which Soustelle had just exited.

He struggled to rise but could only get to his knees. In vain he tried the handle, but the door was locked.

Suddenly from the other side he heard a wretched scream that he knew at once to be his wife's.

"No! Dear God . . .!" he wailed, pounding a feeble fist on the door. "No . . .!"

Still the screaming went on, all but drowning out the dull thuds from Soustelle's blows.

The last sound he heard, before falling back onto the floor in blessed unconsciousness, was a horrifying laugh from Soustelle, mingled with an hysterical shriek from his dear wife.

Logan buried his face in his hands. He could not believe Lise's words.

"They are dead, Michel . . ."

Despite the shakiness of his relationships with Lise and *La Librairie,* which now had to be re-forged, Logan had begun to think things would smooth out. He had already managed to forget the reality of disaster. And how much worse that disaster should strike others because of his momentary blunder. L'Escroc, indeed!

". . . dead, Michel. Do you hear me?"

Paul had not succeeded in his mission. Logan's warning, Paul's attempt to warn them—everything had come too late. And Logan knew he was to blame.

He remembered when the Gregoires' son, now safely out of France and fighting at de Gaulle's side for Free France, had described his parents. "They are like children in wrinkled skins . . . incredibly innocent," he had said. "They are not stupid or naive! Oh no!" He had chuckled softly at the notion of his father being naive. "But they have somehow managed not to be corrupted by this cruel world of ours."

Now the picture of those dear old souls at the mercy of Soustelle and the Gestapo rose up, a stinging self-recrimination before Logan's mind. Had they been sacrificed so that his own skin might be saved? Even if such had not been his conscious intent, his over-confidence had made him careless, numbed him to realities.

"Michel," Lise's voice broke into his thoughts, "you must not blame yourself."

"Why should I not?" he asked bitterly.

"Because this is war. When you're involved in war, blame and guilt only lead to insanity. You do what you must do. You survive. If you manage to help some people one day, you cannot carry the burdens of an evil world on your shoulders the next."

Logan lifted his head so that his eyes met hers. "Then whose fault is it, Lise?" he asked. "When do people have to stop and take responsibility for their actions, even in a war?"

"You tried to save them the moment you could."

"That sounds like rather a *trusting* comment to make. What if it was all a ploy on my part to make my charade that much more believable, while all the time I was in league with Soustelle?"

Lise smiled. "I suppose that is a possibility. And a chance I must take. But I hope I read your reaction to this news with more insight into human nature than that."

"Nevertheless, I should have done more."

"If you had done *more*—sacrifice yourself, perhaps—you might only have brought many more others into danger."

"So the lives of two old persons is a small price to pay for the safety of *La Librairie,* is that it?"

His voice was harsh, meant to bite, though not directed at Lise personally.

"I did not mean that," she replied, hurt. "Surely you know me better than that by now, whatever side you are on."

His tone softened as he reached out and took her hand.

"I'm sorry," he said. He wanted to weep, but shedding tears was one ruse he had never practiced much.

"You must forget all this," she said, trying to assume a businesslike attitude as she slipped her hand from his.

"For a moment, Lise, I thought we could go back to the way it was."

"What do you mean?"

"We were friends before," he replied. "There was trust. We could talk. In a world of lies and cover-ups and darkness, I thought we were able to understand each other . . . trust each other."

He paused, rubbing his hands across his face.

"I need that, Lise," he said. "I don't know if I can dangle out there alone anymore. Though I suppose in this kind of work, trust, attachments, caring—they are the kiss of death. Sometimes I don't know where Michel Tanant leaves off and Logan Macintyre begins."

"Don't say that name to me!"

"Can't you just for a minute forget *what* we are?"

"It's dangerous to forget."

"No, I think it's just *easier* not to forget." Logan sighed. "Lise, I have caused two innocent people to die. How can I ever forget that? That is not something the fictitious Michel Tanant did, which can be wiped out of memory like an imaginary name. *I* did it, do you understand? Me—Logan Macintyre! And *I* will never forget. When this war is long over, I will still have to deal with that fact. I will have to look into my child's eyes and remember all that happened here in France."

"Is that why you never carry a weapon and so carefully avoid violence?"

"Ha! I fear even those standards will soon be gone. Like I said, where do Michel and Logan start to be different?"

"What do you mean?"

"Today Soustelle was following me. I grabbed him and threw him up against a brick wall. I attacked him! I probably would never have been able to break his neck as I threatened. Good acting has always gotten me by—and it'll probably be my demise, too. But what if before this is over I find myself in that same situation with a rifle in my hand? What if I *have* to kill?"

"I wish I could help you in some way, *Logan.*" She spoke his real name for the first time, softly, poignantly, perhaps not even aware that that alone could be enough to help sustain him for a while.

"Thank you," was his only reply.

In her heart Lise knew that he understood. It was a great sacrifice for her to break her code by imprinting a comrade's true name into her mind with her voice.

"I wish I could help you smile again, too," she added. "But it has always been your job to bring smiles and laughter. I'm afraid I fail miserably in that area."

"Someday," said Logan, "the war will be over and we will all be able to smile and be happy again."

"Perhaps there will be happiness for others," said Lise. "But for those who survive this dark life of Nazi occupation which France has plunged itself into by its own stupidity . . . I don't know. I think we will be too changed to be happy anymore."

Logan was silent. He wished he could refute her morbid statement. But he knew he couldn't. He had said just the same thing when he had spoken of his daughter. It was a fact that lately seemed constantly haunting him. Jean Pierre had spoken of changing in a positive way. But Logan was not sure it could be so. His own depressed state over the Gregoire deaths had blinded him to the spiritual realities operating within him, and to the beauties of change. For the moment he only knew that if ever he was so lucky as to see his wife and daughter again, he would he a far different person from the one they had known before.

From his present vantage point, he could not see how such an altered Logan Macintyre would be someone they would even know . . . or love. But in one thing he was correct—he would never be the same Logan Macintyre again.

45 ✠ *Nathaniel*

ALLISON FELT HAPPIER than she had for months.

Nathaniel was home on leave after more than a year away. Actually he wasn't really *home,* for time did not allow for him to get all the way north to Stonewycke. But since Allison was in London, that was almost as good. He had been able to arrange a flight for Joanna to join them there, so it was going to be as near a reunion as the war-torn family had had in quite a long time.

Allison and Nathaniel had driven out to the airport in an army car to meet Joanna's plane, only to receive the news that it was an hour behind schedule. Allison didn't mind the delay, for it gave them time together as brother and sister they had seldom had, even prior to the war.

"It's funny," Allison said as they found seats on the wooden benches in the busy airport. "For so long you were always my baby brother. But now it seems we have caught up to each other."

"Ye mean I've finally caught up to *you*!" said the red-headed Nathaniel, his freckled face breaking into an unabandoned grin that was so much like his father's.

"I don't know," said Allison thoughtfully. "I may have been older, but in so many ways you were always far and away ahead of me. You always knew who you were and what was most important in life. I seem to still be struggling with the things you mastered years ago."

"But I can already tell, Ali," Nat replied, "that ye've got yer feet back on the solid foundation, as Grandma nae doobt would say."

Allison had to smile. Nat and Alec were the only members of the family to cling to the heavy Scots burr, and it was delightful to hear once again after Allison's long exposure to the southern accents.

"I hope you're right, Nat," she replied. "And I think I am close to God again, closer than ever before. Being alone, and having things go against me for a while, really forced me to examine parts of my life that I'd never looked at before. I suppose Logan and I approached our marriage like we did being Christians—a one-time decision that we thought would carry us through. I guess I'm finding out—in both areas—that there's a deeper commitment needed, something strong and enduring enough to last for years . . . forever. Being alone, and on my own, has opened my eyes to some of these things, especially to how shallow I always was. It's hardly any wonder Logan finally got tired of me."

"Ah, come on, Ali, give yersel' a break! Ye canna hae been all that muckle bad!"

"Maybe you didn't know me very well, Nat. No one did. Because I didn't even know myself."

"Weel, I'm right glad for ye noo, anyway."

"Do you remember Sarah Bramford?"

"Ay . . . a friend o' yers frae home?"

"Yes. She and I've been attending church together. It has been so good for me to have someone to talk to. She's grown a lot over the years, too. Yet there are still times of struggle when I really doubt my ability to make the kind of commitment to God I want to. And there are times when I wonder if it's not come too late. If only I had seen some of these things years ago, my marriage might have been spared."

"But ye canna give up hope, ye ken."

"All the hope in the world will be of little use if I never see Logan again."

"The Bible says that hope doesna disappoint."

Allison sighed. "You're right. But it's so discouraging to realize that in so many ways I drove Logan away without realizing what I was doing, all the time blaming him. Oh, Nat, I knew so little about what marriage was *really* meant to be, that love is serving, not receiving."

"Ye'll hae yer chance to make it right again."

"Oh, I hope so!"

"How long has it been?"

"Several months." But even as Allison spoke the words, she suddenly realized it had been a whole year, for it was now spring again, and she had last seen Logan in spring a year ago. It was 1942. In a few months they would have been married nine years. Yet she did not even know where her husband was. Each month she received the anonymous check in the mail; she assumed it meant he was all right, assuming of course that the money was indeed from him. Without realizing it she found her thoughts drifting toward their old channels: had Logan grown so cold and callous as to let their marriage disintegrate into nothing but the sending and receiving of a nameless check month after month? She could not believe he had changed that drastically.

Nat reached out and took Allison's hand in his. How large and warm they are, she thought. So much like Daddy's—comforting and reassuring. She smiled bravely at her brother. After all, this was his leave and she did not want to spoil it with her morose meditations.

"I'm surprised ye haena gone back to Stonewycke," said Nathaniel. "At least bein' oot frae under the shadow o' war would make life more tolerable."

"Then I wouldn't have been here for you!" Allison tried to laugh, but it wasn't much use. "But to tell you the truth, Nat, the shadows that are over my life would follow me wherever I went. And I suppose a part of me is afraid that if I did go, Logan might come back and think I didn't care enough to wait for him."

"But surely he'd ken ye was at home."

"Maybe. But I doubt he'd come there for me," she sighed. "He doesn't feel he belongs there."

"I'm sorry to hear that," said the young man sadly. "Why, Logan's always been family to us, e'en frae that first day we met in front o' Miss Sinclair's place."

"I believe that deep down he knows that. But there are things going on inside of him now that he's probably not clear about."

Allison still recalled vividly how confused he was that day he had left Stonewycke last spring. "But who am *I* to talk? If only I could *see* him," she went on emphatically. "I know that now I could understand him better."

"Ye can ne'er say what God will do."

"A while back I thought I might be able to find him," Allison said, going on to explain her sleuthing attempts with Billy and her eerie encounter with Gunther. "But I guess after that experience, I'm almost afraid to see Logan. Who knows *what* he might be involved in?"

"Why do you say that?" asked Nat.

"That man sounded so German," answered Allison, "and there have been so many unanswered questions—"

"What can ye be sayin', Allison?"

"I hate myself for even thinking it!"

"And ye should, too," Nat gently remonstrated. "I dinna ken Logan as weel as a wife ought to. But I ken enough to say wi' certainty that he couldna be mixed up wi' the enemy." His friendly eyes flashed momentarily with the Ramsey fire. "Allison," he went on, "if ye do naethin' else, ye must believe in him. A man needs that frae his wife, more than anythin'."

"And you still a bachelor," she teased, trying to lighten her sense of guilt. Then she added earnestly. "But such a wise bachelor!"

"I dinna ken aboot that," he replied, embarrassed at the compliment. "I think maybe I jist can give ye the man's perspective. And when ye do see Logan again, he'll ken what's in yer heart—and the one thing he'll want to be certain o' is that ye love him enough to believe in him—perhaps nae matter *what* he's been involved in."

"Love has so many aspects," mused Allison, "almost none of which a young couple getting married is aware of. I'm learning so many ways in which it's different than what I always thought it to be. You always think *love* is an emotion you feel toward another. And to now come to realize it's not that at all but rather how you behave toward others—it's quite an awakening, to say the least. And to think that in our eight years together, I never really *loved* Logan in a true sense, never really put him before myself, despite all the so-called *love* I felt for him."

"He probably never really loved you in that way either, or I doobt he'd ever hae left," said Nat. "Love, as weel's partin', is always a two-way street."

"I wonder if we'll have the chance to start again."

"I'll not stop prayin' fer ye both."

The conversation waned for a few moments, as brother and sister each lapsed into their own private musings. But time was too precious to waste on things that could wait until they were apart. Allison felt an urgency upon her to make this time together especially meaningful for them, a time of cementing the bonds that were growing between them now that they were able to relate as adults on an equal plane of relationship.

"I hope my experience hasn't soured you on the prospect of marriage, Nat," said Allison, anxious to know more about his life.

He grinned sheepishly. "Na, na," he said. "Ye couldna do that."

"But there's no one special?"

"The Lord kens best what's to come o' my future," he replied. "But He'd hae to go some to find a lady to match up wi' the women I think most highly o'—oor own mother, Lady Margaret, and e'en yersel'!"

For an instant a faraway gaze passed through his eyes. It quickly passed, however. "Oh, but there's plenty o' time fer that! War isna the time to be thinkin' o' romance. Too much can happen. I mightna live through it, ye ken."

"Nat, please!"

"'Tis true. Everythin's uncertain in war. But if I make it through, when it's all o'er, then . . ."

"I know you'll find someone as special as you are," replied Allison, and again the two fell silent.

Allison cast a quick glance to her left, and studied her brother momentarily with admiration. He had inherited his father's tall good looks, though he was not as brawny as Alec. No doubt many girls' hearts would throb over him, but his manner was so unassuming that he would never believe they would think of him in such a way. He had much to offer a woman; he would make a grand husband someday.

At the thought a chill ran through Allison's spine as she recalled his words: *I mightna live through it, ye ken.*

She didn't want to think about such things! Not now. Not ever! He does indeed have the potential to be a good husband someday . . . and he would fulfill it, she told herself. Yes, of course war was awful. But it was unthinkable that its evil shadow could extend itself even over Stonewycke.

She glanced at Nat's face again. The boyishness was still there. But at twenty-two, there were faint hints around his eyes of the hard edges the war had forced upon him. War, as well as difficult marriages, matured men and women more rapidly than perhaps they would have wished.

"I suppose all our lives must wait till the war is over," sighed Allison. "It seems such a waste of our youth."

"Wi' God, naethin' is wasted," replied Nat. "He always uses the tragedies to make o' us all better. Ye mind what Grandma Maggie always told us aboot her years away frae Grandpa Ian."

"I know. But to hear her tell the story, it always took on almost a romantic air. You forget how heartbreaking it was for the two of them. And maybe that's why when the heartache comes to us, we forget that it's meant for our good, for the deepening of our faith."

"Weel, we all saw that in Grandma and Grandpa. I jist hope we o' the next generations can allow the Lord the same grace to do that work in us."

"I can see that already in you, Nat," smiled Allison. "We're all so proud of you. When the 51st Highlanders so distinguished themselves at Dunkirk, you should have seen Daddy."

"Weel, we had to live up to the standard set in the Great War," replied Nat, beaming at the thought of his father's pride. "The Germans called us the 'women o' hell,' not kennin' hoo prood we was to be wearin' the kilt. It was a fine unit to be a part o' that!"

"Well, you were all from heaven as far as we're concerned," said Allison. "And where to now, Nat?"

"'Tis all secret, ye ken."

"Secrets!" exclaimed Allison with a downcast frown. "If I hear that word one more time, I'll scream!"

Nat hesitated a moment, then appeared as if he was going to speak, but all at once a voice over the loudspeaker interrupted him.

"Flight Fifteen from Glasgow now approaching the runway."

The conversation seemed over, or at least suspended as Allison and Nat rose to walk outside to watch the landing of their mother's plane. A cold stiff wind met them and Allison had to hang on to her hat to prevent it from joining the aircraft overhead. They watched on the other side of the fence as the plane lowered its landing gear and made its approach.

"I hope Mother's flight was good," said Allison. "She does not relish the idea of flying and only did it this time for you."

"The moment I see her she'll ken hoo much I appreciate it," said Nat. "I never know when I'll be back, or if—"

He broke off suddenly, ashamed of himself for almost voicing his fears to his already burdened sister. "You both will never know how much it means to me to be able to see you now," he finally added.

Allison reached up and placed her arm around him, giving him a loving squeeze.

"Oh, Nat," she said, "forgive my selfish outburst before. I don't care where you'll be or how many secrets you have. I will be praying for you every day."

"Thank you, dear sis," he said. "You know Grandma always said that we ought to pray as specifically as possible."

"Yes . . . I remember."

"Weel, maybe I ought to give ye some help in that particular area . . ."

He paused and smiled. "I'd like ye to ken, Allison. I canna tell ye anythin' exactly. But I can say that for the next several months, I'll nae doobt be eatin' lots o' spaghetti."

"Italy?"

"Ye didna hear it frae me," he replied with a wink. "Noo, *you* hae a secret to keep! And I'm glad ye ken. I willna feel sae alone noo. The Lord will be wi' me, and I always ken that. But I think He understands my meanin'. 'Tis nice to share that kind o' thing wi' someone close to ye."

"I wish you didn't have to go, Nat," said Allison. "I wish we could go back to the time we were all just 'wee bairnies'—running on the sand, exploring the Dormin . . . Oh, I don't know! You shouldn't have to be going off to . . . who knows what!"

She looked up at him and touched his cheek with her hand. There was hardly even a stubble of beard. Yet something deep in his eyes said he was fully a man, coming of age too soon.

"It doesn't seem fair, dear, gentle Nat—"

Her voice broke down and tears rose in her eyes.

Nat bent down and gave her a kiss on the forehead. "I love ye, Allison. Ye're a dear sister. Things may be lookin' a mite dark noo. But I ken they're gaein' to improve, especially for you. Logan will come back, and the war'll be over one day, and the two o' ye will hae the kind of marriage that will match both o' yer wonderful hearts. Especially wi' all ye seem to be learnin' frae the Lord's hand. In na sae very long, we'll all be sittin' together wonderin' why we were so untrustin' and downcast during these times o' trial."

His last words were spoken with almost a distant tone, as if he were trying somehow to convince himself too of the hope of his words in the face of his coming assignment.

"And noo," he went on, "we better dry oor eyes, or Mother will wonder if we're na glad to see her."

The plane touched down, and when Joanna debarked and walked through the gate, there followed a tender reunion of a mother and the children from whom she had long been separated as poignant as such a gathering can be in a time as fearful and uncertain as wartime.

Allison's were not the only tears that flowed.

46 ✖ *House of Cards*

IT HAD BEEN a nerve-wracking five-hour train trip from Paris to Reims, only eighty miles.

Logan knew the French railway system had deteriorated drastically since 1939, no thanks to some of his own operations in recent months. But he had not expected to spend half the day traveling.

Then in Reims he had run into some difficulty contacting the local Resistance cell that had promised a vehicle to carry them the final leg of their journey, the twenty miles to Vouziers. They now had less than an hour to get there and set up their radios in time to catch the European wavelength broadcast of the BBC.

As the old bakery van jostled and bounded along the rutted dirt road through forested terrain, Logan tried to relax by reviewing the important particulars of this current assignment. But the moment he tried to concentrate, the van bounced with a horrible thud into a huge pothole.

"Can't you keep out of *some* of those holes, Claude!" he shouted over the deafening roar of the ancient engine.

"Not if you want to get there by seven!" rejoined the surly Claude sharply.

"It won't matter if we break our necks in the process, or attract a Boche escort."

"Never satisfied, Anglais!" Defiantly Claude jammed on the brakes.

Lise, who was seated between the two men, flew forward, and had her reflexes been a fraction of a second slower, she would have smacked her head into the windshield. However, her hand grabbed the dashboard in time to prevent disaster.

For the next three minutes Claude drove the van at a snail's pace, while Logan sat, fuming at his comrade, silently bemoaning the fact that Claude was the only one available to accompany him and Lise on this particularly urgent mission.

"All right!" snapped Logan at length, unable to stand it any longer. "You've had your fun, and your little joke on me. Now get moving!"

Claude neither looked at Logan nor spoke, but merely rammed his foot to the accelerator. Instantly the old van lurched forward at its former pace, though Claude kept a diligent eye on the road ahead.

Logan seriously wondered how they were going to pull this thing off under such uncooperative conditions. London had made the operation sound easy enough: During the next moon period they were to meet a Lysander at an abandoned airfield five miles southeast of the little town of Vouziers. It would deliver into their temporary care two important Gaullist agents. They were to tune into the BBC every evening at seven p.m. sharp to listen for the message: "On ne fait pas d'omelette sans casser des oeufs. You can't make an omelette without breaking eggs." When *that* came, they knew that night they must meet the plane. Their cover, while they awaited the signal, would be to appear as vacationers.

The whole thing might be plausible enough at the beginning of July. The little village of Vouziers, with the Aisne River at its back door, would have enough of an influx of tourists that three more should be able to go unnoticed. That is, if no one paused to question two men and a woman traveling in a beat-up old bakery van. And if they could somehow put a veil over Claude's foreboding features and eyes full of sinister intent.

All at once, as if the irascible driver had read Logan's unkind thoughts about the glare of his eyes, the van's wheels collided with another trenchlike gouge out of the road. Logan opened his mouth to upbraid him again, thought better of it, and said nothing. Only Lise saw the look on his face, and simply shook her head and sighed with impatience at these unfortunate relations between them. In all the months they had been together, one would think Claude might have modified his prejudices. But any trust that might have developed between him and Logan had been completely negated by Logan's association with the Nazis. Back then, six months ago, his stature with them all had been on very precarious ground. . . .

Lise found herself reflecting back to the events of the previous December. Michel had been arrested just two nights prior to the bombing at Pearl Harbor. When she had gone to meet him that first time, she had indeed felt betrayed—deeply and personally, even more than she had let on to him. On her way to the Left Bank Cafe, she had fantasized that if it were true, then *she* would appoint herself his executioner. She tried to convince herself that the reason for her passionate initial reaction was that Michel had done something few had been able to accomplish since the war—he had won her trust. She had believed in him, and entrusted herself, as well as the cause she was fighting for, to him. For him to violate that was unconscionable. That was all. She forced from her mind all the other anguished and confused cries of her heart. There was only the Cause—she had no other feelings.

Of course, she could never let him know any of this. She had *wanted* to believe in him still, and tried to give him the benefit of the doubt. She would send his message to London, and would do what it might take to back his ruse with the Germans. Because of Jean Pierre she had been willing to give him a chance. But inside, her emotions balanced on the thin line between trust and deception, and it would take some time for her to refocus her feelings. And when they met in the cafe, despite her calm, even sympathetic exterior, Michel never knew that in her purse she had carried a loaded revolver. She told herself she could have, yet even now, she did not know if she *would* have been able to use it on him if he had proved a traitor.

Fortunately, she had not been given cause to find out.

When the word of the arrest and deaths of the Gregoires came to them, she had read his eyes carefully. The anguish of his invisible tears was more real than any Nazi could have put on merely to wear. She considered herself certainly that good a judge of character. She would have no use for the revolver at present, not to use on Michel Tanant, at least.

The others, however, took more time to convince. They had not seen his eyes. Claude still warily watched his flank, and seemed bent on bringing the despised Britisher face-to-face with some harm that would put an end to their mutual involvement once and for all.

A tense week had followed. Michel had so desired a meeting with Henri. But the gentle old bookseller would not risk it—protecting the operation, he said. Lise knew he was afraid to look in Michel's eyes, fearing perhaps that he might see the ugly truth of betrayal there. The strain, on both the young man and the old, was visible. The two had grown close in the months they had worked together—as close as two people could in this murderous life. And now suddenly the relationship that had been a source of sanity to both of them was gone.

A communication from Michel's London chief, Mother Hen, a week before Christmas had done much to bridge the rift and bring him back "in" for all but Claude. The communique had instructed *La Librairie* to follow Tanant's lead, doing nothing whatever to compromise his position with the Nazis. He had the complete support of British intelligence, the report read emphatically. There could be little doubt that the message was genuine. A personal note at the end had cautioned Michel to "have enough sense to know when to fold! We can get you out of France on twenty-four hours' notice if necessary."

The final re-cementing of Michel's position with *La Librairie* had come at the hand—literally!—of the boisterous Antoine. The big Frenchman had been sitting in a cafe waiting for a rendezvous with Michel. It was the end of December or the first week of January, thought Lise as she recalled it now.

Suddenly without warning the place was swarming with French police, raiding it by order of the German command in the city to gather "volunteers" for the labor camps in Germany. Antoine had been brusquely lined up against the wall with all the other likely candidates when Michel had stumbled onto the scene. Without hesitation he had stepped up to the inspector, whom he had recently met in relation to his connection with von Graff.

"What's going on here, Inspector?" he had asked with authority.

"You know how it is, Monsieur Dansette, we have quotas to meet that the Germans give us." He chuckled nervously, by all appearance reacting with some deference to Michel, according to Antoine's later recount of the incident.

"Of course," replied Michel. "I was speaking with General von Graff only yesterday about that very thing, and about resistors as well—they're more *my* line, if you understand me, Inspector," he added with a wink.

"Mais oui, Monsieur Dansette. I hear you and the general are on the trail of L'Escroc!"

"Keep it to yourself, Inspector," said Michel with a meaningful glance.

"Oui, Monsieur! You can count on me!"

Michel then gave the group lined up against the wall a casual onceover.

"You know, Inspector," he said, "that man"—he cocked his head toward Antoine "—he looks like someone I've been after. A dangerous Frenchman. He may have a clue I need. Have him taken to a back room; I'd like to question him privately."

"But of course, Monsieur!"

The inspector complied without further question.

When they were left alone in the back room, Antoine had not known whether Michel's true traitorous face had revealed itself, or if he, Antoine, had been saved from deportation to Germany.

"You're going to have to jump me and escape," said Michel as if in answer to Antoine's puzzled expression. "I know it's not a great ploy, but it's the best I could come up with on the spur of the moment."

"What do you mean . . . jump you?" asked Antoine, still confused.

"I mean knock the bloody daylights out of me, then beat it out that window!"

"You can't mean . . . ?"

"I can, and I do—make a good show of it!"

"They may not buy your explanation, and then you'd be in danger," protested Antoine. "I could only face labor camp—you could be—"

Suddenly there were sounds in the hall.

"This is no time for a debate!" said Michel. "You're going to be on your way to Germany if you don't. I'll fake some explanation. Now *do it*!" he ordered, presenting his jaw to his comrade's powerful fist.

Antoine had derived no pleasure from pummeling Michel's face that afternoon, not because he was squeamish, but because just before his fist had made contact with Michel's cheekbone, he had *known*. It was something he had caught in Michel's voice . . . in the look of his eyes . . . some intangible sense that assured Antoine's keen spy's instincts that Michel was one of them. And if that were not enough, Antoine knew that in setting him free, Michel stood in danger of losing much more than he could ever gain.

Claude, of course, had heatedly debated Antoine's whole interpretation of the day's events.

"You're just a sentimental French fool!" he blasted out. "Can't you see he arranged the whole scenario, just to win your trust, and through you, ours!"

"Perhaps that is what *you* would do, Claude," said Antoine calmly but passionately. "But L'Escroc is much too clever for such a clumsy, obvious ploy. He was just as shocked as I when he walked in and saw the French police."

"Please, this arguing must stop!" intruded Henri. He knew Claude, and knew the discussion would get them nowhere. It was not good for the organization. It was time for a firm decision on *La Librairie*'s policy regarding Michel Tanant, alias L'Escroc, Englishman, leader in the French underground, and now, by accident it seemed, also a double agent in counterfeit league with the Germans. As he spoke, Henri's eyes swept around the small room, and in that moment they were as hard and intractable as Claude's. *"We must be unified!"* he said. "Thus, from this time forward, Michel Tanant will be fully accepted. I believe that events on the night of December 5th happened exactly as he represented them to us, and that he is still wholeheartedly with us. *All* of us will give him the same cooperation and loyalty as before. I am prepared to take full responsibility for this decision, so if you denounce Michel— you denounce me! If you cannot accept this, then make it known now, and be off!"

Thus *La Librairie* weathered the formidable storm of the testing of Michel Tanant's loyalties. He was restored to his place among them, though with a great deal more care now paid to secrecy. And if Claude remained bitter and surly, it was no more in evidence than it had always been.

It should have been a time of great victory for the organization, now that Michel was able to filter intelligence directly from the Nazis. But Lise remembered that their coup was not without its difficulties. Any information Michel obtained could not be used without its being passed along the underground chain and acted upon in such a way that it could not be traced back to Michel. As a result of this constriction, many choice tidbits had to be overlooked completely; any resistance knowledge of them could only have come from extremely limited sources. They were forced to create coincidental-appearing triumphs over Nazi schemes so far removed from Michel's involvement that often more time was necessary to set up the deceptions than they had.

Still, much vital intelligence passed out of S.S. headquarters into Allied hands those months, with no one the wiser, except the British War Office, whose cause—sometimes independent of the French underground altogether—was helped tremendously.

Another factor that always had to be figured into the formula of Michel's double-identity charade was the simple fact that he had to prove himself to the Nazis as well. He had to feed them enough accurate information about the Resistance to make himself useful and to validate his loyalty to the Reich.

This was understandably the most difficult aspect of the deadly game. For if his information always proved bogus or came just a day or an hour too late to do the Nazis any good, eventually their suspicions would be aroused. Many a late-night session was spent with Henri and the others, concocting scenarios that would play to von Graff, which would give the appearance of dealing deadly blows to the cause of Free France and the Resistance Movement, but which in fact would do neither, and in which never the life of a comrade was endangered. The task was not an easy one.

Michel had played the double-agent game in England as Trinity. But when he fed the Abwehr information, only inanimate objects had been endangered—a few decoy ships or planes, anti-aircraft weapons the British could do without, an airfield, an out-of-service railway, an ammo dump from which ninety-eight percent of the stores had been relocated. But now with the Resistance, playing the double-loyalty game—at one time as Michel Tanant, another as Lawrence MacVey, then as Trinity, and to certain Parisians loyal to the Reich as Monsieur Dansette—involved people. He could not sacrifice human beings. Yet that was the most valued quarry sought by the Germans, who knew the underground had nothing if it did not have its leaders. Thus he had to betray without truly betraying, and risk as little as possible to individuals, appearing to give the Nazis much, while in fact giving them nothing.

All the while, the rumors surrounding L'Escroc gradually grew, assuming the proportions of legend. Logan pretended to be moving ever closer. Soustelle's hatred of MacVey intensified, and his determination to eliminate *The Swindler* grew to a passion.

Lise had often wondered, in the months since, how Michel walked this precarious tightrope without cracking up.

As the weeks passed into months, however, she began to see the fine lines of his face etched more and more with tension. No doubt he lived in constant fear of the inevitable moment when it would all crash in upon him. He once told her about a house of cards he and a friend had constructed in a London pub. Precisely leaning cards against one another, some vertically, some horizontally, they had built a tower almost two feet tall and employing some three decks. It had taken them hours to build, but in less than a second a gust of wind from the opening door had toppled their work of art into nothingness.

He had to say no more. She knew it was exactly that fear which constantly gnawed at him day and night, that from some unforeseen corner a sudden change in the currents of his fortune would blow unsuspectingly upon him, unmasking the subtle charade he had so carefully built over himself.

His own collapse perhaps he could bear. But by now he realized that he was the single card at the bottom-center of the tower. He cherished no vaunted ideas that the Resistance depended solely upon him—it would go on long after L'Escroc was a mere memory. But too many lives were now wrapped up in his game If he made a mistake—a shady plan, a phony betrayal, a linguistic slip-up—lives would be lost. If he played the charade too close, tipping his hand, bluffing when von Graff held the winning hand, he could lead the Gestapo right to Henri's bookstore. The Germans were said to be experimenting with drugs that *made* you talk, even against the determination of your own will. If he were captured and interrogated . . .

Yes . . . Lise could see all these things weighing heavily upon him.

When Michel had first come to Paris, she had sensed the thorough enjoyment he felt for what he was doing. She could still recall the boyish gleam in his eyes as he and the two British airmen had left Mme. Guillaume's building right into the arms of the gendarmes. He couldn't have enjoyed the ruse more!

But it was different for Michel now. Lines of anxiety had begun to crease his forehead. She could read sleepless nights in the dark hollows under his eyes. The *élan* she had rightly attributed to him was still there, but it had become a mere frame in which a different kind of picture was now taking shape.

She was both eager and afraid to see it completed. She had watched the underground life turn men into animals. Was not Claude a prime example? She hoped it didn't have to be that way. She hoped somehow Michel could escape such a fate.

Lise stole a glance at him as they bounced along the road toward Vouziers.

He was staring intently ahead, as if he expected danger, even on this sunny July afternoon on an idyllic country road. Why did he intrigue her so, and cause her stomach to do strange things when he was near? She *had* to retain her distance. She could not allow herself to become so vulnerable—it was not healthy for either of them in their present circumstances. Yet, perhaps it was too late.

Suddenly, even as her eyes were fixed upon it, Michel's face paled, and his whole body tensed. "What's this!" he groaned.

Lise jerked her head around. Her eyes fell upon the most distressing sight imaginable. Directly ahead of them, stretching across the dirt road, was a German checkpoint.

47 ❈ *Vouziers*

WHEN LOGAN HAD reconnoitered the area two weeks ago, he had not seen so much as a bowl of sauerkraut. The only thing resembling authority in the region was a pudgy, middle-aged police inspector who, though no patriot by any stretch, collaborated with the utmost laziness. He had not even so much as asked Logan for a look at his papers, and Logan had enjoyed complete freedom to examine the town and study the airfield to insure that it still fit RAF specifications. He had even contacted the local Resistance, which consisted of an elderly farmer and his kindly wife.

Now there were Germans everywhere.

Had word of this mission somehow leaked out? Could he be approaching the final Waterloo for L'Escroc, as he had been fearing for weeks?

Claude pulled the van to a stop behind an ancient truck, his features taut but more with malice than fear.

"Claude," said Logan from where he had crouched down in the back, thinking the three of them together might appear more suspicious, "can't you try to look more like a vacationer and less like you've just slit a Boche throat?"

Claude harrumphed angrily. "You just keep out of sight and leave this to me!"

Lise shook her head and gritted her teeth against her own angry retort. Couldn't they just once lay aside their animosity? True, Claude could be unreasonable, but why did Michel antagonize him at every opportunity?

The truck coughed and sputtered on its way, and Claude pulled up into place.

"Qu'est-ce qui se passe? What is happening?" he said, in what seemed a genuine effort to assume an appropriate attitude.

The soldier, however, had no intention of answering such a question, and instead replied with the most dreaded of German commands.

"Ausweis!"

The demand for identity papers should not have bothered these three, for everything they carried for travel and identity purposes was perfectly in order, having, in fact, been obtained through due process from the proper German departments in Paris. The anxiety rising in each stemmed more from the fact that secreted beneath a false floor in the back of the van were three wireless sets.

Claude and Lise, in the front seat, handed their papers out the window and the soldier gave them a perfunctory glance, then handed them back. Claude reached for the gear shift, but the soldier was not finished yet.

"What is in the back of the van?"

"I don't know," came Claude's unimaginative answer.

Lise immediately leaned toward the window. "We borrowed the van from my uncle in Reims," she said, "so we could tour the countryside, you know. We are on holiday from Paris."

"And that tarp . . . what is it covering?"

Lise hesitated only an instant. "My brother," she said, "he is asleep. He works all night in a factory. He was very tired."

"I must see his papers too. Wake him up."

Lise climbed in back and pretended to awaken Logan, who groggily rolled back the tarp. Lise took his papers and handed them forward.

The guard seemed to scrutinize them a moment or two longer than the others, then handed them back inside.

"Get out and open it up."

With but the faintest hint of a groan, Claude complied. Lise resumed her seat. Logan threw aside the tarp but remained where he was, praying that no one would want to search under the floor where he was sitting.

The guard opened the back of the van, poked around, shoved about a couple of boxes they had placed there as decoys, cast Logan a final wary look, and finally closed the door and waved Claude ahead.

Claude pulled the lever down into first and jerked back into motion, while his two passengers exhaled tense breaths.

In another quarter mile they entered the little village of Vouziers. There were German soldiers everywhere it seemed, although those walking the streets paid them little heed. It was hardly a comforting prospect to think of trying to complete their mission under such circumstances.

While dining in the restaurant of one of the town's two hotels, they learned the cause of the sudden German interest in the area. An army contingent had arrived the day before responding to reports of the presence of several escaped prisoners-of-war in the area. Actually, the German command in Paris had received rumors that this little out-of-the-way village had become a regular link in the underground escape route. For two days all roads had been blockaded and patrols were combing the countryside. No one could say how long they might remain, but the hotel concierge complained that it was already cutting severely into the tourist trade.

After dinner the three discussed what to do. Unfortunately, the radios they now had hidden in their rooms were only receivers brought for the specific purpose of intercepting the BBC broadcast. They had no transmitter; thus there was no way of contacting London about this hitch in their plans. They were all too worn out to consider a return to Paris only to have to turn around for another drive out to Vouziers. Therefore, they deferred their decision until morning.

By the time they awoke, however, it seemed their problem had been solved in spite of their uncertainty. Two escapees had been recaptured some time during the night, and the Germans had pulled out before dawn.

The successive days, while the weather continued fair, were peaceful ones, at least for Logan. Four days passed with no message, and he saw no reason why this excursion could not at the same time be viewed as a bit of a holiday for the beleaguered spies. Even Claude relaxed a little, though he spent most of his time in the cafes drinking too much black-market wine.

Logan and Lise took full advantage of the great weather and the lovely countryside. Leaving the van parked to conserve precious fuel, they rented bicycles at an exorbitant price and explored the banks of the Aisne River and the woods surrounding the town. Except for the tense hour every evening when he bent over his wireless listening for the BBC, Logan gave himself over completely to the holiday atmosphere of the place. At times he practically forgot his reasons for being there and the necessity for a man in his position to remain constantly vigilant.

He first spotted the youth after he and Lise returned to the hotel late one day after a picnic and swim. Lise went up to her room for a rest, while Logan tarried in the lobby exchanging pleasantries with a clerk. The coarsely dressed farm lad looked badly out of place in a hotel lobby, despite all his efforts to appear casually interested in a Paris newspaper.

The natural paranoia of his occupation, coupled with the fact that Logan thought he recognized the lad from earlier that morning, put him immediately on his guard. When he bid the clerk adieu, Logan exited the hotel, keeping his own casually camouflaged watch behind him. It seemed better to verify his suspicions sooner than later.

As he expected, the youth followed him. Logan ditched him easily, circled around the block, and came up behind the boy as he stood puzzling over which way his quarry had taken. The moment Logan firmly grabbed his arm from the rear, he nearly cried out with fright.

"Take it easy, young man," said Logan as he propelled him into a recess between two buildings where they would not attract attention. "I don't want to hurt you, but I *do* want to know why you are following me."

"They told me to be sure," panted the lad, who looked to be about sixteen years old, and completely unaccustomed to his present calling. "Who you were . . . and . . ."

"And what?" demanded Logan.

"It's . . . it's so hard to tell, and they didn't have a very good description," rambled the youth, "and they said I had to be sure. And with the Nazis here, I didn't want to—"

"All right, lad," broke in Logan, trying not to chuckle at the poor boy's discomfiture. "You haven't found a Nazi, and I doubt that I have either. Now let's see just what we *have* found. I believe we both know Monsieur Carrel."

Carrel was the farmer and resister Logan had met briefly on his last visit to Vouziers.

The boy nodded his head vigorously. "Oui!" he said, much relieved. "You are Monsieur Tanant, non?"

"I am," replied Logan. "Now, why did Monsieur Carrel send you after me?"

"My father knew you were returning during the moon period," said the young Carrel. "But you had both agreed not to contact each other unless it was an emergency. So he sent me into town every day to see if you had arrived."

"We've been here four days already."

"I did not look so hard when the Germans were here," admitted the boy sheepishly. "And you were perhaps out in the country often?"

"Oui, that's true," said Logan. "So what does your father want?"

The boy glanced fearfully this way and that before speaking. "He has what the Boche were looking for."

"An escapee?"

"Oui."

"And he'd like some help getting him out?"

"Very much so, I think."

48 ✵ The Escapee

THE FIRST THING Logan noticed on stepping into the Carrel home was the warm, earthy atmosphere. He had been too rushed and disoriented the first time to pay much attention. But now, in a calmer frame of mind, he realized that he had not been in a place like this since the last time he was in Port Strathy and had visited Jesse Cameron's cottage. Madame Carrel was busy kneading bread in the kitchen area, while a young girl of about ten or eleven was thrusting a log into the cookstove fire. In the corner by the stove a calico cat was lapping milk from a bowl.

Mme. Carrel greeted Logan with a ready warmth, no matter that it was wartime and the enemy had occupied her country. She was, and would always be, a simple, open-hearted farm wife, and might well have greeted General von Graff in the same manner.

"Come this way please, Monsieur Tanant," said her husband.

Logan regretted being led away from the friendly kitchen. Yet it remained in view, for the rest of the large central room—consisting of a dining and sitting area—was merely an extension of the kitchen.

Now for the first time Logan's eyes fell on the figure sitting toward the back of the room in a large rocking chair with his feet propped up, facing the brick hearth. The fellow's back was to Logan and his first impression of the man was of a brilliant shock of red hair.

"Monsieur le Lieutenant," said Carrel to his other guest in faltering English, "I have brought a visitor."

"Wonderful!" said the man, also in his native tongue, turning in his chair. "Forgive me for na risin'."

Logan had stepped forward to shake his countryman's hand—for from the accent he knew immediately Carrel's guest was a Scot—but before the fellow had finished speaking and fully turned, Logan stopped and gasped.

"Nathaniel!" he exclaimed.

"The Lord be praised!" said Nat, now making a concerted effort to stand. "Confound this leg," he muttered.

But Logan had reached him in an instant, and, bending over the chair, gave his brother-in-law an exuberant embrace. How good it felt to be so close to someone from home—to family!

"I see you two know each other," said Carrel, this time in French, grinning at the happy scene. Briefly Logan translated his words. Then, almost in unison, both men exclaimed—one in English, one in French:

"Indeed we do!"

"Then I'll leave you to yourselves, while I finish up my chores."

Carrel went outside and Logan pulled a stool up next to Nat.

"What in the world are you doing here?" he asked.

"I was jist goin' to ask ye the very same thing!" said Nat.

"It's a long story, Nat," replied Logan. Suddenly he felt very uncomfortable, and his smile faded. He looked away, pretending interest in the fire.

"Listen here, Logan," said Nat. "Ye dinna hae to be that way wi' *me*! I'm Allison's baby brother, remember . . . the wee tyke who worships the ground Logan Macintyre walks on!"

Logan smiled and faced Nat again. "I'm sorry," he said. "So much has happened . . ."

"But never so much that we'd stop bein' brothers," replied Nat. "And ye ken, Logan, that no matter what, that's hoo I'm always goin' to think o' ye."

Logan laid his hand on Nat's shoulder. "Thank you," he said, not without a great deal of emotion in his voice.

"Noo," continued Nat in a lighter tone, "let me get my story over wi' so I can hear yers—which'll nae doobt be the more interestin' tale."

Logan nodded his agreement with the plan, though he wasn't so sure he wanted to get into his own story. But Nat was talking.

"I was transferred frae the 51st Highlanders after Dunkirk and got into a commando unit. Dinna ask me why I did it—I suppose on account o' my C.O.'s sayin' I'd be good at it. But he'll nae doobt change his mind when he hears hoo this assignment went. I was off trainin' Partisans in Italy—quite a trick wi'oot kennin' a word o' Italian! But we managed pretty weel, and I think we had a good outfit. That was, what, about three months ago—just after seein' Allison and Mother in London. As I was sayin', it went weel enough, until this new fellow joined us. 'Twas my fault, 'cause I liked him and wasna so careful as I should hae been. The bloke wound up betrayin' the whole lot o' us to the Germans. They had me in San Remo prison for a while; then they were plannin' to transfer me to Buchenwald. On the train I kept lookin' for me chance to escape. But we got to Germany before that chance came. Then the train was derailed, and in the mayhem, five o' us slipped away. We've been on the run for a month, though by the time we got here, we was doon to three. We ran into a German patrol aboot a week ago, and all took off in separate directions. That's when I took this bullet in the leg. I dinna ken what's become o' the other two—an American pilot frae Texas and a lad frae British intelligence."

"I heard the Boche caught two escapees about four days ago," put in Logan.

"'Tis a shame," said Nat. "They were good lads. I suppose they'll jist hae to start o'er again."

"How bad is your leg, Nat?"

"It'd feel a lot better if that bullet weren't still floatin' around in there—"

Nat winced in pain, even as he said the words. When the spasm passed, he went on with a wan laugh—

"But I had more pain when I was a lad o' ten and got a fishhook caught in my shoulder!"

"What does the doctor say . . . or have you seen one?"

"Carrel doesna trust the local fellow, but Mme. Carrel has been keepin' it clean. I can walk, wi' a crutch we made—that is, if ye hae plenty o' time to wait for me."

He paused, then said, "And what aboot yersel', Logan?—Though I think I can guess at some o' it."

"Well," said Logan, deciding that some story must be given. "For openers, I suppose you ought to use my code name, especially when there's anyone about. My comrades in the underground have never even heard the name Logan Macintyre. So when you hear the name Michel Tanant, it's me they're talking about."

"Then I'm right—ye're wi' Intelligence."

Logan nodded.

"There's really not much more I ought to tell than that," he continued. "I got into it almost by accident, recruited by a friend for one simple assignment that only lasted an hour or two. They needed someone and I happened to fit the bill. But it was at a time when I was floundering—you know, Allison and I weren't doing too well, I hated my job. So when the chance to get more deeply involved came along, I took it . . . and here I am."

"How long hae ye been in France?" Nat asked.

"Quite a while, I suppose," replied Logan, then paused reflectively. "Longer than I ever expected to be, that's for sure."

He stopped again, reticent to talk about himself. "I don't know, Nat," he went on at length. "Suddenly none of it seems so important. Right now, you don't know how *good* it is to see you! I've felt so lost lately, but seeing you—"

He stopped and shook his head slowly. "I'm sorry," he said. "I never used to be this downcast."

"I imagine we've all hae to do a fast job o' growin' up in these last few years," said Nat. "I'm sure it's been no easier for ye than me."

"What I'd really like to know is, how is . . . everyone back home?"

"Ye're meanin' Allison, o' coorse?"

"Yes."

"Why didna ye tell her aboot what ye was doin'?"

"You know how it is—security . . ." Even as he spoke, Logan could see by Nat's pointed look that he would never accept that pat answer.

"All right," he continued resignedly. "I didn't tell her because I wanted her to believe in me—just in *me*. It seemed, to me at least, that the only way I could live down my past was knowing at least one person—Allison—trusted me completely, even without knowing every detail. I suppose maybe I was wrong. But that's how I felt then."

"She's only human, ye ken."

Logan nodded.

"'Twas a lot o' pressure ye put on her, Logan. And she felt it more'n she let ye see."

"I know that . . . now. I put so much on her. I tried to validate my whole existence through her. I'm surprised *she* didn't walk out on me first. She would have had every right."

"Are ye, Logan? Are ye truly surprised?"

Logan hesitated. "No, I suppose I'm really not. Allison was always strong . . . never a quitter."

"I saw her jist afore I left on this assignment," said Nat.

"What did she say?"

"That she loved ye."

"I never doubted that."

"She's changin', Logan. Changin' wi' the kind o' changes God makes—as I think maybe ye are yersel'."

"I only hope it hasn't come too late," sighed Logan.

"Allison said the exact same thing."

"Did she?"

It was such a small thing—the two of them making the same statement. Is it foolish to place a hope in it? Logan wondered. Have I come to the place that I can let myself hope again, let myself believe that I might somehow fit once more into a life with Allison? Part of him yearned to be able to answer *yes*. That same part of him longed for her, and for all the things in his existence she represented—all the things he had repudiated in his own mind the day he left Stonewycke.

It had all come upon him again suddenly the moment he laid eyes on Nat. How desperately he wanted to be part of that life again! Yet at the same time he was afraid he had already gone beyond the point of no return.

"I don't know anymore, Nat," Logan said after a long pause. "I'm not afraid to tell you the whole thing confuses me more than a little. I'm so—"

He stopped again, suddenly feeling uncomfortable pouring out his innermost feelings to the younger brother he had always striven to impress with his maturity and worldly wisdom. *Anyhow,* he reasoned to himself as he tried to bring his emotions back under control, it's not right of me to burden him. He's got enough troubles of his own right now.

But Nat had little concern for his own problems, for he knew the Lord was in control of them. Instead, his focus remained zeroed in on the struggles of his brother-in-law.

"Ye dinna hae to be afraid," he said sincerely, reading in Logan's eyes what his pride could not express, "when ye belong to God."

"Who said I was afraid?" asked Logan defensively.

"I can tell."

"How did you know?"

"I've battled enough fear mysel' lately to be able to recognize it in another—it's ne'er far frae ye when ye're crouched doon on the battlefield. But I hae a feelin' yers is a more difficult kind o' confrontation because the source o' yer fear comes frae within' yersel'. But ye dinna hae to fight alone, ye ken that, dinna ye, Logan?"

"I want to know—" he replied, before his voice broke off suddenly. Tears rose to the surface of his eyes, and his voice became strangled.

He jumped up, turned away, and strode to the stone hearth, keeping his back to Nat.

"Listen," he went on after a moment, "it's too bad this war doesn't leave us the luxury of mulling over the complexities of life. In the meantime, we've got too many more urgent things to talk about than all my woes."

"*I* dinna agree, Logan," countered Nat with resignation in his tone, looking and sounding more like the battle-worn soldier he was.

"Well, I don't want to talk about it now," said Logan, "or I'm liable to turn into a blubbering fool."

"There's nothin' wrong wi' a few tears if they bring healin' to yer heart."

"You sound just like Lady Margaret."

"'Tis nae wonder. Her blood runs through me, and she gave o' her great wisdom to all o' us. And the blood runs through *you* o' one frae whom she learned a great deal o' what she told the rest o' us. So I ken ye understand what I'm sayin'."

"In this case, however," said Logan stubbornly, "there's *everything* wrong with that particular bit of wisdom about tears and healing. It's different out here. There's no healing to be had on the front lines, Nat."

"The front lines o' life are exactly where healin' must begin," urged Nat. "When everythin's easy and there's nae tryin' o' yer faith, life takes nae inner strength. When it's all easy, ye can manage yersel'. But when things are tough, when ye *are* on the front lines, that's when yer true need shows itsel'. Ye're right—it's different here. But here ye need God *more,* not less!"

"Out here control is life—and that's one thing I can't lose, Nat: control . . . of myself."

He turned to face Nat, almost as if in unconscious challenge.

But Nat had learned something else from his great-grandmother, and that was when to leave off and allow the Spirit to perform its surgical work inside the heart of another.

The tense moment passed.

Logan immediately regretted the severity of his response. He hadn't meant to direct it toward dear Nat at all. Somehow he sensed that his brother-in-law understood. When Logan spoke again, it was in a lighter tone, as if announcing his intention to forget all that had gone before. But Nat's brow remained creased for some time, with a deep ache for his brother-in-law.

"Now," said Logan, "why don't we begin talking about how we're going to get you out of France?"

In the days that followed as they met together and began to formulate a plan, the conversation never again touched upon such personal ground. It would take a still greater tragedy than his own personal need to bring the full thrust of Nat's words, and their deeper implications, back into Logan's troubled mind.

49 ✖ Aborted Shortcut

TWO MORE NIGHTS passed without word from the BBC. But on the third evening after Logan's visit with Nat, the message finally came through:

"On ne fait pas d'omelette sans casser des oeufs."

They could expect the Lysander sometime tonight between ten p.m. and three a.m.

Logan ate dinner at the hotel with Claude and Lise, and somehow the three managed to pass the time until the hour when they would at last embark upon this long-awaited mission. Since the Carrel farm lay in the opposite direction from the airfield, they decided that Claude and Lise should go directly to the field, just in case the plane was early. Logan would retrieve Nat from the farm and take him with him to rendezvous with the others, in hopes that he could get him on the plane and safely on his way back to England.

It was nine o' clock when Logan arrived at the farm.

"Are you ready to go, Nat?"

"It's tonight, then?"

Logan nodded, and Nat flashed a grin through his pale features. Pulling himself painfully up from the chair, with Logan's assistance he hobbled to the corner where his pack lay ready and waiting.

"It is still amazin' to me," he said, "hoo my arrival in Vouziers could hae been timed so perfectly—jist in time to catch a plane ride back home."

He attempted a soft laugh, but it only ended in a painful cough. The festering wound was clearly taking its toll on his body's strength.

As they stepped out of the house, Carrel's son René volunteered to go along, and Logan gladly accepted the offer. An extra pair of hands might come in handy with Nat if they ran into any problems.

They climbed into the van and set out for the airfield, a seven-mile jaunt from the farm. A full moon shone on a clear summer's night, perfectly conducive for a Lysander landing. Logan was glad they had the boy along, for without the luxury of the van's headlamps, due to the blackout, he would have been hard put to find his way on the unfamiliar roads, even in the moonlight.

After ten minutes Logan said, "I thought it was only about seven kilometers from your place to the airfield," worried that he had not yet seen any familiar landmarks indicating they were approaching their destination.

"Perhaps as the crow flies," said the lad. "But the road veers quite a bit to the north before it meets the airport road that you probably took out of town."

"I must have misread my map," said Logan. "We don't have time for delays!" It was not quite nine-thirty, but Logan was worried that he was cutting it too close. Though the plane could be several hours later, he didn't want to take any chances of Nat's not getting on board. "Is there a shorter way?" he asked after a moment's thought.

"There is an old dirt road up ahead," replied René, "not much more than a path, actually. It cuts through the woods and is very rough. But before the war it was not unknown for a young man to take his sweetheart down it in whatever vehicle he could get."

"Is it wide enough for the van?"

"Oh, oui! You should have seen some of the trucks that got through!"

"How much will it save us?"

"I don't know exactly—three or four kilometers perhaps. It's maybe three kilometers through the woods, and the airfield can't be but another kilometer or two beyond that. But the road, I would guess, is eight or nine kilometers still to go."

"We'll chance it! Where is the turnoff?"

"It should be coming up . . . there it is!"

His hand shot out the open window. Logan braked, and swung the van hard to the right and into the densely wooded area.

The road was exactly as René had described it—perhaps worse. It was soon obvious to Logan that they would probably save no time at all. But by the time the realization came they had gone too far to turn back. He therefore continued to push hard, determined to save every minute possible. He knew he had no one to blame for his poor decision other than himself.

The old van bumped and rattled along, now in nearly pitch darkness on account of the forest. Occasionally Logan heard muffled gasps from Nat. Still he drove on, squinting to see the road in the scant rays of moonlight that reached the ground.

Suddenly the sound he dreaded most to hear, next to the report of a Gestapo pistol, came unmistakably through to his ear—the sickening hiss of a tire breathing its last. He slammed on the brakes with disgust. He would now have to pay twenty minutes for the ten he had hoped to save! He climbed out of the van and walked around to the back to get the spare. With incredulity a moment later he opened the tool compartment to see nothing but emptiness!

With tires as old and threadbare as the van's, it seemed incredible that anyone would have driven it without a spare, even despite rubber rationing. But what was most disturbing of all was that he had not checked out this detail in advance. *How stupid of me!* he thought.

Sulkily, he informed his companions of their plight.

"It can't be more than two or three kilometers to go," offered René hopefully.

Logan climbed back in, seemed to debate with himself for a moment, then started the engine.

"There's no sense worrying about this wheel now," he muttered. "We may as well just see if we can push it through!"

He shifted down into first and lurched forward.

Now the ruts and potholes and deeply worn tracks of the road were next to impossible to negotiate, steering a tire with no rubber. In less than two hundred yards Logan was sweating freely with the effort of trying to control the wheel, which behaved as if it had a mind of its own. In the darkness he could not even see the rock, much less try to avoid it. Suddenly Logan's arms were wrenched from the steering wheel and the van careened into the ditch at the side of the road.

"It's my fault," groaned Logan. "I'm sorry, mates." Glancing at his watch, he saw they would never make it by ten. At least they had not yet heard the sounds of approaching aircraft.

Slowly Logan opened the door and got out. The night was still and quiet. Had there not been a war on, René's observation was probably most apt—this *would* be a romantic place. But what was he to do now?

"Let's strike oot on foot," said Nat cheerfully.

"How could you possibly make it?" asked Logan.

"I got this far, didna I? Dinna forget, that plane's my ticket home. I'll make it, I tell ye!"

"If you're up to it."

"'Tisna but a wee bit o' a walk," said Nat encouragingly. "Wi' the two o' ye to help me, we'll get there."

"Let's just pray that the plane doesn't set down at ten and want to be back in the sky by five after."

"Aye!"

The going was painfully slow, but they moved doggedly ahead. In eleven or twelve minutes they had covered about a kilometer and the forest had begun to thin somewhat, offering more light for their path as they advanced. Nat was braced between Logan and René, and Logan was heartened with their progress when suddenly he stopped and signalled them both to be quiet.

"Did you hear that?" he whispered.

The others shook their heads. They were, however, not inclined to argue when Logan silently led them off the path into the deeper cover of the pine wood. Crouching down behind an old tree stump, with held breath they waited to see what would come of whatever sound Logan had heard.

"Monsieur," breathed René.

Logan kept his eyes toward the road, but indicated silence by raising his finger to his mouth.

"Monsieur," repeated René in a scarcely audible whisper, handing something to Logan.

"What's this?" said Logan as he took the object. As soon as his hands closed around it, he knew the answer to his own question.

"My father saw that you carried no weapon," explained René, "so he gave this to me. But I do not know how to use it."

"Well, I doubt we'll have need of it," replied Logan, reluctantly jamming the Webley revolver into his belt. "Let's go . . . I think my imagination is too active tonight."

They arose from their hiding place, inched their way forward back to the widened path, and continued on their way. In another ten minutes they had cleared the woods. The ground appeared to level out before them and the road widened perceptibly. The going had been rough for poor Nat, but now Logan hoisted him a little more strongly upon his shoulder and whispered whatever encouragement he could think of to keep his spirits up. In the distance he was sure he could make out the vague shapes of buildings.

The airfield!

"Come on, Nat!" he said, "we're almost there!"

Suddenly the disaster every agent fears struck without warning.

As if springing up from the earth itself, two German soldiers loomed up before them, blocking their way. The next instant a flash of brilliant light blinded Logan's eyes, accompanied by the sharp commands of German voices. Instantly Logan knew that all the wit in the world would not avail him this time, for he could never explain away the weapon in his belt, much less his limping, red-headed companion who carried no papers, making for a deserted airport in the middle of the night.

50 �֎ *Tragedy*

LISE LOOKED TOWARD the road for the tenth time in the last half hour.

Since Logan had the van and she and Claude only bicycles, she had fully anticipated Logan to arrive at the airfield at nearly the same time as they, despite his detour to the farm. But she and Claude had already been there thirty minutes and still there had been no sign of the van.

She strode over to the runway where Claude was busy clearing away scattered brush and rock from the airstrip.

He glanced up as she approached. "We should have come out here days ago to do this," he grunted.

"Michel didn't want to draw unnecessary attention, either to us or to this place." She bent over, picked up a branch and flung it away. "It's not so bad, and we still have time." She could hardly believe the condition of the landing surface was Claude's only concern. "Aren't you worried?" she finally asked.

"Yes, I'm worried," he answered coldly. "We are going to have a job of it signaling the plane with only two of us."

"Claude!" exclaimed Lise angrily. "Don't you care what happens to Michel? What if he's lying dead in some ditch!"

"It is one less pair of Anglais boots to lick."

"He has never lorded it over any of us—especially you!"

"I'm going to pace off the lamp positions," he said, ignoring Lise's words. "It's nearly ten."

"You plan to do nothing about Michel?"

"I am going to do what *has* to be done, what we came here to do."

"And what makes you think we can go ahead and signal the plane without knowing what trouble there may be out there?"

"The stupid Anglais is probably just lost."

Lise grabbed up a large rock from the ground and hefted it in her hands with fire in her dark eyes. Even Claude might have felt some trepidation at that moment had there been daylight to reveal the flash from those angry orbs. But it was dark, and an instant later she heaved the rock in the air and well away from him.

"I'm going out to look for Michel," she said resolutely.

"Don't be foolish. You have no idea where he might be."

"If something happened he would try to make it here however he could—even on foot if necessary. If the road was blocked, he would go out across country, maybe through the woods. Nothing would stop him except a German patrol."

"And there are none in this area. *He* said that, remember?"

"Things can change. The Germans know this airfield is here, too. They have maps. Who knows but that they might keep it under watch? Michel may have missed something. I just know I don't like the delay."

She turned and walked off, intent on skirting the circumference of the old airport.

"You could never hope to find him out there!" called Claude after her. "It's a foolhardy attempt."

"*You* are the fool, Claude," she spat back as she wheeled around. "You revel in killing your Germans, but when the war is over, what will it all be for? Friends? Country? Ideals? You don't care about any of that. It's all for hatred. And when the last Boche is dead, what will you have gained in return? They will be dead, but you will still be carrying your hatred with you. I do not intend to turn out that way. I won't!"

She turned again and started off, but Claude threw down the armload of branches he held and called out for her to stop.

"Pace off the lamp positions," he ordered. "I'll look for your Anglais." He grabbed up the rucksack that held his Sten sub-machine gun and stalked away. But before he had gone ten paces, he stopped and turned back momentarily to face Lise. "But you are wrong. You *will* end up like me—all of you will if you want to survive. There is no other way."

Then he tramped off into the night, not realizing the stark contradiction between his present action and his words of hopelessness.

Lise watched him as he disappeared into the field that surrounded the airstrip on all sides. Was it possible that her words had actually penetrated? He didn't *have* to go. Had she just witnessed a genuine act of selflessness on the part of the seemingly unfeeling Frenchman? Maybe Claude was human, after all.

She shook her head at the unlikely notion. He had probably done it just to shut her up!

With a sigh, Lise returned to the task at hand. They might not have need of the lights, but they had to be ready nonetheless. She tilted her eyes up toward the star-studded sky, then back to the woods that fringed the fields in the distance. It would be just like the Germans, she thought, to keep a patrol out there—invisible, just inside the trees, waiting, watching, trying to lure the Resistance into using what appeared to be nothing but a long-forgotten and abandoned strip of concrete.

Please, she silently cried in her heart—*please, let everything turn out all right!*

"Your weapons!" ordered one of the soldiers.

Logan took the small pistol out of his belt and threw it into the dirt.

The soldier pointed his rifle at Nat and René. "Weapons!" he repeated.

"They're not armed," said Logan in his inept German.

Keeping his rifle roving between the three and his eyes glaring at them for any sudden movements, the soldier nodded to his partner.

Logan squinted into the spotlight still pointed directly into his face to see if he could determine anything about their plight, but he could see nothing. A moment later he felt hands frisking him. The second soldier then moved on to Nat and René. When he was satisfied that they had been armed only with the handgun, he stepped back with his rifle.

"What are you doing here?" demanded the first soldier.

The question seemed oddly inappropriate to Logan. Why not just haul them into Vouziers, or to their commanding officer and let Intelligence handle the questioning? But something about these two seemed peculiar . . . hesitant.

If he could just stall them somehow, thought Logan. The longer he could keep them from taking action, the more time he had to figure out something.

"My name is Michel Tanant," said Logan. "From Paris. I have travel papers."

"And do you have papers for that?" The soldier cocked his head toward the Webley. "I've seen no such weapons except what we've confiscated from the underground."

"This is all a mistake," Logan went on, hardly thinking about what he said, just trying to buy some time. "We found it along the road. We were coming to turn it in."

The young soldier smiled. Not a cruel smile, but rather one displaying profound amusement at the audacious attempt at such a ridiculous lie. The two soldiers exchanged meaningful looks from which Logan was at last able to guess what was troubling these two.

Could they be lost? he thought to himself.

Here they were, with three prisoners of war, and yet with no idea how to get them back to their unit.

"And your friend there?" asked the Nazi, indicating Nat. "He's just out for a stroll in these deserted woods, with a bad wound like he's got?"

"He's my brother-in-law," replied Logan, the truth spilling out without his even pausing to think about it. "Yes, you're right, he's wounded. Got into a scuffle with a Resistance agent. I was trying to get him into town, but our van broke down and we lost our way."

"Why are you not on the main road?"

"Because if those Free France maniacs get hold of us, they'll slit our throats. You know how they are. It's just lucky we ran into you two! Can you help us into—"

But before he could say anything further, the blinding light which the German had trained on his face was suddenly extinguished, seemingly from the sharp blast of rifle that echoed through the night.

Logan dropped to the ground. More gunfire exploded all around him. Voices shouted out in a multitude of languages. In the confusion he could understand none of it.

He scrambled around, trying to locate his gun where it had fallen. "Nat!" he called. "Nat . . . where are you?"

The only answer that met his ears was more gunfire, this time from close by. The two Germans were firing, but not at him, it seemed. More volleys sounded, this time from farther away, toward the airfield.

Logan heard a scream. It sounded like René, but he could not be sure. He still had heard nothing from Nat, but then Nat was already weak and was probably trying to conserve his strength.

More gunshots, explosive bursts of fire lighting the night, followed by blackness. Another scream of pain, followed by the throaty cursing of a German voice.

Out of the corner of his eye, Logan suddenly saw a figure spring forward. It was Nat, lurching toward one of the German soldiers who had the sights of his gun leveled directly at Logan's head. He hardly heard the quick succession of shots that followed.

Indistinctly aware of the danger he was in, Logan rolled, his fingers closing around the Webley as he did so. Another bullet whizzed within a fraction of an inch from his head. Another quickly followed, spraying dirt at his shoulder. He spun around, trying to make out Nat's form, and while dirt and grass were still spattering up into Logan's face from a third shot, he fired the revolver almost blindly in the direction of the other soldier. Even as he squeezed the trigger, something in his confused brain expected his wild shot to be followed immediately by a fatal slug from one of the Nazis which would end this sudden nightmare.

But no shot came. Everything suddenly fell silent.

Logan pulled himself to his knees, gripping the pistol in one hand and rubbing the dirt from his eyes with the other.

As his vision cleared and the moonlight brought the battlefield into focus at his feet, his whole body convulsed with the sight that met his eyes.

Three bodies bloodied the ground around him.

51 ✻ The Landing

I SHOULD NEVER have made Claude go, thought Lise frantically to herself. Now they were *all* separated, perhaps *all* in danger. What was worse: Lise was now stuck at the airfield alone. She did not dare leave it to search on her own, lest they return and find *her* missing.

What could have happened to Michel . . . to Claude? Was it merely some silly miscommunication they would all laugh about later? Something inside told her otherwise.

Lise paced back and forth, every now and then glancing up into the sky. At least the plane had not yet come. She was concerned for Michel's friend. Who could tell when another chance like this would come for him to get out of France so easily? His wound would make any other route impossible, even fatal.

All at once Lise heard sounds. Instinctively she glanced up into the sky again. But she realized immediately it was not the sounds of aircraft she heard. They came from far away, carried to her ears probably by a trick of the breeze.

They were short, sharp blasts—the unmistakable sounds of gunfire.

Lise scanned the fields in the direction Claude had gone, her heart trembling within her. More shots penetrated the night air. She could see occasional flashes of gunfire off in the distance, perhaps a kilometer away, at the edge of the woods.

Without even thinking her actions through, Lise started running toward the sounds, dreading what she might find. She could hear more gunfire, and shouting.

Several more shots; then all fell silent.

Lise stopped. What if the gunfire had nothing to do with her comrades? To continue on, if what she had seen and heard was indeed from a German patrol, might only attract Boche attention toward the airfield.

But what if Michel and Claude were hurt or in danger, and needed her?

She glanced back toward the airfield, then again at the now silent darkness ahead of her.

Slowly she decided to inch ahead. If she heard anything from the airfield, she would turn immediately and hasten back to it. In the meantime, remaining as cautious, quiet, and out of sight as she was able, she *had* to try to find out what had prompted the gunfire. If her comrades were wounded or dead, the plane would mean little to her now.

Slowly she made her way forward through the uncut grass, crouching now and then to keep out of sight. Minutes passed. Still she saw and heard nothing. Still she seemed no nearer her destination.

Then in the distance came the sound she had been half-dreading. Faintly overhead came the distant whine of the single-engine aircraft.

Logan crouched on the ground, numb. Gradually he awoke from his stupor, his hands shaking. About a foot away lay the revolver where it had slipped from his fingers.

Suddenly he remembered. A young German soldier lay dead, probably less than ten feet away. He could not make out whatever expression had been fixed on his face when Logan's reckless bullet had snuffed out his life. Logan could not see past the circle of blood in his chest. He turned around, lurched, and was sick.

A moment later he felt a gentle hand on his shoulder. He started half to his feet, turned, and nearly shrank away. He looked up into René's stricken face. The boy had tears streaming down his dirty cheeks. Logan couldn't cry. The devastation wracking his brain was too tormenting for weeping to wash away.

There were other bodies nearby, but Logan was afraid to look at them. He knew one was Nat's.

Less than two minutes had passed since the first rounds had been fired. He didn't want to face more death. But he had to. Nat was there.

He forced himself up to his feet, then to his brother-in-law's prostrate form. He laid a hand on the lad's chest. Was there a faint movement he felt? Nat slowly opened his eyes.

"Logan," he whispered weakly, "ye're all right, then?"

"Nat . . .!" cried Logan, but whatever other words he felt in his heart caught in his throat.

He tore off his jacket and pressed it against the wound in Nat's abdomen. Then he slumped down beside the wasted form, staring blankly ahead.

Some flickering remnant of who he was, or who he was supposed to be, kept trying to force its way into his dulled consciousness. He had to *do* something! The shots might have alerted the rest of some German patrol; they had to get moving!

"Your comrade is coming around," called René into the blur of Logan's mind.

"What?"

"Your other comrade," said the youth. "It was he who surprised our captors, off there in the field."

Logan gently laid down Nat's head and went in the direction the boy pointed. Claude had a deep gash on his head, whether from the gunfire or from striking a nearby rock as he had dived for cover Logan couldn't immediately tell. But he would survive, with only another ragged, ugly scar to add to his morbid collection. Logan reached a hand out to help him as he tried to rise, but Claude shook him away.

"I can manage," he growled. "What happened to the Boche?"

"You killed one," replied Logan. "I owe you my life."

"Save your thanks for someone who needs it! And the other?"

"I killed him," said Logan.

"You, Anglais?" exclaimed Claude in derisive disbelief. "I didn't think you had the guts!"

Logan did not reply.

"We'd better get out of here!" said Claude.

Still Logan just stared blankly forward. How could Claude think so clearly after all that had just happened? But then, this wasn't Claude's *first* killing. Did it get easier? Would he one day be able to gun down his enemy without a thought? Such a prospect was even more fearsome than the act of killing itself.

What finally forced Logan back into action, mechanical though it might have been, was the thought of Nat. He was still alive! If they could just make it to the airstrip and get him aboard the Lysander! He had to get Nat home—home to Stonewycke, to his mother, to Allison.

They walked back, and with Logan and René carrying Nat, and Claude stumbling ahead, they managed to get on the move again. Whatever their difficulties had been before, they were multiplied tenfold now. Though Nat should never have been moved, Logan knew whatever chance he had at all depended on that plane. Fortunately, by this time Nat was beyond pain.

"Faster," urged Claude, starting to outdistance them. "It's not far."

But the words were barely out of his mouth when they heard the sound of the plane. In another moment it came into sight in the light of the moon, though it carried no lights of its own. The little Lysander buzzed once over the airstrip, the pilot probably checking his coordinates to assure himself that this dark area was indeed the right field. It circled once more, dipping low enough to make out whatever figures might be below, if there were any.

By this time Lise was sprinting back toward the runway. Suddenly Logan's numbed mind snapped back into action. That plane represented Nat's only hope! It might circle one more time, but then it would take the lack of activity as a sign that the mission had been scrubbed. They had to signal the pilot.

"René," said Logan hurriedly, "run on ahead to the field and help Lise signal the plane."

"There may be a Boche patrol out there, fool!" said Claude. "We must let the plane go!"

"I don't care if the entire Wehrmacht is out there!" cried Logan "Go, René—now! You too, Claude."

Perhaps in his weakened condition Claude had no more heart to argue. Perhaps the thought of Logan in the hands of the Boche again wasn't such a bad idea after all. Whatever the case, he trotted off as quickly as he could.

By now Lise was almost back to the strip, but she still did not know if it would be safe to light the lamps.

Logan picked up Nat, carrying him in both arms, and, staggering under the weight, continued on one slow step at a time.

"Logan," Nat breathed, his voice barely audible, thin and pale. "We've got to stop . . . the pain—"

"It's not far, Nat! Can you hear the plane?"

"I'm na goin' to make the plane—Logan—got to rest—"

"No," said Logan. "We'll make it!"

He quickened his pace only to stumble over an exposed root. He crumpled to his knees, easing Nat as gently to the ground as he could. Immediately he got his arms around Nat's shoulders and under his knees and tried again to stand, though his own strength was all but spent.

"Please, Logan . . . rest . . ."

"You're almost home, Nat. Just a bit farther."

"I'm on my way home, Logan, but na to Stonewycke."

"You can't die, Nat! Hang on!"

"I love ye, Logan! But let me go. 'Tis all right, ye ken . . . I dinna mind sae much as long as I ken ye and dear Allison will be together again."

"We will be, I promise."

"Ye was always a big brother to me—I'm glad it's you that's wi' me noo . . . at the end." He winced sharply in pain, but struggled to go on speaking: "Do ye remember when the old Austin was stalled and ye—?"

But young Nathaniel MacNeil said no more. In the arms of his sister's husband, he calmly slipped away into that rest he longed for, with the smile of a happy memory of their first meeting on his lips.

The moment Claude and René had arrived, Lise had left them to greet the plane and its delivery of the two Gaullist agents. Then she shot off to help Logan in whatever way she might.

Before she had run twenty yards into the darkness, she heard the bitter groan of Logan's voice in the distance, crying his brother-in-law's name. Logan's heartfelt agony and self-recrimination was too keen to accept the reality before him. Neither could he even begin to comprehend the peace on Nat's dying face.

When Lise approached she found Logan hunched over Nat, his body shaking in a convulsion of weeping.

52 ❈ *Duplicity*

NOW IT WAS no longer a game to Logan Macintyre. No more jocular cons. The whole thing had soured, and the business turned dirty.

Lise had seen it coming. Perhaps he had sensed it, too. Now all his reasons for being where he was had faded into reality, and a hollow emptiness settled over both Logan Macintyre and Michel Tanant.

He had always mastered the art of distancing himself from death. Claude and Antoine and others in the underground had done the killing. Nat and Alec and two soldiers in a Vouziers wood faced the bloody battlefields of the war. But now Logan *himself* had tasted the guilt of blood on his own hands. Days later the thought of what he had done turned his stomach. True, he had grabbed the gun and fired out of the sheer instinct for preservation of life—both his and Nat's. But such reasoning could not quell the self-reproach in his heart. It would never erase the horrible picture of the blood-spattered German soldier lying at his feet.

Nor would he ever be able to forget the awful helplessness of holding his dying brother-in-law in his arms.

Lise tried to convince him it wasn't his fault. And of course, it wasn't. But Nat's death had been a truly heroic one—a wounded man, throwing himself at an enemy soldier, saving the life of his brother-in-law, his hero, by taking the fatal bullet in his own chest.

What had he ever done himself that could compare in heroism? Nothing! His life was marked by duplicity and falsehood. His own wife didn't even know where he was, and with her brother dead at his feet, all he could do was load the battered body onto the plane and watch it soar back into the night sky for England.

The facts may not have indicted him. But he could not escape the feeling of culpability. That night in the Vouziers wood had been a night of death, and Logan would never be the same again.

Logan gazed around the crowded cafe where he had just met Paul and passed some messages on to him for Henri. Paul was gone now, and Logan too should be on his way. He had to meet with von Graff in half an hour, and that surely was reason enough to linger. He watched absently as a group of drunken patriots sang *La Marseillaise* in celebration of Bastille Day.

Allons, enfants de la patrie!
    Hark! hark! what myriads bid you rise!
Yours children, wives, and grandsires hoary,
    Behold their tears and hear their cries!

But Logan's patriotic fervor could not be nudged. In the past year he had been in France, he had become as much a Frenchman as any Scot could hope to become. He should feel a pride in thus having united himself with his country's ancient ally. With what pride would not the grand dame of Scottish legend, Mary Queen of Scots, look down on him for his efforts to help the kinsmen of her mother! Now, like so many noble Scotsmen of past times, he had even killed for the glorious cause.

But there was no joy in the heart of Logan Macintyre today. And as he sat listening to the rousing song, all he could think was that those poor blokes were likely to end up in front of a firing squad for their efforts.

Wearily Logan rose. He could not prolong his meeting any longer.

Von Graff wore an unhappy expression, one that seemed to mark his aristocratic features more and more of late.

"You were gone from Paris a whole week!" he stormed.

"My girl wanted a holiday," Logan replied stoically.

"Yet you did not see fit to inform me?"

"I didn't see that it was your business."

"Everything you do is my business!"

Logan shrugged.

Von Graff rose ominously from his chair.

"Anyway," Logan went on defiantly, "I thought we agreed that I would have no watchdogs."

"And I kept our bargain," said the general, sitting back in his chair more composed. "*This* is how I found out."

He held up a document which Logan assumed was his application for travel papers.

He eyed it indifferently.

Von Graff laid down the application, and after studying Logan's expression for a moment, spoke again.

"What's wrong with you, Herr MacVey?" he said in a more sympathetic tone than he had yet used. "Are you growing weary of the double game—mixed loyalties—betraying your own countrymen—all of that? It happens, believe me . . . only too often."

Logan followed von Graff's lead. After all, it was more than half true.

"I think the week in Reims helped," he replied. "Sometimes it's just nice to forget about everything. I guess that's why I went without saying anything."

"There was Resistance activity some forty kilometers from Reims last week."

"Oh?"

"Is that all you have to say?"

"I try not to blow up trains when I'm on holiday."

"It was not a train."

"What then?"

"Nothing was blown up at all, Herr MacVey. I thought you might already know that important fact."

Logan lifted up his eyes to squarely meet von Graff's. "After all these months," he said, "I think I'd be somewhat immune from these tiresome cross-examinations."

"No one is immune," replied von Graff. "Even I must face them."

"You, General?"

"When the Jewish section chief, Herr Eichmann, visited Paris recently, I was hard-pressed to make as good an account of my months here as I would have liked."

"Had you up against the wall, did he?"

"I hoped I might be able to report more significant arrests."

"But at least you didn't have as many *significant* escapes," said Logan optimistically. "You must admit I've done that much for you."

"Perhaps. But the escapes *do* go on, and L'Escroc remains unapprehended."

"L'Escroc has been lying low lately."

"True, but by now I had hoped to see more results from your operations."

"I've set you up with several ideal opportunities," parried Logan. "Can I be blamed if your strong-arm boys haven't kept up their end?"

"All right, MacVey, no blame is laid," conceded the general. "But tomorrow night we may all have a chance to reprieve ourselves."

"A new assault against Free France, eh?"

"Not exactly. A new thrust which Hitler apparently feels is equally important to the subduing of resistant regimes: there is to be a raid on Parisian Jews. Some thirty thousand are scheduled for arrest."

"Thirty thousand Jews!" exclaimed Logan in unmasked shock.

"It's all part of Herr Eichmann's Final Solution. It should come as no surprise really. Berlin's racial loyalties, shall we say, are well known. It would come as no surprise to me if this is merely the beginning."

"Such an action will play havoc with the terms of the Armistice," said Logan. "The Führer will lose much support."

"The Armistice is a sham and always has been. Even Pétain knows that. As far as the Führer's popularity goes—I doubt it will suffer much. He's never been popular with the Jews anyway."

Herr von Graff attempted a chuckle, but even he was capable of realizing how inept humor seemed at that moment. "Besides," he went on, "the French police will conduct the raid—no German soldiers will be involved at all."

"So why are you telling me all this?"

"I want you on your toes," replied von Graff. "An event of this magnitude is likely to bring the underground out in droves—especially its leaders. We could make quite a score in addition to the Jewish scenario—perhaps even L'Escroc will show his face."

"Shall I dangle this information about today, and see if I get any bites . . . stir up the pot, so to speak?" Logan knew he would have to warn the underground of the raid; he hoped with von Graff's affirmative answer to be able to protect his Trinity cover at the same time.

"We prefer the utmost security," replied von Graff. "However, we know there has already been some leaking. Not enough to endanger the scheme, however."

"No mass exodus of Jews?"

"Where would they go? Most are marked well enough by their foreign accents and identification papers. All the railroad stations and exits from the city are being stringently watched. And the punishment for getting picked up with false papers is far worse than the prospect of a labor camp."

"That's where they will be sent, then?"

"That is my assumption. What else would they do with them?"

"But I cannot imagine facilities large enough for such an army of prisoners."

"No matter. What happens to them after the raid is not our concern, now is it?"

53 ✖ Vouziers Once More

THE FINE SUMMER day gleaming over the Vouziers countryside went unnoticed by Arnaud Soustelle.

He had not come here on holiday as Trinity had claimed so convincingly to General von Graff. The general was a fool, for some idiotic reason mesmerized by the smooth-talking Anglais.

Soustelle, however, was neither mesmerized nor convinced. He did not like his influence being usurped and was determined to rectify the situation. He had argued stoutly against the chances of such a coincidence occurring. But von Graff insisted on believing his double agent. Perhaps von Graff has come to the point of being forced to support MacVey, thought Soustelle. If Trinity turns out to be counterfeit, it will reflect very poorly on the S.S. General who recruited him, especially at the very time his fortunes were sagging on other fronts. Nonetheless, Soustelle was going to bring down Trinity, even if it meant taking von Graff with him.

"Stay away from him, Soustelle," von Graff had warned. "Don't let that calm exterior deceive you. MacVey is nobody's patsy!"

"Bah!" replied the Frenchman. "You think I fear such a snail!"

"I doubt you have the senses to fear him," answered the general. "I'm simply telling you that if you insist on carrying on this petty little rivalry, I cannot help it if you bring trouble upon your own head."

"I will do what suits me, and even you cannot stop me, General!" sneered Soustelle.

Von Graff smiled. "Do not tempt me, Soustelle," he said, evidently pleased at the thought of Soustelle crossing the line and going a step too far.

Soustelle said nothing further, only turned and left the general's office, more resolute than ever.

Thus it was, now knowing the content of the conversation between the general and the Anglais, that Soustelle had taken the next early morning express to Reims—a quicker ride than Logan had enjoyed. Working a couple of local connections, he had been led to a certain bakery which, hardly a surprise to Soustelle, turned out to be a cog in the Resistance network. Three agents had been arrested and interrogated. No telling what gems would be dragged from those three before they were finally shot, thought Soustelle with grim pleasure. He had walked away from the interrogation proceedings, leaving the rest of the questioning in the hands of the local Gestapo chief the moment the first important bit of information had been obtained. A bakery van had been taken to Vouziers.

The pieces were fitting together nicely. MacVey goes to Reims, supposedly on holiday. Then, what do you know? A Resistance van departs to Vouziers, only a few kilometers from the underground operation that had taken place in the area. Soustelle wanted to know: who was driving that van? He could have hung around Reims until the information was forced out of one of the captured agents. But that could take days. Vouziers was a small enough village; it would be a simple matter to circulate a description of MacVey about.

Soustelle glanced at his watch as he bounced along the back road in a commandeered Gestapo automobile. He'd drive back to Paris after he had finished in Vouziers; he'd be there some time tonight.

"Ha! ha!" he said almost merrily. "Before tomorrow I will have Trinity in irons!"

He had already decided to gather his evidence and grab Trinity before saying a word to von Graff. He would handle the whole thing on his own, except perhaps for a few well-placed Gestapo agents to make sure he didn't slip away from him. But he wouldn't chance the stupidity of others to foul his coup. Besides, if he nabbed MacVey himself, it would give him time to rough up that pretty face a little before having to turn him in. Above all, he didn't want to allow that Anglais-loving Nazi von Graff to take the glory for himself of exposing Trinity for the traitor Soustelle knew him to be.

Soustelle popped a licorice drop into his mouth, revelling in fantasies of his great victory.

He turned into the town. His first stop would be the French police inspector. He happened to know him from his own days as a gendarme—a fat, lazy excuse for authority. But he could be easily bought.

54 ✖ On the Scent

IT WAS AFTER ten p.m. when Soustelle arrived back in Paris from his successful foray to Vouziers. The drive had been wearing, but he wasn't about to pause in the hunt, not when he was so close.

Lawrence MacVey had indeed been to Vouziers, not only in the company of a woman but also with a sinister-looking man, so he had gathered from a number of interviews. As far as the ex-policeman was concerned, *that* was plenty to accuse him of his double game. But he was prepared should von Graff insist on even more evidence. There were a couple of low-lifes in the town whom he had paid handsomely to swear they had seen MacVey in the vicinity of the abandoned airport where a British plane was reported to have landed at the time when MacVey had been around. Soustelle knew the Anglais was guilty, no matter what the soft-bellied general said. If he had to manufacture a few facts to support it, then so be it.

Unfortunately his successes had come to an abrupt end the moment he entered Paris. He'd driven directly to MacVey's apartment, but the scoundrel wasn't there. Then had begun several more hours of wearisome detective work in an attempt to track the traitor down, but to little avail. He'd gone to the cafe he knew to be a favorite with Trinity. He'd rousted several persons out of bed for questioning. He had canvassed the neighborhood. He came back to the apartment, picked the lock, gave the place a thorough search, but saw that the British agent was extremely careful—the rooms were spotlessly clean, except for a book of matches from one of the many Left Bank cafes. He tried that cafe, hung around till it closed, questioned the employees, but learning nothing more than what he had already been told: MacVey had been seen two or three times in the company of the same woman.

At length, before departing to follow a new tack, Soustelle called in a couple of S.D. agents particularly loyal to him, whose silence he knew he could trust. He picked them up, drove them to the apartment, stationed them across the street to watch the building, then ran inside and up the stairs one more time himself. In several moments he emerged back onto the street, crossing it slowly to his cronies.

"Still no sign of him," he said. "He must be beyond worrying about curfew. It's almost two a.m."

"What do you want us to do if he comes, Herr Soustelle?" asked one of the men.

"Make sure he stays inside. Don't apprehend him unless he tries to leave again. If he goes in, lay low and wait for me. This traitor is mine! If he tries to go out again, nab him. But don't hurt so much as a hair of his head. That pleasure, too, will be mine!"

"You will be back soon?"

"I don't know. You just watch the building and wait. I have one other lead to try."

With that Soustelle turned away and walked down the street quickly into the Paris night. This Trinity, whoever he really was, had proved more slippery than he had anticipated. But if he was not home yet, there could be but one other place he was spending the night. It now seemed this woman with whom he had been seen so often might be his only lead. He knew well enough where to find her. He should have gone straight there in the first place! Where else could the fool MacVey be?

Lise had left Logan and returned to her apartment just before midnight. She and Logan and Antoine had spent the entire day spreading the alarm about the coming roundup of Jews, as quickly yet discreetly as possible, so as not to endanger Logan's cover.

She would still be about that business had not Michel insisted she return to the safety of her home. There was no telling what might befall a Jewish girl on the streets that night.

She lay down on her bed, not intending to sleep. She had not even changed her clothes. She had worked hard knocking on doors, passing along secret messages, warning of the raid. She only hoped no Nazi agents had seen their activities. It wouldn't take much for them to put two and two together, she thought. Her association with Michel was well known. Yet there was a time to cast caution to the wind. And tonight, with thousands of Jewish lives in the balance, seemed like just such a time.

Reflecting on the day's events, Lise fell into a deep sleep.

Some hours later, she was suddenly awakened by a sharp sound. She started up, glanced quickly about, and tried to collect her wits.

It was still dark. All was quiet. It must still be the middle of the night.

She had been dreaming vaguely of gendarmes pounding on Jewish doors, dragging them off to violent deaths. Slowly she lay back down, breathing heavily and perspiring freely.

There came the pounding again! This time it was no dream! Someone was beating on *her* door, and the angry yells that accompanied it did not sound friendly. Even with all her precautions, was *she* going to be raided and hauled off to Germany?

Shaking with fear, she jerked up again and leaped from her bed. Flight would be foolish. She would have to confront them, whoever it was.

She threw a bathrobe over her clothes as a precaution, so as not to look like she had been out, then crept to the front room. Desperately she tried to shake off the remnants of sleep and organize her mind. The knock was not one of the prearranged Resistance signals. It could be no friend. Even as she realized it could be only the Gestapo or the French police, she tried to gain confidence thinking how Michel, with his bravado, would handle the situation. "There's always an angle," he would say.

She switched on a light, then turned the deadbolt and opened the door, squinting sleepily.

"What is it?" she said in a thick, sluggish voice not too difficult to assume at that hour.

"You are Claire Giraud?"

"Yes, I am," she answered. The name was an alias she had used to rent the apartment.

The man who spoke seemed vaguely familiar to her, a Frenchman to be sure, judging by his lack of accent. He was a large, barrel-chested man with a strange odor hanging about him that she could not immediately place. He was not Gestapo, but there was something about him . . .

Then she remembered. Arnaud Soustelle.

"You are acquainted with Michel Tanant?" he demanded rather than asked.

"I—" She rubbed her eyes groggily. "It's so late. What is going on?"

"Do not play games with me, Mademoiselle! I know you are his woman!"

"Is he all right?" she asked. It would have been futile to deny knowing him.

"Quit stalling!" barked Soustelle. "Tell me where he is!"

"I don't know. Has there been an accident?"

Without answering, Soustelle shoved her aside and stalked into the apartment. Roughly pulling apart drapes, throwing aside bedcovers, and flinging open closet doors, he made a hasty search of the three small rooms. Then he turned on Lise again.

"The man is an enemy agent!" he spat. "Though I have few doubts that piece of information is news to you! And he will be captured . . . tonight! If you do not want to join him, you better tell me where to find him! "

"An agent? What can you mean?"

"Bah! You are a fool for protecting him!"

"I can't believe it. He told me—"

"Where is he?" yelled Soustelle, losing his grip on what little patience he still possessed.

"I—I assume he is at home in bed, where every sane person ought to be at such an hour."

"Tanant is neither at home in bed, nor is he a sane man for attempting his dirty double-cross."

"This is all such a shock," said Lise in a trembly voice. She ran a frustrated hand through her hair. "I just don't know anything."

"You *must* know that Tanant is not his real name!"

"I thought he was—"

"Thought he was what?" interrupted Soustelle.

"He told me he was from Lyon," said Lise, praying it was the same story Michel had told the Germans. "He said he was a bookseller."

Soustelle eyed her thoughtfully for a moment.

"I wonder . . ." he mused. Then in a sudden, lightning-quick move, he grabbed Lise by the arm and spun her around so that the arm twisted up painfully behind her back. The act caught her completely by surprise and she gasped in genuine pain.

"I could force the information from you, you know!"

"P—please," sputtered Lise. "We've gone out a few times—I know nothing *about* him. A few cafes, that's all. You must believe me."

"Which cafes?" She gave him two names, neither of which she or Michel had ever been to.

"Who are his friends?"

"I know none of them."

Soustelle gave her arm a cruel jerk.

"Don't you think I would tell you? It was always just he and I—alone. I thought maybe he was married, and so kept our relationship very discreet. Please! I am telling the truth." Real tears flowed from her eyes. But the act did not seem to move Soustelle.

The Frenchman ruminated a moment over her words, then loosened his grip. But before letting go completely, he gave her a harsh shove and she crumpled to the floor.

"You are lying!" he sneered. "I can smell the deceit in every word! And do not think you will escape! I will be back when I have time, and will take more thorough steps to extract the information from you!"

Soustelle spun around and stomped away. Lise remained a moment longer where she sat on the floor, still stunned that he had left without arresting her.

But there was no time to spend enjoying her momentary triumph.

She had to warn Michel!

Yet, how could she? She had no more idea where he was than Soustelle did! But she had to do something!

In a sudden moment of resolve, Lise jumped from the floor, grabbed her coat and put it on in place of the robe, paused another minute to take her revolver out of hiding, dropped it into her handbag, and flew for the door. If she couldn't locate Michel to warn him, she at least had to keep an eye on Soustelle. If Michel had been found out, everything could tumble down. She had to keep the Frenchman away from him!

As she exited her building, Lise caught a fading glimpse of Soustelle's black Renault rounding a corner in the distance. She jumped on her bicycle and hurried in pursuit in that direction. It was going to be difficult keeping him in sight. She would have to stay in the shadows and watch her every move. Not only was it well beyond curfew, but of all nights, this was not a safe one for a Jew to be abroad in the streets of Paris.

55 ※ *"La Grande Rafle"*

AT THREE A.M., July 16, 1942, nine thousand French policemen were dispatched to conduct the Great Raid.

Truckloads of police roared onto the rue Vieille du Temple and other Jewish districts of Paris. They poured through the narrow streets and stormed the buildings, where, inside, their terrified, helpless victims crouched in dread.

Thousands had been able to heed the warnings tirelessly spread by the underground, but many simply had not the means or the strength or the capacity to believe that such a horror was possible.

Many men fled, leaving wives and children behind, believing they would be spared as they had always been in the past. But the gendarmes beat down doors and dragged them out—not only the men they could find, but women and children also. One frenzied Jewess, clutching her infant child in her arms, leaped from her upper-story window, carrying them both to their deaths on the street below rather than face what she now realized must be their only alternative.

It was a new reign of terror in Paris, and somehow as Logan trudged down a darkened back street with Antoine, he could not find much solace in reminding himself of the thousands that had been saved. Later, when he saw the statistics on von Graff's desk, he would know the bold facts: almost thirteen thousand Jews would be arrested before this Nazi operation was over, with over four thousand of that number children.

But on that sultry summer night, his eyes saw what no statistics could tell. Hundreds of human beings were prodded like cattle down the street before him, some with suitcases or hastily assembled bundles of their meager belongings.

At one point as Logan watched from the shadows, a woman struggling with three children and two clumsy bundles, shuffled past. One of the children stumbled over a loose brick in the sidewalk, and, skinning his hands and knees, cried out to his mother. Instinctively Logan began to step forward to help, but Antoine grabbed his arm and yanked him back.

"Don't be foolish," hissed the Frenchman.

Logan wrenched his arm from Antoine's grasp, but it was too late. A gendarme had grabbed up the child and shoved him toward his mother.

"Keep moving!" he shouted, jabbing each of them in the back with the butt of his rifle.

The sad parade continued past. Neither Logan nor Antoine moved, for they both realized they could do no more. Why they even stayed, watching the procession well beyond the curfew as it was, they could not tell. Perhaps their utter feeling of emotional helplessness had made their legs unable to move also. Perhaps because something deep inside them hoped that the impression of such a sight into the hearts and minds of sane men might prevent it from ever happening again.

In another few minutes an aged rabbi hobbled by, a prayer shawl peeking out from beneath his drab coat, his white sidelocks dripping with perspiration from the intense strain of this late night ordeal. Sewed to the front of his coat was the yellow star all French Jews had recently been forced to wear. But above the star, he had defiantly pinned his Croix de Guerre and Legion d'Honneur medals—a hero of France marching in disgrace, herded aboard a truck like a sheep to the slaughter.

Logan watched, feeling the shame any sensitive man must certainly feel at such a sight. But before he had a chance to reflect on the plight of the old rabbi further, at his side Logan heard a strangled cry. He looked around and saw that Antoine's face was twisted with agony from the sight. Tears coursed down his cheeks.

"Mon Dieu!" he breathed, his hands clenched into fists at his side.

The old Jew heard Antoine's words and paused, looking directly at the two Resistance men. His penetrating gaze, to their surprise, was not one that spoke of defeat, but rather was filled with pride, and even displayed a courageous attempt to comfort his countrymen.

"Hear, O Israel, the Lord our God, the Lord is One" was all he could say before he shuffled off with his people.

Antoine started forward out of the shadows. Now it was Logan's turn to restrain his friend.

"What are you doing?" asked Logan.

"Going with my people," replied Antoine.

"Your people?"

"That's right . . . I qualify as one of them," he returned bitterly.

"What?" said Logan in alarm.

"I have a great-grandfather, though always it was hidden because we were good Catholics."

"Antoine, I can understand this must be hard for you. But you cannot do what you are thinking."

The Frenchman's sole response was to take another step forward.

"We need you, Antoine!" Logan called desperately.

He turned his large, shaggy head around. "I think perhaps now is a time when they need me more," he said. "Who knows, maybe I can do some good there." He turned back around and stepped out in line with the slow procession.

Logan said nothing further.

Perhaps Antoine was right. What might not the vibrant, passionate patriot be able to accomplish among these Jews just now to hearten them, perhaps even somehow to help deliver them? He watched as Antoine picked up two struggling children in his strong arms. No, Logan could not stop him, despite the emptiness he felt inside at the loss of his friend.

As soon as this group was past and no more gendarmes were in sight, Logan turned and walked out of his hiding place and in the opposite direction into the night.

Antoine seemed to have found his way—his special path, as had Jean Pierre. Logan wondered if he would ever find his. Tonight he had helped to save many lives, yet he could still not feel the satisfaction that should have come had what he was doing been right—truly *right*—for him. He had even ceased to have that tingling sense of exhilaration he had always experienced before. He was like a dead man—no past, no present, no future, no sense of who he was or who he ought to be.

But his thoughts were interrupted, as they often were these days, the next instant. At the end of the street he spotted a gendarme. Quickly he sprang into the cover of a dark building. His heart pounded and his body pulsed with the overpowering instinct of survival. No matter what his head tried to tell him, his emotions were *not* dead. Something was keeping him from complete despair, stubbornly stirring the embers of life inside him. He *wanted* to live. *Is it possible,* he wondered, the thought flashing through his brain in the very moment of his fear, *that even though I have gone my own way, God has kept His tether tenaciously around me—this far from home, this far from my past life? Is God still there, still loving me as I felt ten years ago?*

Back then life had seemed simple enough. He was a one-dimensional being. Now it had all grown so complicated. His wife . . . his daughter . . . this horrible war! Back then it had been relatively easy to say *yes* to God. But through the years it had proved more and more difficult to bring God into the daily struggles of life. And now . . . ? Now suddenly it seemed that so much time had passed . . . and gradually his life with God had evaporated as if it were only a distant memory. He felt as if he were a prisoner of events, herded along just like the poor Jews he had tried to save. He too was being prodded and pushed by circumstances and times and people outside his control, toward an unknown and fearsome future. For him, as for the Jews, there seemed to be no way out. What could he do to change it? People depended on him. He had cut the bonds to the past.

Yet . . . was he truly being pushed against his will? No. He was not like the Jews. *They* were victims; he was not. He had created his own prison—his own death camp. He could not blame the war, he could not blame Allison, he could not blame God. He knew there was only one person to blame.

The gendarme passed.

Logan had several more blocks to go before he was out of the Jewish district. His need to be especially vigilant forced his probing thoughts once more into abeyance. For the moment he must concentrate on getting home, where he would then be safe to explore the paths of his frustrated mind. By now, however, he had learned that self-examination could sometimes be no less perilous than walking the dangerous streets of Nazi-occupied Paris.

Once he had distanced himself from the Jewish sections of the city, Logan encountered no obstacles as he made his way through the deep, moonless, quiet night. Everything around him was still, even peaceful. There was, however, an eerie aspect with which the tall stone buildings were clothed. The city itself seemed to take on a sinister feel when Logan reminded himself of the awful and cruel upheaval to so many lives occurring only a kilometer or two away.

But in less than fifteen minutes Logan turned onto his own street. Soon he would be safely home, where he could rest his weary body and tormented mind.

56 ✠ *In for the Kill*

BREATHLESSLY LISE STOPPED short at the end of the street.

She had managed to catch up with Soustelle after leaving her place, but in the dark, both staying with him and avoiding his detection was not easy. It did not take long for her to realize that he was heading directly for Michel's. She would literally have had to fly in order to outdistance the ill-intentioned Frenchman and warn Michel before his arrival, even taking paths his auto could not traverse. So she contented herself to follow as closely as she dared. She only hoped some way help would present itself. Now she was almost to Michel's apartment.

Soustelle braked his Renault and stepped out. Lise could proceed no farther because her prey had not gone directly to the building. Instead, he had crossed the street and was now conferring with two agents—either Gestapo or S.D., she couldn't tell from where she stood—who had been hiding in the shadows directly across from the building. Soustelle was not in this alone; the suspicions must be more widespread than she thought if they had the whole place under surveillance!

Lise waited where she was and watched.

After his brief conversation with his comrades, the French detective turned toward the building. Michel cannot possibly have returned by now! she thought. In desperation she had phoned him ten minutes ago, nearly losing Soustelle as she had paused at a phone booth. But by then she had been sure of his destination and decided to risk the delay. In any case, there had been no answer. What was Soustelle up to? Did he plan to wait for Michel inside the building?

While she was puzzling over what to do, suddenly Lise saw Logan approaching from the opposite end of the street. He was already closer to the building than she, unaware of the two agents watching opposite, who had ducked out of sight at his approach. Lise couldn't call out a warning now without alerting the enemy too, and there was no telling how many agents Soustelle had posted about the place.

She had to warn Michel of the trap awaiting him!

While the watching agents were hidden, Lise, now on foot, darted across to the same side of the street as the apartment, edged her way closer, trying to keep out of view. By now Logan had already entered the building.

Lise hastily scrambled her way around a corner and to an alleyway she knew. There was only one thing for her to do now—she had to try to get to Michel *inside* the building, and before Soustelle got his hands on him. If only she wasn't already too late!

Once out of sight from the front, Lise tore down the alley and to a side entrance to the building she and Michel had used several times. Once inside she quietly ran along the corridor to the main staircase, turned, and sneaked hurriedly up the stairs toward Michel's apartment.

Logan's senses were keenly enough honed that he should have sensed his danger, even if his eyes did not *see* it.

But it was four in the morning, and he had been on his feet for twenty-four hours. All he could think of was a hot bath and a few hours sleep.

He turned in to his building, unconscious of all the eyes upon him, and trudged up the stairs to his second floor flat.

He unlocked his door, pushed it open, and entered.

Suddenly his dull senses sprang to life. A faint whiff of something lingered in the thick, dark air . . . a strange odor he had noticed on one or two other occasions. Where had he been when he had detected it before? Hadn't it been when he and von Graff—

But the moment Logan remembered, and thus recognized his danger, it was too late.

Licorice!

In the very instant of the realization, suddenly the large hands of Arnaud Soustelle grabbed him from behind, wrapping a vise-grip around his shoulders and neck.

"So, Anglais!" he growled menacingly. "We meet again! But this time it is I who seem to have the advantage."

Logan struggled to free himself, but he was no match for the overpowering bulk and street-trained skill of the Frenchman. Soustelle laughed scornfully at the attempt, then threw him crashing up against an adjacent wall, twisting Logan's arm up mercilessly behind him. The moment Logan felt the cold steel of a blade against his throat, he ceased his writhing to get loose.

"I would like to save you for the Gestapo," rasped Soustelle, panting from the effort of his attack on Logan, "but it would grieve me not the least to slit your throat here and now!"

"What do you have against me?" asked Logan, his voice choking from one of Soustelle's muscular arms.

"Nothing I do not share against all Englishmen!" replied Soustelle, hatred oozing from his tone.

"I thought we were on the same side, Soustelle!" said Logan, though all his instincts told him the charade was over.

"I know all about you, MacVey, or Tanant, or Trinity, or whatever your name might be."

"I don't know what you're talking about."

"It's all over, don't you understand? I know you are a British agent!"

"Even von Graff knows that! Why do you think I'm so useful to him?"

"You are through playing games with me!" sneered Soustelle. "It's over, I tell you. You're *still* a British agent, through and through. And I think I can also prove that you are L'Escroc."

"That's absurd, Soustelle! Wait till I tell von Graff that you—"

The Frenchman pressed the knife against Logan's skin. "Shut up, you miserable Anglais! You may swindle the stupid Germans, but the game is up with me. Perhaps you would like to confess now, and save us the trouble of interrogation, eh?"

Even as he spoke, Soustelle began to drag Logan toward the door of the apartment and onto the landing. Once there, he didn't much care whether the Anglais went voluntarily or if he had to kick him tumbling down the stairs. He had him now!

"So, how did von Graff find out?" asked Logan, trying to buy time.

"Von Graff, bah!" spat Soustelle as he kicked open the apartment door and began dragging Logan toward the head of the stairway about ten feet away. "As far as that witless Nazi is concerned, you are still his little pet!"

"Well, I'm impressed, Soustelle," taunted Logan. "I never thought you had it in you."

"Why you filthy—!" Soustelle raised his knife ominously into the air. "I'll kill you now—"

All at once a shot rang through the quiet corridor.

The first thought that raced through Logan's bewildered brain was that the Frenchman must have an accomplice. Then the heavy body of his attacker slumped, and he felt the grip of his arms loosen before the ponderous heft of the ex-detective collapsed lifelessly to the floor.

The next instant, before he had a chance to collect his wits, the door below burst open and the building was filled with shouting German voices.

"The shot came from upstairs!"

"Follow me!"

"Two of you, around back!"

Logan had no time to think. He could only react as the sounds of booted feet clamored onto the stairs and toward him.

He ran hastily back into his apartment, pausing only long enough to bolt the door. Then he turned, ran to his window, and climbed out onto the fire escape.

He could hear shouts and attempts to break in the door as he scrambled down, leaping to the hard cobbles only a moment before the Gestapo agents reached the alley.

Meanwhile, upstairs two other agents bent over Soustelle's body, one pressing two fingers against the dead man's carotid artery. He looked up and shook his head.

"What was the fool up to anyway?" he said, "coming in here by himself?"

"He probably didn't think the suspect would resist," answered the other.

"More likely he overestimated his own skill."

"Wouldn't be the first time."

"And now he has a bullet in his back for his foolhardy independence."

"What was he after, anyway?"

"He said nothing to me. Just wanted us to watch the building."

"I'll find a telephone; you see how the others are doing."

While both men exited and walked back into the street, a slim figure stirred from a dark recessed corner of the upper corridor.

Still trembling, she rose, dropped the warm revolver into her handbag and crept from her hiding place. She stole to the landing, stepped over the massive body, and tiptoed down the stairway, now deathly silent.

She tried not to think of what had just happened. Like Logan, before this moment she had never killed. But though she felt the same revulsion at taking another's life, Lise experienced no tormenting self-recrimination.

There would be no regrets for her. She had done what she had done for a worthy cause. And she had saved the life of the man she now knew she cared more about than anyone she had ever met.

57 ❊ Outbursts

AT SIX A.M. Logan stormed into von Graff's office.

Even at that early hour, the general was in, awaiting preliminary reports on the progression of the raid.

"I'll tell him you are here, Herr Dansette—" said his secretary, who had also been pressed into early service.

But Logan did not give her the chance. He rushed past her desk and burst into the inner room where the general sat. The moment he had fled his apartment, he had realized there would be but one way to save his neck and keep his position with the Nazis secure. He had to take a strong initiative, act as the aggressor, and never give von Graff the opportunity to form any conclusions of his own.

"What is the meaning of this, MacVey?" said the general, not a little taken aback by the rash intrusion, not to mention Logan's wild and disheveled appearance.

"I am the one to be asking *that* question, General!" Logan shot back.

"I'm afraid I do not understand you."

"I've had it with you, von Graff!" shouted Logan.

"Please, calm yourself," replied the general, a little alarmed. He rose from his desk and hurriedly closed the door to his office. "What can be so wrong to have upset you like this?"

"We had a deal, and you reneged!" exclaimed Logan, turning on the general with a look of vengeance.

"Sit down and collect yourself," ordered the general calmly. "I don't know what you are talking about, but I'm sure we can—"

"I told you what would happen if you had me followed—and I was nearly killed!"

"Sit down," repeated the general. He then took his own seat, glad to have his desk to serve as a barrier between himself and this wild man.

Logan complied with his order, but he remained on the edge of his chair, still fuming.

"But it looks as if the only one dead is Soustelle," continued von Graff calmly.

So, thought Logan to himself, the general knows everything already. It was indeed a good thing he had played this little rant-and-rave routine rather than trying to play dumb.

"He's dead, then?"

"Come now, MacVey . . . are you trying to tell me you *didn't* know?"

"I thought as much, but couldn't be sure."

"The word that came to me two hours ago was that *you* killed him."

"*Me!* That's ridiculous!"

"Tell me what happened."

"I'm not even sure myself," answered Logan, making an apparent effort to control his ire. "Soustelle attacked me at the door to my place, pulled a knife on me, started making all kinds of wild accusations. Then suddenly a shot fired out of nowhere and Soustelle fell. I figured someone in the Resistance may have seen us and was trying to get me, or maybe both of us."

"So, did you see who fired the shot?"

"Are you kidding? I got out of there!"

"You ran, MacVey?" said the general with a smile. "Hardly sounds like the daring courage of a double agent."

"For all I knew a second shot meant for me would follow on the heels of the first. And in two seconds the place was crawling with blokes—Gestapo or Resistance, who knows? I didn't wait to find out!"

"What's important is that you are still alive."

"No!" exploded Logan, playing his hand out to the full. "What's important is that you went back on your word. You knew Soustelle well enough, didn't you?"

"I knew about his crazy suspicions," admitted von Graff. "But I warned him not to follow you. What more could I do?"

"You could have warned *me!*"

"You were not to be reached—and by the way, what were you doing out at such an hour?"

"You told me to keep my eyes and ears open last night. I just hope this little fiasco hasn't jeopardized my place in the Resistance."

"Might it?"

"Soustelle had a knife to my throat," said Logan, "and the killer may have seen that. Since that's hardly the act of a compatriot, perhaps my cover is still intact."

"Good," said von Graff optimistically. "I would hate for an otherwise successful day to be spoiled."

"Then the raid turned out well?" Logan only barely managed to keep the distress from his voice.

"It's too soon to tell for certain. Many have escaped, of that I am sure. But the successes I mentioned come from a slightly different quarter than the raid itself."

"Oh?"

"Three underground safe houses were raided last night."

"And everyone taken?"

"Yes. Besides the Jews they were harboring, we arrested eight Resistants—probably not the big fish I should like, but arrests are arrests. It'll make my report look good, and who knows what our interrogators will get out of them. We may get a lead on L'Escroc!"

"Very good!" was all Logan could force himself to say. Inside his heart ached, wondering who had been arrested, fearing for his friends.

58 ❊ Sacrifices

LA *LIBRAIRIE* MET LATER that same afternoon.

For security reasons they made use of the offices of Dr. Jacques Tournoux, a sympathizer who offered his rooms on occasion when the group needed greater precaution. It did not arouse suspicion for an unusual mix of men and women to come and go from a doctor's office.

The doctor ushered each one of them in turn from the reception areas and to a private room on the second floor. Then he left them alone. Logan arrived late, for he had taken extra pains to insure he was not followed. The only others present were Henri, Lise, and Claude.

"Where's Jean Pierre?" asked Logan, a gnawing fear suddenly coming into his mind.

"He's been arrested," answered Henri bleakly.

"Who else?"

"We have heard nothing from Antoine."

"He's been arrested as well," said Logan. "That is, he voluntarily went with the Jews. He thought he could help them—I don't know, maybe he can."

"Then we are all that is left."

"I'll get Jean Pierre out," declared Logan flatly.

"But," said Henri, his cherubic face grim and taut, "we must prepare for the worst."

"Jean Pierre will never talk!" exclaimed Lise.

"Nevertheless, we must all relocate and change our names."

"Whether L'Escroc does it, or Trinity," said Logan, "I'm going to get him out tonight."

A silence enveloped the group for several moments as they tried to absorb the stunning blow that had struck them. Such things were to be expected. But it was made all the more difficult when it happened to good men like the faithful Antoine and dear Jean Pierre. Both had provided a kind of stability to *La Librairie* that only the spirits of those remaining could bear witness to.

Claude at last broke the silence. "At least we have lost a dangerous enemy," he announced. "Arnaud Soustelle was killed this morning."

Then he leveled his dark gaze on Logan. "But perhaps you were planning to tell us all about that, Anglais?"

"Funny, Claude," rejoined Logan. "I was going to ask you the same question."

"Ha! I only wish it *had* been my bullet to cut him down!"

"What happened, Michel?" asked Henri.

Logan proceeded to tell about his run-in with Soustelle. "I never saw who did the shooting," he finished. "I'm still not sure whether the slug was meant for him or me."

"But he admitted he knew all about you," said Claude.

"Yes," sighed Logan, "but I'm sure he hadn't told anyone. I think the scoundrel was afraid to blow the whistle until he had positive proof. Von Graff has too much invested in me to be easily convinced. I've already seen him and cleared myself."

"Very convenient!" mumbled Claude darkly.

"Quiet, Claude!" snapped Henri. "There will be none of that—not now!"

Claude slumped back in his chair and said nothing more.

"I wonder who did it," mused Henri, "and why? Of course a man like Soustelle would have no dearth of enemies—"

"Who cares!" cut in Lise, with more emotion than seemed necessary. "The vermin is dead—another enemy is destroyed! Who cares why or how? We are rid of him, that's all that matters!"

For a moment no one said anything, unable to respond to the uncharacteristic outburst. Then Henri's concern showed through.

"Lise . . . what is it? Are you all right?"

"No! I'm not—I will never be right again!"

With the words she jumped up and fled the room.

Logan and Henri exchanged puzzled glances, then Logan rose and went after her. She had only gone to the end of the hall, where she now stood in a small windowed alcove of the bay window overlooking the pleasant street where Dr. Tournoux's office was located.

Lise was gazing out, though she hardly even noticed the lovely summer scene below. When she heard the footsteps approaching behind her, she did not turn. But she knew it was Michel. As much as she longed to be near him, she was also afraid to face him.

She had already decided not to tell him what she had done. She was a killer now. She knew how distasteful violence was to him, despite what had occurred in Vouziers. He could not help but look on her differently now. If she had secretly hoped for love, she knew now it could never come about between them.

Neither could she tell him what had happened in order to win his gratitude. Her very act of supreme loyalty might well win his love, or else foster a sense of obligation that might be confused with love.

But she could not have his love that way—she could not have it anyway. That was clear now.

Perhaps it might have been possible with Michel Tanant. But never with Logan Macintyre, the man that still dwelt within him—the man who, in what seemed an altogether foreign world, another lifetime from this, had a child, a wife.

She could not turn and face him. She could not look into those eyes so filled with vitality and sensitivity.

"Lise . . . what's troubling you?" he asked quietly.

"Nothing." Her voice was as thin and empty as her lame response.

"You're concerned about Jean Pierre?"

"Yes . . . that's it."

He sat down on the window seat next to where she stood.

"He'll be fine," he assured her. "I'm going to see to it."

"I believe you, Michel," she said. "I believe you can do anything you set your mind to."

He shook his head in weary denial.

"It's not true. It never was. Maybe I was lucky. But no—it wasn't even that. For some reason, God seems to have been with me. I still can't figure why He bothers. I suppose it won't be long before He realizes I'm a lost cause."

"No, Michel. *That's* what is not true. God must not give up because He sees your heart. It is a good heart. It is only a little mixed up right now. But *you* are a good man." She sat down, and finally faced him.

"A little mixed up—that is an understatement." He rubbed his hands despairingly across his face.

Lise looked at him intently. "Someday . . ." she began, then without thinking she reached out and gently touched his cheek.

He laid his hand over hers.

"Oh, Michel," she murmured, "what is to become of us?"

They looked deeply into each other's eyes for what seemed an eternity. Then suddenly Logan squeezed his eyes shut and turned away from her gaze.

"Michel," said Lise quietly, "you know how I feel . . . you know that I—"

He lurched to his feet, as if not wanting to hear what she was about to say, and yet something inside wanting to say the same thing himself.

"Blast this war—this life!" he exclaimed.

"I'm sorry, Michel. I shouldn't have—"

"It's not your fault." But now it was he who could not look at her.

"Don't you see, Lise," he went on after a moment. "I feel the same way. In another time, another place, we might have . . . you must know what I mean. You and I . . . it's there, Lise.

We both know it. But this isn't the real world. This is only a moment of time . . . when our paths chanced to cross, and—"

He stopped, searching for the right words, but knowing there were none.

"This war!" he exclaimed in a moment. "It has robbed me of everything! I've given my identity for it. I've lied for it. Dear Lord, I've even killed for it! There's only one thing I have left, though I'm hardly even sure of that anymore. Oh, Lise! Allison is the only part of who I *really* am that still exists. Sometimes it would be easy to lose myself completely in Michel Tanant, and never go back—"

Now he turned to face her again.

"—so very easy, Lise! But I can't. She is my wife, and if I destroy that, then I've destroyed *everything!*"

"Do you love her, Michel?"

Logan thought for a minute or two.

"Yes . . . yes, I do," he finally replied. "Of course I do."

Even as he spoke Logan realized that Allison was his lifeline, the source of stability which God had provided to see him through this time.

"There has never been a question of loving her," he added. "The problem was inside me— my discontentment was with myself. But never with her. Yes, I love her . . . more than anything."

Though he thought he had left England to run away from her, Logan saw that all the time he had carried her with him, not as some chain of guilt around his neck, but rather as a precious link to who he was. Not only as Logan Macintyre instead of all the other fictional selves that had made their claim upon him. It went even deeper than that. His very personhood had its roots in her love for him. Everything he was as a man, even as a man of God, was wrapped up intrinsically in their relationship. Everything Logan wanted in life was there . . . with her—he knew that now.

Lise was a gentle, beautiful island in the crazy, dark, unreal world of horrors where he finally realized he did not belong. To reach out to her now, in the wrong way, whatever immediate comfort it might provide, would mean sacrificing all he truly was, for a mirage.

Though at this very moment it all seemed hopeless, somehow Logan Macintyre would rise from all the mire of his double life and deceit. And when he did, he wanted only Allison to be there reaching out to him.

59 ❄ A Family Parting

ALLISON LOOKED OUT the window at the busy London street below. Somehow the flow of this place never ceased. A woman walking her dog, children bouncing a ball, a boy selling newspapers—no doubt each one had felt the stab of pain and loss inflicted by the insanity of war.

Yet each continued on with life, as Allison also had done.

Dear Nat was gone . . . for eternity. Her brother Ian and her father were thousands of miles away, and Logan too was gone—perhaps forever.

Still Allison managed to survive. She knew now, more than ever before, about the sustaining hand of God. He had indeed enabled her to weather the heartbreaking separations of the last year. But sometimes she could not help wondering what use it was. Why go on trying to be strong?

She did not have to look far for answers. First of all, there was the indefatigable Ramsey blood that flowed in her veins. God may have given her the ability, but her heritage had set the example. She could not break down even if she wanted to. The instinct to survive, and to conquer, was too deeply ingrained.

But there were even stronger reasons, found in the persons of her child and her husband. Her daughter depended on her. Not that Allison any longer thought she had to put on some false front to live up to her name for the child's sake. The season for facades in Allison's life was long past. She had wept sufficient tears in the company of her daughter to attest to that. Yet a child, especially one without a father, needed the security of her mother. Allison could not withdraw into herself no matter how often she wanted to turn away from *everything*. Allison also had a remote feeling that Logan needed her as well. It would sound ridiculous had she dared voice that feeling to anyone. After all, he had left her, disappeared without a trace, cut himself off without a single visible regret or thought of her.

But deep inside she knew that was not true. Somewhere Logan was suffering in his own way. In his pain and confusion he had, she was sure, convinced himself that the only answer was to banish himself from those closest to him, those who could help. He had probably convinced himself they were all better off without him.

But strong within her woman's heart beat the sense that he *wasn't* gone forever, and that something would happen . . . and soon. Was it instinct, or mere wishful thinking? She couldn't tell. But she knew right now she had lo do what he had always wanted her to do—trust him. She had to keep loving him, trusting him in spite of everything shouting out that he wasn't worth it, and believe with all her strength that the dark tunnel of their separation would soon be past.

Yes, she thought, Logan needs me. She was sure of it. But she knew now it was not in the way she had always thought he needed her. He didn't need her abilities, her sense of responsibility, her money, her family name.

Logan needed *her*—the person she was. He needed her love, unconditionally and selflessly.

That had been her mistake when they were together. She had given him everything but the one thing most vital to a marriage—the commitment of her very self. She had said the words, but never until recently had she realized how much she was holding back. Now that her eyes were open, however, she had to believe that even if Logan chose never to see her again, he would still be able to feel that love. That was what he needed most to receive, and what she needed most to be able to give—the knowledge that even across the miles of separation, love was reaching out between them.

Sounds at the front door slowly nudged Allison from her thoughts. She looked up just as the door opened. It was her mother, preceded by her cheerful, bouncing namesake.

"Hello, sweetheart!" smiled Allison as her daughter bounded into her arms.

"Mama!" exclaimed the girl, "Grandma buyed me flower!" She held out her hand, and now Allison saw she was clutching a pink lily, still pretty, though a bit wilted from constant handling.

"It's beautiful, honey," said Allison.

"I bought a whole bouquet," put in Joanna as she laid her bundles on a table. "I hope you don't mind."

"Of course not, Mother. We could use some brightening up around here."

"I thought so, too." Joanna went to the kitchen for a vase.

In a moment she returned with a crystal vase. Allison fleetingly recalled receiving it for a wedding gift, though it had hardly seen much use since.

"This should be perfect," said Joanna. She unwrapped the bouquet and began arranging it in the bowl. "The last of the summer blooms will be blossoming at Stonewycke. Dorey's nursery will have some lovely ones, probably for another month or so. He was always able to coax life out of his flowers clear into October and beyond."

"Are you homesick, Mother?"

"I suppose I might be." Joanna looked up wistfully. "September is when the heather blooms on the hills," she added.

"I'm keeping you here, aren't I?"

"I needed to be away for a time," replied Joanna. "Even the happy memories were bringing tears to my eyes. With May in America and you here, the place had almost become like I found it that first time I walked up the hill to the foreboding old place, as an uninvited housebreaker!" She paused, recalling the passing of the years with a melancholy fondness. "Yes," she went on with a sigh, "I needed to be away. But now . . . perhaps it *is* time."

"I've been so happy to have you with me, Mother," said Allison. "But I don't want to keep you. I'll be fine whenever you are ready to go back."

"I know you will be."

Joanna left the flowers and walked to the sofa to sit with her daughter and granddaughter. She took Allison's hands in hers.

"Dear Allison . . ." She smiled, though tears had begun to fill her eyes. "I have no worries about you. Not anymore—except of course the usual motherly ones. I know those things that are most important have come together for you in your heart. Still . . . if I returned to Stonewycke, I would so like you to come with me."

"Oh, Mother," sighed Allison. "I miss home, too! But you know why I must stay. And lately, I've been feeling much more strongly that I'll see Logan soon. I know it sounds silly, but—"

"I understand," answered Joanna. "They say a breakthrough in the war could come any time."

"You miss Daddy too, I know."

Joanna smiled. "Perhaps both our men will be home soon."

"We can pray so."

"Sure you won't reconsider about coming with me? It will be so empty having that huge place all to myself."

"Go to Grandma's house!" piped up the enthusiastic voice of the child nestled between the two women.

"You'd like to go, wouldn't you, pumpkin?" said Allison, giving her a tender squeeze.

"We are all country girls at heart," said Joanna.

Allison was quiet for a moment as an idea began to take shape in her mind.

"You know, Mother," she said at length, "I've been keeping pretty occupied here with my job and the volunteer work. The pace of activity has been good for me. I have to stay here, for a while longer at least, until I know something about Logan. But I was thinking, perhaps, that you and . . ."

She let her look and knowing nod complete the thought for her.

"Jo loves Stonewycke," Allison went on. "And I have been concerned with keeping her here with the renewed bombing. Now that we are attacking Germany, they say it can only get worse. There've been attacks on rail lines, army depots, and even a few near London again. What do you think? Would you like to take her to Stonewycke?"

"I can't think of a more delightful prospect! But are you sure?"

"I think it's the perfect solution. What could possibly happen to her there?"

Allison paused and glanced down at her daughter, who was clapping excitedly. "Look at her! She can't wait—Stonewycke is in her blood, too."

"So, the decision is made!" exclaimed Joanna with a laugh.

The following days were spent making preparations for the trip. The nurse, Hannah, had to make arrangements of her own for the lengthy absence. Though she would be returning to London as soon as a suitable nurse could be hired in Port Strathy, it was possible she could be away a month or six weeks. Therefore, it was a week before the train tickets could be purchased.

At last the day of departure arrived. Allison tried her best to be stoic. This had been her idea, after all. But as the time neared, she began to anticipate the loneliness that was bound to surround her once these two dearly loved companions were gone. The temptation to change her mind might have grown overpowering except for the joyful glow on her mother's face. The prospect of returning to Stonewycke, and having her three-year-old granddaughter with her besides, set her spirit positively shining. Just watching her mother was a healing balm to Allison's grieving heart.

It was the best answer for now. And who could tell? Before very long both Allison *and* Logan might be able to join them!

The morning of their departure came, and Allison sat in her room dressing her daughter for the trip. They had chosen her pretty heather-colored frock in honor of the return to Scotland. Allison tied the sash at the back into a bow, then spun the giggling child about in admiration.

"You look absolutely lovely in that color!" exclaimed Allison. "It was Lady Margaret's best color too. She always loved the heather, and its mysterious shades suited her perfectly."

She turned pensive a moment, then smiled again at her daughter. "A wee Scottish lassie ye are, my bairn!" she said.

They both giggled together. "Come, let me brush your hair."

Allison boosted her up onto her knee and began brushing the silky amber locks

"Will you come to Grandma's soon, Mama?" asked the girl, as she snuggled close to her mother.

"Oh yes, I will," answered Allison. "I couldn't be away from you for too long."

"Daddy too?"

"We must keep praying for Daddy. I know he wants to, dear. We must give him time."

"Daddy know I love him?" she asked pensively.

Tears struggled to rise in Allison's eyes. "Yes, dear," she said softly. "Daddy knows that. And you keep loving him with all your heart. He needs that from us now more than anything."

"Will he get hurt like Uncle Nat?"

A knot suddenly tightened Allison's throat.

"We must trust God, my wee bairn," Allison replied in a trembly voice. "Whatever God does is because He loves us and wants the best for us—even sometimes being apart from those we love. But that doesn't mean forever. It was the best thing for Uncle Nat to be with Jesus. Just think how happy he is right now!"

She wrapped her arms around her daughter and hugged her tight. "Jesus is with Daddy, honey! Daddy will be back with us soon, just like you and I will be apart only a short time. We'll see each other again before you know it. I promise!"

Allison shook off the sorrow trying to envelop her at the thought of parting with her daughter. She wanted this day to be a happy one.

"I've got a special present for you, honey!" she said.

"Oh, goody—what, Mama?"

Allison opened a drawer in her dressing table and took out a small velvet-covered box.

"This has been in Mama's family for a long, long time," she said. "Long before you or I, or even Grandma was born."

"Ooooh!" exclaimed the wide-eyed child.

"Many years ago, when your great-great grandmother, Lady Margaret, was a girl, Great-great Grandpa Dorey gave this to her," continued Allison. "They were in love, and were going to be married. He wanted to give her something special. And this was it."

She opened the box and lifted out a delicate gold locket.

"Before Lady Margaret died, she gave it to me. It's always been very special to me ever since. Now, I'd like you to keep it for me a little while—so *you* have something special to remember me while we're apart."

Tenderly she placed the chain of the locket around her daughter's neck.

"Will you take good care of it, and think of me a lot?"

"Yes, Mama." She put her arms around her mother's neck and planted a wet kiss on her mouth. "Thank you, Mama!"

"I will pray for you every day," said Allison in a husky voice, filled with emotion.

"Me too, Mama. I pray for you, too."

"Thank you, dear. I love you."

When the train chugged slowly away two hours later, Allison did not try to hide her tears. Suddenly everyone she loved was gone from her, and she could not help but doubt her decision.

But she was being selfish again, she chided herself as she walked out of the station. This was the best thing, and it would do no good to get melancholy over it and start feeling sorry for herself. Certainly she would be lonely. But what she had told her mother was true; she had much to keep her occupied here in London.

Back out on the street, the sounds of aircraft winging overhead reminded her that this was wartime and her services to the needs of the country were vital. It reminded her, too, that London was never completely safe these days. Her daughter would be better off at Stonewycke, far removed from harm.

She was glad they weren't flying. At least the trains were safe enough.

Shaking off thoughts of war, bombs, and explosions, Allison turned and hailed a cab.

60 ❈ Glances Forward and Back

AS THE TRAIN slowly pulled out of London on its northern journey, Joanna's thoughts were not far divergent from her daughter's.

Her anticipation of being home again was tempered with ever-present reflections on the war. Sometimes she felt she could not bear another single moment of it. And she prayed she would not have to bear another loss as a result of the fighting! How could she? Yet she knew the answer. Her Father in heaven had always upheld her, and would continue to do so whatever further blow this nightmare of world war might send their way.

Oddly enough, one of the most difficult aspects of the ordeal of Nathaniel's death had been the brevity of Alec's furlough for the funeral. After so many months apart, the time should have been a joyous one. But more than the tragedy of their son's death had marred it. Alec had tried to put on a brave show, but Joanna knew him too well; plainly, the years of war were wearing away at him.

In an unguarded moment he had shared with her about the bloody battle of Tobruk that June, just weeks prior to the funeral. Rommel had captured the stronghold and the 8th Army was pushed back all the way to El Alamein, after sustaining fifty thousand casualties.

"Fifty thousand men, Joanna!" he had exclaimed. "I still canna believe it. All I could think when I saw the dead an' wounded was that all those lives were lost fer nothin'. Even if we hae hung on to the city—what was it all fer? 'Tis hard oot there t' keep sight o' a madman in Berlin. There are some o' oor troops who actually tend t' admire Rommel an' his Afrika Korps. 'Tis crazy . . . senseless! When I heard aboot Nat, I wanted to hate, to find some revenge. But I couldna—it jist wasna there!"

"You couldn't, Alec," said Joanna, "because such feelings are foreign to your nature— foreign to the Spirit of God within you."

"Then why am I oot there at all? Am I not bein' a mite hypocritical?"

"Perhaps it's *because* of who you are. If there were no men like you on the battlefield, I'd hate to think of the kind of insanity it would become. Aren't good men needed everywhere, even in the most ungodly of settings? Maybe *especially* there!"

Alec sighed and shook his head. "'Tisna sae easy to understand—when ye're oot there in it every day."

"I don't know what to say, Alec. I suppose there will always be lingering doubts."

"Ah, Joanna—it wouldna be sae hard if ye were wi' me."

He put his arm around her and drew her close. "Fer all yer retirin' ways, my dear wee wifie, ye are strong an' wise beyond my ken. I knew it that first day I met ye. Ye were all green about the gills watchin' old Nathaniel's cow give birth, but ye stuck it oot."

"Probably more from stubbornness than wisdom or strength," said Joanna. "I was not about to let an ill-tempered veterinarian get the better of me!"

"Despite mud an' manure on yer fine city dress!"

"Oh, the smell of that byre!" laughed Joanna.

Alec threw his head back and roared.

It had been one of the few times during their brief time together that Joanna had seen that side of her husband surface. And now Joanna tried to keep that pleasant memory of Alec in her mind.

Oh, Alec, she thought while gazing out the train window watching the concrete of the city as it began to give way to the more open spaces of the countryside, *one day we will laugh again!*

Though three years of war, with its sorrows and separations, might do its best to sap them of their very lives, Joanna clutched her Father's promises firmly in the depths of her heart: "Weeping may endure for a night, but joy cometh in the morning."

Still, she did at times wonder what tomorrow would hold for her and her family. She did not question the future as one might who had no hope. She did not look ahead in fear, but rather in a kind of anticipation. Despite its grief and pain, each day held promise for Joanna. To her belonged the uncommon privilege of being aware of God's purposeful moving in the lives of men and women, not measured in mere weeks, months, or even years, but rather in the very generations of her predecessors.

For some fifteen years, since she suddenly awoke to the realization that her grandmother Lady Margaret would eventually die and the legacy of her life be gone, Joanna had been keeping a careful chronicle of the Ramsey clan. It had begun with the memories of Lady Margaret's life, as the older woman passed the details of her story on to her beloved granddaughter. But the more the two women shared and talked, the more intrigued Joanna became to record for her posterity the saga that involved others of the family as well, even stretching back into times long past to the very beginnings of Stonewycke. As it grew, her writings were not simply a recounting of events—births, deaths, marriages—but rather an attempt to trace spiritual and emotional journeys as well, telling tales of growth and development, heartaches and joys, that could never be measured by years, by statistics, by money. And every moment Joanna recorded from the past helped give her hope for the future.

She gazed down at the child, now sound asleep, nestled in the crook of her arm. This little one was part of that future. What would the coming years hold for her? If she did not someday become the literal heir, she was certainly bound to inherit the tradition handed down through the generations of women who helped keep alive the family bond with the ancient estate of Stonewycke. This child, in less than four years, already had an attachment to the land with its rugged seascapes, hills of scraggly heather, moors of barren heath, and lush green pasturelands. She would carry on for the austere Atlanta, for dear Lady Margaret, and even for Eleanor, Joanna's own mother, who had never even set eyes upon the heather hills. Yes, and for Joanna too, and Allison.

Was it too much to place the burden of such a legacy on a woman? Especially on a child, scarcely more than a baby?

It had nearly destroyed Allison. Yet, whenever it seemed the spiritual traditions were about to be swallowed up in the passage of time and in new generations, God had always stepped in faithfully. He had miraculously brought Joanna herself to Scotland. He had restored Margaret and Ian to their rightful places despite their advancing years. He had brought Allison into the fullness of her mother's and father's faith. And now, after ten years of God's refining fires in Allison's life, that faith was becoming deep enough for others—especially this little daughter—to be able to draw from.

Joanna recalled Lady Margaret's prophetic words of many years ago, spoken on the day Allison had given her heart to the Lord: "I do not doubt that as the history of Stonewycke continues down through the years, Allison, you will play a pivotal role in it. And as you look back, it may be that this moment when we three generations of Duncan women can join in oneness with our Lord will prove an important crossroads."

God was faithful.

If for nothing else, the Ramsey clan could proudly claim they mirrored that one abiding truth. And as the Stonewycke legacy would carry on despite death, despite separation from loved ones, despite turmoil and war and loss, so would the eternal legacy of God's unfailing love continue on throughout all eternity.

That thought alone was enough to make Joanna content. And soon she would be home, a bonus she could only at that moment appreciate. Grief and loneliness had forced her away for a season. But now she could anticipate her return with true Ramsey/Duncan zeal. Of course, the presence of her little granddaughter would help immensely!

When the conductor ambled by a while later announcing dinner in an hour, Joanna could hardly believe they had been traveling for nearly two hours. All signs of the city were well behind them now. The hues of autumn clung to the Middlesex countryside. Off in the distance she could see a lovely picturesque little stone bridge, its sides, about waist high, arching over a bubbling burn. Beyond it, in a crook made by the sides of two adjoining grass-covered rises in the terrain, sat a cozy-looking little thatch-roofed cottage, constructed out of the same stone as the bridge. Out of the chimney a thin wisp of smoke curled skyward. Inside, no doubt, thought Joanna as she watched the pleasant scene pass, a homely farm woman is kneading out her ration of flour into a fragrant loaf of hearty bread.

Yes, Joanna was truly a country girl, although when she had first come to Scotland thirty-one years ago, she had hardly been able to tell one end of a cow from the other. But now the thought of the earthy sights and sounds and smells of Port Strathy warmed her heart as it could only to one who truly belonged there heart and soul.

All at once a horribly discordant sight intruded upon the pleasant scene. Ugly lengths of chain-link fencing stretched out in the midst of the rolling countryside. The ten-foot-high fence was topped with three or four rows of barbed wire. There was no sign identifying the installation, but it needed none. Joanna recognized the fenced area as one of the revolting by-products of war—an ammunition dump, most likely.

Joanna sighed. What a contrast! A storage dump for ammunition to kill thousands sitting just across the tracks from such an idyllic country scene of peace.

Joanna was just vaguely aware of the sounds of aircraft whining over the monotonous clatter of the train when she was distracted from the unpleasant scene by a friendly voice in the aisle to her left.

"Lady MacNeil! What a nice surprise!"

Joanna turned with a reciprocal smile on her face, when she saw who it was that had greeted her.

"Why, Olivia!" she said to Allison's old school chum, Olivia Fairgate, "this *is* delightful!" She knew Olivia was married now, but could not for the life of her recall the girl's married name. "It's been a long time . . . I forget how you young people grow up."

"Yes, we do. Why, I've got four children now."

"My goodness!" exclaimed Joanna. "But you are traveling alone now?"

"Oh no! Everyone's two cars over. I was just seeing about having some formula warmed for the twins."

"Twins! . . . I didn't know."

"Two months old tomorrow—what a handful!"

She began rummaging through her purse, but then stopped. "I was going to show you a photo," she said. "But why don't you come and see the real thing—or things. I should say?" She giggled at her unintentional joke.

"I'd love to," answered Joanna, realizing that it would feel good to stand. "I need to stretch my legs a bit."

She turned to the nurse. "Hannah, you don't mind, do you?"

"Not at all, mum."

Gently Joanna eased her granddaughter out of her arms and into the lap of the nurse. Still asleep, the child snuggled into the nurse's arms and sighed contentedly.

"I should only be a few minutes," said Joanna; then she walked away with Olivia, both chatting, filling in the gaps of the years since they had seen each other.

"Was that Allison's daughter you were holding?" asked Olivia. At Joanna's nod, she added, "What a precious child. We really ought to get together more often. My little James is just about her age."

They made their way through the next car, and on to the one beyond it. Joanna had little trouble picking out Olivia's brood—in that particular corner of the railway car, all the activity for the entire train seemed concentrated. A four-year-old lad was sitting on his knees, backward on his seat, straining to see everything that was going on. Next to him, an older boy of about seven was occupied with a book, though only about a minute out of every three was spent reading. Above the clacking of the train's wheels along the tracks could be heard the unmistakable infant cries of two hungry babies. A frazzled nurse looked up with pleading eyes as the two women drew near.

In all the mayhem of the moment, Joanna no longer noticed the drone of approaching aircraft, now much louder than before.

"Hey, Mother," called out the seven-year-old as Olivia walked up, "look at those airplanes! They're coming right toward us!"

But before Olivia could reply, suddenly an ear-splitting explosion burst through the air, forcing their part of the world into chaos and upheaval. There was but an instant for Joanna's sensations to register her shock and terror. She did not even have time to think about Hannah and her granddaughter two cars away.

The train jerked violently, knocking her from her feet and into unconsciousness.

61 ❈ A Higher Plane

JOANNA AWOKE WITH an audible gasp. All around her were the white, antiseptic sights and smells of a hospital room.

She struggled to rise, but a firm hand settled her back into place. She opened her mouth, but no words would come. Her bedclothes seemed drenched in perspiration. In her groggy state, scenes from her long, traumatic sleep assaulted her mind—wild, terrifying bursts of deafening explosions, blinding flashes of light. And always the screams, especially the one childish scream she could never seem to reach.

Now she was being wheeled along a corridor. Voices spoke softly above her, but she could see no faces. Was this but a horrifying nightmare?

But more flashes of memory continued to penetrate her consciousness. The nightmare *had* been real! Snatches of the scene came back to her. Scenes that would forever haunt her, in sleep and in waking, from that awful day.

Suddenly she remembered an earlier waking. How could she have forgotten? A porter, his uniform smattered with blood and torn in many places, was leaning over her.

"Are ye wakin', mum?" he asked compassionately.

"My granddaughter . . ." was all Joanna could say. "My baby . . ."

"'Tis many youngsters in this car, mum, but none dead. We'll find her."

"No . . . not this car . . . two ahead . . ."

Suddenly the man's tender expression became stricken with pain.

"Two cars ahead, ye say?"

But Joanna, clutching at the man and ignoring the pain from injuries she would later discover, tried to pull herself up.

"I have to get to her!"

"But, mum—"

Paying no heed to the man's entreaties, Joanna staggered to her feet, then attempted to run, stumbling along and climbing through the debris to make her way through the appalling disaster. All the while the kindly man hurried after her.

Somehow she managed to get free of what was left of the railway car and into the open air. She ran along the dirt where already the injured and dead were being dragged out and tended to.

Suddenly she stopped. The porter who had been close on her heels came up sharply at her side.

Several cars, one on its side and half blown apart, were engulfed in uncontrollable flames.

She started to run toward the blaze, screaming, "No!" But the porter grabbed her firmly.

"'Tis no use, mum," he said wearily. "Them cars ahead o' yers took a direct hit."

With the fatal words of the porter still ringing in her ears, mingled with the incoherent voices of nurses and doctors, and the blurry whiteness of an unfamiliar ceiling spinning around above her, Joanna lapsed again into unconsciousness, and remembered no more.

Sarah Bramford came the moment she had received Allison's call. She had been out of town, however, and could not be reached for nearly twenty-four hours after the accident.

The moment she walked in, Allison's appalling appearance told more than any words could. Where she sat in the brassy light of the hospital's waiting room, with dark hollow eyes and pale skin, she appeared so lost, like a stranger in some bizarre foreign land where all was against her. She had often complained about her dreadful pallor, calling it the Duncan curse. But the look on her face went far beyond any familiar inheritance..

Sarah rushed immediately to her side and threw her arms around her friend.

Allison said nothing, but burst into fresh tears.

Both women held each other tight and wept; then Sarah finally managed to speak through her tears.

"Your mother . . . is she—?"

Allison nodded. "She'll be fine," she replied haltingly. "A mild concussion, a broken arm, some broken ribs—"

"Oh my!" exclaimed Sarah, "the poor woman!"

"She's just come out of surgery and is asleep—oh, Lord! I don't know what I would have done had I lost her, too!"

Gently Sarah stroked Allison's head, her own tears of heart-wrenching compassion flowing without restraint.

"Oh, Sarah!" sobbed Allison, "what am I going to do!"

Thirty minutes later some calm had been restored to Allison's grief-stricken heart. She looked at Sarah, still with that empty, wasted expression of loss on her face. But she had to talk; it seemed the only way to accept the reality of what had happened.

"The bombers were apparently after some military installation on the other side of the tracks," she said, her voice cracked and tentative. "But some of the bombs came in low, and . . . hit the train—"

She stopped and could not go on for several minutes.

"My little Joanna was in one of them," she sobbed. "Mother had left for a few minutes . . . to visit Olivia in another car—"

"Olivia Fairgate?"

"Yes, she was on the train . . . she and her children. But they're all fine. Their car wasn't . . . they didn't get a direct hit—"

The words caught on Allison's lips. "Oh, Sarah!" she moaned, then was silent for several minutes.

"You don't have to tell me now, dear."

"No . . . it's all right . . . I've got to get it said . . ."

"Tell me whatever you want to," said Sarah tenderly.

"It took them hours to account for everyone. Some went to nearby farms for first aid . . . the Army came out to help, but of course they had their own casualties. . . . But now they know—I just heard it—over two hundred injured . . . sixty-three dead. . . ."

Again the two friends fell silent. Sarah waited, silently ministering the tender sympathy of true compassion.

"God knew what He was doing when He gave you to me for a friend," said Allison, speaking at last. "Thank you, Sarah."

"Let's go get something to eat," said Sarah brightly. "When's the last time you had a good meal?"

"I honestly don't remember," answered Allison. "I haven't been hungry."

"Come on," urged Sarah, rising. "You must have something."

"Well, maybe I could use a change of scenery."

Arm-in-arm they left the tiny, comfortless room, found the stairs, and eventually located the dining room. The tea proved adequate, but everything else was bland and tasteless. Allison toyed with a bowl of soup until it was cold besides. The tea was soothing, however, and when Sarah poured out a second cup, Allison accepted it gratefully.

"I should probably get back upstairs," she said, "in case Mother wakes up."

"I'm surprised she's here in London," commented Sarah.

"There were no adequate facilities in the rural area where the bombing took place," said Allison. "So they brought most of the casualties back to the city."

They both concentrated on their tea for a few moments.

Then Sarah reached across the table and gently placed her hand on Allison's.

"Why don't you come stay with me while your mother is in the hospital?" she said. "Even after she is released, you would both be welcome. You know I have scads of room."

"Thank you, Sarah," Allison replied. She proceeded to stare into her cup a moment. "But I . . . I . . . feel I should stay at the flat. I can't leave. If Logan should come, I must be there."

"But we can leave word for him."

"No, I have to *be* there. I don't know how this will affect all we might have had. I don't even know if I'll ever see him again. But I just know I have to stay there."

"Of one thing we can be sure," said Sarah quietly. "God doesn't *cause* such tragedies, but He can *use* them in ways we in the midst of our grief can never imagine."

Allison smiled, for the first time in many hours.

"You have grown so much, Sarah. I can't tell you how much it means to me to have you right now. I don't have much to cling to, and I'm so thankful to God that I *do* have you."

Over the next days and weeks, Allison did manage to endure the emptiness of her grief. Sarah stayed with her in the Shoreditch flat until Joanna was released from the hospital nine days after the accident. After that, Allison's loneliest moments were relieved in eager service to her mother. By the time Joanna was ready to return north, Allison too seemed back on her feet emotionally, at least enough to go on with life.

God had, and would, continue to use her grief. He was calling her to a higher level of faith, a new plane of trust in Him.

She had heard about such things many times from her great-grandparents. Her own mother and father had told her that the pain of loss and separation was the very thing which had cemented the young love shared by Maggie and Ian into an eternal legacy of love. She had heard, she had read—so many times, in fact, that the truths had little impact for her personally.

In her spirit now, however, she began to discern that the truth of those words was what her own life now desperately required if she was to grow through this time and be strong again.

Now was the time when her trust in God, her love for Logan, and her belief in God's ultimate goodness in the face of black circumstances all around must be stretched to humanly impossible limits. Now was the time when she would have to decide to what extent she was willing to give God her trust. Daily she opened her New Testament to read the words at once so painful and yet so full of hope:

"We rejoice in our sufferings, because we know that suffering produces patience, and patience produces strength of character, and strength of character produces hope. And hope will never disappoint us, because God has poured out his love into our hearts by the Holy Spirit. . . . Consider it joy when you face trials, because you know that the testing of your faith develops perseverance, which must finish its work, so that you may be mature and complete, and lacking in nothing."

To allow this process to work its maturing and strengthening in her heart, she needed to depend upon God more than she ever had in her young life.

"Father," she prayed one evening in the quiet of her room, "following your ways has never been easy for me. Please—help me, dear Lord! I want to trust you, I want to believe this is all for the good! I want to believe that that scripture is true, and that you are working it out in my life. Help me, even if not to *believe* it completely, at least help me to *want* to believe it! Help me somehow to trust you in spite of my own unbelief. I want to trust you, Lord, but I am weak on my own! And more than anything, please, dear Lord, keep your loving hand on Logan. He needs you, too. Let these separate paths we are on help us both to see the light of your Spirit illuminating the way before us."

62 ❈ The Paris Express

THEY CALLED THIS rattletrap *The Berlin to Paris Express.*

Some express! The word was more likely a euphemism for simply making it a thousand kilometers without encountering a bomb! The phrase could certainly have nothing whatever to do with speed! Thus concluded Jason Channing with a disgruntled smirk.

He wondered about the necessity of his current decision to travel to Paris. If for no other reason, he was going because the Führer had encouraged him to see the city—how did he phrase it?—under the "guardianship" of the Third Reich. Hitler may have been a maniac in many ways, but he did possess a tenderness for the arts. Probably it was his way of deflecting attention from his common birth, and perhaps relieving the sting from the memory of being twice rejected by the Academy of Fine Arts in Vienna. The struggling young artist had turned instead to surviving as a street painter in the Austrian capital, and now, thirty-four years later, fancied himself a connoisseur of things fine and cultured. He carried with him such a bloated impression of his own skill that several years ago he had gone on a campaign to round up and destroy what he considered forgeries of his own early work. As if any of them were good enough to forge! And now in his vision for the Reich—purified, as it was, from the stains of both Jews and forgeries—he perceived Paris as the crowning glory.

Besides, the Führer was not a man to be refused; even Jason Channing had the sense to recognize that.

Hitler's major goal with Paris had been to see that the cinema, the theater, and other arts should continue to thrive. The world would see that the Reich did not ultimately bring destruction, but culture.

Well, thought Channing, perhaps the tyrant has succeeded. Even in the midst of the war, France led the world, even America, in publishing. The stage still attracted some of Europe's biggest names. The Louvre was still the world's greatest art gallery and the Left Bank still attracted many up-and-coming new artists. Parisian night life seemed to be flourishing. Jews were *verboten,* of course, from participating in any of this. But who needed their money? There were enough other Parisian artisans and German financiers to keep the creative hub of the world bursting with the appearance of health and happiness. The peasants had no bread, but the Führer saw to it that they had art in abundance.

Channing was no sentimentalist like the Führer. He would never have made this ghastly train ride just to see some ridiculous pictures on canvas, or to hear Karajan conduct *Tristan and Isolde,* although he would no doubt be willing enough to take advantage of some of the other diversions Paris offered a man of the world.

Most of all, however, he had endless business deals to cement. "Thank God for the war!" he was known to have said on occasion. He was scoring a bundle. He may have been black-listed from American industry and unwelcome in certain parts of Britain, but who cared? Germany had proved a veritable gold mine. After the crash of '29, he had taken a chance with his remaining bankroll and invested in aircraft. His associates all called him crazy, but Channing's greed smelled another war in the not-so-distant future. If everyone else back then chose to ignore Germany's steady buildup of armaments, Channing was not one to be duped by soothing words. He knew what was going on, and where the world was headed.

It had been rough at first, until the government contracts began pouring in near the end of the thirties. Now he couldn't produce enough *Messerschmitts* or *Hurricanes,* not to mention his growing contracts with the Japanese.

Because of the war, Channing was now a millionaire in just about any currency he chose.

And since he wasn't a patriot, it caused him no particular qualms that the fortunes of the Third Reich were steadily plummeting. All along he'd known the arrangement would end one day. He made sure not to invest too much of his own money in the factories, at the same time funneling the cash profits in his own direction. When the end came he wanted to make sure he would be able to beat a hasty retreat to some nice neutral spot like Morocco, out of sight of the Germans, out of sight of the Americans and English, and live like a king while setting up some new ventures.

And the Third Reich did seem to be plummeting. Last month the Eighth Army had squashed Rommel at El Alamein in Egypt, a major victory for the British, insuring Allied protection of the Suez Canal. And only a few days ago, on November 8, of this pivotal year of 1942, the British and the Americans had launched their long-awaited invasion of North Africa. Churchill had recently declared, "This is not the end. It is not even the beginning of the end. But it is, perhaps, the end of the beginning."

Why couldn't the pompous snob come right out and say it? thought Channing. The Reich was doomed. Not only in the south but in the east too. There they were slowly crumbling before the rallied might of the great Russian bear.

But to Channing none of the world's political fortunes mattered. He had his wealth secreted away in the safety of a Swiss bank. No matter which way the war went, he would come up smelling like a rose.

So much for the business end of this visit to the City of Lights.

He was also looking forward to seeing his old acquaintance, Martin von Graff, now a general in the S.S. For beyond business and finances, there was a still more vital thrust to Channing's existence: power. It was his reason for being, what kept him driven with the passion of men thirty years his junior.

To the end of possessing power over men and situations and circumstances, Jason Channing had over the years developed a finely honed network of international "eyes and ears." He had in his clutches more dirt on more well-placed personalities than he could ever use in one lifetime. But even if it went unused, the mere fact of its possession was what really mattered. You never knew when it would come in handy to expedite a deal, or encourage a man of influence to close his eyes at the proper time. To know more about another than he knew you knew gave Channing a hidden measure of control. And with control came power!

One of the focal points toward which he had directed his spying activities was none other than his old nemesis, Stonewycke. By now Channing's vendetta was not limited merely to that feisty snip of a girl who had laughed in his face thirty-one years ago, and then run off to marry a ridiculous, manure-sloshing animal doctor. That affront he would *never* forgive! He would carry out his revenge on anyone associated with the place. Of course, the pressing demands of the war had limited his diligence in this area. But he had instructed his people at least to keep a watch for any unusual behavior.

And what could be more unusual than a nervous young woman slipping out in the dead of night to rendezvous with a sinister German at a deserted pub near the Thames shipyards? The daughter, no less! To have something on her might even be better than a direct hit. Parents were so sentimental! That was the perfect way to really make them hurt—get to their children!

Yes, sir! You just never knew what was going to turn up! The noble *Lady* Joanna MacNeil's own daughter meeting with Germans!

Channing *had to* know what it was all about! This was fraught with cunning possibilities!

Thus he directed his antennae toward that little part of the globe. He kept a man watching the girl—what was her name? Allison. But he'd come up consistently empty. He'd stuck a man immediately on the kraut, too. That was more promising.

The name was Gunther. His code name, at least—in reality his informant identified him as one Rolf Pingel. Not that his real name mattered. He was a double agent, ostensibly working for British intelligence. However, the man was a slippery fellow; even Channing was not sure which side of the fence he really called home. Probably *both* sides. "I like the guy already!" Channing laughed to himself.

Channing put his best man on Gunther. But even at that they had a beast of a time keeping up with him. They lost his track several times, but then caught a whiff of him again as he boarded a plane for Lisbon. Suddenly things began to look up. For in Lisbon, who should he meet but Martin von Graff, just before von Graff switched his lot to the S.S.

From the submarine off the northern coast of Scotland—where Channing himself had returned with his dredging equipment some time later—and now to his association with a spy who had links to the MacNeil daughter, the name of Martin von Graff seemed to keep bearing in on the fortunes of Stonewycke, and Channing's schemes.

What might the general possibly know? Channing never could come up with any details on the Lisbon meeting—both men were prime intriguers and knew how to keep quiet. And Channing didn't want to risk spooking any potential leads, so he adopted a wait-and-see posture. Then other priorities occupied his attentions for a while—after all, he still did have a business to operate. The Führer demanded his presence in Berlin for some time, and he could not think of refusing the man whose war was so nicely lining his pocketbook.

But the incident with the Macintyre girl did not cease to churn about in the recesses of his warped brain. He'd followed the society pages enough—and kept his subscription to an Aberdeen paper open for just such a purpose—to keep limited track of the whole brood of them, including that ne'er-do-well husband of hers. He had been troublesome during the whole episode with that fool Ross Sprague. Luckily, it had all turned out satisfactorily in the end. Channing would get to the bottom of this new development at the first opportunity, and then use whatever information he gained to bring down that whole arrogant family.

Getting the Ramsey treasure wasn't enough. It hadn't even bothered them that it had been found and lost again so quickly. Confound those people! What could you do against idiots who didn't even care about money? They were impenetrable, like that spy Gunther! And for all the good that big heavy box had done him, he might as well have left it at the bottom of the drink. It certainly hadn't improved his fortunes much!

Oh, he had been able to gloat for a time in that small victory. But without her to *know* he had won, it was a hollow triumph, indeed. And from a monetary standpoint, it was no easy thing turning a profit from a cache of thousand-year-old relics. He'd no doubt have more luck fencing the stuff after the war.

In the meantime, there they sat in their castle on that blasted hill covered with ridiculous and useless heather. They acted as if they were as impregnable as their feudal ancestors. But this German connection—it could be their Waterloo. And even if it meant nothing, he might still be able to parlay it to his own advantage.

First, he'd pump von Graff. The general no longer had any loyalties to the Abwehr. He might be more willing to divulge some of their more minor secrets. Such as, who was this Gunther? What was his connection to MI5? Who were some of his contacts? And what could he possibly have to do with young Allison Macintyre? Was there any chance her husband was involved somehow?

If the general was reluctant to talk, Channing could always utilize his close relationship with the Führer to loosen him up.

The train whistle sounded a shrill note. Channing caught a glimpse of the Marne outside. He would soon be in Paris.

63 ❈ *A Visit With Henri*

A GUSTY AUTUMN wind accompanied Logan as he walked down the rue de Varennes. He remembered the first time he had made his way down this very street, so confident, so untried. Lise had said that first day they had talked, "You are so naive! But you will learn your lessons soon enough."

Three months ago in Vouziers he had passed through the graduate school of his brutal underground education. Had it really been that long? It hardly seemed possible! Already three months since he had snuffed out the life of that German, and held his dying brother-in-law in his arms.

After such a hideous experience, how had he managed to continue?

He'd been given the opportunity to go back to London. Atkinson had offered.

But Logan held on. Perhaps it was wrong of him to do so. He knew a part of him had lost heart, and thus the danger of becoming sloppy was even more possible. Not only did it place him in more danger, it endangered the lives of others as well. Now Logan knew beyond a doubt that he did not belong here.

Yet something else kept him. It had to do with his conversation with Atkinson before he came to Paris.

"You lack discipline," the major had said. "And you lack staying power. According to your record, the only thing you've ever done that's lasted longer than a year is to get married—and now it appears as if that is failing also. . . ."

A year ago Logan had bought into France's cause. To abandon it now that it had soured for him would be in the act of the old Logan Macintyre—the man who thought nothing of walking out on a marriage the moment it failed to suit his fancy. If I am going to learn the kind of commitment necessary for a marriage, he thought, what better place to start than right here and now? If he ever did make it out of France, and Allison would still have him, she would deserve some assurance. Maybe he needed that, too—needed to know that he had it in him to weather it when life got rough.

So here he was walking again down the rue de Varennes, still in France, still playing his double and triple roles, still helping escapees get safely to Britain. Sometimes he seemed merely to be going through the motions. But he was trying to be faithful to the commitments he had made, yet now looking forward to the day when it would end.

How long would he need to remain to prove his commitment? Logan didn't know. But he had been praying about it. He had been spending a lot more time in prayer these days. And he felt an assurance that God would direct him, that somehow the Lord would let him know when the time was right.

Logan arrived at the bookstore, opening the door to the familiar clang of the overhead bell. He had been looking forward to this meeting with Henri—there had been too few since he had become Trinity again. He liked the man, and enjoyed their time together whenever circumstances would allow. He had gradually established himself at several bookstores around Paris, so an occasional visit to *La Librairie* would not be suspicious.

An old gentleman was browsing among the stacks. When Henri entered from the back, both men deliberately down-played their greetings.

"Ah, Monsieur Tanant," said the shopkeeper politely, "I have the books you ordered in back. I'll be but a moment; they are still packed."

"Merci," replied Logan. "Can I be of assistance?"

"If it is no trouble—the boxes are rather cumbersome."

They retreated to the back room where, though keeping their voices subdued, they were able to greet one another properly.

"How good it is to see you, Michel!" said Henri, giving Logan an affectionate embrace.

"Likewise, Henri."

Still in his reflective mood, Logan recalled the day Henri had promised him a peaceful cup of real coffee when the war ended. He longed for the fulfillment of that invitation now more than ever.

Before they could continue, the customer from the front called to Henri.

"Help yourself to some coffee," said Henri as he ducked out through the curtained doorway.

Logan took a cup from the rack on the wall and poured the coffee. He had just settled himself on one of the crates when he heard the bell sound. He hoped it wasn't a new visitor. But in a moment Henri reappeared.

"We are alone now, mon ami," he said, "so we must use the precious time judiciously. Though I would rather chat," he added with a laugh. "At the very least, I must know—are you well, Michel?" The question held in it more than the mere exchange of pleasantries.

"Yes, Henri," Logan replied in the earnest tone that was becoming more characteristic of his speech lately. "We survive . . . we must. Have you heard the latest news, that the Boche have moved in to occupy all of France?"

"Oui. Their way of retaliating for the invasion of North Africa. Let them have it. It won't be theirs for long!"

"True, Henri," said Logan, thoughtfully sipping his coffee. "But even if the war lasts only another year or two, they can—and will—make those final years ones of living hell for us. Already the execution posters have become a more frequent sight. Arrests are increasing, and I recently heard a rumor that a French militia is to be formed—blokes that will make Arnaud Soustelle look like an angel. These Frenchmen will be able to spy on and ferret out their countrymen like no German ever could. And if they can't, then the new Family Hostage Law will—"

"Inhuman!" exclaimed Henri bitterly. "Executing male relatives and condemning females to hard labor if so-called terrorists do not surrender themselves. I do not like to even consider the possibilities for betrayal this brings to the entire underground movement. But, Michel, what are you getting at?"

"Just because the Boche seem to be losing the war at the moment," replied Logan, "we cannot think we can just relax. It can only make everything worse—bring out the latent beast in our enemy."

"Latent!" spat Henri. "Ha! it has always been visible enough."

"Well," sighed Logan, "I suppose it makes little difference. It will not alter what we must do—except that we must be all the more careful."

"Oui."

The conversation lagged a few moments as the two men drank their coffee and pondered their unpredictable futures.

"We can only be thankful, Michel," said Henri at length, "that our families are safely away from here. I feel for those who will have to make such a choice."

He set down his cup. "But we must get to business—perhaps we can shave a few months off this war."

"Even a few days might be worth our efforts."

"I have the report from Claude that London wanted on the drop sites," Henri went on.

"Good. I'll get that to Lise immediately."

"Now . . ." Henri hesitated a moment before beginning again with more resolution in his voice. "I have a task for L'Escroc."

"I thought we had put him to rest."

"We may have our chance to get Jean Pierre," said Henri.

Logan leaned back. He remembered his confident declaration about freeing the priest on the night when he had been arrested. But his words had turned out to be impotent thus far. The S.S. were not about to let their prize slip easily through their fingers. Logan had worked on von Graff as much as he dared to learn anything that would help them get to him, but to no avail. The general was especially tight-lipped about his captive. Trinity got nowhere. And L'Escroc had had no luck either.

Jean Pierre was being kept in solitary confinement under special guard. He'd been locked in Cherche-Midi for about a month, and Logan hadn't been able to get near him, using any personality or disguise—though he had made some gallant, and as it turned out, humorous efforts.

He did manage to learn that Jean Pierre had not broken under interrogation and, to his relief, that the Nazis were exercising restraint in their handling of this particular prisoner, whether out of respect for his priestly collar or because of the influence of his brother, no one knew. Logan remained constantly on the alert for some breakdown in the general's guard, but when his only opportunity came, he missed it. He knew a transfer would have been the perfect moment, but when they moved him to Fresnes, it had been cloaked in such secrecy that Logan did not learn of the action until after the fact.

As time passed, Logan's interest did not so much flag, but the desperation of the situation seemed to lessen. This, coupled with the fact that they had tried without result, gradually lowered the priority in their minds of making an all-out escape effort. Jean Pierre would not be shot, and he was not going to talk. Moreover, the Germans seemed to be satisfying themselves with the mere victory of having him under lock and key. At this point it seemed the risks of rescuing their comrade outweighed the risks of capture and certain death. For whatever leniency they demonstrated toward the priest would certainly never carry over to anyone caught trying to spring him.

There was more to it than that, however. Logan knew it would take nerve to walk into Fresnes and extract their prize catch. Risk was one thing, and he had always been willing to take certain risks. But with his mind more and more on getting back home, on Allison, on his *real* life, he wasn't sure he had what it took to put it all on the line many more times. He did not think it had as much to do with courage as it did with that *élan* Lise had once spoken of.

Logan looked up toward Henri. He had to listen to the proposal.

"They are going to transfer him again," Henri began.

"How did you manage to learn that?"

"Straight from von Graff' s desk," grinned Henri . "Sometimes a janitor is more effective than a double agent, eh?"

"I have no argument there," said Logan.

"We have people in high *and* low places," Henri went on.

"And sometimes equally effective! But are you sure it's reliable? We were so blind last time—could this be some sort of trap?"

"That is always a possibility."

Henri sighed, then reached for the coffeepot and refilled their cups. "Perhaps it is wrong of me to take this so personally, but Jean Pierre is a special man and a dear friend. I cannot bear to see him in *their* hands."

"I'm sorry, Henri. I suppose all these months have finally dulled my sensitivities. Though the very thought of it appalls me, too."

"You are troubled, mon ami. Might it help to talk about it? I have not Jean Pierre's wisdom, but I am able to listen."

"Time is too pressing," hedged Logan.

"I think it is a necessary risk."

"Like rescuing Jean Pierre?"

"Perhaps."

Henri paused, then said softly, "Sometimes, Michel, all the secrecy drowns us. But we each have our own personal breaking point."

"I don't think I'm quite there . . . yet," replied Logan, then stopped. He took a scrap of paper from his pocket and handed it to Henri.

Henri studied it a moment, then looked up at Logan. "Congratulations!" he said. "But you do not seem overjoyed."

Logan took the paper and glanced at it again. It was from London, Atkinson in particular. It read:

HAVE YOUR CAPTAIN'S PIPS IN DRAWER STOP PROMOTION
JUST CAME THRU TODAY STOP KEEP UP THE GOOD WORK END

"No . . ." said Logan slowly. "I'm not overjoyed, though I know I should be. Here I never thought I'd get into action at all, and now suddenly I'm a captain! But I guess what really matters to me has changed recently."

"Perhaps you just need a furlough—you have been under much pressure."

"If I went now, Trinity would be blown. There is no way I could go to London and cover my tracks."

"Trinity cannot go on forever. Maybe it would be best for you to eliminate him before the Boche do. Drop out of sight and leave von Graff forever wondering who you were and where you have gone. A satisfying final move, it seems to me."

"Except not being able to see his face when he *knew*—that would be a great sacrifice."

"Ah, oui! That would indeed be the *pièce de resistance!*"

"I've thought of the possibility," said Logan, "of simply disappearing. And no doubt it will have to come to that in the end. I'm trying to be attuned to the right moment to fold."

He paused and sipped his coffee, now lukewarm. "You see, Henri, there is another reason why I must stay, and it's in that wire. I have to prove something to the man who wrote it. Even more, I've got to prove something to myself. I cannot leave France until I'm certain my work here is finished. I can't walk out on it like I've done with so many other things in my life. I can't retreat when the going gets rough. I've got to see it out. Yet at the same time, I'm not sure I'm up to something as big as Jean Pierre's escape."

"You will do fine, mon ami. I am certain. And you will not be alone. You will be one of many, and together . . . you will do it!"

64 ✠ *Springing the Priest*

LOGAN CAUGHT A brief glimpse of his reflection in the window as the train sped through a short tunnel.

The image that stared back at him was momentarily startling; the disguise was certainly effective. His hair, topped with a black wool beret, was streaked with gray, as was his moustache. Wire-rimmed spectacles outlined deep-set eyes, created with the judicious application of makeup and not a few sleepless nights. He wore an ill-fitting and frayed dark suit that might possibly have been in style twenty years ago. He appeared in every way as the venerable educator to which his papers bore witness, off for a month of sabbatical.

To his left, in the seat across the aisle, sat young Paul Guillaume, who appeared absorbed in this morning's edition of *Le Matin*. Logan, however, could detect his discomfiture regardless of his extravagant attempt to mask it.

Who could blame the lad? Besides the dozen or so German soldiers scattered throughout the car, there were three extremely vigilant S.S. soldiers. There was a sufficient show of German force to daunt anyone, especially a young underground agent barely dry behind the ears. Logan had anticipated the heavy German presence; after all, the trains to and from Paris were jammed with soldiers going back to the Fatherland on leaves, or returning to their assignments.

The S.S. were different, of course. They were the ones to worry about, for it was the S.S. who were guarding Jean Pierre. It had been good to see the priest after so long, even if they had only two seconds to exchange covert glances and establish recognition.

The three months in Fresnes showed clearly on his debonair features. Logan thought his hair seemed slightly grayer and his skin was pale and sagging, especially around the eyes, which had became cavernous hollows. But despite all that, a brief smile had flickered briefly across his face as he beheld Logan's outfit. Three months had not broken his spirit. That fact was all the more evident in the time since the train had pulled out of Paris. The suave cleric had spent a good part of the time in animated conversation with his guards. They had no idea that the coy priest was more interested in distracting them than in pleasant conversation.

Logan wondered if he had understood, or even received, the cryptic message he had managed to get to him. It merely read: *"W.C. five minutes to Coulommiers."*

He had no doubts, however, in Jean Pierre's ability to carry out his performance in this life-and-death scenario, if he *had* received the note. But his own part had begun to unravel the moment he had boarded in Paris. His contact in the railroad had given his word that the

S.S. and their prisoner would be in car number 7, that abutting the baggage car. How he could be sure of that Logan did not know, but he had had little choice but to accept his guarantee. When the boarding was complete, however, the S.S. wound up two cars away, and Logan had to improvise some way to get Jean Pierre through to the next car.

They had rigged up a false wall in the water closet of that particular car. All Jean Pierre had to do was step inside, where even the S.S. might give him a few moments of privacy. A few seconds later he would step on to the outside platform of the car, and thence into the adjoining baggage car, where he would be as good as a free man.

Simple enough. But the timing had to be precise. He had to start for the W.C. no sooner than five minutes before the train made its brief stop at Coulommiers. They would have about three minutes to get Jean Pierre out of the bathroom and off the train before the guards would get suspicious. Once he made it to the baggage compartment, there would be a crate awaiting him that would be unloaded with all the other cargo scheduled for the little village located seventy kilometers east of Paris.

Logan hoped that by the time the Gestapo were alerted, there would be so much confusion that the simple crate would go unnoticed until Jean Pierre could be removed. There were risks everywhere; Logan fully realized that. But then, every escape plan carried with it the imminent risk of failure. It was part of this business.

But in this present instance, Logan had tried his best to cover every angle: he and Paul would oversee the car; there were two men in the baggage compartment, and he had two other men stationed at the depot in Coulommiers. Besides these, a conductor and a coalman were patriots who would be willing to run interference in a pinch. Each man was under strict instructions that if the thing went sour, they were to scatter everyone on his own; one agent alone was harder to track down than a hoard of eight.

That final injunction against disaster had been fairly routine, not given out of some sense of premonition. But now Logan wondered. He didn't like starting out on the wrong foot. It wasn't as if the switched cars were an insurmountable barrier—he had already thought of a remedy. But it just did not set well.

He glanced at his watch. Fifteen minutes until Coulommiers.

He rose and made his way slowly down the aisle, taking awkward, careless steps, playing his role of absent-minded bookworm to the hilt.

He reached the water closet and entered. Now came the risky part. To jam the door's lock effectively, he would have to do so from outside. Most of the passengers would all be facing the other direction. But if someone chanced by, or some stray eyes fell his way, his innocent little act of sabotage would be undone.

Logan grabbed a small piece of the waxed onion-skin they tried to pass off as toilet paper, crumpled it into a tiny wad, reopened the door a crack, threw the lock shut, then removed a small tool from his pocket. With it he proceeded to stuff the wad of paper into the lock mechanism from the inside, as well as a small piece into the keyhole on the outside of the door.

So far so good. No one had come by.

Now he walked back out into the aisle, pulled the door to him and closed it with a quick jerk, which made more noise than he was comfortable with. But the lock had engaged! Just a few seconds more! Another tiny wad of paper jammed into the lock! He tried the door. It was shut fast!

The job was done. The door would not budge. Whoever tried to make use of this W.C.— including Jean Pierre—would have to go on to the one in the next car. He hoped Jean Pierre picked up the improvisation in the plan!

Slowly Logan turned and ambled the few steps toward the rear of the car, opened the door, stepped onto the landing outside, crossed into the next car—number 7—and continued through it, past the W.C. in which they had installed the false wall, and outside onto the landing. There he paused. Jean Pierre would soon be following right in his footsteps, through car 6, where he would try the disabled W.C. door, on into car 7—no doubt by this time with his guards growing touchy—and into the bogus bathroom there. The plan was admittedly thin, but it was all he had.

Logan waited. In a few moments, even over the racket of the train clacking down the tracks, he should hear Jean Pierre enter the tiny stall on the other side of the wall. From where he stood between the cars, his visibility was limited, but the station could not be much farther. Yet the cold November wind stung through the thin fabric of his cheap suit, and the minutes dragged by.

At last he heard the sound of the door opening, followed by sounds from inside.

All at once Logan realized a minor flaw in his carefully thought-out plan. He had devised no way to insure that it was in reality Jean Pierre in the W.C. If he opened the false door at the wrong time, it would prove not only highly embarrassing, but would also destroy the rescue. Furthermore, what if his attendant guard took it in his head to get some fresh air while waiting and joined Logan on the platform?

Well . . . so far there was no sign of a guard. Logan decided to try one of the signals they had used to indicate friendly callers at safe houses. Two long, followed by three short knocks. If it was Jean Pierre, he would surely catch the signal and make himself known.

Logan knocked, and waited but a moment until he heard another of their codes in response—very light, to be sure, but recognizable.

Quickly Logan opened the false door, Jean Pierre stared at him, a bit incredulous. But he wasted no precious time with talk. He hurried out onto the landing. Logan quickly refastened the door; then they hastened into the baggage car, just as the engine sounded its whistle and began to slow for Coulommiers.

"You shouldn't have done this," Jean Pierre said, speaking for the first time.

"This is not the place to argue," replied Logan. "Besides, you are practically free now. Get in here." He lifted the lid to a large wooden crate.

Realizing the futility of a protest at such a point, the priest obeyed. While his two men closed and re-nailed the top. Logan tore off his professor's garb and hitched on a worn pair of overalls and wool coat to look the part of a freight loader.

The instant the train stopped, Logan pushed open the baggage door about a foot. He quickly scanned the depot area. His two other men were not immediately visible; perhaps they were still inside. Then he saw Paul step off the train from the door to car 7. But the lad froze the instant his feet touched the ground. Logan snapped his gaze to his left.

Gestapo! He could see them inside the depot; several appeared to be searching those inside. They would have his own men there in custody within moments and be heading for the loading dock.

Logan groaned inwardly. They had walked into a trap!

Paul caught his eyes for a brief moment and Logan answered his questioning look with a sharp jerk of his head. Paul got the message—they were all going to have to clear out as best they could. Paul headed in the opposite direction.

Don't break into a run! Logan silently cried, as if Paul might be able to hear his thoughts.

But he couldn't tarry watching Paul. There were others whose safety he also had to worry about. He turned back into the baggage car and closed its door.

"Gestapo!" he said. "Let's get the priest out and then we'll have to make a run for it through the rear door and hope to get away from the station through those fields."

In a moment they were outside crowded on the small platform between cars. The first man jumped from the train toward the depot. The Gestapo were still inside and his disguise was good. He walked straight toward them.

What are you doing? Logan wanted to yell after him. But he soon knew well enough. The man had always been a devil-may-care sort, and this was his way of insuring the escape of his comrades. If anything went wrong, he would figure out some way to detain the Gestapo.

But there was no time to waste! His other companion stepped off the train platform in the other direction, and hurried off to the right and into the large field that bordered the station.

Jean Pierre was next, but his cassock caught on a broken metal fitting as he made his leap. The fabric tore, but not in time. It threw off his landing and his foot twisted painfully under him. Logan jumped down and straight to where his friend lay on the ground next to the track.

"Come on, I'll lift you," he said, grabbing Jean Pierre under his arms and shoulders.

"No!" said the priest. "I will slow you down. I'll try to follow, but you must go."

"But—"

"Now it's you who must do as I say. You have no time to argue," countered Jean Pierre. "It is important you get away. I will be all right, but they will kill you. Your danger is far greater."

"I won't leave you."

"You must, Michel! I will always appreciate what you have tried to do here, but the game is up."

"No! We can still make it!"

"You can still make it! But not with a crippled escapee hobbling behind you. Now go! Don't despair, Michel! I am content. God has me where He wants me, and He will use this time—that is what matters. I will not be harmed, of that I am certain. Now go! Hurry!"

Logan hesitated, then dropped to the ground and embraced Jean Pierre.

"I am so sorry," he said as the sting of tears filled his eyes. Jean Pierre kissed his cheek tenderly. "Go with God, my dear son."

"Au revoir!" said Logan, meaning the words in the depth of their literal sense—*Until we meet again!*

Suddenly shouts and the sounds of Gestapo boots broke from the depot area. In the distance Logan could see one of his comrades three-quarters of the way across the field and beating his way for the woods that lay about half a kilometer from the tracks. In the other direction, walking casually along a country road as if he hadn't a care in the world, was the man whose escape had taken him through the depot and under the very noses of the Boche. He saw no sign of Paul.

Logan jumped up and headed for the field.

"Au revoir, mon ami!" came Jean Pierre's voice behind him.

Logan could not even turn to take one last look at his friend. But somehow, perhaps it was in the sound of the priest's voice, Logan was certain they *would* meet again.

Each of Logan's companions had taken off in separate directions, and Logan too shot off on his own. He hoped the men in the depot, as well as Paul, hadn't been taken. But now all he could think of was making it to those woods! One of his companions, several hundred yards to the south, had just made it to the protection of the trees, and now Logan saw that the other had veered off the road he had been strolling along and was heading for cover as well.

Suddenly a barrage of Gestapo gunfire erupted behind him. Logan flew toward the woods, all but certain that the next shot would end his frenzied retreat.

Miraculously, he was still alive when he reached the leaves of the overhanging trees forty seconds later. He stopped for a moment to glance behind him. The shooting had stopped, but he could see a half dozen S.S. soldiers starting out across the field toward him. Behind them, two or three others appeared to be helping a black-robed figure to his feet.

Logan turned back into the forest, and though tears and sweat mingled in his eyes to blur his vision, raced away as fast as he could run.

65 ❊ *Unexpected Encounter*

"A GLASS OF schnapps, mein Herr?"

"Thank you, General. The offerings of your hospitality have certainly changed since our last meeting on the submarine."

Von Graff took a bottle and two crystal glasses from the antique liquor cabinet behind him and poured out two generous measures.

"I hope you are finding Paris pleasant, Herr Channing," he said as he handed a glass to his guest and then resumed his place.

Both men were seated comfortably in tapestry chairs in von Graff's office. Channing brought his glass to his lips and sipped the strong liquor. He had already been in Paris two days—he hadn't wanted to appear overzealous in looking up von Graff. He was glad he had waited, for von Graff had changed from those days when he had commanded a Reich U-boat. He seemed more deliberate now, with perhaps a cunning edge. He would take careful handling. But nonetheless, Channing was certain he *could* be handled. Time and power had made him both vain and greedy for still more power—or at least to hang on to what he had. Power was what drove him—one of those twisted human thirsts for which there is no quenching.

"Paris is an entertaining city," replied Channing broadly. "I really must consider opening a branch office here. The Führer may have his cultural center, but there is no reason for not developing the industrial potential of the Rhine and the rest of France."

"How is the Führer these days?"

"Optimistic."

"Aren't we all?" Von Graff's question carried with it a definite probing quality.

"Are we, General?" countered Channing. "It's not an easy mentality to maintain these days, what with Churchill prattling on about the end of the beginning and the turning of the hinge of fate, or whatever he calls it."

"So you agree that the Reich is doomed, Herr Channing?"

"I prefer to remain a neutral spectator in these matters."

"But a man who hobnobs with Adolph Hitler can hardly be considered *neutral,* especially—God forbid!—should the war turn against us."

"I've never been one to back myself into corners," replied Channing. "It's a smart man who keeps his options open, wouldn't you agree?"

An ironic smile flickered across von Graff's face. "As a general in the S.S.," he said, "I am hardly the man to talk to about keeping out of corners. I, too, have a duty to remain optimistic."

"But supposing Germany did lose the war?"

"Such a statement could be construed as seditious."

"Do you think the Führer sent me here to trap you, General?"

"It might be an interesting possibility."

"Come, General," said Channing, leaning forward confidentially, "can't we talk off the record for a moment? Surely you have given the question some thought. Or at least you must have considered your own future. The war cannot last forever."

"Am I mistaken, Herr Channing, or are you not building up to some kind of proposition?"

The man is definitely shrewd, thought Channing. *He could be useful in more ways than one.*

"Channing Global Enterprises is growing rapidly, General," replied Channing, "and after the war I am going to want some good men in the operation. To be quite honest, I've had my eye on you since that first time we worked together—remember?"

"You commandeered a German U-boat for some urgent mission off the coast of Scotland," said von Graff. "Your contact's boat, as I recall, sank and he was lost."

"Well, no matter. It all turned out successfully in the end. But that is neither here nor there." Channing leaned back and drank from his glass. "I sensed even then that you were a man I could use."

"Use?" repeated von Graff, his eyebrows arched with deep implications.

"In my company," returned Channing quickly. "You'd have no argument against a thirty-thousand-dollar-a-year job after the war—twelve thousand pounds, a hundred fifty thousand marks—I'll pay you in whatever currency you like. Of course, your mark may not be worth much by then," added Channing almost as an aside.

"But if our cause is doomed, as you so subtly imply," said von Graff, "I may well be occupied less pleasantly after the war."

"I never took you for the bullet-in-the-head type, General."

"It might be better than the other options, like rotting in some British or American prison."

Channing did not respond immediately, but instead nursed his drink. Then he continued. "No one need be caught in the debris and wreckage of a falling Reich. I plan on protecting my own."

"Your family?"

"I have only a six-year-old daughter who is quite safe somewhere in America. I was thinking more in terms of my friends."

"I see . . ." The general drew out the word with deliberate extravagance. "And you are offering me your *friendship*?"

"For a price, of course."

"Of course."

At that moment the intercom on von Graff's desk buzzed. He rose, went to it, and flipped the switch.

"Herr MacVey is here to see you, General," came the voice of his secretary.

"Have him wait," said von Graff. "I'm with someone."

He paused, and was about to flip down the switch when he changed his mind and added, "On second thought," he said, "send him in."

He then turned off the intercom and said to Channing, "I hope you don't mind the interruption. I think you might find it a stimulating interlude. I have the feeling my caller is your kind of man."

Von Graff strode to the door just as Logan was about to reach for the handle.

"Good afternoon, Herr MacVey," said the general "Do come in."

"Good afternoon, General," replied Logan. "Have I caught you at a bad time?"

"Not at all. I have someone here I'd like you to meet."

Von Graff directed Logan to the sitting area of his office. "Jason Channing, please meet Lawrence MacVey . . ."

Von Graff had not the vaguest idea of what hornet's nest he was stirring into life with his seemingly benign introduction. The two men shook hands, neither betraying even the faintest hint of recognition.

Logan knew the name *Jason Channing* instantly. Joanna's stories about first coming to Stonewycke were well-recounted family lore. Though he had never seen the man's face and could not be positive this was the same Channing, his inner ears perked up and the rest of the interview took on heightened significance. Joanna's Channing would be somewhere in his late sixties, maybe seventy by now. This man *looked* younger, and extremely fit . . . but he *could* be about the right age. Such were Logan's thoughts in the brief seconds following von Graff's introduction.

On Channing's part, his keen eye had recognized the face before him the moment Logan walked in, even if the name that fell from the general's lips was an unfamiliar one. He had seen photos of the new young graft into the Stonewycke line, and would not easily forget the man Ross Sprague had shadowed for him ten years ago. He would especially not forget a man who had almost gotten the better of him. He wondered if this Macintyre knew him or had heard of him. It was doubtful. Best keep his own counsel for the time being; no telling how a chance meeting like this could be of use in his machinations against the Scottish family he had come to despise.

"Charmed," said Channing, offering his hand.

"The pleasure is all mine, Herr—what was it . . . Channing?—" said Logan brightly, shaking his hand firmly.

"Herr MacVey is one of my agents," went on von Graff, oblivious to the stirrings within his guests, "who is aiding us in the capture of a desperate French criminal."

"Desperate criminal?" said Logan, a bit perplexed.

"L'Escroc," said von Graff, and turning toward Channing, explained further, "an underground leader in the Resistance." Then to Logan again he said, "Surely you have not already forgotten him?"

"We haven't heard from him in so long, I thought perhaps he was no longer a threat."

"We have reason to believe he came out of hiding last night. That is why I had you called."

"So," said Logan, "who have you lost this time?"

"An attempt was made to rescue an old friend of yours, the priest, de Beauvoir."

"I'm sorry you lost such a prize."

"You misunderstood me, Herr MacVey. We lost no one—the attempt was foiled."

"My congratulations, General," replied Logan brightly. "But that doesn't sound like the work of L'Escroc."

"Perhaps it is presumptuous of me to ask," put in Channing, "but who is this fellow? He sounds intriguing."

"*L'Escroc* . . . the name means *The Swindler*," answered von Graff. "He is a low-life British agent whom the ignorant people have turned into a folk hero."

"I thought you said he was French?"

"French . . . British—who knows? One time he is reported to be one, the next another. One rumor came in that he was Hungarian. But the most reliable word is that he is indeed British. Unfortunately, we can't seem to get our hands on him to learn his identity for certain."

"We don't even have a reliable description," added Logan, playing his part so thoroughly that the humor of his words hardly fazed him.

"But after last night's fiasco, we're closer than ever," said von Graff. "We captured two of his compatriots—men who worked with him and know him."

Logan masked his surprise and dismay. He had arrived in Paris only a few hours ago, after a grueling night trying to elude the Gestapo. He had fallen asleep in his room; when he awoke, the desk clerk gave him the message from von Graff to come by his office. He had not taken the time to make contacts that would sort out the aftermath of the ill-fated rescue, for the others would no doubt have had to stay away from the city longer than he. Thus he had seen no one since they all separated at the depot. He had assumed—*hoped*—that all had made it.

Perhaps, had he known more of how things had ultimately turned out he might have delayed this meeting with the general. But there should be nothing to fear: none of the men working with him yesterday knew him as anything but a bespectacled old man. And none knew the name Michel Tanant . . . no one, that is, except—

But just as the thought crossed his mind, the voice of von Graff intruded into his reflection as if he had read his very thoughts, "And these two *will* talk," the general continued, "before we shoot them."

"What makes you think," said Logan, revealing no hint of strain from the sense that all at once everything was closing in on him, "that you haven't got L'Escroc himself?"

"Our police described one of the men who escaped—a gray-haired old man who ran like a youth!"

Von Graff's eyes narrowed and his mouth tightened. "That was him—I know it! He is too smart to be caught so easily. Besides, of the two we captured, one is a boy and the other doesn't fit the vague description we do have of the so-called swindler."

Poor Paul! thought Logan. *I should never have left him alone!*

But in his anguish over the lad, Logan momentarily forgot his own imminent danger. For Paul knew Michel Tanant. And from his capture and the events of the previous day, the Germans could well trace Logan's underground identity. Indeed, Paul knew plenty—enough to convince von Graff that Logan's true allegiance lay to the west, not the east.

Logan realized that as of now he would have but a matter of days, perhaps only hours, to get permanently underground and out of von Graff's clutches for good. The jig was now assuredly up. But he had to know still one more thing before he began to beat his retreat.

"What of de Beauvoir?" he asked.

"He'll be questioned when he is released from the infirmary," replied von Graff. "He broke his ankle in the attempt."

"And then shot with the others?"

"You appear uncharacteristically concerned over the man's fate, Herr MacVey."

"He was a likeable chap," replied Logan without flinching. "It would seem such a waste."

"Well, rest easy. Baron de Beauvoir still calls the shots where the priest is concerned." He chuckled. "No pun intended."

It was a small comfort that at least Jean Pierre might still make it. He would have to take some immediate action to see what could be done about freeing the others. Only one thing was positively clear in his mind—he would never enter this building again. His stint as a Nazi was up.

When Logan left von Graff's office a few minutes later, he had all but forgotten about Jason Channing in the wake of the news of his friends. Before he had stepped onto the avenue Foch, he already had the beginnings of a plan in his mind for another rescue attempt. When reason prevailed some time later, however, after a serious talk with Henri, he saw that the time for his involvement in such things had passed.

"We will get them out, Michel," his friend had assured him. "But the game has now changed. L'Escroc is dead and must never resurface. Neither can Michel Tanant or Trinity. Until we have Paul safely back, and learn from him what the Boche know, we must take every precaution. Your life is in danger."

"But I must—"

"No, Michel! You must *not*. The season of your valiant service to our cause is past. It is time you began preparations to return to England."

"But, Henri," protested Logan, "there is still—"

Henri calmed him with his silencing hand. "Please, my friend," he said, "do not make this more difficult for either of us. In your heart you knew this time was coming. And now, as leader of *La Librairie*, I tell you, it *has* come. You have done all you could do. You have fulfilled your mission."

66 ❊ *Channing's Realization*

JASON CHANNING DINED with friends that evening at *Shéhérazade*.

He had by no means forgotten his encounter with Logan Macintyre. Though the remainder of the afternoon had been occupied with various appointments and business matters, Macintyre remained on the edges of his consciousness the whole time. Without Channing's even being aware of it, his intuitive, suspicious nature had been probing, doubting. wondering. He had a sixth sense about these sorts of things. And he could detect the faint smell of deception in progress, though he hadn't even taken the time to examine the precise reasons for his uneasiness.

As conversation lagged, however, he found himself giving it fuller consideration. He had said nothing to von Graff about his knowledge of MacVey's true identity. On the surface it did not seem to have any bearing on matters with the general. Von Graff undoubtedly knew MacVey to be an assumed name; no one in the spy business used his real name. So Channing knew Macintyre's family—what of it? von Graff would say.

But the strongest reason for his silence was simply that Channing had not yet figured out how best to use what he knew. He would not divulge information prematurely. And in this present case, he was still not sure he grasped fully the complexities of what was going on.

What *was* going on? That was the question. Something smelled wrong. He hadn't liked the look in Macintyre's eye. His responses to von Graff were . . . he couldn't quite put his finger on it.

For years he had been on the prowl for some bit of slander to use against the Stonewycke brood. On the surface it would seem he had been dealt the very cards to bring down their spotless name—one of their own number a German spy! The scandal could cause an uproar in Scotland and bring down the high and mighty Joanna once and for all.

That had always been the problem—they were all so confounded above reproach. He'd thought he had them when that Macintyre married into the family ten years ago. But no— the whole matter was treated openly as a matter of public record. Imagine, an elite family of the British nobility admitting a confidence man into their number, a common swindler becoming one of the family; the facts of his past, even his run-ins with the authorities, couldn't be used against them!

There is no justice, mused Channing to himself.

Now, it seemed as if he finally had something really good. He had stumbled upon a major discovery, one even more powerful if Macintyre didn't realize who Channing was—which was certainly possible.

But Channing had grown wary over the years. Those infernal MacNeils had a way of coming out on top, and he had learned to show more caution than usual where they were concerned. Their son-in-law a Nazi! What a find! It was enough to disgrace any British family. Yet those people were such oddballs—it probably wouldn't bother them. They'd accepted him as a swindler, why not as a Nazi?

And still there was that something stirring in his gut which said things were not what they seemed.

Channing brought his glass to his lips. Again his train of thought shifted back to the encounter in von Graff's office. There was something there, something he could use. He knew it.

Some indefinable peculiarity of MacVey's interaction with the general had set his subconscious to work. Was Macintyre completely on the up-and-up? He had shown a bit too much concern for the captured priest—even von Graff had noted that.

But no, there was something else. Was he too eager, too cocky, too unflinching?

They had talked about the rescue of the priest, the captures. But what was it they had mentioned before that? A fellow they were after, a British agent whom no one could even describe?

L'Escroc, that's what they had called him. The Swindler . . .

Channing leaned back, the word spinning with gathered momentum in his brain. L'Escroc . . . British agent . . . master of disguises . . .

Suddenly Channing set his glass to the table with a thud.

The Swindler! Of course!

A swindler and a con man had married into the highbrow Stonewycke clan. And now that same man was swindling the Germans! It is almost too fantastic to believe, thought Channing, an evil smile of mingled esteem and scorn spreading over his cunning lips.

Macintyre playing a double game! He could almost admire the man. If it weren't for his in-laws, he might try to find a place for *him* at Channing Enterprises after the war! But as it was, this was his key to bringing down the whole lot of them!

Of course, he could never prove any of it to von Graff. The man had obviously bought Macintyre's act hook, line, and sinker. And all he had to go on himself was his intuition and his ability to read people's motives, sometimes even better than they knew them themselves. But he had learned over the years to trust that intuition. It had served him well. And this present discovery would make up for that one glaring time when his perceptions had failed him, when he had sought to make an innocent young lady his own, and been rebuffed for his efforts.

Yes, his revenge would come at last! And would be all the sweeter in having taken so long to bear fruit.

67 ❁ *End of the Charade*

THEY MET IN the back room of a cafe belonging to one of Claude's friends. It was now too dangerous to go to *La Librairie*.

Claude sat on a bench against a grimy wall cleaning and oiling a rifle. Henri was seated at a plain wooden table with an untouched glass of wine in front of him. Logan paced the floor in front of him. There were only three of them; the war had brought many changes.

Logan didn't know why he was so agitated. He wasn't nervous. He didn't think he was afraid. Yet he was unable to sit still. Perhaps it was because he knew he had something to do, but everything was taking too much time.

The air in the small, dimly lit room was pungent with the odor of cigarette smoke and cheap wine, and jovial voices drifting in from the cafe. It served to remind each person present how isolated he was from a normal existence—now more than ever.

Logan paused in his pacing and looked at Claude. "Why did you bring that thing in here?" he asked peevishly. "It's bad enough that the place is crawling with Germans tonight."

"It's a pretty specimen, non?" returned Claude, purposefully ignoring the thrust of Logan's remark. "A friend found it in the sewer and made it a special gift to me." Claude almost let a smile slip across his scarred countenance. "Those criminals in the old days did not know that when they dumped their incriminating weapons, they would be arming the people for a revolution."

"'Divisés d'interêts, et pour le crime unis.' 'Divided by interests, and united by crime,'" quoted Henri dryly.

"Bah!" spat Claude. "Even your de Gaulle has called the French people to revolution. That is the one good thing that will emerge from this war—a new France!"

"The *old* France was not so bad."

"What do old men know?"

Henri merely grunted, apparently deciding that his time was best occupied with his wine. Then he looked up at Logan.

"Please, mon ami," he said, "sit down. You are making us nervous."

"It's just that I had come here prepared to say my final goodbyes."

"I know," replied Henri. "But the delay could not be helped. Your new identification papers are not yet ready. And as I told you, Lise got word to me that she could not come. She was being watched and thought the danger to you would be too great."

"I know," said Logan, at last taking a chair. "And Paul?" he said after a pause. "Have you heard anything?"

"Whether he has talked? No, we have not heard. He is young and untried."

"I hate to think of what they might do to him!"

"Then do not think of it," said Henri. "You must trust us, that we will get him out. In the meantime, while we are making preparations for that, you must bide your time. You must remain until the new papers are ready, otherwise you will never get out of France. The rest of us have done what we can to protect ourselves."

"Besides," put in Claude flatly, "you and Lise were the only ones he could betray."

"Do not fool yourself, Claude," said Henri. "When one is in danger, all are in danger."

"Philosophies!" muttered Claude as he cocked the rifle several times to work in the oil.

The room fell silent. This would be one of their last times together, yet the gathering lacked essential warmth. It would have been better, thought Logan, if Claude hadn't come. But no, it was as much his fault as the Frenchman's. He had been tense and short-tempered too. Mostly he was angry with himself for bringing about this catastrophe. He had played it too close—not just with the Jean Pierre rescue, but the whole Trinity business. He had started out too sure of himself, overconfident. Then when the reality of the dangers involved had gradually become clear, he was in so deep it seemed it could only end one way. He should have taken Henri's advice and pulled out before it came to this.

But he hadn't. He had been waiting for God to show him. Was this now God's answer?

Even if by some miracle they got Paul out before he talked, he could not go on. Only last night he'd remembered that Paul not only knew a great deal about his operations in the French underground, he also knew Logan's real name from that blunder he had made months ago when talking to the Scottish flyer they had helped escape. Too many threads were coming unraveled. In a way it was a relief. It would be over soon—it almost didn't matter *how* it ended, only that he would be able to go back to a somewhat normal existence. Henri was right—he knew that now. His days as Michel Tanant were past.

But now that the die had been cast, it only added to his present tension to prolong the inevitable. It had been two days since Paul's arrest. Logan had not been back to his room. He had already contacted Atkinson, but the major's reply had been far from encouraging. A plane could not be spared; could he make it out over the Pyrenees? They'd keep trying on the aircraft, but just in case, he ought to get things rolling on the other option. Things had changed; the war was heating up. It wasn't as easy as it used to be.

The prospect of still *another* identity to cope with, as well as weeks of travel through the south, now also occupied by the Nazis, was not an appealing one. It was nearly impossible to find guides willing to risk the Pyrenees crossing now that there were heavier German patrols guarding the frontier. Some were charging as much as 100,000 francs for the job, and Logan feared he would have to resort to his old shady life to garner that kind of money.

Well, maybe Atkinson will still find a way to dredge up a plane, thought Logan. But in the meantime, the uncertain waiting was hardest of all. Before he realized it, his thoughts had him pacing once more.

"I thought we'd have more to discuss," said Logan, jamming his hands into his pockets and glancing around. "Maybe it wasn't as necessary as I thought to get together."

He paused. "I wanted to make sure I had a chance to say goodbye," he went on. "But then Lise isn't here, and the papers aren't ready."

"We will meet again in two days at this time," said Henri. "You may see her then. I know that is what you are waiting for."

Logan nodded. "The papers?"

"Hopefully by then as well, my friend," replied Henri. "You have decided to travel south?"

"I must not remain any longer than absolutely necessary," replied Logan. "If Lise doesn't bring a message from London guaranteeing a plane, then I'll leave as soon as I get the papers. I have a couple contacts in Lyon and Marseilles. Maybe by the time I get that far, London will have come up with something. But it will be best for me to keep moving."

"Forty-eight hours, then," said Henri, rising and putting a hand on Logan's shoulder. Logan nodded, and they left the room, Henri to exit through the cafe, Logan to follow the corridor in the opposite direction and out through the rear door into the narrow alley.

Claude remained seated where he was several minutes more, a cynical gaze in his eye. Slowly he raised the rifle to his shoulder and took imaginary aim down its barrel. Gently he squeezed the trigger till the hammer released and clicked down upon the empty chamber with a resounding metallic echo that reverberated through the small darkened room.

68 ✠ *An Insidious Plot*

THE FOLLOWING MORNING, while Logan finalized plans for leaving the city within a day or two, Channing again walked into von Graff's office. The general was in high spirits and broke out his best bottle of cognac.

"Never mind the hour, Herr Channing," he said buoyantly. "I am in the mood to celebrate!"

"What . . . has the Reich taken Stalingrad or repelled the Allies from the shore of Tripoli?" quipped Channing as he took the offered cognac, not in the least squeamish about a shot or two of good brandy at ten in the morning.

"Better, much better!" replied the general. Von Graff sat back and savored his drink a moment.

"I can't imagine."

"I've got L'Escroc!"

"You've captured him?" said Channing in surprise, suddenly solemn. If von Graff saw anything unusual in Channing's strong reaction to something he had heard about only in passing, he made no mention of it.

"Not exactly in my hands . . . but it is only a matter of time now," answered the general. "One of our prisoners has talked. It seems this fellow—a mere boy, really—acted as a courier for L'Escroc, picking up and leaving messages at a certain mail drop. I've sent a unit to watch the spot, and have every reason to believe it will lead us directly to L'Escroc himself, or at least someone high up in his network."

"It would seem congratulations are in order," said Channing, wondering to himself where this latest bit of information fit into his own schemes.

"And now I know for certain that he *is* indeed a British agent: I've learned his true identity! It seems his name is Logan Macintyre, a Scotsman. I can have my contacts in Britain get me a physical description. I anticipate having him within the week!"

"What good will a mere description do you?" said Channing. "The man will surely take precautions. And Paris is a city of several million."

"We will find him," insisted von Graff, "if I have to track him for months!"

"If he knows one of his operatives has been captured, he will no doubt try to leave the city."

"Are you trying to spoil my celebration, Herr Channing?" said von Graff with a frown. "Besides, precautions take time. According to this Guillaume, he did not contact L'Escroc on a daily basis. Thus he may not even know of the boy's arrest—we have kept it quiet."

"Precautions take time, but so does tracking down a swindler when you have nothing to go on. And how can you be certain the lad is telling the truth?"

"Herr Channing, have you ever had your teeth filed down, one by one? Or had a spiked belt gradually tightened around your chest? Such methods do not foster a lying spirit."

"All of which does nothing to satisfy my question: Even with the information you possess, how do you intend to locate this L'Escroc, this Macintyre, especially when in all likelihood he will be out of Paris for good inside the week?"

"All of a sudden, mein Herr, your interest strikes me as something more than causal. You seem to have something on your mind."

"What would you say, General, if I were to tell you that I came here this morning with none other than your L'Escroc on my mind? What would you say were I to tell you that I could deliver him to you with ease, and save you days, even weeks, of grief?"

Von Graff's eyes glinted as he carefully set down his drink. He knew that Jason Channing possessed resources and contacts beyond imagination. Was it possible he had known of L'Escroc all along?

"I would say that I am intrigued," answered von Graff coyly.

"I had certain suspicions which you have just confirmed," replied Channing. "My personal gut feeling in matters of this kind is something I have learned to rely on. Still it is beneficial to have supporting evidence. And I assure you that I am just as keen as you to see this swindler in irons. However, I think I may have a more effective means to that end."

"Do you plan on making this a guessing game?" asked the general caustically. "You implied that you knew what would put this Macintyre into our hands. Do you intend to drop hints and then dangle me along like one of your lackeys?" Von Graff had never really trusted Channing, and now he definitely did not like this little game of his, or the tone in his voice, for that matter.

"Not at all," answered Channing. "I am merely reluctant to proceed further because I don't know how you will respond to what I have to say."

"Come now, Channing, we are not children!"

Channing cleared his throat and raised an eyebrow, as if to say, *So be it.* Then he spoke:

"Have it your way, General. You want your L'Escroc, alias Logan Macintyre? Well, he is none other than your own Lawrence MacVey!"

Channing's words hit von Graff like a thunderbolt. "That's impossible!" he declared. "He has worked with me almost a year, providing valuable information . . ."

But though his first words were ones of denial, his voice quickly lost its vigor and faded into a stunned silence. Almost immediately he knew it was true. He had been standing at his desk and now sank back into his chair—for one of the first times in his life utterly daunted. He did not need to ponder the implications of the situation long to realize what it meant for him. He had stuck his neck out for MacVey, while all along the vermin was slowly slipping a noose around it. Unless he delivered MacVey's head on a platter, his own career as a German commander would come to an abrupt end. He had no delusions. Himmler was hardly the forgiving sort.

"I'll kill him!" seethed von Graff, all his patrician refinement swallowed in animal hatred.

"You have to catch him first," Channing reminded him.

"What do you know of this matter?"

"I have had dealings in the past with Macintyre, and with people very close to him. I recognized him the moment you introduced us the other day, but it took some time to fit all the pieces together."

"But you said nothing."

"I had my reasons. I had to be sure. Believe me, I want to get my hands on him as much as you do, General."

Gradually von Graff began to pull his wits back around him. Channing was wrong—no one wanted MacVey worse than he! If he was going to succeed, he had to think straight. He was a soldier. He had fought in two wars. He was trained to use his head. It was the only way to remain effective. He had to keep control.

Von Graff straightened in his chair, pulled his shoulders back, and focused on Channing.

"What did you have in mind, Herr Channing?" he said slowly, deliberately.

"We may have both grossly underestimated this Macintyre," began Channing. "I thought he was nothing but a third-rate con man, and you thought he was someone you could control. Well, perhaps we were both wrong . . ."

Von Graff shifted uneasily in his chair, but said nothing. Channing continued.

"He follows no patterns, and it's no use trying to second-guess him. What he lacks in finesse he makes up for in sheer audacity. He is L'Escroc—The Swindler—and he won't easily fall for tricks from others. If he is still in the city at all, you may be sure he will not return to any of the places where you might think to look for him. Neither will he look like the MacVey you know. He has probably already adopted one of his many disguises. And he will certainly never walk into one of your snap controls. He knows his man has been arrested, and so is probably already making arrangements to leave the country, even as we talk."

"You make it sound rather hopeless," said von Graff cynically.

"All these preparations will take time, even for L'Escroc."

"So what do *you* propose, Channing?" Von Graff's voice rose as he spoke, on the bare edge of control.

"We would be fools to go after him," replied Channing smugly. "He's too cagey. But he does possess one weakness, which might bring him *to us!*"

Channing smiled, his cunning eyes flashing triumphantly. "He has a family—"

"Of course!" exclaimed von Graff. "It's inspired! But can we do it? Is there time, before he returns and whisks them to safety?"

"I have a man on his wife at this very moment."

"You already knew . . . I'm afraid I don't—"

"As I said, I have other interests in his family. I've had a tail on her for some time, even before Macintyre stumbled across my path. One call and I can have her here in twenty-four hours."

"Then what are we waiting for!" exclaimed von Graff, jumping up and pulling a telephone toward him. "We'll call—now!"

"There is still the matter of how to contact Macintyre once we have our prize and the snare is set."

"No problem! We'll be able to get a message to him!" said von Graff eagerly. "Just grab the girl and leave the rest to me!"

He rubbed his hands together in anticipation. This *was* an inspiration! Small wonder that Channing was such a successful businessman! After all this time, L'Escroc had been under his nose all along! Well, now he would walk right into his arms. This would be better than just putting a bullet through him, though he'd enjoy that pleasure too. But in addition he would have the man's wife to use as leverage. What information might not he be able to drag out of the traitor! It would more than exonerate von Graff in the eyes of Herr Himmler! And when L'Escroc had spilled his guts, *then*—and not before—he would put a bullet through his heart . . . with his wife looking on! Ah, the revenge would be sweet! It would almost make it worth having been temporarily played for a fool!

The general was practically drooling with evil anticipation as he lifted the receiver to ring the switchboard.

"Get my radio man in here," he said. "We have to contact London immediately."

69 ❋ *Logan's Decision*

IT WAS FIVE in the afternoon when Logan again made his way into the alley and through the back door of the cafe. He'd been wearing the disguise of a French beggar all day and the beard itched terribly. He hoped good news would be awaiting him.

Claude was sitting silently in the same chair as before, the rifle across his lap, looking as if he hadn't moved in forty-eight hours. Logan merely nodded, then shook Henri's hand where he stood on the other side of the small room.

In answer to Logan's unspoken question, he held up a handful of papers in front of him, smiling broadly.

"Yes, Michel, they are here. I have your papers!" he said.

Logan sighed deeply. "It is a sad day, Henri," he said in reply after a moment. "A sad day in which to bid friends farewell. Sad . . . but necessary."

"Yes, Michel. You must go."

Unconsciously Logan glanced toward the door.

"She will be here, my friend," said Henri. "I spoke with her around noon. She knows you leave Paris tonight."

"Then there is still no word of an airplane?"

"Not as of then."

A noise at the door forced the two men into sudden silence. They did not move for a long moment. Then came a soft knock—

"It's me . . . Lise," whispered a voice.

Logan strode to the door, unlocked and opened it just wide enough to let her in, then shut and bolted it again.

She looked at each man, but there was no friendly greeting in return to the probing warmth of anticipated farewell in Logan's eyes.

"I take it there has been no message?" he said.

"Not the one you have hoped for," answered Lise solemnly.

"Then you *have* been contacted?"

"Not by London!"

"What are you telling us, Lise?" asked Henri.

"It looks as if Paul has talked," she said bluntly.

"Poor boy!" sighed Henri.

"Are you certain?" said Logan.

"I went to my mail drop before coming here," she replied. "Paul uses it sometimes. I had hoped perhaps—"

"I had forgotten about the mail drops," groaned Henri.

"I picked up the messages—actually there was only one—and started to leave," Lise went on. "Then I realized I was being followed."

"Followed?" said Logan. "You mean no attempt was made to arrest you?"

"I know what you are thinking," she replied. "They hoped that whoever picked up the mail would lead them to the whole nest. But I lost them."

"Are you certain?" put in Claude sharply.

Lise ignored his question. "The odd thing," she added, "is that this message is addressed to *Logan Macintyre.*"

Slowly Logan reached for the small paper Lise now held out to him. He stared at it a long while before he finally tore open the envelope. He quickly scanned the message.

"Dear Lord!" he breathed as he sank into a chair, handing the folded paper to Henri.

Henri looked at the words, shook his head, then read them aloud:

"Greetings, Logan Macintyre—alias L'Escroc, alias Trinity, alias Lawrence MacVey! Yes, mein Herr, we know who you are! We know all about you. And we also know that within twelve hours you will freely *unarmed and alone* walk through the doors of S.S. headquarters and voluntarily give yourself up. How do we know this? Because we have at this very moment in our possession something you will desperately want. We have your wife, Herr Macintyre! If you do not believe us, her signature at the close of this note is all the proof we will provide. You have but a matter of hours to decide. At five a.m. of the morning following the date of this communique, she will be shot as a spy if you have not made your appearance."

So, thought Logan, *the nightmare has come full circle.* It hardly seemed possible that Allison could be dragged into this world which had so occupied him these many months. But he knew even before he saw her handwriting that von Graff was not bluffing. His gambler's instincts had not dulled over the years; he had always been good at sniffing out the false show of a worthless hand. This was not one. Von Graff held the cards.

And now, at last, Logan had his answer. He had been praying for guidance about what to do. Now he knew. There would be no storming of the gates, no escape plans, no daring rescues, no more deceptions. It had to end—here and now. *Help me, Lord,* he said silently, *to have the courage to trust you now, rather than trying to do it by myself.*

Resolutely Logan stood up.

"What are you doing?" said Lise.

"I am going to the avenue Foch."

"Michel! They will kill you!" she almost shrieked. "And probably never let her go even if you do give yourself up."

"We must try to get her out," interjected Henri. "I have other people we could use. You would not have to—"

"No, Henri," said Logan. "I can't do it that way. The time has come for me to lay down my arms. The fight is no longer mine, but the Lord's. He will protect and deliver her."

"You speak of ancient myths when the Nazis are holding your wife!" spat Claude. "You have lost your senses!"

Logan looked around at his friends. How could he make them understand all that was going on within him?

"The power of God is greater than a division of Nazis," he replied. "I cannot explain it. I only know that I must do what I must do. You may each be called differently. But right now, at this moment, this is my destiny. I *must* go."

He turned toward the door, but Claude's voice intervened from his dark corner.

"So, Anglais, it has come to this! You intend to walk straight into the arms of the S.S.?" It was a challenge, not a question.

"I have no choice."

"Here is your choice!" shouted Claude, wielding his rifle in the air in a defiant fashion. Then, with a quick motion, he tossed it across the room to Logan.

On reflex, Logan caught the weapon, just as he had Major Atkinson's gun that day so long ago in England. For a moment he held the rifle in his two hands, staring down at it; then he glanced back toward Claude. But for an instant he did not see the Frenchman, or indeed any of his present surroundings. Many images raced through his mind—but not the images of a crook named Lombardi, or even of a dead German soldier in a blood-stained French wood. He saw instead images of a man who had spent his life hiding behind one role, one charade, one con game after another. A man who had been careening along his own path for years, grasping at the only way he knew, a way of self-sufficiency and independence—afraid to let it go, afraid of what might happen if he relinquished control of his life, afraid of the path that had beckoned to him more than ten years ago . . . fearful of the way God might want him to follow.

Suddenly Logan realized that his way of life—having to trust solely in his own strength—had become an awful burden, dragging him down like a giant millstone. As a Christian he suddenly saw that it hadn't had to be that way, that he could have chosen to trust in God, but he had not *wanted* to see that path. He had *wanted* to go his own way, to be his own man. It had been easier to blame everything on externals—on Allison, on the marriage, on his lousy jobs, on his prison record. On anything but his own blind self-reliance!

He looked down again at the gun. It suddenly seemed to represent the solution the old headstrong, stand-on-his-own-feet, bold Logan Macintyre would have chosen—storm the citadel of the enemy, if not with might like a man such as Claude, then with cunning and with plans of his own devising.

But the charade was over. He could no longer be somebody unreal, some imaginary Trinity or Tanant or Dansette—no more L'Escroc, no more *swindler*. Storming the complexities of life with his own pitiful *self* was over. He had to be Logan Macintyre again. The time had come to allow God to take command!

He tossed the rifle back to Claude.

"No, Claude," he said. "That is not the way. Neither is L'Escroc. Not this time. This time I will put my fate in God's hands, not my own."

"Bah! You are more of a fool than I thought! You speak the pious words of a child!"

"You may speak more of the truth than you know," replied Logan. "Perhaps a child is what I should have been all along," he added with a thin smile.

"You are an idiot! You think you will go in there and sacrifice yourself to satisfy some . . . some insane urge inside your twisted brain! You will do nothing but betray us all!"

Logan turned beseeching eyes toward Henri. "You understand . . . don't you, Henri?"

The old bookseller nodded. "I understand, mon ami. I would perhaps do the same were I in your shoes."

"Never!" shouted Claude. In an instant he leaped up and took aim at Logan's head down the long barrel of his rifle. The others now realized that while he had been shadowed by the dim light in the corner of the room, he had slipped shells into the chamber.

"Think, Claude!" pleaded Henri, knowing the angry Frenchman well enough to realize that his distorted emotions were taut and that he might do anything. "One shot will have half the Wehrmacht on you."

"What do I care? We are as good as betrayed anyway!"

Quickly Lise stepped in front of Logan. Henri, scrambling from his chair, joined her.

"Then kill us all," she defied.

"Why shouldn't I?" he returned.

"Because then you would be no better than the murdering Nazis you have fought so hard against," argued Henri. "What could your life mean if you were just like them?"

They stood thus for several seconds that seemed to each as an eon, the tension palpable. Then with an angry curse Claude threw down the rifle and stalked toward the door. There he paused and turned, glaring.

"You are *all* fools!" he spat hatefully. "I am done with you!"

When he was gone, Logan looked down for a moment at the gun where it lay on the floor, sighed, then turned with a heavy smile of thanks to his friends.

"I cannot promise anything," he said, "but I will do my best not to talk. I wish I could give you more assurance for all you have done for me. But this is something I must do, come of it what may. The Lord has many ways to deliver His people."

"We need no more assurance, Michel," said Henri. "We have no fear."

After speaking quietly together for a few final moments, Logan placed his arms around the old bookseller in a warm embrace.

"I doubt I will see you again, mon ami," he said, tears standing in his eyes. "But I will never forget you. Please do what you can for Allison if you have the chance. Adieu, dear friend."

"No, Michel," replied Henri, "not *adieu,* but *au revoir* . . . something tells me we will yet again look upon each other's faces."

Tenderly he kissed Logan's cheek.

Logan turned to Lise. They exchanged poignant gazes. War had thrown them together, forcing upon them forbidden desires and painful sacrifices. But out of it each had grown, and out of the rubble of what could never be had blossomed a friendship that would remain forever in the memory of both, though they would never lay eves upon each other again.

"Adieu," Lise said to him, and Logan knew she had chosen the word purposefully.

"Adieu, Lise."

Logan exhaled a deep breath, took one last loving look at his two friends, then turned toward the door.

70 ❄ *Full Circle*

THE SMALL ROOM was icy cold.

Allison shivered and drew the coarse wool blanket more tightly about her shoulders. She glanced at the barred window. It was dark out, but she had no idea what time it was—probably nine or ten at night.

What a fool she had been! She realized that now.

But it all seemed so different yesterday when the two men had stopped her as she walked home from work. "We can take you to your husband," one of them said. She hadn't even paused to think it over rationally, hadn't thought to ask for an explanation or some kind of identification. She still did not suspect foul play when she had mentioned that she should notify her mother and they insisted there was no time, a slight sinister edge creeping into the second man's voice.

Stupidly, irrationally, thinking only of seeing Logan rather than the dangers of wartime, she got into the car with them.

It was too late for sensible thinking once they drew guns and hustled her aboard a private plane. They'd landed once in Lisbon, but she had remained inside the plane the whole time, dozing occasionally, cold, hungry. And now here she was in France—she had seen the Arc de Triomphe from the car window on the way from the airport.

She had been kidnapped, that much was clear, and put in this room, or prison cell, she couldn't quite tell. Until two hours ago she had had no idea why, or if it had anything to do with Logan or if she would in fact see him.

Then she had had visitors.

The door had opened and Allison shot up from the bunk where she had been lying. Two men entered. One appeared to be in his late forties, very refined looking, dressed in a trim black uniform, obviously a German officer, though Allison didn't know enough about their insignias to tell his rank. The other man was considerably older, probably in his sixties, though vigorous enough. He was handsome for a man of his age; dressed in an expensive blue surge suit. He also appeared quite distinguished, though with an entirely different air than the German officer.

The officer stepped forward and held out his hand graciously. "I am General von Graff, Frau Macintyre," he said politely in well-cultivated English. "I trust you are doing well."

"What do you expect me to say, General?" she answered petulantly. "I am hungry and cold. I have been forcibly taken from my home and locked up like a common criminal with no idea—"

"Forgive me for these accommodations. I wish we could provide something more fitting your station."

"They said I would see my husband."

"That is yet to be seen," answered von Graff.

"But I thought—"

"It is entirely up to your husband, Mrs. Macintyre," put in the other man, whose accent now further identified him as an American.

"What is this all about?" asked Allison. "I don't understand."

"Perhaps I might introduce myself," went on the older man. He held out his hand as if he were trying to mimic the general's earlier gesture. "Jason Channing, at your service!"

Allison's brow suddenly creased. She immediately recognized the name, but her perplexity stemmed from the fact that it came so unexpectedly, almost as if she were meeting some historical figure from the distant past.

"You are familiar with my name?" he asked in an almost jovial tone, clearly enjoying the moment so richly satisfying to his vengeful nature. This might not quite settle the old score, but it would certainly help him at least sleep nights with a smile on his face!

All at once in her mind's eye Allison saw her mother, young and untried, standing in a meadow of Port Strathy, facing an influential, debonair man of the world, a man who had flattered her with empty words, a man who had lied and cheated and had tried to bring destruction upon the whole town. In the vision of her imagination—just as her father had described to her many times—she could see her then shy, retiring mother pull back her shoulders and denounce that man before all the residents of Port Strathy.

And now here he was again, with that same arrogant look upon his face that Joanna had so aptly described to her family. Allison wondered that she hadn't recognized him just from that smirk on his face even though she had never seen him before. *How could he be mixed up in all this mystery involving Logan?* she wondered. Was he still, after all these years, striking out against the family of the woman who refused him? One look into his eyes gave her all the answer she needed.

But Allison was not to be cowed. In her veins flowed the blood of Lady Atlanta and Lady Margaret, the same blood that had given her mother courage in her moment of crisis. Allison stuck out her chin, every inch of her small but hardy frame emanating that feisty Duncan stock.

"Channing . . ." She appeared to muse over the name. "Yes . . . it does sound vaguely familiar, though I must say it warranted hardly more than a passing mention."

Channing's eyes sparked at the barb like steel against steel. But he was too proud to show that the wound had penetrated. He, too, was suddenly thrust back in memory to that same Strathy meadow facing the only person who had ever dared refuse him—a frail, worthless, bumpkin of a woman at that! This ridiculous girl was just like her mother—haughty in the face of superiority, fearless even when facing imprisonment or death! But her arrogance would only make his vengeance all the sweeter!

"Have your moment, my dear," he said coldly. "It will be your last."

"What do you want with me?"

"For myself," replied Channing, "it is just a bit of sport. But for the general here, your presence is of purely utilitarian value."

"It is nothing personal, Frau Macintyre," put in von Graff, "for *me*, that is," he added, casting a quick glance toward Channing. "You were simply an extremely convenient way to obtain what I really am after."

"And that is . . . ?" said Allison.

"Your husband, actually."

Allison closed her eyes as the full reality of her circumstances finally dawned upon her. She was being used as bait! But she tried not to show the faltering of her courage, though when she spoke again, her voice was weaker than before. "I'm afraid I still don't understand . . ."

"You need not understand anything further, mein Frau. But Herr Channing was anxious to meet you. He insisted that you know something of the situation."

Von Graff clicked his heels together and bowed slightly. "We will take our leave now," he said. "It is entirely possible that you might also be free to go as soon as your husband graces us with his presence."

Von Graff turned smartly and opened the door. Channing lingered a moment.

"It has truly been a pleasure, Mrs. Macintyre," he said with a smile. "You are every inch your mother's daughter, and I must say that makes the satisfaction of meeting you all the sweeter."

Then he turned and followed von Graff out.

That had been at least two hours ago, maybe four, for all Allison could tell. In anguish she had spent those hours praying that there might be some way to warn Logan. For no matter how long they had been apart, she knew he would turn himself in immediately upon learning these men had her. Knowing he was safe, she could endure this place. If only she could warn him somehow!

71 ❈ Together at Last

S LOWLY LOGAN MADE his way down the darkened avenue Foch.

He had been along here many times in the past months as a supposed German informant. But never in the middle of the night.

After leaving his friends he had returned to his room. He knew it was being watched, just as he knew he had been followed ever since. But none of that mattered now.

He had needed a little time alone, to think, to collect himself for the ordeal that was sure to come. Time to solidify his commitment, both to Allison and the Lord, and to gather strength through prayer for the path he had chosen to walk—a path he had little doubt would lead to his ultimate death. When he left a few hours later he knew he was ready, for the first time in his life, to face the final consequence of war. He was at last ready to lay down his life, in quite a literal sense, for his wife. He was finally a man at peace—with himself and with his God.

On a more practical level, he had wanted to pay his final bill as well, and to scour his room to make sure all traces of any connection to *La Librairie* or any of its people were utterly gone. That done, he glanced around one more time. His personal effects, of which there were few, hardly mattered now either. He made sure he was dressed warmly, bundled up in his overcoat, then turned and headed out into the night.

There would be only one more stop—at the cafe where he spent so much time while in Paris. There was time for a good hot meal. Who can tell? he thought grimly. It would probably be his last.

When he finally began the long walk down the avenue Foch, it was just after ten p.m.

Thirty minutes later, he stood before the somber outer walls of the S.S. garrison. He walked toward the guardhouse, where two uniformed men were stationed. As he approached, they poised themselves with rifles ready.

"Logan Macintyre to see General von Graff," said Logan simply.

"Ah yes, Herr Macintyre," replied one of the men, relaxing his weapon. "We were told to expect you. I will call and tell him you are here."

Even as he spoke, the other guard walked around behind Logan and began binding his hands.

Logan said nothing further, and made no resistance to his captors.

When Channing and von Graff left her, Allison lay back down and tried to sleep. The bed—a thin mattress over a wooden bunk—wasn't much. But she was too exhausted to care. Within moments she was sound asleep.

Suddenly Allison started awake. She had no idea how much time had passed. It was still the dead of night. Sounds outside the door had roused her. She sat up.

The door opened, and light blazed in from the single bulb in the corridor outside. Allison squinted as she looked toward the door. A German soldier stepped in, followed by a man dressed in civilian clothes, and another soldier who held a drawn pistol.

Suddenly Allison's face came aglow and seemed to lighten the darkened cell where she sat. "Logan!" she cried, jumping up. "It *is* you!"

"Oh, Ali," he said softly, "I am so sorry it has to be this way!"

Tears of joy streaming down her face, Allison rushed forward, but instantly the two guards closed ranks around Logan. She stopped, and for the first time beheld her husband's appearance.

She could tell at once that he had changed, yet not in the way she had always feared. He had not hardened, but rather—in spite of the visible strain and the toll of the past year—seemed softer, at peace. It was as if a mask had been removed and she was at last seeing into the depths of the real man—the man she had always known was there but which had remained hidden below the surface. She felt that she was seeing *into* him, as she had always wanted to be able to do. What she saw on his face made her glad and ache all at once. There was love, and yet pain and sadness in his eyes. Something had happened to him since leaving London, and she saw that the changes had not come easily.

Logan turned to one of the guards. "Neumann," he said, "can't you give us some time alone?"

Neumann hesitated, glanced from Logan to Allison, not so much assessing their potential capacity to escape, but rather with a kind of pity. Then he looked at the other guard. "Warten für mich draussen," he said. The guard about-faced and left the room. Then to Logan, Neumann said, "Five minutes, Herr Macintyre; that is all." And he too was gone.

Allison and Logan stood still a moment longer, gazing upon each other, then as if of one mind each took a step. Allison opened her arms to embrace her husband, then saw that his hands were manacled together. She fell into fresh weeping and threw her arms around him, resting her head on his shoulder.

"I'm so sorry for getting you into this, Ali," he said tenderly.

"Oh, Logan . . . dear Logan!" she sobbed through her tears. "I'm just so happy to see you!"

He took a half-step backward, then raised his bound hands and cupped her chin then—that sweet, soft, determined chin!

"Logan . . . I want you to know—"

"Ali," he interrupted, "there's so little time, and I must tell you something—I may not have another chance."

He paused, as if he thought she would protest. But he too saw a change in his young wife.

"Ali," he went on, "I was a selfish fool. I know that now. I had everything so wrong, so turned around. Lady Margaret tried to show me, and Dorey, and even your parents. But I wouldn't listen. I don't know why. I guess I was so stubborn I had to learn the hard way—"

"Logan, please! Don't—"

"Hear me out, Allison. It's all true. I didn't have the slightest inkling what love meant, that it goes beyond happiness and feelings. The kind of love that makes a marriage work is so much different than anything I ever thought. But God is showing me, Ali. He's finally opened my eyes to see that the commitment we made to each other goes beyond all that."

He paused and smiled at her. "I know it's too late now, but . . . as poorly as I'm explaining this, I had to try to make you understand. I never was much good at expressing what was in my heart—I suppose I never really knew my heart before. But, Ali . . . will you forgive me?"

"Oh, Logan, we both had so much to learn," Allison replied. "So much of it was my own fault too. But you know I forgive you."

"I wish we could have the last nine years back, Ali," he said. "I want nothing more than the chance to try to do it right . . . but these five minutes might be the only second chance we have—"

"Logan, no! Don't say it!"

He motioned to the bed. "Let's sit down."

"We must be strong," he said as they sat together on the edge. "But then you never had a problem with that. I suppose it's me I'm worried about. I can be strong too . . . if you'll help me, if I know you'll be all right after I'm gone—"

"Logan, please! There *must* be some way out of this!" cried Allison.

"Oh, if only there were, my darling," sighed Logan. "But you know what they do with captured spies."

"Spies?"

"I've been part of the French underground all this time, acting as a German double agent. They just discovered my identity a few days ago. They grabbed you so they could lure me out of hiding. But having seen you again, and knowing that you still love me, I think I can now face death calmly."

Allison threw her arms again around Logan, her tears flowing freely.

"And our daughter—" Logan went on. "I wanted so much to have the chance to be the right kind of father to her. Please at least tell her that, as miserable a fellow as her father was for a while, he loved her, and . . . Allison, what's wrong?" As Logan spoke, Allison suddenly let out an anguished sob, pressing a hand against her mouth.

"Oh, I wasn't going to tell you now," she wept. "I didn't want to add even more to your grief, but . . . but . . ."

Again she broke out in a mournful cry.

"Please, Ali, share your pain with me. Whatever it is, I've got to know."

"Oh, Logan, it's not just my pain!" she sobbed.

"What is it?"

"Oh, Logan, little Joanna—she's . . . she's dead, Logan! She was with Mother; there was a bombing . . . the train was half destroyed! I'm so sorry to have to tell you!"

Logan was silent a moment. Then he said, "And Joanna . . . ?"

"She had to be hospitalized," replied Allison, trying to calm herself. "But nothing serious. She's all right."

"Oh, Ali . . . if only I could have been more to the two of you!"

He wanted desperately to take her in his arms, but his hands were cuffed. He wrenched at them in frustration.

Allison held him in her arms instead as much to comfort herself as him. Neither spoke for several moments. Never before had they been closer than during these several silent seconds that passed. But their unity did not stem so much from their shared grief—though that had perhaps given focus to it—but rather from the mutual turning of their hearts at last to the God whose desire had always been to bring them together as one. Each was praying for the strength of the other for the trials they knew were coming.

Soon their quiet was interrupted by a sharp tap on the door.

"Two minutes," called Neumann.

Logan shook his head toward the door with a sigh. "I must tell you something else," he said. "I haven't even given you a chance to talk, but I think I know now what you might have said to me, and that will have to be enough."

"This war seems so unfair," said Allison.

"We're in God's hands, Ali. Lady Margaret would say nothing happens by accident." She smiled. "I love you, Logan. And you're right—I can just see her saying that very thing."

"I love you, my dear Ali—more than ever!"

He paused, with another sigh, then continued almost begrudgingly. "Oh, how I hate to spend our last moments on *business*. But even if my fate is sealed—"

"Logan, I won't accept that! There must be some way!"

"If only there were! But please . . . listen to me. I must know that you're going to be safe. That's all I have right now. I'm pretty sure von Graff will let you go. I dropped some hints to him that you knew more about the underground operation than you do, so he'll cut you loose, hoping you will lead him to my associates. There's no way to eliminate the danger.

Just be careful, and warn the others that you are probably being followed. But it's the only way I can be sure you'll get home safely. Now, go to the hotel on—"

"No, Logan! I don't want to go! It's all too complicated! Let me stay here and die with you!"

"Allison, please. Don't you see? I've failed as a husband. My own foolish life has gotten me into this mess. I have nothing left but to try to save you, and to die with honor. That's all that can now give meaning to a past life that has been anything but heroic. I have to know that I have not given my life in vain, that you will live on and maybe remember me once in a while as a man in the end you could be proud of."

"Oh, Logan . . . I *am* so proud of you!" But Allison could say no more through her quiet weeping.

"Now, in the morning go to the Hotel de Luxe on the rue Saint Yves. Do you have that?"

Allison nodded, but Logan was not sure. Her mind hardly seemed focused on the details. The Lord would have to bring it all back to her—there was no time to say it all more than once.

"The rue Saint Yves. Remember . . . it's important. Hotel de Luxe. There's an old woman out front who sells flowers. Buy a bouquet from her, then go to the little park on the corner and sit on a bench. You should arrive by ten a.m. A friend of mine will contact you—he'll know you by the flowers. You'll know him when he uses the name *L'Oiselet.* He will get you out of France."

"Let me stay with you, Logan," Allison pleaded. "I've waited so long for us to be together."

"Dear . . ." He kissed her gently. "Don't you see? The only way I can face what's ahead is to know you are safe. If you remained here, they could use you as leverage. They might torture you to get information out of me. I could stand anything but that. I knew that risk when I turned myself in. But I had to see you. And I had to hope that my gamble with von Graff would pay off and that he would release you. I know they're going to kill me in the end, but if your life were in the balance too, I might betray friends and cause much suffering. With you safe, I can be strong . . . and keep silent."

"Logan! I can't . . . I can't face life without you!" sobbed Allison.

"You will, dear Ali. God will give you strength. He is with me, and He will be with you. You can trust me to Him without fear."

All at once the door burst open and the guards clattered into the room. Neumann held the door while the other marched abruptly up to Logan, grabbed him by the arm, and jerked him to his feet.

"I love you, Ali!" he called hurriedly as they yanked him away. "Be strong . . . the Lord will watch over me!"

"I love you, Logan!" cried Allison through tears of agony. "I will always love you!"

She watched helplessly as he disappeared from sight and the heavy door was thrown shut and bolted after him.

Thirty minutes later, Allison's tears of anguish had spent themselves. She took several deep breaths in an attempt to regain her control, then slowly sat up. She *would* be strong! She would honor his memory by carrying out his last wish. She would remember all he had told her, and would do as he said. He deserved that much from her. She would be brave and strong . . . for *his* sake! Could she do anything less for such a courageous husband? If he were to die with honor, then she would honor him in life. She would not even let the Germans follow her! She would do her best to protect his friends!

Allison sank to her knees beside the bed.

"Oh, Lord," she prayed quietly. "Give me the courage to be strong. Help me to trust you . . . and to trust Logan to you. Give him grace to endure, Lord. Protect him in your love."

72 ❈ *L'Oiselet*

THE WOMAN APPEARED so old and frail, it seemed a miracle that the biting November wind did not whisk her away. She glanced up at Allison, and her wrinkled, brittle face cracked into a toothless grin. Even if Allison had not been instructed to purchase a bouquet from her, she would have done so merely from pity. She took a coin from her purse and bought a bunch of brown and orange mums.

"Merci beaucoup!" said the old flower-lady, nodding profusely.

"De rien, je vous en prie," Allison replied, trying to recall some of her French from school. But *thank you* and *you're welcome* were about the extent of it.

As she continued on her way, she noticed the man in the black jacket. He had followed her last night from S.S. headquarters, and there had been another man standing in front of the hotel. Logan had been right—they were keeping an eye on her. She had made a few vain attempts last night to lose the man. This morning, feeling gradually braver, she determined to do better.

Did they really think she would lead them to the underground? General von Graff had been most gracious about releasing her, even offering to call a hotel. She told him she preferred to stay in a hotel she had used before the war. He made a vague noncommittal reference to her returning to London, but she said she wanted to be near her husband. He said he understood, and she would be welcome in Paris as long as was necessary, pretending that their "little difficulty" with Logan would soon be resolved. She knew he was lying, but said nothing.

As she walked away from the front of the Hotel de Luxe, Allison tried to think of what she might do so as to be alone when she reached the park. Above all, she did not want to endanger any of Logan's friends. Her one possible advantage would be that the man shadowing her would never expect any sudden moves. If she acted quickly, the element of surprise would be on her side.

But what could she do? She knew nothing about this sort of thing.

Ahead she spotted several shops, a cafe, and another hotel. As she approached, she stopped to look in one of the store windows. Yes, the man was still behind her, about half a block away. She could see his reflection.

She turned and continued on. On the other side of the hotel stood a small motion picture theater. That might be a possibility. Back in London, such places always had rear exits. And it was open—a matinee was playing! Without thinking further, she ducked inside, bought a ticket, and hastened into the darkened auditorium.

Now came the moment she had to act quickly. By the time the man behind her bought a ticket, got inside, and became accustomed to the dim light, she would be long gone!

She ran down the right aisle, spotted at the far end the emergency exit, and without a hesitation tried the door handle.

It opened! She stepped through it, closed it quickly behind her, and suddenly found herself in an outside alley that ran behind the hotel. She ran to the end, glanced up and down the street, turned to her left, ran the half-block to the next intersection, turned left again and ran all the way to the next cross-street, where she crossed the wide boulevard and turned up the street to the right. At last she paused to catch her breath.

If that man can find me now, she thought, he deserves to know where I'm going!

Nearly an hour later, Allison, by many circuitous routes, finally arrived at the park Logan had told her about. It was thirty minutes past the appointed time and she hoped she was not too late. The day was a chilly one, but the park was still filled with people. The sun was shining brightly, and that was apparently enough to entice the Parisians out-of-doors. She had not seen her German tail since the theater, but still strolled about for a while, trying to make it appear that she was here for no specific reason, just in case any unwanted eyes *were* still upon her. She was certain Logan would not lead her into danger. She had the distinct impression, as she recalled his words, that he knew exactly what he was doing in setting up this meeting.

She found a bench and sat down, idly watching some children playing ball, trying very hard not to glance about.

In five minutes an old gentleman ambled up and seated himself on the bench that backed Allison's. Before long he began reading a book—Allison could not see his activity, for she still sat facing the opposite direction, but she heard him leafing through the pages. Then she heard his soft voice. At first she thought possibly he was mumbling or reading to himself. Then she heard:

"Madame Macintyre—do not turn or speak."

The urge to do just those two things was nearly overwhelming. But Allison managed to complacently keep her gaze on the children.

"I know you by the flowers," the man went on in English, though with a heavy French accent. "You will know me by the name L'Oiselet. Listen closely. In a few moments lay down your flowers and freshen your lipstick. Then rise, leave the flowers behind you, and walk on."

That was all. The only other sound from the gentleman was that of another page being turned.

Allison followed his instructions, squelching the dozen questions that immediately rose to her mind. She laid the flowers down, took up her purse, added some fresh color to her lips, and, looking in the mirror of her compact, also gave her hair a quick pat. When she had satisfactorily given the impression of a woman fixing her face, she rose and started off. It was hardly the kind of meeting she had expected. She was leaving knowing no more than when she had come.

She had gone about fifty paces when she heard a child's voice calling after her.

"Mademoiselle! Voici vos fleurs!"

Allison turned and a little boy ran up to her waving the bouquet in the air.

"Merci," said Allison with a smile, taking the flowers. She turned and began on her way again. She felt rather than saw the paper wrapped around the stems of the flowers.

Fighting the urge to grab the paper and read the note she was certain would be there, she continued on. She couldn't relax yet. It was entirely possible von Graff had put two or three men on her.

Allison walked straight to her hotel, climbed the stairs to her room, and, once inside, tore the paper off the bouquet. The message read:

"Spend afternoon shopping, with a casual stop at the bookstore *La Librairie,* 124 rue de Varennes, 3 p.m."

73 ❈ *Comrades*

WHAT THE GERMANS would think of her shopping while her husband lay in prison a condemned man, Allison could hardly imagine.

Her follower, who had managed to get back on the trail when she returned to her hotel for a rest, would report that she had spent the afternoon distracting herself in the shops, a perfumer's, a dress boutique, two or three bookstores, making a few idle purchases, not appearing to enjoy herself overly much.

At a few minutes before three she wandered onto the rue de Varennes and entered her third bookstore of the day. Her shadow paused outside across the street. The man behind the cluttered counter appeared about sixty years of age with a pleasant, friendly face. When he spoke, she realized it was the same man from the park, though she had not had so much as a glimpse of him then.

"Bonjour, Madame," he said. "I see they are following you."

"I tried to be discreet," said Allison. "I gathered that to be the intent of your message."

"He appears none too suspicious or concerned," said Henri. "Michel has taught you well, eh?"

"Michel?"

"Your husband . . . oh, but I forget! I ought to get used to his real name—the pseudonym is of little use now."

"He said you were a friend of his."

"And I am honored to be counted as such," Henri replied warmly, though a sadness crept into his eyes. "Come, let us browse among the books over here."

He led her to a shelf toward the back of the store. "Your Boche might get suspicious if I took you into the back, so this will have to do."

Suddenly Allison tensed. All at once she became aware that they were not alone in the small shop, and yet the man spoke freely and seemed to take not the slightest notice. A woman stood leaning against the wall between the high bookcases. When Allison came into view, she stood straight and faced her and Henri as they approached.

"Ah, Lise," the old man said in a subdued tone, "she has come!"

He turned to Allison, motioning her to speak softly. "Madame Macintyre, may I present another of your husband's friends from our small band? This is Lise, and I myself am called Henri. We are glad to have you visit us, though we wish it could be under more pleasant circumstances."

"Bonjour. Madame Macintyre," said Lise, stepping forward and offering her hand.

"I am happy to meet you, Lise," said Allison, accepting the handshake. As their eyes met, the peculiar sensation pulsed through her that the sad, intense, beautiful eyes of the French woman were assessing her merit. She returned the look steadily, until Lise's lips twitched into a half smile, and released her hand, apparently satisfied with what she saw. Allison returned the smile.

"Time is short," said Henri, snapping Allison out of her momentary reverie, "for how long can one be expected to stand in a bookstore? Now, Madame, of primary importance—which Michel was most concerned with—is that papers are being printed for you and arrangements are being made to smuggle you out of the city and back to your home. After that—"

"What about my husband?" Allison cut in abruptly.

Henri shook his head regretfully. "Dear Michel," he sighed. "We want nothing more than to help him, but he is under even closer guard than another of our number, Jean Pierre."

"But you can't just let them kill him!"

"Don't you think we would get him out if we could?" rejoined Lise sharply. "But there is no possible way! We've already discussed everything!" Then she glanced away and appeared embarrassed at her outburst. "I'm sorry," she said, "I did not mean . . ."

"We are all very upset by the situation," said Henri.

But Lise would not accept Henri's attempt to give her a reprieve. "If my English is better," she said, "I am perhaps able to explain that nothing is more important to us than helping Michel."

"Your English is fine," said Allison. "I suppose since you are all strangers to me, it is hard to realize you can be as concerned for Logan as I am. I also apologize."

"Your husband is a remarkable man," said Lise. "He has sacrificed much for our cause, taken many risks. He is very brave, and has rescued countless Frenchmen and Britons and Americans from the Boche. But now that he comes to face the ultimate sacrifice, we must stand helplessly by. It makes our hearts . . . je ne sais pas quoi—" She stopped short, searching for the correct way to express her thoughts. "It is difficult," she added at length.

"He made us swear that we would attempt nothing until you were safe," added Henri.

"Surely you don't always just sit by when one of your people is in danger?"

"No, of course not. Michel was one of the boldest in planning rescues and carrying them out. But you must understand the dangers. Just recently an effort to gain back one of our dear friends failed. Not only is our beloved priest still in prison, he is being guarded more closely than ever. Two others are dead, a young boy has been tortured, and all has led to the imprisonment of your husband. You see, the consequences for failure are severe. It is entirely possible that to leave Michel to rely on his own wits with the Germans he is already well-acquainted with will be the safest course of action in the long run. To try a frontal assault to break him out would only get some of our own people killed; it would probably endanger him far worse."

"What could be worse than a firing squad?" said Allison, starting to cry.

"I'm simply saying, my dear Madame Macintyre, that I cannot risk your life and the lives of others who depend on me. I would gladly risk my own life for him . . . I'm sure Lise would, as well. But until you are safe, and until I know more how my life might be used to gain his release, I see nothing that I can do."

"I am as safe as anyone in Paris," said Allison determinedly. "Thus you have kept your word to Logan."

"Not until we have seen you safely *out* of Paris."

"Time enough for that later," replied Allison. "But I will not leave without him!"

"I think," smiled Henri, "that you are maybe as remarkable as your husband."

"No, Monsieur," replied Allison, "just *very* stubborn. It's a family trait." She returned Henri's smile; wiped away her tears, and took a deep breath. "Logan told me, just before they took him away, that I had to trust God for him. I suppose I have to learn to trust the instincts of his friends, too. But if you're waiting for him to bring his wits and silver tongue to his own aid, I have to tell you, he sounded resigned to martyrdom. I don't think he's going to lift a finger on his own behalf. I think he's made peace with himself, with God, and now with me . . . and is ready to die."

Just then the doorbell rang. Henri hurried away, in case the newcomer was an unwelcome patron. His familiar greeting told the two women all was well, but they remained where they were.

"Did you know Logan well?" Allison asked Lise, following a moment of silence.

"We worked together for over a year," answered Lise. "Henri and I and several others. A few are now in prison. One is a Jew who was taken to a camp in Germany."

"How horrible!"

"War is ugly."

"I would so like to understand what it was like for him here," said Allison earnestly. "If only to grasp more fully the changes that took place in him."

Lise smiled, apparently lost in thought for several moments. It was not a particularly warm or cheerful smile, yet Allison oddly sensed there was something in this melancholy woman she could trust.

"Madame Macintyre," said Lise, the smile fading from her lips, but lingering as a new warmth came into her eyes, "I thought many times that Michel's wife must be a very lucky woman. I am now beginning to see why Michel always held you in such high regard, and spoke of you as fondly as he did. Seeing you helps me understand much about the man I grew to care for."

"It sounds like the two of you were . . . close."

"Yes, Madame Macintyre. I would not be truthful to say otherwise. Your husband—Logan—was a close and dear friend. Before he came I had grown bitter from the war. He helped me in many ways to . . . to be a *person* again. He will always be special to me. But you need have no fear. No one could ever replace you for him. He was an open-hearted man who loved all those he met. But toward the end, I could tell he longed for you terribly. He had many friends, but only one Allison."

"Thank you, Lise," said Allison softly. "You don't know how much your kind words mean to me. But now I think it is time for me to go. I will be back. I hope we may have the opportunity to talk again."

"I will look forward to it," replied Lise.

74 ❊ *Incommunicado*

THE WALLS TOLD the story.

Logan passed the long hours trying to make sense out of the poignant statements, some legible, some merely undecipherable scratchings, etched into the plaster around him with a nail or sharp rock. The prison graffiti told of courage and bitterness and fears, the final pre-death messages of those who had gone before him in the dungeon-like cells of Fresnes Prison.

Some spent the final moments of their lives making clear to anyone who cared their political stands.

Death to Pétain! one had scratched boldly. *Long live de Gaulle!* wrote another, and *Long live the Red Army!*

Others seized the moment to decry their bitter disappointments: *Jean Aubrac—betrayed by a friend!* mourned a Frenchman condemned to the firing squad. And, *Marie Bonnard—I hope my little Suzanne is well,* lamented a patriotic mother; an unidentified cynic simply said: *I don't mind dying; it's a rotten world, anyway.*

An American flyer took the opportunity to calculate the pay he was saving by sitting in prison. And below his computations was an especially odd inscription: *Sgt. Helmut Mölders, to be shot for aiding and abetting the enemy—but my only enemy is the Führer!* "An interesting point of view for a German sergeant to hold," murmured Logan. Yet he realized at the same time that in a sense Germany too was an occupied country, with many inside its borders also struggling to regain their freedom in different ways.

Some of the inscriptions attempted to lend hope to future sufferers. One, quoting World War I poet Rupert Brooke, especially touched Logan in his melancholy moments: *If I should die, think only this of me: that there's some corner of a foreign field that is forever England.* It was signed, *Lt. Bruce Dexter, Flight Officer, RAF—condemned to die, March 10, 1941.*

A priest had painstakingly etched the Lord's Prayer into the wall, and Logan read the words over and over, grateful for some piece of the Scriptures to sustain him. How he wished he could remember more than mere fragments of an occasional verse here and there! But he used the long, silent hours trying to force back into his mind the bits he was able to recall.

I ought to leave something behind too, Logan thought. A man contemplating death can hardly avoid the urge to pass along some "final message" as a statement of his own enduring personhood. But as yet nothing had come to him. So he passed day after day—he soon lost count—in the cold, filthy cell, the only break from his solitary confinement coming when they dragged him out for interrogation.

"I am Captain Logan Macintyre, service number GSDQ 985617," he would say doggedly, over and over, revealing nothing more, despite their brutal questioning. He would never betray his friends. He was ready to die. But when the moment came, he would die alone. He would take no one down with him.

Von Graff himself officiated at the sessions on frequent occasions, though two brawny S.S. sergeants were called upon to perform the actual beatings and other tortures at which they had become highly skilled.

"Who is your commanding officer?" demanded the general.

"I am Captain Logan Mac—"

A swift clubbing from one of the sergeants was his only reward for such determined stubbornness.

"Who is your Paris contact?"

"I am Logan—" But another vicious thrust drew blood from his eye.

"Your hometown, I believe, is Glasgow. What is your address?"

"Logan Macintyre, service number—"

This time an ironlike fist to the midsection doubled Logan's body and he crumpled to the floor in semi-consciousness.

"Come now, Herr Macintyre, why do you put yourself through this? We already have names—Lise Giraud, Jacques Nicolet, Jacques Tournoux, L'Oiselet—Why suffer these needless daily ordeals? You have only to give one word of confirmation."

"I know none of these you speak of," gasped Logan in a faint whisper.

Von Graff grabbed him by the scruff of the neck and, with the help of one of the men, yanked him back up into his chair. Then he angrily took him by the throat and shook him violently. "You're running out of time, you idiot!" he cried. "Don't you care that I am a general in the S.S.? Talk before I give the order to have you shot!"

"I doubt anything I say will change your plans, General," replied Logan, gaining back his breath.

"And you care nothing for life?" shrieked von Graff. "Talk, I tell you . . . save yourself!"

"I care for life, General . . . but I am also prepared to die."

"Bah! You are a stupid fool!" yelled the general, striking Logan's cheek with the back of his hand. "You *will* tell me what I want to know. And then you *will* be shot for your insolence!"

Von Graff turned to leave, saying to his henchmen as he walked away, "Give him some more motivation, then return him to his cell."

An hour later they dumped Logan in a heap on the hard, comfortless stone floor of his tiny cell.

He tried to muster up some pride in himself for not talking, even if only pride enough to give him strength to endure another day's beating in silence.

How easy it would have been just to say the names . . . Henri Renouvin, Major Rayburn Atkinson, Gunther. Thank goodness he didn't know Lise's real name! Of course, maybe Henri wasn't Henri either. No doubt they had both changed their names by now, anyway. Henri could hardly leave his bookstore, but Lise would be long gone from her apartment. Poor Henri! thought Logan. What if he has to abandon his dear books to the underground?

So many times his friends were right on the tip of his swollen tongue—names, places, addresses, plans, code words. They would understand if he talked . . . how much could a man bear? They would have changed everything! Why shouldn't he tell what he knew? They would all be safe by now. . . .

But then in the midst of his thoughts of capitulating, he would catch a hazy image of someone's face, and he would remember—he loved them, and he *could* die for them!

So instead of pride, his feelings turned to mere thankfulness.

He had made it through another day. Maybe by tomorrow the general would finally give up and the execution squad would come for him and he wouldn't have to face it again. Yet it seemed that every day, when the booted feet of death made their daily ritual march down the outside corridor at five a.m., they always stopped at some other poor bloke's cell. He wondered if the men they took instead of him had been tortured to the extent that they looked upon a bullet through the heart as a welcome relief, or as a terrifying moment of eternal doubt.

He was glad that he was at last prepared to die. He hoped when the boots stopped at his door, he would be able to walk out into that open yard with head held high.

Many times in the dark, solemn hours his mind had turned to old Dorey Duncan. How close he felt now to Allison's dear old great-grandfather! Logan had spent enough time in other jails in his past. But now he thought of Dorey, perhaps because, like him, he did not deserve to be here. He wondered what Lord Duncan had thought about during his months of imprisonment. He had never spoken much about that time. But he must have thought of Maggie, from whom he had been so cruelly separated. He knew that Dorey's time in prison had ended in something close to insanity, thinking he had lost her forever. Logan could see how this existence could foster insanity. Yet he had enough to hang on to keep his brain somewhat intact. He knew how it would all end. He didn't have the anxiety of uncertainty. He knew Allison was all right and that she loved him. And Logan finally had his relationship with God to sustain him as well.

He had told Allison that she could entrust him to God without fear, and now he himself must cling desperately to the truth of those words.

He gave his spiritual state before his Maker a great deal of thought in those quiet moments. But he couldn't shake one nagging fear. Eleven years ago, he had turned to God another time when he lay dying. He had felt so sincere back then. Yet the years that followed only served to reveal how shallow his commitment had really been. He had given himself to God in becoming a Christian in much the same way he had given himself to Allison in marriage—with surface emotions and mere mental assent to the truth of the Christian gospel. He had said "I believe," yet had held back his deepest self. He had never confronted the surgeon's scalpel in God's hand and willingly said, "Remake me according to *your* pattern . . . cause my character to reflect the image of your Son." In short, Logan now realized that though he *had* prayed the prayer of belief, he had never truly given his heart—totally and unreservedly—to the Lord. He had given a piece of himself, but not all. He had misunderstood the Christian life just as he had misunderstood the basic nature of marriage, by never grasping the foundational necessity of total, sacrificial commitment. Thus after eleven years, both as a Christian and as a husband, he was still essentially the same Logan Macintyre. The transformation of his character to reflect his Maker—the fundamental essence of spirituality—had still not begun.

He was afraid, therefore, that as he now sat in prison, his thoughts of renewed commitment toward Allison and toward the Lord might be but another last-ditch effort to reprieve himself. Whether the rest of his life was a matter of weeks, days, or possibly even hours, he wanted, even in that short time, to make what beginning he could to surrender his *whole* being to the transforming might of God's love. No more bits and pieces of his personality, no more convenient commitment, no more halfhearted prayers, no more keeping his own image of himself intact. He had played so many roles, worn so many masks, been called by so many names. It was finally time to lay them all down in order to become the man he had *really* been meant to be all along. No more running from one unreal identity to the next. The time had come to become the Logan Macintyre of God's perfect design.

Again his thoughts turned to Dorey. It had been years since he had recalled that day just before the old family patriarch had died. He'd called Logan into his room, and Logan remembered thinking it odd that he should be thus singled out. Dorey had, of course, spoken with every member of the family of that day, but at the time he hadn't even *been* a member of the family. Lord Duncan lay on his bed, the life slipping slowly from his worn-out physical frame and into the new body awaiting him.

"Did I even tell you how much you remind me of myself when I was a lad?" he had asked in a weak, yet still determined voice.

Logan shook his head.

"I could laugh at life," Dorey went on, "and I was such an expert at running from it when necessary. But you're starting out on a better foot than I—you've seen your need for God while you're yet young. You'll likely be just fine, lad."

He paused and let out a long sigh, which revealed that there was more on his mind than he had let on.

"But . . ." he continued in a moment, struggling to voice his concerns in a way the young Logan could grasp, "maybe because we're so alike, I fear more for the pitfalls of life that you may face. I'm ending my life, and you're just starting yours, and . . . Oh, but perhaps it's wrong of me to be so gloomy."

"I respect what you have to say, sir," said Logan.

"I guess what concerns me, lad, is that I think we are both adept at finding the easy way of life," Dorey continued. "I did it with a joke, a dance, and a glass of ale. You had your schemes and gambling tables. And I wouldn't for a moment suggest that God would ever want to take away that twinkle in your eye and your love for a good time. Yet sometimes the way God lays out for us is not an easy one. But it will always be the best one."

"I know that now, Lord Duncan," Logan had affirmed confidently, "now that I'm a Christian."

"I pray it is so," the old man had replied in a retrospective tone. "But *becoming* a Christian is only the beginning of the road, not the end of it. That step is but a door that opens into a new way of life. It's easy to walk through the door and then stop. Many people do just that, continuing in their natural ways, thinking that they have taken some miracle cure with the step of salvation, and that's all there is to it. I ran from God before I knew Him. But there are some who run from Him *after* they know Him. We all have our ways of avoiding what God wants to do with us, inside our hearts."

"Are you saying you are afraid I'm not sincere in my decision?" asked Logan.

"If only sincerity were all we needed!" Dorey replied. "My father used to say, 'The road to nowhere is well-paved with good intentions.'" He chuckled softly at the memory from so long ago. "'Tis a long road ahead of you, lad. You'll be needing *daily* refills on that sincerity to make it last, especially on those uphill runs when the going gets hard."

How right he had been!

But at the time Logan had accepted his words with the cocky confidence of a new believer. He had, despite Dorey's warning, assumed that his initial decision would propel him along. When its power had waned, he had taken it as an indication that he had gone as far as possible with his life as a Christian. It had been easy to rely on his own power. Yet it wasn't sufficient to keep the dissatisfaction from gradually creeping in—with his jobs, his marriage, his home . . . and with himself. Without even realizing it, he had started to run again, just like Dorey said—a Christian running from God. His very life of intrigue, which contained so many ready-made identities, served him with a wealth of hiding places. His real self *never* had to surface if he so chose.

But that was yesterday.

Finally his eyes were opened to the true nature of his need. His time might indeed be short. Nothing could change that now. The consequences of the life he had chosen were his to face, and his alone. But from now on he could make the decision to follow God's way rather than his own, even if the arena for such a change had to be lived out solely in his own attitudes from within a tiny prison cell. Dorey had said there would be no easy way.

So if the execution squad came for him tomorrow, he knew with assurance that they would not be taking out the same man that had been deposited in this cell so many days ago. They would not be blindfolding Michel Tanant, or Trinity, or L'Escroc, or Lawrence MacVey—poor von Graff would be robbed of his moment of victory. For the man who would go to his death was a new man. Not born again, for that had happened eleven years ago. But a man at last aware enough of his own weakness to surrender his *whole* heart to the One who had called his name back then on the road to Stonewycke. Now he could pray, with whole worlds of deeper meaning and firmer intent, the same prayer he prayed then: "Help me, Lord, to become a *true* man."

Logan glanced at the grimy, stained wall of his prison cell. He found a rusty old nail that had fallen into a crack in the floor, probably left by some other chronicler of the past. He reached up and pressed its point into the ancient plaster, recalling to mind an old hymn.

"I am Logan Macintyre," he wrote. "I was lost, but now am found. I was blind, but now I see. I was dead . . . but at last I am ready to live!"

75 ❈ The Approaching Sound of Heavy Boots

FOR TWO MEN who had seen their designs so successfully concluded, von Graff and Channing appeared particularly glum.

"I'm afraid," said von Graff dolefully, "if a man doesn't talk in two weeks, the chances are slim that he ever will."

"Time always works for the victim," offered Channing, puffing grimly on the Cuban cigar von Graff had provided. "I never thought he had it in him."

"You yourself said we had underestimated Macintyre."

"The scoundrel! You'd think he really was one of *them*!"

"What do you mean?"

"Nothing," Channing replied. Yet he could not get out of his mind how the infernal Duncan clan always managed to get the upper hand. And now, even in the death of the blasted woman's son-in-law, they were about to do it again! Just knowing he had failed to thoroughly *break* the principled fool was enough to twist this at least half into a victory for *them*!

"I dare not torture him further," said von Graff. "It would take all the meaning out of the firing squad. A man has to be in his right mind as he stares down the barrels of those rifles, knowing he's only moments away from eternity. It's that look of terror in his eyes that is the ultimate triumph."

"You don't fool me, General," chided Channing. "You don't want to torture him further because you are still sentimental about your protege."

"Ha!" Von Graff savagely ground his half-finished Havana into an ashtray. "I'm only afraid he'll drop dead under the whip and cudgels and deprive us at the last of watching him shot."

"Yes, I suppose you're right. We must have that, at least." Channing studied the burning end of his cigar a moment. "And how much longer must we wait?" he asked.

"I was still hoping his wife would provide us with something," answered von Graff.

"She's still in Paris?"

"Yes. I've had men on her constantly. And I must say her movements are a bit strange for a woman about to become a widow. But nothing suspicious. And certainly nothing of any use to us. Apparently she was telling the truth, and does, in fact, know nothing about her husband's activities."

"Then why is she still here?"

"Probably waiting to take the body home—who knows?"

"You're going to give her the body?"

"I thought you suggested that earlier—something to do with your old feud with her family?"

"Ah, yes! How considerate of you."

"The point is, the girl will be of no use once her husband is executed. Perhaps we've played them both to the limit, and it's now time to have done with them."

"That would be my vote," said Channing with something akin to glee.

"Then let's pull the Macintyre woman back in, and proceed with her husband s execution."

"Yes! Yes!" agreed Channing enthusiastically.

Von Graff leaned over to switch on his intercom. "Please send in Captain Neumann," he said to his secretary.

In another five minutes a brisk knock came and von Graff told his aide to enter.

"Captain Neumann," he said, "will you inform Fresnes that they are to prepare the prisoner Macintyre for execution at Montrouge."

He turned to Channing. "How does seven a.m. tomorrow morning sound?"

Channing nodded with a lusty puff of smoke billowing through his lips.

"He is to face the firing squad?" said Neumann.

"Is there some problem?" asked von Graff sourly.

Neumann snapped to an even smarter attention than he had already been assuming. "Nein, mein General!" he rejoined obediently. "I shall make all the arrangements, sir."

At six-thirty the following morning the winter sky showed no signs of the approaching dawn. The five persons exiting the S.S. headquarters, however, paid little attention to the portents of the sky. The two S.S. officers at the lead of the group walked with precise military gait. They paused when they reached the S.S. staff car parked at the curb. The lieutenant stepped forward and climbed in behind the wheel, while Captain Neumann opened the rear door for the three others of the small entourage.

Channing climbed into the back seat first, followed by Allison. Von Graff slid in beside her. Neumann briskly shut the door, then opened his front passenger door. Before climbing in, he glanced momentarily over the roof of the automobile, as if scanning the area for something, probably just the first hints of coming daylight and an end to this assignment. Then he, too, ducked into the car.

The automobile proceeded east on the avenue Foch, then south down the avenue Marceau, crossing the Seine at the Place de L'Alma. The dark streets were quiet; the City of Lights had not yet come to life on that chilly Sunday morning. It was a ten-minute drive over the uncongested streets to Fort Montrouge. The black of the sky had begun turning gray with the first light of dawn, and a mild drizzle had begun to fall as the car turned into the old fort.

The stone walls of the fortress had seen more glorious days; now age and disuse coupled with infamy to tarnish its reputation, for here the Third Reich performed many of its grim executions. Allison gave a shudder as they drove through the gates. To her left stood the execution post, with its two deadly shot-riddled scars in the wood, one at eye-level for bullets to the head, and one lower down for bullets to the heart.

Dear God, she prayed silently, *be very near to us now!*

The car slowed to a halt and soon the car doors were opened. Allison was ordered to get out. Von Graff and Channing stood next to her, the rain beginning to fall more earnestly now, but hardly dampening the spirit of their triumph.

In another moment her concentration was distracted from the morbid sight as two "Black Marias" rumbled through the gates, just moments after she and von Graff and Channing had stepped out of their vehicle. The two vans stopped next to the execution site some fifty feet from them.

Out of the back of one of the vans clambered eight armed German soldiers. They jogged to the execution post where the prisoner would be tied, then turned and paced off their positions. They then stood attending to their rifles. At the same time the driver of the second van had emerged; now he walked around to the back, opened the wide door, and reached inside to haul out his passenger.

Allison could not hold back a gasp as Logan was dragged out and forced to stand beside the van. When he had been nearly dying from the gunshot wound he had received eleven years ago, he had not looked so dreadful. Even in the dim pre-dawn light, she could see that during the two weeks of his imprisonment he had lost a great deal of weight. His hollowed eyes were ringed with dark circles, or perhaps bruises, Allison could not tell. A definite wound, festering and dirty, crossed the side of his cheek. Dried blood was evident from a wound on his arm, and he walked with a painful and unsteady limp. The injured arm hung limp by his side.

Allison glared at von Graff, her eyes dark and searing.

"How can you do this to fellow human beings?" she demanded. "You must be an animal!"

Von Graff's eyebrows raised and his jaws tightened, but he made her no reply. Her words were perhaps too disquieting to one who had always considered himself a cultivated man. This war was indeed turning men into beasts, but he could not pause to consider the implications of her statement just now.

Logan paused, perhaps hearing a familiar voice through the hazy morning. A look of distress passed across his sallow face when he saw Allison. He jerked his eyes to von Graff.

"Why did you bring her here?" he demanded sharply, though his voice was so weak it lacked force.

"I would not want to deprive a wife a last moment with her husband," replied the general.

But Logan had turned his attention back to Allison and was slowly limping toward her. The guards made no move to stop him.

"Be brave, Ali," he said. "It is not really so bad—I will die with honor. God is with me."

At last, prompted by a jerk from von Graff's head, one of the guards grabbed Logan's arm and pulled him roughly away.

"Logan . . . have faith!" called Allison. "I love you!"

The guard jerked him forward, but he called over his shoulder, "I have always loved you, Ali—"

His words were cut short by a sharp blow to the back that sent him to his knees. Allison stifled a scream, her eyes at last filling with tears. Painfully she watched as the guard yanked Logan back to his feet and slammed his back up against the firing post. While the guard was securing him, von Graff turned to his companions.

"Herr Channing," he said, "why don't you and Frau Macintyre retire to that guardhouse over there where you will have a clear view and remain dry at the same time. This cursed rain is becoming annoying. I will join you momentarily."

"Capital idea, General," said Channing.

Von Graff left them and strode to where Logan was now tied securely to the post.

Logan spoke first.

"Von Graff, I don't care what you do to me, but you have no reason to harm my wife. Let her go back to England. She knows nothing of all this."

"I cannot promise anything," replied the general. "You should know by now that I am not my own man."

"She knows nothing, I tell you."

"After watching her these past two weeks, I am inclined to believe you. She is a woman with peculiar shopping habits, and with a tendency toward odd associations. But one day with her confirms that she is no spy. She is of little use to us. I assume she will go unharmed."

He paused, then held out the blindfold to Logan.

Logan shook his head.

"The stoic to the end?"

"No stoic, General. Just a man who is finally prepared to face life as it comes to him, without trying to hide behind any masks. Life . . . *and* death."

"An admirable point of view, for anyone but a man facing a firing squad."

Logan did not reply.

"I want you to know, Macintyre," von Graff continued, "that despite this unfortunate end to our relationship, I have nothing personal against you. Actually, I have a great deal of regard for you. You played well, Macintyre." He paused and sighed. "But, alas, we were both always fully aware of the rules of the game."

"I know now, General, that this was no mere game," said Logan.

"Dying men always have their 'revelations.' But tell me, Macintyre, now that it is over, and you are about to die an ignominious death which no one will ever know about—tell me, do you have any regrets?"

All was silent for a moment about them. Thirty feet away the execution squad stood resolutely at attention. Not a sound could be heard throughout the semi-deserted compound.

"Regrets, General?" said Logan at length. "Sure I regret that I lived my life so long for myself. Regrets, perhaps—but no doubts. For I know that my life is not now given without meaning. I am laying it down for my wife and for my God. And there are few causes worthier to die for than helping rid the world of your kind of evil."

Von Graff smiled, thinking back to their first conversation aboard the sub in the North Sea. "You are a fanatic, after all, Herr Macintyre. As much as I admire you, I have to admit to some disappointment."

"I apologize for nothing, General."

"I would hardly expect it."

"One last thing, General," said Logan.

"Yes?"

"Though it may not matter to you, I bear you no malice. As God forgives you, so do I."

"You waste your last words on such sentimentalities."

"Perhaps someday they will mean something to you."

Von Graff shrugged, then turned to go. Almost as if an afterthought had just occurred to him, he paused and looked back.

"You will want a word with the priest now I assume," he said.

"Priest?"

"The priest you requested."

"Yes, certainly, but I—" replied Logan, puzzled. He had asked for no such thing. But by now von Graff was fifteen steps from him and walking briskly away.

The general had nearly reached the guardhouse when a new figure stepped out of one of the "Black Marias." He was tall and walked with a practiced poise, marred only by a slight limp, his black cassock trailing out behind him. A thick graying beard and moustache covered his face, and wire-rimmed spectacles perched on his finely chiseled nose.

He approached close to Logan and laid one hand on his shoulder. In the other, Logan saw he clutched a missal and a rosary.

The priest looked deep into Logan's eyes.

"God be with you, my son," he said.

"And with you, Father," replied Logan, his eyes opening wide in dawning awareness.

"Take courage, my son . . . this is your final performance."

Logan's dulled senses suddenly sprang fully alert as he recognized the voice of the only priest in France he had ever known.

76 ✠ *Tour de Force*

INSIDE THE GUARDHOUSE, Channing had taken up an advantageous position in front of the window. At the moment, however, his gaze was fixed on Allison, who had retreated a safe distance away.

"Come closer, my dear," he said in a smug voice. "This is your husband's moment of honor—probably the only one he has had in his crooked and dishonest life."

"My husband is worth a hundred of you, Mr. Channing!" declared Allison proudly.

"You might cause me to enjoy this less," sneered Channing, "if you made some attempt at contrition. But then, I forget whose daughter you are."

"A daughter whose father is a true man alongside snakes like you!"

Channing stepped toward her, grabbed her arm, and forcefully drew her nearer the window.

"You *will* watch your husband die!" he growled. "Then we will see what comes of your Scotch stoicism! I'll see you on your knees before this day is through, and then your mother will know to whom the final victory belongs!"

Allison watched as the priest approached Logan. Then von Graff entered the guardhouse, distracting her attention.

"It won't be long now," he said. "Blast this rain keeping us from a clearer view."

"It will be clear enough, won't it, my sweet?" taunted Channing.

Allison stuck out her chin and straightened her shoulders, but said nothing.

"You're just like that cursed mother of yours," muttered Channing. "We'll see what good that stubborn pride does you now!"

But before Allison had the chance to utter the biting reply that sprang to her lips, the dreaded command filtered into the guardroom from outside in the yard:

Ready!

Eight rifles were instantly readied at shoulder level.

Aim!

All at once Allison saw from the corner of her eye that Channing's gaze was fixed, not on the window nor the proceedings outside at all, but on her. He cared nothing about Logan—alive *or* dead. The true focus of his malicious revenge was centered only on her, and the family she represented.

Fire!

Instantly a salvo of shots rang through the morning air.

Logan's body slumped over on the post, kept from falling by the ropes that bound him.

A piercing scream escaped from Allison's lips.

"Logan!" she cried, making for the guardhouse door.

But Channing grabbed her arm and kept her from running out into the compound.

"Not so fast, my haughty little heiress!" he said with self-important satisfaction. "Stay here with us to complete my celebration!" He wrenched her backward and threw her against the far wall of the small room, where she fell on the floor.

Channing looked outside again to see several men removing Logan from the post to take him away.

"Well, General," said Channing, "it would appear that we have done it!" His voice was jubilant.

"So it would appear," replied von Graff in a subdued tone, his eyes casting some doubt on the extent of his triumph.

They turned away from the window toward the middle of the room.

"I took the liberty of making some small preparations for this great moment," said Channing as they approached a small table. On it stood a bottle and two crystal glasses. "It deserved at least a minor ceremonial remembrance. Will you join me in some champagne, General?"

"Of course, Herr Channing."

Channing uncorked the bottle and poured out two generous measures of the bubbling liquid.

He took one of the glasses, then handed the other to von Graff.

"May I propose a toast?" he said.

Von Graff nodded, as if to say, "The moment of victory is all yours."

Both men raised their glasses as Channing spoke: "To the now-departed L'Escroc. We have outswindled the Swindler!"

Behind them an unexpected but familiar voice broke through the morning air:

"Ah, L'Escroc . . . it was indeed one of my finest roles!"

Spinning around in shock, Channing's glass fell to the floor with a shattering crash. Logan stood before them in the doorway. Allison jumped up from the floor.

"Logan!" she cried.

She ran to him and threw her arms around his wet and bruised body.

"So sorry to disappoint you, General, Mr. Channing," said Logan, "but my comrades asked me to break in on your little victory party. We are—I'm sure you can understand—in somewhat of a hurry to be away from this dreary place."

He paused long enough to bend over and kiss Allison lightly, keeping his eye on his prey.

"I was almost afraid something had gone wrong," she said.

"The only thing that might have gone wrong is that I could have died of a heart attack standing there in front of those guns!" said Logan. "Why didn't you let me know?"

"We couldn't get word to you," said Allison.

"So," seethed Channing with mingled wrath and chagrin, "you knew of this all along! Now I understand your blasted calm!"

"Yes, Mr. Channing," replied Allison. "And your recapturing me was just a decoy, with which you cooperated very nicely. You see, I had no heart to rob you of your one imaginary moment of success. But that, I am afraid, is all you will have."

"Ha!" laughed Channing with scorn. "Do you actually think you can hurt me with your ridiculous little productions! Jason Channing cares nothing for such trivia! I am the ultimate victor. For I still possess the legendary Stonewycke treasure!"

A look of astonishment passed over both Logan and Allison's faces at the words.

"Ha! ha! ha!" gloated Channing with perverse glee. "Surprised? Ha! ha! That idiot Sprague was worth all I paid him, and more, though the fool was so stupid he couldn't even keep himself alive! You just tell your mother, little Miss Stonewycke, that I have her grandmother's priceless Pict box, and that she'll never lay eyes on it. Ha! ha! ha!"

As Channing spoke, already von Graff was thinking of self-preservation. He had inched his way toward a corner of the room, where a rifle sat propped against a wall.

"Not so fast, Monsieur General!" came a voice from the doorway. They turned to see a German soldier standing with rifle poised on von Graff.

Von Graff squinted in sheer confusion. Not only was the man with the drop on him too old, but he was uncommonly small. Yet the gun in his hands discouraged argument.

"You really ought to get to know your soldiers better," said Logan to von Graff. "Perhaps then you could tell good *Frenchmen* from Boche!"

Von Graff jerked his head around toward the window. Outside, the eight supposed soldiers of the execution squad now held their weapons on the four or five real members of von Graff's S.S. detail. The new prisoners were being prodded toward the guardroom.

"Good work, my dear," said Henri to Allison. "Your elaborate plan appears to have come off with scarcely a hitch."

"Her plan?" repeated an astonished Logan.

"Mais oui, Michel," said Henri with a twinkle in his eye. "Did you think all the savvy for intrigue in the family was yours? She refused to let us sit still for your imprisonment. What you once told me is true: *'The Lord has many ways to deliver His people.'*"

Logan laughed. "Ah, me fair lass. Ye done yer man prood!"

"Come," said Henri, "it is time to be off!"

Clinging closely to one another, Allison supported Logan's weary frame as they retreated out into the compound. Allison glanced back for one last glimpse of Channing. Unlike the defeated general, Channing's eyes yet glowed with the embers of red-hot fire—sufficient even for a man of seventy to give proof that he would be back again.

As Logan emerged again into the open air, his eyes caught and held those of one of the captive German prisoners. Neumann returned his stare only momentarily, but long enough to say, "I wish you well, L'Escroc Macintyre." And perhaps also in his eyes was the parting request, *Pray for me sometimes, when I am brought to your mind.*

But this meeting of minds lasted only an instant, and then was past. Henri tarried at the guardhouse until the contingent of Germans was locked securely inside with Channing and von Graff. Then he turned and trotted to where Logan and Jean Pierre were enjoying a more thorough and warm reunion.

"It's not much of a story," laughed the priest in response to Logan's wondering inquiries.

"I couldn't believe my ears when I heard your voice!"

"My brother took great pity on me," went on Jean Pierre, "after my injury. So you see, your rescue attempt on the train *was* a success! He interceded on my behalf, and here I am! Perhaps there is hope for him, after all."

"I never dreamed all of us would be together again except in eternity," said Logan.

"I told you we would meet again," laughed Jean Pierre.

"As did Henri," added Logan. He paused and glanced around, suddenly aware that someone was missing.

"Where is Lise?" he asked.

"She realized this was not her moment, Michel," said Henri. "But she asked me to tell you that she wishes you Godspeed."

"Tell her the same when you see her, Henri. Tell her I will pray for her. And give her my thanks."

"I will, mon ami," said the bookseller. "Now . . . let us be off! That"—he cocked his head toward the locked guardroom—"won't hold them for long."

They ran toward the van they intended to use. Henri paused long enough to spray a round of bullets into the tires of the staff car and the other van.

Then the group of a dozen resistors scrambled into the remaining van. Henri slipped in behind the wheel, ground the vehicle into gear, spun it around, and sped through the gates.

77 ✼ Fait *Almost* Accompli

LOGAN SAT BACK against the jarring wall of the careening vehicle. His body was ready to collapse from the onrush of unexpected events, yet despite the fatigue, his mind remained keen.

"The telephone," he said all at once, not knowing who other than Allison at his side could even hear him above the engine. "We should have cut the line to the guardroom."

"Rotten oversight!" said Henri from the front. "And we are headed right past the main prison. They're sure to be waiting for us."

He slammed his foot on the brake in order to negotiate a u-turn and head in the opposite direction.

"Wait!" cried Logan. "Keep going! The last thing they'll expect is for us to drive right past their backyard. They'll figure us to be going south, away from the city, not back past the prison!"

Henri laughed as he pressed his foot back on the accelerator. "L'Escroc lives!" he cried. "We will dare it! Right past Fresnes!"

"We must breed a new L'Escroc to take your place," said Jean Pierre.

"Monsieur L'Oiselet was not doing so bad a job before L'Escroc came," said Logan. "And I have a feeling he will continue long after L'Escroc is but a passing memory."

In another five minutes the prison came into view. Almost immediately the speeding van encountered several German vehicles roaring past them, all storming westward to Montrouge.

A great cheer went up inside the van.

"Our ploy will give us but a momentary advantage," cautioned Henri. "We still have two stops to make. They will discover their error and overtake us before we know it."

Before long the van drifted to a stop. The larger part of the group jumped out the back. Logan had not even noticed that they had changed out of their German uniforms, under which they had been wearing their normal French attire. "There's a farmhouse just over that field," explained Henri to Logan. "They'll put our people up and get them safely back to the city."

One by one the men ran around to Logan's side of the vehicle, each shaking his hand warmly. He thanked them all, not without deep emotion. Then within moments they had retreated into the wood and the van pulled onto the road again. It now carried only Henri, Jean Pierre, Allison and Logan.

"Next stop for you two . . . England!" shouted Jean Pierre. "And in case I do not have the opportunity to say it later," he added, "God's blessings be upon you! I will think of you often, and when I do, be assured that prayers of grateful remembrance will pass my lips!"

"Oh, Jean Pierre," said Allison, "thank you! Thank you for helping take care of my Logan all this time. And you too, dear Henri! Thank you both so much for delivering him back safely to me! I will never forget you, dear friends!"

"Where are we going?" asked Logan.

"To an airstrip," answered Allison before either of the Frenchmen could respond. "Actually, Henri says it's hardly more than a smooth meadow."

"But where? I never knew about any airstrip out here."

"It's rough, mon ami," said Henri. "But all we could manage. It's about thirty kilometers from here."

"A plane is waiting for us," added Allison.

Logan smiled.

"So, Mother Hen came through, after all!"

He glanced over at Allison. "You are really something!" he said. "How did you manage all this? Is it true, what Henri said back there, that this was *your* plan?" His pride was evident even as he asked the question.

"I didn't do much really," she answered. "I just kept prodding, and trying to figure something out, and asking Henri and Lise questions, until finally the whole thing started to unfold. Jean Pierre's release was a big help, too!"

"Do not let her fool you, Michel," put in Henri. "She lived up to every inch of your reputation!"

"I'm only sorry you had to stay behind bars so long! But we had to wait till word reached us they were moving you."

"Are you kidding? It was worth every gray hair it may have caused to see von Graff's and Channing's faces! What a grand story it will make to tell your mother!"

"There was just one moment, when the guns went off, when for an instant I wondered if everything *had* come off. Those men firing the guns looked *so* German! I wasn't sure our plan had succeeded until I saw you in the doorway. You were so brave—though I never doubted you would be."

" 'Twas naethin', me lass!" grinned Logan, then closed his eyes and let his head rest on Allison's shoulder. "I'm just glad to be alive—and with the woman I love."

They drove on in relative silence for about ten or fifteen more minutes, Henri keeping to a conservative speed so as not to attract unwanted attention. Suddenly he groaned.

"I think we have company," he said. From the rearview mirror he saw four vehicles bearing down upon them from behind, including what looked like a Gestapo staff car. They were about half a mile back.

"Hang on!" he cried, and pressed the accelerator to the floor. The van surged forward.

Gradually he lengthened the distance between them. Ahead lay the meadow.

"Here we go!" said Henri. "Grab whatever you can!"

He turned the steering wheel and the van careened off the pavement, smashing through a rickety wooden fence, and hardly slackening speed as they flew over the grass toward where the Lysander sat in the middle of the field, looking incongruous amidst stacks of hay from last year's harvest.

The pilot saw them coming, realized they were being chased, and ignited his engines. The propellers of the small plane whirred into motion.

A barrage of shots pinged off the sides of the van.

The distance was still too great for the bullets to hurt them unless they happened to hit either a window or a tire. The retiring bookseller at the wheel did not falter but kept his nerves steady as the van bounced and crashed over the uneven ground.

"How will you two get away?" shouted Logan. "We can't just leave you here!"

"Not to worry!" replied Jean Pierre. "There's a road we'll catch on the other side of the meadow. All we'll need is a hundred-meter lead. After a bend in the road, we'll jump, the van will crash over a high embankment, and we'll escape through the woods. When the Germans round the corner, all they'll see is the van tumbling down over the side. By the time they've gone down to investigate and find no bodies, we'll be halfway back to Paris. There's a friendly farmhouse only about a kilometer from there through the forest. So you see, it's all been arranged."

Logan looked up. He could hear the Lysander's roaring engines. Henri sped onto the runway, maintaining top speed until the very last moment. Then suddenly he slammed the van to a screeching halt.

In less than an instant he and Jean Pierre were outside and opening the doors to help Logan and Allison out.

Explosive bursts of gunfire sounded behind them.

"Hurry, mates!" yelled the pilot from the small plane. "If we take one of them slugs in the tank, we're all goners!"

"Come with us!" said Logan.

"We can still be of use here," said Henri.

"Look at him!" laughed Jean Pierre. "We couldn't drag L'Oiselet out of France!"

In the distance, the German cars were wheeling recklessly across the meadow toward them. Out of every window leaned soldiers firing wildly.

"Go, dear friends!" said Henri.

"You too!" replied Logan. "Drive like the wind, Henri! I want to see you two after the war!"

Logan took several more seconds to throw his arms first around the bookseller, then around the priest—companions and friends he would never forget. With tears in her eyes, Allison gave them each a hurried hug.

Then, leaning on Allison for support, and hobbling as rapidly as Logan was able, they raced to the plane, while Henri and lean Pierre scrambled back into the black van.

Hands reached down from the fuselage door, grabbed hold of Logan's shoulders to hoist him inside. The plane was already moving when Allison jumped onto the small stairway and climbed up. The pilot closed the doors and thrust forward the controls and the plane taxied across the meadow.

Behind them sharp reports of gunfire vainly tried to stop the takeoff, but already the Lysander had picked up speed and was nearly out of range.

Logan pulled himself up to a window just as he felt the plane lift off the ground. Already the van with Henri and Jean Pierre was speeding toward the opposite side of the field and into a wood. The German cars had stopped momentarily, with soldiers pouring out to draw better aim on the ascending British plane.

Then Logan saw two figures emerge from the staff car.

He could not see the expressions on the faces of the general and the businessman as they watched their precious quarry wing out of firing range. But he could well imagine their fury and bitter dismay.

Then just as suddenly as they had stopped, the four vehicles filled again, and sped off across the meadow.

Logan slumped back in his seat, realizing all at once how weary he was. Gently Allison took his hand.

He glanced toward her, smiled, and let out a long breath. She too exhaled a long sigh of relief, as if to say, "Whew . . . we made it!"

"We'll soon be home, Logan," she said after a few moments.

"Home to Stonewycke," he murmured drowsily. "I can hardly believe it." He closed his eyes, and with visions of the beloved estate floating dreamily in his mind, he was soon fast asleep.

78 ❈ An Honorable End

ATKINSON WORE A particularly smug look on his face—almost an expression of fatherly pride.

But it was I, thought Kramer with his own vain grin plastered firmly on his countenance, *who saw Macintyre's potential right from the beginning.* Though he had to admit, if only for honesty's sake, that it was the major who had stuck up for Macintyre when the cards were down.

Not that he wouldn't have himself, of course. But someone had to play the devil's advocate.

Thus Kramer had wrangled the privilege of joining Atkinson to receive their Captain Logan Macintyre who had arrived from France a week ago. He had spent the ensuing days in a hospital recuperating from his brutal torture by the Nazis, but was now fit enough to be debriefed and to consider a lengthy leave.

"This is the best part of the job," commented Atkinson.

"Seeing one of your chicks safely home, eh, Mother Hen?"

"Exactly!" smiled the major. Then his eye grew momentarily introspective. "It doesn't happen often enough," he mused. "I pray they will all be coming home soon."

"It won't be long, what with the way our boys are beating the tar out of those Nazis now!"

"I wish I could be as optimistic as you," said Atkinson. "But I think the Nazis have a few more tricks up their sleeve yet. I think we're looking at years rather than months, Arnie."

Kramer's eyes gleamed and he leaned forward. "How would you like to put some money on that, Ray?"

Before Atkinson could respond, a knock at the door interrupted them.

Logan did look fit. At least better than he had a week ago when he had climbed out of the Lysander, taking his first step on British soil in over a year. As Logan now stood framed in the doorway, Atkinson suddenly realized it was the first time he had seen Macintyre in uniform. It made him look quite different. And though he wore the uniform of his country with a glow of pride, it looked rather incongruous on him.

But Atkinson could see that the changes in Logan went deeper than a mere uniform. He no longer wore that look of defensiveness about him. Whatever else had happened in France, there was no doubt in the major's view that Logan Macintyre had found himself.

"Good morning, Captain Macintyre."

"Good morning, sir," replied Logan, shaking Atkinson's extended hand, then turning to Kramer. "And to you also, Major Kramer."

Kramer stepped buoyantly up to Logan.

"Forget that *Major* business!" He grabbed Logan's hand and shook it vigorously, while slapping Logan's shoulder with his free hand. "We're all proud of you, Logan!"

Atkinson picked up a small box from his desk and held it out.

"This is for you, son."

Logan opened the box and gazed down on the sparkling George Cross inside. He was too surprised, and humbled, to speak.

"You earned it, Logan," said Atkinson.

"Thank you, sir," replied Logan. Atkinson's words meant as much as the medal itself.

"It's all got to be kept unofficial for now," added Atkinson. "Security and all that, you know."

"But after the war," put in Kramer, "you'll be a hero of Britain. Of France, too, for that matter!" Then a coy grin erupted on his broad face. "Why, you'd probably be able to win a seat in Parliament!"

Logan smiled at the outrageous idea.

"All I want to do now is go home and live a normal life for a while."

"You shall have that, my boy," said Atkinson.

"But the war isn't over yet," said Kramer. "We can still use you."

Logan knew the demands of war would continue to be felt for some time. Yet at the same time, the mere thought of returning to the kind of existence he had led in France made him cringe.

Atkinson noted the faint shadow that had passed momentarily across Logan's face. "I do have something in mind for you," he said. "*After* a long time of recuperation. It's an extremely vital job in the intelligence effort, and one which I think you'll be perfectly suited for with your firsthand experience. Of course it would be up to you. I think you've earned some say in your next assignment."

"What did you have in mind, sir?"

"We desperately need instructors in our training program, Logan, and I think you'd have a great deal to offer the chaps just starting out. What do you say?"

Logan grinned, both relieved and honored.

"Thank you, sir," he said. "I gladly accept the offer."

Notwithstanding Arnie's crestfallen face, they all shook hands warmly before Logan set about making his report of his time in France.

When he left an hour later, it was with a sense that his sacrifices over the last year, the emotional and physical pain he had undergone, had not been wasted. He had served his country, if not with great distinction, yet with integrity and virtue. He knew at last he could stand with pride alongside his Stonewycke ancestor, old Digory MacNab.

79 ❧ *A Bittersweet Christmas*

NEVER HAD THE somber gray walls of Stonewycke, with snow now piled up against them, seemed more like home to Logan as they did that Christmas of 1942. How good it was to be back! He knew now—in a deeper way than ever—what it meant to be part of something greater than himself—a cause, a family, a faith. He knew they were worth the sacrifice of commitment, the surrendering of his whole self.

He stood by the crackling blaze in the hearth of the family room, watching as Allison strung the last bit of tinsel on the tree.

It was a somber holiday season. There had been great suffering and deep griefs. Alec was still in Africa. Ian had managed to obtain a furlough, but would not be home until the first week in January. May's presence—home from her studies in the States to announce her engagement to a young American law student—added a spark of gaiety to the festivities. Yet the joy pervading the small gathering at Stonewycke that Christmas Eve could not help but be of a rather quiet kind.

Logan saw the contrast most visibly on Allison's face. The outward show of Christmas happiness could not keep an occasional tear from trickling down her cheek. He walked over and placed an arm around her waist. Despite the trembling of her lips, she smiled up at him.

"She always used to grab at the tinsel," she said, "because it was so sparkling and pretty."

"I suppose this time of year will always be the most difficult." Logan knew she spoke of their daughter.

"Last year, in London, it was just the two of us, you were gone. It was such a sad, bleak time. But we decorated the tree, and . . . oh, Logan, if only I'd known it would be our last Christmas together!" Allison stifled a sob.

Logan gently stroked her hair while holding her tenderly.

"I have thought often of the gospel story and of Mary since then," Allison finally went on. "The moment her son was born was a time of joy mixed with sorrows too. Losing our daughter has helped me understand maybe a little of what she felt in her heart. What does it say in *Luke*? 'Yea, a sword shall pierce through thy own soul also.' She knew the true meaning of bittersweet joy. I am so happy that you are alive, Logan, and that we are at last together. Yet I cannot help feeling sad also."

"I know," said Logan gently. "There is something about Christmas that always brings out the extremes of feeling, the happiness that *is,* the memories of what *was.*"

"Will it always be so?"

"Right now our wounds are still raw and tender. But one day, Ali, we will be able to lift up each precious memory of our dear little Joanna, and those visions of her will be to us the pure joy that God intended. God doesn't mind a little sorrow for a season. But we mustn't allow our grief to force us to abandon those memories."

"It's just so hard, especially when I remember her smiling, happy face."

"I know, dear," replied Logan. "But you have to remember, we do not live in this world only. She *is* alive. God has chosen us for a great honor. For those who have lost a son or daughter can feel, in ways we cannot know except through such loss, part of the enormity of what God did in allowing *His* Son to die. Even in our sadness, and in your mother's grief over Nat, we are able to partake in the divine grief of the universe—the shedding of God's blood for the sins of mankind. It is a privilege to know that kind of heartache, and then be able to give it up to His care."

"You're right, Logan. Where did you get such wisdom?"

Logan laughed lightly. "I don't know. I guess sorrow has a way of forcing people into greater understanding of things they can't see when life is perfectly smooth. I don't think God is as concerned with giving happy endings to our lives as He is forcing us into greater depths of laying down of self. Of course, that's where true joy originates—not from surface happiness, but from giving ourselves up to Him. I suppose if there's anything I've learned from this past year, it's that. *Begun* to learn, I should say! I'm still such an infant, Allison, in trying to see from a new perspective."

"Oh, Logan, I *am* thankful for what God is doing in our lives. But the growth can be so painful."

"It usually is. Progress never comes without a struggle."

"And I am thankful for *you*, Logan!"

At that moment Joanna came in carrying a tray of refreshments.

"I made some wassail for us to toast the season," she said, setting the tray on a table and pouring portions of the punch into four glasses.

"Where's May?" asked Logan.

"In the kitchen putting the finishing touches on some scones. She'll be here in a minute."

While they were waiting, Joanna walked toward the large window and stood looking out into the black night. Behind her the warm fire crackled cheerily, oblivious to the stormy winter night outside. Tiny white flakes of powdery snow swirled and danced against the darkened pane, collecting against the bottom corners of the windows. When she turned back toward the others, her face wore the same mixture of emotion Allison and Logan had been feeling.

"You know," she said softly, "I haven't felt much of a holiday spirit this year. It's not been an easy time for any of us, these last months. But just now, as I was thinking, I remembered my first meal in this place. I suppose the fire reminded me of it, though it was in the old banquet hall. That was the day I first knew that Dorey was my grandfather."

Joanna paused, and sighed deeply. Clearly the memory was filled with feelings of many kinds.

"Poor Dorey and Maggie were separated for over forty years," Joanna went on. "Our heartaches can't begin to compare with theirs. Yet look what kind of people they became in the end! Who wouldn't want to radiate love like they each did? Yet the price is high. Suffering is often the price we have to pay for true joy . . . true compassion. They paid the price, and their characters reflected the result. I want God to do that kind of work in my heart too, yet I resist and complain just to be separated from my dear husband for a year or two. Yes, I've lost a son, yet not really lost him—only given him back to God for a while."

She stopped. Allison went to her.

"Oh, Mother," she said, "you seem so strong to us. When I think of Lady Margaret's faith, I think immediately of you, too."

"Thank you, dear," said Joanna, wiping a solitary tear from her eye. "You are a daughter to be proud of.—God, help us all to give ourselves to your work in our hearts!" The mother and daughter embraced warmly, while Logan silently looked on, his own tears rising.

All at once the door leading toward the kitchen burst open.

In walked May, a bright smile on her spunky twenty-year-old face. "The scones are ready!" she announced as she bore the wooden tray to the table. "Complete with fresh butter from the Cunningham farm, churned today, and the berry jam Mrs. Galbreath sent up from town!"

"Ah, May!" said Logan, "how glad we three are that you could come home to join us! What would Christmas be without scones . . . and at least one carefree face among us? Right, ladies?" he added, with a grin toward Allison and Joanna.

They laughed.

"Come," said Joanna, "it is time to remember what the season is about."

They each took their glasses and lifted them toward one another.

"To those," said Logan, "whom we love who cannot be with us."

"May the Lord bless them, one and all," added May, "and give them peace."

"Help us to remember them in prayer," said Allison.

"And," added Joanna, "may the new year see us together again! Thank you, Lord, for the birth of your Son!"

The new year was not to bring the kind of reunion Joanna had hoped for. The war was to rage on for nearly three more years.

There were, however, major Allied advances throughout 1943. By midyear the Allies controlled the Mediterranean and most of the major sea routes. Alec was able to spend a week in Scotland during the summer before being sent to a new assignment. Ian, now twenty-five, had to continue to postpone his university studies.

In September, Italy surrendered unconditionally, and in the following year, June of 1944, the long-awaited invasion of Europe finally took place. Many of Logan's trainees played a vital role in preparing the way for the advance of troops which followed the landing. On August 24 the first Allies reached Paris, and the next day Charles de Gaulle drove through the city in an open car, to the wild cheering of thousands of Parisians. In the months that followed a million arrests were made in France of Nazi collaborators, with tens of thousands of summary executions. It would be many years before real peace would be restored to the torn nation.

The "thousand year Reich" finally collapsed in May of 1945, with Japan capitulating a few months later in the wake of the world's first nuclear explosion on a massive scale.

Thus the glories of victory continued to be mingled with the ongoing horrors of war. But the millions of returning soldiers did not need newspaper accounts of the destruction of Hiroshima to remind them that the world was forever changed. They were changed men. Some were emotionally destroyed, some had allowed the experience to broaden them. Relationships had been forged which would never be forgotten. War had caused both strengths and weaknesses to surface. Most had grown, all had changed, and they well knew that the world they now faced was changed, too.

In Britain, the old ways, long slowly fading, were now all but gone. Though she had, almost single-handedly, kept back facism from taking over Europe in 1940, Britain would never again be the economic and military powerhouse she had been in the pre-war years. New alignments of power would soon emerge, which would change the political and military landscape of the twentieth century forever.

The post-war years would bring these new times, with their accompanying stresses, to the northern Scottish estate of Stonewycke as well. Though the soldiers returned, they did not bring with them a return to the world of the 1920's. A new era had dawned.

80 ✲ Homecoming

A STIFF SEA breeze bent the purple heads of heather.

The sky shone blue and vivid, the air felt crisp and clean. The fishermen predicted a storm to blow in tomorrow, but today the shore and hills and fields were bright and welcome. The world was at peace.

Alec had arrived home the day before. For good! He had spent the evening getting reacquainted with his family and swapping tales with Logan. Now this morning one of the first things he had wanted to do was get out for a long walk with Joanna.

So today they would delight in the sunshine. And if the storm did come, they would enjoy it also. They were together again at their bonny Scottish home; a few drops of rain could not dampen their joy.

Alec clasped Joanna's hand tightly as they crested the final hill on their way back to the ancient family home. Both waking and sleeping, during those long, lonely years in the desert and on other assignments, this very picture had dominated his dreams—his dear wife, the glorious hills of purple, the gray stone walls. He had held on to his loves of family and wife and home and country with such a passion that they were able to sustain him, though it sometimes seemed he could not bear to wake to the grim smell of heat and sand and battle.

"We'll have to cancel our picnic tomorrow if it rains," said Joanna, slightly out of breath after the climb.

"They're sayin' 'twill be a braw storm," Alec replied, glancing toward the sea.

"Why, Alec MacNeil!" laughed Joanna, "I do believe you're actually looking forward to it!"

He laughed with her. "After the Sahara, ye'll ne'er catch me complainin' aboot a wee drap o' rain again!"

They paused to take in the view. The Strathy Valley spread out in lovely panorama before them. Though the summer was just past, like most of Scotland it remained a lush green, accented by the gently waving fields of golden grain, ripening for the soon-coming harvest. The little town of Port Strathy lay about two miles distant at the ocean's edge, from which the shoreline spread out, curving slowly toward the jutting point of land in the hazy distance.

"I never tire of coming here," said Joanna wistfully. "Just seeing the land, the valley, the little farms . . . it keeps me aware of our heritage. I don't know exactly, but something in me doesn't ever want to forget the past, the roots, those who came before. The legacy they left us is too important to let slip away as new generations come along."

"Which is why ye're so devoted t' that journal o' yers," said Alec. "Ye probably added three or four hundred pages since I left fer the war."

Joanna laughed. "Not quite that much, dear! But those long, lonely nights around here did give me plenty of time to work on it. I finished writing about my coming to Scotland, and meeting you, and all that happened then. Now I'm in the midst of trying to put everything Lady Margaret told me through the years into some kind of order. I'm rewriting her childhood from all the stories she gave me."

"And ye still hae t' tell aboot Dorey's comin', an' their sad partin'."

"Yes, not to mention all the years since, and the new generations. Our Ian's at Oxford now. May's engaged to her lawyer and planning to live in America. And Nat, now with the Lord, has left a legacy in the gentle spirit that will always be part of the ongoing heritage of the family. And Allison! Remember when I was so worried about her?"

"Aye, do I!"

"Her struggles before and during the war have caused such a growth and maturing in her. I see her really coming of age as the next heiress of Maggie's legacy. How could I have ever doubted the Lord's power to work in her life? And of course, who could forget her Logan!"

"Who indeed! What a blessed character o' the Lord's creation! I think he'll always hae that foxy twinkle in his eye!"

"Oh, Alec, we *are* fortunate! God has been so good to us! And what stories there are still to tell about this family and this estate!"

"But tell me noo honestly, do ye think anyone's gaein' t' read all ye're writin' besides yer lovin' husband?"

"Oh, Alec," exclaimed Joanna, "it hardly matters! Some stories just have to be told. Even if nobody reads them, they're still important . . . to me! But of course, I'm writing it for the children . . . and their children—for future generations, so that they'll remember the legacy of their ancestors. We mustn't forget our roots, Alec!"

"An' speakin' o' oor children an' their husbands, an' the stories they hae t' tell, look who's comin' yon across the way."

The warm breeze bringing the scent of ocean spray to the land had also beckoned to Allison and Logan; they had taken their way on horseback in the opposite direction from Allison's parents. They had ridden south, across the desolate heath known as Braenock Ridge, down into the valley, through several meadows to the bank of the Lindow, then back across the valley down through the ravine separating it from Stonewycke, up the other side, and were now walking their two horses across a wide moor toward the little summit on which Alec and Joanna stood observing them. Allison held both reins, listening to Logan who, as he walked, read from a letter received only that morning from Henri.

. . . life is so changed, mon ami, from the dark days of the Nazis. Our nation remains in much turmoil, but I have faith that what was always good in France has not been destroyed by the war and will emerge again. As for me, I am happy. My dear wife and children are with me once more, people are once again starting to think about reading, and as they do they are buying books. L'Escroc and L'Oiselet will now live only in memory. But rest assured, Logan, whom I will always think of as *Michel,* that my fondest memories of the war are of those times spent with you. As for the others, Antoine returned unharmed to France, Jean Pierre is still . . . well, he is still himself! Always with a cause, with people to help. Now *he* is trying to keep his brother from death because of his assistance to the Nazis! How the fortunes of time change the political landscape! Lise has gone to Israel. A new cause has ignited her passion, and now her dedication is bent on helping the many Jews released from concentration camps—including her sister—find new hope in Israel. I had a letter from her only last week. I can tell she is, if not yet quite *content,* at least happy for now. Claude I have lost track of. The last I was able to find out, he was in some difficulty with the authorities, some problem with the Russians, I believe. And you, my dear Michel—my apologies again! I must be growing old, I forget so quickly!—I almost forgot to congratulate you on your receiving of the *Croix de Guerre.* Now two medals, one from each country! You are indeed a hero of France, as I said you would be! . . . God be with you, mon ami!

Logan sighed deeply.

"You loved them, didn't you?" said Allison softly.

He nodded. "I guess I would have to say I didn't feel a great affection for Claude," he replied reflectively. "Yet even with him there was, I don't know, another kind of bond, even in the midst of the conflict. You don't go through a war with people, putting your life on the line for them, without attachments forming that will always be with you."

"I knew them only for days," returned Allison. "But I can almost feel a little of it with you."

"But that was then," said Logan. "Now it is time to look to the future . . . to our life truly *together* at last."

"Logan." Allison looked up at him after a moment, her eyes filled with gratefulness. "Thank you for not deserting me. I hardly gave you much of myself. I hope I now know better."

"It is *I* who owe *you* thanks! I was so blind, Allison, so caught up in my own self. I'm so thankful you stuck by me."

"Marriage is such a precious, yet fragile thing," Allison mused. "God has been good to us, Logan. We could have thrown away all we had if He hadn't somehow managed to get through to us."

Logan took his horse's rein, then slipped his arm around Allison's shoulder. Together they walked on up the hill.

"Ho, Alec . . . Joanna!" called out Logan as they approached; "watching for the storm coming in?"

"We'll hae nae talk o' storms today, laddie!" said Alec, reaching out his hand and giving Logan's a vigorous shake. "The wee wifie here winna hae me spoilin' tomorrow's plans wi' talk o' rain. Aye, but it's good to see ye, man! Ye're lookin' as well in the sunlight as ye did last night!"

"And you, Alec! The war hasn't changed you at all."

"Ah, ye should ken better than that!" replied Alec. "Ye may be a smooth talkin' enough city man t' beguile my daughter. But ye canna lie to a cagey auld vet like me! Why, man, jist one look at all this gray on top o' my head'll tell ye I'm no the same man I was in '40! Why, I turned sixty last year, and didna e'en hae me wife wi' me t' feel sorry fer me!"

Logan threw his head back and laughed heartily.

"One thing that hasn't changed is your sense of humor! And you know what the Bible says about gray—it is the sign of wisdom and honor."

"Amen to that!" laughed Joanna.

Silence fell for a moment as each of the four gazed upon the scene spread out before them. There they stood for several minutes more, the one couple arm-in-arm representing the generational link to the roots of the past, the other—holding hands as if still newly in love, as indeed they were—the symbol of the generations of the future.

Then, as if with one accord, they turned and began to make their way together down the hill, toward the ancient family home known as Stonewycke.

Epilogue ❈ London, 1969

WHEN THE HONORABLE Logan Macintyre exited Number Ten Downing Street that chill spring morning, he had every reason to be in good spirits. A pat on the back from the Prime Minister was no small thing.

However, though he wouldn't refuse the praise, he knew that yesterday's session of the Commons merely represented the result of his doing his job as Minister of Economic Affairs. Morton Giddings represented a block of votes Labour needed, and Logan had simply steered them in the right direction.

"Only last week," the Prime Minister had said, unable to keep from gloating, "Giddings said he'd never go our way."

"I suppose a great deal can happen in a week," Logan replied modestly.

"Not with Giddings! He's the biggest diehard we have."

Prime Minister Wilson leaned forward and winked. "Come now, tell me—how did you pull it off, old boy?"

"You really don't want to know, Harold."

"You know I'll find out sooner or later. Surely you of all people didn't pull something shady, did you, Logan?" The Prime Minister grinned conspiratorially.

"It was completely on the up-and-up, I assure you!"

"Never doubted you for a minute—all you need to do is turn on that Scottish charm of yours, do a little song-and-dance with that silver tongue you were endowed with, and things always seem to happen."

He paused. "But I have a feeling it took more than that with Giddings," he added at length.

"Well," Logan answered after another moment's hesitation, "you know how Giddings is constantly bragging about his prowess at cribbage . . . ?"

"Indeed!" exclaimed Wilson with a knowing look. "He bores everyone to distraction and has cleaned out more than a few new boys—"

Suddenly he stopped as realization dawned on him.

"Logan, you *didn't!*"

Logan smiled sheepishly.

"You played for his votes?" pressed the Prime Minister.

Logan nodded.

Wilson laughed outright. "You rascal," he said through his mirth. "And he wasn't aware of your—ah, how shall I phrase it?—your *expertise* with a deck of cards?"

"It's a matter of public record, isn't it? But you know I haven't gambled for years. Gave it up after the war. This was just an innocent game of cribbage."

Wilson continued to chuckle. "Giddings was never very good at doing his homework. I must say this is one of the most ingenious ways you've ever thought of—and you've had some gems!—to cajole your colleagues into voting your way on something you believed in. Come, old boy, this calls for a bit of a celebration."

Yes, Logan was satisfied with himself, and satisfied too with the path his life had followed since the war. Parliamentary wheeling and dealing was a most fulfilling use both of the talents God had given him and his personality, which enjoyed people and activity— especially when worthwhile causes lay in the balance. He had found his place in life during the past twenty years, and in it had gained the respect of his peers—as a man, a statesman, a humanitarian, and a Christian. Those who knew him, as well as those who knew *of* him, saw clearly a man who gave himself for others, not only out of Christian duty—though he was an outspoken national figure for the practical living out of the Christian faith—but also out of plain ethics and morality as a human being. He was a man who honored goodness and desired to see it operating between men—for the sake of goodness itself, and for the sake of God. Yet, being in the national spotlight had in no way dimmed the twinkle in his eye nor the love of an old-fashioned good time. There were still moments when he thought about a reckless scheme—for a worthwhile enterprise, of course!—just in memory of the good old days!

Logan was about to hail a cab, but then decided the day was too beautiful to waste. Besides, it was only a short walk to his office. He pressed down his hat against a gust of wind that persisted in spite of the sunny blue sky. He neared a newspaper vendor and dug a coin from his pocket and tossed it to the boy, who caught it deftly.

"Mornin', Mr. Macintyre!" said the lad above the din of traffic. "'Ere's yer paper."

"Thanks, Joe."

"An' don't ferget yer change, sir."

"Not a bit of it, Joe!"

"Thank 'ee kindly, sir!" said Joe, grinning at the tip. "An' by-the-by, me mum ain't soon goin' t' ferget what you did fer me in that business with the constable last week. An' neither am I."

The youth had run afoul of the law for supposed possession of marijuana. When Logan, who had been buying *The Times* from him for two years, heard of it, he took the matter in hand, interceded on the boy's behalf, and eventually discovered that Joe had been mistaken for a vendor a couple blocks away whose newsstand was being used for small-time drug deals.

Logan had expected no thanks, however. It was the most natural thing for him to do. He well remembered what it was like for a boy trying to live on the streets.

"Well," Joe continued, "she—me mum, that is—she wanted to invite ye t' dinner, but I said as how an important man like yersel'—"

"I'd love to come!" interrupted Logan. "You know my office number—you just call me and let me know when."

"I sure will, Mr. Macintyre! Me mum'll be pleased pink when I tells her! "

Logan tucked the folded newspaper under his arm and continued on. In another ten minutes he reached his office. His secretary, Agnes Stillwell, middle-aged, efficient, and devoted, greeted him warmly.

"You've several messages here, Mr. Macintyre."

She picked up a pad and followed him into his private office.

"James Callaghan in the Home office called and wants to meet with you before this afternoon's session," she began.

"Fine. Go ahead and set up a time with him. Anything else?"

She briskly flipped a page of her pad. "Your wife called to remind you about your dinner guests from Aberdeen tonight. And Alexander Hart of the BBC wanted to know if Monday would be convenient for the interview—"

"Oh, I forgot all about that! How does Monday look?"

"I think we can clear the afternoon."

Logan grinned. "I'd be lost without you, Aggie!"

It was difficult for Mrs. Stillwell to continue to look efficient while beaming under her boss's praise, but somehow she managed.

"And then there's this last message from a Hannah Whitley," she added, straightening her glasses self-consciously.

"Hannah Whitley . . ." Logan repeated thoughtfully. "Who's she?"

"I don't know, sir. She had a most down-to-earth sound . . . almost like a domestic or something. I can't imagine what she wanted."

"I don't think I've ever heard the name," said Logan. "What was the message?"

"Rather odd, really," Mrs. Stillwell replied. "She said she needed to speak with you and wanted to know when you would be in. I asked her to leave her number and said you would return her call if she wished. She seemed reluctant, but finally consented. Here's the number."

"Doesn't sound too odd," remarked Logan, taking the slip of paper his secretary handed him. "I suppose it was mostly in her tone."

"Well, let's see." Logan pulled his phone across the desk toward him, glanced at the paper, and dialed the number. After a silent pause, he hung up. "Now that *is* odd," he said. "The number is out of service. Didn't she just call?"

"I wonder if I could have copied it down wrong. I'm terribly sorry."

"Impossible, Aggie. But don't worry about it." He carelessly tossed the paper into the "incoming" basket on his desk. "If it's important, I've no doubt the matter will catch up with us another time."

TREASURE
OF
STONEWYCKE

To those of God's people who are seeking to impact history and their own posterity, by building into the generational flow of God's dealing with man on the earth, according to Psalm 78:5–7.

"I, the Lord your God, am a jealous God, punishing the sins of the fathers to the third and fourth generation of those who hate me, but showing love to a thousand generations. . . . Know therefore that the Lord your God *is* God; he is the faithful God, keeping his covenant of love to those who love him and keep his commands. . . . Tell this to your children, and let your children tell it to their children, and their children to the next generation. . . . Let this be written for a future generation, that a people not yet born may praise the Lord."

—Deuteronomy 5:8, 7:9
Joel 1:3
Psalm 102:18

CONTENTS

❈ Introduction

FROM THE EARLIEST beginnings of time, God uniquely ordained the family as the primary human organism to transmit His life. The entire structure of ancient Israel was founded upon family. Chief among the commands of Moses to those under his charge was: "Teach these things to your sons and daughters."

The Scriptures make abundantly clear that God's intent when He created the family was that His life be carried down through time, *through the family,* forever—for a thousand generations. Each individual was designed to be nurtured by roots which reached deeply into the soil of the past, giving strength, which then in turn extended into the future.

In Satan's devious cunning, however, he infiltrates and cuts off that umbilical cord of inner life which God implanted within the ongoing and extended family institution. When he is thus allowed to destroy family roots, this many-generational process is undone, and the result is that every successive generation or two, men and women have to discover faith anew. The ongoing vitality and strength of a permanent, life-giving root system is made impotent.

God has given us, however, a responsibility to infuse a heritage into the generations—a heritage involving both the past and the future, a heritage far broader in scope than our own mere lives. God desires permanency from his people, an ongoing fight against Satan's ways, a continual breaking of the chains of evil from the past, even to the third and fourth generation back, and a passing on of the mandate of obedience to God to a thousand generations ahead.

Few apprehend the legacy which has been given us to pass down. We leave the treasure of God's life buried. This parable of Stonewycke is but the universal story which God has been working to infuse within the human chain of generations with every family on the face of the earth. The heritage of God's life within us is a legacy for *all* families, for *all* times.

This is not merely Maggie's story, or Atlanta's, or Joanna's, or Allison's. We *all* must step into it at our own time. Some are born into the bloodline, others (like the fictional Alec and Ian, and the Gentiles of whom Paul speaks) must be grafted in. But the life of God's Spirit moves mightily throughout time, and every man and woman must one day face their *own* place in that life, in that legacy, just as do the characters in the story you are about to read. God takes us where we are—wanderers, orphans, in need of a Father, in search of our true Home—and makes us an integral part of that legacy.

Maggie "became" more than she could have been alone because the stream of God's purpose (of which Stonewycke is a shadow, a type, an illustration) swept over her, drew her into it, and made it *hers.* The legacy is God's life, not Maggie's, but through her obedience was sublimated, and thereby passed on, into future generations.

At every time, in every era, within every human heart, the decision must be faced whether to accept one's place within that legacy. Will we abandon ourselves to God's plan and life for us, or will we ignore the river of the Spirit sweeping over us and let it pass without bringing us up into its inherent life? In every successive generation, every person must face the choices which will determine the impact God's lifeblood will have in his or her own existence, and whether it will move through them into the future, or die. At every turn Satan will try to steal the inheritance which has been given us. Forces will infiltrate our families telling of false priorities, false ambitions, false attitudes which are not God's. But we are commanded and impelled to stand firm, to walk in the calling of the one *true* legacy, and to pass on His heritage to those who come after us in the ongoing flow of generations.

The facts in the story of the Stonewycke Legacy may not be real. But this is a *true* story, in that the truths of God's legacy within His people *are* real. There *is* a treasure, a life, a land, a home, and a heritage that is easy for earthly eyes to lose sight of. As Jesus said, the mysteries of the Kingdom of God are hid, like parables, so that only those with eyes to see and perceive, may truly apprehend them. In so many families, in so many generations, the treasure is buried, hidden, sometimes for centuries. Yet that treasure forms the very strength of God's family, and the ongoing flow of God's life in the world. It is a treasure awaiting discovery by every family, by every man, by every woman, by every child of God in every new generation!

God bless you one and all. It has truly been our joy to experience the life of Stonewycke with you.

1 ❧ Mourners

A GRAY SKY hung heavy over the dormant heather. But from the blanket of black umbrellas gathered at the graveyard, it appeared that the misting October drizzle had deterred not a single resident of Port Strathy from bidding their beloved matriarch farewell.

Donald Creary found himself at the front of the throng pressing in around the grave.

He clearly recalled the first time he had laid eyes on Lady Joanna, though he had been but a wee bairn at the time. He'd possessed nerve enough only to steal a glimpse from behind his mother's dress. Yet even then, his childish intuition had sensed she was someone special. She had come with Doc MacNeil to tend his papa's favorite sow. Of course back then she had been only a stranger in town with a foreign sound to her tongue—that was sixty years ago. But young Donald had needed no property deeds or lawyers to tell him that here stood royalty, or close enough to it.

Lady Joanna didn't need to say so either—nor did she. He never knew a humbler soul. The reverence of the Port Strathy folk sprang from deeds, not words. Never had she put on airs, never had she acted the part of head of the region's most important family. Why, her behavior during the Queen Mother's visit fifteen years ago had grown into legend throughout the valley. Joanna had slipped away in the early morning hours while the dear old lady still slept and had driven (herself, with no thought of a chauffeur!) halfway to Culden to take Mrs. Gordon some medicine for her ailing daughter. After helping the widow milk her cow, she had shown back up at the castle just in time for breakfast with mud and who could tell what else all over her frock! The Queen Mother's delight was so great over the story that both women went down into the valley that very afternoon and had tea with Mrs. Gordon in her humble stone cottage.

Memories like that, which were not uncommon, had through the years made Joanna as highly thought of along Scotland's northeastern coast as the Queen Mother herself. Sixty years of selfless love and compassion expressed in her every act of kindness toward the folk of her land had brought out nearly every man, woman, and child in the valley to pay their respects and say their last goodbyes.

The Rev. Macaulay had begun to speak. Donald had to turn his full attention to the voice dulled by the increasing rain and the canopy of umbrellas, not to mention Macaulay's own personal sorrow.

"*But I would not have you be ignorant, brethren,*" he read from First Thessalonians, "*concerning them which are asleep, that ye sorrow not, even as others which have no hope. For if we believe that Jesus died and rose again, even so them also which sleep in Jesus will God bring with him.*"

Donald ran a hand over his damp cheek. His tears mingled freely with the Scottish drizzle.

Creary's fond memory of Lady Joanna stemmed not merely from her ministry to Mrs. Gordon, her enthusiasm for helping her husband with his animals, nor the esteem in which she was held at Buckingham Palace. His feelings ran far deeper than that. For it had been Lady Joanna who had helped him get right with the Lord.

The war that had cost him his leg had also left him embittered toward just about everything in life. In the years following he had managed to make things miserable not only for himself but also for his wife and children. Lady Joanna had not failed to visit them every day for months after his homecoming, notwithstanding her own grief after the loss of her son and baby granddaughter. But never an angry word had come out of her mouth toward the so-called fate Donald was so fond of cursing. She had taught him about hope, and gradually led him to a sustaining faith. Because of her, Donald understood Rev. Macaulay's words today.

He stole a glance at the family. Yes, they understood too. He saw the deep grief in their faces. After all, her death had come as a great shock. Four days ago she had been active and vital, hardly showing her eighty-one years. Then, literally, the next day she was gone, suddenly stricken with a cerebral hemorrhage. But despite the sadness in their eyes, he could tell they knew she had passed into a greater life, an even deeper vitality.

"For this we say unto you by the word of the Lord, that we which are alive and remain unto the coming of the Lord shall not prevent them which are asleep."

Donald looked in turn at the faces of Lady Joanna's offspring. All the children had come, just as they had for their father's funeral the year before. No distance would prevent members of this family from saying their final farewells to such loved and revered parents as Lady Joanna and Alec MacNeil.

Lady Margaret MacNeil, now Mrs. Reynolds, had come in yesterday, all the way from her home in Boston. Her brother Ian had been in Greece writing a book when he had been wired the news. He had taken the next plane home.

And of course, there stood Mr. Macintyre and Lady Allison, the undisputed new heiress to Stonewycke now, in the forefront of them all. Donald had to admit that as new overseers of the estate, they would be quite different than Lady Joanna and Doc Alec had been. More cosmopolitan, he supposed, more modern. Doc Alec had remained a country man, notwithstanding that his son-in-law was one of the most influential members of Parliament. And Lady Joanna never lost her simplicity of spirit.

Lady Allison and Mr. Macintyre moved to a faster pace of life. Just last year the Prime Minister himself had come to Stonewycke for a visit! And though Mr. Macintyre's career required that they spend a great deal of time in the south, the sleepy little northern region had become, if not exactly a hub of activity, yet an area well aware of its close links to the centers of power in Britain.

But Lady Allison and Mr. Macintyre were like their predecessors in many ways as well. They loved the land, the people, the heritage, the sense of roots no less than the older folks. That was always clear. They cared, and would do anything for you.

Creary would never forget that night his prize bull had taken sick, and the look of grief in the Doc's eyes when he told him there was nothing he could do. Then, a couple of days later, Donald had been down at the harbor with some of the other men, lamenting the hard times, the lack of money, and he had been especially down on account of his bull. Just then Mr. Macintyre rounded the corner, alone, apparently out for a stroll in Port Strathy, though as usual he was dressed as if he'd only that moment walked out of the Houses of Parliament. He'd approached the small group, greeting each of the men warmly with a shake of the hand and a slap on the back, listening in turn to the tales each had to tell.

But before turning to go back the way he came, he'd unobtrusively handed Donald a small folded envelope which Donald, sensing that it was meant to be private, hastily shoved into his coat pocket.

When Creary was alone an hour later, he sat down, opened the envelope, and read the words: *I hear you'll be needing a new bull, and I always did have an urge to invest in livestock. Buy us the best one you can find and we'll share the profits.* The letter was simply signed *L. M.* Folded up inside the paper were two hundred-pound notes. Donald knew Mr. Macintyre had no more thought of taking half the profits than he would of dismantling Stonewycke. That had merely been his way to insure Donald didn't try to give him back the notes.

Even as one of the former Prime Minister's closest confidants, Mr. Macintyre was still a con man of sorts. There were those in Port Strathy, close friends like Donald Creary and others his generosity had found clever ways to befriend, who saw through the exterior. They knew Logan Macintyre never once forgot he was one of them, never forgot he had started out as nothing more than the estate's mechanic.

In those days he had rubbed elbows with more than a few of the menfolk around the grimy tables at Hamilton's, dealing a pretty fast game of cards. The years might have reformed him in that area, but he always seemed to enjoy mixing with the townspeople, no matter how important he grew in London society. And he was still not opposed to a con now and then, if by it he could do someone good without making that person feel small.

Yes, it was a different world now—the 1970s! Changes that had been slowly coming for decades had now worked their way fully into the complete fabric of life throughout Britain, from the top to the bottom of the social scale. A nobleman couldn't live off the land anymore, not as an aristocrat whose rents from his tenants kept him living well. Those times were well past. The common man had risen, and now those on top had to struggle to make financial ends meet just like everyone else. No doubt it cost the family a great deal to keep up the old Stonewycke place these days. Doc's veterinary practice and Macintyre's political career were more than mere sidelines. They were necessary to pay the bills. The gentry still played an important role in maintaining tradition, but these men were now just like all the rest of them. They, too, had to work for a living or else go broke trying to maintain an ancient estate that had become a financial albatross.

Creary's eyes strayed to the closed coffin sitting beneath an awning to protect it from the rain.

Life, despite all the changes, had to go on. Lady Joanna never pined for the past, and she had as much cause as anyone. But Lady Joanna understood what was truly important in life. Perhaps that was why her passing was so deeply mourned.

Rev. Macaulay closed the graveside services with the Lord's Prayer. When the last words had died away, the family began to file past the coffin on their way to the waiting cars.

Creary watched a moment, then filed slowly out through the black iron gate with the other silent townspeople. Halfway across the adjacent field he paused to glance back. The rain was coming down more earnestly now. The ancient cemetery with its moss-encrusted gray stones and markers would soon be still once more. As he took in the scene he noticed a stranger pausing beside the coffin.

"Who d'ye suppose that is?" Creary's wife whispered, leaning toward him.

The woman was tall and slim, in her early thirties, and her black cashmere suit was well-tailored and fashionable. Creary couldn't manage a good look at her face, shadowed as it was beneath a floppy-brimmed black hat, but the hair flowing out from under it was the color of a haystack in a field catching the last rays of an amber sunset. It was an unmistakable attribute, even in this dismal weather. She walked with grace and assurance, and you could tell at first glance that she was a woman who knew what she was about. But what could she be doing here? he wondered. He had never seen her before, and he knew every person in Port Strathy.

"I dinna ken," Creary whispered in reply.

"No one o' the family is she?"

"They didna seem to be takin' no notice o' her."

"'Tis muckle odd," mused Creary's wife.

As they looked, the stranger paused only a moment at the casket and laid on top a lovely red rose she had been carrying. Then, just before walking away in the opposite direction from the family, she appeared to say something. But Creary was too far away to hear.

Indeed, the words she spoke were barely audible, intended for no ears other than those who could hear earthly voices no longer:

"If only I had come sooner. . . . "

2 ❧ Hilary Edwards

HILARY EDWARDS WAS the sort who thrived on the activity generated from being part of an organization on the go.

The rhythmic clicking of typewriters beating out their cadence, indifferent to the unbroken ringing of phones and the hum of a dozen different conversations, was to Hilary the one constant of this place. She liked the sound, found it relaxing, as another might the steady breaking of waves on a shore or the unremitting fall of rain upon an attic roof.

Granted, tomorrow was deadline, which made the appealing noises about the place more frantic than usual. If the editors, typesetters, layout and graphics people, and advertising personnel of *The Berkshire Review* were going to loaf, this was not the time for it. Putting out a monthly magazine with a short staff on a thin budget left little time for goldbricking; and if a momentary breath could be inhaled for a couple of days after tomorrow, it would only be succeeded by the immediate renewal of activity brought on by the next month's assignments.

Hilary glanced out the glass walls enclosing her private office and could not resist a smile. She loved the accelerated pace of approaching deadline. It was at just such times that every feature of good journalism had to fit together.

As editor-in-chief, she was proud of her magazine and her staff. This crew in particular was the best she'd had in a long time, and it told—not only in increased circulation, but also in growing acclaim from some of the other literary journals in and about London.

After a brief lapse into such musing, she quickly returned her attention to her typewriter, where the next issue's editorial still reposed half finished.

"*East End Redevelopment: Who Really Benefits?*" read her caption.

It was a familiar story: old neighborhoods torn down and replaced by high-rise buildings where the rent ended up being three or four times more than the old residents could afford. "It's called 'cleaning up the slums,'" she typed, "but the only ones who *clean up* are the Slum Lords."

Hilary's colleagues had warned her away from the cause. "It's yesterday's news," they insisted. "Who cares anymore—especially among our readership? They want highbrow causes. Who is going to care if a hundred-year-old, rat-infested tenement house is torn down?"

Hilary was not deterred. If they didn't care, then they ought to, and she would make them.

So she'd visited the place, taken a room, stayed three days, interviewed people around the neighborhood, and talked to the residents. Certainly *they* cared, even if they were but a handful and hardly the kind of people the rest of the public paid much attention to. Yet these folk, soon to be displaced from their homes, were citizens too—and had a right to be heard. If their representative to Parliament was deaf to their appeals, at least *The Berkshire Review* was not.

After two weeks of investigation, Hilary had uncovered some interesting, even startling facts. Excitedly she'd tackled the story after arriving home from her trip, relishing the discomfort this month's issue of the *Review* was going to cause several highly placed individuals.

The phone on her desk rang. She paused, tucked the receiver under her chin, then returned her fingers to their resting position on the keys of her IBM, as if still hoping—even in the midst of a conversation—that inspiration was suddenly going to strike.

"Hilary Edwards," she said, then paused to listen. "No, I can't come now, Murry," she went on after a moment. "Sure . . . of course I want to see it. But I've got to be over—" She glanced at her watch. "Oh no! I didn't realize it was so late. That press conference starts in fifteen minutes! I have to go. I'm anxious to hear what you've found, but you can update me later."

She hung up the phone, switched off her Selectric, and jumped to her feet. Where had the morning gone? She'd been at the magazine since seven a.m., and had been confident she'd have no problem getting to the interview at Whitehall. But a dozen unexpected things had cropped up. Now she'd barely make it.

As she rushed toward the door, she took a minute to make sure her gray linen suit was in order and that her blue silk blouse was properly tucked in. She quickly freshened her lipstick, gave her nose a powder and her pale amber hair a quick pat. The effect was well spent, but by no means necessary. Hers was the kind of beauty that needed no such assistance. In fact, had she depended too heavily on such devices, she might have detracted from, rather than enhanced, her natural attractiveness.

At thirty-two Hilary Edwards had a fresh, almost girlish look that stood in sharp, though not unpleasant contrast to the high-pressure, cut-throat world of journalism. Well-defined cheekbones, full lips, and luminous blue eyes tended to offset the vulnerability of her pale skin and hair. The combined effect was interesting, occasionally enchanting, and to the unsuspecting, even a bit deceptive. For however girlish her appearance may have been, she had succeeded in her career by her incisive, unrelenting, determined nature. At first glance she may have looked like a college co-ed, but she could hold her own in any company.

From a London working-class family that lived not far from the neighborhood whose cause she now espoused, Hilary was no stranger to hard-fought victories. She attended the university at a time when that ancient, tradition-bound world still belonged primarily to men, working her way through as a waitress, a department store clerk, a governess, and a handful of whatever other menial jobs came along—and managed to graduate near the top of her class.

After that came a string of newspaper jobs, her apprenticeship for what lay ahead. *The Birmingham Guardian, The Manchester Times,* and two obscure London sheets were found on her list of credits when *The London Times* hired her. In that capacity she met Bartholomew Frank, publisher of the flagging *Berkshire Review.* Back then the *Review* had been a scholarly, often stuffy, decent quality but little appreciated magazine, offering highbrow treatises on current events, which drew its limited readership from Britain's intelligentsia.

Frank offered Hilary the position of chief editor and, though the magazine was likely to fold in six months barring a drastic turnaround, she took the job. It was too great a challenge to resist. Neither of them had anything to lose, so Frank gave her *carte blanche,* and she proceeded to revamp the publication. Her inaugural issue showcased an upbeat yet still intelligent style that, while it continued to appeal to the dons and scholars, made a successful bid to capture the interest of a wider range of the public.

She continued to broaden the *Review*'s base, brought in several key people who shared her vision of what the magazine might become, and in a year had doubled the circulation while at the same time fearlessly tackling many controversial topics.

That was five years ago. Today *The Berkshire Review* was making a profit, and she had insured herself a place of respect among her peers.

Hilary grabbed her coat on the way out of her office, then paused at her secretary's desk to leave some last-minute instructions. In three minutes she had descended in the elevator and was outside in the chilly London air of early autumn.

The Strand was particularly busy that noon and it took several minutes to find a cab. She wound up five minutes late for the press conference, but luckily the Members of Parliament who were scheduled as the object of the press's attention had not yet arrived either.

Two or three of her colleagues waved greetings as she took a seat about two-thirds of the way to the front of the crowded room.

"Now we can get started!" one said in a jovial tone, thick with an Irish brogue. "The *real* muscle is here."

"Hardly," laughed Hilary. "The traffic was treacherous. I'm lucky to be here at all," she said, taking a pad and pencil from her purse.

"You'll have to blast the Ministry of Transportation next week, Edwards!"

"Oh, Bert, I'm not that bad," she replied. His only response was a hearty laugh.

Bert O'Malley was a veteran newspaperman with *The Daily Telegraph.* He had won acclaim for his coverage of World War II from the front lines and had been among the vanguard of the press corps at the liberation of Paris. He was tough, boisterous, and generally a nice fellow who smoked cheap cigars and seemed to possess a singular aversion to wearing a properly knotted necktie. Everyone liked him, and Hilary was no exception.

"What do you suppose the Parliament boys are going to pull over on us today?" asked Bert, blowing a puff of cigar smoke in Hilary's face.

She coughed and pointedly fanned the air with her pad. "You mean *try* to pull over on us?" she said.

"That goes without saying, me dear," returned Bert. "No one can put anything over on the press, eh?" He chuckled ironically.

"We had better keep our guard up anyway," said Hilary.

"You're not becoming a cynic, Eddie, me dear!"

"Don't worry, Bert. A cynic distrusts everything and everyone. I reserve my distrust for those most deserving of such scrutiny."

"Do you now?"

"It's been my experience that most cynics find their fulfillment in just being critical. They have nothing to believe in, so they make it their business to tear down everyone else's values and beliefs. To me that's lower than believing a falsehood. Cynicism in and of itself is nothing but emptiness. That's not why I'm in journalism. I do have things I believe in. My motives aren't to tear down, but to get some good things accomplished. At least I hope that's what comes of it. I'm a believer in what I'm doing, Bert."

"Maybe you should be the politician, Eddie!"

"No thanks, I prefer to be just a writer who thinks a little public scrutiny, focused with the aid of the printed page, is the best way to keep our leaders tuned in to the true interests of the people they are supposed to represent."

"'Power, like a desolating pestilence, pollutes whate'er it touches,' eh, me dear?"

"I wouldn't go that far." She paused thoughtfully. "But let's face it, Bert, too many of our officials have forgotten what it really means to be members of the human race."

"And if anyone can set them straight, it will be you, me girl!"

Bert took two gusty puffs from his cigar, sending a thick cloud of smoke into the air. "Well, let 'em have it, Eddie," he said. "Here they come."

Several expensively dressed men entered from a side door and strode confidently toward the front of the room. As Hilary glanced up, she shifted uncomfortably in her chair, nearly dropping her pad.

"You all right, Eddie?" whispered Bert.

"What?" said Hilary distractedly. "Oh, yes . . . fine. I just didn't expect to see *him* here."

Before Bert could ask what she meant, the room grew quiet and the three new arrivals took seats behind the long front table on which sat microphones and glasses of ice water. All were Labour M.P.'s. John Gelzer and Logan Macintyre represented veteran politicians, both shadow ministers in Harold Wilson's Opposition Labour Party since Wilson's ouster from Number 10 Downing Street by Edward Heath a year earlier. The third man was a relatively new back bencher, Neil Richards.

While they were settling themselves, Hilary quickly thumbed through the notes she had penciled in her pad earlier that morning, an exercise made the more difficult that her hands were suddenly perspiring and cold. Gelzer and Richards had previously agreed to appear before the press following their recent party conference. Macintyre was a new addition, and seeing him unexpectedly walk into the room was the source of Hilary's present discomfort.

She wondered if his presence indicated that the Parliament members thought they were going to need more clout. After all, they represented a current faction arising within Labour that was staunchly bucking the rest of its party's anti-Common Market stance. That summer Heath's Conservative government had launched a blitz of sorts to win the nation's approval for entry into the European Economic Community. Now, in October, Parliament was at last prepared to make the momentous vote.

After some years of vacillation and pressure from the Trade Unions, Wilson was ready to lead his Labour Party in opposing Heath. But there was a solid element in his party, including some influential front benchers, who firmly backed Britain's involvement in the Common Market. A serious split threatened within the party when, during the recent Labour Conference, Wilson and his deputy party leader Roy Jenkins leveled harsh words at one another. Hilary guessed that the three representatives now present, all supporters of the Common Market, were going to try to placate the public, not to mention their leader, Harold Wilson.

Soon a loud hum from an activated microphone filled the room. Richards tapped his mike, nodded toward the sound men, cleared his throat, and spoke.

"I believe we are ready to begin," he said. "Mr. Gelzer will start things off by reading a brief statement."

Gelzer shuffled some papers, straightened his horn-rimmed eye glasses, and then read from one of the sheets in a practiced oratorical tone. He went on for about ten minutes with the usual rhetoric about country, party, and motherhood, closing with a five-minute pitch for the Common Market.

Hilary had to force herself to pay attention, and sighed with relief when he finished. *They would have done much better,* she thought to herself, *to have had Macintyre or even Richards deliver the message.*

The question and answer period proved much more stimulating.

Cauldwell from the *Conservative Daily Express* pressed right to the heart of the issue:

"Can you comment on rumors regarding the possible formation of a new Social Democratic Party?" he asked, pencil ready.

"I can only say," replied Lord Gelzer, "that it is news to me."

"What about reports that Wilson and Jenkins aren't speaking to each other?"

"Surely," sighed Gelzer with great effect, "with so many vital issues before us, there must be more germane topics we can discuss."

Hilary's hand shot up.

"Perhaps you'd like to comment," she called out, "on the fact that the polls still indicate less than half the population favors Great Britain's entry into the EEC."

"You are ignoring the equal number who are in favor of the Common Market," rejoined Gelzer smugly.

Hilary rankled at the glib reply and was about to rebut when Macintyre interceded.

"You are voicing a valid argument, Miss . . . ?"

"Edwards," she replied to his questioning pause. A sudden tight, dry sensation arose in her throat.

"The will of the people, Miss Edwards," he went on, "is vitally important to us. The fact that the percentage you have quoted was substantially lower three months ago is still nothing to hoot about. What do *you* suppose we ought to do when our nation is in such a dilemma?"

He paused, as if expecting her to answer his question. The room was silent.

Hilary returned his gaze for a moment, as if waiting for him to continue. She tried to write off his statement as more rhetoric. But there was a quality in his tone far different from Gelzer's. He was not delivering a pat speech; rather, he seemed to be talking to her as he might if he met her on the street. Still he said nothing.

Finally Hilary shook her head. "I'd rather hear your answer," she said.

He smiled.

"I thought you'd never ask," he said lightly, gently dismissing the tension that had begun to build. "And in reality the answer is a simple one—so disarmingly simple that neither the public nor its leaders think of it often enough. When we come upon the horns of a dilemma such as this one, we employ a tactic that perhaps ought to be taken a little more seriously at all times in Parliament—we try honestly to assess what we feel is best for the nation . . . and then we vote our conscience. Hopefully our constituents will pardon us!"

A soft ripple of laughter spread through the room.

Then Macintyre's amused expression turned solemn. "Miss Edwards, I have folks in my district who voted for me simply because they believed I cared. They don't always agree with my politics, but they knew I'd try my best to do right by them. That's how it works in a representative government. Now, here's an issue over which there is a great deal of division. And I personally believe a positive vote, though it means going against my own party's leader, is the best thing for our nation. So I've got to vote for it, because that's what my constituents expect me to do. They don't want a yes man to blindly do their bidding—or the bidding of a party leader. They want a man of principle and conscience. I may not always succeed in that area, nor will I always succeed in pleasing them, but I do always try."

"Is that what you told Mr. Wilson?" asked another reporter.

"Yes, as a matter of fact that is exactly what I told him."

"Is your dismissal from his inner circle, or even from the party, a possibility?"

"Mr. Wilson is a reasonable man," answered Macintyre, "whom I—we all—deeply admire. He understands such principles as loyalty and conscience, and I am confident the Labour Party will rise above our current difficulties."

The grilling went on for another forty-five minutes.

Hilary spent the time listening, for the most part. There were a dozen questions she'd intended to ask, but somehow their urgency diminished. Before she knew it the three members of Parliament were packing up their briefcases and making their exit. She shook the bemused expression from her face in the realization that the session was over.

"Why, Eddie, me dear," said Bert in a tone filled with good-natured taunting, "you disappoint me."

"What did I do?"

"'Tis what you *didn't* do, me dear!" exclaimed the veteran reporter. "I've come to expect you to go for the throat. But you sat there gentle as a bleedin' lamb!"

"Well, I . . ." she began, trying to make some excuse. She was even faintly disappointed in herself too. But then she realized she had no excuse to make. She wasn't certain about the cause of her docility either.

Hilary bid Bert goodbye and left. There was a less purposeful lilt to her step as she walked out—not exactly hesitant, but definitely thoughtful. Her slower gait seemed to indicate that her thoughts had been diverted, and were now too intense to concern themselves with the triviality of placing one foot in front of the other.

Almost without realizing it she found herself walking to Charing Cross Station. She hadn't intended on taking the tube. Nor had she intended to leave the city. But her feet seemed to know her will better than her mind at the moment. After a couple of transfers, she was soon on a train for Brighton.

3 ❊ *Afternoon With a Friend*

THE SKY HAD reflected a hue of autumn gray since morning, but by late afternoon it had turned foreboding. The clouds hung low and the air smelled heavy and ominous with the imminent storm. The dismal pall spreading over the earth somehow suited Hilary's quiet mood, and the air away from the pressures of the city was refreshing—for the moment, at least. Hilary wouldn't want to stay away long. But just now the serene atmosphere of a half-deserted resort town in late fall suited her.

She and her friend Suzanne Heywood strolled along the beachfront, making small talk about the endless rows of two- and three-story houses fronting the shore, poking now and then into a shop whose window had drawn their interest. On their right, a steady stream of waves rushed at the shore, their white-tipped crests offering the only contrast in color between the greenish-gray of the sea and the blackish-gray of the sky. Indeed, where sea and sky met in the distance, the horizon beyond which lay France and the Continent, the green and the black joined in an almost indistinguishable blur of slate.

"This place can be soothing, can't it?" said Hilary, pausing to inhale a breath of the heavy air.

"Sometimes," replied Suzanne. "But not in the summer when it's crawling with tourists."

Hilary laughed.

"That's why I like winters here best," her friend went on. "We great, would-be writers need our peace and quiet, you know."

Hilary smiled but said nothing. That's what she liked about Suzanne—she never took herself took seriously. That was also probably one of the reasons she had sought her out on this day. In Suzanne she had always had a sympathetic ear, someone who understood, someone who would listen.

How can two such different people remain so close? Hilary wondered. They had become friends over ten years ago when both were students at the university. There had been more similarities then, and their affinity did not seem so unusual.

They found their common ground on the field of social and political battle. In the late 1950s they had been at the vanguard of the dawning social awareness that blossomed fully in the next decade. Hilary had been the firebrand, the central figure in every campus debate, the one standing on corners passing out handbills and button-holing passersby to espouse her cause. Suzanne came at protest from another direction. Where Hilary would have been comfortable commanding the troops of their activist band, Suzanne was its poet laureate, the mystic, the esoteric champion of causes more cognitive than practical. If world hunger were at issue, Suzanne would have been more likely to put herself on a starvation diet than join Hilary on a soapbox or march in a rally.

Their different backgrounds had contributed, no doubt, to such divergent approaches. Hilary, from the working class, was bent on changing things in real and visible ways. Suzanne, from a wealthy and affluent family, daughter of a lord, was satisfied to voice her discontent with society using the more abstruse imagery of a poetic and largely quixotic nature. Her most practical act of protest back then had been the disavowal of her noble ties, and with that, her father's money as well.

She had joined Hilary in the latter's stand against the aristocracy, even going so far, for her, as to circulate petitions advocating the dismantling of the ancient tradition. Such a position was short-lived, however, for as Suzanne reached her mid-twenties, she discovered it much easier to take the support her father offered than continue a penniless existence fighting against it. Lord Heywood had long since given up trying to convince her to get her head out of the clouds, and contented himself with providing the means to help her get on with life.

Through the years both young women had changed, and both, curiously, had gravitated toward writing—Hilary attempting to change the world for the better through journalism, Suzanne working on a book-length collection of verse and scattered narrative of vague intent.

But Hilary had learned that Suzanne, for all her flowery flummery about the earth, the sky, Greenpeace, and saving the whales, had a more than decent head on her shoulders. Though Suzanne was still occasionally apt to float in and out between realism and fancy, reminiscent of the months following her pilgrimage to Haight-Ashbury in 1965, Hilary had come to appreciate her depth of sensitivity and her willingness to be still and listen.

Since the death of her father six months ago, Suzanne had been, unknown to Hilary, reflecting on a good many issues more solid and more traditional than either would have thought possible ten years before. The poet in her was at last awakening to see in a new light the world in which she had been raised.

This dreary fall afternoon the burden of talking and listening had been equally divided between the two, but the conversation had focused on lighter topics, mostly filling the gaps since they had last seen each other. Hilary had come to talk with her friend and pour out some of her recent conflicts. But now that she was here, she grew reticent, wondering if she could share her secret even with her best friend.

Hilary paused at one of the shops and nudged Suzanne inside. The Oriental style boutique was clearly attempting to cater to the current fashion craze. Absently Hilary pulled a dress from one of the racks, a coarsely woven sari with an Indian print design.

"Are you thinking of changing your image?" laughed Suzanne.

Hilary gave the dress more cogent attention, then smiled. "It is more you, isn't it?"

Suzanne took the dress and held it up in front of her body. "I rather like it," she said.

Hilary stood back and gave the effect serious scrutiny, musing that she and Suzanne had certainly come toward the mainstream over the years. She had mellowed more obviously than Suzanne, though she defended her acquiescence to the so-called Establishment with the argument that most newspapers were not willing to hire sandal-shod hippies. And through the years she had to admit she had become comfortable with a role she once might have spoken against.

Suzanne, on the other hand, still appeared at a glance to be offbeat in her approach to life. Even at thirty-one, she still bore the progressive look that this dress represented, with straight, long blond hair, often with a flower tucked behind her ear. Her large, intense eyes needed no assistance from makeup to give them depth. She made a point of keeping her exterior self plain, yet such a practice could not hide her lovely features.

"Should I buy it?" asked Suzanne.

"The price is outrageous."

"My contribution to assuaging hunger in India."

"No doubt the profits will just fill the pockets of some fat Indian lord or prince." But even as Hilary spoke the words, she recalled her own current dilemma. The reminder made her all the more unprepared for Suzanne's uncharacteristic response.

"Oh, come on, Hilly," she said as they exited the shop and continued down the walk, "you don't still seriously believe that all the world's ills are because of fat lords and princes?"

"What! Is that you, Suzanne?" exclaimed Hilary. "Standing up for the nobles?"

"Times change," said Suzanne quietly. "I've been thinking a lot lately. You know, post-twenties re-evaluation of values and attitudes."

"It sounds serious. What brought all this on?"

"I suppose my father's death. He was a good man, trying to do some good things, and I guess maybe for the first time I'm beginning to see his life and what he stood for in a true light."

"I'm sure your father was very respectable and had admirable qualities," replied Hilary. "But of all people I'd think you would know that the nobility is responsible for so much of what is wrong in the world. That's what we were always fighting for, remember?"

"The environment's getting ripped off and the tuna and seals are being killed just as much in countries where they have no aristocracy at all. The world's problems go deeper than the policies of Parliament."

"But its policies aren't helping matters."

"Politics is a whole different scene. Peace, helping the earth to survive, Hilary, it's an inner thing. When I became a Christian several years ago, nothing much changed. I just kept on with my life as it was. I believed differently, but I didn't live any differently. But as I've grown since then, my outlook has gradually shifted, especially lately. I don't want to blame people like my father anymore for problems we all have a responsibility for."

"Of course, of course. But don't we as Christians have a duty to change society for the better, to bring our values to bear on politics? What can possibly justify how out of touch some of those men are? The House of Lords is hardly a body representative of the people."

"No one ever accused it of being such. That's what the House of Commons is for."

"Hardly a great deal better."

"Give it time, Hilly," Suzanne replied calmly. "Look how far it's come! A hundred years ago women couldn't vote, and there was no such thing as a Labour Party. A woman like you would never have been able to raise herself up so she had a legitimate voice in current affairs. The fact that you do have an impact perhaps speaks for our system rather than against it. There's even talk of a woman Prime Minister someday."

"Interested?" said Hilary. "The way you're going I wouldn't be surprised to see you in the running! I never knew you had such political leanings."

Suzanne laughed. As she did, there was a faint hint in her eyes and in the musical quality of her voice which revealed that perhaps, in her quieter moments, she had given such notions a few fleeting thoughts. But she would admit to nothing.

"You ought to know better than that," she said at length. "Me? I'm the society dropout, don't you know? So my father used to say."

"You don't fool me, Suzanne. You're more in tune than you let on. Why else would you devote so much time to your book?"

"Just poetry, dear."

"Poetry with political undercurrents, if I judge your changing interests correctly. I make an innocent comment about Parliament being out of touch, and you launch into a sermonette about the importance of waiting for change."

"Not a bad solution, in most cases. If a nation or a government is moving in a healthy direction, time usually takes care of many problems without the need for revolt and dissent and bloodshed. The activists like you would raise people to action, while I would rather see people focus on inner realities, and let time heal the wounds of society."

"There you go again, Suzanne! You're impossible," laughed Hilary. "You are full of contrasts! Ex-hippie lauds praises of Parliamentary system—I can see my next month's article now! But doesn't it bother you that even the House of Commons, even the Labour Party itself, is full of noblemen?"

"I don't have a problem with noblemen. I'm the daughter of one, remember? It's not the system that's bad, just occasionally how we choose to use it."

"But only in rare cases does that system—the House of Commons particularly—ever genuinely represent the man on the street. It's the nobility, I tell you. They've got a lock on everything."

"Always it comes back to the nobility with you," laughed Suzanne good-naturedly. "You've really got a problem with it."

"Not a problem," Hilary shot back defensively. "I just thought I'd find more support from you, that's all."

"Support?" repeated Suzanne inquisitively. "About what?"

"Never mind."

"It's just not that big a deal. There are so many more important battles to fight, Hilly. I wish I could give you a dose of my so-called blue blood so you could see it works just like your own."

Hilary was quiet for a moment. The thought of blue blood running through her veins was not an issue she wanted to face squarely.

"You think I'm prejudiced," she said at length.

"I didn't say that," replied Suzanne. "I simply think you're allowing yourself to see only one side of a very complex question."

Again Hilary did not reply. Then, after a brief silence, she attempted to shake off the melancholy mood that had settled over her. "I underestimated you, Suzanne," she said. "You're no counter-culturalist at all! Underneath the disguise, you're nothing but a political philosopher!"

"You better keep it to yourself. I do have my reputation as a hippie to preserve."

"What would your father think if he heard you now?"

"I've often wondered that."

"I'm sure he would be pleased," said Hilary. "Probably more than I am to hear the words that are coming out of your mouth."

Now it was Suzanne's time to grow introspective. "I often wish I'd begun to think things through sooner. Now that he's gone, it's too late for me to tell him so much I feel."

"You were only doing what you thought best," said Hilary.

"I suppose. But I had such blinders on. All I could see was my own little world. When I moved into that commune in Soho after I got back from San Francisco, I think it really hurt him."

"Didn't he get you out of there?"

"No, he pretty much let me do my own thing. But that scene wasn't for me. Everyone sat around talking about having their own 'space,' writing weird poetry, singing Hindu songs, and smoking marijuana. They talked about making the earth a different place, but they were all so caught up in their own little private worlds—just as I was. I really did want to make a difference, in my own way, not just sit around and prattle about it while listening to some Maharishi's nonsense. I wanted something I could sink my teeth into, you know?"

"And Carnaby Street?"

"Yeah, my father was involved in that. By then I'd done a flip-flop and came to him asking for the money. And he gave it to me. He'd come to the point where he was content to let my self-expression run its course. Time, you know."

"I never did quite understand why you quit the boutique. It seemed like a good thing."

"In a way, I suppose it was. I made enough money to eat on, trying to convince myself I was being self-supporting and independent from my father. But the Carnaby Street scene was another trip all its own. Just like Soho, only on a different plane. And King's Road. You remember I tried that too?"

"How could I forget!"

"At Carnaby you had all the tourists, and then all the boutique owners trying to be hip and pretend they were marching to the proverbial 'different drummer.' It was so *in* to be weird in '68 and '69. *Sgt. Pepper,* you know—if it seems cool, it must be great. If it looks strange, wear it. If it sounds trippy, like some Tibetan monk may have said it, then embrace it. The little Carnaby Street subculture was in a world of its own, yell all the while chasing after the power of the almighty quid like the bigger businesses round the corner in Piccadilly. No, that wasn't for me either. I've been happy since I moved down to Brighton. I've got my little flat, and I can do my writing without being hassled."

"And carry on the legacy of your father with your budding political and philosophical notions of blending protest with tradition?"

"I suppose so."

"Waiting for the chance to change the world in your own way?"

Suzanne laughed.

"Do I get first peek at the manuscript—exclusive serialization rights for my magazine?"

"When it's ready, you're the first one I'll call. But I know you didn't come all this way to hear me recount my odysseys of the past ten years."

Hilary exhaled a deep sigh. At first she had wanted to talk to Suzanne. At this particular crossroads in her life, she needed the reassuring presence of one who was simply a friend. However, now she wasn't sure they would be able to talk about the things concerning her most without ending up on opposite sides of what was for each an emotionally charged issue.

"It looks as if it's going to rain any minute," she said, as if to steer away from a conversation that had not even begun. "I've got to catch the 5:15 back to London."

"I'm surprised you are here at all," said Suzanne. "Didn't you say tomorrow was your deadline?"

"They can get along without me for a few hours."

Suzanne stopped short and stared with raised eyebrows.

"What's wrong with that?" asked Hilary, defensiveness creeping into her tone.

"It doesn't sound like you."

They continued walking. "Don't worry about the train," said Suzanne. "I'll drive you back."

"You sure?"

"It'll be fun."

"Thanks. A drive through the South Downs is just what I need."

An hour later they passed through the sleepy little village of Arundel and headed north. The drive was unusually quiet. As the silence lingered, there came with it the sense that it was covering up things that needed saying. Suzanne finally ventured to breach it.

"What's troubling you, Hilly?"

"Nothing," replied Hilary, a little too quickly. She knew her answer was too frayed to be sincere. She studied the rolling green countryside out her window for a moment, then sighed.

"It's the same old thing," she said. "You know how we have always fought our country's system of peerage. Well, suddenly it's much more personal to me. The question of the nobility's place in our society is no longer one I can examine from a distance."

"Why's that?"

"I can't tell you—not just now, at least. Maybe it's time for my season of re-evaluation—just like you. But I need more time to sort it all out."

"Sounds serious."

"For me it is."

"You can't have come fifty miles out from town to not talk about it."

"Well . . . I thought I wanted to talk, but I don't anymore." She paused, then added, "I'm sorry. There've been some things on my mind. But it's too complicated . . . and I'm not sure what you'll say now . . . now that you're looking at it from the other side of the fence, so to speak. I know I'm being silly and illogical. I think I just needed to get away from the office, to have a friend beside me."

Again silence descended upon them as the little blue Volkswagen sped its way through the rolling hills and tiny woods which broke up the otherwise open landscape of Sussex. The rain had begun in earnest, and the only sound was the rhythmic thump and swish of the car's windshield wipers.

"Why can't life be simpler, Suzanne?" said Hilary after about five minutes.

"Sometimes it is," she replied, "but the problem is we don't often know what kind of simplicity we want, or need."

"The philosopher again," laughed Hilary.

"Sorry."

"I envy my parents," Hilary went on. "My mother always knew just how her life would be. She spent her youth learning to cook and sew and clean, in preparation for the day she would marry and have children. That was the focus of her whole life—marriage and raising a family. She had no other dreams or expectations. Simple."

"Are you trying to tell me, my dear girl, in your roundabout way, that you're thinking of marriage! Is there a new man in your life, Hilly?"

"No," replied Hilary. "It's just that . . . I've found myself thinking about my own future—not because of a man, but . . . well, what would happen if I met someone, say, who *was* a nobleman. What if, all of a sudden, I found myself on the other side of the fence."

"Is it really so cut and dried, Hilly? I mean, is the division really so sharp?"

"That's what we've been preaching all our lives."

"My father's death has changed my outlook. I spent most of my life rebelling against everything he stood for. Why the dear old man didn't disown me, I'll never know. I deserved it. But he didn't. And now I find that everything that was his is now mine. All these changes have helped me see that he was who he was regardless of his position or title. A *lord* or an *earl* in front of one's name doesn't change intrinsically who a man is, nor does a lady. I thought I'd die the first time someone called me *Lady Heywood* after my father died. But then all at once one day I realized it was the same me. It was only a word, after all."

"So you have no conflict with being a lady?"

"I never trouble myself about it. It never enters my head that I am Lady Heywood. I am who I am, that's all."

"I could never be content as Lady anybody," said Hilary. "My readers trust me to be who I am. I represent something to them. They count on me to speak for the middle classes, for the working people. And whatever readers I have of the so-called elite, they also expect me to address issues that matter in this day and age. To change that, to put a Lady Hilary So-and-So on my byline, would be a sell-out."

"Why all the fuss? Aren't you making much ado about nothing? Or *is* there a man, but you just can't tell me about him? Is that what all this uncertainty is about?"

"No, honestly, it's not a man. Let's just call it an intellectual debate I'm having with myself over the state of our society, and my position in it."

She paused and Suzanne seemed content to let the silence linger. Hilary knew her friend didn't buy her intellectual-debate excuse.

"Why can't people just be themselves, and nothing more?" said Hilary at length, almost as if to herself. "Why couldn't you be just Suzanne Heywood, without the title, without the Lady, without . . . all it represents?"

"But that's what I've been telling you—I am just myself, and nothing more."

"No, Suzanne, there is a difference. I know maybe you don't give much weight to your title. But there are still too many out there who do. I don't care if this is 1971 and some people like you say such things don't matter anymore—they do. There is still segregation in British society, and the line falls right between you and me."

Suzanne chose not to reply further. She knew their friendship was not at stake, and that Hilary's questioning was about something other than that.

Hilary exhaled deeply. "Why do things have to change?" she sighed.

Suzanne's eyebrows arched in surprise. "I thought your goal in life was to change the world."

"The world, yes. Me—no." Hilary hesitated. "I'm not making much sense. Nothing seems to make sense these days."

"Now you're the one running over with philosophical quandaries. But something tells me all you want to do today is pose the questions, not analyze the answers."

"I don't know. You're probably right. I've always been so sure of who I am, what I want out of life. Now everything is muddled. Am I supposed to be a wife or a worker or an aristocrat? Am I supposed to be Hilary Edwards, journalist, daughter of working parents, or . . . something else?" She spoke in a halting voice, then went on after a moment. "How can I be true to my readers when I don't even know what my byline really means? Who I am is important to me, but I don't even know who that is. My mother—" Her voice finally broke and she hid her face in her hands.

"God help me! I don't even know what that means anymore. I don't know—"

She stopped, unable to continue.

Neither spoke for some time.

At last Suzanne said simply, "I'm ready to listen, if it will help."

"I'm not sure I can talk about it yet. It's . . . just too sudden . . . I have to come to terms with it first myself."

"You're not having trouble with your mother, are you?"

An odd look of irony crossed Hilary's face. "If only it were that easy," she said, then fell silent and looked away out the window.

"Well, are you going to make the deadline with that article you were telling me about?" asked Suzanne, trying to lighten the air.

"I don't think I'll even try," replied Hilary. "It will have to wait till next issue." Her lips twisted into an attempt at a smile. "This looks like a perfect evening shaping up for a fire, a pot of tea, and curling up with Lady Hargreave. Tonight I'm going to ignore my typewriter . . . and my thoughts!"

"You're still reading that stuff? What will your professional colleagues think?"

"Sherlock Holmes is now regarded in some circles almost as literature. And Lady Hargreave is every bit as intellectually stimulating. Besides, none of my colleagues are aware of my penchant for murder mysteries."

"I've never read one myself, but they're all the rage down in Brighton."

"You and I should do so well with *our* writing! You really ought to try one, though I suppose a Lady Hargreave mystery hardly fits in with your new avant-garde intellectualism."

Suzanne laughed.

Hilary gazed out at the lush green countryside. The rhythm of the car speeding along the two-lane highway was all too reminiscent of her long train journey of only a week before. If it was not then that her troubles began, that earlier trip had certainly intensified them. She had indeed spoken truly when she said that unexpected change had come upon her, for her world was suddenly upside-down.

Hilary continued to stare blankly out the window at the fields and cottages passing by. Then she drew in a long breath and let it out slowly.

If only she could see what lay beyond the horizon, around the next bend in the road, in the future where she did not know if she dared to go!

4 ❈ A New Era

THE TINY DEAD buds had long since turned brown and begun to fall from the wiry stems which held them. Only a short time earlier these same buds had been the glory of Scotland, crowning its barren hillsides, its mountains, its desolate moors with a majestic robe of royalty. But now, portending the approach of winter, a season which came with unusual fierceness to this rugged northern land, the heather's purple had faded, leaving but tiny husks of death as a memory.

Even on a day when the sun chose to reign over the land in the splendor and warmth of autumn's grandeur, the dying heather spread over the hillsides a solemn coat of unsightly brown. But on a day such as this, when the sun was hidden by an impenetrable blanket of gray stretching for hundreds of miles in all directions, the landscape took on a hopeless complexion of despair.

In the distance, ascending to the crest of a grass-covered knoll, standing out like an island of color amidst the sea of gray-brown dying heather, two middle-aged women walked alone. Just as they reached the top of the small hillock, a chilly gust swept in off the sea, sending the light hair of the one and the dark black hair of the other streaming away from their heads as if to loose it to join the bitter north wind in heralding the end of autumn.

Unconsciously, both women shivered and pulled their coats more tightly about them before starting down the other side. They were seeking a little-used but time-worn trail that would lead them farther away from the North Sea at their backs, inland away from their ancient family home, toward a desolate strip of useless ground. Forgotten now by all but the oldest of the region's natives, the area was known as Braenock Ridge. It was not a pleasant day to stir up memories from the past. But they had put off this encounter, and at last there was no time left. By tomorrow at this time they would again be worlds apart. They had visited their mother's grave one last time together, and now had to arrive at an understanding between them. Both women sensed it, though there were no ready words for the occasion. This was new ground for each. Neither had spoken since leaving the house.

Allison picked at the shriveled sprig of heather in her hand, brushing away the dead fragments of blossom until nothing was left but a slender brown twig. The gray earth, the gray sky, and the dying heather seemed particularly suited to her mood. Her mother was gone, the land was dying, there was no sun, no warmth, no hope, and it seemed as if—after centuries of life—Stonewycke itself was about to breathe its last.

Finally she spoke.

"I m afraid, May."

Her sister did not reply immediately. She knew her duty for the present was to provide a sensitive listening ear. This was primarily Allison's struggle. May could best serve her by hearing her heart and by understanding her fears. There was no way Lady Margaret MacNeil Reynolds could fully share her elder sister's burden. For tomorrow she would be on a plane back to Boston.

"Everything was so different before Mother died," Allison went on. "I knew someday she would be gone, but I never considered the implications. *Really* considered them, you know—what it would mean . . . to me."

"I understand, dear," said May quietly.

"Oh, May, what am I going to do? Mother's been gone only a week, and already I feel voices from the past calling out to me, loading me with guilt for not measuring up to all the other fabled Stonewycke women. It's 'expected' of me now to assume the mantle, to step into Mother's shoes, just as she did when Lady Margaret died. But, May, I don't know if I can occupy the role all of them did . . . or even if I want to. Times have changed. I've got a life of my own that's not tied to this place. Logan and I are happy in London, and I don't know if—" She stopped.

They walked on. May placed a reassuring hand on Allison's arm. "If it's any consolation, I want you to know that I have no exalted expectations of you. To me you have always been a dear sister, the best sister a woman could wish for. I will love you no less, whatever you decide to do."

"Thank you, May," said Allison, a tear forming in her eye. "You don't know how much that means to me right now. With Mother and Dad gone, and with Ian off to Greece again and Logan called back to London, it really is just you and I. I'd never be able to endure this alone."

Margaret smiled. "But you realize I have to leave tomorrow?"

"I know."

"There are things we have to discuss."

Allison sighed. "I know, May. And I know it rests with me."

"You are the eldest. And you are . . . here. Even London is closer to Stonewycke than either Greece or Boston. Of course Ian and I will support you as best we can, but ultimately—"

"I know, dear May . . . I know. What happens now does have to be my decision. But the thought of leaving the old place desolate, or worse, of letting it out . . . or even selling it! It's just too horrible to think about. Yet Logan and I . . . live in London."

"Have the two of you talked about it?"

"Oh yes. But you know Logan—ever the optimist. He doesn't see what the problem is. 'Lots of people keep two houses up,' he insists. 'Besides,' he says, 'the life of a politician is never secure. You never know when they'll vote you out and you'll need to retreat back to the family farm.'"

"Maybe he's right."

"Logan will never be voted out. The people up here adore him."

"Times change."

"Perhaps. But our home has been in London for so long, I don't know if we'd come back, anyway. Logan and I are city people now—Logan always has been."

"Has any of that changed for you, now that—well, these last several months . . . I mean, now that the past has suddenly turned everything around again for you? Do these recent developments make you think of returning permanently to Scotland?"

"I don't know, May. I had been beginning to feel a security, a peace, as if we might be able to experience some of what we've missed. These last two months have been wonderful—riding again, and I'm learning to paint! Although I must admit the pace seems to be catching up with my years; I haven't been feeling so awfully well lately. Content, but a bit weary."

"I thought you looked a little pale."

"Probably just the strain. Change, even positive change, can be stressful."

"Is there any chance she'd be able to keep the place up after you and Logan return to the city?"

"I don't want to apply pressure—especially not now, not after all we've been through."

"Why don't we postpone a final decision for now, keep the staff on, make sure the castle and grounds are maintained? You and Logan can come up every several months and check on things, and we'll see what happens. That will give you all the chance to see what you want to do now that things are so different."

"I suppose that's the best option, but it sidesteps the real problem—for me, that is. The problem of how I'm supposed to respond to Mother's passing."

May sighed. "I was trying to make it easier for you."

"It's the legacy—that's always been Stonewycke's strength."

May nodded.

"I don't mean to sound like a feminist. And I'm not one either. But we all know that there is something special God has done through the women of Stonewycke."

"An anti-feminist? That hardly sounds like the Allison I remember from years ago."

"I didn't say I was an anti-feminist, May. But I've learned some things about marriage—learned them the hard way. And I finally understand what I don't think the women's lib advocates do. Just because the Stonewycke legacy has come through the women doesn't mean that we don't need the men God has given us. Each of the noble, wonderful men in this family has played an essential role in the ongoing life of Stonewycke. Without them in their God-given roles, this family would not have maintained its strong and holy heritage."

"Many women would deny that we each have God-given roles to fulfill, Allison. Especially in this family, which has for generations supported a strong matriarchy."

"I forget," laughed Allison. "You are an American now. My Victorian views on marriage must go down hard for you. After all, America's where feminism is really in vogue."

May laughed, too. "Allison, you couldn't be a Victorian if you tried! All your life you've been your own person—that is what has prepared you to step into the role Mother has left to you."

"And that's probably also why God knew I needed a strong man like Logan as my husband. He encourages me to be myself, and he shows me the respect of equality as a full partner in our marriage."

"That sounds too good to be real."

"You know it didn't come without sacrifice on both our parts. But now I don't have to worry about equality, because he gives it freely. His authority is no threat because it makes me feel all the more secure as a woman."

"You ought to write a book. Everyone does these days it seems. Olivia Fairgate did—have you heard? Pure feminism, very popular in America."

"I think I did read something about it. But anything I had to say about marriage would be instantly banned by the modernists as too old-fashioned."

"Probably so."

"But all this is beside the point about Stonewycke. Despite the wonderful men God brought into the line—Grandpa Ian and Daddy, and now Logan and your Mr. Reynolds, not to mention dear old Digory—we've always known that the bloodline flowed through us women. And now here I am—fifty-six years old, and I never really stopped to consider that someday the legacy of Atlanta's and Lady Margaret's and Mother's was going to come to rest . . . on me."

"Do you suppose we could talk Ian into giving up his travels and coming back here permanently? Maybe we could shift the birthright onto the men for the next few generations."

Allison laughed at the thought.

"That would be wonderful! But it's no good—it would never work. I tell you I can feel the weight of this matriarchal ancestry sweeping over me from the past. In a way it's got nothing to do with what we may decide to do with the property. We could sell Stonewycke, and I think it would still be there. It's a heritage . . . it's in the blood. I can sense it filling me. And I know there's no escape. Besides . . . Ian has such a wanderlust in every bone of his body, settling him down would be like asking for a winter in Scotland without snow."

"It's already on the way, isn't it?" said May. "I can smell it in the wind."

They walked on for several more steps in silence. By now they had come to the trail and had followed in the direction it led, though its way was often obscured by overgrown weeds and heather. The moor they were crossing was not a pretty one. Scarcely a tree was to be seen, only brown heather, rocks, and a few bristly shrubs.

"What they say," Allison went on at length, "about bloodlines, about generations, about the firstborn—like the patriarchs of the Old Testament. There s really something to it, I think. I'd never really considered it before, not in depth anyway. Of course Mother would say things to me, and I've read the stories of Abraham and Isaac and Jacob and Esau and the genealogies of Jesus, and I realize it's important in God's economy. Yet until this week it was all distant. But I tell you, these last few days have made an impact. I'm seeing that those truths were not reserved just for ancient Bible times but are real today. I scarcely paid it any heed, except in theoretical terms, until recently. But I can feel something happening to me . . . "

"And you're not sure if you like it?"

"I don't know . . . " mused Allison. "Like it? It doesn't seem it's a question of liking it or not. Let's just say I was unprepared for it, and I don't know what to do with it. Maybe I don't feel worthy of wearing such a mantle."

"But you remember hearing Mother talk about her coming to Scotland in 1911—how timid she was."

"But Mother was of the mold, so to speak. I've never been cut out of the same cloth."

"You are of the same cloth—we all are—even though we have our individualities. Who says every line of women in every generation of Stonewycke should be exactly the same?"

"But they all had something—something special."

"So do you, Allison," said May seriously. "Perhaps you aren't able to see it. But I do. And from what I remember being told, you are more like Lady Margaret when she was Maggie than Mother was."

"But what if . . . what if I make wrong choices? What if, after all these years, I can't keep Stonewycke afloat? The financial burdens of the place are steadily growing. Mother did prepare me for that. Logan and I have had charge of the money for years. I can tell you, the outlook isn't good."

"Ian and I will help. That goes without saying."

"But will that be enough? What if I—"

Allison paused, glancing away off in the distance. May knew she was fighting back emotions that were new and frightening to her.

At length she tried to continue, but her voice was husky.

"Oh, May, don't you see? According to the Scriptures, they're all watching—Mother, Lady Margaret, Atlanta, and who knows how many others? They're watching me! And—I'm so afraid . . . that I'll fail them!"

She broke down and sobbed as the last words left her lips.

Gently May took her elder sister in her loving arms and held her. They were silent a long while, the only sounds those of Allison's quiet weeping and the rising wind whistling all about them.

"I'd always just assumed," Allison said after she had regained control of her voice, "because of how things were since the legacy would end with me, that it would pass instead to you. After all, you have a son and daughter. Now everything's changed. But for some bizarre reason I'm still afraid I will be known as the one who let it die—after centuries. May . . . I'm just so frightened. I don't want this thing."

"But what you said is true," soothed May, still holding Allison and stroking her light hair in spite of the wind. "It's not you or I or any single generation. It s bigger than that, bigger than either one of us. Besides, we have no choice in these things. The Lord knows best. It is in His grand design how He orders families. Nothing comes by chance. Everything is to a purpose. We cannot alter that you are the firstborn. I cannot change that. Ian cannot change that. Neither can you change that. It is no accident. The Lord has chosen you—not me, not anyone else—to walk this path, to receive the blessings and to carry the burdens of your position."

May paused and looked intently at her sister. "He has chosen you for His purpose that good may result. He is in control. Stonewycke had passed into the hands of those who had no respect for its heritage sixty years ago. But then the Lord brought Mother here, miraculously restored her in the lineage, healed my namesake Lady Margaret, and gave them long and happy and fruitful lives. These may indeed be new times, and you may be a unique individual all your own. But that does not alter the fact that the Lord's hand is on you. His life is in you, and His loving design is still over Stonewycke and all that lies in its future.

You do not have to feel that everything rests upon you. It doesn't, Allison dear. It rests with the Lord, our God. We can trust Him to guide our steps, and to do good. He can do no other."

Slowly Allison released herself from May's arms, stood back, forced a smile, and wiped away the tears with her hand. "You are right, May. Thank you," she said. "Let's walk on a little farther," she added, drawing in a deep breath to steady her shaky voice.

The two women walked on. It was cold, and the wind bit cruelly through their wool coats, but they did not seem to mind. They were, as if by common yet unspoken consent, on a mission—seeking together to retouch ancient familial roots, remembering at this time of earthly loss those who had come before them, and calling to mind memories their ancestors held dear.

Fifteen minutes more they walked. Scarcely a word was spoken. Nothing more needed be said.

At last they reached the crest of a small rise and could see their destination some hundred yards away, where the ground sloped down toward a sort of hollow in the otherwise mostly flat ridge.

"I haven't been here in years," said Allison.

"I don't think I've been out here since that day Mother brought us, remember?"

"How could I forget?" replied Allison, staring ahead.

Before them rose several irregularly shaped stones, piled and leaning against one another in what at first glance seemed like a random aberration of nature. To one who was not acquainted with their history, they would have appeared as nothing but giant boulders in the midst of a dreary Scottish moor. On closer inspection, however, for one who had the perseverance to clear away some of the moss and overgrowth, the stones would begin to take on a decidedly hewn appearance, not unlike some of the more well-known monoliths scattered throughout the British Isles as reminders of peoples long forgotten to the march of time. These stones, however, had been lost to archaeologists and historians for centuries. They possessed a history, but as yet no one had made the discovery that would unlock the secrets of their past. And thus they stood, as they had for more than a century of decades, silent sentinels to a history for the present forgotten, but for the future waiting.

The two women paused, looking toward the stones.

"It was just after Lady Margaret died," said May. "I can hardly believe it was—let's see . . . forty . . . no, thirty-eight years ago. I was only eleven, you were eighteen and just married."

"I remember," smiled Allison. "Mother had been working on her journal all that day—"

"All that day, and the day before, and the day before that!" laughed May. "The moment Great-grandmother died, she seemed almost feverish about it, as if she would forget things she'd been told if she waited so much as a day."

"I'll never forget the walk out here. She was so solemn."

"If what she said is true, I can see why. Remember the tone in her voice when she said: *'This is where it all began'?*"

Allison nodded. "It's hard to believe that seventeen-year-old Maggie—our great-grandmother—and Logan's seventy-year-old great-great-uncle Digory could have found that treasure and lugged it all the way back home. To think that our ancestors were here, on this very spot, over a hundred years ago."

"I wonder whatever happened to the treasure?"

"When those thugs took it after Logan first came here, we thought it was gone forever. Then we ran across Channing during the war and learned that somehow he'd got his hands on it. Logan's tried to get back on his track several times since, but never with any success."

"Whatever the treasure was, I'm sure it was spent years ago."

"It's never been retrieving the treasure so much as it is the history. It's just too bad for a man like that to make off with something that's part of Stonewycke."

"Channing's no doubt dead by now anyway."

"I'm sure." Allison paused reflectively for a moment. "Well," she said in almost a distracted voice, "it's not the treasure really. It's this place. I just had to come out here again. As difficult as all this is, I suppose something inside me had to try to touch Mother's spirit however I can, and Maggie's, and Atlanta's. If I am destined to be the next in line, then I have to know how they felt about this spot of ground, this valley, this land . . . about Stonewycke and all it represents. I needed to come out here, if, like Mother said, this is where it all began. I really have no choice—I must be faithful to their dreams, their heritage."

"And leave the future in God's hands."

"As hard as that is . . . yes."

"You are now in the first rank of Stonewycke's women. You may not be entirely comfortable with it yet. And it doesn't even matter if you go back to London to live. It's in your voice. I can see Mother's eyes in your face, and hear her voice as you speak. I imagine Maggie's in there someplace, too. The mantle is upon you, dear sister, and you will wear it with honor."

They stood silently gazing upon the stones whose ancient story they did not yet know, then turned around, faced the wind, breathed deeply of its chilly freshness, and started back toward home.

They had not gone far before Allison stopped her sister with her hand. May turned toward her.

"May," said Allison. "Thank you. You are as dear a sister as a woman could wish for. I will miss you now more than ever. Thank you for helping me through this time."

May only nodded.

It was now her turn to feel the tears as they began slowly to fill her eyes. The legacy was in her blood also, and suddenly Boston seemed so very far away.

5 ✖ In a Dark Corner of the City

RAUL GALVEZ DUCKED inside the Cheapside pub several moments too late to prevent a thorough dousing from the sudden cloudburst outside. He jerked off his hat and gave it an angry snap, sending a spray of moisture in the direction of several of the pub's other patrons.

One of the men cursed him loudly and threatened physical violence. Galvez replied with a sufficiently venomous sneer to effectively discourage the cocky fellow. Galvez then pushed his short, muscular frame through the crowded, smoke-filled room.

As he moved, his squinting close-set eyes darted back and forth over the place as if he were looking for someone. But all he saw were foreign pale faces speaking a disagreeable tongue that only served to remind him that he was getting further from home every day. He shoved his way up to the counter, thinking only of taking the edge off his disgust.

"Cerveza!" he ordered in a throaty, unfriendly tone.

"Wot's that, mate?" asked the bartender.

"Beer, estúpido!" retorted Galvez. "And make it strong and dark."

"Comin' right up, but you don't 'ave to get so bloomin' nasty about it," mumbled the man as he turned to fill a glass.

Galvez took the drink without any thanks and, after dropping his money on the counter, stalked away to an empty table. As his chunky body fell into its chair, he continued to scan the noisy room, now focusing most of his attention on the front door through which he had just come. He drained his tall glass and was starting on a second when he paused, the beer halfway to his lips, to take particular note of a man just entering the pub. He was tall, broad-shouldered, and stood as if he'd walked off the set of some cheap Italian western, wearing a cowboy hat, shiny tan boots, and a sportcoat with deep, contrasting leather yokes. He, too, scanned the pub as he entered, but his vigil was rewarded quickly as he locked eyes with Galvez.

"Que paso, amigo!" called the man as he drew near. His inept Spanish was thickly accented with a Texas drawl.

He lowered his lanky but taut frame into the chair opposite Galvez and immediately began waving his hand in the air for service, which he received post-haste.

"Bourbon, honey," he said to the girl waiting tables; "straight up." He threw her a leering wink and reached out his hand playfully toward her. Her reflexes were too quick for him, however, and she was soon out of reach.

"What do you think this is, Mallory," growled Galvez sardonically, "Saturday night after the cattle drive? Why don't you announce our business while you're at it!"

"Aw, shut up, Galvez! What's eating you, anyway?"

"This whole place stinks, that's what!"

"I dunno. I thought it was a pretty classy joint myself." At that moment his bourbon arrived and in his preoccupation with his drink, the Texan forgot his earlier interest in the waitress.

"Bah!" spat Galvez. "We have better cantinas in Patquia. But I am speaking of this whole town. It is cold and wet and dirty. The fog never lifts. Rotten, I tell you! And I'm sick of the place!"

"Yeah, and where you come from it's just dirty, huh, amigo?"

Mallory laughed at his own wit, not at all troubled by Galvez's icy grimace. Then he added with a wink, "The money's okay though, huh?"

"Perhaps the General is paying you more than he is me," groused Galvez.

"Maybe so. . . . " returned Mallory in his easy drawl. "But I been with him a long time—seniority, you know, amigo."

"Well, what dirty work have we got to do now—break into another office building to steal some files on the competition?"

"Nah, no burglarizing. He says it's not business this time. We gotta take the evening train to Oxford."

"Madre de Dios!" exclaimed Galvez. "It goes from bad to worse."

"I thought you couldn't wait to get out of this place."

"At least in London there are senoritas to be found."

"The fence is in Oxford, so that's where we go."

"Who is this fence?"

"I dunno. Some egghead who discovered he makes more bucks moving high-class stolen merchandise than pounding education into a bunch of preppies."

"Why this man? There must be a dozen fences right around—"

"'Cause he knows his stuff, and that's what the General told us to do, comprendo?"

Galvez twisted his lips in disdain. "Okay, okay! You gringos and your short fuses! Let's go and get it over with."

"We got time. It's two hours before the train leaves." Mallory raised his hand to signal for a refill. "Relax, Galvez. Loosen up. Remember, this is merry ole England."

In a moment the waitress returned with another bourbon, but this time she was not quick enough to avoid Mallory's bony paw.

"Come on, honey," said Mallory, "all this cowboy wants is to have a good ole time."

The girl didn't resist. As distasteful as his attentions might be, giving in for a moment was better than causing trouble. She was used to Mallory's type and would find her opportunity to squirm free soon enough.

Galvez sat back and scowled at the whole scene. He took a long swallow from his glass of beer, all the while thinking that his grimy, poverty-ridden little village was looking better and better.

6 ❈ Back in London

HILARY WAS BACK in London from Brighton a little after six-thirty. After making their way through traffic, Suzanne dropped her in front of her office building, and at 6:57 she walked through the doors of *The Berkshire Review,* intending merely to check her mail and go right home for the evening.

Suzanne had pegged her correctly, and her surprise at Hilary's leaving the magazine at the busiest time of the month was well justified. Though she had a competent staff, she was not the type to easily leave the work to others. Delegation was perhaps the most difficult aspect of her job. She always wanted to be fully apprised of every facet of the magazine's progress, from research to copy-editing to typesetting to production to promotion to sales.

As she entered, the earlier frenzy of the office had quieted considerably, but several staff writers were still busily engaged at their typewriters or phones. They threw her friendly greetings, no one appearing particularly concerned that she had been absent the entire afternoon.

Hilary exchanged a few words with her personal secretary Betty, and her hand had just touched the door latch to her office when one of her writers, hurrying through the press-room, called out to her.

"Perfect timing!" he exclaimed, his compact frame of about Hilary's own height hurrying toward her. "I'm glad I didn't miss you."

"I just got here myself, Murry."

"I know. I saw you come in just as I got off the elevator. Do you have a minute?"

"Of course, come on in," Hilary replied.

Murry opened the door for Hilary, then followed her into the office. The young man was Murry Fitts, an American expatriate who had attended the University of London, and had decided to make his home in England where a promising job awaited him. Now four years out of the university, he was an enthusiastic and skilled writer, as well as a daring investigative reporter. He possessed a reputation for his somewhat flamboyant style and received not a little criticism from his more conservative colleagues for his shoulder-length hair and bushy beard. But he was just the kind of employee that had helped turn *The Berkshire Review* around, and Hilary had never had cause to hold his particular "style" against him. Besides, long hair and other seeming "oddities" were almost the norm in these days of Magical Mystery Tours and "feelin' groovy." Whether you were straight or wore your anti-Establishment prejudice on your sleeve, you were less likely to look twice at long hair and funny clothes than you might have in '64. And to Murry's credit, he made a point of usually wearing a sports jacket and necktie to assuage his more narrow-minded peers. But Hilary wouldn't have cared if he had dressed in a Nehru jacket and beads. He was a solid young man, forthright and sincere, and, in addition to being a friend, was an ace reporter. He and Suzanne had a lot in common, and Hilary wondered why she had not yet gotten around to introducing the two. She made a mental note just before she spoke.

"What is it, Murry?" she asked after they had seated themselves, she behind her desk, and he in one of the other two chairs in the small cubicle which was her office.

"I've got a couple projects I need input on."

He paused, took his notebook from his pocket, flipped back several pages, and began again.

"I haven't had much time, but at this point I'd stake some pretty heavy odds that there might be more to this East End affair than meets the eye."

"Like what?"

"Code violations, unjustified evictions, possibly even collusion with building officials about the redevelopment."

"Do you have anything solid?"

"Not quite. It's just a sense I get. I think it definitely bears further investigation."

"Hmmm," mused Hilary. "Must have been providential that I decided to call off the story for this issue."

"Come on, you're not going to start giving me that stuff again about God leading you! This is the 1970s, Hilary!"

"I've told you before, Murry, and I'll tell you as often as it takes to sink into that liberal, semi-open brain of yours—God does lead His people just as much today as when the Jews were wandering across the desert with Moses. His ways just appear more subtle now, that's all."

"Okay, okay," laughed Murry. "You'll make a believer of me yet! But you're right, I think it would be wise to hold on to your story and see what happens. I want to poke around a bit more."

"What do you have?"

"Probably nothing more than the proverbial gut feeling."

"The reporter's most valuable stock-in-trade," said Hilary.

"Maybe they'll have plausible explanations for everything," Murry went on, "but I have to ask the questions anyway."

"Anything else?"

"You probably heard about the fire out there a few days ago?"

"Vaguely, yes. Is that tied in?"

"Again, who knows? But it's just too coincidental for comfort, so I looked into it—just for fun. The owner of the building stands to profit a cool two hundred thousand pounds from the insurance company." Fitts made his final statement with pointed emphasis.

"Well, keep at it," said Hilary. "What was the other project you needed to talk about?"

"It's the antiquities piece." Murry scratched his head sheepishly. "It's going a bit slow."

"The piece or you, Murry?"

"Well . . . "

"You're one of my best writers, Murry, and I hate to waste you on something you have no interest in. But it is your turn to do the intelligentsia beat, and you know how important it is that we keep open these contacts and do a museum article now and then."

"I know, but history was never my strong point."

Hilary sighed with understanding. "I can't have the others think I'm playing favorites. But if you don't want the St. Ninian's story, I do need someone to cover an item about a woman who claims to have given birth to an alien baby—"

"Spare me! I'll dig through the archives and keep interviewing the old historians in tweed suits!"

Hilary smiled triumphantly. "Who knows? You might even turn up something startling— some hard news. Some of the world's great sleuths wear tweed suits just to throw people off. You never know what might really be behind the horn-rimmed glasses and tweed of those men you interview."

"I'll see what I can find. At least I'll give it my best shot."

A short pause followed and Hilary took the chance to glance at her appointment book.

"You know, Murry," she said after a moment, "I was just thinking again about the East End thing. Maybe we ought to run out there tomorrow. Have a look at the fire locale, talk to a few people."

"Tomorrow's deadline—it's bound to be hectic around here."

"I know, but we want to look into this fire while it's still fresh. A hot story—as it were— waiteth for no man . . . or woman."

"Then I'll get right on it," said Fitts, jamming his notebook back into his pocket and rising.

"Tomorrow, Murry. Tomorrow! And I'll join you. In the meantime, you have my permission to go home first, maybe even get some sleep," laughed Hilary.

Fitts chuckled at himself. "Yeah. Nothing we can do for this issue anyway." He opened the door. "See you in the morning."

"Good night, Murry."

After Murry had closed the door, Hilary sat back and reflected on the events of a full day. It had begun, seemingly, with that Whitehall interview, moved on to Brighton and her thought-provoking conversation with Suzanne, and finally ended with this stimulating interchange with Murry. At least there was no lack of diversion to keep her from sinking too far into morose melancholia. Tomorrow she would be busy wrapping the next issue of the *Review,* going with Murry to investigate the fire . . . and . . . well, there were hundreds of pressing matters to keep her occupied, not including the new and unexpected.

It was 8:15 by the time Hilary arrived at her flat that evening, after stopping by an all-night delicatessen for something to eat.

7 ❈ The Dream

HILARY KICKED OFF her shoes, put on water for tea, then sat down leisurely in her favorite chair to eat her cold cuts on bread with a side dish of vegetables. She was hardly aware of their taste, however, and when she rose to tend to her tea, she went through the motions methodically as if her mind was far away. As indeed it was. She picked up the book beside her and tried to read.

It was no use. Somehow her discussion with Suzanne seemed bent on intruding more forcibly into her thoughts now that she was in the quiet of her living room. It wasn't so much what either of them had *said*; it was the very persistence of the agitating question. As intently as she tried to steer her mind in another direction, whether she liked it or not . . . whether she was prepared to admit it or not . . . eventually she knew she was going to have to confront the nobility issue head-on. Suddenly it was far more pressing even than Suzanne suspected. Their conversation that afternoon had carried overtones that Hilary's friend could in no way suspect.

She tried to shake the fantasies from her mind. She liked her life. She enjoyed her independence. Why this sudden surge of discontent? She wouldn't have to give it up. She could ignore what had happened. Why not merely go on as before? Business as usual. She wasn't obligated to restructure her life just because some stranger happened to think . . .

Was it indeed her visit with Suzanne this afternoon that had triggered this string of thoughts? No. Such anxieties had been pestering her relentlessly for two weeks. She had sought out Suzanne only as someone to talk with about what was already swirling around inside her.

Hilary liked Suzanne. But their longtime friendship could not alter the reality of her friend's aristocratic birth. It was a fact Hilary had always been aware of as one of the given parameters in their relationship. She had been comfortable with it, comfortable in who Suzanne was, and comfortable in the person she herself was.

Until recently. . . .

Now, suddenly, everything was changed. Suddenly she no longer knew who she was, or who she wanted to be. Suddenly all the things she had told Suzanne through the years about the differences in their stations were no longer valid. Suddenly the firm foundations of the world she had learned to rely on were all gone. She felt as one cast adrift . . . without a lifeline . . . without any sense of where the harbor lay.

The eternal philosophical quandary—*Who am I?*—was suddenly a very practical and real concern.

Hilary had always been pretty certain about the person living under her skin—until two weeks ago. And as she sat in her easy chair that evening contemplating her afternoon with Suzanne, she knew that the turmoil in her mind and emotions stemmed from more than any point her friend had raised.

She tried to ignore the other reason, block it from her mind, hide from it, pretend she had imagined it . . . but to no avail.

Since the funeral it had become all the more pressing and insistent. Because since coming back from Scotland, she realized that now everything was up to her.

The decision had been placed directly in her lap. The only other person on earth who knew was now gone. She could ignore the whole episode, pretend it never happened, go on with her life, and try her best to forget it . . . if she chose to.

Hilary rubbed her eyes wearily.

It was ten o'clock, and she had already tackled too many emotional dilemmas that day to face another—especially this one.

Leaving the remnants of her supper and tea on the table, she rose and went to her bedroom.

Yet even after changing her clothes and crawling into bed, she knew her reason for trying to empty her mind and going to bed had more to do with "escape" than sleep. She did not want to think any more about her unexpected visitor, or about the incredible implications of her words, or about the funeral, or about all the turmoil this was bound to cause in her life. Despite the churning of her thoughts, however, to her relief she soon found herself drifting away as sleep overcame her.

Suddenly Hilary awoke with a shuddering gasp. It was the middle of the night. She was drenched with perspiration.

It seemed her eyes had been closed a mere moment, but in reality she had been asleep for two hours. She had been awakened by the horribly real sensation of ear-splitting explosions, and the sounds still clung to the edges of her consciousness as if they had occurred just outside her window rather than in a dream of a remote and distant time.

She found herself shaking with fear, as if she were the little girl of the dream—forlorn . . . helpless . . . alone . . . running madly away from the awful sounds in sheer panic. Running . . . running . . . crying out for help but with no one to hear . . . stumbling over a stone and falling . . . picking herself up and trying to run again . . . across the little bridge . . . away . . . away from the ugly sounds behind her.

Hilary brushed an unsteady hand across her damp brow and groped in the darkness for the lamp switch. She squinted against the light—this time real, and so comforting after the bursts of blinding flashes in her dream. It was after midnight.

By the time she slipped out of bed, she had for the most part regained her composure and was fully awake. She knew she would not be able to return to sleep for a good while; she wasn't even sure she wanted to. Instead, she climbed out of bed and made her way through the darkened rooms to the kitchen. The unsettling midnight disturbance called for the eternal British cure-all—another hot cup of tea.

While the kettle was heating on the stove, Hilary wandered out to her desk in the living room. She sat down, vaguely thinking that she might work on some of her correspondence. *Who am I trying to kid?* she thought after a few minutes of staring blankly ahead. Soon the whining teakettle drew her back to the kitchen.

As she prepared the tea, images of her dream, against her will, began to filter once more into her mind. It was the same dream as always, hardly altered from when she was a child. Years ago it had haunted her more frequently. Once or twice a month she would wake up in the middle of the night screaming and would not be able to sleep again until her mother took her in her arms and rocked her, gently humming hymns into her ear.

It was always the same . . . vague, shadowy, frightening images of light, and loud sounds, and confusion—and always the little girl running to escape, whose tear-streaked face seemed so real she wanted to reach out and dry the dampness on the terrified little cheeks. As the girl ran, farther and farther from the explosions and jumbled confusion that made up the background of the dream, Hilary was not merely watching events as an observer—she *was* the little girl, and felt her panic with every fiber of her being. Every time she woke up trembling.

As Hilary grew older, the dream came with less frequency, making its unwelcome appearance mostly during times of stress. She had not thought of the little girl for at least two years. Usually she had no idea what brought it on. But tonight's episode was a different story. She knew all too well why it had intruded into her dreamy subconscious now.

Her only surprise was that the dream had not come sooner, the night after—two weeks ago—when she had found the unexpected caller waiting in her office.

8 ❈ *An Unexpected Visitor*

THERE HAD BEEN a morning interview that day on the other side of the city, so Hilary had not arrived at the office until nearly nine-thirty.

As she thought back, Hilary wondered how different things might have been if she hadn't come in that day at all, or if . . .

Probably no different. The lady had been determined and would not have given up easily.

She remembered seeing the woman seated in her private office with her back to the glass enclosure the moment she walked into the pressroom.

"I didn't know I had an appointment," she said to her secretary.

"You didn't," replied Betty. "She apologized for coming without one, but said it was important. She asked if she could wait."

"Who is it . . . what's it about?"

Betty shrugged. "I don't know. Maybe she heard about your article . . . " Betty's voice trailed off, leaving the thought to finish itself.

"That's probably it."

Hilary looked toward her office and gave the woman closer scrutiny. At first glance she did not appear the type to join a cause. Even as she sat, from her back Hilary could almost detect a kind of inbred nobility in the elderly woman. She doubted she was from the East End, after all. Her very bearing seemed to indicate another world altogether. She appeared to be about eighty, but sat with a poise and grace Hilary would not have associated with age. Her silver-gray hair was pulled straight back from her face into a bun at the back of her head. Her carriage certainly would suggest aristocratic blood. Could she be here about the last piece she'd done for the magazine blasting the nobility? No, that had been too long ago, and neither did the woman seem of the sort to make a petty protest.

The woman's face was turned away from the glass, but Hilary saw by the position of her head that she was studying the personal items on the office wall. She seemed to spend some time examining the photo of Hilary with the U.S. Army's "Charlie Company" while she had been a correspondent in Vietnam two years before. Then the woman's eyes shifted in turn to the university diploma, two journalism awards, another photo—this one of Hilary and Suzanne during their student days—and finally lingering on Hilary's pride and joy—an oil portrait of Gladstone. Not only was the famed Prime Minister one of the few politicians Hilary could honestly admire, but the painting had been done while he lived. Only the fact that the artist was somewhat obscure had kept the portrait within her budget.

When Betty quietly cleared her throat Hilary realized she had been staring silently for an inordinately long time.

"Do you want to make a quick getaway?" she asked somewhat coyly.

"Oh no," Hilary chuckled self-consciously. "She looks harmless enough."

But as her hand reached the latch, a sudden wave of adolescent nervousness swept over her. Some sixth sense seemed to be warning Hilary that the encounter which lay ahead was to be no ordinary one. Even then she could not have dreamed how momentous it would really be. She opened the door.

"I see you've noticed my Gladstone," said Hilary as she entered.

The woman turned her eyes from the painting, rose, and smiled. It was a warm, personable gesture, though there was something disquieting in the lady's eyes—a kind of intensity that seemed bent on probing Hilary's depths. She seemed to be trying to integrate the look she had seen in the photographs about the office with Hilary's actual face which was now before her.

"It's quite good," said the woman, her eyes straying once again—almost reluctant to leave their scrutiny of Hilary's features—to the painting. "I haven't heard of the artist, but he has captured a very human quality in the Prime Minister, so rare in most official portraits."

She paused and turned back to Hilary. "Do you collect art, or are you only partial to Gladstone?"

"My budget hardly permits me to collect," smiled Hilary, "but I splurged on this because I think Gladstone was a great man, a true defender of the common man, one of very few politicians with integrity." She stepped toward her visitor and held out her hand. "I'm Hilary Edwards."

The other woman reached out her gloved hand and took Hilary's, pressing it rather firmly for a long moment, trembling slightly.

"I am Lady Joanna MacNeil," she said.

"*Lady* . . . MacNeil," repeated Hilary thoughtfully, "please . . . be seated."

Joanna resumed her seat and Hilary took the chair at her desk.

"I've read your magazine," said Hilary's visitor as if making a casual observation. "You must be a woman with strong political convictions."

"I've never been accused of being a rebel *without* a cause."

"No," Lady MacNeil chuckled softly, "you seem to have no lack of issues to keep you occupied." She paused, as if in thought. "I've never been very politically minded myself," she continued, "but I think there are more men of integrity at Whitehall than we give credit for. I know of at least one."

"One is a rather small minority," countered Hilary congenially, her natural defenses put off their guard by this disarmingly pleasant old woman, yet nevertheless responding to political matters in her habitual manner. "But if there is one, I would like to meet him. Perhaps I should interview him for the magazine."

"Yes . . . " The woman's voice faded off a moment and her eyes grew introspective.

As Hilary observed the change, she had a brief opportunity to study her visitor. The features she noted in the aging Lady MacNeil were fine and delicate. Hilary could tell that in her youth she must have been quite lovely. Her pale skin was creased with many fine lines, and her brown eyes were clear and gentle, but for all her delicacy there was a definite firmness about her chin, a strength, a sense of determination, even forcefulness. Oddly, the look was familiar to Hilary; but as she took an extra moment to analyze it, she was unable to recall where she had seen such an expression before.

The pause lasted a mere moment, and as quickly as it had come, Lady MacNeil's eyes became focused once more.

"But I'm sure you didn't come here to talk politics," said Hilary after the brief silence.

Apparently amused at this notion, the woman chuckled softly, her eyes momentarily growing merry, framed in oft-used crow's feet.

"That is quite true," she replied.

"How may I help you?"

Lady MacNeil grew solemn again and drew in a deep breath, seemingly as much to gather courage as oxygen. "I am here on what might be almost a bizarre quest. I realize I have come without an appointment, though I hope you will understand my reasons for this later. Yet my . . . business may take some time."

"I happen to have some. Please go on."

"For the past several weeks I have been looking for someone," said Lady MacNeil. "As unusual as it may seem for a person of my age, I hired a detective, and I followed what clues I had. And in the end, my search has led me here."

"It must have been a roundabout journey," said Hilary. "If I didn't know better I would think you were from the States, yet your accent is a curious mixture of American *and* Scottish."

Lady MacNeil smiled, oddly again. "That is another story. Perhaps one day I will have the opportunity to tell it to you."

"Who are you looking for, and how do I fit in?"

"With your permission, before I answer your questions, I would like to ask a few of you. Just in case I am on the wrong track, so to speak. We don't want to stir any emotions unnecessarily."

She paused, as Hilary nodded for her to continue.

"Thank you, Miss . . . Miss—Edwards," she said, speaking the name with apparent difficulty. "First of all, I was curious about your name. The nameplate there on your desk reads J. Hilary Edwards. May I ask what the *J* stands for?"

"Joanne—" Hilary answered.

Hardly noticing the sharp breath drawn in by her guest, Hilary went on. "—or Joan. Apparently I had a slight lisp when I was a child, and my parents were never exactly sure."

A clear look of confusion spread over her visitor's face, but nothing was said, and Hilary continued.

"Besides, they preferred my middle name, and I suppose I got used to it."

"I see," replied Lady MacNeil, her brow still creased in thought. "And when were you born?"

Hilary smiled. "I'm afraid that question is not so simple either, but its answer will clear up your confusion about my name as well. You see, I have no idea exactly when I was born. I celebrate my birthday on February 10, the day my parents officially adopted me, but we never knew what the true day should have been. Neither did we know my actual given name for a certainty."

"You were adopted, then?" The lady's voice quivered slightly.

"Yes. I was a war orphan."

"And you know nothing of your real parents?"

"Nothing."

A knot slowly began to form in Hilary's stomach. "I was orphaned under rather unusual circumstances," she went on. "It wasn't so uncommon during wartime, especially in occupied countries. We didn't have so much of it here in Britain, though we did come in for our share during the bombings. I was somehow separated from my parents and was apparently too young to say where I belonged. I was taken to a shelter, but my family was never located. It was assumed they must have been killed. There had been a German raid, bombings, explosions, but somehow I was spared. Eventually I was adopted."

"How—how old were you?"

"About three."

"It must have been difficult for you."

"Children have an incredible capacity to adapt," answered Hilary. "I was at an age before solid memory patterns form. I really don't remember anything of that time—except for a peculiar dream I sometimes have. I suppose I must have cried a lot for missing my real parents, but I have no clear memories. Whatever grief I must have experienced was soon absorbed by a new life, and . . . well, you know how it is with children—they mold to their surroundings."

Lady MacNeil nodded, not without a quick brush of her white handkerchief past one of her eyes.

"So . . . you have no memory of your real parents?"

"None."

"Have you ever wondered . . . ?"

"Every adopted child wonders," said Hilary. "How can you help it?" She paused uneasily, half afraid of where the conversation was leading. "I take it you are leading to something specific?"

Hilary's discomfort brought a certain edge to her voice that she immediately regretted. "I'm sorry to seem impatient," she said. "I suppose I'm not much used to being on this end of an interview."

"It is I who should apologize for being so cryptic." Lady MacNeil paused. "If you'll indulge me a bit more, I'd like to relate a story to you."

"Do go on," replied Hilary, folding her clammy hands as calmly and patiently as she could and resting them on the top of her desk.

"I told you I was on a quest," continued Lady MacNeil, "and the story of how it came about begins during the war with a young couple. Like so many others at that time they were separated, and while he was on the Continent, she remained in London with their child. The bombing had quieted considerably after the Battle of Britain, and they were relatively safe.

"But in late 1942 the Germans stepped up the raids, and this young mother of whom I spoke felt she ought to remove herself to a safer haven. Yet she was torn by a very real need to remain in London. The details of her situation do not really pertain to the story at this point. In the end it was decided that the child and her grandmother would return to their family estate in Scotland while the mother joined them later.

"The irony is that they might have been safer had they remained in London, but only in hindsight are such things visible. For on the way north the train bearing the child and the grandmother was bombed two hours outside of London. The grandmother had left the child in the care of their nurse while she visited a friend in another car, and it was at that moment while they were separated, that the explosion occurred."

Hilary closed her eyes.

She had not had the dream for years, yet all at once the very word *explosion* conjured up a host of nightmarish images in her mind's eye. She did not even notice that her hands were gripping each other like opposing clamps of a vise, turning her knuckles white.

"The trivial acts in our lifetimes go largely unnoticed." Lady MacNeil continued; "that is, until some catastrophe changes everything. You cannot feel guilty or ashamed, for you know there was nothing intrinsically wrong in what you may have done. Yet you know the choice will always haunt the deepest recesses of your heart. This is but scratching the surface of the many soul-searching and agonizing memories and regrets the grandmother had to face in the years following. But in the end, neither the grandmother nor the parents ever saw the child again, for the car she was in received a direct hit from the enemy's plane, and there seemed no doubt she had been killed.

"I need not describe their grief. Only their faith in God sustained them in their loss. And only time was able to dull its painful edge, the Lord using their tragedy to draw the young husband and wife closer together than they had ever been previously. They had no more children, for this one birth had been a miracle in itself.

"As the years passed, their lives managed to go on. That one void, their childlessness, could never be filled; but they nonetheless lived full and happy lives, expending the great love in their hearts in service to others."

Lady MacNeil paused. Both she and Hilary, almost in unison, took a deep breath. The time to seek one another's eyes, however, had not yet come.

"Fortunately, the story does not end there," went on Lady MacNeil. "About two years ago, the father of the lost child received a telephone call from someone unknown to him, yet well known to the grandmother, but whom she had not seen in twenty-eight years. When the caller first identified herself as Hannah Whitley, the father had no idea that the name was none other than the nurse who had been with his child on the day of the terrible accident. Indirectly as a result of that call, other people were drawn into the stream of events, which eventually led the grandmother to enlist the help of an investigator, and ultimately fill in many answers she had wondered about for years.

"After the bombing, Hannah Whitley had lived her own private nightmare, unknown to any of the rest of the family. By some miracle she and the child had been thrown clear on the first moments of the explosion, and had survived what appeared to be certain death, wandering dazed, unnoticed, farther and farther from the train. In the bedlam following the blast, all attention was focused on locating the dead and trying to drag survivors free of the wreckage. Apparently the nurse and the child wandered off into the countryside. Miss Whitley had a severe head injury and was no doubt in shock. In her benumbed state her only thought was to get away from the horrible fires and continuing explosions. They walked for some time, finally ending up at a farmhouse several miles away.

"There she abandoned the child, though even she could not say why she did such a thing. Perhaps in her fear and confusion, she thought it was the best course of action. The farmer's wife discovered the child the following morning, sleeping peacefully in a pile of straw, and brought her into the house, cleaned and fed her, but was unable to make out anything from the child's babbling. In due time they took the child to a shelter in the nearest town, where all attempts to locate her family ended in futility. Eventually she was sent to an orphanage in London.

"By some coincidence Hannah made her way to the same town, though she arrived long before the child. There her wanderings of the one kind gave way to new and more fearful internal ones. Her injuries finally took their toll. She collapsed in delirium and was hospitalized. She was later shipped to London for more intensive care and some surgery. Hannah's mind never completely recovered. Nothing could be made of her ravings either before or after going to London. The surgery did not seem to help, and she lapsed into a coma, in which she remained for two years. When she came out of it, her amnesia was so total that it took years for her to begin to reconstruct who she was. It took much longer before she began to remember what had happened that awful day. When finally bits and pieces did return, she was afraid to come forward after so long. She feared she would be blamed by the family for somehow losing the child.

"She might have remained silent to this day, except that, experiencing a sudden wave of conscience, as I said, two years ago, Hannah made a halfhearted attempt to contact the child's father. She lost her courage almost immediately, however, and never did actually talk to the man, only his secretary. After that, Hannah dropped out of sight again, though it now appears other parties concerned may have run across her somehow. In any case, more recently many long-forgotten links to the past seem beginning to come to light."

"Why—why did she change her mind? Why was she reluctant to come forward?" asked Hilary in a dry, taut voice, relying on her natural journalistic instincts to force her forward where her emotions were afraid to tread.

"I can only guess. But the father had become a rather important man in the government," answered Lady MacNeil, "and I suppose she was intimidated. She was, after all, still suffering from her own measure of guilt in the affair, and to a degree still afraid of what they might think."

"What happened then?"

"The grandmother began her own investigation into the matter."

"And . . . ?"

"And, as I said, her path has led here."

9 ✻ *Confirmation*

A LONG, HEAVY silence hung in the air between the two women.

Hilary glanced around at the glass walls of her office. Outside, the busy pace of her staff continued as usual, though little noise penetrated the soundproof enclosure, making the awkward quiet feel even deeper. This hardly seemed like the right setting for so momentous a meeting.

She let her gaze fall to her hands, still tightly clasped together on top of her desk. As if suddenly aware of the tension that had come over her body, Hilary let her hands fall apart. She rose and walked to a small table that held an electric coffeepot and all the related necessities.

"Would you like a cup of coffee?" she asked in a voice so normal that its sound almost startled her.

"Thank you," answered Lady MacNeil, "that would be nice."

"Cream or sugar?"

"Yes, both."

Hilary poured out two cups, methodically adding cream and sugar to one which she then handed to her guest. Leaving the other black, she picked it up, but remained standing where she was.

"I suppose I need not ask," she said after a brief pause, "if you are the grandmother in your story."

"I am."

"And you think . . . that is, you have come here because—" Hilary stopped, staring into her coffee.

Joanna looked up, her eyes filled with gentle compassion. "I believe . . . " Her voice quivered and her eyes filled with tears; she could not help but call to mind her own fateful luncheon encounter with Ian Duncan so many years ago, when she had been even younger than Hilary. "I believe," she went on, "that you are my granddaughter."

Joanna had unconsciously edged forward in her chair as if she wanted to go to Hilary, but something seemed to hold her back, and Hilary made no move toward the older woman. She remained rooted to the floor where she stood, staring down into her cup, not knowing whether she wanted to run or cry or scream.

Hilary sensed that she must reply. But it had to be a sane, rational response. After all, this must be a mistake. The kind old lady had somehow gotten onto the wrong track, Hilary told herself, grasping after straws to relieve her own inner sense of need. She would have to let Lady MacNeil down gently.

Try as she might, Hilary could get no word out of her mouth.

Finally Joanna's lips twitched up into a soft smile. "I'm afraid I could think of no subtler way of putting it," she said. "I suppose there are no halfway words in which to say such a thing." She paused and sipped her coffee.

"You—" Hilary licked her lips, "—you must have the wrong person."

"My granddaughter's given name was Joanna Hilary."

"A coincidence," Hilary replied weakly.

Joanna said nothing, simply gazing at her with those probing, gentle, liquid eyes.

"I mean," Hilary went on in a frayed, defensive tone, "what more proof have you but a string of—well, coincidences?"

She set down her cup and strode across the room, turning sharply when she reached the far wall. That she was agitated was clear, but her reporter's blood had begun to flow once more now that the shock had subsided a bit. "Surely you can't expect me to accept what you say on such, if you'll excuse my candor, such flimsy evidence. In my business we have a saying: one source, doubtful; two sources, perhaps; three sources, confirmation. You have a name, nothing more." She did not think it necessary at the time to give the details of her dream. "I would need something far more substantial."

"You have no desire to become acquainted with your real family?" Hilary tried for the moment to ignore the wounded tone in Lady MacNeil's voice.

"It's not that," answered Hilary with added sensitivity, remembering her earlier resolve not to hurt the lady. "I just haven't given my real family, as you put it, much thought. I *have* a family I have considered my own for almost thirty years. They love me and I love them. I'm content with my life. And now you are asking me—well, you couldn't possibly understand."

"Perhaps I might, more than you realize."

"How could you? How can you know what it's like to find a grandmother—a family— you never knew existed?"

An odd look flitted across Lady MacNeil's face.

"I know this must be difficult for you," she said at length. "I can think of no way to make it easier. But for my part, you must see that I can't simply walk out and forget the whole thing. It has taken me thirty years to find you."

Hilary sighed, turned away, stared out her window for a moment, then said, "I'm sorry. I suppose I'm not making this easy for you, either. It's just that it comes as quite a shock."

She shook her head, drew a hand through her hair, turned back toward the room and began pacing behind her desk. She hadn't wanted to remember. The dream had been so terrifying, yet even as a child she had somehow known that it was the bridge to her old life. And if her old life had been so hideous, who could blame the child in her for wanting to forget?

In her subconscious childhood pain and confusion, there had always lingered a vague sense that she had been deserted by her parents when she had needed them most. The little girl in the dream had cried so frantically—alone, bewildered, afraid . . . yet no one came to help her. As an adult, Hilary possessed the intellectual capacity to analyze and understand childish misconceptions. Still, it was no easy thing to transfer that logic to the seat of her emotions and unlearn the deepest hurts of life. Though her mind was capable of telling her one thing, her heart did not always readily go along.

Suddenly her hand went unconsciously to her throat.

She had almost forgotten the one small link she had always had to a family . . . to a past life she had begun to think never really existed.

Her eyes darted toward the lady. For a brief instant, Hilary entertained the notion of not mentioning it. It could only complicate the matter.

But why be so deceptive? What was she afraid of? Wasn't seeking the truth the very thing she had dedicated her life to as a journalist?

In almost a sudden defiant response to her silent self-interrogation, she worked her fingers under the collar of her blouse. In another second or two she lifted out a delicate gold chain—one she had bought to replace the original, which had broken when she was ten. On it hung a heart-shaped locket.

The moment it rested between her fingers, there came the sound of a thud and splat as Lady MacNeil's cup slipped from her hand and crashed to the floor. Hilary stared, then hurried to the coffee table, where she grabbed a serviette and stooped down to clean up the spill.

She had not even finished wiping up the coffee when she felt a slim, aged hand reach down to her head as she knelt on the floor, and gently caress her hair. She froze, then slowly turned and lifted her eyes to meet those of the old woman's.

"It's true, then?" Hilary said in a barely audible whisper.

"The locket belonged to my grandmother, Lady Margaret Duncan, and it has been passed down to succeeding generations of women in our family. My daughter, on the day of the train accident, bidding what she thought would be just a short farewell, gave it to her daughter."

Quiet tears flowed from Hilary's eyes.

The fears and confusion of her childhood, and her mature struggling to come to grips with her own identity, had by no means hardened her heart. As she knelt there at the gentle woman's feet, it was almost as if the little girl in the dream had finally been found . . . rescued from the horror of the unknown. The part of her that had always, however subconsciously, felt like a stranger; helpless, and reaching out for something to fill the emptiness only an orphan can know, was now—suddenly and unexpectedly—comforted. Here was her *own* grandmother, a woman who could surely love and protect a lost little child. The tears that ran down her face were the tears she had been waiting thirty years to shed.

At the same time, another piece of Hilary's complex self remained hesitant, fearful of returning the older woman's loving gaze. The mature young woman she had become was real. She was a child no longer. She had adult anxieties and confusions of her own. She could not hide herself in this lady's arms and forget who she was. She already had a family, a life, a job, a future, and she hadn't been looking for any other. She had dealt with her past by putting it behind her. What was she to do with a past she had never known, now that it had come seeking her against her will?

"Hilary," asked Joanna softly, as if she had read her granddaughter's thoughts, "why are you afraid?"

Hilary brushed her fingers across her wet cheeks. "I suppose I'm afraid of change," she said.

She smiled ironically. "I've a friend who is fond of pointing out my vast inconsistency in this area," she went on. " 'Hilary,' she tells me, 'you want to change the world, but you fight personal change ruthlessly.' To tell you the truth, I don't know why I'm like that. All my life I've had this feeling deep inside that I had to make it on my own. An independence, I guess. Maybe it's common to orphans, I don't know. I've never been comfortable unless I was in control of my surroundings, in control of my own destiny, so to speak. And now to find everything so abruptly turned around, so . . . so . . . beyond my control—it's hardly a pleasant feeling. It's going to take some getting used to."

"What makes you think we would expect you to change?"

"I'm not from your world. I'm not even sure I want to be."

Joanna nodded in understanding but was silent for some time.

Hilary pulled herself to her feet, despite shaking knees, and took a seat beside Joanna. "It's all going to take some getting used to," she finally repeated with a long sigh.

"Would you like to know who your parents are?" Joanna asked. Her tone, though free of expectation, held quiet entreaty.

"Did they send you?"

"They know nothing of my quest."

"I merely assumed that they—"

"I made the decision when I first began this to keep it to myself until I was sure. I spoke briefly with my son-in-law to begin with, but shared with him only some of my concerns with, shall we call it, the situation as it then stood. But I wanted to explore the mystery before saying anything to them. It turned out to be a wise decision, for there have been many dead ends, and my feeling of hopelessness after each failure has been . . . well, you can imagine. I sometimes began to think I had dreamed up everything, or was remembering events and places and landmarks incorrectly. I am getting on in years. I even wondered if senility was starting to creep in!"

"And now you will tell them?"

"You do not wish me to?"

"Of course," replied Hilary, defensively again. "What kind of person do you think I am?"

She rose, turned her back on Joanna, and began pacing the small room again. After a moment, she turned around slowly, her face clearly reflecting that she was torn between her adult fears and the deep hopes of a little orphan child. "I'm—I'm so sorry," she said. "I didn't mean to sound that way."

"Think nothing of it, child," replied Joanna. "I do understand, as difficult as that may be for you to grasp. I hope someday to have the opportunity to tell you just how deeply I understand what you are going through—and why."

Hilary smiled, tears again beginning to fall. "What are their names?" she asked in a soft, shaky voice.

"My daughter is Allison—Allison Eleanor MacNeil. That is her maiden name, of course . . . "

But Hilary hardly heard her last words. The moment she heard the name a strange sensation swept over and enveloped her. Allison . . . the mother who had borne her, given her life, cradled her, and then wept over her and grieved for years after her supposed death.

". . . you resemble her, you know," Lady MacNeil was saying when Hilary became again conscious of her voice. ". . . the hair and eyes. I knew I had found you the moment you walked in. It was all I could do to keep from shouting *hallelujah*! and rushing to you!" She gave a little laugh at the thought.

Hilary returned her smile.

"And your father's name is Logan Macintyre . . . " Once again Hilary's consciousness trailed away . . . *Logan*—what a solid, yet unusual name . . . the father whose manly heart must surely have softened and melted at the touch of his baby daughter, who must have smiled down at her as she lay safely in his strong and protective arms.

These were her parents—*her* parents! who had lived these many years with an emptiness just like her own. Surely they had been haunted all their lives since that awful day by nightmares of their own just as she had been.

Macintyre . . .

Suddenly Hilary recalled Lady MacNeil's earlier statement: *The child's father had become a rather important man in the government . . .*

Of course! No wonder the name sounded familiar! She could have written off the similarity as a mere coincidence but for that comment. Her father a politician! She could almost laugh if the thought weren't so dreadful. The man was indeed high up—a minister in Wilson's Labour government before the Conservatives unseated it last year . . . in the news recently for his opposition to Wilson's Anti-EEC policies . . . bucking his own party's stand against the Conservatives along with Roy Jenkins, the Shadow Deputy Minister. *That* was her father!

The very thought was unbelievable—humorous, in a way, were the shock not so stunning. She knew something of Macintyre's history. A decorated war hero who had caused a bit of a stir back in 1950 when he ran for his first term in Parliament. His opposition for the seat had tried to make an issue of his low-level criminal record prior to the war in spite of his full exoneration by the Crown. Somehow Macintyre had won the seat. It was said he had been a confidence man before the war. The question was then asked by those skeptical of his victory whether he had simply conned his unwitting northern constituents. If such was indeed true, he must be very good at it, for he had managed to retain his seat these twenty years and rise to the inner circle of power in Whitehall.

What kind of a family have I fallen into? Hilary thought to herself with mingled astonishment and dismay. Her mother of aristocratic blood . . . her father a politician! *What other thunderclaps would this day bring?* she wondered in disbelief.

"I've heard of him," she said aloud, rousing herself from her reverie, but unable to keep the tremor from her voice.

"Your father is a good man," said Joanna, "and your mother is a kind and gentle woman." Her words were not mere motherly sentimentalities, but were filled with conviction.

"He's the politician you thought I should meet?"

"For more reasons than one," smiled Joanna coyly.

"Yes, I see that now."

"I'm aware of how difficult this must be. Some of the stands your magazine has taken in matters political are not unknown to me."

Hilary forced a smile, but said nothing.

"When would you like to meet them?" asked Joanna.

"You must realize," Hilary hedged, "this is really quite a blow to me."

"I do know. Do I take it then that you are perhaps considering *not* telling them?"

"No," sighed Hilary. "They have a right to know. It's just that—"

She hesitated, then struggled to continue. "—it's just that I need some time . . . to think . . . to get used to all this. This will change my—my—whole world . . . the way I've grown accustomed to looking at things. And not only for myself, but my mother—my adoptive mother—she must be told. I'm her only child, so you can imagine the emotional adjustments this will cause for her as well as for myself. She has given more than half her life to me, Lady MacNeil. Your daughter and her husband—I'm sure they loved me dearly, but they had their baby only three years. I realize that where a child is concerned, it is more than a matter of time, that the bloodline counts for a great deal, but you can see—"

"I understand, Miss Edwards," interjected Joanna with more compassionate understanding than her mere words could indicate. "How much time do you think you will need?"

"I—I don't know."

Joanna reached into her handbag and withdrew a small white card which she held out to Hilary.

"This is how you can reach me," she said.

"Thank you," replied Hilary, taking the card. "Then you will wait until I contact you?"

"You have my word, Miss—no, that will never do," she said in a quick aside almost to herself. "You have my word, *Hilary*," she continued, "on one condition: that you *will* tell them in good time."

"I will—I promise."

Joanna rose and held out her hand in a parting gesture. This time, however, as Hilary took it she began to grasp the depth of emotion in the woman's intense gaze—a grandmother looking upon her granddaughter, now a grown woman, for the first time in nearly thirty years. She sensed the anguish her tentative and uncertain response must have caused in the gentle, soft-spoken old woman. In an effort to somehow make up for her own seeming lack of enthusiasm, Hilary laid her free hand over Joanna's, clasping her dainty hand between her own two.

"I'm sorry I have been so . . . ambivalent," said Hilary. "I guess I'm not very good at this kind of interview. But I do thank you—for finding me—for not giving up. I know I will learn to . . . to love my family . . . and to love you, the more I know you all."

Joanna smiled—a kindly, noble smile. Then, as if her stoic restraint had suddenly broken, tears spilled from the corners of her eyes. Before Hilary realized what she was doing, she had dropped her hands and had her arms around the older woman's slim figure, herself weeping quietly. Joanna returned the embrace, lifting up—in the depths of her being—silent prayers of thankful rejoicing to God.

The tender reunion lasted only a few moments. But perhaps the two women would not have fallen apart so soon had they known this was to be their first and last embrace in this world.

Five days later, while Hilary was still struggling with the dilemma of how to proceed, Lady Joanna MacNeil succumbed to a sudden cerebral hemorrhage.

10 ❈ Uncertainties

HILARY STIRRED A teaspoon of sugar into her second cup of tea.

She had wandered from her kitchen and was now reclining on her sofa. She marveled at how she had forgotten not a single detail of her meeting with Joanna MacNeil. Every look, every word was by now printed indelibly in her memory . . . and upon her heart.

She glanced outside. Everything was black. The night was still and quiet. I have to sleep, she thought. Tomorrow will be a big day. Drinking tea was probably the worst thing to be doing, but she couldn't help it. She had to give her thoughts some company, even if it was only from a teapot.

She could not unfocus her mind from that day in her office. It was to be the last time she would behold that loving, gentle face. *How much have I missed?* Hilary asked herself with more than a twinge of sadness. But the greater part of her sorrow sprang from the painful fact that she could have had at least five more days with her grandmother had she not been so vacillating in her response.

Yet it was foolish to lament the delay now. Her need for time had been valid, if selfish. Even now, she wasn't sure she had fully accepted the startling revelation that had walked into her life in the person of Lady Joanna MacNeil.

Impulse had driven her to attend the funeral. She had taken the train to Aberdeen and then rented a car for the final two-hour drive to the sleepy little village of Port Strathy. During that lonely drive, she first began to consider what she would actually do once she reached the place. She had come all this way without really thinking through her motives, giving hardly a thought to what would come once she arrived. Was she on her way to Lady MacNeil's home to claim her long lost family? Was she going as a relative, as a member of the inner family . . . or as an observer? The answer was far from simple.

When she had first heard about Lady MacNeil's death, Hilary had hoped, or feared—she couldn't tell quite which—that her parents would contact her. She assumed that, knowing death was near, the grandmother would have felt compelled to break her word and tell her children that their daughter lived. But it seemed the suddenness of the woman's collapse had precluded that communication.

She now knew that if she did approach them, it would necessarily be "from out of the blue," so to speak. How much easier it would have been with Lady MacNeil at her side! Notwithstanding the show of confidence and aplomb she was able to manifest when talking in a professional setting with important people in London and throughout Britain, this would take a kind of courage with which she was not intimately acquainted. She wished it all didn't depend on her.

For the first time the unthinkable idea of keeping silent began to nag at her. It was certainly a possibility now. No one would ever know. She could go on with her life unchanged. Logan and Allison Macintyre would be no worse off for her silence.

Even as the notion came to her, however, Hilary shook it off. It *wasn't* a possibility. How could she even consider such a thing? Where would her integrity as a truth-seeker be if she turned her back on one of life's most fundamental duties: honor to father and mother? Besides, she had given the lady—her grandmother—her word.

When and how to do what she must eventually do, she didn't know. This was uncharted ground. Was it shyness? Was it fear? Was it uncertainty over how she would be received? Hilary shrank from the very weakness all these questions suggested. Now more than ever she would have to be strong.

Yet as she stood at the woman's graveside, watching the stream of strangers file by—friends, and the people who were now supposed to be her family—any nerve she might have been able to summon quickly vanished. *I must say something to someone,* she thought. Yet as the black-garbed crowd slowly and silently disbursed, leaving her standing there alone in the countryside of an unfamiliar Scottish setting, no one seemed to pay her much notice, and her mouth was far too dry to speak. She *couldn't* just . . . just walk up and . . . and—and what?

It wasn't difficult for Hilary to convince herself of the utter foolhardiness of her marching up to these strangers and declaring herself their missing daughter. At best they would think her a crackpot. At worst, a boldfaced fraud hoping to catch them at their moment of weakness in order to get her clutches on a piece of the dead woman's estate. They would never believe her.

With such a conflicting set of thoughts in her brain, and an even more frenetic jumble of emotions in her heart, Hilary—timid, disappointed, and feeling every inch a coward—let them all pass silently out of sight, then made her own way back to her car, drove to the inn to pick up her things, and then and began the return drive to Aberdeen, and thence back to London.

If she had hoped to find inner peace in the frenzy and anonymity of the city, she was to be disappointed on that front as well. In a matter of a few short days after her return came the Whitehall interview where Logan Macintyre unexpectedly turned up. Why he didn't seem to recognize her, she never knew. Was it a hidden longing to have her secret discovered without she herself having to boldly step forward that impelled her to confront the M.P.'s as she had, rather than cowering down into her seat in silence, hoping he wouldn't see her? And then on the heels of that came the nightmare that had spurred this late night reflection.

The ancient Greeks would say that the Fates were willing her toward her destiny. She knew better, of course. But the truth of Romans 8:28 was hardly more comforting at this point. It still meant she was being guided by a hand stronger than her own, toward a destiny, a plan, a purpose she couldn't see and over which she had no control. Many years ago, as a teenager, she had entrusted her life to God. As she had matured, she had learned to recognize His guidance in her life. She had even tried to explain the phenomenon to Murry. But never had anything of this magnitude confronted her.

If this were indeed His doing, why hadn't He given her the courage and resolve to do the right thing?

"Lord, what do you want me to do?" she prayed aloud.

The only answer she received was the still quiet of her apartment.

She knew she needed to be more patient where things of the Spirit were concerned. But sitting back and waiting had never been her forte.

"Oh, Lord," she sighed, "I want to be the person you want me to be . . . I'm just not sure who that is." Then she added in barely more than a whisper, "Give me the strength . . . yes, and the boldness to do what you show me."

Hilary glanced around, sighed tiredly, then shivered, realizing for the first time how chilly her flat was at that hour. She looked up at the clock over the television. Two a.m. She pulled a blanket up over her shoulders, not really intending to sleep there on the sofa, yet hardly relishing the idea of even the short walk back to bed. In five minutes she was asleep; her last thoughts before dozing off were a vague determination to spend some time in prayer, and an even vaguer anxiety that her nightmare might return if she fell asleep.

11 ✴ *The Parcel*

THE THREE-BLOCK walk to the Underground station helped clear Hilary's head, still functioning obediently after only four hours' sleep. By the time she reached her office at 7:30 a.m., she was—assisted by the growing effect of three hastily gulped cups of strong coffee—fully alert and ready to meet a vigorous day.

Her morning was consumed with meetings—an hour with the people in graphics, another with the budget department, a lengthy and somewhat heated discussion with the printer over increased rates, and finally several individual conferences with members of the editorial staff. When she returned to her private office at 11:30, it was for the first time since she had hung up her jacket and purse four hours earlier. Betty followed her in with the morning mail, which consisted of a stack of letters and one parcel. She barely had begun to glance through them when Murry Fitts knocked on her door. She looked up, then beckoned him in.

"We still going out to the East End?" he asked, poking his head in. "Maybe have a look at that fire site?"

"I hadn't forgotten," Hilary replied. "I even dressed for it." She waved a hand in front of her to indicate her casual clothing—khaki trousers, peach polo shirt, and brown leather oxfords. "Are you free now?"

"Yes, I kept the afternoon clear."

"Great. Then let's go," said Hilary, jumping up, glad for the diversion of continued activity. "If we get out of here now, we might even be able to grab a bit of lunch."

A short while later they were seated in the back of a black Austin. As the taxi snaked its way through London's congested noon-hour traffic, Murry filled Hilary in on his activities during the hours since they had last met. He had spent the morning poring through the Fire Brigade records and had the bleary eyes to prove it. He had also spoken to a building official regarding the permitting process for the various redevelopment projects in the area.

"Hmm. That is interesting," mused Hilary when Murry took a break in his enthusiastic monologue. The contrast, however, between her indifferent tone and her words was not lost on her companion.

When he was through, Hilary turned her attention to the passing view outside the taxi window. They were approaching their destination, and she marveled that despite all the postwar reconstruction in the area, the East End had retained its look of dingy squalor. This section of London had received the worst of the Luftwaffe attacks, probably in part because Hitler had hoped that it would incite the poverty-stricken inhabitants to revolt against their government. It had produced quite the opposite effect, however, among the stalwart residents. Most East-enders liked their little corner of London, despite the fact that some labeled it a "slum."

Hilary remembered the friendly neighborhood in Whitechapel where she had grown up. It may not have been pretty, but she had always felt secure there. Beyond her own mum, there were always at least five other motherly matrons looking out for her and the other youngsters roaming the streets. She recalled the kindly missionary lady who would set up her little wooden archway on a street corner where any child with a farthing, and not too tall to pass under the arch, could receive a precious packet of small toys.

And there were the street games invented by children who thought nothing of trash-strewn alleys or wartime rubble as a playground offering as many mysteries and delights as any more rural setting. All of it was set against the musical twang of the bawdy Cockney tongue; unfortunately, years of education had obliterated all but a trace of the dialect from Hilary's speech.

The sense of nostalgia came upon her so suddenly she hardly had time to brace herself against the quickly following surge of renewed inner turmoil. The ties of a girl named Hilary Edwards to her home of so many years went deep, and she wondered if she could ever make room in that same heart for a stranger named Joanna Hilary Macintyre.

Murry's down-to-earth voice broke into her thoughts, rescuing her—for the moment at least—from further having to ponder her fate.

"There it is," he said, pointing ahead to where the burned-out skeleton of an apartment building stood eerily against the gray overcast sky. The premises were all cordoned off well back of the debris.

The cab pulled to a stop across the street. Hilary climbed out and paid the cabbie while Murry gathered up his camera bag and followed. They waited for the cab to pull away, then crossed. Hilary shivered involuntarily.

"You okay?" asked Murry with genuine concern. "You seemed pretty quiet in the cab."

"I'm fine. Just got some things on my mind, that's all. And there's something depressing about a burned-out building. It's such a waste. I've never much liked fires. Come on, let's walk around a bit."

While Murry snapped pictures, Hilary gradually made her way about the perimeter of the building; and by the time Murry caught up with her again, she was deeply involved in an impassioned discussion with two residents of an adjoining tenement.

They did not get back to the office till after five.

"How about grabbing a bite of dinner?" asked Fitts as they walked inside.

"Thanks, Murry, but I . . ."

She paused, then added, "Yes, that sounds great. I will."

"I've got to drop this film off at the lab, and then make a call or two."

"Don't hurry on my account," laughed Hilary. "I've got a dozen things to check on! But I'll try to have it wrapped up by 6:15 or 6:30. That be okay? I doubt if I'll even have the chance to look at my mail."

"Six-thirty's fine. If we make it, that will be the earliest you've left here within memory!"

In reality they did not get away until 7:10—still a record. But the extra forty minutes had still not gotten Hilary anywhere close to her day's mail. As they drove the four miles to Murry's modest two-bedroom home in his aging Renault, Hilary chose not to mention that part of her reason for accepting his invitation was the thought that it might provide just the sort of escape she needed from her tormented emotions—something she had been trying to accomplish the entire day. She knew she would have to make a decision regarding Lady MacNeil's revelation, and soon. But until something solid presented itself, or at least some appropriate course of action became clear, she had to go on with her own life. And she certainly didn't relish an evening alone in her flat. She had been praying, and an answer would come. But until that time there was no reason to beat herself with anxiety. Or so she told herself. But the only way she could keep the unpleasant thoughts at bay seemed to be with continuous activity.

By the time she arrived back home, it was 10:30 and the previous night's lack of sleep had finally caught up with her. She fell into bed and slept soundly and dreamlessly until morning.

The next day was like the previous one; though the people and topics and situations were different, Hilary managed to pack as much into the day after deadline as she had the day before it.

The Common Market vote had been taken the previous night in Parliament. Though she tended to oppose the move, she was not so much upset by the resounding victory of assent as she was by the morning's television reports of the event, which included several shots and two brief interviews with Logan Macintyre.

Seeing his face had been more disconcerting than any political event! Over and over in her mind kept tumbling the incredible words: "That man is my father!"

The very thought had tied her stomach in knots, all the more so in the knowledge that her silence was doing him a great injustice. She had attempted to counter that realization by rationalizing to herself that she was not that great a catch as a daughter—maybe the Macintyres would just as soon never know.

She knew that could never be true, and it hardly helped pacify her uneasiness about keeping silent. Always Lady MacNeil's face would intrude upon her attempts at pragmatism, and then Hilary would feel more deeply than ever her own deceit at keeping her startling revelation to herself.

She had made a gallant effort to bury herself in her work, in unending calls and interviews, and even attempts to pick up her article where she had left it several days earlier. But by late afternoon she had to admit to herself that the effort had not been successful. She could not hide from it.

She grabbed her coat and left the building—for what destination, she had no idea. She couldn't go home. She turned up the sidewalk and began to walk. Unconsciously she went wherever her feet chanced to lead her. Three hours later she was still walking, still thinking, oblivious to pangs of hunger. She had been the length and breadth of Hyde Park, through Kensington Gardens, then past Buckingham Palace and finally the Houses of Parliament and back to the office. By the time she returned, it was 8:30, and the place was deserted. She had a stack of work she convinced herself she ought to take home. She'd get it, then grab a taxi back to the flat.

Hilary unlocked the door and walked through the darkened and empty pressroom directly to her office. There she switched on her light and stood gazing about. Her desk was a cluttered mess. She had been so caught up in activity lately that she had been neglectful of daily office business. It was clear Betty had done what was possible to keep it orderly, but there were two or three days of unopened mail and correspondence sitting in a stack that seemed at least eight inches high!

The sight made her realize more clearly than ever that she had to get her life back in order.

She opened her briefcase, thumbed through the files on her desk, laying the most pressing articles inside. She could probably make some headway this evening in the quietness of her apartment. She wanted to work yesterday's interview with those people across from the fire into the article. Good thing she didn't require eight hours sleep every night.

She picked up what was at least two days' worth of mail and gave it a quick scan through to see what was the most urgent. It was not until she picked up several manila-envelope-sized pieces that she noticed the parcel at the bottom of the stack. Now she remembered; it had come yesterday.

It was nearly as large as a ream of paper, and quite as heavy. It was no ordinary packet, for it appeared to have traveled a great many miles, judging from its battered condition and many official stamps.

Closer inspection revealed no return address, but one of the postmarks had originated in Scotland and she could find none from any farther away. Another postmark read Leeds, dated several days after the one from Aberdeen. Whatever the package was, and wherever it had come from, it had certainly taken a circuitous route in finally winding up at *The Berkshire Review*. The earliest date stamped on the package was from some two and a half weeks earlier. Hilary pushed aside her other mail and, sensing the rising tide of some unforeseen emotion within her, tore open the brown paper wrapping.

Inside, her hands clutched a box. Slowly she lifted off its lid, and her eyes fell upon what could not have been a more unexpected sight. Hilary found herself gazing upon a thick, handwritten manuscript bearing the name: Joanna Matheson MacNeil.

The title beneath the name simply read *Stonewycke Journal.* Under those profoundly significant words, centered in the page, was a single sentence of scripture from Psalm 102:

Let this be written for a future generation, that a people not yet created may praise the Lord.

Tucked between the first two pages was a small folded sheet of light blue stationery. Hilary picked it up and read:

Dear Hilary,

I believe I can somewhat understand many of your present confusions and hesitancies. It is a difficult upheaval in your life you are faced with, and one, I know, which came to you unsought. Although I would never ask you to relinquish or in any way alter your attachments to your adoptive family, it is a reality we cannot change that you now have another family as well. I hope and pray that in time you will feel some affection for us. Thus it came to me the other day that it might help you to perceive our family better if you could understand some of the heritage that is now yours—should you choose to have us. When we met I told you that I hoped I would one day have the opportunity to tell you my story. It would seem that now, perhaps, that moment has come.

So, after much consideration, I have decided to send you this manuscript. It is a journal I have kept over the years chronicling as much of the history of the Stonewycke heritage and the lives of its people as I have been able to learn myself. As you will see, I too came to this family as a stranger. But as I learned of my predecessors, this heritage took me into itself and made me one with it, as I have no doubt it will do to you as well. This is by no means polished or professional by the standards you are surely accustomed to. But I entreat you to read it, and perhaps through it find your own place within the family that is, for better or worse, a part of you.

> With deepest affection,
> Joanna MacNeil

With silent tears streaming from her eyes, Hilary sank down into her chair, still grasping the precious letter. The note was dated the day before Lady Joanna's death, and Hilary could not help but sense that these were her last words to her granddaughter as surely as if Hilary had been called to the dear woman's deathbed.

Again a great sadness swept over Hilary. She was struck once more, as she had been the day she learned of the lady's—her own grandmother's—death—with the terrible emptiness of "what might have been."

She looked down at Lady Joanna's journal, and with trembling fingers turned to the first page.

I came to Scotland a stranger, it read, *with no past to speak of, and an uncertain future. My quest was a vague one, and never would I have presumed to think that it would radically change my whole life. For my journey led, indeed, to life—full and complete life in the Spirit of Christ. And with this, God added to me an intensely fulfilling past, and a future brimming with promise. He gave me people to love, and people who loved me. He gave me a family, a heritage that will always demonstrate to me God's unwavering presence with His faithful ones. And this is what gives meaning to the story of the Stonewycke legacy.*

It is so clearly exemplified in the life of dear Maggie Duncan—my own grandmother— who will always be the matriarch of matriarchs. Her pilgrimage of faith perhaps began that day—if such a moment can ever be sharply defined—when as a child of thirteen she went into her beloved stables to find that her father had sold her dear horse, Cinder. Ah, how I remember the day she told me the story of Cinder, how the tears of mingled pain and joy and thankfulness spilled down her old cheeks at the memory which was then almost sixty years old, and how her eyes came alive when she began to reflect aloud on the depth of love and judgment passed to her from her own personal childhood sage, the groom who took care of the family stables. . . .

Suddenly the lights in the pressroom flashed on. Hilary's whole body jerked with a start as if she'd been awakened from a trance. She looked up with a dull expression. The janitor had wheeled his cleaning cart into the big room and, looking up to see Hilary still in her office, he waved a greeting and ambled to her door.

"Workin' late tonight, eh, Miss Edwards?" he said, poking his head into the doorway.

"Yes . . . I suppose so."

"I can wait to do these rooms if you like."

"No," said Hilary, gradually coming to herself. "I only have to gather up a few things; then I'm off. You go on with your work."

"Thank you, miss. If it's all the same to you, I'll do just that."

Hilary watched him shuffle away, then stood, laying the journal in her briefcase on top of the other work. As she snapped the clasp closed, however, she doubted she'd get anything else done tonight. She had tried so hard to fill her life with diversions lately, but this uncanny arrival of the journal—many, many days after it should have gotten to her, served as a powerful and unavoidable reminder that she could not run forever from the destiny that awaited her. The thing she had tried to hide from was now too tangible and present to elude. It was as real as the papers she had just held in her hand, as real as had been the kind, noble countenance—and now, as she recalled the face, she realized it had contained another expression as well, an expression of nothing more, nothing less than a deep and personal love—of Lady Joanna MacNeil, her namesake . . . and her own grandmother.

By the time Hilary had reached her flat, all thought of work had vanished. Her mind and heart—indeed, her entire being—was focused on one sole object—a place called Stonewycke, and the life's blood that had been coursing through the inhabitants of its stone walls for over four hundred years.

Before she nodded off to sleep that night some time after two a.m., Hilary had become familiar with names she would never have dreamed could move her so—names which, in the distinctive and significant hand of Joanna MacNeil, took on character and personality and meaning far beyond the actual words printed on the page. In the very handwriting of her grandmother, they seemed to come to life, filling Hilary with a sense of mingled longing and fullness which her intellect could find no possible way to describe. She felt herself gradually being caught up into something far beyond the confines of her own little world.

Here were Atlanta and Maggie, with whom she suddenly felt intimate, and a rebellious young nobleman they called Ian, and a wise old groom named Digory—her own great uncle by several generations past—who, through the miracle of after-years, had been grafted into the family line to an even more significant degree than his master and nemesis, James Duncan. And most poignant of all to Hilary as she read was the touching story of Joanna's own arrival in Scotland, a stranger in a foreign land, whose uncertain future and perplexity of heart certainly outweighed anything Hilary herself had yet had to face.

As Hilary read and read, she began to see more than a mere recounting of events. She gradually realized that the most vital thread which wove through the fabric of the Stonewycke story was the ever-present hand of God moving in the lives of these people—her own ancestors.

This was *her* family! And it was no ordinary one. God had been active among its people for years. And He was moving still!

12 ❈ Hilary's Resolve

WHEN HILARY AWOKE at 7:30 in the morning, it was all as fresh in her mind as if only moments and not hours of sleep had intervened.

The events of the previous night had been imprinted forever on her heart—they had penetrated into the very depths of her very soul. No more could she run or hide from the destiny that was pursuing her. No more could she deny who she was or turn her back on this family from which she had sprung.

With the reflections that came with morning's light, she knew as clearly as if she were standing gazing into a clean Highland loch that she must, before anything else, face the two new scions of that family—her own parents, Logan and Allison Macintyre.

Hilary knew what she must do.

Though she dressed with particular care that morning, she did so hastily, and with fingers perspiring and cold. She skipped breakfast. She could not have eaten even if she were willing to spend the extra time on it. What she must do she wanted to do quickly—not just to get it over with, but because she was suddenly eager to do so.

She caught a cab a block from her building in a surprisingly short time, and it was only as the cabby asked, "Where to, mum?" that she realized she did not have any idea where the Macintyres lived. It was a silly detail to have forgotten, especially since she had had more than two weeks to look it up, and even drive by if she had wanted. But she had never wanted to before this moment. And now she didn't want to waste the time trying to find the home address. Therefore she answered the cabby with the single word:

"Whitehall."

This would probably be the best way after all, she reasoned with herself. A man could be so much more stoic and level-headed in matters such as this. So, by approaching her father first, she thought, they might be able to avoid an emotional scene. Though why she was worried about that now she didn't know; her emotions were already such a jumble! But hopefully she'd be able to get through it without making a goose of herself. After she spoke with Mr. Macintyre, he could call his wife and prepare for a later meeting. Yes, this was just the thing.

By the time the taxi pulled up at her destination around 8:50, she once again felt collected and, if not exactly confident, at least prepared for what lay ahead.

She located Logan Macintyre's office in the Parliamentary administrative buildings, walked inside, and stepped into the lift as she had done many times before, as if this were no more than an interview with a politician. But this interview would be more—far more—than that. This would be like no interview she had ever had in her life! Before the lift came to a stop, a dreadful fluttering had crept into her stomach, driving out all traces of the composure she had felt earlier.

She stepped outside and began slowly walking down the corridor, aware that her knees had begun to tremble. As she lifted her hand to turn the latch and open the door and walk into Mr. Macintyre's suite of offices, she found it was shaking.

Hilary paused a moment, took a deep breath as if to regain her equilibrium, but instead her head began to swim airily and she had to grab the door latch all the more firmly. What was wrong? She had never felt such sensations before! The thought occurred to turn and flee, except at that very moment she heard the sound of voices approaching behind her in the corridor. Feeling suddenly foolish standing there leaning against the door, she opened it the rest of the way and walked inside.

It was a small miracle she could even speak. Though at that moment her voice was small and sounded thin and hollow.

"May I help you?" asked the receptionist.

"Yes, I'd like . . . I'd like to see Mr. Macintyre."

"Do you have an appointment?"

"No—no, I don't . . . I came rather . . . suddenly."

"Well, you see, today is Saturday and Mr. Macintyre doesn't usually come in, and besides—"

"Oh—" interrupted Hilary almost in a daze. For the first time the day of the week dawned on her. No wonder it had been so easy to get a cab! She hadn't even noticed the quiet streets.

"Perhaps I can reach him at home," she said, regaining her resolve. She had come too far to be easily turned aside.

"It would be of no avail anyway, miss. As I was about to say, Mr. Macintyre has returned north to Scotland."

"Scotland?" A deflated sense of despair was evident in Hilary's tone.

"Yes, to his home."

"How long will he be gone?"

"It is difficult to say. There has been a recent death in the family, and he had only returned to London long enough to participate in the EEC vote."

"Mrs. Macintyre is in Scotland too?"

"That's right, miss."

Without another word, Hilary turned and exited the office. She felt as though an icy hand had clamped itself over her resolve. What could she do now?

As she wandered out of the building onto the sidewalk, she felt a great emptiness inside. If I came here on a kind of impulse, she thought, it was no mere whim. There was a purpose to it, a purpose I cannot ignore. Despite this momentary setback, her course was set. There could be no turning back now. She must follow wherever it led. She *must* fulfill her promise to Lady Joanna!

Sensing a sudden new resolve, Hilary hailed another taxi. This time she instructed the man to take her home. There, she told him to wait while she went inside. In less than fifteen minutes she emerged carrying a small suitcase and an overnight bag. She raced down the few steps, across the sidewalk, and jumped back inside while the cabby put in her bags.

"Driver," she said, her voice as intense as the light in her eyes, "take me to Euston Station!"

13 ❈ *North Toward Destiny*

SHE WAS NEARLY to Northampton before the import of her sudden decision finally dawned on Hilary.

She was returning to Scotland, to the land of her heritage.

What an impulsive thing to do, she thought to herself, grab the first train out of London to Edinburgh! But the call of her past had beckoned with compelling urgency, and this was no time to be dictated to by a railway schedule.

As Hilary pondered the implications of her decision, she wondered what it would be like to face her parents. That was the question which burned in her brain more continuously than any other. That would be the one thrilling, terrifying moment. Would they open their arms . . . or wish she'd never come?

Of course, once Lady Joanna made her "discovery" of Hilary's identity, the encounter was inevitable. Why had she fought it so long? The exhilaration she felt at having finally surrendered to the destiny set before her—in spite of the dreadful uncertainty—was invigorating. At long last she allowed her mind to explore the possibilities.

What would these people be like? What would it be like to be a part of their family—*her* family now? She thought of her adoptive mother; what would her reaction be? She imagined Christmas dinner with the daughter of the elegant and aristocratic Lady MacNeil sitting beside Hilary's simple, earthy, working-class mother. She had no doubt the wise and solid Mrs. Edwards would be able to hold her own in such company once she overcame her initial awe.

What would her parents' reaction be? Surely the daughter of such a woman as Lady Joanna could harbor no snobbery or prejudice. Then for the first time it dawned on Hilary that Logan Macintyre came from a working-class background himself. Had he traveled too far from his roots to remember, and to feel with such decent and simple people?

With that a more fearsome thought formed in Hilary's mind.

Would they be able to accept *her*? Not only because of her upbringing, but also because she was now a grown woman, with personality and character and values and attitudes already set? They certainly wouldn't agree with many of her social and political views. It did not necessarily follow that just because she was their daughter, they would automatically *like* her. She might not even like them.

She thought of all the chances she had taken over the years—the pursuit of an education against financial and social odds; taking over the management of *The Berkshire Review* despite its precarious position. Not to mention the many causes she had been quick to espouse—the more unlikely her chances for success, it sometimes seemed, the more deter-mined she was to fight on the side of the apparent underdog. Yes, she had tackled many difficult obstacles in her life, yet this simple act now before her of meeting her parents loomed as by far the most formidable.

At that moment a train steward approached her seat. She pulled herself from her reverie and glanced up.

"Ma'am," he said with a smile, "the dining car will be opened only fifteen more minutes if you wish luncheon."

"Thank you," replied Hilary, her voice distracted and as far away as were her thoughts of food. "I'm fine for now. I'll wait for dinner."

He nodded and moved on down the aisle. Her eyes followed him disinterestedly for a moment. She had to change trains later in the afternoon. Maybe she'd get off and have some-thing to eat in Yorkshire before the night train to Scotland.

Slowly Hilary turned her gaze out the window. The countryside rushed past in a blur of fields and farm houses, country roads and telephone lines. She wondered if this was the same route her grandmother and she had taken that fateful day thirty years ago. For the first time Hilary reflected back on those earlier events as something she had actually been part of. Her dream would seem to indicate that, in her own way, she remembered the terrible holocaust of death and explosion as vividly as did Lady Joanna. Perhaps it might not have been too far from where they now were, and the realization sent a shudder down Hilary's spine.

Had her grandmother on that day been looking out on this same tranquil scene, perhaps anticipating her return home, made even more joyful by the presence of her little granddaugh-ter? What mysterious necessity had kept Allison behind in London, leaving her daughter to go off without her? Wartime had certainly forced the change of many priorities. Yet what could have been so important for a mother to send off a young child on such a long trip at such a precarious time?

Unconsciously Hilary's gaze fell to the box on her lap. Perhaps the answers were in Lady Joanna's manuscript. She lifted the lid and almost reverently took out the bound pages. Last evening, after skimming through various parts at random, Hilary had begun to read through it continuously, wanting to gain the full impact of the story as it unfolded historically. And now, as she sat on the train, she resisted the urge to skip ahead to whatever parts might con-cern her more directly, and instead opened the pages to where she had left off in the small hours of the previous night.

She had read of Lady Margaret s reminiscences of her childhood, of her love for the Strathy Valley, her love of riding. She had read of old Digory and his tender, compassionate fond-ness for the young girl. She had read of Maggie's stormy relationship with her father James, and of the caring, yet almost solemn, unspoken love between Maggie and the fascinating yet mysterious and impenetrable Atlanta—a woman who seemed in many ways to hearken back to the lost peoples, lost times, and faded memories of Scotland's silent past.

She read, too, of that fateful day when Maggie left her home, neither herself nor her mother realizing what poignant grief the memory of that parting would later bring to each. Hilary could feel the emotion even as she read the words her grandmother had written.

Then Atlanta, holding the envelope she had prepared, gave it to her daughter. Lady Margaret would never forget her mother's words on that, the last day they would ever see one another: "Maggie," she said, "I want you to take this with you. You need not open it now; you would scarcely grasp its significance if you did. But I want you to have it, in the event that something should happen to me, or in ease you are gone longer than we antici-pate. It is the promise not only for your return but for the safety of this land we love. This will always be your home, whatever happens. Do you understand me? It is yours!" Those final words never faded from Maggie's mind and heart even after forty years of exile.

Joanna then went on to recount, according to the memory of Lady Margaret late in her long life, the separation from her beloved young Ian, the voyage to America, the heartache of loss, the trip west, and many memories of that sad but strengthening time which had for so long remained locked in the heart of the aging woman.

Hilary set down the manuscript, closed her eyes, and tried to imagine what it must have been like for Maggie Duncan, only seventeen years old, newly in love, torn between father and mother and lover, to have been wrenched from her home so violently by events beyond her control.

But the significance of that moment had extended far beyond simply a young girl's leaving home. If nothing else was clearly evident as she read on in this chronicle of a family's heritage, one thing was certain—Stonewycke was *more* than a mere home. Stonewycke and the parcel of earth surrounding it, and all it had come to represent among the people of the region, had grown to the proportion of something almost sacred, pulsating with life. There was nothing that could be considered hallowed in the land or the castle themselves. It was only as God worked in and through them, and gave meaning to places and events by virtue of His greater workings in the hearts of men and women, that Stonewycke began to throb with what seemed a spirit of its own, which was nothing more nor less than God's Spirit himself.

As she wrote, at times, Joanna would pause in her telling of events to reflect on this strange phenomenon of Stonewycke.

How can a piece of real estate, a mere chunk of ground, an ancient castle take on such meaning in a region's life? Sometimes I fear we of this family have elevated the importance of this place all out of proportion. I have at times wondered if God is pleased. But then I recall that it is God himself who has infused this life into Stonewycke, and that it is none other than His life—in us, in our hearts, not in the land itself—which gives rise to these feelings. And in so doing He has indeed put something special here. I had no idea how— when I first came to Strathy as a timid and insecure outsider—this place would draw me into itself.

Lady Margaret often confessed that she felt this love for the land flowed in her blood as if it were part of her cellular makeup itself. Then a look would come over her, and I could almost imagine that she was Maggie again, not my seventy-five-year-old grandmother who had been through so much—a look would come over her of such innocent happiness. She would say, "It is something like the love one has for a child"—and I knew as she spoke, for her eyes said it, that she was thinking of me. "You love that child with all your soul. Yet at the same time you realize she is a gift from God. And surrendering her to Him, your love is not reduced, but made something even greater."

Then again her years would become visible in the far-off gaze of wisdom and maturity in her eyes, and she would say, "It is only as we grasp our possessions to ourselves, without giving Christ lordship over them, that they become millstones instead of blessings. That's why the heritage of Stonewycke never could really pass to my father. He never knew the true Source of life. That is why I have, for these last twenty years, never ceased praying fervently that those who come after me would never lose sight of God's work in and through this place. That, and not we ourselves, is the life that passes down from generation to generation." And at such times I could not but wish I had known her, really known her earlier. Yet God's ways are for the best.

As Hilary paused in her reading, she sighed deeply. Is not that my own response? she wondered. *"If only I had known all this sooner . . . if only I had known her sooner."* How perfectly Joanna's reflections on her grandmother Lady Margaret now expressed Hilary's feelings toward Lady Joanna! Now she was following in her grandmother's footsteps, making this pilgrimage back to the land of her birth, having no inkling what future awaited her.

The land, passed down from generation to generation through a line of stalwart women— still it remained, immovable, silent, enduring. Atlanta was gone. Maggie was gone. Now Lady Joanna was gone. But the land remained the one constant in the turbulent history of this Scottish family. Now she was going there.

But no, Hilary thought suddenly. That wasn't true. The land *wasn't* everything. Lady Joanna had made that clear in what she had written. The land was merely an external manifestation of something deeper. The land, no matter how much it was loved, served only as a stage upon which life was lived and choices were made. It was that life and those choices, as they progressed down through time, adding one upon the other, from son to daughter, from grandmother to granddaughter, which led to Life, or away from it. The ongoing daily choice through the years to live in obedience to God's ways, and to make Stonewycke a citadel to preserve a witness to His goodness—this was the true driving force behind this family.

Lady Joanna's faith was clearly evident. Yet it could be seen as an ongoing expression of the faith of Margaret and Ian Duncan, perhaps even owing a good deal of its vitality to the faithfulness of their prayers. Before them had come Anson Ramsey, of whom only a little was said in the journal, but who seemed a bulwark in the family's fortress of belief in God. There had been ignoble ones, too, who had carried the name Ramsey and Duncan. But as bent as some of them had seemed on assaulting the walls of faith, God seemed always to pull the family up and forward through His obedient ones.

What of her own parents? Hilary wondered. Do they, too, carry the lineage of godliness in their veins? She knew that politically Logan Macintyre was reputed to be a man of integrity and uprightness. Now that she thought about it, hadn't she read a profile on him somewhere about his being a Christian too, occasionally outspoken concerning his beliefs?

Suddenly Hilary thought of her own walk of faith. It was not altogether impossible that she was sitting here as a Christian herself, able to grasp the spiritual significance of Lady Joanna's words, because of something deep within her she had never realized existed. There was certainly nothing in her childhood to have stimulated her toward the Lord and His ways. The belief of her adopted parents was nominal. Her father had been a good man, but he had never attended church or thought about spiritual things. His not uncommon view was that religion was for women. Her mother went halfway regularly to Church of England services, but her motivation came from tradition rather than from any hunger toward God in her heart. If she believed in a personal way, the only indication came at times of stress. There was nothing in Hilary's early home life to have planted the seeds of true personal belief in her heart.

But something had always drawn Hilary toward, and never away from God. Even when she branched out, left home, and entered the highly secular university world, and later the active, modern world of London business, there was always a tug in her heart that spoke of a deeper life. She could not remember a time when she had *not* believed, though over the years that belief matured as she grew—from a vague childlike sense that God cared for her, to the firm adult conviction that the Lord was her intimate friend, guiding the direction of her life.

When those occasional times of doubt and insecurity had come, God had always faithfully provided people to help and support her at the crucial moment.

Was it possible that not only the physical but the spiritual blood from the Ramsey and Duncan lines flowed through her veins? Could it be that the pull of her heart toward God, the hunger she had always felt to make Him her friend and live according to His ways—could those desires be the answer to generations of righteous lives and prayers offered up by her predecessors in this unusual family?

Did God really work that way? she wondered. Could life in the spirit be *passed on*? No, she thought, that could hardly be. Every individual is accountable to God for himself. The choices I make must be mine alone.

Yet . . . there might be some internal predisposition *toward* or *away from* God. What about the blessings and curses of God extending to the third and fourth generation? What about the time-demolishing power of righteous prayer? Was it not a fact in God's kingdom that time was of little consequence, and that prayer was not bound by it?

Had Maggie's and Joanna's prayers reached across time and space and thirty years of separation and . . . touched *her*?

The very thought was too incredible to fathom—that she, all her life, had been, without the slightest awareness, affected in a daily and significant way because of the prayers and spiritual disposition and progenetive strength inherent in the lives of people she had never known!

Hilary sighed again. It was indeed too much to comprehend. Was it possible that during all those years God had been preparing her for this moment? Preparing her for . . .

The half-formed thought trailed away as she let herself be distracted by a scene out the train window. A boy was herding a small flock of sheep over a little grassy knoll, probably heading for the stone byre in the distance. It seemed as if the twentieth century had hardly touched the place. Yet they could not be more than two hundred miles from London.

Then Hilary noted the descending sun. She had been traveling most of the day, so intently reading and deep in thought that she had hardly noticed the passing of miles and hours. She would be in Edinburgh in several hours, and from there it would be north to Aberdeen.

She took off her glasses and rubbed her eyes. When a porter called for dinner, she decided to eat on the train rather than wait. She rose, walked to the dining car, and there enjoyed a meal of broiled perch, squash, and boiled potatoes. She was hungry and did not even mind her talkative table-companion, a retired schoolteacher from York who miraculously managed to keep up a nonstop conversation and still consume a hearty meal.

"Bound for Scotland, you say?" said the woman, dabbing the corners of her mouth with the linen napkin. "Beautiful country, I'm sure, but a bit . . . ah, rustic, is it not? Even nowadays. What did you say was taking you north?"

"Well . . . family, I suppose you would say," answered Hilary with an uncertainty her companion took no note of.

"Funny, you don't have a Scottish accent—though there is a bit of something in your voice that's not entirely London. I've got rather a cunning for this sort of thing. I was in Bangkok last year on a Far East tour and met a couple from America. I guessed right off they were from Pennsylvania, and they were astounded!"

Hilary smiled, and the woman seemed to require no further encouragement to regale her with another half-hour of stories from her travels. Hilary could not help wondering what the touring schoolteacher would think of her story—a classic Dickens tale of a poor East End girl who suddenly discovers herself of noble parentage.

Hilary finally took her leave. When she returned to her own car and walked to her seat. there was the journal, as if it were waiting patiently, allowing her the distraction of dinner but then persistently bidding her return.

Within two hours she had made her northbound connection and was seated again, alone with her thoughts. Outside, the dusk deepened, gradually enveloping the speeding train. Hilary read on.

How clearly I remember that day Dorey invited me to his house—The House, as we were accustomed to calling it—for tea. I was escorted into the banquet hall where the great, long table was all decked out with silver candelabra and bowls of the loveliest of spring flowers, along with the finest china and glassware. And there sat Dorey, looking in some respects so lonely and forlorn, yet, dressed as he was in formal attire, I could immediately see this was no mere gardener. That noble look I had caught in his eyes once or twice now returned full force. . . .

I unfastened my grandmother's gold locket and held it open to him. "This is you, isn't it?" I asked through a knot in my throat. Tears formed in his eyes as he wrapped his fingers around the precious reminder of his youthful love.

"At least there's one thing," he said. "There's you. Perhaps it is true that God is merciful. I thought she was dead. That is what they told me. She, along with the child . . ."

Then the truth began to dawn upon me, though it should have long before this, as it had with Dorey. It was more than I could have dared hope for when I had set foot on that ship in New York harbor as an innocent young girl cast adrift into the world. But I knew in my heart it was true, that here—thousands of miles from what had once been my home—I had found my grandfather!

Quite unexpectedly Hilary found tears rising in her own eyes.

So Lady Joanna did know what she herself was experiencing! Joanna, however, had come to Scotland seeking her roots; Hilary, on the other hand, had stumbled unwittingly, even unwillingly, upon them.

How cruel her ambivalence must have seemed to her grandmother! How desperately Hilary wished she could now repent for all that. Of course, it was too late. Though her present journey would perhaps make up for it somewhat, and in some measure fulfill Lady Joanna's final quest, it would never gain back those precious lost days and hours.

Continuing through the manuscript in her grandmother's careful hand, Hilary learned that Joanna had had many years with her grandparents to recapture lost time. It was clear they were rich years too, for Maggie and Dorey were not only noble in the aristocratic sense, but they carried noble hearts in their breasts, abundant with godly wisdom. For a long span of years Stonewycke stood like a light on the hill, spreading beams of goodness and caring throughout the Strathy Valley.

Even during the depression of the thirties, a kind of peace had pervaded the financially suffering valley. With the recounting of those years, Hilary began to read the story of Allison and Logan.

She read on, not without some trepidation. All of a sudden she herself was part of this compelling saga. She could no longer maintain a distance as she found herself swept up in the drama surrounding Logan's past life and his activities during the war. As with so many who had come before him, he too had felt the peace which dwelt at Stonewycke, eventually surrendering his life to the Creator of that peace. Nor could she keep from a strong identification with her mother—strong-willed, arrogant, confused about her place in this noble family—and it was with not a few tears that she read of Allison's finding her peace too, and of the renewed commitment of love in her parents' marriage following what they assumed to be their only daughter's death.

As a seasoned journalist, Hilary was attentive to the honesty of Lady MacNeil's writing. Though every word was filled with tender love, there was no attempt to whitewash individual weaknesses or to paint a glowing but unrealistic picture of the family. Lady Allison MacNeil Macintyre had clearly been no angel in her youth. *That must be where I come by my own strong will*, Hilary mused with a smile. There were even those who had from time to time actually called her arrogant. *Must run in the genes*, thought Hilary. And she was certainly confused about *her* place in that same family. Maybe her mother would be able to empathize with her struggles in a way no one else could. And now, after reading of her coming to Scotland, Hilary realized how deeply Lady Joanna must truly have grasped her conflicting emotions, much more than she gave her credit for during that first meeting. *If only* . . . Hilary thought, but the rest of the thought was cut short as she reached up to wipe away the lone tear that had begun to fall.

Before long a porter came down the aisle and offered Hilary a pillow. She took it, but any thought of sleep was far away. Nevertheless, as she stuffed it behind her head and leaned back against the window, the alertness of her brain began to flag, succumbing to the effects of being emotionally keyed up all day.

The train droned on, the hours of the evening passing with a kind of dreamy quality—the reality of the journal mingling with snatches of dreams that invaded Hilary's subconscious as she dozed and reawakened over and over.

But always the words of Lady Joanna's *Journal* drew her back without fail. Page after page she read until, coming abruptly to a sheet that did not even seem to complete Lady

Joanna's thought, she realized there was no more. With a deep sense of disappointment, almost of loss, and wondering what had happened to the rest, if there was more, Hilary placed the book in her lap, then laid her head back and closed her eyes.

14 ✸ *The Pan Am Red Eye*

THE DUSK WAS an hour later to descend over Heathrow than it was upon the express coach that sped north from Edinburgh to Aberdeen. Nevertheless, as he made his way across the concrete walkway to the waiting white plane, the solitary traveler shivered as if night had already fully come.

I'll be glad to get out of this miserable hole! he thought. *Fog and rain and cold . . . I hate the place!*

As well he might, judging from his attire, which seemed almost comically out of place. Amid veteran London flyers who pulled heavy wool overcoats, mufflers, and gloves more tightly about them to fend off the November chill, he made his way clad only in a thin white linen suit and a straw hat, which would have done little to keep an August breeze off his graying blond head, much less a bitter winter's blow. Small wonder he was cold. Rather than cursing the weather, one would think he might have dressed more warmly.

The climate would change soon enough, however. He knew that by the time he reached his destination it would likely be 80° or more. It would, in fact, be summertime, and by noon might even reach 100°. Then it would be his turn to laugh at these ridiculous limey businessmen in their tweed overcoats. How they ever won the war, he would never know.

The thought did not console him, however. Rather, it served as a reminder that when the plane touched down, it would be not midday but three or four in the morning, depending on how long their layover in that African vermin preserve lasted.

No wonder they called this the "Red Eye." Every time he took the idiotic flight, it took him days to recover. How bitterly he resented that they always booked him on such low-budget crossings. Sure, he had to make the commute several times a year, but what would a first-class fare hurt once or twice? If anyone might afford it, his boss could.

Carrying only a small metallic briefcase, which he'd declined to check into the plane's baggage hold—"You guard that case with your life," he had been told; "don't so much as let it out of your sight!"—, the man walked up the portable stairway and into the forward compartment of the jet. Without speaking to the stewardess who greeted him, he made his way toward the rear of the plane and found his seat.

He sat down, placed the briefcase on his lap, fastened his seatbelt, then unsnapped the two latches of the case, lifted the lid, and peered inside. What all the fuss was about, he could not for the life of him imagine. How those things could have any value whatsoever was beyond him. And why his boss would entrust something of such potential worth to a couple of imbeciles like Mallory and—what was the name of that lunkhead Mexican or Colombian or wherever in blazes he was from? Chavez . . . Gervez . . . ? What did it matter? They all looked alike anyway, with their dark skin and black hair. Why didn't he just go up to Oxford himself, meet the man they called "The Professor," and then be about his business? Quick and simple. But no. They had to pass the stuff around at night. As if anybody would care enough to tail him!

No doubt there were reasons. There were *always* reasons. As much as he might complain about it inside, he kept doing his duty, and always would. He was still a good soldier who knew which side his bread was buttered on. So though he might inwardly grouse about the system, he would not buck it, for he had become an intrinsic part of it. There were generals and there were corporals. Generals gave orders; corporals obeyed them. It was how things worked.

So he had made his connection with the Texan and the South American and given them the goods, and then had waited. Three days later, Mallory was back at his hotel, handed him the briefcase, and said, "Here you are, pal. The report's inside. The Professor says it all checks out—whatever that means."

What a fool! If he was a corporal, then Mallory was only a private. And as for Galvez—that was it, Galvez!—why, he wouldn't even qualify as that!

Knowing Mallory, he'd probably tried to figure out what was going on from the Professor's report but couldn't read it.

He took out the single sheet of paper from inside the case. Nothing much was there. A few dates, two or three names and addresses, a description of the goods themselves, and estimated antique value.

Slowly he placed the report back inside and closed the case. He hoped this satisfied him. He didn't relish another visit here anytime soon, though before the entire episode could be brought to a conclusion, he would no doubt have to—

His thoughts were immediately curtailed as the taxiing airplane suddenly accelerated toward takeoff. *Well, at least I'll soon be out of this cold*, he thought. The sight of the tarmac speeding by under them with several abandoned hangars in the distance reminded him of the unexpected preflight business that had distracted him an hour earlier. He supposed his boss *did* know what he was doing. As innocent as the whole affair had sounded, somehow he had picked up a tail after all. Well, that was all taken care of now. In another moment he felt the tires leave the runway.

The plane banked around sharply to the left, and was soon climbing to 33,000 feet, on a heading that would take them over Portugal, and then along the western coast of Africa to their refueling stopover. But he would not see anything. It would be dark all the way until just prior to their final touchdown.

15 ❊ *The Bluster 'N Blow*

AS HILARY STEPPED out of her rented Fiat, she could not help wondering how much this scene had changed from that time sixty years ago when her grandmother Joanna had first beheld it.

It was just past one o'clock in the afternoon. She had found a hotel last night in Aberdeen, on Union Street not far from the station. This morning she had rented a car, and then driven the rest of the way to Port Strathy. Now she stood, breathing deeply of the clean salt air, in front of the Bluster 'N Blow.

The sturdy stone walls, clean and smooth from the constant exposure to the sea spray and northern winds, the high windows that, as she recalled from her stay the night before the funeral, let in so little light, the ancient and worn oak tabletops, the huge stone fireplace—it had no doubt changed little in the past hundred years.

Hilary glanced in the opposite direction, down Port Strathy's main street and chief region of commerce. There had been no automobiles when Joanna had arrived; now a half dozen or ten of varying ages and makes could be seen. Yes, times had changed. Yet here she stood, just as had Joanna so long ago—equally uncertain about how to proceed, with her future before her, wondering what it might possibly hold.

Well, Hilary thought to herself, *this is my story, not Joanna's. It's a different world now, a different Stonewycke. I may as well see what awaits me. . . .*

With these thoughts, and the realization that her own part of whatever story lay ahead would never find its way into Joanna's journal, Hilary turned back toward the inn, and walked inside.

A Mr. Fraser Davies ran the Bluster 'N Blow these days—a likable fellow in his late fifties, soft-spoken and almost genteel in his manner. Hilary knew little about him, however, for she had studiously avoided unnecessary encounters with the local folk during her previous visit. This time she purposed to be a little more friendly.

No one was present in the lobby, if such could be called the rustic entryway, with its oak halltree and single padded bench. Toward one side opened the expansive Common Room filled with tables and benches. Straight ahead a flight of stairs wound to the first floor. She set down her luggage and tapped at the bell on the desk. Before long its sharp note brought a response.

Wiping his damp hands on a dishcloth, Mr. Davies strode with easy, unhurried steps in through a door behind the counter, which Hilary assumed led to the kitchen.

"Good afternoon to you, miss," he said. "Can I help you?" His tone carried a definite Scottish burr on its edges, yet there was at the same time a certain refinement in his soft voice. He paused, seeming to study her for a moment, until recognition dawned. "Why, 'tis Miss Edwards, isn't it? I remember you from last month, though I didn't get to see much of you, I'm sorry to say."

"Yes, Mr. Davies. You're right, I'm back," answered Hilary. "And I'd like a room, though I'm afraid I don't have a reservation again."

"Hoots! You won't be needing one this time of year. Don't think I'd know what to do with a reservation if it jumped out at me."

Hilary laughed, but Davies went right on.

"We were a bit busier than usual then on account of the funeral, you know, but a full house of guests is hardly the norm around here. It'll pick up some years at the Yuletide, then not again till spring. But today, Miss Edwards, you may have your pick of any room in the place."

He brought out a thick black ledger-book from underneath the counter. "Just sign here," he said, flipping the pages open.

Hilary saw that there had been only two other guests to stay at the inn since she had last signed. She jotted her signature and address on the next empty line, while Davies sorted through a box of keys.

"Here you go," he said, handing her one on a round brass ring. "Same room as last time, if that suits you."

"That would be fine, Mr. Davies. Thank you."

He hurried out from behind the desk, took her two pieces of luggage, and led the way up the stairs behind him to her room. Hilary was relieved he was not an inquisitive man, or at least too polite to probe about her present business in Port Strathy. He merely opened her door, set her cases down inside, and asked if she would be wanting a late luncheon.

"Yes, that would be nice," answered Hilary. "Perhaps just a bowl of soup and a slice or two of fresh bread, if you have it."

Davies nodded, then left Hilary alone, pulling the door closed behind him.

As Hilary kicked off her shoes and lay back on the clean, soft bed, she could not keep her mind from straying to Lady Joanna's first stay at the Bluster 'N Blow. What a shock it must have been, as shy and retiring as she was then, to have gone back downstairs that first evening of her stay to discover that the conversation among the men concerned none other than herself. How mortifying to find that she was the center of local speculations!

Port Strathy had grown considerably since then, boasting a population of some 1,600 today, compared to the 750 back in 1911 when Joanna had arrived via hay wagon over the hills from Northhaven. Fortunately, thought Hilary, my own arrival seems to have gone completely unnoticed by everyone except the innkeeper.

Without realizing it, Hilary soon dozed off. When she awoke, she found herself feeling uncharacteristically timorous as she freshened up and prepared to descend the stairs to the Common Room. Had Joanna's ghost visited her while she slept, leaving a dose or two of timidity behind as a reminder of that earlier time? But no knot of gossiping Scotsmen greeted her. Instead, a cheery fire burned in the hearth, warming the room furnished with a half dozen or so old English style dining tables with their high-backed benches. Mr. Davies was the only one present in the room and was blowing the fire to life with a small hand-held leather bellows. He heard Hilary's step and turned to give her a friendly smile.

"Hello, Miss Edwards. I was wondering what became of you." He hung the bellows up on a hook over the hearth.

"I'm afraid I fell asleep," replied Hilary.

"No harm done. The soup's still warm."

"Oh, thank you. It will feel good."

"Nothing like it on a day like today. There's a storm brewing up out there. The temperature's already dropped ten degrees since you arrived."

"I hadn't even noticed. But now that you mention it, I suppose it is a bit chilly."

"You get attuned to such things when you live in a fishing village. Here the weather can make or break a man. You're from London, if I recall?"

"Yes. As you might expect, I've had very little experience with country life."

"I do understand. My own background is certainly not agrarian either."

"I thought I detected a hint of refinement in your voice," said Hilary.

Davies laughed. "A shrewd bit of detective work! But after twenty-five years in Strathy, I am probably in danger of losing all vestiges of my former life. A life, I might add, quite different from this one."

"You intrigue me. I'll have to probe that mystery later. Did you take over the inn from Sandy Cobden?"

"Ay! That I did. You know some of our history, do you?"

"Not as much as I'd like to."

Davies grinned and his brown eyes twinkled eagerly. "Don't be saying such a thing if you're not meaning it, miss!" he chuckled. "I've been known to bore the socks off many an unsuspecting traveler who offered me less of an invitation than that."

"But I *am* interested," said Hilary. "I'm a reporter. I wouldn't be surprised if there's potential here for an interesting story."

"If you don't mind me asking, is that what has brought you to our little town?"

"Not exactly, but I certainly wouldn't ignore a good story if one should come along."

"Whom do you write for?"

"*The Berkshire Review.*"

"Ay. I've read it. You must be the editor then, now that I put the names together."

Small town innkeepers were hardly the *Review*'s prime market. Yet she should not have expected anything to meet normal specifications in this unique town.

"That's right. I really would love to learn whatever of the Bluster 'N Blow's history you'd care to tell me."

"Let me get your soup, and then I can lecture to your heart's content."

Davies turned and disappeared into the kitchen, returning in a few minutes with a tray bearing a large bowl of steaming potato soup, along with several generous slabs of hearty brown bread. But it was the pot of hot tea served afterward which Hilary enjoyed most, for Davies, with her "kind permission," brought another cup and sat down to join her.

"I don't mind saying," he began, stirring cream and sugar into his tea, "that I love this old inn. That's why I go on and on so about it at the least provocation. It seems to hold the heritage of the town together in a way, almost as much as the castle up on the hill."

"Well, if you don't mind my saying," said Hilary, "though you do a wonderful job of it, you somehow don't fit my expectations of a small village innkeeper."

She paused and sipped her tea. "You remind me instead of a museum curator I once interviewed," she went on. "There's a kind of reverence in your manner, as if this place means more to you than a building to get a glass of ale and rent a bed."

Davies smiled, obviously taking Hilary's observation as a compliment. "You are a very astute judge of character, I must say. The Bluster 'N Blow is much more to me than that. All the more that I nearly did not measure up to its standards, precisely because of my un-innkeeper-like character."

"Do you mean it took a while for the townsfolk to accept you? I take it you had a city background?"

"It wasn't the townsfolk themselves as much as the laird himself, or old Doc Alec, as the people still called him all his life, God rest his soul."

"Oh?" Hilary arched an eyebrow. What could there have been in this gentle-appearing man for her grandfather not to approve of?

"You see, Lady Joanna and Doc Alec were looking for a different sort after Sandy died. More the type you were expecting, I think." He paused for a swallow of tea. "Sandy left no heirs, so it fell to Doc Alec to find someone to run the place. He wanted—how should I put it?—an earthy sort, a humble farm type. Maybe a local man and wife whom the people already knew, whom he could be sure would keep the traditions of the place alive. I was an Assistant Professor at King's College in Aberdeen at the time, and I hardly fit the bill. They were wary of having an intellectual. They didn't think the local folk would accept me. Fortunately my years on the school debating team served me well, and I was able to convince them to give me a try."

"How did you change their minds?"

"My love of history helped, along with changes in my heart following the war. I suppose the same thing was happening to many returning soldiers. Priorities change, and the meaning of life changes too. For me, I found that the cloistered life of the university no longer had its former appeal. Oh, there are advantages to a life in the city. But the older I grew the more my childhood roots began to beckon me. Having come from a family of innkeepers, I had always harbored a dream of one day retiring from teaching to operate an inn. Well, when I chanced to hear about the status of the Bluster 'N Blow, I asked myself, 'Why not now?' So I took an early retirement from the university, and embarked on a second career. The cream on the cake is that this inn is a veritable heaven for a lover of history such as myself. I believe the MacNeils were finally able to see this love in me, and to see that part of my vision for the inn was to preserve its historical integrity."

Davies paused to refill their cups. "So your curator analogy is actually quite apt."

"Does the estate control all of Port Strathy, then?"

"Of course at one time all the lands, even the environs of the town were owned by the estate and governed by it," answered Davies, growing more comfortable now that the conversation had shifted from his own history to that of the region. "Over time, however, the control of the various properties was gradually released, probably for economic reasons. Then in 1911, Lady Margaret and Lady Joanna, in a decision that quickly became local legend and endeared the family to everyone in the area even more than before, relinquished a huge portion of the land, granting full ownership to the individual resident crofters."

"But the inn was excluded from this?"

"The Ramsey and Duncan clan never exactly owned the inn. Through the years it has exercised a controlling influence over major transactions and changes in ownership. The family has retained this authority, as I mentioned in my own case, right up to this present day. But the inn is actually owned by its individual operator. The Bluster 'N Blow has always operated on its own charter. Back in 1741 Colin Ramsey deeded the property that was to become the site of the inn to his friend, Archibald Munro, to whom he owed a certain debt of gratitude. But no Ramsey, except the Ladies Margaret and Joanna, ever gave away a chunk of their land without attaching strong conditions. Such was especially true back in the eighteenth century. That was just four years before the '45, you know—significant times in Scotland's history!" He paused, grinning sheepishly at his tendency to stray from the point.

"But as I was saying," he continued, "Colin's motives may have been purely economical, for, besides the land, he invested a large portion of cash in his friend's project. Thus, a provision was written into the title that should the inn pass from the hands of Munro's direct descendants, the estate maintained the power to choose the new owner, or, if expedient, to reclaim the property. The family has exercised that right ever since, but I think Lady Atlanta Duncan was the first to use that prerogative for purely aesthetic purposes. She cared a great deal for the land, not only for its economic yield, but also for the heritage bound up in the land in and of itself. That devotion has passed down through the generations ever since."

"And Lady Joanna wanted to be certain that the character of her beloved valley did not change," said Hilary thoughtfully. Even as she said the words the memory of her grandmother's face rose into her mind from that day they met in her London office.

"Changes cannot be avoided," Davies went on like the historian he was, "and Lady Joanna knew it. She wasn't adverse to change as such; the transfer of the property gave evidence of that. She wanted to see Port Strathy prosper, and in the twentieth century, you can't remain static and prosper too. The coming of new times has brought new economic demands on landowners. But the Bluster 'N Blow is a landmark, though you won't find it in any tour book. And that is what she wanted to preserve—the sense of history. I mean, if the London Bridge can be sold to an American, anything can happen in this day and age."

Davies drained off the last of his tea, then smiled at Hilary. "If you're not completely bored, you might be interested in seeing my pride and joy."

"With pleasure," said Hilary.

They rose, and he led the way to the back wall of the Common Room, which Hilary had not noticed before. Hanging on the wall was a series of finely carved wooden plaques, each boasting engraved gold plates underneath, one plaque honoring all of the various owners of the inn all the way back to Archibald Munro. Below, framed in glass, was a brief written history of each owner with a pen-and-ink drawing of his likeness.

"This is wonderful!" exclaimed Hilary. "And you did all of this?"

"I had a time of it with some of my predecessors, of whom I had only a name and vague hearsay as to their looks and physical features. But I felt from the very beginning that my job here entailed more than simply providing food and beds."

Hilary was still examining the wall as he spoke. "Queenie Rankin . . ." she mused aloud. "Why, she's just as I imagined her!"

"You do know more than the average person about our little corner of the world, Miss Edwards!" Davies was both pleased and curious.

"Yes . . . I suppose that's true," was all Hilary could think to reply.

"But I don't recall ever seeing you here before the funeral."

"No, I . . . that is . . . well—" but she broke off, flustered, and unable to come up with a quick lie.

"I'm sorry, Miss Edwards," Davies said quickly. "I didn't mean to pry. Please forgive me."

"An apology is not necessary, Mr. Davies. I've been plying you with enough questions, you're surely entitled to a few." Then, because she could think of no reason not to, Hilary added, "I met Lady Joanna recently. She showed me a journal she had kept about the history . . . of her family."

"Ah . . . you've seen her journal." He spoke as if that suddenly placed an indelible bond between them. "It's wonderful, is it not? She honored me, though she would never think of it in those terms, by showing me it also. I've done a bit of writing—nothing important, just university papers—and she wanted advice. She also felt it would help me in this endeavor," he added, gesturing toward the wall.

They were silent a few moments and Hilary returned her attention to the wall. At last she saw the final plaque. It was of Davies himself. But the moment her eyes rested upon it, he began to shuffle awkwardly, giving an embarrassed cough or two.

"I know it must seem a bit presumptuous . . . " he began.

"No," said Hilary. "You are part of this now, and always will be. Not only do you deserve a spot on this wall, but it is your duty to take your place alongside the others."

No sooner had she spoken the words than Hilary realized their application to herself as well as the innkeeper. Like Davies, she was also intrinsically being drawn into something greater than herself. It had begun to come into focus on the train, and now the feeling returned even more forcefully. Being here, standing on the very land that had been in the family of her ancestors for so many generations, so many centuries, she saw more clearly than ever the depth of love, the yearning Lady Joanna had held in her heart toward her—not only as a granddaughter returned from the dead, but also as an integral part of the Stonewycke heritage.

And Hilary was also a link to the *future* of that legacy. Perhaps she would not find her way into Joanna's journal, but might she not be able to do something to help keep the tale which had flowed from Joanna's pen alive for future generations? Might there be a role for her to play in the ongoing story of Stonewycke?

Suddenly, even as she chatted distractedly with Mr. Davies, Hilary knew that she had indeed not come here by accident, that she was not being swept into this saga by mere chance. As a knot tightened within her, she knew that the course of her future had suddenly all changed. She knew there could be no halfway measures. As there had been a Lady Atlanta, Lady Margaret, Lady Joanna, and Lady Allison—so too must there one day be a *Lady Hilary* as well.

Feeling all at once detached and unreal, in a shambling way Hilary thanked the innkeeper as politely as possible, and broke off her conversation. Her voice sounded strangled in her own ear, and she could feel her heart pounding hard in her chest. A hot sweat broke out over her forehead and her knees began to shake.

Hilary had never fainted in her life. Even in the violent jungles of Vietnam, she had kept her wits about her. But she had never felt this kind of lightheaded sensation, and before she made a complete fool of herself, she realized she had to get outside and into some fresh air.

16 ❈ *Uninvited Thoughts*

HILARY STEPPED FROM the door of the Bluster 'N Blow and inhaled a deep draught of the chilly air.

A storm was indeed brewing. The wind off the North Sea whipped at her face and easily penetrated the thickness of her Shetland wool sweater. It quickly restored her equilibrium and forced a thread of practicality into her distraught mind. But still she could not go back, even for her coat.

Gray waves slammed fiercely against the smooth sand that stretched out in front of her before giving way to the rocky shoal at the far end of the promontory in the distance. Overhead the sky was a solid gray mass with little variation of color, except along the distant horizon where a black bank of sinister looking clouds portended the approaching rain. And judging from the wind, coming relentlessly from offshore, the clouds were heading this way and would arrive some time that night.

This northern coast of Scotland was wild and unpredictable. She vaguely remembered Mr. Davies telling her at the end of their conversation that a storm of hurricane proportions had nearly brought down the entire inn over a hundred years ago. Glancing behind her, the inn seemed as solid as the rocky coast upon which it was built. She peered back at the sea, raging in good earnest now, and then toward the harbor. All the boats were tied securely, but that could hardly keep their masts from bobbing up and down and sideways in a frantic symphony of windy, wavy motion.

She began walking along the shoreline toward the harbor. With the physical exertion came some relief from the cold. Her head felt clear now, and it was refreshing to fight against the elements.

Yes, this was a glorious land. She had thought so when she had come twelve days earlier. She had walked along this same beach then too, when the weather had been calmer. She supposed they even swam here in the summertime. What a land of contrasts! It all looked so different now. Not because of the storm. It looked different to her *inner* eyes—the difference between gazing upon an image in a mirror and finally beholding the real thing. Now this wild, beautiful, gray, green, rugged expanse of coastline meant something to her that it never could have before the journal.

Everything was suddenly changed. Now there were so many others whose presence she felt, others who had walked this same way once, others whose feet had passed over this same sand, others whose very blood was part of her own makeup. How many times had young Lady Margaret walked, or more likely ridden her magnificent black Raven along this very shore? And Joanna, too, had come here for consolation during those dark days before she discovered who she was. And here, probably within sight of where Hilary now stood, she had also met her dear Alec.

Once more—the comparisons seemed so frequent lately—Hilary found herself following in her grandmother's footsteps, and seeking the solitude of the sea. Now it was her turn to find consolation, to wrestle with quandaries too complex for the conscious mind to fathom, to ask questions that seemed to have no answers . . . and perhaps—as her predecessors had learned to do during their times of trouble—also to pray.

The truth of her birth had suddenly been laid bare. Not just who she was; she had known that simple fact for three weeks. Now there was much more to face. Now it was a matter of what it all meant.

She had been prepared to accept Logan and Allison Macintyre as her parents. Once the initial shock of Lady Joanna's revelation had sunk in, there had even come a dawning thrill at the thought of being a member of such a fascinating family. Even while reading Joanna's journal, as many tears as that reading had evoked, she had managed to keep a small part of her heart detached from the implications of it all.

But she had not, until standing there in front of Mr. Davies' special wall, realized what membership in this family would mean . . . to her. For just as the heritage of the Bluster 'N Blow had been passed down, though not by blood, from owner to owner, so too the legacy of Stonewycke was no mere static legend that could be relegated merely to the pages of some dusty and archaic journal. It was a living, breathing, ongoing inheritance that went beyond times, places, wills, houses, and earthly possessions. It was a legacy that pulsated with life from generation to generation—a legacy made real, made alive, made imperative, and made inescapable by the journal and the lives of which it told.

Hilary's mind went back to Joanna's note which had been tucked inside the journal. Her grandmother had hoped that Hilary's reading of the words she had written would help her ". . . find your own place within the family." Now at last she discerned what Lady Joanna had truly meant with those seemingly simple words.

And suddenly—strong, decisive, woman of the world that she was—Hilary found herself afraid.

It was not merely the thought of her becoming a member of the so-called aristocracy. That certainly would involve a shock to her system. But it could be dealt with, ignored even if she wished. Surely times of great soul-searching were bound to come in that regard, but it was not that which troubled her most at this moment.

On her mind instead was her innocent conversation with the innkeeper. It had to do with walls and plaques and histories and landmarks, with this shoreline and town, with boats bobbing in the water and the homey little cottages she had passed on her way into town.

Even more than these things, it had to do with people . . . with four incredible women—those women who had fought and suffered and wept and prayed for this land. And had loved it beyond human understanding.

It had to do with the frightening, terrifying, bewildering realization that she was one of them. Fear . . . because she was *not* like them.

She did not love this land the way they did. Yes, the coast was grand, the mountains, the rivers, the Highlands more scenic than anywhere in Britain. Its villages were quaint. Its history was colorful and intriguing. But the depth of *feeling*, of personal devotion, was simply not in her. How could it be? She possessed more affection for the grimy tenements of the East End than she felt for this coastal fishing village, however lovely it might be.

Couldn't she become part of the family and forget the rest? Couldn't she simply slip in, as it were, unnoticed, without a fuss? Besides, there were other grandchildren who might feel ill-used, being so abruptly usurped from their position. If her parents were the kind of people she imagined them to be after her meeting with Lady Joanna, they would surely be able to understand that she was not equipped for anything more. She could never stand tall enough to rank alongside the memory of her predecessors as being in the direct line of heirs. In fact, stranger that she was, they might not even want or expect such of her.

Everything practical, everything logical, told her that such reasoning was right. No one would . . . no one could expect it.

Yet all logic was swept immediately away with the overpowering memory of Lady Joanna's face that day in her office. As that face rose before her mind's eye, something deeper than she could hope to explain with mere words stirred to life within Hilary's heart. Could it be only her imagination, or was there indeed more behind the sensitive features of that face than the simple joy of finding her granddaughter?

Hilary kicked at the sand under her feet. She had walked well beyond the harbor and now stopped and looked again toward the sea. The gray of the sky had already changed. The black clouds were halfway toward the shore, continuing to tumble over one another as they grew larger and larger. However, behind them, faint hints of deep orange and purple now smeared along the horizon. Somehow the rays of the setting sun had managed to penetrate the thick cover. It would be a lovely, fierce, short-lived sunset that would give way within the hour to the approaching blackness. In the distance, though she wondered if her eyes were deceiving her, she thought she spied a small sloop trying to make the harbor, in spite of the elements seemingly bent on preventing its success.

Hilary looked back toward the town, the inn, the houses of gray stone that all seemed impervious to the perils of wind and wave and rain. Here she was! This was not London. She was in Port Strathy, at the very gates of Stonewycke itself. A decision must be made. She had been so certain of her course of action on the train, so sure of what she must do. She could not now get cold feet and turn around again! But could she do it . . . did she have the inner strength it would require to stand before that imposing place, to knock on the door, and say . . .

What would she say to them? If only there were some other way!

Hilary sighed. There was no other way. All the questions were really unnecessary. She knew what she must do. She had given her word to Lady Joanna. What became of it, she could not know that. But she would present herself to her parents. That much she knew. She had to . . . she wanted to.

Hilary bowed her head. It was time to do what she had done all too seldom of late.

"Dear Father," she prayed quietly, her voice making barely a sound in the lashing wind, "give me courage to step into the future you have marked out for me. None of this was of my design. I know your hand is in it all. Forgive me for forgetting. I know you must have been preparing each of us for this moment. Help me to be receptive to whatever your will for me is. Help me to follow as you lead."

She exhaled a deep breath, then turned sharply back toward town and began walking crisply forward. It was time to face her destiny.

17 ❄ *Unsought Heroism*

AS HILARY STRODE through the wind, it was clear evening was descending. Approaching the harbor, she now saw clearly what she had taken for a phantom a few minutes earlier: a small boat was indeed making for the dock. But with every dip into one of the troughs between the waves, it was lost to sight and she feared it would capsize any moment.

Before even thinking why she did so, Hilary broke into a run. Reaching the harbor area, she ran onto the nearest dock, then out toward the end. On either side of her were moored boats of all sizes and shapes, securely tethered, yet making a racket as the incoming waves beat against their sides. Hilary slowed, struggling to keep her feet on the swaying dock.

She could see the little boat clearly now. Its single sail flapped furiously in the gale, and the man sitting astern could barely manage to keep her from tipping, with his right hand on the rudder and his left attempting to keep the sail in position. In front of him, on the floor of the tiny sloop, sat a small girl. She couldn't have been more than seven, and the terror in her face was visible even from the distance where Hilary stood.

On they came, slowly, yet inching ever closer to the outermost railing to which the man might secure his fragile craft. Hilary stood, as one helpless, wanting to help, yet without so much as a rope she might throw them when they got closer. Every wave seemed intent on destroying any hope of survival, but the look on the man's face told of an equal determination to triumph in the struggle.

As he crested a small swell, the man saw Hilary on the dock. The mere sight of another human being, helpless though she was, seemed to fill him with hope, and he wrestled all the more powerfully against the stubborn rudder.

"Come on! You've almost made it!" shouted Hilary. Her voice sounded thin and weak in the midst of the gale.

"We'll try to throw ye a rope!" shouted the man in return. "Hang on to it for dear life!"

He spoke to his daughter, who then crept onto her knees and made her way to the front of the craft, laid hold of a bunched rope, then knelt. Swinging it as mightily as her tiny frame would permit, she let loose the rope in Hilary's direction.

But Hilary did not have the chance to see whether it would have reached her, or whether with it she might have helped attach it to the mooring. For the moment the girl's arm was outspread, a gust of wind took evil hold of the sail. The boat lurched violently, and the seaman's tiny daughter was thrown overboard into the angry sea. All thought of the rope was suddenly gone.

"The lass canna swim!" cried the father in a despairing voice, half rising.

But even before he had the chance to act, Hilary instinctively knew that if he so much as took his hand from the rudder for an instant, he would lose his boat to the sea. Without further thought Hilary plunged into the icy water.

A huge white-tipped wave crashed over her head the moment she regained the surface. Sputtering, she tried to grope her way through the turbulent waves toward where she thought the child had gone under. All about was only water—freezing, churning water. She tried to swim, but her body was tossed about and she was powerless to resist it. Another wave doused her, and as she felt herself sinking beneath it, her feet kicked something solid.

All she could think of was the child, though in her benumbed state she could hardly make her arms and legs obey. She struggled to the surface, took a huge gulp of air, then plunged under in the direction from which she had come. Down she went, with eyes closed, thrashing madly with her arms.

There it was again! Her hands felt something . . . something soft . . . yes! It was the girl!

Wildly Hilary grasped at the invisible form, clutching at the girl's clothing, kicking her own feet, trying to swim back to the surface. But, oh! the cold! Her hands were numb now, so numb she could no longer tell whether she still held the child. All about was darkness. She could see nothing. The wild windy gale began to grow distant in her ears. She squeezed her fingers tightly around . . . around what? She could no longer feel anything. With arms outspread she reached out . . . then she felt the burden go from her grasp. Her fingers relaxed . . . the girl was gone.

In mingled despair and a sense of finally giving in to the powerful elements, her body relaxed. All sound ceased. She could no longer feel the thrashing of the waves over her. The cold was gone now too. A strange peace began to steal over her. Out of the blackness, in the distance she perceived a tiny light. Larger now, it was coming toward her . . . a single light surrounded by blackness. Light . . . and warmth . . . and blackness . . . and then a soft voice, approaching her. And then Hilary knew no more.

When wakefulness began slowly again to invade Hilary's consciousness, it was with a continuation of the same vague sensations. While her eyes were yet closed, she was aware that she lay in a darkened room. As she lifted her eyelids a crack, in what looked to be the distance, but was in reality but a few feet, she saw a light approaching, a flickering light.

Closer it came. From it warmth seemed to be coming. This was just like the dream she had had before falling asleep . . . if she had fallen asleep! Maybe she was dead! A figure stood behind the light! It grew larger. She struggled to rise. A voice spoke. She felt a hand pressing her gently back down where she lay. She looked at the light again. It was something she recognized. It was . . . it was . . .

It was a candle! Of course. She could see it now. A woman stood beside her holding a candle. She was speaking, though she had not heard the actual words until now as they gradually began to sift through her mental fog.

" . . . lie still, dearie. Jist lie back . . . "

The gentle woman's voice soothed her. Slowly she began to take in her surroundings. Beyond the candle in the woman's hand, a soft glow and a deliciously radiant sense of heat was coming from a stone hearth that held a bright but subdued fire. The room in which she lay was a small one; it contained no other furnishings besides the bed, which was of a most peculiar composition but comfortable enough. The ceiling was low, and seemed once to have been painted in something resembling white but had over the years darkened considerably, no doubt from the smoke, not all of which, Hilary's nose now told her, managed to escape up the chimney. She lay, in dry bedclothes, beneath several layers of heavy quilts. The entire result was one of dreamy well-being, though Hilary hadn't a clue where she might be.

Her attendant saw wakefulness coming back into her eyes, and spoke again.

"I hope ye dinna mind bein' here yer lain, miss," she said. " 'Tis the best spot we had where we thocht ye'd be comfortable."

"Yes . . . yes, this is very nice," Hilary managed to reply, though her voice sounded weak.

"Ye see, my man he built this extra room some years back. I hope ye dinna hae objection to a peat fire an' a bed whose mattress be naethin' but the stems o' dried heather. 'Tis the auld Scottish way, I alloo, but folks like us, we grow accustomed to the auld ways."

"It's wonderful," said Hilary, forcing a smile. "I can't remember when I've slept so well."

"Nae doobt!" exclaimed the woman. "Ye gave us quite a scare. 'Tis little wonder ye slept so sound; ye was maist likely deid, or so I thocht, when my man broucht ye here in his ain arms, hangin' limp an' wet ye was. Oh, dearie, my heart warms to see ye lookin' at me oot o' them big blue eyes o' yers!" She leaned over the bed and gave Hilary an unexpected kiss on the cheek.

"But, I don't understand . . . " said Hilary. "Where am I?"

"Ye're in the but-end o' oor tiny hoose," answered the woman with a laugh. "Ye're aboot a mile oot o' Strathy, where my husband brocht ye last night. Brocht ye wi' tales o' heroism t' tell me o' yer leapin' into the sea, an'—"

Suddenly the events of the past evening came back into Hilary's memory.

"And the little girl?" she said in alarm.

"Oor little Kerrie's jist fine. She's sleepin' noo too, in the ben-end, and none the worse fer her spill. An' 'tis you yersel' we've got t' thank fer her very life! But I'm fergettin' my manners. The name's Frances MacKenzie."

She thrust a fleshy hand toward where Hilary lay in the bed.

"Hilary Edwards," replied Hilary as she took it. She felt as though her entire hand were swallowed up in the grasp of the hardy woman's affectionate handshake. "I'm from London."

"Ah, winna my little Kerrie be plumb beside hersel'! The first thing she'll ask is if ye ken Prince Charles."

Hilary laughed.

"She cuts oot his picture frae the magazines, an' can tell ye all aboot when his grandmother stayed in Port Strathy. Though 'tis mysel' who should be tellin' ye that. I was here, ye see, an' 'twas my ain aunt she visited wi' Lady Joanna frae the Hoose. Jist yonder, o'er the valley a couple o' miles. Oh, we didna talk aboot anythin' else fer days an' weeks on end!"

Just then the door opened. In walked a large man whom Hilary immediately recognized. Squinting in the dim light, he spoke softly to his wife.

"Is the lass still sleepin'?" Then as his eyes grew accustomed to the room, he saw that she was awake and looking at him.

"Ah, lass," he said, "I'm right glad to see ye lookin' so fit! Karl MacKenzie, at yer service, mem," he added.

"Oor guest's name is Hilary," said Mrs. MacKenzie. "Hilary Edwards . . . all the way frae London!"

"London, ye say! Weel, that is some way. But I'm jist heartened ye was on the Port Strathy dock last night, mem."

"What happened?" said Hilary. "I can hardly remember—"

"I was a fool, that's what happened!" interrupted MacKenzie in a passionate voice. "A blamed fool fer thinkin' I could take the lass oot fer a ride in the new boat wi' the storm comin' like that!"

He began to stride around the room. "What would o' come o' us if ye hadna come along, lass, I darena think!" he went on, wringing his hands.

"I hardly was much help," offered Hilary.

"Na, mem, 'tisna true! Ye leaped into that water wi'oot thocht fer yer ain safety. When I saw wee Kerrie go ower into the water—"

He stopped abruptly, hiding his face for a moment in his hands.

"Then before I could think what was to be done," he went on, "into the water ye went, divin' an' swimmin' aroun' till ye got yer hands on the wee bairn an' pulled her up an' tried yer best to hand her to me. I managed to get Kerrie back into the boat. An' though I couldna lift ye, I got the rope tied aboot one o' yer arms. In but anither two or three swells I was crashin' in against the edges o' the dock. I had but to get Kerrie oot o' the boat an' pull yersel' in an' then lug ye oot o' the water an' carry ye both t' the truck."

"What about your boat?" asked Hilary in a concerned voice. "Were you able to save it?"

"Hank Shaw was jist comin' outta the inn. He saw ye run oot an' jump in after the bairn. He came as fast as he could, wi' a couple o' men besides. They pulled the boat into the harbor while I was tryin' me best t' get ye back here where my wife could love the life back into ye."

"I'm so grateful," said Hilary with a sigh. "You're both too kind."

"Hoots, Miss Edwards!" exclaimed Mrs. MacKenzie. "Ye saved oor Kerrie's life! What's too kind alongside that?"

"Well, in any case, I should be getting back to the inn."

"Nonsense!" exclaimed Mrs. MacKenzie. "Yer clathes arena yet dry. An' ye already spent the night wi' us. A few more hours willna matter."

"But Mr. Davies will wonder what became of me."

"My man's already been to tell him. An' I winna hear o' yer leavin' wi'oot joining us for midday dinner."

"We'd be honored, Miss Edwards," added her husband. "An' we'd be pleased if ye'd consider makin' this humble room yer home so long as ye hae business in Port Strathy."

Hilary thought for a moment, then smiled up at the sweet couple from where she lay. "It is I who would be honored," she said at last. "I would love to have dinner with you."

"And the room?"

"I don't know how long my business in Port Strathy will last. I have but one urgent matter to attend to, and that I must do, possibly this afternoon. Beyond that, I have no plans. But I will most gratefully consider your offer."

"Thank ye, Miss Edwards," replied Mr. MacKenzie, "'tis all we can ask o' ye."

"Then I'll ask one more thing of you, if you don't mind," said Hilary.

"Anythin'."

"You must call me Hilary."

The two nodded their smiling agreement, then turned and left her alone. As they exited the room, Hilary closed her eyes, a great contentment stealing over her. Something inside had begun to change, though Hilary herself hardly was aware of it yet. A gap had begun to be bridged, vague and undefined though it might be, in her heart.

The God of her forefathers was slowly drawing her into the life of this valley, softening a corner of her heart toward these simple Scottish folk from whom her ancestors had come.

18 ❈ Allison and Logan

ALLISON MACINTYRE, NOW matriarchal head of the Stonewycke household, carried a silver tray of tea into the family parlor. The warmth emanating from the bright fire in the hearth felt good, especially after making her way through the chilly corridors from the kitchen. Pushing aside a copy of the *Daily Mirror* and two or three magazines, she set the tray on the low table in front of the sofa.

"I see you have given up on the newspaper," she said with a sympathetic smile.

Logan, who had been reclining on the sofa, leaned forward and helped her arrange the tray.

He gave a disdainful glance toward the *Mirror*. "I don't know what is worse," he said, "when they rake Roy and the rest of us over the coals or when they do it to Harold."

"At least it's over now," Allison replied. She poured steaming tea into two china cups. "The vote is done and everyone can move on to other matters."

"If only it were that simple," sighed her husband.

"It's not?"

"I had a call from Roy this morning. I didn't have a chance to mention it to you yet. You were busy with your painting, and I was out looking over that acreage with Ferguson."

"What did Roy have to say?"

"He said Harold laid out a pretty uncompromising agenda for repairing the so-called party split. Went public with it yesterday. No more maverick voting, no more abstentions. When the debate begins on the separate clauses of the Market legislation, we had better all toe the line. That sort of thing. In essence, he expects us to undo all we have risked so much for in the first place. At least that's how it looks to me."

"Surely he knows you better than to think you'd agree?"

"Roy is going along with him, and so are many of the others. I suppose if it hadn't been for Mother's death, Harold would be extracting a decision from me by now too."

Allison handed him a cup and saucer.

"Thank you, Ali," he said, laying his hand over hers and smiling.

She picked up a spoon from the tray to stir her tea. Suddenly it dropped from her hand with a clatter.

"How clumsy of me!" she exclaimed in frustration, clasping her right hand with her left and rubbing it. "I don't know what's wrong with me lately!"

"Here, let me take a look."

"No, no, it's fine. But I've been doing this too much this last week. A couple of my fingers have been numb." She rubbed at her troubled right hand as if trying to stimulate the feeling back into it.

"Why don't we have Connally take a look at it?"

"I'm sure it's nothing but the cold. Still, I don't like it."

"Maybe you're right," said Logan good-naturedly. "Winter is coming on, you know."

"I'm sure that's it," agreed Allison, sounding far from convinced. "It wouldn't be so bad if I had more energy. But I just haven't been myself recently."

"So tell me," Logan went on, making an attempt to cheer up his wife, "how did your day go? I haven't seen you since morning."

"Oh, it's been a pleasant day. We painted some."

"She's turning you into a regular artist!"

"I don't know about that. But after all this time it's nice to have something to share, interests in common. And then did I tell you about Patty Doohan?"

"No, what?"

"She became a grandmother today."

"You don't say! Well, that is grand." Logan paused and suddenly a startled expression came over his face. "Ali, don't tell me that you—"

Allison's merry laugh stopped him. "No . . . no midwifing for me. I paced outside while Dr. Connally delivered the baby. I haven't had much stomach for such affairs since that day the elder Dr. Connally was out of town and my mother pressed me into service."

"Your many other talents more than make up for that singular lack, my dear."

"Thank you, Logan. I've often wished I could follow my mother's footsteps as a compassionate dispenser of healing. How well I remember her being called out in the middle of the night with her little black bag in hand. What a team she and my father made—he tending to the cows and goats and pigs and horses, she to the coughing and feverish children of Strathy. I think the women of the community trusted her for some things over the doctor."

"Well, tell me about the new bairn."

"A sweet little girl, Logan. So tiny, so precious. And dear Patty was every bit as proud as the parents."

Allison brought her cup to her lips, steadying it with her left hand, and drank.

"I did something else today," she went on after a moment. "I decided to get out Mother's journal. I don't know why I hadn't done so before now."

Logan reached out and laid his hand over hers.

"I suppose I have been avoiding it," Allison went on. "And perhaps it was still too soon."

"It was bound to stir up old memories no matter when you read it," said Logan.

"I know," replied Allison. "But I thought, you know, with the way it's all turned out these last two months, the changes, the reunion—I thought maybe it would bring tears of joy rather than sadness."

"So . . . which did it bring?"

"That's the strangest part of all," answered Allison. "I couldn't find the journal. I looked everywhere."

"Hmm, that is peculiar."

"But once I was thinking along those lines, about Mother's posterity and what the future holds, I found it hardly mattered whether I was reading her words or not. Seeing the new baby made me think afresh about what lies ahead. I wonder what the future does hold, Logan? What will become of this place and the legacy it represents? For so long somewhere in the back of my mind, I had struggled to come to terms with the possibility of its ending with us. But now that my hope has blossomed anew all at once, I find myself so conscious of the present-day crumbling of long-established traditions. Oh, I don't want Stonewycke to lose its sense of the past, of history!"

"Those things that are truly precious and worthy of permanence will not crumble, Ali. But perhaps I'm not really the one to talk, since I've never been much of a traditionalist."

Allison let her serious expression soften into a smile and patted Logan's hand. "But you know what things are worthy, and that's what matters. I need to pray for that sense too, especially now. I don't want to put on pressure. We might not *all* have the same expectations for Stonewycke's future."

They fell silent for a few moments, each seeming to contemplate the blaze in the hearth. At length, not wanting this quiet time together to end, Allison spoke. "Would you like more tea?"

"Yes, I would," answered Logan, then added quickly as Allison began to lean forward, "Let me this time." He poured a quick blob of milk into her cup, then added the tea, and finally dropped in one lump of sugar, stirred the mixture, then handed her the cup.

"The past seems calling out to me every day now," said Allison as she watched Logan prepare his own cup in like fashion.

"Wishing you had a little granddaughter?" asked Logan.

"I can't deny that a spark of envy did try to intrude. But only for a moment. God gave us full and complete lives, and I am content. Besides, now the story may wind up with a surprise ending. But when I think of Mother and what we shared together during the years I was growing up—"

Tears suddenly surfaced in Allison's eyes and she hurriedly retrieved a handkerchief from her pocket. "I'm glad I keep this handy." She dabbed her eyes and sniffed. "I should never have said anything."

"No, Ali. We decided long ago we wouldn't wall up our memories. There can be no regrets. Remember Lady Maggie's time away from Ian? The Lord always brings things full circle. As he is now doing with us."

He paused, musing to himself.

"That word *wall* just made me think of Maggie's nursery," he went on thoughtfully. "Remember Mother describing how she and Alec cut through the wall?"

"Nothing had been touched, and it was all covered with cobwebs and dust."

"Whenever I think of their adventure exploring this old place, and discovering that lost nursery, I can't help but think of when our own little Joanna was a baby. You know that picture of her I have kept in my office all these years—her sweet little face? Sometimes I can almost still hear her small voice as it was back then, and feel the delicate skin of her cheek when I find myself glancing up at that picture. We can't let ourselves lose such memories, despite all those years of loss. We mustn't allow dust and cobwebs to swallow them. Those intervening years are part of the legacy too, as dear Maggie taught us all."

Allison slid over toward Logan and put her free arm around his shoulder.

"Oh, Logan," she said, "God's greatest blessing to me is *you*! Everything is going to come out right, isn't it?"

"He has not failed us yet, Ali. Though I've long since learned that He doesn't always bring things about in the way we might expect."

19 ❉ Into the Future

HILARY DECIDED TO walk the mile to Stonewycke.

Perhaps it was in part because of Joanna's similar walk sixty years earlier. If she was to fulfill her own destiny, it seemed somehow fitting that she follow in the footsteps of the grandmother who had set this odyssey in motion.

Also, she needed the time alone. Not so much to think, for her course of action was at last settled in her mind. Rather, she needed time to soak in the surroundings of this place, to tune herself in to them so that when she did reach her destination, she would not feel like such an outsider.

The day with the MacKenzies had been so peaceful, just the tonic her turbulent spirit needed. Little Kerrie had endless questions about London and Prince Charles and the Queen and Buckingham Palace. Mr. MacKenzie quietly hovered about, shyly protective of the young lady whose life he had saved, and whom he credited with the saving of his own daughter's. Mrs. MacKenzie bustled about the three-room little cottage as if the Queen herself was expected for dinner! A smile spread over Hilary's face at the memory of that gathering around the plain pine table three hours ago. The beaming faces of the three MacKenzies, so proud to have her in their midst, the pot of steaming potatoes, the plate of cold oatcakes, the boiled cod. Oh, they were dears! thought Hilary.

It was a fine afternoon as she walked through Port Strathy and on up the hill to the east. The sun was already low at her back, though it was not yet three o'clock. The air could not be called warm, yet there was in it a lingering whisper of the autumn now quickly passing. The storm had moved through rapidly as she slept, leaving behind only scattered patches of gray clouds that were now randomly distributed through the pale blue brightness of the sky.

Within an hour the sinking sun would send out shoots of red and orange and pink and purple, lining these same clouds to herald the approach of sunset.

Notwithstanding the sunshine, Hilary wore her coat, knowing she would need it later on. She had returned to the inn from the MacKenzies' to change clothes. It would probably have been more practical to wear slacks and sturdy shoes, since she would be doing a good deal of walking. But instead she wore a brown tweed suit with gored skirt and coral-colored silk blouse, along with low-heeled pumps. Her feet would be sore by day's end, no doubt, but she was meeting her parents after thirty years, and she couldn't help wanting to make a good impression.

She'd toyed with the idea of calling ahead. But then, what would she have said? "Hi, I'm with *The Berkshire Review*, and I wondered if you'd be so kind as to grant me an interview?" She could hardly just blurt out, "I'm your daughter you thought was dead. Could I come for a visit?"

There wasn't going to be an easy way to do it. Walking up to the door unexpected didn't seem altogether "right" either. But this was something that she had to do in person, as awkward as it would be.

To her left the sea spread out to the horizon. The climb was brisk, and she stopped when she reached the top to look back down upon the village, then over Ramsey Head just ahead of her and off the bluff to her left. Then she continued on, leaving the road and turning inland toward the estate. A large iron gate stood open, to one side of which had been placed a large stone of granite, in which were chiseled the words: "Welcome to Stonewycke." Hilary passed inside and continued on, through the wooded grounds of the castle. The wooden bridge over which Joanna had walked had long since been replaced by a sturdy, wide stone bridge able to accommodate automobiles and trucks. Every stone had been hauled to the site by Alec MacNeil and Walter Innes from the quarry on the Fraserburgh Road. The trees had grown older since Joanna's day, but little else had changed. Only the distant sound of machinery, and perhaps a car climbing the hill out of Strathy every ten or fifteen minutes, would reveal that the year was 1971, not 1911.

Hilary drank in the air as she walked, enjoying the sight of every oak, every birch, every mountain ash, as well as the green fields that extended out on both sides of her, up toward higher hills to the east, and downward toward the valley of Strathy to the west. This was such lovely country—so quiet, so peaceful, so green . . . so different than anything she had ever had the chance to enjoy in London.

Well, she thought, whatever lies ahead for me will be found at the end of this long driveway. It can't be much farther.

The insistent ring of the phone sounded from across the room. For the first two rings he tried to ignore it. This was the fourth call of the day, and he hoped it wasn't for him. Logan had gone to the sun-room to read, privately hoping to avoid further interruptions.

Still the phone persisted. Then as the ringing stopped, realizing the housekeeper had no doubt answered it and would have to run up the three flights of stairs after him, Logan was invaded by a dutiful sense of guilt. He laid down his book and went out to meet her halfway.

I probably should have instructed her to take messages, he thought. What good could he be to Allison during this difficult time if his responsibilities in London continued to hound him so? He had let his work separate them once before, and it was not an experience he wanted to repeat.

When he had returned to Stonewycke immediately after the Commons session last week, they had both known he might be forced somewhat to divide his time. It was an involved month; he had many irons in the fire that would not cool just because he went north. And, of course, Allison understood. She was part of his work now. They considered themselves a team. Many of his associates had joked more than once that the Honorable Mrs. Macintyre had through the years garnered at least half his votes for him. Logan was proud of that fact— proud of her.

The housekeeper met him as he came to the first-floor landing. She had only had to climb halfway up the bottom flight of stairs.

"Telephone for ye, sir," she said, showing her gratitude at being spared a longer trek.

"Thank you, Flora; I'll take it in the library."

Logan turned and strode down the corridor to the great double oak doors of the room that had served as Stonewycke's library for over a hundred years. Allison had always insisted that the fragrance of musty, aging books was stimulating, both to the mind and the senses. Personally, he didn't care much for it himself. She often teased him that he would no doubt prefer moving his office out to the room above the stables that had belonged to old Uncle Digory. Could he help it, he would joke back, if an uneducated bloke himself finds the fragrances there more invigorating?

By the time he reached the desk and lifted the receiver, Logan was smiling at the comparison of the library with the stable.

"Hello," he said, "Logan Macintyre speaking."

A brief pause followed.

"Ah, yes, George . . . of course, of course . . . certainly, I know you wouldn't have called otherwise. What is it?"

A lengthy interlude ensued in which Logan nodded, shook his head, and responded verbally at periodic intervals.

"I see . . . yes, good work."

As he was gradually caught up in governmental matters, the smile faded from his face, replaced by a keen glow of enthusiasm, visible not on his lips at all, but rather in his eyes.

"And so you've found five possible violators?" he asked at length. "Which companies are they?"

He nodded his head, then let out a sharp breath. "Trans Global Enterprises? I had no idea our fishing expedition would land such a big catch! But as you say it's still too soon to know. We have to remember we're still in the speculating stages."

After listening for another moment, he added, "I agree, it's a sticky situation, but we have never let money and power intimidate us before . . . yes, of course, discretion must be the byword. No coming on like gangbusters, as they say in America. But there are subtle approaches we can make use of."

He paused while the other spoke, then chuckled.

"Thanks, George. I'll take that as a compliment!"

Another brief pause was followed by an outright laugh.

"I don't know about legendary. But there have always been those to make more of my reputation than reality would justify. In the meantime, we had better do our homework thoroughly. I'd like complete profiles on each company—"

He stopped, clearly interrupted, nodded, then continued. "Good man, George! I should have known you'd already have started. Terrific! I want to be well-armed if this thing proves out and I take it to Ted Heath. . . . When will I be returning . . . ?"

The question required more consideration than he had time for on this long-distance call. Nor was George Ringersfeld the one with whom to discuss what to Logan were complex alternatives. He and Allison had talked and prayed, but both were reluctant to make any definite moves just yet. Neither could deny anticipating their return to the activity of the city. But the peace and tranquillity of Stonewycke, not to mention the sudden turnabout of family considerations, had been more a soothing balm to their spirits on this particular occasion than for many years. Especially with Joanna now gone, they were more strongly torn in the two directions that pulled at their loyalties, as they knew they always would be.

"I don't know, George," Logan said at length. "In a few days, perhaps. Probably a week at the outside. Keep me posted if you turn up anything startling. All right, then . . . thanks for the news . . . goodbye."

Logan hung up the phone, then leaned against the edge of the desk in thought. What a time for this to come up! He should be in London to direct the investigation. Yet he knew he belonged here—for right now, at any rate.

He had begun investigating allegations of illegal practices at the corporate level a year ago during his tenure as Minister of Economic Affairs under Wilson. The change in administrations when Edward Heath's Conservatives had ousted Labour from power had abruptly forestalled his work until the new Prime Minister had suggested to his own Minister that he work with Logan on the problem. Then the furor over the Common Market vote had interrupted progress again, though a month ago renewed murmurings had encouraged him to reopen his investigations. He had never expected that he might have to do battle with a giant like Trans Global.

The fight itself did not worry him. He had taken many an unpopular stance on the Parliamentary floor through the years. He could almost relish the thought of a good clash where the issues of right and wrong were clearly defined. At any other time, he would have welcomed the challenge. But Joanna's death, coupled with the rift in the party and, unavoidably, in his friendship with Wilson, as well as family uncertainties—it had all taken a toll on his emotional reservoir.

A soft knock on the door called a halt to his reverie. Allison opened the door a crack and poked in her head. "We were just going to have some tea downstairs. Would you like to join us, or am I interrupting something?"

"Not at all. I can use a pleasant diversion."

"Troubles?" she asked as she came into the room.

"Just the usual," answered Logan. "I only wish they weren't all happening at once."

"What's the newest?"

"You know that corporate investigation?"

Allison nodded.

"It seems Ringersfeld may have uncovered some shady dealings within our borders, in one of our largest and most respected companies."

"Isn't that more a matter for Scotland Yard, or perhaps Interpol?"

"If it develops into something truly illegal, maybe so. In the meantime I have to decide whether to stir up that kind of fallout. If I do, this particular company is powerful enough to put up a real battle. They could make life miserable for me . . . for us all. It could jeopardize my reputation; they might even move to unseat me. Yet if I don't move on it, you can believe my other convictions are going to be called into question when the press gets hold of it. You know I'm just a stooge for big business and such rot."

"Anyone with an ounce of sense would never believe such a charge!"

"You know the fickle public mind," he said.

She laid her hand lovingly on his shoulder. "You'll do the right thing," she said. "I know you will. You know you've never been one to put your reputation ahead of doing what your convictions tell you."

"Yes," he sighed. "I suppose what I have to do is clear. I only hope we turn up something that will put the odds a little more in our favor. You can't try to uncover the skeletons in the closets of a multi-billion dollar company without some pretty heavy artillery."

"The answers will come, Logan. I don't know where you'll find them, but you will."

He kissed her lightly on the cheek. They linked arms and were just exiting the library when the echoing of the front door chime met their ears from downstairs.

20 ❊ A Long-Awaited Meeting

THE HIGH STONE walls of the huge gray edifice rose suddenly before Hilary as she rounded a curve in the road.

A tight grove of trees, mostly larches, and the steep incline of the hillside around which the road bent, had obscured it from view on this particular approach. Majestically visible for miles around from nearly any vantage point, the magnificent yet sobering citadel known for centuries as Stonewycke remained, until the last possible moment, hidden to visitors making their approach along this main access road.

What startled Hilary most, however, was not the suddenness of its appearance, but rather the sight itself. This was indeed an ancient castle! All of Joanna's descriptions could not have fully prepared her for what now met her gaze. Rising at least four or five stories in the air, with wings attached spreading on either direction from the main structure, replete with towers, turrets, and various stone-carved ornamentations, the imposing stronghold was certainly something out of *Macbeth* or *Camelot*. She couldn't quite tell, at first glance, whether the castle's grimness or its mystical allure was more dominant. Probably the legends surrounding it were due to a healthy dose of both.

Another iron gate stood before her, this time stretching across the road.

One final wave of reluctance swept through her. But Hilary was determined not to turn back now. She walked forward to the wrought-iron barrier, hesitated merely a moment, reached out, and lifted the latch. The gate opened to her touch. She slipped inside, then closed it behind her. Nothing would divert her from the path she knew was hers to follow.

As she approached the courtyard, Hilary was greeted by the perennial view of the rearing horse in the center of a free-flowing fountain. The splashing water was the only sound to be heard in the tranquil setting. No person was visible on the grounds, no barking dog greeted her as she walked.

She paused a moment to study the regal statue, muscles flexed powerfully across the equine shoulders. The nostrils at the end of the stately head flared, the full mane flying back as if the creature had been caught by Medusa's gaze, captured in full flight rather than carved in stone.

The sight brought to Hilary's mind the horses she had so recently read about in the journal, those marvelous creatures that had been such a vital part of young Maggie's life. At the same time it reminded her how unsuited she was to step into the life this august place represented. Her very attire spoke of how out of place she was for the country life, much less that of a country lady. She had ridden a horse only once in her life!

Nevertheless, after her brief stop, she proceeded around the tiled pool of the fountain and drew near the front doors of the castle—doors containing more inherent grandeur than any she had ever seen.

Swallowing hard, she took a deep breath, then reached up toward the bell.

Logan glanced instinctively at his wristwatch at the sound of the chimes. After four telephone interruptions, a caller at the door, whatever the hour, seemed only appropriate as befitting this day.

"Are you expecting anyone?" he asked as they walked toward the stairs.

"No. I can't imagine who it might be."

As they descended, Flora appeared at the bottom of the stairway.

"Mr. and Mrs. Macintyre," she said, "there's a caller for ye."

"Who is it?" asked Logan.

"A stranger, sir. She said her name is Hilary Edwards."

"Edwards . . . " mused Logan, trying to place the familiar sound of the name. "Is she a reporter?"

"She didna say, sir."

"Thank you, Flora. I'll be right there."

Logan turned toward the front door, while Allison headed back toward the kitchen where she had been preparing the tea herself.

"Beggin' yer pardon," Flora added, "but she asked for the *both* o' ye. Right insistent aboot it, too, I might add."

Allison glanced back toward Logan with a puzzled expression, then turned to follow him. "I suppose the tea will keep for a few minutes."

"She's in the drawing room," Flora added before taking her leave.

Allison took Logan's arm and together they walked toward the drawing room.

"I think I know what this might be about," said Logan. "I'll take care of it quickly. Then maybe we can sit down and talk over that pot of tea. It's time we began thinking about some of the decisions we have to make."

Wondering about the tenacity, not to mention impertinence, of a reporter tracking him all the way to Scotland, Logan opened the doors of the drawing room.

He at once recognized the woman seated on the brocade divan as a journalist he had encountered a time or two, most recently at a press conference prior to the Common Market vote, if he remembered correctly. Now that he thought about the incident, he seemed to recall that she had been rather persistent in her style of questioning. But when she looked up at him, he saw none of such qualities. Instead, he perceived a vulnerability. The instant their eyes met, he knew beyond all doubt that she had not come here to grill him. His posture toward her immediately softened.

"Miss Edwards, I believe," said Logan warmly, extending his hand toward her.

Hilary rose and shook his hand.

"Mr. Macintyre," she said, "thank you for seeing me."

"This is my wife, Allison."

As the two women shook hands, Logan could not take his gaze from the eyes of the newcomer. As she looked into Allison's face, the young woman's blue eyes filled with tears that seemed about to overflow down her cheeks.

"You've come rather a long way for a story, haven't you, Miss Edwards?" asked Logan after a moment.

"Actually," began Hilary, turning back toward him, "I haven't come to get a story at all, but rather to *tell* one." Her voice seemed to gain strength as she spoke. "My mission, if such it could be called, is more of a personal nature. And my name isn't exactly Miss Edwards— that's what I've come to talk to you about."

"You have my curiosity thoroughly aroused," said Logan good-naturedly. "Please go on."

"The story I'm going to tell you you may find difficult—even impossible—to believe. I didn't believe it at first myself."

"Try us. We're good listeners."

"About three weeks ago, I received a visit from your mother," Hilary began. As she spoke she turned toward Allison. At the words a puzzled expression spread over Allison's features.

"She told me of the loss of your daughter during the war," Hilary continued, "and of her own recent search to locate her granddaughter when she suddenly became convinced the girl was alive."

Here Logan and Allison looked at one another in surprise.

"We knew of no such search," said Logan.

"Yes, Lady Joanna told me she had said nothing to either of you."

Hilary paused, struggling with previously unfelt emotions rising from within her.

"Oh, how I wish she were still here!" she said. "But I promised her I would come to you, and . . . as difficult as it is to say such words, I must tell you . . . I must try to explain as best I can the incredible story that Lady Joanna told to me."

Again she stopped. By now Logan's jocular expression had turned deadly serious, as both he and Allison listened in rapt attention.

"Without going into every detail Lady Joanna related to me, I would simply say that . . . oh my, I don't know how to say this! . . . what she told me was—"

Hilary took a deep breath, as if to gather courage.

"—she said that I was . . . that she had searched many avenues and had been led at last to me, and that . . . that I was—her granddaughter . . . that the two of you were my own parents!"

In stunned silence both Logan and Allison stared at Hilary, then toward one another, then back at their guest. The moments before anyone spoke seemed interminably long. In reality the shocked stillness lasted but a second or two.

It was Allison's voice that broke the silence.

"But that's impossible," she said. "Our daughter is in the kitchen waiting for us right now. She's been with us ever since she was located, several months ago. . . . "

21 ❆ First Arrival

IT HAD BEEN a dreary summer in Port Strathy. That day three month's past in mid-August proved no exception.

A heavy rain fell with a stiff wind driving the torrent diagonally, knifelike, into the gray castle walls. Inside, even the fire in the hearth seemed a willing accomplice to the black weather. It had been nearly impossible to light, and twice had burned down to cold dead embers before it could be revived. Even then its gloomy warmth could not begin to penetrate the raw chill pervading the ancient masonry. Now and then the swirling wind took the chimney for its trumpet, sending the smoke back into the house in silent puffs. Then, its gusts once more righting themselves, it sucked the smoke back skyward through suddenly glowing coals and a whistling flue.

Outside, that same northerly gale made sport of the trees, shaking them about as if it would pull them out of the ground and toss them into the sea. Indeed, only in a land like Scotland could such a day come during a season bearing the name summer.

Allison pulled back an edge of the curtain and looked outside. She still held a small hope that her eyes might detect a hint of clearing in the dark, ominous sky. But the storm beat down relentlessly. Only large drops pelting the windowpanes greeted her. It was certainly no day to be afoot.

Fierce, deadly streaks of lightning shot across the evening sky followed by deafening explosions of thunder. One of the wicked bursts of light suddenly illumined a moving vehicle, its headlamps barely discernible in the jagged glare of nature's beam. It came through the open gateway into a courtyard prematurely darkened by the mass of clouds, finally pulling to a stop in front of the fountain.

A visitor *was* expected at Stonewycke, though not for two more days. Allison was expecting no callers today, especially at seven in the evening and in such weather. Why someone would be braving the elements at this hour, Allison could not think.

All at once she felt her heart contract. Their preparations had been focused two days from now. Might there have been some mistake? Could this be the moment instead?

She hurried out into the entryway just as the heavy brass knocker struck the exterior of the door. Allison tried to catch her breath but her heart was racing. Slowing to a steady walk, her hands trembled as she reached out to open the oaken portal.

The instant it swung wide another grotesque stab of lightning slashed across the bleak northern sky. Its ethereal glow framed the caller's face for a brief instant, outlining the hair and shoulders but rendering its features momentarily invisible. Immediately the flash passed, however, leaving in the wet dusk a young woman whose precise age was difficult to determine from the youthful innocence staring out from the face, though Allison quickly recognized that she carried herself with a certain degree of maturity.

Intuitively Allison knew that before her was standing the expected visitor come ahead of time. This could be none other than the object of the telephone call they had received but a week and a half ago. . . .

A clipped, businesslike voice had, after identifying preliminaries, delivered the startling news: "We believe your daughter has been located—"

"But that's impossible; our daughter was killed—"

"Do you know a Hannah Whitley?"

The memory of the rest of that conversation would not be easily erased from Allison's mind, nor of the days that followed. They were days filled with endless legalities and calls and meetings and discussions. Logan's London solicitors had conferred with the man in Glasgow, credentials had been verified, several calls to the United States had been made. In the end all the cold, hard matters of law had been satisfied. When Logan was certain everything was in order, he told the gentleman in Glasgow they were ready to meet the young woman, and the final arrangements were made. He and Allison traveled north to Stonewycke, where they had arrived only two days ago. The plan had been for Logan to pick her up at the Fraserburgh train station on Saturday. Now here she was on Thursday night.

"I hope you don't mind my showing up early and unannounced," said a pleasant voice out of the darkened entryway.

"You must be . . . " But even as she tried to speak, Allison's mouth went suddenly dry, and further words were impossible.

"Yes, I am your daughter." The voice contained a delicate, almost breathless quality, sweet and feminine, mellowed yet further with an intense sincerity.

Allison stood before her speechless for another instant. Imagining this moment over and over in her mind throughout the previous week, she had never pictured herself dumb and paralyzed like a schoolgirl. Finally, with great effort, she shook off the spell. She could not leave the poor girl standing with her back to the rain. Something had to be done.

"Come in . . . please," said Allison in an unnatural voice.

"I just couldn't wait another two days," said the young lady, stepping inside, rain dripping from her umbrella and raincoat. "That hotel in Aberdeen was enough for one night. Yet I did not want our first contact to be by telephone."

"I understand," said Allison, finding her voice again.

Then suddenly the tears came. All week she had held them in check, not wanting to let herself believe the unbelievable. But now—after thirty years . . . her own daughter . . . here . . . standing before her!

The young woman put down her suitcase and stepped toward Allison. "Mother . . . " she said in a voice trembling with emotion.

With the word she thought she would never hear in this life, all reserves at last broke down. Allison moved toward her, and as if of one mind the two women embraced. The tender reunion was marred, if only indistinctly, by the barely noticeable stiffness in the arms that encircled Allison. But how could it be any other way? Though perhaps they shared the same blood, as adults they were still strangers.

When they fell apart, Allison half-laughed as she brushed a quick hand over her eyes. "It's wonderful to have you at Stonewycke . . . again," she said, smiling. "Come, I'll take you to meet the others."

Allison led the way into the family parlor, where before long they were seated with Logan and Lady Joanna enjoying a fresh pot of tea. While they sipped from delicate china cups and Logan engaged his daughter in quiet conversation, Allison took several moments to study the newly found Joanna Macintyre. Her auburn hair glimmered in the reflection of the fire, now at last blazing in the hearth. It shone somewhere between the fiery auburn of young Maggie's and the richer, more subdued tones of Joanna's when she had first come to Scotland. Lady Joanna herself, her own hair now gray, sat quietly observing as parents and daughter acquainted themselves, and the similarity of hair color was not lost on her.

She was no carbon copy of her predecessors. How could she be? Yet the resemblances were more striking than might have been anticipated. Still, her eyes were much darker and her skin not so pale as Allison s. Of course, they must not forget to reckon Logan's side of the family in the girl's heritage.

Young Joanna, or Jo, as she said she had grown accustomed to being called, demonstrated complete poise and courteous mannerisms. Her movements were gracious, almost feline at times, measured but purposeful. They learned that she had attended the best boarding schools and graduated from Vassar near the top of her class. Her adoptive father, a banker, was British by birth but had moved to the States after the war.

"That explains the accent," said Logan.

"Having grown up in America," Jo replied in an almost apologetic tone, "I'm afraid I have lost too much of my British heritage."

"We're open-minded," laughed Logan, "even toward the Colonists." Then he added in a more serious tone, his eyes deepening with intensity, "We are just glad to have found you." Even as he spoke his eyes clouded over with tears.

Jo rose and walked toward him with that calm assurance and steady gaze of her dark eyes that they would soon come to know well. She took his hands into hers.

"Oh, *Father!*" she said, emphasizing the word, "I never dreamed that finding my real parents would be this wonderful. You can't know what it's like for me. I feel that my life is at last . . . fulfilled."

"Perhaps we *can* know a little of what you feel," Logan replied with a kindly smile that hinted of past pain. "We lost a daughter, too, just as you lost your parents."

The days following that momentous evening were indeed filled with great joy. When the weather permitted, Logan, Allison, and Jo could often be found walking upon the hills and paths of the estate. The parents wanted the daughter to see everything, and to feel the importance of the land as her heritage. Jo took it all in with a deep awe.

"This is more beautiful than I would have been able to imagine!" she exclaimed one day as her eyes, wide with girlish delight, swept the landscape.

"Do you remember anything from before?" asked Allison.

Jo hesitated as she thought. "Just vague images," she answered at last. "I remember the castle, I think. I mean just the look of it from the outside. And the landscape seems like something I've seen before, almost like it was part of a dream."

"You were very young."

"Oh, but I'm here now at last! And it's so clean and pretty everywhere. I'll have to paint it sometime."

"You're an artist?" asked Allison, realizing for the first time that, though she was an eager and attentive listener, Jo modestly spoke little about herself.

"I sometimes feel presumptuous saying it, but, yes, I suppose I am. Though I am still learning."

"You should be proud of your talents. They are from the Lord. Do you sell your paintings?"

"Occasionally."

"But not enough to make a living at?"

"No, hardly that."

"And you've no hankering after the struggling Bohemian lifestyle?" offered Logan with a smile.

Jo laughed—a soft, almost musical laugh that was pleasant to the ear. "I would never have been a starving young artist trying to eke out an existence somewhere. I have my adoptive parents to thank for that. They were very kind and generous to me."

"We have never had an artist in the family," said Allison. "It will be a delight to see this beautiful land captured on canvas. Perhaps you might even pass along some of your talent to your mother. I've always wanted to learn to paint."

"With pleasure!"

During their quiet moments Allison and Logan found themselves marveling at the blessing their daughter was proving to be, at how the village children followed her about with admiration, at how freely she seemed to adapt to life at Stonewycke. In just a short time she became a special part of their home and community. When Logan found it necessary to return to London, she seemed completely content to remain in Scotland with Allison, who felt she should remain behind, at least for a while.

Only Lady Joanna seemed reticent toward her namesake. It was difficult at her age, she told Allison, to accept change easily, even when it did come in such a wonderful package.

But for the next few weeks Allison's mother kept more to herself than usual, absorbed in her journal, distracted, sometimes going out for solitary walks on the grounds. She even went off oddly once to Aberdeen by the Fraserburgh train, and a time or two to Culden to visit a man by the name of Ogilvie, the son of an old friend, she said, who had taken over his father's practice. When she returned her face wore a troubled expression.

Allison tried to ignore Joanna's frequent quiet moods, determined as she was to enjoy this happy time of reunion. And after three months, only the sudden death of Lady Joanna had marred young Jo's homecoming. The unexpected hemorrhage was accompanied by not a few pangs of guilt in Allison's heart. Yet even then, Jo kept a bright countenance. She proved so supportive, so sympathetic, that Allison wondered if she could have faced the loss of her mother without her newly found daughter.

So what was she possibly to think when all of a sudden another young woman turned up on her doorstep claiming to be their lost Joanna Hilary? What, indeed, but that the newcomer was sadly mistaken in her information.

22 ❊ Altered Plans

SITTING IN THE guest parlor, Hilary did her best to cope with this sudden nightmare.

Sipping the cup of tea that had been offered her, she graciously nodded attentively as Allison recounted briefly the events leading up to Jo's coming some months before. But inside she was paying little attention. She could not keep her mind from playing over and over that scene with Lady Joanna in her own office. How could the woman have been so convincing if it was nothing but a gigantic mistake? Even as she had spoken to Hilary in London, this other daughter—apparently the real daughter—had been here, at Stonewycke, fully known to her grandmother the whole time. What could it all mean?

It was a mistake, that's what it meant. A huge blunder! Her believing the farfetched story in the first place . . . her coming here! She should have trusted her instincts. She knew in her heart of hearts that she, Hilary Edwards—for that was her name after all—could never be part of all this!

And now here they all were—nice, courteous people that they were, who could deny it?— trying to soothe her frayed emotions. Oh, it was all too awful! She had to get back to the city. That was her real life.

"I know how I would feel had this happened to me," said Jo, who had entered the room and was sitting opposite Hilary. Her voice was so delicate, so sweetly consoling.

All Hilary could do by way of response was to set her china cup down a bit too hard. With an awkward chinking sound, its contents spilled over the edge.

"I really should go," she said, rising.

"You can understand our reaction," said Logan in a calm, reasonable tone, despite the tension etched in his face. "We are every bit as bewildered by this sudden turn of events as you must be. That's why we can only hope that by a thorough explanation of everything, we can somehow sort it out."

"Yes, of course, I understand." Hilary, too, attempted to inject calm and reason into her voice.

"Believe me, we want to get to the bottom of this. But we have already gone to such lengths poring over records and documents and verifying the history of . . . of . . . our daughter here"—as he spoke he motioned toward Jo—"that without concrete proof—"

"I only know that Lady Joanna MacNeil came to me several weeks ago with the most startling revelation I could possibly have imagined."

"Why did you wait so long to come?"

"Why did I wait . . . ?" Hilary began to feel control slipping from her voice. "I don't know. It . . . it all took me so by surprise. I wasn't sure I wanted any part of it. The upheaval . . . the change. I tried to come to you once. I came up for the funeral, but in the end I talked myself out of a confrontation."

"Surely, then, you must have realized our daughter had already returned?"

"I spoke to no one. I slipped in at the very end of the service. My mind was so preoccupied I hardly took notice of my surroundings."

"But didn't you—"

"Please," interrupted Hilary, her voice thin and strained. "I had better leave. I am not prepared for a cross-examination. I have no proof—only . . . only the look in a dear old woman's eyes. I've been a fool. You have your daughter."

Hilary turned and fled from the room.

Behind her retreating figure she could hear a clamor of protesting voices, all so sympathetic, wanting to help ease her gently back down into the reality that she was nothing but an adopted working-class woman. But right now she could accept no sympathy, especially from them. She had had to gather courage from within herself to come here in the first place. Now she would have to cope with this unexpected crisis of identity in the solitude of her own soul, and nowhere else.

She ran out into the crisp autumn sunlight, now regretting her decision to walk up to the estate. On foot her getaway would be too slow, and might allow those compassionate people to come after her so they could persist in pitying her foolishness.

She broke into a run, exited the gates, then turned sharply to her right. There was a path somewhere along here, if it still existed. She had read about it in the journal. It didn't lead directly back to town, but at least if anyone did try to follow, they would not think to come in that direction.

She skirted the walls and hedge that surrounded the castle, and after some minutes came to a steep, rocky path that led down into a gorge before finally jogging upward again and out onto a broad pasturelike heath. In summer the grassy expanse would have been lush and green, but now it spread out brown and decaying, awaiting the covering of snow that was not far off.

Hilary slowed her pace to a walk, crossed the barren field, and in about twenty minutes came to a road, one she had not been on before, wide but unpaved. Two or three vehicles passed, each offering her a ride into town. But Hilary could bear no human contact just then.

Walking along the rough, uneven dirt surface, Hilary continued on in the direction in which the sea must lay. She would return to the inn, pay her bill, get in her rented car, and leave this place. How could she have so badly misread all the signs? She was sure God had been leading her to come here. What had gone wrong?

What did it matter anyway? She hadn't really wanted any of this in the first place. To find she was not the daughter of an aristocratic family should be an immense relief. She could now return to her life—the life she had grown to love, the city she loved—and resume being the person she had grown content to be.

Yes . . . she should feel relieved, she said to herself again. This had been unpleasant . . . but it would be better this way.

The road wandered north for about a mile, finally intersecting the coastal road just east of the entrance to the estate that Hilary had taken earlier. She walked down the hill, looking out on the sea, icy blue and calm today, so unlike the stormy expanse that had given her solace yesterday. She needed no solace now, only escape. Before realizing it, she found her feet carrying her down the rocky hillside and across the sand to the water's edge. She couldn't face the inn right now either—she had to be alone.

Perhaps it was only to take one more walk along this magnificent shore. She would never return here. This was not her home. It belonged to another—a sweet, beautiful, lovely young woman rightfully named Joanna. This was her home, her heritage—her Stonewycke. She even *looked* like she belonged here.

She would miss the MacKenzies, thought Hilary. She had wanted to visit them again.

But she couldn't think of all that. If the name Stonewycke forced its way into her thoughts once more, she would crack. Forgetfulness would not come easily. The days, weeks spent in trying to accept the truth about her birth—they might have been put to better use consulting attorneys and researching the authenticity of Lady Joanna's claims. She was a practiced veteran at such things, ferreting out bogus leads from real ones. In the face of the woman's intense sincerity, it had never occurred to her to doubt. Yet what if she had been off in her own little world, and her claims nothing but an ironic game of her aging imagination?

"You are my granddaughter." As Hilary walked, her thoughts drifted back to that day in her office. Lady Joanna's face was still as vivid as it had been that afternoon. Hilary had known the words were true, though every logical, practical reaction inside her had cried out against it.

"How could I have been so wrong?" she silently implored.

The only answer she received was the steady pounding of the waves alternatively slamming against the sand and rocks, then slipping back into the sea. The sight did possess a calming effect. Perhaps it came from the eternal consistency of the sea—surely one of the most awe-inspiring elements in God's majestic creation. She could easily grow to love it, if only . . .

All at once Hilary realized all the changes she had been through over the past days were still with her. Despite her concerted attempts to thrust them from her mind because of how foolish she felt, the images and emotions and tuggings upon her heart conjured up by the journal remained. She could not help still feeling intrinsically a part of the sweeping saga of this incredible family. And, in a way she had never before experienced in London in all her life, she felt somehow a part of the land and its people too. The memory of Frances MacKenzie's large, simple, sparkling-eyed face began to take shape in her mind, and the delicious peace in which she had felt wrapped while lying in her cozy bed of heather. Why, that had been only this morning! One didn't meet faces of compassion and hands of humble service like that very often in London. What did it all mean? What was her part in all this?

Slowly, from some distant place—either deep within her spirit or from outside her, she could not tell which—began to form the incredible thought: *But what if it hadn't been a mistake?* What if that look on Lady Joanna's face signified that she was indeed her true granddaughter? What if . . . what if the case of mistaken identity actually rested with the girl still sitting up there in the castle . . . sitting there with *Hilary's* rightful parents?

The thought was too inconceivable! And if it was true, what could she possibly do about it? How could she think of dealing such a blow to the other—what should she call her?—the other claimant? She had already been at Stonewycke almost three months. She was already part of the family. It would be too horrible for her now to discover that she had been part of a mistake. That look of innocence in her eyes—Hilary could never do that to her! To tell her that her whole life and past had been uprooted, but that it had all been a cruel mistake, that the lawyers had somehow mistaken all the evidence.

What am I thinking? Hilary suddenly said to herself. *This is absurd! She is Joanna Macintyre . . . not me. How can I even consider the risk of being made the ultimate fool by going back there and . . .*

The thought did not finish itself. As she played devil's advocate with herself, she had no plan, no barometer to steady her conflicting emotions.

I'm getting away from here! she decided resolutely. *That's the only sane thing to do!*

She continued on down the rugged shoreline, making her way over the occasionally rocky shoal toward the harbor, Port Strathy, and the wide expanse of level beach on the other side of the village. At length she climbed a large rock that sat at the water's edge, scampered up, and perched herself on top, gazing down at the swirling water as it ebbed and flowed beneath her. At last her mind let loose its futile debating and her thoughts turned to prayers.

There was an answer in the midst of all this. Something assured her of that. She just had to make sure she didn't miss it altogether in the muddled mass of her own confused perplexity. Only as she gave up trying to rationalize the whole dilemma out did a peace steal upon her—and out of that peace the answer would come.

"Guide my thoughts, God," she whispered. "Show me what I'm supposed to do."

Again Lady Joanna's face stole into her mind's eye. This time she saw an aspect of her countenance she had never seen before—neither the day of the fateful interview, nor in her memory since. Beyond the assurance, there had been an imploring in her aged, yet tender, loving eyes. Almost as if she were asking for Hilary's help!

"You give your word that you will tell them?"

Had there been a desperation in her tone beyond that of a grandmother who feared her newly found granddaughter might opt to keep her identity a secret? But why?

Why would the old woman have come seeking a daughter when a perfectly good one—one who bore such a distinct family resemblance, and wore such a sweet countenance—sat at home the whole time?

Two hours later Hilary walked back toward the inn. Dusk was settling over Port Strathy. She had already resigned herself to one more night here. She would return to the inn, take a bath, then perhaps walk over to the MacKenzies' cottage and spend the evening with them.

Approaching about a quarter mile from the inn—she could see it gleaming white and inviting on its perch above the cliffs that extended out to the east—Hilary saw a figure coming toward her. In the gathering darkness of the late afternoon, she could make out no details except that the form walked like a man.

In less than a minute, however, they had moved near enough to one another for recognition. It was Logan Macintyre.

All Hilary's emotional equilibrium began to flutter, and, except for great determination of will, would have fled entirely. She walked steadily on until they came close and stopped.

"Hello," said Hilary simply.

"I hope you don't mind my seeking you out like this," said Logan.

"Of course not."

"Davies said he hadn't seen you. But your car was still parked out front, so I took a chance I might find you somewhere along here."

"Is this where everyone in Port Strathy comes to think?"

"Very nearly." Logan's eyes laughed, but he only let a brief smile flicker across his serious expression, a smile that Hilary felt rather than saw. "My wife and I spoke together after you left," he added.

"I'm sorry if I caused—"

"You caused nothing, Hilary—if I may call you that—except a good deal of confusion. No less for yourself, I'm sure. Please, let's walk." He gently touched her arm, nudging her into motion.

"Thirty years ago," he began once more, "we lost our daughter. In time we resigned ourselves to never seeing her again. But now all of a sudden we have two perfectly lovely young women, both of whom appear justified in laying claim to that position. If you think you are confused, try to imagine our predicament. It would have been enormously easier had we not read such sincerity in your face. But we could hardly deny it. In addition, there is the little I know of you from London, all of which speaks highly of the honorability of your intent. You are a somewhat well-known woman of growing reputation. Thus, it strikes me that you would have much more to lose than to gain by any attempt to deceive us—which I do not for a moment believe you are trying to do. And believe me, I have some knowledge in such matters." He paused, gazing into the gathering darkness.

"But this only deepens our dilemma. For you see, our daughter—Jo, that is, whom you met—has come to us with the most impeccable of credentials and has already been with us nearly three months. I can hardly believe that the people who initially contacted me about her discovery—men of high repute—could have been so grievously in error. Especially after all the checking that was done. And I cannot help fearing the effects of such a blow to her, now to discover she was uprooted and torn from her life in the United States—for nothing but a dreadful foul-up of some kind in interpreting the evidence and records."

"I'm not sure what you are saying."

"If Lady Joanna did indeed come to see you—"

"She did."

"I tend to believe you, my dear," sighed Logan. "At the time you mentioned, she did travel to London. There was some small row about it here, in fact, for none of us wanted her to go alone—at her age, you know. But she insisted. She was to all appearances in perfect health, so eventually we gave up our protests. She was extremely cryptic about her reasons for the trip, however. But the point remains that she was in London at the time you said."

"I think one question should be asked," said Hilary. "Forgive me for it, but I have to know—was she in her right mind?"

Logan seemed on the verge of a quick response, but he stopped himself and did not speak until after some consideration. At length he said, "If you indeed did speak with Lady Joanna, then you would know the answer to that question."

They fell silent for a moment. Hilary was the first to speak again.

"Yes, you are right. I do know the answer. Because, as it turned out, that one meeting with Lady Joanna is going to have to last me a lifetime, I have not allowed myself to forget a single detail of it. She was a remarkable woman. Perhaps one of the most sane persons I have ever met."

"Then why would you raise the question?"

"Because I'm as desperate for answers as you are, Mr. Macintyre. That would have simplified everything, wouldn't it?"

"I believe we must forget about finding *simple* answers."

They were nearing the path that led up to the inn. Logan paused at its foot momentarily and Hilary took the brief lapse in their conversation to study him. It was difficult to reconcile this mature man with silvery hair and moustache with the rakish con man and daring undercover spy of Joanna's journal. But then maybe not, when you looked deeply into his eyes, outlined with distinctive crow's feet now, often deeply introspective. Even in the failing light Hilary imagined hints of wry amusement, even a little mischief. All the features that had made him handsome in his youth had combined now, at age sixty, to give him a markedly distinguished air, mellowed with a sensitivity that had not come except through suffering and hard-fought spiritual victories.

Hilary could not deny the uneasy fluttering within her heart. For against all analysis, she realized this man might be her father! If so, she knew she would be honored to be called his daughter. He was a far deeper and more sincere man than she imagined when she first stood to interview him a week and a half earlier.

But he had begun to speak, and she jerked her wandering mind back to matters at hand.

"In answer to your question, Hilary," he was saying, "I have an interesting, perhaps unusual, suggestion to make. I have spoken to my wife, and we would both like for you to stay with us while we sort this all out."

Hilary gaped silently at Logan. *Interesting* was far too mild a description of the idea!

"I . . . I couldn't," she finally stammered. "It would be—too awkward. I couldn't do that to your dau—to Jo."

"So you will return to London then, and just forget the whole matter?" Logan asked pointedly.

"I don't know. That would be best for everyone, wouldn't it?"

"Then perhaps that answers all our questions. For if you sincerely believed Lady Joanna's claim, then I doubt you'd give it up so easily."

"It almost sounds as if you are *looking* for a challenge, Mr. Macintyre."

Logan sighed. For a brief moment the creases on his youthful face deepened, and he looked old. "I sincerely wish we weren't having to face these baffling questions, Hilary," he said. "But now that they have been raised, we cannot merely turn our backs. Allison and I can never rest until they are resolved." He paused and leveled his gaze steadily at her. "Regardless of what you decide to do, I cannot let this go."

"But you were so sure before."

"Perhaps we still would be if it wasn't for Lady Joanna's part in all this—of which we knew nothing until today."

"She has that much influence, even though she is gone?"

"If you come to know us at all, Hilary, you will soon learn that in this family the women are accorded much respect. For several generations they have been endowed with great wisdom and godliness. The men who have come into the family, such as myself and my father-in-law Alec, we have learned to recognize and honor that wisdom, and never to take it lightly."

"Like the mantle being passed down from one woman to the next."

Logan's head shot around, his eyes suddenly appraising her as if trying to detect if there could possibly be a hint of mockery in her words. But when he saw none, he simply nodded and remarked, "That is an odd thing to say."

"Lady Joanna wrote something to that effect in her journal."

"Her journal?"

"Yes. She sent it to me. Actually, that is what prompted me finally to approach you."

"She *sent* you her journal?" He was obviously stunned by the disclosure. "No wonder it was missing," he said aloud, but as if thinking to himself. Then he turned his gaze from Hilary and focused on the wide sea beyond them.

Logan began walking again. Hilary had to half-jog to catch up. But he said nothing until they had negotiated the short but steep climb up the bluff. When they reached the top, he continued along the flat path for a few brisk paces, then stopped and turned suddenly.

"I believe," he said with decision, "that it is imperative you accept my invitation."

"It would be too strained."

"I might think you were afraid of something, but you hardly strike me as a person who frightens easily."

It was now Hilary's turn to fall silent and momentarily introspective. Perhaps she *was* afraid. Yet her inborn nature had always compelled her to confront her anxieties rather than hiding from them. The same internal force that had urged her to make her first trek to Stonewycke now prevailed upon her to heed this man's words. Neither could she just return to London and forget. The haunting image of Lady Joanna and the stirring words of the journal would never leave her.

"You are right on both counts, Mr. Macintyre," she said, turning to him. "And because I see no other solution, I will accept your invitation."

He nodded, pleased, but remaining grave and thoughtful. They continued on to the inn, where Hilary paid her account, picked up her things, and departed with Logan.

23 ❋ *The Oxford Connection*

A FURTIVE FIGURE dashed out of the shadows, lumbered across the deserted street, darted into an adjacent alley, then stopped.

Clearly unused to the effort, his panting was the only sound to be heard. After a few moments he resumed his flight, crossed the next intersection and continued at as fast a pace—something between a hurried walk and a labored jog—as he could manage for two blocks. His loose frame gave every appearance of rebelling against the sustained exertion. Sweat had already matted his hair, which was a little too thin on top, a little too long on the back of his neck, and was dripping from his high forehead and down his heavily jowled cheeks. Under the shabby wool overcoat, his shirt was already drenched under the arms.

Halting again, he tried to still his aching lungs, listening all the time for the footsteps he was sure were following. There were none to be heard, but he knew the man was out there—somewhere . . . waiting . . . for him!

He had to get back to his flat! There he would be safe—at least until he could decide what to do.

As he moved once more out of hiding and down the cobbled street, terror was visible in his eyes. He knew the stakes of this game. When he had given up his tenure for more lucrative pursuits, he'd known there were risks. And though he'd met many shady and dangerous characters along the way, and managed to hold his own with them, inside he was still a scholar at heart. He would never be altogether like the men he did business with. That's why he'd adopted the practice of protecting himself by always having information on his colleagues at his ready disposal. *Know your adversaries—and your allies* had long been his code. *You never knew when they might turn out to be one and the same.*

Protect your flank. It was the only way to survive. That's why he'd hired his old gumshoe friend Stonecroft to watch out for him, keep his eyes on his clients, tail them if necessary, learn what he could of their background, who was working for whom, where was the money coming from, motives. Call it insurance.

Maybe it was too much for an art broker to take upon himself. The thought made him realize anew how bitterly he resented being known as nothing but a common fence by some of his seedier clients. He had left the university in order to involve himself more directly in his true first love—*objets d'art*. And through the years he had built up a clientele that included some of the richest men in the world. His name would never show up in a *National Geographic* article. But if people in the know wanted information about what was "available," what was hot and what was not, or how to acquire a given piece and how much it was likely to run on the black market, they knew he was the man to ask. In fact, he had been interviewed a time or two, though his name had never appeared in print.

At least one Sheik's gallery in Arabia, a collection of Egyptian relics in Amsterdam, and a truly historic display of priceless firearms in Sweden had been put together almost entirely with his help. He was not adverse to an occasional plebeian assignment of moving a cache of stolen rifles, or perhaps jewels—drug-related jobs, however, he refused to touch. It kept his bank account at the comfortable level of liquidity he liked.

But it was the sophisticated and rare objects of artistic magnificence and even perhaps what he might call historical value, which gave him the greatest satisfaction. It had given him the chance to lay his eyes and hands on beautiful treasures he would otherwise never have been able to see. At the same time, he managed to build up a rather nice collection of his own. And he felt a bit of pride at the fact that a time or two his own former colleagues at the university had contacted him with a thorny historic art puzzler they hadn't been able to decipher.

He hadn't acquired the handle *Professor* only as a nickname designating his one-time profession. He still ran his business, as he chose to think of it, in a studious manner. If he was going to charge his clients the fees he did—he never liked to think of them as crooks on the one side and black market buyers on the other—he had to know everything he could about them, and about the merchandise they brought him to move or asked him to locate. It kept him in the know . . . and out of trouble. No sudden surprises. He liked it that way.

Now all of a sudden Stonecroft was dead. And it wouldn't be hard to trace him back and link them together. Everyone on the streets of Oxford knew the Professor and Stonecroft were close friends. Though he had been part of this world long enough to know how to blend into the intelligentsia around here, Stonecroft stood out like a sore thumb. There'd never been much reason to hide it before, and their relationship went back fifteen years, before either had gotten involved in this business. But now, suddenly, his connection to Stonecroft had become a lethal liability.

His friend was dead! He could still hardly believe it! No wonder he hadn't been able to locate him for the past forty-eight hours. Now *he* was likely to be next! He had to get back home. He had to sit down, behind double-locked doors, and think! Perhaps have one last pleasurable gaze over his treasures.

This kind of thing wasn't supposed to happen at Oxford. This was supposed to be a quiet little town. That's why he'd remained here.

He'd known those two bumbling idiots Tex and Mex were flunky underlings the moment they'd contacted him. "Your contact's a Mr. Smythe at the Shrewsbury office of Trans Global," the Texan had said in his annoying drawl. "Anything comes up, Mac, and you need to get in touch with us, you just call them up and ask for Mr. Smythe with a *y*. You gotta say it like that, 'Let me talk to Mr. Smythe with a *y*,' and they'll know what you mean. You got that, Mac?"

What a positively irritating chap! Why they'd sent a mismatched pair like that, he could never understand. He couldn't imagine a respected company like Trans Global employing such nincompoops. Sure, a company of Trans Global's repute might have a division in its operation financing an archaeological dig someplace. It would be good PR for them. And they might well come to him to evaluate their find. But surely the people involved would be of a higher caliber than those two buffoons!

That's why he'd put Stonecroft right on them. He had to know who was really behind this thing. If Trans Global, then who in Trans Global . . . and why? It was obvious from the first that the assignment was far bigger than the little tokens they'd brought him to evaluate. But he never dreamed who his friend would turn up.

Stonecroft had called from London two afternoons ago with the startling news that Tex and Mex had turned the goods back over to none other than Pingel.

Pingel! He hadn't heard of him for years. This truly was turning into an international operation! And if he was involved, unless there had been some dramatic upscale change in Pingel's loyalties, it meant that none other than the General was behind it all, funding and directing the strings of whatever was going on.

He'd never dealt with the man directly. And he didn't want to start now. But his reputation in the nefarious circles in which the Professor often had to circulate was vast.

The General connected to Trans Global Enterprises, one of Europe's most prestigious firms . . . it was incredible! Just last month he had read that the Prime Minister had cited the chairman and directors of Trans Global as particularly to be commended for their valiant fight against pollution, calling Trans Global "a company that sets a standard for integrity in this changing industrial age, of which the nation is proud." Edward Heath did not dish out such compliments lightly.

This was not only unbelievable . . . it was a dangerous piece of information to possess! If Interpol got wind the General was involved with Trans Global, it would seriously damage the company's prestige. Especially if—but no, that was too fantastic a notion even to consider . . . that the General was actually running Trans Global behind the scenes!

The General was not the sort of man you tangled with. The minute he'd hung up the phone he'd known what he must do. He had to get out of this transaction altogether. The General was known for dusting off people who crossed him. Pingel was the man who usually enforced that policy.

Even before he'd had the chance to figure out how he was going to do it—a man like the General didn't like cowards either, or fences who reneged on deals—Stonecroft had called again, this time from Heathrow. He was watching him right now, he said. He'd learned his destination from a ticket agent he'd slipped a few quid. The name of the city confirmed everything! Hardly surprising, said Stonecroft. It's where all those guys went. He'd see him safely onto the plane, then hustle back to Oxford with a full report.

That was the last time he'd heard from his friend.

Now suddenly, just minutes ago, he'd learned that his body had turned up at the airport. out behind a pile of carts near a deserted hangar.

The moment he'd heard, a cold terror had seized him. The only question that still remained was whether Pingel had gotten on the plane. Probably by now the General himself knew the Professor had put Stonecroft onto his men. The General wouldn't like that.

He had to get home, and then to safety. Maybe to Dublin, Scotland . . . even the Continent. Pingel had never taken that flight. He was here . . . somewhere. He knew it.

He could feel his presence . . . stalking him!

I've got to get out of here . . . away from Oxford! thought the Professor one more time to himself. Then he flew out of his temporary hiding place. He did not stop again until he was safely inside his flat, doors securely locked behind him.

Nervously he made his way to every window to make sure all the shades were pulled. Then he cautiously turned on but one small lamp, and at last, all precautions taken, collapsed on his bed in exhaustion.

24 ✸ An Accident

TIMIDLY HILARY OPENED the door of her room.

For so long she had been used to being in charge. She had had to make her way in life by a determined self-reliance that did not cower in the face of opposition. When she walked through the doors of *The Berkshire Review*, eyes turned toward her in expectation. She was the center of focus, the one who set the magazine's momentum.

Now here she was feeling like a thirteen-year-old suddenly thrust into a new boarding school where she was a stranger amid long-time friends. She was reluctant to so much as walk downstairs alone. She had never felt so out of place in her life.

She stepped out into the corridor, glanced in both directions, then turned to her left. That much at least she was certain of, though it would take some time to familiarize herself with the maze of hallways, rooms, courtyards, parlors, and staircases that comprised the great castle of Stonewycke. She had been fortunate enough to sleep past breakfast, though Logan had come to her room in midmorning and had taken her out and shown her around. They had seen none of the rest of the family. Allison, he said, had remained in bed too, with a severe headache. She would join them for lunch later in the dining room. Now, Hilary only hoped she could remember his directions of an hour and a half earlier.

Her footsteps echoed ominously as she walked. Around any corner she half expected to encounter Lady Macbeth or some Dickensian ghost from a past generation.

At least she did not feel entirely alone in this respect. It seemed that Allison and Logan Macintyre, as little as she had seen of them, seemed a bit out of place as well. Perhaps it was only because they were so much a part of the contemporary world. At the same time, Logan had appeared completely at ease this morning as he showed her several ancient paintings in various corridors, and a five-hundred-year-old vase probably worth tens of thousands of pounds. He seemed comfortable in both worlds, the old and the new, maintaining a kind of casualness toward the house, mingled with not a little respect as well. Actually, the only one who seemed entirely in keeping with the surroundings was Jo, who, with her demure refinement, looked more the part of a Victorian heroine than a Baltimore debutante.

Hilary reached the first-floor landing, hesitated a moment to check her bearings, then started down to the ground floor. There she turned to the right, walked past the family parlor, and arrived at last at the door of the dining room.

Well, she thought, *this is it. Time to make my first "appearance" with the family.*

She reached out, turned the latch, pushed open the door, and walked inside.

"Ah, Hilary," said Logan cheerfully as he rose and walked toward her with a smile. "I see you've found your way."

"Your directions were very clear," she replied.

"Well, I know the hazards of being a stranger in this place," he went on. 'I'm not too old to remember my first days here, and I can tell you it was an intimidating experience, even for a streetwise youngster like I was."

Hilary quickly took in her surroundings. Besides Logan, only Jo was in the room, seated at Logan's left hand. She smiled warmly in acknowledgment of Hilary's arrival, but neither spoke to the other.

"Please, Hilary, sit down," said Logan "My wife will be here soon. She felt better an hour ago and decided to take her morning walk."

Hilary moved around the table to a chair opposite Jo's. "Come now, Mr. Macintyre," she said lightly as she seated herself, "I can hardly picture you intimidated, even by a centuries-old castle."

Logan laughed, but before he had a chance to respond, Jo spoke up. "Just wait till you know my father better, Hilary," she said. "He's full of surprises."

An uncomfortable silence filled the next moment.

Logan cleared his throat. "And that, I'm afraid," he said as his face turned serious, "pinpoints, as it were, our present awkwardness." He took a deep breath before going on. "I don't know how to make this pleasant, for either of you," he paused, glancing in turn toward each of the women. "But the fact of the matter is clear enough: my wife and I had but one daughter. And now, after all these years, it seems suddenly we have two! We're going to do all we can to resolve this confusion as quickly and painlessly as we can. We're going to have everything checked and rechecked. I've already contacted your solicitors in Glasgow"—here he turned and looked in Jo's direction, then glanced around toward Hilary—"and we're going to have to do what we can to trace Lady Joanna's last weeks to see if we can verify what she apparently turned up."

A puzzled expression flitted across Jo's face, but it passed quickly and she said nothing.

"But," he went on, "as much as I am concerned for each of you, the point remains that somewhere a most distressing mistake has been made. I just hope in the end we will all be mature enough to handle the outcome in a Godly manner."

"Are you certain I ought to remain here?" asked Hilary, finally voicing the question that had been haunting her all day. "It might be easier for you all if I just stayed at the inn, or even perhaps if you just notified me in London once it is resolved."

"We had this same conversation last night, as I recall," answered Logan. "Believe me, Hilary, we *do* want you here." As he emphasized the word, Hilary thought she detected a hint of sternness, a side of himself Logan Macintyre had not shown her before. "Besides," he added more jovially, "there is no reason we cannot be hospitable. However this turns out, think of yourself as our guest. After all," he added with the old gleam in his eye, "you and I both have to return to London and, if not exactly work together, at least coexist on opposite sides of the press-Parliament debate. For that reason alone we ought to be friends!"

"You are very persuasive," said Hilary.

"Come, both of you," he said as he rose and took a coffeepot from the sideboard, "let's have a cup of coffee while we wait for Allison. I can't imagine what's keeping her."

"Hilary," said Logan as he filled their cups with coffee, "I was wondering one more thing about your conversation with my mother-in-law. This morning you told me—"

But the sudden look that passed over Hilary's face arrested him in mid-thought. "What is it?" he asked.

"I'd completely forgotten!" replied Hilary in an animated expression. "I can't imagine why it slipped my mind. But when you mentioned Lady Joanna again, it all came back!"

"What came back?"

"The locket . . . she and I talked about the locket!"

"What locket?" asked Jo.

"A locket I've had since before I can remember," said Hilary. "The instant Lady Joanna saw it, the strangest look came into her eyes. She said . . . "

As Hilary took a breath, the silence in the room was deep.

" . . . she said it used to belong to her, and that she'd passed it down to your wife."

"By Jove!" exclaimed Logan as his hand crashed down onto the table to the resounding sound of tinkling china and silver. "That could be the solution to this whole thing! Do you still have it?"

"Yes, yes!"

"Where? Are you wearing it?"

"It's in my room. I don't think I ever took it out of my overnight case." She laid her linen serviette on the table. "I'll get it right away."

"By all means!" said Logan enthusiastically. "We'll have Allison in here to take a look and once and for all—"

Before he could finish, the sound of a commotion outside in the hallway met their ears.

"What in blazes?" said Logan as he hurried to the door and out into the corridor. Hilary and Jo followed him.

A knot of household employees was making their way toward the dining room from the direction of the kitchen. The cook and housekeeper hovered about, while Jake the stableman walked up, carrying Allison in his arms. Logan rushed forward, concern evident throughout his features.

"I'm all right," said Allison as he approached. "I took a bad fall and Jake insisted on carrying me."

"Bad canna be the word for it, sir," said Jake. "My leddy's lucky to be alive. Ye must fetch the doctor here sure. It wouldna surprise me if her ankle be broke."

"Posh, Jake!" insisted Allison. "I'm fine, I tell you. Set me down."

Begrudgingly Jake complied. Allison took Logan's arm.

"Will one of you please tell me what happened?" said Logan, his stern voice now showing through clearly.

"I slipped on the footbridge," said Allison.

"Slipped ye didna, my leddy," argued Jake. "The bridge gave way, an' 'tis only the grace o' God that ye're no lyin' at the bottom o' the creek right noo."

"I was out there just yesterday," said Allison, "and it was perfectly sound."

"Ye go oot there every day," insisted Jake, "and I doobt ye'd be fallin'—"

"Are you sure you're all right?" asked Logan.

"Yes, it will be fine," Allison replied. "But I've interrupted luncheon."

"Don't worry about that; we hadn't even begun."

"I shall go call the doctor," said Jo.

She turned and hurried away, while Jake ambled off in the direction from which he had come, muttering something indistinct about not being able to keep pace with the deterioration of a place this size, while the cook and housekeeper made their way back toward the kitchen with heads together buzzing.

Logan led Allison, limping, into the dining room, where he gently set her down upon the settee.

"Perhaps a drink of water, my dear?" said Logan. Allison nodded and took the glass he offered. Only after a long swallow did Allison first seem to notice Hilary where she stood about ten feet away. She smiled up at her.

"Hilary," she said, "I haven't had the chance to see you since you came back with Logan last night. Welcome—once again—to Stonewycke."

"Thank you," she replied.

Hilary had taken in the whole scene like the reporter she was, as if her eye had been the lens of a camera, objectively observing the passage of events, followed by the reactions of the principal characters involved. She could hardly help the unconscious attempt to locate the proper angle for an article. It would no doubt fall into the category of human interest, focusing perhaps on the love she had read in Logan's eyes, or the genuine concern and devotion of the employees for their mistress. Colorfully intriguing was Jake's gruff insistence that seemed to imply some sinister motive afoot, quickly dismissed by the more level-headed master of the house, leaving the disgruntled handyman walking off alone with no one to grouse at but himself.

"But how could I forget!" said Logan, coming to himself. "Hilary may have solved the entire mystery in one fell swoop, my dear," said Logan to his wife. "She was just telling us that she has a locket . . . *the* locket, according to your mother, that used to be yours."

Before the impact of Logan's words fully reached Allison's mind, the door opened and Jo walked quickly in.

"Dr. Connally is on his way," she said. "I'm sorry I was so long. How are you feeling, Mother?"

"Oh, I'm fine," replied Allison. "Now, go on with what you were saying about the locket."

"She has it here," said Logan. "Please," he went on, turning toward Hilary, "go get it . . . right now."

Hilary obeyed, and left the room.

When she returned ten minutes later, her step was slow and her face told what words hardly needed to say.

"I . . . I can't imagine what happened. But the locket's not there."

25 ✾ Mustering a Force of One

THE LOUD RINGING of a phone split the midnight air.

Muttering a curse, the occupant of the room struggled into wakefulness and fumbled for the receiver. The moment he heard the voice on the other end of the line, his body snapped almost as if to attention and sat up on the edge of the bed. All drowsiness instantly vanished.

"It's *you*!" he said. "I didn't expect . . . no problem . . . no, I was just, er, lying down . . . time difference? It's, let me see, two-thirty in the morning. . . . "

He was silent for some time as the voice on the other end spoke, nodding his assent occasionally, a grave expression on his face.

"Hmm," he said at length. "Yes, that should work . . . a clever way to introduce myself . . . they would have no way of knowing . . . right, couldn't check . . . yes, I'll use that. . . . "

Silence again. Another several nods.

" . . . I understand . . . I'll get up there as soon as I can . . . getting into the house, that might be difficult, but . . . no, no, rest easy. We'll handle it . . . what could go wrong? . . .

In response, the voice of the caller shouted a series of threats which the man softened somewhat by removing the receiver from his ear and holding it back about three inches. Then, without his speaking another word, the line went dead, and he hung up the phone.

Well, he thought, this is an interesting twist to the schedule. "Get up there immediately," his boss had said. "An unexpected setback . . . a complication . . . an unknown person entering the scenario."

He'd have to cancel his plans to go hunting with the earl. But then, this assignment would not be without its potential compensating rewards. And his caller was not a man to be refused.

Now, if only he could get back to sleep. There were preparations to be made, and tomorrow would be a full day.

26 ✾ Small Talk in the Parlor

THE REMAINDER OF Hilary's first day had gone by uneventfully. She'd spent every free minute searching her room for the locket, but it was nowhere to be found. Logan drove her down to the Bluster 'N Blow, but neither did a thorough turning over of the room she had occupied reveal a trace of it.

Jo was away a good deal of the day, so Hilary felt somewhat a greater freedom to walk about the house and grounds, visiting with the staff. She and Allison had enjoyed a talk together—admittedly light, but without the strain of their first meeting the previous afternoon. Dinner had been a rather stiff, yet endurable affair—the conversation stilted, no doubt, on account of Hilary's *faux pas* over the locket.

The next morning she had arisen early and walked to town and on to the MacKenzies', where she enjoyed a visit and a simple lunch. Now here it was the afternoon of her second day at Stonewycke, and time was beginning to hang heavy on Hilary's hands. About three o'clock she wandered in to the family parlor. A fire burned cheerily in the hearth and the room was warm. Logan sat to one side reading a newspaper, with a pen and notebook on his lap with which he was jotting down notes from time to time. Kitty-cornered from him across the room Jo sat, a piece of needlework idle in her hands, staring vacantly into the fire. As Hilary entered, Logan glanced up with an inquiring expression, as if to say, *Well . . . have you found the locket yet?* Jo did not move.

The furnishings in the parlor were modern and comfortable, the color scheme bright and upbeat, and there were no ancient vases to be troublesome to the occasional absent-minded guest. A television sat in one corner and a low coffee table held stacks of magazines and newspapers. A great variety was represented, including every single London daily. It was clear Logan made a point of keeping abreast of current events and editorials and the shifting tides of public opinion. *The Berkshire Review* was among the offerings on the table, and Hilary could not help feeling a twinge of pride that an important man like Logan Macintyre would choose to read her magazine. She restrained an urge to pick it up and thumb through it, notwithstanding that it was last month's issue and she already knew every article backward and forward from supervising them all through the different stages of production. Seeing the magazine did serve as a reminder that she ought to check in with the office. She had reported in when she left the inn. They were managing well, which was a good thing since they just might have to get the next issue out without her services at all. But she should call every couple of days regardless.

She picked up yesterday's *Daily Telegraph*, sat down on the sofa opposite Logan, and began to leaf through it.

"Did you have a nice visit with Frances and Karl?" Logan asked.

"Yes, very pleasant."

"They're good folks, the sort that make this little valley so special."

"I can tell. So hospitable. They keep trying to get me to come back down and stay with them, in their little but-end room, as they call it."

Logan laughed. "That is like them!"

"She's always talking about the people 'up on the hill.' She seemed especially fond of Lady Joanna."

"Oh yes! Mother always had a special place in her heart for Frances MacKenzie. As do I. She shares my mother's name, so I've been rather fond of her."

"She said it was her aunt the Queen Mother visited with Lady Joanna."

"That's right," chuckled Logan. "Frances is fond of that story—tells it every chance she gets! She was old MacDuff's granddaughter. MacDuff—he was the chap—"

"Yes, I know," said Hilary. "I read all about it, remember?"

"That's right, of course. In any case, I think Joanna's love for Frances stemmed more from the soft spot she always had in her memory for her grandfather, who first brought her into Port Strathy."

The door opened and Flora's face appeared. "Ye've a telephone call frae Lonnon, sir," she said.

"Thank you, Flora," said Logan, rising. "You ladies will excuse me. I'll be back in a few minutes. In the meantime, it'll be a chance for you to get better acquainted."

He left the room and silence fell, broken only imperceptibly by the thin crackling of the fire. Hilary feigned interest in her newspaper, trying to think of some appropriate question to ask. It was the first time she and Jo had been alone together.

It was Jo who spoke first, however, rising and sauntering slowly toward the fire. "It's so cold outside! Cook said the back-door thermometer read 23 degrees this morning. She said it will snow soon."

"That will be a nice change," offered Hilary.

"It will be like home for me," Jo sighed dreamily. "I'm from Baltimore, you know. In Maryland. I've been dearly hoping for a white Christmas."

"You should have no worries here in Scotland—even Bing Crosby would be pleased."

Jo laughed softly, and Hilary noted how much the sound resembled tiny bells that seemed in perfect harmony with thoughts of Christmas.

"Do you miss your home?" asked Hilary after a short pause.

"Sometimes, I suppose. Britain is so different in many respects. But I have no real home back in the States any longer."

"Your adoptive family no longer lives there?"

"My parents—my *adoptive* parents, that is—were killed in an auto crash three years ago."

"I'm so sorry . . . I didn't realize."

"There was no way you could have known," replied Jo.

She sat down in an upholstered chair adjacent to the sofa and folded her hands in the lap of her navy cashmere dress. Her lips twitched into a tentative smile as if she were debating some problem in her mind involving the present conversation. Then, apparently deciding to go ahead, she spoke again.

"Hilary," she said with feeling. "it was such a special thing for me that the Macintyres came back into my life when they did. I had been so devastated by my parents' deaths and was so very much alone. It's bad enough to be orphaned once, but twice! I really didn't think I would be able to survive it."

Hilary could think of no appropriate response, so said nothing. A brief silence fell.

"Do you mind my asking you something?" Jo asked after a moment's pause.

Hilary shook her head.

"I'm only curious, so please don't read any other meaning in this, but I heard you say that you spent some time debating whether you would even approach the Macintyres. I wondered what changed your mind?"

"I made a promise to Lady Joanna."

"You knew her quite well then?"

"We only met once."

"Hmm . . . I see."

"Even though she died before I fulfilled it, I knew in the end that I must be true to what I pledged to her."

Hilary paused before continuing. There was another reason she had come. Suddenly she felt a strange hesitation about mentioning it. But just as quickly as it had come over her, she shook it off and went on. "I think it was mostly the journal that convinced me that this whole thing went beyond my personal likes and dislikes and hangups."

"The journal?"

"You don't know about Lady Joanna's journal?"

Jo seemed to consider her response a moment, then slowly shook her head.

"For years she has kept a record of all the events in the life of the family. It begins with Margaret Duncan's life, and is brought up to the time just prior to Lady Joanna's death."

"A history of the family?" asked Jo. "Births, marriages, deaths—that sort of thing?"

"That, but much more too."

"More, you say. Like what?"

"I don't even know how to describe it. A chronicle of . . . of life—emotional, spiritual, as well as historical. It's so much deeper than a mere factual recounting of events. Lady Joanna's impressions come through on every page. It conveys such wisdom, such truth about . . . oh, I don't know, so many things . . . Lord and Lady Duncan, others who touched their lives, how the family was sustained through the years."

"Then she must have written about us—my arrival, her visit with you?"

"That's the peculiar thing. There's no mention made of any of that. Knowing how Lady Joanna wrote down what she thought about everything, I can hardly believe she would omit something so crucial. It's like the last three months were removed from it altogether."

"Removed?"

"The journal ends abruptly, in mid-sentence, actually. It's very odd. But she was getting up in years. Perhaps they were just misplaced."

"Do you still have it?"

"Oh yes. And after misplacing the locket, I've made double sure I don't lose the journal. I've got it safe and sound."

"Would it be an imposition if I asked if I might have a look at it?" Jo's tone was hesitant, demurring, yet a trace of tension could be read in it also.

"I don't know," Hilary began to answer haltingly. "It seems perhaps we ought to ask Mr. Macintyre if he thinks we ought—"

Before she had a chance to complete the sentence, Logan returned and walked briskly back into the room.

Appearing relieved, Hilary said no more, glancing down at the paper that still sat in her lap.

"Well, what have you ladies been talking about?" asked Logan lightly, masking his obvious interest in that very thing. He did not like to have left them so long alone.

"Nothing much," answered Jo. "Just girlish parlor talk, you know."

Logan was at that moment looking toward Hilary, and did not see the momentary flash of defeat that flitted through Jo's eyes, belying the calm nonchalance of her words.

She sauntered toward the chair she had previously occupied, disinterestedly picked up her needlepoint, and then a moment or two later left the room.

Logan resumed his seat, scanned the notes he had written earlier, quickly jotted down the gist of his phone call for future reference, then laid his papers aside and attempted to engage Hilary in easy conversation.

She did not appear interested, however, and remained quiet. Though her apparent reaction to her talk with Jo concerned him, Logan did not press her. In a few moments he rose again, excused himself, and left the room, this time with a determined look of mingled uneasiness and decision etched on his face.

27 ❈ A Visit to the Stable

THE RUSTIC OLD loft over the stables had not changed much in fifty years. In fact, it had probably hardly changed in the more than one hundred years since its most revered occupant lived there.

The steps were relatively new, at least by comparison, and remained in good repair. Logan had built them himself in 1931. They were good, solid steps and barely creaked as he now ascended them.

When Logan reached the door, he had to brush away cobwebs from above the entry, a reminder that it had been too long since he had come to his dear uncle Digory's humble home. The door creaked when he pushed it open, straining upon its rusty iron hinges. But that scarcely lessened the awe the place held for Logan, for it was a reminder that a hundred years before, Digory too had shoved open this same door every day—though not to the sound of creaks, for he was known to keep his equipment well oiled. Inside, everything was just as he had found it that first time, though a bit cleaner perhaps. A small shaft of the late afternoon light pierced the corner of the single small window high up on the western wall. It wasn't much, but enough to illuminate the small room and even smaller alcove.

Logan ambled idly about for a few minutes, brushing down a cobweb or two, running his hand along the sparse furnishings, absorbing the ambiance of quiet peace this room would always hold for him. He did not come here nearly often enough, he told himself. Though since it was usually times of uncertainty or crisis that drove him here, perhaps he ought not to rebuke himself too harshly.

The last time had been more than a year ago when he had been seeking direction for his career. Wilson's long and successful Labour government had been surprisingly voted out, and for a time Logan seriously thought he ought to take that fact as a personal mandate indicating that it was time for his own retirement from public office. He had tried to tell himself he was getting too old to jump back into the fray of running for Parliament again, with all the strain it entailed.

But after time in prayer in the stable loft, he had realized his reaction was due to bitterness, not age. In six years the Labour Party had brought economic health—at least the strong beginnings of such—to Great Britain, yet the election of 1970 had turned into a rejection of the party. It was difficult not to take the rejection personally, for he had played a key role in the formulation of many of the party's policies. But once he recognized the bitterness for what it was, he had been able to ask God sincerely for a change to occur in his heart. With the answer to that prayer came renewed enthusiasm for his job, and renewed faith in and love for his constituents. When he had told Allison of his decision to re-seek his seat in Commons, she had sighed with relief.

"I hadn't wanted to push you before," she said. "It had to be your decision. But I wondered when you would see through that excuse of being too old. Why, sometimes I think it's the political battles that keep you young, Logan! You love the 'fray' as much as any part of the job."

How well she knew him!

Logan was not the sort whose job consumed every aspect of his life. Yet he had to admit that his job was an important part of what kept him going. He loved what he did, and felt he was making a contribution as a Christian to society and to his fellow man.

His position had come as a gift from God, a true answer to the prayers of a returning veteran, coming home from a war that contained many dark hours for those in the thick of it. He had desperately needed direction to his life back then, for even if his faith and his marriage had been substantially healed, he could not keep from fearing stumbling into the pitfalls that had been the catalyst of his personal deterioration before the war.

The first few years had been tenuous, at best. Though he and Allison were at last able to trust one another fully, Logan found himself still lacking in marketable skills. Arnie Kramer had secured him a position in public relations in his father's shipping company. Logan enjoyed the work well enough, yet not to the extent that he was able to envision it as his life's vocation. But the hard-learned lessons of his war years served him well and he stuck with the job for four years. As a result of his tenacity, in the course of his assignments he became associated with members of the Trade Commission and thus first tasted the outer spheres of political life. He knew immediately this was something he liked!

Arnie had been the first one to jokingly mention his running for public office. Logan had scoffed at the notion. But Arnie wouldn't let it go, and began to bring it up with increasing frequency, and with deeper and deeper sincerity—with at least as much seriousness as the old windbag could muster.

"Logan," he exclaimed one day, "everyone knows that politicians are nothing but legalized con men! You'd be a natural at it, old boy."

To Arnie, Logan merely laughed. But inside the suggestion took root. He struggled with the possibility for a long while. He no longer cared to submit to his "natural" instincts, whatever they might be. A wise priest had once told him: "Certain things are truly natural because they come from God. Others are not natural because they originate in our so-called 'natural' man."

He had prayed a long while, over the course of many months, right here in Digory's old room, before he gradually became certain that God did indeed desire him to embark on this new career. And after that first election, which had been a battle worthy of the name, he first understood what Jean Pierre had meant when he spoke of giving oneself wholly to what one is called to do. Becoming a member of Parliament had indeed provided direction in his life. And more, it gave meaning—something he had not found in any of his previous *natural* endeavors.

Yes, Logan had come to this stable loft in the wake of many crises, and to face many difficult decisions. And thus he had come today, even if it had been a year since the last time. The problem facing him this day was unlike anything he had ever confronted, and was a question filled with many complications.

A heavy oppression had grown upon him these last two days since Hilary's arrival. It only made his confusion of late greater. He knew the source of the pressure—it came from the host of unpleasant questions that had been bombarding him. It was not hard, therefore, to associate the oppression with Hilary herself and her arrival.

But when he went deep down inside himself, he had to admit that it had begun even prior to her coming. He had not been able to pinpoint it. Then she had come, and his disquietude took on wider dimensions. Yet somehow he viewed Hilary more as a victim than an instigator. Still, her presence in and of itself raised even more questions. It had come to a head just moments ago in the parlor. Seeing the two young women together, alone, both of them in a frightfully awkward position toward one another—at that moment he had known he had to do something—and soon.

But what? Ultimately, it all seemed to come back to Lady Joanna.

Why had she gone to see Hilary? And without mentioning a whisper of her intent to anyone? It seemed too far-fetched a story for Hilary to have fabricated. And how else could she have gotten hold of the journal? Joanna had admittedly become quieter than usual about two weeks after Jo's arrival. But if she'd had questions, why had she kept them to herself? If only he knew what she had known, whom she'd talked to, what she'd learned and where, maybe some of his own questions would have come into focus. But it was too late to find such things out. She was gone, and her secrets with her.

He and Allison had hoped that by inviting Hilary to Stonewycke, their own instincts and discernment would have the chance to get at the truth; that somehow seeing the two women together for an extended period of time might reveal which one was truly their daughter. But each bore distinctive family characteristics, and after this afternoon he realized he had to take some greater form of decisive action.

He was sure the whole mix-up would in the end be explained by some clerical blunder—either by Jo's Glasgow lawyers and investigators, or by Lady Joanna in her oddly-timed quest that had landed her in Hilary's London office. On one side or the other, there had to be an easily explained error.

Yet another terrible suspicion nagged relentlessly at him. And down inside perhaps this was the crux of his recent anxieties. It was so unthinkable he had not even mentioned it to Allison. But if he was going to get to the bottom of this it had to be considered. Was it possible that one of these women could purposely be attempting to deceive them?

The very thought made him tremble. For if it were true, then the level of such duplicity was incredible. Logan was well known for his ability to read a man's face—one of his attributes as an ex-gambler that served him well. But in this present dilemma he could not venture so much as a wild guess who the impostor might be. If there was indeed hypocrisy, there must be evil genius behind it. Which was why he could not bring himself to believe such a thing. It was too fantastic for even him to swallow.

Perhaps his talent for probing the depths to discern hidden motives did not extend to *women's* faces. Or was he just too personally involved to be properly objective?

He did not dwell on that train of thought for long. He remained convinced that somewhere an enormous mistake had been committed. But in any case—foul-up or fraud, innocence or deceit—he had to do what he could, and take what precautions lay open to him.

He walked into the alcove where the table and chair Digory had used still sat. He eased himself down into the chair, propping his elbows on the table, then bowed his head in prayer.

28 ❀ *Help from a Friend*

WHEN LOGAN DESCENDED the steps from the old loft some thirty minutes later, at least some of the peace he had been seeking had come to him. While he didn't have a complete answer to his dilemma, he did know what action he must take next.

He breathed deeply of the homely, wholesome, earthy animal smells around him. Though he didn't ride, he was glad they still kept a few horses. It was part of Stonewycke's heritage. This would always be Digory's stable, he supposed, though many grooms, mechanics, and handymen had come and gone since his great-great-uncle's time. Logan reminded himself that

Digory's peace had not come because the stable was a quiet place where the anxieties of the world seemed far away. His peace came from a higher Source, and so did Logan's. Because he felt God had spoken to him just now, he walked with a lighter gait and a ray of hope in his eyes.

Logan briskly crossed the back grounds and gardens, entering the house by way of the kitchen. The cook was slicing two cold steamed chickens for a late tea; dinner that day had been served at one in the afternoon; Hilary had been with the MacKenzies at the time. The cook threw Logan a cursory greeting, mumbling something about the impossibility of preparing a *proper* menu with unexpected guests appearing every other day, and with the grocery order being late.

Logan chuckled to himself. Three months ago she had been complaining about how quiet the place had become. *I might not be able to give her warning about our next guest either,* he thought. *Not just yet, anyway.*

He mounted the stairs to the first floor, turned purposefully down the hall, and came to the library. He opened the door, stepped inside, and glanced about carefully before closing the doors behind him. Certain that he would not be disturbed, he went to the phone on the desk and picked up the receiver.

"Long distance," he said when the operator came on.

He gave her the number, then waited while the connection was made.

In a few minutes another feminine voice answered. He identified with whom he wanted to speak.

"May I say who is calling?" she asked in an efficient receptionist's tone.

"Logan Macintyre."

"One moment, please."

There followed a brief pause. Then she came back on the line. "He's just finishing with an appointment. Can you hold a moment?"

"Yes," answered Logan, "I'll wait."

He took the interval to move around the desk to the chair, where he sat down and took some papers from a drawer that needed attending to. He had barely looked at the first one when he heard a masculine voice in his ear.

"Logan, what a pleasant surprise!" it said. "I'm sorry for having to make you wait."

"I know the rigors of a public life," laughed Logan. "Always busy. But I would appreciate it if I could steal a few minutes of your time."

"Of course!"

"This one's personal."

"Go on. What can I do for you?"

"I have rather an unusual problem," Logan replied. He laughed again. "Actually, that's an enormous understatement, as you'll see. It's an extremely delicate matter, and I need some outside input."

"From me?"

"I need someone I can trust, my friend," said Logan earnestly. "So on that count you are my top choice. But I need your keen analytical mind as well. Along with your other, shall we say, non-erudite pursuits—about which you are so bloody closemouthed that even a friend such as myself can't uncover what you are up to!—don't you have a chum in Scotland Yard to whom you've lent your wisdom upon occasion?"

Now it was his friend's turn to laugh. "You make me sound like a genuine mystery man! All from one unguarded comment I made four years ago. I tell you, Logan, you're imagining the whole thing. I'm just what I appear to be, nothing but an innocent—"

"I know, I know!" interrupted Logan. "Always the same answer! And you've got the credentials to back up what you say. But someday, believe me, I'm going to find out what the deuce you are up to!"

"A pointless sleuthing exercise where the object is nothing more than the boring chap he appears to be."

"I don't believe that for a moment. But tell me, isn't what I said about your having a friend at the Yard true?"

"Yes, but my only contributions have been for the sake of mental calisthenics. He's made me privy to a few of their cases, and sometimes by sheer luck, he solves one when I happen to be around. It is a rather stimulating breather from my boring routine, if nothing else."

"Quite, quite! As is this snow job you insist on shoveling my way. Well, perhaps I can propose another 'breather' for you, if you are interested."

"Proceed. You have my curiosity aroused."

Logan briefly outlined his situation, then went on to explain what he hoped his friend might do for him.

"I'm afraid," said Logan, "that I have become incapable of being objective. I must be missing something—perhaps the very thing Lady Joanna saw but kept so silent about. Thus, I thought it might be helpful if someone neutral could observe the situation. An outsider, so to speak, sifting through the evidence, helping me to see what perhaps my own eyes are unable to."

"There's no fault with the credentials?"

"No, none on either side. Everything on the complete up and up. I've had everything double, even triple checked. I verified that Lady Joanna did indeed visit the offices of *The Berkshire Review* at the specified time. And the Edwards girl does indeed possess the journal; the only way she could have obtained it is directly from Joanna. If there is deception involved in any way on her end, it would extend all the way back to my mother-in-law's being fed spurious information. Yet if that is the case, I can hardly believe the girl herself knows about it. She seems to have been genuinely moved by her encounter with Lady Joanna. All indications point toward complete innocence."

"And the other—what did you say her name was?"

"Jo, after Joanna. That was our daughter's name."

"Yes . . . and what about her?"

"Nothing much to say. Everything checks out. She seems innocent enough, too. Allison's been quite taken with her."

"Hmm," mused Logan's friend, "you do indeed have a puzzle on your hands. Have you consulted the police?"

"Heavens no," replied Logan. "No crime has been committed, for one thing. It has to be a muff somewhere down the line. But even more than that—and this is the crux of the matter, after all—one of those women is apparently my own daughter. That alone necessitates treading somewhat lightly."

"I see . . . and you would like me to—"

"Just get to know them, even just socially at first, see what your instincts tell you about the two of them."

"That should be an enjoyable exercise! Tell me, what do they look like?"

"Both beautiful," replied Logan laughing. "But you would need to come up north for a few days. I know your schedule is—"

"Nonsense! A vacation will be a welcome diversion. I need to get away!"

"So you'll do it?"

"I'll have to clear a few things up, but I'm sure I can manage it. At this point, I'm too curious not to."

"There is one last thing I ought to mention," said Logan. "It might be best if we kept a low profile on your reasons for being here. No need to cause undue tensions. The women will be more open if they are unaware of our connection, and you've never met my wife. So I think it would be best if your coming was made to appear purely accidental, and if you and I keep our past association in the background."

"Yes . . . I see what you mean. Any suggestions?"

"You are a clever fellow. You'll figure something out."

"Surprise you, eh?"

"Right! I can't tell you how much I appreciate this, old chap!"

"Then don't. Wait to see if our efforts bear fruit."

After solidifying a few more arrangements, Logan bid his friend goodbye and replaced the phone in its cradle. He laced his fingers together behind his head and leaned back in his chair.

For some reason he felt relieved. Probably because he had finally taken some action, done something concrete. A solution seemed much closer now than it had several hours ago.

29 ❧ Postponed Interview

HILARY HAD NOT slept well since her arrival at Stonewycke.

Part of her temporary insomnia was definitely due to the tension surrounding her visit. It was augmented by the intense quiet of the place once darkness descended. She could hear it now—the sounds of absolute stillness . . . nothing. No night wind was blowing. They were too far from the sea to detect any sound from the shore. The horses in the stable were still. Everyone in the house was in bed. The tranquillity was not broken by so much as the occasional chirping of a cricket, for the cold had driven the creatures into hiding.

Hilary was accustomed to being lulled asleep to the constant accompaniment of sirens, blasting horns, and the screeching brakes of London's taxi system. Her city-acclimated mind could not allow the peacefulness of the country to penetrate beyond her surface senses.

But when she crawled into bed an hour ago, she thought she would have little trouble drifting off to sleep. For the first time in days she felt some release from the burden of confusion that had been weighing her down. For that she could thank Allison.

Shortly after dinner, following two more rather tedious days at the castle, during which time the temperature had dropped even further, Hilary had ventured up to Lady Macintyre's room. Allison was still recuperating from her fall, though she had been out and about some today. The doctor had been in, and upon examining the swelling and discolored ankle had remanded her to bed for a minimum of twenty-four hours, prescribing elevation and ice. Jo had been most diligent in tending Allison and bringing in cold packs ever since. She had, in fact, been in almost constant attendance upon Allison, which was the primary reason Hilary had waited so long to visit the patient. But at the first break in Jo's ministrations, she took the opportunity to pay her own respects.

"I would have come sooner," explained Hilary, "but I didn't want to get in the way. I do hope you're feeling better."

"Much, thank you," replied Allison. "But I have absolutely no patience with being laid up. I'm more frustrated than anything. I'm no good at all with the helpless woman role."

"I understand that," said Hilary. "Activity is certainly part of my profession."

"That's right, you're a career woman."

"I suppose that's as appropriate a term as any."

"I'm sure all my activity drives everyone crazy at times. My poor mother, as tolerant as she could be, was often scandalized at my outspoken participation in Logan's campaigns and work. But it just doesn't pay to try to be something one is not."

She paused and shifted her position in bed. "Please, sit down a minute."

"Don't let me wear you out."

"Don't worry about that. I feel fine. Better, in fact, than I have for two weeks—if it just weren't for my ankle. But I haven't had a chance to talk with you since your arrival. Perhaps the Lord brought about this accident to force me to be still a while."

Hilary pulled a chair to the bedside and sat down.

"I must admit," Allison was saying, "that something inside me has been avoiding this conversation. I had no idea what I would say. In fact, I still don't. The whole situation is filled with so many emotions, many that I have yet to identify within myself. I want to get to know you. But at the same time I have to admit to some fear, for I've become very attached to Jo these last two months. She's become, well . . . if not a daughter to me, then certainly like one. Now suddenly . . . your coming—it's all very befuddling. I feel like pulling back from everything, from both of you, but I know that won't solve anything, either."

"I understand," replied Hilary. "I would like nothing better than to run back to my own secure little world. Believe me, I resisted coming back that night Logan met me at the inn. The only reason I decided to stay was that I had already invested so much of myself in my decision to come to Stonewycke in the first place. I couldn't walk away from it. Besides, after my initial hesitation, I have come to believe quite strongly in everything Lady Joanna told me."

"Logan says you have read my mother's journal."

"Yes, and that journal, and the portrait she paints of your family through the years, played a significant part in my decision."

"It does seem peculiar that she sent it to you. . . . " Allison seemed to muse over the thought before continuing.

"I asked her several times if Jo could read it," she went on. "She agreed whenever I brought it up, but it was always, 'Let me finish this one section,' or, 'I'd like to polish up a few paragraphs first.' So she never got around to it. She died so suddenly."

"She possessed great wisdom, and a wonderful way of expressing herself. The people she wrote about, even you and Mr. Macintyre, are all very real on the pages. I feel as if I know you all."

"She is the one who comes through more than anyone else."

"I wish I'd been able to know her better."

A short silence followed, each reflecting on the confusing turn of events. Finally Allison asked, "Hilary, do you mind my asking about your beliefs . . . your spiritual values? Are you a Christian?"

Hilary smiled. "I suppose you always hope someone won't find that question necessary, that the way you visibly live will be answer enough. But yes, I am. I have been walking with the Lord since I was a teenager, though every year it seems the growth works its way a little deeper."

Hilary paused, wondering how far to open herself to this near stranger who just might be her mother. At length she plunged ahead. "I suppose that accounts for a good deal of my present confusion. I prayed and was sure God was directing me here. Now it seems perhaps I was wrong."

"Are you certain of that?"

"No. I'm not certain of anything anymore. But if God was leading me here, I cannot help wondering why things have turned out as they have."

"Nothing has 'turned out' yet at all. We are all confused. Nevertheless, if there is a single principle that shouts out of my mother's journal above all else, it's the simple truth that God can take the bleakest of circumstances and, for those who are walking in His way, transform them wonderfully so that good results. I am sure God brought you here for a reason."

What a boon those words had been to Hilary—exactly what she needed to hear. They enabled her to shift the weight of the present confusion into God's infinitely more capable hands. Everything that had come about must indeed be part of some design greater than her small mind could fathom. She was here at this very moment for a purpose. Perhaps that was why sleep had eluded her this night, for an anticipation was gradually creeping over her since her conversation with Allison. For the first time since her arrival, she found herself eager for what God had in store. Moreover, she was not so willing to turn tail and run as she had been when she first discovered Jo's presence.

If God had brought her here, then He *would* direct her path and make the way into her future clear.

30 ❧ Snowy Rendezvous

HILARY ROLLED OVER in her bed, squeezed her eyes shut, and tried to force sleep to overtake her.

But it would not come. Many years ago she had learned the futility of fighting a temporary bout of insomnia. During such times it was generally her habit to get up and do one of two things: spend time in prayer, or seek out her typewriter. In either case, the night hours always proved profitable.

But on this particular occasion, as she had already spent a good forty-five minutes in prayer, and as her typewriter was four hundred miles away in London, she had to settle for the third option: a cup of tea—hot enough to be relaxing, weak enough not to send sleep even further away.

She rose from her bed, wondering if she dared roam about the house at nearly midnight, much less rummage through an unfamiliar kitchen. But the worst that could happen might be a scolding from the cook, who, Hilary could already tell, possessed strong territorial feelings toward her domain.

Hilary crossed the room to retrieve her robe from a chair. As she glanced out the window, suddenly all thoughts of tea faded from her mind. It was snowing!

She rushed forward and pressed her face to the windowpane. The white flakes must have been falling for some time, for already one or two inches covered the ground, casting over the countryside an eerie luminescent glow. The boughs of tall firs were just beginning to bend under the weight, and the absence of wind allowed the slender piles of whiteness to grow high upon the branches before falling silently upon the powdery blanket below.

"No wonder it was so quiet outside!" exclaimed Hilary.

With a childlike sparkle in her blue eyes, she threw down the robe in her hand, slipped out of her nightgown, and quickly stepped into her slacks, pulled a sweater over her head, put on her shoes, and grabbed her heavy overcoat as she headed out the door and into the stillness of the corridor.

She could scarcely remember the last time she had been out in a fresh snowfall. The bustle of London usually turned what scant snow did fall there into brown slush before nine in the morning. But she had always enjoyed the snow. Even as she hurried down the staircase, another night came to her mind when she had been about ten years old. The night had been a similar one to this, although she had slept well. In the middle of the night she had awakened suddenly, almost as if some inner voice had told her something extraordinary, beautiful, magical was at that moment taking place in the forbidden midnight hours. The instant she had seen the white gleaming cover spread out over the streets, reflecting the glow of a pale moon peering through a break in the cloud cover, she knew she must venture forth.

Creeping from her parents' flat and down the single flight of stairs, grimacing at the loud creak as she landed on the next to last step, opening the door as noiselessly as she was able, soon she was outside.

Notwithstanding the presence of the moon, snow was still falling, and huge lightly textured flakes brushed against her face, upturned in awe. What a glorious moment that had been for the city-bred youngster, made all the more wondrous in the realization, as she first looked down toward her feet, that neither milkman nor bus nor workers returning home from factory graveyard shifts had yet marred the perfect, velvety mantle.

Funny how things come back to memory, she thought. The uncanny silence, the ghostly illumination. It had been these sensations, more than the sight of the snow itself, which had triggered the memory. It had been many years since that night had come into her mind. As a child she had determined to keep her adventure to herself. But then the terrible cold that resulted two days later forced a confession of her errancy to her worried mother. Mrs. Edwards had smiled gently, and in her eyes could be detected a certain camaraderie which seemed to say that she, too, held memories of one or two childhood journeys such as Hilary's.

"Well, tonight I'll not catch cold," said Hilary to herself as she opened the great front doors and stepped outside.

Her face was met, not with a blast, but yet with the impact of the cold. Huge flakes fell unhindered from the midnight sky—soft, noiseless, gentle.

Hilary held out her hands in unabandoned delight, letting the mystical crystals glide through her fingers. She started down the steps, and was all at once overcome with the curious sensation that she had been there before, standing on those very steps, standing just as she was now, looking out into the sky, with snowflakes fluttering all about. For the briefest of instants, snatches of a dreamlike childhood passed through her mind, with images altogether distinct from the more lucid memories of London. Then came the picture of a small girl again, standing in the snow, with just a trace of high-pitched giggling floating, as if audibly, in the air about her.

Just as quickly as the obscure images had come, they were gone, leaving behind only the sad melancholy of something very precious being lost. Trying to shake the feeling, Hilary continued down the steps and began to cross the courtyard.

She smiled as she went, looking behind her at the footprints she left feeling the thrill of being the only one in on nature's delightful secret. She made a wide circle around the fountain, then wandered aimlessly toward the gate across the entry road some hundred feet away.

Suddenly she stopped. There again was the faint sound. Maybe it hadn't been merely a dream of childhood! Though now there was no giggling, only the faint muffled sounds of voices drifting toward her across the snow. She was not alone in the pre-dawn world after all! Peering ahead, barely visible in the midst of the white earth, Hilary spied two figures. They stood just off the roadway, beyond the gate, in a grove of silver birch. If they hoped for the cover they might afford, the barren, leafless trees offered none. Only one of the figures was identifiable.

Jo stood facing the castle, whispering with emphatic gestures, apparently in heated dialogue with a man whose back was toward Hilary. The usual impassive serenity of Jo's face was flawed with tension to accompany her motions. Even in the night, Hilary thought she could see her dark eyes flashing.

Instinctively Hilary stepped to one side of the gate, wondering what she should do. Before she had the chance to contemplate long on the question, however, the couple embraced, then stepped apart.

Hilary knew she could not get back into the house without being seen, and her footprints would give her away in an instant. She stepped farther into the shadow of the gate, knowing even as she did so that the last thing she could do was hide.

The dilemma of an encounter was forestalled, however, and then Hilary realized why there had been no footprints but her own in front of the house. When the man disappeared back along the driveway, Jo turned and walked through the trees, where a breach in the hedge at the side of the house admitted her to the garden area. There she crossed the relatively short space to the kitchen door, adding a new set of footprints to the ones she had made earlier, and was soon inside.

Breathing a sigh of relief, Hilary waited another five minutes where she was, then walked back across the courtyard—by now feeling the effects of the cold—into the house again, and back up the stairs.

Long after she had climbed once more into the warmth of her own bed, Hilary asked herself for the twentieth time what the strange meeting could signify. If Jo had a lover, why the secrecy? Surely Logan and Allison would not deny a romantic interest to a thirty-two-year-old woman. If not romance, then what other reason could have driven her out in the snow in the middle of the night to meet a man?

She had no way of answering her question, however, and eventually fell into a deep sleep, whose only interruption was a silly dream about two snowmen crossing a large field of ripening grain together. The larger of the two began to melt, causing the smaller great dread. Before long there was but one snow figure left, a child of a snowman, made with two balls of snow rather than three. When she arrived at a village after walking a long distance, there were no other snowmen to be found. And when all the people asked her name, the little snowgirl couldn't remember. When asked where her mother was, all the little snowgirl could answer was, "I don't know where I'm supposed to be."

31 ❈ Fortuitous Encounter

WHEN HILARY AWOKE the following morning, she felt oddly refreshed. Never would she have guessed that her night had been interrupted by snowfalls, secret trysts, and wandering snowmen.

At breakfast everyone seemed to have been similarly affected by a positive wave of good cheer that had come with the snow. Jo entered the dining room, glowing and full of enthusiasm. "It snowed in the night! Isn't it grand?"

"Indeed!" agreed Logan heartily as he dished up his plate from the trays and bowls on the sideboard.

"I should like to take one of the horses out for a ride today," Jo continued. "The day is too gorgeous not to be out in it."

"This terrain's difficult for a horse even in the best of conditions," said Logan. "It might be a bit tricky. Have you ever ridden in the snow?"

"You know I'm quite an adequate horsewoman."

"So you've shown yourself, I admit."

"Why don't you join me, Father?"

Logan laughed. "Surely you know by now that the extent of my association with horses lies in the area of wagering, not riding—and even in that regard I've grown a trifle rusty these days."

"And you've no desire to learn the equestrian side of life at the track?"

"None whatsoever."

"And you call yourself the progenitor of the Ramsey-Duncan strain?"

"I call myself nothing but a humble Macintyre, sprung from the common, yet noble blood of grooms. Don't you know," he added with a wink in Allison's direction, "it's the women who wear the pants in this family?"

"I'd not be adverse to joining you if it weren't for this silly ankle," Allison put in. "But I'll not stay indoors on such a day," she went on with some defiance in her tone, and a coy, sidelong glance at Logan. "I think I shall try my hand at painting a winter scene. I'm feeling good, and I haven't painted in days!"

"I didn't know you were an artist," said Hilary, settling down at the table with a plate bearing half a stewed tomato, a couple of smoked kippers, a piece of toast, and a soft-boiled egg.

"I am merely a student," replied Allison. "Jo is the real artist among us, and she has encouraged me to take it up as a hobby."

"Don't let her fool you," said Jo. "She has quite a talent for it." She paused, then brightened suddenly. "I've a splendid idea! Mother, I'll get you all set up with your paints. Then, Hilary, you can join me for my ride. You haven't yet had a proper chance to see the countryside."

"I'm not much experienced with horses either," said Hilary. She would have been closer the mark had she said she'd only been on a horse one other time in her life, and that was fifteen years ago. But she let her statement stand.

"Say you'll come," prodded Jo. "It will be the perfect opportunity for us to get to know one another better."

Hilary suppressed the urge to say that what she was really interested in was knowing Allison and Logan better. But again she kept quiet, and in an hour thus found herself dressed in riding habit borrowed from Allison, browsing through the horses in the stables. Jake followed after her, pointing out the merits and idiosyncrasies of the half dozen beasts. She finally settled upon a sedate-looking chestnut which Jake then led from its stall and saddled. In the meantime, Jo had chosen her favorite, a spritely dapple gray mare.

The two women mounted. Side by side they provided an interesting contrast. The chestnut, which in the sunlight showed a fair smattering of gray in her coat, hung her head low and, to Hilary's great relief, seemed barely capable of more than a slow trot. Hilary, however, sat bolt upright, looking confident, the reins held expertly in her hands, exactly as Jake had placed them. It was not the first time in her life as a reporter she had had to feign expertise where none existed. She'd snagged many a good news story that way. She knew how to watch and listen, and pick up appropriate clues from others. Why she did so now she couldn't quite explain, except that perhaps she was growing weary of being the odd person out at Stonewycke.

She had no delusions that she would fool Jo with her act once they began to move. It was obvious Jo knew her way around horses from the masterful way she sat the gray. There, atop the powerful mount, Hilary thought she detected an almost imperceptible change in the look of her face. Was it something in the tilt of her chin, or the glint of her dark eyes? It seemed that the animal energy of the gray mare was being conducted through the saddle and up into the rider. Demure and passive the effect would not be called. Untamed, stormy, perhaps. A hint of wild challenge, a daring, supreme self-reliance.

Before Hilary had time to evaluate this hidden person, Jo jabbed her heels into the gray's sides and was off at a trot. Hilary followed as best she could.

Jo led the way at a spirited pace. They headed west for a short distance; then Jo turned sharply toward the south. The night's snowfall had deposited several inches of white covering, but many patches of brown earth showed through, and dormant shrubbery and boulders otherwise spotted the landscape. The pale morning sky, more than half filled with thick gray clouds in front of a backdrop of white, gave every indication that it would not be long before snow dominated the entire countryside.

They continued on for about half an hour, following a rough, narrow trail that surely saw little general use. The air grew colder, and the wind, which had been but a chilly breeze lower down near the sea, turned icy and whipped fiercely at the two riders and their steeds. The chestnut's flanks heaved with the added exertion, but Hilary dared not slow for fear of falling too far behind. Eventually the ground leveled off, and to Hilary's relief she saw that fifty yards ahead Jo had reined the gray to a stop. Hilary trotted up next to her.

"I thought we might need a rest," said Jo, brushing a strand of hair from her face.

She might just as well have said *you*. But Hilary swallowed her pride, gratefully nodded her head, and dismounted. The solid ground had never felt so good. She rubbed the chestnut's white face.

"You are a nice beastie," she said, "but I think even you will agree that we were not made for each other."

Jo swung easily off her mount. "I rode nearly every day in Baltimore," she said, striding over to where Hilary stood. "My adoptive father had a fine stable, even a few thoroughbreds."

"All my father owned was a mangy yellow cat," laughed Hilary. "But she was a good mouser, and that was a valuable possession in Whitechapel."

"Whitechapel?"

"Where I grew up . . . London—the East End."

"Ah."

"I have a feeling that you and I had quite different upbringings. Whitechapel is far removed from all this, believe me." Hilary swept her hand through the air to indicate their surroundings. "In more ways than one."

"It will grow on you."

"But surely you must hope it doesn't." Hilary purposely kept her tone light.

"I hate to think we are rivals," Jo replied.

"But we are, aren't we?" asked Hilary, the interviewer in her surfacing.

"You may look upon it that way. But I feel no sense of competition. I know my credentials are irrefutable. I only feel bad for the mistake that will ultimately be uncovered in Lady Joanna's investigation. It's only a matter of time, I'm afraid." For a brief instant her eyes narrowed and sent out a dark flash. Almost immediately that icy glance was replaced with the gentle breeze of a smile. "I am sorry, Hilary. I really am. I so wish you could be spared the pain."

Hilary walked on in silence, leading her equine companion with the reins in her hand.

"You should see this place in late summer," said Jo, when she caught Hilary again and came up beside her. "It's a sea of purple. When I first arrived, I was just mad to get it on canvas."

"Might I see some of your work sometime?" asked Hilary in her most sincere attempt at friendliness.

"Of course, if you are really interested," Jo answered with apparent shyness, unable at the same time to mask her pleasure. "Look, there's a rock rose bush. Two months ago I painted a gorgeous late bloom right there. Now it's just a tangle of thorns."

"What's that over there?" asked Hilary, pointing toward a huge pile of stones about a quarter mile distant.

"Oh, nothing much. I think they said it was the ruin of an ancient village of some prehistoric people."

"The Picts," said Hilary. "So that's it," she added, almost to herself. Suddenly mesmerized, she began walking toward it.

"Wouldn't you rather ride?"

"Not at the moment," Hilary called back.

"Go on then. I'll bring the horses."

Hilary continued walking as if she were stepping out of the year 1971 and into an ancient fairy tale. Before her stood the ruin where a thousand years ago, maybe more, a marauding band of Viking warriors had slaughtered an entire Pict community—man, woman, and child. Or so the legend went according to Joanna's journal. But the pillaging Scandinavians had not found the treasure they were seeking. That was left for one George Falkirk to unearth a millennium later, only to lose it again in a sordid tangle of murder and deception. Here is where it began—Falkirk's murder, Ian's imprisonment, and Maggie's tragic exile from her homeland. Here too a carefree London con man had been swept into the drama of the Ramsey-Duncan clan, nearly losing his life in his own personal search for the missing treasure.

Yes, so much originated here, perhaps even in my own history, thought Hilary. For so long she hadn't wanted to accept this change in her fortunes. Then once she had come to accept it, suddenly she was having to compete for it.

Jo's intrusive voice was almost a relief. "We ought to be getting back. It may begin to snow again."

Reluctantly Hilary mounted the chestnut. The horse seemed suddenly skittish, more reticent about the arrangement than earlier. The animal snorted and stamped one foot in a most irritable manner. Already the distance between the chestnut and the gray had widened. Not understanding the finer points of a horse's temperamental psyche, Hilary gave her mount a little kick with her heels in an attempt to catch up. The horse broke into a trot and Hilary struggled to hang on. The first time she bounced in the saddle, however, coming down squarely upon the animal's back, the mild mannered chestnut whinnied and reared like a wild stallion, then suddenly shot off in a frenzied run. An experienced rider might have been able to bring the creature quickly under control. But all Hilary knew to do was hang on and hope she wasn't thrown off onto the rocky ground.

The animal tore past Jo, who gasped in surprise. Immediately she urged her gray into a gallop as she sought to overtake her companion. But the chestnut seemed determined to make it a worthy race. Suddenly she was running like a two-year-old thoroughbred rather than the old nag she was. She took no thought for the icy, rock-strewn terrain under her hooves, but plowed ahead, wildly splattering snow and dirt up behind her churning feet. In unmitigated terror Hilary clutched the reins and horn of the saddle, only wondering how much longer she could stay on the horse's back and into which ditch she was going to fall, battered and bruised and broken, and most likely dead!

Behind her Jo trailed on the gray, but did not appear to be gaining ground. Ahead, less than thirty yards away, the ground sloped off into the precipitous descent they had labored to ascend only a few minutes earlier. Once the animal crossed the edge of the ridge there would be no stopping, for the sheer momentum of the descent.

Suddenly in the blur of her panic, Hilary saw a horse galloping toward her. But it wasn't the gray!

She tried to scream for help, as if her distress might not be clearly evident, but no sound would come from her throat.

She flew past the rider. They tumbled past the precipice and now bolted more steeply downward!

The sound of hoofbeats from behind distracted her attention. She tried to glance back, but could only make out fuzzy images of animal flesh and snow. The rider had wheeled his own steed around the moment Hilary had torn past and was now charging after her, and gaining ground.

In another moment, out of the corner of her eye Hilary saw a hand reaching for the chestnut's bridle. Side by side the two horses galloped! Then first she felt a change in the pace. At last her horse was slowing!

It was some time before they came to a complete stop. Even as they did so, notwithstanding its exhaustion and heaving flanks, the chestnut continued to snort and paw the ground. All Hilary could think about was getting off the crazed animal, and in her haste she cared not in the least how clumsy or awkward her dismount appeared! She threw herself down, but even before her feet touched the ground her rescuer was at her side offering a strong arm.

"Thank you," was all the gratitude she could manage, still shaking from head to foot and barely able to stand.

"Come," he said. "I see a rock over here where you can sit."

Beginning to catch her breath, Hilary took his offered arm. "I can't imagine what I'd have done if you hadn't come along," she panted. "I must have looked pretty foolish!"

He led her to the rock, where she sat down and continued to breathe deeply.

"On the contrary," he replied. "Foolish you did not look. Panic-stricken . . . yes! But beautiful on your runaway mount, if I might be so bold as to add."

Hilary laughed. It felt good. She hadn't laughed in days. "Panic-stricken I certainly was! And I'll forgive your forward compliment, under the circumstances."

Now it was the stranger's turn to laugh.

As he did Hilary first took note of her rescuer's accent, and she forgot her own brush with disaster long enough to give him closer scrutiny. He could not have more perfectly epitomized the stereotype of the tall, dark, and handsome hero. Accustomed to looking past the surface for deeper qualities of character, in another setting Hilary's first response toward such a good-looking man might have been suspicion. Yet given what had just taken place, she forgave him his dashing appearance; perhaps he might have the character to match, she thought. His dark brown hair was smooth and well-groomed even after the harrowing ride. Dark green eyes glinted like emeralds in the winter sunlight, and the tanned skin of his well-proportioned face could scarcely have acquired such golden tones anywhere but on a southern summer beach. A neat black pencil-thin moustache, above ivory-white teeth always poised on the edge of a smile, completed the face, lending to the foreign mystique of his Germanic accent.

"May I introduce myself, Fraulein?" he said. Bowing ever so slightly he went on. "I am Viscount Emil von Burchardt, at your service!"

"I am very glad to meet you. I'm Hilary Edwards." She held out her hand, which he took and, bowing again, kissed gallantly. "But it is I who should be at your service."

He chuckled softly. "Ah, you modern women are so delightful."

At that moment Jo rode up and dismounted. She glanced at the stranger and smiled.

Feeling much steadier, Hilary stood to make introductions. "Herr von Burchardt—"

"Please, please. You must call me Emil—all the women I rescue do!"

Hilary laughed and continued. "Then, Emil, I'd like you to meet Joanna . . . Macintyre." Hesitating over the last name, but knowing no alternative, she forced herself to use it. "Jo, this is Viscount von Burchardt."

"Emil, if you will, Fraulein," said the Viscount, bowing once more and kissing Jo's hand. "I had no idea the north of Scotland would display such beautiful women."

"And where might you be from, Emil?" asked Jo sweetly.

"I am of the Austrian von Burchardts; you have perhaps heard of us?"

"No, I'm sorry. But then I am from America and I'm afraid we don't keep much abreast of the European aristocracy."

"Ah, yes. You Americans have such a penchant for throwing out traditions."

"Only some of them. But I do want to thank you for your timely intercession today. I was afraid to press my own horse harder for fear of finding myself in a similar predicament."

"What brings you to Scotland, Emil?" Hilary asked.

"I decided to put in and let my yacht weather in your fair harbor of Port Strathy," von Burchardt replied. "I have been touring the British coast for some months. But today a great yearning for solid ground overcame me, and besides yachting, my second favorite sport is horseback riding."

"It's fortunate for me your legs tired of the sea," said Hilary.

"But I do not want to detain you ladies longer in this cold air. Please, may I accompany you safely home?"

"Thank you very much," replied Hilary.

"May we thank you even further, Herr von Burchardt, by inviting you to lunch?" asked Jo. "I would be honored!"

They returned to their horses. The chestnut showed further signs of agitation. Von Burchardt insisted that Hilary ride with him; he had just the kind of saddle that would make it comfortable, he said. Hilary consented with a smile. In the meantime, Jo had a quick look at the chestnut's hooves, commenting that she thought the animal might have taken a stone. She took its reins and followed behind the Viscount and Hilary, who talked amiably the whole way back to Stonewycke.

Hilary was much relieved to deposit the horse into Jake's care. As the three riders walked to the house, Jake led their animals away, speaking soothingly to his charges and patting them as he removed their saddles and dug out a handful of oats that he let them eat from his open hand.

As he lifted the chestnut's saddle he paused, his wrinkled brow knit in concern. "What be this, lassie?" he mumbled tenderly, rubbing his hand over a sore on the animal's back. Examining the spot closely, he picked out several sharp thorns. "Noo, whaur did ye get these? Sma wonder ye went a wee bit off yer chump when she landed on ye."

He carefully cleaned the tiny wound, rubbed in some salve, then led the weary chestnut back to her stall.

32 ❊ Afternoon Tête-à-tête

THE VISCOUNT VON Burchardt proved himself a charming guest.

He was witty, an adept conversationalist, knowledgeable in whatever direction the discussion went, well traveled with an abundance of stories to tell, yet at the same time perfectly gracious in drawing out discourse from others, in which he seemed to display a profound interest. Logan expressed great fascination with his yachting exploits, asking him question after question. When the viscount would answer, Logan leaned back with a smile which seemed to contain more meaning than its owner would let on, and replied, "You don't say!"

Von Burchardt was vague about his recent itinerary, but when pressed by Logan, who said he hadn't recalled seeing a yacht in the harbor yesterday when he was in town, the viscount merely laughed, saying, "Well, you know us continental gadabouts—we never like to be too tied down, and I only just arrived this morning." Smiling oddly again, Logan let the matter drop.

Allison was the only one who did not seem to be taken in by his charm. Throughout lunch she was grumpy, complaining of a headache that had come upon her during her morning's session with her paints. She found the viscount's mannerisms annoying, and finally excused herself and left the room on unsteady legs.

Logan jumped up to follow her, caught her in the corridor, lent a steadying hand, and saw her to their bedroom, where he sat her down on the edge of the bed.

"What can I do for you, my dear?" he asked tenderly.

"Nothing, nothing at all!" Allison snapped. "Just go back to your idiotic guest Bergmark, or whatever his name is, and leave me alone!"

"Can I make you more comfortable?" said Logan, maintaining his cheery countenance and fluffing up the pillows under her.

"No, no . . . I'm fine. It's just . . . that stupid painting! I couldn't get anything to come out—"

She stopped and suddenly burst into tears.

Logan sat down beside her and tenderly wrapped her in his arms.

" . . . my hand wouldn't go right, and I couldn't keep from mixing colors where they didn't belong," she sobbed, "and my fingers wouldn't stop shaking. The moment I took the brush from Jo's hand this morning I began to feel sick again. Oh, Logan, I hate it! Just when I was starting to feel good again. I so wanted to paint that little stream trickling through the snow, and now I've ruined that canvas and the painting's a mess . . . and look—I've still got paint on my fingers—"

She held out her hands imploringly like a little child, her eyes red from crying.

Gently Logan stroked her hair, speaking softly into her ear. Gradually she calmed, and he laid her down on the bed. In a few moments she was fast asleep. Logan remained at her side a few minutes longer, his hand resting gently on her back, his mouth speaking barely audible prayers on behalf of his troubled wife to the Father of them both, who was watching all, and understood.

Meanwhile, Hilary and Jo were doing their best to keep up the dialogue with their guest, hardly difficult when the guest was a man like Burchardt. By this time he had bent his charms fully upon the two attractive women—with a definite emphasis, it seemed, in Hilary's direction. For her part, Hilary found him pleasant enough, certainly handsome and courteous. She wondered, however, if he might be just a bit too polished. She did not try to analyze the viscount or his motives too deeply. For the moment she opted to put her reporting instincts in the background so that she might simply enjoy the diversion his presence offered. She took him at face value, and for the present that seemed sufficient.

They were just finishing a light dessert of sliced apples and cheese, with oatcakes and butter, when Logan reentered the room.

"I apologize for the interruption," he said.

"How is Mother?" asked Jo, her voice laden with concern.

For the briefest instant, Logan's eyes seemed to recoil with her presumptive use of the appellation. But almost before it had come, the look was gone, and he answered without comment.

"She's sleeping now."

"Oh, I'm so glad. Whatever is the matter?"

"The same thing as last week—nausea, headache, irritability. I think she's frustrated with the painting."

"I really should take some more time with her," said Jo in a concerned voice. "She was doing so well, I thought she would rather experiment on her own."

"Perhaps," replied Logan thoughtfully, "but I'm wondering if she shouldn't give it up altogether. It doesn't seem to be doing anything but upsetting her. Who knows, maybe she's allergic to the paints. She began having these headaches almost the very day you began with her."

The same dark flash passed quickly through Jo's eyes, but when she spoke her voice remained one of expressed concern. "Some people do have such a reaction to the oils," she said. "That's why I usually take Mother out-of-doors when we paint. She was outside this morning, in fact."

"Yes, I suppose you're right," said Logan noncommittally. "But now—come," he went on in a sudden shift of tone, "let's take our guest on a tour of the house!"

"A splendid idea!" remarked von Burchardt with enthusiasm.

"I have, let me see," said Logan glancing at his watch, "until two o'clock when I must meet with the factor. That gives us about an hour. If we move quickly, that should do fine."

He led the viscount out, commenting to him lightly and confidentially as they walked, and the two young women followed.

They had not gone far along the wide corridor when Jo moved up alongside Logan, slipping her hand through his arm, and smiling up at him. On the other side, Hilary quickened her pace until she drew even with von Burchardt.

"Ah, Fraulein Edwards—"

"Hilary, remember!"

The viscount laughed. "Touche!" he said. "I was about to comment to Mr. Macintyre that this maze of corridors and stairways is enough to confuse even the most skilled of cartographers. Judging from the outside, I would never fathom the intricacies contained within these walls."

"I am only just learning the way around myself," replied Hilary. "I have been here less than a week."

"Yes, your—er, Mr. Macintyre, I should say, was just telling me something of this intriguing dilemma facing you all. I must say I have never before run across quite so—"

But at that moment he was interrupted by the sound of Logan's voice.

"If we turned down that hall," he said, "we would come to the East Wing of the castle. It has been out of general use since before Lady Margaret Duncan's time. It's in a serious state of disrepair now and is locked off because of the hazard it presents. We are, however, engaged in the process of restoring it, whenever the townspeople are short of work. We will make a good deal of progress this winter, but it is a slow process. We have never been able to afford a wholesale reconstruction, so we do what we can every year and try to keep ahead of Mother Nature's tendency to tear away at old places such as this."

"When was it last used?" asked Hilary.

"In the old days it was occupied for the billeting of the clan army; legend has it that Bonnie Prince Charlie hid out here after the disastrous battle of Culloden Moor. More recently, James Duncan, Lady Margaret's father, kept a private office there. But that was the last attempted use of the place, for a portion of the roof caved in about fifty years ago, discouraging further use. It is that roof, in fact, which we hope to shore up sufficiently this winter to keep the spring rains out."

Down another corridor, Jo took the lead, motioning them into a large room with high ceiling.

"We call this the heirloom room," she said. She waved her hand about the room, indicating the many glass cases that held precious family memorabilia and clan relics. Positioned about the floor were several mannequins displaying various of the patriarchs' Highland garb. "Lady Joanna prepared this room herself," Jo went on, "expressly for the benefit of the visitors that come to the house, both from the village and as a result of Father's position in London. There are a few valuable objects here, but their chief worth lies in their historical significance. There is a tatted handkerchief with a primrose design, given to Margaret by Lucy Krueger, and several of Lady Atlanta's stitcheries. In fact, over here"—she motioned them toward a particular case—"is one that is reputed to be her very first stitchery, done when she was ten years old." Jo beamed with pride.

"My, but you certainly are well-versed on Stonewycke's history," Hilary found herself commenting.

"I am so fascinated with it all," replied Jo in her glowing and innocent voice. "I hang on Mother's every word and am constantly nagging her to tell me more."

When no one spoke further, she resumed the dangling thread of the tour. "In this case here is a more recent find—architects' prints dating to the sixteenth century when Stonewycke was first constructed. They bear Sir James Hamilton's authenticated signature. He was King James V of Scotland's own architect and personally supervised the building of Stonewycke."

She paused a moment to allow her audience to fan out through the room. Logan disengaged himself from her arm, and wandered aimlessly toward the far wall, focusing more on his own thoughts than on any of the items in the room, with every one of which he was intimately familiar.

An odd mix of emotions rose in Hilary as she moved about—a strange mingling of detachment and reverence as she studied all the treasures in the room. Part of her felt like a member of a tour group walking through one of the great mansions of Surrey, viewing mere historical relics—antiquities from a time as far removed as ancient Rome or Babylonia. Yet in another corner of her heart, perhaps even her soul, a strange stirring was bubbling into life. She wondered if Jo felt the same way, that same sense of involvement, of personally *belonging* to this history. Maybe it all stemmed from nothing more than having read the journal. But no analysis could still the palpitating of her heart when she actually beheld with her own eyes Atlanta's stitchery and Maggie's handkerchief.

They departed the heirloom room and continued on. Walking on ahead, Logan had grown uncharacteristically quiet, seeming distractedly to have left von Burchardt alone to the ladies.

As Logan rounded a corner ahead of them, to her right Hilary glanced inside a door that stood partially ajar. It appeared to be a large open hall, but they passed by so quickly she could see few details.

"What was that room?" she asked as they continued to walk.

"That was the gallery," Jo replied.

"Might we stop for a moment?"

"I'd love nothing more than to show it to you," said Jo, "but it would take quite a while to do it justice, and I think we have already monopolized far too much of Emil's time. It is almost two o'clock."

"I would not want to stand in the way of the lady's wish," said von Burchardt grandly.

Jo's eyebrow shot up almost imperceptibly; then she turned toward Hilary and smiled. "Let's wait until we can do it properly, Hilary. It is a very special place, and I know you'll want to be able to appreciate every painting fully." Jo's steps did not slow as she spoke.

They followed Logan around the corner, and in a minute or two came to a stairway which they descended, soon arriving at the guest parlor. Jo swung the door wide open, the perfect hostess, and allowed her guests to enter. Logan was inside.

"I have already seen to the preparation of tea," he said. "Make yourself comfortable, Herr von Burchardt. Jo," he said, turning toward her, "would you mind helping Flora with it? She's in the kitchen."

Hesitating only momentarily, she turned and fluttered away. As soon as the door had closed, Logan said, "I hope you don't mind if I excuse myself. It has been a pleasure having you." He extended his hand to the viscount.

"I appreciate your hospitality!"

"I hope I have the opportunity to see you again," said Logan. "But for the present I must leave you in the company of my two—lovely friends."

As Logan exited, von Burchardt took up a position standing by the marble mantel. Hilary seated herself on the rose-colored brocade divan.

She was about to ask about his family when he first broke the silence with apparently the same idea in mind.

"I am still rather confused about you two ladies," he said. "Mr. Macintyre's attempt to explain it all left me quite confounded. But perhaps I am prying."

"I think it is an honest curiosity," said Hilary. "I would be surprised if you *weren't* puzzled by it. I am still rather baffled myself."

"But you both have documents to prove your relations to the Macintyres?"

"Actually, I have no such documents."

"But you have other, shall we say, evidence?"

"I don't know. That might even be too strong a term. I really have nothing at all now that the locket is missing."

The viscount's face clouded over momentarily, but he apparently thought better of pursuing that line.

"How does one sort out such a mix-up?"

"I believe Mr. Macintyre is looking into it all."

"Incredible!"

At that moment Jo returned carrying a tray of refreshments. She set them on the low table in front of the divan and began pouring out tea, quite naturally assuming the role of hostess in the absence of either Logan or Allison.

Taking his tea and settling into a chair opposite the divan, von Burchardt spoke. "I was just commenting on what an interesting dilemma you both have found yourselves in."

"Very unfortunate," replied Jo, sitting down next to Hilary. She laid her hand on Hilary's as if to comfort her.

Hilary cringed involuntarily at the chilly touch of Jo's fingers. She glanced into her eyes as if to assure herself she would still find warmth in the other's smile. It was there, but somehow did not reassure Hilary. It was the warmth of October, not of June.

"Where will you be off to when you depart Port Strathy?" asked Hilary of von Burchardt, attempting to sound upbeat and move the conversation away from their family situation.

"Wherever a fair wind blows, Fraulein," laughed the viscount. "But seriously, my journeyings are drawing to a close. After a stop in Aberdeen, we shall make as straight a route as possible for Bremerhaven. I gave my family my word I would be home for Christmas."

"Your wife and children?"

"No, no," replied von Burchardt with an amused chuckle. "My parents and two brothers. I have no wife at present, and certainly no children. I'm afraid I've never been the sort to settle down. There is too much of the wide world to see."

"I've always been rather a homebody myself," said Jo.

"And you," he said, turning toward Hilary, "perhaps in the spring you would join me on my yacht? Have you been to Buenos Aires?"

Before Hilary had a chance to respond, Jo's cup suddenly rattled in its saucer.

"Oh, clumsy me!" she exclaimed, brushing away the spill from her riding habit. Hilary whisked a serviette from the refreshment tray and tried to help her blot up the stain.

"I'd better take care of this right away," said Jo, rising, "or it will never come out."

Von Burchardt stood also. "It is time for me to be on my way as well. There are some repairs to my boat I must oversee."

"You are welcome to visit us any time for as long as you are in Port Strathy," said Jo, momentarily forgetting her mishap.

"Thank you very much. It will prove a most pleasant diversion, I am sure." He took Jo's hand, bowed slightly, and kissed it. Then he turned toward Hilary. As she stood he took her hand also, but she noted that he seemed to linger a bit longer than was necessary as his lips brushed her hand.

"Auf Wiedersehen, my dear ladies," he said.

"Let me walk you to the door, Emil," said Jo. "I have to go that way myself."

Hilary watched as they took their leave, then sat back down and finished her tea, pondering the intriguing interchanges of the afternoon.

Emil von Burchardt . . . a captivating fellow! she thought. *Full of mystery, and—who could deny it?—romance.*

She could not restrain a slight smile at the notion of falling in love with a courageous horseman who had rescued her from disaster.

Good thing I am no romantic, thought Hilary. *I've got to keep a level head on my shoulders. Besides, I have too many other complications in my life right now to add the confusion of love to it. Not to mention the man's noble blood! Even if I'm going to turn out to have blue blood in my veins, that certainly doesn't mean I have to fall in love with a nobleman, too!*

She stood and began gathering up the tea things, thinking how appropriate it was that Jo should play the part of the hostess while she acted the servant.

33 ✖ *Stadium Appointment*

THESE BRITONS DID love their football—though ex-patriate American Murry Fitts would never get used to calling soccer football. It had its exciting moments, he had to admit, though the game itself could never compare to watching the passionate crowds thronging the stands. The stoic English gave all for their game.

Much as Murry would have liked to concentrate on the rousing action on the turf below, he had come here on other business. The call he had received this morning had been tantalizing as only a journalist could appreciate.

"Meet me this afternoon if you want the biggest story of your career . . . " had come the enigmatic voice on the other end of the line.

What reporter could pass up a hook like that?

He'd met the caller once before, only a few days ago, one of the blokes he had interviewed at Oxford for his antiquities article. That's where the sensational call began to lose some of its credibility. Why else would he be calling except as a follow-up to their earlier conversation, and what could be so earth-shattering about a bunch of clay shards or ancient swords?

Now the fellow was fifteen minutes late and Murry was beginning to wonder if he'd been stood up. Glancing down at his watch again, he was trying to decide how much longer to give him when a nervous man passed in front of him.

"I say, is that seat next to you taken?" he asked.

"Yes, it is," replied Murry.

"Are you quite certain?" persisted the man, looking squarely at Murry, then sitting down in it nevertheless.

All at once recognition dawned. If the man's canvas sport hat and dark glasses were intended as a disguise, they had been quite effective. The noise of the crowd made it nearly impossible to be heard. A nice setup, Murry mused. Even if someone was sitting three feet away, he could never tell what we're talking about.

"I'm sorry to be late," the man was saying. "Had to be sure I wasn't followed—as much for your sake as mine."

"What's this all about, Professor?" asked Murry. "Surely not archaeological finds or ruins of ancient cities?"

"No, no!" cut in the Professor sharply, as if he had no time for tedious explanations. "It has nothing to do with any of that. This is, as you reporters say, hard news. This involves crime in the highest corporate echelons."

"Why don't you go to Scotland Yard?"

"Because there are certain . . . aspects of my life the Yard might call into question. I don't want to end up in prison myself."

"You, Professor?" said Murry, with a semi-gleam in his eye.

"I don't have time for your foolish banter," snapped the other, shifting nervously in his seat. "Do you want the story or don't you?"

"What's in it for you?"

"I hope it will save my life."

"Explain. Why have you come to me?"

"I came to you because you were convenient. I had just seen you. I knew how to reach you. I could go elsewhere, but it would take time. That much I will say. But I will explain nothing until I have your answer."

Now it was Murry's turn to shuffle uncomfortably. He wanted no part of an attempt merely to air some personal grievance. Yet if this guy were on the level, with a legitimate story of such magnitude, perhaps involving the underworld, then it might well be of the importance he claimed. It would also mean his fears were on the level too, and that if Murry listened he might be implicating himself in the danger as well. At length he sucked in a deep breath.

"Okay, let me have it," he said resolutely. "What kind of reporter would I be if I weren't willing to take a risk? But I reserve the right to bug out if it gets too heavy."

"Fair enough."

The Professor glanced surreptitiously about before beginning again. "I can't give you many details or facts because I don't have them all myself. But if you look in the right places, you will find all you need. The other day I found out something, and now my life is not worth a farthing. I know running is useless; he will find me no matter what rock I hide under. Nevertheless, once this interview is over, I am gone. It will be pointless to try to look for me. My only hope is to get to him before he gets to me. That's where you come in."

"You're talking about killing someone?" asked Murry incredulously, half rising. "You've got the wrong guy to help you there, pal!"

The Professor laughed humorlessly. "No one could get close enough—I doubt the entire Queen's army could get near him—to kill him. The only way to *get* to him is to expose him. Bring the structure he represents down on top of him. An exposé of the highest order, do you understand? That's why I need a reporter."

"You want me to get the goods on him, then make it public, is that it?"

"Right on target! But you must hurry. I cannot stay out of his clutches interminably."

"So who is the bloke?" asked Murry.

"Have you ever heard of *the General?*"

"What general?"

"*The* General," snapped the Oxford man irritably.

Murry shook his head.

"He keeps hidden, extremely low profile," the Professor went on. "No one really knows who he is. It's probable a fourth or a fifth of the world's big underground racket deals—gun smuggling, narcotics—pass through him at some stage. He controls multiple billions of dollars in underworld activities. That's a conservative estimate."

"And he fronts it all with a legitimate operation?" queried Murry.

"Putting it mildly," mused the Professor almost to himself. "His legal enterprises are clean beyond reproach. Very respected, very profitable. And until a short time ago no one knew of the connection. As far as I'm aware, I may be the only one at this moment who does."

"What connection?"

"The connection between—are you ready for this?—the General and . . . Trans Global Enterprises!"

Murry let out a long, incredulous whistle.

"*The* Trans Global?"

"The very same!"

"How did you find out?"

"That's not important. Let's just say they hired me for a job and I found out more than I was supposed to. And lost a friend in the process."

"That's a rather remarkable accusation," said Murry. "T.G.E. is right up there with Lockheed and Dow and all the other multi-national corporations. You're talking about tangling with some powerful boys."

"Do you want to back out? I can find someone else."

Slowly Murry shook his head. "But how can I touch them, knowing as little as we do?"

"Sometimes it takes a David to bring down a Goliath," replied the Professor.

"That's easy to say when you're not the David and don't intend to stick around for the battle."

"If I could help you, I would. But now it is I who must keep a low profile—an extended vacation, as it were. Far away. Besides, you Americans are better at this sort of thing than we are."

"What do you expect me to do now?" asked Murry.

"You're the investigator. Investigate! You must have friends. Sources, don't you call them? I tell you, Interpol has a file on the General as thick as your wrist. I don't know what you should do. If you turn over enough of Trans Global's rocks, under one of them you're going to find a scorpion. But watch out—his sting is lethal."

"Do I thank you or curse you for this perilous assignment?"

"Time will tell. Now I must go," the Professor said hurriedly, already rising. "I've already been here too long, I fear. If you pull this off and I live to tell about it, I'll repay you for your efforts."

"I'm not doing it for you, Professor."

"Ah yes, that American independence and forthrightness again! Well, I hope you get a bloody good story out of it—the Pulitzer Prize and all those other accolades you writers so admire!"

With those parting words, the Professor turned and squeezed his way along the aisle and soon faded out of sight in the mob of spectators.

Murry sat back in his seat and exhaled a long sigh, hardly aware of the noise or the game. *What have I fallen into?* he wondered.

Pulitzer Prize, indeed! He silently remonstrated himself. *I'll be lucky if I just get out of this without ending up at the bottom of the Thames in a cement overcoat.*

But imagine. What if it *could* be pulled off? If Hilary were in town, he'd talk to her right away. But she wasn't, and—danger be hanged!

He smiled to himself, and knew immediately he was caught!

34 ✻ *Another Arrival*

S NOW FELL AGAIN during the night. Though she slept soundly, when she rose the following morning, however, Hilary felt unrefreshed. It had been five days since she had come to Stonewycke, and there were as yet no signs of a resolution.

As she dressed, she determined it was time to speak to Logan in a more straightforward manner. Murry was doing a good job filling in for her, but the *Review* remained her responsibility. I can't keep my life on hold forever, she thought as she tugged her sweater over her head, for what is beginning to seem nothing more than an illusion—if for no other reason than that I am so frightfully short of clothes! She hadn't planned to stay more than a day or two and, at that, her packing had been hasty.

Breakfast offered no break from the mundane schedule. The Macintyres were unusually taciturn, and Allison appeared more pale than usual, with dark rings encircling her eyes. Hilary wondered aloud about the ankle, but Logan said it was on the mend.

Throughout the meal it seemed all were content left to the privacy of their own thoughts. The clanking echo of silver against china became nearly as unbearable as Jo's usual banter about the table.

Hoping to nab Logan immediately after the meal, Hilary was foiled when he was called away to the telephone and did not return. Dispassionately she agreed to join Allison and Jo in the solarium, which, since Jo's coming, had been converted into a small studio. But after they took up where they had left off the previous afternoon on a still life, Hilary grew restless.

"Would you like to try your hand?" asked Jo cheerily. "I'll set you up with a canvas and palate."

"I don't think so," she declined.

"It's fun, Hilary," urged Allison, "although I think I get more paint on my hands than the canvas." Her voice sounded hollow as she spoke. She did not look well.

"But you remember what I've told you—artistry doesn't worry about neatness," laughed Jo. "Come now, Hilary, how about it?"

Hilary shook her head and excused herself. The only way she could paint pictures was with words.

She set out for the library, hoping Logan might be there. When she walked in she saw him sitting at his desk in one corner poring over several documents. He smiled when he looked up, but it quickly faded once he saw her solemn expression.

"What is it, Hilary?" he asked with sincerity. "Is something wrong?"

"How can you ask such a question?" she snapped, all the frustrations of the day gathering in her sharp tone. "Everything is quite wrong, and I see no change in sight. I can't stay here forever. I have a magazine to run. This whole thing is beginning to look hopeless."

"I understand," he replied sympathetically.

"Do you? My whole life has been turned upside-down, and I have no idea what I'm supposed to do to right it."

"I do understand, Hilary," he said again. "Though it may be hard for you to believe just now. And it may not help knowing this, but there are others whose lives are also in a state of confusion over this." The rebuke in his tone was gentle, fatherly, even kind.

Hilary was silent a moment. She knew he was right.

"I'm sorry," she said at length in a calmer tone. "I didn't mean to be so blunt. I just don't cope very well with being in limbo like this."

"Nor do any of us," sighed Logan. "We each have our own ways of hiding the frustration, the uncertainty. But I think we are all feeling the strain."

Hilary nodded with a sigh, then turned away to glance over the books on a nearby bookshelf. The titles on the spines, however, did not even register to her brain as her eyes scanned them, for her thoughts were far away.

"Perhaps it would help for you to be assured that I am taking action," Logan went on, trying to sound upbeat. "I have some excellent men in London on it at this very moment. I have taken other steps also. But I realize you do have responsibilities. I cannot force you to stay here."

"Please don't take me wrong," said Hilary, turning back to face him. "It's not that I don't appreciate your dilemma, or the efforts you are making. I realize the delicacy of the situation, especially for someone in your position. But . . . perhaps it might even help if I returned to London. It would ease the pressure on everyone around here. Jo and Allison could do their painting without having me underfoot, and you . . . well, at least you wouldn't have to worry about entertaining me. Maybe I could even put some of my own resources to work to help sort this out."

A cloud passed over Logan's face. Now it was his turn to avert his gaze momentarily, looking down at the papers on his desk. Somehow the thought of Allison and Jo spending even more time alone together painting did not reassure him. But he could not voice his reservations aloud. What we need is a diversion, he thought to himself. An event. A ball . . . an open house . . . a live concert—something to get the focus off the problem. He looked back up and sought Hilary's eyes.

"Do what you feel you must," he said finally. "But if you could find it within yourself to give it a couple more days . . . " He hesitated. "I would like you to stay," he went on earnestly. "Consider it, if you will, a personal favor to me. If nothing has been resolved . . . then at least we will have done what we could."

Still reluctant, it was a long pause before Hilary answered. "I suppose another day or two won't hurt," she said finally.

"Thank you," he said. His tone carried in it the sound of relief. His eyes held hers for a long moment; then he went on in a lighter, friendly voice. "Please feel at complete liberty to use our phones as often as you need. I know you have business concerns. And if you wish, you are perfectly welcome to call upon the resources you mentioned even while you are here." A restrained smile played at the corners of his lips. "You might well do better than my West End lawyers!"

"Thank you very much. I'm sorry to have grown surly."

"The tension is telling on us all. Everyone could no doubt use a break." He mused upon his words for a moment. "Yes," he continued, "I will definitely have to give that some serious consideration."

That afternoon, while they sat enjoying an informal tea in the family parlor, Flora entered with the announcement that a caller was at the front door.

"I'll see to it," said Logan, rising.

In less than five minutes he returned, followed by a younger man.

"Ladies," he said, "may I present Ashley Jameson." Then turning to his wife, he explained further, "A colleague of Ian's at the university, Allison." Then to Jameson, he added, "This is my wife, Allison. And these are our two houseguests, Hilary Edwards from London, and Joanna Braithwaite from Baltimore."

Jameson nodded politely to each, then smiled wanly, directing himself toward Allison. "It seems I have made rather a fool of myself," he said. "Do forgive me for intruding on you thus. I appear to have gotten my dates rather badly confused."

"Apparently Ian made arrangements to meet him here," explained Logan.

"I was just telling your husband at the door that Ian and I had planned a bit of collaboration on that book of his. I had no idea he was back in Greece."

"Ian was to come here?" said Allison with noticeable enthusiasm, " . . . again? He was home only three weeks ago for the funeral."

"Well, that's no doubt where the confusion comes in. I spoke with him then and there must have been a mix-up somehow. He always told me when we were working together at Oxford, 'If you're ever in the north of Scotland, you simply must go by the estate,' and now it appears as though I put that rather general invitation together with mistaking the time and place of our supposed meeting, and so I show up at your door unannounced looking like the absent-minded professor Ian always calls me!"

"An honest mistake," laughed Logan. "No harm done, I assure you."

"I tried to carry around a pocket date-book for a while. But I was forever losing it until it scarcely seemed worth the effort. My secretary tries valiantly to keep me on track. But there is only so much even that worthy soul can do." He chuckled, and though he appeared genuinely embarrassed at his *faux pas,* he also seemed at ease enough with himself to take it in stride.

"Won't you join us for tea?" said Jo, stepping forward into the hostess role.

"I don't want to impose further."

"No more talk of imposition," said Allison. "Any friend of Ian's, you know. I'll tell Flora to get a room ready immediately. You must spend the night with us at the very least. Even a day or two."

"Oh, I couldn't put you out like that. You already have guests—"

"Nonsense!" interrupted Logan. "You can't possibly think of starting back to Aberdeen. It's four o'clock in the afternoon, and nearly dark, with snow on the roads."

"We insist," added Allison.

"That's most kind of you," pondered Jameson, thinking how much easier this would make his job. "It is certainly more than I had counted on . . . or deserve under the circumstances."

"Any friend of Ian's is always welcome in our home," said Logan.

"In that case . . . thank you very much."

Logan pulled a chair forward and Jameson sat down between Logan and Hilary. Jo rose quickly from her own seat to pour him a cup of tea from the pot, eyeing him carefully. Her scrutiny did not pass unnoticed by Hilary. She made her own observations more inconspicuously.

The newcomer looked to be about thirty-five, and Hilary hardly needed to be told of his scholarly background. He had academia written all over him. Already she had observed that he carried his tall slender frame carelessly, with an ease which indicated that his thoughts moved on too bookish a plane to worry about mundane pursuits like walking or dressing. His tweed jacket and corduroy trousers were hardly the most fashionable; indeed, the whole effect of his wardrobe gave the impression that dressing each morning was probably an afterthought. At the same time, however, there was a precision about the man that almost belied the bemused and distractable image he tried to put forward. It could be seen best in his sharp, probing gray-green eyes, which at times, Hilary noticed, reflecting an innately wry sense of humor. He spoke in an easy tone too, Oxfordian and refined.

"So what do you do, Ashley?" asked Logan, once the visitor held his tea in his hand.

"Actually, Ian helped me through during some of my rugged earlier years, and now I teach where he left off when he abandoned the university to write his book. Ancient classics . . . Grecian history, that sort of thing."

"What is it you and Ian work on together?"

"Ancient Greece, mostly. He's more the archaeologist, I the linguist."

Jameson's modesty obscured the more notable fact—which subsequent conversation and Logan's probing questions revealed—that he already had three acclaimed translations of Greek classics to his credit, and his name as a collaborator with Ian on a book jacket would do nothing but enhance the book's prestige. Though Logan fairly had to drag any personal information from him, it also came out that Ian, who had been for the last several years involved in biblical archaeology, had in the course of his research turned up some interesting finds in Greece which he felt could benefit Jameson's work as well. For a number of reasons, therefore, their guest concluded, they had remained in close touch with respect to their mutual projects.

"Actually," he said, "I was looking forward to a bit of a busman's holiday. Ian has always said you have marvelous country up here. I've never been north of Aberdeen, but the brief glimpses I've had so far would certainly seem to confirm his words."

"It will all still be here next week, or the week after that, or whenever you and Ian do manage to get together," laughed Logan.

"Unfortunately, I won't," replied Jameson. "I have to be off to a conference in a few days. That's why I was so certain Ian had said this week."

"Well, we'll just have to do our best to entertain you," said Logan, "and give you that holiday you're after. We've had so many other guests lately, besides Jo and Hilary—what was the name of that chap yesterday?" he asked, turning toward the others.

"You mean von Burchardt?" answered Jo.

"Yes, Burchardt! An interesting fellow! Anyway, one more guest will be no problem. The more the merrier, don't they say?"

"Well then, under the circumstances, I accept your hospitality," said Jameson with a smile.

35 ⁂ Suspicions Aroused

WHEN HILARY DOZED off later that same night in her room, she was fully clothed, and an open book still rested in her hands.

She awoke an hour later with a shudder. Her old childhood dream had just begun to intrude upon the outer edges of her subconscious. But her sudden waking prevented its closer and more terrifying approach. She nevertheless felt the heavy discomfort of one who has been roused too soon from a nap. Her mouth was dry and tasted foul, her neck ached from the awkward position in which she had been sitting, and she was chilled to the bone.

All at once her body snapped straight up in the chair. Was that a sound she heard out in the corridor?

Perhaps it had not been the dream that had awakened her at all, but some noise within the castle walls! A door closing . . . the drop of some object on the stone floor.

Intently she strained to hear. She heard nothing more. Rising from her chair, she walked quietly toward her door, placed her hand on the latch, then opened it a crack, doing her best to prevent the hinges from betraying her. Wider she opened the door, then slowly leaned her head out, glancing up and down the hallway in both directions.

At the end of the corridor a retreating figure glided along, then rounded a corner and was out of sight!

Hilary's view had been so brief in the darkened passageway that she couldn't begin to identify the late-night walker. Without two moment's hesitation, she was in the hall. Leaving her door ajar so it wouldn't slam shut and give away her presence, she moved swiftly in the direction of her unknown visitor.

Her room was the only one occupied in this particular part of the house—whoever it was must have known that. Jo was in another wing. It could have been she . . . but why? And if she had intended on paying Hilary a visit at this late hour, why then had she turned back? Perhaps she had been trying to come upon Hilary unawares, and her plan had been foiled by whatever noise it was she had inadvertently made. Or had someone else created the disturbance and frightened her away? It couldn't be Allison; she had gone to bed feeling sick late in the afternoon. She doubted Logan would sneak around in his own house. One of the employees? She didn't know in what room they'd put Ian's friend.

Carefully Hilary approached the end of the hallway, stopped, then peered round the edge of the wall. She could see nothing, but in the distance a faint sound, as if from shuffling footsteps, reached her ears. The figure, whoever it was, was either making for the main stairway or another part of the house. She would never catch the person now without making a disturbance herself.

Slowly she turned and walked back to her room. Once inside she closed the door behind her, locked it securely, then found herself drawn to the window by the glimmer of moonlight coming in from outside.

The snow had ceased falling, and a full moon reflected off the white blanket covering the ground, causing the night outside to look almost like a Scottish summer's gloamin'. The window of her room faced west onto a wide stretch of well-maintained yard, which in late spring and summer would boast a lush, manicured green lawn. On this night, however, a thick soft covering of white stretched from the castle walls to the great hedge that surrounded the castle grounds proper. Hilary recalled Allison telling her it was this section of the grounds which boasted a fine rose garden every spring. It was out there, no doubt, where Lady Joanna had first seen old Dorey and had wrongly taken him for the gardener. Allison hadn't detailed the story to her, but it wasn't necessary; Hilary recalled every moment of the legendary interaction from Joanna's journal.

Before she realized it, Hilary found herself caught up again in memories and images from the past. Sitting at the window with a blanket over her knees, she glanced once more through the precious journal that she had recovered from its hiding place among her things. Alternately reading portions here and there, then lifting her eyes to gaze outside into the peaceful night, she let her thoughts roam back in time.

Of all the intriguing members of the Duncan clan, the enigmatic Dorey, or Theodore Ian Duncan, seemed the most difficult to understand. As she read of his suffering the familiar aristocratic, second-son syndrome, Hilary ruefully thought how this was just one more reason for doing away with the stifling institution. Ian's father didn't even pretend to care for his younger son. A wild and frenzied lifestyle had resulted, until a soft ray of hope, in the person of a Scottish lass by the name of Maggie, shone upon the lad's troubled life. But the irony of the whole drama that followed stemmed from an age-old mythical fatalism: poor Ian proved both the catalyst and the victim of woes which, in certain measure, he brought upon himself.

How I would have liked to know him! thought Hilary, setting down the manuscript and looking out again on the tranquil winter scene below. What an interesting man he must have been in his later years, after he had come to know both himself and God, and had been reunited with his dear Maggie! What a contrast between his youthful boisterous and shallow personality, and the humble demurring introspection of his later years. What wisdom must have worked its way into his character as a result of that transformation! And to have such a man for a great-great-grandfather. . . .

Suddenly Hilary became aware of the folly of her wandering train of thoughts. She could no longer assume he was her ancestor!

In the last few days since her arrival at Stonewycke, Hilary had made great efforts to distance herself from all the ties that she had previously allowed to form within her as a result of reading the journal. This was the first time in days she had given over to serious speculation of the personalities of the family and her potential relation to it.

"I can't think of all this now!" she said to herself. Tomorrow the call could well come from London informing Mr. Macintyre that the entire substance of Lady Joanna's visit had been a mistake, that she had, for whatever reasons, gotten her facts and her interpretation of them badly confused, and had drawn Hilary into this little episode, though in reality she had no possible connection to Stonewycke or the Macintyres.

Hilary wanted to keep a level, practical head about her. She simply could not allow her emotions to give way.

Exhaling a bewildered and frustrated sigh, she began once more to consider the possibility of sleep.

Then without warning, again all her senses sprang to life! This time she was not struggling to disengage herself from sleep. She knew exactly what she saw.

A figure was walking across the snow-covered lawn below! She shot a quick glance at her bedside clock; it was 11:30. Though she had not been able to catch a good look at the furtive hallway visitor of a few minutes ago, something in the walk told her this was the same person. It was certainly not Jo, she could now see, but a man.

Immediately in her memory arose the vision of another night—only two nights ago—when she had seen Jo and an unknown stranger outside the gate together. Could this be the same man? The height seemed about right, though her view of Jo's companion had been dark and incomplete.

Whoever this was, what was he doing out at such an hour? What had he been doing in her hallway? Had he mistaken her room for Jo's, and was now correcting his error? The walk was familiar . . . could it . . . yes! It reminded her of the viscount!

Something about him had puzzled her from the first. He seemed too suave, too—

But before she had time to finish her conjecture, all at once the man down on the snow stopped, then turned, glancing directly up at her window!

Instinctively Hilary pulled away and ducked into a shadowed recess, hoping the small light in her room would not betray her face. It had almost been as if he had known she were there, and was looking for her. But whatever the cause of his sudden turn and probing of the night for her eyes, at least she now knew the identity of this night prowler. For in the split second following his turn before she had backed completely out of sight, the reflected moonlight had shown full on his face, and there could be no mistaking the man. It was not the Austrian.

It was the professor from Oxford, Ashley Jameson!

What could this new houseguest possibly be doing meandering about the house in the dead of night?

After a moment she sneaked another glance out the window with one eye peering round the edge of the window frame. Jameson was nowhere to be seen, but his footsteps in the snow made a clear track to the door toward which he had been heading.

Slowly she put away the journal and climbed into bed, the paradoxes and questions of the night's happenings plaguing her until sleep at last swept her away.

Throughout the following morning she could not shake a heaviness that seemed bent on weighing her down. If she had been uneasy around Jo before, now everything was magnified ten times. Every look, every chance word spoken, especially from the mouth of Jameson, seemed to hold multiple meanings. Added to this, to further blur Hilary's perspective, was a call about eleven o'clock by the Viscount von Burchardt. Applying his charm both toward

Jo and herself, in no time he had wrangled himself another invitation to luncheon, to which he heartily agreed.

"One o'clock, then!" said Logan, once the arrangements had been confirmed. "For the past half hour they had been gathered in one of the West Wing parlors. "Now I have to see my factor, Moryson, about some things." He laughed. "I get up here so rarely that when I do, he tries to get me as much as he can so all his questions and problems can get cleared up. I'll be back before long."

Hilary, too, excused herself. The viscount cornered Jo and plied her with his charm—an exercise to which she did not seem adverse—and meanwhile the mysterious Oxford don wandered outside alone. Allison had still not made an appearance all day.

Hilary went straight to the library, where Logan had directed her when she had asked him about making a call. With the others occupied, she hoped there she would not be disturbed.

She dialed the number and felt oddly relieved as she did so. It felt good to take some action, even if it was nothing more than making a simple phone call.

"Hello, Murry," she said when the magazine switchboard put her through to her associate. "How is everything?"

"Smooth as glass," he said, then chuckled. "Betty told me to say that no matter what, she doesn't want you to worry about anything."

"What's wrong?"

"Nothing, really. Only the usual snags." He paused, and she could tell even across hundreds of miles of phone line that his next statement would not be pleasant. "Well," he went on, "there is talk of a printer's strike—but I have already lined up some scabs."

"Scabs?"

"Finks . . . strike-breakers, you know."

"Is it serious?"

"Right now they're just blowing off hot air. The contracts aren't up for renewal for a couple of weeks."

"It sounds as if you have everything under control." She smiled to herself. Suddenly in the face of her personal concerns, even the news of an impending strike did not sound terribly earth-shattering.

"By the way," added Murry, "I've got to thank you for that antiquities assignment."

"Oh . . . ?"

"Hanging around Oxford's been very stimulating."

"You met a new girl?"

"Don't I wish! But no, I was speaking of a great new story my Oxford source put me onto."

"What is it?"

"Too early even to tell you about. Let's just say it's either going to be a bomb or a bombshell!"

"Well, then, since you're hanging around Oxford, I have a bit of a favor to ask of you."

"Name it."

"Do you still keep in touch with that fellow from Scotland Yard?"

"Once in a while. I have to keep my contacts greased, you know."

"Could you ask him to run a name through the Yard's computers?"

"Sure," answered Murry, "but what does that have to do with Oxford? Say, what's going on up there, anyway?"

"I can't go into it now, Murry. I'm not even sure I know." She then gave him Jameson's name and what little she knew of him. "You might check around next time you're out at Oxford, a little street research to go along with the official report."

"I'm not sure I'll be going back soon. My guy's flown the coop for a while. Insists his life's in danger."

"That *is* interesting. Your guy *leaves* Oxford just as my guy arrives in Scotland from Oxford!"

"Coincidence?"

"I don't know. Find out for me, Murry, will you?"

"I'll do what I can."

"And, throw the name Emil von Burchardt into that police computer while you're at it. He's an Austrian viscount."

"You *are* meeting some interesting chaps up there!"

"Let's put it this way—the one *says* he's an Oxford professor, and the other *claims* to be a viscount. And when you call, Murry, don't leave me any messages. Talk directly with me."

"Gotcha. It might take a couple of days."

"Put a priority on it. Thanks, Murry!"

Hilary slowly put the receiver down.

She sat back in her chair, reflecting briefly on what she had asked Murry to do and wondering if her suspicions were totally unfounded. Deciding that his efforts would be worthwhile regardless, even if she only discovered through them that everyone was on the up and up, Hilary rose and walked toward the library door.

As she opened the door toward her, Hilary's entire mental focus remained intent on what she had just done. As she swung into the hallway, she found her loose hand taken and then pulled upward in a familiar grasp.

36 ✠ *Hidden Complexities*

"AH, FRAULEIN EDWARDS . . . what a pleasure it is to see you again!" said Viscount von Burchardt, kissing her hand.

"Emil!" replied Hilary, "I did not know you were so nearby."

"I'm afraid I startled you. Forgive me. Actually, I was on my way to see you. I had a feeling you might be in the library."

"I thought you and Jo were deeply engrossed in something."

"A mere facade, I assure you. I was watching you out of the corner of my eye."

"Should I be flattered?" said Hilary, regaining her poise.

"Take it any way you wish," replied von Burchardt. "But I would be less than truthful if I told you anything but that I returned today particularly in hopes of finding you alone."

"For whatever reason?" asked Hilary coyly.

"Surely you don't mean to suggest that I am the first man to seek you out?" said Emil, a gleam of mischief in his eye.

"The first viscount," countered Hilary.

"So then," said von Burchardt, offering his arm and starting down the hall as Hilary took it, though lightly, and followed, "tell me more about this intriguing situation here. You and Jo, both vying for the loyalties and fortunes of the Macintyre domain, is that it?"

"A bit crudely put. And perhaps that captures the gist of it. But I would not say we are 'vying' for anything. The truth about our relative status within the family is merely unknown. It's really quite simple."

"Simple, quoth she," said Emil with a grin. "Don't you know that simplicity is but a surface manifestation of hidden complexities?"

"Shakespeare?"

"I'm afraid not. Von Burchardt, actually."

Now it was Hilary's turn to laugh. This man was too straightforward to be other than he seemed!

"You laugh as if in scorn," he added lightly. "You do not agree?"

"About simplicity hiding complexity? I don't know. What do you say to trying out your theory on Jo? What do you know of her?"

"Your temporary *sister,* as it were?" said Emil. "I know nothing about her."

"I thought, perhaps, that you knew her from somewhere else?" probed Hilary with pretended innocence. As she spoke she gazed deeply into the viscount's eyes.

"Me? I've never been here before in my life! But now let's take *you*, Hilary." he said. "You seem soft-spoken enough. Perfectly without motive. Yet something tells me there is much more to you than meets the eye at first glance."

"Merely an illusion," she answered off-handedly.

"I doubt that sincerely. No, you are more intricate a young woman than you would like people to think. I've watched you as you sit back and observe the rest of us, sizing up the other players in this knotty little scenario. You do not say much, Hilary—unlike Jo, who is constantly talking in that carefree voice of hers. But you are always thinking. I can see it in your eyes. And how dearly I would love to know what is going on inside that brain of yours."

Hilary's only response was a half-smile, which said that now she had to give consideration to his remarks.

"You see! There you are again—trying to size me up on the basis of what I've just said! There's no denying it! I am right about you!"

"Perhaps, Herr von Burchardt," replied Hilary, still smiling. "But if what you say is true, you would be one of the last persons I would tell what was going on inside my brain. After all, I know nothing whatsoever about you."

"Except that I saved you from a nasty spill off your horse."

"Yes, of course. And that is no small thing. I am grateful. But that still tells me nothing about *you*—who you *really* are."

"Ah, but that is the beauty of it! I am nothing more than I seem!"

"An Austrian viscount touring the coast of Scotland?"

"Precisely."

"And how are the repairs coming to your yacht?" asked Hilary.

"Repairs?"

"You mentioned having to weather here in Port Strathy on account of some repairs."

"Ah, the repairs—of course! Quite well . . . almost completed. Shipshape of a crew I have!"

"And you've never met Mr. Macintyre either?" queried Hilary.

"Never. Why would you ask? I told you, my coming here is purely happenstance," replied von Burchardt.

By now they had reached the parlor where they had previously been. As no one was there, and as the sun had come out over the winter's landscape, they slowly made their way to one of the outside doors.

"So tell me," said the viscount, seeking again to divert the attention off himself, "how did you come to be here? I find the whole thing terribly fascinating. You were visited by Macintyre's mother-in-law in London, was that it? And I understand there is a journal someplace which sheds light on all this."

Hilary nodded noncommittally, wondering where he had heard about Joanna's journal. Wracking her brain to recall whether it had been part of any conversation to which he'd been privy, in the distance all at once they saw Logan enter the grounds through a gate in the hedge.

"Ah . . . our host!" exclaimed von Burchardt. "Will you excuse me? He promised to let me have a look at the horses!"

"Of course," replied Hilary.

"We will have to continue this discussion later," said the viscount, walking away. "I must know more of what is inside that beautiful head of yours . . . and what brought you here."

37 ❉ *Of Ovid and Aristocrats*

THROUGHOUT LUNCHEON von Burchardt, strategically placed between the two, managed to keep up a steady and inquisitive conversation with both Jo and Hilary. On the opposite side of the table, Professor Jameson observed the proceedings with what was now an amused twinkle, now a look of concern in his eye, following the flow of dialogue from one, then to the other. He and Logan lapsed occasionally into discourse of their own, but it seemed stilted and was broken by long silences. They both appeared content to let the viscount carry the ball, and gained what entertainment was possible from his probing. The Austrian appeared intent on unraveling the mystery of "the two daughters," as he termed it, on the basis of asking question after question, then carefully scrutinizing the faces as they responded.

When the meal was nearly over, the door opened and Allison made an appearance. Logan jumped up from his chair and went to meet her.

"You look much less pale, my dear," he said. "How are you feeling?"

"Better . . . much better. At least I was able to pull myself out of that horrid bed for a while."

"Won't you join us, Frau Macintyre," said von Burchardt, rising and going to meet her.

"Thank you, but nothing to eat for me. I just didn't want to be a completely negligent hostess."

When they had finished eating, Hilary excused herself, Jameson went outside, Jo said she was going to the drawing room, the viscount, continuing to make himself engaging, went with her, and Logan followed, with Allison on his arm, at some distance.

The sun had come out, and, notwithstanding the cold, the day was an inviting one, made all the more so by the thin layer of snow that covered the land, though paths and roads were by now appearing through it. Hilary, determined not to remain cooped up in her room the entire afternoon, went upstairs and changed into the warmest clothes she could find—a white wool Norwegian sweater, blue jeans, a royal blue down parka she'd borrowed from Allison, thick wool socks, and leather boots—and then made immediately for the main front door of the house. It would be good to get out, she thought. The landscape was so lovely, and even the cold would feel good on her face. She needed something invigorating to snap her back into life.

She had hardly taken two steps after closing the door behind her, when around the wall walked the professor, nearly knocking her over.

"Why, Mr. Jameson!" she exclaimed.

"Hello, Miss Edwards," he replied in the easy tone that seemed characteristic of him. "I'm afraid I wasn't paying much attention. I didn't expect to find anyone else out braving the elements."

"I couldn't resist the sun shining on the snow."

"Well, I was myself just off for a bit of a stroll about the grounds. Perhaps you would like to join me?"

Hilary hesitated but momentarily, then nodded an affirmative smile, and the two headed around toward the garden in the direction Jameson had been walking. He was dressed in a heavy plaid wool coat, casual corduroy trousers, and heavy walking boots.

He led across the snow-covered lawn, then struck out across the footbridge on which Allison had fallen a few days earlier, and which Jake had since repaired.

"Careful here," he said, "these wooden planks might be rather slippery."

Hilary negotiated the bridge easily, and within ten minutes they had left the castle's immediate grounds and were making their way across the wide, untouched landscape—expansive common, dotted with bracken, rocks, and what would have been browning grass except for the snow—east of the house.

"How long have you been here, Miss Edwards?" Jameson asked casually after some minutes of silence—noticeable, though not awkward.

"Only a few days."

"Has it been enjoyable for you?"

"That's not exactly the word I would have chosen to describe it," replied Hilary. "It's beautiful . . . peaceful—of course. But the circumstances are awkward."

"Yes . . . I can see they must be."

"Tell me, Mr. Jameson," said Hilary, turning the conversation around and assuming the initiative, "I would have thought you'd be back on your way south by now, busy man that you must be, since your plans have fallen through."

"The Macintyres invited me to stay on—just for a day or two more. And since I haven't had a holiday in some time. . . ."

He let his tone finish the sentence.

"That is the only reason?"

"Yes . . . why? What do you mean?"

"I thought perhaps . . . I don't know what put the notion into my head exactly," said Hilary, trying to sound her most innocent, "but somehow I had the idea that you might have known Jo prior to coming here."

"What . . . Jo? No, I've never seen her before yesterday," he replied quickly, sending an uncertain glance in Hilary's direction. "Why would you think that?"

"I don't know. Just my reporter's inquisitive mind, I suppose," replied Hilary with a laugh.

"An *over*-inquisitive mind, I would say."

"That's the only kind of mind a writer can have—that is, if he's worth his salt as a writer. You should know that. You're an author, though; perhaps it's different when you're writing history." She paused, waiting for him to take up from her lead. But he seemed willing to let the subject drop.

"Would you agree?" she asked.

"About what?"

"Writing . . . history writing being different from other kinds, requiring less inquiry."

"*Less* inquiry, Miss Edwards? Heavens no! Good history requires more inquiry than any other kind of writing."

"Is history the only writing you've ever done?" she asked.

Again, the question seemed to throw him momentarily.

"Why . . . yes . . . er, history is, of course . . . it's my field."

"So you've never thought of trying your hand at something else, a contemporary article . . . the here and now, rather than ancient Greece?"

"No . . . that is to say, I'm not sure I quite understand you. As I said, my field is history, and that is what I write about."

Hilary let the subject drop. It was leading her nowhere, although Jameson did seem flustered by her questions. There was more to him than met the eye, and she was determined to uncover it. He too, like the viscount, was full of questions.

"But, Miss Edwards," he went on before Hilary could decide what tack to take next, "I find myself puzzled by one thing. If this Lady Joanna—Macintyre's mother-in-law, I believe it was—if she came to you, identified herself as your grandmother, gave you her family locket, entrusted you with her precious journal, apparently had documents to show the legal connection . . . in the face of all that, why is there this apparent doubt in the minds of the Macintyres as to the veracity of your position?"

"You know about the locket?" Hilary's tone was sharp, and she looked intently into Jameson's face.

"It must have been Macintyre who told me about it, and the journal."

"Then he must also have told you that the locket has apparently been lost . . ."

A grave look passed over Jameson's face.

". . . or if not lost, then misplaced. In any case, it's not in my room. And Lady Joanna's dead, so no one knows of the 'legal connections,' as you put it. There were no documents. Yes, there is the journal, but the ending pages of it are missing. If they reveal anything about the search she made and her reasons for undertaking it after Jo had already arrived, that knowledge is lost to the rest of us."

"Has there been a search initiated for the locket or the missing pages?"

"Not a formal one, to my knowledge," replied Hilary. For a moment she considered bringing up the late visitor to her wing of the house the previous night, but then thought better of it. "As to the missing pages," she went on, "no one's ever *seen* them. There's no evidence to suggest that there *are* pages definitely missing. When I said that, I was perhaps saying more than I should have. I only assume she must have written more than she sent me."

Jameson nodded, in apparent thought. "That *is* interesting," he mused. "If we could just find that part of the journal," he added in a mumbling tone almost to himself.

"Now *you* seem the one with the over-inquisitive mind," said Hilary playfully, but with design behind her light tone. "Are you sure you only write history? If I didn't know better, I might think you were a mystery buff."

"What's that! A mystery buff? Ridiculous!" replied Jameson, flustered. "I tell you I'm nothing but a dull Greek historian."

"I don't believe that for a minute! There is more to you than you want to let on, Mr. Jameson. Or perhaps I should call you *Dr.* Jameson! Is that what your colleagues call you?"

"No, no, please. *Mr.* will be fine."

"Then you must call me Hilary. No offense to history as a field of study, but I loathe the archaic modes of expression."

"I take it you must be quite the progressive woman, then . . . Hilary."

"Progressive? Perhaps. I don't think of myself as a modernist, but on the other hand I don't think my Creator expects me to wear black and walk dutifully ten paces behind a man, demurring to his every whim."

"God, you say?" said Jameson thoughtfully. "What is it you think God *does* expect from you?"

"He gave me a good head on my shoulders, and some wits, and I think He expects me to use them," she answered firmly. "Which is what I am trying to do as, if you'll pardon the expression, a career woman. Beyond that, I think His highest expectation is that I love and serve Him without getting so muddled with the inconsequential."

"You sound like someone whose faith means a great deal to you."

"That's because it does."

He gave her a quick, sidelong glance, which she pretended not to notice. However, she could not help but wonder at the cause for his apparent astonishment.

"That's very interesting," he said, after pausing to give the statement deeper consideration. "A rare enough thing in today's world."

They walked for a few paces in silence.

"Look!" said Hilary suddenly, pointing ahead. "Isn't that a wheatear?" All Jameson could see besides snow and shrubbery was a small bird perched upon a low branch sticking up out of the snow.

"That bird over there?" he asked.

"Yes. It's really rather late in the year for it—most of the others must surely have migrated by now."

"I see you are an ornithologist as well," commented Jameson.

"Not really. I once covered an ornithology convention. Not very stimulating, I must admit, but I learned a few things in spite of myself."

They had stopped in their walking and Hilary continued to gaze at the little bird with interest. "There's nothing like an outdoor hike on a cold day for invigorating the senses and making fascinating discoveries," she said.

"Walking is the one form of exercise I highly endorse," agreed Jameson. "I try to walk several miles a day."

"Even at night?" The words escaped Hilary's lips before she even knew it, though the question sounded casual.

"If I find no other time," he replied, faltering ever so slightly—as if he had sensed her motive in the question, or as if he was thinking of hiding something.

"I saw you out last night," said Hilary, plunging ahead.

"It is—walking, you know—an excellent antidote to insomnia." There was a trace of something in his tone, Hilary thought, a slight inflection that sounded too glib for truth.

"You have trouble sleeping?"

"Occasionally. And so must you if you were also up at that hour."

"I have ever since I arrived here. Does prowling through the hallways cure insomnia just like the outside air?"

"My, but you are suspicious!" he replied with a laugh. Was it a nervous laugh or an innocent one? Hilary couldn't tell. *"Prowling,* Hilary? Come now, I was merely walking off the effects of my journey, hoping not to disturb anyone. So I purposely avoided any contact with those who were trying to sleep."

A very plausible explanation, thought Hilary to herself. Who can tell, maybe it is even the truth. They began walking again.

It was the professor who first spoke.

"Logan tells me you were reluctant to come in the first place, even after speaking with Lady Joanna?"

Hilary looked askance at Jameson. Everyone around here seemed filled with questions!

"Lady Joanna's revelations came as a great shock to me," she replied finally. "I simply could not imagine myself part of such a—well, *this* kind of family.'

"This kind of family . . . ?"

"Aristocrats, you know. I had the commonest of upbringings."

"Rags to riches—what's wrong with that?"

"Nothing, I suppose, for fairy tales. But I happen to think the nobility is archaic. There's *my* two pence worth of your history! Perhaps a noble institution for two hundred years ago. Outmoded and even dangerous today."

"Pretty strong words."

"I believe them."

"So you couldn't face the fact that maybe you were an aristocrat yourself?"

"Imagine the shock."

"I get your point," he replied, an amused smile hidden from view.

"And not just plain aristocrats, mind you. This family lives in a 400-year-old castle, entertains the Queen Mother, and occupies a seat in the Shadow Cabinet!"

"But as I understand it, Logan is the one member of the family who is of common stock." He cleared his throat dryly, as if he had made a point. "So if you turn out to be a member of this family, you will be only *half* an aristocrat."

"That's quite enough, thank you."

"You do have a serious problem about this, don't you? For a seemingly open, Christian, modern young woman, I must admit that surprises me. I admittedly do not know you very well, Hilary, but it smacks of prejudice."

"A class-conscious society, my dear Mr. Jameson, is doomed to extinction in this age. And Britain is one of the great class-bound societies of the world, though we refuse to admit it."

"That almost hints of Marxism." His tone was not argumentative, at least much less so than Hilary's. But he sounded as if he enjoyed the prospect of a debate.

"I would never go that far," replied Hilary. "But you must admit that when the masses are repressed, it's only a matter of time before the fabric of society bursts apart at the seams."

"We have survived as a nation longer than just about any other on earth."

"Yes, but just look at Victorian England," said Hilary, "when British power was at its apex throughout the world. The squalor of the majority of the population was reprehensible— all while the nobility amassed huge wealth."

"But when did British world dominance begin to collapse?" he asked, then went on to answer his own question, still in a casual tone. This was no argument to him, merely an exercise in logic. "In the twentieth century, coming on the heels of sweeping social reform, enfranchisement, and the welfare state."

"You blame that on the lower classes!"

"Not at all." He smiled. "But I think you would blame the nobility for just the opposite reaction."

"Whose fault is it, then?"

"Must blame be apportioned at all?" queried Jameson rhetorically. "If so, perhaps it ought to be taken to a higher plane—that of spiritual need, of the depravity of man."

"Spoken like one who also possesses spiritual convictions. But even accepting what you say, there is still something intrinsically wrong with a system that says one person is higher than another on some arbitrary scale of worth simply by chance of birth."

"'Nam genus et proavose et quæ non fecimus ipsi, Vix ea nostra voco,'" was Ashley's reply.

"I don't understand a word of Latin," groaned Hilary ruefully, "but I have the feeling my argument has just been doomed."

"Hardly," chuckled Jameson. He seemed to be thoroughly enjoying Hilary's discomfiture. "You see, even Ovid agreed with you: 'Birth and ancestry, and that which we have not ourselves achieved, we can scarcely call our own.' And I wouldn't say that I don't agree also. But it would be a mistake to thoughtlessly throw it out altogether. They tried that in France, and the Reign of Terror was the answer. The nobility may have been corrupt, but Robespierre was nothing but a terrorist. It has nothing to do with class, Hilary. It has instead to do with the state of a man's heart."

"I see your point," she answered reluctantly. "But what benefit then does the aristocracy have at all?"

"Perhaps it has more to do with aesthetics than politics. Think of the nobility as a thread in the larger fabric of society. Don't judge right or wrong, but rather consider what would happen if you pulled out that thread suddenly. The warp and woof of the cloth itself would be noticeably weakened, as it would if any other thread were removed. What would happen to society if suddenly there were no laborers, or if you took away the educational system, or if Parliament suddenly ceased to exist? The nobility is the same—it's an intrinsic part of what makes society function—with its good points and its bad points, like every other aspect of civilization."

"You seem to have thought this through very carefully."

"History does have its contemporary application. But in another way, it's all just a matter of simple logic."

"I don't know—you sound like something more than an impartial proponent of the aristocratic order."

"Perhaps I am a bit of a traditionalist. I suppose I have even been accused of being stuffy by some. That's what comes of being hidden away in a place like Oxford."

Something in his tone seemed to indicate this admission of stuffiness was a smoke screen. That there was more to this man, there could be no doubt. Hilary hated to admit it, but she rather liked his style. He was so confident and self-assured, but with such an absence of pretense, that he could not help but be intriguing. Still, she reminded herself, she could not drop her guard.

Hilary's reverie was interrupted as Jameson spoke again, maneuvering the conversation back to its original point.

"I think I now begin to understand the answer to my original question about your reluctance in coming to Stonewycke," he said. "But then, what did finally change your mind?"

Hilary thought for a moment. That was not easy to say. She still wasn't sure herself. "I suppose," she answered at length, "that I found myself having to confront my own prejudice, as you so pointedly put it. Part of me still feels as I always have about the nobility. But then another piece of me way down inside, the part of me that does want to be open, says, 'Maybe you haven't thought through the whole story yet, Hilary!' Perhaps it's my conscience. But whatever it is, that little voice has been growing stronger recently. And one day, as I was wrestling with what Lady Joanna said, and with what I knew of Logan Macintyre from my professional dealings with him, that little voice stood up and shouted, 'Go to Scotland!'"

"I see . . . very interesting."

They had by now come back to the castle grounds and were just approaching the little footbridge.

They walked back toward the front door to the house. Theirs were still the only footprints across the snow on the lawn. After a few more moments of light conversation, they opened the door.

38 ❈ A Visit to Town

"AH, JAMESON . . . FRAULEIN Edwards!" exclaimed von Burchardt as they walked in. "We were hoping to meet up with you!"

Behind him stood Logan and Jo, bundling up with overcoats and scarves. "We were just heading out," said Logan. "If the two of you are game, we thought we'd drive to town and have a look at Emil's yacht."

"Sounds like an interesting proposal," replied Jameson, "although I must admit my feet are nearly frozen. We've just been out for a tromp through the fields to the east of the castle—beautiful enough, but covered with snow!"

"Yes, please," shivered Hilary, hardly noticing the cold until she was now back inside. "Do let us warm up a few minutes first!"

"I'll go and tell Flora to have some hot tea waiting for us when we return," said Logan. He left while the others continued with readying and warming. In a few moments he returned from the direction of the kitchen.

"And Mrs. Macintyre?" asked Jameson. "Will she be joining us?"

"I'm afraid not. She went back to her room to lie down. Well . . . shall we?" he said, indicating the door with his hand.

Five minutes later the five were seated in Logan's gray Mercedes, Jameson, his long legs pulled up in front of him, seated between Hilary and Jo in the backseat, von Burchardt keeping Logan company in the front. Snow still covered the estate driveway, broken only by the tracks made earlier by the viscount as he walked up the hill from town, and Logan inched along carefully. When they reached the highway, however, the road was clear down into the village. Logan parked in front of the Bluster 'N Blow, and the small party made their way toward the harbor. It was obvious immediately which boat was von Burchardt's.

Pure white, sleek, some eighty feet in length, the yacht boasted the daintiest of little portholes just above the level of the water indicating cabins below, and an upper deck, mostly open, around which a three-foot high rope railing stretched. About two-thirds of the way toward the bow rose the enclosed control room, surrounded on all sides by spacious windows from which the crew could maintain a 360-degree lookout.

"I say, Burchardt!" exclaimed Logan. "Good show! She's positively stunning—easily the most magnificent craft ever to grace our little harbor!"

"Coming from you, sir, I take that as the profoundest of compliments!" replied the viscount graciously. "Come, I'll take you all aboard."

He led the way, offering Hilary his hand, which she took to step up onto the deck. Jo followed, assisted by Jameson, and finally Logan stepped aboard.

"Oh!" squealed Jo with delight, "it's a shame we can't take her out!"

"What kind of repairs are you making?" asked Logan.

"Oh, nothing much really," replied von Burchardt. "In fact, the crew is mostly finished, and I gave them the day off."

"It looks shipshape enough," said Jameson. "Why, I don't see any evidence of work at all."

"Tut, tut, Professor," said the viscount. "Merely internal difficulties. Nothing visible to the novice."

"Then you won't mind if I have a look around?"

"Not at all! Make yourself at home!"

Meanwhile, Logan had wandered toward the control room, while Hilary peered down the narrow stairs which led below deck.

"Would you like to see the cabins?" asked von Burchardt, offering Hilary his hand. "But hold on tightly, these steps are steep."

They made their way slowly downstairs, followed by Jo. Jameson, in the meantime, meandered toward the stern of the craft, then made his way to the back railing and stooped down and peered over the edge. Walking toward it from the dock he had noted the yacht's registration sticker and identifying numbers. Now he examined them more closely. When he stood up a moment later, ruminating to himself, he mumbled something inaudible and rubbed his hand across his face in puzzlement. Spying Logan fore, he walked briskly toward him, but was interrupted by the three others as they emerged from below.

"Find anything interesting, Mr. Macintyre?" asked the viscount as he deposited the two ladies back on the deck.

"I'm not much of a sailor, I admit, Burchardt," answered Logan. "But you certainly seem to have nothing but state of the art equipment."

"Where was she outfitted?" asked Jameson.

"Bremerhaven."

"Everything?"

"Mostly. It is my home port. Actually I bought the vessel in Trieste."

"Ever take her further south . . . the south Atlantic . . . coast of Africa?"

"No, no," laughed von Burchardt. "I'm no world traveller!"

Jameson nodded knowingly, but said nothing.

"We don't want to let that tea get too cold," said Logan. "Before we go, von Burchardt, won't you explain your instrumentation? There are a good many I've never seen."

"With pleasure!" replied the viscount with a broad smile. "Won't you join us, ladies . . . Jameson?" he added, leading the way back toward the front cabin.

Fifteen minutes later the small party piled out of Logan's car in front of the castle.

"Well, that was certainly a pleasant diversion," said Logan. "Thank you, Burchardt, for the whirlwind tour!"

"Perhaps if the weather turns for a bit, I might take you out, say a run up to the Orkneys for a day or two?"

"You are staying around then?"

"Oh, not much longer, but making plans that are too definite always makes me feel tied down. I merely have to return to the Continent before Christmas."

When they were seated in the drawing room and Flora had served tea along with some oatcakes and a tray of shortbread, Jameson picked up the thread of conversation.

"So you're headed back toward Germany then, Herr von Burchardt?" he asked.

The viscount nodded as he sipped at the hot tea. "And then by train down to Vienna," he added. "But tell me, Macintyre," he went quickly on, "I'm intrigued by this whole situation of your mother-in-law's journal. Seems that such a document would shed a great deal of light upon your present dilemma, especially if she documented her contacts and associations, which, as I understand it, turned up different, shall we say, 'evidence' than your own?"

"You're right, I daresay," replied Logan. "But the journal itself, the main part of it, that is, which Hilary received from Lady Joanna and still has in her possession"—as he said the words all eyes involuntarily glanced in Hilary's direction then back to Logan—"is not of particular significance."

A questioning look on the viscount's face invited further explanation.

"Perhaps you would like to explain what I mean, Hilary. You have read it more recently."

"Most of what Lady Joanna recorded was family history, detailed lives of her ancestors and a recounting of her own life and coming to Scotland," said Hilary. "There is no mention of recent events."

"That's because the ending is missing," put in Jo. "Can you believe it? Isn't it mysterious?"

"Missing pages!" von Burchardt exclaimed. "And you've no idea where they might be?"

He seemed to direct the question to Hilary, but then turned back and focused his innocently inquisitive gaze toward Logan.

"Such a pity," he added quickly, "that such a precious family heirloom should be lost or left incomplete."

All at once Logan realized he had given the ending to Joanna's journal no more than passing consideration. Suddenly the truth dawned upon him that she well may have documented her final thoughts and travels in a most revealing way.

"Might we have a look at what you do have, Hilary?" said Logan.

Hesitating awkwardly, Hilary replied, "I really would rather not, right now. This just doesn't seem like . . . the proper time."

Slightly annoyed at her rebuff of his request, Logan nevertheless kept his reaction to himself, thought for a moment, then rose. "Excuse me," he said, "I'm going to dash up and see how Allison is feeling."

He returned in only two or three minutes, Allison with him.

"I have asked Allison about the journal," began Logan as they entered the room, "but she has no more idea about the pages than the rest of us."

"They could be anywhere," said Allison. "But I have never known Mother to be careless, especially where her journal was concerned. Whatever she did with the final entries, I'm sure it was well-thought out."

"There would be hundreds of places around here where she might have hidden them," said Jo.

"Hidden them?" repeated Logan. "I wonder if we're getting a bit carried away. It may be but an oversight of some kind." His voice was wary.

"Perhaps we might have a look about the place, split into groups . . . we would want to start with the most likely places frequented by Lady Joanna," said the viscount enthusiastically.

"I appreciate your concern," replied Logan coolly, "but this is a matter for my wife and me to resolve. Hilary was right, this isn't the proper time."

"Of course! Please forgive me," said von Burchardt. "I've rather gotten carried away with myself, haven't I?" He chuckled softly. "I suppose I cannot resist a good mystery."

Jo seemed disappointed at the chilly turn of the conversation away from the pages. Hilary was relieved. Logan's forehead showed unexpressed thought and concern. Allison looked tired, and Jameson was saying nothing.

"So, do you read mysteries too, Emil?" asked Hilary after a few moments had passed, "or merely try to solve them?"

He laughed. "I'm a doer not a reader," he replied.

"And you think the two mutually exclusive?" asked Jameson, rising slightly out of his chair. This sounded like the beginning of a discussion more to his liking.

From there the conversation strayed innocuously off into a discussion of Sherlock Holmes, Agatha Christie, and the newest British creator of mystery, Lady Hargreave.

When Hilary ascended to her room later that evening, she found she was very tired. It had been a full day, and the time outside, probably the cold, had sapped her energy. Reflecting upon the day's events, what remained most vividly in her mind were the two conversations she had had with the two visitors, Ashley Jameson and Emil von Burchardt. Both were fascinating men, although as different as the very worlds they represented—Emil with his polished savoir-faire and striking good looks, Jameson with his unassuming refinement and casual manner. Both were capable of catching one off guard—the viscount with the direct, cheerful, upbeat approach, the professor by the many subtleties which seemed to quietly radiate out of his character.

Why compare them at all? Hilary asked herself. If for no other reason than they both seemed up to something. Why would they show up at the same time, and then hang around incessantly, always asking questions? Something felt peculiar, and she was right in the middle of it!

She sat down on the edge of her bed, thought for a moment, then rose and went to the suitcase, stuffed under the bed, where she still kept the journal. She pulled out the case, reached to the bottom, and pulled out Joanna's manuscript. She had been meaning to give the book to Allison, but somehow had continued to avoid doing so, even at the risk of appearing possessive of it. She knew her insistence on keeping it seemed peculiar to others in the family, yet somehow she felt it important she not relinquish it just yet. There remained much to resolve, and—who could tell? She might yet be called upon to play an important role in the unfolding of events.

The missing pages . . . Joanna's final words—they seemed to be the key. But where could they be? Again Hilary thumbed to the last page of the manuscript. Nothing had changed. Again she began to read, realizing as she did that she had never *really* read Joanna's final entry, never really perceived what Joanna was trying to say. As she continued her eyes widened. Yet Lady Joanna's words, if anything, served only to deepen the mystery:

August 27, 1971—Today and for the last several days it has been stormy like I have seldom seen on this north coast. Perhaps that explains my mood. I usually love these wild Highland blasts. But not today. I am chilled to the bone, and we cannot even keep a fire in the hearth. But what If feel goes beyond mere climatic conditions. It is a heaviness that has come over me, almost a sense of foreboding, as if some evil presence were incarnate in the storm itself. It is a feeling I have had only on rare occasions in my life, and the memories are too unpleasant to recall. Suffice it to say that I recognize the feeling and to this day am repelled by it.

I am not one to give heed to such ethereal notions, but can it be that the Lord is trying to tell me something? Warning me? Perhaps the hour of my death is near. With that in mind I have spent the last hour in prayer, and though no specific answer has come, I do sense a peace invading my heavy spirit, as though the evil may be present in the storm, but His almighty presence IS in and throughout the storm. Indeed, He made the storm and rules over it yet, and even now is preparing His messenger to combat the forces that would destroy what He has built. A Scripture continues to come to my mind which I know is from Him, but I do not yet understand its significance. "The angel of the Lord encampeth round about them that fear him, and delivereth them." Perhaps I do not need to understand just now— it is enough to know that He is indeed with me, and that He will lead me to—

And there the final entry of the journal broke off.

Unexpectedly tears welled up in Hilary's eyes. "Oh, Grandmother!" she whispered to herself, not even considering that it might not be so. She felt Lady Joanna's spirit with her, and remembered the lady's loving embrace. She had *felt* the love emanating from the dear lady! But was that enough to make her Hilary's grandmother?

Again she glanced at the date of the passage. *I wonder what might have happened that day to put her in such a dark mood?* Hilary asked herself. *I should question Mrs. Macintyre about it.*

She laid the journal back on top of the other things in the open suitcase on the floor, then sat down in the chair next to the window. Tonight there was no light, and although it was still relatively early, only nine o'clock, outside it was pitch black. The moon was still several hours away.

She was so tired—she had to get to bed. Yet she was too keyed up to sleep. The castle seemed unnaturally quiet, as if some mischief were abroad, awaiting the stroke of midnight to unveil itself. She could not keep from imagining noises, first outside, then above her, as though someone were walking softly in a room directly overhead, and then in the hallway outside her door.

With each imagined sound, she strained to hear more and each time was met with only a deeper silence.

For a long time she was undisturbed, and gradually drowsiness began to overtake her. Indeed, the unknown guest in a small sitting room—not above her room directly, but on the next floor and across the hall—was making no more stealthy noise in his stocking feet. The Viscount von Burchardt, whom everyone had bid goodbye about six o'clock, at that moment lay reclining on a sofa, having been let back into the house at a side entrance by his secret accomplice, awaiting the deeper slumber of the occupants of the castle that he might be about the real business for which he had been summoned to Port Strathy.

All remained still. Hilary had just lapsed into semiconsciousness when suddenly a loud knock sounded on the solid wood door of her room.

With a jolt she sat up in her chair, the fear of sudden waking upon her face.

39 ❊ Late Tea

"PARDON ME, MISS Edwards, for disturbing you so late . . . " came the voice when Hilary opened the door.

In disbelief she found herself staring at Ashley Jameson.

" . . . but I couldn't sleep, and I wondered if you would care to join me for a cup of tea?"

"But it's . . . it's . . . "

Still disoriented, Hilary glanced down and tried to focus the hands of her watch.

"It's nearly ten o'clock. I apologize again. I only thought—but if it's not convenient—"

"No, it's not that," Hilary interrupted. "You startled me, that's all." Coming to herself, she added, "Yes, I'd enjoy some tea. Just let me put on a sweater."

In another minute she was back in the hallway, closed her door, and they walked toward the main stairway, speaking softly as they went, as if their very presence in the quiet corridors indicated some sinister intent.

The hallway was chilly and dark except for dim nightlights at each end. As they padded down the deserted passage, Hilary began to have second thoughts about her decision. To her knowledge she was the only one quartered in this particular wing. Jo's room was around several corners. Logan and Allison occupied the master bedroom not far from Atlanta's dayroom. She did not know where Jameson's room was or from which direction he had approached. As they passed closed doors she felt an eerie sensation, as if from the darkness at any moment might spring wild images of wraiths. Hilary was flooded with relief when they turned the corner of the lengthy passageway and saw the stairway at hand. She glanced down in the direction toward Jo's room, but all was quiet and the lights were out.

Neither spoke as they flitted down the staircase, as if by common consent they knew the night air did not want to be disturbed. Jameson led the way to the kitchen, and upon entering Hilary saw that the lights had already been switched on and a teakettle was already on the stove.

"I see you are already prepared," she said.

"I hoped you would join me," he replied, "but I must confess I had my heart set on some tea regardless."

The room was furnished with modern conveniences—two refrigerators, an electric stove, a long wide tile counter with two spacious sinks at either end, and several other appliances. The cook still burned a wood fire in the brick hearth, however, now chiefly for heat, though at one time that same hearth had been used for huge pots of water and boiling oatmeal and potatoes. At the moment the fire was banked for the night, but still emitted a pleasurably warm radiance.

Hilary found a teapot and the tea. Jameson tended the water, and in about ten minutes they were seated at the rustic thick pine table, each with a warm cup in hand.

"So I take it you were not suffering from insomnia tonight, Miss Edwards?" he began.

"It started out so," she answered. "I had just drifted off when you knocked on the door. However, it would appear the affliction still plagues you?"

He smiled in that easy, unaffected smile she did not yet know how to interpret. "So it would appear."

As Hilary sipped the strong black brew, she determined to find out once and for all what this fellow was about, even if it meant she had to relinquish some of her own privacy and aloofness to do so. She had to sort out these people and their motives. Chances are she would learn nothing conclusive from Murry, in which case she was on her own. This story, if there was a story to come out of her sojourn to Stonewycke, would be hers and hers alone to write.

"I enjoyed our conversation of earlier," she said. "I have missed that level of mental stimulation since coming here. Some of what you said forced me to think."

"I'm surprised you haven't cornered Logan—I should say, Mr. Macintyre. I would think with your political interests and leanings, and his position, you could strike up quite a rousing discussion with him." He smiled wryly.

"The situation hasn't quite been conducive to that sort of dialogue." She paused and shook her head thoughtfully, almost regretfully. "I would have liked that though, to really talk to him."

"Perhaps you may still have the opportunity." He stirred cream and sugar into his tea.

"I'm beginning to doubt it. I don't think it will be long before I pack up and return to London."

"You sound disappointed."

"Crazy, isn't it? For someone who didn't want to come here in the first place, you'd think I'd be glad to go." She raised her cup to her lips. "There is something about this . . . place. The quiet, the stillness, the openness of the landscape . . . and the people. You should meet this lovely family I've become acquainted with down in the valley!"

"Perhaps you can introduce me."

"Maybe one day we can do that," said Hilary almost wistfully. "But as I was saying, there is something about this place that grows on you, gets under your skin. Part of me doesn't want to leave. It has nothing to do with whether I'm a member of this family or not. It's . . . it's something bigger than that! At the same time, there is something about this family too . . . "

"Yes, it is a truly incredible family."

"I thought you had only just met them." Suddenly Hilary was on the alert again.

"But naturally I have heard things—through Ian, you know."

"Yes, I'd forgotten. Have you known him long?"

"We've been associated at the university for years. He was my professor when I was a student."

"When was that?"

"I first came to Oxford in 1955. I completed my post-graduate work in 1962."

Hilary made a mental note of the dates. She'd have Murry do some double-checking next time she spoke with him.

"Then it must be quite a thrill now to collaborate with your former mentor," she said, as if she were baiting him.

"An honor, to be exact." The look of admiration in Jameson's eyes seemed genuine enough. "The man is highly renowned in his field. I don't know how much of your . . . what should I call it, your 'potential' family, you know about. But Lady Allison's brother Ian is responsible for several important archaeological finds."

Hilary again found herself aware of the prestige of this clan. In addition to a famous politician, it appeared the noble blood had produced a noted scholar as well. Hardly a surprise, though, she thought. Every one of them, if Joanna's journal was a correct mirror of character, seemed to have been bestowed with some inexplicable measure of . . . what was it? Godliness, character, integrity . . . ? What *was* the ingredient that set apart the people she had read about? She had sometimes felt as if she were reading the lives of a family of Old Testament patriarchs . . . or matriarchs, in many cases. Lady Joanna would no doubt have attributed it to the blessings of God, the result of prayers directed heavenward on behalf of future generations. Hilary could not help wondering what more she would continue to discover.

The voice of her companion interrupted her momentary reverie. "What are you thinking?" he said. "The oddest look just came over your face."

"Oh, forgive me." She gave a light, though hollow chuckle. "I was thinking again about this family. As you said, they grow more and more remarkable. "

"But surely you have noticed how down-to-earth they are."

"That doesn't alter what they are."

"On the contrary," he rejoined, "I believe it *is* what they are. The other—the position, the titles, the notoriety, the public spotlight—that's all peripheral to what these people really are. I do believe they could walk away from all that and not change an iota."

"Yes, I suppose I have seen that," she remarked quietly, thoughtfully. "Mr. Macintyre is a different sort of politician than most I encounter. There is a reality to him even I find refreshing. But you must understand that I grew up on the East End in nothing much better than a tenement. My father worked hard for a living—twelve, fourteen hours a day—to put bread on the table and a little besides—for me. I was an oddity on my street when I went away to the university. True, in recent years I've rubbed shoulders with some important people, and traveled to places my parents would never have dreamed going. But it doesn't matter a great deal where I was actually born. I don't even know that. Whether it was here, or in London, the roots of my being, the person I have become, still spring from simple folk. That's my point of reference to life. I can't change that. I don't think I even want to."

"But what if those London experiences aren't your roots? What if you were transplanted there? Don't you want to know from what stock the taproot of your life truly comes, independent of the sort of tree you may have been grafted onto before you can even remember?"

Hilary was silent a while. "You have a very good point, Mr. Jameson," she finally said.

"Ashley . . . please."

"Nevertheless, that was very deftly put. You do have a way with logic, I must say. I suppose I didn't want to examine that taproot in my own life at first. I was content with who I was and didn't want to discover that in reality I was someone different."

"Doesn't truth dictate that you have to find out?"

"Truth, Ashley?"

"Yes. If something is true, aren't we bound to find out, to learn whether it is, and to order our lives by it?"

"Bound by whom, by what?"

"By . . . integrity . . . by truth itself! To refuse to seek after, and know, and live by truth would be complete and total inconsistency. To me truth must be the guiding principle no matter what your other philosophical leanings."

"Strong words."

"But true words. Truth is the foundation stone for life, for rational thought, even for emotions. To deny truth, in even a small area of your life, is to deny your own personhood, and thus become a nonbeing. Truth—seeking first to know it, and then to live by what you have discovered—is the essence of life. There's no such thing as what you said earlier—ignoring who you really are so you can keep being someone you're not. Don't you see? That's nonpersonhood, nonbeing. The opposite of truth isn't falsehood, as the theologians and philosophers would have said a century ago. Neither is it different truth for you and me, as the modern theologian and philosopher quacks would say today. No, the opposite of truth is emptiness, nonbeing . . . ceasing altogether to have meaning."

"You are very convincing. What you say makes sense. I see I have not thought this through nearly enough." She paused; an odd flicker passed through her eyes, then she added, "I do want to live by truth, Ashley, however it may appear to the contrary."

"I believe you."

"If my taproot, as you say, comes from elsewhere than I had anticipated, even from such an unlikely source as the nobility of northern Scotland, then I will have to deal with that. You are quite right, it is not a fact I have the option of ignoring."

"Perhaps you won't have to make that decision. It may well turn out that Jo is the daughter, anyway, leaving you content with your East End upbringing."

Hilary peered over the rim of her raised cup at this peculiar professor. Was he mocking her with this sudden twist to a serious discussion? Or was he—consistent with what he had just been saying—merely speaking the truth without malice or motive?

From his passive expression, she couldn't tell.

But she did suddenly realize one thing. She had intended on grilling him for information, yet somehow he had turned the tables and she had been the one on the receiving end. The same thing had happened this morning.

She really shouldn't talk so freely—at least not until she had figured out just what he was up to.

"Yes, you're right," she said at length; "my worry may all be much ado about nothing, as they say."

After ten more minutes of inconsequential conversation, Hilary yawned and declared herself ready for bed.

"I think I might have another cup, myself," replied Jameson. "But I'd be happy to walk you back to your room."

"Oh no, don't bother," said Hilary, rising. "I can find my way. What harm could be afoot on a peaceful night like this when everyone else in the place is asleep?"

"No doubt you're right," he laughed. "Thank you for joining me. Good night."

On her way upstairs, Hilary reflected on their talk. He was on the mark, of course. She might not be Logan and Allison's daughter after all. As emotion-charged as had been her time with Lady Joanna, and notwithstanding the locket and the journal, the lady's visit could have been nothing but a misguided mistake. If so, it would not be long before her life would get back to normal. She would continue on as Hilary Edwards. Then she would have to face no major changes, no emotional upheavals in coming to grips with her identity—just as she had wanted in the first place.

Yet even as she tried to convince herself that maybe such a turn would be for the best, she realized that now she wasn't so sure she wanted it that way anymore.

She entered her room and sat down on the bed, still deep in thought. She really ought to return the journal. There had been so much discussion surrounding it, everyone had wanted to see it, she should give it safely back into Allison and Logan's hands.

Hilary stood again, walked around to the other side of the bed, knelt down beside the suitcase, and almost without conscious thought reached for the journal.

It was not there!

A quick panic seized her. Hastily she rummaged her hand through the few items on top of which she had set the manuscript, but Joanna's pages were not in the suitcase!

She jumped up and frantically scurried about the small room until she suddenly spied the manuscript lying on top of the dressing table. She grabbed it up with both hands and held it to her breast, exhaling a long sigh of relief.

With the journal still clasped to her, she sat down in her chair as one suddenly delivered from a nightmare, leaned back, and closed her eyes. The locket was bad enough; she could not lose this journal! It was too precious, and as if to assure herself once more of its reality, Hilary opened her eyes and gazed once more on the handwritten signature on the cover, and the words she had grown so familiar with: *Stonewycke Journal.*

She sat for some minutes, quietly rocking, still holding the book to her, reflecting on her visit with Lady Joanna. But as the initial alarm subsided and she was thinking more clearly, she began to question just what the journal was doing on the table. Hadn't she placed it in the suitcase on the floor just before Ashley had knocked on her door?

Yes, she was sure of it! But then that could only mean—

Was it possible someone had been in her room?

The idea seemed incredible, yet as Hilary stood and began to walk slowly about, there was one of the drawers not quite closed. She never left drawers like that. Alarm coming over her again, she rushed to the wardrobe in which she had placed her few clothes.

Everything seemed in order. Yet they did appear shoved more to one side than she remembered. Had someone been through her very clothes, actually snooping through her pockets? She shivered with the thought.

Retracing her steps, she returned to the dresser, opening one drawer at a time, now bringing all her reporter's instincts to bear on a thorough examination of each, struggling to recall precisely where every item had been placed when last she had used each drawer. As she methodically made her way from one drawer to the next, a resolute look of confirmation gradually came over her.

Yes, there could be no doubt. Someone definitely had been in her room! Everything had been carefully put back in order, but not until it had been ransacked first. Someone had been looking for something, and then tried to make the room look just as it had been.

Had it not been for the misplaced journal, Hilary would never have known!

Who could it have been? The thought plagued her, although the choices were extremely limited. The viscount had left the house hours ago, and she was with Ashley. That left only Logan, Allison, and Jo . . . or one of the maids, or Jake. No one seemed a very likely suspect. If they had wanted to read the journal, why hadn't they simply asked?

But no, she thought suddenly. If it had been the journal the interloper was seeking, then why had he left it? And why had the rest of the room been disturbed when the journal was clearly visible?

Whoever it was had clearly been after something else! What could it possibly be?

But even with the question, immediately Hilary knew the answer.

Of course . . . the missing pages! The ending to Lady Joanna's manuscript!

No doubt the intruder had glanced quickly through the journal itself first to see if she had been telling the truth about the ending. Then, not finding any substantive information there, he had laid it down and quickly gone through the remainder of the room, forgetting to replace the manuscript in the suitcase.

Suddenly for the first time came the question: How had her unwelcome guest known she would be gone from her room?

And in the same moment came the frightening thought that perhaps the culprit had merely waited, somewhere close by but out of sight, until an accomplice succeeded in getting her out of the way for twenty or thirty minutes! Perhaps with an invitation to tea!

So—perhaps those around her were not as transparent as they seemed!

Sitting down again, the journal still clutched in her hands, Hilary resolved anew to be on her guard.

Professor Ashley Jameson waited ten minutes after Hilary left the kitchen.

He rose slowly, cleaned up the few tea things, then exited himself. He moved quietly along the darkened corridors, came to the main staircase, which he ascended, being careful not to make a sound. But instead of continuing up to the third floor where his room was located, he paused and turned to his right. He passed stealthily through two long hallways, around a corner, and came finally to two large oak doors at the end of the hallway.

Here he paused, glancing both ways, then pulled out a large old-fashioned iron key. He inserted it into the lock and turned the latch. The door opened with only the hint of a creak, and Jameson walked inside.

It was pitch dark. He groped about carefully for several moments before his hands found the lamp he had been seeking, nearly knocking it over before his fingers were able to switch it on.

The light flooding the chamber revealed a spacious sitting room, decidedly distinct in its French provincial decor from the heavier, Elizabethan furnishings in the rest of the castle. In daytime hours the room must have been light and airy with abundant sunlight streaming in through the French doors that opened onto an outdoor veranda. But the damp, chilly atmosphere of the place indicated that it had probably not been opened up in months, perhaps years.

Well, he thought to himself, there may or may not be anything in *her* room—I will have to find that out later. He still had to look through the library more thoroughly, as well as in the other places Allison's mother would have been likely to frequent. But here possibly he would find something to at least point him in the right direction.

Whether Jameson realized the historical significance of the room he had just entered was doubtful. For he had just entered Lady Atlanta Duncan's own personal sitting room.

He walked directly to the French provincial desk situated near the French doors, sat down at the chair still there, and immediately went to work.

40 ✻ Hostilities

THE NEXT MORNING Hilary was late coming down for breakfast. When she arrived in the dining room she found it empty, although platters and covered bowls still sat on the sideboard. Ambling to them, she lifted a lid or two, but found the contents lukewarm and unappealing. Suddenly she wasn't very hungry anyway.

Trying to decide whether to have a cup of coffee at least, she turned to see the cook walk in.

"'Tis all cold by noo," she said in a slightly remonstrative tone. "But I can be warmin' it up for ye, dearie."

"Thank you, no. I don't think I'm going to have anything after all."

"'Tisna guid t' be goin' wi'oot yer breakfast, ye ken."

"I'll be fine. But where is everyone, Mrs. Gibson?"

"Here an' aboot. I heard talk o' a drive to toon later."

Opting to go without coffee, Hilary wandered out, just in time to see Logan walk by.

"Good morning, Hilary!" he said cheerfully. "Did you sleep well?"

"Yes, thank you. Once I got to sleep."

"Mice in the walls?" he asked with a laugh.

"Actually, more like persons unknown in the halls," she replied.

"Oh?"

"I think I had an uninvited visitor in my room last night."

"You think?"

"While I was gone from my room for a few minutes."

Logan grew grave. "I'm sorry to hear that." He paused, appearing deep in thought, then said, "Who else knows of this?"

"No one," Hilary replied. "I've seen no one since. I only just now came down." As she spoke, her journalistic instincts scrutinized Logan's eyes—after all, he was one of the persons who would have had a strong motive for unearthing the end of Joanna's journal.

"I'm on my way to the library, Hilary," he went on. "Won't you walk with me?"

She nodded, and they continued down the corridor. For some time neither spoke. Then at last Logan began.

"I've wanted to talk with you, Hilary," he said. "I realize the awkwardness of this situation, and there are times I repent of having twisted your arm to come. I worry that I may have done you an injustice."

"No harm has come to me yet," said Hilary lightly.

"Nevertheless, I feel bad that we—perhaps I should say *I*, for my wife is quite unlike herself these past few days—have been so lacking in hospitality and have left you more or less to fend for yourself. It has not been intentional, I assure you. But with Allison's sickness, which continues to grow worse and baffles the doctor, and with these other guests, not to mention ongoing business I have to tend to, I'm afraid I've just been rather swamped. I'm on my way to return a call to London right now."

"I understand. I know you're busy."

"In any case, please accept my apologies. It was my hope we could get to know one another better. Unfortunately that has not exactly happened. And there is of course the uncertainty of it all as well, which I had hoped my inquiries would have cleared up long before now. But alas, that has not happened either, and we appear no further toward a solution than before."

"I take it then that *you* did not send someone to my room?" Hilary said with a laugh, intended to sound humorous while still getting at the truth.

"That's a good one!" chuckled Logan. "But if I'd have wanted to find something, I'd have just come and asked you."

She knew he was right. That is exactly what a straightforward man like Logan Macintyre would have done. How could she doubt him?

"How is Mrs. Macintyre?" asked Hilary in a new vein.

"Not good," he replied with a serious expression. "She is up today, and even talking about driving to town with Jo. But she is pale, and I am worried. I can't imagine what is the problem."

"Her ankle?"

"No, no, it can't be something that small. She's had little injuries of that kind before, but nothing to knock her so out of sorts."

From what Hilary had read in the journal, Allison Macintyre did not seem the sickly sort. On the contrary, she came across as having inherited a full dose of the family spunk. Perhaps the fall had taken more of a toll than anyone—including her husband—realized.

"Well, here we are at the library," said Logan, "if you'll excuse me. But we'll talk again . . . and soon. I promise to make your stay here more pleasant than it has been. In the meantime, please make yourself at home. Go anywhere you like. Not only do I want to know you better, I want you to know Stonewycke."

With that he disappeared inside.

Hilary continued on, wandering aimlessly through the deserted corridors. It came into her mind to have a look inside the portrait gallery past which they had gone the other day. She stopped, tried to get her bearings, and then set off in the direction of what she hoped was the East Wing. That should get me close to the gallery, she thought. In fact, maybe I'll have a peek at some of the mysteriously unused rooms down in that section, too. Everywhere she turned this ancient castle held fascination!

Before she reached the East Wing or the gallery, however, Hilary found herself standing before the door of the heirloom room. She opened the door and walked inside.

The first sensation to come over her was the intense quiet, not unlike the awesome hush of a great cathedral. There was a sense in which she was indeed walking upon hallowed ground, if not spiritually then in the familial sense. Many of the same feelings she had had during her previous brief visit welled up within her, though now Hilary was alone and had the chance to let the feelings in her heart have fuller sway.

Slowly she walked about, retracing her steps from before, now giving her full attention to each item she saw—clan tartans, young Maggie's seventeenth birthday dress, ancient swords and *skean-dhus* and firearms, and a lovely music box given as a birthday gift to Maggie by her father.

Immediately the music box arrested Hilary's attention, drawing her eyes to the mantel where it sat. In another moment the tiny wooden box, so ornately carved, the gift from James Duncan to his daughter Maggie, was resting delicately in the palm of Hilary's hand. This same box had traveled to America with that young Maggie when she had been forced to flee from her father's wrath.

Carefully Hilary lifted the lid. Instantly the strains of Brahms' Lullaby, faint yet clear and bell-like, undiminished with age, filled the air of the large room.

Hilary stood as one enraptured by the sound, transported in her mind back through time, as if she were that little girl one hundred and twenty years earlier. When the tune ran down, she wound up the box again and listened once more to the familiar melody.

Suddenly a voice broke the stillness of the huge room. "Oh, there you are!"

But Hilary did not hear the words. Jolted so unexpectedly from her reverie, her startled jump sent the music box out of her hand. The next moment she was on her knees beside the poor thing, which had landed with a discordant crack, and was examining its broken leg.

Behind her Allison rushed forward.

"Dear Lord!" she cried as she lurched forward and sank to her knees also. A strangled sob broke from her lips. "What have you done!" she cried. Tears streamed from her eyes, and her shoulders shook with anguished sobs.

"I'm so sorry," said a stunned Hilary, shattered by the sudden disaster. Glancing about, she found the broken piece, picked it up, and as if in mute appeal for mercy for her heinous deed, held it out to Allison.

Allison snatched it from her hand as if she were rescuing it from the clutches of the Evil One himself.

"You!" she shrieked. "You broke it! You destroyed my music box!" Her voice trembled with pent-up passions as if they had been simmering for days. "It's your fault! You destroyed everything! Why did you have to come here! Everything was all right until you came!"

"Allison, stop!" The voice was Logan's, coming from the doorway where he had just entered. He rushed inside, followed by Ashley.

Both women looked up at the intrusion of the sharp voice.

Logan rushed forward and laid a strong arm around Allison's shoulders, gently urging her up. "Allison," he said softly, "what's come over you?" Though filled with beseeching, his voice was gentle.

"She's ruined everything, Logan!" sobbed Allison. "We were happy before!"

"I'm so sorry," was all Hilary could manage to say through her own tears of stinging pain. Then she turned and fled the room.

Feeling utterly helpless for one of the few times in his life, Logan glanced back toward Ashley as one paralyzed.

"You stay here," said Jameson in response to Logan's unspoken entreaty. "I'll see what I can do." With that he turned and followed Hilary from the room.

Turning back to his distraught wife, Logan sought to comfort her. She was always so strong and in possession of herself, he hardly knew what to say. He had never seen her like this.

"Ali, dear," he said softly.

"Oh, look at it, Logan! Look at it . . . after all these years. Maggie will never forgive me! I tried so hard to keep it safe . . . "

"Ali," said Logan, "it can be fixed." He lifted the lid. Much to his relief, the tune played just as before. "With a bit of glue, this leg will mend like new. No one will ever be able to tell."

"No, no! It will never be like it was!"

Logan realized the broken music box was only part of the problem. But what *was* the problem? What was happening to his Allison?

Tenderly he brushed back the tears on her cheeks. "Ali," he said, almost whispering, "it's all going to come out right in the end . . . and very soon. We must just be patient a while longer; then it will be just the way it used to be—"

"No, Logan! It will never be the same again! I know it!" But now her voice sounded faint and hollow, losing its fight. "I'm afraid, Logan . . . afraid . . . "

She collapsed, weeping like a child, into his arms. In another moment she was asleep—whether from exhaustion or a fainting spell, he could not tell.

He lifted her like a baby and left the room. When he had deposited her safely into bed, he hastened to the phone to call Dr. Connally. He knew what would be the doctor's reply, but he couldn't stand by and do nothing.

As he went, Logan thought to himself how pale Allison's face was, and how cold her body felt.

41 ❊ *Duplicity or Veracity?*

ASHLEY FOUND HILARY in her room. She had hoisted her suitcase and another bag onto the bed and was frantically throwing her belongings into them.

"You're leaving?" he said quietly.

She spun around, her eyes filled with mingled anger, hurt, and confusion. "What else can I do?" she replied heatedly. "I don't belong here—I never did!"

"I didn't take you for a quitter."

"What do you know?" she retorted sharply. "You've only just met me."

"I suppose it is presumptuous of me to say such a thing, though I still believe it's true."

"Well, it doesn't matter anyway. I've given it plenty of time, and things are only getting worse." She sighed, her anger easing slightly. "They already have the daughter they wanted."

"Do you really believe that?"

The question took Hilary off guard. It was not the question itself, but rather the tone in which he had spoken it. There was a probing hardness to his voice, with just enough emphasis on the *really* to make Hilary wonder about its intent.

She regarded him seriously for a moment. Suddenly it dawned on her that she didn't know his intent. She continued to fix her gaze upon him, her mind ruminating on all the possibilities that had occurred to her during the past few days, but arriving at an endless string of questions in the end. The outburst that finally escaped her lips, however, was altogether unexpected.

"What business is it of yours, anyway?" she asked.

He faltered, momentarily taken aback, then groped for words with which to answer. "Perhaps none," he said, "but I care about—"

"Truth?" she shot back. "Is that what you were going to say? Ha! Truth indeed!"

"I meant those things I said before."

"Oh yes! Truth and integrity . . . ordering our lives consistently by those principles— bosh! And you're telling me that's what life means to you?"

"I never said I lived truth perfectly," he replied calmly. "But that takes nothing away from the fact that such is my desire, and such I attempt to do to the extent I am capable."

"I see! And is that why you always seem to appear just at the most appropriate times, to start grilling me with questions?"

The interview was going much differently than he had planned. He took a deep breath, considering the best way to respond, but Hilary hardly gave him the chance.

"And while we're on the subject, Mr. Ashley Jameson, supposed Oxford professor, I would just like to know what you're doing here in the first place."

"I made no secret of that. I was here to meet—"

"To meet Ian! Of course! Who just happened—conveniently and coincidentally—not to be here and to be off where he couldn't be reached."

"I'm sure if Mr. Macintyre had any doubts, he could easily—"

"But there are no doubts about you, are there? Mr. smooth, polished, studious, soft-spoken Jameson whom everyone adores! Well, I would still like to know how you managed to appear just at the right moment! And while we're on the subject of your mysterious presence, what were you doing snooping around so late last night, wandering around the place? I suppose you just *happened* to want some tea, and then just *happened* upon my room!"

"It was all just as I said, Hilary," replied Jarneson, his voice still calm, but a deep look of concern filling his eyes. "Yes, I did simply want a cup of tea, and thought I would enjoy your company, notwithstanding the hour."

As he spoke, he scrutinized her face, as if inwardly assessing what he saw, weighing the fluid features of her emotion-filled eyes, the flare of her nostrils, the slight lift of her right eyebrow, the curvature of her forehead, the angle of her chin, the intonation of her words— all given form and a thousand nuances of subtle expression by the shape and ever-changing movements of her mouth and lips.

Just as he spoke the words "notwithstanding the hour," a sudden look as of revelation filled his countenance. With an inward gasp, he caught his breath.

Hilary, however, remained too caught up in her own tirade of frustrated emotions that she saw none of what passed across his face.

"How convenient! How convenient!" she fired back. "Get me out of the room and down to the kitchen so someone else could search my room undisturbed!"

"What?" he said.

"I suppose you knew nothing of it!"

"Nothing, I assure you."

"No doubt, no doubt! The fact remains that *someone* ransacked my room while we were in the kitchen last night!"

A grave expression came over Ashley's face. Things were taking a serious turn. He hoped he could patch it up with Hilary later, but right now there was one more piece of confirming testimony he needed—even if it would be equally subjective to the one he'd just received. And then, once he was sure in his own mind, it was time to let his accessory in this little game fully in on what he had discovered.

"I truly am dismayed to learn of this, Hilary," he said. "But for right now, I think it best I leave you alone. It would be fruitless of me to say anything further."

He turned and left the room. Hilary watched him go, then turned back inside, her emotions calming in the wake of her outburst. She glanced over her things strewn about on the bed, then sat down and sighed. *What should I do?* she wondered. *What should I do?*

Thirty minutes later Hilary still sat on the edge of the bed, still pondering her fate, though by now beginning to recriminate with herself for the vicious verbal thrashing she had given Ashley. After all, he had not really been the object of her frustrations at all; rather, she had been angry at herself over the accident with the music box . . . angry with herself for coming here in the first place. Something down inside her had responded favorably to Ashley from the very beginning. The fact remained that she believed him when he spoke to her of truth. His bearing, the tone of his voice, told her that he was speaking from his heart. And Hilary prided herself on being able to read people accurately. She had not risen in the journalistic ranks by being a pushover. She knew people. She was no easy mark for a huckster. In fact, she possessed not a little of the audacity of a street con herself, and had more than once plied such a trait to her advantage.

Everything in her experience with people told her that this Ashley Jameson was either everything he claimed, consistent on the surface as he appeared to be, indeed, probably just as he said, a lover and seeker after truth—he was either all this, or else he was the most bold-faced, skillful liar she had ever met, a hypocrite beyond compare, who was able to look deep into her eyes and hoodwink her utterly.

The thought almost frightened her. But there were no other options. He must be one or the other.

She rose and walked slowly away from the bed, chiding herself for being so hard on him. He was just trying to help, she thought.

As she approached the window, Hilary looked out on the lawn below.

She could hardly believe her eyes!

There were Ashley and Jo, walking slowly toward the back of the castle, close together, lost in what to all appearances was a lively discussion!

He is a liar, after all! she cried, half audibly. How could she have been so easily duped? *Why, he's nothing but a spy for Jo!*

Hilary spun around and ran from the room. She flew along the hall, down the stairs, and out the front door. Before she realized where she was going, she had left the gates of Stonewycke behind her and was walking hurriedly along the estate driveway toward town.

42 ✾ The Old Garden

As HILARY CAME around one of the sharp bends in the driveway, paying little attention to her surroundings, in front of her she spied Emil von Burchardt walking briskly toward her.

"Ah, Hilary!" he exclaimed in the greeting she had already come to associate with him. "A pleasant morning to you!"

She smiled, forcing down her vexation with Ashley, and approached him. "This is a pleasant surprise," the viscount went on. "As a matter of fact, I was just on my way to the castle for a visit, hoping to see you, I might add, but I did not anticipate so immediate a granting of my wishes as to meet you while I was still on the approach!"

"I was out for a walk," said Hilary lamely.

As von Burchardt reached her, they stopped and shook hands. His look took her face in for a moment or two, then spread over with concern.

"But you look upset, Hilary! Or perhaps just flushed from the walk? May I be so bold as to ask if there is anything wrong?"

"No, nothing! Thank you," answered Hilary, rather too quickly. "Yes, I'm sure it is the morning exercise. I've been walking fast," she added, puffing as if in confirmation of her words.

"I can see that," said the viscount, still seeming to peruse her. "Well, would you care to accompany me back to the castle?"

Hesitating only momentarily, Hilary replied, "Why, yes, thank you," turning as if in resolution. She took his arm and began walking back the way she had come, as if secretly hoping to encounter Ashley that she might make a show of her own independence and disinterest in him.

Beaming with his good fortune, von Burchardt strutted forward with the aplomb of a peacock in full feather, crowing to himself for the fine piece of work he had done in winning over this lovely chickadee. In less than five minutes they passed the gates and entered the courtyard, chatting amiably. Hilary's reactions were perhaps a bit too animated and her laugh a little too loud to suit von Burchardt's half of the dialogue. When she saw that they were alone on the grounds, however, her tone and exhilaration abated slightly.

"So tell me, Hilary," said von Burchardt, "have there been any changes in your fortunes?"

"Only that I am planning to leave soon."

"Oh?"

"There have been no changes, so I think it's time for me to beat a retreat. It was probably a mistake to come in the first place."

"Hmm. Now that is an interesting turn," said the viscount, his matter-of-fact tone revealing far less interest in the disclosure than he was feeling inside. "Then perhaps I might interest you in that cruise aboard my yacht, after all."

"What, Emil? No attempt to talk me into staying?" rejoined Hilary, cocking one eyebrow as she glanced in his direction.

"Why should I do that?" he replied jovially. "It's your life, not mine."

"I suppose I expected it because that's all I get from the other two men around here— exhortations to stay till it is resolved."

"You mean Mr. Macintyre and that Jameson fellow?"

Hilary nodded.

"Ah well, as I say, it's your life to do with what you will. It seems to me that everything would be rather neatly tied up, so to speak. You and I could sail off for a couple weeks. I could deliver you back to London. And we could leave these people here with their problems. What do you say?"

"I don't know. I didn't say I had made up my mind yet."

"A little of the fight left in you?" he asked, throwing her a glance meant to be merry but full of meaning. "Protect your interests, eh?"

"I don't think it's that. I just have to be sure, that's all."

By this time they had walked around by the side of the castle. Hilary had been paying little attention to the direction their steps took, and all at once they found themselves abreast of a small iron gate toward the distant back of the house. Through its bars they could see a little-used garden that neither had visited before. Hilary paused before the gate, then suddenly reached up into a broken piece of rock in the stone wall to which it was fastened, where, in a crevice, her fingers clutched an old and rusted key.

"I see you have become quite familiar with the estate," commented von Burchardt.

"No," said Hilary in a bemused tone. "Actually, I have never been to this place."

"Quite a lucky stroke then, finding the key."

Hilary glanced down at the key in her hand, just as an unsought image flickered through her brain, lasting but an instant:

Standing before a gate, which appeared to be this very one, a little girl grasped the hand of an older woman. Then the child wriggled free from the larger hand which held hers, and began jumping up and down in front of the iron bars, reaching up toward the broken stone in the wall. But even her outstretched arm fell far short.

"Grandma! Grandma! Key! See garden!"

As quickly as it had come the phantasm faded. The faces of the two figures had been turned away from her, and Hilary had been able to discern no details of either person or dress or mannerism. Yet something within her shivered with a recognition of the older woman which she felt rather than saw. The apparition had been but a fleeting snatch of something whose purpose or origin she could neither ascertain nor guess. She turned her perplexed countenance toward von Burchardt.

"I must have read about it in Lady Joanna's journal." she said, then jammed the key into the lock. "Shall we go in and have a look about?" As she spoke Hilary's attention was fixed on the insertion of the key into the old gate. She therefore did not see her companion's reaction to her momentarily lapse. He had read more of the truth in her eyes than she would have guessed possible. For the Viscount von Burchardt—like Hilary herself—was no mean judge of character, and was especially well-versed in reading between the lines of the feminine psyche in all its mystifying complexity. When he saw what passed through Hilary's eyes, over von Burchardt's face spread a look of resolve. He knew the time to act was drawing near.

Hilary found the lock troublesome and stubborn, and it took several attempts to persuade its ancient workings to give way. When it finally surrendered, von Burchardt opened the gate, and then followed as Hilary entered. Both were silent for some time in the hushed atmosphere of overgrown willows and birch trees, under whose wings spread out in all directions lawns and hedges, and bordered flowerbeds.

In the very center stood a gnarled and hoary birch—its great, twisted roots scoring the earth for many feet in all directions, making the ground uneven and rough in its vicinity. In the winter, with its branches barren, the tree took on a mournful air; but Hilary tried to imagine it in summer, covered with greenery, presiding over the lush vegetation on the ground beneath it, with flowers gracing the beds rather than black earth. Even in the garden's present desolation, Hilary could sense that the place was pregnant with unseen life.

Had there indeed been mention of such a garden in the journal? There must have been, she thought, for she felt she already knew the spot so well, though something inside told her it had once been even more unkempt than it was now. How mysterious and wild it must have once been! she thought.

At each end of the enclosed space sat two stone benches, heavily weathered, one displaying a prominent crack. Hilary walked slowly to the far end, the viscount following her silently, and sat down. He joined her.

"It's like entering another world," he said.

"I think that if I were a young girl growing up here," said Hilary dreamily, "I would come and sit on this bench every day and gaze at that grand birch, maybe even try to climb it, and dream to my heart's content."

"What would you dream?" asked von Burchardt.

"I don't know. When I was a girl I used to fantasize being swept away by dashing young men and sailing away to exotic lands." She smiled suddenly feeling silly. "I was quite the romantic in my youth."

He laughed. "And now, look at you!" he said. "Here you sit with—well, as to being dashing, I will make no comment! But as to the exotic lands, you have only to say the word, and my vessel waits to spirit you away!"

Now it was Hilary's turn to laugh. "*In my youth,* I dreamed of such things."

"But no more?"

"Such fancies hardly befit a hard-headed magazine editor."

"Come now, Hilary. You do not seem the hard-headed type."

"You've not seen me crack the whip the day before deadline! But you might be right. Perhaps I am still a romantic after all, though I hope by this time in my life it's tempered with some good sense. And how about you, Emil? You strike me as too much a man of the world to have escaped the clutches of some ravishing beauty this long."

"We marry late in my family—something to do with being fully apprised of the field."

"And that's what your travels are for, to scout the 'field' of eligible heiresses throughout Europe?"

"I hate to balk at family tradition," he replied with a slight laugh.

"Well, you seem to have landed on your feet here," said Hilary. "You have two of us to choose from!"

He laughed, nervously, she thought.

For a time neither spoke, a palatable silence enveloping them as the peculiar magic of the garden weaved its enchantment. Here one could escape the modern age without so much as leaving the grounds. Emil had commented on its being like another world—it was that, and so much more. Everywhere her gaze fell Hilary sensed history overflowing her, in much the same way she had when reading the journal—personal history, real history . . . the reality of being in a place that was part of her very being . . . her roots—like the roots of the huge tree in front of her.

Again, as she reflected within the quietness of her own soul, von Burchardt quietly scrutinized her, and again read more of what was passing through her spirit than he let on. *It is indeed time to act,* he thought. *The moment has come.*

"Come," he said, rising. "Let me take you to town. The yacht is ready to sail, the weather is favorable. If you won't agree to let me take you back to London, then at least join me for the afternoon."

Hilary remained seated. "I hate to leave this place," she said at length, as if she had not heard him. "I feel as if I am under a spell."

"Yes . . . I feel it too. But come," he added, reaching out and taking her hand, "I won't take no for an answer."

Hilary exhaled a long breath and looked up at him with one last lingering hesitation in her eyes. Then she recalled what had driven her out-of-doors in the first place—the incident with Allison and her irritation with Ashley's chicanery. At least Emil was what he seemed, she thought—no more nor no less.

"All right," she said finally. "You're on."

43 ❈ *Aborted Voyage*

IT WAS ABOUT two in the afternoon when Ashley entered the sitting room.

"Has anyone seen Miss Edwards?" he asked. "I must see her."

The only ones present were Jo and Logan. Jo did not look up, and Logan replied that he had only a moment earlier come in from outside and had not seen her. He asked if he had tried her room, to which Jameson nodded in the affirmative, adding that he had been throughout the house and no one had seen a trace of her.

"Has Herr von Burchardt called today?" he asked, divining a measure of what he feared might be the truth.

Logan had not seen him. Jo said she thought he had planned on dropping by today, but she had seen nothing of him yet.

Ashley thanked them and left the room.

Within a few minutes, before he had had time to reason out his actions logically, he was sitting behind the wheel of his car and driving toward Port Strathy. Something told him danger was afoot threatening to thwart his mission.

Aboard the viscount's yacht, everything had been made ready to cast off.

Von Burchardt had retrieved his crew from the Bluster 'N Blow and from Hamilton's. They had gone through the preliminaries of a thorough voyage, even though the Captain, as they called the viscount, repeatedly stressed the fact that they were only going out for an hour or two, a little shake-down cruise. While they made their preparations, von Burchardt gave Hilary a more extensive tour of the vessel. They were both standing before the controls at the bridge, waiting for the first mate to cast off, the engine idling in readiness, when Jameson's car pulled up at the dock and Ashley jumped out. He quickly ran out on the platform.

"Ahoy," he called up. "Miss Edwards . . . I must see you!"

Still irked from the events of the morning, Hilary looked down, debated within herself whether to ignore him or accede to his request, then turned to the viscount and said, "I'll only be a minute. Don't leave without me."

"I wouldn't think of it. Just make sure he doesn't twist your arm for an invitation and wind up joining us."

Hilary laughed. "Don't worry! I wouldn't think of it! If he goes, I stay!"

She left von Burchardt standing at the helm, carefully climbed down the steep stairway to the main deck, crossed it, then addressed Ashley from where she stood.

"Yes, what is it?"

"Please, I must speak with you."

"So, here I am. Talk."

"I mean down here . . . privately."

"What is it that's so important that it can't wait till we return? I'll be back to the house in a couple of hours."

"Are you sure of that?"

"We're only going out for an hour, then back in."

"And you're certain the viscount doesn't have anything more extensive in mind?"

"Don't be ridiculous! At least *he* plays it straight with me."

"I won't bother to ask you what you mean by that. The point remains that I simply must see you in private immediately."

"Well, if you can't say what you have to say to me here and now, then it will have to wait."

She turned and began walking away.

"Miss Edwards . . . *Hilary!*" he called after her in an imperative voice. "You are wanted at the house. I'm afraid it can't wait two hours!"

She stopped and turned to face him.

"Wanted? For what?"

"That I cannot tell you. But you simply must come with me."

"Who wants me?"

"Mr. . . . . Mr. Macintyre," replied Ashley, his voice shaky.

Convinced at last, Hilary hesitated only another moment, then said, "I'll go tell Emil and be right down."

"Please, Miss Edwards," Ashley enjoined, "say nothing to him. He must not come up to the castle . . . not today."

"Why not?" asked Hilary, her irritation returning.

"Again, I'm afraid I cannot tell you. But I implore you to climb down and come with me at once."

Hilary sighed, obviously not pleased with this turn of events, and even more displeased with Ashley himself, but then waving up at the viscount where he stood watching the proceedings, called out, "I'll be back as soon as I can," and then walked down the short gang-way to where Ashley stood on the dock. Quickly he began whisking her away, to Hilary's extreme annoyance, before von Burchardt, who had immediately run off the bridge and down to the deck to protest this interruption to his plans, could get close enough to make his displeasure known.

Ashley opened the passenger door of his car for Hilary, but did not wait to close it himself. While she was still climbing in, he ran around to his own side, watching out of the corner of his eye as von Burchardt followed down the gangway and onto the dock after them. Scarcely had Hilary pulled her door shut before his BMW had spun around and was heading past the Bluster 'N Blow, leaving a red-faced Burchardt standing in a cloud of dust silently cursing the professor's untimely interference.

Inside the automobile the tension between the abductor and abductee was thick enough to cut. Not until Ashley had crested the hill overlooking Port Strathy to one side and Ramsey Head on the other did he abate his speed. Then he pulled off to the side of the road and stopped the car.

"What is this?" asked Hilary in a piqued tone.

"I'm afraid we have to have a little talk before we get back to Stonewycke."

"What about the urgent message Mr. Macintyre has for me?" she asked, growing more exasperated with this man by the moment.

"That's what we have to talk about. I'm afraid Mr. Macintyre didn't send me after you at all."

"What! You lied to me!"

"I apologize. I'm afraid I've never been too good at thinking on my feet. I had to do something to get you away from there, and before I realized what I was doing, out it had come."

"How dare you!" snapped Hilary, reaching for the door latch.

Ashley reached across and held her hand firm.

"I simply must not allow you to go back down there."

"What right do you have—after all that talk about truth? It's all just hogwash to you! I can't believe a word you say!"

"I'm sorry you feel that way. I hope someday I can show you otherwise."

"Let me out of here! I will not sit here and listen to you insult my intelligence, or the intentions of my friend Emil. Either you let me go my own way or I'll—"

"I will not let you go back to that man," said Ashley. "I'm sorry if you think me cruel or unreasonable. But I have my reasons."

He started the car before she had a chance to protest further, ground it into gear, and sped up the road. In the passenger seat, Hilary sat with face red, silent but inwardly fuming. She would get out of this idiotic place the instant she was packed, she said to herself, and never set foot here again!

44 ❊ Detour and Diversion

WHEN THEY REACHED the turnoff into the Stonewycke estate, Ashley accelerated right past. He didn't know exactly what he was going to do, but of one thing he was sure: if Hilary had the chance, in her present mood she would run right back to von Burchardt.

"Where are we going?" she asked with venom in her tone.

"I'm not sure," replied Ashley. "Somewhere you can cool off . . . and where I can think."

Thirty minutes later they drove into Fraserburgh. Though the drive of less than twenty miles had been silent and uneventful, by the time they reached the town of some ten thousand, Hilary had calmed considerably, and Ashley thought he might get her safely back to the estate without risk of her running away. He drove to the middle of the small village and stopped.

"Why don't you have a bit of a look about?" he said, trying to sound friendly. "I've got to make a phone call. There are several rather nice shops within walking distance."

"How do you know? I thought you had never been to this part of the country."

"I'm very well read," he said, a small mischievous smile playing at the corners of his mouth.

She said nothing in reply, merely grunted and folded her arms across her chest.

"You may as well make the most of this," he prompted. "It may not be Carnaby Street or Piccadilly, but who knows, you might find something you like."

Hilary opened the door with an exaggerated *humph* and stepped out.

"I'll meet you back here in an hour," said Ashley. His sentence was punctuated with a forceful closing of Hilary's door as she walked off in the opposite direction without another word.

The smile Ashley had been restraining with great difficulty now escaped and spread across his lips. "Well, Professor," he muttered to himself, "you've got yourself in the middle of a fine pickle now!" But the hour by herself should help settle her ruffled emotions and injured pride, he hoped—not to mention giving him time to consider how best to handle this delicate situation once they arrived back at Stonewycke. After all, he had abducted the Macintyre's guest for no more reason than that his instinct told him trouble was brewing. If an issue were made of it, he could find himself hard pressed to explain his behavior.

An hour later he was parked back alongside the same curb when Hilary walked up the sidewalk toward him, carrying a package. He jumped out and ran around to open the door for her, which attention she accepted with a nod as she climbed into the passenger seat.

"I see you found something, after all," said Ashley cheerfully as they drove away.

"Nothing much," said Hilary with a deadpan expression. "A dress."

"Well, let's have a look."

"What interest could you possibly have in a woman's dress?"

"Actually the fashion industry is quite fascinating. Believe it or not, I've even been to a fashion show."

The incongruity of a stuffy university professor sitting watching a parade of models sauntering by displaying the latest in outlandish French design caught Hilary so off guard that a smile escaped her lips.

"You, Professor?"

"Are you shocked?"

"Let's just say . . . amused."

"So . . . do I see your new purchase or not?"

"All right, you win," consented Hilary with a sigh, opening the box that sat on her lap. "I'm still angry, you understand. What you did was inexcusable, and you have not heard the end of it. But I'll show you the dress."

"A truce, then?"

"For the time being."

Jameson smiled to himself. *The detour to Fraserburgh has been a capital stroke,* he thought to himself, *even if I didn't exactly plan it!*

Hilary pulled out the dress and held it up as best she could, unable to avoid the fact that buying it *had* made her feel better. The man was insufferable, but that was no reason she should not make the best of the situation.

She had never worn this particular color before—a subdued and subtle mixture of purple, gray, violet, and pink. She had always leaned more toward muted, earthy tones. But the moment she had held this dress—whose label identified the shade as "Heather in Bloom"— in front of her and gazed into the mirror, she had been surprised by the effect.

"It's beautiful!" said Ashley, glancing over from his driver's seat. "Positively stunning!"

"The clerk kept trying to push off a cream-colored frock on me," said Hilary, inwardly pleased with his enthusiastic response, yet trying to hide it. "But I loved this immediately."

"I can see why. You will look smashing in it . . . just lovely."

"Thank you," replied Hilary with a half smile. "But don't think you can win me back over with compliments. I have not forgotten what you did."

"I was not trying to win you over. I *do* like the dress."

"Fine. Just so long as you know I'm still angry with you."

"Understood." *This young woman is really too much,* thought Ashley with an inward chuckle. *I'll never be able to live this down!*

But if Ashley's *intended* indiscretions were not enough, he soon found himself facing a most unintended one. About three-fourths of the way back, when they could not have been more than five or six miles from the estate, all at once without warning the BMW's engine began to cough and sputter. Ashley slowed and down-shifted but the automobile did not respond. His gaze fell on the instrument panel and he immediately pulled off the road.

"What's wrong?" asked Hilary.

"I am afraid," he said with a forlorn sigh, "that I have committed the classic blunder."

"What do you mean?"

"It appears we are out of petrol." He attempted a light chuckle, but his humor fell on deaf ears.

"I really can't believe this," said Hilary. "I should think a man of your intelligence would plan his kidnappings more carefully."

"I will be sure to do so in the future. But this is my first time."

"So . . . what do you propose we do?"

"I see nothing for it but to get out and walk."

"Walk? It's freezing out there!"

"It will soon be freezing in here, too. The distance can't be too far. We can make it. If you'd prefer, I'll go myself, and send someone back for you."

"Never mind." Hilary opened her door and stepped out. "How do I know you wouldn't just leave me here to rot?" She started on her way down the road.

Ashley climbed out, locked the car with Hilary's purchase inside, then jogged to catch up with her.

"I thought we had a truce," he said somewhat breathlessly when he reached her.

"I changed my mind." She hurried on ahead of him.

I am a patient man, thought Ashley to himself, hurrying to keep pace with the insufferable woman. But he was no villain, and had just about had his fill of these barbs.

They walked on in silence. The cold and the wet snow began to make its mark felt on Hilary's pace after three or four minutes, and soon they were once more walking side by side. Another ten minutes passed in silence as frosty as the ground upon which they were walking. They had covered perhaps a mile when finally Ashley spoke.

"I am terribly sorry about all this," he said. "I suppose half of what you think about me is justified. But what I did today, no matter how it appears, was for your own good."

"You deprived me of a delightful sail. I am freezing. I have frostbite in my toes, and my shoes are ruined. And you say all this is for my own good!"

"I fear that your delightful sail, as you call it, would have proved something a little more ill-fated. I do not trust that man's—"

"What right do you have to pass judgment on another?" she said, stopping and focusing full on him. In her eyes was the look he had expected. "Moreover," she added, "who are you to dictate my preferences?"

"So you think von Burchardt had only sailing in mind?"

Hilary chuckled. "You were attempting to protect my honor?"

"You are a grown woman," Ashley replied, "quite capable of doing that for yourself. I simply thought—"

His words were cut short by the loud roar of a vehicle approaching behind them. As they turned they saw a truck, possibly of late forties vintage, braking to a stop. Its battered body showed every rough, backroad mile indicated on its odometer.

"Mr. Mackenzie!" Hilary exclaimed as the driver stepped out. "You are heaven sent!"

"What a coincidence meetin' up wi' the twa o' ye oot here," he said.

"I'm afraid we ran out of gas back there," said Ashley, extending his hand. "I'm Ashley Jameson."

"Karl Mackenzie, at yer service. So 'twas yer fine new car I seen back aboot a mile?"

"I'm afraid so."

"Weel, ye'll be needin' a ride, so aboard wi' ye."

"It seems I am always cold and wet when we meet," said Hilary, climbing in.

Mackenzie laughed. "Nice excuse to have ye for a cup o' hot tea." He threw the truck into gear and the ancient vehicle lurched into dubious motion. Neither Ashley nor Hilary, however, were in any mood to disparage their good fortune. "The wifie will be so pleased to see ye again, mem! Ye will join us for a bit tea before we rescue yer auto?"

"We'd be honored, Mr. Mackenzie," replied Ashley. "You're most kind."

Thirty minutes later the two wayward travelers found themselves seated on the floor of the Mackenzie's cozy cottage, bare feet propped up toward the fire to gain the best advantage of the warm hearth. Struggle as she might, under the circumstances Hilary found animosities difficult to maintain, notwithstanding what Ashley had done. Frances Mackenzie's broad, friendly smile and hugging welcome as if Hilary had been her own daughter did not help Hilary to nurse her grudges either. Soon pleasant conversation began to flow among them, covering a wide range of topics, though conspicuously avoiding any mention of the house on the hill.

"What do you grow here, Mr. Mackenzie?" asked Ashley.

"Oh, whatever I can make my wee plot o' land produce. Potatoes, wheat, oats, sometimes barley."

"And you raise livestock?"

"Na that much. A half-dozen nowt—"

"Nowt?"

"Cattle. An' two or three pigs, a handful o' chicks. My byre's nae so big."

Ashley questioned his host further, and before long they were deep in a discussion of spring planting, the fickle Scottish weather, and the delights and hazards of fishing off the north coast. Little Kerrie hovered about, awaiting every pause in the dialogue to question this new representative of the wide world about her favorite crown Prince.

"I think yer shoes an' socks'll be aboot dry when I return," said Mr. Mackenzie at length, standing up. "I'll jist be off to town to fetch ye some petrol."

"I'll join you," said Ashley, jumping up off the floor.

"Ye'll do nae such thing, yoong man," expostulated Mrs. Mackenzie. "Ye'll sit right where ye are an' drink another cup o' tea."

"I'm well able to handle a bit cannie o' gas," said Mackenzie. "So ye jist heed my woman, an' I'll be back 'round shortly."

He left the room and Mrs. Mackenzie walked back into the kitchen to set more tea brewing, Kerrie following her. Ashley and Hilary were left alone.

Ashley sighed. "They're marvelous folks," he said. "I can't help thinking that this is what it's really all about."

"What what's about?" said Hilary in a relaxed tone, her previous anger by now forgotten.

"Life, I suppose." He paused, reflecting on his words before continuing. "I don't know. You meet so many people. And the pace of the twentieth century in places like London, even Oxford to a degree, is so fast, so impersonal. Everyone caught up in his own life without much regard for what's going on about him. But then you step into a place like this . . ." He stared at the bright tongues of flame licking at the slabs of dried peat in the hearth. "My first reaction is that it's from another world, another century. Yet . . . I cannot help but think that *this* is the *real* world and all that—out there—is the illusion. I have my Greeks, and I love them. I have learned a great deal about character from them. Yet the study of Classical Greece, the bankers and investments of London, the political decisions around which the world revolves—none of it could get along, none of it would have meaning without people like the Mackenzies."

"Lady Joanna was constantly saying that very thing in her journal," said Hilary. "The people are what makes the land what it is. They are its life, she said. Had I not met the Mackenzies, I probably would not understand what she meant. I still don't fully know what she meant, because she spent so much longer here than I have. But perhaps I will learn."

"The place is growing on you?"

"How can it not? Stonewycke is no longer just an estate, a castle. Now everything about the whole region has more meaning—the Mackenzies, Mr. Davies over at the inn, even this weather, the wild sea, the desolate moors. I am beginning to feel a little of what Lady Joanna wrote about, I suppose." She paused. "I will be sad to leave," she added.

"And you think it will come to that?"

"Someone will have to go."

A brief silence fell before Ashley replied.

"I sense, Hilary, that you belong here," he said. His voice was deeply earnest.

"A city girl like me? I wonder."

"It has nothing to do with that," said Ashley. "It has to do with something deeper. The Macintyres, Logan and Allison, probably have to live in London. Perhaps they prefer it, I don't know. Yet they *belong* here no less. They are an intrinsic part of it, and it is part of them. I'm sure it's bound up in birth and ancestry. But it's more than that too. They *love* Stonewycke and its people and all it represents. I think what I sense is that same deep love growing within you."

Hilary grew restive and cast Ashley a long serious glance.

He was making it very difficult to maintain her anger, justified as she still considered it. Was all this just his clever way of soothing over his true intent? She couldn't tell. His words fell pleasantly on her ear. Yet she didn't really know what he intended. Perhaps she would have to watch herself more carefully—around both von Burchardt and Jameson.

They arrived back at the estate about an hour later. Hilary spent the rest of the afternoon in her room.

Dinner that evening was rather a tense affair. Hilary sat in relative silence. Though her ire against Ashley had subsided, she was still confused and wary. Ashley seemed more introspective than usual and said little. Allison was present, looking pale and worn. She ate hardly at all, and did her best to make an apology to Hilary over her outburst in the heirloom room. But her words seemed so detached and feeble that with Hilary's remaining caution preventing any genuine warmth from showing itself, the whole display came off as forced and unreal.

Midway through the meal, Logan stood to make a surprise announcement, which he hoped would clear the air, put the events of that morning behind them, and enliven the gloomy atmosphere that seemed to have descended upon the place.

"I've been thinking it is time for a bit of a change of pace around here. It is no secret that we have all been under varying degrees of stress, and I believe such is sufficient reason for us to lay aside our mourning of Lady Joanna's passing for a few hours—I'm certain she herself would give us her blessing. Therefore, I have decided that Stonewycke shall host a small 'soiree' for our friends, neighbors, townspeople, and perhaps a few of my political associates—a thorough mix, just like a creamy Scottish trifle. What do you all say? We'll have some music, kick up our heels a wee bit. Of course we'd insist on you remaining with us until then, Jameson. How about it?"

"Splendid idea!" replied Ashley. "I'd be delighted."

"Allison, dear, what do you say? I'll have Flora, and maybe Jo and Hilary, help take care of all the arrangements. You won't have to do a thing but be your charming self. Mrs. Gibson can ask some of the village ladies to help with the food and drink."

Allison seemed to have some difficulty focusing on him. Then her quivering lips bent into an attempt at a smile.

"Good! Good!" Logan grinned, rubbing his hands together. How much of his buoyancy was an act intended on bolstering his wife's suffering only he himself knew.

"I'll send Jake around town and to some of the farms first thing tomorrow," Logan went on as if running through a preparations list in his mind. "I'll call some of my own cronies in the area. Moryson can drive over to Culden and down to Huntly—I'll want the Gordons and Blacks to be here if they can. Professor Jameson, perhaps you'll be kind enough to help us set up the large hall, furniture out of the way for dancing, tables set up for refreshments, that sort of thing?"

"Certainly—my pleasure."

"You'll invite the Mackenzies?" asked Hilary.

"Of course!" replied Logan. "And what about that von Burchardt fellow?" he added. "He seems to have rather taken a liking to you, hasn't he, Hilary?"

"I hadn't really noticed," she answered, flushing slightly.

"As a matter of fact, he was here earlier asking for you, but apparently you were out with the professor here." He motioned toward Ashley. "Seemed almost frantic to see you. But after cooling his heels in the drawing room for half an hour, he finally left. You entertained him a while, Jo. Did he say anything about what he wanted?"

"Uh . . . no, nothing," Jo replied, taken off her guard by the question. "Just small talk, that's all. No, he said nothing."

"Yes, well . . . in any case, we ought to try to contact him on his yacht. Anyone planning a trip into town?"

Before Hilary could volunteer, Jo answered, "I have to go down to one of the shops tomorrow morning. I'll see if I can find him and invite him."

"Fine! Now, there's a great deal to do, and we'll all have to pitch in. So let's get a good night's sleep. Tomorrow will be a big day. There are many preparations we have to make. I propose, if we can get everything in order soon enough, that we don't delay. Let's have our—let's see, what shall we call it? Our 'Goodbye-to-Fall-Welcome-to-Winter' party two evenings from tonight, on Friday."

45 ※ Astonishing News

FRIDAY CAME.

All day the usually quiet castle was a beehive of activity, cars and vans and delivery trucks arriving at regular intervals, the telephone ringing almost constantly. It had been no small matter to notify and then prepare for over fifty guests in such a short time. But Logan had been determined to divert attention off their own personal concerns, and hard work seemed to be the answer.

As the day wore on and as things shaped up, he could not help being pleased. Every time he walked by the kitchen, where the cook was superintending a makeshift crew of six of her friends from the village, Logan chuckled to hear her complaints about the impossibility of the task, "When ye're no gi'en enoch hoors in the day t' make what ye'd conseeder *proper* preparations."

Yet whenever he saw her in the hall, tiny beads of perspiration on her forehead, he gave her a pat on the back and a "Well done, Mrs. Gibson! We'll make it on time!" And by midafternoon the faithful woman was beginning to take on a lively glow as the fruit of her labors began to appear in the form of completed trays and dishes of food ready to be carted into the hall.

In the big hall itself, all furniture had been removed except for the long rows of tables to one side, which would display Mrs. Gibson's wares, and some forty or fifty folding wooden chairs set up around the perimeter of the room for the guests not inclined to dance.

About two o'clock, a small band arrived and began setting up their equipment. There was not a great deal to be done, in that the band consisted of one accordion, two fiddles, a pianist, a drummer, and a vocalist who doubled on the penny whistle. To Logan's chagrin, the bagpiper had taken a sudden illness and was unable to be there.

A glorious day had dawned for the party. The autumn sun shone bravely, warming the frozen earth to almost 50 degrees by noon and melting the last remnants of the snow about the grounds. Though it would be dark by five o'clock, Logan made sure that the grounds would be well lit and hoped the warmth would linger long enough into the evening that their guests would be able to enjoy a walk outside or in the garden. The great hall opened out into an inner courtyard to one side and to the south lawn on the other.

At 4:30 Hilary drew herself a hot bath and slid into the soothing water with a contented sigh. It had been a hectic day, yet she anticipated the evening which lay ahead. Logan's idea had indeed been just what the situation called for. She had not seen Emil since leaving him bewildered on his yacht. And now that her emotions had had a chance to cool, she wasn't sure if she wanted to, or what she would say to him when she did. Of only one thing she was certain—he would be here tonight.

She had conspicuously avoided Ashley for the past two days, and he seemed to be likewise avoiding her. Why he had done what he had, she had not a clue. She would find out what he was up to, but not until after the party. He was too much a puzzle to be able to walk straight up and have it out with him. In the past two days her wrath had changed in character to a smoldering irritation that she did not quite know where to direct. Therefore, she kept to herself, watched his movements, her suspicions still in place, though she saw nothing more to increase her mistrust of his motives.

Once back in her room she laid out her new outfit and nodded her head with approval. Whatever the circumstances surrounding their madcap little drive to Fraserburgh, at least she had to admit that it had proved serendipitous for her. She had a new dress to wear to the party.

She dressed leisurely. It was not yet five and the guests were scheduled to arrive between six and seven. She spent more time than usual on her hair, then finally took up her dress and slipped it over her head. Its lines were simple, as she liked, but soft and feminine. The silky skirt flowed in gentle folds, its subdued colors entwining in a manner reminiscent of heather swaying casually in a mild September's breeze. She had purchased a strand of simulated pearls, but as she clasped them around her neck she could not help thinking how nicely the locket would have complemented this particular dress.

At 6:20 she left her room and made her way slowly down the corridor. At the top of the main stairway she paused. On the floor below, Logan stood among a half dozen guests who had just arrived. Hilary noted the contrast between them—a farmer and his wife, a single man wearing an expensive dinner jacket, a merchant she recognized from Port Strathy, the postmistress, Mr. Davies from the Bluster 'N Blow, and another couple, only that moment arrived, who had been brought to the door in a limousine and whose tuxedo and jewelry matched the extravagance of their ride to Stonewycke.

With each one Logan was at ease, and made them all comfortable with one another. *He really has a gift,* thought Hilary, *of putting people at ease and making them feel they are important to him.* The small group was laughing, and Logan had just slapped the farmer on the back. Now he proceeded to introduce the new arrivals, treating them all, despite their widely varying stations, as equals.

A moment more she paused, taking in the scene, reflecting how appropriately Logan's behavior at that moment epitomized what Lady Joanna would have said Stonewycke represented—its people and the ministry of the estate to the community of the surrounding region. She was proud of Logan, whether he turned out to be her father or not—just for the man he was. *He is a good man,* she thought, *a man of character, a man of depth, a man of compassion.* How little she had truly understood him when first they had spoken on the day of that London press conference!

Suddenly, as if with one accord some unseen force prompted them to glance up, Hilary became aware that the small knot of guests at the bottom of the stairway was looking at her.

Flushing slightly, she began her descent, feeling strangely self-conscious. The amber tresses of her hair, which she had curled for the occasion, bounced as she went, giving colorful and correspondent motion to the graceful movement of her dress.

"You look lovely, Hilary!" exclaimed Logan, bounding up the stairs two at a time to meet her. He offered her his arm, which she took lightly and gracefully, and he continued the descent with her.

"Ladies and gentlemen," he said formally but jovially, "may I present our esteemed houseguest of the past week, Miss Hilary Edwards, of London and *The Berkshire Review.*"

"Bravo, Macintyre!" said the single gentleman, first with a glance in Logan's direction, then extending his hand to Hilary. "Where do you come up with such beauties?"

"A trait that runs in the family," said Logan, throwing Hilary a quick wink.

"Hello, Mr. Davies," said Hilary, moving from one to the other. "How nice to see you again."

Once introductions and pleasantries had been sufficiently exchanged, Logan said, "Hilary, I was just going to escort our guests to the ballroom. Would you care to join us?"

She smiled, took his arm again, and they turned and led the way down the corridor, Logan's face beaming with pride.

"Oh, Moryson," he called out to the factor, who was at that moment approaching from the far end of the hall. "Will you watch the door for a few minutes and greet our new arrivals? I'll be back shortly."

When they reached the ballroom, Hilary saw that most of the guests were already present, clustered in small groups about the hall, nibbling on the lavish spread of cold cuts, sliced cheeses and fruits, small sandwiches, smoked fish of many varieties, and of course at least a dozen platters each of oatcakes and shortbread, brought in by many of the local women who cherished each her own private recipe which she lost no opportunity to show off. Logan excused himself just as the accordionist and fiddler began with a rousing rendition of "Scots Wha Ha'e," and returned to the front door to play the part of host to the last-minute arrivals.

Slowly Hilary began making her way around the room, introducing herself, greeting the few people she knew, keeping an eye out for Karl and Frances Mackenzie, whom she had not yet seen. Neither had she seen Allison.

Jo was on the other side of the room, surrounded by several young men who were at that moment laughing at something she had apparently just said. Unconsciously Hilary began moving in the other direction, not wanting to encounter Jo without the protective cover of Logan's presence. Ever since arriving at Stonewycke she had had the feeling that Jo was too nice, too perfect. Now all at once, even though she could not see her face, Hilary felt a sense of foreboding as she looked in Jo's direction.

Even as she was reflecting on what might be the reason for the peculiar sensation, she heard a voice beside her.

"Miss Edwards?"

She turned around to see Flora the housekeeper.

"Ye hae a telephone call, mem."

"Now?"

"'Tis long distance, mem. The yoong gentleman didna want to leave a message."

"Thank you, Flora. Where shall I take it?"

"The parlor'd be the closest, mem."

Hilary followed her out of the hall. Who could it be but Murry? she thought, though it hardly seemed he'd had long enough to get the information she had requested already.

She opened the parlor door and walked to the phone. To her relief the place was empty. She picked up the receiver. It was Murry.

"Hi, Hilary," he said. "How ya doing? I hope I didn't catch you at a bad time."

"Oh no, Murry. We're just in the middle of the biggest social event of the year around here!"

"You're kidding!"

"Actually no," she laughed. It was refreshing to talk to someone from her old life, someone who represented the stability that had been so suddenly taken out from under her feet.

"There are fifty or more people milling around here even as we speak. But go ahead. I want to know what you have for me."

"Well, I'm really onto something big. I wish you were here, because I can't go into it over the phone. I'll let you know specifics as soon as I can. Let's just say in one of our next issues we're going to take on a corporate giant that will make Goliath look like a gnat! But that's got nothing to do with what you asked me to look into. It's an outgrowth of that dull piece you asked me to work on last month. Man, you won't believe what's turned up!"

"Come on, Murry! What do you have for *me*?"

"Okay, I don't have all the stuff you wanted yet. But I do have the goods on the guy you first asked about, though I can't imagine why you'd want *him* run through the police computer. There are no goods on him. He's squeaky clean—"

"Who, Murry? Which name?"

"Jameson . . . Lord Deardon. If you'd only have told me about the Deardon business right off, I could have gotten this to you even quicker."

"Deardon? I don't understand. I don't know that name."

"Your Ashley Jameson is Lord Deardon. Inherited the title a couple of years ago. Aristocratic blood further back than you can see. Pretty low-key bunch, but nonetheless up to their ears in dough. Deardon . . . or Jameson—he keeps to his civilian name—sticks to his university pursuits. Thirty-six years old. He even relinquished his seat in the House of Lords to devote himself more fully to his Greeks. A real scholar, renowned in his field, I gather. More into his studies than playing the part of a nobleman. I'm surprised you hadn't heard of him— but then neither had I. I suppose Greek tragedy just isn't our bag."

"You're certain about all this? I would never have dreamed this guy would have a dossier so . . . I don't even know what to call it—impressive."

"It's all pretty much public record stuff. All I had to do is throw his name around Oxford. Didn't even have to trouble my pal at the Yard."

"I must say, I am astounded. This guy up here's been acting peculiar, doing strange things." She stopped for a moment, thinking. "Do you have a physical description?" she added.

"You think someone's impersonating him?"

"I doubt it. But I wish I had a photo."

"Well, here's what I got off his university files," Murry went on. "Six-one, about a hundred seventy pounds, or rather twelve and a half stone, light brown hair, gray-green eyes, drives a '69 BMW—"

"That's him. . . ."

"I'm surprised Logan Macintyre couldn't have supplied you with all this information," commented Murry.

"Why's that?"

"They are old chums, as I understand it."

"What!" exclaimed Hilary, incredulous at the unexpected revelation.

"Worked together on a couple government projects, and the professor's also worked with Macintyre's brother-in-law."

"How can that be?"

"Hilary . . . what is it?"

"The oddest thing! Those two have been dancing around here for days pretending they don't even know each other!"

"Why the charade?"

"I can't imagine! I knew there was something going on, but I would never have guessed it fell in *that* direction! I wonder where Jo fits into their little subterfuge," she added as if talking to herself.

"Jo?"

"Never mind, Murry. It's too complicated to explain. I'll fill you in on everything later. Anything else?"

"I'm sorry I've been dragging my feet on this. As I said, I've kind of gotten hooked into something else—but I'll get on von Burchardt right away."

"Okay. Thanks, Murry."

Hilary hung up the phone, her mind reeling. She could not even begin to assess the implications of what Murry had told her. Suddenly there were more doubts than ever with the revelation of his connection with Logan!

Why would they possibly keep that secret? And with all their talk about the nobility, why would he have kept back the significant fact that he was of aristocratic blood?

Of course none of this startling news in the least explained Ashley's bizarre behavior of spiriting her off Emil's yacht.

Beneath it all, Hilary's brain spun round and round with the question: *Why the ruse?*

Slowly she turned and walked from the room like one in a daze. For the moment she had completely forgotten the party. She exited the parlor and walked down the hall in the opposite direction from which she had come, aimless, with no destination in mind.

She had to think. Suddenly everything was upside-down. With Logan's candor now called into question, she no longer knew *whom* she could trust. If anyone!

46 ✵ The Gallery

FOR MORE MINUTES than she could keep track of, Hilary walked.

Paying little attention to her direction, she followed corridor after corridor, went up and down staircases she had never been on before, and met no one. All the family and guests were occupied in the other wing. Without even realizing she was retracing her steps toward more familiar regions, all at once she stopped before a door she recognized.

Quickly her mind came awake. This was the door to the gallery, which she had been wanting to see but had still never been inside.

For several moments she remained standing, merely contemplating the door. Then she slowly reached out, turned the latch, and swung the huge door open on its silent hinges. She stepped inside, fumbled about the wall nearby for a switch, found it, then flipped on the lights.

Immediately a subdued quiet overcame her, as if she had entered the cloistered chapel of a monastery. A great intimate hush permeated the very walls, intensified by the high vaulted ceiling. At first to Hilary it seemed the silence was due merely to the absence of sound. As she began to glance about her, however, she realized there was a more profound reason for it than what could be explained on the mere physical plane. Dozens of unmoving eyes filled the walls, pulsating with vibrant yet undisturbed motion, every face deepening the intense stillness, emphasizing the silence in the midst of their voiceless entreaties. If ever a "cloud of past witnesses" was visible, Hilary now found herself standing in the midst of it.

Holding her breath, she began to make her way slowly around the room. All about were family portraits, mingled with others of Scottish historical significance, with here and there selections that had obviously been acquired purely on the basis of pleasure and enjoyment. The owners of this hall were clearly collectors of art with a discriminating flair.

Gradually Hilary took in many paintings by masters—Raeburn, Wilkie, Gainsborough she recognized particularly. The far wall held but one painting, an enormous eight-by-fifteen foot exhibition of the battle of Culloden, surrounded by a one-foot wide gilded wood frame. To each side of it, enclosed in glass cases and sitting silently on brass pedestals, were two marble busts—one of Mary Queen of Scots, a replica of that which was housed in Edinburgh Castle, and one of the Bonnie Prince Charlie, whose full figure looked down upon the proceedings from his desperate perch in the painting above.

On the walls hung fierce Highland chieftains, delicate ladies in waiting, children in Eaton jackets and knickers or frilly crinoline. Hilary read each nameplate, finding many of the names familiar from her reading of the journal. Others were new; all held fascination. She paused at each, forgetful of time, lost in the solemn import of the moment.

Andrew de Ramsay, the original scion of the Stonewycke line, the builder of the castle, overlooked the descendants that had sprung from his stock from a portrait so old it was encased in glass to protect it from the air. His fiery red hair struggled, even while posing for the dignified painting, to break from the restraints of his plaid bonnet. Everything about her reminded Hilary that the Ramsays were of warrior stock, fierce Highlanders come down into the low-lying coastlands only lately in their genealogy to people the northern coast of their land, yet always but a violent breath or two removed from the savage Pict and Viking heritage which first spawned their energy and dynamism.

The independent nature of the family was clear on every face, whether it was Thomas Ramsey's insistence on changing the spelling of the family name, Colin's running off to die in Prince Charlie's ill-fated cause, or Anson Ramsey's attempt to deed the family property over to his tenants. Such a headstrong self-reliance seemed to have been the most prominent trait passed down through the years—either as a blessing or a curse, depending on how each recipient of new Ramsey blood chose to use it—right down to the carrying out of Anson's wish years later by two of the most remarkable of this breed, Lady Margaret and Lady Joanna.

Reading the journal could never alone give her the awe-inspiring sense of the flow of life through generation after generation as did gazing upon these portraits, though reading it had certainly prepared her for this moment. But as Hilary stood looking upon the faces of those who had come before—who could well be her own ancestors—she was caught up in the life that their faces conveyed. The room fairly exploded with silent vitality and power. As she gazed, there gradually emerged from each face a uniform consistency of expression—something in the eyes, the hair, the twist of the lips, the shape of the jaw . . . something which said, "I know what I am about, and I know from what roots I come. For I am a Ramsey. And my heart is proud of the Scottish blood that runs through my veins."

This look, this expression of defiance, boldness, and self-sufficiency had clearly been translated from the fierce males to the females who continued the direct line from Andrew down to the present. In the softer faces of the more delicate sex, the expressions of independence were more subdued and subtle, not quite as easy to identify amid the exterior trappings of outward feminine beauty. Stare as she might, Hilary could not exactly identify what she saw. But whether the portrait was four hundred years old or forty, something in each face made her very aware that these people were all of the same blood.

For several minutes she stood before the two most recent portraits to be added to the gallery—those of Logan and Allison Macintyre—scanning every detail. Both were appealing faces, full of life, full of love, full of zest. But there could be no doubt through which of the pair the blood of the Ramseys flowed. For while it was the hint of a roguish smile around the edges of Logan's mouth that drew a viewer's attention, when one's gaze fell upon Allison it could not be easily pulled away. It was not her mouth nor her beauty, however, that arrested further thought. In Logan the suggestion of mischief made you smile. In Allison the silent force of her eyes held your gaze, compelling you to look beyond, until you were drawn into the invisible vitality of the generations that had come before.

At length Hilary exhaled a long sigh and turned from the painting. She wandered back again through the room. She returned to the portrait of Lady Joanna she had already seen. The painting must have been done when she was in her mid-forties—from the style of clothing, probably some time during the depression. How lovely she was! mused Hilary, though no artist could ever capture the true beauty that was Joanna MacNeil's. Age and wrinkles and gray hair may have altered the exterior, but the lady who had visited her only a short time ago still felt life as she had when she had sat for this portrait.

"How I wish you were here now, Lady Joanna," Hilary murmured aloud to the lifeless figure. "I know somehow you would be able to help me with my confusion."

She found herself trying to compare this younger Joanna with the woman she had met so briefly in her office. So many similarities remained—the quiet refinement, the reserved dignity, that look in her eyes which she had obviously given Allison.

Hilary moved to the next painting immediately to her right. Central on the wall, in a place of honor, rested an early painting of young Maggie.

Hilary had already become quite familiar with two other paintings of the family matriarch. A picture of Maggie at nine or ten hung in the parlor. Another, which must have been commissioned after her return from exile, showed Lady Margaret at age seventy or so. It hung in the entryway to the castle, just to the left of the great stairway.

The one upon which she was now gazing, however, had been painted when the girl was about seventeen, no doubt just before events had conspired to force her to leave her homeland. Hilary stared at the portrait, probing every detail of the face, an inquisitive expression building on her own countenance. Something was there . . . something she couldn't quite identify. She had seen it before . . . somewhere.

She glanced quickly around. Was it in the portrait of Allison? No, she didn't think so. She looked over at Joanna's face again, then back to young Maggie's. What was it?

Suddenly the dress Maggie wore jumped off the canvas at Hilary, making her gasp audibly. Of course! That's why it looked so familiar! She's wearing a heather-colored dress . . . just like mine!

She laughed to herself. What a coincidence! She turned away and began to leave. But even as she walked in the opposite direction, Maggie's eyes seemed to bore holes in the back of her head, compelling her to turn back. *The dress isn't all,* Maggie seemed to say to her, though Hilary felt rather than heard the words. *There is more! Don't turn away until you have discovered it! Gaze upon my face, Hilary,* an inner voice seemed to say. *Gaze until you know . . . until you know!*

Hilary stopped, then slowly turned back to face the wall. Still silent, young Maggie returned her gaze, drawing Hilary closer, ever closer, by the eyes she had passed down, first to Eleanor, then to Joanna, and at last to Allison, whose eyes were even this moment looking at her from the adjacent wall next to Logan.

It *was* more than the dress! But it was more than the eyes as well. The familial similarities found in each of the women all were focused in this one youthful, commanding, unyielding, rugged, sensitive face—the vulnerability of the sensitive nose, the pale skin that subdued the other features and highlighted the shades of the hair, the strong cheekbones, the high forehead that allowed the robust eyebrows full expression, the eyes that always seemed looking into the distance, contemplating the depth and the grandness of life.

It was more than all these features. As Hilary continued to gaze at the portrait before her, suddenly it came into focus. The thing she recognized more than anything else was the chin!

She remembered the meeting with Lady Joanna. She had noticed it so clearly. It had looked strangely familiar in that first moment of their meeting, though subsequent developments caused her to forget. But now all at once, seeing it again in Maggie's face, offering a fitting foundation to the mouth, lips, eyes, and cheekbones that rose up from it, there again was that distinctive chin! Hundreds of people could possess such a combination of distinguishing physical traits. But only one person she knew!

No wonder they had jumped out at her all at once off the canvas! Those same eyes, those same cheekbones, those same eyebrows, and that same chin had been staring back at her for as long as she could remember, whenever she looked in a mirror!

And with the stunning realization came back into her mind the words of her reporter friend, the Irishman Bert: "If it weren't fer that chin, Eddie, me dear, I'd think you was the essence of naivete. But between the chin and those eyes, I know you're not one to tangle with!"

Unconsciously Hilary's hands went to her cheeks as she gasped again, this time audibly. For several moments she stood as one in a trance, unable to take her gaze away from the incredible face that had at last revealed the truth of its secret.

Behind her, she had not heard another enter at the door she had left ajar, nor was she aware of the presence which now stood beholding her, statuelike, as she stared upon the wall. But to the one observing, the scene as it spread out on the other side of the gallery could not have been more bitterly poignant, for to her too, more than resemblance of dress had been revealed.

"So . . . at last you know." Jo's voice echoed like a thunderclap through the silent gallery.

With a frightened start, Hilary spun around. Speechless, she opened her mouth, but no words would come.

All the effort in the world could not have wiped away the truth from Hilary's face. Their eyes met and locked together. For a long, uncomfortable moment they held one another's gaze in silence.

Then gradually a mask seemed to fall from Jo's innocent, well-controlled countenance. All shams abandoned, her eyes suddenly narrowed. Her mouth, which had always been so quick to trace a sweet smile, hardened with vehemence.

"It doesn't matter, you know." Her voice was as icy with harsh disdain as it had once been with musical simplicity. "They will never believe you. Allison loves me. She is so ill that a little shock could kill her. You had better watch what you say!"

"She is not that ill," said Hilary, finding her voice.

"She is *very* ill!" spat back Jo. "If I were you, I would be careful not to do anything to upset her. Anything, do you hear? I do believe she is quite suicidal."

"You don't mean to say—"

"I mean watch your step, Miss Edwards, so that no harm comes either to the woman you may think is your mother . . . or to yourself! Just remember—before you say anything to anyone, they will never believe you. I will make sure of that!"

Before Hilary could say anything further, Jo spun around and left the gallery.

47 ❈ Outside the Ballroom

THE GATHERING WAS in full swing when Hilary wandered back into the great hall, still in too much of a stupor to pay much attention to those about her. She must have been gone for more than an hour before Jo's untimely appearance. The band was in the middle of "The Flowers of Edinburgh" and the floor was filled with at least five highly animated sets of dancers. Yet even with forty persons dancing, the floor could easily have contained another five sets. Laughter and pleasant conversation echoed throughout the room in spite of the music, all of which fell almost discordantly on Hilary's keyed-up, flustered senses.

Logan stood at the far end of the room, chatting with friends, now and then clapping in time to the music and adding a rousing *whoop*! or yell to the accompaniment. Beside him stood Allison, looking drawn and strained, a mere shadow of the hardy woman of the portrait Hilary had just seen. Beside Allison stood Jo, showing her every attention, lavishing upon the ailing woman the care and tenderness she seemed to require.

Slowly Hilary began making her way toward them. She had no idea what she would say or do. Something inside her sensed danger. But whether she could avert it, and whether she had any who might be allies in this house, she did not know.

She had walked about halfway around the perimeter of the room, her brain gradually clearing as she considered what action to take. But her thoughts and her steps progressed no further.

Suddenly von Burchardt was at her side, and in a flurry of ebullient greetings had firmly taken her arm and half-led, half-propelled her into a St. Bernard's Waltz which had just begun.

"Emil, this is a surprise!" she said.

"So I would assume," he replied, smiling broadly, his white teeth flashing. "After your desertion the other day, I assumed you wanted to see me no more."

"That's not fair, Emil," said Hilary, attempting to turn on what charm she could muster. "You saw what happened. That horrid Professor Jameson grabbed me off your yacht."

"You appeared walking willingly under your own power," persisted the viscount, his smile unable to mask the cynicism in his tightly controlled voice.

"He lied to me, Emil. He told me I was needed urgently at the house."

Ruminating momentarily, von Burchardt nodded thoughtfully. "I see," he said. "Yet when I called only a short time later, neither of you were there. I could not help fancying myself the fool."

"I'm sorry, Emil. He kidnapped me. I had no choice. I was positively furious at the man."

For the next couple rounds of the waltz they danced in silence, though on neither part did there appear any desire toward a more intimate embrace. Stiffly they went through the motions, each lost in his own private thoughts regarding the other. Emil contemplated recent days, the interference of this busybody Jameson, and whether or not he could work his way back into the good graces of this little vixen in his arms. If he could, was there time for such a ploy to do any good, or were stronger measures called for? If he could not get her onto his yacht voluntarily, perhaps a forceful abduction would prove necessary after all, just as his accomplice had suggested in the first place.

He should have listened. Now there was going to be the devil to pay for letting her slip through his fingers right when he had been just minutes away from casting off and eliminating the source of their difficulties for good.

For her part, Hilary found herself struggling with remaining last-minute uncertainties about where loyalties lined up around here. The professor had been too easily absolved in one convenient stroke by Murry's call. What if his presence here was part of some evil scheme? What was more likely to follow than that he would have covered his tracks with a well-documented cover? She could not escape the fact that he had lied to her, and had been seen at least once alone with Jo, whose motives she now had reason to suspect as well.

Perhaps I should confide in Emil, she thought. *What harm can it do? If he is merely a disinterested visitor to Port Strathy, his knowing a few more of the family secrets would cause no trouble. He already knows as much as anyone else anyway!* She had to get it off her chest, and besides Logan—who was too close to the situation to be objective, she said to herself—there was no one else she could trust.

"Emil!" she said as the dance ended, "perhaps we could talk somewhere. More seriously."

"Certainly!" responded the viscount, thinking to himself that getting Hilary away from this crowd was the obvious first step toward his yacht. If they cast off tonight, they could be standing outside Newcastle by morning.

"Shall we go to my yacht? We will have all the privacy there we could desire. I have an automobile, and we could be there within minutes."

"I'm not ready to leave the party just yet," replied Hilary. "How about a walk outside?"

Hiding his displeasure, von Burchardt nodded, then led the way with a wave of his hand. As they approached the door, out of the corner of her eye Hilary saw Ashley enter the ballroom from another door with a small group of locals. Unexpectedly her heart gave a little leap at seeing his relaxed, friendly countenance. Was it fear or relief that prompted the unsought flutter? She could not tell, but in spite of all logic, her instincts told her his motives had to be honest and that, all unexplained actions aside, he was a friend.

Before she had opportunity to reflect further, however, they were out the door and into the chilly evening air.

They walked some distance on the lawn in silence, Hilary pondering how to express the concerns on her heart. Without realizing it, she allowed the viscount to lead her inconspicuously toward the front of the house. As they went he commented innocently about the weather, the coming of winter, the conditions of the sea for sailing, asking here and there a harmless personal question, displaying all the charm which had endeared him to the inhabitants of the house after his first appearance. Hilary carried on her share of the conversation, while underneath her mind debated with itself, trying to sort out the new events this evening had revealed. Before she knew it, they had left the courtyard and were passing the gates.

"Hadn't we better turn back, Emil?" said Hilary with a shiver.

"Nonsense, my dear," he replied with a laugh. "Let's just enjoy a little walk among the trees along the drive."

"Please, I think—"

"These firs really are magnificent," he persisted, now clutching her arm more firmly and walking on. "You will see what I mean once we get beyond the glare of the lights from the castle."

"Emil, please! You're hurting my arm!"

"Come, my dear, let's walk a bit farther," he replied, not relaxing his hold.

Recognizing herself powerless to resist, but still not divining the extent of her peril, Hilary submitted, and they continued forward.

All of a sudden, from out of the dark in front of them, a figure stepped onto the road.

"Ah, my good man, Herr von Burchardt! Splendid evening for a saunter about the grounds."

It was Ashley!

Unable to believe her ears, for she had only moments ago seen him absorbed in conversation in the ballroom, Hilary felt a great surge of relief at the sound of his voice, rising above the viscount's muttered cursing of the blackguard meddler!

Still puffing from his dash through the trees, Ashley walked toward them, gave von Burchardt a rousing handshake, turned, and fell in on the other side of Hilary. He had seen them exit the hall, had followed them long enough to spy out the direction in which they were headed, and then had gone back through the house, out a door on the opposite side, run across the lawn, through a break in the hedge, through the grove of trees that extended out from the courtyard, finally winding up beyond the walkers at the point where he met them on the road.

"Where are you two headed?" he asked with cheerful innocence.

"Merely out for a walk, Jameson," replied the viscount with forced calm, "which I hope you'll allow us to continue by excusing us."

"I was just going to ask Miss Edwards to join me for a dance when I was in the hall a few minutes ago."

"As you can see," said Burchardt, "she is at present occupied."

"Indeed. But it really is rather cold out. What do you say, Miss Edwards—do you feel like warming up to a quick-stepping reel?"

"Why, yes, thank you," replied Hilary. "That sounds—"

"Now look here, Jameson," interrupted von Burchardt, his temper at last getting the better of him. "Do you make it a practice of going around interfering where you're not wanted?"

"I'm sorry, Burchardt. I only thought the lady might—"

"The lady is fine! And she is with me!"

"For the moment. But she says she would like to dance . . . with me."

The viscount stopped and turned to face Ashley. "If you are serious about your meddling, Jameson," he said with scorn. "Then perhaps we ought to have it out right here and now between the two of us!"

"I have no desire to fight you, Burchardt," said Ashley. "But I will not allow you to take Miss Edwards another step from the house."

"You will not *allow*!" yelled the viscount, laughing in derision. "You expect to stop me from doing as I please? Ha! ha! ha!"

"Hilary," said Ashley softly, turning toward her, "go back to the castle . . . please."

Hilary retreated a couple of steps, but was arrested by the viscount's voice. "Stay where you are, Miss Edwards! I want you to see your supposed hero's true valor after I have punished him as he deserves!"

"Go, Hilary," repeated Ashley.

Hilary walked farther back toward the gates. Von Burchardt stepped menacingly toward Ashley.

"If you so much as lay a hand on him, Emil," shouted Hilary from where she stood, "I swear to you I will bring every truth-loving man from inside that hall out with my cries. And then it will not go so well with you, I think!"

Von Burchardt stopped.

"Come, Ashley," said Hilary. "Will you please accompany me back inside?"

With one final glance in the direction of the esteemed Viscount von Burchardt, Ashley turned and rejoined Hilary, leaving Emil standing in the middle of the darkened roadway in a white fury.

Hilary slipped her hand through Ashley's arm and held tightly.

"I'm glad he didn't hurt you," she said.

"I don't think he would have."

"But he might have."

"That was a chance I had to take."

"Does this have anything to do with that hairbrained abduction you pulled at his boat the other day?" asked Hilary with a laugh.

"I suppose," he replied. "I was sure he was up to no good. I can't prove it, but I'm certain he has been trying to get you away from here . . . permanently. I couldn't let that happen. Not only for your safety's sake, but for the sake of Logan and Allison. That's why I've been watching you so close, both then and tonight."

"All this time I thought you were his ally . . . or Jo's!"

"Me . . . hooked up with von Burchardt?" said Ashley incredulously.

"I thought you must have lured me away from my room that night so he could come in and prowl around."

"That's a good one!" laughed Ashley; then his face turned somber. "Hmm, though perhaps you're onto something."

"What do you mean?"

"Just before I arrived at your door that night, I thought I caught a faint whiff of perfume lingering in the hallway. At first I dismissed it as yours. But then when you opened the door it was not there. If von Burchardt did indeed have an accomplice that night . . . "

He let his thought trail away unstated.

"You're not Jo's ally either? You've been spending a lot of time with her."

"Not so much, really."

"I've seen you together."

"Just sorting out the evidence. I have to spend enough time with the both of you so that I know you. How else can I—"

He stopped, realizing he had gone too far.

"How else can you what?"

"I suppose not much harm can come from your knowing, now that we have come this far. Without spending time with the two of you, there's no way I can make an accurate report."

"A report? You make it sound so clinical. Whom do you have to report to?"

"It seems only fair that you have some explanation. I hope he'll forgive me." Ashley paused, took a breath, then said, "I am here at Logan's request. He wanted someone he could trust to act the part of a neutral party. He thought perhaps he and Allison were too deeply involved in the situation emotionally to judge accurately between you and Jo—if no concrete evidence presented itself. At the same time he felt the two of you would feel reticent around someone you knew was his friend. Thus the charade. He asked me to come incognito, as it were."

"Well, you certainly pulled it off! I was so suspicious of you that I even called an associate in London to have you run through the police computer."

Ashley chuckled, amused at the idea.

"You were completely exonerated, as far as it went. I should have known all along that your intentions were noble, or at least genuine."

"Noblesse oblige and all that, eh?"

"That is a subject we are going to have to deal with one day, Ashley," laughed Hilary. "But something tells me this is not the time."

They walked on a few more steps in silence. They were again nearing the house, and in the distance voices could now be heard of the merry-makers. Overhead the night sky was speckled with pulsating stars, appearing crisper, even closer, in the chilly air. Rising through the trees to the north of the castle, the moon was just now making its appearance felt. Both Hilary and Ashley inwardly found themselves wishing the circumstances surrounding this moonlight stroll had been different.

"I did not have the chance to see your new dress for long inside," said Ashley at length. "But now that we get nearer the light, I must say my first assessment was correct. It is beautiful. I should say you are beautiful in it!"

"Thank you." Hilary was glad for the cover of darkness, for she felt the red rising in her cheeks.

"Are you warm enough?" he asked, seeing her shiver.

"We'll be in soon. What about you? Or do those midnight walks of yours give you such a hardy constitution that you scoff at the cold?"

"My, you really have been suspicious of my actions!"

"Do you blame me?"

"Maybe not. But am I entitled to no secrets at all?"

"You owe me no explanations whatsoever . . . unless you want me to trust you."

"All right then," said Ashley. "Yes, I have been about at night a couple of times. On that particular night you saw me, I wanted to have a closer inspection of the bridge where Lady Allison had her fall. I have also been snooping around the place in search of both the missing locket and the missing pages of Lady Joanna's journal, but without success."

"Do you suspect—well, that the fall was not an accident?"

"I haven't known what to think. Logan told me to leave no stone unturned. And you know what Sherlock Holmes wisely instructed—'Once you have eliminated the impossible, what you have left, however improbable, must be the truth.'"

"You go in for that sort of cloak-and-dagger thing?"

"Another secret we unfortunately have no time for."

"I'm afraid something we must take time for," said Hilary, "is Allison's well-being. I'm worried about her."

"So have we all been."

"I don't mean from her illness." Hilary paused, running the brief conversation with Jo in the gallery back through her mind. At length she spoke again. "Ashley, how well do you know Allison? Do you think she could be suicidal?"

"What! Impossible! No truth whatever! Why would you ask that?"

Hilary recounted Jo's words of earlier.

"It was not the words themselves," she concluded, "but the way in which she spoke them that frightened me."

"Dear Lord!" breathed Ashley. "We've got to get back inside, and fast!"

"You actually think she could be capable of—"

"I don't know. But I shudder to think what might be afoot."

He turned, grabbed Hilary's hand, and walked quickly toward the door to the ballroom. "Whatever happens from now on," he said, "you keep near Allison if at all possible. I don't know what I may have to do."

Hilary stopped him. "Ashley, there's just one other thing I have to know. Did you meet Jo, out there near where we left Emil, in the trees, two nights before you arrived?"

Ashley looked earnestly into her eyes, still clutching her hand. "The only young lady I've been with under the stars since coming to Stonewycke is with me this very moment." He paused, still taking in the light reflected in her eyes. "Now, come," he went on, "we must go in. Things have begun to move quickly, and we must be vigilant."

48 ❧ The Rakes O' Glasgow

WHILE HILARY AND Ashley had been occupied outside, Jo walked up to Logan and slipped her arm affectionately through his.

"Father," she said, "I am worried about Mother." Her soft voice almost quivered with its distress.

"We are all concerned," replied Logan.

"Something happened yesterday I must tell you about."

"What is it?"

"Mother was working on a particularly involved landscape—"

"She painted yesterday? I thought I told you no more painting until she was feeling better."

"She seemed a little more perky," said Jo demurely. "She asked me to let her paint."

"Go on," said Logan.

"All of a sudden she became frustrated and threw down her brush. I tried to encourage her. 'It's coming along fine,' I said. But she shook her head with such despair and then said, 'It's not just this. It's . . . it's everything! Life! I am miserable . . . I can't go on like this any longer!'"

Jo stopped, then glanced up into Logan's face with all the sincerity she could bring to her command, and said, "Oh, Father, I am so frightened for her!"

"Those were her exact words?"

She nodded. "I am hesitant to mention something like this, Father, but don't you think it might be time to consider some kind of therapy?"

"That's preposterous! Allison is strong. We will work this out."

At that moment, at the far end of the hall Jo spied Hilary and Ashley entering through the door. Whether or not the look on their faces told her the truth, her eyes flashed darkly. She quickly recovered, however, and went on. Logan had seen nothing of what transpired, and did not yet feel the urgency in her tone.

"This kind of depression is not uncommon after the death of a loved one," Jo said convincingly. "Perhaps the right psychiatrist could snap her right out of it. But if these feelings of hopelessness are allowed to deepen—"

She paused, but only momentarily. Out of the corner of her eye she saw Ashley approaching.

"—they can lead to self-destructive—" she continued, but Logan cut her off.

"Not Allison. She would do nothing of the kind."

"There have been cases of insanity in the family, have there not? I do not like to mention such a thing, but it is a fact that these tendencies are often inherited."

"Dorey's case was entirely different." Logan paused and appeared to ponder her words. But just then their conversation was brought to a close by Ashley's appearance.

"I say, Mr. Macintyre, might I have a word with you?" he said.

"Professor Jameson," replied Logan, shaking Ashley's hand. "Of course, of course. But I must tell you, I promised Allison you would have a dance with her, and she is quite tired. Perhaps you might oblige her that pleasure first, and then we'll have a little chat."

"With pleasure! Where is your wife?"

"Let me see . . ." said Logan glancing about. "Oh, there she is! Over there, talking with Hilary."

Ashley left Logan and walked in that direction. A few minutes later the Viscount von Burchardt entered the hall, though as he made his way toward where Jo stood he kept as much as possible to the shadows. Their brief tryst involved no more than a few whispered words and was unseen by anyone.

Meanwhile, Allison safely occupied with Ashley, Hilary approached Logan with a smile.

"You look radiant tonight, my dear," said Logan.

"I've just been outside," replied Hilary. "I suppose my cheeks are hot from the walk."

"They're just forming up sets for 'The Rakes o' Glasgow.' Won't you join me?"

"These Scottish country dances are mostly beyond me," laughed Hilary nervously, attempting to mask her internal agitation.

"Come on. I'll lead you through it!"

Logan offered his hand and they walked out onto the floor.

"Here . . . we'll just slip in with Mr. Jameson and Allison. They seem to need a fourth couple for this set."

As they settled into place, Logan waved down to the other two couples. "Creary . . . nice to see you!" he said. "Jones, you're looking fit tonight!" Then suddenly the music was underway.

"You are quite proficient with our dances, Mr. Jameson," said Allison when the dance was about halfway through.

"It is not the first time I have been to such a gathering, but I must admit they are rather complicated." Even as he spoke Ashley missed a step and had to skip and shuffle to get back in time.

"I've made you lose your concentration."

"It doesn't take much, Lady Allison," laughed Ashley. "I am glad to see that your ankle is recovered."

"Yes, it mostly is. I only wish I weren't always so tired."

Ashley found himself staring at the hand which was at that moment clasped in his. Even as they moved across the floor, his brain zeroed in on the fine lines of Allison's fingers. Then his attention was arrested by the paint stains on her hand, as if she had not cleaned up thoroughly from her last session. *Funny,* he thought to himself, *that she would leave herself so.* But now that he thought of it, she had had bits of colored pigment on her hands and fingers ever since he had come. He had just never consciously noted it before now.

In the midst of his reflections, the music stopped.

"Good show, Jameson!" shouted Logan. "Thank you. I'm sure my wife is very grateful!"

"I doubt that! You are talking to a man with two left feet!"

"You did yourself proud, Mr. Jameson," said Allison with a sigh, "but I really must sit down. I am positively exhausted."

Logan led her to a chair. "I'm sorry," she said, looking up into his face with almost a forlorn expression of sadness. "I'm just not myself. I don't know . . . " Tears began to well up in her eyes. "Logan, I just don't know what's wrong," she said.

Logan took her hand and gave her a reassuring smile. But she was right, and he knew it now. Something *was* wrong.

49 ❧ *The Oxford Don*

ASHLEY HAD TO move quickly.

He glanced around. Allison was with Logan. Hilary was engaged in a lively conversation with one of the farmer couples not far away. He should be able to sneak away for a few minutes.

He inched toward the main door, then casually slipped unobtrusively into the corridor. Not a single one of the guests noticed his departure. His stealthy movements had been noted by only one member of the house, who now realized the curtain was coming down on her three-month engagement. Whether her performance achieved her final goal or ended in failure depended on how skillfully she played this final scene which was about to commence. She checked her pocket, then slid across the dance floor, forcing her mouth into a pretty smile.

Meanwhile, Ashley Jameson moved cautiously and quietly on his way through the house. The situation was serious. He knew that. In spite of this however, he could not prevent the excitement that rushed through him as he began to reason through the mystery now facing him. This was not a plot he would write. Actual lives were at stake!

In many ways, Ashley Jameson was a simple man, despite his intellect, his position, and his noble upbringing. He was a renown authority on Classical Greece, and was also beginning to gain a reputation in the study of the antiquities of his own country as well. Besides his translations of *Euripides* and *Aristophanes,* he had published several scholarly essays, and had lectured widely, most notably at Harvard and Berkeley. But he viewed his pursuits as natural extensions of himself, and not a few of his colleagues envied him the ability to handle it all with such ease and matter-of-factness.

The academic life particularly suited Ashley. At thirty-six years of age he had found at Oxford the perfect environment to nurture his interests. He thoroughly enjoyed intellectual debates with fellow dons as well as his students, and was most content with a good book in hand in front of a crackling evening fire.

But there was another Ashley Jameson, one the public never had the chance to view— one unknown even to his colleagues. This was the man who reveled in the intricacies of unraveling a good mystery. Call it a closet interest, a hidden passion, a secondary vocation. Whatever term one applied to the phenomenon, Oxford professor Ashley Jameson had all his life been fascinated with criminology, as his friend, Chief Inspector Harry Arnstein could well attest. They had put their heads together on more than a few knotty London crimes. And though Ashley allowed no credit to come his way, he had been highly instrumental in solving several cases in Arnstein's file. He was glad to let Harry take the bows, for the Chief Inspector threw plenty of material his way too, even if Ashley had to change the names and circumstances before any other eyes saw it. It was, after all, Harry himself who had first propelled Ashley in the direction of his secret obsession, his private endeavor that gave him such pleasure, but which must always be kept from the public eye.

He only hoped that his peculiar talent, when put to the test of real life, as it was tonight, would serve him as it had in other areas. He prayed that right here and now his senses would be sharpened and his eyes opened. Logan was his friend. Allison was Ian's sister. He had promised Logan he would help him, but thus far he felt as if his mind had been on a treadmill. No clues seemed to lead anywhere. Now he knew that his loyalties had extended beyond his friendships with Ian and Logan, but had come to involve Hilary as well. For all their sakes, he prayed he would find something which would uncover the truth.

Ashley was no romantic in the strictest sense. Perhaps it was unfair ever to expect a woman to compete with his scholarly pursuits and his criminological avocation. He had come to accept the single life as one of the necessary drawbacks to the hermit-like existence within the confines of Oxford, where his books, his typewriter, and his collection of Doyle, Christie, Gardner, Sayers, and Chesterton, were his sole companions. He had always considered that it would be asking too much for a woman to enter that world with him. But was it possible he had simply been waiting for the right moment to open the doors of that world to the right woman? Before he could allow himself to even think about such things, however, he had to solve this mystery at Stonewycke, which seemed to be growing more portentous by the minute.

He rounded a corner, walked up a flight of stairs, down another long corridor, up still another staircase, and at last arrived at his destination. From his pocket he pulled out a ring containing perhaps a dozen keys that Logan had given him. He had already used half of them, at odd moments in various places throughout the castle searching for the journal. But to date he had not been in this room.

He found the key, inserted it into the lock, turned the latch, stepped inside, and flipped on the lights.

Ashley took a quick look around, walked across the room, switched on a low-wattage bedside lamp, then returned to the door and turned off the overhead. He doubted the light would penetrate the heavy draperies even if there should by chance be someone outside to observe it, but he could not conduct a proper search without some light, though the less the better.

He paused to take in a general impression of the place. It certainly had a lived-in look, tidy, yet full, nicely decorated and arranged. It was obvious Jo planned to stay for a good long while!

The furnishings were all of antique walnut, rather dark, but Jo had apparently added touches of color to brighten the dreariness of the medieval decor—a frilly pink pillow on the bed, baskets of flowers, and several paintings on the walls. Ashley moved about slowly to take in a closer look at these last items. They were mostly all Jo's own work, and in spite of himself Ashley found he was impressed.

He halfway expected someone of her nature to create art of a shadowy, surrealistic variety, hinting at ominous intent, like the flash of her eyes that gave mixed signals of warmth as well as deceit. But what he met here was rather a Renoir-style adaptation, where children, gardens, country settings, and simple people predominated. He was particularly struck with a vivid scene of a local Scots woman milking a cow while her two barefoot children looked on. But then as Ashley examined it closer, he realized the signature on the corner of the canvas was Lady Allison's. She possessed clear talent too, though as he understood it, that ability had remained undiscovered until Jo's arrival.

"Perhaps some good will come of all this in the end," he murmured to himself as he moved on.

There were no suitcases to be seen. All Jo's belongings had long since been put away into the wardrobe or one of the dressers. Ashley pulled open the doors of the massive oak wardrobe and ran his hand randomly through the dresses and slacks, skirts, sweaters, and jackets hanging inside. Nothing of apparent interest presented itself, although toward the back of the closet sat a closed suitcase.

He removed the case, set it on the bed, and opened it. All that was inside was a rolled-up canvas. He took it out and spread it open. It was a painting of Jo's, of the same style as what he had already seen, except the setting was very different. Scotland was nowhere to be found in this scene of an old adobe building with a red tile roof. "Hmm," mused Ashley to himself, "looks like Mexico or Central America somewhere." A large dog was sprawled out on the porch, sound asleep.

He wondered why she hadn't put it with the rest. If he were himself ever inclined to purchase some of her work, he would have chosen this particular piece. The dog was uncannily lifelike, and even in sleep, rather endearing. Her work was good, he had to admit. He could not help hoping his worst doubts would prove wrong.

Replacing all as he had found it, he next moved to the dressing table. The top was dominated with the usual variety of women's accoutrements. He picked up several items and looked them over. Most were American-made, though some had been purchased in Britain. To one side of the mirror sat two tubes of oil paint, one a cobalt blue, the other China white. They rested on a small tray along with two small plastic cups and a palette knife, apparently awaiting mixing. He began to turn away when it occurred to him that he had seen no other art supplies or equipment in the room—neither brushes nor spare canvas nor kits nor easel. He recalled someone saying that the solarium on the fourth floor had been converted into a studio. He glanced again at the small tray in puzzlement. *Why two tubes of paint, and nothing else?* he wondered. Aside from their apparent isolation, he could see nothing unusual about them.

Next he began a search of the drawers. This process was the most distasteful of his entire enforced burglary. As his hands rummaged through Jo's personal belongings, he felt more than ever the common sneak-thief. Just as he reached the bottom drawer, suddenly his hands stopped dead.

Had that been a noise in the hallway!

He cocked his ear toward the door. All was quiet.

Ashley tiptoed to the light, turned it off, then crept to the door and opened it a crack. The hallway was deserted.

He returned inside, sat down on the bed in the darkness, and waited. For five minutes he listened intently, but no other sound came. At length he switched the light back on and resumed his search by resolutely pulling out the top drawer of the second dresser.

It was filled merely with a few handkerchiefs and hair combs. He pulled it out as far as the drawer would come, but nothing else was revealed. It occurred to him that if Jo was clever enough to orchestrate such a cunning deception as had apparently been planned, she would not be so dull-witted as to leaving something incriminating out in the open where any visitor to her room might notice it. Surely she would have destroyed all ties to her true identity; even the initials on her luggage had been in keeping with the ruse: J.B.—though that might indeed be her real name.

If she had been so careful, what was he hoping to find, anyway? The room was bound to be clean.

Ashley was about to push the drawer back in when he suddenly recalled a ploy he had used himself a time or two. An amateurish trick, to be sure, certain to be discovered by any master detective. But it was worth a try—Jo was no doubt herself an amateur.

He smiled smugly to himself as he pulled the drawer out again, this time all the way out of its rails until he held the drawer in his hands. He examined the underside with one hand. Disappointed to find nothing, he stood a moment longer, then quickly turned and set the drawer down on the bed. Then he spun around, bent down, and scanned the vacant cavity of the dresser where the drawer had been.

Yes! There was something there, along the back side of the dresser.

He reached far back. His fingers felt a small white paper packet. He pried it loose and brought it out and set it in the palm of his hand. He opened the unsealed flap of the tiny envelope, sniffed, then peered inside to see about a teaspoonful of a white, crystalline powder. He moistened his finger and took up a few grains to taste, thought better of it, brushed them off, and sniffed it again. It smelled bitter, but even the most innocent of concoctions could be that.

More to the point, was this envelope Jo's? And why was it thus concealed?

Ashley examined the packet more closely, noticing for the first time a tiny bit of handwriting on one corner. He had missed it before because the words were few, written small, and in a light pencil. He had to hold it under the lamp to read it clearly. There were but two words: *Friar's cowl.*

Ashley rubbed his chin in contemplation. Where had he heard that name before?

He set the question aside for the moment as he realized he might now be able to determine ownership. If he could find a sample of Jo's handwriting, he could at least clear up that part of the mystery.

Going on hastily to the next drawer, he was rewarded in his quest as his eyes fell upon an appointment calendar. Thumbing through it quickly, the pages were oddly blank through August, the first notation being August 27: *Arrive Port Strathy.* Other engagements followed that: *Dinner at Smiths. . . . Market with Mother. . . . Lady Joanna to leave for London.*

It was clear this belonged to Jo. Ashley wasted no more time. He took the calendar and packet together, held them up to the lamp, and even in the poor light there could be no doubt the handwriting was the same. It did not answer every question, but at least he now knew that whoever the calendar belonged to was also the owner of the envelope of powder.

He removed his handkerchief from his pocket, poured out a small portion of the substance from the envelope into it, then carefully wrapped up the handkerchief. He wished he had something less porous to put it in, but this would have to do. He dropped it into his pocket, then carefully replaced the packet in its original hiding place, making sure the tape held it firm, then picked up the drawer off the bed and slid it back into the dresser.

Still puzzling over the words on the envelope, Ashley went on with his search. He examined the remainder of the bureau, drawer by drawer, though the contents were scant. In the bottom drawer, however, hidden inside a stocking and shoved far to the rear, his fingers felt something Logan had mentioned in a quick whisper to him the day he had arrived, and which he had later heard about from Hilary's own lips. Of course, in and of itself it would hardly be incriminating. Yet it was an interesting place to find it.

He closed the drawer, sat down again, still perplexed by the nagging uncertainty of the strange envelope. If only he could place that powder! He should know it. He had done extensive study of—

All at once Ashley jumped to his feet.

He spun around, his hand on his forehead.

Of course! he exclaimed half-aloud. *That's it! Dear God, I hope I'm not too late!*

He rushed out of the room, forgetful of the lamp still on and not even locking the door. In a full sprint he ran down the corridor, turned and flew down the stairs two at a bound.

50 ❊ *Conspiracy Uncovered*

IN THE BALLROOM, the moment "Scotland the Brave" had begun from the band, Logan interrupted Hilary's warm visit with the Mackenzies with the request for her favor on the dance floor, to which she assented with a smile and curtsy.

"I don't know very many of your northern dances," she confessed. "Though I'm having a good time trying."

"'The Gay Gordons' is one of the easiest and most enjoyable of all," said Logan, "especially to the national anthem. I never tire of it."

"You'll show me what to do, then?"

"Just keep in step with me, and watch the other couples as we move in a large circle," said Logan, taking her left hand in his left, and her right hand as his arm came over her shoulders. "And when we need to turn, I'll give you a push or pull. Okay . . . here we go . . . right, left, right, *turn* . . . back, two, three, four. Change directions! . . . two, three, *turn* . . . back, two, three, four. Now I spin you slowly with my right hand . . . once, twice, three times . . . and now waltz position for a little quick-step around . . . perfect! You see, nothing to it!"

Hilary laughed.

"Now, here we go again!"

By the time the song was half over, they had gone through the dance four or five times and Hilary's feet were obeying her smoothly. But in the middle of the next two-step sequence, Ashley suddenly burst into the large room, glanced around hurriedly, then rushed toward them the moment he had found them among the many guests and dancers.

"Logan!" he called out, breathless, trying to keep his voice down so as not to arouse suspicion, yet obviously worked up. "Come with me."

"Why, Mr. Jameson—"

"No need for that any longer, Logan. She knows. But you must come . . . immediately! There's no time to lose!"

Leaving Hilary alone in the middle of the floor without even an explanation, Ashley led Logan back the way he had come, not even pausing to allow the latter to explain the hubbub to the astonished guests nearby.

Once in the hallway, Ashley began to grill Logan with questions as they made their way toward the stairway.

"I have been observing a great many things," he said as they hurried along, "not the least of which is your wife's deteriorating emotional state. It has occurred to me that the problem may have other than an emotional cause. Tell me, has she been taking any medications lately?"

"None that I know of. An aspirin or two perhaps."

"Anything for her ankle?"

Logan paused in thought. "The doctor did give her a liniment."

"A liniment . . . hmm. That's interesting. I suppose it could . . . "

"But all this began long before she hurt her ankle."

"Can you say when, exactly?"

"It came on gradually. Perhaps around the time of Lady Joanna's death. Well, no—actually I recall some incidents even before that . . . nausea, depression. But I couldn't give an exact day."

"Perhaps two months ago?" asked Ashley, still walking rapidly along.

"That could be. Mid . . . late September. Yes, I suppose that's about right."

"What about von Burchardt? What do you know of him?"

"Only what he told us. Seems a nice enough chap."

"When was the first time you saw him?"

"Just the day before you got here, Ashley. Why?"

"I don't know, Logan. I don't know. I'm still trying to piece all this together. I'm grasping at anything."

"Why the urgency?"

"I may not have the full picture yet, but I have found some things that will interest you. For one thing, do you recognize this?"

Ashley pulled the locket from his coat pocket.

"Thank the Lord!" exclaimed Logan. "That's the locket . . . the one Allison gave little Joanna thirty years ago! Where did you find it?"

"It may or may not surprise you to learn that it was in a drawer in Jo's room."

"But I thought Hilary—"

"I did not say how it reached Jo's room," rejoined Ashley. "I just said that's where it was. We'll have to figure that out later. What about Lady Joanna. Just why did she go to London?"

Logan hesitated a long while before answering. When he at last spoke it was not without sadness in his tone. "She never said exactly. But though I've never wanted to admit it before, I think the reason was indeed just as Hilary's story implies, that she had doubts about Jo from the very first."

"You think your mother-in-law apprehended something deeper than you did?"

"I'm embarrassed to say it, but I think I blinded myself to what she saw because of how Allison took to Jo at first. She was so pleasant, made Allison feel happy and whole. I wanted to think everything was resolved. Joanna tried to tell me once. She got as far as suggesting that we ought to investigate Jo's credentials further, and I nearly blew up at her. It was the first time I can recall us having *words* with each other. After that, Joanna kept mostly to herself, probably thinking that if something was to be done about the situation, she would have to do it herself."

"And what became of it?"

"Well, you know the rest. One way or another—I don't know how—Joanna located Hilary . . . their meeting . . . the journal. But Joanna's secrets died with her."

"Then Hilary showed up here . . . and you called me?"

"Yes," said Logan with a sigh. "I think I always sensed something amiss, though I couldn't put my finger on it. That's probably why I insisted that Hilary stay."

By this time they had arrived in the corridor that led to Jo's room. "Well, we're almost there," said Ashley. "I can guarantee what I have to show you will not be pleasant."

Ashley opened the door. It was exactly as he had left it.

He walked straight to the bureau, pulled the top drawer out, again set it on the bed, then said to Logan, "Look in there."

Logan obeyed.

"Take it out. I want you to find it just as I did a few moments ago."

Following Ashley's example, Logan reached in, unfastened the small envelope, and brought it out into the light.

"What's inside?" asked Logan.

"I'll tell you in a moment. But first I must ask you just a few more questions. First, is there *anything* Allison has been taking besides aspirin? Think, man—*anything!*"

Logan was silent, shaking his head slowly.

"All I can say is that *I* know of nothing."

"Okay, then perhaps . . . I don't know. It could be the liniment," he said, speaking softly almost to himself. "But then there's the time problem. Still, it could absorb internally."

"What's this all about, my friend?" asked Logan.

Pondering but a second more, Ashley looked up, took a breath, then plunged ahead with his startling revelation.

"Logan," he said, "what you are holding in your hand is one of the most lethal poisons in existence. Just two milligrams of aconite internally is instantly fatal."

"But Allison's fine! What does a deadly poison have to do with her?"

"I said *internally* that's how it works. The point here is that Allison is not fine! She has been more ill than we have had any idea—that is, if I am correct."

"You think this white powder is responsible?"

"Yes, I do believe so. Aconite can also be absorbed through the skin. In past times they actually used the stuff in lotions and potions, in minuscule amounts of course, as a pain killer, for things like neuralgia—to deaden an area of muscle tissue."

"But how would Allison—"

Before Logan could say a word further, suddenly Ashley's hand shot to his head as if remembering the missing piece to the puzzle.

"Logan!" he exclaimed. "When I was dancing with Allison just a while ago I couldn't help noticing that her hands had paint stains on them."

"She's been painting with Jo whenever she feels up to it."

"But why doesn't she clean it off her hands?"

"She always said it was the mark of a true artist to let some of the color remain behind."

"That's bunk! What artist have you ever heard of who only cleaned his hands halfway! What do Jo's hands look like?"

"Now that you mention it, they're always pure white."

"Precisely my point! That's got to be it, Logan!" He glanced almost frantically about the room, his eyes coming to rest on the top of the dressing table. The two tubes! . . . the palate! . . . the small cups! Of course! That had to be it! She mixed the poison right here!

"Logan!" he exclaimed. "It's the paints!"

"But how could—"

"In strong enough amounts, even a little on the skin, for a prolonged period of time . . . the cumulative effect!"

The swift rush of evidence bombarded Logan's consciousness, ripping the scales from his eyes. In another instant he was jolted into potent wakefulness.

With an outburst of righteous fury his hand slammed down upon the desk beside which he was standing. Without another word, he turned, flung wide the door, and—his hand still clutching the deadly packet, his eyes filled with fire, and his nostrils flared in indignation— strode from the room as a man possessed, prepared to do battle.

Ashley followed behind, not even pausing for a backward glance at the chamber from which such vile deception had secretly originated.

Had he looked in the opposite direction down the corridor, he might have seen a silent witness to their discovery, who had followed them, hiding in waiting, watching from a secluded shadow as Logan exited. The full effect of the revelation registered plainly upon his face; then he stealthily returned by another route to the room where his co-conspirator was at that moment attempting to consummate her wicked design.

51 ❈ *Flight*

LOGAN STORMED INTO the ballroom with such a fierce expression on his countenance that almost immediately the music ceased and all heads turned in his direction. As he strode purposefully into the room, he seemed to grow in stature, until the very resplendence of the ancient clan chieftainship came to dwell bodily upon him. With eyes aglow he quickly scanned the faces of his loyal people, searching for the tares among the wheat, that he might root them out and bring them to a righteous justice.

From where she stood, once again engaged with Frances Mackenzie, Hilary perceived at once—however calm and good-natured a man her father was—that the kettle of his wrath had boiled over. She rushed toward him.

"Where is Jo?" his voice thundered, not at Hilary, but to any who might care to listen.

All eyes scanned the hall. She was not to be seen.

"Has anyone seen the Viscount von Burchardt?" growled Logan. "I have evidence of a plot in my home, and I want to speak with him!" He gestured with his hand as he emphasized each word.

There was no sign of the Austrian.

As if in a single moment, Hilary, Logan, and Ashley each became aware that neither was Allison present. They glanced at one another, dawning dread in their eyes, then all three rushed toward the door into the main corridor of the house.

As he went, Logan shouted out orders.

"Hilary, you check the west wing—ground floor, then first floor. Ashley, go to the library."

Before he had well finished his words, they were gone.

"Jake," Logan went on, "I have no idea where they might be. Take a look outside . . . the stables . . . the barn. Moryson, run down to the kitchen and tell the cook that Mrs. Macintyre is missing. Tell her to enlist what help she can to look in that quarter of the house."

The two men went.

"Now, let's see . . . Creary, come with me. Mr. Davies, would you wait out by the main stairway, in front of the door? If anyone brings news, dispatch it about the house that the rest may be brought back. Let's go, Doug!"

They exited, leaving the ballroom in a storm of buzzing and bewildered anxious questioning.

Logan ran first to the drawing room, then the dining room, then the family parlor. Each was empty.

When he and Creary ran back along the corridor toward the front door, Hilary was just descending the staircase. In another moment Ashley ran up from the direction of the library.

"Moryson told me to say he went to look in the East Wing," said Davies.

"The East Wing?" repeated Logan. "There's nothing there but—"

At that very moment the sound of a revving car engine was heard, then the grinding of spinning tires across the graveled courtyard.

Logan spun around, as if debating whether to go after it.

"There is a little sitting room just where the East Wing connects with the inner courtyard," said Hilary. "I think I've seen Jo there a time or two."

"It's worth a try!" said Logan, leading the way. "We'll have to let the car go."

The small band followed him, but had difficulty keeping up. By the time they reached the spot and walked in the open door, Logan was already kneeling beside Allison where she lay on a sofa at the far end of the room.

"Jo brought me here to help me rest," Allison was saying in a weak voice. "She was just about to give me this"—she pointed to a glass sitting on a nearby end-table filled with some colorless liquid—"when that man rushed in. She said it would help me sleep."

"What man? Von Burchardt?"

"Yes . . . him."

"What did they do . . . where are they now?"

"I don't know. He said something to her about the game being up," she went on in a weak voice. "Then she tried to come back over and was going to give me the medicine. But he grabbed her hand and pulled her away. He said, 'We've got to get out of here!' "

Logan spun around. His eyes sought Ashley's, and in another moment the professor was on his way outside to check the car garage.

Slowly Logan took Allison in his arms. "Well, my dear," he said with a smile, "let's get those hands of yours cleaned up, and then put you to bed."

Just as they reached the hallway outside the room, Ashley returned.

"I don't know which car it was that drove away a minute ago," he said. "But there's only one missing from the garage . . . Jo's. Do you want me to go after them?"

Logan pondered for a moment.

"No," he said at length. "They're long gone by now. Once they're on Burchardt's yacht, we'd never be able to stop them. We'll have to find some other way."

52 ❄ *Faraway Alliance*

IN THE LATE morning quiet of what had once been the proud command post of a high-placed generalissimo, now only one of a dozen such rundown villas stretching between the capital and Punta Norte, a man sat stirring his morning cup of coffee.

The weather here is downright fine, he thought to himself. Even after all this time he was still not tired of the sunshine and the 80-degree mornings, though he could not for the life of him acclimate himself to the inverted seasons. Summer in November and December—the thing was ridiculous! But he'd learned to live with everything else in this backward, rat-infested place—why not the seasons?

He paused in his reflections to sip the strong brew the servant had brought him.

"Fine weather," he muttered, "but these blasted provincials still can't make a decent cup of coffee! Crying shame, too—this close to where they grow the cursed beans, it ought to be better!"

He took another sip, grimaced, glanced at his watch, looked around, then added: "Where is that confounded idiot with the mail?" As if any of these foreigners could understand him anyway!

This sedentary life hardly suited him, though he had long ago managed to accustom himself to the inevitable. For one who had thrived on exercising his power over others, such a transition had not come easily. However, seated in the east garden of the villa, with servants at his beck and call—he would have been pleased to know that *they* at least still trembled at his command—he did manage to maintain a remote suggestion of the appearance of a retired country caballero surveying his range. But his expensive white linen suit was draped over an emaciated, almost wasted frame, and the rakish white straw hat shaded mottled, wrinkled skin from the searing sun. His mind these days was more occupied with reliving past glories, not to mention fomenting of past hatreds, than with the contentedness that should instead have come with old age.

With a bony hand, yet remarkably steady, he poured more cream into his cup, followed by one more cube of sugar, as if thinking to mask the bitterness of the concoction. It was a ritual he amused himself with every morning, realizing its futility all the while, yet choosing to play out the diversion as one of the few ruses left with which an old conniver could indulge himself.

His dark thoughts were interrupted by the approach of a servant, also attired from head to foot in white, but whose three-day growth of beard revealed that he was not a valet or house steward by profession. He, too, had once trained for what he regarded as better things. But in these days, with the Fatherland so Americanized, one had to go where one would be safe, and do what one could to get by. Such a strategy of pragmatism bound the inhabitants of Villa del Heimat together in an amalgamation of loose symbiotic relationships of convenience, seclusion, and survival.

"Die Post ist here," he said. "Shall I bring it to you, mein Herr?"

"Yes, of course, you fool!" exclaimed the other. "I'm expecting an important letter from—never mind from where! Just bring it here!"

Three minutes later he grabbed away from the hand that delivered it a single letter addressed in the handwriting he had been hoping to see, a flowing hand with which he was intimately familiar. Yet as he ripped open the envelope, the distinctive fire in his eyes reflected venom rather than love.

Hastily he scanned the two onionskin sheets. This was no time for dilly-dallying with familial pleasantries; he wanted news, even if the letter was dated a week earlier!

At length he put the letter down and gazed into the distance. The confounded new arrivals at the place had certainly thrown a kink into their plans. But it would all be over soon, and he would have what he had so long coveted. "So," he mused half articulately, "in the end it is I who remain." The hint of a smile crept over his aging lips. "And in the end it will be I who achieve this one final conquest. Not this time will you—"

His dark thoughts were interrupted by the crisp step of an approaching visitor. Glancing up, his face displayed immediate recognition.

"Ah, Herr Gunther."

"Mein lieber Kommandant!" replied the new arrival with a faint grin.

"I've told you not to call me that," croaked the other with as much visible anger as he could summon. "You know my title! Word must not leak out about my past identity."

Gunther laughed.

"You and your eccentric notions!" he said. "No one down here stands on protocol. No one cares about us. The world has forgotten, don't you know?"

"But *I* have not forgotten! I will never forget. And I will have my revenge!"

"Yes, yes, and I will do your bidding and help you keep fighting your private little war. But at least I suffer from no false delusions. Even your own company goes on without us."

"They do *nothing* without my consent!" squawked the old man, leaning forward in his chair as if he would wring the neck of his right-hand man for such an impertinent suggestion. "They will yet pay for humiliating me! I will make them pay!"

"Ah, General, look around," said Gunther in a highly uncharacteristic moment of philosophy. "This is a time to enjoy the fruits of our labors. It's not such a bad life. Better at least than that sardine can of a sub where—"

"You don't need to remind me of the past—I remember every bitter minute of this wretched existence I'm supposed to call life."

"You were glad enough for that existence thirty years ago when you stole the Reich's U-boat and made your escape."

"I well remember the incident!"

"Then you should know that you are fortunate to still be alive. Many of our comrades have not been so lucky. You know what happened to our friend—"

"I don't pay you to preach to me!"

With a sigh, which indicated that he knew how things were, and that he would continue to wield the General's gun and carry out his designs of treachery despite his words about pausing to enjoy life, Gunther pulled a yellow envelope out of his pocket. "I have been to the village," he said. "There was an important communique there for you—an urgent telegram."

"Give it to me!" demanded the old man, his shrieking voice cracking with the effort of the words.

The moment the paper was extended toward him, he snatched it away with a swiftness that contradicted the feebleness of his body, reminding the onlooker of the lightning-quick stroke of a frog's tongue snatching a fly out of midair. The old man ripped open the Western Union envelope and held its contents up before his rheumy eyes. Then he swore angrily, dropped the letter in his lap, and began groping on the table, knocking over the pitcher of cream in his exasperation.

"Where are those absurd spectacles?" he shouted.

The younger, albeit graying, man stepped forward and quickly located them on the table, then handed them to his employer.

The old man shoved them on his face, then grabbed up the telegram again. His lips moved, ruminating silently on the words his aged eyes beheld:

IGNORE PREVIOUS LETTER STOP PLAN EXPLODED STOP IDENTITIES IN DANGER STOP HAVE FLOWN COOP STOP FULL REPORT UPON ARRIVAL STOP.

His face flushed, his eyes bulged with incensed wrath.

"They cannot beat me again!" he screamed, his entire body now shaking with the culmination of his passion as he threw the telegram from him.

"Calm yourself, General," said Gunther, concern etched on his hardened sinister features.

"Shut up! I will never be calm! I will never rest! Not until they pay for this!"

He bent over in an attempt to retrieve the telegram, but lost his balance, and would have toppled from his chair had Gunther not been there to steady his emaciated frame.

For thanks the old man spat a barrage of profanity at the man—who now had been with him twenty years—and continued in a steady stream even as another paroxysm of coughing possessed him, his heated face growing red from mingled anger and exertion.

Gunther turned and walked into the house, leaving the once mighty leader gasping for breath. He sent the servant for the doctor, then left the villa, wondering how much longer the old man could cheat death out of its due.

53 ❧ *Time of Reunion*

THREE PEOPLE IN Stonewycke's family sitting room enjoying tea together was not an unusual scene.

Two women shared the divan, while the acknowledged head of the family stood in front of the sideboard on which he had just placed the pot from which he had poured tea.

A familiar setting, an afternoon chat in the sitting room, it was indeed. But never before in the lives of these three had there been a gathering quite like this one. And never would there be again.

Allison had been in bed since the evening of the party, and had only a short time ago come down for the first time. She was still frail, but a smile had returned to her lips, a hint of the real Allison already beginning to reemerge.

Since that fateful night, Logan had spoken to Hilary only briefly, and more casually than he would have liked. It was clear from the upbeat mood about the place that everything had suddenly changed at Stonewycke, and he had looked for an opportunity to bring it out into the open. However, he had driven to Aberdeen the following day in order to set investigations in motion. In addition, he felt it fitting that he await his wife's recovery for this emotion-filled moment.

Logan turned and cleared his throat.

"I don't really know what to say . . . " he began.

The two women chuckled and glanced at each other, a nervous release for all the feelings pent up inside.

"That's a switch, isn't it?" he added. "Logan Macintyre at a loss for words!"

Now they laughed outright, and Logan could not help joining them.

"I *don't* know what to say, Hilary," he went on more seriously. "I'm sorry I was away yesterday. But maybe it's better this way, since now that Allison is feeling better we can all have our first tea together."

"I couldn't help keeping to myself yesterday either," said Hilary, staring down into the cup she held in her lap. "I had a lot to think about, and I almost found myself avoiding this moment. It's all so new to me. I didn't know what to do at first. I felt like a shy schoolgirl on her first date."

"Well . . . here we are at last," said Logan. "And I've not been able to avoid the feeling that some sort of more formal—I don't know . . . apology, perhaps, was called for on the part of Allison and myself—"

"Please," interrupted Hilary, "you know that's not necessary."

"It is necessary," he repeated. "At least it's necessary for us. We did not behave to you when you came as we now wish we had."

"You couldn't have known," protested Hilary.

"Nevertheless, we are sorry it was difficult for you. Needless to say, we grieve over the years since you were . . . lost to us . . . that we did not do more—somehow . . . " He stopped, took a deep breath, and struggled to continue. His voice was gruff and uncertain.

" . . . that we did not do more . . . to confirm the reports . . . of your death—though we exhausted what resources we knew of."

Still Hilary gazed into her cup, her thoughts far away. Her eyes were clouding over with tears.

"Thankfully," said Logan, laboring to keep his voice intact, "those long years and these last uncertain months are now behind us. As frivolous as it may sound after all we have just been through, we mean it with all our hearts when we say we want to welcome you back into your family."

"Thank you," Hilary whispered. A lump rose in her throat. "I . . . I don't know what to say either," she half laughed.

Allison's hand reached toward her. Hilary clasped it and held tight. Even as she did so she lifted her eyes, and they met those of the man she now knew she loved, not merely as a statesman or a friend . . . but as a *father*.

Logan set down his cup of tea and slowly approached his wife and daughter. Suddenly, Hilary was out of her seat and in his arms. Without restraint, her tears of thirty years flowed out onto Logan's chest, while his strong arms wrapped around her shoulders and pulled her tightly to him.

For a moment they stood—silent . . . weeping. Allison rose and walked toward them. Without words, Logan gently loosened himself from Hilary's embrace so that mother and daughter might join their hearts as well.

Hilary turned. There stood Allison gazing upon her, her recently beleaguered countenance now overspread with a radiant smile, tracks of tears falling down her pale cheeks.

"Oh, Mother!" exclaimed Hilary, rushing forward to embrace her.

"I'm so sorry I doubted you!"

"It's over now, Mother," breathed Hilary softly.

"Oh, but I feel like such a fool," wept Allison, "being taken in like that when my own daughter . . . shouting at you like I did . . . I'm so sorry . . . "

She could not continue, but broke down, her shoulders convulsing with sobs.

Hilary held her close, while Logan now stretched his arms about the two women, his own tears flowing freely.

"We all have to live with the pain of our regrets," he said softly. "How deeply I wish I had been a better father when you were with us thirty years ago!"

"I weep in my heart to think that I nearly rejected what Lady Joanna told me," said Hilary. "I almost did . . . I didn't want to see my life turned upside-down."

"All our lives have certainly changed . . . and will change," said Logan. "And though perhaps all three of us will have to bear these pains yet a while longer, they will be healed. Our Father will use them to strengthen the bonds of our love which we are only beginning to discover."

Gradually the tears began to lessen and they resumed their seats around the fire.

"I want you to know," said Hilary after a moment, "that I no longer have any doubts. I'm . . . I'm *glad* you are my parents."

"We love you, Hilary," said Allison.

"Thank you . . . Mother," replied Hilary, tears rising in her eyes afresh. But she brushed them back and tried to laugh.

"I don't even know what to call you," she said to Logan.

"Call me whatever you are comfortable with . . . Logan suits me fine."

"Then I'll call you Logan," said Hilary with a smile, "until the word *Father* comes a little more naturally."

"And what do *we* call you?" asked Allison. "I must admit it's going to be difficult to think of you as Jo or Joanna now. But I love the name Hilary too; that's why we chose it for you."

Hilary laughed. "It's served me well for many years!"

"I think our daughter will always be Hilary to me from now on," said Logan. "Hilary— one who brings joy! I can't think of anything more suitable. It was as Hilary we came to know you. But tell me . . . *Hilary,"* he went on, "when did you first know? I mean really *know* . . . that is, after you arrived here?"

"In the gallery. But I haven't yet told you what happened the night of the party, have I?"

"No. Tell us, please," insisted Allison.

"Oh, but we've got to be there! It can't really be told at all. What I experienced that night has to be seen!"

"By all means then," said Logan enthusiastically. "Let's go to the gallery!"

"We'll have to go by way of my room," said Hilary, "so that I can slip into another dress."

"Whatever you say!"

Logan led the way to the door, opened it for the two ladies, then, with his wife on one arm and his daughter on the other, escorted them down the corridor and to the stairway.

Only the daughter was prepared for what awaited them. Indeed, had the husband and wife been aware of the astounding revelation which was shortly to greet their eyes, they would much earlier have realized in whom the legacy of young Maggie Duncan had flowered.

54 ❧ *Confirmation of Intent*

"THE LOCAL DOCTOR has kindly given me permission to use the small laboratory in his surgery," Ashley said to Hilary when he knocked at her door the following morning. "Would you care to join me for a drive into Port Strathy?"

"Sure," answered Hilary. "What do you need a lab for?"

"The packet. Thus far I have only speculated on the contents of what I found in Jo's room. It's imperative not only for the police investigation but also for Allison's continued treatment that we identify it precisely. I want to run some tests."

Hilary grabbed up her coat and a hat, then joined Ashley in the corridor.

"Can't the police do all that?" she asked as they made their way downstairs.

"Logan is still uncertain how far to bring the authorities into this. He's made some discreet inquiries of his own, but he wants to know more before it turns into a full-blown public investigation."

"And you're his sleuth, eh?"

"No comment," said Ashley, a boyish grin tugging at the corners of his mouth. "Let's just call it my little hobby."

Hilary threw him a sidelong glance as they walked down the stairs, finding it difficult to keep her curiosity in check.

Once out in the open air by a side door, they walked around to the front of the house where Ashley's car awaited them. Ashley opened the passenger door of the BMW for Hilary and saw her comfortably seated, then went around to the driver's side and slid in.

A few moments later Dr. Connally emerged from the house, climbed into his own car, and followed them into town. In ten minutes the two automobiles pulled up in front of the doctor's office on Port Strathy's main street next to the mercantile. Dr. Connally ushered them in, led them down a narrow hallway to the back of the building, then, switching on a light, welcomed them to his laboratory.

"It isn't much," he said, "but it does save me having to send out many of my samples and specimens. It takes at least forty-eight hours to use the Aberdeen facilities."

He began to clear a place on one of the counters. "Here you go, Mr. Jameson. I hope we have everything you need. I'm not exactly equipped for this sort of thing. I'm not even certain I could make such a test without using a reference book."

"I'm sure we'll manage fine," said Ashley.

"I'm still rather curious where a Greek historian comes by a knowledge of forensic medicine."

"So am I," added Hilary with a raised eyebrow.

"Just picked it up here and there," said Ashley, coughing nervously. "Now, let's see," he went on, changing the subject, "what will we need?"

With the help of the doctor, he gathered a petri dish, a vial of phosphoric acid syrup, sodium molybdate solution, and a Bunsen burner. He poured a portion of each of the chemicals into the dish, then sprinkled in some of the powdered solution from the envelope. He gave the concoction a stir then, clamping the dish with a handle, held it out over the flame, moving the dish gently back and forth. Before long the substance in the dish began to turn color, eventually becoming a brilliant violet. The three observers exchanged meaningful glances.

"Just as I suspected," said Ashley. "This confirms aconite. Now to see if my further speculation is true. By itself, perhaps, the mere presence of poison would not be considered incriminating by a court of law, but . . . "

He did not finish the sentence, but instead took from his pocket a small container of the blue paint he had removed from Allison's own palette in the solarium. He had taken two other colors also, but had particularly chosen the blue because of the tube he had found in Jo's room, which he assumed was sitting on her dressing table awaiting its fatal addition.

He repeated the procedure he had used on the powder.

Because the paint was a diluted concentration, the change when it came was not so startling, but there could be no mistaking the change to violet when the mixture was held over the flame.

"I can hardly believe it!" said the doctor.

Ashley had spent too much time prowling about Scotland Yard not to believe it; long ago his naivete about human nature had been abandoned.

"The tests will be finalized," said Connally, "when I have completed the analysis of Lady Allison's blood sample. That will take somewhat longer. I will also send a sample to Aberdeen to confirm the testing."

"Will she recover from all this?" asked Hilary with concern.

"Yes," replied the doctor, "but it will take time for all the effects to work their way out of her body."

"We are fortunate in one respect," said Ashley. "Had Jo been in a hurry and administered this substance orally, Allison would have died almost instantly—especially in that she possessed the crystalline variety, which is ten to fifteen times more poisonous than other forms. I only wonder where she could have gotten it. Aconite is obsolete these days, extremely difficult to come by."

"I have a colleague," offered Connally, "who served as a medical missionary in Central America. He was appalled at the outmoded drugs still to be had there."

"Central America, you say?" pondered Ashley. "Hmm . . . that is interesting."

"What is it?" asked Hilary.

"Oh, I don't know . . . maybe nothing. But when we were having a look about von Burchardt's yacht, I took a good look at the registration sticker."

"And?"

"I can tell you it wasn't registered in Austria or Germany. Nowhere in Europe at all. That was when I began to have extreme doubts that our friend Emil was telling the truth."

"Where was the boat from?"

"It was carrying an Argentine registration."

Hilary let out a long, low whistle.

"Argentina," thought the doctor aloud. "Yes, I suppose it's possible. In fact, it wouldn't surprise me a bit if you could still come by such compounds there."

"Let's get home," said Hilary, turning to Ashley. "I don't want to be away too long."

"Are you coming back to the house, Doctor?" asked Ashley.

"I have another patient to see in a few minutes. Then I want to prepare some medication for Lady Allison. I'll return in about an hour."

"Thank you again for the use of your facilities."

Back in the car, Hilary turned to Ashley as he started up the engine. "It continues to amaze me—the wide range of your knowledge," she said. "You're a regular Renaissance Man! How do you fit everything in?"

"All in a day's work, you know."

"Something tells me there's more to it than that."

"You're not a mystery buff, are you, Hilary?"

"On the contrary, I love mysteries. Unraveling them is one of my jobs as a reporter."

"It's my job too."

"The mysteries of the past?"

"Yes . . . of course." He paused, carefully considering his words. "But I am highly interested in present-day mysteries too."

"The clues . . . the poison . . . going about the house at night looking for manuscripts and lockets and evidence?"

"Have I really been so obvious as a prying would-be Sherlock Holmes about the place?"

Hilary laughed.

Suddenly Ashley seemed to grow very serious, as if pondering some weighty matter. He drove up the hill out of town very slowly, his mind far from the actions of his hand. At length he spoke again.

"So, Hilary," he said, "you like journalistic mysteries."

Hilary nodded.

"Do you like to *read* mysteries?"

"You mean stories?"

"Yes. Mystery novels."

"Conan Doyle . . . Ellery Queen? Yes, in fact, I do."

"Would you think it peculiar if I told you I do too?"

"No, I don't think so." She paused, then laughed. "Is that what this is all about? Renowned Greek scholar secretly a devotee of pulp mystery novels! It's my scoop of the decade!"

"I'm afraid it's more serious than that."

"They're not going to defrock you because you enjoy a good story. Everyone needs a diversion."

"But as I said, it's a more serious compulsion for me than that."

All at once he pulled the car to the side of the road and ground to a stop. "Come with me," he said. "Let's go for a walk."

They got out of the car, crossed the road, and continued walking in the direction they had been headed. They were only a hundred yards or so from the crest of the hill, toward which they now made their way, the vast blue North Sea spreading out below them. For a long time Ashley was silent, and Hilary did not press him.

At last he drew in a deep sigh, exhaled, and then spoke.

"What I'm about to tell you only one other person in the world knows. It's one of the best kept secrets in the modern publishing world, and you've got to promise me you'll never tell a soul."

"Is it all really so serious, Ashley?"

"For me . . . yes, it is. My private life is important. Sacrificing it is not something I am willing to do."

"Then I promise. But you don't have to tell me this. I promise, I won't press if you'd rather—"

"I *want* to tell you," he interrupted, emotion obviously building within him. "I have known I would have to tell you for some time . . . ever since that day I wasn't exactly truthful with you."

"You had to keep the truth from me, Ashley. I hold none of what happened against you."

"I don't mean about Allison or my knowing Logan or what I was doing here or the ruse about meeting Ian. I wasn't altogether comfortable with that, but I accepted that I would have to play such a 'role' so to speak in order to get at the deeper truth of what was going on. But there were other times, when we were talking more personally, when I could not escape the feeling that I was lying to you."

"Oh, Ashley, don't torture yourself with guilt over such little things."

"But don't you see? Everything I said that day about truth mattering—it really does matter a great deal to me. Living by truth is my whole life. I've not had the chance to share with you as much as I would like. But I am a Christian—"

"I knew that."

"How?"

"It's obvious. By the way you live, the way you care. You're a very compassionate individual, Ashley Jameson."

"Then maybe it won't come as such a surprise for me to say that the little things are important to me. And I haven't been able to get out of my mind that day when we were walking out in the snow. Do you remember?"

"How could I forget?"

"You asked me if I ever wrote anything but history."

"I remember."

"I said no. I lied to you—point blank. It had nothing to do with Jo or Logan or my so-called investigation at the house. I just lied. And I've been uncomfortable with it ever since. Your question caught me off guard. I fumbled around for words, and before I knew it, I'd allowed myself to tell you something that wasn't true. So now I have to try to make it right."

"I understand," said Hilary. "Just so long as you know that you have in no way injured or offended me."

"Understood," said Ashley. "Besides," he added, stopping and looking into her face, "now I want to tell you. I want you to know me, because . . . well, the revealing of a close secret to a friend is a rather personal thing to do."

"Ashley, is this your rather Victorian way of saying that you care for me?"

"I suppose it is." He cleared his throat and chuckled awkwardly. "Of all my varied areas of knowledge, affairs of the heart is one arena in which I am an unskilled and inexperienced participant."

Hilary chuckled softly, then slipped her hand through his arm. He smiled, seemed to gather strength from her simple yet heartfelt gesture, then plunged ahead.

"Like I said, I like mysteries."

"As do I," added Hilary, her heart bounding as she walked by Ashley's side.

"Not only do I like to read mysteries, I like to try to solve them. I have a friend in Scotland Yard. Sometimes he lets me in on his cases. That's how it all started, in fact, years ago, when we were both students in the university. But that caper is another story altogether!"

"Promise you'll tell me someday," said Hilary.

"Promise. But not only do I like to get involved in real cases, I then . . . " He paused. This was more difficult than he had anticipated. He took another breath. " . . . I then write down my experiences."

"A mystery journal. What a great idea!" exclaimed Hilary.

"Not exactly a journal. I . . . I change the facts around from the way they really happened . . . add color here and there . . . change the setting . . . change the names."

"Ashley! Are you trying to tell me you're a closet mystery writer, with a drawer full of short stories taken from the police files?"

"In a manner of speaking . . . yes."

"That's exciting! I love it! Why would you be embarrassed to tell people that?"

"Because I've even had some of my work published."

"You have? That's great! But I've never seen your—Of course!" she exclaimed. "You use a pen name!"

Ashley nodded sheepishly.

"Ashley Jameson the historian turns out to be none other than a whodunit mystery writer! No wonder you wanted to keep this under wraps! So, what magazines have your stories been in? I'd like to see them."

"They haven't been in magazines, actually."

"What then . . . a book . . . an anthology of short stories?"

"I didn't say I wrote short stories."

"Long stories then . . . what?"

All at once a portion of the truth broke in upon Hilary.

"Ashley . . . you don't mean you write mystery books . . . novels?"

"I'm afraid so."

"That's fantastic! Please, stop beating around the bush. What's your pen name?"

Ashley sighed. "I've come this far, I guess you might as well have the whole enchilada, as they say on the streets of New York. Well . . . here it is—but I'm afraid you might recognize her name. And then what will you think of me?"

"I'll think none the less of you!" pleaded an exasperated Hilary. "Just be out with it before I—" Suddenly she paused. "Did you say *her*?" she asked.

Ashley nodded.

"She! Your pseudonym is a woman!"

"Rather a well-known one I must confess. The name was first given me by my friend at the Yard. I've since thought of having him drawn and quartered."

"Ashley, you don't mean . . . ?"

Again Ashley nodded modestly.

"But, Ashley, she's one of the best-selling mystery writers in the country. Over a dozen books! You can't be . . . but, you are serious!"

"Now you see why I've got to keep it quiet."

Hilary's mouth hung open in dumfounded amazement.

"I can't believe it!" she said. "I just can't believe it! Ashley Jameson, my toe-in-the-sand, tweed suit, soft-spoken Ashley Jameson, stuffy old Greek scholar, is none other than—Lady Hargreave herself!"

Ashley did not reply. His mind was too full of the revelation he had just made, and his heart was too full of the woman at his side, for words to be possible just now.

Hilary clung to Ashley even more tightly, then slowly rested her head upon his arm, a quiet smile of contentment on her lips.

Together they continued walking, in silence, long beyond the gates of Stonewycke, eventually discovering a long disused path down the bluff to the sea. They talked about many things, not the least of which was their future together.

It was well over an hour before they returned to the car.

55 ❊ *Loose Fragments and Plans*

"WELL, I'LL TELL you when I first knew something was up," said Logan. "During that very first luncheon with our old friend von Burchardt. I had a nervous feeling about him all along. Do you remember how he slipped around all my attempts to pin him down?"

He and Ashley were seated across the table from Allison and Hilary in the inner courtyard where they had just finished a light lunch. The sun was shining and the air, protected as it was from any breath of wind, was unseasonably warm. Ashley and Hilary had arrived back at the house just as Flora was setting the table.

"I was confused all along," said Hilary. "Just when the viscount would flash that smile of his, making me sure he was up to no good, I'd see Ashley walking off across the lawn with Jo, and grow so suspicious and infuriated with him that I'd begin to succumb to Emil's oily charms."

"I've explained that," laughed Ashley. "That time we were talking in your room, just after the incident with the music box when you were so distraught—"

"When I berated you for all your truth and integrity talk—"

"That's the time! You were so upset, passion written all over your face, your eyes aglow. . . . Suddenly it dawned on me whose face I was seeing in yours. It was Logan's! In that moment I knew beyond any doubt that you were his daughter."

"So why then did you rush right out and take up with Jo again?" asked Hilary with a twinkle in her eye.

"Because before I said anything I had to be positively sure. I had to look at her face again. I even tried to bait her with some leading questions, seeing if I could get a rise out of her, seeing if I could detect anything whatsoever that reminded me of either Allison or Logan. I had seen such confirmation from the flash in your eye that I had to gather my final bit of evidence from Jo's face."

"What did you find?" asked Allison, clearly feeling much better.

"Nothing. Not a trace. She was a cool one. She could almost have fooled me if I hadn't gotten to know Hilary so well."

"Of course I had to keep my distance from you," Logan said to Ashley, "when anyone was around. It wasn't easy getting you off by yourself so we could compare notes. And von Burchardt was a complication I'd never counted on when I called you."

"Speaking of von Burchardt," said Hilary thoughtfully, "do you remember, Ashley, that I told you I asked my friend at the *Review* to check up on you? At the same time I gave him Emil's name."

"And?"

"He hadn't found anything out when we last talked. I ought to give him a call."

"Why don't you, right now?" suggested Logan. "We need to know who we're up against in this plot against us. And what are their motives."

"I will," said Hilary, rising. "I'll go call him right now."

She left and walked to the library. Fifteen minutes later she returned.

"I have some most interesting news!" she announced.

"You got through?"

"Did I ever! I'm not sure where this leaves us, but one thing is certain—we're up against something bigger than merely Jo and Emil."

"Out with it, Hilary," chided Ashley. "We're on pins and needles!"

"Okay. My associate on the *Review,* Murry Fitts, did an investigation on our friend the viscount. He hadn't called me yet, he said, because there were some other names he was trying to get that he thought might tie in. In any case, here's what he has so far."

She paused, flipped through the small notebook she had been holding, and then began. "Emil's story, as far as it went, is true. A titled Austrian family whose wealth goes back many generations. However, they lost everything during the depression and were quick to espouse Nazi propaganda. The elder viscount was made a minister in the Nazi regime formed in Austria in 1938 when Hitler annexed that country. This von Burchardt was eventually promoted to Hitler's own inner circle in Berlin. At the end of the war he escaped with many other war criminals and disappeared. He was thought to have wound up in South America."

A whistle escaped Ashley's lips.

"What is it?" asked Logan.

"I was just telling Hilary this morning that von Burchardt's yacht was not from the Continent at all, but bore an Argentine registration. It had a Buenos Aires port of entry emblem just below the registration."

"Most observant of you," said Logan, impressed.

"He is rather remarkable. isn't he?" added Hilary coyly. "I think I shall have Murry put his name in the police computer after all."

"The results will be quite boring, I assure you!" rejoined Ashley.

"I doubt that!" said Hilary. "But I wouldn't doubt that the implication of your discovery regarding the yacht is correct. Emil has indeed spent a great deal of time in South America. But—and I can't imagine how Murry got this; I'm afraid to ask—the Israeli Mossad has tried to trace Emil to possible war criminals, but have come up consistently empty. Nevertheless, it does make one wonder."

"War criminals," mused Logan. "Will it never end?"

"The old Nazis are dying off," said Hilary. "But I suppose their progeny must be accounted for."

"The sins of the fathers, and all that," said Ashley. "But it would be blind on our part to fall into such a trap."

"I fully agree," said Hilary. "On the other hand, it would be unwise to become lethargic as long as even a remote possibility exists. In Emil's case, however, there is no such direct evidence. He is doubtless a liar and a deceiver, apparently even an accomplice to an attempted murder. But that does not make him a Nazi, too."

"What *does* it make him?" asked Logan pointedly.

"That is the substance of my chat with Murry," answered Hilary. "Murry has been involved in his own investigation of a seemingly unrelated matter. Now all of a sudden the paths of these two sets of circumstances have intersected in a most interesting fashion—intersected at the common point of our friend the viscount."

"What is Fitts's story about?" asked Ashley.

"A contact of his—a man, I might add, who is running for his life, supposedly because of this very information he possesses—came to him with an incredible story that connects one of Europe's most influential international companies, Trans Global Enterprises, with syndicated crime."

"Logan, that's the company you told me about after Ringersfeld's call," said Allison, who had been paying closer attention to the course of the conversation than her scant contributions would have indicated.

"Yes . . . I know," said Logan soberly. He gave a thoughtful nod, still pondering the implications of what he had just heard. "It appears perhaps there are more intersecting paths here than any of us realized. My staff has recently begun its own investigation of that company. But go on, Hilary."

"Have you heard of an underworld figure known as 'The General'?"

"Seems to ring a faint bell," said Logan. "Like something I heard when I was talking to a chap from Interpol."

Ashley shook his head. "I probably should know the name. But I'm sadly out of touch with things—you know, the cloistered Oxford lifestyle."

"Not as much as you think, Ashley," said Hilary. "Murry's contact is an ex-Oxford don himself, an art expert who now deals extensively on the black market, high-stakes stuff. Murry didn't take the time to tell me how all this relates, if he even knows yet himself. But this General is an enigmatic figure whom Interpol and other intelligence agencies have been after for years. No one knows who he really is, where he operates from, or exactly what he's into. But he's suspected of racketeering in everything from drugs to weapons to diamond smuggling—you name it. So then all of a sudden this Oxford fellow of Murry's quite by accident stumbled upon a connection between the General and Trans Global—a connection which, if true, is front-page stuff that would have a thunderous impact on the stock market, government contracts, and all kinds of economic implications."

Logan sat as one transfixed. As recent Minister of Economics, he was intimately familiar with the effect news such as this could have, and could not believe what he was hearing.

"So Murry has been burrowing his way into the maze of that company," Hilary went on, "as quietly as possible, to say the least. And in so doing he chanced upon the piece of news that concerns us—our very own Emil von Burchardt, it seems, is a product consultant for that organization, actually a vice-president in charge of international marketing, or some such title. Of course, that could mean just about anything."

"An impressive, though shady, dossier to have come up with in such a short time. Your man Murry must be quite a guy."

"He's a workhorse. I couldn't run the magazine without him," said Hilary.

"Considering von Burchardt's record," suggested Logan, "it's entirely possible that his so-called position could be little more than a front that allows him free movement all over the world."

"Exactly!" said Hilary.

"And that yacht of his is the perfect cover," added Ashley. "Who knows what he might be carrying in that thing?"

"He could easily be a liaison between the General and the more legitimate side of the operation," said Logan, thinking aloud.

"Which, as farfetched as it sounds, could be Trans Global," said Ashley.

"A big assumption, I realize," admitted Hilary. "But what a journalistic coup if it is true. Can you imagine the story?" Her eyes glistened with the thought.

"And you'd like to be there with Murry when it comes off the presses?" laughed Logan.

"I have a feeling my thirst for adventure will be sufficiently fulfilled right here."

"Where does Jo fit into all this?" asked Ashley.

"Unfortunately, that's all Murry has at the moment—just this connection between Emil and Trans Global. He's trying to find some other names that tie in. Whether we'll get a line on Jo and who she is and what part she plays, I don't know. He promised to call back the minute he has something more."

The small group fell silent.

"I don't know how all these fragments of information are going to tie together," said Logan at last. "But I have the strong sense that we are only beginning to unravel them. Where they will lead us in the end, only the Lord knows at present."

"Well, I need some air," announced Ashley. "Hilary . . . how about a stroll outside?"

"I have an even better idea," she replied.

56 ✵ A Ride

"WHY WON'T YOU tell me where we're going?" asked Ashley.

"You'll find out, all in good time! It's a mystery—you should enjoy being kept in the dark!"

At Hilary's insistence, she and Ashley had taken two horses out and were now crossing the desolate heath south of the castle. Jake had carefully saddled the two animals, checking their blankets twice for any foreign materials.

"I dinna want to see nae runaway creatures for the twa o' ye, Leddy Hilary," he said.

"The last time I took out one of the horses," she explained to Ashley, "I nearly broke my neck. Someone had put a thorn under my saddle when I left the horse for a few minutes. At least I do owe that much to Emil. He saved me from a horrible spill."

"Do you think they planned the whole thing?"

"Who knows? I'm now convinced she knew he was coming. It had to be the two of them I saw together in the woods. Then the next day he showed up just in time to rescue me and begin trying to charm me. Whether the thorn and the rescue were part of the scheme, or just a spur-of-the moment nicety on Jo's part, I don't know."

"They sure didn't let on they were acquainted. I'd never have guessed it at first, though as time went on and I watched them both more closely, I began to wonder about some things."

"Almost as secretive as you and my . . . father."

Ashley looked over at her. "It has a nice ring to it, Hilary," he said. "I truly am happy for you."

She reached across, took his outstretched hand, gave it a squeeze, then smiled. "Thank you."

"You know, what Jake said a while ago is true—you are a 'lady' now. How does it feel?"

Hilary did not respond for some time. The only sound to be heard was the rhythmic clip-clop of their horses' hooves over the damp earth.

"It's scary," she said at length. "Everything I resisted for so long is suddenly a part of me . . . who I am. It's not just the nobility itself, it's everything this family is, all it stands for—there's such a spiritual heritage. Scary . . . but I have to admit there's an excitement to it, too! What might God have in store for me as . . . as a Macintyre, a Duncan, a member of the Ramsey clan! Oh, that reminds me—I have to call Suzanne! She won't believe all this!"

"Suzanne?"

"Suzanne Heywood—a friend of mine. Daughter of a lord. You might have known him. She lives down in Brighton. But to answer your question, I don't really *feel* a lot different. But this will take a lot of sinking in. It's going to alter the way I view my job, my writing, my perspective on the country—everything!"

"You have time to get used to it," said Ashley comfortingly. "You've been through a great emotional upheaval."

Again they fell silent.

"You know," said Hilary at length, "you sit that horse pretty well. If I didn't know better, I would think you've spent some time in the saddle."

"Us renaissance men, who double as mystery writers, like to indulge in a wide range of experiences—grist for the mill, I believe it's called. Like riding horses and attending fashion shows."

"Will you ever cease amazing me? Well, I'm no horsewoman, I can tell you that. But I had such a good time the other day—before the thorn, that is. And the horses were always such an intrinsic part of Stonewycke. I thought it fitting that we go out for a ride."

"Then how about a little canter!" As he spoke Ashley urged his mare forward into a gentle trot. Hilary's mount followed.

"Ohhhh!" she yelled, hanging on to the horn as if for dear life.

Within another thirty minutes, with some perceptive pointers from Ashley, Hilary was becoming comfortable with the old-fashioned mode of transportation. They had traversed through the outlying farmlands southeast of the castle and were now circling south onto the bluff where only sparse vegetation was visible.

"Your question about my adaptation to life as a *lady* has other implications than just my life at Stonewycke," said Hilary as they rode along. "It also adds to my puzzlement of what I am to do with you in my thinking."

"Because you are a *lady*?"

"No. Because you are a lord."

"What has that to do with anything?"

"I don't like the aristocracy, remember?"

"Rather a difficult position to maintain now, I would think."

"Just because I have to accept myself as of noble birth doesn't mean I have to automatically change all my associations."

"I see. So you are going to continue holding my birth against me, even though I had no hand in planning it, but as for your case, you will allow yourself to be absolved completely?"

"I see nothing so unreasonable about that."

"Spoken with the logic of a woman," said Ashley, who then broke into a good-natured laugh.

"Ashley Jameson, you are determined to infuriate me!"

"Hilary, be reasonable. Jesus went about with the poor, with the middle class, and with the wealthy. Just as He did not hold poverty against a man, neither did He hold riches. How can we do any differently? God looks at every man's and every woman's heart, be they poor or rich. To discriminate against the nobility in attitude is as unacceptable to God as the rich keeping the poor downtrodden under their feet. Both are errors of extreme."

Hilary thought for several moments.

"I should know better than to expose my quirks to you, Ashley. How can you be so reasonable . . . and so right?"

"I've thought about these things."

"Do you think everything through?"

"I suppose I do."

"Why? Don't you ever just react spontaneously?"

"Of course I do. But even then, I think about my actions, even after the fact. It's part of my stewardship as a Christian. To me, every detail of life is to be submitted to Christ's lordship. Therefore, I have to think through the details of life so I can be aware of those areas where I need to focus my prayers more intently."

"I would not have known that about you just by looking."

"You once said you could tell I was a Christian by seeing how I did things. I'm glad of that. But at the same time, my faith is something I don't go spreading about all the time."

"Is that why you said nothing to me about it for so long?"

"I've always felt that matters of belief, heart attitudes, are an intensely personal thing. I'm not comfortable sharing on that level until I genuinely know someone, and they know me. Very few of my colleagues at Oxford know that I pray for them as I walk in their midst across campus, or that I start every day with prayer, or that my tiniest actions I hold up to scrutiny against the commands of the Bible. Those are personal things. It's not that I think any of them would laugh or consider me a kook. That hardly concerns me. It's simply that my priority in life is to *live* by what Jesus taught, to model my life after His, rather than to talk about spiritual truths. In other words, I want to live my faith first, talk about it second."

Again Hilary was silent. It was some time before she spoke again.

"Being with you is showing me many things about myself," she said quietly. "I've been a Christian for years. I take my faith seriously too. But I think I have never really weighed the necessity for taking my belief into the tiniest details of life, as you said. There has always been within me a—I don't know . . . a feeling, I guess, that God was in complete control of my life and everything in it."

"That's faith too. A wonderful, strong sense of His hand undergirding all of life. There's nothing wrong with that."

"Yet perhaps God does want more from me. More of that daily, moment-by-moment, detailed sort of awareness of what really comprises godly behavior—in *every* interaction, *every* attitude, *every* decision."

"I think He wants that from us all. That's why I do think through my actions and attitudes—as unspontaneous as it may seem! Because I think God is worthy of my dedication to Him at the deepest levels of everything I say and do and think."

"Ashley, you are something!" sighed Hilary. "I think I could very easily become attached to you!"

"I'm not sure how to take that," replied Ashley. "As I recall, you were rather taken with von Burchardt, and look at what he turned out to be."

"That's not fair! I wasn't taken by him for a minute! I couldn't stand the fellow. I was only trying to see what you would do."

Ashley threw his head back and laughed. "There's that woman's memory to go along with your woman's logic! Think now, Hilary. You couldn't stand me!"

"Well . . . maybe just for a while there I was a bit confused." She threw him a coy grin. "Oh, but look!" she exclaimed. "We're here!"

"Where are we?"

"This is where I wanted to bring you."

"All I see is a deserted hillside with nothing visible for miles."

"But that's the beauty of this place. Come this way. There's something I want to show you. As a historian, I'm sure you'll appreciate it."

"I still see nothing."

"The stones are obscure from this distance. They blend right in with the rest. But when we get closer, you'll be able to pick the ruins out easily."

"Ruins? I'm intrigued already!"

"Just wait till I tell you the story!"

57 ❊ *Lady Joanna's Quest*

LOGAN HAD BEEN watching impatiently for the return of the two riders. While they were still in the stable turning over their steeds to Jake, he rushed out to them.

"We have found the missing pages to the journal!" he said as he ran up. "I could hardly wait until you got here to read them!"

"Where . . . what do they say?" said Hilary all in a rush.

"I don't yet know what they say," answered Logan. "We decided to wait until we could all be together. Come . . . I'll answer your other questions on the way inside."

He led the way as the three crossed the lawn, entered at the kitchen door, and proceeded upstairs to the drawing room.

"It was Allison who unraveled this particular mystery," he said. "She was lying in bed, her mind idly wandering about over all the family stories. She wasn't even thinking about the journal at the time. She had been reflecting on her mother's coming to Scotland and the difficulties she had faced. Suddenly it came to her: Both Atlanta and Maggie had hidden very important items in the framing and backing of a favorite picture, actually a stitchery Maggie had done as a girl. Where else would Joanna have hidden something special in her life?"

"In Maggie's stitchery of the family tree!" exclaimed Hilary. "Of course! But where is it? I don't remember ever seeing it . . . though come to think of it there were some stitcheries in the heirloom room."

"Those are different ones. The family tree was hanging in Joanna's own room."

Logan chuckled. "Dear Joanna was a sly one!" he said. "A place so obvious, yet it was the last place we thought to look. I even had Ashley right there hunting in her secretary when what we sought was hanging on the wall just a few feet away all the while."

"So did you get it?" asked Hilary excitedly.

"Yes, yes! But not without having to pry apart Maggie's poor stitchery once again!"

By this time they had reached the drawing room. Entering, they saw Allison sitting on the divan, manuscript pages on her lap, tears streaming down her face.

"I couldn't help myself, Logan," she said. "I had to read Mother's words. Oh, it's so hard to have to live through it all again! But I suppose it's good for me too, for the Lord is working healing in my heart in so many ways already. I want you to read it to them . . . aloud."

Logan nodded, then walked to his wife, kissed her tenderly, and took the pages from her hand.

"Hilary, come . . . please," said Allison. "Won't you sit beside me for this?"

Hilary walked forward, sat down, and Allison took her hand. "Now then," said Allison, "we are ready."

Ashley found a seat. Then Logan took up the pages written in Joanna's fine script and began to read.

. . . whatever truth He chooses to reveal to me. What I am to do, He will make clear in His time. One thing I do know, that the Lord our God surrounds and protects and delivers them that are His people.

"That section makes little sense," said Logan. "It was apparently a continuation of something that came before."

"I am sure it continues just as it is from the end of the last page that I have," interjected Hilary. "Shall I go get it from my room?"

"Not now," answered Logan. "We can compare them later. The most important section—indeed, the reason I believe Joanna hid this portion of her journal—is still to come. I think she was fearful of the result should this have chanced to fall into the wrong hands."

"But she knew we would find it eventually," said Allison. "I know she knew, dear Mother! But go on, Logan. I want them to hear it."

"The next entry is dated September 16," said Logan. "But after that there are no more dates and the story flows together." He paused, took a deep breath, and began to read.

I could not have anticipated that the small act of opening a door could so alter the lives of so many. But when, on the evening of August 27, a young woman stepped out of the past and into our home, many unforeseen changes were immediately thrust upon us. Logan and Allison's daughter, as we had been told a week before, was suddenly come to life in the person calling herself Joanna Braithwaite. Our dear, lost Jo was suddenly restored to us after almost thirty years!

Oh, what a day of joy it should have been. And I cannot say I was not swept up in the exuberance at first. The atmosphere about Stonewycke was positively buoyant for days. I scarcely think I had seen Allison so happy in memory, especially when she and young Jo began to do things together—ride, paint, walk in the garden. I was happy for them, yet something began to eat away in my spirit, something I was reluctant to identify at first. The change came over me gradually. I might not have even noticed, or might have brushed it aside as irrelevant, except for that day—that single moment—in which a single unguarded look escaped from Jo's well-schooled demeanor.

Allison had pressed me to recount for Jo some of my experiences when I arrived in Port Strathy, also a stranger, after a long absence. I had been reluctant. In fact, since Jo's very coming I had been hesitant to share with her about our family history. I didn't know why; it was such a peculiar reaction for me to have. I never did mention my journal to her. But on that particular day Allison was persuasive, and I gave in and began to tell Jo about the events of that summer when I arrived at Stonewycke.

She listened attentively until I arrived at last to that fateful day of the town meeting in the meadow when Dorey came miraculously through the crowd to my side, and Alec galloped to our rescue a heroic knight, and how I gathered my courage to walk forward and denounce Jason Channing to his face, while Palmer Sercombe slunk away unnoticed. At that moment in the tale, I chanced to glance up at Jo, and the look on her face nearly struck me speechless. In her dark eyes flashed the venom of hatred. And as often as I recall the incident, I have not been able to account for it. Allison was seated so that she could not have seen it, and even had I attempted to describe it, I doubt Allison would have believed it possible. I might not have myself had I not been witness to it. Somehow I managed to finish the story, and by that time Jo was, to all appearances, back to normal.

After that it seemed my eyes were opened. I began to see so clearly through the facade that Jo presented so expertly. I began to wonder if those odd forebodings only hours before her arrival had been God's way of warning me, or at least preparing me for this terrible intrusion into our lives at Stonewycke.

But what could I do? Allison had completely accepted Jo as the daughter lost to her for thirty years. I could not blame her for that. All the documents had been verified. I hated myself at times for my suspicions. But just as I would be on the verge of thinking I had made up the reasons for my doubts, then I would see that flash from Jo's eyes again, as if warning me against causing a stir. There was something in her look I seemed almost to recognize, but I could never put my finger on it. Sometimes I even wondered if for some twisted reason, Jo purposefully revealed her true nature to me in these subtle ways, perhaps to encourage discord between myself and Allison and Logan, which it did in fact accomplish before long.

Finally, I could live with my doubts no longer. I approached Logan. I hoped I could reason with him. And I could not blame him for becoming upset. I had no facts, only the vague feelings of an old woman. Everyone—the maids, the neighbors, the village children—was taken with Jo. I stood alone with my doubts. But I knew as long as they plagued me, I could not live with them. I knew at last that I must find proof of some kind, either that she was or she was not who she claimed to be. I had to know.

That was when it occurred to me that the best proof—if indeed Jo was not their daughter—was to find the real daughter. If Jo had documentation stating that she had lived through the crash, then perhaps the real daughter was alive. I knew that the whole charade could have been made up and that it could turn out that my granddaughter really had died as we had long thought. Yet Jo had so many facts correct that cast no small amount of truth upon her tale. It certainly seemed to bear investigating.

Where was I to begin? I had no knowledge in such matters. Therefore I spoke one day, using only generalities, to our local constable—a man whose discretion I could trust, especially after I swore him to secrecy.

"How does one go about finding a missing person?" I asked him.

"Weel, m'lady," he said, "they ought to be missin' for twenty-four hoors afore the police can do anythin'. But in yer case, perhaps—"

"It has been much longer than that."

"That bein' the case, I can fill oot a report."

"I'm afraid it has been many years," I said. "I doubt a report would be of much help." I could not help feeling rather sorry for him trying to make anything of my cryptic explanations. "I'm not even sure the person is alive," I added.

"Hmmm . . . 'tis a puzzler, to be sure, m'lady." He paused and scratched his stubby beard. "Noo, on the television," he went on, "they're always hirin' them private investigators— private eyes, ye ken."

I smiled. "I hardly watch much television these days." The mere thought of me, at eighty-one, traipsing all over who knows where with someone dressed like Humphrey Bogart was too bizarre. Especially when I was looking for a needle in a haystack—a needle that might not even exist.

But in the end I found myself asking for his advice in securing such a man, as silly as I felt to do so. He put me in touch with a friend of his from Glasgow, a good man who had been a policeman but retired early because of an injury to his foot, taking up the less demanding occupation of private detecting. We arranged our first meeting in Culden. I had Logan drive me there to visit a friend, and at my friend's house, I first met Caleb.

Logan paused to smile at the memory. "Why, the cagy old fox!" he said to himself. "She put that over on me but good!" He then went on.

If ever God directed my steps in this old-age adventure of mine, it was in the finding of Caleb Boyle, a faithful and trustworthy friend. He could instantly upon hearing my story have written me off as a senile old woman. Sometimes I even had doubts about my sanity myself! But Caleb took me seriously, believed in me, and worked like a stout horse on my behalf.

It was his suggestion that we forget for the time being trying to discredit Jo, and concentrate instead on discovering whether another daughter—the true daughter—was indeed still alive. To do this I had to take us back thirty years and relive that awful nightmare of the day our little Joanna was lost. It was not easy for me to keep making excuses about my unexplained absences, and the travel was taxing, but I felt I had to go back in time myself, and lay my eyes again on the places involved, hoping something—miraculously—would present itself that we had overlooked before.

The incredible story told by Jo's solicitors contained so many details which rang true, I could only conclude that they had truly made contact with Hannah Whitley at some time after her call to Logan in London. Whether she actually changed her mind about talking to him, or else spoke to someone perhaps she shouldn't have in an unguarded moment, I don't know. The fact remained that poor Hannah was never heard from again, and then Jo appeared at Stonewycke with a story based entirely on Hannah's testimony. Therefore, we began with the assumption that much of Jo's story was true, and then went back to attempt a reconstruction of events ourselves to see if we might get on a track Jo's people had not taken into account.

What was always curious about Jo's story was the lack of detail. I sat in a couple of times on discussions Logan had with the solicitors, prior to her coming. And though I said nothing, it struck me that none of the people involved knew exactly where the events following the crash had taken place.

Thus, as Caleb and I began looking into the matter, I knew we had one fact no one else did—I had been there during the crash. If only, I thought, I could remember something that had not surfaced before!

We went to the site of the accident. Many changes had taken place in the ensuing years. The railway now bypassed that area, running five miles to the south. I have strong doubts that Jo's people ever located the crash site, because it took us days to do so ourselves. Over and over we rode as I scanned the surroundings. But nothing seemed familiar. All at once, Caleb thought to check with the railroad. That is when we discovered about the line being changed. We hadn't seen anything because we were on an altogether different track! Caleb managed to uncover a thirty-year-old map of the area, and finally we drove to the site of the old ammunition dump. It was of course no longer there, but the moment we were in the vicinity, I knew we had come to the right place. What a thrill it was when we stepped out of Caleb's automobile and walked over to the old track bed where once the train had gone, now grown over with weeds and brush.

Two days we spent close by the crash site. Caleb applied no pressure, but drove me about, walked with me, let me look and think and remember. And gradually images of that fateful day began to come back to me. I recalled certain farmhouses I had seen from the train window just before the bombing, and then when at last Caleb and I came upon the pretty little stone bridge with the stream beneath it, and a matching stone cottage just beyond, I knew we had found the exact spot. "This is it, Caleb!" I shouted. "I remember! We passed this bridge just before the explosion!"

It was a long shot, Caleb said (his colorful language is so intriguing!). But he began to canvas the entire area, walking to every farmhouse within sight. Most of the residents had come since the bombing. Others remembered but had seen nothing. Some had been little children at the time and their memories were garbled and dreamlike and of little use. The lady in the stone cottage with thatched roof, however, remembered the day clearly and had heard rumors from the direction of the village to the north about survivors who had been seen wandering about.

The time came when I had to return to Stonewycke. But Caleb diligently continued his painstaking survey of the area. I did what I discreetly could to inquire how much Jo's lawyers had actually learned from Hannah and whether she was still in contact with them. But in neither attempt did I find out anything new. I am, I fear, worried about Hannah.

One day Caleb telephoned me. I will never forget his words. "I have news," he said. "Big news. Go down to the town and call me back when you can talk." If I hadn't been so anxious to hear what he had to say, and had the situation not been so tense, I probably would have enjoyed all Caleb's cloak-and-dagger precautions. But I was too nervous to have fun.

"I found them!" he said excitedly the moment I had him back on the line from the phone at the Bluster 'N Blow. "An older couple. They knew nothing about a train wreck or a bombing. Their little farm is miles away! There is no way anyone else could have found these people! They are in the exact opposite direction from the new train line, and two miles from the town."

"If they know nothing about the crash," I said, "then what have you found out from them?"

"Just this," said Caleb; "they woke up one morning thirty years ago to find a lost, bewildered little girl sleeping in a pile of straw just inside their barn door. They took her in, but had no idea where she'd come from. The child talked about a nurse bringing her there, but the old couple saw no evidence of anyone else, could make out nothing more of the child's story, and eventually took her to a shelter in the town."

"My granddaughter is alive!" I exclaimed, hardly able to breathe. "Oh, Caleb, how will I ever be able to thank you?"

"You can save your thanks until I find her for you," the dear man replied .

"And what now?" I asked, hardly able to contain my joy.

"I'm off right now to the shelter. I'm going to go through their records and follow every lead until I find your granddaughter, Lady MacNeil. I can smell it. I know we're getting close!"

As I hung up the phone I'm afraid I felt too much like screaming for happiness to be able to go back to the estate. Instead, I went for a walk down along the shore to collect my thoughts. It was then that I decided that I should continue to keep my quest secret, even from Logan and Allison, until I knew for certain where it would end. In due time they must be told, but not until I had the full story. In the meantime I determined to be more faithful than ever to my journal and to write down what we were learning. Whether my decision will prove to be a wise one, only time will tell.

Logan paused in his reading to take a deep breath and glance around the room. On the divan Hilary's head rested on her mother's shoulder and Allison wept softly. In a voice which seemed to indicate that had he not had to continue reading, he too would likely have given way to tears, Logan continued with Joanna's words.

The records Caleb found were scanty, but they did speak of the child that had been found, and then documented her later placement in a London orphanage. He followed the trail to London, where the course of events became difficult to trace in that there were several orphanages involved, one of which had been closed down in 1946. Why more was not done to locate the parents of these children lost during the war, I do not know. But there was much confusion, many records had been destroyed, shelters and orphanages set up during the war were temporary at best, and in our case, because of the reports following the crash, we never even considered that our young Joanna Hilary could be alive.

How thankful I am for dear Caleb for disproving that error once and for all! After many weeks in London, he gained the following information. First, he had surprisingly run across some scanty news of Hannah again. She had apparently been hospitalized in a delirious state in the same town to which the child had been taken. She was sent to London for more thorough care, lay in a hospital for some time, and when she was finally released was suffering from amnesia. Caleb could find out no more about her, and everything else we know has come from the direction of Jo's solicitors.

Secondly, in London Caleb eventually isolated five possible candidates from the records of the final placement papers for children during the time period in question, of the right age. I interviewed two of these before the fateful moment, just three days ago, when I walked into the offices of The Berkshire Review.

The moment I laid eyes on Hilary, I knew she was my granddaughter. I'm sure God was causing the truth to leap within my mother's heart, yet one look in her face sent the truth shouting at me as well. There, in a glance, I could see my dear grandmother, Lady Margaret, and so vividly the features of my own daughter Allison. And yes, not a little of my own face as well! Such a beautiful young woman she was, reflecting the very heritage of which she was a part, yet which she did not know.

If only Allison and Logan could lay eyes upon Hilary, I thought, then they would know beyond any doubts. Yet then I realized that Jo's face, too, contains many similarities to Hilary's—uncannily so. It causes me to wonder how long this deception has been planned.

I want so desperately to tell of my discovery to Logan and Allison. But Hilary has asked me to wait and I will honor her wish. In the meantime, I am not sure what to do about Jo. Is she an impostor? Or is she but the victim of a regrettable error?

I do not want to push, yet I am anxious for this affair to end and for truth to prevail. I feel more fatigued than I have in a long while. Inside there is a glorious contentment in my heart. I am joyful, exhilarated. Part of me feels young again, just in the memory of those moments of reunion with Hilary. Yet another part of me is very tired. That part of me wants only to embrace my dear granddaughter again, and then have a long rest.

As he read the final words, Logan could contain himself no longer. Tears overflowed his eyes and he wept without shame.

After a moment he laid the papers aside, then walked softly toward his wife and daughter. He fell to his knees on the floor before them, clasped each of their hands, and—gazing first deeply into Allison's face, then into Hilary's, with a huge tear-stained smile on his own—said, "Thank God! . . . Thank you, Lord, for preserving our precious heritage . . . in spite of our own weakness!"

58 ❈ *Pieces Fall Together*

"HOW I WISH I hadn't been so reluctant to accept grandmother's revelation," said Hilary, "so that I would have been able to embrace her again."

Logan had taken a chair opposite the divan, and Ashley had left the room, thinking the family should share this time alone.

"We all had our reluctance and our blindness," said Logan. "I as much as anyone."

"That is all past," said Allison. "Now we can rejoice that half of Mother's final wish was fulfilled—for she has indeed now found eternal rest with her Lord."

A brief silence followed; then Allison spoke again, voicing a thought that had only just then occurred to her.

"Mother's journal is complete," she said. "I feel as if an era has ended. I cannot help but be saddened. Yet I see now that this journal was Mother's life's work. It truly counted for something important, perhaps more than we will ever know."

"I have no doubt," said Logan, "that it will reach into the future and deeply touch yet unborn members of this clan."

"Might Lady Joanna have even wanted it to continue beyond her lifetime in a more tangible way?" suggested Hilary. "This journal is so rich, not only in family history, but in a documentation of events to do with this land, with Stonewycke, with the Strathy Valley, and especially in capturing the spiritual perspectives that have been woven in and through the lives of such a diverse range of individuals. Might it not be a legacy, in its own way, to be passed on to the two of you, in order to continue the keeping of the family record—an ongoing tribute to Grandmother's dream?"

"I hadn't thought of that," Allison replied.

"It's a great idea!" said Logan. "Hilary, you are the writer. I think Joanna's journal would be best left in your hands. She passed it on to you for a reason. A good one, I think. Who knows how many lives might be blessed by the events recorded by Joanna through the years if you were able to chronicle the story in a more organized way."

"Do you really think so?" asked Hilary, thrilled at the very prospect. "But I have been so removed from events for so long. I wonder if I am qualified?"

Allison again took Hilary's hand in hers. "For years," she said, "an unusual phenomenon has operated in this family. I have thought about it often and have wondered why it has been so. When I question the Lord concerning it, He repeatedly drives me back to the principle in Scripture of the desert as symbolizing the purifying time of preparation. Moses was exiled in the desert to ready him to lead his people out of bondage. Then the children of Israel spent forty years in the desert to prepare and humble them for the taking of the promised land. After his conversion, Paul spent years in the desert as the Lord prepared and strengthened him for his ministry. And before His public preaching and teaching began, Jesus spent forty days in the wilderness."

As she spoke, Allison's countenance took on a distant look, as if she were gazing down the long span of history. "All this may seem far removed from Stonewycke," she continued, bringing her attention back to the present, "but the principle still applies. I am the only woman since Atlanta who has lived here at Stonewycke, or even in Scotland, continuously since birth. And even I was emotionally separated from my heritage for several years. Maggie and Joanna were in America for large parts of their lives. You spent thirty years in London, separated even from the knowledge of your roots. But I believe God uses those times of exile to strengthen the legacy of what this family has come to represent, to deepen within us our love for the land, and especially to cement our faith in a mighty and loving God."

Allison paused, gazing deep into her daughter's eyes with a look of love that had not before now passed between them, the love not only of a mother but also of sisterhood. "Hilary," she concluded, "I think you will find that your separation makes you as much one with us as anything possibly could. However, it is a family characteristic that I pray will be passed on no further."

"Thank you, Mother," said Hilary, tears forming in her eyes again. She leaned over and put her arms around Allison, and both women wept together.

A soft knock on the door temporarily interrupted the family gathering. Logan immediately stood and answered it.

"I'm sorry to disturb ye, sir," said Flora, "but Miss Hilary's got another telephone call."

Reluctantly Hilary rose and followed the housekeeper out. By the time she reached the library, her equilibrium was restored and she was able to present a normal voice to Murry on the other end.

She returned about ten minutes later to the drawing room. Ashley was now with Logan and Allison.

"Your associate on the magazine again?" asked Logan when she entered.

Hilary nodded. "With some additional information. Although none of it makes much sense to me."

"Don't keep us in suspense," said Logan eagerly.

"Basically all Murry had for me this time was a list of names." She turned back a few pages in her notebook. "These are other prominent figures in Trans Global's hierarchy. If Emil is tied in to TGE, then perhaps other of Jo's accomplices are as well."

"The only accomplices I could think of would be the lawyers," said Logan. "I had them checked and rechecked, and everything appeared on the up-and-up. But I did not know at the time to investigate whether there might be ties to TGE. That is something we should do immediately. But let me see your list, Hilary. Perhaps something will ring a bell."

He reached over, and Hilary handed him the open notebook. Logan sat back and scanned the list of about ten names.

Suddenly Logan froze, his eyes fastened to the seventh name on the list. After a moment's hesitation, he shook his head in disbelief, took his reading glasses from his pocket, put them on, and read the name again.

He stared at the sheet of paper. How could it be? But there the name was in the middle of the list, like a ghost from the past!

It couldn't be! No one could possibly know!

Slowly he looked up and glanced around at the others.

"This is incredible!" he said slowly. "A mere coincidence, perhaps . . . yet something tells me . . . "

Still shaking his head, he held the notebook up for them to see, pointing to the seventh entry.

"This is a name I have not heard or seen for thirty years!"

"Who is it?" asked Hilary.

"It is no one," he replied. "A fictitious nonentity."

"Then what did the name mean when you knew of it back then?" asked Ashley.

Logan drew in a deep breath, then exhaled as he answered, "It was *me*!" he said incredulously. "Monsieur Dansette, merchant from Casablanca, a man without even a first name, a supposed Nazi sympathizer. The man never existed. It was a cover I used during the war while I was in France . . . a cover conferred upon me by an officer in the SS . . . a *general*!"

"Logan, what are you saying?"

"Perhaps I am making a quantum leap here, based on mere speculation. But instinct tells me differently. The name is just as we used it back then! Yet, why would he resurrect that name? You would think he would make every attempt to erase all possible links to the past."

"Who, Logan?" asked Hilary.

"His name was—or is?—Martin von Graff. SS officer and escaped war criminal. If he is still alive, he'd have to be in his late seventies, early eighties . . . " He stopped and thought for a moment. "But now that I recall," he went on, "I remember reading a report from the Israelis several years ago listing him as dead. I thought then that that segment of my life was officially behind me completely."

"Could he be alive . . . could he have masterminded Jo's deception?"

"He certainly would have had motive," answered Logan. "Motive against me, at least. I'm afraid my activities put quite a black mark on his SS record. I heard that following my escape from France, von Graff was suddenly transferred to the Russian front. He would have had plenty of motive to seek revenge."

"There was also the matter of my rescuing you from his firing squad," put in Allison.

"And no small caper it was, my dear!" laughed Logan. "Yet I just can't see von Graff coming against us after all this time. As insidious and subtle as he could be, he was still from the old school. A man of some honor, I always felt, lurked beneath that Nazi skin. Had circumstances been different, I could even have imagined us friends. Had he wanted revenge, I would have thought him the type to choose a more direct approach—pistols at dawn, that sort of thing. After what we did to him, he had every reason to hate us, that is true, but . . . "

He shook his head. Something still didn't fit. When he continued, his voice sounded like one debating within himself.

"The Mossad are pretty thorough about their war criminals. If they say he is dead, then I would think it must be true."

"Yet here is a name," reasoned Ashley, "a major executive in a company with links to a criminal called 'The General.' It makes one wonder."

"And," added Hilary, "Emil von Burchardt, Jo's own accomplice, sits right in the middle of it, with known ties to the Nazis. It would appear von Graff could be behind it. But we must not forget whom we are really after."

"I wonder . . . " Logan rubbed his chin, his mind racing with the staggering possibilities. "It is entirely conceivable that Jo is only a soldier, dispatched to perform a task in the cause of the General. If that is the case, then it truly is *The General,* whoever he is, whom we are after."

"I think you may be right, Logan," said Hilary. "But I cannot forget that look I saw in Jo's eyes when she discovered me in the gallery. It was just as Lady Joanna described. It was not the look of a mere underling. For some reason, I am sure Jo has a personal stake in all this."

Later that afternoon Logan walked alone into the library.

He had made several phone calls, one of which had confirmed that his information about von Graff was correct—the Nazi general was dead.

Where does that leave me? Logan wondered. *Where could the name Dansette possibly have come from? What is the connection to this modern-day general? Might von Graff have used the name Dansette before his death, which reports confirmed to have occurred in 1959? Why, then, did the name remain on the company roster? Why had von Graff used the pseudonym at all, if he had indeed used it?*

Logan leaned back in his chair at the library desk, laced his fingers together behind his head, and allowed his mind to wander once more over the discussion of earlier with Hilary, Ashley, and Allison.

The General . . . Nazis in hiding after the war . . . von Graff . . . Trans Global Enterprises . . . an attempt to infiltrate the estate, their very lives, with an impostor . . . revenge . . .

How were all these factors related?

More importantly, how were they connected to Stonewycke, especially with von Graff dead? He seemed the only link tying Dansette and the General to Stonewycke. Yet he had been gone twelve years, and the plot against them hatched only recently.

Logan's mind drifted further back. . . .

SS Headquarters, Paris. . . . There came into his memory the scene of von Graff entertaining his protege Lawrence MacVey. The suave, urbane aristocrat staking his entire reputation as a Nazi on an ex-con man. Yes, von Graff had reason to be bitter . . . but he was dead.

All at once the panorama of Logan's thoughts widened.

They were not alone in that elegant SS office. Another man was there, not dressed in a uniform at all, whose chilly presence Logan began to feel even before he moved out of the shadows of Logan's memory into view. But as he stepped forward, he seemed to emerge from further out of the distant past than Logan's thoughts could take him.

Jason Channing!

Logan snapped upright in his chair. Could it be possible?

The notion was unthinkable! Yet Channing always seemed to turn up in the life of Stonewycke, his malicious figure perpetually lurking in the shadows like a tiger stalking its prey.

Without a shred of proof, without a scrap of evidence, in that moment Logan knew beyond any doubt who was his adversary. It *had* to be Channing who had leveled this latest attack against his old nemesis. But the man would have to be a hundred years old! Logan would never forget the fire in Channing's eyes that day he had been foiled in the guardhouse of Fort Montrouge. As love and honor sustain Godly men, so do malice and vengeance possess and sustain men who give themselves over to evil.

Yes, the whole twisted masquerade of Jo's deception and attempted poisoning of Allison reeked with the malevolent aroma of Jason Channing!

There could be no doubt . . . the man was alive!

He had not forgotten that hideous day which had tormented him for sixty years, when a shy, untried girl had thwarted his greedy scheme and denounced him boldly in front of hundreds of witnesses.

Channing would *never* forget! And the memory would goad him until he tasted revenge.

59 ❊ *Parental Vile*

SHE HAD ALMOST forgotten what the heat in Buenos Aires could be like at this time of the year. Leaving the winter of northern Scotland to find herself suddenly in the middle of a southern hemispheric heat wave was shock enough. Dread for the reaction awaiting her, however, was an even worse torment.

Jo dabbed her damp forehead for the third time as Emil wheeled the Jaguar around the final curve of the drive up to the villa. Ahead she could see the tile-roofed main house of the villa's sprawling complex. Well, she thought with a sigh, home at last.

The flight from London had been ghastly enough, exhausting after their hurried departure from Scotland, though she should have been grateful to have gotten out of the country at all. Then they had been delayed at the airport due to some mix-up with what little luggage they had. Finally, the ride to the villa had been hot and uncomfortable, no matter that they had picked up Emil's Jaguar in the city and driven in some elegance. But however she looked at it, home was not a welcome sight. After all, her mission had not been successful. She looked over at Emil, who was now braking in front of the empty fountain that stood before the house.

"You will go in with me, won't you?" she asked with uncharacteristic nervousness in her tone.

He glanced over as if the request surprised him, then gave his moustache a careless pat. He is looking rather superior and smug, she thought, especially for one who has failed no less than I.

"Well?" said Jo crossly.

"My dear, you are more than capable of handling this yourself." He paused to turn off the ignition. "Besides, he will only think less of you if you display weakness now."

"And what about you! No last-minute heroics?"

Von Burchardt smiled. "I do not have as much at stake, now do I, my dear *Jo*?"

"I do not want to hear that name again—ever!"

Angrily she pushed the door open and jerked herself from the car. "Don't think you will get off scot-free, *my dear*!" She slammed the door and stalked away toward the house.

Kicking the dust up toward one of the dry cactus plants that bordered either side of the walk, she approached the door. The servants had seen the Jaguar approach, and now a houseboy opened the door to welcome her deferentially.

She inquired about *El Patron*. The boy's face turned solemn.

"El señor has taken to his bed, señorita," he said.

Jo's brow creased—whether with concern or disguised relief, it would have been difficult to determine.

"How long ago?" she asked, increasing her pace.

"Two days, senorita."

"How bad?"

"Not bad. Only weak. The doctor, he come twice a day."

"Send someone out to get my things from the car and then take them to my room. I will want to be alone with El Patron for a while. Comprendes?"

"Sí, señorita, yo comprendo!" replied the servant, who then hurried off to be about his assigned tasks.

She continued on her way, traversed a long corridor, arriving at last to a closed door. She paused, took in one last deep breath as if preparing for her fate, then raised her hand to rap briskly on the door.

"Who is it?" came a weak but still gruff voice from inside.

Instead of answering, she turned the latch and entered.

The room was dark, the drawn shades allowing in only tiny splinters of the sunlight from outside. Even though a ceiling fan was churning overhead, the air was stifling—both hot and too well used. Without waiting for her eyes to accustom themselves to the subdued light, she walked straight but calmly to the bed and bent down near the figure lying there with covers pulled up about his chin.

"I'm back," she said.

The notion crossed her mind briefly of giving the wrinkled cheek a kiss, but she thought better of it.

Jason Channing's eyes flew open and glared wrathfully at her.

"How dare you!" he cried, though his fury lost a great deal of its intended menace as it passed through his debilitated, ancient vocal chords. "How dare you come and show your face!" fumed the old man.

"I'm sorry I failed," she replied, with attempted contriteness.

"Don't put on that sweet vulnerability! I know it is a mere act! Remember, I am the one who paid to give you the best lessons money could buy."

"Then, what would you have me do?" she said, a hard edge now in her voice. "Shall I slit my throat for you right here?"

"For all you have given me, it might be a good start!" Channing's tone was cold, giving no evidence that his words were anything but what he intended.

She turned and walked a couple paces from the bed.

"I should have made my getaway the moment that woman showed up," she said petulantly. "Everything was going so well until then. But I knew how important this was to you, so I stuck it out—"

"You ran at the first sign of trouble!"

"I stayed well beyond the limits of safety!" she countered, spinning around to face the bed again.

"I thought you had more guts than that!"

"To the very last instant I even tried to pour the poison down her throat, but Emil—"

"Bah! You flew like a frightened rabbit!" shouted Channing, rising shakily from his pillow. "You ran like the cowardly swine you are!"

She sucked in a ragged breath. She had known this was coming, but was still not quite prepared for it.

"I did the best I could," she said.

"Well, it wasn't good enough!" he shrieked.

"It never is!" she hissed bitterly.

Channing shifted in his bed and tried to hitch himself up on the pillows, swearing angrily when the activity exhausted him.

"Curse those fool doctors!" he muttered, "coming in here with their antiquated remedies to do nothing but weaken me and keep me in this absurd bed! Blast them all!"

She reached her hand around his shoulder to help him. The action seemed to mitigate his anger momentarily. He shook his head mournfully.

"All that work," he moaned. "Two years! Plastic surgeons and theatrical coaching for you . . . buying off those muddleheaded lawyers . . . setting the plan up in such detail—all wasted! What a poetic victory it would have been!"

"It may not be too late, Father."

But Channing waved an impatient hand. "Does it matter anymore?" he lamented. "I thought we had them when I learned about that old crazy woman—what was her name? Whitley . . . something Whitley—the loony old woman trying to get up her nerve to tell the Macintyres about their daughter. It was my moment!" He sank back, his voice losing its force. "Now it looks like I had the old goose put away for nothing. But what does it matter? She's beaten me again!"

"It was a beautiful plan, Father," she said, sitting down on the edge of the bed.

"A coup!" he rejoined, half rising again. "The coup of the century! Installing my own daughter as the unknown heiress to their precious Stonewycke! I could have gone to my grave a contented man. But that snip of a Joanna Matheson did it to me again!"

"Perhaps we can yet undo what she has done."

But Channing was no longer listening. Hearing the name from his own lips that he had hundreds of times vowed should never pass from his mouth again seemed to send him into a trance. Suddenly he was many miles and many years removed from the Villa del Heimat.

"Oh, Joanna," he moaned. "Why do you hate me so?"

"I do not hate you, Father."

"I don't mean you, you fool!" spat Channing, lurching back to the present only long enough to denounce his own daughter for her stupidity. "I mean *Joanna* . . . the only woman I ever loved!"

"What about my mother?" Jo shot back. "And what about me?"

"Your *mother*"—Channing's lips twisted cruelly around the word—"was a mere convenience. I did, after all, need to be respectable among my peers. You were the result of that union—my only joy, my only hope for—"

"For what?" Jo spat the words at him. "For revenge against Stonewycke? How can you speak of *love*? You have never loved me—you have only used me. I doubt that you ever for a moment really loved your precious Joanna Matheson! You only wanted to possess her, to use her the way you use—"

"Shut up! Why else do you think I gave you her name? It's *her*, I tell you! *She's* the cause of all the grief that has ever come to me!"

Again his eyes glassed over. He continued to gaze at his daughter, but his voice had again passed backward in time, erasing six decades in an instant of his own dementia.

"I could have given you everything, Joanna," he said, his voice rising with passion. "The world was mine! Together we could have reigned over it. But no! Your damnable pride would not be broken! You and your stiff-necked notions of honor! You and that oaf of a ridiculous manure-tromping lout you called a man! Hah! Oh, Joanna, how could you have been so blind! What possessed you to say those things about me to the town? I hated you that day! But in that very act you showed what you were made of. Ironic, isn't it, my dear? The day I swore eternal vengeance against you was the very day my heart was forever spoiled for another. That day I despised you, yet I also knew I could have no other woman. How I hated you, but could not live without you. Joanna . . . Joanna—"

"Father," broke in Jo sharply. "You mustn't go on like this!"

Jolted as if slapped in the face, Channing stared at her blankly, trying to focus his bewildered eyes.

"And stop looking at me like that! I am not that Joanna. It's enough that I have to bear her name. Don't speak to me as if I were her! She is dead. And I wish to heaven all the rest of her brood were dead too!"

"Dead?" repeated Channing, still stupefied.

"Dead! Do you hear me?"

"She will never die," he said softly, his face contorting in the macabre agony of his self-inflicted insanity. "You will not die before . . . before . . . I—"

Jo watched with horrified fascination, aware that Channing was losing all grip on reality.

"I can see you . . . Joanna, you will not go away . . . before you and I . . ."

His voice trailed away and he glanced toward the door as if looking for someone.

"Perhaps you are right," mused Jo icily, almost to herself. "She lives on in that daughter of hers—Allison Macintyre—still sitting on that hill, mistress of all she surveys! Gloating over their victory! Sitting where *I* should be sitting! I have borne that hateful name, cursing it every day of my life! Stonewycke should have been mine!"

Without warning Channing's dulled eyes suddenly came into focus and he was himself again.

"They do not know I was behind the masquerade?"

"Of course not," replied Jo. "But they still hold Stonewycke."

"Yes . . . yes." Channing's eyes narrowed, his head rolling from side to side, agitated. "They still hold Stonewycke, but perhaps they have not won yet. I hate them . . . I hate *her* more than them all! I will yet vanquish them! I will not rest! Oh, what a pleasure it would be to break her proud spirit . . . and then watch her die!"

"For me the moment of triumph would be to grind that pompous Hilary under my foot in the dirt!"

"There might yet be time . . . "

Channing closed his eyes as his features grew taut, while evil machinations consumed his thoughts. His aging brain was once more sharp and in control.

"I want her!" he cried passionately at last, rising from the pillow. "Bring her to me! Ha, ha! I will find a way to crush them yet!"

"*We* will find a way," said Jo. "We will have our revenge or die. Neither will I rest until it is done."

"Get back up there immediately! But be on your guard. This time they will be alert for trouble."

"I will be wary. Don't worry. I know every inch of the place."

"I *am* lucky to have a daughter such as you," said Channing, in a voice not of love but rather shared cunning. His pinched lips twisted briefly into what might have been interpreted as the semblance of a smile. He grasped her hand in his and closed his eyes, for the moment assuaged in the delicious taste of anticipated revenge.

60 ✠ Father and Daughter

EVEN AS CHANNING and his daughter were planning the final act in a diabolic and empty vendetta, their chief adversary puzzled over his own role in this unsought drama of hate and retribution.

Logan sat alone in the loft above the stables.

He still could not believe it was Channing! The man's malice against the Duncan clan had spanned six decades, growing each year like an unchecked cancer, never healing, becoming more and more destructive with age, leaving only misery, perhaps even death, in its evil wake.

It had to stop!

Not only for the sake of Logan's family, but for the future of Stonewycke, Port Strathy, his own posterity . . . and perhaps most of all for the sake of Channing himself. He had to be rotting inside—both physically and spiritually—from the effects of his own pernicious hate.

No longer, Logan now realized, could he sit passively and allow it to continue. Channing was a dangerous man who had wrought much havoc in the world through his greed. Unless it were stopped, his organization would continue to plunder and destroy lives long after the General's death. The entire network had to be broken.

Whether there was hope for Channing himself, only God could know. In himself, Logan doubted it. But that could not alter his course. What God put in his hand to do, he must do, however unlikely results might appear. There was always the possibility God intended him to be the instrument of the man's repentance.

Notwithstanding spiritual concerns, however, Channing had to be stopped. There was no question about what had to be done. The problem was *how* to go about it without being ensnared by the vicious workings of Channing's machinery, which appeared to have arms and eyes and ears everywhere.

Logan spoke to the Chief Inspector of the London branch of Interpol. They wanted the General and would do whatever it took to get him, but they had already been futilely on his cold track for twenty years.

"These things take time," said the CI regretfully. "He works entirely through blind intermediaries. Probably no more than a handful of men have ever *seen* him, and these are so bloody loyal that even if we managed to get our hands on one, we'd have him dropping on the floor with half a cyanide tablet falling out of his mouth before we got a word out of him."

"You need something—or someone—to bring him out in the open," suggested Logan.

"And I need a secluded little spot on the Riviera and a fifty-foot yacht!" scoffed the detective. "But I doubt I'll live long enough to get them."

"I have a plan."

"You, Mr. Macintyre? Sleuthing about in our bailiwick, that's hardly in the province of Members of Parliament, is it?"

"Do you want the General or not, Mr. Rollins?"

"I want him!"

"Enough to give me carte blanche?"

"I don't know . . . there are dangers—"

"I can get him for you. The man and his methods are not entirely unknown to me—"

"You know the identity of the General!"

"Let me put it this way: I have a strong and educated speculation."

"Then you must tell us!"

"Not yet. I have an idea, but I must work alone—one whiff of the law, as it were, and his inner circle will bolt so fast it will take another twenty years to ferret him out again."

"This is highly irregular."

"*Regular* methods have yet to be successful."

"That is true." Rollins paused in thought. "I'll bring the matter before my superiors. One more question: are we to be absolutely uninvolved, or may we arrange for discreet backup?"

"I will not turn down a safety net, but it must be *very* discreet, and utterly invisible. One more thing—there may be some problems with extradition. That is something you could look into and help me on."

"Consider it done."

"Good," Logan replied briskly. "I'll get back to you tomorrow," he added, hanging up the telephone before the man could protest further.

That had been two hours ago, and Logan now wondered about his assumed confidence on the phone.

A plan indeed!

He didn't even know where to find Channing! He could be anywhere from Siberia to Monte Carlo for all he knew, although Logan had been giving the location of the man's hiding place a great deal of thought.

Of one thing he was confident. He *would* have a plan. He *would* come up with something, and somehow he *would* put a stop to this sixty-year war Channing seemed intent on waging.

He leaned back in Digory's old chair and closed his eyes.

Dear God, Logan prayed silently, *keep my heart pure. Don't let me fall prey to the very malignancy I am trying to halt. Give me wisdom, O Lord. Guide my path. Open my eyes to subtleties and details I might otherwise overlook. And somehow, Lord, as difficult as it is to say, I pray too for Jason Channing. Infiltrate his twisted heart with your Spirit that the man may see the futility of his bitterness. And make me willing to be your instrument in the answering of that prayer.*

Logan heard a soft rap on the rough wooden door, and opened his eyes.

"Come in," he said, looking up. He smiled when he saw Hilary.

"Allison said you might be here," she said. "I hope you don't mind my intruding."

"Not at all."

"I have never seen this place, and I thought it might be a good spot to talk, though it could have waited."

"I'm glad you came. I am happy to share my great-great uncle's little home with you. But then Digory is your uncle too—let's see, how many greats would that be? I tend to lose track." He laughed.

"What was he to us exactly?"

"He was my mother's great uncle. Brother to her great-grandfather MacNab. He never married. His possessions went to my mother's grandfather when he died, and later to her, where they remained buried for years in an old trunk."

"Until you came along?"

"Almost," laughed Logan. "But that's another story!"

"You'll tell me someday?" said Hilary with an affectionate smile. "That is one area where Lady Joanna's journal is a bit scant on detail."

"No doubt!" rejoined Logan. "Yes, perhaps one day I shall tell you all about my discoveries and my coming to Stonewycke. There's Digory's Bible," he added, pointing to a small table. "I keep it here—sentimental reasons, you know."

Slowly Hilary walked over and picked up the ancient black volume. She held it silently for a few moments.

"This isn't such a remarkable place, really," Logan said at length. "But then, I believe it is that very thing which makes it so special to me. A haven of simplicity in a world that can at times seem overwhelmingly complicated."

"I can't picture you as one easily overwhelmed," replied Hilary, setting the Bible down and rejoining Logan, taking a seat in a plain wooden chair opposite him.

"Is that a daughter or a journalist speaking?"

"A little of both, perhaps."

"Well," said Logan with a thoughtful sigh, "all my life I have been too adept at putting on fronts, even when I don't intend to. That's how I made a living, that's how I managed to stay alive during the war—donning one facade after another. And now for the last thirty years I've been trying to break the habit. It is an aspect of my character God deals with constantly. But early patterns die hard, and I still have to work to be just myself. Every once in a while I find myself slipping unconsciously into one of my old characters whom I've missed."

"Don't you ever find it, I don't know—fun?"

"Sure. I'm not one who necessarily despises my old life. God gave me a fun-loving personality, and yes, I enjoy who I am." He paused, smiled, a twinkle in his eye, then chuckled lightly. "I still laugh when I think of some of the crazy things I pulled. At the same time, I know God intended more for me. That's why I am thankful to Him for bringing me out of the *need* to wear a facade in order to more deeply develop my true personality in Him. Yet still, after all this time, I am often overwhelmed, or would be without God's steadying hand."

"It sounds as though you are thinking about this on more than merely an abstract plane."

Logan sighed. "I hadn't really stopped to consider why this is so heavily on my mind today. You're right. It's no doubt because I have a feeling I'm going to have to slip into a disguise of some sort in order to get to the bottom of this thing with Channing. But I want to do it under the direction of the Lord, not in the power of my old nature. I guess what I'm battling with is whether that's possible."

"Why wouldn't it be? Surely God is able to use us as He made us to accomplish His purposes."

"I think you're right. But where the flesh is involved, it always pays to walk warily. The battle I'm waging within myself could too easily requite malice with malice. I mustn't let that happen." Logan stopped and rubbed his hands across his face as dark memories from the past intruded into his thoughts. "Jason Channing has brought much pain into my life, and he has haunted those I love like a demon wraith. My human desire is to lash back at him. But, thank God, I am being purged of that desire."

"What will you do, then?"

"I must confront Channing and make him stop. He is an evil man, a politically and morally and socially dangerous man. He must be stopped before he hurts and destroys further. I know he will not quit until he sees us destroyed. But the confrontation I speak of must grow out of the power of God to work righteousness, not the power of the flesh to seek revenge."

"The thought that his own people were *here* among us is enough to make my skin crawl when I'm lying in bed at night."

"We have to be aware of the fact that your presence is now an added irritation to Channing, making you a target as well."

Hilary shuddered. "Murry called again this morning," she said. "Do you remember his man in Oxford—the fellow who first put him onto Trans Global?"

Logan nodded.

"He was found murdered yesterday. A suspect has been arrested, an Argentine national, a man named Raul Galvez. The police have tied him to the General, but Galvez knows nothing. He was merely hired to do the job."

"The guy in Oxford got too close and Channing had him killed," said Logan flatly.

"And now Murry is more than a little concerned about his own safety. I told him to back off the story."

"This is just one more reason, is it not?" asked Logan.

"Reason for what?"

"For me to find and stop Channing."

"You mean for the police to stop him."

"No, Hilary, I mean *me*. Channing as the General has eluded the police agencies of the world for many years. He will be even more cautious now as he senses the walls beginning to close in on him. Only one thing will force him out of whatever hole he is hiding in, and that is the hope of retaliation against the clan he so despises, the family that has once again foiled his designs. He must be lured out into the open."

"If I didn't know better, the journalist in me would think you were hatching a plan using yourself as bait."

"Do you know anything else more likely to draw him out than the thought of turning his defeat around and gaining control of Stonewycke? I am the perfect decoy."

"But he's already tried to kill you once!"

"Twice, actually," corrected Logan. "A few years ago I learned that Channing was involved in my capture by Chase Morgan's blokes during the depression."

"You nearly died because of that!"

"But I didn't. The firing squad failed, too. The Lord will protect me again." A faint smile flickered across Logan's face. "I only hope the saying *Third time's a charm* has no basis in fact."

"How can you joke about such a thing?"

"Sorry. I suppose once I felt the Lord saying I had to confront Channing, a bit of the old con man in me began to surface. As long as I keep my motives straight, I might as well enjoy it, wouldn't you say?"

"One last big sting?"

"Not exactly how I might have phrased it . . . but that's the idea."

Hilary did not say anything for a few moments, clearly in thought.

"It's not just you Channing is after," she said at length.

"True enough. His wrath is leveled at all of us."

"Then let's take no chances," Hilary went on. "We must make the hook absolutely irresistible."

"What do you mean by that? Who is this *we*?"

"I am doing this thing with you."

"You are most certainly not," declared Logan.

"I read in Grandmother's journal," said Hilary, "that when Channing and von Graff had you before that firing squad, Channing was not looking at you or anticipating your death as much as he was watching Mother—gloating over her distress, relishing her anguish as she watched you die—as if through her he was really getting to Grandmother."

"That's right."

"It will be a Stonewycke *woman,* then, that will be the true *piece de resistance* in whatever scenario you are cooking up. A woman from Stonewycke will be the one inducement he will not be able to resist."

"I ought to feel offended," smiled Logan. "Reverse chauvinism, you know! But I am proud. I do not know how I could ever have doubted that you are our daughter. But I still have strong reservations about letting you in on this one. This is no light undertaking. I cannot overemphasize the danger. Channing means deadly business."

Hilary rose and walked toward Logan. "Please," she purred, placing her arm around his shoulder. "I won't be in any danger with you there to protect me."

She was conning *him* now. And Logan knew it!

"I have just found you, Hilary. I do not want to risk losing you again."

"And I have just found this family. I have wondered about my place in it. Now I believe it is this—fighting for those I love, and for the land, as so many generations of women have done before me. I am not a little girl. I am a grown woman able to take care of myself. Please . . . Father, I want to be with you!"

Logan hesitated, pondering her words.

"Father and daughter side by side, eh? One last fling together for the good guys!" He glanced up at Hilary, the old twinkle lighting up his eyes.

"That's it!" she said, reflecting the same sparkle.

"I know that look! You got those eyes from me! Unless I miss my guess, what they're saying is that I might do my best to stop you, but I'd never succeed. You'd follow me anyway!"

"You're absolutely right!"

"My eyes and the Duncan feistiness!"

"Can't help myself. It's in my blood!"

Logan laughed. "Then who am I to refuse?"

"So what is your plan?" asked Hilary eagerly, sitting down again.

"Plan? Whoever said I had a plan? We'll have to wait for the Lord to show us one."

"I still don't like the idea of you being bait," said Hilary. "Channing might decide to have done with you right then and there."

"That's a possibility," Logan replied. "But if I were still a betting man, I'd lay odds against it. That is not Channing's way. He prefers a slow death so he can watch the suffering. Look at the elaborate ruse with Jo. She could have killed any of us at any time, but that would not have suited Channing. Besides, he won't kill me as long as he thinks he can further extend his power over us. That's exactly what we'll use against him. We'll make him think he can still gain the ultimate victory. But now we have to get down to thinking through the details. I have a feeling we might be able to use Ashley. At this point our only real connection with Channing is through his Oxford so-called 'colleague.' It's a place to start."

"I hope you're right about Channing playing along," said Hilary, trying to match Logan's smile with a courageous bravado.

"He will. I know him. But before we do anything further, we must commit our way to the Lord. Let's pray, not only for boldness, but that His will may be accomplished through our actions."

61 ※ The Hook

GUNTHER'S AUSTERE FEATURES were particularly grim as he strode purposefully through the portico. The heat wave of last week had given way to several days of rain, and now, though the temperature had dropped eight degrees, the air was muggy and humid. The General was seated at the far end of the open veranda in a high-backed wicker chair, a blanket laid over his legs in spite of the warm, sticky air, and a young boy was seated on the floor at his feet slowly waving a large leafy fan back and forth.

Still entertaining his delusions of grandeur, thought Gunther sourly, as if he were Caesar or—God forbid!—Hitler himself. Well, maybe he is a neo-führer, after all, he thought. He had set them all up after the war—with his money, his power, his worldwide connections, keeping them all safe and hidden from prying eyes.

But Gunther shook his head as he glanced at the newspaper he held in his hand. It could not last much longer. *He* would not last much longer. By all normal standards he should have died long ago.

"Mein Herr," said Gunther as he approached.

Channing's eyes opened. Gunther noted that they were still sharp, clear, and incisive no matter how debilitated his body appeared.

"What do you want?"

"You are looking particularly well today," answered Gunther.

"Forget the banalities!" rejoined Channing. "I want news, not flattery. What do you hear from my daughter?"

"Nothing yet, mein Herr. But no news is good news, eh?"

"It better be!" snapped Channing.

"Speaking of news," Gunther went on, "this came today." He stretched out the newspaper toward Channing. "Look at the lower left-hand corner."

Channing grabbed the paper in his gnarled hand, laid it in his lap while he dug out his eyeglasses from his pocket, then quickly scanned the columns until he finally focused on the specified place. The headline glared unpleasantly at him.

GUNSHOT VICTIM: POSSIBLE LINKS TO UNDERWORLD

Oxford, England—Ex-Oxford Professor, Mitchell Dodds, is in critical condition following a shooting Friday not far from his residence on Windham Street. Dodds remains comatose, but informed sources believe Dodds had dealings with a notorious underworld organization, headed by the enigmatic international criminal known only by the cryptic title "The General." The General has eluded Interpol and other national and local police and investigative agencies for two decades, but Interpol's London chief Rollins is confident that if Dodds survives, he will be able to lead police closer than ever before to the infamous crime lord. Queens Hospital sources, however, remain guarded about Dodd's recovery.

When Channing finished the article, he lifted the paper in his hand and flung it away from him.

"Fools!" he screeched. "Those two bumbling idiots! I hope they rot in jail!"

"Only one has been captured," corrected Gunther. "Mallory got away. At least Galvez knows nothing."

"Everyone knows *something,* you fool!" shouted Channing. "Why did you hire such imbeciles in the first place?"

"Galvez will not talk."

"I want him taken care of anyway! Where is the fool of a Texan?"

"I don't know. Probably in some cantina in Galveston."

"At least he was smart enough not to show his miserable face around here."

"I will see to it that he remains away," said Gunther coldly.

"Yes. You know how I hate loose ends. Find him and dispose of him. I do not want Scotland Yard getting on his trail."

"And the Professor?"

"The same, of course. But this time, no bungling! Take care of it personally!"

"They will no doubt have him under tight security."

"That newspaper is almost a week old. He might be out of the hospital by now."

"I doubt it. The paper said he was comatose and in critical condition. By now he may have died and saved us the trouble."

"Or lived and talked!" Channing ran a hand through his white hair. But before he could utter any further imprecations, Gunther cut him off.

"I will attend to it immediately, mein Herr!" Gunther turned to go, but Channing's failing voice stopped him.

"And, Gunther—" Channing croaked with menace, "do not fail!"

Gunther nodded, then continued out, while in his chair a fit of coughing overtook his aging chief. The exertion from the heated conversation had overtaxed his weakened system. The boy ran for the nurse, and within ten minutes Channing lay again in his bed, silently cursing all the fools around him, and himself for being at their mercy.

62 ✠ *Final Gambit*

ASHLEY JAMESON HAD dreamed up many an eccentric scenario as Lady Hargreave. But this real-life drama was the most incredible of all.

No doubt it struck him as incredulous because he happened to be, for the moment, right in the middle of the plot. It was one thing to set characters of a book into motion doing crazy things. But when it was your own life on the line, all romantic notions suddenly fled, and all that was left was pure, undiluted fear.

Yes, here he was. Ashley Jameson, dull university professor, closet mystery writer . . . but certainly *not* a detective—here he was, sitting in a stranger's flat—a dead stranger's, no less!—waiting to be discovered by a ruthless killer. And here he would remain. For he had, in a moment of insanity he now thought, actually asked for this particular role in Logan's scheme.

With the assistance of Interpol, Professor Dodds had been resurrected from the dead via a bogus newspaper article planted in *The London Times.* In the role of Dodds, Ashley hoped to throw a curve to whomever the General sent to finish the job someone else had botched. If it worked, Logan would find himself with an invitation to meet personally with his old nemesis, Jason Channing himself.

The entire scheme, with all its twists and subplots, was a long shot, as Logan would say. But Dodds was the only possible link to Channing's location. Thus Ashley had stepped into Dodds' now vacant shoes, spent a few days at the hospital, and then, after an astounding recovery, was released. For three days now he had been living in Dodds' Windham Street flat. He only hoped that when Channing's assassin came for him, he would be ready. The police had men staked out around the place at a safe enough distance so as not to scare off their prey. Ashley himself remained indoors as much as possible.

Ashley glanced at the clock. It was ten p.m., Dodds' usual bedtime, or so Ashley had established over the last several days. He laid aside the book he had been reading and rose from the leather easy chair.

Nights were the worst. Although it had been arranged for a policewoman in a nurse's uniform to come in daily while he caught a few hours' sleep, he could not keep from becoming extremely drowsy at night. How much longer such an upside-down schedule could go he wasn't sure.

He turned out the lights, then walked toward the window, careful not to make an easy target in front of it. Pulling back the shade a crack, he glanced outside. A light rain fell. The streets glistened with moisture, but were otherwise dark except for the occasional passing of an automobile with its bright headlamps.

I don't know what I expect to see, Ashley mused to himself. Surely no professional killer was going to hang about under a streetlamp with his trenchcoat collar pulled up over his neck, waiting for the whole world to see him.

Sighing, Ashley turned back into the room and sat down again in the chair in the darkened room. The hands of the clock on the wall loudly ticked off the minutes. Logan warned him the waiting would be the worst part. He had been right.

Ashley tried to divert his mind into more pleasant channels. He recalled the last time he had seen Hilary several days ago. They both had been a bit too eager to point out that their parting was not a *real* goodbye, and that they would be parted for only a brief time. They each realized, of course, that they would have to stay clear of one another while he was "undercover," though Hilary had smiled when he had used that oddly out-of-place term.

"I think you are rather enjoying all this, Ashley," she had said.

"An exciting change of pace from the grind, you know."

"You will be careful?" she said as she wove her arm around his while they walked under a full winter moon over the snow-covered university paths.

"Of that you may be certain!" He took a small package from his coat pocket, simply wrapped in brown paper. "Perhaps this will help the hours pass more quickly," he said.

"Ashley, a present! You are a romantic, after all!"

"The well of the scholar runs deep, my dear."

"I am only beginning to discover just how deep!" Hilary tore off the paper and found her hands clutching a clothbound book. She smiled as she read the title: *"The Mystery of the Designing Debutante:* A Lady Hargreave Mystery."

"Hot off the presses, as you journalists say," said Ashley. "Perhaps it may serve in some small measure to explain my interest in the fashion industry. And you are the first person in all of Britain to possess a copy."

"Autographed, I hope?"

"Certainly not! Lady Hargreave never signs her books—a quirky sort of lady, you see. My publisher seems to think that the mystery surrounding the lady sells as many books as her stories themselves. I myself prefer to think it is pure creative and artistic excellence, but I see no reason to burst the old fellow's bubble."

"I shall simply devour it."

"I hope it won't entirely keep you from thinking of me."

Hilary drew closer to him. "It could never do that, Ashley, don't you know?"

Even sitting alone in the black apartment, Ashley could not restrain a pleased grin as he recalled her words. A year ago he would have thought that at such a seasoned age in his life, it would have been impossible to fit a woman into his staid and ordered bachelor routine. Yet now he found himself wondering if it would be possible to imagine his life *without* the daughter and niece of his two old friends, Logan and Ian.

The university tower clock striking the quarter hour pulled his thoughts back to the present. Ten-fifteen. Still no intruders.

Ashley began to wonder if they had made it *too* easy for Channing's man. Logan said there was always a fine line between a good piece of bait and a tip-off.

Ashley began to reflect on everything else Logan had told him before he set out on this madcap task—a crash course in the confidence game! Logan would have been so much better in this part, to be sure. Or an undercover detective, if things got too rough. But Channing, and possibly his men, knew Logan. And those kinds of men had an uncanny knack for smelling the law no matter what the disguise. Or so Ashley had argued when he had wanted the assignment, even though Galvez insisted he was the only one to have had face-to-face contact with Dodds.

Logan had pointed out one other factor, too, probably trying to convince himself of the rationale of letting an untried scholar confront a hit man:

"After all, Ashley," he had said, "you already know all the professorial lingo. Your very inexperience and authenticity will give us an edge against Channing, who will be on the alert for a setup."

They both knew there were many risks. The plan could unravel at any number of points. But it was all they had. Logan was counting on its one most important feature. Channing would *want* Logan now more than ever, and in his blind obsession he was liable to overlook practicality. "His wanting me will be our foot in the door," Logan said. "The dodge can only work when the mark desperately desires what you're offering him. Remember, Channing doesn't know what *we* know. That's our ace."

Suddenly a noise out of the night met Ashley's ear.

He listened intently. Had it been his own overwrought imagination, on edge, waiting for something . . . *anything* to happen?

There it was again! A faint creak on the third step outside. He noticed it himself every time he entered the flat.

He swallowed hard. His whole body tensed as an inner sense told him this was it. He opened a drawer in the table next to the chair where he'd placed the automatic pistol Inspector Rollins had issued him. He'd done a good deal of hunting on his estate in Cornwall, and was a fair shot. But he'd never be able to use a weapon against a human being.

Logan had assured him he wouldn't have to. They wouldn't expect him as the scholarly type to be a killer. But they'd have no way of knowing for sure. His very unpredictability would throw them off guard. Ashley wrapped his fingers around the hard cold steel handle of the revolver, withdrew it, and pointed the weapon at the closed door.

He swallowed again. His throat was suddenly very dry. The only thought his brain could focus on was the possibility that both Lady Hargreave *and* Ashley Jameson had at last bitten off more than they could chew.

63 ❈ *The Professor and the Assassin*

WHOEVER STOOD OUTSIDE the door was good. Ashley hardly detected another sound. Had he been asleep in his bed, as was supposed, he would have been an easy target. But Ashley would not be a victim tonight, not if he could help it.

A faint scraping could now be heard. The intruder was picking the lock. In another minute the door inched open.

Ashley sat like a statue, daring not even to breathe. When he acted, it had to be fast and unexpected, and perfectly timed. His left hand was poised by the switch to the lamp that would send its blinding light toward the door. His right still held the gun.

A moment more and a dark figure, tall and rather trim, slowly shouldered its way into the room. It turned to close the door. For a brief moment its back was to Ashley.

Now!

He flipped on the switch, bathing the man in light and momentarily disorienting him.

"Don't move a muscle!" said Ashley, in the shaky voice of one unaccustomed to such scenes. "Don't even think of turning around. I am holding a gun on your back."

"You are insane if you think you will get away with this," said the intruder in a menacing Germanic accent.

"Nearly getting killed sometimes does that to a man," replied Ashley. "I may be insane, as you say. But that does not lessen the potency of this gun in my hand. Now please, drop your weapon."

"So you can kill me?"

"Good heavens, no!" exclaimed Ashley. "Unless of course . . . but you wouldn't do that, would you? I do so hate the sight of blood."

Gunther hesitated another moment, then dropped the pistol he held onto the floor with a thud.

"Now, you may turn around," said Ashley.

"What do you want?" asked Gunther impatiently as he turned and did his best to take in his surroundings while squinting against the light. He did not like being on this end of an attack.

"Come in and have a seat. We may as well be comfortable as we talk."

"And I suppose you'll want tea too?" scoffed Gunther.

"That might be nice, but I suppose we'd best get down to business first." Ashley motioned with the gun toward a chair directly opposite him.

Gunther sat down, looking cold and superior despite the fact that an inept professor had so easily gotten the drop on him. As he did so, Ashley rose, moved toward the door while still keeping his visitor in the sights of his gun, retrieved Gunther's pistol from the floor, then resumed his seat.

"What is this business you want to discuss?" Gunther asked in a blunt, irritated tone.

"Well, I expect you have come here to finish the job those other two chaps started." Ashley paused as if expecting a response from Gunther. But the German remained impassive. "I suppose you want to kill me," he continued, "before I tell anything to Scotland Yard. Was that your thinking?"

Still Gunther did not reply.

"As you can see," Ashley went on, "I have been out of the hospital for several days, and though I am still weak, I have said nothing."

"Why should I believe you?"

Ashley thought for a moment. "I see what you mean. That does make it a bit sticky, doesn't it?" He paused. "Well, for argument's sake," he went on, "let us just accept that for now, what do you say?"

Gunther did not protest, when Ashley went on.

"Good! Now . . . I haven't talked because, to be perfectly honest, I have my own business interests to protect."

"What interests?"

"All in good time."

"And what about the story in the *Times* saying you had connections to the General? He was very angry to read that!" As he spoke Gunther shifted threateningly in his chair.

"Sit back please," said Ashley, gesturing with his gun.

"He wants you dead, Dodds! He does not like his name appearing in the newspaper!"

"I do apologize for that. I rather lost my head when I first realized I might be dealing with the General. But you can't really blame me, can you? I'm afraid I mentioned something to a reporter before I slipped into the coma. Later, when they released me, I denied everything. And as it was the word of a respected Oxford professor—well, actually an ex-professor—against an overzealous reporter . . . well, the poor newspaper fellow was left with a bit of egg on his face."

"We try to kill you, and then you turn around and *protect* us?" said Gunther skeptically. "Why should I believe you? I *don't* believe you!" Again he half rose, as if the weapon in Ashley's hand were a mere toy that concerned him not at all.

"You really must relax. I'm not at all used to guns, and I wouldn't want you to frighten me into using this before I have had my say."

Again Gunther sat back. His face wore the expression of a caged tiger awaiting the merest momentary lapse that he might spring upon this nincompoop of a dim-witted professor.

"As I said, I was protecting myself every bit as much as I had any noble notions regarding your employer," said Ashley. "I saw no reason to jeopardize any of our positions when we could all benefit so handsomely from an alliance that keeps us all healthy."

"Just what do you mean by *benefit*?"

"Quite simple, actually." Ashley relaxed, lowering the gun slightly. "I think I have something the General wants. Besides my silence, of course."

"What might that be?"

"The reason he contacted me in the first place was to analyze and possibly dispose of some rare and ancient artifacts."

Several days earlier a careful search of Dodds' flat had turned up a file containing descriptions of several items delivered to the Professor for inspection by two men named Mallory and Galvez. It was easy to assume that this had been the reason for the initial contact between the General and Dodds. But the moment Hilary had read Dodds' descriptions of the few sample relics, she knew she had seen something of the same sort before.

Lady Margaret Duncan was one of the few persons in recent times to have ever seen inside the ancient Pict box which had lain undisturbed under the great stones on Braenock Ridge for a millennium. Later in life, after the box had long been lost track of, she described some of the pieces, as best her aging memory could recall, to her granddaughter. These found their way into the journal, and the descriptions were still fresh in Hilary's mind. When the search of Dodds' flat turned up the list, Hilary immediately noted distinct similarities. The fact that Channing, the last known possessor of the box, was now mixed up with Dodds seemed to corroborate the correlation. Ashley now planned to use this knowledge as his trump card.

"Before my unfortunate *accident,*" Ashley went on in a carefully measured tone, keeping a mistrustful eye on Gunther's every move, while continuing to nurture the image of an absent-minded buffoon, "I was able to conduct a little research, along with my preliminary tests. I concluded that what your General possesses is extremely valuable indeed, very rare, very ancient. I also discovered an interesting fact that I did not put in my original report."

"And what is that fact!" spat Gunther, growing weary of this simpleton.

"Just this. That it is also—how shall I put it?—very *hot*. The relics appear part of a collection belonging to the Stonewycke estate in northern Scotland. They were stolen some forty years ago, and besides still being an open case, that theft is connected to an unsolved murder."

"What does that have to do with me?"

"Perhaps nothing . . . perhaps a great deal. I understand that items of this kind pass through many hands over the years. In my business it does not usually pay to look too closely at the histories of the items which I am paid to deal with. But I assume the General came to me because he hoped to unload this cache of his, which no doubt has been a rather difficult undertaking for him due to the circumstances of the theft and the antiquity of the items."

"As you said, such things pass through many hands."

"And as I have been *trying* to say, I have a client who is interested in purchasing this collection of relics, and will ask no questions regarding how your employer came by them.

He happens to know that the original—what should I call him—*guardian* of the goods following the theft is now dead. He is only interested in retrieving them."

"You have been quite busy for a man only just risen from his deathbed."

"I daresay, Mr.—by the way, I don't think you mentioned your name."

"I didn't. It is unimportant."

"Ah, yes. Of course. Well, as I said, I do have a party interested in the sale, and had already begun initiating these arrangements before the—ah, the shooting. That has, I'm sure you can appreciate, slowed me up somewhat."

"Bah! You are a fool!" said Gunther. "There was never any talk of a *sale*."

"Isn't that what all this was about? I naturally assumed—"

"The General is not a man to make careless assumptions about! He was merely having the items valued and authenticated. I doubt he would sell them at any price! He is sentimentally attached to the ridiculous things."

Gunther paused a moment to reflect on Channing's obsession. "He lets no one near them," he went on. "I've never even seen them."

"Surely he must keep such priceless objects displayed in some fashion?" Ashley lowered the gun unconsciously as he became more absorbed in the interchange.

Gunther threw his head back and roared, in part hoping to make Ashley drop his guard even further, but also amused at the humor of his last remark.

"On display! They are so locked away, or buried, no one knows what he's done with them! Occasionally a peculiar mood comes over him and he goes off in private, sometimes for hours on end—once he was gone all night—muttering all the while about his treasure. But no one goes with him. It's . . . but never mind all that! No one knows where they are, and wherever they are, they're not for sale!"

"Then why contact me in the first place?"

"I only follow orders—and right now my orders are to kill you!"

With a sudden movement, Gunther jumped to his feet. He had been watching his captor with the eye of an eagle, and the moment he perceived he had relaxed and grown overconfident, he wasted no time in attempting to seize the advantage.

He had not counted on Ashley's quick reaction, however. Nor had he believed this droll professor would have the gumption to use the weapon he had held so inexpertly in his hand. Ashley, on the other hand, had been waiting for a counter-attack. His only surprise was that it had taken so long to come. The moment Gunther lunged forward, Ashley fired the automatic. The slug missed Gunther, as Ashley intended, but it was close enough to make him wonder.

At the unexpected blast from the pistol, the German fell back. He gaped at Ashley, momentarily stunned that this unassertive professor had the guts to pull the trigger.

"Dash it all!" yelled Ashley. "Don't force me to do something nasty! Can't we approach these negotiations like gentlemen?"

A dry, hard sound, somewhat resembling laughter that had grown rusty from disuse, escaped Gunther's lips. "Gentlemen? An interesting idea." He scratched his head thoughtfully, then eased back into the chair. "Well then, what is on your mind, Professor?"

"I have a proposition that could make your employer a wealthy man."

"Ha!" mocked Gunther. "He will be warmed to hear of your offer! Ha! ha! It will prove to him that you do not know his true identity. For he is too rich ever to see a fraction of his wealth."

"Be that as it may, my prospective buyer would be willing to part with a tidy sum to make the acquisition."

"I tell you, he will never sell. He will go to his grave with the treasure still in his possession and its location unknown."

"Just tell him my buyer is anxious."

"How tidy is the sum we are discussing?"

"In the millions, if the other pieces are of the same quality as those I examined."

"What do *you* want out of this?"

"I should think my life would not be too much to ask—that, and my usual ten percent, of course."

"You *are* audacious! That is one thing I can say for you."

"I am also holding the gun." Ashley waved it for effect.

"You cannot sit up nights indefinitely," replied Gunther. "Your guard will have to relax eventually. When it does, nothing will prevent me from doing what I came here to do—some dark night, long after your business with the General is concluded."

"I am fully aware of that possibility," said Ashley, "and thus I have taken the precaution to invest in a bit of insurance—in the form of a safe-deposit box and a letter containing its key which has been entrusted with a friend. In the box are documents revealing everything I know. Whether or not you and your employer had anything to do with the events that occurred in Scotland forty years ago hardly concerns me. But I think Scotland Yard will find highly interesting the General's connection to Trans Global, various other crimes and murders that have taken place over the years, the transporting of certain stolen items of great value, as well as your possession of the Stonewycke treasure itself and your part in my own murder. All this will make fascinating reading, and will be made public upon my demise."

"You *know* the General will not be toyed with!"

"I do indeed, from personal experience." Ashley patted his stomach as if to indicate his wound. "Believe me, I am not toying. I live, and the General and I benefit mutually. I die and . . . well, we both lose. Simple logic, actually."

Gunther leaned back, folded his arms together, and appraised Ashley carefully.

"All right, Professor," he said at length, "for the sake of argument—as you would say—let us just assume my employer *was* interested in selling his precious relics. Who is this buyer of yours?"

Ashley paused. If the bait was to be dangled, he had to give it just the right touch.

At last he opened his mouth to speak.

"Logan Macintyre," he said matter-of-factly.

Gunther jerked forward again, but this time in stunned shock.

"What are you trying to pull, Dodds?" he roared.

"Logan Macintyre, Member of Parliament," Ashley repeated. "I see nothing so irregular about a man, if he is willing to pay, attempting to purchase back something of which he was the original owner."

Gunther hesitated, thoughts running rapidly through his mind. If Macintyre was involved, questions could not help being raised. . . . Why now, all of a sudden, was he interested in retrieving what had once belonged to the estate which he had inherited by marriage?

"You had better understand, Mr. Dodds," Gunther warned, "that if this is any kind of a ruse, you are a dead man—whatever your threats of exposure!"

"Why would I risk my life unless I am telling you the truth? Really, must we be so barbaric?"

"It's a shame my old general is not still around," mused Gunther. "*He* would have appreciated your pluck." A look almost of sentimentality momentarily disturbed Gunther's iron-like visage. Quickly his features hardened again. "Unfortunately he is no longer here, and you have five minutes to convince me you are on the level. How did you make contact with Macintyre?"

"*On the level* is a rather inapplicable phrase for men in our business it seems," replied Ashley. "But to answer you—this is how he contacted me. Before my accident, I had already put the word out—discreetly, of course—for persons interested in rare artifacts of this kind. I have certain clients who are particularly loyal customers in various categories of merchandise. Thus it got around—nothing that could be traced, you understand—that certain old relics of possible Pictish connection might soon be available. Macintyre is not one of my clients. But apparently he has had his own word out for years now in hopes of relocating his goods. So by way of the underground grapevine he has found me."

"Was anything said to him about the General?"

"Good heavens no! I already learned my lesson on speaking that name too freely."

"Did Macintyre mention any names?"

"None. He wants the family heirlooms back where they belong and is willing to pay. That's all he said. He is unconcerned with ownership or specifics of where they have been through the years."

Gunther rubbed his forehead, his brow deeply creased. He had not expected this. It would seem Macintyre would have enough on his mind these days, what with phony daughters and attempted poisonings, to concern himself with that treasure.

But if the Professor's story was true . . . then all this had been in the works long before Jo and Emil had been forced to flee. It might even be that Macintyre had intensified his search *because* of the daughter, wanting the restoration of the family wealth to pass on, soon after Jo's original appearance.

Dodds would have no reason to lie. For all his stuffy ways, he was a shrewd businessman, with his own profit his major interest. This could be the very thing Channing had desired for years—a prime opportunity to get to Macintyre. The beauty of it would be that Macintyre would walk right into it not even realizing he was stepping into Channing's stronghold.

Still, there was the possibility Channing might think otherwise. Gunther had his orders, and Channing did not like his orders disregarded.

Could he afford to take the chance of not informing him of this new development in the scenario? He didn't think so. Gunther well knew of Channing's consuming passion in life—not that he cared anything about it himself; he thought the ancient vendetta was ridiculous.

But he knew Channing would want to be told of *anything* regarding the Stonewycke clan. He would not be happy if Gunther acted independently in this matter.

Gunther looked up at Ashley.

"All right, Professor, it looks as though you have talked yourself into staying alive for yet a while longer," said Gunther. "I will relay your proposition to my employer."

64 ❈ Contact Is Made

BRITISH AIRWAYS FLIGHT 829 touched down at Ezeiza Airport on schedule. The fine skyline of Buenos Aires, the largest and most cosmopolitan city in South America, was bathed in a luxurious warmth of a humid 72°. Not bad for early December, thought Logan as he collected his suitcase from the conveyer. Allison and he would have to try it sometime for a vacation. But thoughts of pleasant times would have to wait.

As Allison came to mind, not for the first time in the last days, a knot tightened in his stomach. She was going to be all right, and had already thrown off most of the effects of the poison. But he had to struggle to prevent a bitter anger from rising within him when he thought of Channing's attempt to snuff out her life. He had to continually remind himself what his true motives were in this attempt—to destroy the cancerous feud, not be drawn into it himself.

He strode across the tiled airport baggage dock to customs, where his government position allowed him to pass through quickly. Outside, the heat was even more noticeable, but not unpleasant after Britain's chill. He hailed a cab.

His instructions from Channing's man, with Ashley acting as intermediary, were simple: Fly to Buenos Aires, register at the Grand Hotel Royal, and await further instructions. Though the man's absolute insistence that the Professor's interested buyer come himself, in person and alone, was an unusual request, they had expected it. Ashley had feigned hesitation when the requirement was made part of the deal. He had taken enough time to fake a call to Logan, and in the end had reluctantly agreed.

Channing had taken the bait, they had played the little game of being indecisive over his terms, and in the end—once Gunther had relayed his employer's final message: "You tell him if he wants to buy those relics, he comes to me in person!"—had consented. The deal was set.

At least half of Logan's mission—finding the General's whereabouts—would soon bear fruit. They now knew Channing was in Argentina, probably near Buenos Aires. But this was a metropolis of several million. Even Interpol had come this close. Channing could be anywhere within a fifty- or hundred-mile radius. They still had to get to his door.

The taxi dropped Logan at the hotel. A bellhop took his luggage at the curb, no doubt expecting a generous tip, which he got. He was escorted to the front desk, where he registered.

"I'd like a room toward the front," said Logan, "with a window facing Florida Avenue." He didn't know if such precautions would be necessary, but he wanted everything covered.

He went straight to his room, made two phone calls, then kicked off his shoes and stretched out on the bed. It felt good to relax after the tiring flight and he knew he'd better take advantage of these moments while he was able. He hoped Channing gave him the chance to have a good long sleep before contacting him. But no, Channing would not be so considerate. He would want Logan as frayed and out of sorts as possible. Logan closed his eyes and was soon dozing soundly.

An hour later he awoke to the sound of a sharp knock at his door. He tensed momentarily, then recalled he had ordered a meal through room service when he registered. The waiter brought in a tray; Logan paid him, then sat down in one of the simulated leather chairs to eat. Hungry, he consumed what had been delivered, despite the fact that the food was poor and he was restless. When he finished he soon found himself pacing the floor of the small room.

He glanced at his watch. He had been here two hours already. No doubt the hotel concierge was under orders to notify Channing or his intermediary the moment a registration was made under the name Logan Macintyre. How long would he wait before he made contact? No doubt he'll make me sweat first, thought Logan. But that wouldn't take long in this heat; the air conditioning in the Grand Royal did not seem to be working.

Logan paused in his pacing in front of the window. It was midafternoon. In the outlying villages, no doubt, siesta time would have quieted down the pace. But in the heart of Buenos Aires, the streets full of tourists and traffic, one would never guess this to be other than the international center of over five million it had become. He noted the hotel directly across Florida, the Richmond. The view of the street was better from there, but that detail might not matter should Channing's man decide to come upon Logan unawares. He had to consider that possibility, for he would definitely be taking counter precautions to prevent being followed.

Logan turned back into the room and continued pacing.

At half past five, the summons finally came.

The soft knock on Logan's door was in itself unportentious, but Logan answered it not without some trepidation, and with a silent prayer on his lips. When he swung the door open, he found himself face-to-face with an unexpected ghost from the past.

"Gunther!" he exclaimed in true amazement.

"We meet again, Herr Macintyre." Gunther's mouth twisted in a half smile, his delight in Logan's discomfiture obvious.

"Where . . . how in the world do you fit into all this?" asked Logan, now remembering that Ashley had mentioned that his late-night caller had spoken with a German accent. Logan had never even guessed that Ashley had been face-to-face with the old double agent with whom he had worked in the war. Had he realized Ashley was going to confront Gunther, he would never have let him pose as the Professor! His estimation of Ashley's bravery suddenly increased tenfold.

One look told him that Gunther had not changed much over the years, except for gray hair and a few more wrinkles. His features were still hard, and his countenance as lethal as a steel saber.

"We can talk over old times later," said Gunther. "We have a small journey before we reach my employer."

"Then it is not you I am to deal with?"

"I am still only a hatchet man."

"For whom?"

"All in good time, Macintyre."

"Von Graff?"

"He's dead."

"So I heard. Who then?"

"I do what I must do."

"Still working both sides of the fence, eh?"

Gunther's eyebrow arched. "Expediency was and is my motto, Macintyre. It has kept me alive, healthy, and financially well off for many years."

"I, too, am alive, healthy, and well off, my friend," said Logan pointedly, "but from following a different creed."

"Will you preach to me, Macintyre?"

"As you said, we have a journey ahead of us. Surely there will be much to talk about." Gunther grunted sullenly.

"So . . . you cannot tell me who your employer is?" continued Logan.

"I think he would prefer to remain anonymous a while longer." Gunther paused. "Get your things. It is time to go."

"I will not be returning here?"

"Not in the near future," Gunther replied cryptically.

Logan gathered up the few items he had unpacked, dropped them in his suitcase, latched it, grabbed the handle, and followed Gunther out the door. As they stepped into the corridor however, he stopped.

"Wait!" he said. "I forgot my razor."

"You can get another."

"This was a good one. It will only take a moment."

Logan ducked back inside, closing the door behind him. He hurried to the bathroom and retrieved the cheap single-blade razor he had put on the sink counter. Walking back through the larger room, he paused long enough to pull the curtains almost shut, leaving a one foot gap of open space, then rejoined Gunther in the hallway. He opened his suitcase and tucked the razor inside.

The two men continued down the corridor to the elevator. As Logan feared, they followed a surreptitious route out of the hotel, keeping to rear hallways, finally exiting through a service door. They continued on foot down an alley, Gunther glancing about.

"Still the cautious one, eh, Gunther?" chuckled Logan lightly.

"It has not harmed us yet, Macintyre," replied Gunther. "Besides, in dealing with a *swindler,* would you not be cautious too?"

"I see what you mean. But many years have passed since those days. I am now a respectable politician!"

"A contradiction in terms!"

Gunther nudged Logan forward. They turned left from the short alley at the rear of the hotel into a semi-deserted street that appeared used mostly for deliveries. Logan glanced about, as if trying to get his bearings. A black Lincoln Continental was parked about half a block away. They walked to it. Gunther paused, took a ring of keys from his pocket, then unlocked the passenger door for Logan. Without pausing to open it, or to help Logan with his luggage, he walked around to the driver's side.

As Logan swung his suitcase inside, out of the corner of his eye he noted a young Indian boy, a street waif by the look of him, who had been standing at the farther end of the block eyeing them, dash off and out of sight. Getting his luggage situated, Logan seated himself and closed the door. Gunther started the ignition and pulled away.

Logan rolled down his window just as Gunther stopped at the first intersection. Then the huge automobile pulled out quickly through traffic, as Gunther wheeled his way east onto a large boulevard.

"What's this street called?" asked Logan.

"Avenue Corrientes, but what does it matter?" snapped Gunther. "Roll up that window!"

Slowly Logan complied, but not before he had taken a good look up and down the street, spotting the avenue called Florida as they sped across it.

Around the corner, only moments before, a woman exited the Richmond Hotel. Though not tall enough to attract attention by it, she was lanky, and her movements were made awkward by the bulky camera bag strung over her shoulder and the bulging Indian-weave tote bag in her hand. Her pink-rimmed sunglasses, in combination with her brightly embroidered peasant outfit, such as were at that moment being offered in any of three dozen bazaars within a mile, marked her as the consummate tourist, probably an American by her ostentatious display of purchasing power.

She shambled down the hotel steps, paused a moment to speak with a breathless young street beggar, then jogged south along Florida. Her paraphernalia bobbing about, she reached a rented Volkswagen sedan, threw in her gear, then jumped in with surprising ease behind the wheel. As Gunther's Lincoln cruised by, she started her engine. The VW eased its way into traffic, turned onto Corrientes, and settled into the late-afternoon rush, four cars behind the Lincoln.

Within two hours she had returned to the Richmond. Leaving her cumbersome baggage in the car, she hurried up the hotel steps, purposefully crossed the hotel lobby to where a bank of pay telephones stood. She inserted two coins into one, then dialed the operator.

After a moment she spoke into the handset:

"Overseas assistance, por favor."

65 ✻ *In the Spider's Lair*

FIFTY MINUTES AFTER departing Buenos Aires, the black Lincoln pulled through the gates of the villa.

Logan was quick to note the armed guards posted at the gate. He wondered how many such sentries there were about the place. But his attention was soon diverted to the villa itself. By the look of it, Channing had not made much of a point to showcase his wealth. Men in his position were better off keeping a low profile; perhaps that extended to the security too. Still, armed sentries were probably not an uncommon sight about the homes of wealthy patrons in these third-world republics.

Gunther braked to a stop. They had not even stepped out of the car before a servant appeared from the house. He took Logan's suitcase, while respectfully keeping his distance from Gunther. Inside, the entryway to the villa was spacious and well kept, though sparsely furnished.

Logan found himself wondering what had filled Channing's years since they had last met—what besides the obvious obsession with vengeance and hate. During the drive Logan had continued to attempt conversation, but Gunther had proved his usual taciturn self.

"Would you care to go to your room, Herr Macintyre?" Gunther asked formally.

"My room? I assumed we would make arrangements for our transaction and then you would take me back to the city."

Gunther smiled. "I have a feeling your business may take somewhat longer than you anticipated, and that you will be spending the night."

Logan eyed him carefully. This could be more dangerous than he planned on.

"Well then," said Logan, "let's do get on with it. I am rather anxious to be about our business—and not a little curious besides."

"I thought so," said Gunther. "My employer is anxious also, and if you were up to it, wanted you taken directly to him. Come this way."

Toward the end of a long corridor they came upon closed double doors. Gunther paused and knocked.

"¿Quien es?" The voice that came from inside was scored with age, but contained no less self-important arrogance than it had thirty years ago when Logan had last heard it.

"It is I . . . Gunther. I have our guest."

"Ah, very good! Come in!"

Logan entered behind Gunther, and beheld a man standing with his back to the door in front of a marbled hearth. No doubt wanting to make the most of the surprise revelation of his identity, he remained several moments after the door clicked shut exactly where he was. He wore a tan-colored smoking jacket, and was supporting himself with a cane. The back of his head still contained probably half its original quantity of hair, but it was pure white, as was his skin, giving himself away as clearly not at home amid the dark-skinned natives in this climate where the sun shone hot.

Slowly the lean, wasted figure turned. On his face was plastered a smile of insidious delight, which, notwithstanding his physical impotence, yet emanated a malevolent power.

"Channing!" exclaimed Logan in disbelief, his stunned tone, now that his eyes actually beheld his adversary, only half an act.

"Who else do you think would possess the legendary Stonewycke treasure?" returned Channing wryly, hardly able to contain his delight to find Logan Macintyre at last within his resourceful grasp.

"But . . . but . . . I thought you were dead! I thought . . . I assumed . . . "

"You thought I had unloaded it, eh? Ha, ha, ha!" croaked Channing, his elation curbed only by the evil in his soul. His laugh did not ring with joy, but rather struck the dissonant chord of wicked vindication. "Ha, ha! That's a good one, Macintyre!" he went on, savoring the moment. "Surely you didn't think me such a fool?"

"So . . . you have kept it all these years?"

"I once fancied the notion of selling it," replied Channing, wiping his eyes and still chuckling. "But then I realized the only interested buyers would be one of *you* fools from that backwater northern province. Besides you cursed sentimentalists, only legitimate historians would take a second look at it. And I certainly couldn't have pawned it off on any reputable historical buyer without having to answer too many questions. Besides, what could I have gotten for it? Worthless bits of scraps, nothing more." He sighed purposefully. "But I have over the years grown rather fond of it."

"And now . . . what has changed your mind? Why sell it now?"

Again Channing began to laugh—at first softly, then rising in volume.

"Excuse me, Macintyre," he said through his laughter, "but this really is too humorous! You are more of a fool than I took you for!"

"I merely asked why all of a sudden you want to—"

"Ha, ha!" roared Channing. "Oh . . . that's a good one, eh, Gunther? Ha, ha, ha! Sell it! Ha, ha! I have no intention of selling it, Macintyre!"

"But I thought . . . then why this elaborate ruse to get me here? I thought I was coming here on a legitimate business deal."

"Oh, Macintyre! You really must stop! Ha, ha! All this exertion is going to be the death of me! Ha, ha! Don't you yet get it, Macintyre?"

"Get it? What are you driving at?"

"The treasure is not for sale. Macintyre," replied Channing, calming.

"Then why am I here?"

"Don't you know, Logan? May I call you Logan? Why, you are my friend. I merely wanted to see you again! Come . . . sit down."

Channing waved Logan toward one of the expensive chintz-covered chairs situated before the hearth. "I will have some refreshments brought."

Logan sat down, as one recovering from a great shock. Channing took the adjacent chair, then glanced up at Gunther. All humor was gone from his countenance, and his eyes were again empty of life. "See to the refreshments, Gunther," he ordered in a deprecating tone.

Gunther made no response, either silent or verbal; he merely turned and exited the room.

Channing turned fully toward Logan. "I'm certain this change in your plans will be somewhat disconcerting," he said benevolently. "But we will do our best to make it up to you. Dinner will be served soon. You have been traveling the better part of the day and must be fatigued. So I am having our finest guest accommodations prepared for you."

"I assure you that's unnecessary," said Logan.

"It's not the least trouble."

"If you'll simply have Gunther drive me back to town after dinner, I'd be most—"

"Please, Mr. Macintyre. I wouldn't think of it! You are my guest!"

"I've never known you to be so hospitable, Channing," said Logan.

"I've never before entertained a Member of Parliament in my home."

"I see," said Logan, pausing thoughtfully. "I seem to recall an old proverb to that effect. Something to the effect of, 'Visit the spider in his own lair before you judge his character.'"

"Exactly! But you misquote, Macintyre. The saying is in regard to a wolf, not a spider."

"I didn't know you were a literary man, Channing."

"I am full of surprises, Macintyre, even at my age. But the point of the saying is well taken. One never knows when one will find the wolf, so to speak, a congenial sort. You've read your Kipling, I assume."

"Yes, of course. Well, I hope you're right, Channing."

At that moment a servant entered with a tray containing coffee service. He set it on a table and served each man submissively. Logan did not see Gunther again until dinner.

"So, what became of you after the war?" Logan asked, sipping his coffee.

"I kept busy. I aided a few of my German friends."

"You mean Nazi friends?"

"Yes, that too. I helped some relocate. I found myself quite out of favor with several Western governments, and it became beneficial to all of us to find a place far from the madding crowd, as it were."

"Here?"

"And other places. We are quite diversified, you know."

"So I had heard."

Channing cast Logan a quick glance, but let the remark pass.

"I reorganized my company under a new name, set up a figurehead chairman and major stockholders, while I continued to exercise control. I gave my expatriate friends new identities and positions within the company hierarchy. I even took a couple of new identities myself."

"What about von Graff?"

"Oh yes, him too. He didn't fancy a firing squad, and he was perfectly suited to operate the U-boat I stole from the German Navy just before the end of the war. He died twelve years ago—a massive heart attack. Never knew what hit him."

"At least he deserved that much," commented Logan. "Von Graff would not have been the type to put up with a long enfeebling illness."

"We *all* get what we deserve, Macintyre." Channing's emphasis of the word had a sinister edge.

"What about you, Channing?"

"Prosperity and long life . . . just like a saint." He chuckled dryly. "I wager you never expected me to last so long!"

"And happiness?" said Logan, ignoring his final comment.

"Thank God I was never sentimental about such tripe."

"Have you known peace, Channing?"

"Bah! Don't preach to me, Macintyre!" Channing challenged sharply. "I've heard of your grating religiosity and moralism. No doubt you think I've been a bad sort and will burn in hell.

You have probably even prayed for my soul! Well, you are a fool! I don't care what happens to my soul—I don't believe in such rubbish. I've had everything I wanted out of life."

"Everything?"

Suddenly Channing's cup rattled in its saucer while his face turned red. His eyes glared, flashing like sparks from hot metal. The muscles in his wrinkled face twitched violently. All at once he looked old and on the verge of collapse, and his voice weakened into a hoarse gasp from the rage that had seized him.

"I will have everything before I die!" he spat with choking venom.

"I hope so, Channing. I truly do." But as Logan spoke the words, he knew full well that he and Channing were speaking of things as different as black and white, as far removed from one another as heaven and hell.

Logan and Gunther dined alone. Channing did not appear. The word was that he had taken to his bed.

The meal was quiet and uneventful. Logan could not help wondering if he had been wise in allowing himself to be brought here. Channing was unpredictable. He could fly into a rage at any moment and order Logan hanged or shot. He could also die without warning. There were too many variables for Logan to feel entirely at ease.

After dinner he was escorted to his room.

Bidding him a cool good night, Gunther closed the door behind him and walked away. Immediately Logan placed his hand on the latch and turned. It was locked tight.

He walked across to the only window in the room and pulled aside the faded shade. The window was firmly encased in steel bars.

Even if he had planned on getting back to the city, now there was little chance left. He had known this might happen, while still praying against it. The reality of the situation was that he was a prisoner in Channing's home.

He only hoped he got out of here alive, and hadn't indeed, of his own volition, entrapped himself right in the middle of the spider's web.

66 ❈ L'Escroc's Curtain Call

THE FOLLOWING MORNING Logan was let out of his prison-like room by a servant. He breakfasted alone, deprived even of Gunther's chilly company. Another man, however, maintained a somber vigil over him the entire time. Logan decided the time might be right for some reconnaissance.

"Do you speak English?" he asked as the man poured out his coffee.

"Un pocito, señor."

"Tell me, where is—uh—the master of the house? He is feeling well, I assume?"

"Sí. He well, but he want no veesitors."

"I will see him today, perhaps?"

"It is not for me to say, señor."

"Yes, of course." Logan paused, buttered his bread, and wondered if Channing had his people too well trained for him to expect them to talk freely. "What about Mr. Gunther?"

"Zee tall German, he come and he go."

"He is gone now, I presume."

"Sí."

"How long will he be gone?"

"I do not know his business. I am criado—servant. Nada mas." He snapped his mouth shut and Logan knew he'd get nothing more out of him.

He had learned one thing from the conversation. Gunther could present a problem. Not knowing where and how people moved around this place had created a number of loose ends.

Gunther's presence in the villa was perhaps the worst of the batch. He could show up at any time, and they would have no control over what he might do.

Logan quickly offered up the problem in prayer. No plan was foolproof, but he was thankful at least that he had a God who *was* in control no matter what. In control of their very lives, if it came to that.

Immediately after the meal another servant came and escorted Logan to a patio garden where Logan encountered Channing once more.

"I trust you passed a comfortable night, Macintyre?" he asked from where he sat in a wicker chair, basking feebly in the morning sun. His voice was soft, though he put on a bold front. He did not look as though *he* had slept well, but he would never admit that Logan's presence in the compound unnerved him.

"As comfortable as one can in a *locked* room," returned Logan.

"An unpleasant but necessary precaution."

Logan drew up a chair opposite Channing's. "I came here thinking to conclude a business deal," he said. "Then you tell me you never had any such thing in mind, but merely wanted a visit with me. An odd arrangement, I must say, keeping a guest under lock and key."

"You insist on humoring me, don't you? These trivial little jokes. Surely you get the picture now, Macintyre. I have *plans* for you! As you correctly surmised, I did not have you brought here for no reason."

"I have wondered what you were going to do with me."

"You are worried for your life? How nice!"

"The last time we met," said Logan, "you made a nearly successful attempt in that direction. But I would not say I was worried. Merely curious."

"If you give me what I want, I may even let you live."

"Luckily the last time my wife was there to foil you."

"Your wife . . ." Channing's voice shivered over the words. Logan could only glimpse the raw edge of his hatred, kept scarcely at bay beneath his show of mock cordiality. "She will come to your rescue no more, Logan Macintyre. This time it will be *I* who emerge victorious!"

"That's what it's been about all these years, isn't it? Defeating us. That's really all you want. Most men would have given up long ago."

"That has always been your foolish error, Macintyre! Thinking that I was like most men. But I do not give up! Oh, you may think you have defeated me. But those past battles were mere insignificant skirmishes. Soon the war will culminate, however, and I will be the conqueror! Do you realize, Macintyre, that with you in my power I now possess the leverage to force that arrogant wife of yours to give me whatever I ask, even to signing over Stonewycke?"

"So that's your game, Channing! Lure me down here, and then hold me as ransom for the estate?"

"A brilliant maneuver, wouldn't you say?" Channing leaped shakily to his feet.

"It will never work!"

"It will work!" shrieked Channing in an unexpected outburst. "You don't know the half of what I will bring to bear against you! I will win, I tell you!"

"My wife would never do such a thing."

"Not even for her precious husband?"

"Perhaps you've overestimated even *our* sentimentality."

Regaining his control, though his lower lip still quivered, Channing gazed down his nose with a superior sneer. "I think not. But this is more than a simple case of blackmail. As I said, I have something a little more certain in the works."

"Haven't you tormented us enough?"

"Oh no! Not by a long sight!" Channing's voice broke with wrath. "Don't you understand? I plan to have it all—each and every one of you at my mercy, and all that is yours in my possession! It's so simple! Ha! You're a sentimental fool, Macintyre. The game is over! I have you . . . I have it all!"

"Why, Channing? I will never understand why you are so obsessed with us and with Stonewycke. What could it possibly mean to you?"

"It's *her* . . . she's the cause of it all!" Channing was raving now. "Tormented *you*? What about the torment she's caused *me*! My money was dirty . . . not good enough for her—the haughty little vixen! But I will show her! I have the treasure where she will never lay eyes on it! I have her arrogant politician of a son-in-law! And soon I will have—"

He stopped, his eyes aglow with the fire of cunning, and rubbed his hands together in warped anticipation. "Oh yes, the war is finally over. I've waited sixty years for this moment . . . and my victory is at hand!"

He fell back into his chair as one expended.

Logan shuddered at the man's diseased passion. He attempted to divert the tone of the conversation.

"I thought the so-called treasure was worthless," he said, with as much control as his own voice could manage.

"Worthless on the black market," replied Channing, his tone calming. "But in the esoteric world where people care about such absurdity, I suppose it is priceless—my man in Oxford verified that. When I can bring it out into the open *legally,* who knows what price I will be able to command for it? You yourself were willing to part with a sizable sum for it." Channing rubbed his wrinkled chin. "I still can't figure where you would have been able to produce that kind of money."

"We were willing to do anything to get it back where it belongs."

"Ha, ha! It will not return to Scotland until I am master of Stonewycke!" he laughed wickedly. "Ruminate on that a moment, my high-and-mighty Mr. Macintyre!"

At that moment a servant appeared at the patio door. He walked across the flagstones to where Channing sat.

"Excuse my interruption, sir," he said, "but a message has arrived." He handed Channing a Western Union envelope.

Channing tore into the paper like a starving beast, his bony fingers trembling as he put on his glasses and then held the paper up close to them. His eyes devoured the words with elation; then slowly his twitching lips began to part, his yellowed teeth glinting through the wide smile of delirium that spread across his face.

Finally he looked up and leveled the ludicrous expression of wild-eyed ecstasy upon Logan.

"There . . . you see!" he cried. "Just as I said—I *have* won! You snivelling simpleton . . . you imbecile! Did you really think you could keep me from my due? I have won, I tell you! You and your idiotic family, and your precious worthless treasure, and your ridiculous valley full of bovine dimwits! Mooncalves, all of you! Fools! To think you could stop Jason Channing! I've won! At last . . . at last I've beaten you all! *It's all mine!*"

With the last cry of triumph still ringing in the air, he flung the telegram at Logan.

Logan picked the paper off the floor where it landed. The brief message was simple:

EVERYTHING HAS GONE AS PLANNED STOP WE'VE DONE IT STOP ALLISON MACINTYRE IN CUSTODY STOP ARRIVE B.A. TOMORROW STOP STONE-WYCKE WILL SOON BE OURS STOP

Logan's hand dropped limply to his side. Propping his forehead in his other hand, he slowly shook his head.

"You can't do this . . . you can't do this, Channing," he murmured, all strength draining from his voice.

"I have done it, Macintyre!" gloated Channing. "I can hardly believe they pulled it off," he added almost as an aside to himself. "They sneaked back in there and made off with her right under their noses! I didn't think that fool Burchardt had it in him!"

Becoming aware of Logan again, Channing addressed him once more, as if he had only just then thought of the idea. "There is, of course, always the possibility of a trade. What do you think, Mr. Proud-faced Politician?"

"What do you want?"

"You *know* what I want!"

"Then you should also know I cannot give it to you."

"You have no choice now, you fool! I have your wife!"

"It is my wife, not myself, who controls the Stonewycke property. She will never give it to you, even to save her own life," said Logan, looking at Channing with a forlorn expression as tears rose up in his eyes.

"Perhaps not! But when she sees the rope around your neck and me standing ready to give the order, she will relent!"

Logan said nothing in reply.

"Ha, ha! I've done my homework. I know Stonewycke has no cash. All your bleeding-heart notions of doing good. You give away half your income! You're a sucker for every sad-storied beggar who comes along! You gave away the land to those moronic peasants you have such ridiculously fond notions about! Where has it left you? Fools! Now I have your treasure *and* your wife, and your own life in my power! You have nothing to bargain with, nothing to trade to get her back. You have nothing! She has nothing! Nothing but . . ."

As he spoke a sickening leer spread across his face, again revealing his remaining yellowed teeth: " . . . nothing but the deed to Stonewycke! And if either of you want to leave here alive, that is my price!"

Logan slumped back in his chair, rubbing his face in agony.

After a long and painful moment, he finally looked up and stared Channing full in the face.

"You *have* won, Channing. You can have anything. I will talk to Allison. Just *please* . . . *please* don't hurt her."

Channing threw back his head and laughed mercilessly. Unfortunately the exhilaration brought on by his moment of supreme triumph was too much for his frail body. After only a few seconds of uncontrollable laughter, his voice broke like an ancient hinge, and his mirth ended in a paroxysm of fitful coughing.

Logan glanced around, spotted a pitcher of water, hastened to it, poured some into a glass, and brought it to Channing. He took it, struggled to sip the liquid, but could only swallow with difficulty. When the seizure had subsided after a few moments, he attempted once more to speak, but by now his voice came out in a mere whisper.

"You call your solicitors, do you hear?" he croaked. "Begin having the arrangements made."

Again he began to cough and sent out his thin, wasted hand toward the glass of water.

"Can't you give me a few minutes to take all this in? In the name of all that's true, Channing, even you must have *that* much humanity left."

"I have nothing left for you but impatience! You have made me wait for years . . . for decades . . . for what has always been rightfully mine! You talk of patience! I am out of patience . . . and you are out of time. You will make that call!"

"Not until I have seen Allison and am sure she is safe and that no harm will come to her."

Logan eyed Channing steadily, as if to say, *On this point I will not back down.*

At length Channing glanced away. "I suppose that is how these things are done," he conceded.

"Now please, let me go," said Logan. "I just want to return to my room and be alone."

Channing waved him off. "Try nothing foolish, Macintyre, or it will go badly for your wife."

Logan turned and walked defeatedly toward the door. As he went he sighed raggedly. "I don't know what . . . " he began to mumble to himself, just loud enough for Channing to hear. His voice was disjointed and he rubbed his face and eyes as he spoke.

" . . . I don't know what this news will do to my mother-in-law," he went on. "I doubt she'll be able to hold up when I tell her. It will probably kill her. . . . "

67 ❊ Malice Unhinged

CHANNING'S HEAD JERKED forward.

The impact of Logan's words caused what little color was left in his withered cheeks to vanish instantly.

"What?" he cried, though his voice was pale and worn. Leaning forward, his thin fingers clutched at the arms of the wicker chair until the bones seemed about to pierce through the skin.

Logan turned back toward him with a confused look. "My mother-in-law . . . she's not well, you know."

"What are you saying?" demanded Channing. His face was ghostly white, his red eyes bulging out of his head.

"She will be devastated."

"Who?"

"My mother-in-law . . . Lady Joanna MacNeil."

"Why . . . why that's impossible! What are you talking about?" Channing laughed, but it was a hollow, desperate attempt. "You've finally snapped, Macintyre! She's dead—died four or five weeks ago. I read it in the paper." As he spoke, Channing began to breathe heavily, and his eyes seemed unable to focus on Logan.

"She was very ill," said Logan. "Even failed to register a pulse rate at one point. The news hounds grabbed the story prematurely. But in the end she pulled through."

"Impossible! I don't believe a word of it!" Channing continued to suck in deep draughts of air as if his lungs were suddenly too small to contain what they needed.

"She was always a strong woman. I suppose they don't keep abreast of our local news down here," Logan went on.

"This is madness!" raved Channing. "I read it in the *Times*! She cannot be alive!" His voice shook with passion and disbelief.

Slowly Logan reached into his pocket and took out a folded newspaper clipping. "I keep this as a reminder of my many blessings."

He handed it to Channing.

The headline over the two-column article read: LADY JOANNA MACNEIL RECOV-ERS MIRACULOUSLY FROM NEAR-FATAL HEMORRHAGE.

Channing crumpled the paper into a wad in his fist and threw it on the floor. He glanced around wildly, attempting to make the worn-out circuits in his brain focus this bewildering new information. "But why didn't . . . " he muttered to himself. " . . . how could she . . . but, no . . . then why didn't she notify . . . unless . . . but it could be a fake. . . . "

Again Logan turned to go.

"Wait a minute, Macintyre!" yelled Channing after him. "You can't go now! You've got to . . . got to tell me whether it's true! I don't believe it for a second . . . the article's a sham!"

Once more Logan paused and looked back. "Look, Channing," he said weakly, "the last thing I would want is for you to know Joanna is alive." He stopped for a moment and sighed. "But now it is all changed. Suddenly we are on the brink of losing everything. Under the circumstances, I know she would want to see you one last time, talk to you—"

"*See* me . . . she would want to see me—how . . . ?" he stammered incredulously.

"She is here."

"What . . . I don't . . . how . . . ?" As he struggled to find any coherent words, Channing's tottering body trembled with involuntary emotion.

"She came to Argentina with me. She had to be here to verify the authenticity of the treasure."

"But we had you under surveillance!"

"I had no idea what kind of people I was about to deal with—we all know the Professor did not gain his reputation by singing in choir. You don't think I would let her near any danger, do you? I insisted we travel separately, so if it turned rough, she would be well in the clear."

"She . . . she . . . is *here*?" Channing's words were labored as he continued, trying to cope with disbelief and a fierce eagerness.

Logan nodded.

"I must see her! The swine! . . . I will make her pay!"

Logan closed his eyes.

"I must! Do you hear me!"

"I was afraid it would come to this," Logan whispered in a voice filled with distress.

But Channing was hardly heeding him. His fiery eyes rolled about in his head while he muttered gleefully to himself, rubbing his hands together in sick anticipation, "The impudent hussy . . . she will be the best prize of all! Grovel—that's what she'll do! I'll make her beg . . . beg for her precious Stonewycke! And it will still be mine!"

He laughed cruelly. "The fool . . . to think she could keep it from me! I told her I get what I want. Curse her for not believing me! Curse them all! I will destroy her . . . topple her from that proud perch where she sits with that lout of a farmer looking down on me! I'll show the little jade what real men are made of! I'll show—"

"Please," interrupted Logan, "don't make her come here. Keep Joanna out of it. I'll do anything you ask. I'll sign the deed."

"Silence, you fool!" screamed Channing. "You think any of that is important now? Only one thing is left . . . the only thing that ever mattered! Oh, you'll sign the deed! But first I will see her beg in the dust before me! Get her here—now!"

"I will need a vehicle—"

"Not you! I can't send you!"

He heaved himself up from his chair and began hobbling forward, but his thin cane could hardly support his agitated frame, and his shaking hand did little to steady it.

"I have to think," he mumbled, "—Joanna . . . here! Unbelievable, yet—yes, it is fitting . . . this is how it should be!"

He turned toward the door. "Mario!" he shouted. "Mario!—where is that fool?" he added to himself. "Order a car immediately!" he yelled again.

68 ❧ *Reunion Out of Time*

THAT SAME EVENING a black limousine wheeled easily through the villa gates.

The dark glass of the windows obscured sight of any passengers, but when the automobile stopped at the guardhouse, it was waved quickly on. It proceeded down the drive, finally coming to a stop before the house.

The driver jumped out, hurried around to the passenger door. He opened it and reached in. A slender gloved hand emerged from the darkened recesses of the limousine, lightly took the offered assistance, and in another moment an elegant woman stepped out.

As she stepped onto the brick pavement, it was clear in an instant that she was graceful and shapely, dressed in a tailored gray linen skirt and pale rose silk blouse with long sleeves and a demure purple bow at the neck. A wide-brimmed, pale pink hat shaded her delicate skin from the late yet still hot Argentine sun, but it could not hide her rich auburn hair, streaked with gray and pulled back from her face. At first glance the woman gave the appearance of youthfulness, but closer inspection revealed lines about the eyes and forehead. She might have been forty or sixty, maybe even seventy. The subtlety of her movements made it impossible to tell.

The driver escorted her to the door, her hand on his arm. When another servant appeared at the door, the driver bowed slightly before departing in deference. The house servant then led her through several corridors, finally stopping at the double doors of the room where Logan had first met the master of the house.

A voice from inside instructed them to enter. It sounded anxious, cold, with almost a disguised hint of nervousness.

Two men stood inside to receive her: Jason Channing and Logan Macintyre. The eyes of both were fixed on the door as it slowly opened.

The woman entered and stood. Exhaled breaths from both men indicated their reactions upon at last laying their eyes upon her.

Channing's stunned response was a gasp he struggled to mask. In speechless shock he gazed upon the object of his combined attachment and bitterness. For sixty years his depraved mind had misguidedly told himself that he loved this woman. His warped emotions had desired her, yearned for her, lain awake nights dreaming of this moment when he might behold her once more, if only to convince himself she had not all along been some phantasm out of a youthful nightmare. He had never loved her, though even now, as he stood there, his failing heart beat wildly—too wildly to last much longer. He had never loved at all; his was a self incapable of truly loving. He could only possess . . . take . . . control. What he could not possess and control, he desired—desired all the more that he could not have it! This desire, he tried to convince himself, was love.

Now suddenly before him stood the one thing, the one person, in all his life, he had not been able to control, not been able to possess, not been able to buy. If he felt anything beneficial toward her—he was not a man absent of emotion; he was well-endowed with an abundance of keenly-cultivated hate—it might have been something akin to a respect for her determined strength of will, an inner power of character he did not meet in the circles with which he was associated. Certainly he did not meet it within himself.

Meeting such an unknown—a strength that stood up to him, resisted him, denounced him!—was too great a threat to the inner world of a man like Jason Channing. His heart, his mind, his very soul could not cope with being rejected . . . defeated. He was familiar with inner power. Corrupted, Joanna's strength could have almost offered an equal to his own. Uncorrupted as it was, pure, guileless, determined to turn her back on him, she had become a fixed obsession in his twisted brain, blinding him to all reality.

Silence hung in the room for several moments. The sounds of the ticking clock, a buzzing fly, even the breathing of the three persons standing there quietly, were magnified unbearably as time itself stood still. At last the woman's voice broke into the hushed stillness, more like the gentle tap of a wave against the shore than a hammer against rock.

"Jason Channing," she said. "It has been many years."

Channing licked his parched lips. She should be older, he thought. But he wasn't surprised. She was still beautiful! In his mind's eye she would forever remain the lovely young woman who had boldly stood up to him that day in the meadow at Port Strathy. Incredibly she was even wearing the same outfit!

"You are alive!" he murmured at last.

"I doubt your eyes would deceive you," she answered.

"You look . . . wonderful," said Channing, his breath coming in short spurts. "You have hardly aged!" His eyes began to fill with tears.

"Thank you. You're very kind to say so."

"Oh, Joanna! Why did you do it? We could have been so happy—could have had so much together. The world lay at our feet! It is still not too late! You may still share it with me! Joanna, come back with me. We will together have what we should have had long ago."

"It was impossible then, Jason, and it is equally impossible now. I did what I felt I had to do."

Channing looked deeply into her face. Suddenly his eyes narrowed. "You have not changed," he said. "Still proud . . . still impudent . . . I can see it in your eyes."

She sighed. "But all my pride will not help me now, will it, Jason?"

His mouth twitched, violently fighting against conflicting passions—rage, what seed of love might be attempting to sprout within the stone he would have called his heart, triumph, revenge, bitterness. From somewhere deeper than them all, the most distressing thought he had ever had was knocking on the door of his consciousness—the dawning awareness that even now, in the moment of his supreme and final triumph, he had still not really won over these people; the sense that they were from another world, and that he could do nothing to conquer them, that even in death they would defeat him.

He blocked the hideous notion from his mind, forcing instead a sneer upon his face.

"You admit it, then!" he cried, barking a hard laugh. "You *are* defeated, and at my mercy!"

"Yes, Jason. After all these years, you at last have your victory. All the life is gone out of Stonewycke and it is now ultimately in your power. The granddaughter I thought I had found has suddenly disappeared. My son-in-law is your prisoner—"

"I have your daughter too! I have everything, Joanna!"

The woman's hand clasped her mouth in shock, and she staggered back. Logan caught her and gently led her to a couch. Channing remained where he was, as if the very act of standing before her emphasized his triumph.

"Yes . . . I suppose you do, Jason," she said quietly. "Even the treasure. It is still in your possession?"

"Of course! Your fool of a son-in-law thought he could buy it from me!"

"We should have known it was too good to be true."

Channing's eyes again grew blurry as the awareness of time vanished from them. "Joanna," he said softly, approaching the couch and reaching out to take her hand, "don't you see? It is not too good to be true. We can still be happy together. It can be *ours,* Joanna! Yours and mine—Stonewycke . . . the treasure . . . all we wanted . . . we can share it."

He struggled to pull her up from where she sat, but was in danger of toppling over himself. "Come, Joanna . . . come with me . . . we will get the treasure; we will take it with us back to Stonewycke! We will be happy there . . . together!"

She rose. "Thank you, Jason," she said. "That will be nice. I would so like to see the treasure."

"Come . . . come with me," he said, leading her toward the door.

Just as they reached it, he glanced back at Logan, who had followed them. "Stay where you are, MacNeil! This does not concern you. She is mine now!"

Logan hesitated. Channing continued to eye him carefully.

"Why do you look at me like that, MacNeil? But wait—" As he stared the fog began again to clear from his befuddled brain.

"—you're not . . . no, of course! You're not the clodhopper!"

He spun his head around for a moment toward the door, as if to insure himself that Joanna was still there, then back into the room.

"Macintyre! What are you doing here? But . . . I see it now . . . it's a trick—you're trying to make me think you're that fool who passes himself off as her husband! Well, it won't work, Macintyre!"

"No, Jason. This *is* my son-in-law, Logan Macintyre. You have known him for many years."

"Of course . . . I know that! What do you take me for, a dottering old fool?"

"Might we go now, Jason? Grant me the one last pleasure of allowing my eyes to look upon the treasure that has for so long been yours."

"No! I am not such a fool as to fall for your chicanery. I know you, Macintyre! Bring your wife's mother in here to beguile me into revealing where I have that worthless parcel of relics! Well, you will not find me such an easy mark! Your lost granddaughter, indeed! You fools! You don't even yet know the truth: your precious Jo, that you took into your hearts, was my *own* daughter! Ha, ha, ha! What do you think of that, Joanna! And now she and I will rule Stonewycke! My daughter, Joanna Channing—named after you, my sweet— how do you fancy that? Joanna Channing, mistress and heiress of Stonewycke! Ha! ha!"

Logan caught his breath at Channing's stunning revelation. Joanna staggered back away from the door and again sought the couch.

"It is true," she said feebly. "My days are over. I have nothing else to live for." She cast sorrowful eyes toward Logan. "I am sorry for bringing this upon you, my dear son. So very sorry." Then she turned back toward Channing. "Where is my daughter?"

"She will be here soon."

"What will you do with us, Jason?" she said in a pleading tone.

"I don't know," he said with superiority, folding his arms. "Perhaps if I yet see the proper compliant attitude, I *might* show mercy." He spat out the words with the contempt he felt for the very idea of clemency.

"I will go to my grave destroyed. Will you not grant me the dying wish of seeing the treasure that has been our undoing?"

"Never! No eyes but mine shall ever see it again! The thought of you all going to your deaths wondering where I've stashed it away warms my aging heart!"

"Perhaps this is but a ruse," suggested Logan, "and you don't have it at all."

"Oh, you would like to believe that, wouldn't you, Macintyre? But you are wrong. I fished it from the bottom of the ocean in 1936—*your* ocean! You never even knew what was going on just a mile from your blessed coast!"

"What would it hurt for me to see it now?"

"Hurt! You dare speak to me of *hurt*! Well, suffer, Joanna! It is *your* moment to feel the hurt you have inflicted upon me all these years! Suffer . . . as I have suffered!"

He tightened his grip on his cane, turned away, and hobbled from the room.

Logan and the woman exchanged quick, questioning glances. But before either had the chance to speak, two servants entered and bade them follow.

They were taken to separate rooms, and the doors locked behind them.

In the dark of the night Jason Channing paced like a caged lion back and forth across his bedroom floor.

His old bones seemed suddenly enlivened, as if from some fiendish fire burning from deep within. Notwithstanding his apparent energy, the glow came from the dying embers of life. The very lust of his victory was consuming the last remaining vitality from his spirit. In the core of his being sat a cold stone, and thus the peace that should belong to a man who has gained his heart's desire was instead to him mere emptiness. The passion of his hate fed upon itself, leaving only death in its wake.

His agitation intensified through the night.

She had returned from the dead, but still she would not bend her proud neck before him! Even in defeat, she haunted him! Why could he not, even now, erase from his memory that picture of the proud, majestic, despicable girl in that confounded meadow? Why could he not see her on her knees? Even in his mind he could not make her bow in front of him!

She *had* been vanquished today! He had defeated her. She had even admitted as much! Yet still that look remained in her eyes—that smugness, that lovely, irritating, beautiful tilt to her chin! Even as she said the words, "You have your victory, Jason," inside she had still not been broken. She was still—she would always remain—her *own* woman!

Would the memory of her face *never* leave him in peace?

Just before dawn, he collapsed in an exhausted heap upon his bed. He slept like a cranky child, who only gives grudgingly over to fatigue.

69 ※ *Final Stroke*

CHANNING DID NOT awaken until about nine.

When he appeared for breakfast, he looked wasted and feeble. He had nothing to eat, only drank black coffee and ordered trays sent to his guests' rooms.

He still did not know what to do about them. Though he could hardly admit it to himself, he could not bear just yet to see *her* again. Soon his victory would be complete. Then he would stand before her to mete out his wrath.

At 10:30 the phone rang.

He listened a moment. "Bring her immediately!" he barked into the receiver. "Gunther . . . what do you need him for?"

He paused and listened. "Well, he's not here. How much help do you need with a woman? Get her here now—I want no more delays!" He slammed down the receiver with a crash.

Some time after lunch had been brought to his room, Logan heard the key once more in his door. He was wanted by El Patron.

He followed the servant who delivered the message. Halfway along the corridor he met another servant escorting the Lady of Stonewycke. He cast her a heartening smile, but they dared exchange nothing beyond the commonest of pleasantries in front of Channing's people. Soon they were back in the salon where Channing had the habit of receiving his visitors.

"I thought you would want to be present with me as I greet my new guests," he said.

"I tell you, Channing," Logan said hotly, "if my wife has been harmed in any way!"

"You will see for yourself in a few moments." He waved a tired hand toward the chairs. "Make yourselves comfortable in the meantime."

Joanna took a seat on the couch. Logan remained standing, too tense to relax. Channing sat in a chair opposite Joanna, his eyes leaving her only when the knock came to the double doors.

"Enter!" he called out, turning his head from her with effort.

Allison stepped in first, her arm in the firm grasp of the Austrian viscount, von Burchardt. He held a .38 revolver in his other hand.

Channing grinned lecherously. "Welcome to my house, Allison Macintyre." Then he looked sharply at Emil. "Well, von Burchardt, I see you managed *this* job without bungling it!"

He scrutinized him for a long moment, taking in the viscount's eyes, pencil-thin moustache, and expensive, fashionable white linen suit. "You've lost weight," he mumbled off-handedly.

Emil snapped his heels together smartly and bowed in that grandiose fashion for which he was known. "My labors for you, Mein Herr," he said in his oily German accent, "take precedence over all else—even eating!"

Channing grunted, unimpressed.

"Where is Jo?" he asked.

"There was an important matter in the city she had to attend to. She does not anticipate being detained long."

"There is nothing more important than this!" fumed Channing. "She should be here!"

"She sends her regrets, and will be here shortly."

"Well, I won't wait!" Channing bellowed. He turned his attention to his guests.

"So, here you all are—all of you . . . together!" He flashed a lopsided grin. "Touching, is it not, Emil? And kind of me to arrange this little family reunion."

"Allison, have they harmed you?" asked Logan, hurrying toward her.

"Not so fast, Macintyre!" said Emil, pointing the gun toward Logan.

"I am fine. We can be thankful at least for that. And you, Mother?" she asked.

The older woman nodded but said nothing.

"I should have hired a photographer!" gloated Channing, filled with the moment he had so long desired. "Ah yes, a photograph would be perfect—to capture this momentous occasion for our progeny to remember—especially since my daughter could not be here!"

"Your daughter!" exclaimed Allison.

"Oh yes! You did not know? Ha, ha! Had my original plan succeeded, it would have been the tour de force of my life. My own daughter installed as heiress of Stonewycke, while all the time you were taking her to your hearts as if she was one of your own! The poetic beauty of it!"

"Jo is . . . your daughter?" said Allison in disbelief, glancing toward Logan. He merely nodded sadly.

"Oh, no doubt she would have told you eventually—perhaps when you were on your deathbeds, helpless to do anything about it. Ha, ha! But I begin to think it better that she failed. Had our design worked, only she would have been able to exult in our triumph. This way, I too am able to see your faces in defeat! Ha, ha, ha! I must admit, it makes every one of the past sixty years almost worth it to see your despair on this glorious day!"

"And what now, Channing?" said Logan.

"What now, you ask! What do you think? You will give me Stonewycke, and in my compassion I will allow you to live. If you refuse me, I will have you all killed, here and now, while Jo flies back to Stonewycke to claim the inheritance as *your* daughter!"

A soft voice came from the couch, speaking to him for the first time. "Jason," it said quietly.

Channing stopped and turned his head. His gaze was arrested by a penetrating stare from the eyes he had dreamed of so long. Deeply they probed his mind, unflinching, commanding his own eyes to remain and not look away. Gradually an involuntary twitch of mental distress began to flit about the edges of his mouth.

"Jason," the voice beckoned again. "It is I you want. Is that not true?" Still her eyes held his.

"You are all I have ever wanted," he replied, the tenacity of his will losing its grip.

"Now you have me, Jason. I am here . . . " As she spoke he was helpless to resist the magnetism of her eyes. "Let my family go, Jason."

"I—I cannot . . . he will—"

"No harm will come to you, Jason, I assure you. None of us would hurt you. We care about you, Jason."

"*Care* about me? Why, that's—but . . . but of course you do! You must! I am the new master of Stonewycke!" His voice contained none of its former power. His eyes fought to look away, but could not. She had gained mastery over him, and now held him fast.

"We *do* care about you, Jason," she said, her voice still hushed, "in a way you perhaps cannot grasp. All of us in this room—"

But at last he succeeded in looking away, and the spell was broken.

"And care you shall! For I will soon be in Stonewycke . . . I am preparing for our journey even now! Come, Joanna," he said, rising and grabbing his cane, "we are going by ship, just as we did last year from New York . . . only this time without that busybody, Mrs. Cupples!"

He made for the door. "Come, Joanna . . . come! The steamer is sailing this afternoon . . . We must gather our things!"

"You will take the treasure with you?"

"What's that, my sweet?"

"The treasure, Jason . . . the treasure of Stonewycke."

"Yes, yes . . . of course. I shan't forget *that*! It must go back with us! I'll go retrieve it now. Come! You must help me . . . it is heavy!"

She rose. He half-grabbed her arm and led her with what force he could manage out the door. Once they were outside, the others rose also, exited the room, and followed slowly down the corridor. Emil trailed behind, still carrying the gun.

70 ✥ The Truth

CHANNING LED THE way through several corridors, toward the back of the elongated L-shaped house, through servants' quarters, past the kitchen, and finally out into the hot, humid air. The small entourage crossed an open dirt quadrangle, and arrived at length at a run-down adobe structure that looked like little more than an unused shed.

Still Channing hobbled gamely along, though once inside, in the darkness, he found the footing more treacherous. Immediately after closing the huge oak door behind them, he turned sharply to the right, traversed a narrow corridor, then arrived at another heavy, iron-studded door that faced left.

Channing stopped, pulled out a large ring of keys from his pocket, selected an old-fashioned one, well rusted, inserted it into the door, and shoved it open. With his free hand he pulled the chain on a dim lightbulb that hung from the ceiling, illuminating a narrow stone stairway which descended under the earth. Led by Channing's faltering step, which every moment appeared ready to collapse beneath the weight of his body, they made their way down in single file.

At the bottom, a maze of underground passages spread out before them. Though they passed several locked doors, and others with bars across them that appeared to be cells of some ancient dungeon, it was obvious the more recent use of the place had been as a wine cellar. On either side of the corridor, which gradually opened wider and wider, revealing long narrow, low-ceilinged rooms, sat rows upon rows of barrels and casks and crates of bottles filled with wine.

"It won't be long now," said Channing. "There is one special room here . . . of my very own. No one else has a key. And no one knows what a special wine I keep in storage," he added with a gleam in his eye. "Come, Joanna . . . we will be there shortly!"

The echo of his voice seemed to disturb him. He looked about and, though he had been aware of their presence as they descended the steps into the cellar, he seemed now all at once to see the others for the first time.

"What? But, Joanna, I thought we were alone . . . we have to—"

He paused, focusing on Logan. Gradually the dawn of recognition spread over his face, and with it came back to his eyes the demon of hatred.

"Macintyre, what are you doing here!" he demanded. "This is private business between Miss Matheson and myself!"

"I keep no secrets from my family, Jason."

"But, Joanna, who . . . who are these? I don't understand." His eyes narrowed and he squinted at her, then glanced at Logan, then back at her.

"—I see it now!" he shouted. "It's a trick! You were only trying to trick me into showing you the treasure! Well, I've spoiled your little game! What do you pack of fools take me for?"

"We take you for nothing more than what you are," said Logan, who had had his fill of the trick they were perpetrating. "That is a man in need of healing, in need of what can give life. Believe me, Channing, we want nothing but life for you. This life of yours, this enmity and hatred, is no life. It is a living death."

"How dare you preach to me, you pathetic fool! Let me out of here! You will never see your blessed treasure! I will take it with me to my grave!"

"The treasure is meaningless, Channing, alongside your life."

"Good . . . good! Meaningless it might as well be, for you'll never lay eyes on it!"

"You may scorn my words, Channing. Though you hate me, I cannot bear to see this cancerous bitterness destroy you." Logan took a deep, sorrowful breath. "Yet there must be hope for you. Will nothing make you listen?"

"Hope! Ha! You *are* a fool!" he cackled vilely. "Well, I have had enough of you—all of you!" He tried to push Logan out of the way with his cane, then, failing that, went around him and began hobbling off in the direction from which they had come. "Von Burchardt," he cried, "shoot them! Each one of them, right here—now! I'm finished with them!"

He took two more paces, stopped, turned back, and saw the viscount standing, making no move to carry out his order.

"Shoot them, I tell you!" he shrieked. "Or I will shoot you!"

"I'm afraid I cannot do that, Mr. Channing," the man replied.

"Cannot . . . what? How dare you disobey me!"

"I *must* disobey you." He let out a prolonged sigh, glanced toward Logan, then lowered his gun and let go of Allison. With the hand that was now free, he reached up to finger his moustache. Then to Channing's horror, he peeled it off.

"What! . . . von Burchardt, what are you . . . oh, God . . . no!" cried Channing as the truth broke in upon his benumbed consciousness.

"May I present my friend, Ashley Jameson," said Logan calmly. "I'm afraid he was the one who helped me apprehend your friend the viscount in the attempted kidnapping of my wife. The real von Burchardt, as well as your daughter, are at this moment in the custody of the police in Aberdeen."

"What have you done? It is an evil trick . . . Joanna!"

"And this—"

Logan held out his hand to the older woman, who now had a handkerchief in her hand and was proceeding to wipe away the cosmetic wrinkles on her face. "—this is my daughter, Joanna Hilary Macintyre—my *real* daughter, as even you can see by her resemblance to my mother-in-law, who has indeed gone to be with her Lord."

"No . . . it cannot be true!" Channing stammered as he staggered back against the dirty stone wall.

"It is true," said Logan with feeling in his voice. "It is over, Channing."

Channing looked away, walked a few steps, then turned back to face the two men and two women. His skin was ashen. His eyes stared in disbelief. For several moments all was silent. Slowly he slumped to the floor.

"It cannot be true," he repeated. "The victory must be mine! I cannot let you defeat me again!" But even as he spoke, the vitality of life slowly drained from him.

Logan sighed, then approached him. When he spoke again, his voice was full of compassion for the broken man who would have killed him.

"*We* do not defeat you, Channing," said Logan. "It is the devil of hatred, the demon of bitterness who would defeat you. *They* are the enemy, not us."

"But who set them on me?" he whimpered. "It was her! *She* forced them on me!"

"We bring them upon ourselves. Hatred comes from within, Channing. No one can force it upon another."

"Well, she did her best of it!"

"I'm sure she did do her best. She tried to turn you to the truth."

"What! By turning the whole town against me? By making me look the fool?" he cried, struggling to his feet. Then grabbing his cane, he began to pace around.

"By keeping you from cheating the townspeople, which was the best thing she could have done for your soul, if only you had allowed it to start you down the road of truth."

"My soul! It's precious little she ever cared for my soul! Tormenting me day and night for sixty years."

"I happen to know that she prayed for your soul, Channing, during all of those same sixty years."

"Prayed for me! What rubbish! That's just the sort of thing she would do! Prayed that I'd repent, no doubt. It's rubbish, I tell you!"

"It's truth. Repentance is the door into life."

"Telling God you're sorry, I suppose," Channing spat.

"And that you want Him to remake you in the image of His Son."

"Well, I'm not sorry! I've lived my life and I had my way with it. And it's low I'd sink before I'd ever ask to be made like that fool they call his Son! Going around preaching that nonsense they call the gospel, and then letting them kill Him without trying to get away. If God had a Son He would have more power than that! Nonsense, I tell you."

"It's truth."

"It's humbug!"

"His Son's power was of another kind than can be seen by the eyes of this world. You've probably heard the story of how He conquered death, and walked away from the grave?"

"A fairy tale!"

"A historical fact," asserted Logan.

"I suppose you believe it?" asked Channing.

"Not only do I believe it, I base my entire life upon the fact of Jesus' resurrection. By His victory over death are we given power to live."

"*I've* lived, I tell you—and no doubt much better than if I had spent my years trying to be religious and worrying about my conscience pricking me every time I turned around!"

"Have you lived, Channing? Really lived?"

"I have, more than you, Macintyre! I'm a rich man!"

"And powerful too, from what I hear."

"Yes, powerful! A formidable opponent they find Jason Channing when anyone tries to cross me!

"Rich and powerful," mused Logan. "And happy?"

"As happy as any man can be! We've all got to go sooner or later. In the meantime we might as well get what we can!"

"Which is what you did?"

"Certainly!"

"And now?"

"What do you mean *now*?"

"What will you do with all that you have? Your greed has gained you wealth and might. Can you take it with you?"

"Of course not! I'm no fool! Neither can you take your precious Stonewycke with you! I'm not a religious man, mind you, but I know my Scriptures. Dust to dust, ashes to ashes. I know we go the way we came!"

"Ah, but there *is* something we can take with us into the next life, Channing."

"Poppycock! Where'd you get an idiotic notion like that?"

"From the Scriptures."

"And just *what* can we take with us?"

"Our soul."

"Oh, well . . . if you believe in that moonshine!"

"Whether you believe in it or not, Channing, your soul *does* live on. And it takes with it the character it has become during life on this earth."

"The soul has a personality? That's absurd!"

Logan's heart leaped within him at the mere suggestion that, even in his anger and pain, Channing had dared to ask a question about the eternal being of man.

"What is the soul, Channing, but the essential *you*—that innermost part of your personhood which is left when everything to do with this world suddenly vanishes. You have been fashioning the essential personality of your soul all your life long, by every word you have spoken, by every choice you have made, by every action you have taken toward another fellow human being."

"And now my soul is damned to hell, I suppose!"

"God only knows, Channing. All I know is that it is never too late to begin making marks of selflessness and goodness upon your soul. You cannot make yourself pleasing to God only by doing good. But every kind deed, every gracious word, every repentant attitude—they all reflect the state of your soul—whether or not you are genuinely seeking to discover and live by the truth God has revealed."

"Even if I believed what you say—which I don't for a moment!—there's no time. It's too late for me!"

"It's never too late. As long as there is one gasp left in a dying man's heart, it is not too late for him to begin."

Channing stifled a cry of mingled anger and despair. "I *am* a dying man, Macintyre. I can feel death stalking me. God help me, I hate it!" he cried. "And I hate Him for bringing me to this. I'm not ready to die!"

"You may hate Him, but He loves you. He's the only one who can help you face what is ahead. It's true, Channing; it's never too late to begin."

"A poor beginning that would be—ten thousand black marks on the soul, and one death-bed mark on the other side. Foxhole religion, Macintyre—what good is it?"

"When you face Him, God will not tally up a scoresheet. He will only want to know in which direction you were trying to move. It is never too late to change directions. That's what repentance is, turning around and going the other way."

Channing was silent a moment and seemed to be thinking. Again he slumped to the ground and sat, breathing heavily. His face was pale, his skin cold. In his eyes could be seen the exhaustion from the inner struggle.

"You think I'll see Him then . . . face-to-face?"

"We all will."

"And he'll condemn me to hell, no doubt! I thought He was supposed to be forgiving. Sins white as snow and all that claptrap."

"*He* does not condemn us. We condemn ourselves. *He* offers us life. It is up to us to receive it."

"When did He ever offer *me* life?"

"Every day you lived, He was trying to speak to you. Did your conscience never bother you?"

"Oh, a time or two, I daresay, but I put a stop to that early enough. A man with a touchy conscience will never get far in this world."

"There you see—He was speaking to you, but you refused to listen. The world is upside-down from true reality, Channing. Getting on, as you call it, in the *real* world—the world of spiritual reality, the world we will all suddenly become part of the moment we die—getting on in that world means denying this world around us now. It's all backward. The more we strive to get ahead here, the further behind we will be then. The last shall be first, you know."

"Leaves a man like me in a bit of a pickle, I daresay, who was told nothing about all this!"

"We've all been told, Channing. Jesus came two thousand years ago to tell the world. His followers have been telling us ever since."

"No one told me! If they had, maybe I'd have been different."

"We all know the truth in our hearts. Even if no one tells us, the truth of reality—the truth of God's character—is all about us and inside us. The world He created, and the conscience He put inside us, they are there to tell us about Him all day and night, every moment of our lives. No man can say he has not been exposed to God's truth. No man will *dare* say it when he faces Him. In that moment we will know that we knew the truth all along, but we chose to turn our backs on it. Every man, every woman—we all make the choice, whether consciously aware of it or not."

"Rather an infernal mess that leaves me in, if what you say is true."

"There are consequences to what we do with our lives."

"So how is a poor fool like me to get out of such a predicament?"

"By doing what He has been telling you all your life."

"Being good, I suppose!"

"That's a good thing, but not the starting point."

"Don't toy with me! What am I to do?"

"Lay it all down. Your bitterness, your hate, your unforgiveness. Lay it down that He might heal your soul."

"And then keep the Commandments and be a good boy, is that it? There's no time for all that! Look at me, Macintyre! I'm a dying man!"

"There's only one command you need worry about, and there's always time for that."

"And what is that?"

"To believe in the Lord Jesus Christ."

"Poppycock! That's nothing you can *do*!"

"You can *do* nothing *until* you've done that."

"My life's behind me, I tell you!"

"A life of greed, of thirsting for power, of hurting others, a life of bitterness and unforgiveness."

"How dare you speak to me like that!"

"The day will come when you *must* face what you are, Channing. Better you hear it from my lips, while there is still time, than from His."

"Curse you, Macintyre! To speak so to a dying man! If I could just stand—this wretched cane!" he exclaimed, struggling to rise, but falling back as the cane slipped under him. "If I could only—by heaven, if I were a younger man, I'd kill you myself!"

"Channing," pleaded Logan, "do you ever want to see *her* again—face-to-face?"

The question sobered him and he fell back.

"Of course I do! But it's too late for that too. She's dead."

"Her soul is not dead. And I'm sure she wants to see you again. What do you think she would say to you? Will she forgive you for the misery you've brought her family?"

The unexpected question bit deep into what was left of Channing s blunted conscience.

"She will, when I explain how I loved her."

"Did you love her, Channing?"

"Of course I did! Why else would I offer her the world? Why else—"

"Why else would you scheme and kill in order to destroy all she held dear? What kind of love is that?"

"How dare you!" he shrieked.

"I dare speak the truth to you because you will soon face your Maker, and He will speak the truth to you . . . and more! He will not be put off, Channing! You must face reality. The only path left you, the only *life* left you, is to lay down the demons of hate and vengeance and greed and selfishness that have ruled in your heart."

"She will forgive me, I tell you!" he screamed.

"Indeed, she will. She does forgive you! And so do I, so does my wife, so does my daughter. We harbor you no malice, Channing. For what you have done, our hearts are open with forgiveness toward you."

"Then God will forgive me too! Can His forgiveness be any less?"

"Infinitely greater in every way. But neither our forgiveness nor the forgiveness of God can enter your heart while it is yet full, blocked by the hate that has kept you in bondage and misery all these years. Until the bitterness is gone, there is no room for the forgiveness to enter."

Channing thought for a moment. His body was still, his mental and physical energy nearly spent. His breathing came in short, weak pulses, and when he again spoke, Logan had to strain to make out the words.

"So what you're telling me is that I have to lay down everything I've lived for—"

"Only your *self*, and the bitterness and unforgiveness you've carried with it all these years."

"And then believe, you say, in Jesus Christ? What am I to believe about Him?"

"You need believe nothing *about* Him. We must believe *in* Him."

"How do you do that?"

"By laying down your self, your past, your *own* desires, that you might trust Him to give you life. Give yourself into God's care, Channing. The moment you open the door of your heart to let *out* the sin and evil you have harbored there, in that moment His forgiveness enters and all is changed. In that moment, your soul becomes forever His."

Channing did not reply. His eyes were wide open and clear, but his thoughts were far away, reliving the many years that had led up to that moment he was about to face. The damp, darkened wine cellar was hushed like an underground cathedral as each person present was aware of the internal and eternal struggle then being waged within the mind and heart of the old sinner.

Gradually Logan felt the grip of Channing's hand tighten.

"I . . . I see," he struggled to say, but his voice was a mere whisper and he was having difficulty gasping for air. "They are coming . . . I see them . . . but—where did that bright light come from? Macintyre . . . Logan—are you still there? I'm . . . I'm going . . ."

Logan felt the withered hand slowly relax. A long final breath of air escaped Channing's lips. Logan looked long upon the face. The eyes were closed. The twitch was gone from the lips. He was dead.

Silent tears fell from Logan's eyes as he released the lifeless hand and sat back upon the floor.

Slowly Allison walked toward him, knelt down, and laid a hand on his shoulder.

"You did all you could, Logan," she whispered.

"I will always wonder," he replied. "There is always so much one *wants* to say."

Hilary and Ashley drew near and knelt down also.

"Dear Father in heaven," Logan prayed aloud. "For this man's soul we now offer our prayers. Whether or not he made his peace with you, only you know. We just ask that you cleanse *us* of any remaining bitterness or unforgiveness. Let us truly know your forgiveness, O God! Jason Channing made his life a grave filled with dead men's bones. I pray, Father, that Channing's hate will stop here, that the chain of his corruption and evil will be broken, and that the hold he must surely have on his own daughter be undone. For Jo we pray too, that your healing forgiveness might pour itself out on her. Dear God, your love still prevails, and has the power to heal—let each one of us experience that healing now."

71 ✠ Vintage '36

"IS IT OVER, Logan?" asked Allison. "For us, as well as Channing?"

"I don't know, dear," he replied. "I think so. Though the Lord will never be through with our lives, nor with the work He wants to do in our family."

"What are we going to do . . . now?"

"We are going to trust God . . . and believe He will deliver us."

Logan and Allison still sat with Hilary and Ashley in the corridor where Channing's body lay slumped on the ground. They had been praying together for some minutes.

"We have committed our way to Him," said Logan, "and He will guide our steps."

"I do not think Channing's men will simply let us walk out of here, Logan," said Ashley.

"But I am so sick of the guile we are using," replied Logan, "while speaking to Channing about truth."

"You mustn't forget that we prayed before undertaking this venture, and asked God to guide us," said Hilary. "You knew you had to face Channing, stop the evil and let it go no further, and talk to him, as a man, as a brother, about his soul. How else could you have done that but to get him alone, in a state that he would listen? I don't see how it could have been achieved any other way."

"It simply seems that there might have been a more straightforward way . . . I don't know."

"*If* God had opened the doors in that direction. But He gave you *this* idea . . . and it worked."

"Did it? Channing is dead."

"He died hearing of God's love, and with four Christians with him praying for his eternal destiny," replied Hilary. "Under what other circumstances could such a thing have occurred? You did not misread the signals from God, Logan. Even though this was, in a sense, a con on the unsuspecting man, I think God knew it was the only way to break in upon the hardened crust of his heart. You prayed for guidance, and I think He gave it to you."

Logan sighed. "Perhaps you're right."

"Besides," added Allison, "look at it practically. Had you tried to stop Channing any other way, more out in the open, there would surely have been bloodshed. He was a wicked man. Confronting him could have meant death for innocent people, even for yourself or any of us. You had to protect your family, too. The legacy of this family is not over. I, for one, want time to spend with my daughter!" As she spoke, she smiled at Hilary. "God used you, Logan, in His way, which might at the moment seem a little peculiar, to confront Channing and to protect your family. I thank God for what you did."

"It's not over yet," reminded Ashley. "We may still have to con our way out of here."

"Wise as serpents, eh, Ashley?" said Logan.

"And innocent as doves."

"I only wish we'd have found the treasure," sighed Hilary. "It is part of the legacy too."

"Not so important, however, as how Channing spends the *rest* of his life," said Logan. "It will not seem such a great loss in the light of eternity."

"Who said it must be a loss?" asked Ashley. "We have to be close. I think we can spare a few minutes before we plan our escape."

"Of course!" said Hilary. "It must be in one of these rooms nearby!" She jumped to her feet and continued through the cellar, pausing before every door and opening each to look for clues.

"What exactly are we looking for?" asked Ashley, rising also and following.

"Who knows?" answered Logan. "None of us have ever seen it."

"Mother's journal spoke of a large box. That's all Maggie said."

"Channing spoke of historical relics," said Logan. "That could mean just about anything."

Hilary had run on ahead, excitedly probing every corner of the corridor.

"Here . . . come here!" she called out. "There's another large room!"

The other three followed, reaching the end of the passageway they had been in, off which two doors opened. One led only into a small room filled with empty barrels. The other led into a large, open room which was nearly empty.

"There's nothing here," said Allison.

"But look, Mother," said Hilary. "At the far end—another door! I tried the handle, but it's locked."

"It's hard to believe they would have installed electricity down here unless they had an important reason."

"Didn't Channing mention something about another room . . . a key?" said Logan.

"Yes, he did!" exclaimed Hilary. "A special room, he said. And no one had a key but him!"

They glanced around at one another.

"A bit quirky, perhaps," said Ashley. "But do you suppose it might be in order for me to borrow Channing's keys for a minute?"

Without awaiting an answer, he turned and ran out of the room and back along the corridor. When he returned he carried Channing's ring of keys.

It took several attempts to find the correct one, but at length his patience was rewarded when one of the keys slid in. He turned the latch and gave the door a shove. Its rusty hinge scraped from the friction; it had not been oiled in years, and was apparently not often used.

All four heads peered into the black opening.

"Stand back," said Logan. "Let me."

He took a step inside, nearly falling as he did so. "It's another set of stairs," he said, recovering, then gradually disappearing downward. "I'm feeling the walls," he called back, "but there appears to be no light switch."

The others continued watching, but in another moment or two he had disappeared into the dark cavity. All they could hear was the sound of his feet probing their way downward through the blackness.

"Ah, here it is. I think—yes, that's it!"

Suddenly a light flipped on, revealing the treacherous narrow passage. Logan stood at the bottom.

"A rather ingenious way of discouraging visitors, wouldn't you say?" he called up. "Placing the switch at the bottom! Well . . . what are you waiting for? This has got to be the place!"

Eagerly Hilary skipped down the stairs to join him, followed by Allison, then Ashley.

The passage in which they now found themselves was extremely narrow, allowing but one to pass at a time. To either side were occasional doors, unlocked, in which were housed various vintages of wine, undoubtedly rare, presumably from Channing's private stock. The fourth door they reached was again locked.

"Ashley . . . the keys!" Logan called back.

Ashley handed the ring forward.

Logan fumbled with them a while. At last the door yielded. He walked inside, found the light easily, and switched it on.

The room was perhaps ten feet by twelve feet, with a low ceiling. Against one wall were stacked three or four cases of wine. Three large wine barrels lay on their sides at the far end. The four detectives spread out in silence to examine the contents.

"Curious," said Hilary, picking up a bottle from one of the chests. "Every bottle here, though from different vineyards from all over the world, is labeled 1911. There's probably a small fortune here, just in the wines!"

Logan was thumping at the three barrels.

"Do that again, Logan," said Ashley, approaching.

Again Logan knocked against the casks.

"Do you hear that," said Ashley. "This one has an altogether different tone. I'll wager you there's no wine in that cask. It's as empty as a hollow log!"

Quickly Logan glanced about. "There must be a crowbar, or something we can use to pry off that lid!"

As he looked around in the darkened light, meanwhile, Ashley was examining the label on the barrel. He stood before it stumped. This was certainly no wine, and no vineyard he was familiar with.

"*Steenbuaic—1936*," he murmured aloud.

"What is it, Ashley?" asked Hilary, coming up beside him.

"This label . . . it's most unusual. If I didn't know better, I'd think it was—"

"Ah ha!" exclaimed Logan, interrupting his thought. "Just what we need. Probably left here for this express purpose!"

Ashley and Hilary stood aside as Logan approached. He plied the crowbar to the questionable barrel of curious vintage. The lid fell away, and all four gasped simultaneously at what they beheld.

It was not wine.

72 ✠ Trail of the Reliquary

THE HEIRS TO Digory's and Maggie's legacy stood on the cold earthen floor of a dungeon-like room. Before them sat the ancient box that had been the object of such greed, such hopes, such mystery, and such speculation, where Logan and Ashley had placed it after lifting it out of the barrel.

For several moments each of the four was too awed to speak. Gradually they began to examine it more closely.

The metallic box was no larger than a small steamer trunk, perhaps one foot by two feet, and some eighteen inches high at the peak. Most of the exterior was of some kind of enameled metal—certain iron rivets and other fasteners were rusted, parts displayed the green corrosion of copper, but most seemed made of bronze. It had held up well through its wanderings over many hundreds of years.

A pyramidic lid of four slabs—two isosceles triangles and two isosceles trapazoids—were hinged to the box itself, joining at a peak where an ornate bar fastened each of the lid pieces to one another, apparently serving as a handle for two men to use in carrying the box, which Ashley judged to weigh some seventy or eighty pounds. The surface was richly engraved, and within moments, unable to restrain his historian's curiosity an instant longer, Ashley was on his knees examining it all over in minute detail. He ran his hand over the rough surface of the once smooth and shiny metal.

"This outer layer appears not an original engraving at all," he said, "but rather taken from a mold of some sort."

"Let's open it up!" said Hilary, her eyes glowing with anticipation.

Logan turned to Allison. "This should be your honor, my dear."

She smiled, but quickly became solemn. "After witnessing Channing's lust for this thing, I almost don't care what is inside. Yet it is such a part of my heritage, at the same time I feel compelled to know once and for all what it contains."

Encircling the outside of the box were several lengths of heavy chain, obviously a new addition, probably Channing's fitting legacy. A padlock held the chain links together and it required another search of Channing's ring to locate the proper key. Ashley handed it to Allison, who inserted it easily into the lock. It must have been kept in good repair, for it snapped open readily. They pulled away the chain; then Allison took hold of the bar, unlatched the hooks binding the portions of the lid to each other, slid out the bar, and slowly spread back the sides of the lid and opened the box.

Inside, it was lined with the same thin enameled metal. Two large woolen blankets took up a good amount of the space, though they were mostly decayed with age. They had apparently been used to pad the other items. They seemed newer than the relics they had been used to protect, but by the look of the plaids they were probably not put there by Channing. Perhaps Digory had added them, suggested Logan.

Carefully Allison unfolded the blankets. There were a dozen or so items of some size, as well as miscellaneous small trinkets, a few coins, spoons, knives, two penannular brooches, some scraps of silver, and several smooth polished round stones almost resembling marbles. Of the larger items, several were of obvious value, and others appeared purely commonplace. Most were of ornamented silver alloy, including four bowls, a gilt pommel, one chape, three silver chalices, a pair of heavy candlesticks, two sword hilts, and an odd looking piece of fine silverwork that resembled a sword hilt but was at the same time quite distinct. This last caught Ashley's attention and he lifted it out.

"This is marvelous!" he breathed in awe. "Positively unbelievable! At last the pieces of this ancient mystery begin to fit together!"

"I could see the gears of your brain turning furiously as you eyed the outside of the box," chuckled Logan. "Can you regale us with your expertise? But please, we are mere laymen. Keep it simple."

"Look at these engravings," he said, pointing to the exterior of the box and tracing his finger along the lines of the filigree. "I had a suspicion when I first saw it, but the reproduction is not of the best. You see here"—he pointed with his finger—"you can tell that the box itself has been plated with what we see. If we could see the original underneath, I'm certain the engravings would be much more detailed. Nevertheless, you can see here what looks like a *chi-rho* monogram. The Greek letters *chi* and *rho* are known as the Chrisma, a symbol

"Oh, not much, really—as pure gold, that is. Let's see, sixt
perhaps a thousand ounces . . . that's—I don't know, three, ma
sand pounds. A lot of money, to be sure, but nothing alongside
of a find such as this. One of the original owners of the box r
to cover the gold and hide its wealth."

"I wonder if Channing knew?"

"I doubt it," said Logan. "He would have melted it down

"I wonder who made it . . . and why?" sighed Hilary, "an
Braenock stones?"

"There is probably much we will never know about the h
tainer," sighed Ashley. "But it makes one hungry to travel b
early era, and try to discover where things like this had thei

"We always thought," said Allison, "that the treasure b
had been wiped out in the eighth or ninth century—or at le
"It probably was hidden at that time."

"It is possible the beginnings of its history go back much
dred years earlier than that! Oh, the journeys it must have t
must have held it, the stories it could tell about our cou
Stonewycke's beginnings! All before it came to be buried
of Braenock Ridge. My mind simply reels!" exclaimed A
the mere speck of time since Maggie's days!"

"George Falkirk, wasn't it," said Logan, "who first dug
"With his henchman Martin Forbes," Allison replied. "
same cloth as Channing, became greedy, and that was the
them discovered about the gold underneath the thin layer of
Falkirk, and then he himself met his end falling from the

"All the intrigue surrounding that murder nearly destroy
said Hilary, remembering clearly what she had read in Jo

"Then dear old Digory, after he and young Maggie so
out of the ground and load it on the back of a horse and bri

"Maggie told me once," broke in Allison, "in one of l
the treasure—I'd completely forgotten this until now!—
and put them in two bags, thinking to more evenly distr
weighed just as much empty as it did full."

"It's a wonder they managed it!" remarked Ashley.

"I had just been thinking of Digory's loyalty to the
spare them, he dug it up from the garden where he and M
it again in a place no one knew."

"Where was that?" asked Ashley.

"At the top of Ramsey Head," answered Logan. "I'
flicted with the disease—the desire for the kind of fulf
would bring."

"There were no riches of that kind here anyway!"

"But your quest, however misguided, did bring you t
with a smile. "And to me." She paused, recalling the s
met. "All this makes me think that perhaps our concept
all along. Digory meant well when he tried to hide it.
attribute intrinsic evil to the treasure itself.

"From its very beginnings it was intended for some
even draw a heathen nation closer to His Son. What a v
it refused to stay hidden—from its burial on Braenock
to the bottom of the sea where Channing somehow l
dungeon of a wine cellar in Argentina! But always it

used by early Christians in the period of about the fourth to the sixth centuries. This box is very similar, almost a replica, of one I've seen at the Scottish Museum of Antiquities. It would not surprise me to learn they had the same origin. That one is the Monymusk Reliquary in which King Kenneth MacAlpin carried the personal belongings—perhaps even the remains—of St. Columba from Iona to Dunkeld."

"The patron saint of Scotland," said Hilary.

"I believe that title more officially belongs to St. Andrew," said Ashley. "But Columba was one of the major forces in bringing Christianity to Scotland and is certainly revered to this day."

"Ashley," said Logan, "are you saying this box is somehow linked to the spread of Christianity through early Scotland?"

"An old wine cellar in an Argentine villa is hardly the place to make such pronouncements," said Ashley. "But I would stake a heavy possibility on it. The items inside are quite indicative. This"—he held out the odd-looking item—"looks like the top from a pastoral staff. And some of this other silverwork could be vestments from some early church. I don't know about the sword hilts. They look of Pictish make. The rest, these smaller items, could be nothing more than some family's belongings, even a child's treasures. I don't know. It will take a great deal of time for someone more knowledgeable in these matters than I to go through and analyze each one. But I cannot help but be reminded of the discovery beneath the floor of the little church on St. Ninian's Isle in, let's see, when was it?"

"In 1958, I believe," said Logan.

"That's right. Well, some of this bears a striking resemblance to that find at St. Ninian's. So I would assume Pictish origins for much of it, probably in connection with some early monastery or Christian hermitage, perhaps along the northern coast there, or even upon what were once Stonewycke lands."

"What you said about the engravings . . . and the connection to the Picts—" Hilary's voice was breathless with excitement. "Do you mean it's possible this box could date from as early as the fifth or sixth century?"

Ashley nodded. "I would say no later than the eighth. Perha

"It's older than any of us ever thought," said Allison.

"Were there any old churches, monasteries. or the like, a Lossiemouth and Fraserburgh?" asked Ashley.

"There are stories of a St. Aiden," replied Allison, "who tra disciple of Columba who was sent out from Iona to establish known of him. But as a child I remember hearing tales of ruin a monastery or church of some kind, I don't know. Nothing Ramsey Head and the Old Rossachs Kyle were mentioned in

"Hmm," reflected Ashley. "Churches in those days were o of many kinds. But then that made them all the more subjec explain how the box found its way inland—to escape, perhap that would have come from the sea, and for which there wou vance warning. It will take a great deal more research, not to the bottom of the history of this reliquary."

"If the casket in the museum," Hilary asked, "once held t this have been put to a similar use? Perhaps for a different s

"It's very possible," answered Ashley. "That could expla ago such relics as these, especially relics with any religious esteem. There were those who even attributed supernatural p carried into battle as a talisman. If it contained a possession o the better. Some were indeed reported to carry bones or ashe I can't wait to get home. There I'll be able to compare both the museum pieces, and perhaps even to ancient descriptions we l

"Isn't it wonderful," said Allison, "that this box, this so-c to the very roots of Christianity in Scotland? A box full of so meaningful!"

As they spoke, Ashley had been slowly rubbing his ha the reliquary.

"Hullo!" he exclaimed all of a sudden, "what's this!"

He bent down, then lifted up one end of the box.

"Logan," he said, "hold that up there for a minute, wo

Logan complied.

With his finger Ashley continued to probe at one of small edge of the plating material peeling away," he said ners seemed to have borne the worst of the wear and tea how well the thing has weathered."

He continued to pick at the bit of torn metal, then l light. Finally he stood back up and let out a long sigh.

"You can set it down now, Logan," he said. "Well, Alliso ing across his face, "you may have spoken more prophe

"Why . . . what did I say?"

"Bend down there . . . look at that corner."

Allison did so. Hilary and Logan bent down as well

"Why, it looks like—!" exclaimed Logan.

Allison was still looking intently. "It's a different

"Bright, yellowish."

Suddenly the truth dawned on her. She spun aroun

He nodded. "That's right," he said. "Gold!"

They all looked at one another, stunned.

"The whole box!" asked Hilary in disbelief.

"I would guess," Ashley replied, "that would acco

"What would it be worth?" asked Allison.

of God's truth! Though it has been connected with violence, corruption, and greed, it has also acted as a catalyst to lead people to the Lord."

They all stood silent for some time, reflecting on Allison's words. Each one, in his or her own way, felt as if he had personally traveled with the box over its many miles and centuries of journeys. Within each of the four hearts beat the elation of fulfillment and completion, as if the quest of the treasure for a peaceful and final resting place was nearly at hand.

But they could tarry no more, at least for the moment, reflecting on the still-to-be-revealed mysteries of the antiquities before them or the current implications of their find. They were trapped in an armed villa, whose master was now dead, but who still wielded power over his servants.

It was time to think about getting out.

73 �֎ *Escape*

LOGAN AND ASHLEY re-secured the lid and bar to the box.

"I think we should put it back into the barrel," suggested Logan. "As heavy and bulky as that will be, it's our only chance of getting it out of here."

"You're probably right. You and I ought to be able to handle it."

"But I'm afraid, once we get out there in the vicinity of the guards," answered Logan, "we're going to have to have Hilary's assistance with the barrel, even though the weight could be a problem."

"I don't mind," said Hilary.

"And me?" Ashley shot a puzzled glance at Logan.

"I have something else in mind for you, my friend."

"How will we get it past the guards?" asked Allison.

"That's the plan," said Logan. "Ashley, you will have to use your pistol again and once more don the role you earlier pulled off with such finesse."

Ashley took the .38 from his pocket and looked down at it distastefully. "I will be glad to return this to the Inspector," he said.

"Soon enough," said Logan sympathetically. "In the meantime, we will become your prisoners again. Oh yes, and you'll need that charming moustache too."

Ashley pasted the thin moustache back in place.

"You make a better viscount than Emil!" laughed Hilary.

"Ah, Fraulein! At your service!" Ashley clicked his heels and flashed a toothy grin.

"Are we ready then?" asked Logan.

The underground passages seemed much quieter. Perhaps it was from the knowledge that Channing's body now lay in its temporary repose—or the awareness that unexpected danger might lie around any corner. Logan had always known that getting into Channing's fortress would be far easier than getting out again.

In ten minutes they had reached the narrow flight of stairs which would take them back out into the sunlight. Here Logan paused.

"As soon as we get it to the top," he said, "you and I are going to have to manage the wine cask, Hilary. Ashley, you cover us from the rear. Remember, the secret to a good con is confidence. That's what the word means. So walk steadily, and you especially, Ashley, have to look as if you know what you're about. Don't let any of the servants or guards cow you. You're about Channing's business, which is to take us out the main gate, and you're unconcerned about any of them."

"Got it."

"I suggest that instead of going back into the house itself, we just move through the compound, around the house, and to the gate. The way will be more direct, and from what I've seen, we'll run into fewer people. I'll lead, but, Ashley, you've got to make it look as though you're calling the shots."

Logan and Ashley carried the bulky wine cask up the stairs and set it down at the door. "Okay . . . places, everyone," said Logan. "Here we go!"

He and Hilary hoisted up the barrel. Logan shoved the door with his foot, and into the compound they slowly walked. At first the sun was blinding, but not a soul was to be seen as they made their way slowly along. Outside the kitchen a few servants came and went, but beyond an initial glance or two, seemed to pay little attention to the unusual entourage. No cars were to be seen within the precincts of the house itself, thus their most likely means of escape would be Ashley's rented automobile, which still sat where he had parked it at the front gate.

At the door to the servants' quarters, Logan spotted one of the Argentines who had been with Channing a time or two. The man eyed them carefully as they passed, said nothing, but seemed to stare with particular interest at Ashley's gun. As they approached, Ashley gave Allison an irritated shove with his left hand for good measure. She winced in apparent pain, carrying out her share of the ruse to annoyed perfection, and stumbled forward.

As they went, something began to nag at the back of Logan's brain, a feeling he couldn't pinpoint as if something important had been forgotten, overlooked. But as often as he replayed the events of the last two hours over in his mind, he could fix upon nothing.

They were by now approaching the outside corner where the two wings of the villa's L-shape joined. Once around it, they would be only some seventy-five feet from the gate, and in plain view of Ashley's car. Hilary's arms were tiring, but she bravely held on, the only sign of her fatigue being large beads of perspiration on her forehead.

Logan was fixing in his mind what to say to the guards at the gate when, just as they rounded the corner, a figure came striding briskly toward them. His appearance was so unexpected that the four escapees were brought up short. All of a sudden Logan was brought face-to-face with the unknown loose end he had forgotten to reckon with in his escape plan.

"Well, Gunther," said Logan calmly, "I've been wondering where you had gone to."

Taken just as much by surprise as they, Gunther was quick to size up the situation. Logan, of course, he knew immediately. The women he didn't recognize, though the older one appeared vaguely familiar from long ago in his past. But it was Ashley who garnered his longest scrutiny. He was familiar . . . but there was something out of place . . . the moustache—of course! It was none other than the Oxford professor in some ridiculous disguise. Why would he be holding a gun on these people?

"It looks as if I've returned none too soon," replied Gunther. "What are you up to, Macintyre?"

"He's up to nothing!" barked Ashley, feigning the best German accent he could muster. "Now out of the way, mein Herr. I've orders from Herr Channing to get these people out of here!"

"What are you talking about?" replied Gunther, unimpressed. "You're no more German than I am English!"

"I am the Viscount von Burchardt!" replied Ashley. "No doubt you've heard Herr Channing speak—"

"You are no such thing!" growled Gunther. "I know perfectly well who you are! Do you think my memory's that short? What kind of idiot do you take me for?"

"Nevertheless, I *do* have the gun," said Ashley, now in his own voice.

"Channing is dead, Gunther," said Logan. "My companions and I feel it would not be appropriate for us to continue our visit any longer. We are leaving, and I hope you will—if not for old times' sake, then for prudence on your own part—stand aside and let us go calmly."

"What do you mean, Channing is dead? Did you kill him? I didn't think you had it—"

"He died because his time had come, Gunther. His own hate had weakened him beyond recovery. Whether he died still clutching it, or having released it to his Maker, I do not know. You will find his body in the wine cellar. Now, if you will step aside—"

"You are jesting!" scoffed Gunther. "You do not think I will let you walk right out of here!"

"Ashley," said Logan, "if you will be so kind."

Ashley waved his gun in Gunther's direction.

"You are fools if you think you can get out of here alive! This place is surrounded by a dozen armed guards. Their orders are to protect Channing. If they believe he has been compromised, even if I tried to help you, nothing would stop them from doing their duty. You're a dead man, Macintyre!"

"We will take our chances," replied Logan. "We'll worry about them when the time comes. But remember, for now we have the gun on *you*."

Gunther laughed, in that dry, hard sound which contained no hint of joy or humor at all, only mockery.

"You will never shoot me, Professor—or whatever you are!" he said, eyeing Ashley disdainfully. "I let you get away with it before because I was curious about what you had to say. But I read it in your eyes then, and I see it now—you haven't got what it takes to shoot a man!"

As Gunther spoke, Logan and Hilary set down the cask. Logan stepped up near Ashley and relieved him of his weapon. Though everything Gunther had just said of Ashley was equally true of Logan, perhaps *L'Escroc* might call upon one more supreme bluff, for old times' sake, to gain freedom for his family.

Logan took the pistol firmly in his hand. Unlike Ashley, he knew well enough how to handle such a weapon. Moreover, the .38 *looked* secure in his grip, and Logan possessed half a lifetime's practice in making his eyes convey a steady and unblinking confidence. Now he would have to call upon that old experience once again.

"You are right, Gunther," he said. "Ashley is too intelligent and sensitive to harm another human being. But I am an old street punk who grew up with crime. I may have reformed in my latter days. But down inside that impertinent swindler is still part of me. Look into *my* eyes, Gunther, and you will know that I am not bluffing now. Do not forget, my old wartime colleague, that I killed back then and am no stranger to danger."

He paused and stared deeply into Gunther's eyes, holding them in his grip. His words had been measured and forceful. At length he went on, in a low tone that contained not a thread of detectable pretense.

"I *will* use this if it comes to that," he said. "I hope it does not. I could never live with having to kill again. But here are my wife and my daughter and my friend. And make no mistake. Gunther . . . *I will not see them harmed*!"

Several agonizing seconds passed. Logan knew Gunther was mentally assessing all the possibilities, not the least of which concerned the likelihood that, for all his bravado, Logan was indeed bluffing. But this had to be balanced against thoughts for his own safety. Gunther well knew all von Graff's illuminating stories about Logan's stint in Paris. The General used to laugh and say his friend Trinity, or MacVey, or whoever he was, could talk a charging rhinoceros into lying down for a nap.

But in matters of familial loyalty and protection, you could never tell what a man might be driven to do. He continued unflinchingly to hold Logan's steady gaze. There was an edge to the man's voice that hinted at the truth. These women *were* his wife and daughter, as he said, and even the mildest man was known to be able to kill to protect those he loved. Even if it had been thirty years, Logan still knew his business, still knew how to survive.

At last Gunther spoke. "This was Channing's battle anyway," he said. "I certainly have no intention of getting myself killed for it."

"Then if you will be so kind as to accompany us," said Logan, taking Gunther's arm, "we will be on our way."

With Allison now free to assist Hilary with one end, Ashley lifted the other end of the cask, and they continued slowly on toward the gate.

"I am curious about one thing," said Gunther as they walked. "You obviously planned this thing from the beginning. Planting the phony newspaper article, and the phony professor—"

"I'm actually quite a real professor," interjected Ashley.

"I thought you played the part too well," said Gunther. "But, Macintyre, did you know Channing would be here?"

"Yes," answered Logan. "We discovered his daughter's masquerade, and also learned of his identity as the General, and the connection to Trans Global Enterprises."

"So you came to Buenos Aires knowing full well what you were walking into?"

"In a manner of speaking. But I was not without people keeping an eye on me. My daughter here"—Logan indicated Hilary with his free hand "—planted herself in the hotel across the street. I signaled her with the curtains in my room before leaving with you—"

"And I had the back of your hotel being watched," put in Hilary, "and my own car parked so I could keep an eye on both hotels and the alley."

"So you followed us here, and that's how you all learned the whereabouts of the villa," said Gunther, with reluctant admiration. "I've got to hand it to you, Macintyre. You covered yourself rather well!"

"From you, Gunther, I take that as high praise."

"Just one more question. How did you connect it all in the first place? The General's identity has been safe for all these years. How did you find out it was Channing?"

"Elementary, Gunther," smiled Logan. "A mutual friend of ours left me a thirty-year-old clue."

"I don't follow you."

"A name, Gunther. A single name, still listed on the roster of TGE corporate executives—a name known to no one but von Graff and myself, a name I had used as a cover in France—one Monsieur Dansette. Once I saw that name, I knew there had to be some connection with von Graff. But there is one thing that still puzzles me. And that is—why would von Graff resurrect that name when there was always a remote possibility I might one day stumble upon it?"

"That cagey old rascal!" said Gunther, not without the hint of genuine affection in his voice. Then he glanced up at Logan. "You really have no idea, Macintyre?" he asked.

"None at all."

Gunther did not speak for a moment, obviously caught in his memories of his old mentor. When at last he opened his mouth, his words were nonetheless forceful that they fell so unexpectedly on Logan's ears.

"It was *you*, Macintyre," he finally said. "You always were to von Graff . . . almost like a son. He respected you . . . never forgot you."

"But . . . " said Logan incredulously, "but I was the enemy!"

"One thing you have to understand about von Graff," Gunther went on, "is that a part of him was never cut out for the military life. He could be ruthless, but there remained another side to him."

"Whatever became of him?"

"After the war, the General lost everything, including his own self-respect. Channing gave him a new identity and a position in the company. Eventually he even put him in the figure-head top position. But in the underground operation he was always known simply as *The General*. But von Graff was a man of some refinement. He prized his honor above all else. Though involved with Channing, his ways of doing business were foreign to von Graff, who always, I think, felt a bit guilty about what he did. The General even took to reading a Bible before he died. You were one of the few men he truly respected, Macintyre. He followed your career and many times swore he would go see you one day. Channing would probably have had him killed if he had tried. But when it became necessary to assume a new identity, which it did for all Germans in his position who hoped to get away clean, it's hardly surprising that he would have clung to a reminder of an honorable man he had once known."

Logan sighed deeply, remembering with fondness his old adversary.

"Then why is the name still on the roster?" asked Logan. "Didn't von Graff die in 1959?"

Gunther nodded. "By then the company was enormous—worldwide. It was worth millions. All the while Channing himself had remained completely hidden from public view, pulling strings behind the scenes. It made it easy for him to achieve his purposes when his name and background were nowhere to be found. Von Graff was an executive in the company, going by the name Dansette. But everyone in the shadow organization still just called him *The General*.

It was a comfortable disguise, and by the late fifties all traces of any connection to Nazism were gone. When von Graff died, Channing slipped into this already-existing identity. The facade was so neatly in place, so Channing took on von Graff's identity as 'The General,' in his continued underground activities, thus keeping his own personality still obscured."

Gunther shook his head. "I imagine he kept the name Dansette on the TGE's roster, too, just for convenience, having no idea what it signified. Neither did I. Neither did anyone. A clue out of the past that perhaps helped von Graff recall those days before the war when he had been a man of honor, but which no one else knew anything about. I wouldn't doubt if he secretly hoped someday you would discover the name and destroy Channing's corrupt organization."

Gunther's uncharacteristic soliloquy stirred Logan deeply. He found it increasingly difficult to hold the gun on Gunther in light of such startling and personal revelations.

They were now entering the courtyard. Ashley's car was not far now.

"What will it be, Gunther?" said Logan. "Can I trust you to help us get through the gates?"

"Channing may be dead, but I have my own survival to think of. I can't let you get to Interpol with my name."

"You won't even help us for the sake of the memory of our mutual friend?"

"My own skin means more to me than sentimentalities, Macintyre!"

"I thought as much. I guess we'll have to take you along." Logan nudged Gunther forward. "I'm going to put this gun in my pocket. But it will still be aimed at your midsection. Let's go!"

They crossed the courtyard and reached Ashley's car without incident. The guards standing outside the main door nodded to Gunther but apparently saw nothing so unusual about the strange procession, led, as it appeared, by their well-known comrade.

Anxiously Ashley and the two women removed the box from the wine cask, careful to keep out of view as much as possible, and then loaded the reliquary into the trunk, while Logan prodded Gunther into the back seat, following after him immediately. Ashley climbed in behind the wheel, with Hilary and Allison crowding in next to him. He started the ignition and wheeled into motion.

Ashley drove the remainder of the way across the courtyard, pulling up at the main gate where one of the two guards present waved him to a stop.

"Buenos dias, señor Gunther," he said, peering in. "You are off again so soon?"

Gunther hesitated momentarily, then felt an unseen jab into his ribs.

"Sí . . . sí, Miguel," he replied. "I am escorting some guests into the village. I will be back soon."

Miguel waved Ashley on, and the car passed through the open gates. The instant they had rounded a slight curve in the road and were out of sight, Ashley pressed down the accelerator. Audible sighs could be heard throughout the cramped automobile.

Some two or three miles from the villa, Logan asked Ashley to stop.

"What now?" asked Gunther with some concern in his voice.

"It is time for you to get out," answered Logan. "You have cooperated with us, but I want no further danger to my wife and daughter. I think it is time for us to part ways."

"You are letting me go?"

"Yes," said Logan. "But I know the location of the villa, and enough about Channing's organization to bring it down. I doubt you will be able to remain free for long."

"I will do my best!" said Gunther, with a look that might have been interpreted as a faint smile. Whether a smile of camaraderie or one which merely indicated pleasure that this chump of a do-gooder still had too much heart left for his own good, Logan could not tell. The German climbed out of the car and began walking along the dirt road. Then suddenly he turned back.

"Macintyre," he said, his cold, impassive voice not softening, but his words revealing more than his eyes would let on, "you will see to it that Channing gets a proper burial?"

"Yes, Gunther, I will do that."

"And his personal effects taken to his daughter?"

Logan nodded. "Gunther, I do believe you have a heart, after all!"

Gunther laughed dryly. "A moment of weakness. The first and last you will ever see!" Then he strode away.

Again Ashley pressed on the accelerator and they sped away toward Buenos Aires, where both Interpol and the local authorities were immediately notified.

74 ❋ The Berkshire Review

HILARY DRANK IN the lovely sounds around her—clicking typewriters, ringing phones, the buzz of many voices in a half-dozen impromptu conversations around the room. It did indeed feel good to be back in her office at the hub of the activity she so loved.

But Hilary knew she was not the same person she had been when she left this place so many weeks ago. Much had changed . . . *everything* had changed! Her horizons, both internal and external, had broadened considerably. She had grown to love another world outside the bustle of London.

"I am different," she said to herself. "But I am the same person, just as Ashley said it would be."

She looked down at her IBM and, suddenly inspired, began working the keys. She had been wondering all day what she would write for this editorial. It had to be special, for it would be somewhat of a farewell. For a while, at least.

Something about values . . . change . . . the deeper meaning of life. That's what she wanted to write about. A bit ambitious, perhaps. But after what she had been through, she had to try touching a meaningful chord. She must just focus it down, concentrate on one particular element in all that had come her way.

Yes, it was time for a leave of absence. As much as she loved the magazine, she was looking forward to the opportunity of returning to Scotland to get better acquainted with her new family and their beloved Port Strathy—and Stonewycke. It would be a time to begin a new phase in her life. She smiled when she thought of all that would be happening in the next few months. As much as the rest of it, she was eagerly anticipating beginning to organize the material in the *Stonewycke Journal* in hopes of writing a more orderly chronicle of her family's history. Would six months' leave be enough?

Six months . . . eight months . . . even a year. She would stay in touch. The magazine was still very much a part of her life. And it would be in Murry's capable hands during her sabbatical. As interim editor, he would blossom from a good journalist into a fine manager and administrator, directions she had been wanting to take him for some time. And the new staff writer and columnist-at-large she had hired to fill in Murry's vacancy would no doubt make life at the *Review* interesting. It had taken some smooth salesmanship on Hilary's part, but she was delighted when Suzanne had finally agreed to try journalism as a change from poetry.

"It's only temporary," she had insisted.

"Agreed," consented Hilary with a laugh. "But you'll love it—believe me! Now you'll have an audience to try out those outlandish ideas of yours on!"

"Who knows?" Suzanne said. "A taste of the hard-boiled world might inject new life into my prose *and* my poetry."

The romantic in Hilary could hardly refrain from smiling inside when she noted the special energy flowing between her two friends from the start. "Hmm," Hilary said to herself, "you never can tell what's going to happen!"

She came to the end of the page. removed it from the carriage, and was just slipping in a fresh sheet of white paper when Betty knocked on her door.

"This package just came," she said as she entered. She laid it on Hilary's desk, then left.

Hilary remembered the last time a strange package had come to the office. It had changed her life.

She wondered what this one could contain. The return address was unfamiliar, but it had originated in London. It was not large, perhaps about the size of a small shoe box. She tore off the brown paper and lifted the lid, then pulled out the brief note that lay inside.

"These were among the items confiscated from the Villa del Heimat. The police have no further use for them, and we were told to forward them to you."

It was signed, Chief Inspector Rollins.

Hilary examined the items in the box—a few assorted mementos, some photos. Not much really, when you considered they represented nearly a century of a man's life. A man worth millions, who had controlled financial empires, yet this was the only heritage to be left behind from that life of greed and ambition.

Jason Channing had not built his life with the bricks that lasted beyond death. No gold nor silver nor precious stones here—only wood, hay, and stubble. A business crumbling beneath the revelation of its sordid foundation, a criminal organization now breaking to pieces from the onslaught of the law. The only guests to attend his funeral beyond Logan, Allison, and Hilary—his lifetime adversaries—were a few locals, and a handful of men who had worked for him. Not a single person he could have called a friend.

In the end, he had lived for nothing. And now he had nothing but this small box to pass on to his daughter, who was herself facing a prison sentence. She probably did not even have the memory of his fatherly love. *Not much of a legacy,* Hilary thought.

She sighed sadly, glancing at her watch. She would just have time to stop by Holloway Prison, where Jo was awaiting trial. Then she had to pick up her mother in Whitechapel and catch her train.

Hilary recalled her adoptive mother's reaction to the astounding news of the location of Hilary's parents. The dear woman was simply marvelous, thrilled that the once-orphaned child could now enjoy *two* families!

"But, dear me!" Mrs. Edwards had exclaimed, "what a family! I'll want a new dress to meet them!"

Hilary laughed. "I think we'll *both* need new dresses, Mum!"

Yes . . . her life was changing. But the things that mattered most were still constant, and would always be so. When *she* died, she knew that the sum total of her life would mean more than this handful of mementos left behind by a wealthy man. God had blessed her beyond all the earthly riches a person could imagine—blessed her with love, with family and friends, and with a future of eternal meaning.

With these thoughts fresh in her mind, her fingers began again sailing over the keys. In fifteen minutes the editorial was finished. She re-read it, satisfied, then slipped the first page back into the typewriter and typed in the title she had omitted earlier: "A Lonely Shoe Box."

Hilary rose, gathered up her things, and walked to the door. There she paused and took one last look behind her.

"I'll be back soon," she murmured, then opened the door.

75 ✠ *The Treasure of Stonewycke*

THE MORNING WOULD dawn bright and fair.

It was too much to expect, in this land of contrasts with its inclement and unpredictable weather, that on *this* special day the sun would shine.

But spring had come to Stonewycke, and this day in early May looked as though it would display all its glory. The song of the wren in the budding trees could be heard in the valley. The heather on the hills was green with new life, preparing itself for the burst of purple glory four months distant. The gentle breeze was clean, with just a touch of the tangy salt from the sea and the chill from across the waters to give assurance that this was, indeed, the far north of Scotland.

Hilary had risen early. It was only natural that she would be flooded with a sea of sleep-inhibiting emotions and thoughts. On the contrary, however, she had slept soundly, and when at five she suddenly found herself wide awake, it was with the peculiar sense of having been roused for some purpose. She dressed quickly and slipped quietly out: for whatever compulsion was upon her, she knew it was calling her outside, into the freshness of the northern morning, to be alone.

Notwithstanding that in two or three hours the sun would be bright and high, the clean air was bitingly cold and Hilary bundled herself well. She walked first to the old garden and sat awhile on the stone bench in mingled reflection and prayer.

The treasure once was here, she thought. *Buried in this very spot by Maggie and Digory, though no one ever knew it. Hidden, yet alive, not decaying, nurturing the essential life within, like a seed under the ground, awaiting the moment when its life would again blossom with the coming of dawn.*

How could any of the hands that had possessed, or buried, or sought, or dreamed about, or moved, or thirsted after the treasure know the fullness of what it represented, both to the history of this land and to the heritage of this region?

Slowly Hilary rose. She walked out of the garden and toward the footbridge that led across the stream and south onto the moorland which gave way in the distance to Braenock Ridge. The dawn was advancing now, and she could see her way clearly.

The treasure was on her mind. She was full of the very essence of it, her keen mind probing, as if to discover some hidden significance they had all overlooked in the five months since its discovery.

Slowly she walked, in no particular direction, pausing every now and then to note the progress of the rising sun behind Strathy summit to the east. Mingled in her reflections were images and faces and scenes from Joanna's journal. She had set up a temporary office on the fourth floor of the castle, where on a clear day she might look out over the treetops to behold the valley and even the sea in the distance. There she had been working assiduously on . . . she didn't even know what to call it! Since first reading it, some inner compulsion had said to her that the story of this family—*her* family now!—had to be told. Not in dry, statistical numbers and dates, births and deaths, but as a "story"—a living, breathing tale of *real* people, whose lives, all taken together, left a *living* and vital legacy—not only to their own descendants but to God's people everywhere.

But there was so much to tell! So *many* people were an intrinsic part of the legacy, some for good, others for ill: James, Anson, Atlanta, Talmud, Andrew, Thomas, Robert . . . so many stories . . . so many lives. And then of course Maggie, Ian, and Joanna, and even Eleanor's part, unknown to her . . . Alec . . . her own parents, Allison and Logan.

Oh, thought Hilary, *it is so huge! It's a legacy that* cannot *be told!* In despair she had risen dozens of times from her typewriter in the last few months, vowing to cease her futile effort of attempting to put the story down on paper.

Yet something always brought her back, just as something had called her out on this chilly morning. *He* would not let her rest. It was, after all, not *her* story, not Joanna's story, not Maggie's story. It was *His* story! It was a legacy He had been building into the lives of men and women since the creation of His world, a legacy He had built into the very nature of the ongoing family structure—father passing his heritage on to his son, who passed it on to his own son, and on, and on throughout time; mother giving life to daughter, who in turn gave life to granddaughter, and down through the years, from generation to generation . . . the life of God passing from parent to child, spreading out, deepening, extending itself in wider and wider circles, transforming the world with the news and the impact of God's love and mighty character.

What a heritage! thought Hilary. *The people of God passing on His life throughout the world! And what a family I am part of . . . a family in which that life can be witnessed again and again, blossoming in fullness in one generation, spreading out, influencing many lives, perhaps being lost sight of for a season, then re-surfacing to grow and deepen again. Thank you, Lord, for the faithfulness of my own forebears whose lives and whose prayers for their posterity are so responsible for implanting the seeds of your life into me. Thank you, Lord, for those seeds of faith that never die!*

"It's just like the treasure," Hilary pondered. "Hidden . . . yet always alive, waiting to be rediscovered by every successive generation. The life of God hidden within the human heart—implanted in many cases by prayers and faithful obedience of a righteous ancestry—awaiting in every new generation the discovery by each individual soul whom God, in His timing and in His own unique way, calls into relationship with Him."

Hilary sighed. The treasure . . . the individuals she was coming to know out of her own descent. God had indeed bestowed upon her a rich legacy!

She had been so deep in thought that she had been paying little attention to the direction of her steps. She glanced up. In the distance a figure was approaching.

Allison, too, had risen a great while before day. The same compulsion had fallen upon her, driving her from her bed. She, too, had needed on this day to be alone with her Lord, the God of her ancestors.

She had long ago made peace with God in the quietness of her heart. And she had made peace with the circumstances, painful though they were, of her life. Out of necessity she had neither thought nor prayed much during the years of her middle age about the passing of life on to future generations. She had grown to accept her lot as a mother without a child to build her life into.

Now suddenly all was changed. Now she found herself standing, as had those who preceded her, as representative of the elder generation of Stonewycke women, to whom had been entrusted the passage of the legacy left to her by the likes of Atlanta, Maggie, and her own mother. Now it was *hers* to transmit to *her* daughter—that it might continue beyond her present life.

A formidable responsibility . . . an awe-inspiring blessing!

Like her daughter, Allison had found herself mingling thoughts and prayers concerning the recently discovered treasure with those about her ancestry. She, too, had been walking now for about an hour, though she had left through the front gate and wandered in a large circle to the point where she saw Hilary walking in her direction. She waved, and picked up her pace. How fitting, she thought, that we should meet out here on this, Hilary's wedding day—alone, just the two of us. This is, after all, the traditional day when the hearts of mothers and daughters are often drawn closer than at any other time.

As she walked toward her daughter, she looked upon the face that was smiling back to her in greeting. The sun had just risen, and from behind Hilary now sent its bright morning rays radiating through her amber hair. Around her head a glow encircled her face, as if the light were coming from the auburn locks themselves.

"What a beauty!" murmured Allison to herself. "My own daughter—and so lovely! What a blessing she is, Lord. Thank you! She is more to me than any treasure could ever be! *She* is a treasure!"

With the revelation, suddenly Allison caught her breath in a short, involuntary gasp. "Of course!" she exclaimed inaudibly. "That's it! That's why you wanted me out here, isn't it, Lord? You wanted to show me what it all meant!"

As her mother came forward, Hilary beheld anew the face she had so grown to love, radiant now, both with the morning sun and with a beaming smile of love. Hilary thought she would never tire of gazing upon that face, not only because there were so many years of loving it to be regained, but also because in that face seemed to be embodied the very essence of all the faces she could only imagine in the eye of her mind when reading the journal. But this—her mother's—was a living, dynamic, loving face, a countenance that reflected both the heart of a mother and the glory of God. All the others, whose faces she had not been able to know, lived on in this wondrous face she did know. And she even hoped, in some small measure, the face of her mother would live on . . . in her.

Now upon Allison's face she saw a great smile. Her mother was running toward her with open arms.

Suddenly into Hilary's heart broke a stunning truth which in an instant, in the single flash of a moment, unified all the thoughts she had had since arising on this most special of all days.

"Now I see, Lord!" she cried in her heart. "*This* is the treasure—not the box, not even the abstract heritage of Stonewycke! This is the legacy, the heritage of life passed on through the generations in this family. The box is only a symbol. The *true* gift, the *real* treasure is the life you have passed on—through Maggie to Joanna, and to my own dear mother Allison! And now you are passing on the treasure to me! The treasure is in that beautiful face of my mother!"

With tears streaming down her face, Hilary began to run forward, arms outstretched.

Thirty minutes later the two women approached the footbridge arm in arm. Their tears of joy and mutual discovery had by now mostly dried. The conversation just past, though unheard by any other, was one both mother and daughter would treasure the rest of their lives.

Now what promised to be a long and memorable day was upon them. There was much to be done.

76 ✖ *Celebration of Love*

ALLISON GLANCED AROUND at the guests seated on folding chairs in Dorey's lovely rose garden.

In certain ways this gathering reminded her of Lady Joanna's funeral seven months ago. Many of the faces were the same. But today there was the crisp brightness of a warming spring day instead of the drizzle of late autumn. And today the eyes contained smiles which looked forward with anticipation, rather than tears which lamented the passing of an era. The past was behind, the future lay ahead—as it always would. The life which was in Stonewycke and its people continued to move forward.

Allison smiled at her friends and neighbors. They were here to celebrate with the family a grand and wondrous occasion. A lump rose in her throat when she thought that not so very long ago she had no hope of being in such an enviable position. Yet here she was today, the mother of the bride!

The very thought still sent a thrill through her body. Then she remembered that this bride had *two* mothers. Allison turned and smiled at Mrs. Edwards, and patted her hand affectionately.

Yes, it was a grand day—the day her new daughter would be married to a man of God's choosing. What a pair they made—the imperturbable, traditionalist professor, and the progressive, firebrand journalist. Yet their very differences complemented one another.

Just three days ago the two of them had ridden on horseback to Braenock Ridge. Allison and Logan had driven the car out as far as possible and then had hiked the rest of the way in to meet the young couple. They had come upon them unannounced and had paused a short distance off, unable to resist a few moments silently observing their daughter and her husband-to-be as they poked about the ancient stones. Both were alive with curiosity, talking furiously—not only about the original site of the treasure they were exploring, but about all kinds of things.

It was obvious from watching them—in their blue jeans, boots, and loose-fitting shirts and jackets—that they were going to have fun together. Neither was satisfied to accept superficialities, either in relationships or—as they now displayed as they scrambled about the rocks and earth—in matters of science or history or knowledge. Where Ashley literally dug in the earth to discover the roots of man's historical being, Hilary dug into the motives of human hearts with her literary investigations. They were, in that sense, very much alike after all. Together they would have quite an impact on the world around them.

But at that moment the violins began the wedding march, and Allison's attention was diverted to the front of the colorful gathering. There stood an oaken altar, bordered by large wicker vases full of roses and lilies. Rev. Macaulay appeared from the door at the side of the house and took his place at the altar. Then followed Ashley's best man, a Chief Inspector from Scotland Yard by the name of Harry Arnstein. "Now *there is* a mismatched pair," mused Allison with a silent chuckle. Arnstein appeared the perfect stereotype of the policeman— thick, muscular, with a broad homely face and small drooping eyes. How he and the lanky scholar had ever become such close friends, Allison could not guess. And to her every inquiry they had been very evasive. But again Allison's musings were interrupted as a third man stepped from the side door.

Ashley Jameson, styled Lord Dearden, appeared every inch the noble gentleman now, no matter how much he might choose to downplay it. The black pin-striped tuxedo suited him well; he looked even taller than usual. Even on so momentous an occasion as his own wedding, he walked with more than a trace of his usual casual manner. Yet Allison could note at the same time a purposefulness in his step which revealed immediately there was more to this man than could readily be discerned on the surface. Hilary would have a lifetime to discover all the fine nuances of the personality and character of this man of God who would soon be her husband and the latest of Stonewycke's line of noble family heads.

Allison reflected on the men God had integrated into the family heritage over the past hundred years. In a birthright where women had dominated the line of descent, the husbands of their choosing had in recent times been men of great inner strength and stature. Each added new facets to the vitality of life that passed from generation to generation. Ashley, too, would make his mark upon this posterity, infusing his own genes and character and perspectives into the family bloodstream.

Suzanne Heywood, Hilary's maid of honor, then appeared, her long blond hair set off by a gown of pale blue silk, the wide neckline accented with frilly lace in tones of cream and blue.

All at once the violins struck the chord announcing the approach of the bride. A chill of pride coursed through Allison's heart as she stood. In the seats behind her, in addition to the many neighbors and townspeople, her sister May and brother Ian were on their feet too. Behind them were Hilary's friends from the magazine, Murry and Betty and several others. On the opposite side of the aisle, Ashley's colleagues from Oxford were rising now. Allison could not stop the tears streaming down her face, nor did she want to. Mrs. Edwards quietly slipped a hand through her arm. When Allison glanced toward her with a smile, she saw that the dear woman was weeping too.

At last came the processional. Many moist eyes turned to see father and daughter, arm linked through arm, begin down the aisle under the smiling blue sky.

How handsome Logan looked! Never on the floor of Parliament, thought Allison, could he have been so distinguished! Joy and fatherly pride beamed from his face; the twinkling eyes and broad smile inevitably reminded Allison of the Logan in his younger days. His smiling eyes had always been full of life. But today they were filled to overflowing with the exhilaration of having his daughter s arm through his, and knowing that their love, long lost, was now marvelously and mutually shared to the fullest. His grip on Hilary as they slowly moved forward with the music gave evidence that he might have difficulty giving her away when the moment came.

Logan turned his head slightly and smiled down at her, as if he could still not believe his good fortune in discovering his daughter. At last the tracks appeared down his cheeks. But no one thought the less of him, for his tears were caused by the joy and thanksgiving only a father can know on the day of his daughter's marriage.

Hilary herself came down the grassy walkway the perfect vision of the bride. Though her white gown was simple and understated, the overall effect was nonetheless elegant. The dress was silk, overlayed with lace. The flounced, over-the-shoulder peasant neckline beautifully set off Lady Margaret's gold locket. A ring of spring flowers, all gathered from Dorey's greenhouse or upon the hills themselves, adorned her amber hair, and a short veil hung down to her shoulders. In her hands she carried a matching bouquet.

Allison's lip trembled. Here indeed was the true treasure of Stonewycke! The box they had retrieved could never compare with the wealth that now graced Dorey's garden. It had been with them all along, in the heritage of God's presence abiding within this family, and this land, through the centuries, a pearl of great price now visible for the world to see. No doubt Maggie and Joanna were watching, sharing the fulfillment Allison felt.

Who could tell how far into the future this eternal treasure would extend? God's very life was waiting to be instilled within those yet unborn. The heritage would continue, as His Word promised, even to a thousand generations of those who loved Him and kept His commands.

Logan and Hilary reached the end of the aisle. The violins stopped, and Rev. Macauley stepped forward.

"Who giveth this woman to be married to this man?"

Logan cast a wistful yet loving glance down at his daughter, then smiled through the tears he was not ashamed to show.

In that moment Hilary realized anew that she had become part of something much larger than her limited vision could grasp. She had been swept into an ongoing stream of generations, every one of which had to "choose this day whom they would serve." None who had gone before had been perfect, yet each had left his or her own special mark upon the family. She could not help but wonder what would be *her* stamp of individuality, and Ashley's.

Hilary smiled up at Logan. Perhaps the minister's question was a more difficult one than for most fathers. After all, they had just found each other, and now he was being asked to give her away all over again! But Logan knew he would never lose the companionship which had begun to grow between them.

"Her mother and I!" came his buoyant answer. Then he leaned over and tenderly kissed her cheek.

"I love you, Father," Hilary whispered.

Logan gave her arm a final squeeze, then took her hand and offered it to Ashley.

Hilary and Ashley now moved side by side in front of the altar, and proceeded to pledge their lifelong commitment to one other, before family and friends, and the great cloud of witnesses watching from above.

The village down the hill was quiet and nearly empty. The shoreline stretching west and east was calm; the many vessels tied to their moorings in the harbor sat idle and unconcerned. Little work was being done today in the valley called Strathy. A great hush seemed to have descended upon the land. No soul was present on the foothills to the south, upon whose heather-covered slopes had ridden the progenitors of the heritage that was at this moment being rediscovered anew. In the distance, great silent white clouds hung over the Highlands. All life seemed to have paused in the region and come to rest upon the couple now dedicating themselves to each other before family, friends, and God.

The sun glowed upon Hilary and Ashley, and a gentle sea breeze wafted in from offshore, as if offering a loving benediction from their dear Father in heaven who had unfailingly led them on these converging paths where their lives and love were now joining as one. Also as a reminder that His Spirit would continue with them always.

❈ *Epilogue*

SLOWLY THE LINE of visitors wound its way along the corridor toward the East Wing of the great house.

"As I mentioned," the guide was saying, "this portion of the castle was for many years in disrepair. Only last spring were the renovations at last completed. Mr. Macintyre oversaw most of the repairs."

"I'm from America," said one of the visitors, "and I've toured quite a number of castles. It seems as if you never see anyone, even in these that are listed as still being family homes. *Does* somebody actually live here?"

"Oh yes," the guide replied, "both the Macintyres and the Jamesons make this their home, but only for part of the year."

"Macintyre—isn't he the politician?"

"That's right. Mr. Macintyre just began his twenty-fifth year as a Member of Parliament. However, his schedule does not permit him to be here more than two or three months out of the year. There has been some talk lately about his retirement, and if that does indeed come to pass, he has made it clear that he and Lady Macintyre will spend the remainder of their lives at Stonewycke. In the meantime, the details of administering the estate fall to Lord Ashley and Lady Hilary."

"It was my understanding that Lord and Lady Deardon also live in England?" asked a woman near the guide, her greater knowledge of the family betrayed by her Scottish accent.

"That is partially true. They too split their time between the north and south. Mrs. Jameson still functions as the chief editor of *The Berkshire Review,* of which she is now co-owner. And Lord Deardon remains a professor at Oxford. However, both of them have so arranged their duties and responsibilities that they are able to divide their time between their home in Watlington, the Deardon estate in Cornwall, and here at Stonewycke."

"How do they manage it?" asked an Englishman with a laugh.

"For one thing, they're both very efficient and productive," answered the guide. "But also they have greatly scaled back their commitment of time to the magazine and the university. As some of you may know, Hilary Jameson carries on a rather heavy writing schedule outside the magazine itself, and her husband is involved in several notable archaeological explorations, on some of which his wife accompanies him."

"When are they here?"

"They manage to be at Stonewycke usually about five or six months out of the year, administering the affairs of the estate, as well as coordinating their other projects. Most of their writing takes place here as well. Lord Deardon is a noted historical scholar whose research he documents completely after every project or expedition. For the two or three months out of the year when neither family can be here, usually falling between March and June, they graciously allow the National Trust of Scotland to conduct these tours of the Stonewycke castle. During this time, the grounds and castle itself are maintained by their factor and excellent staff. Now, if you'll all just step through this door here, we have arrived at the Heirloom Room, which is, I'm sure, what most of you have come to Stonewycke today to see."

The guide led the way, followed by the fifteen to twenty people in attendance. The moment they entered, an awed hush fell upon them.

In the center of the room, encased in glass and sitting on a massive bronze pedestal, stood the Stonewycke Reliquary, the most significant ancient historical find in Britain in twenty years, which had, three years earlier, dominated the historical journals, *The National Geographic,* and Hilary's *Review,* as well as gracing the cover of *Time* and being found worthy of a four-page story inside. Once its contents and the box itself had been thoroughly examined by a staff of experts, certain of the items had been given to the British Museum, others to the Scotland Museum of Antiquities, while others had been chosen to remain with the box.

The thin plating that had sheathed the box had been meticulously removed and kept intact as almost a shadow replica of the Reliquary; it was now on display in the Museum of Antiquities along with its sister, the Monymusk Reliquary. The removing of this sheathing had revealed a stunning and minutely complex engraved box, approximately one-eighth inch thick of solid gold, reinforced at all the corners with stronger metals. The box was concluded to be between twelve and fifteen hundred years old. Further research was even at that moment being conducted, a portion of it led by Ashley himself, into a more precise determination of the box's origins and early history.

The guide then began a brief history of what was known about the priceless gold Reliquary and how it had come to be discovered, as well as describing those items that had been found in it, which were displayed to the side. Slowly and quietly the visitors made their way up close to the box to view it while she spoke, then gradually spread out through the room to see the other Stonewycke mementos the family had chosen to let remain for public view.

Since the discovery of the Reliquary and the attendant publicity, both the Macintyre and Jameson families had been the object of far more notoriety than any of the four was comfortable with. Yet they recognized a certain amount of it as their civic and historical duty as persons in the public spotlight, realizing that time would ultimately diminish interest in the recently publicized find. They did, however, take the precaution to make sure that during their months at Stonewycke, no public tours or visits were allowed, thus preserving what privacy was possible to this nationally-known family.

By now Logan was recognized wherever he went, and even on the streets of Aberdeen or Edinburgh was constantly hounded for his autograph. His eyes still sparkled, his step still bounced, and he still bought his papers from the newsboys on the sidewalks of London.

Every day when she was at Stonewycke, Allison managed either to visit one of the women from the valley or have several up to the castle for tea. The stories told in fond tones by some of the farmers' wives began to sound very much like those told of Joanna twenty years earlier.

Suzanne still editorialized for the *Review,* though she had begun to give politics more serious consideration than when Hilary first mentioned it to her. She and Murry had hit it off immediately. Neither had seen anyone else socially for over two years.

Hilary had retold about two-thirds of Stonewycke's story from Joanna's journal and was trying to interest a publisher. She had been trying to talk Ashley into an excavation of the Braenock Ridge area as part of his research.

Logan and Donald Creary had together gone into the business of raising long-haired Highland bulls for export to Germany, and the venture had turned rather lucrative for both.

Ashley's closet obsession with mystery writing remained solely the family's secret. He managed to continue to write one new novel about every twelve to eighteen months, and the diverted royalties helped keep Stonewycke in the black for many years to come.

Let this be written for a future generation . . .

. . . He established the law in Israel, which he commanded our forefathers to teach their children, so the next generation would know them, even the children yet to be born, and they in turn would tell their children . . .

. . . Then would they put their trust in God and would not forget his deeds, but would keep his commands . . . through the generations to come of those who love him and keep his commands.

—Psalms 78:4–7